North Lincolnshire Council
www.northlincs.gov.uk

Library items can be renewed online 24/7, you will need your library card number and PIN.

Avoid library overdue charges by signing up to receive email preoverdue reminders.

To find out more about North Lincolnshire Library and Information Services, visit www.northlincs.gov.uk/libraries

www.northlincs.gov.uk/librarycatalogue

KINGDOM BLADES

This is a work of fiction. The events and characters described herein are imaginary and are not intended to refer to specific places or living persons. The opinions expressed in this manuscript are solely the opinions of the author and do not represent the opinions or thoughts of the publisher. The author has represented and warranted full ownership and/or legal right to publish all the materials in this book.

Kingdom Blades
A Pattern of Shadow & Light Book 4

All Rights Reserved.
Copyright 2016 Melissa McPhail

v1.0

Paperback ISBN: 978-0-990629177
Hardcover ISBN: 978-0-990629184

This book may not be reproduced, transmitted, or stored in whole or in part by any means, including graphic, electronic, or mechanical without the express written consent of the publisher except in the case of brief quotations embodied in critical articles and reviews.

Five Strands Publishing Co. http://www.FiveStrandsPublishing.com

Five Strands Publishing and the "FSP" logo are trademarks belonging to

Five Strands Publishing Co.

KINGDOM BLADES

A PATTERN OF SHADOW AND LIGHT

—— BOOK 4 ——

ALL THINGS ARE FORMED OF PATTERNS...

MELISSA McPHAIL

BOOKS BY MELISSA McPHAIL

Cephrael's Hand

The Dagger of Adendigaeth

Paths of Alir

Kingdom Blades

ACKNOWLEDGEMENTS

WHILE THE ACTUAL writing of a story tends to be a solitary activity, taking a book from conception to publication involves many creative and generous individuals.

I cannot thank enough my many early readers—guinea pigs, some might say—who read multiple renditions of chapters, each time somehow managing to forget the earlier version where the character did something completely different. That you emerged unscathed from this gauntlet is testimony to your fortitude. You have my deepest gratitude!

To my many beta readers, editors, designers and other professionals who lent me their time, skills and knowledge, thank you!

To my husband and daughters, who endured evenings and weekends without my attention so this book could be finished to meet my own ridiculous, self-imposed dead-line, my gratitude knows no bounds.

Finally, this book could not have been written without the wisdom of philosophers, whose enlightened views of existence have shaped my understanding of the world: Ralph Waldo Emerson, Siddhartha Buddha, L. Ron Hubbard, Voltaire, Jesus of Nazareth, Marcus Aurelius…many others. I owe them a debt that can never be repaid.

AUTHOR'S NOTE

IT'S ONE OF those forest for the trees sort of things. Once a pattern has already been drawn-designed-created, you can see it all there in one glance, complete. But try to follow just one strand of it and see where you end up. Then try following two, or three. Then twelve. Imagine trying to follow all of the individual strands that make up the pattern, all at the same time. You very quickly lose the weave—sometimes even when you're the one weaving it.

This was the problem I faced as I was writing *Kingdom Blades*. It's a complicated book, but I wanted it to feel simple to you. I wanted you to tumble along the pattern's threads as upon a river's course and never feel like you don't know where you're going (even if you're not necessarily sure where *I'm* going). I wanted you to see the pattern in its simplicity and have no concept of the complexity involved in weaving it. I hope I've accomplished this.

To make the going a little easier, here's where we left off with some of our favorite characters at the end of *Paths of Alir* (at least, the important things you need to know):

Tanis and Pelas

Tanis, Felix and Nadia were investigating the Literato N'abranaacht (aka Shailabanáchtran) when Shail's allies, the Danes, invade the Quai game at the Sormitáge and take Tanis and Nadia hostage, along with two hundred other Adepts. Felix is left trapped among a pile of others who were caught by the battle.

Later, Tanis and Shail meet over tea, where Tanis is introduced to the Warlock Sinárr, who expresses an immediate (and very unwelcome) interest in making the lad his concubine. Shail tells Tanis that he's invited his brother

Pelas to come and retrieve him, and elicits Sinárr's help in destroying Pelas, with Tanis as the prize.

Pelas meanwhile has been in a tower in Myacene, prisoner of his brother Darshan, and thinking his power lost. Darshan gives a *goracrosta*-bound Isabel val Gelderan to Pelas, triggering Pelas's instinctive compulsion to harm her. Isabel sacrifices her troth to Ean in order to free Pelas from his brother's compulsion. Pelas then frees Isabel and goes to answer his brother's summons.

Pelas arrives in the temple where Shail is holding Tanis and Nadia prisoner. Working in concert, Pelas and Tanis escape Shail and Sinárr's trap and flee with Nadia across a portal through Shadow. Upon arriving back at Pelas's home, however, they find that Nadia has been affected by *deyjiin*. Tanis and Pelas work together to Heal her.

After this Healing, Tanis realizes that he is actually an Adept of four strands, a gift which comes to him via a rare variant trait that he shares with his mother, Isabel. Tanis recalls then that he is the son of Arion Tavestra and Isabel van Gelderan. A trove of memories opens to him, including knowledge of the bindings that still exist between himself and his parents.

Pelas tells Tanis that he would choose a new brother and asks Tanis to bind them. During the blood-binding, Pelas works *elae*'s fifth-strand, making the binding Unbreakable.

Ean, Isabel and Sebastian

In the first half of *Paths of Alir*, Ean rescues his brother Sebastian and then frees him from the matrix of amnesia and compulsion placed upon him by the wielder Dore Madden.

In the last half of *Paths of Alir*, Ean goes with Sebastian and Isabel to the Fortress of Ivarnen in Saldaria to rescue the Captain Rhys val Kincaid from Dore Madden and the Prophet Bethamin (aka Darshanvenkhátraman). In Ivarnen, Ean learns that his loyal men who'd been traveling with Rhys (Cayal, Brody and Dorin) have been made into *eidola* and is forced to fight them.

Every time Ean unworks one of the *eidola*, he makes a beacon for Darshan's awareness. Sensing Darshan coming for Ean, Isabel purposefully strikes Ean into unconsciousness. She gives her staff to Sebastian and warns him that Ean will need to learn how to unwork many *eidola* at once. She tells him to enlist Prince Darieos of Kandori's help in the effort. Then she gives herself to Darshan to give Ean and the others time to escape.

Ean rouses to learn that Isabel is gone. He and Sebastian fight their way through hundreds of *eidola* to escape Ivarnen along with Rhys. The captain is injured during this attempt, and combined with the illness he developed during his captivity, the injury proves too much. The moment they arrive off the node back in Kandori, he collapses into unconsciousness.

Trell and Alyneri

The Sundragon Náiir and the zanthyr Vaile rescue Trell from the Fortress of Darroyhan and the *mor'alir* Adept Taliah hal'Jaitar. Alyneri and Björn Heal Trell from Taliah's dark pattern, which was pulling his lifeforce after hers into death.

Upon waking, Trell realizes that all of his memories have been returned to him, whereupon Björn explains that he removed Raine D'Lacourte's truthbinding.

After Trell and Alyneri reunite, Björn tells Trell about his brothers' activities. In the end, Trell goes with Alyneri to learn the *cortata*.

Franco Rohre and the Nodefinder Rebellion

Franco and Carian were attending a party in honor of Niko van Amstel's candidacy for the Second Vestal when Franco meets Immanuel di Nostri (aka Pelasommáyurek). Carian heads off somewhere with Devangshu Vita, one of the Fifty Companions, while Franco and Immanuel are taken hostage by the Nodefinder Demetrio Consuevé.

Franco helps Immanuel escape from the sea cave where Demetrio has left them to drown. Later, he finds that Immanuel has returned him to Niko's estate, and that the Alorin Seat Alshiba Torinin has Healed him.

Franco feels immediately drawn to Alshiba and swears to serve her. She tells him that Niko has named him as a deputy vestal, and summons him to the cityworld of Illume Belliel.

Carian and Devangshu succeed in their efforts to steal an important work, *The Vestal Codex*, which outlines the rules for becoming a vestal. They return to the First Lord's *sa'reyth* and establish their headquarters for the new Nodefinder Rebellion, which is dedicated to preventing Niko from permanently gaining the vestal seat.

Gydryn val Lorian, King of Dannym

In *The Dagger of Adendigaeth*, King Gydryn val Lorian learns that Radov of M'Nador is conspiring against him. He decides to withdraw his forces from the princedom's war, but he knows that Radov's Consul, Viernan hal'Jaitar, will do anything to prevent this if he learns of it. Gydryn devises a secret plan and sends the young Lieutenant Jasper val Renly off with orders to see it carried out. He also sends Loran val Whitney, Duke of Marion, with the majority of his knights to the abandoned Fortress of Nahavand, which lies across enemy lines, in the hopes of keeping Loran and his knights out of reach of Viernan hal'Jaitar.

As *The Dagger of Adendigaeth* comes to a close, King Gydryn is dying in the desert, the result of a plot to kill him devised by Viernan hal'Jaitar. The truthreader Kjieran van Stone saves the king from death, but then Kjieran mysteriously immolates himself upon a burning pyre. Just as unconsciousness is claiming the king, two Khurds arrive. The one called Prince Farid tells the other to take the king with them.

At the end of *Paths of Alir*, Gydryn wakes from a long bout with fever. While still convalescing, he's visited by Rajiid al Basreh, Prime Minister of the Akkad, who tell the king they have much to discuss.

❖

As always, to assist in your reading, you'll find in the Appendix an updated glossary, dramatis personae, Adept chart, the Sormitáge Rankings, and lists of the Laws and Esoterics.

Cartographer's Notes: As a result of the last cataclysm, circa 3,220 V, and the subsequent rising sea levels in the northern reaches of the Sea of Agasan, the Hallovian coastline has shifted in some areas dramatically from the original charts. Since the maps were last charted, abyssmal reefs have arisen. Many of these reefs are not marked on charts predating the last Age. Coastal maps dated prior to 3,220 V should not be used when sailing the Sea of Agasan off shore of Hallovia.

Sailors have reported unseasonably rough seas in the crossing between Hallovia and Devon in the winter months, especially around 3,7 p V. Captains are advised not to attempt the crossing in the dark months of winter. Sea conditions can be unstable and storms occur.

The Empire has received numerous reports of sea snakes infesting the waters surrounding the islands off the coast of Hallovia. As this archipelago includes numerous uncharted isles, it has been difficult to confirm sightings.

Captains are advised to set course north of the Jamaiian isles or pay ransom to pirates.

Hallovia

Empire of Agasan

Rimaldi

Caladria

Farozhar (the Sacred City)

Sea of Agasan

Tregarion

Islands of Jamaii

N

Shor
Edennar

Calgary
Aracine

Gandrel Forest

Dannyr

Devon
Towermount   Stradtford
                  Acacia

Jeunie

Chalons-en-les Trois

Valdére

Veneisea

Vionne-Sur-Le Valle
                            Rogue Valley

Xanthe

Cair Xeroea   Cair Rethyn

              Cair Palea

Bay of Jewels

              Cair Thessalon

Bem

Kroth

Dheanainn

MAP OF ALORIN

Eastwatch
Wynne
Tambarré
Saldaria
M'Nador
Nahavand
Taj'al Jabanna
Tal'Shira
Sand Sea
Raku
Abu'Dhan
Haden Gorge
Ka'alil
Sakkalaah
Qar'imali
Akkad Emirates
Duan'Bai
Forsaken Lands

Myacene
Fire Sea
Avatar
Vest

The Middle Kingdoms of Alorin

Charted on behalf of the Empress by the Imperial Cartographer on this date of 517aV to reflect the missing island of Cair Tiern'aval, which vanished from the Bay of Jewels circa 497aV.

Additional maps can be found online at MelissaMcPhail.com

The Middle Kingdoms

Shoring Isles
Edennar

Calgaryn
Aracine

Gandrel Forest
Dannym

Devon
Eastwatch
Stradtford
Towermount
Glaiss R.
Acacia
Highlands
Wynne
Elvior
Morwyk
Jeune
Tambarré
Chalons-en-les Trois
Kandori
Saldaria
Valdère
Doane
Veneisea
M'Nad
Nahavand
Taj al'Ja
Tregarion
Sand Sea
Vienne-Sur-Le Valle
Raku
Rogue Valley
Xanthe
Haden Gorge
Olivine
Sakkalaah
Qar'ima
Cair Xersea
Cair Rethynnea
Akkad Emirates
Duan'
Bay of Jewels
Cair Palea'andos

Cair Thessalonia

Shi'ma
Bemoth
Kroth
Malchiarr
Forsaken Lands

Dheanainn

N

M'Nador & Surrounding Kingdoms

45th parallel, where electric
of Mt. Veut have been know

Wynne

...ess Range

...rambarré

Saldaria

Dhahari Range

M'Nador

Tal'S...

Nahavand

Taj al'Jahanna

Sand Sea

Raku

Kutsamak Mtns

Abu'Dhan

Mt. Attarak

Haden Gorge

Qar'imali

Sakkalaah

Cry R.

Akkad Emirates

Duan'Bai

At the tim...
Avatar V...

PART ONE

"You cannot sculpt a piece into a Player. A Player must mold himself out of fortitude and conviction."

–The Fifth Vestal Björn van Gelderan

PROLOGUE

Several weeks ago...

THE NADORI REGIMENT Commander Nassar abin'Ahram stood in his tent beneath the shadow of an overhanging ridge at his high camp of Ramala, trying to discern a dot winding its way across the desert. Even in the shade, the heat was unrelenting.

Why did the desert grow hotter in the last hours of the day? It was as if the earth's fiery core emitted one final enormous belch just before the world pitched into another chilling night.

Nassar squinted through wavering lines of heat at the wandering dot winding its way through a landscape of fissures and dry crevasses as deadly as any that marred the northern reaches. Without a clear heading, it was nearly impossible to find his high campsite, which clung as lichen to the under-shadows of the ridge. The only visitors Nassar saw were hawks…and scouts who already knew the route.

As the dot grew larger, he recognized the Dannish Captain Jasper val Renly. Nassar knew Jasper well, for the captain had the unenviable task of relaying orders from the Dannish leadership to their soldiers scattered in outposts across M'Nador.

When M'Nador's war with the Akkad had been at its height, Jasper's duty had kept him in constant danger. Nassar had often worried for him, and he'd regularly included him in his nightly devotions. But since the Akkadian Emir had brought out his Mage, who in turn had summoned those Sundragons from Azerjaiman knew where; since M'Nador's catastrophic loss on the Khalim Plains, where two thousand men had been reduced to ashes and dust…well, the war produced more stalemates than skirmishes now, though Nassar had heard that the Qar'imali was still seeing its share of battle.

Sundragons...

Nassar was of two minds about the Sundragons. On the one hand, they'd slain some of M'Nador's best captains in the early days of the campaign—*may Inithiya take their spirits to Jai'Gar*. On the other hand, fewer lives had been lost on both sides since the dragons appeared, and Nassar supposed that was to everyone's benefit—*Jai'Gar be praised*.

Still...he would've liked to have put a barrage of arrows into the dragons' hides, one for every Nadori soldier the creatures had slain—*may Huhktu claim their bones*. This retribution seemed only fair. But nothing harmed the beasts short of magic, and even then, Prince Radov's wielders had to endanger themselves working the fifth strand of *elae* to so much as make a dent in the dragons' general indifference.

Nassar had witnessed these battles: daylight skirmishes where explosions of blinding light had engulfed the flying dragons, who responded with fireballs like miniature suns that evaporated entire mountainsides and left craters in the earth; and midnight battles where lightning repeatedly blanketed the heavens, smoldering evening clouds forming the stage for dances of flashing fire.

All of this had imparted to Nassar a healthy respect for the dragons' power. His soldiers warded themselves against the dragons with superstitious marks and talismans, while his officers cursed the beasts and called them demons, but Nassar didn't believe the dragons were inherently evil. They were no different, really, from any other who stood to defend their way of life.

No...war stood out as the true evil in their time—Nassar knew this as Jai'Gar's own will, for his conscience spoke it nightly. War offered opportunity to the worst sort of scoundrels while making murderers of honest men.

The afternoon sun had fallen behind the Ramala escarpment by the time Jasper val Renly came straggling into Nassar's camp, looking as bedraggled as a coyote who'd been weeks separated from its pack.

Nassar observed Jasper as the captain handed off his horse to one of the Dannish soldiers, pulled the cap from his head and pushed a hand through damp, sun-streaked hair. For all Jasper appeared bone-weary, Nassar perceived an urgency within his movements and in his gaze.

Nassar lifted a hand to him, both a welcome and a summons.

The captain fitted his cap back on and trudged uphill to Nassar's command tent. He stopped just beyond the open drapes, pressed palms together and bowed deeply. "*As-salaam'alaykum, al-Amir.*" *Peace be upon you, Commander.*

Nassar pressed palms and bowed slightly as he murmured the traditional reply, "*Wa'alaykum salaam*, Jasper val Renly." He waved his steward to bring a goblet of *siri* for the weary captain. "You have seen hard riding, Jasper of the North. What brings you to this remote pinning between dust and sky?"

Jasper accepted the *siri* and drank it all in a few deep swallows. Then he pressed the back of one hand to his mouth. "Prince Radov and my king go to parley with the Akkadian Emir. By now they should have commenced their meeting beneath the tents of peace."

"Jai'Gar willing," Nassar added with a prayerful glance to the heavens. The Dannish soldiers were often making claims without asking the blessing of the gods. Perhaps the god who ruled in the north cast an indifferent eye to blasphemous oversights, but Nassar knew his own gods were not so forgiving.

He motioned for his steward, and the man came again with the pitcher to refill both their goblets. Nassar raised his. "To peace, and an end to this conflict of brothers."

"To peace." Jasper downed the *siri* again.

Nassar arched brows. Something had the young captain on edge, but somehow he doubted it was a meeting of kings. "Come and join me, Captain." He motioned to a pair of camp chairs. "I would hear what else from Tal'Shira and afar."

"And I would tell you what I know, *al-Amir*, but I must speak with the Lieutenant Evryn val Lynne posthaste and give him this news and more from the kingdom." Jasper placed his hand on the satchel at his hip by way of indicating his meaning.

Jasper often carried letters to the men from their loved ones while upon more important travels for his king and duke. Nassar respected the way the Northmen kept in contact with one another. Soldiers were far more willing to give up their lives for another man's fight when their own personal needs were met.

Nassar snapped his fingers meaningfully, and his steward darted off to fetch Lieutenant val Lynne. "Farouk shall return with your lieutenant momentarily, Captain. At last look, he was inspecting the ridge fortifications and will need some time to make his way back to us. Until then, sit—by Huhktu's bones, you look as if you haven't slept in days."

Jasper dutifully sank down onto the indicated seat. Nassar retrieved the pitcher of *siri* and refilled the captain's cup for a third time himself. Perhaps if the man imbibed enough spirit it would loosen his tongue. Nassar embraced any distraction to alleviate the tedium of his days. A man could only pray so much.

"Now tell me," he eyed the captain as he retook his own chair, "why the haste? Clearly you've been many days ahorse."

"Your eyes do you credit, *al-Amir*—though I suppose my weariness is obvious." He gave an apologetic smile. "Several weeks ago, His Majesty King Gydryn val Lorian summoned me personally to attend him in Tal'Shira. There, he gave me new orders." A flicker of something crossed the young captain's brow upon this memory. "He bade me deliver the parley news to every one of our outposts, so that our commanders might know when the parley began and be heartened by it."

"That is a considerable undertaking."

"Verily. I've been riding solidly for several weeks and have visited nearly every one of Dannym's regiments."

Nassar shook his head. "Would that I had more to offer you than *siri*."

"It is more than many have offered. For your hospitality, I pray Azerjaiman sends you many blessings on Qharp's fair winds."

Nassar's gaze betrayed a certain skepticism. "That I might live to see the end of this war, if Jai'Gar wills it, would be blessing enough." He stroked his dark beard alternately with fingers and knuckles, eyeing Jasper all the while. The man sat calmly enough, but Nassar sensed that inside the captain was bouncing like a jumping bean on a sun-heated stone. But whatever Jasper had on his mind, it clearly wasn't something he intended to share, so Nassar didn't press. An honorable man didn't interrogate his guests simply to assuage his own boredom.

Still…there were topics certain to be safe between them. "You were in Tal'Shira recently? What news from the capital?"

Jasper sipped at his *siri*. "Refugees are flooding in from Abu'Dhan, the Qar'imali and other parts of the south where the fighting continues. Departing Tal'Shira now means hours of navigating through refugee camps."

Nassar exhaled a slow breath. "The Qar'imali…" he shook his head and gave Jasper a regretful look, "wars within wars…this is what we see with the fighting in the south. The tribal blood lives in long tattoos on the arms of such men, recounting their lineage decades back, but ink is all that binds their loyalties now, and ink was ever a weak substitute for virtue."

Jasper gazed long upon him. For some reason, he looked disconcerted by Nassar's observation.

As Nassar was wondering what the captain had on his mind but wouldn't say, he noticed a distant shadow passing among the sparse clouds of sunset. He watched the dragon's passage through the heavens with a slight frown narrowing his brow.

"One has to wonder why the Emir doesn't send his Mage or his

Sundragons south to end the conflict in the Qar'imali," he posed thoughtfully, "or at least to stalemate it, as they have done here."

Jasper noted the direction of Nassar's attention and turned to look over his shoulder at the dark glint of a dragon flying among the violet clouds. "I've seen what they can do. A single Sundragon could vaporize an entire company—perhaps a whole battalion—if it stood unopposed. Combined, they could end this war." He turned a frown back to Nassar.

"But then where would we be," Nassar shifted a sobering look to Jasper, "with a Sundragon as our king?"

A fervent muttering from afar drew both their gazes, and soon the turbaned head of Lieutenant Evryn val Lynne came into view, followed closely by Nassar's servant, Farouk.

Nassar held up a hand in greeting. "Ah, Evryn. Give welcome to Jasper val Renly. The captain has braved the distance to bring news to you from your king."

Jasper stood quickly. His right hand automatically went to the satchel at his hip, as a soldier taking comfort in the presence of his sword. "Perhaps we could retire to your tent, Lieutenant, and leave the *al-Amir* the privacy of his own?"

Evryn looked inquiringly to Nassar. "With your permission, Commander?"

"Of course."

The Northmen departed, and Nassar exhaled a slow, disappointed sigh. He foresaw no stories shared in his tent that night, no new tales brought from afar. *Ah well…* a quiet evening at least offered another opportunity for prayer. Perhaps this would be the night his gods blessed him with an answer.

Nassar thought no more of Captain Jasper val Renly as he went about his evening inspections, nor later as he knelt on his pallet and gave thanks for the many blessings of his life; nor even as he labored through a fitful sleep, awoken several times by unusual sounds out of the darkness.

In fact, he spared barely a thought for Jasper until the dawn light brightened the canvas of his tent and he emerged with a yawn—

And found the entire Dannish contingent had made off like thieves in the night.

Then he thought of Captain Jasper val Renly quite fervently.

ONE

*"He is a plate spinning on Balance's needle,
likely to topple in any direction."*

–Dhábu'balaji'ṣridanaí, He Who Walks the Edge
of the World, on Ean val Lorian

"SHE ASKS THE impossible!" Sebastian val Lorian threw down the charcoal pencil he'd been using and fell back forcefully back in his chair. He scowled across the worktable at Dareios.

The Kandori prince's colorless eyes were fixed on a pattern he was penning with meticulous care, but he arched a triangular brow at Sebastian's comment. The motion wrinkled the dark tattoo of the *Khoda Panaheh* on his forehead. "The impossible..." his lips curved upwards at the corners. "I don't think the word falls within Isabel's vernacular."

Sebastian shifted his gaze to the monolith that was Isabel's staff, which was occupying a corner of Dareios's laboratory. When Isabel had tossed the staff to him back in Ivarnen, Sebastian had believed she was giving it to him for safekeeping, to watch over until she could return to claim it. Now he felt more like the staff was watching him.

It didn't seem overly pleased by his progress.

Sebastian plucked at the stitching on the arm of his chair. "We've been at this for weeks, with barely a scrap to show for our efforts." Indeed, the worktable between them bore marks of dedicated abuse—piles of discarded papers, charcoal dust, ink smears, and everywhere the ash of their failure.

Dareios dipped his pin in a pot of ink and looked up under his brows. "She wouldn't have given us the task if it couldn't be accomplished."

Sebastian grunted sourly. "Would that I shared your faith."

'...*Tell Ean he has to find a way to unmake entire companies of these creatures in one blow. Tell Dareios I said to use* invertéré *patterns if he must...*'

Isabel's admonishment during those last fevered moments at Ivarnen had become a torment to Sebastian. He and Dareios were trying to find a pattern—rather, a matrix of patterns working in concert—that would allow any wielder to unwork an *eidola,* or at least disrupt its connection to its master in such a way that the creature lost animation. They'd been upon the task day and night, ever since Sebastian stepped off the node from Ivarnen carrying a barely conscious Rhys val Kincaide and with his youngest brother as a haunted shell of himself.

And as much darkness as they'd already endured, Isabel's warning only seemed a portent of worse yet to come.

Dareios set his pen on its stand, folded fingers on the table and settled his colorless gaze on Sebastian. "Are you going to go talk to Ean?"

"He won't listen to me." Sebastian shifted his gaze to meet Dareios's, only to realize that the truthreader had been referencing another matter entirely than the one occupying Sebastian's thoughts. Understanding pinched sharply behind his eyes. "Thirteen hells—did Isabel visit your dreams last night, too?"

"*Preyed upon them* might be a better description." Dareios traced his forefinger along one triangular eyebrow. "I fear if it takes us too much longer to get Ean to comply with her wishes, the Prophetess will visit my mother in *her* dreams." He winced at the prospect. "We must head off such a catastrophe at all costs, Sebastian."

Sebastian frowned down at the half-finished pattern on the parchment in front of him.

Dareios sat back in his chair with a sigh. "I never would've given Ean that pattern if I'd known he would use it to keep Isabel from communicating with him."

Ean had been plagued by troubling dreams ever since Ivarnen, dreams that had so disturbed him that he'd finally asked Dareios for a pattern to ward his mind while he slept. Sebastian well understood the malaise of ill dreams. Dore still haunted his.

"Yes," the truthreader murmured, obviously catching Sebastian's thought, "my palace is full of men with ghosts."

Sebastian plucked at the arm of his chair. "If you hadn't given Ean that pattern to ward his dreams, he only would've worked it out some other way." If there was anything he'd learned about his youngest brother, it was that Ean's ingenuity knew no bounds—of imagination, prudence, or even the near side of common sense. Sebastian slid further down in his chair and leaned his head back against the cushion. "I wish I knew how to get through to Ean. Everything I say just glides off his stubbornness like water over an oilskin cloak."

"A mind once set can become as immutable as granite." Dareios exhaled a sigh redolent of personal experience. "Sometimes all we can do is chip away at its immutable face and pray our blows miraculously hit a fault."

Sebastian gave him the quirk of a smile. "Is that another of your Kandori sayings?"

"Nay, Prince of Dannym, it's the experience of a man with eight sisters and an Agasi wife. In Kandori, stubbornness is more abundant than jewels." He winked at him. "Now that *is* one of our proverbs." Dareios picked up his pen. "Go, my friend. Ean needs you, and we need him. In the meantime, I will press on. The steps of today's disheartenment become the path of tomorrow's success."

Sebastian pushed resignedly out of his chair. "I should've been raised in Kandori. You've a saying for every state of existence."

Dareios placed the point of his pen and his attention back on the pattern he was inking. "Never fear, Prince of Dannym." He arched a brow wryly as he drew a curving line. "If you continue courting my sister Ehsan, she will surely educate you in all of them."

With his mind split between worrying for Ean and contemplating when next he would see Ehsan—*thank you, Dareios, for putting the distraction of your gorgeous sister so firmly in my thoughts*—Sebastian set off towards the laboratory where Ean was working.

His brother had claimed the most distant of Dareios's workrooms, supposedly for the safety of others—in case a pattern he was testing went awry—but Sebastian suspected the arrow of Ean's true motives was aimed at solitude, which he seemed to crave since returning from Ivarnen.

Whatever else was plaguing Ean, it certainly wasn't helped by the Lord Captain Rhys val Kincaide's condition. After all they'd sacrificed and endured to save him, if Rhys didn't survive…Sebastian feared what it would do to Ean.

Dareios' Adept sisters had done all they could to shore up the captain's pattern, but he'd contracted an illness during his captivity—which imprisonment Sebastian, as Işak'getirmek, was to blame for—and the malaise had set in deeply; only time would tell if he could make a full recovery. Until they deemed him safe from Death's reach, Dareios's sisters were keeping Rhys unconscious in a Healing sleep.

Still, Ehsan believed that Rhys' prognosis looked promising, and her words had heartened Ean—that is, until several days after they'd returned from Ivarnen. That's when desolation's spear had struck his little brother.

They'd been working the *cortata* together on the sand court, stripped to their waists beneath the warm springtime sun while Dareios's gaggle of sisters watched behind veils that hid their whispers but not their admiring eyes. Sebastian had just been lifting his sword for another swing when Ean stilled, as if suddenly paralyzed. Then his face had become a mask of anguish. His fingers went slack, his blade fell to the sand, and he dropped to his knees while the currents went mad.

Sebastian hadn't known what to do. He'd gone to one knee, placed a hand on his brother's shoulder, and remained silently at his side this way for close to an hour. All the while, the riotous currents had wreaked such havoc on his senses that he'd suffered a headache for two days afterwards.

Following the event, Ean had refused to speak to anyone. Even a visit from Rhakar with good news of their brother Trell's rescue from Darroyhan had failed to guide Ean out of his black overcast.

Over the last fortnight, however, Sebastian had managed to pry an explanation out of his brother for what had occurred that day. Just bits and pieces, what little Ean knew—mostly he'd sketched a rough outline and filled it with conjecture—but now, no amount of reason from Sebastian could make Ean see any other shape than the one he'd drawn.

He found his brother standing on the laboratory balcony with his hands braced on the railing. A late spring breeze was rustling the garden trees and pushing ashen clouds across the sky, but Ean was so encased in the fifth that the wind darted around his form, disturbing neither his hair nor his clothing.

"I eliminated five more patterns last night," Ean said without turning.

Sebastian paused in the open archway. He had no idea how Ean was testing the patterns to determine their effectiveness at destroying *eidola*; he wasn't sure he wanted to know. "Dareios has a dozen more for you to try when you're ready."

"Fine. I'll do them tonight." Ean dropped his chin to his chest. He was gripping the railing so tightly that his knuckles were white.

Sebastian took a tentative step into the raging fifth—it felt like a wall of wind pressing against him. He couldn't tell if Ean was holding the fifth on purpose or if it was boiling in response to his mood. "Are you all right, little brother?"

Ean speared a hangdog stare at him. "How could I possibly be all right?" He clenched his jaw and returned his gaze to the valley, where the crater made by their fall, weeks earlier, made a pock in the fertile plain. "I'm not sure I even know what 'all right' means," Ean muttered as an afterthought, "but I'm fairly sure it doesn't apply to me in any possible sense."

Sebastian frowned and exhaled a slow breath. He well knew his brother's mind. Verily, Ean had shared everything with him—the fullness of his tale from the moment he'd set foot on the mainland to now and all of his dreamed memories—yet for all Ean's recent hard experience, he was still sorely unacquainted with the vagaries of love.

Of course, trying to *explain* this to him...

"Ean," Sebastian sought another route into the quagmire of Ean's obstinate resolve, "you can't *know* that Isabel—"

"I know what I perceived, Sebastian." Ean tightened his grip on the railing. "I sensed it would happen even before she left, and I felt its truth the moment our bond was restored. She's betrayed our troth."

Sebastian winced at the vitriol in his brother's tone. "That's conjecture at best—"

Ean spun him a fierce glare. "I'm *not* wrong."

Sebastian held his brother's gaze. "There is one way to be sure."

Ean grunted and looked back to the valley.

Since Ean clearly wasn't going to release the fifth any time soon, Sebastian braved the tumultuous vortex to join his side. The hairs on his arms were standing on end as he placed his hands on the railing and stood shoulder to shoulder with his youngest brother.

"Isabel visited Dareios and me in our dreams last night. She asked us to deliver a message to you." He cast Ean a sidelong eye. "She wants you to stop warding your dreams so she can speak to you."

Ean worked the muscles of his jaw. "She knows where to find me."

"Yes, and I trust she would've come in person if she could have."

The currents were seething with Ean's indignation. "I have nothing to say to her. She laid with another man."

Sebastian took a deep breath and a firm hold upon his patience. "Let's say you're right, Ean."

Ean gave him a look that said he clearly was.

"Will you deny her an opportunity to explain? She must've had a good reason for what she did—*thirteen hells*, she sacrificed herself to save the three of us! That act alone should secure your willingness to hear her side of things." He searched Ean's face for even a flicker of willingness. "Ean, it's Isabel we're talking about here—"

"Yes, *Isabel*." The currents rippled beneath his sounding of her name.

Sebastian pointed out as gently as he could, "You know she understands far more than we do about this game."

Ean thrust a glare at him, dual-shafted of fury and despair. "Tell me this, brother. If her actions stand above reproach, why does she feel such guilt? Oh, yes," he glowered in response to Sebastian's surprise, "Isabel's side of the bond is *saturated* with regret."

Ean directed his gaze back towards the dark line of the Dhahari Mountains. "Now I'm bound to her and bound to this game…and I would be free of both of them."

"Ean…you don't mean that."

Ean gave him a look that said he absolutely did.

Sebastian searched his brother's face. To his relief, he saw more than a lover's wounded pride there. "It's not just Isabel, is it?" He looked Ean over, trying to decipher the impressions he was getting. "It's not this task she set for us either, so…is it the dreams that have you in such a black humor?"

After a moment, Ean bowed his head, a silent acknowledgment.

Sebastian arched brows. "It's that bad?"

Ean worked the muscles of his jaw, staring off. "In Rethynnea, when Rinokh invaded my thoughts, I was sure my brain was going to explode." He looked balefully to Sebastian. "That was before he broke every bone in my body. And when he licked his thumb and cast his power into me, I could feel it etching my soul, corroding my connection to *elae*…dissolving *me*."

"Shade and darkness, Ean—"

Ean looked back to the view. "These dreams are nearly as bad."

Sebastian stared at his brother with concern narrowing his brows. "And Dareios's pattern of warding…?"

"It works." Ean clenched his jaw. "Some of the time."

Sebastian pushed the hair from his eyes, not knowing what to say. Words were a shallow consolation in any case.

Ean pressed himself away from the railing and hung his head between his arms. "If they were just dreams…I don't know—I'd like to think I could endure them. But these visions are invested with peril and purpose, and a desperate sense of loss so devastating and *real*…"

Sebastian regarded Ean more closely. "What do you mean, 'if they were just dreams'?"

Ean turned his head to look at him. "All the time, Sebastian—they're coming at me *all the time*. I can barely think for the barrage of images. Only the fifth seems to hold them off, so I hold onto it for as long as I can."

He was describing an experience Sebastian himself had known when Dore's patterns concealing his true past had finally burst. His heart went out to his brother. "They're memories, Ean?"

Ean rested forearms on the balustrade. "I told you how so much of Arion's knowledge of Patterning had come back to me, yes?" He worked the muscles of his jaw while staring off. "It hasn't been without cost."

Sebastian leaned his hip against the railing. "Little brother, I've seen you do things with the fourth strand that made even Dareios arch a brow. *Ean*..." Sebastian bent to capture Ean's bleakly absent gaze, "what if this experience is your own doing?"

Ean blinked. Then he straightened. "What do you mean?"

Sebastian tossed his blowing hair out of his eyes. "When you were instructing me in how to escape the Labyrinth, you suggested leaving clues for myself, even as you had done."

"Yes, but—"

"The Labyrinth is a fourth-strand construct, right?"

Ean nodded.

"So...couldn't there be other fourth-strand constructs—layered patterns that bind memories and thoughts together?"

"I suppose, but—"

"Ean, what if these dreams—these *memories* so plaguing you—what if they're something you did? What if binding his memories into a fourth-strand construct was the only way Arion knew to restore his memories to himself—to you—in a future life?"

Ean regarded him with a furrowed brow.

"He could've done it as a last desperate act." The idea was claiming a firmer place in Sebastian's conviction the more he considered it. "That's why the memories have such peril and purpose embedded in them. Somehow you've broken the vessel that contained them, and now they're trying to find their rightful place in your recollection."

Ean's frown deepened.

Sebastian looked his brother over. "Isabel told me that I should try to help you remember your past, and we've been doing that together. But now I'm starting to think you don't need me at all. You only need to trust yourself and let these memories come—however painful they may be. You just need to—"

"Have faith in my path?" Ean's tone held an echo of emptiness.

Sebastian held his gaze. "As Isabel would say, what else is there for us to do but walk it?"

❖

Ean stood on the balcony outside his bedchamber watching the Kandori sky darken behind the Eidenglass Range. He stayed there until all that remained of the day was a fiery line beneath a greenish glow. Overhead, a storm was blowing in and rapidly consuming the clear night, even as memories belonging to another man were overtaking Ean's thoughts.

He'd released the fifth; likewise Dareios's fourth-strand pattern. Now the rising wind buffeted him, much in concert with the images pounding his overtaxed mind.

Had the heterogeneous pictures come with some point of reference, some context in which to frame them, he might've...well, not *welcomed* them, but at least found relief in finally gaining some understanding. But they flashed into being and out again like spears crossing left or right of the mark, leaving him reeling from the confusing echo of their passing.

His father had spoken to him once about different kinds of bravery—on the field of battle, in ruling disparate peoples, in maintaining one's sense of integrity amid the politics of kings—but King Gydryn had never mentioned the inherent bravery of admitting fault, or in the claiming of responsibility for another man's sins.

Inarguably, Ean was remembering actions from Arion's life. Yet if they were not also somehow his own acts, why did he feel such a grave sense of conscience surrounding them? In the same breath he felt entirely disconnected from the man he'd once been yet wholly bound to Arion's choices and deeds. It was so difficult, this odd mishmash of sensations—the vernal hopes of a young man warring against a dead man's failures, with a thorny vein of betrayal threaded throughout it all.

Ean wanted to be able to assign this feeling of betrayal entirely to Isabel's recent treason; yet in moments when clarity and reason prevailed, he deeply feared that this sense of betrayal was an echo of some guilt *he* harbored over Arion's choices—deeds as yet unknown and hidden, their truth denied him. The two layering betrayals had become inextricably entwined, even as his life and Arion's had become, even as he and Isabel were.

He stayed on the balcony until the night turned black—long hours being chilled by the buffeting wind—and only sought his bed when an icy spring rain drove him inside. Then he lay in darkness for another long while, trying not to think about anything, yet over-thinking everything.

Finally, he fell asleep...

And found himself in Isabel's chambers in Niyadbakir.

A wall of mullioned doors stood open to admit the evening breeze, which was fluttering the sheer curtains. Wielder's lamps in wall sconces cast a golden glow across the room, imparting a jeweled quality to the air. Ean looked around, seeing sumptuous couches...

And at the far end of the room, haloed by the diffuse light, Isabel.

It hurt Ean to see her. It hurt him more to feel suddenly denied the right to gather her into his arms, as if she'd become another man's property since they separated at Ivarnen. He stood in the well of his own silence, bound by walls of emotion that found no expression.

Isabel folded an opalescent robe about her form and came towards him, tying the sash. Her chestnut hair draped long across one shoulder. She was not wearing her blindfold.

Why wasn't she wearing her blindfold now of all bloody times? Did she think to encourage his forgiveness with the blessing of her colorless gaze? It only infuriated him more that she'd revealed her eyes to him at a time when such a scar of anger prevented his enjoyment of it. For some unfathomable reason, this hurt Ean the most.

In that moment, if his gaze could have injured her as deeply as her betrayal had wounded him, he would have allowed it to do so. In the next moment, he turned away.

"Ean..." Her voice both entreated and caressed him through the bond with an unwelcome, yet desperately missed, intimacy.

"I've come because you demanded it." Ean felt like his body had been strung along the fine edge of a blade, with betrayal's weighty hand forcing him down along the razor length. "But you've no right to engage with me intimately, Isabel. Not now."

She stared at him for a moment's startled pause. Then she said quietly, "Very well. Thank you for coming."

Ean clenched his jaw. It made him feel no better to injure her as she'd injured him—*damn it all.*

He sensed more than saw her moving closer. "Sebastian told me Rhys is recovering and that you're working to find a way to destroy the *eidola*."

"Is that why you've made me come? To hear the progress I've made on the tasks you assigned me?"

He felt her uncertainty in her hesitation, sensed its tugging along their bond. He'd halted her approach with the venom in his tone. Now she stood five paces away, all but demanding his attention with the stillness of her thoughts.

"At Ivarnen..." Isabel was gazing levelly at him, but Ean got the impression that she stood with her back to the wall, bravely facing a line of archers. "Darshan was coming for you, Ean. He'd latched onto your life pattern when you unworked his *eidola*, and he was following you on the currents. I did what I could to protect you."

Ean turned her a cold stare. "What you did at Ivarnen isn't at issue, Isabel."

"Ean..." the slightest hint of frustration came into her tone, "there are things you need to know—"

"All I need to know is did you lay with him?" his words cracked like lightning through the bond.

Isabel held his gaze, but hers was deeply troubled. "Yes."

Ean clenched his jaw and turned away. Fury boiled violently in his chest; if he'd been in his body instead of Dreamscape, the currents would've been fulminating.

"Ean, will you allow me to explain?"

"What is there to explain?" he returned tightly, barely able to find breath. "You made your choice. You walked your *path*. Doesn't that justify anything you chose to do?"

She cringed beneath the heat in his tone.

Suddenly he felt too full of anger and wanted nothing near him. He headed for the doors and the balcony beyond, seeking the space of the open night, that it might afford him room to breathe.

Isabel followed hesitantly after him. She paused in the doorway while he walked towards the far end. "Knowing what you do now, Ean…if given the chance to potentially shift the balance of the game, but at a great and terrible cost…what would *you* chose?"

Ean grabbed the railing and then pressed himself away from it, hanging his head between his arms. He couldn't care less about Björn's bloody game.

"Ean?"

He swung her a heated glare. "If your choice was justified, Isabel, then why do you feel such guilt over the act?"

She stood in the doorway haloed by the room's golden light. Her face was in shadow, but he felt the apology in her gaze and knew she sought his forgiveness. Her emotions pelted him like rain upon a still pond: contrition, compassion, desire for atonement…

"I knew the choice would hurt you," she murmured, "despite its importance to the game."

"*Despite*…" Ean turned his head and met her gaze, though it hurt to look at her at all. "Do you really think I don't understand that you're a woman of two paths? You've made it abundantly clear, Isabel." Indeed, he knew *why* she'd done it, if not why she'd needed to. Still, walking two paths didn't change the fact that she'd given herself to another man.

No, not another man. A *Malorin'athgul*.

Ean suppressed an oath and pushed away from the railing.

"Darshan gave me to his brother Pelas." Her words chased after him as he stalked away from her—

"I woke in a tower, bound in *goracrosta*."

—lassoed his chest and pulled tight—

"Darshan had compelled Pelas against his will to maim and kill Healers."

—halting him with a sudden jerk—

"He intended for Pelas to kill me as well."

—and rooted him agonizingly to the patio stones.

When Ean managed to turn around, he saw that she'd closed the distance between them. Now she stood near enough that he could see a luminous tracing on her skin between the open folds of her silk robe. From afar, he'd thought the swirling patterns had been stitched into the silk. Now he saw that the light was emanating from etchings in her skin—*carvings*—as if engraved there.

"*Light of Epiphany*, Isabel..." the words barely escaped the vice of his shock. He pushed her robe from one shoulder to view the pattern that covered it. He thought he'd known horror in envisioning the act of her betrayal; the truth far surpassed anything he'd imagined.

When he placed his fingers on the pattern, she flinched and caught her breath.

His eyes flew back to hers. "Didn't Björn Heal you?"

Her lips were pressed together tightly. "The patterns aren't responding to Healing...not in the way we expected."

Ean abruptly released her. "What does *that* mean?" He stared at the silvery patterns in her skin with an unnamable horror. "What in thirteen hells did he *do* to you?"

She gingerly pulled her robe back up over her shoulder. "I'm healing, Ean. Just...slowly."

Ean stared at her uncomprehendingly. "Are you saying *you* don't know—that *Björn* doesn't know how to Heal these marks?"

"They're patterns of Chaos, Ean," she murmured resolutely. "They don't respond to *elae*."

"He carved *Chaos* patterns into your flesh?" Ean shoved both hands into his hair and spun away, desperate to incinerate someone. Pelas would've been ideal. A litany of violent curses chased across his tongue, but he couldn't find the breath to voice any of them. They wouldn't have been dark enough, in any case.

He paced at the end of the balcony with his hands clenched into fists, feeling as if the realm was too small to contain his fury. Then a horrifying thought stilled him. He looked darkly to her. "And when it was all done—he'd carved you up, marked you as his own and bedded you...then what? You just watched him walk away?"

She stood in the path of his wrath, letting it buffet her without protesting, her colorless gaze entreating his understanding. "If I had harmed him for harming me, Ean, it would've defeated the purpose of saving him."

"*Saving* him." Derision sliced his tone. "From *what*, pray, were you *saving* him? He's an immortal being, Isabel!"

"Pelas has chosen a path now, Ean." Clearly she was hoping he could see the reason in her acts. He could tell that his anger was painful to her, that each comment left a pock in her resolve, expanding craters of uncertainty. "He's pledged himself to the survival of this world…to *our* game."

Ean worked the muscles of his jaw. The things he wanted to say were too cruel, and he only wounded himself every time he wounded her. Would that she might've suffered the same affliction.

"And then?" he ground out the words through the millstone of his ire. "I suppose he just blithely carried you back to T'khendar?"

She pressed her lips together, perhaps invoking strength. "I summoned Phaedor."

Her words were daggers in his heart. "You could've called *me*," he scraped out. "You *should've* called me!"

She gave him a desperate look. "It's Phaedor's role, Ean…to protect us."

Ean stared at her, unbelieving. "And what is *my* role in your life?" He stopped her reply with an upraised hand. "No, don't say anything." The same hand pushed the hair back from his face and then fell listlessly to his side. Somehow he'd rounded rage's pinnacle and was now plummeting down the far side of disbelief. His emotions tumbled along behind him in voluminous clouds of malcontent, growing blacker with every breath.

Suddenly all he could think about was how he'd died three times for this game. Ean rubbed his face with both hands and then pressed palms to his eyes…his temples. He looked at her between the brace of his arms. "What is it we're doing, you and me?"

Isabel's expression grew alarmed. Well she knew that tone in his voice. "Ean…"

He interwove his fingers behind his head and lifted his gaze towards a Dreamscape sky, his palms pressing hard against his temples, though they did little to ward off the swarming feeling in his skull. "Are you just patronizing me with your affection, condescending to sleep with me until the man you *actually* love finally raises his head again?"

"Please, Ean, you can't really think I would—"

He dropped his arms and speared a glare at her. "You offered yourself in sacrifice to the enemy!"

"Who is an *enemy* no longer—"

"Because you whored yourself for his allegiance!" He grabbed the railing and pushed away from it again. He didn't think he could take much more of this. "Phaedor…Pelasommáyurek…" His breath came ragged; his heart lay in shards at his feet. "You'd choose stallions for your stable and make a gelding of me."

She caught her breath.

Ean clenched his jaw. "Why did you want me to bind with you anew?"

That time he saw desperation come into her gaze, felt it vibrating along their bond. "I thought…" her voice came faintly, "I thought I would be helping you."

Ean straightened away from the railing to face her, but his jaw felt slack, his body drained of life. She'd devastated him with her choice. "Well…I pray that's the end of it. I don't think I can survive any more of your help."

He gave her one last look. Then, with a grave force of will, he threw himself from the dream.

TWO

"There is no turning back upon the road to truth. One must walk it to the bloody end."

–Morin d'Hain, Spymaster of Dannym

ACROSS THE MIDDLE Kingdoms of Alorin, Old Night had staked her claim. She'd drawn a blanket of clouds over the northeastern province of Saldaria and its sleeping city of Tambarré and now stood a jealous watch, that the nimble Dawn might not disturb these lands too quickly. She ruled the dark with a hag's churlish mood, and the dreams she delivered to Tambarré's sleeping occupants held the sharp tang of her festering resentment.

When the world had been young and the mountains new, Night would come bearing gifts. She would sprinkle the firmament with stars and limn all things in moonsilver. Lovers would dally sweet and long beneath her auspicious gaze. Men became bold, and women more beautiful; babes grew stronger, children taller, and old men found peaceful rest. Bravery, hope, courage, faith—all such treasures were easily found by those who wished for them. The sleeping dreamed of whatever they most desired.

But as the ages turned, Night saw her gifts misused, her blessings twisted to bring harm, her sweet, candied dreams feeding envy and greed. Over the centuries, Old Night beheld too many disappointments: innocence sacrificed, lovers lost; men spilling one another's blood for want of dirt or bits of metal, battling armies taking advantage of her dark veils to advance vengeful atrocities.

Old Night couldn't recall when compassion had left her. It had run away with the jealous moon one night and never returned. In its absence, she'd become distempered, inconstant, vengeful. No longer did she convey ephemeral dreams of sweetness and hope, for men would only twist their fragile constructs into violent shapes. Now she gave them dreams of wrath, for this darkness was all they cared for.

Darshanvenkhátraman, Destroyer of Hope, was no less prey to Old Night's foul temper than the rest of Tambarré's sleeping occupants. As she spread ill across her demesne, Darshan writhed on the bed of his temple chambers, caught in the throes of a torment, part memory, part dream…

"Kjieran…Kjieran what has happened?" Darshan gathered his acolyte into his arms.

Kjieran pushed a jumble of confused images across the bond, each of them blood-tinged and desperate. His thoughts sought oblivion.

As Darshan pieced together what had happened, his fury surpassed the bounds of reason. "WHO DARES ATTEMPT TO HARM YOU?"

"Hal'Jaitar," Kjieran whispered.

Hal'Jaitar. Hal'Jaitar. Always this wielder's name spoken in association with his acolyte's pain.

Darshan pushed a strand of raven hair from Kjieran's forehead, wearing a look of outrage. Their bond had grown thick in the intervening weeks, its stalk dug deep; sprawling roots bound the fibers of both of their beings. To lose Kjieran now would be to lose a part of himself.

The emotions that gripped Darshan were stronger than any he'd experienced in the Void. Unmaking had never engendered such urgency as this need to ensure Kjieran's safety and protection.

He held his acolyte's head with one hand while stroking his hair with the other. "Why did you not call upon me for aid?" The terrible foreboding of losing Kjieran made his tone dangerous and dark, full of injury and accusation when all he really felt was concern.

Kjieran opened his eyes as his lord held him, and in the meeting of their gazes offered a desperate submission that aroused Darshan to new heights. Kjieran reached for him…

—the dream shifted—

"KJIERAN, I DEMAND YOU CEASE UPON THIS COURSE!"

Darshan roared through the magical binding that joined him with his acolyte, yet Kjieran continued to defy him. The truthreader stumbled through the desert sands, refusing to respond. As he neared a pyre constructed of jumbled tents, Kjieran extended his hand and gathered elae *to him. Darshan felt the snap of Kjieran's intent as it formed, and the pyre erupted into flame. He tried then to claim control of Kjieran's body, but the acolyte threw himself onto the pyre in spite of this.*

Darshan's rage thundered like a tidal wave across the bond. Kjieran became the voice of his fury, howling a cry that pierced the sky.

As Kjieran's eidola *body began to burn, Darshan felt his connection with Kjieran thinning. The pattern of binding became a frayed rope lashing two skiffs together in a storm. Such a feeling beset him as he'd never experienced. Later he would come to know it as desperation.*

Then the binding rope snapped, and Darshan felt Kjieran falling away. They were men stranded in separate lifeboats in a storm-swept sea. Darshan watched helplessly as the waves drew him and Kjieran in opposite directions. He could do nothing but fume in silence—

"Why do you plague me with this memory?" In the dream, Darshan shifted irritably in a low-slung chair and looked to Kjieran, who was kneeling at his feet.

They were in the highest level of the Prophet's residence on the Tambarré acropolis. To Darshan's left, an arcade of arches framed the Iverness Mountains and their jagged line of snowy peaks, while to his right, high clouds were casting lonesome shadows across the southern plains. Beyond his shaded temple, the day seemed too bright.

*Yet…*the day was actually night and Darshan's body was asleep. He knew this the way one knows things in dreams.

The Kjieran dreams were coming regularly now. Each time they began with the same vivid memory of Kjieran's final moments. Invariably they left Darshan feeling betrayed anew and kept the wound of Kjieran's treason freshly bloodied.

Always Darshan would wake from the instant of Kjieran's demise into a dream within a dream, where Kjieran's ghost waited to torment him. Sometimes Darshan saw his acolyte's face clearly; other times it was frustratingly obscured. Just then, Kjieran's dark hair had fallen forward, shadowing his eyes.

"Perhaps…" Kjieran whispered, "perhaps it's because you haven't yet learned its lesson, my lord?"

Darshan assessed him critically. "What lesson is there to be learned from betrayal?"

Kjieran braved a glance up at him. "Why else would you be forcing yourself to remember a moment repeatedly, my lord, save to discover some new meaning in its recollection?"

Darshan grunted. "That assumes you're here as some construct of mine, but immortals do not dream."

Kjieran's colorless eyes dropped again. "If this is no dream, my lord… what is it?"

Darshan's gaze tightened. "I suspect it is a haunting."

Kjieran's brow furrowed. "Why would I be haunting you?"

"I suspect you'd know that better than me."

"But I *don't* know!" Kjieran's eyes flew back to Darshan's. "I only know that I'm here with you. Surely this proves it is but a dream—for in a dream, I'm but a construct and might only know what you know."

Darshan regarded him, darkly desirous. "If this were a dream of my construction, Kjieran van Stone, you and I would be doing other than talking."

A faint flush came to Kjieran's features.

Darshan reflected that at least this iteration of Kjieran wasn't saturated with fear, but it bothered him, not knowing whence came these 'dreams.' Were they actually a construct of his own imagination, or the product of some magic worked upon him by his brothers? Or, as they more clearly seemed, communion with a spirit who had not moved on?

The latter idea proposed the most confusion.

When Dore Madden had first given him the binding patterns to work on Kjieran van Stone, he'd told Darshan of the Adept Returning. Dore had described the frail human bodies as vessels holding an immortal being, one whose essence remained the same through an endless succession of shells.

Darshan had thought the concept utter folly—one more of a thousand-again illusory tales that humanity had invented for purposes unfathomable to him; yet Shail similarly claimed that Ean val Lorian, the prince who had become so troublesome to them, was in fact a Returned Adept from an earlier age.

Whether or not he believed Dore and Shail—neither of whom could be trusted—Kjieran's presence in his dreams begged the question: if Kjieran had not been unmade in death, as all things were wont at the fringes of Chaos…where *did* his essence go? Certainly Darshan had intended for their binding to be eternal when he'd forged the working. Had he succeeded in binding Kjieran's *soul* to him, independently of any body that soul was meant to fill?

The mystery troubled him deeply, for it had numerous unsettling ramifications.

Of course it bothers you, brother. If these 'creatures' called Mankind are immortal beings, it proves they were meant to endure. Pelas's unwelcome voice intruded on his dream, his thoughts…his haunting? Perhaps Kjieran and Pelas were both haunting him.

Darshan pushed from his chair. "Walk with me, Kjieran."

Kjieran stood with eyes still downcast and set off with his lord.

Darshan clasped hands behind his back and strolled towards the band of daylight that brightened the world beyond the temple's arcade. He wondered at the odd attachment he had to Kjieran; how even after treason and betrayal, he still desired the Adept's companionship. Just thinking of Kjieran drew a cord of tension through Darshan. Pelas had a name for the sensation.

"It's called love, my lord," Kjieran said quietly.

Darshan cast him a sidelong eye. What did it prove that this specter of Kjieran so clearly knew his thoughts? Unfortunately little—ghost or dream, either could explain it. "Love…" he arched a critical brow, "is an illusion."

"Call it what you will, or call it nothing; still you cannot deny the *experience* of it, my lord."

"Experience." Darshan's eyes tightened. "That's Pelas's word."

But could his brother Pelas have gained the know-how to impose dreams upon his consciousness, even while convinced that his power was gone, even locked away in a tower halfway around the world? Pelas had tricks that defied Darshan's understanding.

He swept Kjieran with his gaze, seeking shades of Pelas in his acolyte's manner. "I don't recall the living Kjieran as ever being so bold."

Kjieran's brow constricted as he thought this over. "If I'm the construct of a dream, my lord, then *you're* dreaming me in this guise. Perhaps this is how you would've wanted me to be. Then again," he said, arching brows resignedly, "a ghost would have no fear of boldness, for what has a ghost to lose?"

A fervent banging on the outer door dragged Darshan from the dream.

He roused to find the three acolytes he'd taken to his bed last night still sleeping among the tangled sheets and that incessant banging reverberating like a gong through his chambers. He aimed thought as a spear and stilled the man beyond the door. The banging ceased.

Daylight was flooding the room, too bright for an early sun. He'd slept longer than he meant to, the ill dream holding him hostage even as Kjieran's memory did. How could he still feel such connection to a man who had betrayed him so thoroughly?

Like Pelas has betrayed you?

The thought came from elsewhere than his own mind, he was certain, for it held a strain of guilt that was an emotion foreign to him. Pelas had earned his fate with his idylls and dilettante ramblings about the realm… with his blatant defiance of purpose. Darshan had been forced to obscure his brother's power for his own good.

"…My lord?" an Ascendant's voice floated diffidently to him from beyond the heavy doors. "The Advisor says they're waiting for you to depart for Tal'Shira by the Sea."

Yes…

Darshan threw off the sheets and shook out his mass of braids as he headed off to wash and dress. His mind was already traveling ahead to the moment he would stand over Viernan hal'Jaitar and determine his guilt or innocence.

❖

The Adept wielder Viernan hal'Jaitar, Consul to M'Nador's Ruling Prince, stood in the shade of a cloistered walkway bordering the plaza known as the Court of Fifty-Two Arches. Before him, three score Talien Knights stood in formation, sweltering in the midday sun while they awaited the arrival of Prince Radov's esteemed guests.

Esteemed guests…

Hal'Jaitar snorted dubiously. He couldn't decide which man he held in less esteem—the lunatic Dore Madden, or that lunatic he served, the Prophet Bethamin.

The Prophet sought followers and minions, looked mistrustfully upon allies, and considered no man his equal. It grated on hal'Jaitar that he had no other recourse but to enter into yet another pact with the Prophet Bethamin. He despised the truths that had driven him to such desperate measures—incredible truths…*incomprehensible* truths.

Gydryn val Lorian had gotten the better of him.

Even in the silence of his thoughts, this admission rang discordant bells of impossibility. Gydryn had taken the point—by *Cephrael's Great Book*, he'd taken the whole bloody match! And the reports only grew more inconceivable as the days progressed. Another scout arrived each hour, it seemed, to report the same news: the Dannish soldiers were abandoning their positions, disappearing from the lines.

How did an entire regiment of soldiers simply vanish overnight as if swallowed by the desert sands? Even when the departing troops left a trail, it invariably wound into the stony mountains where a convoy of trolls could pass unnoticed.

Hal'Jaitar ground his teeth.

His men had trained the Dannish soldiers to blend in, cover their tracks and leave no trace; the Akkad and M'Nador's war was one of ambush and subterfuge, not mile-long lines of soldiers marching towards well-organized death. Now the Northmen were putting their newfound skills to mutinous use. It was galling to imagine an entire army skulking somewhere among the immensity of M'Nador, plotting mutinous departure, or worse, *overthrow*.

Hal'Jaitar had sent his Shamshir'im to the four corners of the princedom in an effort to head off future desertions. They'd intercepted a company of mutineers and were holding them now at the Fortress of Khor Taran in the region of Abu'Dhan. If nothing else, those soldiers would provide some leverage over Dannym's unruly king when they found him…if they found him…if he was still alive.

But Viernan suspected that somehow, against all odds, Gydryn val Lorian was. The val Lorians were far too resilient—they just refused to bloody die!

How had Gydryn val Lorian managed such a coup?

Within the shadows of his black *keffiyeh,* the consul's right eye twitched. Either Dannym's king had come to Tal'Shira with this plan already formed, or he possessed more cunning than hal'Jaitar had given him credit for.

The currents flashed with a surge of the second strand, and the Prophet's entourage appeared in the nodecourt.

First came a procession of Ascendants and their sepulchrally veiled Marquiin—once truthreaders, now golem things so corrupted by the Prophet's power that *elae* brooked no part in them—followed by a diamond configuration of four figures in hooded black cloaks, with Dore Madden at their center. Then came the Prophet himself.

Standing nearly seven feet tall, Bethamin towered over the assembly. A glistening tunic of thin gold disks draped the upper half of his chest, while the bronzed flesh of his muscular midriff disappeared beneath a skirt of leather and gold mail. Hundreds of long braids bound in gold bands tumbled down his back.

Radov's Talien Knights stomped out to welcome the Prophet. Representatives of the Council of Princes followed on their heels, and a formal reception commenced.

Despite having no love lost between them, Viernan held a healthy respect for the Prophet's power and preferred to maintain his distance—preferably a few *kingdoms* distance. Through their limited interactions, he'd learned much about the man—

Man…the consul's upper lip rose in a sneer. Whatever dark life inhabited the Prophet Bethamin, *man* had no part in it.

Viernan found a pleasing justice in letting the Prophet solve the problem of populating their war in the face of Dannym's withdrawal. Over the years, Radov had courageously done Bethamin's dirtier work by eliminating the val Lorians—inasmuch as none of them had actually been successfully *eliminated,* at least all were out of the way—so Bethamin's lackey, Stefan val Tryst, the Duke of Morwyk, could make his play for the Eagle Throne. Yes…'twas only fitting to let the Prophet bear some of the war's weight out of his coffers. Huhktu knew M'Nador's were bleeding for the effort.

After much pomp and circumstance that no one seemed to appreciate except the officials conducting it, the ceremony concluded and the honor guard marched off. As the procession passed hal'Jaitar, the Prophet turned his head and settled his gaze unerringly on Viernan.

He got the unsettling impression that the Prophet's attention had been fixed unwaveringly upon *him* the entire time.

The question was…*why?*

Upon conclusion of the banquet in Bethamin's honor, hal'Jaitar joined his prince and the Prophet in the Dome of the Blossoming Lotus. As Viernan arrived, palace servants were pulling the chains to lower the outer 'petals' of the dome to open the carved soapstone screens that formed the circular inner walls. A cooling breeze off the sea soon came venting in.

The Prophet chose a seat on one of the long, curving couches. Radov already held a glass of absinthe and was orating loudly on the necessity of reclaiming Raku.

Viernan speared an assessing gaze around the room, taking note of Bethamin's Marquiin, and Dore's four hooded creatures standing like ghouls near the doors. Then he made his way down the wide steps to the central circle, where Radov was speaking.

"Ah, Viernan, finally." The Ruling Prince held out his glass by way of acknowledging Viernan's arrival. "Tell them the troubles we're enduring—" Abruptly he swung a half-circle and flung out a finger at the Prophet. "*You* promised us weapons and soldiers but sent us Saldarian trash—mercenaries who prefer drink over duty and augment their pay in stolen maidenhoods. By Huhktu's bones, they're pillaging before the battle's even been fought!"

Hal'Jaitar was impressed that his prince had managed to so accurately capture and repeat the sentiment expressed by his councilors, when the prince personally knew only indifference to the issue anymore.

Dore Madden bowed obsequiously to Radov. "Your Highness—"

Radov silenced him with a severe look. "Hold your tongue, Madden." He waved his glass towards the Prophet. "I want to hear what *he* has to say."

Viernan admitted that his prince commanded a certain ferocity when not playing absinthe's drunken lover. His heavy brow and aquiline nose lent an intensity to his gaze, while the tattoos circling his throat seemed a collar of dark thorns inside his ornate kameez. Certainly the large ruby in the center of his royal agal gave a sense of wealth and state to his person. Yet Hal'Jaitar knew it was only a matter of time before the Ruling Prince of M'Nador melted into a toadying vassal again. No one held dominion before the Prophet.

Bethamin shifted his gaze slowly and deliberately to Radov, a minute change of direction, yet it gave the impression that his own thoughts resided a realm away. "When a dog misbehaves," he posed in his sonorous voice, one that had already gathered legions of followers to a doctrine of questionable logic, "do you punish the animal, or its trainer? Only one course reaps a lasting change in the dog's behavior."

"Saldarians require a hard lash, my prince." Dore crossed one knee over the other—a scarce plug of bone jutting against his robes—and folded fingers around the protrusion. "They must be corralled and dominated, as a pen of hogs." He looked up at Radov beneath his brow, his black eyes little agates of malice. "But as with hogs, my prince, with proper handling, they'll ravage your enemies, flesh and bone."

Radov grunted and sipped his absinthe. "Leadership. The problem is always leadership. Those northern captains couldn't corral chickens, much less men of ambition, such as your Saldarians."

Viernan stifled a sigh. "Saldarians aside," he stepped in before Radov offered the princedom to the Prophet in shuddering tribute, "Raku must be reclaimed or we'll lose the support of the Council of Princes."

The Prophet radiated disinterest. His gaze began shifting away again.

"If we lose their support," Viernan stressed, nabbing Bethamin's attention before it slipped off to another dimension, "the Hadorin line could fall within a fortnight, the princedom within the month." He leveled the Prophet a burning look, speaking only to him. "All which you sought through our alliance will be lost."

The Prophet looked back to him. "Not all."

The consul curled his lips in a poisonous smile. "Enough."

"Viernan, you needn't threaten our guest." Radov threw himself onto one of the couches and spread an arm along the back. "He's our ally. He's come all this way to help us."

Hal'Jaitar bowed in acquiescence, but as he straightened, he aimed a look of warning at Dore Madden. The wielder had his skeletal fingers stuck in a host of putrid pies, and Viernan knew the bakers of most of them. He let it be known with his gaze that he wouldn't hesitate to retaliate against Dore if the Prophet denied them aid.

Bethamin feared naught of Viernan's vengeance; Dore understood better. The latter licked his spidery lips. "What is needed to reclaim the oasis?"

"Soldiers," grumbled Radov.

"Wielders," said Viernan.

"Dragon…bane," Radov finished through a belch. He gestured with his glass. "*Something* to dispatch those damnable Sundragons."

"You have thousands hovering outside your city walls," the Prophet remarked. "Why do you not rout them before you to overrun this oasis?"

Radov snorted. "Peasants. Women and children. Refugees. What do they know of swordplay? Abdul-Basir's cavalry would trample them in seconds—if those bloody Sundragons didn't fry them all first."

The Prophet inspected Radov with his dark eyes like two black holes, sucking the light out of everything that came within their gravity. "These dragons guard the oasis?"

The prince tossed back the last of his absinthe and answered hoarsely, "Not just the oasis. The things are a bloody nuisance all up and down the lines."

The Prophet shifted his gaze to Dore. "Why have I heard so little about these dragons?"

"The *drachwyr* do not pose a threat to you, my lord." Dore licked his lips and looked back to Viernan. "*If* there was a way to…divert the *drachwyr*, what size force would you need to reclaim Raku?"

"At least another five thousand men to augment the prince's forces gathering now at Taj al'Jahanna," Viernan said. "The bulk of the Emir's army is stationed at Raku and they hold the high ground. It will be a brutal and bloody reclaiming." Especially since they'd lost the support of Dannym's army.

"Five thousand." Radov stared at his empty glass. "But no more Saldarian trash." He shifted his gaze to the Prophet. "I want trained soldiers, men who will follow commands and not flee from the lines. And I want the new things. *Those* things." He motioned with his head towards the four hooded men standing by the doors.

Bethamin arched a brow.

Dore seemed to tremble all over. "The *eidola* are the Prophet's blessed children." He cast said Prophet an ingratiating gaze rife with unwholesome adoration. "He does not *sell* his children."

"But he'll trade them, won't he?" Radov glared at Bethamin. "Why'd you bring them today if not to barter with them? Like the first two black-skinned things who came and went so quickly…or that other one—that undead truthreader you sent to spy on me."

Viernan stifled a grimace. He regretted telling Radov about Kjieran van Stone's unique physicality, but he would've regretted more *not* informing his liege. Radov extended trust no farther than his glass of absinthe, and the increasingly paranoid prince was quick to rid himself of suspected enemies.

The Prophet folded fingers in his lap and replied with chilly equanimity, "What need would I have to spy on my allies?" He shifted his attention to Viernan, pointedly adjusting the focus of his inquiry.

It occurred to Viernan in that moment to wonder if Kjieran van Stone had told his master of their mutual interactions, their…altercations? A suddenly disquieting thought, for the Prophet repaid betrayal with his thumb to a man's forehead, marking him with a long, suffering end.

Dore offered meanwhile, "My prince, the *eidola* are here as the Prophet's bodyguards."

Radov snorted with derision. "What need would the Prophet have for bodyguards among allies?"

The Prophet skewered Viernan with his gaze. "Interestingly, Kjieran van Stone thought the same."

Despite himself, Viernan paled.

The Prophet turned his searing attention back to Radov. "You ask for a new agreement, yet I haven't any confirmation that your part of our last accord was completed."

"No—I mean, *yes*, it's done." Radov pulled a flask from his pocket and refilled his glass, much to Viernan's grinding frustration. "You wanted the val Lorian princes out of the way. They're out of the way. You wanted the King of Dannym killed. We eliminated him."

Hearing Radov speaking so openly about these treasons made Viernan's skin crawl.

"These treasons were not committed beneath my name." Bethamin flicked at his muscled knee, as if a spec of dust had dared alight upon it.

Radov frowned into his absinthe. "Well…of course, I mean, on behalf of the Duke of Morwyk. In any case, Gydryn val Lorian is dead." Then he frowned. "He must be dead."

Viernan was not so certain, but he kept this thought to himself.

"The king vanished with all of his…knights," Radov gave another belch, "and then some."

Viernan had not yet told his prince that the entire Dannish army had also vanished. He preferred that his head remained attached to his neck.

Radov leveled Dore a black glare that he then turned on the Prophet. "Whatever your creature Kjieran van Stone did, he vaporized my entire force—including the marauders we sent in to be certain the deed was well accomplished. No-no. Gydryn val Lorian must be dead. Otherwise we would've heard from him…*of* him."

The Prophet crossed a sandaled foot over one knee. "You want troops, and *eidola* among them. What do you offer me in return, Radov abin Hadorin?"

"Not gold. I can spare little enough of that." Radov ran his forefinger along the rim of his glass. "What do you want?"

"The Prophet desires to rebuild the great cities within his governance," Dore said. "Workers are in short supply."

Radov grunted. "Tradesmen, craftsmen…I've put every one I could find to use serving my army."

Dore licked his lips. "You've a cornucopia of refugees outside Tal'Shira's walls."

Hal'Jaitar misliked the dark light of intent burning in Dore's gaze.

Radov frowned. "A nuisance. They want me to feed them, clothe them, suckle their babes…"

"Drive them from your lands!" Dore spoke with a feverish enthusiasm that Viernan knew couldn't bode well for anyone. "Cast them to the north, where *we* will receive them."

Radov turned to Dore. "Even should I," he retorted, assuming a sudden belligerence, "what guarantee do I have that you'll carry out your part?"

The Prophet lifted one long-fingered hand to indicate the four hooded creatures standing by the door. "I leave you with a gift."

Radov spun his head, and his brow furrowed fiercely. "Four? I want fifty!"

"Four for today," Dore murmured. "Fifty in return for your people. A worthy trade, my prince."

Viernan viewed Dore with disgust disfiguring his upper lip. Whatever malignant use Dore intended for M'Nador's rabble, it had the man trembling with ecstasy at the thought.

"You will send the people forth?" Dore prodded.

"Yes, yes." Radov waved irritably at him. "No idea what good they'll be. I suppose you'll find some use for them."

"Oh, yes. *Yes*."

Knowing that dreadful look in Dore's eyes for what it heralded, Hal'Jaitar might've stopped this transaction; but regret, remorse…these were luxuries that neither he nor the princedom could afford. "And the Sundragons?" he inquired pointedly of Dore.

Madden looked to him. "We will give you the means to deal with the *drachwyr*."

"Plus five thousand men and fifty *eidola*," Radov reminded them. He smiled at this contemplation. "Then we have an accord." He stood and extended his hand.

The Prophet drew back from it as if it was a repellant bug.

Radov glared hotly at him. "In my culture, we shake hands to seal a bargain!"

"A curious custom." The Prophet arched an eminently superior brow. "Either a man intends to do what he says he will do, or he doesn't. How does the pressing of flesh change this?"

"It's our *custom*."

Bethamin flowed from sitting to standing and looked down at the Ruling Prince, giving the impression of a god observing his creation and deliberating on whether or not it reflected enough divinity to allow it to live.

With a sort of deliberate dubiety, Bethamin took Radov's hand, but as he gripped the prince's palm in his own, he turned his eyes to hal'Jaitar with a single question burning clearly in his gaze: *And once you've shaken a man's hand and he betrays you, what* then *is your custom, Viernan hal'Jaitar?*

THREE

"A man never learns anything by doing it right."
—Liam van Gheller, Endoge of the Sormitáge

THE NODEFINDER FELIX di Sarcova della Buonara rested his chin on one hand and stared out the open window into a drizzly grey afternoon. There was something about a rainy afternoon that just didn't inspire. A misty morning could still bode well for adventure, but a grey afternoon—Belloth's balls, it might as well be all over at that point. Put the day to bed and hope for a more promising dawn.

A damp breeze teased at Felix's hair, stirring strands of blonde, auburn and dark brown into his eyes—one green eye and one blue, the mismatched pair apparently a gift from the Avieth his mother swore was his *real* father, which was total bollocks. Felix fashioned himself about as daring as they came, and even he wouldn't have the balls to cheat on Lord Davros di Sarcova.

Trying *not* to think about his father—because his stomach was already queasy from eating the very questionable meat pie that his jailors had offed on him that morning—Felix let his gaze idle across the empty courtyard while a slow exhale took its time crawling out of his lungs.

The stone-lined court was the kind of dull, featureless place that might've existed in any city the realm over, but this one was attached to the Order of the Glass Sword's infamous Tower, home of the Imperial Inquisitors; a honeycomb spire of labyrinthine halls and secret rooms playing host to the Empire of Agasan's condemned elite.

Or so everyone said.

Felix had seen with his own eyes the patterns carved everywhere into the stones—patterns which contained the Tower's prisoners far more effectively than iron bars. He could imagine the truthreader spies that were probably even now treading secret passages between the walls; ghostly observers reading the minds of the Tower's occupants when their diligence waned to its lowest ebb—a more effective means than torture for ferreting out the truth.

Or so Felix had decided during his many recent sleepless nights, when the suspected truthreaders scurrying behind his walls had been his only company. He'd spent plenty of bitter hours pouring out his heart to them. He hoped they'd been taking notes.

Felix had also decided that the fact that he had nothing to do during his days but stare out the window was a harsher torture than any inquisition could mete out. And the absolute worst part of all? There was not a node in sight! Which probably accounted for why they'd put him in a room with an operable window.

Felix blew out his breath. Most places, you couldn't spit without hitting a leis. But as far as his eyes could see spread only mundane stone, roof tiles and glass. Not a single portal opened onto the Pattern of the World. Not even a *twisted* node.

This fact unnerved Felix mightily.

They'd put him in a dead spot of the Pattern of the World, a place without nodes or leis, a place that shouldn't exist in nature.

Put a Nodefinder on a dead spot where he couldn't even sense the Pattern, and suddenly he couldn't breathe, couldn't think or reason…the feeling was said to be akin to drowning. A Nodefinder could go mad in such a place.

Felix had heard of dead spots. They were central to the horror stories the second strand *frites* scared each other with in their first years at the Sormitáge. But any Nodefinder worth his salt knew that dead spots didn't exist—*couldn't* exist—leastwise not ones large enough to be the kind of terrifying things described in the stories.

Except…the Order of the Glass Sword's tower had been built on one.

Felix puffed a discontented exhale. He hoped the spies crowded between the walls of his room were as bored of watching him as he was of watching the empty courtyard.

'…*Consider yourself an honored guest of the Empire*…'

The last inquisitor who'd visited had told him that. He'd been a mealy-faced man with a moustache like an oxen yoke and a truthreader's colorless eyes. According to said inquisitor, Felix wasn't in prison—leastwise, that's what they'd tell his family, *if* anyone in his family ever bothered to inquire as to his whereabouts, which Felix was pretty sure would never happen.

The room where they were holding him had a four-poster bed and was exactly ten paces and one foot-length square, which probably aligned with some obscure engineering formula but made pacing bloody awkward. Felix knew this because he'd paced the room a hundred times already. In both directions.

It also had a privy and a massive wooden table, the kind that would kill you if it fell on you, except you couldn't so much as budge the dust off of it, so there wasn't much fear of that.

Felix crinkled his upper lip towards his nose and slid another begrudging exhale out into the damp afternoon. They shouldn't be able to hold him like this, tortured by boredom—and for no bloody good reason!

He wasn't the one who'd vomited up a hundred bleedin' Danes to wreak havoc at the Quai game.

He hadn't summoned that pair of black-faced demons from Belloth-knew-where to throw the stadium into chaos.

And while everything else was blowing up, *he* most assuredly hadn't allowed those Varangian arseheads to quietly spirit a bunch of Adepts out the bloody back door.

Felix was entirely innocent of the things they were accusing him of—which fact, he admitted, rather bolstered his disinclination to confess the things they *ought* to be accusing him of. That the princess had forged a trust-bond with him and Tanis also inclined him in the not-so-forthcoming direction.

Even so, he shouldn't have to depend on fourth-strand workings to uphold his gods-given right to keep secrets. He was the son of a powerful lord! If his father only knew how they'd been treating him—

Actually…he thanked the Sanctos his father *didn't* know. Felix would rather have dealt with the torturous interrogation of the Order of the Glass Sword than be questioned by Davros di Sarcova.

And he'd been 'dealing' with the Order's intelligence people almost as much as he'd been dealing with the High Lord Marius di L'Arlesé's men, Vincenzé and Giancarlo. In the countless days he'd been locked in that room, a dozen blockheads had questioned him, four different truthreaders had read him, and none of them trusted anything he told them. The High Lord's man Vincenzé had paid him a score of visits, each time trying to get Felix to say something different than what he'd said the time before.

Felix had told them everything he knew.

That is…well, he hadn't told them about the book Malin had stolen from the Imperial Archives, one of the apocryphal books from the *Qhorith'quitara*. Felix still had possession of the book—or would, as soon as they returned his satchel to him. But they hadn't asked him specifically about the book, and he wasn't obligated to bring it up.

And he hadn't told them about his pact with Tanis and the Princess Nadia, or their coordinated attempts to uncover the truth behind Malin van Drexel's disappearance—which collaboration had ended with their investigation into the Literato N'abranaacht, aka the Malorin'athgul Shailabanáchtran—mainly because he didn't feel like trying to explain any of *that*.

And he hadn't told them about his variant trait, the one that allowed him to travel on twisted nodes, because...well, he wasn't stupid. Felix just hoped they wouldn't summon his father.

When he'd first awoken in the Sormitáge infirmary with his leg all stuck with Healer's pins and a raging headache, remembering little except having been made into a human sandwich along with a bunch of blokes whose arse hairs he would rather not have met so intimately, well...he *might've* mumbled something about the need to notify his father *then*. But he'd very quickly recovered his wits.

He needn't have worried, in any case. Sormitáge Healers never listened to their charges. They'd simply pushed him back down into unconsciousness so they could Heal his broken leg, and when he'd woken again, his leg was working properly and he was lying in the four-poster bed, wondering where in the blazing Sanctos he was.

In a bloody dead spot on the Pattern of the World, that's where!

Felix's fingers absently rubbed the amulets he wore on a chain around his neck, which boasted the sanctified effigies of his ancestors, who were supposed to be looking out for him. One amulet bore the long-nosed face of his many-times great aunt Frangelica, who'd died of a broken heart, and the other depicted his great-great-great-grandfather Dominico, who'd died fighting pirates. Felix rubbed the outline of his great-grandfather's face between thumb and forefinger and thought of praying to him for deliverance, but he rather imagined that any help Dominico was likely to send him would only get him into worse trouble.

He wouldn't have tried to flee in any case, even had they given him the opportunity. Attempting an escape from the Tower while under suspicion of treason wasn't usually the smartest plan.

Sancto Spirito!

What in the thirteen hells had happened to Tanis and the princess? And why hadn't they come to retrieve him from such totally unfair—if not *entirely* undeserved—captivity? He would have words with both of them when he saw them again.

If he saw them again...

Shadow take that Vincenzé! The High Lord's man had no compunction about threatening Felix with permanent incarceration if he didn't 'come clean' on his alleged crimes. But how was he supposed to 'come clean' on something he hadn't done?

Felix glowered out into the rain.

It might've been an hour or many hours later—it was impossible to tell the time of day beneath such a gloomy sky—that Felix heard the clicking of the stone locks in his door, which signaled that someone had worked the trace seal from the other side. The door swung open on the doleful whine of much-abused hinges to reveal Vincenzé and Giancarlo in the portal.

"Oh, joy." Felix turned his gaze back to the rain.

"We share a similar appreciation of your company, Felix di Sarcova," the truthreader Giancarlo remarked as he shut the door behind their entry. Stocky, and with the corded arms of a sailor, Giancarlo gazed upon the world from a square-jawed face crowned by a mass of unruly brown hair. But though he exhibited all the charm of a forge-worker, his truthreader's eyes revealed a shrewd intelligence.

Much in contrast to his stocky cousin, the taller, handsomer Vincenzé pushed hands on his hips and scanned his bright blue eyes around the room—as if expecting some change from the last time he'd thusly surveyed it.

Felix didn't trust Vincenzé. The wielder had three Sormitáge rings and a dangerous look about him—like one of those Jamaiian pirates, only better dressed. And while he boasted the kind of patrician features distinctive to the Caladrian elite, his dark hair had a decided sweep of daring to its wave, and his hand never strayed far from his blade.

Vincenzé finished his survey of Felix's insultingly sparse accommodations and fixed a shrewd gaze on Felix himself. "Well, Sarcova…" he strode over to the table and hooked a leg over one corner, seating himself on the edge, "what have you to say for yourself today?"

"Where's my satchel?" Felix flung an abused glare in Vincenzé's direction. "I told you I'm not talking to you again until you bring me my things."

Giancarlo pulled Felix's satchel out of a larger pack at his hip. He dangled the bag tauntingly in the air from one hooked forefinger. "And why should you want this so badly, *eh?*"

Felix darted up and snatched the satchel out of Giancarlo's hold before the truthreader could hide it away again. He clutched it to his chest as he retreated to his chair. "I'm not going to escape through it, if that's what you're implying."

"And why should that be what he was implying?" Vincenzé's too-keen gaze took Felix's measure, and the lad did not at all appreciate the evaluation poised there.

Of all of the people who'd come to interrogate him—inquisitors, adjuncts, truthreader spies—Vincenzé posed the gravest threat to Felix's secrets. The wielder had instincts, plain and simple, and with the truthreader Giancarlo ever at his side, Felix couldn't lie to him. It took all of his skill to make Vincenzé think he'd answered his questions when he really hadn't.

"You can't hold me here like this," Felix grumbled. "I've done nothing wrong."

"That's yet to be determined," Giancarlo returned.

Felix leveled the truthreader a rat-faced stare and said nothing.

Vincenzé settled interlaced fingers upon his thigh. "The sooner you come clean with us, Sarcova, the sooner you'll see the other side of that door."

Felix didn't imagine the other side of that door was much more interesting than this side.

"We know you're holding back on us." Giancarlo remarked, whereupon Felix felt the Adept barging into his mind, seeking truths that didn't belong to him. So Felix did something he was very skilled at—he vacated his mind completely.

He wasn't sure if it was another variant trait or just a skill he'd honed out of self-preservation as the youngest of nine Adept boys, but Felix had a way of retreating to the furthest edges of his thoughts and lingering there like a shadow in the corner of the room, leaving all else vacant to inspection. It wasn't the same as trying to lie to a truthreader, or even like a wielder shielding his thoughts. This was more like having *no* thoughts for the truthreader to read.

Felix finally felt the unwelcome steps of Giancarlo's mental probing moving on again, so he slipped back into the space of his own mind, dragging his thoughts behind him like a timid puppy on its leash.

Giancarlo turned to his cousin, pressed his lips into a thin line and shook his head.

Vincenzé scowled. "Now look, Sarcova—"

"I want to see Tanis." Felix clutched his satchel to his chest and glared at the two Adepts. "At least tell me where he is…what you've done with him." He hoped they weren't holding Tanis in the very next room. He wouldn't have put it past Vincenzé to try to play him and Tanis off each other to see what information could be gained.

Vincenzé and Giancarlo exchanged a look. Then the latter turned his colorless eyes back to Felix. "Tit for tat, Sarcova. We tell you something true, you tell us something true."

"You imply I've told you something untrue."

Vincenzé broke into a sly smile. "Well, you haven't been exactly forthcoming with us, have you, Sarcova?"

Felix glowered at him. "You didn't answer my question."

"Yes, an effort you're equally adept at, *eh*? Not so enjoyable when the tables are turned."

"Tit for tat." Giancarlo wandered over and leaned against Felix's bedpost. "Or you can go on not knowing what happened to your friend."

Felix expanded his glower to include both of the men. "Fine."

"Fine." Giancarlo sounded smug.

"Fine." A rather predatory smile presented itself across Vincenzé's face. "We would happily let you see Tanis…if only you might tell *us* where he is."

The room fell silent except for Felix's suddenly pounding heart. Even the doleful rain seemed to take a breath in pause. "…What do you mean?" A sinking feeling dragged at Felix's chest. "You mean…they *took* Tanis?"

"And who precisely would *they* be, *eh*?" Vincenzé arched an inquiring brow.

Felix rubbed both palms against his eyes. His mind returned to those last moments at the Quai game, when everything went mad. He'd hardly been able to keep up with Tanis there at the end, what with everyone in screaming chaos and the stadium exploding around them. Tanis had started running so fast—fair *streaking* from stand to stand, trying to reach Nadia down by the field. To imagine the bastards had gotten him—

Bloody Sanctos on a stake! Had they taken the princess, too?

Felix returned his gaze to Vincenzé's. Now he saw the tension behind the man's eyes for what it boded. Now he understood why both of the Caladrians had been so patient with him, so willing to give him what he asked for. Never mind Tanis—the *Princess Heir* was missing, and they thought *he* knew something about it!

Sancto Spirito!

Gah! The burning truth of it was, Nadia would never have gotten mixed up in any of this, if not for him. She would never have been at the Quai game at all. She would've been safe in the palace!

Felix was the one who'd tripped his way into her rooms…who'd brought Malin's disappearance to her notice…who'd delighted in her interest in helping him in his investigation…who'd reluctantly agreed to take her across twisted nodes so that her guards would never know she was gone…

The fact that Felix possessed an unregistered variant trait and had been using it illicitly to travel on twisted nodes—this fact paled next to the undeniable truth that he'd used his talent to sneak the Imperial Heir out of the palace without her guard.

Felix wished he'd never gone to meet Malin in the Archives that night.

"Is your guilt choking you, Sarcova?"

Felix lifted a burning gaze to Giancarlo, who was regarding him with smug satisfaction, like a diamond-eyed cat with a mouse trapped beneath its paw.

So what if they had him cornered? That didn't make him stupid enough to confess to things they weren't yet accusing him of. Besides which, he didn't know how much he *could* tell them, even if he tried. How far would Nadia's trust-bond protect their secrets? He didn't actually know.

He shifted a look between the two Caladrians. "Those Varangian bastards took Tanis?"

Vincenzé hooked his toe on the room's only chair, spun it around and straddled it, folding his arms across the back. "Why don't you tell us what you know, Sarcova, and maybe we'll tell you a little of what we know, *eh*?"

Felix hugged his satchel closer against his chest. "You first."

"*Prego*." Vincenzé eyed him meaningfully. "The High Lord has been studying the currents." He lifted a finger from his arm and rolled it around at Felix. "Upon *elae's* tides, he found *your* pattern, Felix di Sarcova. He also found the lad Tanis di Adonnai's pattern, and much to his grievous displeasure, the Princess Nadia's pattern as well."

Felix might've gone a little pale at this information, or else it could've been his lunch coming back with a vengeance. It was hard to discern what exactly was making him so queasy.

"Your turn, Sarcova." Giancarlo straightened away from the bedpost with his meaty arms still crossed. "What's your involvement with the attack at the Quai game? How did you help the Danes take the Princess Nadia?"

"*How*—what—*me*?" Felix protested shrilly. "*I* had nothing to do with any of that business! It was bloody N'abranaacht—"

"N'abranaacht?" Giancarlo exchanged a puzzled look with his cousin. "The Arcane Scholar? The same scholar who half of Faroqhar watched fighting a demon?"

Vincenzé held up his hand to pause any further inquiry along that line. "*Your* signature was all over the second strand currents, Sarcova."

"Because I was trying to escape!"

"On twisted nodes?" Giancarlo arched a skeptical brow.

Vincenzé waggled his finger at Felix. "Or else you were helping the Danes."

Felix's eyes went wide. "Why would *I* help those bastards?"

"The ninth Sarcova son?" Vincenzé arched a suggestive brow. "Even in a family of wealth, you don't stand to inherit much. What prospects do you truly have?"

"Well, I certainly wouldn't prostitute myself to the bloody Danes!"

"If you weren't helping them with the invasion, why did the second strand currents carry your signature?"

"I *told* you—"

Vincenzé silenced him with an upraised hand. "I want the truth this time, Sarcova. What were you and Tanis di Adonnai doing at the Quai game with the Princess Nadia?"

Felix bit back a curse. *Damn that Vincenzé!* He was adept at asking the right sort of questions—the specific sort, along the very line of inquiry that Felix didn't want *anyone* walking.

He clenched his jaw and cast a defiant stare back at the man. "We weren't *with* the Princess Nadia."

Vincenzé assumed a humorless smile. "Semantics. Perhaps Her Highness wasn't with you at the Quai game, but *you* smuggled her out of the palace. Dare you deny it?"

Felix did go pale that time.

Giancarlo skewered Felix with his colorless gaze. "Come now…out with it, Sarcova. With what we already know of your activities, continuing to lie to us will only make things uglier for you."

Felix worked the muscles of his jaw and considered Giancarlo's threat.

If they'd truly had anything on him beyond speculation, he wouldn't be enjoying a room with a view. *But*…if he now admitted to traveling twisted nodes…if he admitted to having an unregistered variant trait and using it to carry the Princess Nadia out of the palace, he'd be signing his own death warrant.

Pshaw! Death warrant? They'd make him *pray* for death!

Yet, if he lied here to the High Lord's men, especially with that bullmastiff Giancarlo passing judgment over his words…well, he might as well put a noose around his own neck and jump out his window right then.

Felix hugged his satchel and glared sullenly at Vincenzé. "I'm not telling you anything more until you quit treating me like a traitor."

Vincenzé grunted. "Believe me, Sarcova, if we actually thought you'd betrayed the Empire, this would be a very different sort of conversation. Come clean with us now—last chance, *gatino*."

Both of the High Lord's men were staring at him expectantly. Felix couldn't see any way around answering. He dropped his gaze. "Princess Nadia ordered me to take her from the palace."

Vincenzé shot Giancarlo a triumphant look. The truthreader frowned blackly at his cousin, dug a coin from his pocket and tossed it over. Vincenzé grabbed the silver out of the air and began riffling the coin expertly across the back of his fingers. "So where is she now, Sarcova?"

"How the hell am I supposed to know?" Felix hugged his satchel closer, but thus far it had proven an inefficient shield against Vincenzé's intuition. "Tanis was trying to get to her when N'abranaacht blew up the stadium and Belloth's hell broke loose and half of a column and a dozen blokes landed on top of me, and the next thing I know I'm here being pounded on by you people."

"N'abranaacht." Giancarlo cast a frown at his cousin. "Again the Literato."

Vincenzé kept riffling the coin across his fingers. "Why did the princess order you to take her from the palace, Sarcova?"

Felix exhaled a deflated sigh. "We were trying to find Malin—you know," he flung a glare at them, "the job that *your* people should've been doing."

"And you thought you'd find him at the Quai game?" Giancarlo posed dubiously.

Felix ground his teeth. Giancarlo's comment only emphasized how singularly ignorant they were as to what was really going on.

By the blessed Sanctos, how right Tanis had been! No one understood the threat N'abranaacht posed to them all. Malin had barely *glimpsed* it and look where it had gotten him.

Vincenzé waggled a finger at him again. "How did you get the princess out of the palace?"

Felix shifted a defiant glare to him. "We walked."

Giancarlo snorted. "Right out the door in front of Her Highness's Praetorian Guard?"

Felix shrugged. "They didn't see us leaving."

"And however did you manage that, *gatino*?" Vincenzé's words sounded benign, but he was watching Felix far too sharply.

Felix gave a muted curse. "You know…you kind of shove one foot in front of the other and shift your weight forward, and—"

"That's the crux of it, isn't it?" Vincenzé rose abruptly from his chair. "You didn't 'walk right out the door' with the princess in any sense of those words, did you, *eh*?"

Felix held the wielder's stare and tried not to let Vincenzé see how fast his breath was coming.

Giancarlo fixed Felix with his colorless gaze. "Your silence is answer enough. Don't you understand, Sarcova? The Princess Heir's life may be in danger."

"I'd say so, if those bastards took her," Felix replied tightly.

"Tell us where they're holding her and we'll entreat the Empress for clemency on your behalf."

Felix flung a glare at the truthreader. "I. Don't. Know."

Giancarlo leaned towards him threateningly. "We think you do. We *know* you're holding back on us. What are you not saying, *eh*?"

Felix rolled his eyes dramatically. "What am I not saying? Oh, gee…let me see…the food they forced off on me today smelled like a dog's arse? Oh, here's something that may be important: I woke up with my balls itching this morning, and then the massive crap I took came out in the shape of a goat's head. Do you think that's a portent?"

Vincenzé shoved the chair under the table with an impatient slam. "*Do you know who's holding the Princess Heir, Felix di Sarcova? Do you know where they might've taken her?*"

Felix clenched his jaw and glared at him. "No."

"And if you had to guess?"

"Then I'd say ask bloody N'abranaacht."

"If only we—" Giancarlo began, but Vincenzé's pointed stare effectively silenced him.

When the wielder turned back to Felix, his gaze betrayed not a hint of amity—not that there'd been much to begin with. "If something happens to the Princess Nadia because you were too scared for your own skin, Sarcova, I will personally flay you from forehead to heels and take my bloody slow time about it—the Lady as my witness."

Felix scrubbed at his nose with his forearm and looked sullenly up at him. "Are we done?"

Vincenzé eyed him for a moment longer. Then he dug that silver coin from his pocket and tossed it at Felix. The lad caught the coin just before it struck his nose.

"Give that as an offering when you make your next prayer." Vincenzé ran a hard gaze across him. "Maybe the gods will listen if you bribe them, *eh*? Raine's truth, you're going to need their blessing to make it out of this alive." He spun in a swirl of rebuke and stalked out with his cousin in tow. The stone door growled shut behind them with disturbing finality.

Felix stared after them, feeling drained.

The High Lord's men had no idea how deep they'd all sunk into the stinking bog of N'abranaacht's sedition—by the blessed Sanctos, Felix barely comprehended it himself! And if what Tanis had explained to him was true—which it mostly so far seemed to be—then they all had an Adept's chance in Shadow of doing anything about it.

Felix let out an explosive exhale and reconsidered his reticence to confess. But the truth was, he might've told the High Lord's men everything he knew—*anything* that could have conceivably helped them—and still wind up on the far side of nowhere and only in deeper trouble himself.

Bloody Sanctos on a stake!

He was really going to have words with Tanis when he saw him again.

◆

Vincenzé pulled the door closed and exhaled a forceful breath. The ache behind his eyes was pushing heavily against his lids so that it was a grave effort to keep alert. He'd lost count of the sunsets and sunrises since he'd seen his bed.

The Princess Heir was missing. If anyone dared spare a moment for sleep, the High Lord would ensure their eyes never opened again.

Vincenzé looked to his cousin. "Did you get anything this time?"

Giancarlo mashed his palms against his eyes and then shoved both hands back through his longish hair. "*Gah…*" he leaned his head back in the cup of his hands. "My brain feels as wooden as my limbs."

Vincenzé clapped a hand on his cousin's shoulder. "Nothing then?"

"The boy has a natural ability to shield his mind." Giancarlo dropped his arms to his sides. "I probed as far as I dared, but he's as adept at avoiding my talent as he is at skirting the truth. The House of Lords would love him."

Vincenzé grunted. "A boy like Sarcova is far more likely to wind up on the other side of justice." He started off down the passage.

Giancarlo eyed him sidelong. "Do you really think Sarcova is using an unregistered variant trait? I couldn't pry even a hint of that truth from his thoughts."

"All the pieces fit."

"But Davros di Sarcova wouldn't have dared to keep such a secret from the Sormitáge. He would've reported his son's variant trait to the Office of Recondite Scholars at the time of his enrollment."

"Maybe Davros doesn't know." Vincenzé exhaled a frustrated breath. "*Dios mio*, but Tanis put his finger on the truth from the outset. Do you remember when the lad said that someone with a variant trait could've taken Malin van Drexel from the Sormitáge and no one be the wiser?"

"*Sì*, but Felix can't be behind Malin's disappearance. He spoke a truth when he said he and the princess were looking for the boy. There must be more to it."

"I think there's a *lot* more to it than what few truths Felix di Sarcova lets slip across his tongue." Vincenzé looked his cousin over. "But whatever is really going on, be assured, the princess and her two young knights are deep in the thick of it."

They descended a long flight of stairs and passed a row of armored soldiers, pushed through a pair of double doors, and headed down another set of wide steps into the open air. With the fall of twilight, the drizzle had intensified into a begrudging rain.

Vincenzé pulled up the collar of his coat and upped his speed across the deserted square. The piazza was especially empty due to the High Lord having placed the city under curfew and the Red Guard on high alert. The only people out and about were those working beneath the High Lord's own insignia.

Investigators were still scouring the Quai field like ants, but they'd discovered little more than what everyone already knew—that the Danes had made off with nearly two hundred Adepts during the chaos, including the young truthreader Tanis di Adonnai—who'd been in the High Lord's charge, and which fact His Grace was mightily disturbed over—*and* the Princess Heir, which very few people knew about, and which made Vincenzé dread the Empress's imminent return from Köhentaal as if the forces of darkness were closing in upon him from all sides.

Giancarlo frowned disagreeably up at the clouds. "His Grace suspects that the Princess Nadia and Tanis bonded with each other."

"Clearly they're all three bonded into *something* together," Vincenzé muttered by way of agreement.

"Felix seemed convinced the Literato N'abranaacht was behind the invasion at the Quai game." Giancarlo turned his cousin a curious look. "Why didn't you want him to know that N'abranaacht is dead?"

"The more Sarcova knows, the better he becomes at skirting the truth."

Giancarlo muttered an oath by way of agreement to this. "What else do you think Sarcova is keeping from us? Clearly he doesn't know what happened to the princess."

Vincenzé narrowed his gaze. All the pieces of this puzzle were laid out before his vision, but he couldn't yet put them into their proper order. He glanced to this cousin. "Walk this path with me: first the van Drexel boy steals one of the *Qhorith'quitara* books from the Archives and goes missing. Soon following this, Sarcova comes under suspicion for mysteriously appearing in places he shouldn't have been able to access. Then, *capita a fagiolo*, Björn van Gelderan's zanthyr shows up in the company of a lad with prodigious talent."

Giancarlo made a loop in the air with his hand, a gesture of disbelief. "*Certo*, the only dormitory room Tanis can be placed in is Felix's."

"*Naturalamente.*" Vincenzé opened both palms in acknowledgment of this irony. "For a time, all goes quiet."

"The calm before the storm."

Vincenzé angled him a look of agreement. "Then, *alla stoccata*, the next thing we know, Varangians are terrorizing a Quai game across a twisted node; two demon creatures out of legend are exploding the stadium; a Literato who isn't supposed to be able to work *elae* makes a dramatic show of wielding the fifth in front of half of Faroqhar while attempting to kill one of the demons; and the most important heir in the Empire goes missing—along with two hundred other Adepts." Vincenzé turned his cousin a pointed look. "You think all of this isn't somehow connected?"

Giancarlo shrugged. "I just don't see how."

Vincenzé blew out his breath. "Neither do I. But the Empress will return soon. No doubt she'll get to the bottom of it."

"And good night to the bucket," Giancarlo grumbled, a phrase which implied, *and that's the end of us.*

This almost went without saying. And if they didn't find the Princess Heir before Valentina's ship reached Faroqhar, it wouldn't be just their heads on the executioner's block. The furthest reaches of the Empire would reverberate from the Empress's fury.

FOUR

"Dare not trust Love to lead you. Love will stay the course, even to the edge of doom."

–Valentina van Gelderan, Empress of Agasan

TANIS LAY ON a blanket on a grassy hillside beneath Pelas's Hallovian manor, gazing up into a very blue sky. The breeze bouncing off the sea cliffs stirred his hair, while the sun warmed his face and Nadia's laughter warmed his heart. The spot they'd chosen for their picnic offered a commanding view of the charcoal cliffs and beyond these, the depthless blue sea.

It might've been the wine that was making it difficult for Tanis to concentrate on the conversation Nadia was having with Pelas that afternoon, though he suspected it was more likely the heady sensation of his newly fashioned binding with the Malorin'athgul, which had wakened him to the essence of the cosmos in marvelous, yet unsettling, ways.

'...Through me, you're bound to the heavens, and through you, I'm bound to the earth...'

They'd been just a few days bound now, and with each turning of the hourglass, Tanis gained some new perception. When he chose to sense the world through Pelas's side of the binding, he could discern the density of the air, feel the obdurate pull of the moon—even conceive the far-flying motion of the planets in their propulsion around the sun; celestial bodies caught in a powerful equilibrium of forces.

But Tanis didn't often seek these perceptions, for they held an inherent largeness that disoriented him.

The lad had expected his and Pelas's binding to settle—perhaps into a passive state, like Phaedor's binding of protection, or at least to a quiet awareness, as with the lighter, impermanent bond he shared with Nadia—but as Pelas glowed on the currents, so also did he glow in Tanis's mind, even as Tanis seemed a sun in Pelas's...or so the Malorin'athgul had told him.

They were anchors for each other now, a pair of circling stars creating gravity between them. Tanis suspected they would be able to find each other no matter what impossible distances separated them—across the realm or even on other worlds, through time itself. Even as he and his parents could.

When Tanis had realized that his parents were still bound to him and he to them, his entire view of existence had changed. *So* many answers had been waiting for him behind the veil that had protected his identity.

And when he'd reached out upon their binding and spoken to his mother...*oh*, the things she'd told him! He was still trying to make sense out of much of it, putting context to some things and filing others for future reference, in some instances just trying to conceive of the possibility...

Nadia's sudden laughter drew Tanis's attention to where Pelas was making illusions to entertain her. It reassured him to see color returning to the princess's cheeks, to find her sitting up so easily on her own.

After their mad escape from Shail's underground temple, Pelas had drawn *deyjiin* out of Nadia's life pattern, and Tanis had Healed the results of its destructive touch, but her lifeforce had been drained nearly to an ember. She'd needed time to regain her strength.

They'd all needed time—to recuperate, regroup, reclaim a sense of themselves and each other. They hadn't spoken about what would happen when they did finally return to Faroqhar, as they must, and soon. The Sormitáge would probably still be up in arms from the attack at the Quai game, never mind that the Empress's heir was missing.

And while these shadows lay across the path just behind Tanis, he sensed an even darker storm looming on the horizon. The Danes were obviously planning some sort of revolt—Shail had kidnapped countless Adepts for *some* purpose, after all, but Tanis had no idea what the Malorin'athgul was truly planning. Felix's fate also weighed heavily on Tanis's conscience; had his friend survived the explosion that had caught them both? Yet what sat most unresolved for Tanis was how he'd put Nadia in harm's way by involving her in his and Felix's investigation. He suspected Balance wasn't finished making him atone for that grave error in judgment.

A fluttering unease always accompanied this thought.

"Don't tell me that's actually you there in the painting." Nadia leaned forward to better study the illusion Pelas was crafting for her, a reproduction of one of his paintings from the Sormitáge. "That's *you*..." she gave him a disbelieving look and pointed to a figure wearing an elaborate damask coat and wide-brimmed hat, "right there?"

"Doesn't the coat give him away?" Tanis murmured.

Pelas eyed Tanis humorously. That day the Malorin'athgul was wearing a violet coat that brought a vibrant gold hue to his coppery gaze. "I painted myself into many of my paintings—somewhere inconspicuous, of course, just to see if anyone would notice. It was a game of mine."

Nadia shook her head. "To think all of those years I studied your paintings and wondered about you, the great artist Immanuel di Nostri, and theorized on your muses, and tried to imagine what you looked like, and you were right there all along, just…smiling at me." Nadia shook her head wondrously. "Did anyone ever notice?"

Pelas winked at her. "A very few."

Nadia had been somewhat awed to learn that Pelas was Shail's brother, but when Tanis had told her that Pelas was better known as the artist Immanuel di Nostri, her jaw had dropped. She'd thereafter insisted on calling him Immanuel, which made Pelas smile, as he was smiling just then.

Nadia exhaled a contented sigh. "Will you show me another one, Signore di Nostri? I've never seen such artfully crafted illusions."

Pelas chuckled. "I fear your praise will go to my head, Princess. Soon I will become fat with it, and then none of my hats will fit."

Nadia flung a daisy good-naturedly at him. "I'll buy you as many new hats as you like."

Pelas gave an indulgent sigh. "Very well, Princess. For you, another, and hats be damned." He refreshed Nadia's goblet from a decanter of wine, then reclined on one elbow and blessed her with one of his devastating smiles. "What would please Your Highness this time?"

Nadia settled her goblet in her lap. "Something…different." She glanced to Tanis, inviting his opinion. "Something we've never seen before."

"Something you've never seen before…" Pelas ran a forefinger along his lower lip and gazed thoughtfully off. "This would imply some place you've neither been nor witnessed by way of an artist's hand. For an artistic connoisseur such as yourself, this means we must travel far indeed. Ah…" the finger lifted in a moment's inspiration, "I have it."

Pelas's gaze lengthened, as though across the shimmering ocean. The only indication he was concentrating at all was a slight tightening around his eyes. Then a scene began forming, superimposed before their canvas of blue ocean and cloudless sky.

First appeared the knotty trunk of a vast, white tree. Next followed many fat limbs. But as the illusion became more solid, blocking out the view of sea and sky, Tanis realized he wasn't looking at a tree, but at a *city* crafted in the shape of one, with building stacked upon building, tower growing from tower, until the branches of streets angled off in countless directions. Doors and windows, arches and rooftops gave the trunk its bark-like texture, while hundreds of white twig bridges connected the branching streets and buildings in a leafy sprawl.

Nadia clapped her hands. "It's *magnificent*. It even has fountains—oh, Tanis isn't it glorious?" Nadia exhaled a dramatic sigh of appreciation. "What I wouldn't give to have such an extraordinary imagination as yours, Signore di Nostri."

Because he shared the Malorin'athgul's mind, Tanis understood things Nadia could not. The lad met Pelas's gaze. "Where did you see it?"

Pelas smiled, a soft acknowledgment of the truth Tanis had perceived. "In Shadow."

Nadia froze her goblet halfway to her lips. "In Shadow?" She turned a look between the both of them. "But I thought…" Then she frowned.

Pelas angled her a wry smile. "You thought Shadow was a black nothingness, bleak and devoid of existence?"

"*I* certainly did." Tanis pushed up on one elbow to better look at him. "Phaedor said Shadow was a dimension and that it had no *where*, nor even a *when*."

Pelas vanished the illusion of his tree with a flick of his gaze. "Your zanthyr could likely explain Shadow far more adroitly than I can. My understanding is experiential."

"But you've been there?" Nadia asked. "You've seen this tree city?"

"Indeed, Princess."

She gazed wordlessly at him. "A *city* in Shadow, but…who lives there?"

An odd expression flickered across Pelas's face. "I'm not sure anyone lives there. Taerenhal belongs to a Warlock named Rafael—if it still exists."

Tanis pushed his thumbs to the bridge of his nose. All of the images and thoughts suddenly swirling through Pelas's mind were starting to hurt his head. "*Gah*," he looked up under his brows. "I can't make sense of anything you're thinking."

Pelas grinned at him. "I'll explain what I can, little spy."

He refreshed all of their goblets and then rested an arm across one bent knee. "Calling Shadow a dimension seems correct to me, for it has no substance save for what the Warlocks give to it. Shadow is…energy bound into illusion solidified into form…sometimes—that is, if the Warlocks have chosen to make things solid enough for others to perceive them. When you travel in Shadow…" his gaze took on a faraway look, "…no, it's not so much traveling as *shifting*. Imagine you're sailing in a bank of fog, and then—quite without warning—an island appears in front of you. In those moments, you've merged with a Warlock's...*world* seems an inapt term to describe the universes shaped by their minds. Their worlds are not like this one."

Nadia was listening intently. "Long ago, in the time known as The Before, the Warlocks of Shadow came regularly to Alorin—thousands of years ago, when most of what we understood about *elae* was superstition, before we made contact with the Council of Realms, before Cephrael bestowed upon the First Emperor Hallian the truths of the *Sobra I'ternin*." She gave a little frown. "They were dark times for the realm."

Tanis remembered the Imperial Historian Maestro Greaves lecturing on The Before, but he couldn't recall the historian saying why the Warlocks of Shadow were no longer broadly terrorizing the realm. "What stopped the Warlocks from coming here?"

"The Council of Realms." Nadia looked to him. "My mother says Warlocks work *inverteré* patterns innately and can bind mortals to their will with a single glance. My mother says it's a condition of inclusion in the Council of Realms that a world refuses to have any interaction with the Warlocks of Shadow."

"Yes," Pelas fingered the rim of his goblet, "some Warlocks find this arrangement rather...unfashionable."

Tanis didn't want to be reminded of arrangements with Warlocks. "If Shadow has neither where nor when," he posed, returning them to the earlier topic, which was safer to his mental constitution, "how do you navigate it?"

"Similar to the way we operate in the Void..." Pelas paused, frowned, managed an apologetic grin. "I've never tried to describe any of this before. I beg your forbearance." Pelas rubbed at his chin with a furrowed brow.

Whereupon Nadia said, somewhat awed, "Do you really unmake entire stars, Immanuel?" Pelas looked shifted his copper eyes to her. "It just seems so incredible. I mean, you seem like just a man." Then she dropped her gaze and added blushingly, "I mean, not just *any* man..."

Pelas chuckled. "In the Void, my brothers and I assume a different form, a much larger form. But no form we could assume would approximate the space occupied by a star. To unmake a star, we first have to..." he frowned again, "...it's like we expand our minds to become bigger than the star, or perhaps to..." Pelas rubbed at one ear and winced slightly. "This is challenging to explain."

"No, I think I see." Tanis gazed wonderingly at him, for a marvelous understanding was dawning. He recalled his mother's lessons on Absolute Being—long dissertations on a wielder's need to expand his awareness to encompass the space in which he intended to produce an effect; his father had written entire journals on the topic—and he connected this training with the images in Pelas's mind. "Actually…I think what you're trying to explain is covered in the Esoterics."

As keen to Tanis's thoughts as the lad was to his, Pelas arched a brow and leaned back on one hand. "I really must spend more time learning your Laws and Esoterics. I well recall your mother saying to me…" but he fell silent upon this thought, and his mind became quiet.

Tanis had learned that this quietude meant Pelas was closing off parts of his mind, concealing the thoughts harbored there—clearly thoughts about Tanis's mother and Pelas's mysterious relationship with her. The lad knew Pelas still had some confession to make to him about it, but neither of them had yet felt ready to broach the subject. Tanis laid his head back on the blanket, closed his eyes and tried to dull the swarming feeling that still edged his thoughts.

Nadia meanwhile said to Pelas in a tone tinged with wonder, "Your illusions are so much more elaborate than any I've ever crafted."

"Your rose a bit ago was perfect and lovely, Princess."

"But that rose is something I studied long upon and worked hard to capture," she returned. "You seem able to craft illusions more easily than either Tanis or me—and the gift comes to *us* innately."

"It is merely the product of an artistic eye." Tanis heard the smile in Pelas's voice. "Your talent is far more formidable."

"Tanis," Nadia tapped him on the arm, "do you see how Signore di Nostri flatters me? You could learn from him."

Tanis opened one eye to peer at her. "You would have me learn *more* ways of making you blush?" He emphasized this question by placing certain images in the shared space of their minds.

Nadia pressed fingers to her lips and tucked her chin into her shoulder, blushing vividly.

Pelas chuckled. "I've had many years to hone the skill of illusions, Princess. When working on the Sormitáge's Grand Passáge, I would craft the illusion first for my own eyes and then paint it as I saw it."

"Oh, that makes so much sense! Art historians have long praised the astonishing lack of error in your work." Nadia brushed a strand of hair from her face and smiled at him, but then her expression sobered, as if the breeze had blown a sudden solemnity into the conversation. "Immanuel…did no one ever know you were fifth strand?"

Pelas settled his gaze on Tanis—the lad both felt his attention and sensed it emanating across the binding. "*I* didn't know until Tanis showed this truth to me."

Nadia shook her head. "All those years at the Sormitáge and no one knew."

Tanis opened his eyes to meet Pelas's gaze, both of them struck by the same thought—Shail had spent even longer at the Sormitáge in the guise of an Arcane Scholar.

Pelas held Tanis's gaze. *I still do not know what my brother was doing there for so many years.*

Tanis swallowed. *I expect we'll find out sooner than we'd like.*

With the unease roused by this uncertainty still thrumming between them, Pelas said to Nadia, "When the great wielders of the Fourth Age roamed the halls of the Sormitáge—Markal Morrelaine, Arion Tavestra, Malachai ap'Kalien…your mother—" and he cast an unreadable look at Tanis, "I had to be careful to conceal my nature, but in truth, I was in little danger of being discovered. The greatest men of that Age walked past my scaffolding every day, and not a one ever thought to seek the fifth in my construction. I was but a lowly painter, a mouse among giants."

Nadia choked into her wine.

Pelas cast her a quietly amused look. "The Sormitáge and its sister Citadel had their own aristocracy reigning above the blood of kings. Rowed wielders were the true royalty of that time. The art circles I traveled in were rich but decidedly less illustrious."

Tanis propped his head on his hand again. "Did you know my father?"

Pelas shifted his eyes back to the lad with a look of gentle apology. "I knew of him, of course, but our interactions were limited. Your father walked in the highest circles, for he was the Alorin Seat's closest friend and held the heart of the High Mage of the Citadel." Pelas gave him another smile, reflective of admiration. "Your father was the envy of all who knew of him."

Nadia turned to Tanis, her eyes bright. "Do you know what an amazing secret you are, Tanis? No one knew that Isabel van Gelderan and Arion Tavestra had a son."

"Only the household staff in the valley," Tanis offered by way of absent agreement, his thoughts elsewhere.

"But oh—what a *mystery*." Nadia looked him over as if he was suddenly very intriguing. "Centuries between your birth and now…surely you weren't hidden in Adonnai all that time?"

Tanis exhaled thoughtfully. "All I know is that the zanthyr brought me to Her Grace's estate in Dannym when I was just a toddler."

Nadia squeezed his hand and grinned at him. "*So* mysterious."

"Yes, our Tanis is quite the undiscovered gem." Pelas winked at the lad. "But I think it's your turn to craft an illusion for our pleasure, Princess." He lifted the decanter to fill her goblet again.

"Please, no more!" Nadia laughingly waved away the wine. "My head is far too fuzzy. Tanis, you take my turn."

"Very well, Your Highness, if you insist."

Rolling onto his back again, Tanis clasped hands behind his head and let his mind wander, and as had happened ever since binding with Pelas, his free attention was immediately sucked into Pelas's gravity.

Soon, Tanis felt himself floating amid spiraling galaxies, passing through vast clouds of colorful gasses, sinking into a black sea studded with billions of stars...

One particular section of stars captured his fascination. Tanis began fashioning the pattern of those stars with the fourth strand, positioning each star as he saw it in relation to the next, dotting the landscape of his illusion with points of light. He was so intent upon duplicating the exact relationships and relative distances of each star to its neighbor that he hardly noticed the larger picture he was forming until Pelas sucked in his breath.

Tanis pushed up on one elbow. "What's wrong?"

Pelas was staring at the illusion glowing in the space between them: myriad diamond dots forming multiple designs. "Tanis..." he looked extremely uncomfortable. "Where did you see this?"

Tanis turned his gaze to the illusion. "It just sort of...came to me."

Nadia was peering intently at it. "Why, it almost looks like a wom—"

"Tanis, please let this creation go." Pelas sounded dismayed.

Tanis banished the illusion at once, though its image remained vivid in his mind's eye. He knew, too, what Nadia had intended to say. In the way one can draw imaginary lines among the stars of a constellation to outline a perceived shape, so had the patterns of the stars in his illusion seemed, when viewed as a whole, somehow reminiscent of a human form. What he didn't know was why that form had caused Pelas such discomfort.

"Well...it was lovely, whatever it was." Nadia touched Tanis on the arm. "I think I should rest before dinner. Would you walk me back to the house, Lord Adonnai?"

Tanis stood and bent to help her stand up. "You're really going to keep calling me that, aren't you?"

She gave him an arch look as she took his hands. "The title is your birthright." Nadia shook out her skirts and then looked him up and down archly. "You're not just Arion's heir, you know. You're Björn van Gelderan's also."

Tanis looped her arm through his. "Are you trying to help me feel more comfortable with the idea or less?"

Nadia grinned impishly. Then she turned to Pelas, who had also risen, and bobbed a curtsy. "Signore di Nostri, thank you for the lovely afternoon."

Pelas gave her a lavish bow. "The pleasure was all mine, Princess." His tone sounded light, but he met Tanis's gaze as he straightened, and the lad saw a shadowed concern lingering there, its source concealed in the sudden immense quiet of his mind.

Tanis escorted Nadia back to the manor feeling a welling unease. He attributed it to a perception that had been growing throughout the day, one that he'd come to associate with a calling on his path.

As he saw Nadia into her bed chamber, the unease grew so strong that he feared she would perceive it in his thoughts and wonder at it. He realized then that it wasn't his own feeling but Pelas's, the latter's rising disconcertion overflowing across their binding.

Tanis helped Nadia prepare for her nap, doting on her because he enjoyed it and because she let him. After she'd finished the tea he'd prepared for her—one of his lady's recipes—he sat on the bed at her side until her lids grew heavy and she sank into sleep with a soft smile gracing her lips.

Then he went in search of Pelas.

He found him on the terrace. The early evening sky remained clear, but the ocean breeze was tossing Pelas's long hair into wild designs, even as it had on the night Tanis had met him, free from the influence of his brother's compulsion.

Tanis halted at the Malorin'athgul's side and joined him in gazing out over the sea, whose waters had assumed twilight's mercuric hue. Tanis no longer perceived the darkness that had so often overtaken and possessed his bond-brother in the early days of their relationship, but a grave disquiet thrummed within Pelas now, much in contrast to his mind, which had gone completely still.

After a time, Tanis glanced to him. "It's still there, isn't it?"

Pelas kept his gaze on the distant sea and his hands clasped behind his back. "Yes."

"But you're no longer subject to Darshan's compulsion. That's what you meant before, when you said that acts beneath his compulsion would no longer plague your conscience?"

Pelas exhaled a slow breath and turned to meet Tanis's gaze. The lad had never seen him look so troubled. "I think it's time I explained to you how I learned to overcome it."

Both his expression and the turmoil of his thoughts, which suddenly tumbled forth upon an avalanche of disconcertion, unsettled Tanis greatly. He sought to reassure him. "Whatever it is…I promise I will hear it."

Pelas turned back to face out across the sea. "From the instant of our reunion, I've sought a way to tell you. Now the moment is here...I still don't know how to shape the words."

"It has something to do with my mother, doesn't it?" Tanis didn't need to be sharing Pelas's mind to have gleaned that much. For all the world, it looked like Pelas was bracing himself. "What is it?" Tanis took hold of his bond-brother's arm and made him look at him. "What do you feel so desperately unable to tell me?"

Grave apology darkened Pelas's gaze. He slipped free of Tanis's touch and wandered further along the terrace. When he spoke, his voice was low and tightly controlled. "You know what Darshan's compulsion required of me."

Tanis felt an immediate ill apprehension descend upon him. "Yes." He watched Pelas working the muscles of his jaw, clenching and unclenching, even as his thoughts seemed to alternately clench and slip around the secret he was holding so close, yet was so clearly desperate to confess.

"I don't know how it came to be...perhaps she simply willed it so, after we crossed paths at Tal'Afaq," Pelas spoke as if each word was slicing a piece of flesh from his soul through its utterance, "but your mother and my brother Darshan..."

Tanis suddenly couldn't breathe, his chest was so bound by foreboding. "What about them?"

Pelas turned to him. "For a time, your mother and I were both Darshan's prisoners...together. My brother tortured me into unconsciousness and then worked an illusion to deceive me, so that when I awoke, I was convinced he'd taken away my power. He locked me in a tower from which I had no escape—thinking my power lost—and after a time, he...gave me your mother, bound to the same poles as he'd used to electrocute me—his humorous idea of a gift." Contrition made a storm of Pelas's features as he held the lad's gaze. "Darshan meant me to...he had *compelled* me to..."

Tanis stared at him with the terrible realization and all of its ramifications taking horrifying shape in his thoughts.

My mother? You had my mother *bound and—*

Pelas took him by the shoulders. "I didn't harm her like the others you've witnessed. For days, I tried to resist harming her at all, but the force of Darshan's compulsion bearing against my will—Tanis...I couldn't *stop* myself—"

Tanis sank his head into his hands. This was so much worse than he'd ever imagined. He didn't know how to respond to it—mentally, emotionally...rationally...

"Isabel said she was there to help me." Pelas was begging his forgiveness with his thoughts and his tone and his every breath. "She was my prisoner, yet she said I was *her* path. Tanis…"

Tanis, please…

Tanis felt sick. He pressed his palms to his forehead and tried to breathe around the clenching feeling in his chest. After a time, he managed grimly, "What's the rest of it?"

Pelas exhaled a slow breath. "I harmed her, Tanis. By Chaos born, I wish I'd been stronger! She…" Pelas braced his hands on his knees as if to support the weight of his confession. "She said to use patterns, and I—I… penned them into her flesh with a razor stylus—"

Tanis couldn't hear any more—didn't want to *know* any more, for he saw too deeply into Pelas's thoughts and couldn't endure the images he found there.

The swarming feeling in his brain made his legs unstable. The lad staggered to the closest urn and braced a hand against it while the world spun dangerously. He wanted to flee, to run, to lash out in horror and protest, but he stole some breath back from his incredulity to gasp instead, "How did she free you?"

Pelas remained behind him, radiating dismay. "She taught me how to sublimate the compulsion, how to claim its power as my own."

Tanis, I beg you, please forgive me!

Tanis spun him a stricken look. "Just…" He really thought it might destroy him, knowing this had happened. "I need…some time," and he flung himself into a desperate sprint, running as far and as fast out of Pelas's company as his legs would carry him.

FIVE

'Better to be the wind of change than a leaf blown down the path.'
—An old Kandori proverb

THE PIRATE CARIAN vran Lea whistled tunelessly as he walked a quiet street of Cair Rethynnea with the royal cousin Fynnlar val Lorian at his side. The afternoon sun pushed their shadows in front of them, so that Carian's, with his wild wavy hair, dual cutlasses, and britches bunched up around his cuffed boots, looked reminiscent of a giant fanged beetle; and Fynn, with his Agasi-styled coat flaring above his knees, appeared a tasty mushroom.

"You know," Fynn remarked while Carian was smirking over this comparison, "left to their own devices, things always go from bad to worse. I don't get why you feel such a need to help them along."

"The Nodefinder Rebellion is an act of conscience, Fynnlar."

Fynn grunted sourly. "Conscience and I get along best when I let it go one way while I go another."

Carian pulled out his pouch of tobacco and started rolling himself a smoke. "You and your gold are gonna be parting ways a lot faster if Niko van Amstel becomes the Second Vestal. How does your conscience feel about that?"

Fynn sucked on a tooth and eyed him unappreciatively.

"You think I'm just in this for the fun of the fight?" Carian looked up under his bushy eyebrows and tongued the edge of the paper to seal it. "Niko would make it so that Jamaiians like myself can't even travel freely on the nodes on our own bloody islands. If he has his way, the Espial's Guild will control every node in the bloody realm. That means blokes like you will be paying *Guild* rates for an Espial to move your stolen merchandise, and blokes like me'll be slicing off a cut of our profits every time we use our Maker-given talent."

Fynn veritably gasped. "That's piracy!"

"You bet your pretty silk knickers." Carian puffed his roll alive and exhaled a cloud of bluish smoke towards Fynn. "And not even a code to rule 'em right, or keep 'em on the straight and narrow."

"Shadow take bloody Niko van Amstel," Fynn groused.

A bloody Niko van Amstel formed the gist of Carian's dreams most nights.

Bloody Niko van Amstel...

Carian could do things with the Pattern of the World that many ringed Espials only dreamed of—he'd gained his skills through trial and error and years of bold adventuring, learning how to travel and manipulate the ley lines of the world's magnetic grid with a weather eye and an ample helping of luck—yet *bloody Niko van Amstel* thought to keep *him* from traveling the nodes! Him and hundreds of others without formal sanction, said 'permission' coming by way of a gold Sormitáge ring, or for the weaker-willed or leaner-pocketed—who couldn't afford Sormitáge training—one's name on an 'approved list,' granted for the very low price of one's immortal soul sold to Niko.

By Tethys, if Carian had his way, Niko would've already known the sharp end of his steel, but the Great Master had forbidden him to seek vengeance in his name. Carian knew Dagmar had his reasons, even if *he* sure as silver couldn't see any good ones.

"Bloody Niko van Amstel," Fynn grumbled again. "Would that his mother had seen fit to drown him at birth. Women can be so shortsighted."

Carian grunted his fervent agreement. *Especially that birdie*—speaking of women who lacked vision. If the Avieth had enough to amount to Carian's little finger, she'd see what a catch *he* was. But Gwynnleth was still refusing to return to Alorin with him, despite the fact that he'd given up his lizard lover.

Carian puffed on his smoke discontentedly while inventing several new curses about obstinate, myopic Avieths.

Fynn gave a dramatic sigh. "Tuesday will be over by the time we get wherever you're taking us, vran Lea, and then I'll be of no help to you, because it will be *Wednesday*. In fact, I'm sure somewhere in the realm it's already Wednesday. Why don't we just give up on this doomed-from-the-first-moment-Gannon-bloody-came-up-with-it effort, and I'll buy you a drink back at the good old homestead."

"First of all, you're never the one buying." Carian skewered him with an agate eye. "Secondly, our node is just around the corner, and third and most importantly, Balaji's wine is too damned sweet." Carian hitched up his britches. "You're free to walk away from all of this, Fynnlar, just as soon as you pay me the money you owe me."

Fynn gave an indignant sniff. "You know perfectly well I make a point of never paying anyone the money I owe them—especially my friends. Without binding and contentious financial ties, what motivation would any of us have to talk to each other?"

Carian clapped him on the shoulder by way of agreement. "You are the gooey layer beneath our collective shoes, Fynnlar."

"I'll bet someone could compose a fine song about my altruism."

"Tell your altruism to get its blades ready. The blokes guarding this node ain't the sharpest knives in the drawer, but they know how to aim the pointy end of their swords well enough."

They were approaching a building with the kind of self-important edifice that shouted its desire to get robbed. In another life, Carian might've answered that call, but he felt duty binding him to their cause now as surely as being measured for his chains. Belloth's salty balls, every nodefinder in Alorin would be strung up in gibbet cages if Niko had his way.

Carian pushed through a pair of iron gates and led Fynn along a corridor. Like so many of the 'public' nodes, this one had been established in better days, when Nodefinder brethren were free to travel the grid, regardless of rank or Guild standing. The passage leading to the court was wide enough for two wagons and tall enough for coaches to pass beneath the arched roof without knocking the coachman from his seat.

Nodefinders and Espials alike made their living as facilitators of transport for anyone who could pay their fee. If Niko had his way, those fees would all channel through the Guild, giving them reign over the entire realm's commerce. It didn't take a genius to figure out why the Guild had voted Niko into his current position of authority.

The passage opened onto a wide courtyard framed by arches, out of which a dozen or so guards descended in rapid fashion.

"*You* again!" The foremost of the guards came stalking towards Carian with his hand gripping his sword hilt.

"*Again*." Fynn turned Carian a flat look. "I said no more free-repeaters."

"I told you before," the leader growled as he neared, "this node is *closed*."

Carian exhaled a cloud of bluish smoke towards him. "It's a node, mate. It can't be closed."

"It's closed to *you*, pirate," sneered a second bloke, whose nose jutted out from his face like the Dheanainn peninsula. Carian could hardly focus on the man's words for the massive distraction of his nose.

He blew smoke dubiously in his direction. "I've traveled this node a hundred times. It's never been closed before."

"Well, it is now," growled the leader, "like it was last week, like it will be *for you* tomorrow and every day thereafter."

Several of the other guards began closing the circle around Carian and Fynn. One of them, who had a deep cleft in his chin, looked particularly itchy to draw his sword.

Carian arched a bushy black eyebrow at him. "Draw that blade, mate, and I'll be showing you a whole new way to kiss the gunner's daughter."

The man's expression darkened.

The leader tightened his hand on his weapon. "*Your* kind aren't welcome here."

"My kind…" Carian blew smoke at him, "you mean the Jamaiian kind?"

The man gave a humorless sneer. "I mean the kind without Sormitáge rings, Guild sanction, or balls to account for their stupidity."

Carian puffed out three smoke rings in quick succession as he considered the mouthy leader. "This node belongs to the realm, and I mean to travel it. Now, you and your bilge rats can stand aside, or get intimate with Humiliated and Really Damned Sorry here," and he laid his hands on the hilts of his cutlasses.

The leader shifted his gaze around his twelve-against-two odds and smirked. "We'll take our chances."

Fynn exhaled a long-suffering sigh. "You're *really* making me regret Tuesdays, vran Lea—which is a grave injustice, if you must know. It was the last truly tolerable day of the week."

"You take arse-face there," Carian nodded towards the man with the cleft chin. "I'll handle the rest of them." Then he drew both of his cutlasses in a cross-handed swoop, sang a rebellious, "*All hands ho!*" and made for the leader.

Two men darted into his path.

Carian clenched his smoke in his teeth and performed his favorite *Mujindar* maneuver, Gannet Plunging for Fish, which entailed spinning while slashing, twirling like the bird as it plunged into the sea, his blades as very deadly wings. The men fell.

Behind him, Fynn cursed and danced back from arse-face's descending blade. He fingered a slash in his sleeve and glared at the man. "This was my fourth-favorite jacket to wear on Tuesdays!"

Carian grinned around the smoke clenched in his teeth. "Cleave him to the brisket, Fynnlar." He advanced towards the leader again.

The latter motioned at his men, and four others rushed at Carian, placing themselves aggravatingly once more between himself and his target.

Carian punched one man in the jaw and kicked another away with a hearty blow. Then he swung his right-hand blade at the third man, who he dubbed Duck Lips, while parrying Peninsula Nose's descending blade with the sword in his left.

He fought the both of them for a bit while he tossed the hair out of his eyes. Then he finished off Duck Lips with a spooling circle and a stab, and Peninsula Nose with two slashes and a jab.

The two who'd taken his fist and his boot got wise, picked up their blades and ran off.

Carian looked to the leader.

He blanched.

Fynn finished off arse-face while the last few guards scattered. Then he joined Carian's side, still muttering about his jacket.

The leader darted a wide-eyed look between Carian and Fynn and started backing away, as though he wanted to follow his mates to safety.

"So…" Carian sheathed Really Damned Sorry while keeping Humiliated aimed at the leader's throat. "I've a message for you and your scallywag of a boss, the one as calls himself a vestal."

The man backed himself into a statue and jerked abruptly, whereupon Carian stuck the point of his cutlass beneath his chin and exhaled a cloud of smoke in his face.

"Pay attention now." Carian plugged the fingers holding his smoke into the man's chest while he kept his blade against his throat. "This is our shot across the bow. You tell Niko van Amstel that we won't be letting him hornswaggle the realm into his private coffer. You tell him that for every node he claims, the rebellion will claim two—like we claimed this one today, like we'll claim another tomorrow."

The leader's eyes were watering from the smoke filtering up around his face.

Carian looked him up and down. "You got all that?"

He nodded fervently.

Carian sucked on a tooth and considered him for a moment longer. Then with a few well-placed flicks, he sliced through the laces of the man's pants. They collapsed around his knees.

Carian spun on his heel. "Ahoy, Fynnlar. We're weighing anchor out of here." As he walked to the center of the court, Carian cast a look over his shoulder and pointed with his cutlass at the leader, who was grabbing for his britches. "Just you remember who had you bent over with your pants around your knees, poppet. The next time I come calling, *you* don't want to be here."

Whereupon he wrapped a companionable arm around Fynn's shoulder and escorted him across the node.

The Pattern of the World welcomed him with open arms, an instant cajoling, enticing, roaring river of kinetic life. For a moment, Carian stood with his head thrown back and eyes closed, his smoke hanging forgotten between his lips, while *elae* surged around him.

Come...follow, the wanton river urged. *Claim us, use us, we are yours...*

Carian had taken many lovers in his life. None had ever been as tormenting, as attractive or as tempestuous as the Pattern of the World. She was every Nodefinder's siren call and Carian's lifelong addiction, his greatest passion, his most irresistible, untamable first love.

"How long are you just going to stand there, vran Lea?" Fynn clenched Carian's shoulder by way of emphasizing his discomfort. Carian had almost forgotten Fynn was with him, such was the intoxicating lure of the Pattern.

Ah! Carian lowered his head to view the Pattern with a spark of humor and two shakes of suspicion glinting in his wily gaze. *You wanton strumpet! You'd pin me to your bosom for an unbroken moon with—*

"Vran Lea, this isn't the most pleasant experience for normal people."

Carian glanced over his shoulder at Fynn. The royal cousin stood with his face scrunched in a painful grimace and his dark hair floating in a halo around his head, unruly waves enlivened by the Pattern's static charge. Even the hairs on his unkempt goatee were standing on end. Carian grinned and turned forward again. "Unbunch your royal nappies. I'm just preparing the way."

To his Nodefinder's eyes, the Pattern spread in nearly infinite pathways before him; yet he knew those magnetically charged routes like the lines on his palm, as certain of their connections as the razor edges of Humiliated and Really Damned Sorry.

He found and grabbed the two ley lines he needed and began binding them to one nodepoint. This was somewhat like trying to take two streams of lightning and direct them to the same metal rod, only harder.

Carian finally got the node fixed in his mind and darted a look at Fynn. "Ready?"

Fynn tugged uncomfortably at the seat of his britches. "Just get us off this damned Pattern before all of the hairs on my arse are standing on end."

Carian released the grounding anchor he'd placed upon the node. Energy pulsed, and the Pattern's magnetic induction pulled them along the ley lines he'd bound together. They flew a lightning bolt's jagged path, crossing thousands of miles in a heartbeat.

An instantaneous charge filled Carian but then rapidly drained away, the moment reaching its climax too soon. The Pattern only ever gave her lovers a taste of her, and it was never, *ever* enough.

Oh, my sweet, how you make me crave you…

Fynn's hand felt like a claw on his shoulder. Carian stepped off the node onto a grassy hillside beneath a sky just clearing from a storm.

"About damned time." Fynn headed off down the hill, tugging at the seat of his britches.

In the distance, a collection of cerulean tents nestled in the bosom of three hills. Their bright color stood out vividly against the misty mountains and overcast sky. This valley adjoining the First Lord's *sa'reyth* had become home base for the Nodefinder Rebellion.

Carian knew how to find the place because the Great Master Dagmar Ranneskjöld had shown him how to bind two ley lines together to make it appear—kind of like using a witching rod to dowse for water. But for all intents and purposes—that is, as far as the Greater Reticulation was concerned, such being the official name of Alorin's magnetic grid—the place didn't exist.

Pondering this mystery for probably the millionth time, Carian took a last draw on his smoke, flicked it off into the wet grass, and set off down the hill after Fynn.

The royal cousin's mood had sobered, or at least his blood had—the quality of Fynnlar's disposition much depended on his level of dissipation. As Carian loped up beside him, Fynn was fingering the tear in his coat sleeve. "How many is that they've taken over now?"

"Twelve nodes so far in the Cairs."

Fynn rubbed at his nose. "It's only going to get worse. They'll just keep claiming more nodes, and putting more guards on the ones they know we need to use."

"That's why we need Cassius. With his network, we can travel the length and breadth of the Middle Kingdoms and never touch a Guild node. The man's practically a guild unto himself." He cast Fynn a sidelong eye. "When *is* Cassius joining us?"

Fynn glowered sullenly. "Remind me again why *you* can't meet with him?"

"Well…you may recall hearing that someone was using Cassius's nodes to ferry stolen contraband—which he never would've known about but for Guild investigators showing up at his door."

Fynn stared at him. "You were using Cassius of Rogue's nodes for illicit transport and not even *paying* him for the privilege?"

"Can't say he took too kindly to it." Carian flashed a culpable grin. "So when are you meeting with him?"

Fynn scowled. "I told you, he has stipulations."

"Gannon's going to want details."

Fynn scowled even harder. "I despise that kilted Hallovian truthreader. He has no respect for other people's privacy. I'm sure it must violate some fourth-strand Adept law, the way he goes around eavesdropping on everyone's thoughts."

"He's unorthodox, but you can't deny Gannon's usefulness." Carian elbowed Fynn with a grin. "Who are *we* to talk about orthodox, eh?" He chuckled to himself.

Fynn looked him over sootily. "I like you less right now than I did a minute ago."

They made their way to the central pavilion, which was serving as the rebellion's command center. Carian pushed through the heavy drapes but then just stood there with his hands bracing the poles and a grin on his face, admiring the product of his early efforts.

Fynn ducked beneath his arm and moseyed on over to the wine cupboard, but Carian only had eyes for the massive globe that dominated the center of the pavilion. The planetary grid comprised thousands of silver lines, each connecting through starry points on the sphere's surface. Up close, the ley lines were infinitely complex, branching and crisscrossing in a dizzying display. The thickness of the ley line indicated whether it connected to a weld, a node or a leis, which points appeared respectively as dots of varying widths and brightness on the globe. Touch a point on the grid, and the globe would zoom in or out on specific welds and nodes, allowing a Nodefinder to study the Pattern of the World in three dimensions and minute detail.

The sphere was an illusion, of course, but one that every true son of the second strand should have the blessing to look upon at least once in his life. A weldmap sourced the illusion—*Carian's* weldmap—by way of a map generator, which harnessed *elae*'s fourth strand specifically for this purpose.

Once, weldmaps and generators were in use throughout Alorin. Now, just the maps themselves were as rare as Tethys' mercy when she was in a fury. *Now*, a Nodefinder had to extrapolate his own map, building it in his head through extensive travel and trial and error, or else attend the Sormitáge and spend his first decade memorizing the Greater Reticulation.

Carian's weldmap might've been the last one in use in all of Alorin. Oh, if that old woman Yara had only known what a treasure she'd possessed! Carian would've stolen the entire Kandori fortune for it.

Smirking over this contemplation, Carian headed across the pavilion towards two men who were conferring over a canvas map, the primary minds behind the rebellion: the truthreader Gannon Bair and the Nodefinder Devangshu Vita.

Devangshu straightened as Carian neared. "Well?" He looked up under his severe black brows. "Did they get the message this time?"

Fynn joined them with his nose in a goblet of wine. "Oh, they got it."

Carian hooked a leg over the edge of the table opposite Devangshu and rolled himself another smoke. "We'll have trouble again the next time we go back."

"What?" Fynn protested. "After the beating we gave them?"

Carian licked the wrapper to seal it and lit the roll from a nearby lamp, eying as he did so the carved marble pieces that dotted Devangshu's canvas map—markers for nodes occupied, targeted or claimed.

"Yeah…" he exhaled a cloud of bluish smoke. "That spineless mollusk is descended from a special subspecies of stupidity. Mayhap his self-preservation got the message, but I guarantee his ego didn't."

Devangshu removed a marble piece from the map and pocketed it again with a frown. Carian blew out another cloud of smoke with a thoughtful exhale. "I'm gonna need reinforcements next time."

"Oh, and what am I?" Fynn complained.

"Only available on Tuesdays," Gannon muttered. The heavily bearded Hallovian Highlander had become the Nodefinder Rebellion's unelected yet somehow undisputed leader.

Tall, broad and generally hairy, the truthreader had the look of a rearing bear about him—if a bear had biceps like stacked coconuts and eyes that saw into the back of your thoughts.

Fynn withered beneath Gannon's colorless inspection. "Yeah…well, you'll have to talk to He Who Crouches on the Spine of Humanity about booking more dates on my calendar. I'm his principal wine taster, you know."

"Yes," Gannon was leveling Fynn a steady look, "I know."

Fynn gave him a wan smile. "So…I'll just go see what Kardashian is doing." He made a hasty escape towards the Nodefinder-thief, who was standing across the way.

"Reinforcements." Devangshu pushed hands in his pockets and frowned at the map. He had one of those disdainful, aristocratic countenances that perfectly encapsulated the bored indolence of the Bemothi nobility; but Carian had yet to meet anyone more fervently devoted to ousting Niko van Amstel from the Vestal Seat. "We're spread a bit thin as it is."

Carian puffed out a smoke ring. "I know." He frowned off at the slowly revolving globe projected by the weldmap. It wasn't numbers they needed so much as strength. They had to show these ruffians they meant business.

Now, if the Avieth had been at his side instead of Fynn...*by Tethys' watery tits*, that woman could fight!

"The fact is, we need more men." Devangshu pulled the marble piece from his pocket and began fingering the figurine while his brown eyes scanned the map and his angular brows dipped into a severe V. Then he looked to Carian and Gannon. "We need Franco Rohre."

"Undoubtedly," Gannon remarked as if this was a foregone conclusion.

Devangshu fingered the figurine in his hand in an agitated fashion. "Without Franco, I doubt we'll be able to gain enough support to defy Niko's claim to the Vestal Seat. And you know Cassius of Rogue is going to demand that Franco have the helm before he'll negotiate with us."

"Franco must become the figurehead of the rebellion," Gannon said by way of agreement. "If we stand up Franco up as our candidate for the Vestal Seat, the entire strand will fall in line behind us—Guild and freemen alike."

Carian eyed the both of them with his roll of weed held loosely between his lips and smoke filtering up lazily around his face. "He won't do it willingly." The roll bobbed with his words, shedding ash on his thigh. He flicked at it absently. "The Admiral abhors attention as much as Niko lusts after it."

"He has no choice." Gannon's tone was firm. "Not if he would see the strand spared the rape Niko intends."

Carian took a deep draw from his smoke and considered the truthreader. "Franco is Niko's deputy now, and you want to make him *our* frontrunner? Let's just paint a big target on his back, eh?" He flicked ash from the end of his smoke. "Niko will castrate and gut him if he finds out—or at least have one of his goons do it."

Gannon shrugged. "We all face many dangers in this endeavor."

Devangshu was staring at the figurine in his hand. "If we can't appeal to Franco's vanity, we'll have to appeal to his conscience."

Carian snorted. "The Admiral's got more baggage of that sort than a caravan of Khurds and already a few too many voices jabbering in his head. It's anyone's guess which one of them is in charge."

"All of the Fifty Companions feel the bondage of their oaths to the First Lord, Carian vran Lea." The ghost of dark regret glimmered in Gannon's uncompromising gaze. "Whether they did as the First Lord bade them or disregarded those desperate and reckless oaths given in the Citadel's catacombs on Tiern'aval, rest assured...the chains weigh heavily." He looked him acrimoniously up and down. "Yours may be the only virgin conscience among us."

"Fancy that!" Carian grinned at him.

"But Carian is right, Gannon." Devangshu set the figurine back on the table. "We three will never convince Franco to do it. We'll present him to the brethren instead. Epiphany willing, their combined might will accomplish what ours alone cannot."

Gannon nodded resolutely to this wisdom. He pinned Carian with one of his listen-closely-and-do-exactly-as-I-say stares. "Go and brief Dagmar and ensure that Rohre comes to us as soon as he returns from Illume Belliel." He scanned his colorless eyes across the pavilion, surveying the activities within. His gaze tightened. "It's time Franco Rohre stuck his neck in a noose along with the rest of us."

Carian exhaled a cloud of smoke. Maybe he'd pay birdie a visit while he was in T'khendar. Massively annoying the Avieth would make the trip far more enjoyable. He nodded to Devangshu and Gannon and flicked the butt of his smoke off towards Fynnlar, who glared at him. "Well, you know what I always say, if you're gonna dance the hempen jig, it's best to do it with friends."

Then he headed off to start measuring Franco for his own specially tailored noose.

SIX

"We all stand at the center of our own lives. It's not until we look beyond ourselves that we find cause and purpose."

–Isabel van Gelderan, Epiphany's Prophet

FRANCO ROHRE SLOUCHED in Raine's throne in Illume Belliel with his chin on his hand and his mind elsewhere. He'd tried staying engaged with the Council of Realms' discussion that day, but after countless hours of listening to the same tedious argument reworded a hundred different ways, he'd lost the ability to focus on anything except the growling in his stomach.

Yet he understood the importance of the discussion. The Council had recently passed a measure that would legalize trade between the realms after over a thousand years of prohibiting it. That the measure had passed at all was a monumental feat. No one admitted to voting in favor of it—no one even admitted to *recommending* it for a vote—yet someone with clout had to have signed off on the measure for it to have arrived on the Council's docket. Needless to say, speculation abounded.

More startling still was that the Speaker refused to name the Seat who had initially proposed the measure, only going so far as to say that it had his wholehearted support. Rumors told that the Speaker himself had written it and purchased the votes he needed to see it passed using a variety of currencies, including extortion, blackmail and bribery. Of course, these were only rumors.

The ramifications of the measure were as momentous as they were destabilizing. The measure hadn't even been enacted yet and already the Council had broken into contentious and dissenting factions.

"If we open the welds to anyone," one Seat had posed in reopening the discussion that morning, "how can we possibly regulate travel between the realms?"

Fourth-strand patterns inlaid across the hall had translated what he said so that the *thought* was communicated to those listening, regardless of the language being spoken. It had taken some getting used to for Franco, this double-hearing of translated thought superimposed over vocalization.

The same Seat added rather vehemently, "The Council cannot think to enact the measure until the necessary qualifications and restrictions have been determined and statutes written to regulate Nodefinder travel."

The Council had gone on to argue about the point for most of the morning, even though everyone seemed to be in agreement that regulations would be needed.

This was a different issue from the matter they'd argued several days before, which had centered around the problem of determining the criteria for a Nodefinder to be allowed to travel between the realms.

As the morning's discussion was dying down, another Seat had taken the floor, moving to the front of his section of thrones to address the assembled members. "How are any of the worlds supposed to open trade with one another when our weldmaps have been redacted to remove all of the node points that would allow interrealm travel?"

This had met with a fierce outcry over the general state of weldmaps.

They'd already argued the problem of redacted weldmaps two days earlier.

Another Seat had then launched a further debate on how to establish a single unit of exchange when the materials that were considered precious varied so greatly from realm to realm. This had consumed the better part of the afternoon.

Now the sun was waning, along with Franco's patience. His interest had found another occupation a number of hours ago.

His gaze for the hundredth time that day found Alshiba, who occupied the throne of the Seat. Her light blue eyes were fixed forward and her features were set to impassivity. From an inauspicious beginning where she'd Healed him and then somehow bewitched and beguiled him into swearing himself into her service, they'd developed an unexpected rapport. Alshiba seemed almost to *trust* him.

The Seat across the hall continued droning on about the necessity of establishing a mint in Illume Belliel, which half of the Seats seemed to be in alignment with and half vehemently opposed.

Franco sighed. He cast his gaze around the immense, circular hall, letting his eyes drift across the thousand Seats and their accompanying vestals. They seemed a forest of bright colors gleaming beneath the hall's faceted crystal dome.

As the gathering place of the vestals of a thousand worlds, the Hall of a Thousand Thrones reminded Franco of a great theater entirely comprised of balcony boxes. Each world convened within its own box, which allowed for privacy of discussion while yet keeping every vestal in view of the rest of the Hall.

Which is why Franco was still sitting there trying to look engaged. Most of the vestals nearest him just looked bored, most especially Niko van Amstel, who was sitting in Dagmar's throne on Alshiba's right. Franco could tell from Niko's vapid, unfocused gaze that his mind had clearly traveled elsewhere.

In the middle of the hall, the Speaker sounded a chime, signaling the end of that discussion. Franco, like most others, returned his attention to the Speaker.

The elf Aldaeon H'rathigian sat on his throne atop an alabaster tower carved with a spiral of stairs and worked all over with patterns. With his long, white-gold hair and his sylphlike form draped in pearlescent robes, he looked inimitably statuesque.

"Your concern has been noted for further inquiry and review, Ambassador." Aldaeon's calm voice reverberated deeply throughout the hall. He added with admirable patience, considering how many times he'd already expressed a similar sentiment, "The establishment of statutes governing the new measure, as well as a plan for enacting them, will be the primary mandate of the new regulatory committee."

Another Seat rang a chime to be heard. "Speaker, if I may inquire, who is to be on this committee?"

The monument beneath Aldaeon's throne swiveled so the Speaker now faced the inquirer. "I will be appointing the Chair. The Chair will appoint his or her committee members."

Franco didn't envy any man that position. Chairing possibly the most important and controversial measure the Council had passed since their ruling, millennia ago, to prohibit interaction with the Warlocks of Shadow? It seemed more like a death sentence.

"Speaker?" another Seat chimed in from the other side of the hall.

Aldaeon's tower swiveled again. Franco wondered how the man kept from becoming dizzy with all the round and about.

"This is inarguably one of the most important positions ever established for a Council committee—"

You read my mind, Ambassador, thought Franco.

"—under the circumstances, shouldn't the Committee Chairperson be determined by a majority vote?"

Aldaeon gave a slight twinge of a smile, which Franco noted even from that distance. "That it *is* such an important position is precisely why it will not be determined by a majority vote, Ambassador."

Whereupon hundreds of chimes rang simultaneously—the cacophony of outrage that instantly filled the hall throbbed in Franco's head, its force doubled by the patterns of translation.

Alshiba looked wearily to him. "I think I've heard enough for one day. Shall we go?" She stood, gathered her white silk skirts, and climbed the stairs towards a curtained exit at the rear of their balcony box. Niko jumped up and joined her side, at once bending to murmur in her ear.

Franco pushed from his chair and took up the rear. As he was heading for the drapes at the top of the stairs, however, he couldn't help but notice the Speaker's gaze fixed upon their box. Aldaeon was taking special note of Alshiba's departure.

When Franco caught up with the Alorin Seat in the passage beyond, Niko was walking at her side and complaining, "...*such* an imposition to require us to sit for unending hours listening to problems that don't concern us, when we should be spending that time resolving the very real issues threatening our *own* realm."

Franco shook his head, marveling at the infallibility of Niko's self-absorption. It was a wonder rain didn't bead off the man, he was so saturated by conceit.

The Alorin Seat kept her gaze forward and her stride smooth. "If you find the affairs of council governance too tedious, Niko, I give you leave to remain in Alorin."

"No-no-no, I don't mean that," Niko quickly straightened his shoulders as if to adopt a stance of authority. "I'm fit to serve in any capacity. I merely mean to point out how untimely it is that we should have to spend all of our time here, when we've so much to do in Alorin."

"To lead is to serve, Niko," Alshiba said levelly, but Franco heard the exhaustion in her voice. "My place as the Seat is here in the cityworld; but as a vestal, your duty lies in Alorin, close to the people, to their plight; my eyes and ears."

Niko sighed disagreeably. "The realm is no more pleasant at present." He tugged at his coat as though the cloth was suddenly too binding.

Seems unfair to expect mere cloth to enclose such a massive ego, the mad voice in Franco's head snickered.

"My edict to restrict travel upon the nodes is an important step in imposing control and standards upon the strand," Niko said. "I expected it would meet with some minor resistance, but I'm being challenged at every turn! Why, Agasan's guilds have outright refused to comply, pending their own deliberations." He pushed a hand across his immaculately coiffed hair, shaking his head as he murmured, "It's an intolerable situation."

As ever, Niko only ever saw the illusions cast by his own expectations, to the utter exclusion of reality.

Do you think he'd recognize reality if it beat him on the head with a rock?

Franco rather imagined Niko would merely be confused by it.

What about a bench? An anvil?

Franco was envisioning things he'd like to hit Niko over the head with when Alshiba replied, "If you'd sought my opinion before issuing an edict that affects the entire realm, Niko, I might have advised you this could happen."

The intimation in Alshiba's tone wasn't lost on Franco, but he was fairly sure her subtle rebuke flew right past Niko's notice.

Niko shoved hands behind his back and deflated slightly. "The Free Cities of Xanthe were quick to agree to my edict, but now Rethynnea's Guild is blaming me for all manner of things—as if *I'm* somehow responsible for *their* being robbed."

"Robbed of what?" Alshiba asked bemusedly.

Niko's expression collapsed into sullenness. "Someone stole the Vestal Codex."

The Vestal Codex was a literal tome listing the rules and regulations governing vestalship to the realm. While in itself a valuable work to the vestals and Guild leadership, Franco couldn't imagine what anyone would've hoped to gain from stealing it. It wasn't like you could sell it without making a whopping target of yourself.

Niko threw up an exasperated hand. "Probably members of this purported *rebellion*."

"Rebellion?" Alshiba drew up short and turned swiftly to face him. "What's this?"

Yes, what is this? Franco became instantly attentive.

Niko's face puckered at the word. "Surely nothing to beg Your Excellency's attention. It's probably just a few covetous ill-wishers, no doubt riled by the restrictions I've put in place to make the realm safer for everyone. It will all blow over soon enough." He leaned around Alshiba to better view Franco, who was standing on her right. "Know *you* anything about it, Franco?"

"It's the first I've heard of it, Niko," which was true, though a hinting intuition made him uneasy.

Niko scowled. "Pity. But then...well, you've been here in the cityworld this whole time, haven't you?" His tone made up in resentment what it lacked for in warmth. "Seems like as my deputy, *you* should be the one spending all your time in Alorin mopping up—"

"A deputy vestal is the Seat's deputy, Niko, not the adjunct of another vestal, and I have need of Franco here." Alshiba leveled him a steady gaze. "I expect you to take this rumored rebellion in hand at once, Niko. Make your way to Alorin and do what you must to quash it. We cannot have second stranders becoming fractious with infighting."

"As you wish, Your Excellency," Niko muttered, but his brows had formed a deep V of resentment, and his breath reeked of malcontent.

They'd stopped just shy of the wide staircase that twined down five stories to the Hall's atrium. Alshiba started down it now.

"Ere I depart, Your Excellency," Niko murmured as he trailed behind her, aiming a daggered look at the back of her head, "might I inquire as to the other matter I earlier brought to your attention?"

Alshiba had her skirts in hand and was making a swift descent. "Which other matter?"

Niko aimed a glance at Franco. "About the Fifth Vestal? I believe you'll be surprised and…pleased by the candidate I've found to replace him."

"We're hardly in a position to attempt replacing the Fifth Vestal." Alshiba reached a landing where the stairs branched. She paused there and looked Niko over, her gaze uncompromising. "Concern yourself with *your* candidacy, Niko. Until the Council ratifies you, anyone might stand to challenge your appointment, and a strand in rebellion is hardly a feather in your cap."

Niko barely kept a glower from overtaking his expression; the effort to suppress it resulted in a strained twitching around his eyes.

Alshiba regarded him levelly. "I should think you'd want to depart at once."

Niko's jaw tightened. He seemed to want to say something, but he must've thought better of it, for he gave her a stiff bow instead, his eyes cold now. "Yes, Your Excellency. I should think I would." He spun on his heel and stalked down the stairs to the left, radiating indignation.

Alshiba watched him with a tiny furrow between her brows until he passed out of sight. Then she let out a measured exhale and shifted her gaze to Franco, speaking volumes in a glance, inviting of his company.

He motioned with his hand for her to lead away. She started down the stairs to their right but had hardly taken three steps before her footing faltered, and she swooned.

Franco grabbed for her. He heard her catch her breath as he pulled her back against him, and for a moment they hung in a delicate counterbalance.

Alshiba felt unexpectedly fragile in his arms, as if she was bound to corporeality by tension and determination and little else.

Then she relaxed somewhat, found her feet beneath her, and extracted herself politely from his arms. "Thank you." She gave him a look of gratitude while brushing a strand of flaxen hair from her face. "I don't know what happened just then."

He looked her over seriously. "You're clearly exhausted is what happened."

A fretful smile attempted at her lips, but it vanished without gaining much for its effort. "Perhaps I might have your arm for a bit longer?"

Frowning concernedly, Franco extended his elbow.

She accepted it with another flickering smile.

Silence accompanied them down the stairs. They walked closer than they had before, yet Franco felt propriety's invisible wall now separating them.

Propriety...and a canyon of secrets.

He'd spent nearly every waking moment of the last score of days in Alshiba's company. Each day he found more reasons to admire her; each day he watched her struggling to understand all of the factions in play, and each day he felt more guilt over the things he couldn't explain.

Though she'd subtly acknowledged that he served the First Lord, there were still many secrets that weren't his to reveal; thus, they often danced around subjects, circling the sleeping giant rather than risk the ire of its waking. But in this caprice, the truths that were bound to Franco's tongue became as burning blisters, too painful to release, yet just as agonizing to endure.

The staircase ended in an atrium—vast, sheathed in pretension and awash with Adepts upon their daily tasks. If Franco looked with different eyes, he could see grooves worn into the polished marble floor, the ruts of the same political maneuvers being performed in endless repetition.

Alshiba moved them towards the exit, her intent spoken by the firm hold she kept upon his arm. Franco needed no command to stay with her. In truth, it bothered him how drawn he was to her company.

She was the First Lord's lover for decades, the voice in his head pointed out. *Did you imagine you would find nothing in her to admire?*

But his admiration for her wasn't the problem.

He forced himself to think of other things.

"My lady, what are your thoughts on Niko's comment?" Franco glanced at her as they were heading for the exit doors. "Could he actually have found someone qualified to..." he was about to say *replace*, but who could ever possibly replace the Fifth Vestal?

Alshiba shook her head. "Alorin hasn't produced a fifth strand Adept in centuries."

Franco winced and scratched at the back of his head.

Her gaze sharpened upon him. "*Has* it?"

"Well…"

Secrets, secrets, the mad voice in his head goaded.

"The First Lord…has found a few fifth-stranders," Franco managed with a rather pained grimace. "He invited them to T'khendar to escape the ostracism they were facing in Alorin. And then…well, of course there's Ean val Lorian."

Her brows lifted. "I recall Raine speaking to me of the val Lorian prince. He claimed Björn had Awakened him far past the usual age, but—" Noting Franco's troubled expression, she narrowed her gaze upon him. "What are you not telling me?"

Franco scrubbed a hand along his jaw, wishing he might've avoided this conversation altogether. Why did always it fall to him to tell her the most shocking truths? "I suppose you should know, my lady: Ean val Lorian is Arion Tavestra Returned."

Alshiba came to an abrupt halt, dragging him backwards since she still had hold of his arm. "Arion Tavestra has *Returned*?"

What would she say if you told her this was the third time? The mad voice laughed hysterically at this.

"Does he remember—" but she stopped herself, staring hard at him. Then she shook her head. "What does he remember?"

"Enough, I think." Franco looked off towards the doors leading outside the hall, pining for escape. "I pray enough." He glanced to her with an entreaty to continue walking and she blessedly came without a struggle. "But I guarantee you Niko isn't planning to present Ean val Lorian for your consideration as the new Fifth Vestal."

Alshiba regarded him speculatively. "You think Niko was serious about that."

He gave a sort of grunt.

"Franco…" Alshiba frowned faintly, "you've hardly said an unkind word about Niko since arriving here, but I sense grave conflict in you. I would that you trusted me enough to speak candidly…to speak the truth."

Franco exhaled heavily and shook his head. "Truth is too subjective, my lady."

She really frowned at this, possibly because she felt the same. "Then tell me what appears true to you."

Franco cast her a troubled look.

The Paladin Knights manning the massive doors opened them at

Alshiba's approach, and Franco escorted her outside into the long light of late afternoon.

The Hall of a Thousand Thrones crowned the mountainside around them framed by sculptured pathways that wound through terraced gardens, administrative palaces and manicured grounds; hundreds of acres entirely surrounded by a high limestone wall. Locally, it was known as the Vestal City. Westward lay the expanse of Illume Belliel's azure ocean. Around, below and eastward, back through the mountainous hills, spread the cityworld with its towers and grandiose estates, the embassies of a thousand realms.

Keeping hold on Franco's arm, Alshiba headed down a path leading towards a sculpture garden, with the sparkling ocean dominating the horizon. There was hardly a place within the Vestal City where one couldn't see the water.

She regarded him with equanimity. "I suppose asking for your trust is bold of me."

"Not at all, my lady."

"I assure you that whatever your counsel, Franco, I will accept it."

Franco pushed a hand through his hair and eyed her uneasily. His chest felt tight, the pressure of the hundreds of truths he hadn't confessed all pushing to the forefront at once.

"Several months back, at the behest of the Great Master, I answered a summons from Niko and attended him at his estate. There, he and Dore Madden told me of their plans to depose the vestals, specifically Dagmar and Björn."

He turned his gaze to Alshiba, feeling a resurgence of the fury and horror he'd experienced during that conversation. "This would be bad enough, my lady, but you can't imagine they'll stop there—not those two. Niko's intelligence runs with the mean, but his ambition knows no bounds. And Dore Madden—" Franco had to stop himself from thinking too hard about Dore or his temper would come to a rapid boil. "I've never met a man so vile."

Alshiba frowned deeply at this and became silent.

For a time, they strolled a promenade beneath blossoming trees whose petals covered the path, lending it their delicate purity, yet Franco saw each petal as another truth he'd failed to confess. He was fairly sure there weren't enough petals on path or trees to account for the things he hadn't told her.

Finally, Alshiba let out a slow exhale. "I've perceived Niko's duplicity," she glanced to him, "though not to the degree you imply. But there's one thing I cannot understand. If overthrow is truly his intention, why would he have proposed you as his deputy?"

Franco shook his head. He couldn't understand that decision either, but he didn't doubt Niko hoped to gain from it somehow.

"Does Niko know?" She searched Franco's gaze with her own. "Does he know you serve Björn?"

To hear this truth spoken so plainly…yet not simply, for her statement had rung as a chord of notes—low tones of regret sounding with middle tones of resignation, both resonating disharmoniously against upper tones of bitterness, the latter slightly sharp and out of key. She'd never before stated it so bluntly. It appeared they were no longer skirting the edge of that truth.

Franco's gaze strayed to the trees. Long rays of sunlight were streaming through the blossoming branches. He felt somehow that he was sullying the innocence of that place by his presence. "I don't see how Niko could doubt my allegiances after what happened with Demetrio Consuevé." Six inches of steel piercing his gut rather shouted Demetrio's opinion of him—and Niko's by extension.

And the Lord Abanachtran…a Malorin'athgul, the first he'd ever encountered, except if…but he dared not think on those mysteries now.

Of course, Niko claimed to have known nothing of Demetrio's attack on Franco, but that was a laughable fallacy. Nothing happened on Niko's estate without his sanction.

"Do you think Niko hopes to gain something from Björn through you?" Alshiba was clearly following her own train of logic.

"If he does, he hasn't yet approached me."

"I suppose I haven't given him much chance, keeping him in Alorin as I have. I thought…" but she retreated to silence without sharing what she'd thought. Franco tried not to speculate where her mind might be taking her.

The promenade led into a park that offered incomparable views of the city as well as the mountainous coastline, Alshiba looked hesitantly to him. "Do you mind walking a bit more, Franco? I feel the need to clear my head."

"Not at all, my lady. I could use a walk myself."

She gave him a grateful look and they started off in a new direction. Soon they passed the pillared court of a *soglia're*, one of the many portals that linked the city's public spaces in a chain of easy travel, but Alshiba forewent the nodecourt and headed instead for the outer wall of the Vestal City.

Somewhere between Hall and gardens, Alshiba's Paladin Knight and truthreader, William, had joined their assemblage; but the latter lingered a polite distance behind, out of earshot if within quick reach of her call.

Franco wondered what William thought, seeing the Alorin Seat walking arm in arm with him. Then he decided he didn't care what he thought.

Through the tunnel beneath the wall, Alshiba chose a route that took them over a bridge before a tumbling waterfall. She stopped at the bridge's midway point, between two bronze statues, rested her hands on the wide marble railing and gazed out to sea.

Then she sighed. "What a fool I've been."

Franco stopped close beside her, their shoulders nearly touching. The falling sunlight was glinting off her oathring as like the ocean waves, but all he really noticed was how frail her finger seemed beneath the heavy silver band.

"I fear the events I've set in motion."

Franco turned and leaned back against the marble railing to face her. He crossed his arms and met her gaze. "Niko?"

"I never should've thought to…" She closed her eyes and exhaled a slow breath. "I made a grave error in judgment—a desperate error. You'll laugh at my folly."

"I wouldn't laugh at anything you did, my lady."

Alshiba cast him a dubious look. Shifting her gaze back to the sea, she smoothed a strand of hair from her face and then stared boldly ahead, as if directly into the storm. "Raine had vanished. Seth claimed the Fourth Vestal had been tricked into T'khendar—by *your* hand, in fact." She flicked a gaze in his direction, a stone to ripple the unsettled waters of his conscience. "It was as much as I could take, losing another vestal to Björn's damnable game—still with no *explanation* for any of it!"

Franco stared at her oath ring, feeling a familiar stone of guilt lodged his chest. It hadn't been his idea to steal Raine from her side—he'd only been following orders—but her ring reminded him of the companion rings he'd seen on the fingers of her three vestal brothers, all of whom were now living in T'khendar. Men she'd trusted. Men who for all intents and purposes had abandoned her.

How alone she must feel.

And though her vestals had departed without explanation, though her entire life lay moldering beneath the shadow of that mystery, though Franco stood as a representative of all she didn't understand…yet she hadn't demanded any answers from him. She *could* have—it was within her right—but knowing the truthbindings placed on him, she'd chosen to remain ignorant rather than bring Franco to harm.

The surprise and gratitude he felt over this ever assaulted him. Just that small degree of compassion from her was too much for him to stomach; it just sat there, indigestible, fermenting his guilt.

Alshiba turned and leaned against the railing, as he was. The mountain now loomed above them, lush and elegant, its terraced sides studded with mansions, rooftop gardens peeping through the canopy of ancient trees.

"I had hoped to stir at least *one* of my vestals to take action, and Niko seemed harmless. I had no idea he was capable of—" Alshiba let out a forceful exhale. "By Epiphany's light, of inspiring *mutiny*, Franco? An entire strand in revolt? I never imagined such a thing could happen."

Franco thought mutiny was preferable to apathetic acceptance, though the rumor of a rebellion bothered him on several levels. But the idea that Niko might be trying to replace the Fifth Vestal with his own candidate troubled him far more.

Alshiba pushed fingers to her brow and gazed absently at the waterfall tumbling down its deep and shaded ravine. "Now I'm caught in my own web. Having submitted Niko as a candidate, it's up to the Council to ratify him or not."

They were both praying for *not*.

She glanced to him and then straightened away from the railing. Franco offered her his arm again, and she took it absently.

"When I proposed Niko, I thought it absurd to imagine the Council would approve his nomination, but now…" Alshiba sighed ruefully. "He cares nothing for the work we're doing here; his only interest is in making alliances to solidify his votes—and the worst sort of alliances, with the most powerful and unscrupulous of Seats."

"Mir Arkadhi," Franco muttered, having seen Niko too many times for comfort in the Eltanin Seat's company.

Alshiba gave him a telling look. "I've tried to keep him in Alorin as much as possible."

Franco clenched his jaw. The very idea of Niko van Amstel permanently becoming Alorin's Second Vestal made him physically ill; yet the more he understood of Council politics, the more he realized it was a real possibility. Vestal appointments were meant to be for life, but Dagmar had been gone so long that it was feasible the Council would declare his absence as abdication and agree to replace him.

Alshiba sighed. "Would that there was another candidate to challenge Niko."

Franco gave her a sidelong look. "What do you mean?"

She aimed a glance his way. "Technically, Niko is only nominated to the position of Second Vestal. Until the Council ratifies him and makes his vestalship permanent, anyone can seek the appointment."

Franco wondered what made him more uncomfortable in that moment—the intimation in her words, or the voluminous look she was leveling him.

He swallowed and looked off out to sea. "The Great Master is Alorin's Second Vestal."

"For all the good it does us here."

He frowned deeply at this.

She arched a brow in subtle challenge. "I had hoped Dagmar would hear of Niko's advancement and come with sword at the ready to defend his stake."

No... Franco swallowed, *he just sent me.*

Alshiba placed her other hand on his arm, drawing his gaze back to her. She must've seen the discomfort in his eyes then, for her gaze entreated him earnestly. "I don't *want* to replace Dagmar, Franco, but I need a Second Vestal to advise me," she looked back out towards the sea and frowned slightly, "more so now than ever before."

Something in her tone... Franco connected the memory of the Speaker so intently watching Alshiba's departure that afternoon, and his logic took an unexpected leap. "Are you saying..." he stared at her harder, "Alshiba, are you saying *you're*—"

"Aldaeon has asked me to chair the Interrealm Regulatory Committee."

Franco gaped at her. "And you've accepted?"

"Not officially, but I'm strongly considering it. I voted in favor of the measure. It only follows that I would want to see it fairly enacted."

"That's...brave of you." He shoved a hand through his hair. It wasn't what he'd wanted to say. *Obscenely dangerous* seemed more apt.

And after the outcry he'd witnessed that afternoon, it was abundantly clear that any one of a thousand Seats might take matters into their own hands to ensure their candidate became the Committee Chairperson—even if it meant permanently eliminating any and all perceived competition.

With William always a watchful distance behind, Franco escorted Alshiba back to the Alorin embassy, overlooking the sea. The estate supported many residences, but Alshiba's apartments were a mansion unto themselves.

William opened the entry doors for her. "Is there anything I can do for you, Your Excellency?"

Alshiba gave him a tired smile. "No, William. Thank you."

He nodded and made to close the doors.

"Franco." Alshiba's voice halted William and Franco both. "Stay a moment, would you?"

Beset by a sudden odd anxiety, Franco dutifully turned back. William leveled him a look that spoke volumes—*several* volumes: warning overlapping caution, layered with threat. Then he closed them inside the mansion together.

Alshiba led Franco through a series of palatial rooms and into her study, where a wall of glass doors overlooked a high balcony patio and the sea. She walked to a sideboard while Franco looked over her impressive collection of artifacts, which were artfully arranged on shelves and pedestals around the room—and indeed, more of which he'd noticed on display throughout the mansion.

Alshiba came over and handed him a goblet. As he took the wine from her, their eyes met. Something in the look she gave him…he read it well, yet its message was so unexpected that he became sure he hadn't read it well at all.

They quickly separated again. It was almost painful the way they haunted each other's periphery—tentative, belabored by apprehension, neither one quite brave enough to step into candor's central light.

Alshiba wandered over to the priceless collection of artifacts. "Lovely, aren't they? They're Björn's, mostly." She sipped her wine. "Tributes from the Thousand Realms. Niko has added more in recent weeks."

Franco didn't care about the art just then, for his eyes were pinned on her hand and the way it was shaking as she held her wine. She seemed uncommonly pale in the dying light. "Alshiba—"

She turned a look over her shoulder. "You still don't entirely trust me, do you?"

Franco dropped his gaze to the dark liquid swirling in his goblet. She was adept at reading him—uncomfortably so, considering the relatively short time they'd spent together. "I'm not sure I even know what trust feels like anymore."

Alshiba grunted. "It feels like safety. Both are rare commodities in Illume Belliel." She walked towards the windows and the encroaching night.

Franco perceived a grave weariness in her movements as well as in her speech; even in her quiet exhalations. It seemed to him as if she stood by force of will alone, not even resting in her own home for want of projecting the strength that had become a shield for her. It had never been more apparent to him that *he* wanted to be that shield.

Franco lowered his gaze back to his wine. What had *happened* to him? From death's door, he'd awoken as if to a completely different life, with a new mistress and sudden purpose found in service of her. How had she claimed him so completely?

"For three centuries it was just Raine, Seth and me." Alshiba turned a look back towards him as she strolled the long windows. "Raine and myself, more truly, for Seth as you know, offers intemperate counsel." She touched a hand to the glass and then continued on, trailing regret behind her. Franco wondered what was really on her mind…why she'd asked him to stay.

After a time she exhaled a slow breath. "Do you know why I voted for the measure to allow interrealm trade, Franco?"

Franco lowered the wine from his lips. "No, my lady."

She turned to face him. "I voted for it because Björn would've voted for it." A tragic sort of smile touched her lips and lingered, hinting of regret. "All these years—verily, for *three hundred* years—I've simply been doing as Björn would've done, trying to make the decisions he would've made." Her expression twisted into disharmony. "Ironically, a traitor's remembered counsel still proves the truest."

Franco drank his wine. It would do no good to try to advocate for the First Lord; the betrayals she was speaking of were ones Björn admitted to without justification—*personal* betrayals, deep treasons of the heart.

Franco sensed the fragile filaments of her trust reaching towards him, seeking *him*, so delicate he hardly dared breathe for fear of scattering them. Yet deeper still rooted his own fear of *being* trusted.

"For so many years, I've lived this way," she confessed, an odd hesitation in her manner, "hardly daring to have a thought without comparing it first to Björn's ideal. Living, sleeping and breathing the mystery of his abandonment. But then *you* came—"

She wavered unsteadily on her feet.

Franco rushed over and caught her. He hastily set down his wine to better support her and helped her sit down in a chair. Then he knelt before her. "My lady?" He took the goblet from her hands and set it down.

She looked frighteningly pale and dabbed at her cheeks with the backs of her fingers. "The wine. Perhaps—"

"It's not the wine, Alshiba." Her condition alarmed him. He held her gaze, determined now to get the truth out of her. "Are you ill?"

She stared into his eyes with a furrowed brow. Then she exhaled a tremulous breath and fell back in the chair. "I don't know." Her head lolled to one side. "I'm not sleeping. I can't seem to keep anything down."

This news disturbed him greatly. "How long has this been going on?"

She gave him a rueful look. "I noticed it soon after you and Niko arrived in Illume Belliel."

A host of ill possibilities bombarded Franco upon this news. He searched her gaze with his own. "You've seen a Healer?"

"Of course."

"And?"

"She said my pattern seemed frayed but couldn't find a reason for it."

"But she Healed you?"

"She tried. The Healing hasn't…taken."

Franco's thoughts were rapidly carrying him to dark places. He knew too many ways *elae* might be used to make a person ill. Doubtless Alshiba knew them also—doubtless she'd had Illume Belliel's Healers search for them in her pattern, but if it wasn't *elae* making her sick...

The First Lord must hear about this. He would want to know what's happening to the woman he loves.

Franco gazed disconcertedly at her while considering the ramifications of illness versus ill working, wishing he understood better how to help her. In the last, he handed her back her wine—at least she was keeping that down.

Their eyes met as their fingers met, and Franco glimpsed a naked truth in her gaze. Words crept shyly towards her lips but then fled back into hiding, where his own words remained, thinly shielded by protestations of duty.

She withdrew the goblet from his hand and drank of it, keeping her own counsel behind her silence, making him wonder if his own unexpected desire had merely tricked him into imagining hers.

Feeling an unwelcome anxiety, Franco stood and went to pour himself more wine.

Alshiba followed him with her gaze. Her eyes felt like heat, searing him all the way across the room. "Franco, I hate to impose upon you...but until I understand better of what's happening to me, will you...stay here... with me?"

Franco paused with his hand on the decanter. He'd thought at first... the intimation in her tone...but no, she only meant to have the support of his company, and the mansion had countless bedchambers.

Instinct told him he should leave at once, that he did not want to encourage his own ill-conceived thoughts. But she'd bound him to her that very first day—he still had no idea how—and leaving her side had become an unpalatable choice.

The First Lord's admonishment echoed in mind, relayed to him via a Dreamscape conversation with Dagmar: *'...Tell Franco to do nothing to betray Alshiba's confidence, even should it appear to mean betraying mine...'*

Franco blew out a forceful breath and turned her a look over his shoulder. "Of course, my lady."

SEVEN

"I would rather traverse the valleys of a thousand hells than live a day without desire."

–The zanthyr Vaile

ALYNERI PARRIED TRELL'S descending sword, twice, and again. He forced her back—three quick steps beneath his flying blade. She spun under his next swing and thrust her weapon upwards, aiming for this throat. He reared back, and her blade sang past his ear.

The *cortata* filled her with its tingling, heady power, while Vaile's Merdanti blade hummed in her mind, a constant companion that enticed and encouraged. And *Trell*...matching blades with him felt the sweetest torment.

Trell lunged. Alyneri sidestepped.

She jabbed and he slung her blade away.

Into her opening, he advanced with four rapid blows. She met each of them and then spun out of his line, swiping for his side.

He sidestepped and made an angled thrust back at her. She spun out of his reach, aiming a backhanded stroke as she turned. He swept her blade aside with a scraping ring and lunged for her. She danced back with a laughing gasp.

Who could've imagined that sparring would be so invigorating, so purely enjoyable, so *freeing*? One side of her blade knew exhilaration, the other exhaustion, while desire radiated in each clashing, making her blade hungry for the taste of his.

The more she fought Trell, the more she admired him. The quality of his movement, the power of his focused advances...he wooed and enticed her even while battering her. She felt the threat in his every swing; yet his gaze, pinned unerringly upon hers, invited her ever closer. They courted each other with deadly blades, and never had a romance known a more intoxicating mix of danger and desire.

Now Trell stalked her with his blade held low. A sheen of sweat clung to his chest beneath his open shirt, but its hem remained tucked into his pants. She could tell how hard she was making him fight her by the state of his shirttails.

She brought up her blade with both hands and darted in for an overhead blow. He grinned and parried her with an upward stroke. Steel clanged. Sentient blades sang. Their eyes met but inches apart.

Then Trell hooked his foot behind her ankle and swept her off her feet. As she fell, he caught her hand above her head while his other hand grabbed her around the waist, and he cushioned her fall as they landed together in the grass.

Alyneri felt the length of him pressing atop her and smiled demurely up at him. "I don't recall this sword form, Your Highness."

"Indeed not, Your Grace?" Trell slipped her blade out of her hand and brought her arm down within the confines of his. "I thought everyone was familiar with this form."

To keep herself grounded against the invitation in his gaze, Alyneri swept her mind back through that day's sparring. "Were you using the *cortata* at all?"

Trell smiled. "A little."

"How much?"

He pressed his lips to the back of the hand he still held. "Enough to make it fair."

"If you never use the pattern in our matches, how can I know for certain that you have it?"

"I have it, Alyneri." Trell released her hand and traced his fingers along her collarbone instead, sending delightful shivers through her. He was hardly paying attention—at least, not to the conversation.

To be fair, she was having difficulty concentrating on more than the feeling of his body pressing against hers. She could remain focused when sparring with him, with some *distance* between them, but lying in his arms…

"Soon," Trell ran fingertips down her throat, imparting a lingering tingle in a trail of promise, his smoldering gaze intense upon her, "very soon…" His mouth hovered close to hers.

Alyneri closed her eyes, warm with the connection she felt to him. "It cannot be too so—"

"Why do I always find you two this way?" Vaile's voice chided them.

Alyneri opened her eyes to find the zanthyr striding out of the trees. Vaile wore a dress of clinging green silk, split up the sides to reveal tall boots of the same velvet hue. Somehow, the dress only made her seem more dangerous, as a panther's sleek fur accentuates its lithe power.

Vaile came to a halt above them and arched a raven brow. "It would lead one to wonder if any swordplay ever occurred at all."

Trell lifted his gaze to her. "Alyneri distracted me again."

Vaile's emerald green eyes regarded them amusedly over crossed arms. "Perhaps I should encase Her Grace in armor."

Trell grinned. "That would only invite a different challenge." He sat up and helped a blushing Alyneri to sit up as well. "It's not Alyneri's fault." He brushed a strand of hair back from her shoulder and smiled at her. "She does the best she can, considering my propensity to distraction."

"Yes, I'm well advised of how difficult you've made her task." Vaile retrieved her blade from the grass—the one Alyneri had been sparring with—and looked it over as if gazing upon an old friend. "Sidthe has told me everything."

Alyneri's eyes widened upon the sentient blade. "Everything?"

Vaile cast her a potent look. "*Everything.*"

Alyneri covered her mouth with one hand and turned, blushing, to Trell.

Trell chuckled. "There are no secrets in the First Lord's *sa'reyth*." He pushed to his feet and held his hands to help Alyneri to stand, shooting Vaile a grin the while. "Only subtext."

"Which you are learning to speak with alacrity, similar to your mastery of the *cortata*, I do believe, Trell of the Tides."

Trell gave Vaile a bow. "Thank you, my lady. I bask in your esteem."

"But not so much, I think, as in Alyneri's adoration." Vaile's smile held a feline serenity, quietly approving. She set the toe of her boot beneath Trell's sword and flipped it up to him. He caught it out of the air, whereupon she gave both of them a nod of earnest meaning. "Ramu has returned."

Alyneri exchanged a swift look with Trell. Her heart was suddenly fluttering. "Then…"

Trell wrapped his arm around her and drew her close, his gaze locked upon hers. "Tonight?"

Alyneri smiled…nodded quietly.

Vaile regarded them as a dam observing her kittens. "Come, adored ones. Ready yourselves."

They met again beneath sunset skies upon a hill overlooking the First Lord's *sa'reyth*. As Alyneri rounded the rise, Trell was already there, looking dashing in a cerulean coat trimmed in gold embroidery and with his hair swept smoothly back. She felt her own blue dress too simple by comparison, despite the heavy beadwork decorating it.

Trell held out his hand when he saw her, his gaze admiring. "You look beautiful."

Alyneri looked him over wondrously. "I feel common, next to you."

"A princess of Kandori?" The quirk of a smile hinted on his lips. "Common, you are not."

Alyneri looked down at her hands, held in his, and then nervously back to him. "Are you sure about this?"

His eyes crinkled. "Need you really ask?"

"It will feel…strange. It may hurt. The experience is different for everyone."

"Pain doesn't frighten me, Alyneri."

"That's because nothing frightens you."

"No, that's untrue." He ran his thumb across her lips and held her gaze captive to his. "Living without you…that frightens me." He drew her close and wrapped his arms around her. "This bonding—"

"Binding," she correctly softly, though her mind was fair shouting it and her heart a pounding drum to be heard throughout the countryside.

"—binding," he ran his lips across her hair, "whatever discomfort it involves, I welcome it."

Alyneri still couldn't believe it was happening. They'd spoken of marriage, but with so much in play, so much unknown, with their titles and the responsibilities associated with them momentarily pushed aside but always looming…the prospect of any formal ceremony carried too much complexity.

They both felt their promises to each other more binding than any law, more meaningful than token rings, yet this binding that Trell had so readily agreed to…

Ramu wouldn't be using the fifth, but the intention remained the same. They would be joined more surely than any king or court could adjudicate, their fates entwined, their very paths through the tapestry interwoven. Bindings were the Adept form of marriage and far more *binding* than signatures and seals on parchment. But Trell wasn't an Adept, so before the binding itself could take place…

"Why do you look so concerned?" He took her chin again. "You're fair scowling, Duchess—and on this, our…what do you call it? Not a wedding day, a binding day?" He arched a brow amusedly.

Alyneri forced her expression to relax. "Sometimes I still can't believe Prince Trell val Lorian wants to spend his life with me."

Trell's eyes glinted as he looked her over. "Believe me, Alyneri. I feel the same." He brushed his fingers along her cheek and smiled at the jeweled pins Jaya had put in her hair. "Every day I ask myself what I could've possibly done to deserve a woman so brave, selfless and true."

Alyneri was starting to feel fluttery from the implication in his gaze—never mind her own contemplation of the night ahead. She admitted softly, "Your mother chose better for me than ever I chose for myself."

"Oh, that's right," his eyes shone with a mischievous light, "we're betrothed, aren't we?" He drew her into his arms again, but then his mood sobered. "In some life, anyway."

Alyneri laid her head against his chest. "It feels so far off, doesn't it? Calgaryn, court…a world away."

Trell's chest rose and fell with a sigh. "A hundred worlds."

They were still standing in this embrace when the others arrived. Balaji with Vaile, Jaya and Mithaiya, Carian beside Fynnlar, and Náiir and Rhakar behind them. In the last came the illustrious and rather elusive Ramu.

Alyneri hadn't yet met the 'sometimes' leader of the *drachwyr*, but something in his bearing—not to mention his height—reminded her instantly of Phaedor. The others parted naturally to let him pass.

"Ah, Trell of the Tides," Ramu's eyes were warm as he approached. He took Trell by the shoulder while gracing him with the full measure of his attention. "I've been kept apprised of your adventures. It pleases me beyond words to greet you here again today."

Trell took Ramu's shoulder with gratitude in his gaze. "Your advice has guided me since the moment of our parting."

Ramu nodded graciously to this and shifted his attention to Alyneri. "And here then would be Alyneri, Princess-Heir of Kandori, scion of my brother's line, of whom I have heard so many tales of bravery."

Alyneri pressed her palms together and bowed in the Kandori fashion. She lifted a smile to him as she straightened. "Thank you for coming here for us, my lord."

"I can think of no better interlude to my duties."

Knowing what those duties entailed, Alyneri felt all the more honored—and awed—by his officiating presence.

Ramu motioned the others into a circle and had Alyneri and Trell stand before him, holding each other's hands. "Tonight we attend and bear witness to the mortal binding of Trell val Lorian and Alyneri Haxamanis." He looked between the two of them before settling his intense gaze on Alyneri. "Alyneri, daughter of Jair, do you consent to be bound to this man, who is no Adept, but whose path you would walk as though your own?"

Alyneri's heart did a little leap. She gazed at Trell—wonderingly, still hardly believing the moment was real, that this was truly happening—and somehow found breath to respond. "Yes, I do."

Ramu shifted his attention to Trell. "Trell val Lorian, Prince of Dannym, brother-bound of Björn van Gelderan, do you consent to be bound to this woman, with full knowledge of what this entails? Do you willingly, of your own determinism, choose to walk this woman's path as though your own, until Cephrael parts you?"

Trell's gaze, holding Alyneri's, made her heart dance. "I do."

Ramu nodded to both of them. "So intended, so let it be. Trell," and he motioned for Trell to turn to him. They stood for a moment facing each other, regarding each other, and then Ramu smiled. "It is my honor to awaken *elae* to your awareness. If you will permit me the truthreader's hold…"

Trell stepped closer, and Ramu placed his hand over Trell's forehead—thumb to temple, first and middle fingers to the pressure-points at the bridge of the nose, and ring and little finger pressing into the opposite temple.

Seeing Ramu's hand splayed so, Alyneri immediately thought of Tanis. How she wished the lad might've been there to witness this moment in her life—this astonishing, *impossible* moment—when she and Trell joined their hearts and paths, and Trell was awakened to *elae*! How Tanis would've smiled upon them!

Trell's eyes were closed, his lips set with an almost contemplative smile, as if he was mentally observing the *drachwyr's* efforts and was intrigued by them. Knowing Trell, the fiery awakening of *elae*—a moment described by so many *na'turna* as a most terrifying experience, like unto standing in Divinity's reckoning light—would simply be another marker on the ever-lengthening road of his past, a moment to ponder, or not, as and when life required; possibly a chance for learning, certainly a topic of introspection, yet no more than these unless circumstance bore it necessary.

'*Life comes at you, and you…handle it, Alyneri.*' This was the sum of his wisdom shared with her once. Yet so wise it seemed to her now, having wept and worried and despaired over his welfare for so many long weeks, able to do little more than hope, casting prayers into the heavens doubting anyone heard or cared; utterly isolated in her fear—at times her own life even seeming imperiled by it—with nothing else *to* do but tremble in the shadows of the unknown. Yet Trell, the while, had simply taken each moment, each day, at it came, and *handled* whatever life threw at him.

Alyneri had never known anyone who faced his mortal existence with such simplicity of expectation, yet who, by this very view, placed life so effortlessly under his control.

Moments passed and no one spoke, yet the world was hardly silent.

That gathering of immortals drew the currents as sparrows to a newly seeded field. *Elae* swarmed them on excited wings, and no Adept within miles could've missed its song. Alyneri stood as though within the buffeting wind, feeling the currents fluttering around her. The Lord of the Heavens threaded Trell's awareness with every strand of the lifeforce, waking him to *elae's* melody, until—

Trell started, the barest captured breath, whereupon Ramu released him.

Trell opened his eyes with a powerful exhale and stared at Ramu. Then he looked fast to Alyneri and held out his hand to her, his gaze growing wider by the moment. She took his hand with joyous tears in her eyes.

"A mutual binding is woven by each wielder." Ramu looked to the others. "Who works the pattern for Alyneri?"

Jaya stepped forward with a smile as glowing as the citrine gemstones dangling across her brow. "I will wield the threads on her behalf."

"Very good, Jaya. Take your place at her side." Ramu again looked to the others. "Who stands for Trell?"

"I do." Náiir moved forward and placed a hand on Trell's shoulder. Trell turned him a grateful smile.

Ramu nodded to his brother, then opened his palms and took a step back. "Prepare your workings."

Jaya took Alyneri's hand, whereupon she felt the *drachwyr's* polite mental inquiry, a lady standing on the doorstep requesting admittance to the privacy of her mind. Alyneri welcomed Jaya into the intimacy of her thoughts with gratitude and open arms, and with her breath caught on the joy constricting her throat.

Jaya's awareness flowed as a warm and glowing elixir into the goblet of Alyneri's mind. She saw brilliance and felt sunlight and knew kindness in the grace of heat. She barely heard Ramu's next words for the extraordinary sensation of Jaya's mind melding with—no, *overcoming*, hers.

"What is to be the form of this binding?"

Trell had hold of Alyneri's other hand and squeezed it. He angled her a captivating smile. "A kiss."

Then he pulled her close and his mouth was on hers, and Jaya started Patterning, and Alyneri's world exploded with light and color and the heady sensation of twirling—*spiraling*—through space, feeling strings of herself growing, becoming…intertwining as vines of connection took root. She knew little more than these sensations beneath blinding light and the dizzying wonder of Trell kissing her, until—

He appeared.

Suddenly she cradled his mind in hers, felt hers embraced in his. They knew each other as the daylight knows the sky, their minds made permeable to each other's truths. It took Alyneri a dazed minute to extract her thoughts from Trell's, and she really only managed it when he released her from his kiss.

Trell pressed his forehead against hers and let a sigh escape his lips. "And I thought you were beautiful on the outside."

Alyneri's breath caught. Then she threw her arms around him and hugged him while he laughed against her ear.

Someone—probably the pirate—let out a jubilant whoop.

The last light of the sun passed beneath the curve of the world.

And the *drachwyr* made an offering of fire to the stars.

Alyneri watched over Trell's shoulder as Náiir opened his hands and sent tiny glowing stars floating upwards to illumine the night high over their heads. The other *drachwyr* followed suit, and soon dozens of glowing lights hovered above them, an extension of the heavens.

Ramu opened his palms. "So intended," two orbs of golden fire appeared and floated upwards to join the others, "thus is it so."

As she gazed at the *drachwyr's* floating stars, Alyneri reflected on the miracle of that moment. To have been joined in binding with Trell val Lorian by immortal Sundragons in a ceremony so ancient and holy, and so purely beautiful in its intent! She felt so graced to have *this* man as her partner, and these friends as the enablers and witnesses of their troth. Could she truly be deserving of such happiness?

Then Jaya took her by the shoulders and was smiling and kissing her on both cheeks. "Sweet Alyneri, may Epiphany bless your union." She moved to Trell and kissed him, even as Mithaiya came to bless Alyneri in like manner. By the time Balaji, Náiir, Rhakar and Vaile had all given their graces, Alyneri felt her face must surely be glowing as brightly as the *drachwyr's* stars.

But when Ramu offered his blessing…it might've been a trick of the tears filling her eyes, but it seemed for an instant as if all the stars in the heavens burned twice as brightly and then fell in cascading silver veils, as of diamonds thrown across their path.

Finally Fynn and Carian came sauntering up. Fynn extended his goblet with a wave of his arm and gave her a surprisingly debonair bow. "Welcome to the family, Your Grace."

Alyneri took his hand and accepted his kiss on her cheek. "Thank you, Lord Fynnlar. I trust you won't make me regret becoming related to you."

Fynn arched a brow. "I wouldn't trust that at all, Your Grace."

Carian clasped wrists with Trell wearing a grin. "Who'd have thought when we made our accord in Olivine we'd wind up together here, eh my handsome?"

Trell held his hand and his gaze. "A few times, I was fairly sure that if we wound up anywhere together, it would be on the doorstep of the Returning."

Carian replied with a wink, "Nah, I told you, the ladies have a thing for me."

Alyneri slipped an arm around Trell's waist. "The ladies...?"

"The goddesses of Fortune and Luck," Trell advised.

"Yeah, about that," Fynn nudged Carian with his empty goblet and then waved them all to follow after the *drachwyr*, who were heading back to the *sa'reyth*, "you promised to put in a good word with them for me."

Carian hitched up his britches and ambled into the lead. "Just as soon as you pay me the money you owe me, mate."

"That sounds very much like a bribe," Fynn followed after him, looking aggravated, "and you *know* my moral index requires me to steer clear of bribery unless *I'm* the one being offered the money..."

Trell held Alyneri back to let the vagabond pair disappear over the rise. Then he wrapped his arms around her waist and drew her close. She saw her own happiness mirrored in his eyes, her thoughts mirrored in his, both of them very much enjoying sharing the space of their minds.

"We're *bound*, you and I."

Gazing up at him with happiness flooding into her, Alyneri simply nodded.

"This...connection is wondrous, Alyneri, yet I'm bound to you even more by gratitude. I wouldn't be standing here to know this moment, this miraculous experience, if not for you."

His words resonated as sound in her ears, warmth in her heart and truth across the bond they now shared. "We are become each other's light."

He tucked her head beneath his chin and exhaled a contented sigh that drew a chord of joy through her. "You have long been mine."

❖

Trell sat beside Alyneri at the head of Balaji's banquet table enjoying the merriment taking place around him. More *drachwyr* flame-lights hovered beneath the peaked roof of the violet tent, shedding their sparkling light on those who'd gathered to celebrate Trell and Alyneri's union.

Beyond those well known to him, he saw many Adepts from the Nodefinder Rebellion, whose compound occupied the next valley. Trell knew a few by name: the thief Kardashian, who he'd first encountered on his adventures with Carian; Gannon Bair, one of the few truthreaders Trell had met who hadn't an ounce of innocence about him; the Bemothi Nodefinder Devangshu Vita, in whom Trell acknowledged a solid intellect and competent air; and the ebony-skinned Whisper Lord Ledio Jeroen, who had a quiet demeanor that reminded him greatly of Loghain, another Whisper Lord, whose sensibility and solicitousness stood much at odds with his countenance. Even the oft-bickering *drachwyr* were in solidarity that evening as they gathered in celebration.

But no matter how engaging the conversation elsewhere, his attention always strayed back to Alyneri, seated at his side. She was laughing now with Jaya and Vaile, the three of them as sisters in their devotion to each other. Alyneri's brown eyes were lambent with her laughter, while her thoughts felt quiet in his mind, peaceful. Happiness permeated them.

From the first moment he'd laid eyes upon her after dragging her from Naiadithine's flood with a broken arm, all covered in mud, Trell had felt an uncommon connection to her. As his admiration and respect for Alyneri had grown, of course that connection had strengthened as well, but what he felt now was exponentially so much more.

It was *heady*, this feeling. Being bound to Alyneri, sharing the space of her mind, this offered amazement enough. But Ramu's awakening of him to *elae*—*this* experience, Trell could barely breathe through, even so many hours later.

The lifeforce consumed his awareness, and through it, he kenned a powerful connectedness to the living world. Surely that connection had always existed, but he'd never known it so intimately, so potently. Now, suddenly, to have it materialized in a way that was perceptible…

It was astonishing and humbling.

While part of him basked in the warmth of Alyneri's admiration and pondered their later evening together with glorious expectation, another part of him perched between wonder and reverence. To be surrounded by so many Adepts, each of whom felt this connection every day—oh, Trell recognized they'd likely become inured to the sensation, but to know it at all! To live with it and somehow become at peace with this constant and overwhelming feeling of expansion!

The understanding even gave him a new respect for Taliah—not merely that she could sense this power but that she *used* it. That any Adept would dare to channel it somehow…that they found the hubris in themselves to *command* it…the entire thing inspired his awe.

As the night lengthened, Trell found himself gazing at Alyneri for lengthening spans of time. He loved watching her, loved how his gaze alone could bring a flush to her cheeks. Even her lips seem to swell beneath his inspection, as if in preparation to receive his.

He'd meant what he'd said earlier. During his imprisonment, Alyneri had been the light that promised a dawn to pain's endless darkness. Even before he'd known her well, she'd brought a lightness to his heart.

He'd endured months of watching the way her silk dresses clung and shifted and hugged her form. Now, on the night he would finally have her, he found himself oddly treasuring those last few minutes of wanting, even though he doubted he would ever lose his desire to claim her. Something in Alyneri called to a part of him in a way he still didn't entirely understand.

When he finally extracted her from the gaiety, he didn't feel rushed, yet an urgency underscored his motions. He took her hand and drew her from her chair and they waved their goodbyes to the accompaniment of expected jests, laughter, and well wishes; and then they were walking back down the hill to the *sa'reyth* and Trell's tent, and knew only the silence of the night and the quietude of each other's anticipation.

Trell understood he would not be merely claiming Alyneri for himself that evening but also her maidenhood, which for some reason, women treasured like little boys their wooden swords or a noble his favorite hawk; gods help the man who tried to part any of them from the other.

"Did you just compare my virginity to a bird of prey?" Alyneri's frosty tone only partially concealed her amusement.

Trell turned her a grin. "You weren't supposed to hear that." As he was sweeping aside the drapes to enter the *sa'reyth*, a thought occurred to him, and he turned beneath the parting to bar her entrance. "Have you been listening to my thoughts all night?"

Alyneri clasped her hands behind her back and smiled quietly at him. Never had innocence looked so culpable.

Trell shook his head admiringly. "No wonder you were blushing." He grabbed her close to the tune of her laughter and gazed down at her, wondering if he might take her there and then.

Alyneri caught a fingernail between her teeth. "I think Jaya at least might take slight offense."

Trell growled an oath and swept her up into his arms. He carried her off while she laughingly claimed innocence, blaming him entirely for thinking too loudly into the shared space of their minds.

Gaining his rooms, Trell set Alyneri down on the edge of his bed and then propped his hands to either side of her, pinning her body as he captured her gaze, and thought deliberately, *I cannot think quietly when thinking of you.* To this, he added a host of images, his intentions for the rest of the evening, and was rewarded when a furious blush overcame her expression.

Trell let the hint of a smile manifest, but he didn't release her from his gaze. "I fear you have me at a disadvantage, Your Grace."

Alyneri's brown eyes looked liquid in the lamplight, her lips flushed. Her mind, shared with his, fairly hummed with expectation. "How so, Your Highness?"

Trell leaned closer. She fell to her elbows on the bed. "It appears there is much to be learned about managing this binding, Your Grace. You'll have to instruct me."

Alyneri searched his gaze, seeking deeper meaning to his intent. "Of… of course."

Trell smiled. "Good." He straightened and walked to the sideboard and a decanter of mulled wine. He could feel her startled gaze following him. Clearly she'd expected him to simply throw her on the bed. He threw her a half-smile instead.

With wine in hand, he returned and sat down beside her. "It appears I know how to share my thoughts with you." He extended a goblet to her. "Instruct me in how to keep them to myself."

Still braced on her elbows, Alyneri blinked at him. "You mean…now?"

He smiled and drank his wine.

Alyneri pushed herself upright. Then she took the wine from him, looking confused.

So their courtship found a new channel. Sitting at one end of the couch while Alyneri claimed the other, Trell put meaning behind his gaze but made no advance. They drank wine and ate fruit from the platter Balaji had left for them, and beneath Alyneri's somewhat bemused tutelage, Trell learned how to guard his thoughts.

It wasn't that he wanted to hide things from her, but context framed understanding, and there were still too many of his own experiences for which Alyneri would lack that context. He dared not join with her when he couldn't stop his thoughts and memories from flooding out. Above all else, he needed to protect her from those.

When at last he knew himself capable of withholding what he willed, Trell set down his wine, settled his gaze on Alyneri, and let his mind fill with thoughts of her—of his admiration and respect, his adoration, and his desire to protect and provide for her. When Alyneri's eyes grew glassy, he filled his mind with other thoughts, those darkened by the midnight colors of desire, of longing, and of a languorous yielding upon passion's boundless shore.

These thoughts drew a flush back to her cheeks and made her breath come faster. He watched her bosom rising and falling and placed this vision of her in the shared space of their minds, that she might see and understand how her need drove his; that she might know the depth of his regard, that while he claimed her body for his own, he would cherish her love more.

Alyneri sat for a moment with her lips parted, seeing the vision of herself framed in his eyes. Then she reached for him, even as he reached for her.

Thought became fluid as their hands found one another. Somehow they found their feet. His fingers deftly unworked the hooks of her gown, hers the buttons of his coat. He broke their kiss to pull his shirt over his head but let it fall slowly as he gazed upon her delicate shift—hardly more than a slip of sheer silk edged in lace, yet it cupped her breasts and slid languidly across her hips, sketching shadows beneath her navel.

Trell withdrew the pins from her hair and arranged the heavy locks as they fell until they teased long at her waist. He walked a circle then, admiring her with a subtle half-smile while she stood confidently beneath his inspection. Then he came up behind her and drew her close to feel him rise against her.

"Are you…" she whispered breathlessly, leaning back against him, "do you…"

But he knew she didn't know how to ask him what he truly desired, or if he thought she could fulfill it.

Trell pressed a kiss to her neck. "Everything that's happened to me, Alyneri—all I've endured….I would do it all again to have this night with you."

She knew he meant it. He made sure that was clear in his thoughts.

"*Trell…*"

He claimed her neck and then her mouth, and soon after, the rest of her, and as daybreak claimed the world and he took her yet again, Trell reaffirmed for himself that every word he'd said was true.

EIGHT

*"The truest power there is in this universe is understanding.
It is the greatest force for change."*
—Björn van Gelderan, Fifth Vestal of Alorin

ALL THE NEXT day, Tanis walked the lonesome Hallovian moors, keeping company with the gorse and the wind and his own troubled thoughts. He tried to push images of the Healers he'd seen Pelas torturing from his mind—tried not to imagine his mother in the same situation, or recall too clearly the images he'd caught from Pelas's thoughts—but the constant wind blew ill envisionings into his head.

He was reeling, both from the turbulence that came with the knowledge of what Pelas had done, and from sensitivity to Pelas's acute torment on the other end of their binding. Several times that day Pelas had contacted him, mind to mind, to convey again his sorrow at having harmed Tanis by harming Isabel. He'd begged Tanis to let him explain better of his acts. But Tanis didn't think he could handle knowing more details.

He felt Pelas's dismay as if it were his own. He perceived the man's deep contrition. He didn't even really *blame* him, for he understood how Pelas had suffered beneath Darshan's compulsion—and he knew from his own experience that a Malorin'athgul's compulsion was impossible to deny.

But could he *forgive* him?

How could he forgive him?

After thinking himself in circles for the better part of the day, Tanis finally determined that he needed more information before he could reach any conclusion about what to do, or even decide how he really felt about what Pelas had done. Yet the very idea of listening while Pelas told him more details filled him with dread. He saw then only one path.

Sunset was painting the clouds in shades of violet-rose when Tanis finally found his way back to the cliffs. Sitting down near the crumbling edge, he hugged his knees, gazed out at the dark line where sea met sky, and tried to regain some sense of equilibrium.

Finally, still not ready to face more truth but too emotionally exhausted to endure the indecision any longer, Tanis closed his eyes and cast his thoughts along a different binding…an older bond. His mind seemed to travel *so* far…reaching out across an immense distance, but then…

Tanis, love of my heart.

Mother—

Abruptly his thoughts just started pouring out—a turmoil of confusion, horror, disbelief, even a desperate desire to reject the truth, all of it in a flood of wordless emotion.

He felt her startled silence. Then an ethereal sigh, redolent of regret. *I see he told you.*

Tanis was struggling so desperately to find a way to reconcile what Pelas had done with his own sense of rightness. Hearing her admission gave him an overwhelming urge to distance himself from both Pelas and his mother. He didn't know what he'd do, perhaps just leave—bindings be damned—and flee with Nadia to elsewhere in the realm, just anywhere he wouldn't have to deal with *this*.

Oh, my dearest son, I'm so sorry…

His mother must've sensed the dismay that gripped him, for all at once the world around Tanis shifted, *altered*—

—He found himself standing on a high balcony overlooking an immense white city. The sight was so startling and at the same time so awe-inspiring that he almost forgot his troubles in lieu of the view. Part of its majesty was how *real* it seemed. He had to be dreaming, yet his mind felt awake—*alert* even—perhaps more so than it had just a heartbeat before.

"Tanis."

He started at the sound of her voice—so real, so *close*, as if truly hearing it with his own ears instead of mind to mind—and turned.

His mother stood in the portal between two open doors. She wore an aqua robe of heavy silk, and her dark hair hung in an elegant plait across one shoulder. She looked exactly as she had in his lessons. As he met her gaze for the first time since babyhood, he saw his own eyes mirrored in the shape of hers.

For a heartbeat's pause, Tanis clung to the railing at his back. Then he launched himself across the space between them and threw his arms around his mother.

She caught her breath in a joyous inhale. One hand cradled the back of his head while the other clutched him close. "Oh, my son…my dear, dear boy." She smelled of jasmine and sunlight, just as he remembered.

Though in truth they remained realms away, his mother felt solid and warm in his arms. And being in *her* arms…Tanis was smiling so wide his face was starting to ache.

Isabel pressed a kiss to his cheek and released him from her arms, but only to take him by the shoulders, that she might better look upon his face. "You've grown so tall." Her gaze reflected admiration and a mother's pride. "So like your father."

He met her colorless eyes, feeling a wondrous, welling joy that quite overshadowed all that had been troubling him. Though they'd spoken across their bond, this was their first meeting in the flesh—or as close as they could manage—since he'd left her arms as a toddler. Yet standing there, bathed in the warmth of his mother's adoration, Tanis felt as though they'd never been a day apart.

He looked around again. "Where have you brought me?"

"Dreamscape." Her eyes strayed out across the city, and a softness came to her expression. "Niyadbakir, T'khendar. My home." She looked back to him and cupped his cheek tenderly with one hand.

Then her smile faded, her brow furrowed. "I regret that he had to tell you," she stroked his cheek with her thumb, "but how could he not? You two are bound; there can be no secrets between you." Tanis glanced away at this, to which she added, "And you wouldn't want there to be."

"No." Then he flinched at what it would mean, knowing *all* that Pelas knew.

"Oh, Tanis…" She ran her hand lovingly down his arm. "Say what you would to me. I'll answer what I can."

Tanis pressed a palm to one eye. He wanted to know, but he didn't want to know. He *had* to know yet couldn't bear the knowing, and he certainly didn't want to *ask*—

She stroked his arm. "I'm unsure of the source of your turmoil. Is it fear for my welfare, or do you feel betrayed by him? What is it that bothers you most?"

In their Dreamscape meeting, she was regarding him steadily, but through their binding, the truthreader in her was permeating his thoughts, seeking the answers to her questions—answers he wasn't even sure of himself.

After a moment she caught her breath. "It cannot be…surely you're not concerned for my dignity?"

Tanis's eyes flew to hers. "He *cut* you! You were *bound* and—" Tanis pushed both palms to his temples, wishing he could sear the images out of his head.

His mother stroked his arm again. "I understand why you would have such feelings, and you're right to feel as you do—of course you would. You're my son, my champion. But here I now stand, Tanis," Isabel said gently then. "What harm remains that *you* need worry for?" When he didn't answer, she drew in her breath and let it out slowly. "Would you fashion me as his victim? Who is aided by doing so?"

Tanis dropped his hands and looked at her.

She arched an inquiring brow. "Pelas is not helped, for he becomes the tormentor. I am not helped—indeed, I'm made helpless by the description. Who gains from your pity? Your own sense of dignity, perhaps?"

He frowned at this.

She gave him a telling look, if still a gentle one. "A wielder acts from a place of causation—*always*, in every sense, with every step along the path. I don't see myself as a victim of Pelas's acts, Tanis; I beg you, don't do it in my stead."

"But…" Tanis exhaled a forceful breath. Pelas *had* harmed her. Surely there should be consequences.

Yet even in having the thought, Tanis realized that Pelas had been enduring consequences throughout—he'd been made to do things he hated and regretted, yet without any ability to withhold himself. He'd even taken steps to sequester himself on a remote Hallovian shore, rather than bring more harm he felt incapable of preventing. For centuries, he'd conceived of himself as a monster. The personal cost had been high.

Isabel took up his hand again, and with a look of invitation, drew him towards the railing. "This game is bigger than you or me, Tanis, bigger than any of our personal desires. Bigger even than our personal concepts of justice. The game *isn't* fair in many regards. It is not kind to individuals, and it's certainly not kind to love."

She stopped at the railing and laid her hands on the marble balustrade. His mother radiated calm—no matter the emotions she might've been personally experiencing in that moment, and Tanis suspected they were powerful and intense—outwardly she projected only a sense of serenity.

Isabel glanced to him, and her expression resolved into a tragic sort of smile. "Your uncle has lived three hundred years without the woman he loves. I have done the same; your father has died three times for this game and now lives anew, but as yet without the full knowledge he'll need to survive it."

She didn't tell him what name and face his father wore now, and he didn't ask. It was not the time to go hunting down that path.

Isabel sighed and shook her head. "I would've kept you free of the game if I could have."

Tanis thought of that sense of duty that had initially bound him to Pelas, and the newer feeling that pushed or pulled against him when he seemed to set his will in the wrong direction. "Somehow…" he lifted his eyes to meet her gaze, "I think I've always been bound to the game."

His mother exhaled a slow breath by way of agreement. "Our paths are entwined, yours and mine, even as mine and your father's are, and mine and your uncle's within the fabric of the tapestry."

She looked back out across the sparkling city, and a faint furrow came to her brow. "I couldn't have freed Pelas from Darshan's compulsion if you hadn't begun the process of freeing his mind, Tanis. Pelas would not now be pledged to a path except for what we together have done. And we have all three of us made sacrifices to gain the place we stand now."

She turned him a look of deep concern, yet her eyes were luminous with adoration. She lifted a hand and stroked his cheek. "I think that when it comes to Pelas, you are the last person who needs an explanation of why those sacrifices were worthwhile."

Tanis dropped his gaze, for of course, this was true.

"And he *loves* you." She placed her hand on his arm and squeezed it gently. "When we two were together in Darshan's tower, all was darkness in Pelas's world except the memories he kept of you. Seeing the likeness of you in the shape of my eyes was the thing that allowed him to overcome the melancholia that had claimed him and ultimately to overcome Darshan's compulsion."

Tanis looked desperately to her. "But he *harmed* you—"

"Tanis, that was my path." She took him by both arms and made him face her. "I chose to walk it, even as you must choose to walk yours."

When Tanis still stared at her with the faint shadow of horror behind his eyes, his mother exhaled a measured breath and loosened the sash at her waist. She slipped one shoulder free of her robe and revealed the pattern etched there. The scar lines were thin, barely more raised than a tattoo, but the way the silver lines glowed…they might've been traced in mercury.

"Do you see, Tanis love?" She searched his gaze with a deep meaning in the conflict marring her brow. "There is a truth here that must be acknowledged."

Tanis swallowed and shifted his eyes back to hers, but he quickly looked away again, for the truth she was sharing with him across the binding made him feel wobbly inside. He couldn't grasp all that she was showing him—pieces of past visions, future possibilities still gauzy and insubstantial—so he let her visions seek their own place in his thoughts until such time as the light of understanding might illuminate them.

"He didn't know, you know." His mother ducked her head to capture his attention and pulled her robe back up over her shoulder. "When Pelas was drawing his patterns in my flesh, he didn't know I was your mother."

Tanis's eyes flew back to hers.

She acknowledged the question in his gaze. "Yes, I could've told him. He would've stopped at once if I had. He would probably have freed me immediately and bound himself before harming me again. But then where would we be?" She searched his eyes with her own. "Tanis...I knew my path was leading me to Pelas, and I knew that I would somehow be given the opportunity to bind him to our game, but I didn't know the circumstances under which that chance would appear...only that it would require sacrificing something very important to me."

She took his hand in hers and ran her thumb across his knuckles. "Along my path, I made choices. Some of those choices were..." she frowned slightly, seemed to search for the right word, "unusual. When I saw that those choices had led me to the circumstances under which Pelas and I met...I'll admit I was concerned. But I trusted that I would somehow find my way through. I believed I could still bring about the effect I intended to achieve—application of the First Law—even though I didn't see how I could possibly help him at first."

Isabel released his hand and turned and laid both of hers on the railing. She gazed out over the vast, glowing city. "If I had made my personal safety more important than my path...if I'd told Pelas who I was to make him stop hurting me, where would we be now?"

Tanis lifted a tormented gaze to her.

"I was not a victim in my interaction with Pelas, my son. If anything, I manipulated him to the best of my skill. I made no move to stray from the path until I saw that my postulated outcome would be achieved. It is the First Law, and an unbreakable one."

Tanis exhaled a slow breath and nodded once. "Yes, mother." This was a lesson he would never forget.

Looking him over then, she exhaled a sigh and drew him into her arms again. Holding him close, she murmured at his ear, "Whatever Pelas has done to violate the Balance, whatever forces he's set in motion against himself as a result, *we* need not be the agents of its retribution."

Tanis heard much more in this statement than he understood, similar to the way the zanthyr spoke in dualities, conveying multiple layers of meaning. He hugged his mother closer and rested his chin on her shoulder. "I understand."

"To love and forgive despite anything that is done to us is the truest expression of greatness, my dearest son. It is your choice now how to treat Pelas, your choice what you will feel towards him…but I would like to see this greatness in you." She blessed him with a smile then, and a caress of her fingers along his cheek—

—And he was back on the cliff, hugging his knees and staring out across a mercuric sea while the moon rose slowly in the east.

Feeling somewhat relieved if not exactly resolved, Tanis made his way back to the manor. While he dressed for dinner, he considered everything his mother had told him.

The feeling of her presence remained heady in his mind. He wondered if she'd stayed with him somehow, for he felt an almost gentle prodding away from thoughts of Pelas to ruminate instead on the other truths, ones she'd hinted at as much as ones she'd given him bluntly.

'…*your father has died three times for this game…*'

Three times? Tanis exhaled a slow breath while donning a clean tunic. No wonder the zanthyr had said his father wasn't as he remembered him.

The lad had long suspected that Arion had died, though the zanthyr had never said so exactly, but something in Phaedor's gaze when he'd spoken of Arion, some shadowed duality in his words…Tanis had known.

During his first exchange with his mother across their binding, Isabel had intimated that Tanis and his father would know each other again one day. Tanis was eagerly anticipating that reunion.

Through reading his father's journals, Tanis had grown to admire him immensely. Indeed, Arion's philosophies had shaped the way Tanis worked the lifeforce. Yet even more valuable than any one technique was learning how Arion *thought*. Tanis found himself easily following the same logical paths his father had walked down, finding connections between ideas and action in a way he wasn't sure he could have explained to anyone, yet which Arion had been able to do with alacrity. Arion hadn't just been strong in his talent, he'd been brilliant in its execution.

Like Isabel, but by way of a different gift, Arion could predict events. He could see beyond the curve of causation and posit an outcome, *because he could see patterns in life as easily as he could see them in* elae. Arion could observe myriad paths of cause and consequence and know how each of them would connect at some future point. He could predict outcomes in ways that others couldn't fathom.

Tanis had gained enormous respect for his father through the ideas and thoughts he'd penned in his journals. Now, knowing that his father lived anew…even with a different face and name…even without remembering all that he used to be…suddenly the Returning took on a grave new importance for Tanis. If any portion of that man remained, Tanis wanted to know him.

He chose a coat from his armoire but paused as he slid his arms into the sleeves. It was one of the many coats Pelas had commissioned for him. Looking at it more closely now, something in the arabesques on the sleeve reminded him of the mercuric design etching his mother's shoulder.

Tanis exhaled a heavy sigh and slumped down on the edge of a chair. With Pelas claiming all responsibility and his mother claiming all responsibility, there didn't seem to be anyone left to blame.

He no longer wanted to blame either of them. He just wanted to walk his path, and he wanted to walk it with Pelas beside him and in the fullness of his mother's approval.

Odd that he could've felt so tormented just hours ago and now be able to put so much behind him. His mother's wisdom had grounded and focused him in ways no one else's could have.

Tanis finished dressing and headed out of his rooms. He heard Nadia's laughter while still on the stairs, and he rounded the dining room archway to see Pelas and the princess already seated at the dining table.

Pelas looked up as Tanis arrived. Tanis had never seen him wear an expression so akin to fear as what he saw in his gaze in that moment.

"Oh, Tanis, there you are! Immanuel and I have had a marvelous day—where *have* you been?" Nadia gave him a smile that only lightly chided his absence.

Holding Tanis's gaze, Pelas quickly pushed across the silent explanation that he'd kept Nadia occupied to give Tanis time with his thoughts. Tanis imagined that Pelas, *aka* Immanuel di Nostri, might've been the only personage in the entire realm capable of so distracting Nadia van Gelderan that she hardly noticed Tanis's absence for an entire day.

Nadia continued brightly, "Immanuel was just telling me about a fountain he sculpted for the Maharajah of Anhara-Dadra in Bemoth."

"Oh?" Tanis moved slowly on into the room.

"He carved it from four blocks of travertine that were each as wide as this table and as tall as the ceiling."

Tanis rounded the table and started towards his chair. Pelas followed him with his gaze. "That is certainly impressive."

"It's a *famous* fountain, Tanis." Nadia's tone implied his response had lacked an appropriate degree of appreciation.

Tanis smiled at her as he reached his chair. "I'm sure the fountain is quite impressive, Nadia, but there's just no way its beauty could compare to yours."

Nadia blinked. "Why, Lord Adonnai…" a faint flush brightened her cheeks.

Tanis placed a hand on Pelas's shoulder but said to Nadia, "You told me I could learn much from our host." He squeezed Pelas's shoulder and angled a look his way. "I intend to."

Pelas met his gaze in a heartbeat's pause. In that breath of frozen time, he radiated immense relief, an almost desperate curiosity, bemused wonder…

Tanis…you've forgiven me?

Tanis held his gaze. *We're brothers now, and brothers we will always be.*

Something released in Tanis the moment he said this, as if an absolving wind had blown away the last of his angst and dismay. Logic, reason… these might've dictated a call for restitution, even atonement, but Tanis's heart simply wanted to forgive. He saw nothing to be gained from holding onto the feelings that had plagued him since Pelas's confession—they would only become chains around Tanis's own ankles—and much to be gained by letting go of them.

Perhaps even more importantly, he and Pelas were brothers now, eternally united through the Unbreakable Bond. But that binding was not merely the forging of a permanent connection; it was also a promise of devotion, one so complete that each might take on the other's acts as though they had been their own. Tanis knew that had the situation been reversed, Pelas would not have hesitated—Pelas never would've turned his back on him, no matter what he'd done.

Oh, how truly his mother had known the feelings residing in his heart, even before Tanis had recognized them himself!

Tanis, I am overcome. Pelas's eyes were vivid with gratitude, yet his admiration glowed more brightly still.

Smiling softly, Tanis took his seat.

And the world started again.

Pelas reached to pour Tanis some wine. Tanis settled his napkin in his lap and lifted a smile to Nadia. "So tell me more about this fountain."

NINE

"Sorrows come not as single raindrops but as showers."

–Jayachándranáptra, Rival of the Sun

Ean crouched in the shadow of a gargoyle guarding a tower roof at the Fortress of Ivarnen. A icy wind was whining through the shingles and tearing at his cloak, numbing his fingers as they gripped the gargoyle's stone arm. A capricious moon blinked in and out of view behind scudding clouds, but even when shining it offered an indifferent light. To distant eyes, Ean's hooded form would've seemed but the gargoyle's ill-cast shadow.

A host of *eidola* milled in the courtyard far below him. Their clattering voices raised in agitation sounded like a chorus of angry cicadas. The chittering outcry was a result of a dozen or so of their brethren lying inanimate amid the larger congress. No amount of pushing or cajoling would rouse their fallen comrades. Ean had made sure of that.

Now he readied the last of the patterns he intended to test that night.

The more he observed the *eidola*, the more he pitied them. Men, whether noble or base, should still live and die as men, not as the unnatural incarnations of a madman's perverted imagination. Though it didn't lessen his loss over his loyal men, Cayal, Brody and Dorin, seeing this truth at least helped to mitigate some of the guilt Ean felt at having destroyed them in his effort to rescue Rhys. Surely death was a kinder master than the golem half-life of the creatures milling in the yard below.

As he watched the *eidola* crawling over each other, angry ants with no queen to guide and coordinate their action, he wondered why he kept coming there…why he kept trying to do anything Isabel had tasked him with. He'd told Sebastian he only wanted to be free of the game, and he'd meant it, yet night after night he found himself back at Ivarnen, attempting to find a way to accomplish the job Isabel had assigned to him.

An innate sense of duty rooted Ean to the game. No matter his personal disagreements, he understood that winning it meant survival for the race and losing meant the end of everything; yet he felt just like those *eidola* ants, acting on the queen's impetus—barely more than a golem himself.

So many of Arion's memories had returned now that Ean no longer knew where Arion ended and he began. The picture of his life had become an outline colored in by another man's experiences. He'd become as Arion's ghost, rather than the other way around; merely the receptacle of Arion's essence, Ean's body overtaken and possessed by Arion's memories and thoughts.

Yet even this hadn't been enough for Isabel.

Ean couldn't help but wonder…would she have allowed a Malorin'athgul to mutilate her flesh if Arion had still been alive? Would she have forsaken their bond and given herself to Pelas if *Arion* had been waiting at the other end of that road? And if Arion had been alive to comfort her, would she still have called Phaedor to her rescue?

None of this matters, Ean. His brother's voice echoed back to him from an earlier confrontation, one of many. Sebastian's was always the voice of reason trying to reach him through the noise of his outrage. *You and Isabel are bound, now and forever. Somehow you've got to find a way to forgive her.*

Yes…bound, the prince thought while the *eidola* clattered anxiously over their fallen comrades and a cloud passed before the moon, dripping darkness onto the night. *Bound like these poor creatures who were once men but now are just remnants of themselves.* Had Darshan given them a choice to become as they were?

Ean remembered those early days with Isabel and wondered if he'd even had as much choice as the *eidola*. He'd been bound to Isabel from the moment he first laid eyes upon her, even though he couldn't recognize the feeling for what it was at the time. The secondary binding he'd worked in this life was as gauze tied around a statue's marble leg: an odd and ultimately unnecessary embellishment. Arion and Isabel had worked the Unbreakable Bond. Ean had merely opened one more sluice onto a water wheel already turning.

Oddly, it didn't bother him so much that another man had made the choice to bind himself and all his future selves to Isabel van Gelderan; only that he now didn't seem to know what to *do* about it.

A gust of wind whipped around the tower, tearing at his cloak and threatening his stability on the ledge. Ean held his hood in place against the wind and wrinkled his nose at the *eidola* stench it carried—a tangy, metallic musk akin to the odor of stones pulled from a rancid creek. The wind cut through his heavy woolen cloak to spread a layer of ice along his flesh, but its chill was a reminder of what he'd come there to do—and it wasn't to brood.

At least…that wasn't the primary purpose for his visit.

Ean called up the last group of patterns Dareios had given him to test and formed them into a matrix in his mind. The *eidola* were notoriously impervious to *elae* and gave off no life signature on the currents. It had been challenging coming up with patterns that would work on them.

Assembling the matrix as a three-dimensional puzzle in his mind, Ean made his intent encompass the entire mass of *eidola* and then poured *elae* into it.

As *elae*'s warmth was flooding his consciousness, Ean wondered what the *eidola* thought…that is, if they had any thoughts of their own. Were they stubbornly clinging to life, even as he was, not really knowing why living was preferable to dying, only fearing more the darkness beyond? Was he granting them mercy, or severing their last lifeline of hope? He would never know.

Ean released the pattern. A noxious cocktail flew on an arrow of the first strand.

The prince watched dispassionately from his tower vantage as his matrix hit the *eidola* in the courtyard and spread upon impact like a gaseous explosion. A score of the creatures fell and started convulsing while their brethren shrieked clattering *eidola* shrieks and went into a frenzy.

At last.

They'd finally found a way to make patterns cling to the *eidola*.

Sebastian would be pleased. It had been his idea to try using the first strand. He'd posed the theory that even though the *eidola* showed no life signature on the currents, the first strand might remain within them as a sort of dormant connective tissue. Dareios had designed a pattern that latched onto the first strand and used it as a grappling hook for the rest of their working to cling to.

Having achieved their first goal, Ean now watched to see if *his* patterns—the ones comprising the inner layer of the matrix—would be effective in severing the *eidola*'s connection to their master.

If nothing else, the patterns were certainly incapacitating the creatures. Those afflicted had fallen and were flailing about, while a host of others argued in rattling complaint. Ean had noticed that without a stronger mind actively directing them, the *eidola* were uncoordinated and incapable of reason. This made them more dangerous rather than less.

Come on—work, damn you...

He had only minutes before a sentry spotted him or one of the *eidola* lucids appeared to coordinate a retaliatory action. The lucids were nearly always linked directly to Darshan and often wielded *deyjiin*. Ean preferred to avoid them.

Indifferent to his impatience, the creatures continued convulsing, turning the courtyard into a seething mass of molten—

A rattlesnake hiss sibilated behind him.

Ean spun in a low crouch.

An *eidola* was spidering head-first towards him down the steep roof. Its cold eyes were leveled on him, luminous with *deyjiin*. "You are the one." Its voice sounded like stones tumbling in an urn.

"So you can talk." Ean slowly backed away as the lucid advanced. "That's... horrifying."

The *eidola* reached the ledge where Ean was retreating and straightened to its full height. It was a good deal taller than himself and considerably broader. Darshan had claimed a mountain of a man for this minion.

Violet-silver glinted in the *eidola's* obsidian eyes. "My master wants to speak with you," it advanced dangerously towards Ean, "the Him Who Would Unmake His Children."

Ean took another backwards step and bumped up against a second gargoyle. There was nowhere to go but over the edge.

"Yes, I'll bet he does." The idea of 'speaking' with Darshan felt like worms writhing in Ean's gut. "Sadly, my dance card is full tonight. Do give your master my regards."

He dove off the roof.

The wind sang in his ears while the *eidola* in the courtyard below roused a clattering roar. Ean made a rope of the fifth and swung himself towards a shallow balcony on the next tower. Unfortunately his aim was off. He hit the balcony railing with a grunted exhale and had to haul himself up and over the stone. Not exactly the graceful escape he'd envisioned.

A bolt of *deyjiin* missed his ear by a hair and disintegrated the balcony doors instead.

Ean threw up a shield of the fifth and spun a glare over his shoulder at the lucid, who was standing beside the gargoyle on the opposite tower. "I thought you said your master wanted to *speak* with me!"

The creature flung another bolt at Ean.

The prince threw himself to the stones, just as the balcony disintegrated under him. He tumbled into empty air.

Ean hissed a curse and flung the matrix he'd just used on the other *eidola* towards the lucid on the tower. Then he somersaulted backwards and made the air solid beneath his feet.

He landed in a jarring crouch that reverberated from toes to teeth. He could make the air solid at will; he hadn't quite figured out how to make it *squishy*.

Heart pounding, Ean slowly straightened. He was righting his hood and cloak when arrows began pelting his shield of the fifth. He resisted the urge to flinch and cast his gaze upwards to find archers appearing in windows and balconies and men with spears running atop the fortress walls. But unless they were firing arrows cast in the fifth, they wouldn't stand a…

Arrows cast in the fifth.

Ean stared as the solution they'd been searching for suddenly presented itself to him. Only these arrows wouldn't be bound to the fifth, but to the patterns that severed the *eidola's* connection to their master. With his love for pattern-smithing, Dareios would welcome the challenge.

Ignoring the pelting arrows, which could no more penetrate his shield than a bee could a bottle, Ean made stairs of the air and trudged back up to the shattered doors of the tower, where a leis and his escape awaited.

On the opposite roof, the lucid was regaining himself—Ean had suspected that matrix wouldn't be strong enough to incapacitate a lucid for long.

Reaching the shattered balcony, the prince stepped onto the crumbling edge, grabbed hold of the wall and leaned out to better view the lucid. He saluted it in farewell. "Give your master my regards!" Then he swung himself inside and took his leave of Ivarnen.

Night's blanket still draped Kandori when Ean stepped off the node in the Palace of Andorr. He went in search of Dareios and his brother, just in case either of them were still awake, but finding their laboratory dark, made his way to Sebastian's old chambers instead.

The shattered space still bore the material wounds of their brotherly battle on the night Ean had finally freed Sebastian from Dore's matrix. Ean had spent many recent evenings in those rooms, when sleep either wouldn't come, or when he feared that it would.

He ducked through the drapery cordoning off the rooms and walked across dusty tiles towards the broken outer wall. This he'd begun recreating—*regrowing*—using patterns from Arion's memories. He might've repaired the room more quickly by simply molding the fifth to his intent, but he was using the place instead to test his recollection of Arion's theories and learn anew the individual patterns that Arion had long ago mastered.

Arion Tavestra's knowledge of *elae* had been extensive. He'd trained for centuries to gain the understanding and skill he'd possessed.

It had never been more apparent to Ean why he didn't have time to relearn what Arion had known, how *remembering* offered his only hope. They were in the last quarter of the game—ready or not, he had to play his position.

Almost harder to face was recognizing how his own nature had brought him to this woeful place of ignorance. Had he simply died as Arion and been reborn into the next life, he might've had ample time to study Patterning between that moment and today.

But he'd died *again and again*—likely due to the same brash stupidity Ean had so many times seen in himself, and which Rinokh had so easily capitalized on. Thus, those intervening decades, which might've been spent in study, had been wasted growing to adulthood two times over.

Oh, Markal... Ean shook his head, *I finally understand you.*

No wonder the man had been so brusque and uncompromising, so insistent that Ean had to remember—because Arion had been brilliant. And they needed Ean to be brilliant again.

What must it have been like for Markal...to know what Ean was inherently capable of, yet to watch him fail and fail and *fail*, to see all of that immense knowledge and ability lost. It must've been agonizing.

Even more frustrating to Ean personally was that though he now recalled much of his earlier lifetime as Arion, yet the most important truths remained hidden. What had really happened at the Citadel? How had Arion died? And what betrayal of Arion's sang so sharply in Ean's consciousness that its guilty notes pierced the veil of memory but the song itself remained hidden?

Feeling the punishing weight of these unknowns, Ean sank down on an upended urn, braced elbows on his knees and let his head hang while the currents funneled through him.

Exhaustion had become his closest companion. He felt it always, a downy layer that dampened his thoughts and made his flesh sluggish to respond, but exhaustion's muslin coating at least turned Arion's memories into hazy outlines instead of sharp and cutting recollections full of emotion and regret.

Recalling to mind the patterns he'd been recently practicing, Ean lifted his gaze and focused on the shattered bits of stone spread across the tiles. Then he set to work, binding sand and stone on a molecular level, particle by particle, stacking them in a continuing polarity that magnetized each particle to the next, rebuilding the wall stronger than any forged of mortar and stone.

The patterns involved in this process had required all of his concentration at first, but now the sequence was becoming automatic, leaving part of his mind free to wander.

It wandered, as it often did, into Arion's memories...

Arion Tavestra narrowed his eyes and drew another careful line of the pattern he was sketching in his journal. Mathematical equations written in a neat hand along the journal's left margin put explanation to the pattern's use, while diagrams of each of the pattern's angles gave a complete view of the three-dimensional pattern so it could be wielded.

This pattern melted rock. Arion had formed the pattern with his intent, postulating the possibility against the laws of energy. But the doing was the easy part. Function always monitored structure—thought, *intent*, was in every case senior to action.

Understanding what had occurred as a result of one's intent...that was where Arion's real interest lay. *Why* had this particular pattern caused the rock's molecules to circulate and recombine into a new but equally stable structure?

He'd spent weeks extrapolating backwards from the *doingness* to achieve understanding of what he'd done. In the process, he'd developed the equations that explained this pattern's potential for energy transfer, elemental synergy, and symbiotic molecular realignment. Now the equations could be used to induce and predict further phenomena.

His journals were filled with such patterns and associated formulae.

Laughter rang out from across the room. Arion glanced up beneath his brows to see two of his friends clapping a third on the back in a congratulatory fashion.

They'd gathered in the common room of Malthus, the Sormitáge boarding house so many of them called home. Malthus, with its vaulted ceilings and loftier personages, its venerable halls and its aging Scholars—learned mummies of petrified thought, embalmed of pipe smoke and atrophied traditions.

Malthus, with its massive lion's mouth mantel carved of pretension, and its paneled walls burnished with wisdom yet continuously oiled with the ideals of youth; Malthus, where they discussed the Laws and Esoterics as revolutionaries might argue ideologies.

It was where they made their home, where they studied and debated and dreamed; but for Arion, they might've dwelled anywhere, so long as they were together, for it was these people—his closest friends—who made Malthus what it meant to them all.

Upon this thought, Arion scanned the rest of the room. His eyes crinkled warmly as his gaze alighted on a corner more crowded by ideas than men. Among the five voices raised there in a heated debate, the loudest two were Anglar Tempest's and Malachai ap'Kalien's, two of Malthus' resident idealists, who were ever at odds with their pragmatist opposites—the truthreaders Voss di Alera, Haden van Leister and Raine D'Lacourte.

*Raine…*who had no idea that in a few days' time, Björn van Gelderan was going to invite him to take the Vestal Oath.

"Arion," the truthreader Cristien Tagliaferro waved to him from hearthside. "Come and congratulate young Francois on his recent accomplishment."

Arion looked back to his drawing and started another careful line. "Which was?"

Cristien clapped the dark-haired Francois on the shoulder again, while his colorless eyes looked him over admiringly. "Gaining the favor of Elyse van Gelderan."

"You're wasting your breath, Cristien." Seated by the fire, Parsifal D'Marre held up his goblet to Francois but fixed his amber-eyed gaze on Arion. "Tavestra counts only one accomplishment as being worthy of praise—the kind that comes with a gold ring."

"Not true, Parsifal." Arion finished the loop on the line he'd been penning and looked up. "I congratulate Francois on his display of courage."

"Oh, here we go." Cristien rolled his eyes humorously and headed across the room towards the sideboard and more wine.

"Courage?" Parsifal spread his arms along the back of his leather chair and crossed an ankle over one knee. He made a show of stroking the satyr's chin whiskers he called a beard while he pondered Arion's comment. "I'll grant there's a small degree of bravery in approaching one of the Emperor's nieces, but…"

"Courage," Arion lifted a finger in his favorite manner of erudite mockery, "could be described as first, intending to cause something, and second," he added another finger beside the first, "pressing forward to achieve the effect one intends despite any and all odds, letting nothing and no one stand in your way." He winked at Francois. "I suspect our Francois encountered quite a few people standing in his way on the path to courting Elyse van Gelderan."

Francois beamed at him.

"*Letting nothing and no one stand in your way,*" repeated a deep voice from the room's entrance.

Arion turned his head to see the Maestro Markal Morrelaine, his master, standing beneath the arch of the open doors. Markal's broad frame took up much of the space, and his dignity claimed the rest. A pall of skepticism hovered like smoke around him, the residue of his comment. "Does that mean *harming* anyone?"

"If need be," Arion admitted.

Markal moved on inside the room, whereupon Francois and the others hastily excused themselves—Arion was the only one who enjoyed debating with Markal. The wielder advanced steadily behind the cavalry of his stare. "The ends justify the means?"

Arion set down his pen and folded fingers in his lap, all of them bound by gold Sormitáge rings. "Sometimes."

"Sometimes when?"

"When the end is greater than the sum of its parts," offered a returning Cristien. He sat down at the table next to Arion and pushed a goblet of wine towards him.

Arion gave Cristien a quick smile of gratitude.

Cristien...with his tousled brown hair and poet's mouth, more apt to quote a sonnet than the Laws, yet who was conspiring with the rest of them in the most desperate gambit of all time.

Cristien clasped hands behind his head and leaned back in his chair. "But we're talking about courage, old man, not morality."

Markal arched a mordant black brow; its triangle of dubiety stood out starkly against his head of wavy white hair. "Arion is talking about Patterning with his little speech on courage, therefore we *are* talking about morality, Cristien. The two must be inseparable for a wielder."

Cristien leaned forward and tapped a finger on the table. "Not morality. Ethicality. Those Philosophy literatos want us to think the terms are interchangeable, but they're not—especially not in Patterning. The moral code of conduct devised by the State must always bow to the ethical principles of individual reason."

Markal cast the fifth across the room and lassoed an armchair to his will. Its feet scraped so loudly as they crossed the marble floor that the Adepts debating in the corner paused their heated discussion to glare at him.

Indifferent to their irritation, he seated himself with scholarly aplomb and steepled fingers before his broad chest. Leveling Cristien that particularly menacing gaze he assumed when about to give an upstart student a verbal lashing, Markal inquired coolly, "And pray inform me, Cristien Tagliaferro, what is the difference between morality and ethicality?"

Cristien drank his wine while eyeing Markal over the rim. After a moment, he replied, "What's ethical is not always moral."

"How not?"

Arion gave Markal a hard look. "Must you always advocate for the darker side of reason? You know perfectly well why not."

A smile flickered at the edge of Markal's lips but disappeared before it could manifest, banished for its impertinence. "Yes, but does Cristien?"

Cristien's expression sobered. "If I didn't, do you think he would've asked me to join the Council of Nine?"

Markal grunted. "I don't profess to understand a fraction of what Björn does."

"But you profess to challenge his decisions," Arion observed dryly.

Markal turned him a penetrating stare. "Only the incomprehensible ones."

"When the greater good speaks louder than the individual wrong," Cristien declared with a hint of indignation in his tone. "That's when an act may be ethical without also being moral."

"Stealing the storm to end the drought," Markal proposed broodingly.

"Yes."

"Compelling the iniquitous to a new moral course?"

"Potentially." Cristien drank his wine and gazed deliberately at Markal over the rim.

"Slaying the enemy's army to *prevent* the war?"

"Yes, if you must!"

"And bring Cephrael's gavel falling upon your head, Cristien," Markal growled. "*Ethicality* in Patterning will get you killed."

"*Courage*," Arion stressed, returning them to the original topic, "requires a steadfast, unwavering conviction to achieve the effect one has envisioned despite all adversity—even the adversity of moral conflict, Maestro. This is application of the First Law: *KNOW the effect you intend to create*. Our only true protection in Patterning is a steadfast application of the Laws."

Cristien leveled a vindicated look at Markal. "The Laws—not the arbitrary moral codes of kings and literatos—keep a wielder on the right side of Balance."

Markal pressed and released his steepled fingers as if the bellows of his thoughts. "The First Law: *KNOW the effect you intend to create*." His dark eyes scanned the both of them. "The Law speaks nothing of *achieving* the effect."

Cristien waved him off. "Achieving the effect is implicit, old man."

Markal looked to Arion. "And the achieving of this effect justifies all manner of ills? Is this your stance, Arion?"

"I'm merely seeking to define courage, Maestro."

"No, you're setting a precedent that cannot be maintained. Sometimes the effect shouldn't be achieved—sometimes you don't realize this until halfway down the path of achievement. What one *can* do isn't always what one *should* do, and the far-reaching ramifications of a wielder's actions are not always predictable."

"That's where you're wrong, Maestro. It's the First Law in action. If you can't predict and control the outcome, you shouldn't be Patterning to begin with."

"Glibly spoken when all of your workings to date impact only yourself, Arion. Take those viewpoints out into the arena of the world and see how far-reaching becomes your prediction."

Arion sprouted a grin. "Very well, Maestro, if you insist."

Markal put a hand on his arm. "Despite Björn's predilection for metaphors, this is no game we've embarked upon. We can't predict every far-spiraling thread of the pattern we'll all be working together. We cannot know the final image this tapestry will present to the world, to posterity."

Arion's expression sobered. "Even if it were only a game, I would take it no less seriously." He shook his head and searched Markal's gaze. "What is it you fear? Our success depends entirely on being courageous enough to do *whatever* it takes to achieve the effect we've envisioned, no matter where the path of the game takes us."

Markal leaned back in his chair again. "Morality be damned?"

"You're like a dog with a bone on this point," Cristien groused. "The *moral* consequence is not as important as the *ethical* one. How can it be when we're talking in terms of centuries? What's important to one man in one lifetime is inconsequential when dealing with the future of the entire race."

"Only the outcome matters, Maestro," Arion said by way of agreement, "but that's *because* we're working for the greater good." He sat back in his chair with a forceful exhale. "Look...I freely admit we could debate Balance versus morality until our beards turn white without ever reaching any definitive conclusion. But in the context of *this* game—*his* game—we're working from a premise that means survival or destruction for *every living being*. This is the biggest game ever envisioned, the greatest challenge, with all the Realms of Light hanging in the balance. If we don't adhere to the First Law—if we don't have the courage to *make sure* we achieve the effect we intend, how can we ever hope to succeed?"

Arion glanced to Cristien. The truthreader nodded his agreement, his colorless gaze grave.

Markal shifted his brooding gaze to Cristien. "Forsaking anything to achieve your intended outcome?"

Arion pressed fingertips on the table. "Doing whatever is needed to accomplish our aims—because they *are* for the greater good. Never giving up on the effect we've decided upon until it's achieved. We have to have that level of courageous causation from all of us to win this."

Markal looked Arion over. His eyes were very dark. "I wonder if you really know what that means."

"It means not one of us can waver from our commitment to him or to the game. Not ever, not for any reason."

"Nor for anyone?" Markal challenged with an arched a brow. "And you think you're prepared to make that vow?"

Arion held his gaze steadily. "To my last dying breath."

Markal exhaled slowly. "Yes…that's what worries me."

Ean exhaled a shuddering breath and sank his forehead into his hands. Every memory of Arion's was but a minute variation of another. Always the man was unshakable, determined, certain of his course and willing to do whatever it took. It was his mantra—as much as Markal pledged himself to method and order, Arion had defined himself by his outlook on courage.

Ean had no idea how he defined himself now.

Reckless and brash…what a poor investiture to be all that was left of the magnificent Arion Tavestra.

'You put too much importance on the man you were and not enough on the one you are becoming.'

Isabel's words. Would she have still betrayed him if he'd become the man she needed him to be?

Ean released *elae* and leaned his pounding head back against the wall. He meant to close his eyes for only a moment, but instead fell quickly asleep.

And with sleep, so came the dream…

Arion stood beneath the Citadel's shattered dome holding his bloodied sword. All around him, the marble floor was a littered wasteland. Death's unwholesome song filled the air as it made an evening meal of the innocent.

Arion's hands and vambraces were slick with blood. None of it was his own, yet he felt as if most of the blood shed that night had belonged to him personally, so dear were the ones already lost.

He looked down upon the man dying at his feet: a Paladin Knight in shimmering, *elae*-enhanced armor. He'd come from Illume Belliel to claim Malachai ap'Kalien in the name of the Council of Realms—as if Malachai was fool enough to stay in Alorin…as if Björn would've let them take Malachai to suffer more injustice.

Arion dropped his chin to his chest and exhaled a tremulous breath.

What a travesty it had all become: the flag of their brilliant cause burned to bitter ash by Malachai's war; the needless deaths of thousands of Adepts, and now these Paladin Knights, all of them misled—along with the rest of Alorin—so that the Council of Nine might have time to regroup and recover from the tragedy of Malachi's madness; and lastly, but most germane to the fury that fed through Arion's veins in that moment, this treacherous coup against Isabel, orchestrated by Dore Madden and his craven followers.

'…the brave must ever face the hardest road. I would this bloody job did not fall to you, my brother, blood-of-my-heart.'

Björn's words, spoken just before he and Cristien rushed off to confront the traitors who had attacked Isabel and then fled when justice arrived in the guise of the Fifth Vestal. Arion was determined it would not be the last thing he and Björn said to one another, despite Isabel's foretelling.

He lifted his gaze back to the towering doors. It had taken him less time to slay a dozen Paladin Knights than it had to unwork Dore Madden's binding on those doors.

Ever the vile man held a repertoire of debased and wicked patterns at the ready. Dore was ingeniously skilled at contorting the lifeforce into the worst manifestation of itself. That night he'd crafted patterns of the foulest intent and bound them with debased others, like razor wire, so that Arion had to bloody his honor just unworking them.

Now it was done. Arion scanned the currents one last time to be certain he'd found all of Dore's traps. Then he sent a flow of the fifth to open the massive doors, shielded himself with the same, and moved through their shaded parting into the silent hall beyond.

The pentagonal Hall of Invocation with its hundred thrones and bands of jeweled windows remained serenely untouched by the battles raging elsewhere in Tiern'aval's Citadel. Dore or some other had extinguished the wielder's lamps that should've illuminated the glorious chamber, but Arion saw with the currents in any case.

And the currents…

They sloshed and careened and tore through one another like the waves of a hurricane sea. Indeed, he felt as if he walked amid such a raging storm, for his mind was being constantly pummeled by energies made foul.

Frustratingly, the currents revealed that Dore had fled across the Citadel's weld, which lay not far beyond the Hall of Invocation. But the *other* man, their true enemy…*he* remained close. Likewise, a score of Mages who thought the enemy's nightcloak of *deyjiin* would be enough to fool Arion—*him, w*ho could hear their rank thoughts louder than *deyjiin*'s roar, who could taste their ignoble breath poisoning the air.

Arion cleansed his blade with a thought, hearing a whisper as the blood seared away. Would that he could so easily cleanse his conscience.

"Gerald hal'Gere, Willem Stonewall…" Arion called off the names of the Mages whose life signatures he saw on the currents.

With each new utterance, his anger increased exponentially. Whereas during the earlier battle he'd been fighting a faceless force of many, now he put names and countenances to the acts of treachery against Isabel.

Fury rose on a wave of indignation, and he claimed the tumultuous currents for his own. A single thought of intent stole the storm of energy and rechanneled it back against the Mages.

Power exploded through the room.

The high windows shattered, gilded thrones splintered. The concussion sent a wave rolling through the stone floor, dislodging massive blocks of marble.

"*SHOW YOURSELVES!*" Arion's *elae*-enhanced voice brought to bear the righteous fury of every Adept who'd died that night.

His words were still resounding in the chamber when a deep voice, smoothly contemptuous, stilled the reverberation.

"Go on…" it goaded, equally *elae*-enhanced to fill the chamber, "present yourselves to the *great* Arion Tavestra."

The nightcloaks dissolved to reveal a score of Mages in various states of unbalance as a result of Arion's working. Some were clinging to the walls or each other, others had fallen. Smoke came pouring in through the shattered windows, further obscuring sight, but now the currents revealed to Arion what the nightcloaks of *deyjiin* had been concealing from him all this time.

Compulsion.

Arion felt that truth as an agonizing stab to his conscience.

These Mages were *all* under compulsion.

To dictate a man's actions with a binding compulsion and release him to accomplish one particular task required immense skill, but to compel multiple consciousnesses through decision and action like marionettes? These Mages were clearly still under the control of one individual mind—a *powerful* mind, to actively compel so many determinisms at once. Whether or not the other Mages Arion had already killed were being compelled or had willingly followed Dore, Arion would now never know.

So ordered by their master, the Mages found their feet or righted themselves and started *en masse* towards him. Some carried Merdanti blades; others, talismans to aid in Patterning. Arion saw no remorse in their gazes, nor even any hint of the knowledge of what they'd done, only a black hatred and the will to destroy.

Oh, Isabel…

He'd thought he would be claiming traitors in her honor, but killing a being under compulsion was no better than slaying a dog for obeying its master. These men and women had no choice but to do whatever their master, his enemy, willed. Arion had no way of knowing if they were innocent or guilty of the sedition they'd participated in; their every act might've been against their own determinism, in violent opposition to their will.

Or they might've been wholly in Dore's camp from the start.

Whatever their intentions had once been, they were intent on destroying him now.

Arion saw the currents forming into patterns and threw up his left arm with a shield of the fifth. Even prepared for it, the bombardment of energy drove him to one knee. How could it not with dozens of powerful wielders on the other end of it, their minds and abilities usurped by one individual, their combined mental power focused into a weapon of singular intent?

Grounding himself between violent energy and the immutable base of terra firma, Arion drew deeply on the fifth and engaged gravity's effort to brace and support his own. A continuous onslaught of energy bombarded him as he struggled to stand up, jaw clenched. The currents plunged away from him in gargantuan waves, pummeled by the combined will of the Mages, while Arion stood within a crater of ravaged space, protected only by the force of his own will.

Gaining his feet, he deliberated on his next choice.

His enemy would use the Mages until their minds were a ruinous sludge; yet somewhere beneath the hatred and malice, the true beings remained—tortured, agonized…suffering.

But innocent or no, they stood between himself and the enemy.

Choices spiraled away from Arion like the whorls of an arabesque, but he saw only one path that led anywhere but ruin.

He would have to make their deaths permanent. He couldn't leave an opening for the enemy to reanimate them, as Malachai had done with his Shades.

'*…I would this bloody job did not fall to you…*'

By Cephrael's Great Book, Arion wished the same!

There was no more time to deliberate. He could feel himself weakening beneath the unyielding barrage of raw power.

Forging the fifth into an impermeable shield, Arion grabbed the third strand, raised his sword and sprinted down time's tenuous thread. The Mages wouldn't feel his blade until after it had taken them. It was mercy, of a fashion.

One swing of his Merdanti sword and Gerald hal'Gere's head and body fell in opposite directions. Arion skipped through time. Another swing, another head tumbled. He skipped again. Flashes of seconds, moments stolen between breaths, thought split into fractions. He felled the next Mage, and the next.

Six seconds gone, half a dozen Mages slain. Arion rode the forward edge of time's tumbling wave. He gave them no recourse to their power. Even death couldn't catch him.

And then it was done.

A score of decapitated bodies lay in an ever-widening pool of blood, but Arion was looking forward, not behind. He'd made his choice; he was walking his path. He had no other path to walk.

On the far side of the dead, an archway opened into a long passage leading to the Citadel's weld chamber. Arion cleansed his blade with a thought and started down it.

A haunting chuckle followed him the entire length of the corridor, raising his hackles as a blade dragged along a raw nerve. Mirthless, cold, it raked painfully across his mental shields, a razor-edged plow sowing seeds of indecision, cultivating self-doubt, uncertainty and fear.

Arion sensed compulsion in that laugh—whispering, invisible whorls of intent. A lesser mind would've been easily claimed by it. The currents raged around him, frenzied and frantic. They told him nothing.

He entered the octagonal weld chamber and headed between the massive pillars supporting its vaulted ceiling of jewels and gilt. Slowly descending the wide steps between the pillars, Arion cast his gaze warily around. He knew nothing of his enemy save for the way the man's will churned the tides of *elae*, but he suspected...*yes*, he suspected his nature.

They'd been waiting for the Malorin'athgul to show themselves for a very long time.

A patronizing chuckle disturbed the stillness of the room—a silence that was only apparent to those who couldn't hear the roaring currents.

"*Ah*...the great Arion Tavestra. We meet at last."

A man moved into view from behind a column. He was very tall and broad-shouldered, and he carried a Merdanti blade with the point held low. Shadows clung to his face, obscuring his features.

Arion stilled on the stairs.

"It's a fitting irony, don't you think?" The stranger waved a hand in idle fashion. "That in your attempts to save your Adept race, you go to such lengths to help destroy it?" He moved towards Arion, walking the outer circle of the octagon of pillars. "And most pleasurable yet, to find that here, on the final frontier of battle, *you*—the *magnificent* Arion Tavestra—become the hand of my intent, no less a puppet to my will than those poor fools you've just slain."

Following the enemy with his gaze, Arion clenched his jaw and readied his patterns.

"But then, what choice did you have?" The stranger's tone dripped with malicious amusement while his steady steps brought him ever closer. "If you hadn't killed them, they would've killed you, and living on thereafter, they would've served my will, even as you have done tonight." The stranger pointed his weapon at Arion. "*This* is the lesson learned by mortals who take it upon themselves to challenge their gods."

Arion kept a tight hold on his anger and a tighter hold on his shields. "You're no god of mine."

"But that is the fundamental understanding you lack." His words sounded as the crisp shattering of glass. His blade, pointed at Arion, became the focus of his intent, and *deyjiin* blasted along it.

Arion caught the bolt on his weapon, feeling its deadly *zing* even through his shield, and roughly slung the power to the stones. A huge swath of marble promptly dissolved into sand.

The enemy chuckled. "Do you see? A god doesn't need your consent, your *saccharine* adoration. He *is* power incarnate, as you will learn—"

—the dream shifted, passing through veils of shadowed memories, images flickering in flashes of lightning pain, strings of tortured unmaking… and then—

Arion lay gasping in darkness.

His chest radiated a burning agony, while every other part of him ached with cold. *Elae* was draining out of him, pooling with his blood.

A shadow moved, and the form of his enemy rose above him. He dragged a dagger dripping with *elae* out of Arion's chest.

Arion choked—pain radiated, a thousand times worse than before.

Dear Epiphany!

Breath wouldn't come, for his lungs were full of blood. His gaping chest constricted in futility. Dying eyes stared into the shadowed face of his enemy, but all Arion saw was the man's life pattern glowing on the currents, tormentingly whole despite Arion's best efforts to unmake it.

He managed a threadbare gasp—his mouth was too full of blood. "This isn't…the end…of me."

The enemy leaned closer, coming nearly nose to nose. His dark eyes gleamed in the muted light. He flashed a sharp smile. "Come and find me. I'll be waiting."

Then he licked his thumb and pressed it to Arion's bloodied lips, a taunting, formidable farewell.

And every molecule of *elae* in Arion's body exploded—

Ean jerked awake with a shuddering gasp, his brain throbbing with the latent agony of that final moment, and his stomach sickly. He pushed hands to his head and curled his body forward, pressing elbows to his knees. A low moan escaped him.

The First Lord had assumed the blame for Arion's actions at the Citadel—a loyal, selfless act that had earned him extreme vilification from the other vestals, and most of Alorin and the Council of Realms by extension. Björn could not have known why Arion killed the Mages, yet he'd remained steadfast, determined to support Arion's choices, trusting his decisions to the end.

Ean exhaled a shuddering breath.

He still felt the conflict of that choice. Arion had slain the Mages remorselessly, seeing no other path, yet there was no arguing that he'd killed them in cold blood. Perhaps there had been no better way.

But Ean wondered…had Arion let the Mages live, would they have remained puppets to the enemy's will, or might he have been able to save them from the compulsion at some later time, unworking the binding on their minds? If Arion had taken the road through mercy, would he have stood upon firmer ground when facing the enemy at the last? Had the compromise of slaying potentially innocent people caused Arion's downfall?

And where had come the betrayal Ean still sensed as such a cankerous growth on his conscience? Somehow he didn't think it fed on guilt over the Mages' deaths.

And then there was that vision of the enemy.

The Enemy…

Ean felt cold upon recalling his voice, which was undeniably the voice from his many earlier dreams of unmaking. Would that he'd better seen his face, but whether blurred by dreams or Arion's pain, the man's features seemed but daggered shadows of contempt.

He closed his eyes and let a latent shudder pass through him and away. Then he focused upon a particular thread of awareness.

*Isabel…*he cast the thought to her across their bond, sensing her mind quickly at the other end. She opened herself to him with desperate welcome, but Ean hadn't contacted her for reconciliation.

Isabel, the Mages…they were all under compulsion. Arion saw no other path.

He quickly closed his mind to any offered reply. He didn't want her voice in his head, but he felt he owed her that truth at least. He certainly owned it to Björn.

Then he remembered why he was on the balcony of Sebastian's shattered rooms and the solution he'd landed on earlier…

And he wondered why he still cared.

Dawn had come while he dreamed of Arion's last night. Feeling threadbare on many levels, Ean turned a weary gaze to the valley and the line of eastern mountains. There, beneath the gold clouds of sunrise, he imagined another path leading across the field of a different game. He saw endless possibilities for where his life might take him.

They seemed more unreal than any of his dreams.

Ean stood and went to find his brother.

TEN

*"If you can't escape the skeletons in your closet,
you might as well teach them to dance."*

–An old desert saying

FRANCO ROHRE STEPPED off the node into blazing, painful sunlight and an oven wind raking across him. He pushed a hand over his eyes and gazed out over the immense expanse of T'khendar's Windlass Desert.

Five arches demarked the nodecourt where he'd arrived, their columns of black marble carved with innumerable patterns. To his right, an agonizingly long set of stairs zigzagged up a jagged volcanic ridge where, hundreds of feet above, an obsidian pavilion overlooked the desert.

Franco tried not to look to the south. He knew what he would see there well enough.

Taking a deep breath of determination, he started up the long staircase leading to the pavilion with the sunlight blinding him and sweat soon running down his back. Despite his intention not to look, a constant part of him remained acutely and uncomfortably aware of the violent storm darkening the southern horizon. It was like the damned thing was calling to him, *demanding* his attention. The more he tried to ignore it…the more insistent he became on *not* looking, the more he *had* to look.

When he finally spared a glance southward, he saw a black band of clouds crackling with electrical storms. It raged along the entire visible front. Above the dark tumult, angry red veins striated the sky. The firmament seemed the fragile webbing of a shattered vase and the horizon the mess of sludge seeping from its broken base.

Franco had weathered this very storm beside the Great Master. He'd felt the thinning fabric of the realm; he knew how fragile T'khendar's pattern had become in those aetheric places. At any moment the final filaments could give way to a creature of devastating power who was intent upon unmaking them all.

And he knew it would've been Alorin suffering those storms—*Alorin* being attacked, its pattern unraveled—if not for the First Lord's foresight.

Breathing hard, yet feeling uncommonly chilled—for his Nodefinder's senses were all too keen to the kinetic storm blackening the horizon—Franco rounded the final step on the stairs and lifted his gaze to the obsidian pavilion and its many open-air chambers.

The First Lord had raised the palace directly from the volcanic rock, growing columns, walls and roofs right out of the stones that supported them. As with everything the First Lord created, the palatial structure offered beauty as well as function.

Franco had barely caught his breath before Dagmar appeared from beneath a shadowed arcade bearing an offering of chilled wine and a smile. "Greetings, Franco. It's good to see you in the flesh after so many weeks."

"Thank you, my lord." Franco admitted an equal reassurance in seeing the Great Master standing solidly in front of him. Dreamscape had been their only means of communication since Alshiba had summoned him to Illume Belliel, some weeks ago now.

Dagmar drew Franco into the shade of the pavilion and the protection of Björn's patterns, whereupon the arid desert air became noticeably more comfortable.

In the center of the domed chamber, the First Lord, the Fourth Vestal Raine D'Lacourte, and General Ramuhárikhamáth were standing around a long onyx table studying a map of T'khendar that had been raised in perfect relief out of the block of stone.

Ramu was indicating a strip of mountains and saying as Franco and Dagmar joined them, "…must've been in this area. It was a large tear—easily a league in length."

Björn looked up beneath his brows and gave Franco a smile. "Ah, Franco. Welcome. My oath-sister set you free at last?"

"Not exactly, my lord." Franco approached the map table and observed the many small red markers placed at numerous spots on the relief—so many more than when last he'd seen it. He lifted a look of alarm to the others. "Are these *all* places where T'khendar's fabric is thinning?"

Ramu answered darkly, "If by thinning you mean the Malorin'athgul Rinokh is doing his best to unmake the realm…then yes."

Franco suddenly really needed that wine. He drank deeply of it.

Björn returned his gaze to the map. "Let's see the nodes in that area, Ramu."

The *drachwyr* touched the relief and an illusion sprang into view—a map of T'khendar's welds, projected in three dimensions.

Franco observed it wistfully. Before Malachai's war, weldmaps had been common throughout the realm. Now, centuries had passed since Franco had seen a weldmap in use the way it was intended.

He studied the silver ley lines of T'khendar's map with care, though he knew their pathways intimately by that time, due to his work with Dagmar.

T'khendar was smaller than Alorin, but twice as many ley lines crisscrossed its globe. The First Lord and his Council of Nine had constructed the realm with the strength of a fortress, and a fortress it had become. But even the most stalwart fortress might fall beneath an overwhelming force.

Björn touched one of the nodes on the glowing sphere, and the view zoomed in to magnify that one node and reveal its hundreds of leis, all of them as intricately connected as a spider's funneling web.

"Yes, I see where he's found a weakness." The First Lord's cobalt gaze dissected the web of energy lines. "We can reinforce the weaker area by connecting these two nodes via a new webwork of leis," and he pointed out the nodes in question to Ramu.

Raine knuckled his chin. "Won't that pull too much energy from the lower grid?"

"I don't think so." Björn looked to Dagmar for his input.

"Well, it shouldn't…" Dagmar moved to stand beside Björn and assessed the grid from the same view.

Franco watched the interchange feeling an odd duality of regret and hope.

It had been part of his self-imposed penance to observe the slow decline of Adept arts—impotently, torturously, knowing he had with his own actions contributed to that unanticipated end.

As an oak tree stung by lightning's sharp bite, Alorin was taking a long time to die, but it *was* dying. In its withering, fewer Adepts Awakened each year. Far worse, increasingly smaller percentages of them trained in their craft. What knowledge had remained after the Wars grew musty from lack of use, and much had already been forgotten. Halls of heroes were pilfered for their ancient artifacts, but the thieves never understood that the real treasure had long been lost: the understanding of how to use those talismans of power.

The weldmaps were a perfect example of this. The Espial's Guild had housed the majority of their weldmaps in the Guild Hall on Tiern'aval. When the island had disappeared at the end of Malachai's war, so vanished their maps. What charts remained were considered too priceless now to keep in regular use. The Guild kept them locked behind iron doors and trace seals, or beneath heavy glass cases, protected by patterns they no longer knew how to craft, the maps themselves little more than curiosities now to be observed or gloated over.

In that regard, Niko had been going on and on about Dagmar's weldmap and how *he* ought to have it now that *he* was to become the new Second Vestal. Franco understood why Niko wanted it—that is, he could think of a hundred reasons *Niko* might want it, but not a single one of them would be for the purpose of serving the realm.

Yet to be fair, every Nodefinder coveted that piece of canvas. The Great Master's legendary weldmap was said to be the last map in existence that showed not only Alorin's welds but also the welds that connected each of the Thousand Realms of Light. Dagmar's was the last virgin map, constructed in Alorin during the time known as The Before…a wilder time, when the Warlocks of Shadow still terrorized the Thousand Realms.

Franco might've asked the Great Master for the truth—did the map in fact show the welds to all the worlds, even, some said, into Shadow itself? Did such actually even exist? There were many things he might've asked Dagmar, none of which he'd never been able to bring himself to ask.

Yet, for some reason, seeing T'khendar's map hovering there now gave Franco a renewed sense of hope he wasn't sure he had any right to feel. But it served him to be reminded that not *all* knowledge had been lost when Tiern'aval fell: the Citadel library had been reconstructed in T'khendar's city of Renato; Adept learning continued in Niyadbakir under the tutelage of the inimitable Markal Morrelaine; and the High Mage of the Citadel herself still gazed upon the stars of future to guide their course. With such personages manning the helm, surely all wasn't lost?

The others must've concluded their discussion while Franco was absorbed with these thoughts, for he came out of his internal reverie to find them all staring at him.

"Well, Franco…" Björn pushed hands into his pockets and eyed him inquisitively, "if my oath-sister hasn't released you, some compelling matter must've driven you to us. What news then from Illume Belliel?"

Even though his first piece of news was old by gossip's standards, Franco still had to force it out around a gag of his own incredulity. "My lords…" he ran his gaze around those assembled, "the Council of Realms has voted to enact a measure to allow interrealm trade."

He'd expected surprise, shock, disbelief perhaps. But his news met with a silence so complete, Franco thought he could almost hear individual grains of sand shifting in the desert far below.

Dagmar turned a weighty gaze to Björn. "Then it's begun."

"And long overdue," Ramu rumbled.

Raine sank back against a low cabinet and looked to Franco. "Who put the measure forth?"

"The Speaker himself."

Raine let out a low whistle, while Dagmar muttered, "That was brave of him."

Franco paused his goblet halfway to his lips and lowered it again. "It's odd, though." He looked between the two vestals. "You'd think with a statute so momentous, the Speaker would want to share the burden of source—you'd think he wouldn't *want* to make a target of himself—but despite huge pressure from the Council, he's still refusing to name the Seat who initially wrote the measure."

Björn exchanged a voluminous look with Dagmar before shifting his gaze to Franco. "That's because I wrote it."

Franco choked into his wine.

Dagmar clapped him a few times on the back.

With the spirit still flaming his throat, Franco managed hoarsely, "Forgive me, my lord." He pushed the back of his hand against his mouth and stared at Björn. "But *when*? Three hundred years ago?"

Björn arched resigned brows. "Give or take a few decades."

"This has been a long time in coming," Ramu murmured. Dagmar grunted and walked to pour himself more wine.

"Björn…" Raine's cautionary tone called his oath-brother's gaze to his. "You do of course realize that opening the realms to each other in any capacity necessarily opens them in every capacity. Granting such freedom to the realms challenges the Council's very charter. There are a lot of vested interests who won't be pleased about that."

"We all see it, Raine." Dagmar leaned back against the wine cabinet and inspected the goblet in his hand as if seeing the distant cityworld in its reflection. "The Council has been restricting travel between the realms for millennia, and profiting immensely in the doing."

Raine shook his head. "I can't believe they voted in favor of this. It goes against everything the Council has been pushing—*centuries* of duplicitous warnings against this very course. How did Aldaeon ever get the measure passed?"

Franco fingered his goblet. "Alshiba said it was a near thing."

"Three hundred years of favors and blackmail stored in wait is my wager." Dagmar drank his wine thoughtfully. "However he managed it, it's about bloody time. But he's made a fat target of himself in the offing."

Franco met the First Lord's level gaze. "He's asked Alshiba to head the committee to oversee the measure's implementation."

Raine turned him a swift look of alarm. "She mustn't!"

"I fear she intends to accept, my lord."

"She'll be a good choice if she can survive long enough to see it into action." Dagmar sounded less than optimistic.

Björn considered Franco over crossed arms and with the faintest of furrows between his brows. "She'll need you now more than ever, Franco."

"You can't let her do this, Björn." Raine threw out a hand. "She'll become the prime mark for every vested interest in the Thousand Realms!"

Björn turned Raine a calm but penetrating look. "She's the only one who *can* do it, Raine."

The truthreader's expression hardened. "There are *five thousand* Adepts on that Council—"

"But few with Alshiba's strength of character," Ramu pointed out.

Björn still held Raine's gaze. "Aldaeon wouldn't have chosen Alshiba if he had a better candidate. He understands the danger he places her in."

Raine's expression grew frustrated. "You know perfectly well that he chose Alshiba because of *you*—"

"This is what we've been waiting for, isn't it?" Dagmar's question drew the First Lord's gaze back to him.

The faintest of contemplative smiles came to Björn's lips. "Indeed, brother. Our first step towards a new tomorrow." Then his smile fully manifested, and the glint of opportunity danced in his gaze. "Perhaps I should pay Aldaeon another visit."

"Epiphany bless us." Raine gave Björn a look of tormented protest and sank down on the edge of the cabinet again. "Didn't you say that Aldaeon put you in a *celantia* the last time you showed up in Illume Belliel?"

"Only because it would have compromised his position to do otherwise." Björn pushed his hands in his pockets. "It wasn't personal, Raine."

"It would've felt fairly personal if the circumstances had required all of us to go to Illume Belliel to break you out of gaol."

Björn's eyes glinted with humor. "I certainly would've enjoyed that rescue."

"So, what would be your rationale for going now?" Dagmar swirled his wine contemplatively around in his goblet. "Stir up the pot again and see what floats to the surface?"

Björn shrugged. "Eventually they'll have to follow me."

Dagmar grunted at this.

Not understanding their obscure conversation anyway, Franco stood with conflict twisting in his gut. He knew Alshiba would not thank him for what he meant to do—Björn van Gelderan was absolutely the last man in the Thousand Realms Alshiba wanted to see—but he hoped she would forgive him for it.

"Perhaps...while you're there, my lord, you might pay a visit to the Alorin Seat as well?"

Doubtless catching the concern beneath his words, Björn turned and fixed Franco with the razor point of his attention. "Please explain what you mean by this, Franco."

Franco downed the last of his wine and winced as he lowered the goblet. "I think someone is poisoning her."

"*Poison.*" Raine sounded alarmed.

Franco glanced to the Fourth Vestal and then back to Björn, trying not to cringe beneath the intensity of his gaze. "She said she started feeling ill soon after Niko and I arrived in Illume Belliel. The cityworld's Healers told her that her pattern was frayed, but they couldn't Heal it...or else something is fighting their Healing. She's losing weight, she says she can't sleep..." Franco looked down at his empty goblet, feeling an odd emptiness equally inside himself. "My lord...I fear for her."

"I mislike the sound of this so-called illness," Ramu rumbled.

Björn cast him a sidelong eye. "You and me both, my friend."

"What are you thinking?" Dagmar crossed arms before his broad chest. "*Mor'alir?*"

"Or *inveteré.*" Björn narrowed his gaze thoughtfully. "Either or both."

"There's something else, my lord." Franco stared into his goblet, really wishing he had more wine. "Niko claims he's found a candidate to replace you as the Fifth Vestal."

At this, Björn looked to Dagmar and exchanged a long, silent look. The two of them ever seemed to hold their own conversation within any larger one, with just their gazes speaking in a private subtext.

Raine grunted dubiously. "Alshiba would never consider replacing you." Yet a deep furrow marred his brow.

"Which will only place her in danger from the factions driving Niko," Ramu noted. "They may already be the ones at work against her."

Sill holding Björn's gaze, Dagmar murmured, "She's going to have them coming at her from all sides."

Raine shook his head, seeming conflicted. "We should go back."

"Nay, brother." Dagmar lifted a finger off his goblet and pointed at him. "It's easier to protect one person than three, and we're very much needed here."

Raine leveled him a heated look. "We're very much needed *there!*"

"Illume Belliel will fall," Björn exhaled a heavy sigh and pushed hands into his pockets again, "but the cityworld can be restored. If T'khendar falls, all is lost."

He began walking beside the table. "Alshiba is the one I'm the most concerned about, the only one who still doesn't know she's a Player—the *sole* Player on a field stacked against her."

"First Lord," Franco inquired quietly, "can't you just…tell her?"

Björn looked to him with soft apology in his gaze. "It's a peculiar aspect of this game, Franco: you can't tell a person they're a Player and have it be so. They have to realize it for themselves and choose their own positions." He touched the onyx table and dismissed the glowing sphere from above it. "Any time I've tried assigning someone a Player's role, they've never found their way onto the field."

Dagmar gave a resigned shrug. "You and Arion set up the game that way."

Björn gazed across the table at him. "There was no other way to do it—not and have any hope of winning. A field rotating on Balance's pin, as like to fall in any direction? *Everyone* has to play their positions."

Dagmar waved towards the desert. "Maybe stirring up the pot is exactly what we need. We all expected them to be here by now." He looked Björn up and down. "How does the timing feel to you?"

Björn's gaze danced. "Provident."

"Well then," Dagmar saluted him and drank his wine, as if this answered everything.

Björn shifted his gaze to Raine, clearly seeking his thoughts.

Raine exhaled resignedly. "You know what's best."

Björn gave him a dubious grin. "Do you really believe that?"

"I believe you know it better than I do," the truthreader grumbled. "Go then, and find out who's working their foul craft against our oath-sister."

Björn nodded solemnly to him. "You may depend upon it, Raine." Then he cast his cobalt gaze across the rest of them, smiled in farewell, and took his leave.

When the First Lord had vanished down the steps leading to the nodecourt, Dagmar raised his goblet to Franco by way of gaining his attention. "How long do we have until Alshiba comes searching for her favorite deputy vestal?"

Franco walked to refill his goblet. "She'll be in a Council meeting until late tonight."

Dagmar extended the decanter by way of offering Franco more wine. "That should give you enough time to visit Carian in the Cairs." As he poured, he said with a meaningful look, "Let me tell you what's been happening since you left…"

Franco stepped off the node in Rethynnea's Guild Hall and blinked against the bright light of midday. The sun had been setting as he'd left T'khendar, so the stark daylight of the white-walled city felt sharp against his eyes. The two realms were never quite time-coincident, no matter what part of Alorin he was coming or going from.

"Good day, gov'nor," said a male voice from behind him. Franco turned to see an armed guard approaching. "Might I see your papers—*oh*," he drew up short and promptly ducked a retreating bow. "I didn't recognize Your Excellency at first."

Franco wondered how the guard had recognized him at all.

The latter nudged his cap in a casual salute, added, "A good day to you then," and retreated into the shadows.

Franco watched him walking away with a faint frown narrowing his brow. Then he turned and headed down a cloistered walkway towards the exit.

The sun accosted him again as he emerged into a wide piazza bustling with activity. He pushed a hand over his eyes and scanned the busy square, searching for Carian vran Lea's telltale mane and wishing the pirate had chosen somewhere less populated to meet.

"Admiral?"

Franco winced at the address, while at the same time wishing he hadn't been so certain the voice was addressing *him*.

He turned to find a waif of a boy looking up at him; large, dark eyes staring from an elfin face. The lad seemed about as disreputable as any child could aspire to be—a street urchin of the commonest sort, the type liable to pick your pockets and scamper off if you so much as scratched your nose. Barefooted and dirty, he wore a pair of ragged britches and a beaded Khurdish vest that he'd probably stolen right off a drunken man's back.

The boy grinned, proudly displaying a broken front tooth. "It *is* you, ain't it, Admiral?" His words were shaped with the street brogue common in those parts. "The Cap'n said you'd come 'ventually."

Franco peered at him while reassuring himself that his purse was safely inside his coat. "*Who* said?"

"The pirate—Cap'n vran Lea? Says I'm to bring you to 'im. Offered me a crown for me efforts."

"Is that so?"

The urchin grinned. "Said you'd give me the same."

Franco sighed. "I'll bet he did."

"Will you come, General?"

"It's Admir—oh, never mind. Yes, I'll come." Franco motioned him to lead away. As they were heading across the piazza, he thought again about the Guild's guard recognizing him and inquired of the lad, "How did you know me?"

"The Cap'n told me what ye look like, Admiral."

Franco could only imagine the description Carian vran Lea might've given of him. "Indeed? What did he say?"

The boy flashed a mischievous grin. "Said ye'd be the handsomest man I'd ever seen."

Franco's gaze narrowed. "I highly doubt he said that."

"*Then* 'e said to keep a weather eye for a man who looked like 'e grew up with a noble name but walked like a man who'd traded it away."

Franco frowned at this uncomfortable description. He wasn't sure how he felt about Carian giving it to a street child—or to anyone for that matter. "What else did he say?"

The boy pushed through a mass of people crowding a tinker's stand and shot a grin over his shoulder. "Said ye'd have a minstrel's look about ye."

"Is that so," Franco remarked flatly.

"Oh, aye, 'e said it, 'e did." The boy's button eyes gleamed like bright pebbles. "Also said to watch for a man who walked like the specter of Death was always kissin' 'is heels but kept walkin' anyway."

"He said all of this," Franco muttered. Though for all his skepticism, he couldn't deny how each statement rang with an uncomfortable truth.

"Every word, Admiral. Took a quarter of the 'glass tellin' me it all." The boy's dark brown eyes looked Franco up and down. Then he turned his impish face forward again and said more quietly, "But 'e shoulda told me to look fer a man wearin' a cloak of shame 'cross his tarnished honor."

Franco nearly missed a step.

"A man who built a fortress of ignoble secrets and now hides behind 'em, who locks trust away with the silver and serves 'is friends cowardice on plates of chagrin—"

Franco grabbed the boy roughly by the shoulder and spun him around. "Did Carian tell you to say that?"

The urchin gazed at him with an expression of injured innocence. "Admiral? Is somethin' wrong?" Worried eyes darted to Franco's hand gripping his bare shoulder, fingers nearly white.

Thirteen hells, did I just imagine it? Franco quickly released him. He pushed a hand through his hair and stared hard at the boy. *I truly am going mad.*

You're just figuring that out? his conscience sneered. *Smart as the dog that chases its own tail, aren't ye?*

Be silent!

Franco gave the boy an apologetic look. "I'm sorry, lad. I thought you said…" But he would never again speak aloud those words, for their truth had shocked him.

"Not to worry, Admiral." The urchin turned and led off, whereupon he said in that same quiet voice, "It's hard hearin' what people are sayin' when yer conscience speaks louder than they do."

Franco gritted his teeth. He really had to be imagining it.

After an indecently lengthy walk along the harbor, the boy stopped in front of a tavern with a glossy red door. The sign over the door showed a bearded man's head with an arrow stuck through his temple, mouth hanging open, eyelids slack and tongue lolling. Above the face hung the painted words: *The Duke's Head.*

"This is it, Admiral." The boy held out his hand expectantly.

Franco eyed him with a narrowed gaze, but he gave him a Free Crown all the same. He noted while he did that the head depicted on the coins held a striking resemblance to the rather grim one painted on the sign above the tavern door.

The boy bit into the gold and then, grinning, pocketed the coin with a hearty, "Thanks, Admiral." He darted away.

But as Franco was opening the tavern door, he heard the boy say low into his ear, "Ye may think yer too far over the cliff, Admiral, but the Lady, she's got yer hand, she does."

Franco caught his breath and spun. The boy was walking away—too far to have said something so intimately close. Yet when he felt Franco's attention upon him, the lad turned his head. A knowing gaze that seemed far too old for his years looked back at Franco. Then the crowd closed in and the boy disappeared from view.

Unnerved, Franco headed inside.

Men crowded *The Duke's Head* like hogs at a trough. The air stank of sweat and stale beer and a particular sour odor that such places always seemed to possess, as if the demon smell had penetrated the very planks of the floor and now no amount of cleaning could exorcise it. Franco peered through a haze of smoke and finally spotted Carian vran Lea at a corner table, playing Trumps with three other men.

When Franco reached him, the pirate had the butt of a smoke clenched between his pearly teeth and his eyes concealed behind his cards. Franco had to clear his throat several times before Carian noticed him.

"Oh, there you are, Admiral." The pirate grinned around his smoking tobacco weed, shedding ash on his shirt in the process. "I'd begun to wonder if you were ever gonna show up."

Franco noted the pile of coin in front of Carian—twice what any of the other men boasted. "I see it's been a strenuous wait."

"Now, who would it have served for me to sit on my arse in the piazza waiting on Your Excellency's pleasure?" He said Franco's new title with a particular smirk.

"Certainly not your pockets."

"Vran Lea," one of the men at the table growled, "play yer damn card or fold. We ain't got all day to sit here while you and yer boyfriend make pillow talk."

Carian cast him a gimlet eye. Then he looked back to his cards. Then back to the man, who was still glowering at him, and finally to his cards again. He threw the latter on the table. "I fold, damn you."

The man gave him a black look.

Carian swept up his winnings and pocketed them as he stood. "Let's go, Admiral." He grabbed Franco's arm and dragged him off.

"You owe me, vran Lea!" the other player called after him.

"In your wettest dreams, Jacard," Carian grumbled. Then they were out on the street.

Carian turned them towards the marina and walked with long-legged nonchalance, jingling the coins in his pocket. "So…I take it Lakti found you," he aimed a sidelong look at Franco.

"Lakti?"

"Street gamin, so high." Carian held up his hand about the height of the boy's head.

"Yes, about that." Franco cast him a narrow stare. "What did you tell that boy?"

"So he talked to you, eh?" Carian flashed a knowing grin. When Franco continued pointedly staring at him, he chuckled to himself and turned forward again. "Unnerving little bastard, ain't he?"

"*Carian*," Franco made his tone hard. "What did you tell him?"

"It's his gift, Admiral. He gets all in your head." Carian twirled a forefinger beside his temple for emphasis. "Screws with you something fierce, eh? But if you need somebody found anywhere in Rethynnea, Lakti's your boy."

Franco did feel unnerved. It was like the boy had walked directly into his soul and plucked out its most tender morsels for closer inspection. The things he'd said…Franco would never have admitted them in the quiet of his thoughts, much less put them to voice. "Are you saying you told him nothing about me?"

Carian turned him a grin. "Blimey, the little bastard really got to you, didn't he?"

Franco glared at him. "If by this question, you're referencing the ill cast of my mood, surely it has nothing to do with where I've been and what I've been doing since you and I parted company at Niko's estate—" Abruptly Franco exhaled a measured breath and reined in his irritation, which was serving neither of them. Then he looked around. "Where *are* you taking us?"

Carian cast him a telling look. "You ain't the only one who's been busy, Admiral. Just up here a ways more, and then you'll know all."

ELEVEN

"It matters less what you look at than what you see."

—The Adept wielder Malachai ap'Kalien

A LATE SPRING STORM squatted over the province of Saldaria as if magically bound within the confines of its borders. Rain lashed the plains and fell as snow in the northern mountains; wind buffeted the cities, and lightning struck repeatedly at the Temple of Tambarré, whose Prophet, according to rumor, summoned the storm with his dreams.

Caught somewhere between the waking world and the restful state of true sleep, Darshan stood with Kjieran van Stone in a groin-vaulted loggia, watching the rain. The raging storm of Darshan's dreams seemed an echo of his thoughts—or perhaps a resonance of them cast outward from his slumbering mind to influence both the plane of dreams and the dawn.

Storms, Darshan understood. But this inner turmoil mystified him.

Kjieran stood beside him, radiating dismay. Darshan didn't know why. Each of his dreams seemed a continuation of the one that had come before, yet without any remembered context to explain the place they'd now arrived, only a sense of the long moment connecting to some earlier time, and a feeling of conflict, raw and often explosive.

Kjieran looked up at him through the spill of his dark hair. "Did you love me, my lord?"

The faintest shadow narrowed Darshan's brow. "If love exists, it is a human emotion and therefore unknown to me. How can I say what I felt for you?" He eyed him askance. "Did you love me?"

Kjieran frowned. "I…desired you, at times. But love?" He shook his head. "I don't think I could've loved you when I was so full of fear of you."

"I didn't understand your fear." Darshan glanced to the specter of Kjieran and felt again that familiar pang of loss, combined with the ache of a mystery he might never solve. He both yearned for and dreaded these moments with his acolyte's ghost—yearned for them because he could re-experience the connection they'd shared; and dreaded them, for he always woke to find the bond severed and Kjieran dead on a pyre of betrayal. "I gave you the greatest gift I had to offer."

Kjieran glanced away again, looking troubled. "You bound me to you."

"A connection I shared only with my brothers. I extended this to you, Kjieran, a bond I have never shared with another."

"But you made me *eidola*. You bound me against my will."

Darshan's gaze tightened. "I do not see why this should matter."

"You gave me no choice about it, my lord!"

"Choice? What *choice* is this of which you speak?" Darshan raked his gaze across him. "You exist to die. I gave you immortality—"

"Against my will!" Kjieran interposed.

"—and divinity through an eternal bond with me."

"Where is the divinity in becoming a monster?" Kjieran clenched his jaw and stared bitterly.

Darshan gazed bemusedly at him. "I never wanted to harm you." Darshan felt the truth of these words like a barbed lash, for they defied his basic nature, his most fundamental beliefs. He put his hands on Kjieran's shoulders and turned his acolyte to face him. "I wanted to make you immortal."

Kjieran pressed his lips together tightly. "But you gave me no choice in it, my lord."

Darshan's hands dropped to his sides. "Choice. *Choice*." He turned away, fuming again. "You're obsessed with this idea of choice."

"Every sentient creature is invested with it, my lord."

Darshan spun him a look. "No. You're invested with purpose. These are not the same."

Kjieran dropped his eyes to his feet, enveloped by a cloud of malcontent. "You assume only *you* have choice, but this conclusion stands an uneven ground upon the least inspection, my lord." When Darshan merely stared at him, letting his silence speak his disagreement, Kjieran looked up and said boldly, "Our Adept bodies are not immortal like yours, or like those creatures of the fifth strand—the *drachwyr* and the zanthyrs—but our essence *is* immortal."

Darshan grunted. "You parrot my brother's philosophies. Are you a ghost, Kjieran, or merely an echo of Pelas's thoughts crossing through the bond he and I share?"

Kjieran clenched his jaw and looked out into the storm. "I wish I knew, my lord."

Lightning struck, charging the air with an ozone tang, charging the dream with emotion. Darshan felt the lightning mutate with its expiration; it coursed now through his mind, bringing a critical sharpness to his thoughts and a surge of desire in his core.

That Pelas might be influencing his dreams, constructing these moments with Kjieran to torture or misdirect him…that his brother might be looking on in silent witness of their private interactions…these ideas infuriated Darshan. But it infuriated him more to see Kjieran every night and be denied his touch, and to wake after such dreams, aching and unsatisfied, yearning for a man who was forever beyond his reach.

He willed his tumultuous ire to settle and looked back to his acolyte. His gaze was very dark. "You weaken me, Kjieran."

Kjieran appeared staggered by the statement. "However could *I* weaken *you*?"

Darshan considered him amid the hypnotic drumming of rain on stone. "I cannot compel you here in this place, not even to gain the answers I'm seeking. But even in life, I never sought to compel your desire. I didn't want to control you. Much of what I felt about you—how I treated you—ran at odds with what I believe to be true. I didn't understand it then. I still don't."

Kjieran dropped his gaze to his hands. "This I remember."

Darshan flicked an irritable look over him. "Dore repeatedly advised me to bind you to my will. If I had…if I'd bound you with compulsion from the start…"

Kjieran lifted a tormented understanding back to him. "I would still be yours."

Giving in to his pressing need, Darshan reached for Kjieran and drew him closer. He brushed at a strand of Kjieran's shoulder-length black hair, thinking of their last union, wishing it had happened in the flesh instead of solely in their minds. He looked him over, wondering… "Perhaps you still are."

Kjieran's brow furrowed. "What do you mean?"

"Perhaps you haven't moved on because I can't let you go."

Fear constricted Kjieran's expression. "Because we're bound still?"

Darshan let Kjieran see the raw desire in his gaze. "I wanted to spend eternity with you, but this mortal shell of yours would never have survived in Chaos."

Kjieran turned away, his breath coming faster. After a time, he swallowed. "That's why you made me *eidola*."

"Kjieran, look at me."

Kjieran dutifully met his lord's gaze, though he looked uneasy now. "To us, my lord, the *eidola* are monsters...like your Marquiin."

"So you've explained to me." Darshan caught a lock of Kjieran's hair between his thumb and forefinger. He had no idea what would happen if he let his dream travel to the places he yearned to go, and he didn't want Kjieran to vanish again. "At the time, Dore made a compelling case for your immortality in this guise."

"He doesn't serve you true, my lord."

Darshan arched a sardonic brow. "Yes, I'm increasingly discovering fault in Dore's advice."

Lightning struck again, reflecting Kjieran's colorless eyes as stars. Darshan ran his hand through his acolyte's hair, observing the way it shone in the muted storm-light, admiring the shapely line of his jaw. It thrilled him to see Kjieran's breath coming faster beneath his touch, to see his pulse quickening and his eyes taking on a vivid luster.

Kjieran wakened desires that Darshan had known only in the Void; yet they were not the same desires, for in the Void, he'd thrilled in the act of unmaking, but with Kjieran...

Kjieran, he wanted to endure.

Darshan searched his acolyte's gaze with his own. "Is it so terrible, being here with me?"

For a moment, Kjieran seemed just as captivated. Then he dropped his gaze, looking stricken. "I...don't know."

Darshan traced the line of Kjieran's jaw with his thumb. "What do you feel?" His own desire charged his breath.

Kjieran looked up at him, his eyes brimming with tears. "Lost."

—the dream shifted—

"Hello, brother."

Darshan spun to find Pelas reclining on the terrace wall with an arm draped across one bent knee. Gone was the stormy day...Kjieran. Sundown drenched the world in flame.

Darshan glared at Pelas. "Is all of this *your* doing?"

"How could it be my doing? You have me locked away in a tower, convinced that I've lost my power."

Darshan considered his middle brother with a smoldering gaze.

Pelas straightened to sit on the edge of the wall and braced his hands at his sides. His dark hair fell long about his shoulders. "Has it never occurred to you that these dreams might be your conscience's attempt to raise its unwanted head?"

"Ridiculous."

Pelas smiled. "To imagine you have a conscience? I suppose, yes; yet I haven't given up on you, brother."

"How are you doing this?" Darshan stalked towards him. "Desist from this attempt to manipulate my thoughts. It serves neither your purposes nor my interest."

Pelas got to his feet on the terrace wall and looked down at him. The dying sunlight cast a rim of warm gold around his form, but his eyes were distant and cold. "Things are not as they seem, Darshan. You've been standing too long in Dore Madden's shadow. You see his illusions and call them truth."

Darshan waved off the idea. "Dore Madden—"

Pelas held up a hand. "Yes, I know. He stands in *your* shadow—I recall this tedious speech." Pelas jumped down from the wall and landed in front of him, standing not quite eye to eye. "But my dear brother…" he plucked at the collar on Darshan's robe, idly neatening its line, "what *you* don't understand is that the shadow you're seeing is Dore's own. He's simply convinced you think it's yours."

Pelas looked him over with his dark copper eyes and a self-satisfied smile. "If you ever left your ivory tower, perhaps you'd see the truths you're so plainly missing."

Fuming, Darshan reached for him—

He woke to the reverberation of lightning striking stone. The air hissed with static. Frustration thrummed through his veins.

Darshan threw off the sheets to the rumble of thunder and strode to where the storm raged beyond the open doors of his bedchamber.

Tambarré's high acropolis was seething with current, lightning gathering for another strike. Darshan felt the coalescing energy prickling his bare skin. It roused gooseflesh and brought a heavy resistance to his thoughts.

His thoughts were charged enough without the storm's intrusion.

The unfamiliar feeling of his hair whipping his flesh drew his gaze from the firmament back to his person. His acolytes had spent several hours the previous night unweaving his braids. Now his hair hung long about his torso, its raven ends free to spit and sting his naked form with the wind, the silken masses becoming quickly tangled.

Darshan turned his gaze over his shoulder. Three acolytes lay sleeping in his bed.

Before Kjieran, he'd routinely woken to find bodies cold with death lying beside him, but it had been months since any of his lovers had pleased him enough to warrant his releasing them to the fulfillment of their purpose—a merciful end to the burning torment of life. Once, he'd granted his acolytes their ascension almost nightly. Now he couldn't bring himself to care enough to draw a single one across the threshold.

No part of this world felt the same since Kjieran had sought death over eternity with him. This choice above all else disturbed Darshan, for as much as he wished to deny it, he recognized that it had been a *choice*.

It gravely confused him.

'...*If you ever left your ivory tower, perhaps you'd see what you're missing...*'

Pelas's words were an arrowhead working its inexorable way beneath the armor of his conviction. His brother had goaded him many times to get out into the world, obvious attempts to entrap him into the same lust for experience that afflicted Pelas. Darshan had easily deflected his brother's earlier taunts, but this latest one clung to his consciousness—not as enticement, but in warning.

His thoughts strayed back to the question which had been nagging at him: *was* all of this actually Pelas's doing? Was he somehow influencing Darshan's dreams, even from a remote tower in Myacene, even thinking his power lost?

He suddenly had to know.

Heading back through his bedchamber, Darshan brushed each of his acolytes' minds to wake them—an odd impulse which Kjieran would've described as gentle. Increasingly he found himself meting to others what treatment he'd desired to give to Kjieran. While it didn't ameliorate his loss, his acolytes didn't seem to mind the change in treatment. They'd even ceased trembling in his presence, which made their lovemaking more fervent, if no more pleasurable to him.

The three young men rose and attended him, keeping their minds quiet and their gazes downcast. They combed his hair and brought him his garments, but the Prophet's usual garb didn't suit his purposes that day.

He chose instead a black coat that Pelas had given him years ago, before their variance of purpose had driven a wedge between them. The damask fabric held a subtle sheen, and its arabesque design reminded him of the swirling eddies of Chaos. It would cheer his brother to see him wearing it.

His acolytes brought him black pants and boots in the northern fashion. They spun his masses of hair into an ornamental knot and secured it with long pins carved of volcanic glass. The artistry pleased him.

He sent them away and summoned his power.

Chaos called endlessly to Darshan. He felt its pull in his every inhalation, in a tingling of his skin and a tugging upon his consciousness, which ever sought to return to that maelstrom place where the unraveling fringes met the infinite Void. Long years he'd ached to return there. The more his fervor to unmake this realm, the greater his frustration at Pelas's dilettante comportment.

He'd placed Pelas in a tower in the remote north of Myacene, with its constant snowstorms and limited daylight, because it was the closest this world could come to approximating the Void. He thought it would please Pelas to be continuously reminded of their home.

Yet now…now the idea of leaving Alorin and returning to Chaos, of potentially losing what ethereal connection to Kjieran remained to him…

He couldn't conceive of it.

Darshan sliced the fabric of existence and moved through the darkness of Shadow, traveling from Tambarré to Myacene with a step of thought. He emerged into Pelas's tower room to a dim daylight made darker by a late spring storm. Snow was swirling madly against the windowpanes. Darshan turned with a darkness in his gaze but a lightness in his heart to greet his brother—

—and found the tower empty.

Rage pulsed through the currents. A violent flare of power splintered the swirling snowflakes into minute particles of ice and blasted the clouds into mist for miles in every direction. Sunlight flooded into the room from a suddenly clear sky.

"*How?*" The breath of Darshan's incredulity formed a cloud of frost on the air. He spun in place, seeking any explanation for Pelas's impossible escape.

Then he saw the note.

Darshan tore it free of the dagger pinning it to the wall and read the words written in Pelas's hand.

My dear brother,

Thank you again for showing me definitively where I stand in your esteem. To make my position equally clear, know that I've selected my own path and will be walking it henceforth without your interference.

Brother, your arrogance blinds you. That delicate bird you so generously left me to carve into pieces saw through your elaborate deception from the moment she awakened, and once I released her from the goracrosta, it took but a whisper of her power to overcome your foul illusion and restore me.

Don't bother summoning, Darshan. I shan't be attending you again. I shall be paying a visit to Shail upon his quest for dominion, however, for he has *something of mine that I must retrieve, ere I set off in pursuit of a purpose of my <u>own</u> choosing.*

He'd signed it with the flourished letter of his name.

Darshan clenched his jaw and incinerated the paper with a thought.

While ash fell from his fingers, he turned a dangerous gaze around the tower, seeking…what? He couldn't say. Perhaps some clue to show Pelas was lying about his means of his escape, anything to disprove his impossible claims.

'*…I've selected my own path and will be walking it henceforth without your interference…*'

Every word of his brother's note held layers of meaning.

The first two lines clearly informed him that Pelas would be acting on his own agency. '*Walking it henceforth without your interference*' could only mean that Pelas had found some way to escape Darshan's compulsion.

Impossible! He'd bound that pattern with the elemental fifth. Pelas could not have removed it.

How then? Some new trick offered by Dore's little bird, Isabel?

A little bird who was not so delicate after all, not if she could remove an illusion Darshan himself had crafted—and remove it easily, if Pelas's account bore any truth.

So…Dore had not been lying to him about Isabel val Gelderan's power, which meant that she'd somehow hidden the extent of her ability from him during his inspection of her mind.

Darshan's gaze tightened.

Dore had told him much of Isabel van Gelderan, much he in turn had ascribed to the man's unique paranoia. Now he questioned that disregard.

More germane to his immediate concerns, however, was who Pelas could have allied with *against* him? Isabel? This so-called Prophet of Epiphany, the once High Mage of a lost Citadel?

And what definitive path had Pelas chosen? It was clear in his brother's words that he would be acting thereafter against their purpose. But Pelas could not be acting alone.

Had Dore been correct in his warnings that others were working against Darshan and his brothers? Could it be true, as Dore had so often and emphatically claimed, that this Björn van Gelderan was their avowed and knowing enemy, despite the abounding stories that indicated otherwise? Had the stories been a purposeful subterfuge?

Darshan worked the muscles of his jaw. It disturbed him to imagine he could've been so wrong…so deficient in his understanding.

Disturbed? No, this word did not begin to describe the rage coursing through him.

He walked to a window and looked out over an icebound landscape of jagged mountains and vast glaciers...and summoned his brother Shail. Then he obliged himself to wait.

This setback with Pelas roused a grave conflict in Darshan. Part of him willed that they should all return to the Void then and there. The headiest sensation one could experience in this pathetic world managed only to be a paltry approximation of the rush of unmaking. And while in the Void, he'd never conceived of such base emotions as what had coursed through him in recent weeks—anger, frustration, loss, a hungering desire, and a sense of betrayal that roused a righteous fury. These feelings were so foreign to him that he hardly knew how to interpret them, much less how to craft their proper expression out of the clay of this shell.

Yes, the lure of the Void was strong, if only to escape the feeling of barrenness that currently held him in its grip. Yet to flee the realm without accomplishing their purpose...this failure would become a canker upon his conscience forevermore. This he knew and understood.

No, he must stay and see their duty done. *Except*...destroying this world meant destroying Kjieran.

That he felt at odds with this truth utterly infuriated him.

Darshan was still standing at the window when he felt a tremble in Alorin's fabric and looked over his shoulder to see his brother Shail stepping out of Shadow.

Shail swept Darshan with his gaze, and a contemptuous smile lifted one corner of his mouth. "This is a new look for you."

Darshan was unclear whether Shail's was referencing his clothing or the boiling froth of power surrounding him. He turned to face his brother squarely. "You took your time getting here. Was my calling not clear enough?"

Shail's upper lip twitched. He began wandering about the room. "Would that I could've rid myself of your incessant braying sooner. I do have my own matters to attend to. Oddly, time continues its inexorable march, completely indifferent to your permission." A condescending smile smeared him up and down. "How galling that must be for you."

Darshan regarded him levelly. "Where is Pelas?"

Shail laid fingertips on Pelas's table of knives. "I thought you had him in hand. Wasn't that how you described his position when last we spoke?"

"Don't bandy words with me, Shailabanáchtran. I know Pelas came to you."

"I'm not hiding him beneath my waistcoat like a stolen timepiece,

Darshan. Do you think I would willingly leave him to his own devices when his every breath is taken in action against us?"

Darshan worked the muscles of his jaw. "How long ago did you see him?"

Shail shrugged. "A few days."

Darshan studied his youngest sibling with a critical eye, wondering what possession he'd stolen from Pelas, and how Pelas had managed to steal it back—for it was obvious from the tightness of Shail's gaze and his general distempered demeanor that he did not possess this treasure still. Of course, he was trying to hide this fact from Darshan.

Shail turned a look around. "So this is where you imprisoned our brother?"

"You find it too remote?"

His lip lifted in a sneer. "Too humane." He wandered the room disinterestedly.

"You have some plan for retrieving whatever it was Pelas took back from you?"

Shail shot a piercing look over his shoulder. "You had your chance to take our recalcitrant brother in hand," the words came out in a fractious hiss. "I assure you, *my* methods will be more effective."

"Yes. I deeply wonder what those methods will involve." *For any method you would use to discipline Pelas, you would surely use against me as well.*

Darshan plucked a blade from Pelas's table and thumbed the razor edge while his mind assessed, evaluated, deduced. He looked up under his brows at his brother. "And what affairs of yours has Pelas interrupted, Shailabanáchtran?"

Shail straightened a candle in a sconce. "Why do you care?"

"Call it curiosity."

Shail arched a dismissive brow. "Your interest would be better aimed at the boy Pelas has taken as his paramour." He picked up a silver cup from the mantel and sniffed inside it. "A truthreader, coincidentally, and powerful." He eyed Darshan askance and flicked his gaze up and down his form. "Just the way you like them."

"Such lures away from my question—you fear so much what I'll find if I inspect your activities?"

Upon this utterance, the currents went dangerously still. Shail turned to him with a decidedly unfavorable gleam in his dark eyes. "The moment you step out of that temple of yours, you'll be far out of your depth. Take care of deep water, brother."

"An intriguing warning, coming from you." Darshan set the dagger back in its place. "Did you have anything to do with Pelas's escape?"

Shail snorted. He returned the cup to the mantel. "You think me a fool."

"Yet he went straight to your location."

Shail shrugged. "I had summoned him."

"I assume for the purposes of reclaiming from you this truthreader he's infatuated with? And doubtless which you now intend to steal back again. An inane and childish interplay of 'his and mine.' How exactly is our purpose served by these games?"

"You have your diversions, we have ours."

Diversions indeed. Darshan knew perfectly well that Shail had never taken a single step that didn't somehow serve his own agenda. This *tête-à-tête* with Pelas would be no exception.

'...I'll be attending Shail upon his quest for dominion...'

Pelas had specifically said *dominion* in his letter, but if Shail had been acting upon their purpose, *destruction* would have been a better suited description.

Darshan considered his youngest brother with a dark suspicion forming.

He'd always known that following their purpose was simply a game to Shail. He'd assumed it was a more interesting game than the one Shail had been playing in Chaos, and when this game was done—their purpose accomplished, and the Realms of Light unmade—Shail would simply find another game to play in pursuit of their purpose.

But now Darshan wondered if Shail was pursuing their purpose at all. He traced his fingers along another of Pelas's knives. "I find myself suddenly curious to see how you're filling your days, brother."

Shail moved a candlestick on the mantel a fraction of an inch to the left. "I fear you would find the hours mundane, what with no truthreaders to corrupt or acolytes to compel to your bed…"

"Yet my interest is piqued to see the many ingenious ways you must be acting towards the accomplishment of our purpose."

Shail's hand stilled on the mantel. He turned Darshan a portentous stare. "Meddle in my affairs at your peril, Darshan."

And there it was, as plain a confession as he would likely ever get from his youngest brother.

So Pelas was right. Darshan felt more disappointed than surprised.

He lowered his gaze back to Pelas's table of knives and selected a black-bladed stiletto from among the collection. He observed quietly as he examined its edge, "If you've abandoned our purpose, Shailabanáchtran… nothing can protect you." Then he lashed out with a net of *deyjiin*.

Shail snarled a curse and just caught the upper edge of the net in his upraised fist. The net expanded into a sizzling curtain of silver-violet energy pulsing with intent. Shail's face twisted as he strained his own power to keep the net from closing around him. "You let…Pelas turn your mind against me!" he gasped while his fist grew white and his face red and veins bulged in his neck. "*Why?*"

Darshan approached his brother steadily. In his mind he held firm his intent, so that with each step, he pushed the net more forcefully to close around Shail. "Curiously, I think Pelas is telling the truth."

"*So what if he is?*" Shail shoved his other hand up to help hold off Darshan's confining net. The flickering power cast ill reflections on his features. "Why should we not act as gods to these creatures? We've only to align our will and this world prostrates itself across our path!"

Darshan continued his approach, eyeing his brother inscrutably, his thumb running casually along the sharp edge of the stiletto. "So you choose to become as they would fashion you? A god by a *mortal's* standard? No less and no more than what their minds can envision?"

Shail snarled venomously, "Isn't that what *you* do every day?"

Rivulets of blood were running down Shail's arms, darkening the silk of his robes. Darshan pushed a little harder on his net, and Shail staggered backwards. He sucked in his breath and glared venomously at him.

"It is our *intent* that determines our effect, Shailabanáchtran." Darshan thumbed his blade—Pelas's blade. It was delightfully sharp. "*My* every action has been in pursuit of our purpose. What can be said of yours?"

He shifted the intent in his working, and the blood on Shail's hands sputtered and burst into flames. Shail snarled a furious curse. Darshan caught a glimpse of his intent with the glare in his eye, and—

Power ripped through the room. The tower walls exploded, the roof disintegrated, furniture flew away with screams of rending wood, and the wind came swirling violently through, scattering the deadly detritus of the explosion.

Darshan seared the air clean with a thought.

When stillness settled an instant later, the ravaged tower lay open to the elements, and Darshan stood alone.

TWELVE

*"To succeed as a wielder requires a passionate
and inconsolable obsession."*

–The Adept wielder Arion Tavestra

TANIS STOOD WITH Nadia on Pelas's rooftop terrace watching the sun rising between a molten sea and a stormy sky. The lad thought the storm a fitting portent, for they were any moment due to depart for Faroqhar.

Hallovia was famous for its torrential weather. The approaching storm already had the sea white-capped and the waves in a high fury; yet Tanis had the sense that this storm wouldn't come close to approximating the fury he was sure to face from the Empress of Agasan upon their arrival back in the Sacred City.

A thread of tension bound Tanis, cords of consequence reaching out from a far distant Faroqhar. He already felt chained, as if his past choices had placed the manacles on wrists and ankles, only waiting on time and conscience to draw them tight. Men claimed to be shackled by circumstance, but Tanis felt jailed by yesterday's decisions.

Exhaling a measured breath, trying to ease the apprehension that had his insides knotted up and his hands all twitchy, Tanis moved up behind Nadia, wrapped his arms around her and drew her close. He breathed in her scent and rested his head against hers. He didn't know what would happen once they returned to Agasan, but he doubted very much that he'd be given an opportunity to be alone with her again.

The world felt askew.

Though the sea seemed to maintain its position parallel to the horizon, on some level, Tanis perceived it tilting.

"What are you so worried about?" Nadia shifted slightly in his arms. "You rescued the heir to the imperial throne. You'll be seen as a hero." A look flickered across her brow and she added under her breath, "That is, if they even noticed me missing at all."

Tanis pressed his nose to her hair and breathed deeply of her scent. "You wouldn't have been in danger at all if not for me."

Nadia arched an imperious brow. "I seem to recall that I'm the one who put on a disguise and snuck out of the palace without my guards." She turned in his arms. "I won't have you blaming yourself and leaving me out of it, Tanis."

Simple words, but Tanis heard a far deeper intimation there. He wasn't certain she'd meant for him to perceive it though.

I want to be with you—always.

That time the thought came with an ethereal pinch, for clarity.

Tanis smiled and drew her closer once more. "I want that too, Nadia." He rested his head against hers and gazed off over the ashen sea. "But I don't know where my path is leading."

She pulled away just far enough to look at him. "Why can't it lead to me? You're the son of Arion Tavestra, heir to Adonnai. Do you have any idea the fortune you stand to inherit?" She searched his troubled gaze. "Besides, as I told you, when I'm empress I can choose my own consort. Not that it will matter once my mother finds out who you are—"

"It's not as simple as that, Nadia." Tanis pressed his lips together and held her gaze. He hadn't yet told her that his mother lived, or that he'd spoken with her via their binding.

There was much he hadn't told her.

Making his tone more gentle, he said, "Even if it was that simple, I'm not sure my name is a truth that should be shared. I'm..." *Gods and devils*, there was so much he couldn't say. Tanis shook his head and then exhaled a forceful breath. "I'm not just bound to two immortals, Nadia, I'm bound to an immortal game; my uncle's game."

Nadia must've seen something in his gaze—or else in his thoughts, Tanis didn't know which—for she withdrew from him and took a step back. Her eyes studied his expression while her mind searched his for the truths he'd thus far kept hidden. But Tanis feared sharing more with her; for if he held any certainty, it was that the more Nadia knew, the greater danger she'd be in.

Finding his deeper thoughts closed to her awareness, Nadia frowned. "Is there nothing you'll tell me? Don't you trust me to—"

He quickly enfolded her in his arms again. Pressing his forehead against hers, he murmured, "You know it's not a matter of trust." She was a warm comfort in his arms and a grounding presence in his thoughts. He would've told her everything if he dared. "The zanthyr brought me to the Sormitáge because that's where my path was leading, but somehow I knew from the beginning that I hadn't gone there to study."

"It wasn't coincidence that placed you in Felix's room or brought you into our doomed little investigation. That's what you're saying?"

Tanis exhaled heavily. "I'm bound to a zanthyr and a Malorin'athgul, Nadia, and they're bound to me. That should indicate the scope of what I'm involved in."

Nadia regarded him circumspectly. Then she rested her head against his shoulder and traced the arabesques on his coat sleeve with one finger. "And the zanthyr Phaedor is also bound to you?" Her finger circled, circled on his sleeve. "You never told me this before."

"It never came up. Do you think it's important for some reason?"

"Well, it's certainly intriguing..." She lifted her head to look at him. "Are you familiar with the legends of Cephrael?"

"Not nearly as familiar with them as you are." Nadia was a veritable fount of information on the *angiel*. "Why?"

"Just now, when you so blithely said you were bound to *two* immortals..." she paused to let him note the miraculous aspect of this statement, "you reminded me of a Genesis legend." She cast him a long look while a thought lingered in her mind, unspoken. He sensed it hesitating there like a diver at the edge of a cliff considering the plunge.

A sudden smile hinted on Nadia's lips. "Oh...it's not so enjoyable when others are coy with you, is it?" She slid out of his arms and walked towards the railing, radiating amusement.

Tanis frowned after her. "By this you imply that *I* am coy?" He followed her across the marble tiles. "I am never coy."

She laughed and spun him a look. "You are *fabulously* coy with information you don't want to divulge. I daresay as formidably closemouthed as your zanthyr—if my father's indignation is fair testimony of Phaedor's nature."

She was teasing him, but Tanis felt frustrated. "Nadia, I only want to protect you—"

"I know your mind." She smiled and held out her hand to him, so he took it. "You know," she drew him to stand with her at the railing, "sometimes people can be in just as much danger by *not* having information as by having it, especially when said knowledge might impact their choices."

Tanis shook his head. "If I hadn't let *you* be the distraction while Felix and I searched N'abranaacht's rooms—"

"Tanis, you're walking your path. What makes you think I'm not walking mine?" She held his gaze pointedly, forcing him to conceive of this possibility. "You had your tea with Shailabanáchtran. So did I. Perhaps we were both meant to."

While he deliberated this logic, which he couldn't fault even if he gravely misliked it, Nadia moved beneath the circle of his arm so that they faced out across the ocean together.

"Everyone thinks Björn van Gelderan betrayed the realm." Nadia exhaled a slow breath and glanced meaningfully to him, whereupon Tanis sensed a previously shuttered window in her mind suddenly opening, even as she said, "That is, except my mother."

Tanis arched both brows.

She arched but one in return, both an invitation and a challenge. "You don't have to tell me all of your secrets—especially not the ones you're afraid will endanger me—but Tanis…if Björn van Gelderan works in secret to right the Balance of the realm, as my mother suspects, and if you're helping him, shouldn't I at least know that much?"

Tanis frowned deeply at this.

A rising breeze blew Nadia's dark hair into her eyes, and she turned her head slightly so the wind blew the strands away from her face instead. "There are many legends of the Genesis," she told him while casting her colorless gaze along the jagged line where the Hallovian cliffs met the charcoal sea. "But one of the more famous legends is the story of how our Maker created Alorin and the first races."

Tanis murmured into her hair, "Even I know that one."

"But do you know Cephrael's part?" Nadia gave him a look that was all crisp challenge. When Tanis merely grinned and nodded for her to continue, she regarded him imperially. "After our Maker created the zanthyrs, the Sundragons and the Wildling clans, He brought His blessed children, the *angiel*, into the realm and asked of His new creatures: 'Who would serve my children? Who would bind themselves to my blessed son and daughter, that they might have a protector to aid in anything they required?' And Tanis, do you know who answered Him?"

Tanis grinned. "I'll bet you're about to tell me."

Nadia arched a brow at him. "According to the legend, the greatest of all the zanthyrs fell to one knee before our Maker, and he said, 'I will bind myself to their fates.'" She eyed Tanis meaningfully. "Legend claims that our Maker gave this zanthyr infinite ability so he might be aided in his task of protecting the blessed *angiel*."

She lifted a hand to free a lock of hair from her face, yet the dark strands blowing across her fair skin gave her an alluring quality that Tanis found quite mesmerizing in that moment. He wished she'd have let her hair linger longer across her eyes...her lips...

Nadia caught him staring and gave him a coquettish smile, accepting of his adoration. Tanis wondered if she took a class instructing in the proper smiles to use to woo a suitor—

"Tanis, pay attention."

He smiled. "Sorry. Please continue with your story."

She eyed him narrowly. "It's not a *story*, it's a famous legend that surely has its roots in truth."

He grinned and nodded for her to continue.

"After the zanthyr bound himself to the *angiel*, the other races followed in kind, pledging their troth to Cephrael—the *drachwyr*, the Avieths, the Tyriolicci; some say even the dark races of Shadow bound themselves to Him."

She freed her hair from her eyes again and turned her face back into the wind. "Thus Cephrael came to share in their collective awareness and knew all that they knew. With this vast understanding of the cosmos, he assumed his role as the Hand of Fate, serving all by serving the Balance." Nadia arched a brow as she finished, inviting Tanis's reply, daring him to deny the things she'd implied. Oh, she'd suggested much with the thoughts that had been spinning within her mind while she spoke—wild connections and assumptions that seemed to fit in a certain context, yet could have absolutely no basis in fact. Her gaze hinted that she thought he must surely know the truth of these matters, and the expectant arch of her brow challenged him to share what he knew.

Tanis smiled at her. "It's an interesting theory."

"Oh, you're terribly coy!" she laughed and swatted at him.

Tanis probably would've enjoyed the speculation under different circumstances, but matching Nadia's lighthearted mood that morning was proving a challenge. The closer they came to their agreed-upon time of departure, the more the world seemed askew; he felt like he was walking sideways across a steep hill, leaning into its incline to keep from sliding off.

With this distempered sensation unbalancing him, Tanis tossed the blowing hair from his eyes and gazed off out to sea. The morning wind held the tang of salt, tears of the distant waves. Somewhere another storm was building. He didn't think it was in Hallovia.

A tugging as if on the fabric of the realm alerted Tanis that Pelas was approaching. Suddenly every muscle in his body seized up, as if bracing for impact.

He clenched his jaw and looked to Nadia. "It's time." He turned to face the house just as Pelas reached the open terrace doors.

The Malorin'athgul paused in the doorway. "Ah, the princess and her prince." Pelas's copper eyes were bright, lit by the promise of adventure. "I bid good morning to you both. Are we ready to travel?"

No. Tanis thought as Nadia bobbed a curtsy and said brightly, "Yes, Signore di Nostri."

Pelas caught Tanis's thought and cast a look at him, both bemused and curious. "This was *your* idea, Tanis."

"That doesn't make it a good idea." Tanis was suddenly very sure they should not go anywhere just then; yet when he thought to say as much, he felt as if that entire hillside was pushing down against his chest, preventing him from finding the breath to say anything at all.

"Oh, but I'm excited." Nadia moved to Pelas and greeted him with a kiss on both cheeks. "When we came through Shadow before, I was hardly aware of it. I want to see it this time."

Pelas gave her a humorous look. "I fear there isn't much to see, Princess."

"But there's the experience of it, isn't there?"

He bowed his head to this sentiment. "There is definitely that." He extended his elbow graciously to her.

Nadia slipped her arm through his and then cast a look over her shoulder. "Tanis, are you coming?" Then she frowned at him. "By the Lady, why are you so tense? I told you not to worry."

"Yes, why *are* you so tense?" Pelas looked him over speculatively.

Tanis held his bond-brother's gaze with his hand still holding the railing. *Do you perceive nothing?*

Only your unease.

Tanis pushed a hand through his hair and lodged it there as his mind roamed the paths of perception. Pelas's side of the bond carried only its usual swarming sense of the vast elemental cosmos, while his own had become a wall of force veritably pushing against him, urging him to take that next step.

Tanis scrubbed at the back of his head and then threw his arm down to his side. He started forward to join them. "Let's do this then."

Nadia gazed wonderingly at him. "Light of the Lady, Tanis, you make it sound like we're going into battle. My mother and the High Lord cannot seem that formidable to you."

What do you perceive, Tanis? Pelas placed a hand on his shoulder as the lad reached his side.

Tanis met his gaze. *I cannot say...something.*

Pelas's copper eyes searched his. *If you would have us stay, speak the word.*

Tanis worked the muscles of his jaw.

Last chance, little spy...

Tanis felt such a force pushing against him that he barely ground out the thought, *We have to do this.*

Well and so.

The lad felt a rushing sensation, and a silver-violet line split down through the air.

Nadia inhaled a gasp. "So easy?" She spun a look at Pelas and then leaned to better view Tanis, who was standing on Pelas's left. "But surely—Tanis, don't you think this is how Malin vanished from the Archives?" Nadia looked back to the widening portal and shook her head. "Poor Malin. We still don't know what became of him."

Tanis didn't need reminding of how he'd made such a mess of things. He'd underestimated Shail at every turn. He adjusted his satchel diagonally across his chest and looked to Pelas.

Thus with a hand on Tanis's shoulder and Nadia on his arm, Pelas took them into Shadow. The portal winked shut behind them.

"Why...it's so...*dark.*" Nadia's voice seemed swallowed by the endless void. Tanis felt a sudden nervousness flood into her mind and wished he'd been holding her hand.

"Can you feel it, Tanis?" Pelas asked into the darkness. His words were similarly swallowed.

"Feel what?"

Pelas squeezed his shoulder. "The absence of time."

Tanis was opening himself to Pelas's perception when he felt something shift—

Wrong—no, this is wrong!

Light exploded in his brain.

Pelas hissed and pulled Tanis close against him, but the lad still felt like they were whirling head over heels. There was nothing by which to gauge up or down, neither wind nor gravity to prove they were in motion, yet he knew they were tumbling. He could sense Pelas trying to anchor them again, though he couldn't grasp how he was attempting it.

Then came a jolt, more mental than physical, a light that wasn't light but rather a sudden perception of depth, and Pelas's growl—

A force ripped between them, tearing Tanis from Pelas's hold. He went flying again. Nadia screamed.

Tanis!

The lad felt Pelas mentally reaching for him—

An arm closed around his chest—not Pelas's.

The tumbling ceased. That feeling of unbalance slammed into its proper horizon.

And a voice that had haunted Tanis's dreams many nights since they'd parted murmured close at his ear, "Shadow has no form save what our thoughts impose upon it."

The Warlock's arm tightened around Tanis's body, pulling him against a powerful frame. "And I am more adept at molding it than your White Knight of the Void."

Tanis!

That time Pelas's mental call felt far away. Sinárr had imposed some kind of barrier—Tanis could sense it now like a veil between himself and Pelas. He knew there was no chance of reconnecting with Pelas, even as he knew he would have to go with Sinárr—that this was, in fact, where his path had been leading him.

Whirling together through the dark, Sinárr ran his nose along Tanis's neck, inhaling deeply. Then he exhaled a delighted sigh, and Tanis felt another shift. The sensation reminded him of passing through that curtain of *deyjiin* at Shail's temple.

Then he knew only silence, the feel of Sinárr's arm holding him close, and an endless sensation of tumbling.

❖

Pelas realized what was happening an instant too late.

He flung out his awareness to anchor them and reestablish his own frame of space, but the energy of the two colliding universes was in such turmoil that it wouldn't comply with his intent. He felt Sinárr's bubble of space piercing inexorably through his, sensed the Warlock's established frame of space overtaking—indeed, *consuming*—his own.

Then the two merged. Pelas growled an oath—

A blast of force ripped Tanis out of his arms. He only kept hold of a screaming Nadia because their elbows were linked.

Tanis! Pelas threw out a line of energy to bind the lad to his own space, but Tanis had already been yanked into Sinárr's universe.

Just as Pelas managed to hold his anchors in place and establish a frame of space within which to orient himself, he felt another mind descending—pouncing, *pouring* in—and Shail imposed his own consciousness into the space Pelas had framed.

Pelas mentally struggled to hold his anchors and push Shail out of his space, but his attention had become scattered, and he couldn't summon the necessary force to oust his brother.

An icebound world not of his creation appeared—instantly, as a breath of vapor upon a glass pane. Pelas stood with Nadia on a vast glacial plane, breathing air of crystallized ice that felt sharp in his lungs. High mountains loomed all around, mostly obscured by fog.

Nadia clung to his arm, dazed and frightened. "Lady's light, what's happening?" she whispered.

He drew her closer while he looked out over the bleak landscape. His gaze tightened. "Trouble."

"Where's—" Nadia turned a look around, and her eyes widened while her voice grew fainter. "Immanuel…where is Tanis?"

"With the Warlock." Pelas would've preferred that his tone hadn't sounded so grim.

Nadia caught her breath. "Sinárr took Tanis?"

"I'm afraid so, Princess."

Tanis notwithstanding, they had bigger problems at the moment. Dark shapes were appearing out of the fog. One in particular captured Pelas's attention.

Shail solidified into view carrying his Merdanti blade with the point held low. He wore fighting leathers instead of his usual silk robes, but he hadn't changed his condescending smile. "If you weren't so predictable, Pelas, the process of schooling you would be much more rewarding."

Pelas eyed his younger brother while working the muscles of his jaw. He should've anticipated that Sinárr and Shail would come after them. He should've expected they would use Shadow to do it. *By Chaos born*—he should've at least *tried* to understand the voice that had been whispering ill tidings in Tanis's thoughts!

"Predictability has its place," Pelas remarked while trying to think of a way of escape that wouldn't imperil Nadia. "It's difficult to fight your enemies if you can't find them."

"That's precisely my point, Pelas." Shail idly spun his blade as he continued his approach. "You claim your only endgame is stopping mine, yet what hubris to even conceive of the notion when you're so shortsighted." He stopped before them and settled his condescending gaze on Nadia. "Did you really think I would just let you go, Princess?"

Nadia tried to inch away from him. Pelas tightened his arm around her shoulders, but he knew their chances of escaping together were slim. He had no recourse to his power while Shail controlled the framework of the Shadow-space they were occupying.

Shail arched a brow in cold humor and returned his eyes to his brother. Then his gaze tightened. "What have you done for the last three hundred years, Pelas?" He emphasized this question with a swirl of his blade and began walking a circle around them.

Pelas followed him with his eyes. "Was that a rhetorical question?"

"I'll tell you what you've done." Shail speared him with a contemptuous glare. "You've squandered your time dallying with frilly-frocked natives, immortalizing their pathetic efforts with bits of colored mud."

"That's somewhat of a generalization—"

"And *Darshan*..." Shail snorted as he passed behind Pelas. "He's spent all of his time dwelling in religious fantasy, stroking off on the erection of purpose." Suddenly his voice was close at Pelas's ear, his blade sharp at his back. "But ask me what *I* have been doing."

Pelas saw too nearly his many errors in misestimating his younger brother. He replied in a low voice, "What have you been doing, Shailabanáchtran?"

"*Studying.*" Shail made the word speak with ominous implications. "*Learning.* Piecing together the fragmented truths of this realm's pitiful history into a pattern by which I may rule it—and all of the Realms of Light."

"No one can fault you for ambition." Pelas shifted his eyes to gaze tightly at the other shapes that were emerging from the fog.

There were two races of *eidola*: the ones made out of men from the Realms of Light, and the kind constructed whole-cloth from the aether of Shadow.

The *eidola* of Shadow were also of two natures: those bound to Warlocks as active harvesters of power, and the ones the Warlocks had discarded, remnant entities that had once inhabited the worlds the Warlocks had fashioned; entities that had taken on some form and shape through the centuries but hadn't enough of their own essence to sustain themselves once the Warlocks moved on to more interesting fare. Vampiric creatures, these revenants would latch onto and feed off of anything that held a spark of life within it.

The ones coming towards him now were very definitely the latter. There were at least a hundred, and they all had their black eyes fixed firmly on him.

Shail followed Pelas's gaze with his own and said low into his ear, "Word has it that revenants can feed off an immortal for ten thousand centuries before he becomes too weak to sustain them."

Pelas was really wishing he'd thought to bring his sword. "So I've been told. I can't imagine anyone volunteered to test the theory."

"It will be another first for you, brother." Shail moved around to face Pelas again, his smile blending venom with contempt. Then he shifted his gaze to Nadia, and his expression sobered. "The princess, however, will be coming with me."

Nadia caught her breath.

A silent stream of invective charged through Pelas's mind. He had no weapon that would help him against his brother, and he couldn't work *deyjiin* within the frame of Shail's space. And then there were the revenants to contend with. He'd never be able to escape them while also trying to protect Nadia.

Oh, Tanis, forgive me what I must do...

Pelas took Nadia's wrists and handed her forward.

"*No!*" She flung a desperate look at him, her colorless eyes pleading, *why?*

He pushed his mouth against her ear. "Whatever happens, I will find you."

Then Shail was pulling her into the circle of his own arm. She struggled, but so might a butterfly endeavor against a hawk.

Shail looked Nadia over, and his smile widened.

Pelas ground his teeth. "*Shail—*"

"Now, you needn't worry for the princess, Pelas. I have something special in mind for her." He licked a razor gaze over her again.

Knowing his brother's sense of humor, Pelas imagined he knew exactly what Shail planned to do with Nadia.

Shail's dark eyes were gleaming with malicious amusement as he lifted his gaze back to Pelas. "This is an intriguing predicament. Do you seek your paramour through the endless universes of Shadow, or save his lady love from her own bleak fate? And time...time is ever against you, Pelas." Shail glanced to the whitewashed sky. "Even here, where time can be molded readily to our will, you haven't an infinity of it—for Sinárr can hardly restrain himself when it comes to Tanis, and Nadia..." he shifted his gaze to look her over hungrily again, "let's just say the sands are falling in her hourglass as well."

Nadia tried to pull away from him, but he clutched her so tightly against his side in return that her face constricted with pain.

"For all that your meddling is irksome, Pelas, I do enjoy seeing you scramble as a result," Shail remarked then. "I did warn you that you'd be out of your depth."

Pelas clenched his jaw. The revenants were less than twenty paces away. He could feel their hunger radiating more coldly than the air of Shail's frozen world. "So I recall."

Shail looked his brother over one last time. "Well...I'll leave you to your *experience*."

A silver-violet line split the air. Shail barely gave the portal time to widen before he stepped in, dragging Nadia with him.

Pelas looked to the revenants.

Their black eyes were ravenous.

He had time for one clear thought. Then they swarmed him.

THIRTEEN

"A man cannot be too discriminating in the choice of his enemies."
—The Adept truthreader Thrace Weyland

VIERNAN HAL'JAITAR STOOD at a tall window in the Castle of Ivarnen, looking out over a broad and scenic estuary while Dore Madden threw a tantrum in the next room.

Like Tambarré and other of Dore's acquisitions for the Prophet, Ivarnen had been a center of learning during the reign of the Cyrene Empire, but more germane to Dore's interests, it had also been a base for the Quorum of the Sixth Truth, that coalition of fifth-strand wielders who dominated the realm in the times known as The Before.

Built atop a mountainous isle in the middle of the Enduil Estuary in Saldaria, the fortress retained the elegance of a bygone era. Somewhere deep within the lowest passages of Ivarnen, perhaps among the flooded caverns riddling the island's core, the Quorum were rumored to have held their dark rituals. Researchers of Quorum lore believed the Order's sacred archives remained intact somewhere, possibly at Ivarnen.

Whatever Dore's true motivations for acquiring the fortress, the maze of subterranean caverns beneath the restored castle fulfilled the man's insatiable appetite for private spaces in which to work his twisted experiments.

Viernan hal'Jaitar loathed Dore Madden and his Prophet lord; he loathed that M'Nador needed their aid, and most of all, he loathed how readily Dore took advantage of M'Nador's weaknesses.

Since their new accord struck in Tal'Shira, the man had increasingly imposed upon Viernan to attend his company, as though the chains that bound them in their political troth bound them also into camaraderie.

One might've witnessed these invitations and thought Dore had taken Viernan into his confidence, but Viernan knew the truth: Dore Madden had such a chokehold on him that he no longer cared what wildly vicious and despicable plans of his Viernan overheard. Viernan was the moth with its wing beneath Dore's finger, and they both knew it.

Oh, but Dore's most recent summons couldn't have come at a more inconvenient time. Viernan felt part of himself still sitting at his desk, staring at eleven words that had burned themselves into his mind, his thoughts, his core, his eyes forever etched with the script of their delivery: *invasion at Darroyhan!...prisoner rescued...the enchantress fallen...Dragon... zanthyr...mutiny...*

His agent might've written only those words and Viernan would've understood the whole of it. Verily, instinct had warned him to distance himself from Trell val Lorian while he'd still held the prince in Tal'Shira. Even so, Viernan hadn't expected to be so thoroughly right in his suppositions.

A Sundragon *and* a zanthyr had come to rescue the prince? Viernan admitted himself rather intrigued to learn how Trell had garnered the support of such immortal creatures. But immortal support at least accounted for his unaccountable luck. Countless times Viernan had personally tipped the prince into a raging surf, only to find him rescued off the shores of impossibility. Was the man *actually* blessed of a god?

Now Darroyhan was a shambles, Viernan had lost a valuable interrogator in his daughter Taliah, and he'd lost Trell—*again*. Just as needling was learning that one of his captains had stolen a boat and mutinied, along with his company. The one grace that had come from Darroyhan's fall was ridding himself of the Prophet's *eidola* spies.

Now, instead of tending to his own important affairs—like tracking down the recalcitrant val Lorian prince before he could act against M'Nador's interests—there he stood while Dore Madden carried on with Niko van Amstel about matters that had nothing to do with M'Nador and everything to do with Dore's personal vendettas and obsessions. The man really was as mad as Malachai. Yet in his fervent race towards lunacy, Dore evidently ran neck and neck with Niko.

It was painful listening to the two of them ranting on entirely different subjects—clearly not even sharing the same seditious conversation. If he was forced to listen to them much longer, Viernan feared he'd soon go mad as well.

"We have to do something about her, Dore." Niko's plaintive voice was as grating as a raven cawing outside the window. "I mean, what has she done, really? I mean, what does she *do*?"

"Do? What we must do is destroy the accursed man!" Dore spoke with the clipped and rapid diction he often employed while pacing, as if the meter of his feet must match the meter of his speech. "He's *Returned*, damn him to thirteen hells. Niko—do you hear my words?"

"Yes, but *she* doesn't *do* anything. That's my point."

"Which is precisely why *we* must." Dore growled an oath under his breath. "Never mind his persistent, pernicious destroying of the Prophet's *eidola*—in our very backyard, under our very noses!—but I tell you, he stole Işak'getirmek from me, and that cannot go unpunished. No, Niko—*Niko*, listen to me: Arion must be *punished!*" the word came out in a venomous hiss.

Despite himself, a morbid curiosity drew Viernan over to the archway separating the rooms. In the drawing room beyond, Dore was pacing before a limestone mantel, while Niko sat slumped in a low-backed Saldarian chair with his long legs splayed across the carpet.

The latter sighed petulantly. "I can't see how punishing Ean val Lorian will help depose Alshiba."

Dore eyed him sharply. He was walking with his shoulders slumped forward and his hands behind his back, looking not unlike an opossum pacing in a cage. "*Oh*, but he is deserving...yes, so deserving. You have no idea how deserving, Niko."

"Alshiba is deserving. I'll grant you that." Niko sank his chin onto one hand. Then he lifted it again and straightened. "But—did you say Arion?"

Dore slung a finger at him. "Arion Tavestra is an abomination!"

Niko scratched his head and sank dispiritedly back in his chair again. "I thought he was dead. What did you say about Arion?"

"I said he's *Returned*, you slow-witted fop."

"Arion was...well, he was the best of us, wasn't he?" Niko picked at a fraying thread on the arm of his chair. Then he frowned. "Arion could be a problem if he wasn't dead."

"He will die. He *has* to die—*and* her..." Dore's face twisted with a grimace, as if reliving an unpleasant memory.

Viernan wondered absently what might constitute a *pleasant* memory for Dore Madden, but then he realized he would really rather not know.

"*She* must die soon, but not quickly..." Dore quivered like a thin blade. "No...not quickly."

Niko hit his fist against the arm of his chair. "That's what I've been saying! We have to get rid of Alshiba."

"*And* Ean val Lorian." Dore cast Niko a fearsome glare. "But how to do it? Tyr'kharta, Tal'Afaq, here at Ivarnen...he's escaped all my traps, just like Arion...but they cannot escape me every time. Balance must eventually intervene." He rubbed his hands together slowly. "We'll cast the net wider.

The whole world will be looking for Ean val Lorian. He must pay the cost of the Prophet's Marquiin, of our lost *eidola*..." his eyes went glassy and he slowly ran his tongue along spidery lips, "my lost Işak'getirmek."

"Alshiba is a wielder. That's part of the problem." Niko shifted discontentedly in his chair. "We have to be careful how we go about eliminating her." His lower lip jutted slightly as he thought this through. "You need to handle this, Dore. I named Franco Rohre as my deputy, like you told me to do, but now she's calling *him* to attend her in Illume Belliel and making me do all the work here in Alorin. Franco Rohre isn't even a *vestal!*"

Abruptly Dore spun to him. "You cannot move against Franco until you get the map. Do you have it? Do you have Dagmar's weldmap?"

Niko glowered. "No."

Dore's black eyes shone with dark determination. "Much depends upon it. You must make Franco collect it from the Second Vestal."

Niko shot him a churlish glare. "How am I supposed to do that when he's spending all of his time in Illume Belliel with Alshiba and I'm stuck down here? Anyway, Franco doesn't trust me, and neither does Alshiba—she flat out told me I can't order Franco to do anything until I sit the Vestal Seat. I'm telling you, Dore, something has to be done about her!"

"Did you give her the items I gave to you? *Did* you?"

"*Yes*," Niko grumbled.

"Then you must wait. That is all." Dore resumed his pacing.

Niko gave a dramatic exhale and plucked petulantly at his chair arm again. "To see how little Alshiba has accomplished in three centuries, one would think the vestals were as indolent as the nobility. But it's so much *work*."

"We have our work cut out for us, yes, but Ean val Lorian cannot escape us forever. Mark my words, Niko."

"But how has her incompetence escaped everyone's notice for so long? Just tell me that." Niko pushed abruptly out of his chair. "The realm is dying, our Adepts aren't Returning, the Fifth and Second Vestals have been missing for centuries—*centuries*, Dore! And now Raine D'Lacourte has gone missing as well?" He flung up a hand. "You'd think someone would've at least *remarked* upon it. Questioned her qualifications to hold the Seat... *something*."

Dore spun on his heel and started pacing in the other direction. "A new trap. That's what we need. Oh, but it must be sophisticated. Yes, very elaborate, this trap for the magnificent Arion Tavestra."

Niko turned him a confused look. "I thought you were hunting Ean val Lorian."

Dore waved him off. "No matter, no matter, we will have them both."

Niko arched brows. "Impressive."

"Yes, the realm will be on fire for our val Lorian prince, and then...yes, then we'll draw him to us like a fish on a line."

"That's what we need, Dore. You've hit it. We've got to find some way to draw Dagmar to us—never mind Franco. We don't need Franco if we can get our hands on Dagmar and deal with Alshiba at the same time."

"Oh, we'll deal...we'll deal such a hand that our Arion can't help but play in our game. Pinch points—" he snapped his fingers, "that's what we'll use. We'll find the prince's pinch points and *squeeze* them until the little pustule pops. And when we finally have him oozing in our hands..." Dore's spidery lips spread with the rictus that passed for his smile, "*then* we shall break him like we broke his brother. Oh—oh, *my* yes! Just think of it, Niko. The great Arion Tavestra strapped on my table, soon to become my newest puppet..." His gaze darkened with something so abominable that Viernan had to turn away.

"Viernan, what say you?" Niko looked to Viernan as he was trying to purge Dore Madden's expression from his mind. "Is not the time to replace all of our vestals long overdue?"

Viernan shifted a black gaze to Niko. It was a grave indignity being forced to attend Niko van Amstel and Dore Madden for a legitimate reason, much less to stand and observe this lunacy. "I do not see the need for vestals at all."

Niko drew back his head like a startled tortoise. "Now...now let's not be hasty, Viernan. *I'm* to be a vestal, after all, and the Seat soon thereafter—you'll see. It's all arranged. When I'm in power, things will change. When I have *all* the power....well, you'll see, Viernan." Niko gave him one of his insincere smiles. "Great changes will follow."

"Great changes for whom?"

Niko blinked at him. Then, perhaps because Viernan looked so doubtful, Niko came over and tried to drape an arm around his shoulders. "Viernan, really, I—"

Viernan sidestepped him with a black stare of affront.

Niko looked startled. After a moment, his eyebrows sank into a sullen glower. "You haven't come to any of my dinners."

Viernan regarded him in disbelief for a moment and then turned his gaze to Dore. "How much longer must I wait, Dore Madden? The rest of the world does not revolve around your obsessive quests for vengeance."

Dore turned him a corrosive stare. "The Prophet shows your prince the *eidola* we're making for M'Nador—proof of our fidelity to our mutual troth. I cannot say how long they will share each other's wisdom."

As long as it takes your Prophet to feed on what's left of my monarch's free will, Viernan thought, his eyes very dark.

"You know the kind of people who don't come to my fêtes, Viernan?"

Viernan turned Niko a daggered look of disdain. "People with lives to lead?"

Niko drew himself tall. "People whom I suspect have been Called by the Fifth Vestal."

Or visited by a Whisper Lord, which would seem to me quite preferable to attending one of your fêtes.

Had anyone else insinuated that he served Björn van Gelderan, Viernan would've taken it as a personal affront, but Niko van Amstel was too obtuse to notice that he'd offended anyone, so Viernan replied instead, "The Fifth Vestal remains a threat to all of us."

"I know! It's really a problem." Niko swept a hand across his perfectly coiffed blonde hair and gave Viernan a concerned look fraught with superficiality. "This idea of oaths, for example…it's *so* absurd. I mean, there were dozens of us in the catacombs, and the Fifth Vestal might've given each one of us a different task, or none at all, and none of us be the wiser as to what the others have been set to do, or not to do, and then…*then*—" he waved his hand in the air, "being made to work the Pattern of Life, being denied the right to choose to live on or die a natural death—not that I wouldn't have chosen to work it, mind you, Viernan. Any Adept who hopes to gain his rings must work the Pattern—but it seems unjust for the Vestal to deny us the right to end our lives as we ourselves choose. It's like he wanted to punish us by making us live through the years after the wars and see what became of our acts."

Of course he did, you idiot. Viernan ground his teeth. Niko was upon the topic now like a dog to a bone. Huhktu knew the man would gnaw at it until he'd reduced all of its logic to irreconcilable bits.

"And then…this whole Calling issue all these centuries later, as if we're to even *remember* what he demanded of us…" Niko shook his head and gazed doubtfully at Viernan. "What I mean to say, Viernan, is who does that? How could anyone possibly police that many oaths?"

Staring blankly at Niko, Viernan wondered if Cephrael had somehow already judged, condemned and sentenced him to Ivarnen, for surely this was some new level of hell.

"And then to just come Calling after three hundred years to see if you've done as he bade you…or not, I suppose." Niko pushed hands into his pockets and toed at the clawed foot of a couch. "Or, what if you did what he told you to but you made a mistake? Mistakes happen, Viernan. In such a case, would you still be ripped to shreds?" He turned Viernan an earnest look, as if truly desiring his counsel. "You do see what I mean, don't you? There's just no sense to it."

Viernan gazed at him in mute disbelief.

"But of course you must understand. You…" Niko paused, frowned. "Well…but, *you* haven't been Called have you, Viernan? No, you wouldn't say if you had been. Who would?" He toed at the sofa's clawed foot again, hands shoved deeply into his pockets. "I mean, *I* might even have been Called. There's no way to know, really. The only way to tell is by our allegiances."

"To truly know a man, examine his enemies."

The resonant voice coming from the doorway drew Viernan's gaze, whereupon he saw the Prophet standing there with a piercing stare, as usual, fixed unerringly upon himself. Truly, the man was like a buzzard waiting resolutely for its prey to expire. Viernan was determined not to become that prey.

Prince Radov stood at the Prophet's side holding an empty glass. He looked a little unsteady on his feet, but whenever did he not, these days? He staggered over to Viernan. "Bethamin has shown me some miraculous things today, Viernan. Really, you should take the tour the next time we come."

"I shall count the hours, my prince."

Radov slapped a hand on Viernan's shoulder and leaned heavily into him, breathing the rancid stench of drink into his face. "Bethamin and I have agreed that his *eidola* will rendezvous with our forces near the outpost of Ramala."

Dore came over with his black eyes shining with a dreadful inhumanity. "To dispose of the *drachwyr*, our contact says you'll need to rally M'Nador's entire army there."

"Impossible!" Viernan clucked. "If we withdraw our forces from the southern lines, we'll lose Abu'Dhan."

"You must have all of Radov's forces there at the right moment to draw the Sundragons forth in force." Dore rubbed his hands together. "It's Abu'Dhan or Raku, Viernan. Your choice."

Viernan spied him viperously. *What if I choose to see you boiling in flame?*

"Our contact advises a fortnight—surely no more than two—and then M'Nador must be ready to attack. The battle must commence while the Emir's Mage is gone. My contact says this is the only window when the Sundragons may be effectively eliminated."

Viernan scowled. Had it just been the army of thousands he had to muster and rout, he wouldn't have fretted; but Inanna knew his prince wouldn't agree to be carried to the battlefield in a litter, and it took more than a fortnight's effort to sober up the Ruling Prince of M'Nador enough to sit his horse—assuming Viernan could pry his prince away from that whore, Absinthe, at all.

Radov swayed precariously. "If Dore says we have to withdraw our forces from Abu'Dhan, then do it, Viernan."

Viernan turned him a forceful stare. Was *Dore Madden* running their war now? "My prince," he managed a knifing smile, "the forces in the south are needed to hold the lines." In actuality, the forces in Abu'Dhan were needed to hold a thousand Dannish troops, who were far more significant to Viernan's aims than lines of boundary drawn on a map.

Radov waved airily with his glass. "Let the Saldarians hold the lines."

Viernan gnashed aggravation between his teeth. "The Saldarians will not hold the lines, my prince. They'll start their own little kingdom, making everything either subject or prey." He trusted Saldarians about as much as he trusted zanthyrs and gypsies—which was to say not at all. He was fairly certain the blackguards were all in Dore's pocket anyhow.

Radov belched again. "What do we care about Abu'Dhan? There's nothing but dirt and rabble down there anyway."

Viernan gave a rather sickly smile. "As my prince wishes." He would have to take steps of his own, send one of his Shamshir'im wielders to oversee Khor Taran, for he *assuredly* wasn't leaving the Dannish soldiers in the care of Saldarian mercenaries.

"My prince, you've seen the weapons the Prophet has promised us? You're satisfied?"

"Quite, quite. But now I'm tired." Radov's face swerved perilously close to Viernan's. "I would rest now. Let's go."

Viernan made an obsequious bow. "Your will, my prince," and he gladly turned his back on the madhouse called Ivarnen to take his liege home.

FOURTEEN

"How a man wields his power over others is the truest test of his character."

–The High Lord Marius di L'Arlesé of Agasan

FRANCO STARED AT the impossible while his mind struggled to accept what lay plainly before his eyes. "Is that what I think it is?"

The illusion of a massive globe was hovering in the center of the pavilion tent.

Franco shoved a hand into his hair and lodged it there, stuck on his incredulity. "By *Cephrael's Great Book*..." He spun a look to Devangshu, immediately ruled him out as the perpetrator, and looked around for the pirate.

Not surprisingly, Carian was grinning with proud culpability.

"*Carian,*" Franco grabbed his arm, "how in Tiern'aval did you come by a weldmap?"

The pirate extracted himself from Franco's hold. "Told you I was more than just an improbable combination of irresistibly handsome flesh, Admiral." He clapped Franco on the shoulder, gave him a wink and a grin, and motioned him further on into the pavilion.

Inside, a score of men were working feverishly upon...well, Franco wasn't sure exactly what they were doing. Some were studying the weldmap's glowing globe and making notes, while others were collaborating over various other maps and canvases hung around the tent. They all seemed quite industrious. He recognized many faces.

Carian held out a hand as he strode forward. "Behold, Admiral! The core of our rebellion."

Franco nearly missed a step. He spun Carian a swift stare. *This is the rebellion Niko was complaining about? The one Alshiba tasked him to take in hand?*

"It begins here," Devangshu said more sedately from Franco's right. "We're cataloguing which nodes Niko and the Guild control and determining the most strategic points to disrupt their network. Others are preparing lists of node owners who can be persuaded or bribed to let us use their nodes for travel. Nodefinders who don't fit Niko's profile can travel freely on *our* nodes. We aim to control more nodes than they do so as to assume a position as great or greater than the Guild's."

Carian clapped a hand on Franco's shoulder again. "Think of it as assembling your armada, Admiral."

Franco gave him a pained look. He wasn't sure what to think about their ideas of rebellion, wasn't sure how to tell Alshiba the truth of it. And then there was that weldmap…

He could hardly concentrate for the way it consumed his view. Seeing such miracles in T'khendar hadn't surprised him, but to see them *here*…

He paused just short of the hovering globe, which towered over him at three times his height. Up close, the silver lines that formed the planet's magnetic grid were infinitely complex, branching and crisscrossing in a dizzying display. Seeing it gave him an odd pain in his chest.

Franco walked beneath the glowing illusion towards a plinth supporting the weldmap itself. To the layman's eye, the canvas appeared as a jumbled mess of black ink and crisscrossing lines. A flow of *elae* into the map itself would wake the design to a Nodefinder's view, raising the sphere illusion on a scale similar to what he'd seen at the First Lord's table in T'khendar.

But Carian's map lay upon a thin piece of black marble with milky crystal obelisks attached at each corner, the entire contraption carved with patterns. The black marble base and its attached crystals was a fourth-strand talisman, a generator that woke the weldmap and projected its image in a broad illusion for all to see.

Franco looked back to Carian with wide eyes. "Where in Tiern'aval did you find a grid generator?"

The pirate was rolling himself a smoke. He glanced up beneath his brows. "D'varre wasn't using it, so we took it off his hands."

Franco's face went slack. "You *stole* it from Rethynnea's Guild Hall? Thirteen hells, Carian—when?"

Carian lit his smoke on a lamp and puffed a bluish cloud into the air. "The night of Niko's fête."

You know, Franco's conscience sneered, *that night he vanished with Devangshu to do something productive while you were alternately hiding from* the Alorin Seat and letting Demetrio Consuevé poke you with the sharp end of his temper.

"It's the Thief's Code, Admiral." The red-haired Nodefinder-thief Kardashian interrupted the snide chiding of Franco's conscience as he came strolling up. "The ally of my enemy is fair game for the reaping. We relieved D'varre of a few things he wasn't using." He flashed a grin beneath bead-dark eyes and then touched a hand to one of the node points. The grid zoomed in on the node, revealing hundreds of new ley lines that connected that node with others nearby. He began studying them.

'...*now Rethynnea's Guild is blaming me for all manner of things—as if I'm somehow responsible for their being robbed...*'

Niko's words took on all new context; pieces were starting to find their place in the puzzle, and Franco wasn't at all sure he liked the picture they were forming.

In Kardashian's wake came the truthreader Gannon Bair—tall, burly, heavily bearded, wearing a badge of resolve with the same constancy that he wore the kilt of his clan. Franco admitted he was reeling a bit just from seeing so many familiar faces...from realizing they were all serving the First Lord.

"Franco." Gannon nodded sedately to him.

"Gannon." Franco wondered how many other faces from the past were going to suddenly appear like ghosts summoned by his conscience to haunt him.

"Ah look," Devangshu motioned to gain Gannon's attention, "there is the royal cousin." He nodded towards a man sitting in an armchair at the far end of the tent.

Gannon grunted. "Excellent." He tucked his chin towards his chest and headed that way, looking very much the charging grizzly.

Franco hadn't seen Fynnlar val Lorian since the night of Prince Ean's banquet in Calgaryn—*thirteen hells,* it already felt like a lifetime ago. But what in Epiphany's name was Fynnlar doing at the First Lord's *sa'reyth*?

Gannon drew up before the royal cousin, a rearing bear observing an offensive badger. "Fynnlar, what, pray, are you doing here?"

At the moment, Fynn was sitting sprawled in an armchair with a goblet in one hand. He looked up at Gannon's address. "Oh, hello, Grumpiest Kilt-wearing Hallovian Horseperson. And how are you on this rainy afternoon?"

"Interested in why I'm finding you here, Fynnlar."

"Can't you see that I'm directing traffic?" Fynn waved his goblet at the Adepts moving hither and yon. "Do you have any idea how important my role is? How many collisions have been avoided?"

"How many?"

"Well..." Fynn frowned at him, "none so far. But that's only because these Nodefinders of yours walk in unnaturally straight lines."

"I'm sure that has nothing to do with the fact that they're all *sober*," said an entering Alyneri d'Giverny, who looked a little damp from the rain and was carrying an equally rain-spattered tray packed with silver-domed platters.

Fynn lifted a finger off his goblet to point at the Healer. "You know, I really think you could be onto something there, Your Grace. I've always found sobriety to be overrated myself, but you make a strong case for its having at least one redeeming virtue." He pressed a fist to his chest to ease a belch along. "Providing, of course, that one cares to walk in straight lines, which as virtues go, *is* rather frivolous."

Alyneri paused beside their group and nodded to Franco. "It's nice to see you again, Mr. Rohre."

Franco nodded in polite, if bewildered, reply. "Your Grace."

She gave them all a soft smile and held up her tray. "Food for the troops." She headed off again.

Franco watched her go bemusedly. She hardly seemed the same young woman he'd met in Calgaryn. Then again, he had no clue why these presences from Calgaryn were presenting themselves at the First Lord's *sa'reyth* at all. Between the improbable weldmap dominating the pavilion and the many unexpected presences, the entire night was starting to feel rather surreal.

"And *you*..." Fynn's comment drew Franco's gaze blinking back to him. "*You* caused quite the ruckus in Cair Rethynnea, I'll have you know. Thanks to that damnable zanthyr, I'm unable to talk about it without losing my dinner, or I'd have words for *you*, sir. Never mind that I haven't seen my cousin since you dragged him off to that outlaw realm nobody's supposed to be able to bloody travel to."

Franco stifled a wince. "I assure you, Fynnlar, that night in Rethynnea isn't one of my fondest memories."

"Fynnlar," Gannon called the royal cousin's gaze back to him, "why are you *here* instead of in Veneisea gaining Cassius of Rogue's allegiance for our cause?"

Fynn leaned his head back against his chair and groaned dramatically. "Is it Tuesday again already?"

"*Fynnlar.*"

"All right, all right!" He glared indignantly at Gannon. "I already told you, Cassius has stipulations before he'll meet with me. I'm working on them."

"Yes, I can see you're diligently upon the task."

"Well, admittedly, I would be able to accomplish more if I was available on days other than Tuesdays, but my regular duties are quite formidable."

Franco looked the royal cousin over. "What duties might those be, my lord?"

Fynn puffed up proudly. "I am the sole wine taster for He Who Wanders Around Startling People."

Franco turned a mystified look to Carian, who mouthed in reply, *Balaji*.

Fynn sipped at his wine, swished the liquid around in his mouth, swallowed, and made smacking noises. "Balaji says I have a discerning palate."

Alyneri commented as she passed back by, carrying a different tray, "You're very good at discerning ways to keep from doing anything useful."

"Now, you know perfectly well the necessary role I play in society, Your Grace," Fynn called after her. He lifted an imploring look to Franco. "Surely you understand, Rohre. If all of the inebriates of the realm became upstanding citizens, think of the anarchy it would cause. Our economic stability is predicated on an indolent nobility. Why…entire ecosystems could collapse!"

Fynn grew impassioned and plugged his own finger into his chest. "We inebriates are a delicate breed, and growing rarer by the day! What, with industrious people like Her Grace going around, making mass conversions to the religion of productivity and forcing people into hard work on days other than Tuesdays—"

"Gannon," a bluish haze wreathed Carian's head in the damp air, "haven't you yet resigned yourself to the incorrigibility of Fynn's disposition?"

"You're one to talk, vran Lea." Fynn gave him a sour look. "Besides, my father always told me to embrace my faults, that they could become my strengths. I'm only seeking to apply dear daddy's immense wisdom towards the bettering of my life."

"I doubt Prince Ryan had this particular fault in mind," Gannon grumbled.

Fynn cast him a black stare. "I assure you, my father knew well of my faults." He stared sootily into his wine. "He found time in his busy schedule to remind me of all of them, each and every day."

"Gannon…" Another face emerged from the haze of Franco's unwelcome past as the Whisper Lord Ledio Jerouen stuck his ebony-skinned head into the tent from a near opening. "The brethren are assembling."

"Ah, good." Gannon turned his implacable, colorless gaze on Franco. "Come, Your Excellency. Our strand brothers await your address." His tone dripped with equal parts irony and implication. Franco misliked the measures of both.

As the group was heading off—the whole crew not so subtly encircling Franco, so he wasn't given much choice about going with them—a tall shadow leaning against a tent pole snared Franco's attention. Upon first glance, he mistook the raven-haired man dressed all in black to be the First Lord's zanthyr, but he quickly saw better of his mistake.

The man was of the same immortal race, but this zanthyr stood with muscled arms crossed and a smug sort of smirk on his face, as if thumbing his nose at Mother Nature and everyone else for the fact of his form coming so much closer to perfection than theirs. Something in his manner raised Franco's hackles immediately.

Gannon noted the line of Franco's gaze and grunted. "The zanthyr Leyd. He intentionally radiates dishonesty to conceal his vicious under-layer."

Franco looked back to Gannon. "Why is he here?"

"A very good question."

Taking note of their attention, Leyd pushed off the pole and met them at the tent opening; yet to Franco, the *meeting* more held the quality of a clutch of thieves suddenly descending to block their path.

"Evening, gentles." Leyd shoved thumbs in his sword belt and abraded them with a sharp grin.

"Leyd," Gannon remarked by way of a less than amiable hello. Of any of them, he claimed the best position to challenge the zanthyr; they were at least of similar builds. "What are you doing here?"

"Oh, just helping Vaile's little pussycat bring some 'food for the troops.'" Leyd looked Gannon over, still with that patronizing smile. Then he flicked his gaze across the rest of them. "Where's the party?"

"At the far end of my patience." Gannon's gaze was firm. "State your business or stand aside, Leyd."

Leyd chuckled. "Always so bristly, Papa Bear. You think you're a match for me?"

Gannon's eyes tightened. "I think you're unwelcome here."

Leyd rocked idly on his heels, thumbs jammed in his sword belt, and cast his gaze around the pavilion. "The *sa'reyths* are open to all outcasts, whether or not they're one of your preferred flavors, truthreader."

"This isn't a *sa'reyth*," Devangshu dared comment.

Leyd cast him a dismissive sneer. "It's a stone's toss close enough that one could be mistaken for the other."

What was it Franco sensed in this statement? Something hinted? Something implied? It was hard to discern the truth beneath Leyd's insincere smile. "And yet they are not the same," Franco pinned his gaze on the zanthyr, "just as any two zanthyrs might be mistaken for one another, yet maintain widely disparate loyalties."

Leyd's green eyes shifted to Franco and took his measure in a glance. His smile remained condescending, but Franco felt sure the zanthyr had taken the meaning of his comment, as surely as Leyd had meant something by his.

He rocked on his heels again. "You'd be Franco Rohre, then." Leyd's eyes flicked to the glowing sphere dominating the room. "Is that your weldmap?"

Devangshu's expression darkened. "No matter whose map it is, it's no business of yours—"

The zanthyr speared him with a stare so sudden, his entire form instantly radiating such ferocity, that the hairs on the back of Franco's neck stood straight up in alarm.

"My *business*," Leyd growled, descending on Devangshu, "is whatever I decide it is."

"Well, that's all done!" Alyneri came striding up, brushing her hands against her skirts. "Good evening to you all, gentlemen." She nodded to the men and patted the zanthyr on the arm as she passed. "Time to go, Leyd. Vaile's waiting."

Leyd cast an oily smile across the lot of them, making Franco feel dirty simply by observing it. Then he nodded to Gannon amusedly, remarked, "Another day, Papa Bear," and followed Alyneri out of the tent.

Carian exhaled a cloud of smoke. "What by Tethys' tits was that about?"

The entire experience had left Franco feeling unnerved. He looked to Carian. "Nothing good."

Gannon grunted. "Malice clings like mold to that creature's core." He glanced over the rest of them. "Let's be off. We'll be late now as it is."

One turn of the hourglass later, Franco stood in a back alley in Dheanainn frowning at an iron-bound door while Devangshu tried again to properly activate the trace seal binding it.

"By the Dísir," Gannon growled, "why'd you make it so bloody complicated?"

Devangshu paused his hand mid-script to turn a hard look at the truthreader. "The waves of your irritation are disrupting the pattern—never mind my concentration."

Gannon grumblingly took a few steps back and spread his arms to encourage the others to do the same. "Give him some room, gents."

Leaning a shoulder against the wall across the alley, Carian elbowed Franco in the ribs. "Ready, Admiral?"

Franco glared at him. "For what am I meant to be ready?" Aggravation would've threaded his tone even if the pirate's bony elbow hadn't caught him so near to where Demetrio Consuevé's sword had left its mark.

Franco's attempts to get any of them to explain what they were doing in the seediest part of Dheanainn at the greediest hour of the night had only resulted in an exchange of knowing glances and private smirks.

Carian clapped a companionable hand on Franco's shoulder. "It's time to pay the piper, Admiral."

"What's that supposed to mean?"

The Whisper Lord Ledio Jerouen came striding around a corner from behind them. "All are assembled." He nodded to Devangshu. "You can tell him now."

Franco clenched his jaw. "Tell me *what*?"

"We've just called a few of the brethren who'd like to hear your perspective on this Niko fiasco, Franco," Devangshu replied soothingly, as if anything short of making a swift about-face back to the *sa'reyth* was likely to assuage Franco's edginess.

Ledio meanwhile extended his hand to Franco and nodded a welcome.

Franco clasped wrists with him, but he couldn't stop himself from frowning as he met Ledio's gaze. It had been years since he'd crossed paths with the Whisper Lord, decades since they'd had any conversation. He couldn't help recalling Ledio from their earlier days—misguided years, when all of them had been blighted by an inadequacy of conscience. Now Franco suffered an overabundance of it.

"It's been a long time, Ledio."

Ledio's lips twitched with a smile. "I can tell by your hesitation that you remember our last conversation."

"You made it hard to forget."

Ledio held Franco's hand as firmly as he held his gaze. "Do you ever wonder where we'd be if that fight had ended differently?"

Franco exhaled a slow breath. "Often."

Ledio grinned and released his hand. "I do as well."

Franco frowned at the Whisper Lord. "I can't help wondering why you're involving yourself with all of this. It isn't really your fight."

Ledio's eyes were deeply hooded, but Franco saw strength in his golden gaze, and a certain resolve that all of them bore…that is, those of the Companions who had accepted their Callings. "When once I might've acted, I cowered, Franco, but never again."

Franco considered him with a furrowed brow. He didn't know what Ledio's Calling had been, but he did know that every one of the Fifty Companions who had refused the First Lord's summons had succumbed to a Whisper Lord's daggered gloves.

Franco cast a pained look at the door where Devangshu was still laboring to work the trace-seal, dreading the moment he finally succeeded. He had no idea why any Nodefinders would've come to listen to him, no idea what he was supposed to say to them. He turned to Carian. "What are the strand brothers expecting to hear from me?"

"Just the usual reassurances, Admiral." The pirate settled Franco a particularly untrustworthy smirk.

"Ah ha!" Devangshu turned a triumphant look to Gannon and pressed the latch. The heavy door swung inward to darkness.

Gannon led the group into a large, shadowed space. Far ahead, a vertical strip of light demarked a parting of drapes, likewise indicated by the general chatter of muffled voices floating to them from an adjoining hall.

Devangshu stopped before the drapes and pulled a voluminous tome out of nowhere—or rather, very likely from his *stanza segreta*, known colloquially as a coach, a portable leis that any Nodefinder worth his salt set up the moment he mastered the skills to do so. Then he shoved through the parting, and the murmuring from beyond quieted.

Carian grinned and nudged Franco. "After you, Admiral."

Scratching his head bemusedly, Franco followed Devangshu through the curtains—

—and onto the stage of a dimly lit theater. A *large* theater. And a sea of faces staring at him.

Franco felt a fluttery apprehension blossom inside. He'd been expecting a score of Nodefinders; instead he was gazing upon hundreds. Some nearer faces he even recognized as ringed Espials like himself, men who could travel freely beneath Niko's restrictions.

Carian and the others filed in behind Franco as Devangshu was saying to the assembly, "…friends, *this* is our salvation." He held up the massive book with both hands for everyone to see.

Franco's eyes widened. He hissed to Carian, "Tell me that's not what I think it is!"

"The Vestal Codex," Carian smirked, at the same time that Devangshu announced it to the audience and received roaring applause.

'…*Someone stole the Vestal Codex from the Espial's Guild in Rethynnea—probably members of this purported rebellion…*'

Franco exhaled a dramatic sigh of disapproval. "Don't tell me, you stole the Vestals' sacred manifesto from Rethynnea's Guild?"

Carian shrugged unrepentantly. "D'varre wasn't using it."

Devangshu meanwhile had opened the book to a page he had marked and was saying to the assembly, "…*Codex* states that the Council of Realms has to ratify Niko van Amstel's appointment to make it official, but—" and he looked up under his brows at the audience, "they can only legally do that if they either have proof that the Great Master is dead, impeached, or has personally abdicated."

"Vestal appointments are for life," Gannon murmured, as if that wasn't readily apparent.

Devangshu closed the massive book and cradled it close to his chest. "Now, we have proof that the Second Vestal *lives*."

Another roar of cheering applause erupted.

"Bloody right he does!" Carian hitched up his britches indignantly.

Franco turned him a severe look. What was the man *doing*? And what sort of proof was Devangshu talking about? He turned back to him feeling unbalanced.

The Bemothi held up a hand for silence, and slowly the crowd settled. "Now, I'm pleased to be able to tell you, brothers, that two among the rebellion's leadership," and he extended his hand towards Franco and Carian, "have been to T'khendar. They've seen and spoken to the Great Master personally! They could attest to this under a Telling."

While the audience murmured with surprise, Franco swung a glare at Carian and hissed, "You *told* them this?"

"And why shouldn't I?" The pirate jutted out his chin unrepentantly. "We ain't truthbound on it." Franco was inhaling to snap a reply about prudence and common sense, but Carian cut him off with a hand gripped around his arm and a low caution, "Think about it, Admiral: of all the thousand things the First Lord has bound us to silence about—and he's been thorough, Raine's bloody truth—there're just as many things he *hasn't* bound us on."

Franco stared at him.

"If the First Lord didn't want us spreading these truths around, he'd have bound us. You have to see the logic in that."

The awful fact of it was, Franco did. He only wondered why he hadn't made that connection himself.

"We've lived with some secrets too long," Gannon remarked from Carian's other side. Doubtless Franco had been thinking the thought so loudly that the truthreader had plucked it easily from the aether.

Devangshu meanwhile said to the crowd, "What I wouldn't give to visit that place of unmaking. To look through the dark volcanic glass, as Carian vran Lea has described to us, and see with my own eyes the creature who haunts the fringes of our realm, seeking any way back inside..." He lifted a telling gaze across the sea of faces, quiet now beneath the image his words had invoked. "What I wouldn't give to put a face to our true enemy."

"Malorin'athgul," Gannon said darkly, tasting of the name.

Franco could barely breathe with so much truth all flooding to the surface at once. He spun to Carian. "You *told* them about..." But the words wouldn't form, his chest felt so tight. A great pressure was pushing down on him.

Carian put a hand on his arm and met his gaze with uncommon candor in his brown eyes. "Admiral, Niko is blaming the First Lord for the realm being out of Balance. By Belloth's bloody balls, the bludger is trying to rouse support to invade T'khendar! It's time our brethren knew the *real* cause of the realm's troubles."

Devangshu said in that moment, "Brothers, we *must* rid the realm of the pestilence that is Niko van Amstel!"

To which the audience applauded and Franco's gut twisted with an ill foreboding. Like an ant upon a boulder about to tip and roll, he had the sense of something portentous in the offing, but his mind could only dimly comprehend the enormity of what was happening.

Devangshu held up a hand to quiet the group. "Now, brothers, after a detailed study of the Codex, we've found another factor in our favor." He opened the book and read from a marked page, "It says, '...*a candidate is only nominated to the position until the Council of Realms ratifies his candidacy, at which time the vestal appointment becomes permanent. Until such time as permanency is appointed, the vestalship is open to any candidate.*'" He closed the book and shoved it back into his satchel, where its shape promptly vanished. "Under the circumstances, the Council might require Alorin to choose a new Second Vestal simply because the Great Master has been gone so long. Then what—we're stuck with bloody Niko van Amstel?"

Malcontent rumbled through the theater at this.

"I'm with you, my brothers, and that's where this passage comes into play. What it means is that even though the Alorin Seat gave Niko a vestal ring, technically he's still only *nominated* to the position." Devangshu turned a meaningful look over his shoulder and then back to the audience. "Brothers, we need our own frontrunner!"

This announcement met with an approving cheer—no, a veritable roar.

Seemingly as one, all eyes settled on Franco.

He blinked…and blinked again. Then he looked around in sudden frantic denial. "Surely you don't mean me!"

Devangshu extended his hand to Franco and included the assembled brethren with his gaze as he challenged, "Franco Rohre, I know I won't offend anyone when I declare that you've demonstrated the most talent of any of us assembled here. Who else can say they've personally trained with the Great Master? Who else can say they've successfully plus-crossed a node?"

Franco turned Carian an incredulous glare. "You *told* them about the Sylus node?"

The pirate grinned. "Legendary work, Admiral."

"*Really*," Kardashian added. His black eyes gleamed enviously.

Franco gritted his teeth. "Is there anything you *didn't* tell them, Carian?"

"By all the Gods of Niger," Devangshu was addressing the audience again, "think of it, my brothers: plus-crossing nodes! Who else would dare attempt it?"

"Certainly not Niko," Gannon muttered ungraciously.

Someone called from the audience, "How do you plus-cross a node?"

Carian stepped forward. "It's two doublebacks, mate!"

"That's a myth!" someone else called, while the room devolved into speculative murmuring.

Carian shoved hands in his pockets. "You're right, of course. It can't be done—except the Admiral did it." He turned a grin at Franco and then looked back to the audience. "Avast, all of you!" He waved a hand for their attention, and when they'd quieted, said to them, "Now, we've all heard of a doubleback, that being a forked route. You take the primary ley lines of two nodes and pin them to the same nodepoint. Once traveled, the first point switches off and the second switches on. Two different passes across the same node will result in people traveling to different places. I've crossed one of Rohre's doublebacks unsuspectingly myself.

"But *plus-crossing* now…" he grinned again, eyes bright with candid admiration, "*plus-crossing*, mates, means *four* possible outcomes. It's *four* primary ley lines pinned to the same nodepoint."

"That's impossible!" someone shouted, whereupon arguments bounced back and forth across the theater.

Carian held up his hands for silence again and then pointed at Franco. "I can personally attest that the Admiral has crafted doublebacks *and* plus-crossed nodes. The Great Master himself described Franco's work to me, *and* I've inspected them with my own eyes, my handsomes!"

Upon which statement the audience erupted into shouting—a hundred enthusiastic questions bombarded the stage all at once. Franco glanced weakly over his shoulder and noted dispiritedly that Gannon, Kardashian and Ledio had all lined up behind him, conveniently barring any escape.

As the noise of reaction among the brethren was dying down, someone called from the audience, "Franco…"

Franco reluctantly tore his burning gaze from Carian to look out across the sea of indistinct faces.

The same voice called then, "How many rings do you have?"

"Three," Carian answered before Franco could lie about it—or at least attempt to avoid answering.

"*Three.*" Devangshu and Kardashian said in wondrous unison, while the audience murmured with sibilant awe.

"The High Mage of the Citadel bestowed them upon him herself," Carian announced to them proudly. Then he just grinned in response to Franco's murderous glare.

Franco stared hard at the stage floor with his face burning and unspoken curses singeing his tongue. With every secret that Carian so blithely revealed, he felt like a layer of his flesh was being flayed.

Perhaps Gannon was right. Perhaps they'd lived with these secrets for too long, but he didn't know how to live without them now. They'd become part of who he was-is-would-always-be. He couldn't separate himself from them... he didn't know where he began and they ended.

"Niko has but two rings," someone in the audience shouted, "and he gained his second after the Wars!"

A general murmur of malcontent answered this point, for everyone knew that the trials held since the Wars were inferior to those overseen by the Citadel's High Mage.

"Brothers, there's no question about it." Devangshu quieted them with upraised hands. "If the Alorin Seat is determined to appoint someone to the vestal position in lieu of the Great Master's return, it *must* be our brother-in-arms, Franco Rohre!"

To which the shout of approval reverberated the loudest of all.

"Brothers!" Devangshu held a hand proudly to Franco, hope and possibility making his brown-eyed gaze uncommonly bright. "I give you *our* candidate for Second Vestal: the Admiral, Franco Rohre!"

Abruptly Devangshu and everyone else cleared the stage. Franco found himself standing alone, facing a theater filled with Nodefinders shouting a roaring applause, and the repeating echo of his name:

Fran-co! Fran-co!

By Cephrael's Great Book!

Franco's mouth had gone dry, and a sudden lack of breath made him feel that he was choking on seawater and trapped again in a dark cave alongside Immanuel di Nostri. Would that the man had made his own escape that night and left Franco in that cave to drown! He remembered all too well seeing the stars of Cephrael's Hand through the opening in the cave roof, and later the feeling of Fate's threads reaching out for him, binding him to a new course.

Now, seeing where that course was leading, he knew that somewhere up in the heavens, Cephrael had to be laughing.

FIFTEEN

"Destiny isn't chance but choice. It isn't a thing to be waited for.
It is a thing to be achieved"
– The Adept Socotra Isio, Sormitáge Scholar

ALYNERI WALKED THE path from the rebellion compound back to the *sa'reyth* carrying a tray under one arm and a lightness in her heart. Since binding with Trell, she'd hardly known a moment outside of bliss. She felt him always in her mind, even when he was physically distant, yet he might've shared a chair across the fire from her for how close he seemed when she thought of him...for how easily they could converse.

Of course, she was always happier when she felt useful, and between her training sessions with Vaile, teaching Trell the *cortata,* and caring for the Nodefinders—none of whom seemed capable of mending or washing their own shirts, much less preparing a meal for themselves, yet not a one of them had thought to bring a servant along to their secret hideout to care for their needs—Alyneri was feeling rather gainfully productive.

She hummed a Kandori tune to herself while Farshideh's husky voice sang in her head and her feet kept a steady rhythm on the path.

Once upon a wildling sea,
My love sailed a ship, or three,
And crashed upon my shores, did he
A-weary of his measure

I took him to my breast that day

And held fever's chill kiss at bay
And chased skulking Death away
To keep him as my treasure…

Alyneri rounded a rise, and both tune and feet came to a halt.

Across the meadow, Trell and Vaile were approaching. She might've guessed from the quiet of Trell's thoughts that he was shielding his mind from her, but she'd been too enraptured by joy's dazzling spell to imagine it coming to an end. Now, seeing Vaile's expression, not to mention the silence of Trell's thoughts, Alyneri knew that it had. Still, she looked to Trell for explanation as he neared.

In his thoughts he gently stroked her cheek, while in the world he gave her a kiss. Then he captured her gaze significantly. "Rhakar has come."

Rhakar. The Shadow of the Light. He flew closest to the First Lord's field, occasionally even straying into the game, and rarely ventured into the *sa'reyth* unless duty or one of his siblings summoned him. Alyneri feared this time his presence was due to the former.

She gripped the silver tray to her chest. "Why is he here?" Yet she needn't have asked, for she saw her thoughts mirrored in Trell's gaze.

They'd both known the day would come when Trell would need to resume his place in the First Lord's game. Balaji had told them that the game had intensified, that Players now faced off on both sides of the field. In fact, this knowledge had spurred them to seek their binding, that even in separation they could know each other's minds.

Yet even understanding that Trell would soon be called had not prepared Alyneri's heart for the moment.

"Have you…" she had to force the breath from her frozen lungs, "spoken with him?" She saw in his gaze that he had. "I see." Alyneri summoned her composure and her courage in equal measure to ask in a voice that sounded much calmer than she felt, "When do you leave?"

He brushed a hand across her hair. "Dawn."

Alyneri pressed her lips together tightly and nodded.

"Trell!" Náiir's voice reached them from higher up the hill.

Alyneri turned to see him standing there with Rhakar, the latter radiating his usual formidable air.

Trell waved to Náiir and then kissed Alyneri again. "I'll join you in a moment." He headed off.

Alyneri hugged the tray to her chest and frowned after him.

"Do not fear, *she-sidthe*," Vaile murmured, using her name for Alyneri, which meant 'fierce kitten' in Old Alaeic. She brushed a lock of hair back from Alyneri's shoulder in motherly fashion. "His lifeline extends far."

Alyneri let out a slow exhale. "I no longer worry as much for his life. More I worry for the time we must spend apart, even knowing I can reach him now…" she gave a contemplative smile. "Well, it's not the same as being by his side, is it?"

"We must teach you Dreamscape in our next lessons. It is at least *some* consolation when we must endure a lengthy separation from those who are dearest to our hearts."

"You can *teach* me to weave Dreamscape? I thought it was only available to those with the variant trait."

Vaile took Alyneri's chin between her thumb and forefinger, her emerald gaze darkly enticing. "You can teach most anything to those with the will, *she-sidthe*, but there *is* one thing you cannot teach." She leaned in—

The unexpected kiss caught Alyneri completely off guard. A *deep* kiss. Vaile's lips were soft upon hers, her tongue even more so. Her kiss was confusing and…*electric* and wondrous.

Vaile withdrew and eyed her quietly.

Alyneri felt an odd and marvelous stirring in her core, as a butterfly fluttering ephemeral wings.

The zanthyr smiled a very feline smile. "I have given you the Pattern of Life just now."

Alyneri's breath caught. She stared at Vaile.

"This pattern can only be gained from one who already knows its path. I've bestowed it already upon your Trell of the Tides, on the night Náiir and I took him back from that *mor'alir* witch at Darroyhan. If you both choose to wake the Pattern into being, you may know immortality together. Time will never again be your enemy."

Tears sprang unbidden to Alyneri's eyes.

Vaile cupped Alyneri's cheek and gazed softly upon her. "True love should not be bound to the lifespan of a mortal shell. Now you may pursue it together across the centuries, or not, as you both choose."

Alyneri threw her arms around Vaile. She said in a choked voice, "I have never had such a friend as you."

Vaile stroked her hand across Alyneri's hair, as a mother gently grooming her cub. "If you cannot enjoy living your life with those you love, you've already lost the game. Remember this, *she-sidthe*."

Alyneri withdrew and brushed tears from her eyes with the back of her fingers. As she met Vaile's gaze again, she nodded. It felt a solemn promise. Vaile wrapped an arm around Alyneri's waist, and they walked together back to the *sa'reyth* with the Pattern of Life still fluttering in Alyneri's core.

Reaching the open-sided tent where she'd so often spoken with Balaji of deep and meaningful truths, Alyneri found that He Who Walks the Edge of the World had set out a late luncheon on the long wooden table. Trell ducked beneath the awning just as Alyneri arrived.

Unsurprisingly, Fynn was already seated at the table, perched on a stool with goblet in hand, his unruly dark hair mussed and standing up on one side, and his violet jacket askew. He looked very much like he'd only just awoken.

Trell grinned and clapped him on the shoulder as he passed. "You're starting to resemble something of a wild bird, cousin."

Fynn yawned. "One must occasionally sacrifice a little dignity to serve the greater good. Isn't that right, Your Grace?"

Alyneri left Vaile's side to rejoin Trell's. "Your statement presupposes one exhibits some shadow of dignity to begin with, Lord Fynnlar."

Trell wrapped an arm around Alyneri and drew her close. Amazing how relieved she felt just standing next to him. With the shadow of his now imminent departure looming, each moment sang with a heightened clarity: his touch, his smile, the heady feel of him so near…Alyneri willed each of these moments to become indelible, that she might return to them during the weeks ahead and take comfort in the memories.

Fynn meanwhile screwed up his face. "Don't the Kandori have some saying about dignity? How does it go…" he waved his goblet airily, "*'only the alfalfa takes the measure of the earth's indignation'* or some such?"

"Only the wind knows the truth in the water?" Alyneri offered helpfully.

Fynn lifted a finger off his goblet. "That's it."

"I'm afraid that saying has nothing whatsoever to do with dignity."

"Damn." Fynn scowled. "I was sure I had that one figured out."

Balaji spread a piece of linen on his prep table and looked up under his brows as he was placing figs upon it. "Rhakar mentioned that you'll leave at first light, Trell of the Tides. I'll have a basket ready for your travels before dawn."

"Thank you, Balaji."

Dawn. Alyneri turned her face into Trell's shoulder. Suddenly the sun seemed to be streaking towards the horizon, the hours remaining to them already too short.

Trell took her chin and kissed her.

"*Ah…*young love." Carian vran Lea gave them a lusty grin as he ducked into the tent. He ambled over to where Fynn was sitting, looped a leg over an empty stool and leered at Trell. "It's a fine thing to see you with the little Healer, Trell of the Tides. Such a pretty chase as you, I might've taken you otherwise for a nancy boy."

Alyneri wrapped her arms around Trell's waist and looked to the pirate.

"They say we see in others those attributes we most fear confronting in ourselves, Captain vran Lea."

Carian frowned at her.

Fynn nudged him. "Don't mind her. She's been cooped up day and night with Vaile for weeks now. Spending that much time with a zanthyr can't be good for anyone." Fynn took a drink of his wine. "So where are you off to, cousin?"

Trell glanced to Balaji. "All I know is that my presence is required and I should bring my sword."

"That sounds ominous," Alyneri murmured.

"Or merely prudent." He winked at her.

"Right…" Fynn scrubbed at his hair, which stood up like a rooster's tail, as though he'd slept all night in a bowl. "Looking back on our travels together in hindsight, being so enthusiastic to reunite with good ole daddy mightn't have been such a fantastic idea."

"You don't seem too unhappy with your current position of glorified debauchery," Alyneri pointed out.

Fynn pressed himself taller. "A man of my quality must count his blessings, Your Grace. Don't you realize there are thousands of others equally qualified to fill my shoes?" He waved his goblet in a wide arc. "The job market is saturated with the corrupt and dissolute, while the positions calling for truly honest men are few and far between. Would you rather see me drunk *and* unemployed?"

Trell laughed. "I'm sure my uncle Prince Ryan would be relieved to know you've finally found gainful occupation, cousin."

Fynn belched and lifted a finger to point at him. "Except on Tuesdays."

"Speaking of which…" Carian angled a look at Fynn and then grinned meaningfully at Alyneri. "Have you asked this lovely poppet about traveling with us on our little errand, Fynnlar?"

"No," Alyneri replied firmly, in answer to both questions.

Fynn scowled at her. "You haven't even heard my proposition yet, Your Grace—and you must admit an opening in your calendar now that my cousin is heading off to probably get himself nearly killed again."

Trell chuckled. "I appreciate your vote of confidence, Fynn."

Fynn turned him a look of deep sincerity, even if not of impressive sobriety. "One must be realistic, cousin. How many lives can one man really have?"

Vaile came up behind Fynn and placed her hands on his shoulders, making him jump half off of his stool. She leaned to reply next to his ear with her eternally knowing gaze pinned on Trell, "That very much depends on how many gods are watching over him." She shifted slightly to level her green eyes on Fynn then. "Or have you forgotten how you yourself received the benediction of immortal patronage?"

"No," Fynn grumbled into his wine. He lowered his goblet to glare at her. "When I'm sleeping through the night again, *then* you'll know I've forgotten."

Balaji folded down the top of the basket he'd been packing and came over to Trell and Alyneri. "A meal for you both." He offered the basket to Trell along with a smile, the one that always made Alyneri a little nervous inside. "Go, have your night together. Náiir will call you when time can wait no longer."

Trell took the basket and in return gave Balaji a smile of gratitude. "Thank you, Balaji."

Alyneri leaned and kissed Balaji's cheek, murmuring demurely, "How well you know our minds."

Balaji smiled at them both and replied with a wink, "There are no secrets in the First Lord's *sa'reyth*."

They made their way into the high hills with Trell gripping Alyneri's hand and silence holding her tongue. There was no reason she should fear separation, yet fear had her firmly in its grip. Alyneri tried to think as Trell did and view his return to the game as the next thing life was throwing at them, and they just had to handle it, but somehow this simplicity got tangled in all of the worries she held in her heart.

Finding a clearing with a commanding view of the mountains, the valley, and the depthless blue sky, Trell opened the basket and took out a blanket Balaji had packed inside. "Do you think we're still in Alorin?" He shook out the blanket and spread it across the grass.

Alyneri was holding herself with her arms, gazing out over the vista of green hills towards the jutting, granite peaks—which hovered so close, she thought she might've draped a garland upon their crags. "I don't think so." She hugged her arms closer about herself. "This world just feels…"

Trell came up behind her and placed his hands on her shoulders. "Cleaner?" He enfolded her in his arms and drew her against him. "Clearer?"

Alyneri let out a slow exhale. "I was going to say innocent, though it sounds a strange thing to say about a world. But there's a guilelessness to this place that I can't explain." She glanced back at him and smiled. "I'm glad to know you feel something, too."

"Yes, it's quite perceptible. I recognized it the first time I came here, though at the time I didn't realize what I was feeling."

"Some other realm then." Alyneri leaned her head back against Trell's shoulder and tried to quell the ill anticipation of his departure, tried to enjoy instead the moments that remained. "But which one?"

"Ah...*that* is the question, as Balaji would say." He planted a kiss upon her neck and drew her down to the blanket, adding in his best Balaji imitation, "We must ask ourselves, young Alyneri, in pursuit of this answer, where would the Mage have chosen to establish his haven?"

Alyneri laughed—Trell had exactly captured Balaji's inflection of voice as well as the elusive twinkle in his gaze. She settled down across from him and watched quietly as he withdrew the various bundles Balaji had prepared for them, her mind a whir.

As he was unfolding the meal, she asked him, "Will you see the Emir?"

Trell handed her a cloth filled with figs. "I expect so. I hope so. I need to thank him for his generosity and kindness," he looked up at her under his brows, "and for sending me on a quest that led me to you."

"That reconciliation has been long in coming."

He angled her a smile. "Just so, Your Grace."

Alyneri fingered the collection of purplish fruit and noted the damask design woven into the linen. "Your path has circled so many times...circles within circles."

"Yet somehow always back to you."

Alyneri looked up at his words. Trell was regarding her so intently that she smilingly dropped her gaze again. "I hadn't thought of it that way."

"I have, Your Grace. Many times." He gave her a significant look. "And now we're bound, and I need never leave you again." *For we remain here, together, always.* Into this sentiment he layered intensity of feeling and something more...a touch, as of a kiss, yet whispering all along her core.

Alyneri's breath caught. Heat flamed along the path of his ephemeral kiss. Her eyes widened as she stared at him. "Where did you learn *that*?"

"Náiir." Trell started crawling towards her wearing a devious smile. "His lessons on the more arcane uses for bindings have proven *very* informative." He rose up to take her by the shoulders.

Alyneri fell back beneath him, laughing. The figs were quickly scattered.

Much later, they lay together beneath a bright moon. Alyneri gazed along the line of Trell's bare arm, partially pinned beneath her head, and studied the round scars that marred his flesh. In the starlight, they held a sort of sheen, smoother than the rest of his skin.

She and Trell had spoken of many things since his rescue from Darroyhan, since she'd nearly killed herself saving him. They'd shared dreams and fears; they'd spent hours speaking of the Mage and his game, and just as many reminiscing of Dannym…but of the secret trials of his imprisonment, not a word had Trell spoken. These truths he'd bound into a place of silence, saying only that those wounds were his alone to mend.

Alyneri knew he'd been tortured; more telling than the scars upon his flesh, she'd seen the evidence of it in his life pattern. Some traumas found their way so deeply into a man's structure that his pattern forever retained their impression, even after his body had been Healed.

Yet whatever scars Trell carried on his soul from his months spent in captivity seemed but surface wounds upon his character. Alyneri had witnessed nothing in him to indicate the damage had penetrated any deeper than a few shiny circles in his flesh.

He must've perceived where her thoughts had gone, for he hugged her body closer and murmured in her ear, "None of that matters now."

Alyneri thought of the many invisible scars that threaded through her own soul and marveled that he could say such a thing so easily and honestly. She traced her finger from the scar on Trell's palm to the one on his forearm and asked him softly, "How can you be so free of something so traumatic?"

"What would be the point of keeping it?"

She paused in her tracing. Then she turned in his arms to look at him. "There is no point, is there? But we do keep such memories sometimes, even as painful as they are. They can become as treasures held close, thorny crowns we bear as if to prove some righteous point, while at the same time declaring our desire not to bear them at all."

Trell trailed his fingers along her cheek, thoughtfully, his grey eyes mercuric in the moonlight, lips barely parted, as if sharing his deepest secrets with her on a whisper of departing breath. "In truth, Alyneri, the worst of it remains a blur…those early days pinned to the wall of Veirnan hal'Jaitar's malice." He was regarding her so nakedly, his mind so open to her, Alyneri knew an intensity of connection deeper than anything they'd yet shared.

"In times like that, pain becomes a kind of friend." Trell propped his head in one hand and traced his other contemplatively along her collarbone. "It reminds you that you're still alive; it focuses your energies on remaining so. Pain shows you what you love and brings an acute gratitude for what you have…and for no longer having it, upon its departure."

Admiring of his courage, Alyneri kissed him tenderly.

Trell gave her a fleeting smile and rolled onto his back again. "I think what was done to Sebastian is far worse than anything I endured."

Alyneri trailed a finger down the line of his chest. "What do you mean?"

Trell glanced briefly at her. "When he and I met in the Kutsamak, I could tell that he struggled against another's will. His mind had been overtaken. But all of the torments I experienced…while they were painful, and at times terrifying, I still knew myself while enduring them. It would've been far, far worse to lose *me* the way Sebastian had, to be so overcome by another's will that you couldn't act upon your own." He gave an explosive exhale. "Even when I didn't know my name, I still knew who *I* was. I'm so amazed by my brother's strength. His situation would've ruined me."

Alyneri gazed wonderingly upon him. Trell must've noted the change in her expression, or else the quiet of her thoughts, for he smiled and rose up to press her down beneath him. "Whatever that thought was, Your Grace… you should think it more often." He stroked his thumb gently along her lower lip, his eyes desirous. Then he brought his lips to hers and showed her what else Náiir had been teaching him.

※

An hour before dawn, they made their way back to the *sa'reyth*. As much as Trell felt Alyneri's anxiety radiating across their binding, as much as he wanted to stay forever by her side, he couldn't deny the excitement drumming a distant yet palpable beat when he thought of returning to the game.

This respite had been valuable, necessary for both of them, and he'd made the most of his time—taken advantage of the *drachwyr*'s wisdom and Vaile's benevolence as best he could—but he'd never expected it to last even as long as it had.

Gaining his rooms, Trell packed what things he imagined he might need, wishing he had a better idea of where he was headed or what the Mage was expecting from him. At the last, he belted on his sword and donned his cloak, feeling as though the moment heralded both a beginning and an end.

Then he looked to Alyneri. She was leaning against an armoire, hugging herself and watching him with a faint furrow between her brows.

Vaile called her 'fierce kitten.' Trell could see this trait in Alyneri—perhaps he'd always seen it in her. Vaile had merely shaved off the fur of Northern propriety, which had never clung well to Alyneri to begin with, to reveal the lean creature beneath. Alyneri didn't share Vaile's predatory manner, yet he knew her to have a strength equal to the zanthyr's, in her own way.

A smile teased at a corner of Alyneri's mouth. "What is that look?"

Trell walked over and slipped his hands around her waist. "It's love, Your Grace."

She arched a brow at him. "It seemed a little hungry for love."

Trell grinned and pulled her hips more firmly against his. "Love finds infinite forms of expression."

Alyneri leaned into his embrace and laid her head against his shoulder, and they stood in silence, letting the beat of their hearts and the resonance of their thoughts speak their feelings. After a lengthy span that yet felt too short, Alyneri sighed and tightened her arms around him. "We knew this day would come, but I'm not ready for you to leave again."

He rested his cheek against her head. "And I don't want to leave."

"Yes, you do. You're very nearly eager, if you ask me."

Trell chuckled. "Well…I don't want to leave *you*." She felt different in his arms than she had before their parting in the Kutsamak; lean muscle now sculpted her frame in ways he found very alluring. It was a wondrous pleasure envisioning her without her silk dress, or the garb she wore for their sparring matches—nearly as enticing as actually observing her thusly.

"Promise me…" She drew back to look at him. Her brown eyes were large and lovely…and concerned. She conveyed so well her thoughts with just the faintest tightening of her gaze, he hardly needed the binding to know them. "Promise me you'll be careful. You have immortal friends, but they can't follow you everywhere, and if you're too reckless and brave—"

He chuckled. "Have you ever known me to be reckless?"

Her gaze sharpened upon him. "I grew up watching you, *Prince* Trell val Lorian. I know all of your exploits—venturing out to sea stacks, free-climbing hundreds of feet up the Calgaryn cliffs, chasing Ean across nearly vertical palace roofs—" She broke off and frowned at him. "Why are you smiling like that?"

Trell caressed her cheek with his thumb. "Because I remember all of those adventures."

The furrow between her brows deepened. "Trell…" she exhaled a sigh, "I'll grant you go into situations with more forethought than Ean, but you are every bit as reckless with your life as your brother is."

Trell regarded her quietly. "You'd rather I was afraid?" When she merely gazed at him, he wrapped his arms around her again and said as he pressed a kiss to her hair, "If our every parting is to bear the shadows of our last, Alyneri, the scars of those months apart will never fade."

She fell silent at this, and then she murmured, "I wish sometimes that you weren't so perceptive."

He pressed a smile against her head. "It's a great relief to me to know that you're here at the *sa'reyth*, safe. It would be harder out there, having you with me."

She drew away slightly to better look at him. "Why?"

He brushed his fingers slowly across her hair, his mind suddenly a whirlwind of shadowy memories. "Taliah tried to break me, Alyneri." Amazing how easily he could confess it now, how distant those months seemed, as unimportant as shells crushed on a path behind him. "Many times she came close, but because the game fell only between the two of us, I prevailed. Yet I know now that I would've fallen to her quickly if she'd held you in kind."

He caught his finger beneath Alyneri's chin to hold her gaze. "The idea of Taliah working her craft upon *you*...I couldn't have borne it. I couldn't even think of you in those weeks, because you weaken me."

"I *weaken* you?" She looked dismayed and tried to pull away from him.

But he bound her with his arms and pressed his forehead against hers. "Because I love you so deeply that I would rather die than see harm come to you. But you strengthen me, too. Of course you do." He ran his hand across her shoulder and recalled the many miraculous things she'd accomplished on his behalf, and how true she'd been to him.

"That's what it means to be human, I think," he offered upon a quiet exhale. "To share such a profound yet terrifying connection with someone that they become your strength and your weakness. That they balance your assumed invincibility and temper your deepest moments of inadequacy with the certainty of love."

Alyneri caught her breath. Then she hugged him fiercely.

"Trell, it is time." Náiir poked his head through the parting of drapes, whereupon his eyes crinkled. " *'Oh Love,'* " he pressed a hand to his heart and lifted his gaze to the ceiling, " *'why visiteth thy arrow upon my heated breast? For what sins must I endure thy tormenting caress?'* "

Alyneri dabbed at her eyes and turned to smile at Náiir. "That is one of my favorite passages in the *Kandori Book of Princes*, when Dastan is lamenting the loss of Elaria."

Náiir winked at her. "And well it is that you should know this epic poem, Princess of Kandori."

Trell reluctantly released Alyneri and took up his pack. "I know a few Kandori stories myself."

"Indeed, Trell of the Tides?" Náiir stepped politely back from the parting of drapes to let them pass.

Trell angled Náiir a wry look as the three of them headed off together. "Some of those stories concern you, I suspect."

Náiir beamed. "Oh, then you must tell them to me someday! I very much enjoy hearing stories of myself."

"You're the only one who does," Jaya remarked as they happened by where she was setting out her morning tea.

Náiir turned a look over his shoulder. "Envy is an unbecoming color on an immortal, Jaya."

"So is narcissism," she murmured sweetly back to him.

Náiir shook his head and sighed as they continued on through the connected tents. "All appreciation of life stems first from an appreciation of ourselves, Trell of the Tides. My sister is somehow unable to grasp this fundamental truth. The finding of self-love…it is the greatest of endeavors."

"*Self*-love doesn't sire nine Kandori princedoms," noted a passing Mithaiya, who appeared to be on her way to join Jaya.

"One merely *begins* with self," Náiir cast Mithaiya a look of aggravation, "and expands outwards to embrace the love of others, reaching greater appreciation through each new concentric circle of life."

"It seems very sensible to me," Trell remarked equitably.

"Indeed, so I also feel, Trell of the Tides. Would that my sisters shared our opinion." Náiir pushed aside the final drapery, and they emerged into the dawn.

Trell turned to Alyneri. She met his gaze with hers veiled in silence; he knew what courage she'd had to summon to let him go without complaint or tears.

He took her shoulders. "I think you should go with Fynn."

She blinked at him.

"On this mission of his and Carian's. Who knows? Maybe some of your quality will rub off on them. You can keep me apprised of their activities," and he tapped his temple meaningfully.

Alyneri gazed at him for a moment more. Then she nodded.

Trell leaned and captured her mouth in a fervent kiss. He willed into it everything he hadn't been able to say, and he placed within the shared space of their binding his promise, his honest hope, to be able to say all of it one day—*every* day—for the rest of their lives.

When he released Alyneri, her eyes were glassy, but she smiled bravely, hugged her chest with her arms, and nodded him on.

Trell turned and headed off. Out of necessity, he focused his attention on the path ahead.

Náiir walked with him towards the picketed horses and Balaji and Rhakar. Seeing the two *drachwyr* standing by the horses reminded Trell uncannily of his first departure from the *sa'reyth*, when he'd set out upon another mysterious path into a similar unknown with a task to accomplish for the Mage.

Balaji gave him a smile as he neared. "Ah, Trell of the Tides, a good morning to you!"

"And to you, Balaji." Trell shifted his pack onto his shoulder and his gaze to the other *drachwyr*. "Rhakar."

The Shadow of the Light nodded in reply.

Náiir clapped a hand on Trell's arm. "This is where I leave you, Trell of the Tides. Fair winds, fair skies, and the Lady's blessing upon your path until we meet again."

For a moment as he looked back to Náiir, Trell saw not the luminous dawn but a stone room in a dark tower on a night of storms—and Náiir's eyes, staring into his.

'...*Oh, my friend, this nightmare is almost behind you...*'

Trell took the *drachwyr* into a rough embrace. "Thank you," he murmured at his ear. "*Thank you.*"

As they separated again, Náiir met his gaze with a grave sobriety. "You are brother-bound to the Mage and by extension to us, Trell of the Tides. We would brave the darkness of Shadow in search of you." Then he nodded to all and departed.

Trell watched him go, feeling such ineffable gratitude that he could barely breathe for the space it occupied in his chest.

"Thus we find ourselves at a junction we've crossed before, my friend." Balaji's meaningful tone drew Trell's gaze back to him. Balaji looked him over with his typical enigmatic smile. "When last we met at this crossroads, you asked me about pieces and Players."

Returning Balaji's gaze quietly, Trell marveled that he'd ever thought to suspect the Mage's motives, for the larger pattern seemed so clear to him now. "You said then that a piece becomes a Player by finding out what game he's playing in."

Mystery's enticing light danced in Balaji's eyes. "I did indeed."

"Well..." Trell blew out a decisive breath, "I've found my way onto the field." He looked between Balaji and Rhakar. "What now?"

"Another fair question." Balaji grinned at him. "Pieces jump at the Players' commands without understanding the purpose behind their actions. Players need no orders to decide which way they will proceed, merely a view of the playing field and a weather eye upon the goal." His gaze implied Trell fit decidedly into the latter category.

Trell looked between the two *drachwyr* bemusedly. "You're really not going to tell me anything more about this mission?"

"The Mage has determined it's time for you to take the field again, Trell val Lorian," Rhakar said. "Now you know as much as either of us."

Balaji handed him Gendaia's reins. "The Lady's blessing upon you, my friend."

Rhakar had his own horse's reins in hand, and without another word, he led away.

They'd just reached the trail and were about to mount the horses when a new shadow appeared out of the dawn—Vaile, dressed for sparring. Trell found an unexpected relief in this; Alyneri would at least have somewhere to focus her attention instead of dwelling on their separation.

Vaile's hand captured his arm and her emerald eyes his gaze. "Take care with your life, Trell of the Tides. *She-sidthe* has big plans for you both."

Trell nodded to her. "I will do my best, my lady."

Vaile hugged him, hard and long, evoking a memory of the kiss she'd given him at Darroyhan. He could almost still feel its flutter in his core.

As she withdrew, the zanthyr cupped his cheek with her palm, but her expression was serious and stern. "This war is not merely one of men and nations; it's a symptom of the realm's unbalance. If left unchecked, it will spread like a cancer until it has infected the entire world. We didn't save you so you could go back and fight this war, Trell of the Tides. We saved you so you could *end* it."

Trell stared at her.

"We must away, she-cat." Rhakar was already in his saddle. "We travel in haste. Timing is key."

Trell turned and eyed him silently. *If you know that timing is key, then you clearly still know more than I do*, but with a final glance at Vaile—both of farewell and gratitude—he swung into Gendaia's saddle and gathered his reins.

Rhakar led them fast away into the dawn.

SIXTEEN

"Most people miss Opportunity because it is carrying a shovel and looks like work."

–Yara, an old Kandori woman

WHEN THE MOMENT came, Felix di Sarcova was engaged in a dream, wherein a dryad was guarding a node he wanted to travel and requiring three pleasures of him before she would let him cross. Being that she was a nymph and thereby very beautiful, Felix was all too happy to bow to her wishes.

He was just leaning in to give her the first of what he hoped would become many kisses, when a forceful presence disrupted the dream. Actually, it felt more like an iron hand reaching *into* his dream, taking him by the throat and yanking him out into the waking world—with no regard whatsoever for his mind's current occupation.

Felix roused sputteringly into darkness and batted desperately at the iron hand fastened around his throat. Only…his efforts met with empty air, so he opened his eyes to see what had actually awoken him.

A pair of emerald eyes were glowing above him like two great green moons.

Felix sucked in his breath and sort of crab-crawled backwards and into a semi-seated posture with his spine wedged painfully against the headboard.

The eyes seemed unmoved by this impressive retreat.

"Wh—who are you?" Felix looked around for any other disembodied eyes glowing in his room.

"Get dressed, Felix di Sarcova." With the deep voice, akin to a purr but echoic of a growl, a tall form materialized out of the darkness, shape filling in its proper place around the emerald eyes.

"Shadow take me." Felix's mouth fell open. "You're…why, you're Tanis's zanthyr!"

"I am Phaedor. And your window is closing."

"My—" Felix spun a look at his open window. Then he understood. "Oh, I get it." He nodded wisely at the zanthyr. "You meant that metaphorically."

"There was no metaphor in 'clothe yourself.'"

Felix just stared at him, both fascinated and slightly unnerved. "Have you come to break me out?" He'd lost count of the days he'd been forced to keep ill company with the dust in that forgotten room. Suddenly a new hope flamed inside him. "Did Tanis send you? Did you rescue him, too?"

"Tanis is walking his path, as you must do, Felix di Sarcova." The deep voice around those glowing eyes gave an eerie imagining to what Felix's path might entail. "Doubtless you would prefer to walk it clothed."

Felix frowned at him and slowly climbed out of bed. He tried to reassure himself that the zanthyr obviously wasn't there to harm him—he could've done that easily enough without bothering to wake him up—but it was hard to commit to the idea with those glowing eyes watching him so unnervingly, as if they already knew all of his secrets.

He was just reaching for the light on his bedside chest when every lamp in the room flamed to brilliant life.

Felix winced in the now too-bright room. Shading his squinting eyes with his hand, he turned back to say something and saw the zanthyr in the light. The words froze on his tongue.

Tanis hadn't been exaggerating in describing him. The zanthyr was damned impressive.

Tall as a horse—no, a rearing bear. *Okay*, maybe not one of those ice bears they had stuffed in the Imperial Menagerie, which all the governesses took their charges to see when they were still young enough to be awed and inspired by the vast diversity of the realm's fauna, but which outing had only resulted in Felix and his brothers pretending to throw different types of animal scat at each other and chasing around terrorizing the Menagerie's other visitors, but in any case, *really* tall—and dressed all in black leather.

He was also very intimidating, and bloody good looking. Tanis had failed to mention that. Somehow it had been easier for Felix to imagine Tanis's zanthyr as being fierce and menacing, but finding out he was ridiculously handsome to boot—that just rubbed salt in the wound.

Felix finally noticed that he'd sort of wedged himself between the bedside chest and the bed frame while he'd been staring at the zanthyr. Tanis had told Felix he could trust Phaedor, but the way the man was looking at him, sort of oozing danger from his boots to his wavy raven hair...Felix wasn't so sure.

He wetted his lips. "Tanis...uh, said I could trust you."

The zanthyr made a dagger appear in his hand and started flipping it into the air. "He did, did he?"

Felix eyed the dagger uncertainly and licked his lips again. "Unconditionally."

Phaedor arched a brow. "That is quite a commitment to make on my behalf."

"Okay, maybe he didn't use that word, but he *implied* it."

"You may unconditionally trust in the Empress's ire if you make her wait for your arrival."

"*Okay*, all right, I get it." Felix dropped to his knees on the floor and hunted around beneath the bed for his pants. Finding them, he sat and flopped his feet up and down while pulling them on. "So...where is Tanis?" He paused with his pants around his thighs. "I mean, you must know, right? Tanis said you know everything."

"I see Tanis has been filling your head with his ideas."

Felix eyed the zanthyr speculatively. "But you're not denying it."

The zanthyr flipped his dagger, making it spin three times before catching it by the point. "If a man says the sky is green when it is patently blue, what need to argue? The man is clearly mad."

"So...that's a yes, then?" Felix felt as tense as cat on a fence with barking hounds on both sides, and the zanthyr watching him from between the strands of his wavy hair—so like a predatory cat marking the progress of its prey through the veldt—well, that just wasn't at all helpful. "Will you just tell me this one thing?" Felix gazed up at the man, praying Tanis had been right in all the things he'd said about him. "*Do* the Danes have Tanis?"

The hint of a shadowy smile might've twitched on the zanthyr's lips. He flipped his dagger again. "Not at the moment." Then he fixed those unnerving emerald eyes on Felix, making him feel very much pinned in his sights. "But the Empress may yet turn you over to them if you make her wait."

Felix choked on a swallow. "You mean—she really—" he scrambled to his feet and pressed himself back against the bedside chest. The Empress was summoning *him?* "You mean that wasn't just some metaphor I wasn't supposed to understand?"

The zanthyr looked him up and down. "She would prefer you presented yourself to her suitably clothed, but—"

"*Okay*, you've made your point!" Felix looked frantically around for his tunic and finally spotted it under the table. He rushed over to it. "It's just that Tanis said you talked in riddles."

"Riddles." The zanthyr arched a brow and followed him with that unnerving gaze. Felix just couldn't escape from it. The zanthyr's bloody gaze was taking up so much space in the room that Felix could hardly think around it.

"Okay, maybe he didn't use the word *riddles*." Felix snatched up his tunic and thrust his head through the opening. "I think his exact words were 'cryptic and elliptical truths you won't understand and probably would rather not know.'" Shirt donned, he looked around desperately for his belt.

The zanthyr nodded towards the corner.

Felix saw his belt cowering there and felt a unique kinship with it. He ran over and grabbed it up, whereupon a thought occurred to him. He stilled with his hand on the leather.

Straightening slowly then, he looked over his shoulder to the zanthyr. "Why did *you* come for me?" The words sounded a little broken and embarrassingly shrill. Felix cleared his throat. "I mean…why not the High Lord's men, or the Empress's Praetorian? Why not *anyone* else?"

The zanthyr did smile at him then, a dangerous sort of smile, full of mystery and insinuation. "At last, Felix di Sarcova lands upon a question worth asking."

Felix waited for him to expound upon this comment, but the zanthyr merely eyed him through the veil of his wavy hair and flipped his dagger again.

"But not worth *answering*, I take it." Felix frowned down as he fastened his belt around his hips. "I seem to recall Tanis saying you could be…"

Phaedor arched a brow by way of inquiry into exactly what he could be.

Felix scowled at him. "Never mind." He started looking around for his boots.

The zanthyr pointed his dagger helpfully towards the opposite corner where Felix saw his boots peeking out from beneath his crumpled cloak.

Felix padded over to them. "Obviously you didn't come here to answer a bunch of *my* questions." He glanced at Phaedor for confirmation of this fact as he reached his boots. "Why then?" He sat down while mumbling through the possibilities, "Not to question me—that's a certain text. If you know everything already, what need for that tedious undertaking?"

"Verily." The zanthyr flipped his dagger.

Felix frowned at him. "Tanis said you were sworn to protect him, but that you also were there to keep him on this path—whatever *that* involves. But you said just a minute ago that I had to walk *my* path…" Felix was trying to shove his foot into his boot without undoing all the buckles, so his voice sounded somewhat strained as he continued, "...but *having* a path implies you're walking it, kind of regardless of what you do. So that can't be why you came for me." He grunted as he finally forced his foot all the way in and dropped his heel on the floor. Then he lifted his mismatched gaze to the zanthyr. "Can it?"

Phaedor grinned and flipped his dagger.

Felix reflected that the zanthyr was really skilled at unapologetically not answering any questions. He got his other boot on more easily and grabbed his cloak with one hand as he stood up. "So...?" He straightened and looked to the zanthyr.

Phaedor arched a brow at him.

Felix shifted on his feet. "I mean...*is* that why you came? To put me on my path?"

Phaedor nodded towards Felix's satchel, which was lying on the chair by the window. "Lest we forget the coach to carry you upon this path."

Felix did a double-take at him, and his breath caught. The intimation in the zanthyr's tone...how could he possibly know that the satchel was his Nodefinder's coach? Yet this was undeniably what he'd been implying.

Worse...and this really gave Felix pause, such that he nearly missed a step as he was making his slow way across the room to claim said satchel... did the zanthyr somehow know about the *book*?

By the bloody Sanctos. Felix took up the strap of his satchel and slowly slung it diagonally across his chest. Then he looked down at himself and grimaced at his disheveled appearance. "I wasn't expecting to be summoned into the presence of the Empress when I put these clothes on."

Phaedor caught his dagger by the point and pinned his striking gaze on Felix. "No indeed, Felix di Sarcova, you and Tanis were expecting to catch a tiger with a snare designed for a rabbit."

Felix felt this pinioning truth spear him. He dropped his head, and a hollow feeling opened in his chest. "If I could undo—"

"You shall have your chance for atonement." The zanthyr started towards the door with his long black cloak floating at his heels. Felix stood rooted, thinking of Tanis and Nadia, and even poor Malin, and what a bloody irreconcilable mess they'd made of everything.

The cell door swung open soundlessly before the zanthyr's approach. He paused and looked over his shoulder at Felix. "Offer the Empress your contrition, and she will meet it with steel. Offer her truth, and you may yet find an opportunity for redress."

Felix stared at him, contemplating meeting the Empress with a pounding heart and a mouth gone dry. Most people went their whole lives and never even saw the Empress, save perhaps from a million heads away on the day of the Solstice, when a figure like a tiny diamondine stick waved from a cupola atop the dome of the Summer Palace. And now he was going to stand before her and...what? Be charged with treason? Or worse, blamed for taking the Princess Heir out of the palace?

Suddenly the zanthyr seemed like a guard come to escort him to the gallows.

As if reading of this thought, Phaedor flashed a predatory smile and strode from the room.

Felix made haste to follow. He trailed the zanthyr down a long, vaulted passage that looked more like it belonged in a mountain castle than a prison tower. It had to be late at night—or he supposed, early in the morning—but they passed a lot of guards, who mostly tried not to look at them, or to not look at the zanthyr. And they passed a lot of spies trying to look like normal people, but normal people actually slept at night, so Felix wasn't fooled. Finally they descended a mile of stairs and left the Tower, with Felix all too happy to never visit again, and headed across a plaza beneath an open, starry sky.

About halfway across, Felix saw silvery portals blink into existence everywhere and heaved a shuddering sigh of relief. He wasn't sorry to leave the dead spot forever behind either.

Yawning prodigiously, Felix dared another glance at the zanthyr, who walked at his side like a towering statue formed of shadows. The man was certainly an enigma, just as Tanis had claimed. But then, most anyone would be an enigma if they never said a damned thing except 'indeed' and 'is that so?' and 'hurry the hell up.'

Looking away again, he observed more to himself than the zanthyr, "Tanis thinks of you like a father." He rubbed his nose on his sleeve and took a deep sniff of free air. It smelled suspiciously of old bourbon and garlic, likely a result of the taverns on the far end of the square. "Not that he said those words exactly," Felix amended, sniffing again, "but I could tell. And a *good* father, mind. Not like *my* father, who changes wives with the seasons and forgets which progeny belongs to which dame. He better remembers the names of his bloody hawks than his own offspring." Felix shoved both hands through his hair and scowled at the moonlit pavement stones in front of his boots. "He treats his hawks a good deal better than his offspring, too."

"Hawks learn faster than boys and are quicker to obey."

Felix spun the zanthyr a look. "Yeah..." Hearing the too familiar phrase unnerved him all over again. "That's *exactly* what my father says."

The zanthyr shot him a sidelong smile, elusive and dark, the image of himself.

Felix scowled down at the pavement.

Yet...even with how uneasy the zanthyr made him, Felix still felt like he could trust him—likely as a result of Tanis having spent so much time talking about him. But Tanis had also said that the zanthyr reflected back at people whatever they put out towards him, which bothered Felix, because he wasn't feeling the same trust coming from the zanthyr. Phaedor seemed to regard him more like a bear observing a squirrel that had the misfortune of finding its way into his lair—and the bear was taking its time deciding whether to leave the squirrel to its own harmless devices or squash it for its personal entertainment.

Felix pondered this all the way across the piazza, through a *soglia're* and into the Imperial Palace, where his mental explorations began more resembling justifications, especially as he started noticing how so many places inside the palace looked familiar, which put his earlier explorations on Faroqhar's twisted nodes into a rather rattling new perspective.

They were walking down a marble-drenched passage Felix was supposed to have never seen before when he posed, "But if the squirrel finds its way into the bear's den, he's still only following his path, right? I mean... did the squirrel really have a choice, if all of its decisions along its path are preordained?"

The zanthyr eyed him askance. "The Empress no more subscribes to destiny than she will find any conceivable justification for your hopping around the Sacred City on twisted nodes."

Felix nearly missed a step. He gulped a swallow instead. Unlike Vincenzé, the zanthyr wasn't fishing for a confession. He *knew*.

"*Sancto Spirito*." The oath barely made it across his lips, his breath had fled so fast. "I'm doomed."

"The future is an empty landscape, Felix di Sarcova."

Felix looked up to find the man staring knowledgeably at him. "So you're saying I'm...*not* doomed?" He screwed up his face with the effort of trying to decipher the zanthyr's cryptic intimation. "You're saying our paths aren't fixed?"

The zanthyr looked ahead again. "The future is unfixed, for few men are actually creating it. Most are focused solely on the now, the evident, the pressing. Many cannot see further down time's curve than the length of their gaze, and the majority no farther than the edge of their boots."

"So...that's a no, then." Felix scratched his head. He wasn't sure how this point was intended to help him.

Maybe it's not. Tanis had explained that sometimes the zanthyr just said things to see how people would react to them. Apparently he did this to the High Lord di L'Arlesé a lot.

Felix didn't much like the idea of being the squirrel that the great bear was just toying around with. In hindsight, he wished that he might've come up with a different metaphor to use in framing their interactions…

But you'll want a bear at your side when you head in to battle Shail's tiger.

Felix turned the zanthyr a startled look, for the thought hadn't at all seemed his own. It finally occurred to him that while the man walking at his side both distracted and unnerved him, Phaedor actually *knew* what they were up against. Felix was no longer alone in understanding the truth—in fact, Phaedor doubtless understood it far better than Felix and probably even Tanis did. Felix realized that in the zanthyr, he had a powerful ally.

They were walking a chequered marble floor across a wide gallery where four hallways intersected when Felix asked, "Are we going to go together to rescue Tanis?"

"Tanis doesn't need our help, but others will." He paused just before an impressive marble archway depicting the Lord of the Forest reaching for the Lady of the Rivers. Two long lines of Praetorians stood just beyond this portal, their ranks of shining armor extending far down the passage.

Felix gulped a swallow and stared at them. That is, until the zanthyr placed a hand on his shoulder. Then he gave a little jump and stared at the zanthyr instead.

"Dare not dissemble to the Empress, Felix di Sarcova. To do so would be your last mistake." Phaedor turned and started off again.

Felix wasn't so stupid as to try to lie to the Empress, and in any case, his attention had stuck on something else. "Wait—what did you mean by *our* help?" He caught up with the zanthyr beneath the arch and then followed him between the long lines of Praetorians, who didn't even shift their gazes in challenge, yet whose presence so crowded the huge hallway that Felix felt smushed just walking between them.

As the zanthyr was approaching a pair of massive double doors guarded by four stone-faced Praetorians, he looked to Felix and advised in that low purr-growl, "Select wisely when to play your truths or you will miss your opportunity. These will be no trifling opponents you'll face around this gaming table."

Then he reached the doors and nodded to the Praetorians. The one in charge nodded smartly to the zanthyr and then looked to Felix. "And who have we here?"

The zanthyr placed a hand on Felix's shoulder. "The Adept Nodefinder Felix di Sarcova, to see the Empress."

"She hasn't called for him."

"She will soon."

The Praetorian looked Phaedor over with a deep furrow between his brow. It was the look of a man poised on the brink of a precipice deciding whether or not to jump while an entire tribe of headhunters was chasing up behind him. At the conclusion of this potent deliberation, the soldier grumbled, "Do you vouch for him then?"

"Absolutely not."

Felix started. Then he glared at the zanthyr.

"Are you armed, Sarcova?"

"Armed?" Felix protested. "*No*, I'm not—"

"All right, let's have a look at you."

Suddenly two Praetorians had Felix by the arms and another was pushing his legs apart.

Felix yelped. "*Hey!* What's the big—"

"Find silence, boy." The guard behind him started patting Felix all over—as in really, *all* over. His pats were more like the flails of a housekeeper enthusiastically pounding the dust from a rug.

Felix aimed a rather frantic glare in Phaedor's direction, but the zanthyr was already passing through the doors. Felix was willing to bet *he* was armed to the teeth.

When the many probing hands had thoroughly explored every inch of Felix's body, a final one shoved him forward. He stumbled into surreality then as he followed after the zanthyr into the palatial expanse that comprised the Empress of Agasan's personal apartments.

SEVENTEEN

"The truest wisdom may be found in knowing you know nothing."
—Zafir bin Safwan al Abdul-Basir, Emir of the Akkad

DARSHANVENKHÁTRAMAN DREAMED...
He stood on a marble-paved path gazing at a large fountain with a centaur at its gushing apex. The centaur stood over a reclining maiden, who lay with her back arched and her breast pressed against the point of his drawn bow, as if to willingly embrace the arrowhead about to pierce her heart.

"That's how I feel when I'm with you," Kjieran observed from Darshan's right.

Darshan's gaze tightened. The maiden wore an expression of rapture, but he didn't think this was Kjieran's meaning. He scanned the statue and then the surrounding gardens. "I don't recognize this place."

"I do." Kjieran exhaled a melancholy sigh. "This is the Sormitáge."

Darshan turned and studied him. What did it prove that he was dreaming of a place he'd never been? Unfortunately little, for both Kjieran and Pelas had spent many years at the Sormitáge. Either of them could be weaving its halls and gardens into his dreams.

He returned his gaze to the centaur and surprisingly found much to appreciate in the statue's artistry. "This is a pleasant space for a haunting." He flicked his gaze at Kjieran and then clasped his hands behind his back and strolled the path leading around the large fountain.

Kjieran cast him a slight smile as they walked, perhaps reminiscent of happier times; for Kjieran's smiles never touched his eyes—not in Darshan's dreams. In his dreams, sorrow shadowed Kjieran's gaze, sometimes so deeply that Darshan felt haunted by it all the waking day.

Only...on this day, the dream felt lighter, less angst-ridden and deluged by need. Or perhaps he was coming to accept the dreams. Certainly he found himself wishing for the night all the long day, yearning to return to Kjieran in whatever capacity he could be with him.

No...this should not be.

In his core, Darshan knew he shouldn't maintain such attachment to a mortal. For that matter, he shouldn't have bound Kjieran for the reasons he'd bound him—not to serve their purpose, but for his own selfish pleasure; because he'd wanted to share eternity with Kjieran, because he'd wanted *this* doomed creature to endure.

Unfortunately, what he wanted with Kjieran felt like an egregious violation of his purpose in so many ways, and yet true and correct in the only ways he could bring himself to care about.

"It's dangerous for you, isn't it?" Kjieran lifted his gaze to meet Darshan's as he walked at his side. "What you feel for me."

Darshan looked back to the path ahead. "Yes. Very."

They walked with the sun at their backs. Darshan's shadow fell much longer than Kjieran's. They two were as the clouds that cast their shadows upon the land; together, yet separate. But Darshan had meant for them to be one, even as he and his brothers were one in the Void.

"I don't understand how things can feel so right and wrong at the same time."

Darshan cast him a sidelong eye. "Right, wrong...these concepts are foreign to me."

Kjieran gave a forceful exhale. "How can they be foreign to you, my lord? They're the most fundamental concepts of life!"

"For your race, perhaps. But what use would I have for such concepts?"

Kjieran seemed utterly befuddled by this question. "I can't fathom not understanding right and wrong. Even Dore Madden *knows* which is which, I vow—he just doesn't care one way or another." Kjieran looked quickly back to him. "But I think you *would* care, if you understood them."

Darshan arched a brow. "Very well. Enlighten me."

Kjieran seemed startled by his easy willingness. He turned ahead again and swept a hand through his dark hair. "I...hardly know where to begin. *We* begin practically at birth. A child starts learning right and wrong the moment he reaches for his first toy."

"And what makes an action 'right,' Kjieran? Surely there cannot be a single standard the realm wide."

Kjieran frowned. "An action is right if it agrees with what is good or just."

Darshan shook his head. "Right, good, just...one term defines another and that one the next until they circle back to the first. Your language reflects the inevitability of your lives."

Kjieran radiated frustration. "It's just the opposite. These words reflect a striving towards a better future. Something is *just* because it helps a man live longer, live happier. It's *right* to the degree it assists his survival."

"Ah, *there* is another meaningless word." Rounding the fountain, Darshan seated himself on a stone bench and eyed his acolyte quietly. "Tell me, Kjieran, what use has an immortal for this idea of survival? Why would an immortal employ *survival* as a factor in formulating any reasonable decision or action, when *his* survival is never in question?"

Kjieran blinked at him.

"Right and wrong...these terms were developed by a race entirely mistaken in their purpose, deluded by false concepts like *hope* and *happiness* into thinking there is more for them beyond the simplicity of death. An immortal has no need for wrong and right. Survival and its related concepts are not factors that apply to immortals in any possible sense."

Kjieran's expression faltered and then fell. He seemed to deflate a bit. "If immortals aren't concerned with right and wrong, what does concern you, my lord?"

"Only purpose and its achievement."

Looking defeated, Kjieran sank down beside Darshan. "I see your point, my lord." But he was radiating disagreement.

One corner of Darshan's lips twitched with a negating smile. "Do you?"

Kjieran glared off at the fountain.

Darshan crossed one knee and clasped his hands around it. "That your race talks of right and wrong and is so concerned with survival only proves that you're not immortal, that you were never meant to survive—which is why you're so fixated on the condition. Mankind ever seeks what it cannot possess; the polarities of energy call to their equal opposites."

Kjieran turned with sudden defiance. "Does being immortal make you infallible? Is it so impossible you could be wrong—that is, incorrect?"

Darshan held his gaze with an edge darkening his. "*Wrong*...as I was wrong in trusting you, Kjieran?"

Kjieran clenched his jaw and rebelliously held his gaze. "If it speaks to my point, then yes."

A smile hinted on Darshan's lips. He looked his acolyte over approvingly. "You've become bold in death."

Kjieran held his gaze with determination. "Wrong has another definition, my lord. We use it in describing things that are untrue. And these ideas you have of us…no matter what you think…they *are* wrong."

The Prophet Bethamin stood staring at two long lines of postulants who had gathered in the north transept of his temple to receive his assessment. A score of men of varying ages and racial backgrounds were kneeling at his feet with bare chests and their newly shorn heads bowed.

A haze of incense diffused the daylight pouring in through the high windows. The sunbeams illuminated the postulants with a faint nimbus but draped the Ascendants standing behind them in shadows.

The temple shouted with silence. Yet for Darshan, the postulants' thoughts shouted louder still. Some who knelt before the Prophet were common men hoping to Ascend and find a place on his temple staff; most were truthreaders gathered from across the realm and brought to Tambarré to be cleansed of *elae's* corruptive taint.

Darshan stood before them, reading their thoughts, tasting the emotions that drained out of them like blood, staining the air with wavelengths of disharmony. From those hoping to Ascend, he tasted anticipation's crisp edge on a thin note of uncertainty. From the Adepts, the darker tones of horror, grief, fear.

Always he tasted fear in the minds and hearts of men. The emotion was so prevalent he'd thought it as inseparable from their mettle as flesh and breath to corporeality. But Kjieran had told him that Adepts looked upon his Marquiin as monsters. Now he'd begun to wonder if the Adepts he'd come into contact with all radiated fear simply because they feared him.

Both conclusions had their merits; both held their weight when examined, but only one could be true, and he was coming to suspect it was the latter.

What other conclusions had he falsely formed?

Darshan clenched his jaw. The more he entertained Kjieran in his dreams, the more the Adept's ideas had begun influencing his own.

A dangerous association, indeed.

And now…

Darshan stared at the line of truthreaders. If they were mortal, as he'd originally believed, then cleansing them of *elae* and elevating them to unto death was a merciful act and a true forwarding of his purpose.

But if their souls were immortal, as Pelas and Kjieran both claimed…if in observing solely their frail shells he'd missed the existence of the immortal being inhabiting those shells…if Adepts were actually *meant to endure*… then elevating them served no purpose at all.

What disturbed Darshan the most in this contemplation was the tiny, fragile voice that wanted it to be true; because if Adepts Returned, he might have a chance to find Kjieran again.

Yet if it *was* true…why, it called into question everything he knew! It redefined every action he'd ever taken, subverted his merciful cause into malefaction, made his existence in this realm *purposeless*.

Darshan quivered with violent negation of this idea.

His furious denial pulsed through the currents, making the Adepts in front of him cringe. He declared he would purge the thought immediately from his consciousness and attempted to do so…

But the idea lingered like an ill-conceived weed that no amount of strenuous digging could uproot.

"My lord?" One of the Ascendants dared approach him with clasped hands and downcast eyes.

Darshan knew the sun had moved from one side of the temple to the other while he'd been standing there. He didn't need an Ascendant to tell him what the light plainly showed. He narrowed his gaze at the assemblage. "These men are not suitable to become Marquiin."

The fear that had been radiating on the currents became hesitation, uncertainty… hope.

Hope. Ever with mortals comes this delusion of hope.

Yet *hope* too keenly and uncomfortably described the odd sensations he felt when he imagined finding Kjieran in the Returning.

Darshan clenched his jaw. These were treasonous thoughts he could not allow to continue. He returned his attention to the lines of initiates and their attending Ascendants, who were darting nervous glances at one another when they thought he wasn't looking.

"*Cast these men from my temple.*" He made his voice resound with disapproval. His censure rippled the air, flattening the flames in the near braziers into a precarious flickering and sputtering. The Ascendants uniformly cringed.

"*Nonbelievers.*" Darshan's outrage brought dust showering down from the high vaults to sparkle in the streaming sunlight. "They sully my halls."

Relief flooded the currents. The Ascendants gaped at him.

"But…*m-my lord*," one of them was bold enough to stammer, "we scoured the Middle Kingdoms—"

The Prophet silenced him with a glare of such icy reprimand that he and all of the other Ascendants instantly fell and hugged the floor. The lines of postulants were staring at him open-mouthed, too stunned to realize they should be prostrating themselves also.

Darshan rested a hand behind his back and held out the other. "To become Marquiin, an Adept must have *embraced* my faith." He raked his gaze across his prostrate staff. "You bring me captives. My Marquiin must be captains!"

"Forgive us, kind lord!" the Ascendants murmured pathetically.

"I sent you forth to spread my Word, but what do you bring me in return for the power entrusted to you?"

The Ascendants murmured hasty words of supplication.

"Your mandate is to *disseminate*—broader, farther. Let neither borders nor kings stop you from spreading my word. Be industrious in your proselytizing; bring my truth to the masses!"

"Your will be done, Lord above Lords, Fire of All Hearts…" The Ascendants intoned the Prophet's list of titles and continued on with the ritual chant.

Darshan departed.

Halfway back to his chambers, a familiar voice spoke into his mind, *Brother…*

Darshan's gaze tightened. *Shailabanáchtran.* He let the fullness of his displeasure slice across the bond.

I would approach, if you will receive me.

Darshan's skeptical grunt echoed back to him from the empty passageway. Shail might've adopted a propitiative tone, but Darshan didn't for a moment believe him penitent. He told his brother where to meet him.

Shail was waiting for him when he reached a sundrenched terrace, and he wasn't alone.

Darshan emerged from the shadows of an arcade with dark disapproval cloaking his expression. "You're looking inordinately pleased with yourself, Shailabanáchtran. You take a foolish risk coming here if you intend to continue on a path in denial of our purpose."

"Then I suppose that can't be the path I've chosen, can it?"

Darshan's immediate mistrust rippled the currents. He looked over the adolescent girl who was Shail's hostage. "What's this?"

Shail's smile dripped malice and condescension in equal measure. "*This* is Nadia, a prized truthreader to add to your collection—so few of them are females, you know. Call her a conciliatory gift."

Darshan misliked Shail's superior smile. "What would I want with her?"

"I think you'll find her full of intriguing facts about all manner of things, but especially our brother's recent activities." He took Nadia by the shoulders and moved her towards Darshan. "Perhaps after hearing what she has to say, you'll reconsider your anger."

Darshan looked her over doubtfully. "And Pelas?"

Shail summoned a portal. "He won't be bothering us for a *very* long time. As I explained to you, my methods are effective. Well…" he looked Darshan over with a mocking smile, "enjoy your present," and he departed through his portal.

❖

To Nadia, it all felt a blur.

One moment she was anticipating a rather triumphant return to Faroqhar, and the next she was tumbling into unreality—from utter, disorienting darkness, to a frozen wasteland, to the even chillier arms of Shailabanáchtran, and then, bound in *goracrosta* and held again in an interminable, frightening darkness until…

Blinded by the glaring light of mid-afternoon, Nadia blinked through watering eyes at a shadowed form that was approaching down an arcade. Her muddled mind wondered if Shail had taken her to some other realm, for the man coming towards them hardly seemed human. She strained to focus her eyes, strained to focus her thoughts through the *goracrosta's* mind-numbing bite.

He emerged into the light like a god in human form. Taller even than Shail, he wore white pants low across broad hips that yet seemed too narrow to support his shoulders. A wide-sleeved white robe draped his arms but left his muscled chest bare. A gold torque collared his neck, and wavy black hair cascaded down his back.

Even without access to *elae,* Nadia felt power radiating off of him. His gaze as it shifted between Shail and herself was very, very dark.

Shail and the tall man were speaking, but Nadia hardly heard them once she realized who the man was. Then, all too suddenly, Shail was gone and she was left staring up into the smoldering gaze of the Prophet Bethamin.

The Prophet…who made Adepts into monsters, whose Ascendants had taken Tanis and tried to do the same to him. The Prophet…whose doctrine sowed dissention among otherwise harmonious races. The Prophet, also known as Darshan, who'd placed on his brother Pelas a maliciously evil compulsion that had nearly ruined him.

Now he stood staring at *her* with those terrible eyes, so coldly compelling…so *calculating.*

Nadia swallowed.

The Prophet came towards her.

She felt a sudden desperate urge to run, to scream for help, to *rebel* against whatever he meant to do to her, but his gaze pinned her feet to the stones and her breath to her lungs and even forced her thoughts to freeze in whatever shape they'd assumed.

From the look in his eyes as he towered over her—near enough now to feel the chill emitting from his flesh—she felt certain he intended something terrible, but he only hooked a finger beneath the *goracrosta* that bound her wrists, and the rope whispered into ash.

Elae flooded into her.

Nadia inhaled a shuddering gasp. Then she caught her breath, for the full force of *him* descended on her too. His power wrapped around her, penetrated and entwined her as roses overtaking a statue. Stems of his binding will wound through her mind; sharp thorns sank in to mold it to a shape of their choosing.

He turned and started back towards the building. Nadia's body automatically followed.

Time seemed to jump, for the next thing she knew, she was standing in a windowless octagonal chamber framed by a blind arcade. He sank into a low-slung iron chair in the middle of the room and extended his long legs in front of him, his arms on the leather-padded rests, fingers curled around the knobby ends. The room held no other furniture, no adornment beyond the arches carved into the walls, yet it felt almost too full—filled with the force of *him*.

Now he was just staring at her.

If every man in the Empire had been ogling her in stark nakedness, Nadia couldn't have felt more self-conscious than she did standing before the Prophet Bethamin fully clothed. She knew what he did to truthreaders; she knew what he did to men. And if she'd had any question about his intent towards her, the riotous energy bombarding the room dispelled all doubt. She resisted the urge to cringe by shoving her hands behind her back.

'Let nothing and no man shake your composure.' Her mother's instructions echoed in her mind. *'An empress's comportment is as critical to her success as alacritous thought and attention to detail.'*

But Nadia was sure her mother had never faced off against anyone like Darshan.

Worse than the Prophet's calculating gaze was the feeling of his mind sweeping through hers as a wind across an open plaza, leaving no space unexplored, no leaf of thought untouched.

Mostly to distract herself from the frightening sensation, she worked some moisture into her mouth and braved, "Why did you release my bonds?"

She wasn't sure if he would answer, but after a moment he replied in a deep voice, "I don't need magic rope to bind you."

Whereupon she found herself kneeling on the floor with her arms splayed out in front of her and her forehead pressed low against the tiles. The marble was cold beneath her brow, but not nearly so cold as the feeling of his mind controlling hers.

Oh, to become so malleable beneath his will! She didn't even have any awareness of the action until it was done!

Nadia could've found courage in defiance—in even attempting to defy him, in even *imagining* that she might—but he gave her no chance to think about defying him before compliance was achieved.

Nadia choked back a cry. It caught in her throat while she trembled. She pressed her forehead harder against the floor and bound in a sudden fear-spawned grief with a tight swallow. Is this what it had been like for Immanuel—Pelas—beneath his brother's will? How had he ever resisted? The experience was unlike any compulsion she'd ever heard of.

"Stand up, Nadia."

A heartbeat's thoughtful pause, and then she moved shakily to her feet. He hadn't compelled her. Perhaps he knew he'd made his point.

He tapped a finger against the chair. "What is your full name?"

She heard herself say, "Nadia van Gelderan, daughter of Valentina, heir to the Empire of Agasan," and then she caught her breath as if to suck the words back in.

"What is your involvement with Shail?"

"We think he abducted one of our friends..." the words flowed as water across her lips. She could no more stop them than she might've stopped the selfsame fluid once it left her tongue. She didn't even recall having a thought before the information crossed her tongue to be absorbed by his smoldering gaze.

Nadia had never experienced anything so terrifying. Her mother was a stacked truthreader with four Sormitáge rings, and even she hadn't this kind of control. His was a power beyond her comprehension.

When he'd torn the whole story from her like an offending weed ripped out by the roots, the turbulent energy surrounding him settled, and he observed her in silence, his gaze taking every inch of her measure. Nadia felt like *she* was the weed ripped from all things familiar and tossed into the pail of the inexplicable.

'An enemy is only an enemy while your purposes are misaligned.' Her mother's words became a bastion for her composure.

'In negotiation, trust is a better commodity than pride.' Her father's advice helped her claim a foothold from which to view her position.

'Whatever happens, I will find you.' Immanuel's words. If she trusted him, she had to keep faith with his promise, too.

The Prophet tapped a finger on the end of his chair arm while his gaze roamed across her, making her feel no better than a slave standing disrobed on the block at auction. She could read nothing of his thoughts—even with full access to *elae*. And as for trying her talent on him in return? Well…there was courage, and there was stupidity.

"Tell me what you know about Pelas."

Once again, the words flowed—everything she knew of Immanuel came pouring out. In the last, she finished, "…he promised Tanis he would protect him and said he would choose his own brother this time. They worked the Unbreakable Bond."

His eyes grew darker than the void of a starless night. *"My brother bound himself to a mortal boy?"*

The cold fury in these words brought a dreadful edge to the currents, so that each wave crossing her felt razor sharp. Nadia hugged her arms around her chest, but bone and flesh offered ill protection against his reverberating anger.

"Tanis isn't…mortal," she forced out—*so* discomfiting to have him rip things so effortlessly off her tongue, but when she wanted to craft her own words, the muscle became as unmalleable as hardened clay, "not if he works the Pattern of Life. And even were death to separate them, now that they've worked the Unbreakable Bond, they would find each other again in the Returning. It is proven so."

"*Proven.*" His tone held a leading edge, demanding explanation.

At least he hadn't compelled her answer that time. "There are hundreds of works in the Sormitáge Archives on the Returning: personal accounts, memoirs, biographies and case studies specifically on the Unbreakable Bond. A special order of *Sobra* Scholars has spent centuries researching and documenting the subject."

"*Sobra* Scholars…" his finger tapped, tapped…as if in time to his thoughts, "those who study the work you Adepts prize so highly, this *Sobra I'ternin?*"

"Yes." She swallowed. "It…speaks of you, actually."

His head tilted almost imperceptibly to his right. "Of *me*."

"Of all of the Malorin'athgul."

His probing power swirled around and through her mind upon this utterance, tasting, testing…as a tongue exploring a new flavor. Nadia fought the urge to cringe.

"Speak to me of this."

"A young Nodefinder named Malin van Drexel found your names in the *Qhorith'quitara*—these are apocryphal works kept in the Sormitáge Archives. We think that's why N'abranaacht—I mean, Shail—took him. *If* he took him." She dropped her gaze. "We still don't know what happened to Malin."

His finger tapped a cadence while his eyes considered her with a piercing scrutiny.

She swallowed and pressed on. "My mother said the *Sobra* speaks more of you. She didn't divulge much to me, only that Malorin'athgul are the balance to creation, that you're crafted of both fabrics—*elae* and *deyjiin*—and…" Nadia lifted her gaze back to his, "and that you shouldn't be in our world at all."

That finger lifted to point at her. "Echoes of Pelas's words."

Her gaze followed the line of his finger back along a muscled arm up to his very dark eyes. It was somehow worse that his features were so striking and yet his manner so chillingly indifferent.

"Imman—I mean, Pelas," Nadia's heart was fluttering, "he never spoke to me about your purpose here. I only know what my mother told me from the *Sobra I'ternin*."

His finger resumed its tapping, his gaze its dark assessment of her. "How exactly have your scholars 'researched and documented' the Returning?"

It occurred to her to wonder *why* he was no longer compelling her answers, but whatever his reasons, Nadia was grateful for the chance to think her own thoughts and frame her own sentences. So she answered him as readily and honestly as she could.

"They…have followed certain Adepts through the centuries. Many Adepts don't recall their past lives, but those who have worked the Pattern of Life and then…somehow…lost their life, these often can recall them. It's the binding aspect of the Pattern—it holds open the doors of memory."

Nadia was becoming more sure of herself the longer he let her speak. "Over the centuries, Sormitáge scholars have searched for and studied those Adepts. Truthreaders worked with them to recall their previous lives, while the researchers tried to discover things only those Adepts who died could've known, so as to test the veracity of their recollections."

She hooked a strand of dark hair behind her ear. "The laymen and the masses who believe in the Returning must take much on faith, but those Adepts who have studied discover there is little faith involved. The truths have been proven time and again."

Upon this utterance, the Prophet retreated to his thoughts.

To Nadia, the slight lessening of his attention felt as perceptible as a cloud's shading of the sun. She had no idea how well he'd accepted the information she'd given him or why the subject had intrigued him to begin with.

She pushed another strand of hair from her face and tried to collect herself, to straighten her shoulders and keep her hands from shaking. A moment of boldness struck her and she ventured, "Your brother Shail..." but then she stopped herself.

His finger paused its tapping, hovered, and then started again. "What of him?"

Nadia took a deep breath to fuel her courage. "He knows the *Sobra*. He's been studying it for centuries—he admitted this to us. He said..." Again, she caught her tongue. Oh, if only she could read him better!

The Prophet arched a brow. "Continue, Nadia."

Nadia chewed on her lip, regarding him uncertainly. "Shail...spoke of you when he was holding us in Shadow." She searched his gaze at this, hoping to catch some hint as to how he was receiving her words. "He said that you spent all of your time dwelling in religious fantasy and..." despite herself, she had to drop her eyes to confess, "lecturing about purpose."

"Those are unlikely to be the words he used."

Did he sound faintly amused? By the Lady, he was so hard to read!

"Not exactly...no. But then he said that *he* had been studying and learning for centuries, piecing together Alorin's history so that he could rule it and all of the Realms of Light."

Not merely tapping now, his fingers curled, riffled and resettled on the padded arm of his chair.

Nadia watched him watching her and tried not to worry where his thoughts might be taking him, or where he might be later taking her. The only remotely heartening point was in recognizing that while he'd compelled her answers at first, he'd been surprisingly sedate in his treatment of her since...restrained even.

Her courage waxed as panic waned. "Do you enjoy our fear?"

His head tilted almost imperceptibly to the left. "It is merely the emotion I most often receive from your race."

"Perhaps if you didn't compel us against our will, we wouldn't be so terrified of you."

"A specious theory. Fear is innate to your kind."

"So is boldness."

"Especially with you, it would appear."

She dropped her gaze to her hands and tried to think of some other entry into conversation. He instantly blunted her every advance.

"This unbreakable binding my brother worked with this truthreader..."

Nadia lifted her gaze back to him.

His fingers riffled. "Tell me about it."

She took a deep breath to calm her racing heart. "There are many types of fourth-strand bindings." She suspected the Prophet himself knew most of them. "But the Unbreakable Bond is woven of all of the strands of *elae*. It is most often forged through blood and involves the weaving together of both Adepts' life patterns. They become intimately and inextricably joined."

Nadia glanced down at her hands and then back to him. He gave her no indication of how he'd received this truth. But talking was more comfortable than the deathly silence of his gaze.

"Most fourth-strand bindings are patterned so that they can be broken, but not the Unbreakable Bond. *Elae*'s fifth strand is woven throughout the other strands of the pattern—through the very life patterns of the persons involved. In the case of Tanis and your brother…" she searched his expression, but it remained as stone, "in Pelas's case, because he's natively of the fifth strand, he merely had to will that the binding would endure," thus had Tanis described the experience to her, "and thereby bound them with the fifth, making the bond unbreakable."

The Prophet's fingers riffled as flickering thoughts to be inspected, evaluated and discarded. Abruptly he stood and strode out of the room.

Nadia was standing there wondering if she should follow him when a wall sizzled into being across the archway leading into the chamber. The energy glowed with a cold light unlike *elae* and yet also unlike what she'd witnessed of *deyjiin*. Nadia gazed after him with fear and uncertainty vying for purchase on her features.

The Prophet never looked back.

EIGHTEEN

"*The simplest way to control a man is to lie to him.*"
– Shailabanáchtran, Maker of Storms

PELAS LINGERED IN the interminable dark. Hovering forms blanketed his vision; lassitude, his vigor. Every breath required an effort of will. A hundred revenants were piled atop him in a seething mass, every one of them leeching power from his form. He had become a dying star.

Caught in the timelessness of Shadow, Pelas yet remained aware of every grain of sand falling in Nadia's hourglass, of the minute hand of destiny spinning apace with planetary rotation, time turning in inexorable synchronicity with the ever-weaving pattern. He'd promised Tanis to protect the princess. He couldn't fail in that promise, but escape seemed far beyond his reach.

In the beginning, he'd felt the pain of the revenants' touch. Now all he knew was a numb immobility…and darkness. What light might've once graced that icy place had vanished as a lamp extinguished—as his brother would have his life extinguished—and now the only light came through his memories of Tanis and the faint connection that bound them still.

While the revenants fed, consciousness waned. When they abated, momentarily satisfied, it waxed. It was waxing then.

As Pelas regained awareness of his own mind, he began to fear how long he'd been lost that time. He felt an agonizing need to free himself—less for his own welfare than for Nadia and Tanis's, though to be certain, he didn't relish an eternity trapped in this, his younger brother's well-devised hell.

The writhing conglomerate of bodies atop him shifted. The farthest golems began scrabbling down through the stacks of their brethren to take their turn at the trough of his lifeforce. Pelas wasted a few precious minutes of lucidity cursing his brother. Then he set his intention again towards finding a way out of there.

Minutes passed—or hours…days? It was impossible to say in a place that held no time. For all he knew, the entire game had played out back in Alorin and Nadia had already been lost, poor sacrifice to Shail's enmity.

No.

He wouldn't allow harm to come to Nadia—or to Tanis.

How then to depart this plane?

Bodies squirmed atop him, and the sludge of half-dead things assumed a new grotesque shape. Nameless pressures clung to him; revenant mouths reeking with want affixed themselves to every inch of his form, their minds radiating a gluttonous hunger. Even the tip of one black toe could leech its bit of life from his veins. They only needed an ounce of fleshly contact to suck him dry.

Eternity would pass before they were sated. Without a bond to the Warlock who'd created them, they became as sieves. For a time the energy of life would fill their forms, but it would only drain slowly out again, dissipating into the void, becoming nothingness, wasted.

And you're wasting precious time…

That was the trouble with being drained by revenants. Concentration fled from the horror of it.

Pelas felt new teeth biting into his ear. New lips, fingers or even toes affixing to the back of his neck, his ankle, his stomach, his thigh…pressing or sucking his flesh taut. Everywhere his body knew such pressures. A tingling pain began anew, carrying him upon a rising wave of pain towards unconsciousness's dark shores.

Helpless against the rushing tide, Pelas tumbled within it back into oblivion.

Nineteen

"Illusion becomes reality when collective agreement is achieved on the illusion and when enough agree that the illusion should persist."
 —*Sobra I'ternin*, Section VII.II The Laws & Esoterics
of Patterning, Twenty-Second Esoteric

TANIS ROUSED INTO darkness, then to kaleidoscopic light. Everything around him seemed to spin, combine, and explode again. Pinpoint stars trailed colorful tails as they swirled. He felt disoriented. With no horizon to determine up or down, he couldn't tell if he was falling, spinning or simply lying still while everything else spun.

Instinctively he pushed outwards with his mind, hoping to strike something solid he could hold onto, an anchor by which he might orient himself. As his awareness expanded outward in its search, he sensed…not exactly the *edges* of space; rather a perception of dimension, a framework, and then of things filling the space within that frame.

In the way one seeks to focus through a fog, Tanis tried focusing his mind on the vague forms he was perceiving, to force them to take some shape. Eventually, the spinning light slowed…and *became*—

Tanis clenched his teeth and tried to hold the impressions still in his mind, but it felt like trying to hold in the light of an exploding star—

Suddenly the forms dispersed into crazy spirals again.

Tanis tried once more to force the world to become still. He tried again to perceive the dimension of space and then to sense the things filling that space.

Again the swirling lights began to slow…

After a lengthy span of time, they congealed into wavering shapes. At one point it seemed as if his concept might actually hold and become solid, but

Tanis was pushing against an oddly pliant resistance. It accepted the pressure of his will, but the instant he relented, it sprang back again into the shape it wanted to assume.

Finally exhausted by the effort, Tanis surrendered to the disorientation. He closed his eyes, expecting that sense of vertigo to return...but rather than perceiving the swirling lights beyond his closed lids, he sensed instead a solid band of light that felt bright, almost like...*daylight?* A comforting pressure resolved beneath his back.

Tanis hastily opened his eyes and sat up.

The daybed he was lying on was positioned against one wall of an arcade. Beyond the arcade's carved columns and groin-vaulted ceiling spread a sunlit garden teeming with flora. The arcade adjoined another arm and continued on to form a courtyard enclosure. The surroundings were palatial.

Sitting up more fully to better look around, Tanis saw a woman standing several steps away, staring open-mouthed at him.

Tanis pushed palms to his eyes, took a deep breath and opened his eyes again, but the woman was still gaping at him.

Tanis swung his feet to the chequered marble floor and looked over at her. She was tall and willowy and wore a foreign-looking gown of aqua silk wrapped many times about her form. Her long auburn hair trailed in a braid across one shoulder. Tanis braved an uncertain smile. "Um...hello."

She clapped a hand across her mouth, and her eyes filled with tears.

He had no idea why she was upset, or for that matter, what was happening—what *had happened*—where he was, who she was...

She blinked dual tears and turned away.

Tanis stood and took a tentative step closer. "Have I done something to upset you?"

She was silent for so long, he began to wonder if she'd heard him or if she didn't speak his language. But she finally dabbed the tears from her cheeks with the back of her hands and whispered, "I...thought you'd escaped."

And just like that, Tanis knew her. It was less in her features and coloring than the way her words felt in his mind. "You're the Avieth." He did not say *Sinárr's Avieth*, though it's how he thought of her in that moment.

She turned him a barren look. "I knew he would want you." She dabbed at her face again. "When I saw you in the laboratory...*elae* had all but left me, yet you still glowed."

Tanis remembered their conversation and how ravaged he'd felt upon first realizing she was an Avieth, tethered and bound. Gratitude for her help that day softened his expression. "You warned me to flee."

Her bottom lip trembled and she dropped her gaze.

Tanis took another step closer. "I'm Tanis."

"Mérethe," she whispered. There was something fragile about her, like a tiny bird struggling with a broken wing.

"Where are we, Mérethe?"

She lifted a startled gaze to him. "You mean you don't know? But I thought…"

He angled a curious look at her. "You thought?"

"It doesn't matter what I thought." The sunlight fell across her features, illuminating the hint of freckles on her nose and cheeks. Her heart-shaped face held an elfin quality, but sorrow cast a veil across her beauty. Mérethe clutched at her upper arms, binding herself. "We're in *his* world now."

"Sinárr's?"

She nodded.

"In Shadow?"

She nodded again.

Tanis gazed around, feeling unnerved. "If we're in Shadow…why does it look so much like Alorin?"

Mérethe drew in a shuddering breath. "Shadow has no form except what the Warlocks give to it."

He turned to her curiously. "So he fashions a world that appears exactly like our own—why?"

She shrugged.

Tanis scratched at his head. He sensed an important truth in this information, but the connection eluded him.

He walked to the nearest column and laid his hand on the sculpted marble. It felt smooth, cold and immobile beneath his palm. "Is this place real?" He glanced over his shoulder to where Mérethe stood hugging her chest. "It feels real."

She met his gaze brokenly. "It's as solid as Sinárr wills it to be."

Tanis considered this. Then he wondered…. "Does he will it to be otherwise?"

She bowed her head and swallowed. "Sometimes."

Pondering this, Tanis studied the marble beneath his hand once more. Even the veins of the stone were true to his expectations. "So Sinárr's world doesn't always appear like this?" He cast her a look. "What does it seem like other times?"

Mérethe buried her face in her hands.

It took a moment for Tanis to realize she was shaking with silent tears. Not knowing what else to do, he went and laid his hands lightly on her arms. When she didn't shy away, he enfolded her gently, half expecting her to stiffen, but she clutched desperately at him instead and buried her face in his shoulder.

Tanis held her while she wept, his brow furrowed and anger fomenting in his thoughts. He could only imagine what life had been like for her, trapped and bound to a Warlock, prisoner to his caprice.

After a time, Mérethe attempted to compose herself. "I'm sorry." She dabbed at her cheeks with her palms. "It's been so long since I had anyone to talk to." She wandered over and sank down on the daybed. Tanis sat down beside her.

Mérethe glanced at him. Wet lashes framed deep-set eyes of pale blue. Her ginger brows were the same hue as her freckles. "Your question…" She nodded towards the garden. "Sinárr's world has never looked like this. *This* is…I mean, I thought…" her brow furrowed.

There it was again, that confession half-uttered. He leaned to try to capture her gaze. "What did you think, Mérethe?"

She exhaled a slow breath. "Watching things just before you appeared…" A rueful glance flickered to him and away. "I thought *you* did this."

Tanis drew back. "What do you mean, 'before I appeared'?"

Her bottom lip began trembling. She bowed her head and made knots of her fingers in her lap.

Tanis had a sudden terrible foreboding. "Were you…he *didn't*…" The idea seemed so unimaginably horrible that he almost couldn't speak it. "Mérethe… does he keep you in the formless dark?"

She pressed palms to her eyes and drew in a shuddering breath. "He rarely thinks of me anymore…rarely cares to make things solid for me. I've become uninteresting to him."

Tanis thought of the disorienting void he'd experienced for just a short time and felt sick at the very contemplation. Never mind the lack of human contact, to have no contact even with anything *real*? How long could a person exist in that state without going insane?

His heart went out to her so strongly—if it had been in his power to slay Sinárr and free her in that instant, he would've done it without a second thought.

"I would like to think I've become used to it," she clasped her hands in her lap forlornly, "but Alorin's Adepts weren't made for the dark. I know it has changed me." She must've seen the concern in his eyes, for she gave a little smile. "It wasn't always this way. While my contact with *elae* lasted, he was kind and even generous…of a fashion."

Tanis knew only outrage on her behalf. "How can you say that? He *fed* off of you—"

She spun him a desperate look. "Tanis, don't you see? This is *your* fate now. If I only tell you all the horrible parts—"

Tanis placed a hand over hers. "Mérethe, I'm a truthreader. You can't fool me, not even here…" Then he frowned, for it occurred to him that *elae* had to exist in Shadow somehow, for otherwise how were they both alive?

And if *elae* existed…

He tried listening for Mérethe's thoughts, but heard only the wind in the garden; he tried looking for leis or nodes but saw only the illusion Sinárr had made solid. He tried working a pattern of his father's to reveal the currents, but he could gain no sense of *elae* with which to fill the pattern and form his intent.

But it has to be—the lifeforce must exist here somehow.

If it did, Tanis couldn't sense it. Nor could he sense Pelas, though he had the barest perception that their bond still existed—likewise that connection with his mother—yet trying to cast his thoughts outward to reach Isabel only made his attention wander aimlessly off.

Tanis was frowning over all of these facts when he heard someone approaching from further down the arcade. He and Mérethe both stood at the same time. A page was coming towards them carrying a stack of folded clothes and a pair of shoes.

"Sinárr is trying to impress you." Mérethe dropped her gaze to her fingers, which she alternately entwined and squeezed. "It's been a long time since he bothered with servants."

Tanis gave her a curious look.

She arched a brow, challenging his understanding. "To craft personages whole-cloth, ingrained with the understanding of what food to choose and how to prepare it and serve it? Or to send them here bearing…gifts." She regarded the young page with a sort of vague horror. "It's much simpler for Sinárr to just make the food appear on the table—or the clothes appear on you."

The servant stopped in front of Tanis and bowed with a murmured, "My lord." He bent to one knee and held the items over his head.

Tanis frowned at them.

"Sinárr wants you to believe all of this is real." Mérethe was watching the kneeling servant, looking haunted now. "He's…courting you, I think. The way he once courted me."

The idea made Tanis distinctly uncomfortable. Likewise the page kneeling before him, awkwardly holding up the clothes and shoes. Tanis took them just so the boy would get up again.

Which he did. Then he bowed with another "My lord," and departed back the way he'd come.

Tanis watched him go, trying to find any chink in the illusion, but the boy didn't blur at the edges or fade in strange places, his clothes had wrinkles where they ought to, his hair wanted a trim, which seemed somehow appropriate, and he even walked like a boy would, hitching up his slightly-too-loose-in-the-hips britches as he went.

Tanis looked to Mérethe. "Sinárr's illusions are very convincing."

She sighed.

Tanis assessed the clothes in his hands then. They were made of a sumptuous silk and beautifully constructed, but he felt apprehensive about wearing them. He hadn't minded when Pelas had commissioned coats for him, but the idea of being dressed by Sinárr roused all the hair on the back of his neck.

Mérethe nodded towards the other end of the arcade. "I should let you change. He'll be waiting."

Tanis followed her gaze and saw a set of double doors where only empty wall had been before. He reluctantly started off in that direction, but after taking just a few steps he looked back to her. "If he's weaving this illusion just for me…when we separate, what happens to you?"

"That depends on how solid he wants all of it to remain." She sat down on the daybed again and lifted a hollow gaze to the groin-vaulted ceiling and its frescoed arabesques. "Are you sure this isn't your doing? I've never seen him make anything so elaborate."

Tanis looked at the ceiling. She'd called it elaborate, but he'd seen hundreds like it at the Sormitáge. "If I made it, Mérethe, I have no idea how." He frowned, concerned for her. "Will you be all right?"

"I'll just sit here for a time, Tanis."

Until such time as Sinárr remembers your existence?

The very thought made him clench his teeth, but he nodded to her and made his way to prepare to greet Sinárr.

Tanis stood for a while in his rooms debating whether or not to put on the clothes just to see what Sinárr would do about it, but considering that he was living just then at the whim of an immortal who could very likely snuff his life as easily as pinching out the flame on a candle, prudence suggested a more diplomatic approach.

He'd just finished dressing when another set of double doors appeared on the other side of the room, an obvious request for his attendance. Tanis pushed a hand through his hair and stared at the doors. He rubbed his nose and stared at the doors. He wiped something from his eye and stared at the doors. Then he blew out his breath, stalked across the room and opened them.

Across a loggia, the grand edifice of a white bridge gleamed alluringly, framing a view of…

Well, it might've been one of the most beautiful vistas he'd ever seen.

A marble bridge wound through a forested ravine, passing among steep mountainsides and sheer cliffs. A cold-looking waterfall tumbled down a granite-faced chute and sent mist drifting across the balustrade.

Tanis tried to recall if he'd ever seen such a marvelous place before, even in a painting—he couldn't quite dismiss Mérethe's idea that he'd somehow influenced Sinárr's creation while trying to escape the disorienting void—but the design of the bridge seemed as foreign to him as the mountainous landscape. Never mind that the bridge appeared to simply be floating among the trees.

With apprehension gripping him like a too-tight vest, Tanis started off down the bridge. The mountains soon reared so steeply above him that their tops were lost to his view.

It was so odd, this experience: on the one hand being fascinated by his surroundings and the other wondering how any of it existed at all. He tried not to think too deeply on the truth—that he was lost in Shadow, the captive of an immortal Warlock who wanted to bind him for eternity.

Tanis wondered why he wasn't more afraid. He wondered why he wasn't trying *everything* in his power to escape…

Even as he had the thought, a familiar mental barrier resisted the idea; even thinking it felt like trying to swim a raging river upstream. Tanis knew that feeling well—verily, he despised it at times. But its meaning was clear.

*So…*finding a way out of Shadow wasn't the direction his path was leading him. Then where in Tiern'aval *was* it leading him?

He trailed his fingers across the marble railing as he walked, feeling the smooth stone, noting its temperature, the way it became cool or warm as a result of the sunlight. How could Sinárr capture so many sensations and details? How could an individual mind form an illusion so incredibly complex?

And why didn't it frighten him more, knowing he was hostage to that mind?

In truth, Tanis was more worried about Mérethe's fate than his own. He wondered if perhaps his unusual equanimity had something to do with the perception of immortality he'd gained from binding himself with Pelas. To Pelas, eternity was almost *palpable*. The awarenesses Tanis had gained through sharing Pelas's mind had changed him in ways he never could've anticipated. He wasn't the same person he'd been even a week ago.

Tanis saw the end of the ravine looming ahead, a great V-shaped opening where verdant cliffs juxtaposed against the azure sky. The bridge, like the mountains, appeared to end there.

He emerged from the mouth of the mountain's shadow onto a wide, arching balcony. Beyond its marble railing, an emerald carpet of trees abutted a sea. On the far horizon, a curtain of rainbow mist—shifting veils of color—dominated the vista. High above, variegated clouds blended into a nebula of violet-rose gasses that merged into the void of starry space. It truly appeared as if Tanis was standing on the edge of the world.

"It *is* amazing, what you've done."

Sinárr's voice came close in his ear, even as his black-skinned hands found Tanis's shoulders from behind. He felt the man's cold touch radiating through the silk of his coat.

Tanis realized he wasn't merely standing on the threshold of the world, but on the precipice of life as he'd known it. The balcony seemed to tip precariously, leaving him balanced on its lengthwise edge. One wrong step and he would tumble into the abyss.

Sinárr possessed a powerful presence behind him, radiating not merely *deyjiin*'s telltale chill but a steady flow of some other kind of power. And yet... was he really standing there at all?

Tanis tried to work some moisture back into his mouth. "What do you mean...what *I've* done?"

Sinárr murmured into his ear, "I felt your effort to merge minds with me as I wove this world into form."

In his own realm, the Warlock's voice held a darkly liquid quality. Each word seemed to flow into Tanis's mind and stimulate his perception in a new way, waking awarenesses that felt strange and startling. Tanis wanted to move away, but Sinárr had him pinned.

"I accepted those parts of your creation that seemed to fit with my design. Ah, Tanis-mine, I knew the moment I saw you that our opposing natures would call to one another, but I had no idea you would find your place next to me so instinctively."

Tanis tried to quell the riotous feeling in his stomach, which was less a response to Sinárr than a battle against that unbalanced feeling of almost falling. "I didn't know what I was doing."

"Precisely my point—it came as naturally to you as it does for me. We were made for one another, Tanis."

Tanis was wondering how long he was going to be able to just stand there without falling off the edge of all things sane and reasonable when Sinárr gave a desirous growl and released him. "Ah! But this should not be so quickly over."

What shouldn't be over so quickly?

The Warlock walked towards the railing, a tall form, striking of feature, and oddly...solid. In fact, he appeared surprisingly solid in the world of his own creation. He wore the same black pants and velvet coat as had graced his form in Alorin, but now he'd gathered his long ebony hair into a thick ponytail bound with silver. Tanis didn't for a minute believe this was Sinárr's true form. He wondered, in fact, if Sinárr had any humanlike form at all.

The Warlock spread his hands along the railing and leaned slightly forward out over the world he'd crafted from the aether of Shadow.

Or at least the illusion of a world. Tanis had to keep reminding himself of that.

Sinárr's golden eyes lifted to the unearthly demarcation where the clouds dissolved into rose and violet gasses, with the star-studded backdrop of space opening a depthless void behind. He assessed this point for a long time. Then he smiled, revealing very white teeth, and turned to Tanis with unexpected fervor—

Suddenly he stood directly in front of Tanis.

The lad drew back with an intake of breath.

Sinárr looked him over fervently. For all his smile held a certain aesthetic charm, it was not unlike the predatory grace of a panther or a coiling asp. Its inherent deadliness bled all of the beauty out of it.

"*Ahh*, Tanis…" Sinárr seemed oddly reluctant—to or from what, Tanis couldn't say, but there was a restrained quality to his manner. "Just the *sensation* of you…" he touched Tanis's cheek with his thumb and closed his eyes.

Tanis felt the unmistakable sensation of *deyjiin* flooding into him and clenched his jaw, steeling himself to endure whatever would follow…yet what followed was an opening through which he sensed Pelas across their binding.

Tanis pulled Sinárr's hand down to his heart, hoping the firmer contact with the Warlock might help him sense Pelas more clearly. He pressed both of his hands over the Warlock's own, binding it close.

Sinárr regarded him with startled curiosity, but Tanis cared only that the flow of *deyjiin* had restored his connection to Pelas.

Pelas!

Pelas's mental reply came on a flood of hope. *Tanis!* The lad sensed his bond-brother reaching for him—

Sinárr snatched his hand away.

Pelas vanished from Tanis's mind.

Disappointment stabbed the lad. His bond-brother had felt *so* close, as if their fingers were only inches from touching, inches from reuniting. He lifted his eyes to the Warlock and found him staring at him, which made the moment worse somehow.

Sinárr looked him over again speculatively.

Tanis was fairly sure that nothing good could come from Sinárr's speculation.

"My…but you are a delicious torment. But come, our meal is served." The Warlock extended a hand to indicate a table at the far end of the balcony, where servants were just then unveiling domed platters and pouring wine into crystal goblets.

None of them had been there two seconds ago.

'...*He wants you to believe all of this is real...*'

Tanis pressed palms to his eyes. Sinárr's illusion seemed *utterly* real. It was not unlike the experience of seeing his mother appear in his bedroom at the Villa Serafina, or joining his mother in Dreamscape, and yet *this* experience was so wholly unlike those others that it felt entirely surreal at the same time.

"Tanis, will you have some wine?"

Tanis dropped his hands to discover that he was sitting at the table with Sinárr, who was extending a crystal goblet towards him.

Of everything he'd experienced thus far, this was the most jarring. Tanis resisted the urge to grab the seat of his chair and spin a look around, just to be sure they hadn't also moved into a different realm in the blink of an eye.

With effort, he met the Warlock's gaze—which in that moment seemed infuriatingly benign—and forced a swallow. Then he took the wine. For a moment, he studied the sanguineous liquid that filled the glass. He doubted imbibing an illusion would calm his nerves overmuch, but he drank it nonetheless. It certainly tasted like wine—*really good* wine.

It was terribly confusing.

Tanis lowered the goblet and gazed again at the dark fluid. "Mérethe says none of this is real." He lifted his eyes to Sinárr.

The Warlock sat back in his chair, the wings of which extended above his head. He seemed amused. "What is reality? You tell me, Tanis, Adept child of Alorin."

Tanis was opening his mouth to respond when he realized he'd never actually tried to define the word before. He'd been about to say it was something that could be touched, tasted or sensed, yet by that definition, everything in Sinárr's world would qualify.

The Warlock smiled. "I'll tell you what reality is, Tanis. It is what you and I agree that it is."

Tanis frowned at him. "I didn't agree to any of this."

Sinárr's golden eyes sparkled. "Did you not?"

Tanis thought of those early moments of disorientation when he'd tried to impose some shape upon his perceptions. He didn't at all like the conclusion he came to.

Sinárr chuckled as if hearing his thought. "When you are bound to me, we will create worlds together. Then reality will be what we two share."

Tanis's eyes flew back to his. "You..." he barely found the breath for words, "you want me to *create worlds* with you?"

Sinárr's eyes glinted like sunlight shining through a golden glass. "With such lifeforce as you possess, Tanis—imagine what we could create together."

Tanis felt a desperate protest welling. He pushed his goblet away from him, wishing he was pushing himself away from Sinárr. "What if I don't *want* to be bound to you?" He stared at the tabletop, searching frantically for a coherent thought. His suddenly pounding heart seemed to have chased lucidity away. "If I don't want…*that*…we would find no agreement. We could have no mutual creation."

Sinárr sipped his wine and eyed Tanis hungrily over the rim. "You will be bound to me. My will shall be yours also."

Tanis forced himself to hold the Warlock's gaze. Then he forced himself to take a deep breath and let it out slowly, and thought logically. "If you bind my will to yours, Sinárr, anything made together will only be your creation."

Sinárr frowned at this.

Tanis retrieved his wine and drank all of it in several large gulps. It did unfortunately little to lessen the hollow feeling in his chest. He felt a bit like a condemned man arguing with the headsman, just delaying the inevitable.

Once more he tried imagining a different end than staying with Sinárr—taking Mérethe and fleeing together, Epiphany knew how, or overpowering the Warlock and using some means he hadn't yet discovered to contact Pelas—but these contemplations left him feeling unbalanced. Still, he couldn't believe he was fated to become a Warlock's pet Adept. That *could not* be his path.

Sinárr motioned to the meal. "Why not eat something? I'm given to understand that mortal bodies need sustenance."

Tanis wondered but dared not ask what sustenance the Warlock lived on. He turned his attention to the platters of food: fowl and hare, even a stuffed young pig. Tanis frowned at it, struck by a thought.

"Is it not to your liking?" Sinárr inquired solicitously. "You would prefer some other dish? I was under the impression—"

"The food is—there's nothing wrong with the food." Tanis sank back in his chair with a powerful exhale. "It's…I was just thinking…if *I* had the power to create worlds—universes even—any way I liked…"

The Warlock eyed him speculatively. "Yes?"

Tanis ran a hand along the chair arm. "I don't think I would construct my world in such a way that for any living thing to gain energy, some other living thing had to die."

Sinárr arched brows in surprise. Then he relaxed into another one of those dangerous smiles. "You cannot see how aligned we are already, Tanis-mine. When we are of one mind, you shall weave *elae* into Alorin's native patterns, and I shall weave their *inverteré* opposite, and the two patterns binding together shall form four dimensions—a world that will be *real*, as you say, to anyone." He leaned towards the lad and added with a passionate fervor in his golden gaze, "I *want* this, Tanis."

Tanis pushed a palm to one eye. The prospect of being bound to Sinárr made his stomach feel like worms were writhing in it. He decided to change the subject. "Why do you make your world look so much like Alorin when you could create it any way you want?"

Sinárr settled one hand behind his head and leaned sideways in his chair. "I like your world. I've missed roaming freely there."

"Warlocks haven't walked our realm since the Before, thousands of years ago."

Sinárr arched a brow. "Has it been that long? Your time and mine are not coincident." He gave a contemplative smile. "I well recall the days before your Alorin joined Illume Belliel's Council of Realms. We Warlocks enjoyed many freedoms." Sinárr leaned forward to take up his wine again. "Warlocks cannot tear the binding fabric between Shadow and the Realms of Light, else we would've long returned there to treat with *elae*'s children."

You mean to enslave them?

Tanis rubbed uncomfortably at one eye. The outline of a picture was starting to form, but its shape remained a dim impression, the faintest tracing on a sun-bleached canvas. "I don't understand. If you *like* our world..." it seemed improbable, though Sinárr surely had no reason to lie to him, "why are you allied with Shail against us? He wants to destroy Alorin."

Sinárr arched a brow amusedly and sipped his wine. "Does he?"

Tanis spied him narrowly. "You know that he does."

Sinárr chuckled. "Have you still not realized the truth, not even with all your many gifts?" He leaned forward and pinned the lad with a look as unsettling as it was compelling. "Shailabanáchtran works illusions as readily as any Warlock. Nothing with him is as it seems."

"But he's planning some sort of rebellion with the Danes. He kidnapped hundreds of Adepts for them."

"Are you certain about that?"

Tanis gave him a hard look. "I'm certain he kidnapped hundreds of Adepts. I was there. I saw them."

Sinárr smirked. "Shailabanáchtran doesn't give a whit about the Danes or their war with the Empire."

"But then why did he take all of those Adepts if not for the Danes' rebellion?"

Sitting back again, Sinárr arched a brow and smiled into his wine. "Whyever indeed?"

TWENTY

*"Let the birth of each new day be your own rebirth; grow,
learn, love, admire. Revel in possibility."*

–From the writings of Epiphany's Prophet

GYDRYN VAL LORIAN, King of Dannym, stood on a balcony, gazing across a great walled city filled with glittering domes. The circle of civilization spread as a lake amid the russet land, buildings too bright beneath the brilliant blue sky, sparkling diamonds in a landscape bleached of color by the relentless M'Nador sun.

Little had Gydryn known, as he'd lain shedding his life's blood into the searing sands, that the Nadori sun had been bleaching him, too. Those scalding rays had burned away the lies that had darkened his soul for a decade, cleansing him of false hatreds. Now, like the colorful mosaic walls of his rooms, Gydryn's spirit shone once more with glorious hues.

In the orchard that spread beyond his rooms, white-turbaned men capered among the high palms, their fronds the only green to be seen for miles.

Raku.

How indescribably odd to be standing in the very oasis city his generals had spoken so fervently about needing to reclaim. *Odd?* No...the word did not even begin to describe the bizarre turn his life had taken.

From the moment Spymaster Morin d'Hain's letter had reached Gydryn aboard the *Sea Eagle* with news of Radov's alliance with the Duke of Morwyk and the Prophet Bethamin, events had begun tumbling down an increasingly implausible slope—from a vicious rumor that his middle son still lived, to Viernan hal'Jaitar's attempted assassination of him, to Kjieran van Stone's fiery sacrifice—until he'd suddenly awoken as the honored guest of a man he'd long blamed for the death of his sons...an enemy who appeared to be no enemy at all.

He hadn't been long awake after recovering from weeks of feverish sleep when the Akkadian Prime Minister Rajiid bin Yemen al Basreh had come to see him.

Rajiid bin Yemen al Basreh...who wore a turban of dignity above his cloak of reserve. He was Morin d'Hain's counterpart in the world of espionage, and every bit as formidable in his craft as Gydryn's Spymaster. In all of the king's speculations about who might've gone to such lengths to save his life, al Basreh's was one name he had never even considered.

Sitting at his bedside on that momentous day, al Basreh had welcomed Gydryn and told him several stories. One tale described a line of knights, battle-weary and forlorn of their liege, yet making their determined way across enemy lands.

Al Basreh explained that his Akkadian scouts had observed these men but had left them alone, waiting to see where they would go and what they would do; and in time, the knights had found their way to the abandoned fortress of Nahavand.

Another tale spoke of companies of soldiers scrambling across the rocky mountains as scorpions in the night, yet who were not bred of the desert—Dannym's men, *his* men. These soldiers made no venture to claim new territory, only made their way as rapidly and unobtrusively as possible to Nahavand. The Emir's scouts had observed all of these migrations and many more and had allowed all to pass.

Hearing this, Gydryn knew the inner warmth of an impossible triumph, the feeling heightened by an uncommon sense of vindication. It had been a desperate gamble, sending his men into Akkad-held lands to escape the machinations of Radov abin Hadorin and Viernan hal'Jaitar, but Epiphany had granted his prayers and protected his troops by way of a benevolent monarch he'd had neither reason nor right to hope for.

When al Basreh had left the king that day, Gydryn's heart had been full.

He had not seen the prime minister since.

In the following days...weeks, Healers had come regularly to ensure his improvement, and servants brought him more food than he could ever consume in pursuit of regaining his strength, but what Gydryn most desired were answers.

Even before the Akkadian Emir had gone to such extremes to save his life, Gydryn had known that Abdul-Basir was not his enemy, for Morin d'Hain's letter on the *Sea Eagle* had implied it, and Kjieran van Stone had sworn it with his dying breath.

Oh, Kjieran...

Most stirring to his soul was the question of what had happened to Kjieran during his months in the temple of the Prophet Bethamin. If not for Kjieran's missives—sent secretly and bravely under prodigious threat—Morin d'Hain would not have learned of Radov's pact with Bethamin in time to warn Gydryn. And if not for Kjieran's personal efforts, Gydryn would certainly have died amid the dunes of the Sand Sea, yet one more victim of Viernan hal'Jaitar's perfidy.

Those final scalding hours with Kjieran had become indelibly seared into Gydryn's memory, but they'd also left him with a torrent of questions—he'd watched an entire company of men disintegrate before his eyes while remaining himself untouched; then had come Kjieran striding over the dunes, with his blackened flesh and inhuman strength....

'He sees what I see...'

The memory of those words, scrawled in blood across Kjieran's wasted chest, still haunted Gydryn's nights. And then to have watched the pitiful man immolate himself?

The king tightened his hands around the balcony railing. What horrors had Kjieran endured to drive him to such a desperate end? And yet throughout, he'd remained loyal. It broke Gydryn's heart.

Trying to push these thoughts from his mind, for they only served to widen the fissure of grief rent in Kjieran's name, Gydryn watched the turbaned laborers doing...well, he wasn't sure what the men were doing up in the high fronds, save endangering their lives. Yet, he supposed that whether they wagered their lives in the palms or on the plains of battle, they faced the same peril. The price of a man's life remained constant, no matter how he chose to risk it.

He'd taught his sons that a king must bear the weight of conscience on behalf of his men. He'd tried to teach them that a leader of men must assume the guilt of all, so that mere soldiers might follow orders with a clean conscience and their honor intact. He believed it earnestly and lived by it wholly, but in eight years of war...*oh, such weight* had he assumed! Not merely the deaths of honorable men but of his own beloved sons.

And yet...

One ghost of potential truth still plagued the king relentlessly. It had haunted his dreams during his feverish recovery and lingered still like a vagrant, making allies with the shadows in his room. Viernan hal'Jaitar had tried to manipulate him with it; Gydryn had battled his conscience over pursuing it; al Basreh had offered no information regarding it, yet if anyone would know the truth of this rumor, the Akkad's prime minister had to. If only the man—

A knock came upon the door to his chambers. The king turned from the railing to see a turbaned servant enter, press his palms together and bow. "Peace be upon you, Your Majesty."

Gydryn pressed palms and murmured the traditional reply, "Blessings be upon you also."

The servant bowed yet again. "I have been called, if it so please you and you now possess the strength, to bring you to our *Su'a'dal*, His Imminence, Emir Zafir bin Safwan al Abdul-Basir."

At last!

Gydryn's muscles still shook at inadvertent times, and too long upright brought on a vengeful vertigo, yet he thought he could walk all the way to Calgaryn if it meant getting his questions answered.

He nodded to the servant to lead away.

When the king arrived in the Emir's salon, which overlooked the city via an arcade of mosaic-covered arches, the Akkadian leader stood talking to his prime minister and a younger man who was dressed in flowing black robes. All three men were bearded, all wore grey and black-striped turbans, and all turned as the servant escorted Gydryn into the salon.

The Emir pressed palms together and bowed his head in greeting. "Peace be upon you, Your Majesty. Welcome to Raku."

Gydryn hooked his cane on his arm, pressed palms and bowed his head in return. "Blessings upon you also." Lifting his gaze, he scanned the three pairs of dark eyes fixed upon him. "My gratitude knows no bounds. I live by your generosity."

"And perhaps by Jai'Gar's grace, as well," the Emir's effacing smile made concession to this truth, "for we all live by His will." He placed a hand on the arm of the man standing to his right. "Perhaps you remember my son, Farid."

Gydryn shifted his gaze to the younger man. He recognized his lean, dark features and inscrutable gaze as the face he'd seen leaning over him in the desert, just before unconsciousness had claimed him.

"Farid is my most far-ranging scout, Your Majesty. By Jai'Gar's blessed will, he was born a Nodefinder and rivals the Mage's Sundragons for the distance he can cover in a day. He watches the farthest reaches of our lines, from the Dhahari Mountains in the north to the Forsaken Lands in the far south."

Gydryn nodded soberly to the prince. "I cannot express the depth of my gratitude, Prince Farid. As grievous as my wounds were, you might've left me to die and known no censure for it."

"My heart would've known it, sir." Farid glanced meaningfully to his father, who nodded. Then he bowed and took his leave.

Gydryn was left gazing at the Emir.

Zafir's was an aged countenance, ostensibly shaped through hard years and harder battles—the kind of face where every line had been purchased at the cost of conscience. In Gydryn's years of envisioning the Akkadian Emir, he'd summoned a visage chalked of treachery and misshapen by evil deeds; instead, he found a face sketched of compassion belonging to a man who lived close to his gods.

"Kings receive each other in apartments of state," the Emir said into Farid's departing silence, "but men sharing confidences seek more intimate surroundings." He motioned to a grouping of couches and chairs. "I hope you will forgive me for selecting the latter for our conversation."

"I respect the opportunity to speak candidly." Gydryn meant these words, yet he made no move to take a seat—verily, how dared he seat himself among truth when he'd spent so many years keeping company with lies? He felt as if his grievous misjudgment of the Emir now tainted his every breath, that sharing the space with the Emir at all befouled the many graces the good man had already bestowed upon him. How did one broach an apology for beliefs so wrongly conceived?

Yet no apology would find its way without courage. Gydryn shifted his gaze between the Emir and Prime Minister al Basreh and exhaled a slow breath. "Too long have lies separated our kingdoms."

"Well spoken, Your Majesty," the Emir replied. "I could not agree more."

"Please, call me Gydryn."

The Emir made a slight nod and pressed a jeweled hand to his chest. "And I am Zafir."

They all chose seats.

After he settled, Zafir clasped hands in his lap and searched Gydryn's gaze with his own. "Perhaps events have proven enough my intent, but I would say it outright: our kingdoms need not be enemies. I will share everything I know of this war with you, and I've asked Prime Minister al Basreh to do the same. I would there were no lies between us."

Gydryn held Zafir's gaze amid a welling surreality. For so long he'd known this man only as a faceless target of accusation and acrimony. *So many* years to have everything so backwards and wrong. "I must apologize to you, Zafir." The king's brow furrowed deeply. "My kingdom has held you in the greatest of contempt, and it seems undeservedly so."

Zafir's brown eyes crinkled with forbearance. "The sun has set upon those days, if you also will it."

"Verily, I do." Gydryn shifted his gaze beyond the arcade, and for a moment he saw not the pale city framed through carved arches but a kingdom soiled by treachery and a family by tragedy, and he wondered...

By all the stars in the heavens, he wondered about *so many* things! He had so *many* questions. But the question most burning in his heart won out.

Gydryn ran a hand over his beard. It was a joyless moment, confronting these men with the defamatory lies he had believed of them. "You must know that my council—indeed, my kingdom—has long blamed you for the deaths of my two oldest sons. Only recently I learned that Radov stands behind these acts. Perhaps you know nothing of what truly happened to my boys..."

—By Epiphany's light, it felt like flaying flesh to peel the words off his tongue!—

"but if you have *any* information..." his burning gaze conveyed what his tongue at last refused to.

The Emir and his prime minister exchanged a long look. Then Zafir turned back to Gydryn. "Of your eldest son Sebastian, we have no knowledge." His expression was deeply apologetic, and his tone conveyed a father's understanding of the terrible burden Gydryn must carry in his heart. "But of Trell..."

"Permit me to tell you another story, Your Majesty." Al Basreh settled hands in his lap and his dark-eyed gaze on the king. "Five years ago, a youth washed ashore in a fishing village named Kai'alil..."

The story proceeded in the fullness of truth across the lips of the Akkadian prime minister. With every word al Basreh spoke, Gydryn became more deeply embroiled in an internal war between horror, guilt, and hope. To think of his treasured middle son living for so many years without even the grace of his name...and all that time he'd been in the Akkad. If Gydryn had received the least hint that Trell lived, he would've scoured the globe in search of him.

"...the more we investigated, the more we began to see the shadows of a plot against the Eagle Throne..."

Al Basreh's words left Gydryn feeling hollow, for he knew their truth too nearly.

"...and we felt Trell's life remained in danger..."

As the prime minister continued his story, Gydryn clenched his jaw tightly—against grief, threatening anger, and a confluence of turbulent emotions. The faction within him that battled on the side of guilt wanted desperately to blame these men for keeping his son from him, but the greater part of his heart was rejoicing in a single truth:

Trell is alive!

A rising wind just then brought an echo of distant cheering. The prime minister paused his tale, exchanged a look with his liege and excused himself momentarily.

As al Basreh was departing, Zafir turned back to Gydryn wearing an expression of deep apology. "I understand if you cannot forgive us for keeping knowledge of your son from you, Gydryn." He arched brows resignedly. "I'm uncertain that I should even ask your forgiveness for such an act. But I want you to know that I did everything within my power to treat Trell with the dignity deserving of his birth. I brought him into my house; I gave him responsibilities and privileges beside my own sons; I took him into my confidence. And when Trell asked to take his place in our war, I gave him a company of Converted to command, that he might earn his nobility and prove his honor."

Zafir looked towards the day, which glowed brightly beyond the shadowed arcade, and his expression assumed a cast of loving regret. Outside, the cheering grew louder, closer. Glancing back to the king, Zafir offered an apologetic smile that was yet full of a father's pride. "This, Trell did every day he spent beneath Jai'Gar's eye."

Gydryn clenched his jaw and looked off into the too-bright city.

How cunningly Viernan hal'Jaitar had taken the facts and twisted them to suit his aims. He'd tried to use Trell's survival to manipulate Gydryn into maintaining his allegiance with Radov. His tawdry attempt had failed, but this was testament less to Gydryn's intelligence than to a father's shattered dreams.

"I hoped with time, Trell would regain his memory," Zafir offered, "but he never did." He gazed upon the king with deep frown lines framing his nose and mouth. "No doubt you wonder why we didn't send word to you."

Gydryn arched brows and slowly looked back to him. "I don't wonder." He held Zafir's gaze, feeling his own grow ever darker with grief and guilt. "By then, I thought you my gravest enemy. Any missive would've been denied outright, a certain ruse."

Zafir exhaled a slow breath. "So we believed as well."

The irony of the moment hit Gydryn as painfully acute, twisting his expression into a grimace. "Once, I thought you my enemy…yet as daylight reveals truths overlooked in the night, I find my son and I both owing you our lives."

Zafir opened palms to the heavens and gave him an effacing smile. "The gods work in mysterious ways. I am but their servant." With this, he rose and walked to a table holding a pitcher of chilled wine. He returned with two goblets in hand.

Gydryn accepted the wine with a look of sincerest gratitude, respecting the symbolism inherent in the act of one king serving another.

As he was retaking his seat, Zafir offered, "The last chapter of this story brings us to Radov's request for parley."

Surprise made Gydryn straighten in his chair. "*Radov's* request? Do you mean to say Radov invited *you* to parley?"

The Emir looked him over carefully. "Indeed, Gydryn."

The king stared at him. "Were you aware that my Duke of Marion, Loran val Whitney, received a letter requesting parley—a letter signed by *you*—and that Radov claimed to have received the same letter?"

"That is curious." Zafir's frown deepened as he considered this news. Then he lifted his gaze back to the king. "Let us table the matter of the mysterious invitation for now and look instead to what it precipitated; for whatever its source, the letter of parley forced my hand regarding Trell. I knew he would've wanted to attend the parley, and I would've had no cause to deny him, but I dared not allow it, Gydryn. To bring Trell near Radov, knowing what we knew?"

The Emir shook his head, and his expression became wrenched. "I used Trell's pain to manipulate him into leaving. To my shame, Gydryn, but I saw no other path. The mystery of his name haunted Trell. It cleaved my own heart to keep the truth from him, but I believed with my whole soul that anonymity was the only thing protecting him beneath our gods, and…" he gave Gydryn a look of grave and tragic candor, "by this point, I had come to love your son as my own."

Silence flooded the room as a sudden breeze. Gydryn gazed into his wine and considered all that he'd been told. Beyond the windows, the cheering had quieted. Finally, the king drew a hand roughly down his beard. Hope hovered within his grasp, but he couldn't yet give it purchase in his heart. "And now?" He lifted a troubled gaze back to Zafir. "Where is my son now?"

❖

Trell recognized the road to Raku long before the oasis walls came into view. How odd it felt to him to be riding towards the city again, alone but for an immortal's laconic companionship. When last he'd approached those walls, he'd been riding amid the jesting laughter of his men. Yet he'd *felt* alone then, lost without an identity to hang his hat upon.

As they rounded a rise and the oasis' crenellated walls came into view with guards manning the high ramparts and archers upon the towers, Trell exhaled a measured breath to soften his rising anticipation. Though he didn't know exactly what to expect, he thought it likely that he would see the Emir. How much he wanted to say to his adoptive father; how deep the waters of his appreciation! He was just wondering if anyone would recognize him when a call rang out.

"It's the Lord Rhakar!" The iron-studded gates groaned and began opening to admit them.

Trell cast an inquiring look at the *drachwyr*.

Rhakar shrugged. "There are times when it behooves us to be known simply as men, Trell of the Tides."

Oddly, Trell felt relieved that the *drachwyr* had been the one the men had recognized. The uncomplicated man named Trell of the Tides had worn but one allegiance: to the Emir and his holy war. Yet Trell val Lorian, Prince of Dannym, necessarily wore many allegiances, some of which Trell had yet to reconcile for himself. With his name, he'd also donned a mantle heavily embroidered with the responsibilities of royalty, the duties of a prince, and the alliances of kings. These things, too, he would have to address with the Emir.

Rhakar nodded to the soldiers manning the gates, and then he and Trell were reining their mounts through the long tunnel beneath Raku's wall. The tunnel opened upon a yard where soldiers were tending weapons, sparring, or otherwise at their leisure. Outbuildings framed the wide space.

Trell had barely emerged from the tunnel's shadow into the bright daylight, when—

"*Trell?*" a deep voice rang out across the yard. Then a shout: "It's Trell of the Tides!"

A volley of gazes struck his way. Time took a breath in pause.

Then men came bolting towards him from all directions.

His name shot from tongue to tongue like a stone skipping across a pond. More stones joined the first, until the skipping pebbles formed a torrent of his rippling name. Soldiers mobbed Trell with clapping hands and shouted words of welcome that echoed off the looming wall.

Hands lifted him from his horse onto strong shoulders. Nameless faces led Gendaia away, while others offered him drink and refreshment, but Trell's surprise so choked him that he couldn't have managed even a swallow.

Borne on the shoulders of proud men, Trell reached Raku's main thoroughfare and its promenade of tall palms, whereupon a collective hail rose up from a mass of soldiers jamming the road.

Trell of the Tides! Trell of the Tides!

Friendly hands jostled him every which way. Shouted words of praise bombarded his ears. A sea of faces grinned in welcome.

Ever a shadowy presence at his side, Rhakar kept them moving through the ocean of men until they reached the Sultan's palace. The men carrying Trell lowered him onto the steps as though a true hero, with the crowd maintaining its cheering all the while.

Rhakar led Trell up a long flight of steps.

Feeling heady by the time he reached the top, Trell turned and offered a wave of gratitude. Then Rhakar was ushering him inside the shaded entrance and leaving the whirlwind stirred by his arrival to disperse on its own.

As the doors were being closed, Trell paused in the cool, dim interior and pushed a hand through his hair. He looked bemusedly to Rhakar. "That was…unexpected."

It might've been amusement that glinted in Rhakar's yellow eyes, but he only nodded to acknowledge Trell's comment and motioned him on again.

As Trell headed through the Atrium, he observed the arabesque designs in the tiled floor and saw himself walking upon a spiraling path; oddly, he couldn't tell if the circle was beginning or ending. Had he been brought to Raku to see the Emir, his adopted father, and finally convey his thanks for all that great man had done for him, closing the circle on the last five years? Or had the Mage sent him to Raku—as Vaile had intimated—to take a new role, the vital first steps of another spiral in the pattern of the Mage's vast game?

Most surprising to Trell was his own ambivalence. Whether he faced a beginning or an ending, or was merely joining a course already in motion—*whatever* the Mage needed of him, he would do without hesitation. How different he'd become from the man who'd stood outside the River Goddess Naiadithine's shrine with suspicion as his most trusted guide!

They passed through an archway clogged with the Emir's personal guards and were walking a vaulted corridor when voices floated to Trell's ears as if upon a passing breeze. Yet *this* breeze permeated clothing and flesh into the depths of his chest, where it lodged needles of recognition.

His feet stopped with abrupt defiance.

"…dared not allow it," the Emir was saying, "…to bring Trell near Radov, knowing what we knew?"

Trell stood anchored to the tiles just beyond an archway while the Emir's voice and words evoked a haunting memory: their last conversation of parting, a sleepless night upon the walls of Raku, and then the visit to Naiadithine's shrine and the beginning of a new circle.

Since learning his name, he'd come to suspect the truth the Emir was now confessing to someone, the reason he'd relieved Trell of his command and sent him away in the middle of the war: because Trell would've gone to the parley, only to have Radov potentially recognize him—Viernan hal'Jaitar *certainly* would have—and Trell knew already what end he would've met then.

Only, had it happened upon the course of that earlier path, no immortals would've come to rescue him at Darroyhan.

"...used Trell's pain to manipulate him. To my shame...but I saw no other path..."

Trell swallowed. He heard contrition threading through the Emir's voice; his words were saturated with it, yet Trell knew only gratitude to him.

As he stood there, keenly aware of eavesdropping, yet even more aware of the man standing beside him—Şrivas'rhakárakek, the Shadow of the Light, his personal guide into the next spiral of his future—Trell thought of all that had happened upon his path...and realized that he wouldn't change a single thing.

The Saldarian mercenary Raliax had roped him to a trunk and put him into the Fire Sea; yet for enduring the torment of drowning, he'd gained Naiadithine's grace.

The truthbinding that had so ravaged his memory had yielded a life of continuous awakening to a new and wondrous culture, while the sacrifice of one father and family had gained him another.

And had he always known his name, he never would've made friends of Sundragons or zanthyrs, met Carian van Lea and traveled the nodes, or forged bargains with pirate captains; he never would've come to understand the inviolate shield his integrity provided him, or learned of the depths of Radov and hal'Jaitar's treachery against his family's reign.

And his relationship with Alyneri—a treasure so marvelous that it both weakened and strengthened him—would've been conscripted, their eventual union forced rather than mutually desired. That is, if he'd lived to marry at all.

Oh, no...he would change nothing—*nothing!*—of the past five years, for his every sacrifice had reaped rewards far beyond their cost.

These many thoughts passed in the space of a single exhale. Then Trell was inhaling to make himself known—

When another voice stole the breath just claimed by his lungs.

"And now? Where is my son now?"

Trell's heart was suddenly pounding, apprehension beating counterpoint to an impossible hope.

Could *his father* really be there *with* the Emir? His own kingly father?

Trell had spent so many nights debating with himself, troubling over how he would ever reconcile his allegiance to the Emir with the duties of blood. Now to find his father *here?*

The breath of impossibility finally released him. He exhaled determination and stepped around the corner.

"Your son is here, father."

Silence led a charge through the room.

The Emir rose first to receive him. Meeting his adoptive father's gaze,

Trell tried to convey the depth of his appreciation, his enduring gratitude, his understanding.

Then another man was rising and turning to face him—*Oh*, he knew that visage as dearly as his own! Trell watched his father's expression constrict, watched him swallow, as if forcing back a welling emotion—surely the same combination of joy and impossibility that was flooding Trell.

"*Trell...*"

His name, choked across Gydryn's lips, caused an echo of painful recognition. He knew instinctively that his father had not spoken his name in all of the time they'd been apart.

Trell had to force his feet into motion, force himself through an invisible boundary between himself and his father that had been constructed of the lost pieces of their lives. He was hardly aware of crossing the room, only of the moment when his father opened his arms and they collided in a rough embrace.

For a moment, Gydryn's arms bound Trell as tightly as emotion bound his voice. Then his father drew back and clasped a strong hand at Trell's neck, the other clutching his shoulder. Grey eyes, so like his own, stared into his. "*My son...*" Gydryn's eyes were glossy as they searched Trell's.

Trell held his father's gaze, swallowed...nodded. Smiled.

Gydryn glanced to Zafir—incredulous, ineffably grateful. Then he pressed a kiss to Trell's forehead, rough with things as yet unsaid, and took him by both shoulders and looked him over.

Oh, to gaze upon his father's face after so many years! After so many nights of desperately wishing to know that visage but only seeing shadows! And how miraculous to remember it so well now, to recall from the creases framing his father's eyes the thousands of times he'd seen that smile and known he was loved.

Trell was smiling so wide that his cheeks were starting to ache. He shook his head wondrously. "Father...how are you *here*?"

One corner of his father's mouth twitched wryly. "The light of impossibility is shining on both of us, son, for I stand with equal amazement in view of you." After another searching gaze, he released Trell and held a hand to the Emir, that Trell might greet him also.

Trell looked to Zafir. How wondrous it seemed now to have two fathers, and to so admire them both.

Zafir opened his arms, and Trell went to him. They took each other by the shoulders and kissed once on each cheek, and once again. "Jai'Gar blesses us with your safe return, son-of-my-heart." Zafir's gaze, falling warmly upon him, conveyed far more than a simple welcome. "And...I perceive that your memory is once more whole. Can it be true?"

Staring at him, thinking of their last parting, Trell had so many things he wanted to tell him—to tell both of his fathers. "The Mage saved my life, *Su'a'dal*—twice, by Jai'Gar's grace—and with the second Healing, he removed Raine D'Lacourte's truthbinding, which had held my memory in thrall for so many years."

"*Ah*, no." Gydryn exhaled with dismay. "What happened to you in the Fire Sea?"

Trell released the Emir and looked back to his father. "Saldarians overtook the *Dawn Chaser*. They interrogated me, activating the Vestal's truthbinding, and when I gave them nothing, they scuttled the ship and cast me to the depths with it."

Suddenly ashen-faced, Gydryn slowly sank down on the couch. He looked up gravely at Trell. "Yet you survived."

"By Naiadithine's grace, father." Trell looked to the Emir. "Did you know, *Su'a'dal*? When you sent me to Her shrine for a blessing on my quest, did you know I held Her favor?"

Zafir motioned Trell to take a chair positioned between the two couches. "I suspected." He retook his seat across from Gydryn, giving the king a look of encouragement and compassion, for the monarch seemed overcome. Looking back to Trell, he added, "I hoped it was so. To be delivered out of the sea so miraculously… you were a fable come to life."

"You're favored of a…god, my son?" Gydryn sounded hesitant, amazed, slightly dubious but clearly not wanting to offend either of them by voicing his disbelief.

"I have heard the goddess's whisper in my soul, father." Trell willed his father to see the truth in his eyes.

Zafir clasped his hands together and pressed entwined fingers fervently to his lips. "*Oh*, what did She tell you, son-of-my-heart?" His brown eyes grew bright with unshed tears. "Might you share Her words with me?"

Trell recalled the many times Naiadithine had spoken to his heart and bowed his head, feeling humbled by the graces She'd bestowed upon him. "She said, *Follow the water, Trell of the Tides.*"

Zafir made a sound, half cry and half amazement, kissed his fingers and lifted his clasped hands to the ceiling. "Jai'Gar be praised that the twisting paths of tragedy have yet brought us to this happiness!" He looked back to Trell wearing a rare smile that considerably lightened his usually somber countenance. "Only the gods might've foreseen such an end as this!"

The gods, Trell thought, glancing between his two fathers, *and Björn van Gelderan.*

Finally Gydryn let out a forceful exhale, as if to clear the last of his disbelief. "Perhaps indeed as an agent of his gods, Zafir has saved us both, Trell."

Trell turned a swift look between them. "Saved *us*?"

"By Jai'Gar's will, son-of-my-heart, Farid found your father in the Sand Sea, wounded and near death. He brought him here to Raku for Healing."

Gydryn ran a hand down his beard. "Viernan hal'Jaitar planned to have me assassinated on the road to the parley. A favorite tactic of his, and not entirely unanticipated."

Trell stared at him as he processed his words. "Then…" he searched his father's face, "you know of Radov's duplicity?" He turned his gaze between his father and the Emir with surprise welling so swiftly that it nearly choked off his voice. He exhaled the incredulous hope, faint with impossibility, "Father…is Dannym no longer allied with M'Nador?"

"No more." Gydryn arched brows resignedly. "At least, as far as my reach extends." His tone shockingly indicated this might not be far enough.

"To this very end, the future must be written," Rhakar remarked from the doorway.

Trell had completely forgotten the Sundragon was there.

Zafir looked to him and nodded gravely. "Just so, Lord Rhakar." He extended a hand to the *drachwyr*. "Your Majesty, may I present the Sundragon Şrivas'rhakárakek, the Shadow of the Light."

Gydryn looked at Rhakar. Then he blinked twice and looked at him more closely.

"Lord Rhakar, may I present His Majesty, Gydryn val Lorian, King of Dannym."

Rhakar nodded to the king and then shifted his yellow eyes back to the Emir. "The Mage urges action, Zafir."

"Rightly so, my lord, especially in view of Farid's news." The Emir stood and shifted a serious gaze between Trell and Gydryn. "Let us adjourn to where the others await—Gydryn, Trell, we will share with you all that we know."

As they walked away from the gallery, the Emir and Rhakar strode several paces ahead, by their distance giving Trell and his father what time they could to become reacquainted.

Trell was acutely aware of his father at his side. While the greatest barrier to their reconciliation might've already been overcome, much yet remained to be discussed.

"Trell…" the king looked to him wearing a neutral expression, but Trell sensed a torrent of conscience deluging him. "If I had known—"

"Likewise, father." Then he turned profile again, smiling softly. "Trust that Alyneri has assured me on your behalf of all that need be said to that end."

"Alyneri d'Giverny?" The king sounded bemused, astonished. "How did you and she meet? She was supposed to be traveling with Ean."

"She was until—" But how could he even begin to explain the convoluted paths that Cephrael had woven for him and his brothers? Trell shook his head, still amazed himself. "In the course of her travels, Alyneri has saved Ean's life, my life, Fynnlar's life." He looked back to his father. "When you sent her south with Ean, you were granting a blessing upon all of the sons of House val Lorian."

His father gazed wonderingly at him. "I perceive there is much to tell to this end."

Trell puffed a forceful exhale by way of agreement. "The events of the last single year of my life would take longer in the retelling than all of the five years before." He assumed a quiet smile. "Yet in the moment when I first heard the *Su'a'dal's* voice, and then yours…in that instant did I realize that I wouldn't change any part of my path up to now." He searched his father's gaze, hoping that this truth might give him some solace and calm the riot of conscience that was still obviously plaguing him. "I hope you can understand what I mean by this. I've known such graces as to make even the worst experiences worthwhile. My life has been blessed, father."

Gydryn gave a startled cough. "I am…as amazed by your words as by the man you've become, Trell." Seeming at a loss for words, he turned to stare ahead, frowning slightly. After a time, he glanced to Trell again. "My generals told me of a leader among the Emir's elite staff, a brilliant tactician who thought like a Northman. They faced a host of difficulties as a result of his command." His grey eyes searched Trell's face. "You?"

Trell nodded. He remembered, too, his conflict of conscience in those times. He'd been serving the Emir in his efforts to thwart Radov's allied forces, yet even while still bereft of name, he'd felt and suspected some kinship to Dannym's soldiers.

His father turned profile again and exhaled a measured breath. "You saved many lives, my son."

Trell gave him a startled look.

"Aye…not the words you expected to hear from me, I suspect?" The king angled him a sidelong eye. "Yet when I heard news of this commander—who is finally revealed to be *my* beloved son—from the first, he had my gratitude."

"Father?"

"If you hadn't kept Veneisea out of the war, Trell, my men would've endured a much longer and far more brutal engagement. Instead, by some grace beyond my comprehension, my army is intact and rested for our return to Calgaryn, and my treasured middle son *lives*—" His voice broke upon this word, and he paused and closed his eyes briefly, as if offering a silent prayer.

But not just your middle son...

Gazing at his king father, hearing his words...Trell wanted desperately to tell him of Sebastian. Yet...while he understood that this conflict of kingdoms was but a small ramification of the First Lord's game—that somehow it figured into that greater purpose, formed some part of the final picture—he didn't know his father well enough to know if *he* would understand how deeply their paths had been woven into Cephrael's intricate tapestry.

Lacking that understanding, some things would be nearly impossible to explain to him—Sebastian's misadventures, as case in point—even had they the time, which they didn't. Already they were nearing the hall where the Emir held his war conferences.

For his father to truly understand how Sebastian's path interwove with theirs, Trell would have to explain Ean's role, his Awakening and Return, his connection to Isabel and Björn van Gelderan, Björn's own true actions—*thirteen hells*, he'd have to explain the entire game for his father to be able to make sense of Sebastian's survival and life as a wielder.

Furthermore, Trell couldn't know if Sebastian and their father would ever meet, for the First Lord had said that Trell's eldest brother was a Player, too. Would it be a kindness, then, to tell his father that his eldest son and heir lived when the two might never know each other's faces again? When he couldn't offer adequate explanation as to how Sebastian had survived? When he himself knew only pieces of Sebastian's early torments? And when he knew nothing of Sebastian's current role in the game, or what dangers he was facing?

Noting his silence, Gydryn turned Trell a look of concerned apology. "You're a man in your own right now, Trell. How far you've matured beyond the youth I placed on a ship and cast south bearing all of my hopes. As a man, you've set your own heading, charted your course. I would have you know I respect these decisions, whatever is to come."

Ahead, the Emir and Rhakar passed beneath the carved archway leading into the hall, but Trell stopped and turned to face his father. "Your Majesty..."

He hardly knew how to say the things he felt in his heart, for the feelings were too tumultuous and powerful. Trell looked down at his boots and then up again to meet his father's gaze, his back and shoulders pressed straighter against the rod of new convictions. "Father, I'm sworn to the Fifth

Vestal, the man you know as the Emir's Mage…" he took a deep breath and added, "but I'm also your son, and I will always be your son, if you will have me thusly."

Holding Trell's gaze, Gydryn's eyes grew glassy once more. He clenched his jaw, seeming gripped by emotion. Then he wordlessly draped his arm around his son's shoulders, and they walked with solidarity into the Emir's war chamber.

TWENTY-ONE

"The darkness can hide from the light, but the light can never hide from the darkness."
–The truthreader Mir Arkadhi, Seat of the realm of Eltanin

DARSHAN STOOD BENEATH an arcade at the Fortress of Ivarnen staring out at the rain while Dore Madden paced ruts of malcontent into the tiles behind him. The sky overhead wore a mantle of ash. Mist shrouded the day the way the memories from his dreams enveloped his thoughts. Darshan had hoped the storm would bring some clarity, but it was only a dull rain, reminiscent of melancholy.

His latest dream was troubling him deeply…

"You cannot see through the veil of your arrogance, brother." Pelas had been perched on the merlon of a tower, reclining on one elbow with his long hair streaming on the wind. *"There are facts in front of you so blindingly obvious that you pass them every day and see them not at all."*

In the dream, Darshan worked the muscles of his jaw. More frustrating than these dreamed conversations with Pelas and Kjieran was not understanding how they kept happening—and being unable to stop them. He'd never met helplessness before. So far he wasn't finding much to appreciate in the acquaintance.

He clasped hands behind his back and tried to keep his temper in check—ever Pelas pulled the worst emotions out of him. "What, pray, might these obvious facts be, Pelas?"

"Look around you, Darshan—just look.*" Pelas's tone was as patronizing as Shail's.* "What do you see?"

Darshan exhaled a measured breath. Fistfights with his middle brother were never rewarding, and even less so in his dreams. His eyes grew very dark as he turned to face him. "I see a world waiting to be unmade."

"Nay—Darshan, if you'd actually looked, you'd have seen a world set within the boundaries of time."

Darshan grunted. "I admit such an observation is too obvious to have required my notice. What's your point, Pelas?"

Pelas was dangling a leg over the side of the wall. Something in his nonchalant position irritated Darshan. "Only this, brother: if our Maker intended for these worlds to be destroyed, why did he place them within the framework of time? For this implies they were meant to endure."

Darshan frowned.

Pelas arched a wry brow. "Ah, you see it finally, don't you? Chaos has no time. It exists eternally in one moment, and every moment in each new moment. But these worlds have time, Darshan."

Darshan felt a restless malcontent. Would that it had only been a result of his brother's invasion of his dreams and not from some deeper truth.

Pelas slipped off the merlon and approached him. The wind made dark flames of his hair, while his copper eyes glowed like a fire's coals. Darshan couldn't look away. "Why did the Maker give these worlds time, Darshan—why did He hide them from us—if He didn't mean for them to endure?"

"My lord…"

Dore's servile whine drew Darshan from his thoughts.

Dore had his head tucked while he paced, shoulders hunched, reminding Darshan of the aardvarks that scurried the Saldarian grasslands. "My lord, something really must be done."

Darshan was strongly considering ways to rid himself of Dore Madden. The man was keeping council too closely with Shail these days, and his more recent advice reeked of subversion. He clasped hands behind his back and returned his gaze to the clouds and the rain shedding itself across Ivarnen's broad estuary, yet all he saw was Pelas's burning gaze. "If something needs be done, then do it, Dore."

"Yes, my lord…" Dore licked his lips again, "but *what* to do…this is the issue. Ean val Lorian cannot be allowed to continue stealing in and out of Ivarnen. He's disrupting your good work and destroying the *eidola*."

Darshan turned a chill look over his shoulder. "*Your* work lies here at Ivarnen, not mine."

"But they are your *eidola* he's destroying, my lord." Dore paced with his chin tucked low, as if to hide his eyes from the light.

Darshan turned back to the rain. The burning existential questions he was pondering were far more compelling to him than Dore's obsessions. "*Eidola* promised to a putrefied prince whose rule is nearing its end. I have plenty of *eidola* in Tambarré. These treaties you made with Radov serve no purposes of mine."

Dore shook his head from side to side, his manner quite at odds with his words as he replied, "You're right of course, my lord. You needn't concern yourself with Radov and his war, but Ean val Lorian...he is a thorn—nay an *arrow* shot from an errant bow that claims the king and wins the battle."

Darshan misliked Dore's analogy. "Ean val Lorian is no threat to me."

Wind funneled through the arcade. Darshan followed its rain-drenched scent out onto the terrace to escape the smothering reek of Dore's manipulative breath.

Dore scuttled after him. "The val Lorian prince is a threat to your plans, my lord. He would thwart your purpose, undermine your important work! He and his Isabel, bound with the Unbreakable Bond—he's Arion Tavestra Returned, my lord, and Tavestra..." Dore shook his head emphatically. "Tavestra is no trifling enemy."

Darshan had heard this rant countless times; Dore could spout it endlessly, the words recombined a thousand ways, never saying anything new nor offering any insight of value or consequence. Darshan's interest was waning until he heard, "...found each other again in this life. Now she Awakens him to the powers he once had—"

"Found each other." Darshan spied Dore over his shoulder. "Found each other how?"

Dore's pink tongue trailed across his lips. "It's the nature of the Unbreakable Bond, my lord. The two souls call to one another, they...they *summon* each other across time."

Darshan considered this. "How does this Unbreakable Bond compare to the binding you advised me to work on Kjieran van Stone?"

"They are quite similar, my lord. It is what you asked me for—eternity with the man." He watched Darshan with a dark light in his eyes. "I've only ever tried to give you exactly what you asked for."

Darshan grunted dubiously at this.

"If only you had let me question Isabel van Gelderan." When Darshan said nothing to this, Dore continued, "She could've told us much, my lord—oh, *so* much! She and her brother have been working for centuries to thwart you. Oh, if you had let me question her while I had her bound in *goracrosta*, what truths I could've uncovered—"

"How?"

Dore blinked. Then he reared his head back to look up at Darshan. "How what...my lord?"

Darshan leveled him a piercing stare. "*How* have Isabel and Björn van Gelderan been working to thwart my purpose?"

Dore ducked his head again and shifted agitatedly from side to side.

"They…they have a vast network, my lord, contacts that span the globe. Ean val Lorian—"

"I did not ask about Ean val Lorian." Darshan clasped hands behind his back and looked away again.

"But he is one of their agents, my lord, and you see what chaos he's caused!"

"I see the chaos he has caused *you*, Dore Madden. I do not see how these others are a threat." It wasn't entirely true—Isabel had apparently orchestrated Pelas's escape, but Dore didn't know that.

Dore made a frustrated exhale. "The High Mage sees the future, my lord, and her brother, the Fifth Vestal…" he shuddered, and his eyes grew wider and wider, "he wields powers that would shock the gods."

"Not *my* gods."

Dore gave a sort of quivering wince. The tip of his tongue flickered hesitatingly between his lips and then vanished, as if uncertain of its welcome. His face readjusted into that preening expression he assumed whenever he was trying to be coy.

"Björn knows of *you*, my lord." Dore inched closer. "He knows your powers, your capabilities. His Sundragons have stalemated the war—"

"Radov's war."

"My lord…" a sort of desperation whined in Dore's rising voice, "Björn still has the support of the other vestals—"

"I thought you and Shail controlled Alorin's vestals."

"Soon we shall have our candidates in place, but the Balance is delicate right now."

"Balance bends to *my* will."

"*Precisely*, my lord!" Dore shifted and waggled his body from side to side, like a dog pinned behind a fence. "If you mean to take no action against our enemies, my lord, at least…at least let me move forward with making your army."

Darshan gazed off into the misty day. "I will make no more *eidola*."

"But my lord!" Dore quivered with frustration. "How will we supply troops to fulfill Radov's need if you have no army?"

"I am sure you will find a solution. The problem in either case is yours to solve."

Dore whimpered unhappily. "But…but, my lord, if your enemies rise against you, you will need *eidola* to combat them, and now…but we have everything in place now in Tambarré to work the conversion. Think of it, my lord—*multitudes* bound to you…"

He continued talking, but Darshan had stopped listening. Dore had become his youngest brother's mouthpiece, useful now only in revealing what new betrayals Shail had involved himself in.

"Take the *eidola* away from here." Darshan gave the order without waiting for Dore to pause. "Keep their location hidden, or deliver them early to Radov, I care not which, only that you remove them from Ivarnen and other of my holdings."

Dore's mouth snapped shut. He furrowed his brow deeply and curled his upper lip towards his frowning nose, the two nearly touching.

"You may personally oversee the conversion of the last clutch of *eidola*, lending them your considerable protection. Thus this mortal prince who so plagues your efforts may not trouble you again."

It wasn't the solution Dore had wanted—he salivated over Ean val Lorian's body trussed and bound on his table—but Darshan would no longer willingly supply fodder for Dore's unwholesome appetites.

He had a different fate in mind for Prince Ean val Lorian...this prince who had so many times escaped their traps, who had mysteriously severed Darshan's bond with his Marquiin, who feverishly attacked and destroyed his *eidola*, thumbing his nose at Darshan, mind to mind.

This prince who had worked the Unbreakable Bond and allegedly Returned and found his love anew.

In the many times their minds had brushed as Ean had been recklessly ripping the life out of an *eidola*, Darshan had gotten a sense of Ean val Lorian. He knew that the prince would not stop trying to find ways to destroy his creations. Ean would seek more of them to test his patterns. With the *eidola* gone from Ivarnen and the other castles hostile to him, the prince would be forced to come to Tambarré.

A dark light of intent burned in Darshan's gaze. *This time, Ean val Lorian shall come to* me, *and I will have many questions for him.*

TWENTY-TWO

"Come and find me. I'll be waiting."
–The Enemy, to Arion Tavestra

EAN WALKED A hallway in the Palace of Andorr hoeing vexation through the currents. With his every step, spiny stalks of frustration twined through tendrils of dismay, such that a deadly bramble of energy rose in his wake.

So close! They'd been *so* close, only to come to a staggering halt at what appeared to be an insurmountable barrier. How were they to test the effectiveness of their patterns without *eidola* to test them on?

The night had been a complete waste. He'd traveled all the way to Ivarnen only to discover the *eidola* gone. The worst part was that Ean should've anticipated the move.

He and Dore were waging their own little game within the larger war, a skirmish of vendettas, heirlooms of vengeance hidden for centuries until time and circumstance might reveal them anew. The First Lord's game whirled around them, carrying them towards a final confrontation, but somehow they managed to make moves and counter-moves and keep their own game alive within the broader field of action.

Ean knew Dore thought this way. Without ever speaking to the man in this life, he knew that Dore had been waiting for Arion's Return for centuries—indeed, that their private feud was simply a continuation of one that had come to a precipitous halt at the Citadel on Tiern'aval, when a more powerful Player had stepped onto the field.

'Come and find me. I'll be waiting.'

Ean couldn't shake those words from his head. He *needed* to know what had transpired between Arion and the Enemy in those lost moments of darkness. Where had Arion strayed from the path so as to bring Balance to bear against him? How had he betrayed Isabel and Björn? And why would he ever have done so?

For Ean was sure that Arion had.

He felt it now...that sort of grim inevitability that descends upon a man when he finally faces the spears of his misdeeds without justification's shield. He knew Arion had committed some betrayal. He just didn't know how or why it had come to pass. And until he did...until he dug into the grave of Arion's conscience and beheld that truth, until he could face that moment, he would never again be whole.

By all the gods!

Frustration and regret tolled endlessly in Ean's head. His every failure resonated foully against each of his earlier ones, setting them all to a dissonant clanging, announcing his misdeeds like a chorus of plague bells warning everyone away. Balance was shouting; Ean just couldn't understand its roar.

He pushed a hand through his hair as he climbed a long staircase towards his brother's rooms. Weariness haunted his every step. His nights, he spent hunting *eidola,* for they were a kinder adversary than sleep; his days, he spent dreading the nights.

Perhaps it was just weariness that had caused him to miss the most obvious repercussion of his actions: that if Ean couldn't be stopped, Darshan and Dore would simply move their *eidola* elsewhere, out of his reach. Perhaps his muddled brain held too much kindling and not enough sparks to ignite it properly, but he couldn't help worrying that he'd somehow attracted Cephrael's blighting eye and drawn Balance to bear against himself *again.*

How galling to think that Dore Madden played the game better than he did.

This unexpected thought speared him deeply, dragging his feet to a halt on the landing of Sebastian's floor. Yet how could he deny it? Since Björn had reclaimed him from the paths of the dead, Ean had been guided, ordered, prodded and jostled about, no less a marionette than he'd been while still running for the Cairs, with Raine D'Lacourte pulling the strings on one side and the zanthyr on the other.

'*...Players make their moves at will, reassured only by their own resolve, facing dire consequences, protected by no one, and shielded by nothing but the force of their conviction...*' These were the zanthyr's words, spoken all those months ago.

Perhaps he had claimed some place on the field...but then he'd just stood there letting everyone bash and batter him, making no moves save ones that had nearly cost them everything.

Oh...he'd made so many mistakes! What successes he'd gained had come at a heavy cost. Even in freeing Sebastian and rescuing Rhys, he'd still only been reacting to another Player's actions.

Ean leaned back against the wall and braced his hands on his knees, letting the truth claim him as he claimed it—though Raine's truth, it felt like bitter bile on his breath.

But in this soul-searching, he saw something important, a vital difference between himself and Arion: Arion had trusted his instincts, while Ean grudgingly held in suspicion even the decisions he hadn't decided on yet. But if he couldn't trust his instincts to lead him, he was never going to *be* a Player.

Somehow he had to learn to trust himself again.

A bright dawn had claimed the world by the time Ean reached his brother's apartments and sought him inside, expecting he would just be waking. To his surprise, he found Sebastian and the Princess Ehsan standing close together out on the terrace.

Looking exotically lovely in a beaded turquoise sari, Ehsan was the first to notice Ean's arrival. She turned with a demure smile, pressed her palms together and bowed politely to him. "*Sobh bekheir*, Prince of Dannym."

"And a good morning to you also, Princess." Ean leaned a shoulder against one of the loggia's arches and crossed his arms. The currents were calm, but with the energy obviously circulating between Sebastian and Ehsan, they should've been electrified. He suppressed a smile. "Am I interrupting something?"

Sebastian tugged at one ear and held a hand to the princess. "Ehsan was just…"

"Leaving." She gave Sebastian a decorous look that said one thing, beneath an arched eyebrow that suggested quite another, and nodded once more to Ean as she departed. "Prince Ean."

"Princess Ehsan." Ean looked over his shoulder to watch her glide away. Then he noticed his brother doing the same and grinned openly at him.

Sebastian cast him a sidelong glance. "What?" He returned his admiring gaze to Ehsan's curves.

Ean's grin widened. "How long are you two going to keep this up?"

Sebastian exhaled a slow breath. "As long as possible." He watched Ehsan until she vanished around a corner. Then he shifted his gaze to Ean, whereupon a frown overtook his expression. "Forgive my asking, Ean, but did you sleep at all?" He walked to a sideboard and poured wine into two fresh goblets.

"Not really." Ean gratefully accepted the wine his brother offered him. "Look that good, do I?"

Sebastian grunted dubiously. "Slightly better than death warmed over."

"Sleep isn't much of a friend to me these days." Ean lowered himself into a chair at the table, whereupon his weary, wandering gaze noted breakfast dishes not yet cleared from a meal set for two. He lifted a smile back to his brother. "Should I be asking if *you* slept last night?"

"No, you definitely should not." Sebastian swept him with his gaze as he sat down across from him. "Something's different about you. What happened last night?"

Ean fingered his goblet, frowning. Then he drank his wine and collapsed backwards into the cushion of his seat. "I should've seen it coming." He rolled his head around on the back of his chair. "It was an obvious play."

Sebastian's expression narrowed. "Seen what coming?"

"The *eidola* are gone from Ivarnen."

Sebastian halted his goblet at his lips and lowered it again. "Gone? How gone? *Where* gone?"

Ean shook his head. "Moved, I suspect. I don't know where, but without them I have no way of testing our patterns. No way of knowing if they will work."

"Shadow take Dore Madden." Sebastian glared into his goblet and then drank deeply of it. Staring into the cup as he lowered it again, he muttered, "Would that the Demon Lord had seen fit to claim *him* at birth."

Ean grunted. "Dore would probably have corrupted Belloth, too."

Sebastian lifted his gaze back to him. "So…what do you suggest?"

Ean rolled his head around on the back of his chair again and stared off to the side, over the broad vista of a hazy Kandori morning. Like Arion when he'd faced the Mages, Ean perceived numerous paths spiraling out before him, roads to a new future; also like Arion, he knew there was only one he would choose.

He exhaled a sigh. "What else can we do? We have to find another colony of *eidola*."

Sebastian scrubbed at the back of his head. "Tal'Afaq is out of the question—they'll be on the lookout for you there. Likewise Tyr'kharta… Ivarnen. You've shortened the list of possible strongholds considerably."

Ean had already reached the same conclusion. He arched resigned brows. "Save one."

Sebastian gave him a portentous look of alarm. "Surely you don't mean Tambarré."

"Whatever else Dore and Darshan are planning—moving the *eidola*, probably expecting me to seek them out again and laying some trap in wait—I guarantee they won't be expecting me to come to Tambarré."

Sebastian's eyes widened. "Because no one in the realm would be that stupid!"

Ean met his brother's gaze and held it while he drank more of his wine. "It occurred to me, Sebastian, that the only way I can possibly win against them is to do the unexpected."

"Ean…" Sebastian shifted discontentedly in his chair. "Isabel sacrificed herself so Darshan wouldn't find you. Now you mean to walk right up—not to his doorstep, nay, but like as into his damned privy chamber—and announce yourself?"

"All I mean to do is get in, throw the pattern, see that it works, and get out as fast as I can."

Sebastian grunted and shook his head. "If you work the lifeforce in the Prophet's temple—verily, *anywhere* in Tambarré—the Prophet will know."

Ean frowned at this. "I can do much with my talent innately without causing a disturbance on the currents."

"It's not the currents." Sebastian refilled his wine rather agitatedly. "Dore Madden has linked wards set all around the Tambarré acropolis like a chain of bells. Even with your skill, Ean, you'd never be able to unwork them all. By Cephrael's Great Book—half of them are carved into the very stones. And the *Prophet*…" he sat back again with a forceful exhale, "I can't even begin to describe him to you. Just let me assure you, he *will* know if you work *elae* near his temple. You can't risk it."

"Yet…there may be a way," a new voice said.

Ean turned his head to see Dareios leaning against a column, arms crossed. Their host nodded in greeting. "*Sobh bekheir*, Ean, Sebastian."

Dareios looked resplendent in a royal blue kurta, whose placket and rounded collar were embroidered with jewels in the design of a falling star. With his shining dark hair, the *Khoda Panaheh* marking his brow, and that dangling ruby in his ear, he seemed the quintessential Kandori prince. "Pardon my eavesdropping, but Ean's thoughts were loud enough to perceive far down the hall."

Ean grunted. "I'd invite you to explore the deepest corners of my mind if it would solve this problem."

Dareios' smile implied there weren't too many dark corners he hadn't already explored, but he said only, "My family has contacts in the Prophet's temple. They may be able to tell us when the Prophet is next away. Ean would only need a few hours to get in and out and could do so without attracting Bethamin's eye."

Sebastian muttered, "That would at least be one less evil to deal with," at the same time that Ean asked, "You have contacts in the Temple of Tambarré?"

A wry smile teased on Dareios' lips. "You'd be amazed how many people have 'people' in the Prophet's temple, Ean."

Sebastian exhaled by way of agreement. "The place has more spies than candles."

Ean perked up. "Then perhaps—"

Dareios shook his head. "I'm afraid they won't be of much help to us, save to provide some information."

"He's right," Sebastian said. "There's no deadlier place to serve two masters. No spy would so much as dare to lift his head, lest the Prophet notice him."

Ean thought of the truthreader Kjieran van Stone and the formidable task he'd accepted in becoming Dannym's spy in the Temple of Tambarré. He wondered if the man yet survived, and if he'd managed to learn anything that would help his king father keep the kingdom safe from the Duke of Morwyk.

Ean gave a ponderous sigh. *What a tangled web.*

Dareios glanced at him with understanding in his gaze. "Let me see what I can learn." He nodded to them both and departed.

Sebastian fingered his goblet and stared quietly into the dark liquid within. "All these *eidola*..." After a moment's contemplation, he muttered, "Do you ever ask yourself *why*? What's he making them *for*? What does he intend to do with them?"

"All the time." Verily, for lack of understanding that very important truth, Ean felt like he was already standing at the gallows, with the *eidola* looping a noose around his neck.

Sebastian set his goblet on the table and then sank back in his chair. "I wish Isabel had shared more of her vision with us."

Ean grimaced into his wine. He would rather have had needles driven underneath his fingernails than think about Isabel. He clenched his jaw and stared off into the day, noting how the world beyond seemed very bright in comparison to the loggia's cool shadows and his own stormy humor. "She's a Player in the game, Sebastian..." he murmured discontentedly, "but so am I."

Sebastian considered him with a frown. "Have you made your peace with her, then?" When Ean said nothing to this, only glowered off, he noted, "You can't avoid her forever—"

Ean's eyes flashed to his. "Nor can I just forgive her." He hadn't wanted to bring the subject up again. He hadn't wanted to discuss Isabel at all.

Sebastian absently edged his goblet away from his knife. "I could've sent Trell to his death at the hands of Viernan hal'Jaitar," he observed quietly. "Can you not forgive me either?"

"You were under compulsion and had little choice, as I recall."

"Perhaps she didn't either."

"Isabel herself would argue every free mind has a choice. She chose her path. She chose to betray me while upon it."

"And I chose to send Trell to M'Nador, but you've forgiven me that betrayal. What choices did *you* make that betrayed Isabel?"

Ean clenched his jaw and stared off into the painfully bright beyond.

Sebastian sat forward and leaned elbows on his knees, hands clasped before him. "Here's one to help you, little brother: Arion abandoned Isabel. *You* left her to live her life alone for three hundred years."

Ean flung him a black glare. "I *died*, damn you!"

Sebastian arched a brow. "Indeed." He sat back in his chair with challenge gleaming in his gaze. "And in your knowing decision to walk that path to your death, weren't you choosing the game over Isabel—even as she chose the game over fidelity to you when she bound a Malorin'athgul to our cause?"

Ean held Sebastian's eyes with his jaw clenched. He wished he'd never told his brother any of it, for Sebastian willingly looked where Ean would not. Moreover, his point hit closely to a truth Ean had yet to unveil about a choice he didn't understand.

Sebastian tapped at one arm of his chair. "How were your choices any different from Isabel's, Ean?"

Ean ground his teeth. "She *laid with another man*, Sebastian."

The quirk of a grin twitched in the corner of his brother's mouth.

Ean glared at him. "What?"

"Ean," Sebastian retrieved his goblet from the table, "it's just…she's sleeping with another man every time she sleeps with you." He raised his goblet to him meaningfully and then took a long drink.

Ean just stared at him, feeling numb.

Perhaps seeing that his point had struck center, Sebastian regarded him pensively. "You're both Players, you said. So *be* a Player. Do what you have to do…but don't make the mistake of thinking your choices are any different from Isabel's, or that the decisions you've made for the sake of the game are somehow beyond reproach, while hers are not." He dangled his goblet beneath one draped hand and regarded Ean with concern darkening his brow. "You've both chosen the game over each other. You've both made the game more important than anything else, and maybe…maybe that was and still is the right choice."

Ean wanted to argue, but his brother made things too simple. Out of belligerence more than reason, he grumbled, "One betrayal doesn't sanction another."

A grim smile flickered on Sebastian's lips. "How do you valuate betrayal, Ean?" He fingered the rim of the goblet suspended beneath his hand. "Can one kind of betrayal really hold more weight than another? You betrayed Isabel, she betrayed you…by Epiphany's light, is any of it even *important*? Ah…" He shook his head. "I don't know how to guide you in this."

Sebastian set down his goblet and pushed out of his chair. Shoving hands into his pockets, he walked absently beneath the terrace arches. "You've a right to feel as you feel, Ean. I'm not taking sides against you, only…" he glanced over his shoulder, "only I would have you see *both* sides. It's what our father always taught us—that there are at least two sides to every conflict, and often both feel equally justified in their view. Our power as kings, as diplomats, as leaders of men, comes in being able to assume multiple points of view and understand them. Only in understanding can we hope to positively influence the outcome of any conflict."

Sebastian paced quietly for a time and then turned another sudden, pointed look at Ean. "You know…you're not the same man Isabel made the Unbreakable Bond with, yet she bound herself to you newly in this life without hesitation."

His words felt like crushed glass ground into the wound. Ean glared down into his empty goblet. "What's your point, Sebastian?"

Sebastian turned to him, looking thoughtful. "My point is that Isabel saw in you the man she vowed to love for eternity, even though that man carries a different face and body." He leaned back against a column, hands in his pockets. "I was just thinking…maybe these shells and what's done to them…maybe that isn't so important."

'…We are none of us the shells we wear….'

Isabel's words, given as consolation when Ean had rejected Creighton because he wore a face of chrome.

"I'm not trying to excuse what she did, Ean, or saying that because *we* are not these shells that it doesn't matter how we interact with them. Only… you're seeking some way to forgive her, and it seems to me like deciding what parts of your relationship are most important to you is a good beginning."

While Ean stared broodingly at his goblet, Sebastian blew out a forceful exhale and turned his gaze out over the vista. "How often do you think I've thought about what Dore did to me?"

Lifting his gaze, Ean suddenly saw not his oldest brother, hale and whole, but the naked, broken man he'd found chained to a granite slab in Tal'Afaq.

Sebastian must've observed the latent horror in his expression, for he grunted with understanding and laid his head back against the stone column, letting his gaze drift away. "You have no idea what it was like…the degradation I felt, how utterly ruined I was for so long. Dore worked his damnedest to destroy everything about myself that I respected. He dug himself so deeply into my soul, I thought I'd never be free of his seed. But somehow, despite all of it, I managed to hold onto at least a shadow of my honor."

He looked to Ean with concern furrowing his brow and shifted his stance against the column. "I have to believe this is because honor doesn't reside in our corporeal forms, Ean, but in some, I don't know—" He shrugged absently, searching for the term, "*ephemeral* part of us…the part that continues on into the Returning. If *that's* who we truly are, what does it matter what happens to these bodies we don for a brief span of eternity?"

Sebastian pushed off the column and walked beyond the loggia into the sunlight. The passage seemed to cleanse him of the dark shadows that were gripping both of their hearts. "At least…that's how I have to think of it." He leaned his forearms on the balustrade. "It's the only way I *can* think about it and live on with my sanity intact, knowing all of the things Dore did to me…the things he made me do." At this, he let out a slow breath and hung his head.

Regarding him gravely, Ean understood what his brother was trying to tell him, and Sebastian probably had the right of it. It unfortunately didn't lessen the confusing guilt he felt around the entire affair.

Sebastian turned over his shoulder and regarded Ean with a frown. "We'd better go see what Dareios has learned."

Ean stared at him through burning eyes. "Yes, I guess we should."

As fortune—or fate, Ean couldn't quite decide—would have it, Dareios' spies reported that Bethamin had been gone from the temple for a few days, but they had no information on his expected return.

Not knowing when they might get another chance, the three of them decided it was worth the risk. They spent the rest of the day and evening planning, with Sebastian and Dareios each sharing all they knew about Tambarré, exploring all possible places where the *eidola* could be housed, and delineating escape routes for Ean to follow after he'd accomplished the mission.

"One last thing, Ean," Dareios said as they were wrapping up. "My sources tell me that the Prophet's Advisor" —aka Dore Madden— "has put a bounty on your life to the tune of two hundred gold talents."

Sebastian let out a low whistle.

"A princely amount indeed," Dareios agreed.

"The whole of Tambarré will be on the lookout for you with that kind of bounty on your life, Ean," Sebastian said.

Dareios stroked one triangular eyebrow. "You'll need to get in and out fast and unnoticed."

Ean stood and smiled darkly at them. "So what else is new?"

Long after midnight, Ean returned to his rooms and collapsed onto his bed with an exhausted sigh. He hadn't intended to sleep, but it had been so long since he'd visited with slumber that it claimed him almost at once.

―⁕―

"Dore's planning something." Arion slung himself roughly down into an armchair beside the drafting table where Björn was working. "He's set up his own little version of our Council of Nine. He's plotting an overthrow—I just know it."

Björn was sketching an intricate diagram on a large canvas that took up the entire drafting table. He narrowed his gaze as he carefully connected two lines using one edge of a triangular ruler. The currents were amassed around him in billowing, burnished clouds, flax to his spinning wheel, only this spindle took the form of a glass-tipped pen. He spun several strands of elae to form his magical ink, adjusted his ruler to a new direction, and drew another line. "What does Isabel say?"

"She says she can't see anything on his path."

Björn angled him a look. "Can't see anything of consequence, or can't see anything?"

Arion scowled. "She wouldn't specify."

"An odd ambiguity, coming from my sister." Björn sat back in his chair and considered Arion with a slight furrow between his brows. "Do you think Dore's actions connect to this pattern of consequence you've predicted?"

Arion worked the muscles of his jaw. "There's a darkness at the other end of that pattern that I can't work through. It vanishes into mist as if their objectives are purposefully being obscured." He met Björn's gaze. "Would even our enemy have such power?"

Björn arched brows to admit the possibility. "We don't know all that they're capable of."

"We don't know a tenth of what they're capable of!" Arion shoved out of his chair and stalked over to the windows, pushing hands into his pockets.

"Cause and consequence follow in a logical sequence. Even though I can't see how it all connects, instinct tells me that it does." He turned a serious look to Björn. "I fear Isabel is relying too heavily on her Sight. She's not willing to believe what I've foreseen, though logically the path extends in that direction."

"Providing men make the choices you've predicted they're going to make."

Arion pinned him with his gaze. "I've never been wrong."

Björn returned a shadowy smile. "Neither has Isabel."

Arion frowned at him. "You know, you're really a terrible mediator."

Björn's gaze glinted of amusement. He set down his glass pen and folded hands in his lap. "I thought a mediator's primary mandate was impartiality."

"Except when I'm right. Then it's your duty to help your sister see that." Arion blew out his breath and leaned his head back against a glass pane. He cast a troubled gaze towards the frescoed ceiling. "I have an overpowering feeling that we should be following our instincts instead of depending so much on *elae's* channels to guide us through this bog."

"That's quite a statement, coming from you."

Arion looked back to him. "Do you disagree?"

Björn considered him quietly for a moment. "In theory, I agree with you, but I also think we're going to need to use every resource available to us, pursue every possible avenue, to gain the advantage." He picked up his glass pen again and went back to his chart.

The canvas spread before him comprised hundreds of carefully intersecting geometric shapes. It was beginning to resemble a globe. When Arion looked more closely at it, he saw the grid was three-dimensional. Björn made a motion with his hand, and the three-dimensional figure on the page spun to reveal a new section, only partially sketched in—the beginnings of T'khendar's weldmap.

Björn slid the corner of the triangular ruler into a new position. "I trust that whatever machinations Dore may be working against my sister, you and Isabel will soon have them in hand."

Dissatisfaction thrummed through Arion. He angled a restless look at his brother-by-binding. "Sometimes I think you place too much faith in all of us."

Björn lifted him an admiring smile, one that acknowledged the deep bond of friendship they shared. "I either trust all of you implicitly, or I take every position on the field myself—which you and I both know would open the game to the liability of a single point of view." He gave him an encouraging look and returned to his map. "There's no other way to do this, Arion. I have to trust you and Isabel to play your positions. So play them well."

Ean roused with a start and looked to the windows to find them still blessedly dark. Surging into action, he tossed his satchel onto the bed and began grabbing the items he would need for his journey. The dream remained in the back of his mind, stirring a restless malcontent.

As he took his sword and scabbard from their hook in the armoire, he stilled. His sword felt heavy in his hands, weighted by duty…a sword that Phaedor had remade for him into a sentient Merdanti blade.

'…*You will have need of that sword yet. Much need…*'

Ean exhaled a heavy sigh. He had to wonder, if he went ahead with this course, moving forward as Arion had always done to achieve the effect he intended despite any and all odds…if he chose to pursue a path of unpredictability in the face of Dore's predictions…would he finally be stepping onto the field as a Player? Would he finally be finding his position and playing it well?

A knock came on the door, and Sebastian pushed his head through the parting.

Ean arched brows. "It's late…or I suppose I should say early." He shoved his hair out of his eyes and went back to his packing.

"I couldn't sleep." Sebastian closed the door behind himself. "I just kept having this terrible premonition that you're going to go out there and do something stupid."

Ean eyed his brother tetchily. "Isabel didn't come to you in another dream, did she? Send you in here to try to change my mind?"

"No. Just call it an older brother's intuition, knowing his littlest brother's foolhardy nature."

A smile crept across Ean's features. "Trell was the foolhardy one. I just didn't want to be left behind."

Tragically, thoughts of his middle brother reminded Ean of the many others he'd inadvertently drawn into this game: Alyneri, Tanis, Gwynnleth, Fynnlar. Where were they now? What trials had they endured? Even the problems his mother and father were facing against the Duke of Morwyk seemed somehow connected to him, all of them interwoven into the vast tapestry that encompassed Björn van Gelderan's game.

No…Björn's and Arion's game. He had to remember that.

Ean straightened and turned to his brother. "Do you think I'm making the wrong decision, going to Tambarré?"

Sebastian puffed a forceful sigh. "No. I don't entirely agree with this course, but I support the rationale for why it's necessary." He wandered across the room towards the glass doors and Ean's balcony. "But I've been thinking."

Ean followed him with his gaze. "About Tambarré?"

Sebastian turned him a telling look. "About choices." He crossed his arms and leaned one shoulder against the armoire. Beyond the mullioned glass, the barest lightening in the eastern sky bespoke the coming dawn. "We choose in every moment how to react to the things done to us. In *every* moment, Ean." He puffed out his breath and turned his gaze outside. "Every day I wake up and choose not to let Dore's degradation define me now. Every day I have to fight against those memories. *Every single morning* I push them off and decide to live the life *I've* chosen, not one Dore fashioned for me."

Ean groaned and sank down onto the bed. "This is about Isabel."

"I can't let it go, Ean—I can't let *you* go without speaking my mind."

Ean felt defeated already. He waved to his brother to say what he would.

Sebastian pushed off the armoire and wandered about the room. "All night I've been thinking…if you truly love Isabel," and he glanced up under his brows to emphasize his point, "if you love her, Ean, shouldn't you be thinking of what *she* went through, at least in part? It seems to me that if you were thinking of her instead of yourself—*thirteen hells*, you should be filled with gratitude that she's alive!"

He sank down abruptly on the edge of a chair, leaned forward and rested elbows on his knees to better view Ean eye to eye. "Think on it, little brother: Isabel threw herself in Darshan's path to keep him from finding *you*. She gave herself up to become a prisoner of the Prophet, a *Malorin'athgul*—and thank Epiphany he gave her to his brother Pelas, because he could've given her to Dore!"

A chill pealed down Ean's spine at this heretofore unconsidered idea. He stared at Sebastian, feeling suddenly ill.

"Yes, you see it now too, don't you?" A sort of latent horror came into Sebastian's gaze as well. "Isabel knowingly sacrificed herself to save *you*, Ean." He fell backwards in the chair and grabbed the arms, as if to steel himself against the same convulsive truth. "If I were you, I would be immensely relieved that the woman I love is alive and well and not under a madman's control…not mutilated beyond a few scars."

You didn't see the patterns carved all over her body.

But Ean kept this ungracious response to himself.

He pulled his sword onto his lap and fingered the sapphire pommel stone, wishing it didn't remind him so much of his past mistakes and other things he would rather not think on.

Sebastian was regarding him with a restless unease, as if the words he wanted to say made the chair hot beneath his seat. "*Yes*, she betrayed you, but what about this love you supposedly bear for her?" Sebastian pushed from his chair. "This *boundless* love isn't enough to forgive her for walking her path? At least Isabel found a way ultimately to *survive* it. Could Arion say the same?"

Ean glared darkly down at his sword.

Sebastian came over and laid a hand on his shoulder. "I have to say these things. I have to have a clean conscience letting you go, little brother. I was there when Isabel said goodbye. I saw the look on her face." He squeezed Ean's shoulder. "Besides…I don't know when I'll see you again…*if* I'll see you again."

Ean lifted him a tormented look. "Don't say such things."

Sebastian shrugged. "If it's not you death claims, it could be me." He pushed hands in his pockets and gazed off towards the coming dawn. "I can't shake the feeling that we've got this brief calm before the storm. Any day now it could hit."

Ean couldn't help but wonder if the actions he was about to take in Tambarré would be that beginning, but he kept this thought to himself as well.

"I'd best get going." He stood and donned his jacket and cloak and belted on his sword. Yet now that it was time to take leave of each other, he found it agonizing to part with his brother. He took Sebastian by the shoulders and then embraced him. "I'm so grateful for you," he confessed.

"And I for you, little brother." Sebastian gave Ean an encouraging smile that didn't quite banish the concern from his gaze. "Come. I'll walk you to the node."

Ean took up his pack, and they departed.

It seemed only minutes before they reached Andorr's nodecourt. Ean walked to the center of the tiled space and summoned the patterns he needed to travel on the Pattern of the World.

Then, with a last look of farewell that roused a deep uncertainty, he lifted a hand to Sebastian, watched his brother lift his in return, and stepped onto the node.

TWENTY-THREE

"Never try to teach a bear to sing. It only frustrates you
and really annoys the bear."

–The *Hearthwitch's Handbook*

TANIS WOKE TO the sound of thunder. Rising from a large four-poster bed, he walked to the windows and pushed aside the drapes to gaze out over—

Gone were the mountains of yesterday. Now he looked out from the stern stateroom of a massive ship, if told from the size of the ever-expanding wake it was leaving in the charcoal sea. The waves undulating behind them wore shades of ash, with variegated spots of blue in places where the sunlight still peeked through the turbulent clouds. They were sailing upon choppy waves, but Tanis felt no motion—the only indication that the world he looked upon was actually Sinárr's illusion.

Tanis gazed at the rain-washed sea with a furrow marring his brow. He couldn't help wondering if the night had been allowed to run its course, or if Sinárr had merely created the illusion of night, when in fact the time had passed in a blink. What if the night had not been at all? Had he actually left Sinárr only seconds ago, yet was being made to believe he'd gone to bed and woken as if to a normal dawn? Was Sinárr able to alter Tanis's thoughts about his experience as easily as he molded the experience itself?

It was unsettling to contemplate, and probably unproductive, so Tanis turned his mind to more important matters, like the fact that he was terribly hungry. Whatever else Sinárr might be manipulating, he knew *that* feeling was real.

A knock on his door drew his gaze, and Mérethe entered, carrying a tray. She wore a navy dress that seemed appropriate to their maritime surroundings, with a split skirt and an open neckline that highlighted her shoulders. A strand of pearls collared her neck.

She smiled and balanced the tray on her hip as she pulled the stateroom door closed. "Good morning, Tanis."

"Is it morning?" He gave her an unconvinced look. "I wish I could be sure. But it's nice to see you, Mérethe, whatever the time of day."

"Surely you're too young to be so charming." She gave him a sidelong glance while setting the tray down on a table by the windows. "Sinárr thought you might be hungry."

Tanis eyed the domed platter. "He did, did he?"

Mérethe straightened and pressed out her skirt. "It's difficult to hide things from him in his own universe."

Tanis walked over and lifted the silver dome to find an assortment of savory tarts, sausages and pies. He was so hungry, he didn't care if they were real or not. He set the dome aside. "Will you break your fast with me, Mérethe?"

She cast an uneasy look back at the door. "I…don't think I should."

Tanis pulled out a chair for her. "Why did he send you with my food if he didn't expect us to talk?"

Mérethe kneaded her fingers as she considered him, her blue eyes round with uncertainty. But eventually she sat in the chair he was holding out for her.

Tanis walked around the table and seated himself, observing Mérethe as she served herself a tiny portion of food. He wished she would've taken more. She looked perilously thin.

Tanis reached for the teapot to pour some tea, and—

Froze with his fingers around the handle. Where had the teapot come from? He couldn't recall noticing it until he'd expected it to be there.

Shaking off this unsettling experience, Tanis went ahead and poured tea for both of them. "Has Sinárr told you much about the Warlocks or their history?"

She nibbled at a piece of toast she'd chosen. "Some."

"Did he ever tell you why he models his world after Alorin?"

Mérethe looked at the toast in her hand as if concerned it might become something else. "I never thought to ask him."

Tanis shoved half of a piece of quiche into his mouth. It tasted of sage, mushroom and leeks. *How does he* do *this?* Sinárr even made things *taste* like they were supposed to! For a moment, the immensity of this simple point fully unnerved him. Then Tanis decided he didn't care and ate the other half.

"Warlocks…" he reached for another piece of quiche, "they seem nearly godlike." He considered Mérethe quietly while she ate. "For all intents and purposes, in Shadow, they *are* gods. Don't you think that's true, Mérethe?"

Mérethe nibbled fretfully at her toast.

"I've been wondering, did our Maker create the Warlocks the same as He created the other immortal races—*drachwyr*, zanthyrs…Malorin'athgul?"

She set down her toast, still barely touched, and rested her hands in her lap. "I don't know, Tanis."

Tanis scrubbed at the scruff on his chin and tried to think the idea through. "It follows that our Maker created them. But if He did, *why* did He create them?"

Mérethe gave him a hollow look. "Perhaps they balance something. Isn't that the reason for most everything?"

"Yes," Tanis sat back in his chair and frowned, "that's what I've been struggling with." He looked at her significantly. "But here's the thing: when the Maker created the Realms of Light, Mérethe, He gave the Warlocks access to them."

Which begged the immediate question: *What has the Council of Realms* unbalanced *by denying Warlocks access to the Realms of Light for all these centuries?*

Mérethe was making knots of her fingers in her lap.

Tanis leaned to try to capture her gaze. "What do you know of the Council of Realms? Has Sinárr told you anything about what happened between the Council and the Warlocks of Shadow? There must've been some conflict. Surely he shared something with you about it?"

Mérethe's gaze flicked to him and back to her hands. "I think the problem centered on the *inverteré* patterns the Warlocks use. That is…from the way Sinárr speaks of it, *inverteré* patterns are native to Warlocks in the same way *elae's* patterns are innate to Adepts. When they work their power in the Realms of Light, Warlocks twist *elae* into an inversion of itself." She glanced up uncertainly at him. "You mention Balance, Tanis, but when the Warlocks were in Alorin, there was no Balance in the realm. They subjugated the races of man to cruel whimsy and enslaved Adepts to their will like toys. They made men do frightful things."

"Yes, I've heard the stories."

Mérethe stared brokenly at him. "I wish I could help you, Tanis, but I don't really know anything more. He's never spoken to me the way he speaks to you."

Tanis exhaled a slow breath while he considered the Avieth. She'd clearly suffered so much already, he didn't want to make things worse by pressing her for information, but there were so many things he needed to understand. He felt once again as if he stood on the verge of some important truth, yet no matter how he strained to grasp it, the ledge of understanding remained just out of his reach.

Frustrated with himself as much as the situation, Tanis pushed out of his chair, shoved hands in his pockets—*wait, pockets?*—and wandered over to the mullioned windows.

The storm had completely overtaken the day. Now ashen sheets of rain striped the sea. He watched a heavier line of pelting raindrops coming towards them across white-capped waves, but all he really saw was the nebulous outline he'd formed in his mind. He kept trying to fit the pieces he knew into this outline, but none of them had the proper shape.

"Tanis?"

He turned Mérethe an inquiring look.

"Most of us don't realize how much our senses frame our belief of what is real." She dropped her gaze back to her lap and absently traced a damask design on the tablecloth with her forefinger. "We think if our bodies can feel it, it's real. Sinárr *knows* this." She caught her bottom lip between her teeth and braved a worried glance at him. "All of this is illusion."

It seemed an important truth to her, but Tanis had already reached his own conclusion about reality. He leaned his shoulder against the window sash and regarded Mérethe steadily. "If Sinárr's illusions can feel as solid and real as our own world, Mérethe, who's to say that Alorin wasn't formed in exactly the same manner?"

She looked terrified by this idea.

"Yesterday..." Tanis paused, grimaced, corrected himself, "well, *whenever* it was that I last saw Sinárr, he claimed that reality is basically what we have agreed that it is. The Esoterics even support this idea."

He'd realized this truth as he'd been lying in bed, pondering his conversation with Sinárr. "The Twenty-First Esoteric says: *Reality is monitored by collective thought agreement.* I had always interpreted this Esoteric in reference to the crafting of fourth-strand illusions, but it's clear that the Esoterics apply to the wielding of *any* energy, in any realm."

Tanis pushed off the window and walked back towards the Avieth. "By this logic, Mérethe, Alorin is no more and no less real than Sinárr's world—save that more of us have agreed on its existence."

Mérethe dropped her gaze back to her lap and her voice to a bare whisper. "You shouldn't say such things, Tanis."

"Mérethe, why?" He couldn't understand why she was so focused on making him believe that Sinárr's world was only an illusion.

She flung a desperate look at him. "*Because...*" but her voice broke, and she dropped her gaze again. Tears welled in her eyes and then fell down her cheeks. "Because...he will make you forget what *is* real."

Tanis placed a hand gently on her shoulder.

"The people you love," she whispered brokenly, "the places you hold dear, the things and ideas that meant something to you—you'll turn your back on all of them. You'll forsake them for the illusions he panders."

Tanis had no doubt this had been her experience, though it made him wonder…

He crouched in front of her seated form. "Mérethe, when we met in the laboratory in Alorin, you told me that Sinárr would make me *eidola*, like the others." He put his hands on the arms of her chair. "What others? Has he brought others here?"

Mérethe wiped at her eyes. "Most Adepts cannot survive in Shadow for more than a day or two, even bound to a Warlock. This much he told me."

Most Adepts… Tanis filed this information for later investigation. "But he's made *eidola* out of other Adepts?"

Mérethe cast a nervous look at the door as if it was the ear of Sinárr's mind. "He's made no *eidola* for himself that I know of, but…I think he's made *eidola* for the Malorin'athgul—or helped him in some way."

"For Shail?"

She nodded.

Tanis wondered grimly if Malin van Drexel was one of those unfortunates. Then he asked the question he'd been leading up to. "But he didn't make *eidola* of you."

Mérethe exhaled a tremulous breath. "He brought me here to be his concubine," she lifted him a look of dread, "like you."

"Yes, like me." Tanis made a face. He squatted on his heels, thinking about the idea. Sinárr seemed to have a different concept of a concubine from how Tanis thought of the term. Perhaps the subservient aspect was the same, but Sinárr's interest wasn't sexual—leastwise not towards him.

Tanis pushed to his feet and returned to his chair. Leaning back, he gazed off at distant shapes, trying to focus on the ideas that refused to combine into the answers he was seeking.

After a while, he shifted his eyes back to the Avieth. "What's he waiting for?"

Mérethe gave him a startled, doe-eyed look.

Tanis cast a narrow stare off towards the door, just in case Mérethe knew something about it that he didn't. "Sinárr brought me here; he knows I can't escape. He could bind me at any time." He looked back to her. "Why hasn't he?"

Mérethe stared at him.

Tanis made his tone more gentle. "Is this how it happened for you?"

She pressed her lips together tightly and shook her head. Tears welled in her eyes again.

Tanis exhaled a breath of frustration. He settled a steely gaze on the door. *If you're listening, Sinárr, I would that you answered my questions yourself.*

Instantly two light raps came. The page boy from yesterday opened the door and stood in the portal. "Would you accompany me, my lord?"

Tanis glanced down at his clothing, thinking he would need to dress, and found that Sinárr had already taken care of that.

Something in this disturbed him, but it took him a moment to put his finger on why. He shifted his gaze back to Mérethe and her navy dress. He'd assumed that she'd chosen it herself; now he suspected otherwise.

Suddenly, this seemed terribly relevant. In the next instant, he understood why.

The Esoterics taught that a wielder must operate at a level of 'prime cause.' The moment a wielder allowed another's intention to direct or alter his own, he violated the First Law: *KNOW the effect you intend to create.*

Arion had often written in his journals about the importance of a wielder knowing *exactly* what effect he wanted to create; equally important was the follow-through to achieve that postulated effect. No wielder could succeed who allowed another to make decisions for him.

That's when Tanis understood a devastating truth. How long had it been since Mérethe had been allowed to make her own decisions? How long had Sinárr been moving her about, dressing her as *he* willed, feeding her what *he* chose, *placing* her in time and space like a doll with no thoughts of her own? And how long could a living being endure such treatment, even gently exacted, without losing a grasp upon their own will and sense of self?

It wasn't just Sinárr's keeping Mérethe in darkness that had bled the light of life from her; it was the fact that she couldn't make a single decision of her own.

Tanis knew he had to avoid that potentiality at all costs. When he surrendered responsibility for his own thoughts and choices, he really would become Sinárr's puppet. He cast the thought outward, *I think I'll choose my own clothing, thanks.*

"As you require," replied the servant boy in the doorway. He indicated an armoire with one hand. "When you're ready, my lord, he awaits above." He closed the door as he left.

Tanis looked down at himself and saw that he was wearing his night clothes again. When he lifted his gaze to Mérethe, she was staring open-mouthed at him.

Tanis emerged from below decks into a raging storm. The sails of the barquentine's main and mizzen masts were reefed, while the square-rigged sails on the foremast were fully let out, for they sailed with the wind.

White-capped waves washed around the ship on all sides, and ashen sheets of rain pelted the sea, but only a stiff breeze crossed the deck.

Tanis saw Sinárr standing amidships at the starboard railing. His long black hair with its bands of silver stood out brightly against a wine-red cloak, which was snapping on the wind. Tanis walked to join him.

"A real ship would be pitching and hawing in this weather," the lad noted as he reached Sinárr's side.

The Warlock cast him a sidelong smile. "Yes, but I find that tiresome, don't you?" He looked Tanis over appreciatively, his golden eyes noting the dark blue tunic and pants the lad had chosen for himself—albeit from an armoire stocked with items that Sinárr had created.

At least…Tanis presumed Sinárr had filled the wardrobe with clothes, but the hint of amused approval in the Warlock's gaze now challenged this assumption.

Sinárr looked back to the sea. "It's an interesting experience, having someone else form things in my universe."

"Isn't that why you brought me here?" *Isn't that why you're holding me here?*

Sinárr eyed him hungrily. "Indeed it is, Tanis-mine."

Tanis's fortitude thinned beneath the Warlock's fervent look. He really wished that he might've possessed a sturdier defense against this immortal than his meager wits and unpredictable glimpses of Fate's will. Back in his rooms, Tanis had felt a certain bravado to confront Sinárr. Now that he stood looking up at the tall and strangely compelling Warlock, he found words of challenge much harder to summon.

Sinárr studied him for a moment with the hint of a smile on his lips. "You want to know why I haven't yet bound you." He reached as if to touch Tanis's face but instead held his ebony hand paused before his eyes. "You cannot see yourself as I see you." Fingernails that glinted of gold hovered in front of him. "Even if a mirror existed that could reflect your essence as it appears to me, still you wouldn't see what I see, for we perceive through different lenses."

Sinárr closed his fingers into a fist and lowered his hand. "You are a delicious temptation, don't you see, Tanis? I would not forgo the sensation of our courtship so quickly." He stepped closer to Tanis, still offering that fervent gaze, his body leaning towards the lad as a tree inclining towards the sun. He caught Tanis beneath the chin and lifted the lad's eyes to meet his. "You prefer I should be quick to end it?"

Tanis jerked free of the Warlock's touch, feeling unnerved.

It wasn't the avid look in Sinárr's eyes or even his cold power that made the lad so uncomfortable. It was a sort of *resonance* he felt happening between them. Like two pitch forks tuned to the same note, Sinárr's frequency was eliciting an odd and intensely unsettling recognition in Tanis. He backed away.

Sinárr followed as the lad retreated, forcing him up against the railing. Tanis could feel Sinárr's power wrapped around him and growing tighter with every breath. What disturbed him, though, was this feeling of repulsion and connection—as much as he felt the need to get away from the Warlock, so also did he feel disconcertingly drawn to him.

Sinárr held up his hand as if to touch Tanis's shoulder but again paused just shy of contact. "This feeling," he murmured, "this desirousness that flows upon a sort of delirious energy…it's not something I've often felt outside the raw creation of worlds."

Tanis regarded Sinárr, feeling confused and more than a little panicked. It was absolutely impossible that he could be *attracted* to this creature. So what *was* he experiencing? And *why* was he experiencing it?

He clutched the railing with both hands, feeling like the ship was tossing on the waves and likely to pitch him overboard at any moment. His mind sought any logical thought to cling to and finally landed on one.

"*Often*." Tanis looked up at Sinárr, still braced against that impending fall. "You said you've not *often* experienced this…" he paused…swallowed, "feeling."

The Warlock finally straightened away from him, allowing the lad to recover his breath and his wits. "Yes." Sinárr frowned slightly. "With Mérethe, in the beginning, I felt something similar, though far less strongly so." He looked Tanis over quietly. Then he extended a hand inviting Tanis's companionship and started off towards the stern.

Tanis exhaled a shuddering sigh of relief and followed him.

Sinárr clasped hands behind his back as he strolled the deck with his blood-red cloak snapping on the wind and his golden eyes lifted to the storm. He moved like a predatory cat flows over the mountainside, absorbing leaps and landings in its powerful limbs, seeming nearly to float along.

Actually…comparing Sinárr to a predatory cat didn't seem so far off, now that Tanis thought about it. Certainly the more time he spent in Sinárr's company, the less human the man seemed. Tanis admitted a certain fascination with the Warlock, but even this didn't explain the strange energy that waxed and waned between them.

A flicker of amusement hinted on Sinárr's lips. "You don't like it, this sensation."

Tanis still felt like the ship was heeling beneath his feet and walked with a hand half-outstretched, ready to grab the railing at any moment. "I don't understand it. Do you?"

Sinárr turned him a curious eye. "No, admittedly." His gaze took in Tanis's slightly tilted stance—which must've looked ridiculous, considering the ship was sailing flat in the water—and gave a low chuckle. "Would you like to go somewhere more stable, Tanis?"

Abruptly the lad found himself standing within a grove of oak trees. Dappled sunlight fell on a carpet of leaves and gilded a brook off to the left.

Sinárr asked from beside him. "Better?"

Tanis still felt askew.

The Warlock laughed softly. "Somewhere else then."

The world vanished. Suddenly Tanis gazed into a starscape. Everywhere he looked, he saw stars. What he didn't see was any sign of his own body.

How is this meant to be better? Even without hearing his voice, he knew it sounded shrill.

You will see. Here...this will help.

Tanis felt Sinárr's arms wrapping around his chest.

This is hardly better, Sinárr.

Sinárr chuckled. *Not this part. I know you shy from my touch, but until we're bound, physical contact is necessary for what I mean to show you. Watch...*

At first, Tanis saw only pinpoints of light appearing on a velvet background—distant suns, perhaps with worlds of their own. Then a blackness appeared to spread in the center of his vision until it blocked out even the tiny points of light.

To build a world, it is necessary to first create space.

The blackness rapidly encompassed Tanis's entire view.

We create space by first creating a point to view.

Tanis saw what appeared to be a distant sun blink into existence. Right away, he realized he was *perceiving* it rather than *seeing* it—an odd distinction, yet it felt somehow important to have noticed the difference between sight and perception. Sight used bodily eyes, and the other...well, Tanis couldn't explain where perception came from. It was more a sense of knowing, of receiving back from the world some manner of communication or context of being; it was an *awareness* of things that did not depend on human eyes.

As he let this perception deepen, Tanis realized that whatever else this ball of energy was, it *wasn't* a star formed of exploding gasses.

Between us and the first of our starpoints spans the view of dimension. Now we frame space.

Tanis perceived more starpoints, as Sinárr had named them, blinking into existence to frame the darkness, forming the vertices of a shape that resembled a cube. But what truly excited him was that he could *feel* the space Sinárr had just carved into, or perhaps formed out of, Shadow's aether.

Whereas before, the flat expanse of darkness had held no depth, now Tanis perceived *space* framed within the starpoints.

What shall we put into the space we've formed?

A spark of light appeared in the center of the empty space. The light started spinning and drew other sparks of light into its core, where they coalesced to form a sphere.

A colorful effluence began spreading outwards from the sphere. These vapors distilled into the space around them or were drawn back into the sphere by the gravity of its spin, so it seemed a twirling dancer trailing colorful ribbons of light. As the dancer spun, it gathered more energy unto itself. The lights combined, fused and became magnetized. The center grew denser, darker, as gaseous particles cohered and compacted to form a solid core.

Watching raw energy coalescing into being, seeing what was undeniably a world forming before his very eyes, Tanis knew awe and amazement on a scale that defied description.

Whatever sickly drink he'd imbibed that had made him feel so unbalanced before had faded, replaced by an intoxicating concoction of exhilaration and wonderment and a burgeoning urge to make something so marvelous himself.

Even more incredible to experience was the sense of *largeness* that accompanied this moment. What he saw was no small ball of energy mimicking the creation of a world. It was surely a planet as large as Alorin—perhaps larger. Tanis conceived that the space his mind occupied had become *vast*—so massive as to watch from afar as a true world was forming out of the aether. Of this truth Tanis had no doubt.

We can spin a world into being from the raw energy of Shadow, or...

Sinárr made the spinning orb vanish—an entire *planet* vanished before his eyes!

...fashion something new from our imagination alone.

Suddenly Tanis found himself standing on an outcropping of luminous black stone amid a crescent-shaped waterfall of stars. Sinárr held him close in his arms, but for once Tanis didn't mind the Warlock's nearness. All the heavens were dark save for the sparkling brilliance around and behind them, which was nearly too bright to look upon. The starfall tumbled from unknowable heights into an abyss of velvet dark, and every star promised a new experience, new worlds, new opportunities for *making*.

Sinárr's arms tightened possessively around him. *Changing what we've created is as simple as our decision.*

All at once they were plunging inside a tube of stars—*no*, the stars were falling around *them*. The entire world had become formless streaks of light.

Within the shifting veils of energy that coalesced and streamed around him, Tanis saw endless possibilities.

Imagining himself drawing upon that energy, thinking of what wonders *he* might create, Tanis knew a joy so light and airy—and yet so vibrant and *real*—that he had no idea how to express it in human terms. It made him feel like crying and laughing and—*exploding*—all at the same time; it offered the exhilaration of immense freedom channeled alongside a wondrous sense of *play*. And throughout it all threaded an infinite, nearly impossible feeling of expansion, like simply *being* so much greater and larger and just *more* than he was.

Tanis felt heady. He'd stopped caring if any of it was real. He rejoiced in the overwhelming wonder of the experience, thrilled in receiving—*perceiving*—so many wavelengths of existence, and in observing a kind of creation he'd never imagined possible.

Tanis exhaled a sigh and laid his head dizzily back against Sinárr's chest. *When is it my turn?*

He perceived the Warlock's surprise. *I've never let another guide my intent. But that's what you want, isn't it? To create worlds with me?*

He felt Sinárr's uncertainty…and then a distance, as if a ridge of energy had coalesced to form a wall between the two sides of their opposing thoughts.

Suddenly they were standing once again on the white balcony of their first meeting. A moon was rising beyond the edge of the world, looming close and full between the dawn-colored cosmos and the iridescent, striated sky. A second moon at half phase glowed above the first, higher and fainter, just shy of the gaseous nebula of violet-pink clouds and clustering stars.

Sinárr walked away from Tanis, breaking off their contact.

Loss descended like a predator upon the lad. He'd had but the barest glimpse of making—more observing the experience than participating in it—yet the idea of being denied it now opened a terrible, agonizing void.

Tanis wondered if this was what it meant to be courted by a Warlock: in one moment being devoured by his desires and in the next denied them, returned to what should've felt a blessed freedom but instead feeling tainted by an undertone of loss, the deepest part of you wondering why you missed the heady terror of his attention.

"I've been thinking on what you said, Tanis." Sinárr turned a look over his shoulder. The moonlight limned his features, highlighting the angles of his nose and cheekbones, lips and jaw, while the planes of his dark skin faded into the background, forging him into an outline of himself. "I had never considered the idea before." He arched a brow. "No one ever compelled me to consider it before." Sinárr spread his hands along the railing and looked out over the edge of the world. "I see the logic in your argument, of course—if I truly want the benefit of your ability, your mind must be free to create with mine. Thus there can be only one solution."

The lad barely dared hope—

"You must agree to be bound."

Tanis choked on his own breath. "What?"

Sinárr turned from the railing and started towards him. The wind blew his cloak outwards behind him, and with his dark features limned in silver, he seemed alien and unearthly. "To create a world together that *all* might perceive—a world formed as your Alorin was formed, Tanis, with *elae* and *deyjiin* in perfect balance, a world forged of Shadow and Light..."

Sinárr stopped in front of him. His nearness woke that inexplicable resonance that Tanis dreaded, but his attention fixed on the lad felt oddly... engaging. "To create such a world, Tanis, our minds must act as one mind, working in concert to weave together the identical, inverse patterns that are respective to our natures."

Tanis stepped unsteadily back from him and pushed a hand through his hair. There were at least a dozen things in what Sinárr had just said that made no sense to him—for instance, what was the real difference between the worlds Sinárr created in his own universe and those he intended for them to create together, if all were illusion to begin with? And how could Alorin be fashioned of both *elae* and *deyjiin*? Or, if making a world that anyone could perceive required both forces, how had Björn van Gelderan forged T'khendar without *deyjiin*?

The worst of it was that even though he didn't understand Sinárr or agree with his actions, he didn't see anything fundamentally wrong with his goals.

It was immensely confusing.

Tanis pushed palms to his temples and tried to force the chaos in his brain to take the shape of words. "Let me see if I've got this straight. You've taken me away from everyone and everything I know and love, you're holding me here against my will...but you want my *consent* to be imprisoned and bound for all eternity?" Frustrated by the absurdity of Sinárr's expectations, he flung out a hand towards the world at large. "Shall I lock myself in my cell and place the manacles on my own wrists and ankles too?"

Sinárr looked startled. "This...isn't what you desired, Tanis?"

Tanis leveled him a telling look. "You're holding me against my will in an alien realm, Sinárr."

Sinárr seemed baffled by his ire. "You object to this treatment?"

"More than somewhat!"

Sinárr seemed pinned to immobility by Tanis's unexpected censure. His brow constricted. "I have never understood this view. Yours is a lesser race and therefore subject to mine."

Tanis's eyes flashed. "Lesser by whose estimation?"

Sinárr opened palms to the heavens. "It is an objective truth. Your race is not immortal."

"Immortal by *one* definition." Tanis faced him squarely. "Our bodies may not be immortal without working the Pattern of Life, but the essence of an Adept's being *is* immortal—everything that we *truly* are transfers from lifetime to lifetime: our minds, our experiences, even our memories. Have you heard nothing of the Returning?"

Sinárr turned up his palms in entreaty. "Tanis, be reasonable."

"*Reasonable?*" the lad sputtered.

"Your race cannot work *deyjiin*."

"And yours can't work *elae*!"

"You cannot build worlds—"

"Nor can you, Sinárr!" Tanis was well and truly angry now. Oddly, in the fires of indignation, he found firmer footing. In fact, he felt a force thrusting him further into it and was suddenly quite certain of his path.

A furrow marred Sinárr's brow. "How can you say this when I've just *shown* you—"

Tanis pointed at him in accusation. "You admitted all of this is illusion when you declared that you needed *me* to make your world solid to others."

The Warlock looked taken aback. "Tanis, I thought you saw—"

"Oh, I *saw*." Fury thrummed through Tanis in a way that felt powerful and true. "A moment ago, I saw something marvelous—miraculous, even. So much so it was nearly unbearable." He pushed a hand through his hair, still feeling the vestiges of that experience, the haunting effects of the emotion that had accompanied it, and the pounding ache of its loss. "What I saw made me *want* that more than I've ever wanted anything in my life." Tanis leveled the Warlock a severe gaze. "Now I only see hypocrisy clothed in human garb."

Sinárr blinked at him.

Tanis looked away. "I don't want to talk to you right now." These were the words he said aloud, but he was thinking, *I just need to be alone in my own space.*

Whereupon he found himself back in his empty bed chamber, which was an illusion, and *very* much alone, which was not.

TWENTY-FOUR

*"Any moral man will stand his ground for what he feels is right.
It takes a better man to acknowledge instantly and
without reservation that he is in error."*
—Ramuhárikhamáth, Lord of the Heavens

MARIUS DI L'ARLESÉ, High Lord of Agasan, Consort to the Empress of Agasan…father of a kidnapped heir…laid a hand on the red marble mantel and bowed his head. Across the long gallery, Valentina was receiving a briefing on the attack at the Sormitáge. Surrounding her stood a host of *Sobra* Scholars, several members of the Order of the Glass Sword, and commanders of both the Red Guard and the Imperial Adeptus and their aids.

Every word spoken in explanation of the events at the Quai game felt as a flail abrading Marius's flesh. Every single thing that had occurred was a result of *his* failure to understand the currents. That such an attack could happen at all sat squarely on his shoulders, *his* grave misjudgment, *his* ineptitude.

Valentina sat unmoving in her chair, listening with her chin propped upon her fingers, occasionally lifting her head to ask a question but otherwise keeping her own counsel. The fourth formed a wall around her thoughts, but the flinty hue shading her gaze revealed much of her disposition.

For a time, Marius had stood behind the others, draped in the jagged shadows of self-abasement, silently enduring the reports and Valentina's telling glances as a form of deserved torture. Then he'd stood by the windows and watched the sun setting in a stripe of flame between dual bands of darkness. He'd left the windows when they'd begun to reflect his own beleaguered stance.

So many days since the attack, and they were no closer to finding the truth...no closer to rescuing his daughter—*no closer to knowing where to look for her!* The node the Varangians had escaped across had been irreparably damaged. Pattern engineers from the Imperial Adeptus would have to rebuild its innate pattern from near nothing just to make it operable again. It gave them no clue to where the Danes and their Adept prisoners had traveled.

Marius had immediately ordered the Red Guard stationed in Kjvngherad to search King Ansgar's every fortress and holding across Daneland, but while the reports from those units continued filtering in, so far their searches had discovered nothing...no stolen Adepts, no *trace* of his daughter.

The air in the gallery felt sharp in Marius's lungs. Would that it might've brought the same sharpness to his thoughts. His mind was a whirlwind of spiraling facts he couldn't connect. *Elae's* currents coming out of Daneland carried an incomprehensible stain; they told him nothing. Without the currents to convey magical workings to him, he was blinded, even as Valentina remained blind without her Sight to guide her. And the true cause for either of these ill developments remained as clouded as his wits.

A little sleep could restore clarity.

But the Imperial Heir had been taken. To imagine his beautiful daughter in captivity, held at the mercy of their enemy...to imagine anything *happening* to Nadia...

Surely they knew the prize they held. They would use Nadia for leverage, a jewel to dangle before the imperial bargaining table. They would keep her safe, unharmed.

Yet if bargaining was their aim, why hadn't he heard from them?

Them—them! Who was he even talking about when he used the term? The Danes? Or another faction, as yet unrevealed?

Marius clenched his fist against the mantel.

The love he bore for his daughter notwithstanding, he almost worried more for Tanis di Adonnai, who hadn't the protection of an imperial birth, and whom Björn's zanthyr had left in his charge while Phaedor was protecting the Empress on her trip to Köhentaal. The Empress had now returned, safe and unharmed, while Tanis...

That the lad had been captured while under Marius's protection...*by the Lady's blessed light,* there was just no way to reconcile it! He'd failed in his promise. It was unconscionable.

He dreaded to the very depths of his core the moment when the zanthyr would confront him on this truth—for surely the creature wouldn't hesitate to drag him through the mud of his ineptitude. Pointing out Marius's failings was one of Phaedor's favorite entertainments.

Strangely, the creature had absented himself since Valentina's ship had arrived back in port that day. Marius couldn't decide if this was a kindness to him or an acute form of torture. He certainly didn't need Phaedor's derisive criticism to see the gravity of his own mistakes.

Oh, they'd gotten things in hand at the stadium eventually, but only after those marauding bastards had claimed upwards of *two hundred* Adepts for their Danegeld, due vengeance for the tithe the Empress had placed on Daneland's Adepts.

And the monsters who'd been the invaders' weapons of distraction... *they* were creatures out of legend, out of myth. And far too akin to the hapless Adept that had once laid bound in the Tower's deepest dungeon, chained to a table while his body slowly petrified into enchanted stone.

—*'What would you have us do?'*
'Kill him—while you still can.'—

The zanthyr's haunting warning still prickled Marius at inopportune times. That they'd heeded his caution—under great strain of effort, enough to make Marius wary of ever facing such a creature when conscious—offered ill comfort. It galled Marius immensely to do anything Phaedor suggested.

The High Lord exhaled a slow breath and tapped his fist against the mantel, trying to force a needle of clarity through the rough wool his brain had become. A question he'd asked himself a hundred times kept hounding his thoughts: *how had King Ansgar orchestrated an invasion of such complexity when the Danes had no Adepts with the ability to work the necessary patterns?*

After the last Varangian revolt, during which Ansgar's king father had been slain, Valentina had placed a restrictive tithe upon the province. Nine out of ten Adepts born were to be sent to Faroqhar; only those in civil service would return.

Even Marius had felt this penance too severe and certain to cause friction when the young Ansgar came into power. And he was sure now that it had done that very thing. But the fact remained that Daneland had few Adepts. None were formally trained in the fighting arts; none had more than their first ring—certainly none possessed the skill to untwist a node and then corrupt its native pattern to cover their retreating tracks. Marius could only conclude that if the Danes were indeed behind this attack, they were not acting alone.

This was the needling suspicion that kept him so on edge. It was that *other* who stood behind the king, the one hiding in Ansgar's shadow...*he* was the one Marius truly sought—and who was frustratingly eluding him at every turn!

Across the room, a low feminine voice sounded a pleasing murmur, though her words were far from comforting: Francesca da Molta, Commander of the Imperial Adeptus, was giving her report. Doubtless

Francesca had foreseen this uprising, even as Marius had. She'd been responsible for quelling the last revolt. Her blade had claimed the king.

Marius laid an elbow on the mantel, sank his hand into his hair and let out a slow breath, allowing his tension to ease with the exhalation, summoning calm if not clarity. Too agitated to remain still for long, his feet soon found their natural motion across the rug again. He'd spent much of that afternoon pacing along the outer edge of the assemblage surrounding his empress, but after Valentina had made a comment about his resembling a lion haunting the verge, he'd moved to the other end of the gallery to pace in relative privacy.

Nearby, a marble archway opened into a drawing room where his Caladrians waited upon his call. Would that he'd had a reason to summon them, some new clue for them to investigate.

Would that he had any idea where the Adepts had been taken!

Marius…

Valentina's mental call drew his gaze in time to see a procession of departing personages coming towards him, all of them looking like harassed cats with flattened ears and diverted eyes—looking anywhere but into the face of his own disapprobation. Only Francesca, the Adeptus Commander, glanced his way in passing, her hazel-eyed gaze voluminous with apology.

Valentina reached him in their wake. She placed a hand on his arm and a lingering kiss upon his cheek.

Grateful to be alone with his wife at last, Marius drew her into his arms and exhaled a tremulous breath, rife with things unspoken. They'd not yet had their own time together, no opportunity to discuss what she'd found in Köhentaal, or his other investigations. But the most obvious needed no discussion: *in her absence, he'd failed her.* This truth was an arrowhead beneath his armor, with every breath working its inexorable way towards his heart.

"Do not blame yourself so, *mio caro*." He felt the breath of her low words across his ear. "My Sight failed to foretell these events."

Marius shook his head and clenched his jaw. "We are both of us blinded."

She withdrew to look into his eyes. "Phaedor assures me it is intentional, this blinding. That it has a source, an enemy…a name."

Marius misliked hearing such trust in her voice when speaking of the zanthyr, even though the zanthyr's views agreed with his own—verily, he'd argued that same point endlessly with Valentina; but he found it beyond vexatious that because Phaedor said it, *now* she agreed. He feared the result of his wife having spent so many weeks with that creature. Too, she seemed improbably calm for a woman who'd just learned that her lands had been invaded and her heir taken hostage.

Then the truth dawned upon him, as with the painful glare of sunlight. "*He* told you something, didn't he? Something that changed you? Some arcane knowledge that creature alone possesses?" He took her by both shoulders. "He *knew* all of this would happen?"

Valentina's gaze tightened upon him. "You forget yourself, Marius."

Marius dropped his arms and turned away. By Belloth's unwholesome eye, that creature got under his skin like no one beneath the sun. When he should've been focused on the Empire's wellbeing, all he saw was the red haze of jealousy. And Valentina…

Marius glanced back to her. She stood with her hands at her sides, watching him with the slightest arch of brow, a nuanced inquiry into his agitation, an admission that she was leaving him to the privacy of his own thoughts.

Utterly galling how badly the creature discomposed him. Phaedor wasn't even in the room and he was driving a spear between Marius and his beloved. Verily, the Empire was poised on the brink of what might be the gravest threat they'd faced in three centuries, yet all Marius could think about suddenly was the need to bed his wife.

Valentina extended her hand with tolerance and her gaze with understanding. After a moment, Marius took the former and dropped his chin towards his chest. "My thoughts shame me, Valentina." He hardly felt worthy of her forgiveness.

"You're exhausted, Marius. The mind finds its own path in such moments." She tugged on his hand, encouraging him back to her side.

Marius lifted his gaze, and for a moment, her beauty captured him—her dark waves bound loosely with diamond pins, the straight line of her shoulders, which seemed to bear the pressures of ruling an empire with grace and ease, the elegant curve of her collarbone, framed so alluringly by the wide neck of her damask gown…

As a girl of only sixteen she'd claimed him, heart and soul. He'd watched the years carve the youth from her features and limbs, even as they'd seemed to bring a brittleness to his own; but time's passage through the Pattern of Life had only sculpted Valentina into exquisite shapes, her form forever pinned at the peak of womanhood. He'd never felt deserving of her, and certainly not now—

"So bleak, Marius." She touched his face.

Marius's gaze tightened upon her. "And you're not?"

"I know your mind. You would rather my wrath thundered through the firmament, but I dare not give such emotion sway or we'll all be lost."

Marius frowned deeply at this.

Valentina searched his gaze for understanding. "The currents blind you, my Sight has abandoned me…should we now fixate our attention with the rigidity of anger, we should find our judgment so clouded as to lead us to ruin."

Marius shook his head. Valentina had always ruled with her head more than her heart, even in regards to her children. "You never loved Nadia as I do." Then he winced and turned his gaze away, his jaw tight. "I apologize. That was uncalled for."

"But not untrue." A flicker of a rueful smile hinted on her mouth. "She is your daughter and my heir. For that very reason, neither of us can afford to let emotion rule our heads."

Marius felt too keenly the time apart from his wife. Usually they grounded each other, balanced each other's weaknesses in important ways. The friction of the days spent without her had frayed his patience and fused the gears of his composure.

Valentina tugged on his hand to gain his attention.

When he looked back to her, she nodded towards the archway. "It appears we have one more person to consult."

In the next room, Vincenzé and Giancarlo were on their feet and staring at a figure that was approaching across the marble floor, a dark personage wearing black leather and a cloak of shadows, the image of Night embodied.

Valentina nodded in welcome. "Phaedor."

"Empress." The zanthyr's deep purr-growl elicited a visceral reaction in Marius. He had to force himself to keep his expression neutral.

The zanthyr shifted his emerald gaze to Marius, and there was dark amusement in it. "High Lord."

Marius clenched his jaw and nodded to him.

And then another figure separated itself from the long shadow cast by the zanthyr. The lad was walking with his head turned backwards, looking over one shoulder. "Well, that was bloody unpleasant. Thanks so much for not vouching for me. I think the bastards forgot to search up my arse—"

He looked forward then, and noting suddenly the assembly of gazes fixed upon him, both tongue and feet came to a standstill.

Valentina arched a brow and gave the lad one of her more unsettling smiles, the kind she reserved for haughty princes. "Well, Felix di Sarcova… let's talk about nodes, shall we?"

TWENTY-FIVE

*"He wouldn't know the feeling of truth in his hands
if it took the form of his own cock."*
–The Adept truthreader Gannon Bair, on Dore Madden

SHAILABANÁCHTRAN STEPPED OUT of Shadow into the Fortress of Tal'Afaq's cavernous underbelly. Tumultuous currents at once buffeted him; *violent* waves, shouting a confused protest, the product of *eidola* in conversion. Nothing so outraged Mother Nature as her own patterns misapplied. Ironic that Balance wasn't so easily offended.

While his portal winked closed behind him, Shail cast a summons and then stood for a time, basking in the chaotic currents.

He'd heard a story once, a *drachwyr* philosophy that declared that the divine naming of immortal creatures encapsulated their individual purpose for existence. The concept intrigued him.

Shailabanáchtran, Maker of Storms...

Yes, it suited him.

His brother Darshan viewed their purpose like a child trapped in a dark room; he stood within its shadowed confines, perceiving only the space occupied by the darkness, never bothering to search for a light much less a door leading elsewhere. Pelas, for all his pathetic love affair with humanity, at least had never barricaded himself within Darshan's ignorance.

Then there was Rinokh...*poor Rinokh*. Shail smirked at memories of his eldest brother. Rinokh had been so stultified by archaic ideas that he would only have been a nuisance. Ean val Lorian had rid Shail of Rinokh's irritating presence far more effectively than he ever anticipated.

Three Malorin'athgul brothers...all of them so misguided, so naïve, so *inept*. Shail suffered none of their imperfections.

Lifting his head as if to embrace the sun's warmth, Shail took a deep draw of *elae* at its most riotous. Furious waves washed across him, their crests choppy and sharp with the erratic reversal of opposing polarities. The patterns used to craft golems out of men forced purity to mate with the grotesque, causing a repulsion on the currents. That same repulsion was mirrored in the expressions of the living when they observed the dark product of that copulation.

Shail floated blissfully on these turbulent waters; they were echoes of Chaos, a microcosm of the energies that ransacked the Void. He never felt so alive as when among the riotous oscillations of violent unmaking.

He moved idly off towards the caverns where Dore was making monsters out of men. Halting at the edge, he cast his gaze across a wasteland of death and spoke to the doomed upon the currents. *We have purified you of the light. Now you shall be reborn of darkness.*

Near where he was standing, smoke appeared and coalesced into form. Violet-black eyes, like a raven's iridescent wing, glinted in a visage of shifting planes. A hand solidified out of the dark mist. Then more of the figure— tall, broad of shoulder, trailing wings of smoke.

"Ah, Vleydis," Shail nodded to the Warlock. "Thank you for coming. I thought you'd like to see this," and he motioned to the *eidola* in making.

The Warlock shifted his glittering gaze to assess the dying forms. "It is as you said it would be." His eyes and deep voice both held a hypnotic quality. In their time, they'd captured many a man's will as viscerally as a horn rallying soldiers to battle. "Though I still do not see the need for these precautions. *Eidola* are easy to craft."

"In Shadow, yes, but to forge them here requires time we may not have."

"How not?" The Warlock studied him with his glimmering gaze. "Time bends to your will."

"*Balance* bends to my will." Shail gave a flickering smile. "Time is less malleable."

"A distinct disadvantage of this plane, I've noticed."

"Dore has made these *eidola* with one of the new patterns. I'm testing others as well—patterns that will allow us to convert humans in as little as a few turnings of an hourglass. The supply would be nearly endless."

"*Eidola* are endless."

"In *Shadow*, Vleydis. In the Realms of Light, if you send your *eidola* into battle, you'll be losing strength with every harvester slain. I'm devising patterns that will create pawns who can draw upon the power of Shadow for animation but won't deplete your power if destroyed."

"Intriguing." The Warlock's eyes gleamed with dark possibility. "I would be interested in exploring the advantages of such pawns."

"They will be my gift to you, once perfected."

The smoky planes of Vleydis's face reshaped themselves into an expression of skeptical surprise. "And what do you ask in exchange for so unique a gift?"

Shail clasped hands behind his back. "A trifling thing," his lips twitched with an almost smile, humorless and cold, "a matter of some framed space in Shadow to create as I will."

"*As you will…*" the Warlock's tone held a sharp curl of amusement.

"I have need of a repository for some artifacts that have outlived their usefulness."

Vleydis gave a low chuckle. Mist rippled in waves beneath his laughter. "Artifacts. A curious descriptor." He looked Shail over with his eyes of crystallized darkness. "You would have the space connect to Wylde, I presume."

"If it isn't too much trouble."

"It is no trouble for me, Shailabanáchtran."

"I am fain to hear it." Shail began strolling the cavern's edge. "How go things in Wylde?"

The Warlock followed, a dark pillar trailing smoking wings. "The others are beginning their exits from the world, as planned. But I must tell you, this act will not be well received if they cannot gain the access you've promised them."

"Have I ever failed you?"

"No…" yet his tone hinted of hesitation, "but you promise a thing we've failed to accomplish for millennia. Many believe it cannot be done."

Shail arched a derisive brow.

"Some of us have strongly expressed concerns, especially in light of your brother."

Shail's derision became a sneer.

Vleydis looked him over speculatively. "You dismiss our concerns, yet Rafael has taught Pelasommáyurek much of Shadow—much of *us*. One or both of them could upset our plans."

"I have already taken care of Pelas. He won't be a hindrance to us. Rafael, I leave to you."

"You speak with such certainty, Shailabanáchtran, but the only certainty in the mortal universe is its unpredictability. How exactly have you—"

Shail raised a hand to pause Vleydis's inquiry. He'd noticed a new strain upon the roiling tide, a different form of abhorrent mutation, and it was approaching rapidly.

Dore Madden came scurrying around the corner. He drew up short, rearing back his head. "My lord." He licked his lips. His eyes flicked to Vleydis and back again. "You've come."

Shail eyed him with disdainful reproach. "I am not a dog to be summoned, Dore Madden."

"I would've come to you readily, my lord, but your brother…" Dore looked between the two immortals uneasily. He ever seemed a hyena waiting for the right moment to dart in between the lions and steal its bit of carrion flesh. "You should know what's happening with your brother."

Shail crossed arms before his red silk robes and stared down his nose at the wielder. "And what, pray, is happening with my brother?"

"He's ordered me to stay here until the *eidola* are out of conversion."

"And for this umbrage you've interrupted me from my important work?"

"No, of course not, my lord. I only say this that you might note the symptom of your brother's change." Dore shuffled before them. "Something has changed mightily with him, my lord. He refuses to make any more *eidola*. He won't even speak now of the army he once promised. He's turning away every initiate from his temple. He will make no more Marquiin."

Shail's gaze tightened. The vast loom of his plans was weaving at a rapid pace, combining multiple fibers into one masterful pattern, but Darshan could still upset his fine cloth if he decided to interfere.

It didn't surprise him that his older brother had grown disinterested in masquerading as the Prophet Bethamin; it only surprised him it had taken Darshan so long to tire of it. And yet, if Darshan's interest had at last strayed elsewhere, it begged the question: where had it turned?

One possibility Shail found particularly unpalatable was the idea that Darshan had discovered the truth behind his and Dore's actions all these years. In Pelas's tower, he'd certainly appeared suspicious—no thanks to Pelas for *that* inconvenience. But if Darshan *had* finally roused to the truth… well, it could prove problematic. How problematic depended on how much of the truth Darshan had intuited.

Shail leveled his cold-eyed gaze on Dore. "If my brother ever realizes that you've been lying to him all these years, he will incinerate you from the aether."

Dore gave a sort of unctuous quiver. "*My lord…*" the eyes darted to Vleydis, but the Warlock would offer no safe harbor. "My lord, you *know* I've only ever done what you told me to do. Every pattern you bade me give to your brother, every command you issued—even to the compulsion placed on Pelasommáyurek at *your* suggestion—I have followed your orders always to the letter!"

Shail's upper lip lifted in a contemptuous curl. This servile act of Dore's might've fooled Darshan, who expected men to cower in his presence, but Shail simply found it repugnant. "Cease this quivering charade, Dore Madden," upon which utterance Dore froze instantly. "Does my brother trust you still or not? This is what we must assess."

Dore stared at him out of the shadowed canyon of his eyes. Then his expression curdled. "I do not know." He spun and paced a short line before Shail and Vleydis, hands behind his back, bony shoulders slouching forward. "His mind is elsewhere. He can no longer be led."

Shail's gaze became very, very dark. "That is a pity."

Dore flung a black glare at him. "It's that truthreader, his once acolyte—he's *still* fixated with him, I vow. Since Kjieran van Stone died, your brother has grown increasingly distant. I cannot make him focus on anything of importance to us. We never should have advised him to make the acolyte into *eidola*. I knew it was a bad idea—we should have eliminated the man, as *I* advised."

Shail flicked at a speck on his robe. "You said Kjieran van Stone couldn't be trusted. You said my brother favored him above all and was seeking a way to bind with him. Making the truthreader into *eidola* solved both of these problems, while strapping Kjieran to your table would only have enraged my brother."

Dore grumbled, "My lord, he would never have known—"

"Be that as it may," Shail looked indifferently back to the dying men littering the cavern floor, "that the solution didn't result to your advantage is hardly a concern of mine. I merely gave you the patterns to forge Darshan's troth with his beloved truthreader."

Dore stared at him for a moment's pause, then he spun to pace back in the opposite direction. "But you must advise me more carefully next time—you admit it, my lord." He thrust a glare at him. "This ultimately worked to neither of our aims."

Shail arched resigned brows. "You may be right." He glanced to Vleydis and started strolling again. He would've preferred the Warlock hadn't learned these truths, and yet…if events proceeded as Shail was beginning to think they would, the Warlocks would understand his need for the framed space in Wylde—and be in agreement with his particular use for it.

He drew a gilded feather from within his sleeve and spun it between his thumb and fingertips. "Both Darshan and Pelas have become afflicted by the same corruptive malady spread by the creatures of this world." He flicked a contemptuous gaze from Vleydis to Dore. "That's the trouble with this pestilence you humans call love. It befouls everything it touches; it twists men's minds to serve only *its* desires. Even gods are not immune to it." He plucked at the feather's shaft with his thumbnail, his gaze remote.

"But what do we do, my lord?" Dore shook his head from side to side. "His mind is set. He won't make the army." Dore flung a look at him. "I *need* that army!"

"And *I* need Dagmar Ranneskjöld's weldmap!" Shail's words reverberated in the cavern, casting sharp waves through the currents. He speared Dore with those words as well as with his gaze, grounding the man to a quivering halt as by a spear thrust suddenly and forcefully into the dirt. "The avenue of our bargain runs two ways, Dore Madden."

Dore flinched away. "Yes-yes, of course, my lord. Niko van Amstel is—"

"An incompetent. Don't attempt to saddle me with the burden of his ineptitude. I need the map and I need the portal open to me. *Make it so.*" The currents rippled away from him, serrated saws of warning. He did not have to say, *'or face the consequences,'* for Dore knew well enough what he would face if he failed.

Dore ducked his white-haired head and made sniveling remarks of contrition.

Shail regarded him circumspectly. With Dore, as with any wild animal, obedience was gained through a careful meting of punishment and reward; yet he had to be discerning. Dore only ever fought when cornered and then with the vicious desperation of a creature intent on surviving at any cost. Too much threat would only make the man turn tail and flee…but if empowered in the shadows, his malevolent ingenuity knew no bounds.

Dore glared unhappily at his feet, a resentful dog brought to heel. "And what of my army, my lord?"

Shail considered him. Dore had proven useful over the years—verily, his unrelenting fixation on Arion Tavestra had served Shail's purposes well—but now he wondered if the man's usefulness had permanently waned.

And yet…

This army Dore craved might serve to claim the proverbial two birds with one stone—or pattern, as it were. The more the idea spiraled into shape, the more he liked its potential ramifications.

Shail smirked at the thought. Ever Balance's malleable flesh shifted beneath his intent; ever it opened itself to him, a wanton whore desirous of his impaling will. He turned and strode from the cavern, trailing a smoking Warlock and a frenzied wielder.

"If my brother is so fixated on his dead truthreader that he can no longer be led, let us disregard him altogether." He arched a sardonic brow. "The ship sails as well with or without a figurehead."

Dore shuffled along behind them in Vleydis's misting wake. "But how will I make an *eidola* army without your brother to bind them, my lord?"

Shail clasped hands behind his back and continued walking. "I've been testing a new matrix of patterns that combines *inverteré* and *elae* together and balances their opposing natures."

"*Inverteré*..."

"With these patterns, you might make a man *eidola* while maintaining his own essence. Thus you would have no need for my brother's immediate involvement."

Dore looked riveted by the idea. "The body will change without experiencing death?"

"The body will undergo a metamorphosis that ceases just shy of death; for a time, the *eidola* can subsist on what remains of its own lifeforce. Eventually they will need to be bound to an immortal to remain animated, but they will serve us before this end. The Pattern of Changing requires the same catalysts as any binding and need not involve my brother directly." Verily, Shail could've done it himself—or Vleydis could have, for that matter—but Shail would face unmaking before he'd bind such a revolting creature as an *eidola* to his own lifeforce. "You'll find converts for such an army in ample supply."

Dore waxed a cadaverous grin. Shail hadn't seen the man exhibit such malevolent excitement since the days of their mutual plot against the High Mage of the Citadel.

He strode on with quiet satisfaction. *And when Darshan discovers you've made an eidola army without his consent, his fury will be in ample supply.*

"I will devise a diversion to call your *Prophet* away," Shail drawled the word contemptuously. "Be ready in that moment to fashion this army. It must be done in the shadow of Darshan's distraction."

"I shall set preparations into motion at once, my lord." Dore bowed and departed.

Shail watched the wielder walking away and shook his head. *They make it so easy.*

Then he bade farewell to Vleydis, tore the fabric of the world with a thought, and departed back to his own affairs.

TWENTY-SIX

"There is no greater shield than a man's untarnished honor."
—Rhys val Kincaide, Captain of the King's Own Guard

KING GYDRYN VAL Lorian entered the hall with his arm wrapped around his treasured middle son, still overwhelmed by the impossible truth of Trell's survival and even more by the fact of his presence at his side.

That his princely son had formed his own allegiances during their years apart hardly surprised him, though he admitted a certain bemusement upon learning that Trell had sworn an oath in service of the Vestal Björn van Gelderan. Nevertheless, his son lived! What could truly trouble him in light of such a blessing?

In an era where enemies welcomed each other as friends, Gydryn was beginning to see—nay, to repeatedly realize—that few things were as they appeared. Kjieran van Stone had been transformed into a monster, yet he'd saved Gydryn's life. Against all odds, his men had fled supposedly friendly garrisons to find shelter within hostile territory, and the man he'd thought was his gravest enemy had dauntlessly dragged him back from death's door.

In view of these truths, perhaps Björn van Gelderan was also not as the world believed him to be. Most suggestive of this was Trell himself. Gydryn had already observed the cloak of honor draping his son; he knew Trell would not have sworn himself to anyone undeserving of his support.

Ah, Trell... Gydryn let out a slow exhale and shook his head, *what tragic and confusing roads we've traveled to reach this point together!*

Could it be true that Trell regretted no part of his journey? Gydryn was only now starting to see how it might be possible. Surely he better appreciated—even welcomed—the vagaries of life for having so nearly lost his own.

And Trell...he had clearly traversed a gauntlet and emerged—well, if not unscathed, at least with his conscience intact, which was the most any good man could hope for.

Gydryn tightened his arm around his son's strong shoulders, treasuring the contact, and walked with him into a pentagonal hall. Huge canvas maps concealed the mosaic walls, seeming garish and ill-placed beneath the chamber's elegant dome. It struck Gydryn how desperate war made men, driving them to deface such artistry with rough charts marking death's passage across the land.

Trell went immediately to a large map that dominated an oblong table in the room's center. Prime Minister al Basreh and Prince Farid were already standing over it.

The Akkadian prince nodded to Trell by way of welcome, his dark eyes just barely hinting of an affection that Gydryn saw mirrored in Trell's own gaze; yet Gydryn noticed also a voluminous warning in Farid's meaningful look.

While Gydryn was wondering what ill news Farid was harboring, Zafir walked around the map table and stood behind its western edge. Markers of varying colors studded the canvas, ostensibly representing the locations of each kingdom's forces.

"Gydryn, please allow me to begin with a summary of our positions. These markers show the location of your men," and he indicated the blue markers congregated at the northwestern edge of the mountains, near where the lines between kingdoms became blurred.

Gydryn stopped across the table from Zafir and braced both hands on the lacquered edge. He assessed the collection of blue markers in the north, but also noted a similar marker pinned in the far south. His gaze flicked to the Emir and back to the northern section of the map, towards which he nodded. "That is Nahavand?"

"Yes. As far as we can discern, the majority of your men have assembled there, save these." Zafir tapped the marker in the south. "My scouts have reported that a regiment of your troops is being held under guard at the fortress of Khor Taran, in the region of Abu'Dhan."

Farid offered, "They were part of the battalion holding Radov's furthest southern lines and had the longest march, Your Majesty—time enough for hal'Jaitar's Shamshir'im to act against them."

Gydryn straightened beneath a haze of unease. "How many men have they trapped?"

The stern, yellow-eyed Rhakar said, "Approximately one thousand."

Gydryn kept firm hold on his composure, but barely. "*One thousand?*" He stared at the map with a dark foreboding pressing against his thoughts. How was he going to rescue his soldiers in the south when he needed to be in the north readying his troops for the journey home?

The future of his kingdom hinged upon his rapid return with his forces in hand. He dared not sacrifice the kingdom for a thousand men. Still, the idea of abandoning them brought the taste of char to his tongue.

"You must rally the main army, father." Trell scrubbed at the scruff of beard darkening his jaw, clearly pondering the same problem. "I'll go to Abu'Dhan and free the rest."

Gydryn turned a swift look to his son—his brave, courageous son!

Trell nodded to him, all the acknowledgment needed in that moment, so much conveyed within their locking of gazes, and then he looked to the Emir. "That is, if you can spare some men to aid me, *Su'a'dal?*"

※

The moment Trell learned of the king's captive men, he saw the problem this presented for his father. One thousand Dannish soldiers held at Abu'Dhan, ten times as many in the north awaiting orders to return home...clearly his father couldn't be both places at once.

Until that moment, Trell had been wondering why the Mage had pulled him back onto the field in *this* precise moment. Now he understood. He recalled Vaile's admonishment and felt the weight of her meaning—for already this war had spread its sickness through three kingdoms and threatened to involve even more; it had weakened his own royal house with its treachery and made a laughingstock of Radov's once strong reign.

The idea of these symptoms of unbalance spreading unchecked into the Akkad—never mind where Morwyk and the Prophet would wander, sowing their doctrine of intolerance, unbalancing the world further—he could indeed envision the entirety of the Middle Kingdoms eventually succumbing to chaos.

He wasn't sure how rescuing his father's men from Abu'Dhan would help end the war with M'Nador, yet he felt strongly that freeing those men was exactly what the First Lord needed him to do.

Trell looked up from the map. "You must rally the main army, father. I'll go to Abu'Dhan and free the rest. That is, if you can spare some men to aid me, *Su'a'dal?*"

The Emir turned a deep frown to Farid.

"You must hear the rest of my news, Trell." Farid exhaled a slow breath, heavy with disconcertion. "Radov is rallying his forces at Taj al'Jahanna, *and* he's pulling his men from the southern lines."

Trell's brows lifted. "He'll lose Abu'Dhan."

"Verily, he's lost Abu'Dhan," Farid said, "though we have yet to retake it ourselves. Since Radov withdrew his forces, the region is in turmoil and overrun with Saldarians."

"Godless men." The Emir pressed palms together and lifted his gaze heavenward.

"The bastards are roaming the countryside preying upon Radov's people—never mind our own," Farid added.

Trell considered all of this information, whereupon the truth hit him rather forcefully. "You think Radov's going to try to retake the oasis."

"It *has* been Radov's desire since the moment he lost it," Gydryn murmured by way of agreement, "and a much debated point of contention among my generals."

Trell looked to Rhakar. "Would even Radov be so foolish as to attempt a press on the oasis with the *drachwyr* flying the skies?"

Rhakar gave him a look that clearly said how foolish he thought Radov could be.

"That is the question we've been asking ourselves each night while sleep is eluding us, Trell," Farid admitted.

The Emir regarded Trell with a deep furrow between his brows. "As much as it ails me, son-of-my-heart..." he shifted his gaze to the king, "Gydryn, I dare not send any men away from Raku at this time."

Trell's father looked to him with pain behind his gaze.

Farid knuckled his beard while staring at the map. "What about Raegus?" He looked from his father to Trell, explaining, "*Su'adal* sent him with a company of Converted to take the Saldarians in hand."

Trell studied the map. Abu'Dhan was a region of high, forested mountains that remained cool even in high summer. No territory could've been better designed in favor of bandits and renegades. But he well remembered Raegus n'Harnalt, whose company had replaced his at the Cry, and he knew him to be a capable leader.

He looked up at the others. "How many men with Raegus?"

"Two hundred," Prime Minister al Basreh replied.

"Do we have any intelligence on the situation at Khor Taran?" Trell shifted his gaze between the prime minister and Rhakar. "What kind of opposition we might be facing?"

Rhakar crossed his arms. "It's a large fortress held by at least a thousand Nadoriin, perhaps more. Saldarians come and go."

"How much help can you and the others give me?"

"Scouting," Rhakar answered. "What intelligence our immortal eyes can draw from the currents. Little else. The Balance in the game hinges on a pinpoint."

For a moment Trell held the Sundragon's yellow gaze, feeling as though he and Rhakar stood upon the same overlook, sharing the same understanding of what they saw. "How many men can I do it with?"

Rhakar arched a brow. "To any other, I would say at least twice their numbers, for their position is fortified, and they have the high ground." He looked Trell over with the hint of an admiring smile. "But beneath your command? Two hundred could turn the tide."

"*Two hundred* against a thousand Nadoriin?" Gydryn shifted an incredulous look to Rhakar and then turned it on Trell instead. "*Trell…*"

Trell saw a hollow truth in his father's gaze, a confession that he would rather lose his men than lose him again.

The Emir meanwhile frowned down at the map. "It is a risk, assuredly, Gydryn, but Trell held off the entire Veneisean army with only fifty men. If anyone can accomplish this feat with so few soldiers, he can. I trust Lord Rhakar's assessment."

"It's at least a manageable force to get through the mountains." Trell scrubbed at his growth of beard. "Are we in agreement, then?"

If there were any dissenters, they held their peace. The discussion turned to a plan of action. If the gods were with them, Trell and his father would reunite within a few weeks.

As they were breaking to attend to preparatory tasks, Prime Minister al Basreh laid a hand on Trell's shoulder and said in the desert tongue, "It is good to have you back among us, Your Highness. The Converted have been missing you."

Trell nodded a gracious thanks, though hearing himself named a prince by the Akkadian prime minister still gave him an oddly discomfiting pang.

As al Basreh moved away, Trell's father approached with an open hand, which he clasped about Trell's arm. "Trell…" myriad emotions flickered across his king father's face, but in the end, he shook his head and gave him a smile. "I'm so proud of the man you've become."

"I wouldn't be the man I am today if not for your upbringing, Father."

Looking oddly pained by this claim, the king smiled again, but it failed to banish the shadows from his gaze.

Trell started walking, following the others out of the room. "For so many years, I wondered about my parents. I was always asking my face in the mirror, 'Who are you?'" He exhaled a slow breath. "Philosophers like to say we're all the products of our experiences, but I think who we are is more a result of the ideas that we don to fashion ourselves in our own eyes." He gave his father a grateful look. "Who I am, these qualities you profess to admire...Father, *you* ingrained them in me from the very start."

Gydryn gazed at him in wonder. "I hear echoes of Errodan in your speech."

"And of your wisdom, too, Father." Trell grinned suddenly. "I distinctly remember your telling me—when I was demanding some form of outrageous punishment for Ean over some trivial thing he'd done to me—that my choices would frame the man I was to become."

A smile lightened his father's expression, at last banishing some of the darkness from his gaze. He placed a heavy hand on Trell's shoulder, and for a time as they walked together, they simply let the contact say what words were too inept to capture.

Eventually the king dropped his hand and exhaled a slow breath. "Tell me of Ean." He glanced to Trell, looking him over. "You mentioned meeting Alyneri in your travels. You must know something of your brother, then? I sent him to the Cairs praying he would be far enough away to escape Morwyk's reach."

But not far enough to avoid the First Lord's.

Trell nodded to him. "Though our paths haven't yet crossed, Ean is well by last accounting." He tried to think of what he could say of Ean that would make any sense to his father. "Like me—and the Emir and many others—Ean is sworn to the Fifth Vestal and works to further his cause."

"Which is?" The king's gaze held a curious concern.

"Salvation." Trell stopped walking and turned to his father. "Before I knew well of the Emir's Mage, before I knew him as Alorin's Fifth Vestal, I knew better of those who served him. I saw in them a nobility and strength of character that I only hoped to emulate. I quickly recognized that people of such integrity would never swear themselves into the service of an unworthy leader."

First nodding to this truth, the king started them walking again, clasping hands behind his back. "This sentiment echoes my own observation of you, Trell." He gave him an earnest look. "Whatever confusions shadow the Fifth Vestal's name, I trust you would never serve a man undeserving of your support."

"I would not be standing here but for his compassion, father."

The king gave him a rueful smile. "Yes, I recall your saying so."

They reached the atrium and a splitting of their paths. The king placed both hands on Trell's shoulders, while Trell took his father's in return, and for a time they gazed at one another with words too heavy on their tongues.

"I hope we shall one day be granted the time to know each other again," his father said.

"This is my hope also, Father."

Pressing his lips together tightly, the king took Trell into a close embrace.

In that moment, as he held his father with equal strength of feeling, Trell sensed another circle beginning, a needle threading their paths in diverging arcs. He prayed those stitches would eventually circle around to join anew.

Then the king was joining Farid, who was waiting just ahead before a passage leading left, while Trell turned to his right and the waiting Sundragon who was his guide into the next circle of his life.

TWENTY-SEVEN

"You know what chafes my arse about that so-called prophet, Bethamin?
Who's he supposed to be a prophet for?"
–The pirate Nodefinder Carian vran Lea

VIERNAN HAL'JAITAR'S BLACK robes swirled around his legs as he strode against a damp, buffeting wind up the stairs leading into Niko van Amstel's Bemothi manor.

Viernan loathed Bemoth. The entire kingdom was a fermenting cesspool reeking of verdant, growing things. The humid air was saturated with stench—*he'd* become saturated with it in just the short time it had taken him to walk from the node to Niko's door. His silk robes most assuredly stank of vegetative life.

As he topped the steps, the doors opened to disgorge a butler in liveried black and grey and a shorter man holding several fat ledgers.

"Welcome, my lord," intoned the taller of the pair. "May I have your name and occupation, if you please?"

I do not please. Niko had invited—nay, *demanded*—Viernan present himself at his estate, which really meant that Dore Madden had demanded it; but being trapped in Dore's filthy pocket did not require him to suffer Niko's pretentions.

As Viernan was deciding how he intended to respond, a rotund woman in a crimson gown walked across the hall and happened to glance his way. Her round eyes became instantly rounder. "Viernan?" She rushed over to him like a too-fat cherry and elbowed the butler aside. "Viernan! Why, it *is* you!"

Viernan scowled at the Healer Mian Gartelt.

"Oh, but come in—come in!" She grabbed his arm and drew him

unwillingly inside, informing the butler as she passed, "He needn't be in your book. He's one of Niko's oldest friends."

"Yes, madam." The butler bowed stoically and withdrew with his aide.

Viernan couldn't decide which indignity rankled the most: being dragged anywhere by Mian Gartelt or being named a friend of Niko van Amstel.

Mian roped her chubby arm through Viernan's. "It's so good to see you here at last, Viernan." She pulled him into the stream of guests milling in Niko's halls, fruit of the aristocracy with clearly nothing better to do than wile away their insincere hours upon the decadent pursuits offered at Niko's home.

Mian gave him a cherubic smile and patted him on the arm. "So tell us, what have you been doing these many years, Viernan?"

Avoiding inane conversations such as these. He made a point to avoid fraternizing with any of the Fifty Companions when possible, but especially with brightly colored vipers like Mian Gartelt.

Viernan halted and abruptly disengaged his arm from her piggish fingers. "I've come to see Niko." The emphasis in his tone spoke clearly enough even for Mian Gartelt to get the point.

Her painted expression twisted beneath flashing eyes, but instantly reassumed its sugar-sweet façade. "I see courtesy is still too rigorous an undertaking for you. You always did treat etiquette like a whore's unwelcome get. If this is your liege's idea of decorous comportment, I faint to imagine myself in Radov's court."

Viernan smiled thinly at her. "Likewise, madam."

Mian looked him over icily and waddled away.

Viernan snared a valet and had the man lead him to Niko.

The valet ushered him into a gallery, where Viernan found his host stalking back and forth before a wall of glass doors like an actor playing a dramatic theatrical role. The day outside appeared as night beneath the building storm.

Seated in a chair facing Niko's stage, Dore Madden was saying, "…you *have* a vestal ring—"

"But it only opens the portal for *me.*" Niko threw up an exasperated hand. "This is what I've been trying to tell you, Dore." His gaze fell upon Viernan then.

"There must be another…" Dore noted the sudden shifting of Niko's attention and spun his head. He immediately scowled at Viernan.

"Ah, Viernan." Niko sounded dispirited. "You've come."

Viernan felt no need to reply to this observation. He headed further into the room and heard the doors shutting behind him. "What is so important that it requires my presence in this seething cesspool of a kingdom, Dore Madden?"

"We'll get to that." Dore turned back to Niko. "The ring and the map. Those are his terms. Have you the map?"

Niko cast him an injured glare. "How can you be so fixated on a bloody weldmap when our strand is tumbling into chaos? Have you not heard a word I've said? This rebellion has gotten far out of hand." He turned and stalked petulantly in the other direction. "We've lost a score of nodes to these so-called rebels. I've had to double the watches on the nodes we still control. Rethynnea's Guild is still up in arms over the robbery of their weldmap generator, and the Guildmaster is furious with *me*—"

Dore scowled at him. "It's Tavestra and his lot behind this, rest assured."

Niko eyed him askance, somewhat skeptical. "And now there's talk of some new candidate for the vestalship? This man they're calling the Admiral." He lifted a wounded look to Viernan. "They can't do that, can they, Viernan? The vestalship belongs to *me*."

Viernan thought himself as likely to be confirmed as Alorin's Second Vestal as Niko van Amstel.

"No, no, no." Niko wagged his head and continued pacing. "They're even staging protest rallies outside the Guild halls—*Dore*, are you listening to me? The Guild Masters have sent guards out into the crowd, but they haven't found a single Nodefinder among them. It's like they're all being paid to make trouble for me."

"Very likely," Dore muttered.

Niko halted abruptly and spun to face him. "But I'm becoming *unpopular*."

Dore glowered at him in the throes of rumination. "*You* can somehow travel to and from Illume Belliel. Why can't you take another person with you?"

"I'm telling you, it doesn't work that way." Niko exhaled a frustrated sigh and looked down at his vestal ring. "My ring only allows *me* to travel to the cityworld—I don't know why." He started walking slowly again while turning the ring around on his finger. "Even if I did manage to bring someone across the node with me, we'd arrive to a thousand tons of raw power boring down on us—I've seen the demonstration, Dore. It's no idle threat." Niko tapped the ring with his middle finger. "Maybe there's something wrong with the stone."

Viernan regarded him sootily. *Or perhaps there's something wrong with you.* The vestal rings were widely rumored to respond to their owner's thoughts and deeds, even becoming ruined if a vestal broke their oath of service to their strand.

As if catching a strain of the thought, Niko extended his fist and followed its lead over to Viernan. "What do you make of it, Viernan?"

Viernan hadn't seen a vestal ring up close in three centuries—and if he saw another one in the next three more, it would still be too soon—but he didn't need to look closely at Niko's to notice the milky blur clouding its core. "The vestal rings are aqua clear." He leveled an inscrutable gaze upon Niko. "Yours is cloudy."

Niko flung his hand at Dore. "Do you see? *That's* what I've been trying to tell you! Alshiba gave me a defective ring."

More likely you're the defect.

Dore's eyes glinted like black agates deep in the hollows of his skull. "Our ally grows impatient, Niko. You will do as we've promised—and soon—or face the spear of his displeasure."

Niko stilled. His face assumed a sickly hue.

Viernan cleared his throat pointedly.

Dore turned a glare of annoyance over his shoulder, which Viernan matched with equal venom. He stood taller and drew his robes closer about his form. "Speak what you've called me to hear, Dore Madden, lest I depart without the knowledge."

Dore shifted in his chair, noisily, by way of conveying his displeasure. "Fine, fine, but sit down, will you?" He waved irritably at a seat in front of him. "I am not an owl."

"Nor I a dog."

"Viernan, you needn't be so prickly." Niko rubbed dully at the stone in his ring and looked up under his brows. "We're allies, you know."

Viernan eyed him sharply. "You need not remind me of this unfortunate truth."

Niko exhaled a dramatic sigh. "We do live in unfortunate times." He breathed on his ring and then scrubbed the stone against his coat sleeve. "Here we stand together, bound to the troth of repairing our dying world..." he looked at the stone, frowned, lifted his gaze back to Viernan and immediately assumed, as with the donning of a mask, that pretentious expression he favored when addressing the masses, "yet what do we face but dissention, rebellion, internecine battles, when we should be a unified force!"

Viernan was in no humor to suffer another of Niko's melodramatic speeches. He drew in the deepest breath of patience he could muster, though it still felt thin in his lungs, and growled, "The *news*, Dore Madden?"

Dore glared at him as if he'd spoiled the punch line of a lengthy story. He flicked at a piece of lint clinging to his knee. "Your prince's people have arrived safely in Tambarré."

"*Safe.*" Viernan lifted his lip in a sneer. *Safe* could in no way describe the plight of M'Nador's refugees, not with the luminous malice burning in Dore Madden's gaze.

"The Prophet is ready to complete his bargain and is sending fifty *eidola* to support your assault on Raku." Dore wore a dangerous look of satisfaction. "They're en route to you posthaste from Tal'Afaq and should arrive within a fortnight. Morwyk is prepared to lend you five thousand men—trained soldiers, as your prince required—but there is something else."

Viernan struck a viper's stare towards Dore. "Else? *What* else? Our bargain has already been fixed."

"Events move, Viernan." Dore flicked at his knee again but was apparently unable to dislodge the lint clinging there. He finally pried the offending particle from the cloth with his fingernails. "Gydryn val Lorian is dead, and soon your Prince Radov will regain his precious Raku. But," and he eyed Viernan malevolently at this, "if he means to do it with reinforcements from Morwyk's army, he must make concession of his navy to serve Morwyk in the north."

"Preposterous!" Viernan could hardly believe Dore would dare ask such a thing.

"Events progress, Viernan," Dore repeated with a pointed stare. "Morwyk will soon move on Calgaryn, but he cannot have Dannym's Admiral n'Owain out-flanking him from the sea. He'll need your navy, disguised as raiders, to attack the coastal cities and draw Dannym's warships away from Calgaryn."

Viernan leveled Dore a daggered look. "M'Nador's navy will be needed to protect Tal'Shira while Price Radov is at the front."

Dore scoffed at him. "Who would think of invading Tal'Shira? No, Viernan. Speak to your prince. I believe you'll find him quite amenable to the idea. Doubtless he will see reason where you cannot."

Doubtless your Prophet has reduced his will to that of a sea sponge.

"And what about the Sundragons? Where is this contact who claims—"

"He'll find you at the front." Dore's malevolent stare twisted into Viernan like a fire-flamed corkscrew. "Make haste, Viernan, lest the dust of your passing go unnoticed."

Dore's comment seemed to hold a duality of meaning, an implication Viernan misliked as much as Niko's festering kingdom, one-eyed gypsies, fortunetellers, and zanthyrs of any gender....

And Thrace Weyland.

He spun in a swirl of black silk and wordlessly took his leave, but he couldn't so easily turn his back on that feeling. It haunted his steps all the way to home to Tal'Shira.

TWENTY-EIGHT

"Like bugs to malicious boys are we to the gods."
–The Immortal Bard Drake di Matteo

"*From whence COMETH this power? Is it agent of divinity or demon?*" The Ascendant's baritone voice sounded like the low clanging of a death bell: doleful, interminable, unrelenting. Sitting on her cot, Nadia pulled her knees to her chest and pushed her hands over her ears, but somehow his words still reached her.

"*If it be divinity what fuels their forms with light and fire, if it be pure of intent, innocent of action, their mortal corporealities anointed by the blessed kiss of sanctity...*" he licked his forefinger and turned a page in the *Book of Bethamin*, inhaled a sanctimonious breath and continued reading, "*transcendent souls born of celestial radiance; if this be their genus, for what purpose must they have been put here upon this, our terrestrial plane?*"

Nadia pushed her palms harder against her ears.

The Ascendant stood in the middle of the archway, just beyond the energized wall, forming an obstacle to her view of the Marquiin, who was standing a few paces behind him.

Her eyes kept straying to the latter.

The first two Marquiin who'd come to question her had been horrifying—barely even sane. Their questions phrased as accusations had made little sense to her, and their *thoughts*...it had taken all of her skill to keep their radiating malice from infecting her mind.

She'd feared the Prophet would be angry with what little information she'd given them, though she'd made an earnest effort, but how does one answer such accusations as, '*Why were you sent here to spy for the Empire?*' or

'*What treachery is the Empire planning against our master?*' Their badgering and berating had quickly brought her to tears, especially since she feared angering the Prophet by not answering properly. She would rather have endured the Marquiin's insanity than more of Darshan's compulsion.

She'd been surprised then when the third Marquiin came. The winds of his mind only swept in circles of confusion, without the hatred and desire to harm so prevalent in the thoughts of the others. He'd used a gentle manner towards her and had even spoken eloquently in her own tongue.

Could this be him again?

Why had he treated with her so? It was almost as if Darshan had ordered him to be kind, which begged the question of why the Prophet might've issued such an order.

By Cephrael's Great Book, he was such an enigma!

Nadia leaned back against the wall and rested her elbows on her knees, thinking again through her meeting with the Prophet.

Pelas's description of his brother had led her to believe Darshan was arrogant, indifferent to human suffering, and wholly bent on the destruction of their world. Tanis's description of the Marquiin and the Ascendant who'd captured him in Acacia had further solidified her impression of the Prophet Bethamin. Nadia had envisioned a terrifying man who thought himself a demigod and sent his minions outward to spread a doctrine of horrifying intolerance.

Nadia had been hearing about the Prophet Bethamin in one form or another for years. Reports from Agasan's Order of the Glass Sword named him an insurgent and his Ascendants tyrannical minions; the Marquiin, they called abominations. Her mother thought Marquiin were a worse affront to *elae* than Malachai ap'Kalien's Shades. Of the man himself, the Order had only been able to discern that he wielded an arcane power.

Now that Nadia had met the Prophet, she knew him to be all of these things and yet...not.

A monster wouldn't have held her prisoner in his own temple, or freed her from *goracrosta*. Thus far, Shail had treated her far more monstrously than Darshan had. Yet undeniably, the Prophet had committed monstrous acts. She was staring at the product of one of them right now.

Nadia narrowed her gaze, trying to better focus on the Marquiin. The wall of energy blurred her vision as if through rising heat, but even had her sight been clearer, she still would've had difficulty discerning the Marquiin's features beneath the grey silk shroud covering his face. Out in the world, the Marquiin wore both shroud and veil to '*signify their purity*' and '*veil their true essence from the wretched gaze of the sullied,*' but the shrouds alone apparently sufficed while in their master's temple.

The Ascendant raised his voice for emphasis, as if her quiet thoughts were disturbing his reading. *"For what purpose then have they been put here? Surely for no other than service, for thus is the Maker's will: that all who might serve do so; that divine gifts be used towards the betterment of those less fortunate, asking nothing, giving all, devoted sacrifice of body and will, the alignment of conscience along the path of unrestrained abnegation, expelling all self unto servitude..."*

Nadia shifted with a pained grimace. The words of that book felt like needles in her ears. She might've taken recourse in her talent to silence the awful man, but she wouldn't risk using *elae* in the Prophet's temple just to spare herself a little discomfort. One didn't purposefully annoy a cobra when it lay coiled between oneself and freedom.

After her interview with the Prophet, his acolytes had brought her a cot, an armchair for sitting in while being questioned (or sermonized to—ever Bethamin's Ascendants were vigilant to wake her before dawn with filth read from their sainted *Book of Bethamin*), a table for eating upon (or banging her head against when frustration overcame her), even a privy booth with a connected room for washing, though she wondered if some dark humor was at work behind its construction, for it appeared to have once been a confessional chamber.

Nadia frowned at these thoughts.

A monster didn't give his young female prisoners privy chambers and leave them with access to their Adept gifts.

Maybe he just doesn't want his own residence reeking of excrement.

Then why keep me here instead of in some baser cell? But for this argument, she found no suitable reply.

"Yet if service be their calling..." the Ascendant licked his forefinger and thumb and turned another page, inhaled a deep breath of pretension and continued dolorously, *"why do so many of them seek to rise in ranks, even above their betters? From whence cometh this superior disdain that they use divine gifts only to incur wealth and power? By what right do these lustful creatures dominate, when they were assuredly placed here for servitude?"*

Nadia's attention again strayed back to the Marquiin. This time she rose from her bed and walked towards the iridescent wall, that invisible demarcation of her odd prison. She'd learned how closely she could stand to the barrier without feeling like humming bees were crawling all along her skin.

Trying to ignore the preaching Ascendant, she focused instead on the Marquiin who was standing behind him and slightly to one side. "Brother... may we speak?"

"...slave to those less fortunate..." intoned the Ascendant.

Seeming ghostly in his collared grey robe and close-fitting head shroud, the Marquiin approached Nadia.

With relief, she saw as he neared that he was the same Marquiin as had last attended her. She braved a fleeting smile. "I've thought of other things your Prophet may be interested in hearing."

"*...if from demons, they should at best be bound into service, their terrible abilities conscript to—*"

The Marquiin put a hand on the Ascendant's arm. "Brother, I believe that's enough reading for today."

The Ascendant jerked back from the Marquiin with rounded eyes, staring mightily at the grey-gloved hand resting on his arm. "*Why-why-why* do you presume to touch me?" His stammered words of indignation seemed much at odds with the horror on his face.

Nadia felt a pang of pity for the Marquiin. Even this revolting Ascendant despised him.

The Marquiin slowly lowered his hand back to his side. "The princess has information for the Prophet which I am obliged to hear, brother. You must resume your reading at a later time."

The Ascendant's cheeks flooded with the ruddy color of his anger. He angled a scathing look at Nadia. "Can you not see she merely seeks to evade the Prophet's truth?"

"It is not for us to judge, brother, but to act as we've been given." The Marquiin took the book from the Ascendant's fingers with his own grey-gloved hands and turned to a specific page, from which he read, "*'Do not seek to know thyself. Seek to know my will, for I alone of this world am divine.'* So say the writings of our master." The Marquiin closed the book and handed it back to the Ascendant, his meaning clear.

The Ascendant scowled.

Nadia knew his type—too young to receive any kind of power without abusing it; full of vigor, envy and spite in equal measure.

The Marquiin was still holding out the book. "The Prophet bade me receive the princess's words and answer her questions as my primary mandate. Please, feel free to query our lord directly, should you disagree with my actions."

The Ascendant glared at him for a moment longer. Then he snatched the book from the Marquiin's hand and clutched it close to his chest as he rushed off. The Marquiin frowned after him for a moment, his expression making creases in the grey silk that conformed to his face.

Something in his melancholy manner, in the terrible hurricane storm of his mind, drew a needle through Nadia's sympathy. She felt it threading her to him—by aspect of shared imprisonment, parity through ostracism or aught else, she couldn't say. But he had been kind to her. At the moment, she didn't even care if that kindness came by the Prophet's command.

But whyever would he give such an order?

"He's right," she found herself confessing the moment the Ascendant had gone. "I *was* trying to stop him from reading any more of that…book." Her tongue ached to decry the *Book of Bethamin,* as well as its author, but speaking ill of a god in his own house hardly seemed prudent.

"It doesn't matter." The Marquiin frowned after the Ascendant. "They only do it for spite. If you suddenly embraced the faith, you would never see one of them again."

Nadia perceived within the storm of his thoughts a sudden hint of the innocent Adept chained to a lashing god. She dropped her gaze regretfully. "I would that I did have more to confess to you."

Now why did she say that?

The Marquiin seemed equally surprised by her comment. He took a step closer. "If not confession," he proposed, "perhaps you have questions. My master bade me be truthful with you and answer anything you asked to the best of my knowledge."

Nadia blinked at him. *Why by the Lady would the Prophet do that?* It should've relieved her, but Nadia only found the Prophet's order unsettling. To cover her disconcertion, she grasped for the first question that came to mind. "Do you embrace the faith, brother?"

The Marquiin's eyes were as hollow shadows beneath the shroud that concealed his face, though his dark eyebrows stood out rather clearly against the sheer silk. He looked down at his gloved hands. "When your mind is being torn apart, you can resist or you can succumb. I thought I might escape the worst if I supplicated." His jaw tightened, stretching the silk shroud. "I was wrong."

His confession revealed such naked pain—immediately her heart went out to him. A truthreader's entire existence revolved around the sun of thought. To have one's mind so entrenched in the gravity of another's will would be a truly horrifying state. She tried not to think of how the Marquiin's fate might also become hers; she worried enough about that in the cold darkness of the night, when the Prophet's temple opened its doors to nightmare.

He was still staring at his grey-gloved palms. "After the act is done and irreversible, some embrace the power invested in them. I do not know any who've sought the Fire. I haven't met any who truly believe."

"I'm so sorry." She dropped her own gaze to her hands. He'd been so kind. What must it have cost him to converse with her, another truthreader still in contact with her gifts, her small chamber less a prison than his own apparent freedom? Was it any wonder the other Marquiin had treated her so ferociously? What they must've thought of her, flaunting her freedom at them.

"Does it pain you to speak to me?"

Lifting his gaze, the Marquiin answered, "There's a kind of resolution in accepting one's own acts."

"Your acts? But surely *you're* not to blame for what the Prophet did to you?"

He came closer to the barrier—so close she feared for him touching it. "I might've chosen death when the Fire was raging in my veins." He looked off, as if seeing that moment again, or perhaps some future other than the tragic one he'd chosen. "In that moment, Princess, I could see Death standing just across the threshold, beckoning to me. I cowered from him." He looked back to her. "Now I know Death's arms would've offered a more merciful embrace than the storm that lives forever within me."

"But you seem so sane!" Nadia blurted the words before she could stop herself. Immediately she flushed and dropped her gaze to her hands. "I'm sorry. That was insensitive of me."

"Yes…but fairly observed." He leaned a shoulder against the wall and gazed off along the invisible barrier that separated them by mere inches. His brow furrowed beneath the silk, making odd shadows in it. "A few days ago, you wouldn't have said so, but now…."

Nadia moved closer still, until the static energy coming off the barrier lifted the fine hairs on her arms and made her skin itch. But standing so near, she could better see his features. She realized he could hardly be much older than herself. "You were saying?"

He turned his head back to her. "Caspar."

"I beg your pardon?"

"My name is Caspar."

She offered a smile she didn't feel. "I would we might've met under different circumstances, Caspar."

The ghost of a smile hinted beneath the shadow-silk of his shroud. "We never would've met under different circumstances, Princess."

So many thoughts laced these words of his—astonishingly *clear* thoughts. Intense, *desperate* thoughts projected to her as if a grappling hook thrown in a last daring effort to halt a slide over the precipice. Nadia suddenly saw no monster, only a young man trapped in a monster's cage, urgently craving escape.

Against all judgment, she let the hook pierce her mind and even took hold of it herself to be sure it was properly lodged there. Caspar was anchored to her now, dangling above the abyss—bonded to her.

What chance Caspar had was now pinned to her, as her chances were likewise secured to Pelas. They were both dangling, in truth, two climbers roped to a third who climbed out of view in the rocks above, yet who remained their only hope against a fall.

But with the temporary bond she'd just established came the storm. Into her own mind surged that chaos wind, bringing its dark clouds of insanity, its jagged flashes of lightning pain. Nadia quickly closed a mental door to wall it off, immensely grateful that *she* could, since Caspar could not.

Her heart was suddenly beating faster for knowing what she'd done. *Bonded with a Marquiin!* She managed a dry swallow and focused back on him. "Can you…" she indicated his silk shroud, "*will* you take it off?"

"It is forbidden." Yet he was reaching to unhook the clasps at the back of his head even as he said the words.

As Caspar pulled the silk forward, his dark hair spilled forth. The shroud slid away to reveal deep-set eyes framing a slender nose, followed by a squared chin and jaw. The almond shape of his eyes and his accent indicated his origins lay far to the east. The Marquiin tattoos darkened his eyelids, brow and temples with thorny whorls. When he lifted his eyes, his irises were a murky grey where they should've been colorless.

Caspar let out a slow breath and met Nadia's gaze. Through the intensity of his stare and the shared space of his thoughts, an understanding passed between them. She kenned that he'd thrown that grappling hook consciously, if without hope—he'd had no hope of *his* effort actually working, what with *elae's* touch nearly lost to him—yet *she'd* caught it. *She* had secured the private bond he'd so desperately sought of her and had connected their minds, offering hers as a sort of refuge.

Well…she'd done more reckless things in her life. But not many.

Nadia wondered for the hundredth time why the Prophet had left her with access to her gifts.

Because you're no threat to him. Caspar's thought reached her clearly within the part of her mind they now shared.

Nadia studied him intently. Her hands were shaking, her heart still beating fast. This was an audacious and foolhardy gambit they'd just embarked upon together.

Then the reality of their plight struck home to her, and tears stung her eyes. She gave him a pleading look of apology. *I can offer you nothing!*

He smiled a little. *Only hope.*

Nadia knew how slight a chance that was. Her brow furrowed deeply as she looked at him. *A slim one.*

His smile inched a fraction wider. *When I woke this morning, I had none.*

Nadia searched his face with her gaze. The tattoos around his eyes were clearly patterns, but not like any she'd ever seen. She drew in a deep breath and said aloud, partly in the hopes of calming her racing heart, "How long have you been...like this?"

Caspar removed the neck clasp of his shroud and shook out his hair. Dark locks fell just above his shoulders. He pushed long strands back from his face with both hands. "I was the last one." He plucked his fingers free of their gloves, one finger at a time, and looked up at her beneath his brows. "I think the Prophet chose me because of my resemblance to Kjieran van Stone."

Nadia knew that name. Tanis had told her that the King of Dannym's truthreader had vanished without explanation, an unconscionable act from a ringed truthreader in the service of a monarch. She had suspected from the first that Kjieran had been sent on some clandestine mission—more so after hearing that the Fourth Vestal Raine D'Lacourte sometimes played advisor to Dannym's king.

She'd expressed as much to Tanis then, and now here Caspar was speaking Kjieran's name in association with the Prophet Bethamin. It couldn't be coincidence. But what did Kjieran van Stone have to do with Caspar becoming Marquiin?

"I'm sorry." She pressed two fingers to her forehead in protest of the buzzing energy field in front of her as much as the chaos storm still howling at the fringes of her thoughts. "I don't understand the connection."

Caspar held his gaze steady upon her. "They say Kjieran was the Prophet's favorite acolyte, one of the few of us he never made Marquiin."

She caught the intimation in his tone. "Then what did happen to him?"

Caspar regarded her warily. "The Prophet made him...something else."

"Caspar," she begged forgiveness with her gaze, "you'll have to speak more candidly if I'm meant to understand. I know nothing of these events."

He considered her for a moment with his brow slightly furrowed and his lips pressed together, perhaps deciding if he dared venture the story, or even determining if he could bear to tell it.

After a time, he turned his head in profile to her. "A few months ago, the Prophet called me to attend him. I was newly arrived, still sick from being held below decks during a rough voyage, chained with *goracrosta*." He gave a pained grimace, dropped his gaze to his hands and his voice to the threadbare volume of confession. "First the Prophet took me to his bed. Soon after, he made me...this." He closed his eyes, and Nadia saw his larynx lift and fall with a swallow. "I still don't know if he meant it as a punishment or a patron gift."

Nadia tried to keep the horror from her expression, but she feared she was failing badly.

"No more of us has he made since then." Caspar looked back to her with a grave hollowness behind his gaze. "I don't understand what's happened to him."

These words made her afraid without knowing why. "What do you mean?"

Caspar fingered the gloves in his hands with his brows pinched together. "The Prophet has changed."

"How has he changed?"

He stared off, working the muscles of his jaw. "For a while there was just talk—wild and unlikely stories that the Prophet was turning new initiates away, speculation that he would make no more Marquiin." He looked back to her. "The temple is always rife with gossip concerning the Prophet's possible intentions. No one understands him. Everyone fears him. There's no logic to who he takes to his bed, no reason to who survives such encounters, or who he'll damn into *this* hellish existence. So I didn't believe the gossip until..." Caspar dropped his gaze. "That day I first came to see you, Princess—on that day, the Prophet summoned me to his chambers, and there..." he clenched his jaw and seemed to struggle with the words. "There...he laid his hands on me, and..."

Nadia held her breath.

Caspar looked away along the wavering line of the energy field. "It was like he drew the madness out of me. It hurt so desperately, I thought—at first, I thought he was draining all the blood from my veins. But then a clarity returned to my mind that I'd forgotten could exist." He focused an intense look back at her. "Then he told me what he desired and sent me to you."

Nadia stared at him. "He made you *sane* again? Why? For what possible purpose?"

"I don't know."

She heard the fear behind this statement and decided not to pursue more questions in that direction. "But now you say it's true? He's making no more Marquiin?"

Caspar sank slowly down the wall to sit on the floor. Nadia followed him onto her knees, gazing concernedly at him.

"*Things are not what they seemed.*" Caspar turned her a look. "This is all he spoke in explanation for the grave injustice he'd done me, in apology for destroying *everything*—" Caspar's voice broke and he pushed palms to his eyes. After a moment, he continued barrenly, "But I heard what he *meant* in his way of speaking to us, his Marquiin...speaking his thoughts as entire thoughts complete, without words, like shoving the whole choking melon down your throat with his fist buried in it. He means to make no more of us."

Nadia asked as gently as she could, "Did he say why?"

Caspar draped his arms across bent knees and rested his head back against the wall. "He never says why."

Nadia laid her palm upon the wall, close to the barrier, her only means of conveying the sympathetic touch she so wished to offer him. After a moment, Caspar aligned his hand on the wall parallel to hers. A hair-thin barrier of energized death separated their fingers.

His eyes sought hers. *What do we do now, Nadia?*

Oh, what irony that her captor was looking to her as his only any chance of freedom! *Now?* She exhaled a slow breath, finding courage somehow in his unexpected trust, and a renewed sense of faith within her troth to save him. *Now we wait.*

TWENTY-NINE

"No good deed goes unpunished."
—*The Hearthwitch's Handbook*

LIGHT SEARED INTO Pelas's mind like the midday sun hitting his closed eyelids—blindingly bright, even through the gentle shield of unconsciousness. He shocked back into awareness with a gasped breath, inhaling that plane's cold, thin air along with a powerful sense of—

Tanis!

Pelas perceived the lad through the sun that was Sinárr's glowing presence; the Warlock filled his own universe, but Tanis was a bright star within it. Reaching out along the bond, Pelas swam fast towards Tanis's star.

Framed space shifted in turning cubes, crossing and overlapping—Sinárr's, Shail's, Pelas's own space intersected and held for a breath of time as Pelas's bond to Tanis opened a tunnel of communication through colliding universes. The lad's location became suddenly very clear to Pelas, but *reaching* him...

Pelas drew energy through his bond with Tanis—drew energy from Sinárr by extension—and tried to anchor his awareness in a new context of space, outside of the plane Shail had trapped him in. Pelas sent his mind swimming up through circles of space, seeking a new position in the void's infinite pool.

Just as he perceived the surface of Shail's framed space and was throwing out new starpoints—

Sinárr severed the connection.

Space collapsed.

Pelas tumbled violently back down into a starless plane of writhing darkness: the revenants encasing him. They glommed to his body so densely as to mimic a planet's newly forming core.

Now the pain of their feeding needled into every part of his form. Pelas swallowed back a welling frustration and tried to focus through the pain, tried to anchor his awareness enough to assess what he'd just experienced.

He sensed an important truth in that chance reconnection with Tanis, hints of a way to escape, but pain had him trapped in its jaws and demanded all of his attention instead. He tried to think of other things.

Thinking was painful.

He drew a curtain with his attention and huddled inside it, as a child behind the drapes cloaking a dark window. Concentration came slowly and with a great force of will. He impatiently watched it approaching down the road of his thoughts, the bobbing lantern of lucidity growing brighter but at the agonizing pace of a snail.

No, a snail would've beaten it to his door.

Connection.

At last it came to him. That was the key. He'd been able to use his bond to Tanis to tap into Sinárr's power, because their lifeforces were all currently connected—himself and Tanis via the Unbreakable Bond, Tanis and Sinárr for as long as the Warlock held the lad in Shadow.

Pelas saw the simplicity then, the key to his escape. He and his brothers were bound, as he and Tanis were bound. But did he dare attempt to draw upon his connection to either of his brothers?

Darshan's mind would be too far from his reach. Alorin's substance formed a dense barrier between their minds; he wouldn't be able to penetrate it without his own power—and it was *power* he would be seeking through the bond. But Shail…somehow Shail still held extant starpoints in Shadow; he was still framing the space in which he had Pelas trapped. Thus he had to have kept a portal open somewhere to allow the continuing connection.

Which meant…

The revenant horde started undulating again. Pelas knew he had only a breath of time before they began their next feeding and drained his consciousness along with his lifeforce.

He quickly sought Shail's mind as he would've if they'd been roaming Chaos together. After a lengthy time that showed him just how much the revenants had already drained his lifeforce, he at last perceived Shail's mind—similar to the way he still perceived Tanis's. Both connections were distant and indistinct, pinpoint stars of the faintest dark glimmer.

But Pelas didn't need to *contact* his brother; he only needed to use the bond they shared to siphon some of Shail's energy for his own use, enough to call someone else to his aid. Someone closer by.

Closer. As if the word held any relevance in Shadow, where an infinity of beings might occupy the same space—for in Shadow, *space* only existed between the points each immortal himself framed.

Pelas drew powerfully upon his bond with Shail, with all the force of his will. It felt like sucking energy through a straw longer than the circumference of the world. Finally he succeeded in gaining the slightest prickling of *deyjiin,* a mere whisper of breath.

The revenants were writhing now…coiling, blanketing him, clutching all about his form. He felt what little energy he'd accumulated rapidly draining away and lassitude rushing in again to fill the vacuum left by its departure. With desperate will, Pelas cast forth an image into the void, a card of calling to summon another Warlock. It was pure thought; it had no energy, so it couldn't be trapped by Shail's starpoints, but it had energy behind its impetus.

Then the pain of the revenants' feeding grew too bitingly intense, and Pelas surrendered to the darkness once more.

THIRTY

*"He shouldn't feel such obligation to keep sacrificing himself
for a troth another man made."*
–The Shade Creighton Khelspath, on Ean val Lorian

EAN WALKED THE crowded corridors of Tambarré's *Shadû el-Fnaa* market, marveling at the wonders offered in the City-Within-the-Stone. Part covered bazaar, part local meeting ground, the maze of stalls, shops, stands, stores, and showrooms—all comprising the same connected warren that was the *Shadû el-Fnaa*—easily covered a quarter of Tambarré's Lower City.

Beneath the souk's bamboo roof, one could find mosaic pottery, chiseled metal lanterns, and stall after stall of silver and pewter teapots with curving spouts. Huge ceramic urns overflowed with dried fruits and nuts, or were piled high with an ochre-hued rainbow of spices. Olives filled vats like the treasure hoard of pirates; onions and garlic hung in draped garlands. Kaftans, jeweled slippers and bolts of fabric were stacked in stalls; leather goods of every conceivable make cluttered the air space, while enormous woven carpets and animal skins hung from ceiling beams.

The souk offered a dizzying display of color and texture to accost every sense, and all with the accompanying shouting and bartering of shopkeepers eager to make their next sale.

Within the *Shadû's* warren of covered streets and shadowed alleys, mercenaries strolled behind Tambarréan aristocrats swathed in colorful, billowing silks. They in turn followed in the footsteps of Bemothi traders, discerned by their bejeweled turbans as much as the wicked sabers at their belts. Vestian merchants, with their ominous black veils strung with gold coins, and Dheanainn sailors with pierced ears and brows argued with Avataren slave traders, whose shaved and tattooed heads reminded Ean uncomfortably of Bethamin's Ascendants.

Oddly, the latter were notable mainly for their absence, there in a city now known more for its *al-qasr*—the local name for the temple complex that crowned the Tambarré acropolis—than for the trading hub it had been for millennia.

'*You'll want to enter Tambarré through the node in the Lower City…*'

Ean understood now why Sebastian had suggested that route, for the node had spit him out in a crowded plaza facing the *Shadû el-Fnaa's* elaborate arched entrance, an open invitation to blend in and disappear.

He'd quickly procured new clothing in the Tambarréan style—an embroidered kaftan, turban and cloak of indigo blue over matching desert pants—but for a stroll in the *Shadû el-Fnaa*, he needn't have worried. The place was so jammed with the representatives of different races, languages, dialects and cultures that even his fighting blacks wouldn't have drawn a curious eye.

Ean wore his turban with the hanging end draped across his features, and he viewed his surroundings through the veil of *elae's* currents, alert to patterns that might be attuned to detect an Adept of his particular ilk. But though he assessed his surroundings with a cautious eye, he couldn't quite keep the wonder out of his gaze.

He came to a covered plaza where vendors had set up food stands. Café tables and chairs were set all about a central fountain, whose watery music could barely be heard beneath the louder counterpoint of diverse languages. From one of the vendors, Ean bought *bestila,* a meat pie of layered pastry filled with a mixture of ground almonds, eggs and saffron-infused chicken, the whole of it covered in a rare confectioner's sugar. He retreated to the deeper shadows edging the crowded square and watched the goings on while he ate.

Sebastian had drawn a map of the city for him, but Ean still got lost three times before he found his way out of the honeycombed alleys of the souk. Midday had arrived by that time. After spending the morning beneath the souk's shaded corridors, the high Saldarian sun felt too bright to Ean's eyes.

All around him spread high walls of sandstone, their soft sides carved or stippled into the intricate designs so gloried by the desert kingdoms. And towering over everything, visible from nearly anywhere in the city, the mounding acropolis, ringed by a mile of crenellated sandstone wall, topped by an impressive complex of temples and palaces built first by the Quorum of the Sixth Truth and now home to the Prophet Bethamin.

Ean found his way to a plaza that offered an unimpeded view of the acropolis. While he refilled his flagons, he stared up at the imposing forty-foot walls, with the sun beating down on him from directly above and sweat trickling down his back.

'...*those tricks you performed to get us into Ivarnen...don't try them in Tambarré...*'

They'd spent hours collaborating on ways to enter the temple that didn't rely on his talent, yet now, having seen the place for himself, all of their ideas seemed inadequate. Nevertheless, Ean was committed to the path. He knew the effect he needed to achieve in Tambarré. Now it was a matter of remaining dauntless on his path until he achieved it.

Unfortunately, at the moment, dauntless was feeling a lot like uncertainty.

The prince headed off to seek a higher vantage from which he might view the acropolis and its many temples. Surprisingly he encountered few of Bethamin's minions about the town. Ean knew the Prophet didn't actually rule Saldaria, but he'd still envisioned Tambarré as a rat's nest of Ascendants and Marquiin. The city's only infestation, however, appeared to be feral cats.

The sun was falling in the west by the time Ean reached the city's westernmost edge, where the city walls abutted those surrounding the Prophet's *al'qasr*. A wide plaza opened before the gates leading into the Prophet's compound. Through this impressive portal lay gardens and the famed Stairway of Stars and its lengthy climb to the acropolis rim.

A few hundred paces west of the *al'qasr* gate loomed the city wall and the *Qobbah al-ilah*, or Vault of the God, the most impressive and frequented thoroughfare into Tambarré. Beside this, a set of wide marble steps led to the top of the city walls.

Ean climbed these steps, weaving around people who'd claimed a spot for rest, eating, gaming or debating, and joined many others atop the city's ramparts, where a tree-lined park ran the length of the wall.

Fifty paces brought the prince beneath the shade of tall palms and close to the wall's outer, crenellated edge. But he stopped short when he saw what lay beyond the city.

To his right hulked the mound of the Prophet's acropolis, with its temples and terraced gardens, orchards, vineyards and farms. But directly in front of Ean, the rolling Saldarian plains played host to the ramshackle tents and campfires of thousands of refugees.

Unmistakable among the gathering were the Prophet's minions—Ascendant ants with their torques and cuffs flashing gold in the afternoon sun; Marquiin-like moths wandering what might loosely be considered streets within the camp.

At that moment, hundreds of men, women and children had amassed along the part of the outer wall that also abutted the grounds of the Prophet's *al'qasr*. Most of the refugees stood packed in against one another with their gazes lifted towards the Prophet's westernmost temple, which jutted from a stepped landing midway down the acropolis mesa.

"Nadori refugees," said a female voice from Ean's left.

The prince turned to see a veiled woman swathed in the embroidered tangerine silks usually reserved for Avataren nobility. She had more gold around her wrists than Ean had in his packs. A frothy veil enwrapped her turbaned head and shoulders, but the cloth left her slanted dark eyes free to look him over. Which they were doing with some candor.

"They say not long ago these same refugees collected outside the walls of Tal'Shira by the Sea." She had a sultry voice, deep and low for a woman, and spoke with an accent Ean couldn't quite place except that it wasn't Avataren.

For the moment more intrigued by the refugees than the mysterious woman, Ean frowned off at the patchwork of tents. "What are Nadori refugees doing here?"

"Partaking of the Prophet's hospitality." She laid her hands on the sandstone merlon between two crenels and cast him a dubious half-smile. Her dark eyes swept him again, lingered for a moment on his hand, which he had resting on the hilt of his sword, and lifted back to meet his gaze. A smile flickered on her lips. "Or so some say."

"Curious." Ean thought the word equally described the Nadori refugees and the woman.

The glint in her dark, slanted eyes implied she might've used the same word in description of him.

A rising afternoon breeze rattled through the high palms. The woman lifted her gaze to the sun. "It won't be long now." She leaned out slightly over the crenel. "Come and see."

Ean glanced around. Unlike in the *Shadû el-Fnaa*, affluently dressed women of many nations strolled the breezy ramparts. Some had guards, but others walked alone. This woman was drawing no eyes, yet her casual candor seemed much out of place to Ean. He considered her carefully, recognizing that she could be working for anyone, allied to anyone, but in the last, curiosity won out over caution, and he joined her at the wall.

The vantage did provide a better view of the Prophet's lowest temple. In fact, if he leaned across the crenel, he could just see the base of the outer wall and a large gate facing the assembled masses.

This opened even as he watched, and a procession of Ascendants emerged. A dozen of the shaven-headed miscreants led twice as many acolytes, all of whom were carrying baskets of what appeared to be food.

A cheer rose up from the refugees. They swarmed the acolytes.

A feeling of grave foreboding swarmed Ean.

The Prophet is feeding *these people?* It seemed enormously out of character and deeply in conflict with a Malorin'athgul's intent.

As the food was being distributed, a new cheer erupted among the refugees, even louder than the first. Ean was trying to discover the source of this excitement when he saw the Prophet himself emerge onto a terrace of the lower temple. Bethamin strode to the edge of his balcony and raised a hand, part greeting, part blessing. The cheering became roaring adulation.

Ean felt a cold anger bloom in his chest. *Thousands* of people…and all of them craving the Prophet Bethamin's divine attention?

Bethamin was too far away for Ean to see him clearly, though his height and build presented an imposing figure even from that distance. He wore a long white robe that left his chest bare, and a golden torque collared his throat. His black hair hung in a curtain down his back, untroubled by the wind.

So that is Darshan.

Ean felt gravely conflicted. *I should leave now. As fast as I can.* But he stood rooted.

This was the man who'd given Isabel to Pelas to be tortured and killed, the man who made monsters of truthreaders and demons of men; possibly even the man who'd claimed Arion's life—the faceless Enemy that had turned the Citadel Mages against Isabel and bound them to his will. Raine's truth, the Prophet Bethamin was certainly no stranger to compulsion.

"It happens daily, this devotional," the woman murmured.

"Daily?" Ean stared perplexedly at the cheering refugees. "The Prophet is feeding these people every day?"

She arched a brow as if to share in a curious agreement. "From his own stores, so they say."

Ean cast her a sidelong look. He couldn't well make out her features beneath the embroidered veil, but her accent fell a tone flat of Avatar, and her dark eyes had an epicanthic fold—not a trait common to the Avataren nobility.

She noticed him looking at her and smiled. "It's an intriguing display, no? This, the Prophet's uncommon charity. This from a man who calls the lightning every night in his sleep."

"What?"

She arched a brow. "Have you not heard the stories? The Prophet summons the storms with his dreams. Or so they say. I suppose it could just be the time of year." She shifted a mocking gaze back to the cheering crowd. You would not see actual residents of Tambarré flocking to Bethamin with this level of adoration."

The more she spoke, the more curious Ean became about her. "What *would* you see from them?"

She gave a wry half-smile. "Don't mistake me. I'm not so foolish as to speak ill of the Prophet in his own city." Her even gaze quite belied the insult in her tone. "Even the most ignorant scamp is not so foolish as that. The people of Tambarré treasure the Prophet's disinterest almost as much as his gold."

"I don't take your meaning, madam."

She arched a brow, as if this was only common knowledge. "When he came to Tambarré from Myacene, or whatever dreadful rock he crawled out from under, the Prophet Bethamin flooded thousands of gold talents into Tambarré's economy and purchased by way of his generosity the nobility's indifference and a blind eye to his work."

"You're saying the Saldarian nobility know what Bethamin does to Adepts, and they don't care?"

She shrugged. "Gold's voice is louder and travels farther than a truthreader's anguished cry. The Prophet swore to barter Saldaria's independence from Radov of M'Nador and succeeded. They would've paid him for even the promise of it."

The cheering from the refugees at last subsided. Ean restrained himself from looking again to see if the Prophet had returned inside. He didn't want to look upon that man, or think about Isabel being his prisoner, or consider their eventual inevitable meeting, or any of the other hundred things that infuriated him about Darshan.

"And what business brings you to Tambarré, my lord?"

Ean turned and really focused on the woman then. Whoever she was, he mistrusted her attention. "Nothing of import to one such as yourself, my lady." He nodded politely. "If you'll excuse me—"

"I see you are a true stranger to Tambarré not to know an agent of the *Khashathra-pāvan* of Pashmir."

Ean halted. The Satrap of Pashmir was one of the most powerful rulers in Avatar, claiming nearly the status of a Fire King. He had agents in every known market whose duties were to procure the rarest of treasures on his behalf. They were each autonomous and generally afforded princely status among the merchant classes, for the satrap's appetite for antiquities was legendary.

The prince ducked a conciliatory bow, slight but appropriate, and said in Avataren, "*Ma'zerat mi-khāham.*" *I beg your pardon.* "I fear you've noted my ignorance. We don't greet many agents of the *Khashathra-pāvan* where I hail from."

She regarded him with quiet amusement. "Yet you know how to apologize to one."

He smiled thinly. "The product of a prudent education."

"Or provident breeding."

Ean was beginning to feel increasingly uncomfortable as the object of her attention. Her smile appeared benign, but beneath her overtly casual manner, Ean sensed an oddly fervent anticipation. "I'm just..." he hunted for an explanation that might dull her interest rather than pique it.

"Searching for a plausible lie?" She smirked at him.

Ean's gaze tightened. "Forgive me. My business grows pressing elsewhere." He bowed and moved on.

She turned after him, still obviously smiling. "If you hope to remain anonymous, *my lord*, might I suggest keeping your sword beneath your cloak? Kingdom Blades might be a rarity in Tambarré, but few are likely to mistake them for common steel."

Ean came to an abrupt standstill and turned a swift look over his shoulder. Feeling highly unsettled by her warning, he nodded once more. "Thank you for the explanation. A good day to you, my lady."

"And to you, my lord." She smiled, artfully innocuous, but Ean felt her dark eyes following him all the way down the ramparts.

The encounter had disturbed him. Had the satrap's agent recognized *him*, or just his blade? Could others have put two and two together as well? But no...if she'd known his identity, why had she let him walk away? Surely an agent of the *Khashathra-pāvan* knew Dore Madden had out a bounty on his head.

Ean clenched his jaw and stalked through the park, his mind a whir. The best thing to do would be to finish his mission and get out of there fast, before anyone else connected on his identity. Yet attempting to infiltrate the Prophet's temple with the Prophet in residence would be foolish beyond measure, while the idea of returning to Kandori seemed no less palatable an option. Surely there was some way...some solution...

Ean knew one thing for certain: *Arion* wouldn't have given up that easily.

Ean secured lodging and then spent the rest of the afternoon exploring possible ways into the Prophet's *al-qasr* while grappling with his conscience over the right course of action.

In his previous attempts, Dore had been expecting him; Tyr'kharta, Tal'Afaq—Ean had knowingly been walking into traps. This was the point he couldn't dismiss in his battle with his conscience—that this time Dore *didn't* know he was coming.

And of course, his purpose remained just as imperative—he had to test their matrix to determine if it disrupted the *eidola's* connection with Darshan. This matrix was doubly important, because if it worked like they expected it to, anyone could wield it, and do so without putting themselves at risk to counterattack from Darshan. Previously, every time Ean unworked one of the *eidola*, he risked contact with the Malorin'athgul's mind. This matrix would ensure a degree of separation that would protect anyone working it from Darshan's mental view. Ean knew that in every way, this effort was vital to the game.

Yet Darshan had returned…

Round Ean went on that carousel of *should I or shouldn't I?* But no matter how many revolutions he made, he always stepped off feeling like the opportunity was too valuable to pass up, their need too dire—providing he could smartly find a way into the *al-qasr* and out again.

That was the crux of the problem, and the reason that nightfall found him dressed in his fighting blacks exploring one possible route inside.

The roads in that part of Tambarré were closer kin to alleys than streets, with windowless stone walls that shielded inner gardens, each *riad*, or household, a self-contained oasis. The *riad* walls were high, the streets narrow, revealing the barest slip of the heavens on the best of nights, and that night storm clouds were rapidly overtaking Ean's patchwork view of the sky. He called upon the currents to light his way instead—the barest of workings, a calculated risk.

Sure, calling the currents is a calculated risk, Fynn's voice remarked in his head. *Siphoning off the first strand to keep yourself awake is a calculated risk. Staying in the Prophet's city at all is a calculated risk. Just tell me this, Ean—how long before the sum total of all of these 'calculated' risks adds up to the end of you?*

The Fynn voice had a point, and yet—

If he hadn't called up the currents just then, he might not have noticed the men until it was too late. There were at least a dozen of them coming at him from both ends of the street, thugs of the commonest sort, but they looked properly armed for the close quarters of the Lower City.

Ean inwardly swore. How could he have been so unaware as to let them trap him this way? Had he really been that lost in thought?

This is what happens when you and Sleep have a contentious parting of ways, Ean Alyneri's voice chided. *Awareness tends to take its own hiatus until you two mend your fences.*

Ean rubbed one eye and admitted to the Alyneri voice's point. He admitted also to a slight sense of disheartenment that Dore had found him so quickly. Maybe the Satrap's agent had turned him in for the reward after all.

With his next exhale, summoning focus, Ean drew his blade and spun into the *cortata*. *Elae* quickly flooded into him, strengthening the innate patterns that formed the woof and warp of his Adept composition.

He turned to face the closest of his attackers.

They were grinning at him. Perhaps they thought him mad, twisting and spinning like a dervish in the middle of the alley.

Ean rushed them.

He slew the closest two before they got their weapons up, and a third as he was swinging his. Now the currents sang in Ean's ears. Now he felt the *cortata's* power coursing through him. Having begun the pattern, he could work any part of the long sequence and keep his energy constant.

He whipped a dagger towards a fourth man and spun to engage a fifth. As their blades clashed, his dagger found its mark in the hollow of the fourth thug's throat, and the man staggered back in a fountain of blood. The others closed in on Ean, and for a time he knew only the motions of the *cortata's* pattern bolstering his strength, and the song of his Merdanti blade.

Twelve men? Only *twelve* men? As Ean slew another, he felt an almost indignant irritation. He'd faced off against the Sundragon Ramuhárikhamáth when Ramu was intent—if not on outright destroying him, at least he hadn't been holding back. Even without *elae*, twelve men hardly posed a threat to him. Dore Madden knew this better than most—

No…damn it—the truth hit Ean with a clap of *how-could-you-be-so-stupid?* Dore wouldn't have sent thugs after him. Dore would've sent *eidola*.

Dore would've sent eidola.

This realization brought a tingle of possibility. Suddenly Ean knew how to test their matrix.

He spun and brought his blade down across the chest of the man coming up behind him, elbowed another in the nose and kicked a third into the wall. The last two men wisely backed off, even as a hulking brute came forward between them carrying a scimitar big enough to take down a charging bull.

"There now, little prince," he said in Avataren in a voice as deep as his chest was broad, "you've made a good show, done your duty." He spun his scimitar in an impressive showing that proved he knew his way around his blade. "It doesn't have to end this way for you. Just do what she wants. Work a bit of magic—"

He swung for Ean.

The prince sidestepped and blocked his swing. Even with the *cortata*, the force charging through this clashing of steel sent pain flaring all the way back to Ean's shoulder. A similar clashing of blades followed as the Avataren made a rapid charge. Ean felt suddenly as if the Avataren *was* the bull. The strength of his blows forced the prince on the retreat; the rapidity of his attack pushed Ean to the edge of his ability. Any more, and he'd be forced to work *elae*.

Which seemed to be exactly what the Avataren wanted.

What had the man meant when he'd said 'work a bit of magic'? It certainly seemed like he was doing everything possible to push Ean into a desperate position. Perhaps desperate enough to work *elae* in the Prophet's city?

Ean danced back as the Avataren came at him anew—three, four, five fast slashes of his weapon, each one aiming for the prince's chest, each one only narrowly avoided. Ean took a few steps to try to recover the *cortata*, but the Avataren blocked him as if he knew his intention, as if trained also in its pattern—trained actually to prevent Ean from reclaiming it.

Another barrage of punishing blows, and the Avataren spun and kicked Ean in the chest. The prince hit the ground and somersaulted backwards onto his feet, but he came up with his head spinning and the taste of blood on his tongue. He backed up fast, putting some distance between them while he recovered his breath.

Thunder sounded. The rising wind tore at Ean's clothes. The Avataren's face seemed sketched of shadows.

He spun his blade as he advanced. "I kill you, or I let you live. It doesn't matter to me. But I get nothing if you don't do magic. What's it gonna be then, little prince? You choose."

Ean tried to reason through the situation, looking at everything that had happened and where it might be leading—

And a pattern flashed in his mind.

Not of *elae*, but of action and consequence, the spiraling threads of choices extending forward into possibility. He got the briefest glimpse of this pattern, of its paths of choices as yet unmade, yet it left a vivid residue of certainty of what would become. Ean was tempted to let things play on just to prove to himself the validity of the vision, to determine how far he'd glimpsed into future action.

In fact, he almost *had* to.

The pattern began with a choice—his choice—his step forward upon a specific path of consequence. Thinking no further than the surety of what he'd seen, Ean took that step.

He threw the second strand beneath his motion and in a heartbeat had the Avataren up against a wall and his sword at his throat. The giant's eyes bulged—with surprise, wonder, the pressure of the fifth compressing his lungs, pinning him to rock more surely than Ean's Merdanti blade? Probably all of them.

"Who paid you?" Ean growled in Avataren. He put the fourth into his question—the better to ensure the man's veracity and quick reply.

The Avataren choked out, "She—"

His eyes went glassy in the same moment Ean heard a dull *thock* and saw three inches of a black spike suddenly protruding from the Avataren's temple. Blood slowly drained into his dead eyes. Ean released the Avataren and spun, fast seeking the assassin. A blacker-than-black shadow vanished behind the lip of a roof.

Ean charged after it. He heard the Avataren's body hit the ground even as he was running up a ramp of air. Just as his head cleared the roof, something careened off his fifth-strand shield—probably another of the same spikes that had claimed the Avataren.

Wind tore at the prince as he ran across the roof in pursuit of the assassin. Even as he watched, the man jumped an alley, landed on the next roof and rolled back to his feet with acrobatic ease, and kept running.

Ean put the second beneath his steps and leapt after him. Glancing down, the alley beneath his flying form appeared as a river of bronze to his *elae*-enhanced vision—the currents of the second strand. Ean landed on the next roof and kept chasing.

Above, the sky was solid darkness and boiling with thunder, but *elae's* currents made the city bright to Ean's eyes. The assassin darting across the rooftops appeared as a dark speck against an outline of gold.

The assassin leapt off a roof's ledge and landed a story below on a lower rooftop. Rolling back to his feet, he turned as Ean was leaping after him and flung two more deadly darts. When they struck Ean's fifth-strand shield, they caused an oddly clamorous resonance that he felt in his teeth.

Ean landed and kept running.

The figure sprinted for the edge, threw himself across another alley and tumbled to his feet on the roof of what could only be the *Shadû el-Fnaa*. The souk's countless connected stalls and stores all shared the same roof, making an odd exoskeleton of ridges and angled tiles.

Ean flung the second beneath himself and became a flying shadow across the darkened street. He landed awkwardly and skidded sidelong down the tiles. The assassin was running along the spine of the souk, a dark outline against the darker night. Lightning flared, backlighting his form, and Ean threw a pattern.

The figure tumbled.

Ean darted after it, up and over the undulating rooftop, but when he reached the edge where he'd seen the figure fall, he saw only a darkened street hosting a promenade of shops.

Ean slung himself over the roof's edge and landed in a cushion of the fifth. An easterly wind pushed at his back before tearing on down the promenade, shaking the near fig trees like a mother remonstrating a naughty child. Ean warily cast a pattern in search of the assassin just as lightning split the sky in a searing flash.

'...*The Prophet calls the lightning in his sleep...*'

From the promenade, Ean had a clear view of the acropolis and its glowing temples. Even as he watched, another jagged streak cracked the firmament. Ozone charged through the air. Elemental energy slammed through the currents. Ean felt the molecules splitting, bombarding each other in their attempt to flee the Prophet's furious slumber. He grunted. *And I thought my dreams were bad.*

A darkness streaked towards his head.

He reared back with an intake of breath, and a foot narrowly missed his jaw. The assassin wore black from head to toe; only her slanted eyes showed above a fitted mask—eyes he instantly recognized.

Immediately the foot struck for him again, faster than any mortal should be able to move. She bore after him in such a furious press that for a moment it was all Ean could do to stay out of her reach. Tumbling, spinning, twirling—one fist barely missed his nose before another fist or foot came flying at his head.

Whereupon, Ean realized that she had to be moving so fast by means of some form of innate timeweaving—like Gwynnleth when she'd fought the Whisper Lord back in Chalons-en-Les Trois. That's why Ean couldn't see any patterns associated with her movement—they were intrinsic to the patterns of her thoughts.

There were a hundred ways he could've wielded his power to end her life, but Ean wanted answers. He wanted to test his glimpsed pattern of cause and consequence.

Whenever Ean dreamed of Arion, he recovered some new trick that his former self had known. Now he called up Arion's third-strand pattern—a matrix really, formed of the third and fifth woven together—and stepped off the world's time-stream.

Suddenly he saw the assassin moving as slowly as if she was practicing the *cortata* at half speed. The faces of the Mages that Arion had slain superimposed themselves before the assassin's hooded head, so that Ean felt like he walked time in two places at once. Behind him on that stream, Arion carved a path of death. Ahead of Ean lay a different pattern of consequence, yet somehow part of the same pattern.

In the next instant, he had his hand wrapped around her throat and a dagger poised at the back of her neck, just beneath her skull—a quick death, if it came to that. The assassin stilled with a sharp inhale.

"Whatever game you're playing," he said quietly, backing her into the alcove of a shop entrance, "you picked the wrong opponent."

Her chest rose and fell with her rapid breath, and her slanted eyes grew even more narrow, dangerous. "Look down, Prince of Dannym."

Ean glanced down between them and saw a curved silver blade in her hand, ready to eviscerate. He arched a brow.

She hissed and dropped the weapon, grabbing her wrist with her other hand. A burned palm radiated beneath the seared leather of her glove.

Ean gave her a razor smile. "The benefits of a prudent education."

The curse she spat at him sounded uncomplimentary even in a foreign tongue.

He pinned her up against the wall with the fifth and pulled off her mask. As he'd expected, the Satrap of Pashmir's agent glared blackly back at him. Without the voluminous layers of silk, she wasn't but a wisp of a woman, barely stouter than the braid in her raven hair; but Ean had seen firsthand how deceptive was her impression of frailty.

At least he could assess with some certainty that she was not Avataren nobility. Her slanted eyes and oval-shaped face placed her clearly from the region of Malchiarr, or perhaps the eastern country of Vest, which also better explained her accent.

"Now...who are you?" Ean stepped back and crossed his arms. "What's this all about?"

Pinned against the wall by the fifth, she glared venomously at him. Thunder sounded overhead in emphasis of her defiance.

Ean tightened his intention, and his fifth-strand bounds pressed her more firmly into the wall, eliciting a hiss of pain. "Why did you follow me? Why did you send those goons to attack me? Why did you want me to work *elae*?"

Her slanted dark eyes stared back in silence.

The prince shook his head, his own anger simmering. "Lady, you have no idea what I'm capable of. I've kept you alive for some answers, but if you're set on dying to protect your secrets—"

"Sheih."

He tilted his head to regard her cautiously. "Shay...?"

"My *name*," she snapped, "is Sheih." Her dark eyes strayed to the promenade. "You should release me. Even now the *shaytan'jinn* will be coming."

Shaytan'jinn? It was an Avataren word. "Demons?"

"They are a scourge, the Advisor's personal army. Two weeks ago, my partner went to discuss a complicated matter with the Advisor and never came back."

Ean followed her gaze towards the promenade. He knew well what would be coming for him soon enough, but how did this *Sheih* know about them?

He released her from his bands of the fifth but kept his own shield in place.

She stepped away from the wall and rubbed around the edges of her burned palm, radiating fury and something else…something indefinable; the currents were shouting it, but in a language Ean didn't speak.

He ran a calculating gaze over her. "*Shaytan'jinn*…you speak of *eidola*."

Sheih picked up her hood from where he'd dropped it on the ground. "I've been hunting them since my partner died."

"Unsuccessfully, I gather."

The venom in her gaze as she straightened could've felled an olyphaunt. "The Advisor only sends them to settle his vendettas, and I didn't have any more partners to sacrifice."

Ean thought he was starting to understand. "That's why you wanted me to work *elae*. You made me bait for them." Never mind that this had recently been his same intention.

Sheih arched a critical brow. "Nay, foolish prince. You became bait for the *shaytan'jinn* the moment you set foot in Tambarré."

Ean studied her in silence. Some of her answers fit within the pattern of consequence he'd glimpsed, but quite a few strands of truth seemed to be missing from the whole. "How did you know I was a wielder?"

Sheih rolled her eyes. "Mercenaries talk, but Ascendants talk even more. Rumors out of the *al-qasr* say Prince Ean val Lorian severed the Prophet's connection with one of his Marquiin. They say you killed the *shaytan'jinn* in Ivarnen. They say you can walk on air and turn stones to sand—they say many unbelievable things."

"But you believed them?"

She snorted. "I believe the two hundred gold talents Dore Madden is offering for your head." Sheih moved to the edge of the building and looked up and down the promenade. The howling wind was whipping the trees into a frenzy of flying leaves and rustling branches. "Now the Advisor will know it's you." Her tone revealed a hint of satisfaction. "Now he will send one of his demons, and I shall at last have my vengeance."

Lady, you have no idea.

Sheih thought Dore would only send one *eidola*, but if he thought Ean was in the city—and how could he not, with the performance Ean had delivered on the currents that night?—he would unleash a wave of demons in pursuit.

Ean joined Sheih at the alcove's edge. "We shouldn't meet them here."

She angled a brow upwards. "*Them?*"

Ean cast his gaze off through the storm, but really he was casting it along the currents, seeking a telltale disturbance that would alert to the *eidola's* approach. "Is there somewhere else we can watch for them? Somewhere higher up?"

She regarded him circumspectly. Then she nodded. "Follow me, Prince of Dannym."

THIRTY-ONE

"We are none of us so rich as to afford the luxury of regret."
–The Agasi wielder Markal Morrelaine

BJÖRN VAN GELDERAN landed lightly on the patio of his once-apartments in Illume Belliel, worked the trace seal on the glass-paned doors and slipped soundlessly inside Alshiba's study. Closing the doors behind himself, he looked around.

The space had changed little from when he'd held residence there. It seemed the only real changes Alshiba had made were to remove anything that reminded her too nearly of him.

Gone was the armillary he'd kept upon his desk. Likewise a set of journals—she'd doubtless turned those in to the authorities ages ago. Björn smiled at the contemplation of a team of investigators scouring his rambling musings, looking for some proof of treason.

The room's shelves and pedestals still displayed treasures from the Thousand Realms, tributes collected during his many centuries of service as the Alorin Seat. Alshiba had received some new tributes of her own as well, it appeared.

He moved on inside, scanning the room with his vigilant gaze, searching for patterns not of his own creation—for plenty of those remained. Yet what he saw most were the memories, ephemeral tracings layered upon one another as if a matrix of patterns—conversations, debates, sleepless nights, afternoons spent pacing, *thinking*, while the sun cast long, striated rays through the glass-paned doors. He saw faces, each connected to a series of events trailing into his lengthy past, and each a springboard into spirals of future consequence.

And he saw Alshiba, often in the periphery, sometimes in the background, rarely the central focus but never far from his side, or his thoughts, during those years. There was nothing fair about what he'd done to her. No way, really, to atone for it.

He walked to his desk—Alshiba's desk—and ran his hand along the delicate wood, warm with the fresh sense of her. But underneath...the impression of his own lifeforce remained. The wood was saturated with it.

He'd laid preservation patterns throughout his home. They trapped more than time; they captured the lifeforce, energy bound to objects, objects bound to the time stream of the world's consciousness. Each book on his shelf held an energistic history, every floor tile a tale—or several. The mansion was clogged with the detritus of his thoughts, impressions, emotions...desires.

Never mind the armillary, how could Alshiba stand all the rest of it?

The currents in the room were calm, which meant that whatever malicious craft was being worked against Alshiba likely remained dormant until she appeared. Instinct told him they'd planted some kind of *atrophae*, or cursed object, created with *mor'alir* patterns designed to bring harm or illness. An *atrophae* could be formed of anything into which a pattern could be indelibly inscribed. Any one of the treasures in the room could've been *atrophae*. Many of the common items, too.

Björn started with the newest objects and began systematically working his way through the room, laying his hands on everything, permeating them with his thoughts, searching for patterns within their construction. That he could see patterns made this task much easier, though no less time-intensive, considering the number of items in the room.

The sun made lengthy progress in its trek through the heavens while he was conducting this inspection. He was fully prepared to stop time while he checked every item in every room of the mansion, but he found what he was looking for in a crystal goblet, one of a set aligned beside a corked bottle of wine. She very likely drank from the goblet every day.

Björn felt the sizzle of *mor'alir* the moment his fingers touched the crystal. He lifted it to the light and saw patterns etched throughout, though they would be invisible to anyone lacking his particular variant trait.

Two layers bound the glass. The patterns forming the first layer of the *atrophae* were attuned to *elae*'s first strand and would activate when touched by an Adept of that strand. The patterns of the second layer were designed to disrupt the same.

Every time Alshiba came within range of the goblet, it would activate like a tuning fork, but one that emitted a deadly, draining hum. The goblet was effectively cutting Alshiba off from *elae*'s first strand—a twice poison, for her Healer's nature drew heavily on this creative lifeforce. Over time, she would wither, sicken and grow ill. A cunning and completely untraceable means of eliminating her.

Björn exhaled a slow breath. His cobalt gaze grew hard. A *mor'alir* Adept had crafted this deadly gift—and expertly so. He recalled watching Alshiba drink wine from that very goblet the last time he'd paid her a visit.

Ah…Alshiba, my love. I never meant for things to come to this.

Björn looked over the crystal again, studying its construction. Then he drew upon the fifth to shape his intent. The goblet shimmered, seemed to refract the light differently for an instant, and then solidified back into form with a faint chime, now without its hidden patterns. Björn set it back on the sideboard.

He might've removed the goblet altogether, but it would be a simple thing for the perpetrator to plant another *atrophae* if he found his first one missing. Better he thought his noxious gift still active.

Björn returned to his inspection of the room.

He found four more *atrophae* before he was finished. Each one he altered and left where it lay.

He would need to come back and check the entire mansion. He would need to spend more time in Illume Belliel than he'd anticipated. *Atrophae* were like poison; even after he'd found and destroyed them all, Alshiba would be weak and in need of Healing. And he knew too well the type of predators circling her in wait, watching for any weakness. There were several obvious hyenas hungering on the fringes, but lions, too, of this he was certain.

Björn exhaled a slow breath and set down the last of the *atrophae* he'd unworked. Alshiba hating him was a consequence he could live with, but something happening to her as a result of him was not.

The currents swelled faintly, the ripple of a familiar presence approaching.

Björn walked to a cabinet and plucked two lowball glasses off the shelf. Then he reached into a space that appeared to be empty and withdrew a cut crystal decanter, half full with an amber liquid.

He cast a whisper of the fifth to close the cabinet doors and was striding across the room, making for the patio, when his eyes caught upon a marble King's board with pieces frozen in play.

For a moment, he stared at it.

Then a smile touched his lips.

It was the last game he'd been playing before leaving Illume Belliel on that fateful night when everything had gone awry. He wondered why

Alshiba had left the game as it was—surely this, of anything, would've reminded her of him.

Then he landed upon the reason, and his smile broadened.

Knowing his oath-sister, she would be trying to discern his strategy for winning a simple game of Kings as if it might somehow help her understand the larger game he'd masterminded. She'd probably spent many hours trying to piece together his plan for this game and wouldn't restore the board until she had.

He noted that it was actually his turn.

Björn leaned and made his next move.

He slipped out onto the patio just as the study doors were opening.

◆

Alshiba walked into her study with her head pounding and the hair standing up on the back of her neck like the ruff of an affronted cat. Yet even if she'd been a hissing and growling cat, Niko wouldn't have noticed her irritation.

"…long have those responsible for our race's decline gone unpunished." Niko followed her into the room amid a diatribe she'd heard already once, and that once was a hundred times too many. "Our enemies flourish while Alorin withers. Fewer Adepts are born each year. Now, I must ask Your Excellency, is this fitting? Is it *just*?"

Alshiba somewhat slammed a journal she'd been carrying on her desk and turned him a strained look. "Niko…" she let out a slow exhale, measuring her patience as she counted her breath. "What do you think we'll gain by attacking T'khendar? Do you think that in three centuries Björn won't have planned for something like this?"

Niko looked perturbed by her interruption. "*Perhaps*, my lady," he admitted, sounding dubious, "but surely he can't have planned for two hundred Paladin Knights."

"*Two hundred.*" She stared at him. "How do you imagine you could possibly rally two hundred Paladin Knights to invade T'khendar when the Speaker rarely sends more than fifty at a time, even into the most heated conflicts?"

Niko's brows arched into condescension, resembling the *f* holes on a violin. "For the war criminal Björn val Gelderan? My lady…" his smile was nearly as patronizing as his tone, "he's the most wanted man in the cityworld's history. Sure the only reason the Speaker hasn't already called for his extradition is the problem of how to reach the damned place."

Alshiba laid her hands on the journal, feeling the smooth leather beneath her fingers. She took small comfort in it. The journal was one of

Björn's, part of a set he'd kept by his desk but which she now kept locked in her bedroom.

His thoughts, penned so candidly within the context of his private musings, were the only link she still had to him, her only guide beyond an imperfect memory as to how he would think, react, consider—how *he* would've handled a problem of policy or politics. Björn's journals were treasures far more valuable than any of the hundreds of priceless tributes collecting dust around her chambers.

Unfortunately, they didn't help her solve the problem of Niko. He was a problem she'd created all on her own. She fixed him with a level look. "And you think you have this solved, do you? Some means of reaching T'khendar?"

Niko gave her a condescending smirk. "Isn't it obvious?" He walked to the sideboard and helped himself to some of her wine. Turning with goblet in hand, he smiled. "We have Franco Rohre."

Something in the way Niko said Franco's name made the hairs of her arms stand up in alarm.

Alshiba kept her expression neutral with effort. "I'm not sure I follow your logic." She pulled out her chair and slowly sank down onto it, trying her best to keep him from noticing how exhausted she was, how drained emotionally and physically. Fortunately, the man only really noticed things happening within the radiating circle of his ego.

"Don't you, my lady?" Niko leaned back against the sideboard and crossed his ankles, his manner smug and improperly familiar. "Did you not say that you know Franco serves Björn? Didn't you declare he was holding the other Vestals in T'khendar?"

She had, but not to Niko.

Alshiba felt a trill of unease. Had Niko been listening to her private conversations? Was he *spying* on her? Or had he merely aligned himself with others who were?

She'd been so tired lately…so fatigued. It was making her careless. She would have to be more careful to ward her communication as well as her thoughts. The latter she did immediately, though if Niko had any skill with the fourth, she would eat her own shoes.

Alshiba slowly rose from her chair and walked to the sideboard. A gentleman would've offered to pour her some wine. Niko stepped out of her way.

"Whatever other allegiances he may or may not have," Alshiba said as she attended to her own drink, "at the moment, Franco serves Alorin."

Niko smirked down at her. He was standing far too close for propriety. "He's been Called, my lady. Make no mistake of it." He dared push a lock of hair back from her shoulder and let his fingers linger a little too long by her neck. "Franco Rohre has been to T'khendar, and he can take us there again."

Us?

For a moment, as she stared at Niko, Alshiba wondered what she could possibly have been thinking. How could she not have seen the vile lining of his nature? Admittedly, she'd known Niko was vain; she'd thought those shallow waters were all there was to him. She'd never imagined the river of his comportment concealed so much decay, or so many deep holes of treachery.

Alshiba walked towards the wall of glass-paned doors and air that didn't reek of duplicity. It felt as dangerous as turning her back on a bull. "What do you mean, he's been called?" She aimed him a look over her shoulder. "Called to what?"

Niko blinked at her for a moment. Then he hurriedly drank his wine.

Alshiba arched a brow. *That's interesting.* She would have to ask Franco what Niko had meant by the phrase—she'd no doubt whatever next came out of Niko's mouth would be a lie, if he deigned to answer her at all. "In any case, Niko, I can't see the Speaker agreeing to commit to a military campaign with the Interrealm Trade Measure's enactment imminent and the Council still so divided."

Niko glowered at her. Then he seemed to regroup and crossed the room purposefully. Whatever was driving him was clearly a harder taskmaster than she was proving to be.

He stopped close before her and gazed down, assuming an expression of deepest sympathy. A cobra's calculating gaze would've been more sincere. "You cannot be hesitant to seek retribution for how Björn wronged you." Niko ran his fingers along her arm. "Alshiba…he *betrayed* you."

His advances were becoming more obvious and less endurable. Ever since she'd asked Franco to stay in the mansion with her, Niko seemed to have been trying to worm his way into her household too. Even had she been open to his courtship she wouldn't have trusted his motives. She slipped free of his touch and moved away from him again. "This isn't about Björn and myself, Niko."

Niko stared blackly after her. "No, my lady, no indeed." His tone held all the warmth of a glacial stream. "It's about bringing justice to a man who held ultimate power and egregiously misused it. It's about apprehending a man who let Shades wreak havoc on the innocents of our realm…" He was growing impassioned again—she could tell by the insultingly glib rhetoric he so easily summoned. "No, no *indeed*, not! It's about a man who stood by to let our race be ravaged, and lest we forget, who committed the ultimate blasphemy and dared create a new *world—an entire world,* Alshiba!"

Björn... you created a world!

Three centuries, and the truth still astonished her... still awed her nearly to the point of breathlessness.

Alshiba regarded Niko through a haze of misgiving. She didn't for a moment believe he cared about T'khendar, or Alorin, or even about Björn's atonement. Frankly, she couldn't fathom why Niko van Amstel was so adamant about invading Björn's realm, but his interest certainly couldn't spring from any altruistic purpose.

Alshiba set down her wine on a table and lowered herself onto the chair beside it—the same chair where Franco had confronted her on her illness, where she'd observed something in his gaze...

Alshiba leaned back against the cushion and rubbed her throbbing temples with thumb and forefinger. Her head was swimming, her stomach ever the source of a sickly turmoil. But mostly she felt thin. Wafer thin. *Gossamer thin.* The barest, crackling shell of herself. Not even a sketch anymore, merely a hasty outline on a scrap of parchment long discarded, fading in the sun.

"My lady, are you ill?"

What was it in his voice? Not concern... hope?

No, Niko. I'm not ill. I'm undone.

She no longer cared to understand the thousand choices Björn had made. She didn't have the energy even to try. She only prayed he had things in hand—because *oh,* how she'd mangled it on her end! One of the finest misapplications of the First Law ever witnessed.

KNOW the effect you intend to create.

She'd *intended* for Björn—or in the very least, Dagmar—to return and claim his place on the Council. She'd intended that they would see Niko aiming for the Vestal Seat and experience a driving need to prevent the man's ascension—or at least fear she'd gone out of her mind and feel some obligation to step in and resume their duties in defense of the realm. She'd *expected* them still to harbor at least a *miniscule* concern for the positions they'd once so selflessly and brilliantly held. She'd never imagined she would be stuck with Niko!

"I'll be all right." Alshiba dropped her hand into her lap. "It's just a spell."

Niko looked dubious but gave her a smile, the first time his insincerity seemed appropriate. He wandered over to her Kings board and gazed down at it while sipping his wine. Then he reached a hand—

She gasped. "Don't!"

Niko paused with his fingers just shy of one of the pieces. He turned her a look of puzzled injury. "Is it a game in play then?" The obvious inquiry in his tone asked who she might be playing with.

Alshiba found herself on her feet, not having realized she'd moved at all. She smoothed her skirts and tried to calm herself with a slow exhale. "It's a long story."

She walked to the Kings board, mostly to be certain he didn't try to touch any of the pieces again. "I think I should turn in early, Niko." She tried to put kindness into her tone but probably only succeeded at impatience. "Perhaps you should leave now."

He held her gaze. "Very well, my lady…if that's what you want." His words were very much at odds with his expression, his suggestive tone very much implying that this couldn't actually be what she wanted.

Alshiba dropped her eyes to summon her patience—

Her gaze flew back to his in alarm. "Did you touch it? Did you touch the board?" Her heart was suddenly frantic at the mere thought of Björn having been there—for who else could've made that move, one she'd hardly considered in all her years of careful scrutiny?

A thrill pulsed through her—*damn you, Björn!*

Niko drew back with a look of confused protest. "I touched nothing. I promise you."

Alshiba stared at the Kings board with her breath coming embarrassingly fast. Her heart was frustratingly at odds with her conscience.

She swallowed and looked back to Niko. "Alert the Speaker. Sound the alarm."

❖

Aldaeon H'rathigian, Seat of Markhengar and Speaker of the Council of Realms, closed the doors to his study with a slow sigh. He slipped out of his bejeweled Speaker's robe, hung it in its case behind the door and flowed with the grace of the Elven races around the corner into the main room.

Where he froze, his colorless gaze riveted to a distinctive crystal decanter resting on a low table between a grouping of chairs. "*Where* did you get that?" He lifted incredulous eyes to the man seated in one of those chairs, then looked swiftly back to the decanter as if fearing it might vanish at any moment.

"From my apartments." Björn sipped a caramel-colored liquor from the cut crystal glass he held in one hand, the other being draped along the low back of his leather chair. "Well…Alshiba's apartments."

A ponderous mystification overtook the elf's features. He looked somewhat desperately back to Björn. "I searched those apartments personally from end to end!"

Björn smiled, all culpable innocence. "Perhaps you weren't looking in the right places, my friend."

Aldaeon speared him with a stare of disbelief. "I very nearly tore the mansion apart!"

"Oh, wait—no, that's right," Björn winked at him while swirling the coveted liquid around in his glass, "you must not have been looking in the right *when*."

Aldaeon stood for a moment with incredulity widening his gaze. Then he sank down onto the chair across from Björn with a slow sort of grace. For an elf, it was very nearly a plop.

Björn nodded to the other glass on the table. "Join me, my friend."

Aldaeon settled such a look upon him. Then he stared hard at the bourbon. "As furious as I was with what I perceived to be your betrayal at the time…I was almost more furious for thinking you'd taken this damned bottle to T'khendar with you. But it was here all the time?"

Björn gave him a soft smile. "I would've told you if you'd asked."

Aldaeon picked up the glass and studied the amber liquid within. "I'll remember that the next time you abscond to a foreign realm with the only bottle in existence of my favorite bourbon."

Björn's blue eyes danced. "If I'd known you were missing it so desperately, I'd have sent you a case of it. We distill it now in T'khendar."

Aldaeon shook his head. "Of course you do." He gazed at the amber fluid for a conflicted moment, as if debating the ethics of sharing libations with a wanted criminal. Then he took a sip, whereupon a blissful serenity overtook his expression. He closed his eyes and reclined back in his chair.

Björn leaned and placed a small marble box on the table between them.

At the sound of stone clacking against the glass, Aldaeon opened his eyes and fixed his colorless gaze on the box. "What's that?"

"A gift for you to open later." Björn sat back in his chair. "I heard you got my measure passed."

The Speaker grunted. "Dubious congratulations. I barely survived with my head still attached."

"Thank you for that, my friend." Björn willed that his gaze might convey all that Aldaeon's effort meant to him—his gratitude at what Aldaeon had done, what he'd risked, what he'd potentially sacrificed. He let his thoughts speak this loudly to the truthreader.

Aldaeon arched brows and gave a rueful exhale. "Yes, well…I recall what you said to me when you gave me the measure all those years ago."

Björn smiled quietly over his glass, holding the rim just shy of his lips. "I…may have been a little hard on you then."

Aldaeon frowned thoughtfully. "'When the majority of people are benefited by taking the action,' you said, 'despite all obstacles and odds, you are ethically bound to push it forward.'" He shifted his gaze back to Björn, serious and solemn. "It's become a guiding rule of my reign."

"It has long been mine as well." Björn lowered his arm to the chair with his glass caught beneath his fingers. "Who will you appoint to head the committee?"

Aldaeon looked up at him beneath his brows. "Do not pretend you don't know who I've chosen."

A half-smile twitched Björn's lips. "Has she accepted?"

Aldaeon sighed resignedly. "I would ask you to speak with her, but I doubt your influence would prove beneficial."

"I must agree with you there."

There were times when Björn stood upon Time's undulating pathway and looked both forwards and backwards, seeing choices that had brought him to where he stood then, and others whose full consequences had not yet come to bear. They marched on with him, those decisions, an army spreading in a phalanx at his back—*his* army, forged of judgment and conclusion, moving inexorably forth towards the moment of its intended strike. *Past choices reflecting future action*...both, in a sense, were already behind him on Time's pathway, for he couldn't change them now. The events he'd set in motion had developed their own inertia, the game its own life.

He'd known at every moment, with his every choice, that he was permanently changing the future path of millions. He'd had to be *so certain* when he made those choices. He neither regretted nor second-guessed now the decisions he'd made in the past, but often he regretted the way those choices had impacted others.

Björn lifted his gaze back to the elf. "Has Alshiba spoken to you of her illness?"

"That...yes." Solicitude shadowed the Speaker's colorless eyes. "The best Healers in the cityworld have examined her. I hate to say it, but you may be the only one who can determine what ill is being worked against her."

"I entertained a similar notion."

"Ah..." Aldaeon arched brows in understanding. "So that's why you've returned." For some reason, this seemed to sadden him.

Björn regarded Aldaeon quietly. "You know you'll only be placing her in greater danger if you make her the Committee Chair."

The elf lifted him a swift and penetrating stare. "Are you volunteering in her stead?"

"Trust me, my friend," Björn held up his drink soberly to him, "with what's coming our way, I guarantee you'll want me right where I am."

The Speaker's gaze tightened, the only indication of his unease—with

Björn's intimation, or perhaps with conversing so intimately with an infamous traitor...it was difficult to say which fact more unsettled the elf. "And what is coming our way?"

Björn lowered his glass to the arm of his chair and nodded towards the Speaker's desk. "It's all there in my letter."

"Ah, yes." Aldaeon cast a sooty gaze in the same direction. "By this, you no doubt reference the mysterious letter that literally *appeared* while I was conducting an inquest—what was it...a fortnight ago?" He arched a brow at him. "The timing seems a bit off, especially for you."

"It isn't an exact science, the mailing of letters to arrive centuries in the future."

"But you claim your predictions are." Aldaeon's colorless eyes held a shade of skepticism. "Even knowing you as I do...I needn't point out that none of these predictions have yet come to pass."

"None that I shared with you," Björn corrected with an easy smile. Then his expression sobered. "But they will. It's nearly a surety."

Aldaeon frowned. "You speak with such assurance, your letter, warnings as proclamations...by any other view, they might be construed as threats."

"You know me better than that."

"*I* do," Aldaeon cautioned, "but many others do not. With your absence so notable, the aspersions upon your past...I fear they'll lay upon your head the very villainy you say you're working to prevent."

"There's nothing new in that, Aldaeon."

"Björn..."

Björn lifted a hand to pause the elf's protest. "My reputation is a cheap sacrifice for what we're trying to accomplish." He didn't need to say, *and so is yours,* for this was evident in his steady gaze.

Aldaeon pressed his lips together and regarded Björn with a deep furrow between his brows. Suddenly he leaned forward and hissed under his breath, "Do you have any idea what would happen to me if I proposed even a quarter of what you wrote in that letter? Do you know how many Seats already want my head? If I so much as *hinted* at the possibility of opening negotiations with the Warlocks of Shadow, the Council would *crucify* me."

Björn fingered his glass quietly and regarded his friend in silence, just the hint of his thoughts reflected in his gaze.

Aldaeon sat back forcefully in his chair. "Don't say it," he groused. "I know what you're thinking: why is my head more precious than yours?"

A smile flickered on Björn's lips. "I was contemplating what your handsome head would look like hanging above the Eltanin Seat's mantel."

"Ah, yes," Aldaeon arched a dour brow, "Mir Arkadhi. He is one who makes me wish I had eyes in the back of my skull."

Björn set his empty glass down on the table and sat back again. "I found five *atrophae* in Alshiba's apartments today."

The Speaker blinked at him.

"They were *mor'alir*. The patterns hinted of Eltanin work."

"*Five atrophae.*" Aldaeon frowned ponderously at this. "Do you think Eltanin is behind the attempt on her life?"

"It's hard to say. Eltanin sits behind a lot of things without standing directly behind anything."

"There's a certain text. What did you do with the *atrophae*?"

"I left them where they were, minus a few patterns. There are probably more. I'll need to search the entire mansion." He ran a finger thoughtfully along the arm of his chair. "Whoever intends her harm…you can't think they'll rely solely on *atrophae*."

The elf gave a powerful exhale. "I'll offer her additional protection." He leveled Björn a look of perilous concern. "I do not know if she will accept it."

"Thank you, my friend. We both know Alshiba's importance to this effort." With that, Björn pushed to his feet.

Aldaeon fingered his glass with speculation in his gaze. "And what of her other illness…the one that's been ailing her ever since you left?"

Björn offered a resigned smile. "I'm working on a cure for that one as well." He nodded and started off.

"You know I can't let you leave."

Björn paused—halted more by the apology in Aldaeon's tone than from his words. He turned back to see a host of Paladin Knights flooding onto the balcony. There would be no escape in that direction. Not this time.

The study doors flew open, and more Knights streamed in. They wore *elae*-enhanced armor and were surrounded with shields of the fifth.

Björn looked back to Aldaeon and arched a brow.

Shadows of apology veiled the elf's countenance. "Of course, you understand…I had no choice, my friend."

Björn exhaled a slow breath while eyeing the incoming flood of Knights. "Of course."

The Speaker stared at the bourbon in his glass unhappily. "An honorable man cannot set friendship before duty, Björn."

"I wouldn't respect you nearly as much if you did, my friend." Björn scanned his gaze across the Paladin Knights. There might've been fifty of them altogether, come in the name of claiming him for the Council Inquisitor. An appreciable number—what they might send to a faraway realm to put an end to a conflict of kingdoms—but not outrageous, considering *he* was their quarry.

A smile twitched on Björn's lips. "Impressive." He turned with interest back to Aldaeon. "All of this took time to arrange. How did you know?"

Aldaeon exhaled a measured breath. "Alshiba alerted me. She knew somehow that you'd been in her apartments." He arched a brow. "It appears she may still be vexed with you."

Björn's gaze hinted of amusement. "I think more than somewhat."

"I am sorry, my friend." Aldaeon truly meant this—Björn could see the contrition in his expression, feel it in his thoughts. "But you're wanted for questioning—rather vehemently, I believe." He looked with resignation to the Knights and gave a weary sigh. "Take him into custody."

The closest two moved towards Björn—

Spiraling sapphire patterns burst out around them, forcing them to draw back.

Aldaeon hissed an oath and jumped to his feet.

The same patterns flared around him, shooting forth along an invisible barrier to roughly outline the shape of a cube.

Suddenly the room erupted into a kaleidoscope of dazzling aquatic swirls, as every Paladin Knight tried to move and found himself encased in a *celantia's* invisible box.

Björn looked to the milky stone beneath his feet and thought, *dissolve*.

Marble faded out of existence. He dropped in a whisper of the fifth and landed lightly on the floor one level below.

The Speaker slammed his hands against the *celantia* surrounding him. "Björn!"

Björn looked up at him through the rather large hole in the floor/ceiling. "Of course...you understand, I had no choice, my friend." He pushed a hand to smooth back his hair and then held it out towards Aldaeon, a gesture of gratitude. "Though...I really must thank you for the pattern of the *celantia*. I'm finding it endlessly versatile."

Aldaeon growled a frustrated oath.

Behind the Speaker, the knights were all attempting to escape the *celantias*; Aldaeon's study appeared as a star webbed with tentacles of undulating blue light.

The Speaker at last seemed to take note of the large hole in his floor. He leveled an exasperated glare at Björn. "*This tile* is made of a Starstone that has to be grown from Valerian crystal!"

Björn grinned at him. "Open my gift."

For a heartbeat, the elf stared. Then he swung to the table before him and grabbed up the small marble box. Inside lay a glowing crystal that shone like a star. Aldaeon looked back to Björn. "This took time to arrange." His tone conveyed equal parts admiration and vexation. "How did you know?"

Björn winked. "Because I know Alshiba."

Aldaeon cast an aggrieved look down at him. "I'm keeping the bourbon."

"I would have it no other way." Björn touched his brow in farewell.

"Björn!"

Björn looked back up at him.

Aldaeon pressed a hand against the *celantia*. Spiraling patterns flared all around him, casting flickering blue light across his pale features. "You know you don't help your case with these illicit appearances."

Björn pointed an admonishing finger at him. "Never let our friendship come before your duty, Aldaeon. I'm counting on you."

Then he flashed a smile and rushed away into the dark.

THIRTY-TWO

"When a truth becomes a fact, it loses all its intellectual value."
–The Adept Cassius of Rogue

TO FELIX, THE Empress's personal apartments seemed a small palace. Following a dozen paces behind the dark form of the zanthyr, Felix moved from one gargantuan, palatial room into the next gargantuan, palatial room until all the gilt, velvet and marble began to blur together.

In many locations, he noticed silvery nodes winking at him, and each alluring summons sang a siren's call. These portals were shadowed by twisting, but *he* might've traveled them as easily as any other—and they knew this, the vengeful sprites. Felix eyed the nodes uncertainly as he passed. He was sure they'd somehow all been put there just to test his fortitude.

He thanked the Sanctos—especially his many-times great-grandfather Dominico—that he'd never bungled his way onto any of *those* nodes. He could just see himself stepping off the node and finding the Empress of Agasan in her dressing gown. The thought brought a cold and clammy chill to his flesh. He doubted the Empress would've been as receptive to his charms as her daughter had been.

Though the zanthyr strode many paces ahead, he yet dragged a wake of static through the air such that Felix, walking in his wake, felt like insects were biting him all over. Scratching uncomfortably at his rear end and silently cursing the zanthyr, Felix followed Phaedor beneath a marble-framed archway into a vast gallery that might've easily seated three hundred people with room to spare for dancing and an orchestra, probably an entire troupe of acrobats…

A procession of important-looking personages was heading towards them from the gallery's opposite end. Felix could tell they thought themselves *very* important from the severe upward tilt of their noses. He also noted, with some delight, that all of them were on a collision course with the zanthyr.

When it became clear to them that the zanthyr did not intend to move out of their path, the *Sobra* Scholars in the lead veered out of Phaedor's way with sidelong glares.

Next came a tall man wearing a really expensive coat and the chain link badge of the Commander of the Imperial Guard. He merely adjusted his course to avoid Phaedor and maintained his quiet discussion with his two aides. Felix in turn gave the Commander a wide berth. He never much liked getting too close to any of the Empress's Imperial Guard, and definitely wanted to avoid the notice of their infamously merciless commander.

Last came a woman wearing black breeches and a belted coat, boots to her thighs—all of which framed her curves in all the right ways. She wore her long, honey-brown hair in a complicated braid, and a Sormitáge ring glimmered on each of her fingers.

Felix's eyes widened.

The only woman in the Empire with a full row was Francesca da Mosta, Commander of the Imperial Adeptus. Francesca cast her lovely hazel eyes across Felix as she passed, eliciting all kinds of inappropriate thoughts in the lad, which he had to severely censor from the two truthreaders following in her wake.

Felix turned his head over his shoulder to watch the commander for as long as he could. It wasn't every day that a woman with a body like that wore clothing that showed off her curves like that. Francesca da Mosta was the stuff of fantasy to just about every unmarried male in Faroqhar, and a few too many married ones to boot.

Felix was still looking over his shoulder at the commander's retreating form when he suddenly realized he was catching up with the zanthyr, whereupon he felt compelled to complain, "Well, that was bloody unpleasant. Thanks so much for not vouching for me. I think the bastards forgot to inspect up my arse—"

That's when he looked forward again and saw the assemblage of important personages staring at him—the *truly* important kind, that is, the kind that just *were* important without feeling the need to convince you of it.

Felix's mouth stopped at the same time as his feet, so that he sort of stood there wavering at anchor. His mismatched eyes darted around, recognizing Vincenzé and Giancarlo, who in turn were giving him their usual goon stares.

Just beyond an open archway stood the High Lord, who Felix had only ever seen from afar; and beside the High Lord stood a dark-haired woman of tall stature and graceful bearing wearing a dress worth a small kingdom, with Nadia's diamondine eyes and dark hair, and whose depthless gaze had Felix instantly quaking in his boots.

"Well, Felix di Sarcova," the Empress said in her famously deep and throaty voice, so like and yet unlike the countless imitations Felix had heard of it, "…let's talk about nodes, shall we?"

Felix cast a desperate look at the zanthyr—*he'd* gotten him into this, hadn't he?—but the infuriating creature merely summoned a dagger out of nowhere and cast it flipping into the air.

Whereupon Felix remembered his protocol before the Empress. He dropped to his hands and knees and then pressed himself flat onto the cold stone floor. The chant Nadia had taught him came to his tongue, and he began speaking the words—probably butchering them; who in the provinces actually spoke *Old Alaeic?*—taking care to properly enunciate each of the accented vowels as Nadia had instructed. "*Cuithné no du'or, 'im aenné thuithné cor, du'dé*annae *du'dor…*"

When the Empress didn't offer the expected reply, Felix braved a glance up at her. She was standing with a finger poised beneath her bottom lip and gazing down at him with a faint arch to her brow.

He hurriedly pushed his nose back into the marble and chanted the next verse, "*Amananaé, amananaé, halem-halem amanana*é—"

"What are you doing, child?"

Felix paused his chanting and stared for a second longer at the marble blurring before his vision. Then he lifted his head to the Empress again. "Am…I not supposed to…Your Majesty?"

"The Empress may be addressed as Aurelia," the High Lord advised.

"A-Aurelia," Felix amended. Feeling jumpy and unnerved, he sat tentatively back on his heels and darted a look around at the others. The Caladrians were glaring at him as though they thought him engaged in some ill-conceived joke, while the High Lord looked baffled and the Empress rather amused. The zanthyr just flipped his dagger.

Felix realized the Empress was waiting for an answer. "The, uh… princess said if ever I met you…Aurelia, I was to prostrate myself and say these verses."

"And did my daughter tell you what these verses meant, child?"

"No, Aurelia."

"A children's rhyme…about donkeys." The Empress turned and began walking towards a hearth and two velvet armchairs set near it. The train of her gown whispered across the marble in her wake. "I fear my daughter was having a bit of fun with you, Felix."

Felix felt his face flush and dropped his gaze. "Come to think of it..." he clenched his jaw to hold back his embarrassment, "it *was* after I made a comment about her teeth."

The Empress seated herself in the high-backed chair, which was as grand as any throne, and spread her silk skirts around herself. She settled that disturbing gaze on Felix then—he felt her attention spear him all the way across the room—and motioned him to approach.

Felix sort of shuffled across the marble tiles to stand before the Empress. He felt pea-sized and was worried his voice would sound the same. All he could think about were the zanthyr's words of caution counterpointed with Vincenzé's many threats, which took on an uncomfortable new probability.

She reclined in her chair and rested her hands casually on the arms, but there was nothing casual in the way she was looking at him. "Vincenzé says you'll have nothing to offer me but half-truths; that your every attempt will be to shirk responsibility and divert my attention elsewhere. He believes the best thing I can do is lock you away for using an unregistered variant trait to travel twisted nodes and kidnapping the Princess Heir."

Kidnapping the Princess Heir?

Felix gulped. These truths were accusations for which he had no defense. For the first time, he realized that without Nadia to speak for him, his acts couldn't be even remotely justified. He stood rooted to the floor with a dry-throated panic welling, cinching off his breath so that it came in embarrassing little gulps.

"Marius found evidence of your pattern upon the second strand currents during the Quai game and believes you may have been involved somehow in assisting this unforgivable attack."

Felix darted a frantic look at the High Lord.

"This would be treason of the highest order, Felix di Sarcova, incurring a sentence of execution after a lengthy course of torture."

Felix's swallow felt painful in his chest.

"Yet Phaedor assures me that you will prove yourself valuable," the Empress's merciless gaze pinned Felix into immobility, while her tone felt a searing blade of derision, "as unlikely as that sounds to all of us here. Perhaps you might begin by explaining what has become of my daughter."

Felix couldn't help himself. He heard his tongue whisper, "What *has* become of her?"

"That is precisely what you are going to tell us if you hope to have any chance of living free beyond this night." She lifted a finger to point at him. "You may begin at the beginning."

Her mental nudge prodded Felix's tongue into quick action, and before he knew himself, the words were tumbling across his lips, grateful to be free at last. "My roommate Malin was kidnapped, and no one was doing anything about it—leastwise not the *right* things…"

The story unfolded in its fullness: how Felix had started using the nodes to investigate the names on Malin's fateful list, how he'd inadvertently found himself in Nadia's chambers, and their subsequent pact to find Malin together.

While Felix was speaking, the High Lord came and seated himself in an armchair near the Empress, while his Caladrians took up positions behind him. Felix had no idea where the zanthyr had gotten to. The one time he braved a look behind him, the creature was nowhere to be found.

"Not for thievery, then," the High Lord muttered when Felix was speaking of the several times he'd been caught in the private chambers of Sormitáge faculty while engaged in a search for Malin's abductor.

Felix dared glance to the High Lord. With his shoulder-length dark hair, just barely grey at the temples, his fine crimson coat, and the effortless elegance of his bearing, the High Lord exemplified the ideal Agasi nobleman. Felix felt an utter pauper by comparison. "No, Your Grace." He dropped his gaze. "Though…I suppose…no less illegal."

"We will come to that in a moment." The Empress looked him over with a hardness in her gaze that made him tremble deep inside. Finally, she said, "Giancarlo believes you were courting the Princess Heir. *Were* you courting my daughter, Felix?"

Felix shook his head emphatically *no,* because his breath had momentarily fled him. "I-I think Tanis was courting her, though. I mean… she said he was." After his embarrassing prostration before the Empress, Felix no longer entirely trusted everything Nadia had said to him.

"*Nadia* said this?" The Empress arched a brow and looked to the High Lord. "Tanis…Phaedor's ward?"

The High Lord was frowning severely at Felix. By way of answering the Empress, he arched a raven brow. "A truthreader of immense talent."

Felix snorted without thinking. "*There's* an understatement."

The Empress returned her gaze sharply to him. "Explain this comment."

Felix dropped his eyes with a grimace. Shadow take his wagging tongue! "Forgive me, Aurelia," he whispered. He just knew at any moment the Empress was going to summon her Praetorians to take him in hand, and the second time they laid hands on his person wouldn't be nearly as pleasant as the first.

Why, oh why had the zanthyr said those things to him? What had he meant that he would miss his opportunity? Opportunity for what? To deliver himself to the headsman's block?

"Answer the Empress's question, Felix di Sarcova." The High Lord sounded deeply displeased. "What did you mean by this remark?"

Felix braved a look at him. "You mean...but don't *you* know?" He shifted his gaze between the two adults regarding him so remotely, realized yet again just who he was standing in front of—only the two most powerful people in the damned Empire!—and had to remind himself to breathe again.

"Tanis followed me across two twisted nodes, Your Grace. *By himself*, Your Grace. And at the Quai game, I thought...well, he ran so fast he was a blur. I know for sure that when we were in N'abranaacht's apartments, Tanis timewove to allow us to escape, and then *he* pulled *me* across the node."

The Empress turned an unreadable look to the High Lord. "These are peculiar truths."

"Aurelia, please." Vincenzé leveled a critical stare at Felix. "The boy but deflects our attention elsewhere. In our interviews, he repeatedly claimed the Literato N'abranaacht was behind the attack."

Felix glared at him. "Because he is!"

Vincenzé retorted caustically, "The Literato N'abranaacht was seen by a stadium of thousands battling *against* one of the demon creatures at the scene. Explain that, you lying little bastard!"

The High Lord raised a hand. "Be at peace, Vincenzé."

The wielder's fierce expression at once sobered into apology. He ducked a bow. "Your pardon, Aurelia...Your Grace."

The Empress remarked to the High Lord, "I do not think the boy knows the Literato is dead."

Felix felt all the blood draining from his brain in a long cry of *whaaaaat?*

Panic's hand closed around his throat. He looked for the zanthyr again, but he only saw shadows. The damnable creature had lured him from the safety of a rabbit's den and promptly abandoned him to the wolves.

"Ask him how the Danes used a twisted node, if not without his help," Giancarlo murmured threateningly.

Vincenzé speared Felix with a fuming stare. "Ask him where the Adepts were taken."

"Ask him where the demons came from," Giancarlo said.

"Ask him what treasure the Danes offered in exchange for his traitorous soul." Vincenzé's gaze was hot with accusation. "Ask him what he expected to gain."

The High Lord shifted in his chair. "What say you to these claims, Felix di Sarcova? So far you've offered us little of value." His manner remained remote and dispassionate. Felix felt even less sure of himself beneath the High Lord's gaze than the Empress's. "You have already admitted to taking the Princess Heir from the protection of the palace. What leap then to imagine you delivered her directly to the enemy? Your pattern, alone of any man's, lay upon *elae*'s second strand after the attack. With my own eyes, I saw it riding those ill tides; with my own heart, I believe you to be possessed of unsavory intent."

Upon hearing these words, a hollow opened in Felix's chest, through which all of his breath instantly drained. His hands and face began tingling, and his vision went dark around the edges.

"Speak now if you have something of import to confess, child," the Empress said, "some compelling reason I should not deliver you at once to the Imperial Executioner."

Felix sucked in a shuddering breath and stared hard at the toes of his boots. What could he do to convince them of his innocence when the truth clearly meant nothing to them? What could he do to make them *listen*, to make them *see*...?

'*Select wisely when to play your truths or you will miss your opportunity.*'

Was this the moment the zanthyr had been meaning? Bloody Sanctos on a stake—of course, the creature had conveniently vanished while Felix was being raked over the coals.

"Do you see?" Vincenzé's tone dripped with sarcasm. "The boy knows no—"

Felix made fists at his sides and turned the wielder a hot stare. "If you will permit me to reach inside my satchel here, Aurelia," he looked back to the Empress, "I have something that may be of interest."

Giancarlo snorted. "There's nothing in that bag but pages of crumpled scribbling. I inspected it myself."

Felix kept his gaze on the Empress and his tongue in close check.

The Empress nodded. "Proceed, Felix."

Praying he wasn't making another mistake—like agreeing to meet Malin after hours in the Archives, or making a pact with the Princess Heir, or trusting a bloody zanthyr—Felix opened his satchel and reached—not merely inside the hemp bag, but all the way across a leis into his Nodefinder's coach.

Of course Giancarlo hadn't found anything in the bag. He'd have to be a Nodefinder to even notice the leis, much less be able to activate the pattern that opened the secret door. Thus did Felix retrieve the book of the *Qhorith'quitara* that Malin had taken from the Archives. Recalling too well the feeling of magic the thing possessed, he drew it carefully from his bag.

A riotous alarm sounded. It shrieked in Felix's ears like an entire fleet of banshees, only a thousand times louder.

The High Lord gave a startled oath. The Caladrians swore. Felix shrugged his shoulders towards his ears and shoved both hands with the hated book towards the Empress.

"Giancarlo…take it from him." The High Lord's voice could barely be heard over the shrieking banshee alarm. "Vincenzé, go silence the alarm."

Giancarlo snatched the book from Felix's grasp while Vincenzé ran from the room.

Felix pushed his hands to his ears and stared at his boots until the shrieking ceased. Whereupon, the Empress remarked into the aching silence of his tortured ears, "It seems you did not inspect the satchel closely enough, Giancarlo."

"Yes, Aurelia." The stocky truthreader glowered accusingly at Felix.

"I surmise there is some purpose in your returning this sacred book to us." The searing reprimand in the Empress's tone razed Felix to a nub. "That is, beyond the admission of yet another crime against the Empire?"

Felix pushed his hands behind his back because they were trembling. "There're some papers just inside the cover," he looked pleadingly to the High Lord, who motioned to Giancarlo to hand over the book.

"Tanis is the one who worked it all out," Felix explained while the High Lord was carefully opening the cover. "Tanis knew the names, you see. He called them Malorin'athgul."

The Empress drew in her breath sharply. The High Lord's gaze lifted at once.

Felix did his best not to flinch. "Malin was reading the book and came upon the names first. He…he recognized the anagram of one of them. Look there, you'll see it, Your Grace. At the top of one of those pages of Malin's ciphers…Isahl N'abranaácht. It's Shailabanáchtran, clear as day."

"Your Grace, I must protest—" Giancarlo began.

The High Lord raised a hand sharply for silence. "Shailabanáchtran? Where did you hear this name? Did the zanthyr speak it to you?"

"No, Your Grace—"

"You stand before the Empress. Dare not lie to me."

"Never, Your Grace!" Felix turned an earnest and rather desperate look between them and then added to the High Lord, "Tanis recognized the names the minute he looked at Malin's ciphers. He worked it all out in minutes. You see, Tanis *knew* N'abranaacht—Shail, I mean. Tanis knew what he was capable of."

"Tanis," said the Empress again meaningfully, "the *zanthyr's* ward."

The High Lord frowned deeply at her.

Into this silence, Vincenzé returned and took up his position behind the High Lord, glaring the while at Felix.

When no one else said anything, Felix looked back to the Empress and offered haltingly, "Tanis traveled with one of the Malorin'athgul for many weeks—the one called Pelasommáyurek. You'll see his name there on the fourth page, Your Grace. Tanis had met Shail while traveling with Pelas. And N'abranaacht..." Felix wetted his lips, still feeling a measure of that dry-mouthed panic, "I vow, *he* recognized Tanis even before Tanis knew him."

The Empress was regarding Felix with a furrow narrowing her brow. "How did you come to possess a book of the *Qhorith'quitara*?"

Felix forced a swallow. He couldn't believe what he was actually about to confess. "I...was in the Archives the night Malin vanished." He turned an apologetic look to the High Lord, and Giancarlo behind him, even though neither of them had personally questioned him on *that* subject, "so I knew Malin hadn't run away, like so many others were claiming. Malin had just shown me the book, which he'd taken from the vault when the Imperial Historian wasn't looking, and he was about to explain everything that had been bothering him, when we heard this noise..."

Felix cast a glance around. None of the eyes watching him appeared to be looking any more favorably upon him than they had been before, and two sets of them belonged to *truthreaders*. It was terribly disheartening to discover that the truth actually meant so little.

Felix wiped his nose on his sleeve. "Malin shoved the book at me and went to investigate the noise, but I...I got a really bad feeling, so I followed him. I saw him turn down an aisle, but when I reached it, he was gone."

Felix looked to each person in the room, promising truth with his gaze, beseeching their trust. In the last, not knowing if even one of them believed him, he turned dejectedly back to the Empress and slowly closed the flap on his satchel. He wondered if they'd let him wear it to the headsman's block—but no...the Empress had threatened long, involved torture...

"Why did you not return the book to the Imperial Historian, Felix?"

The lad looked up at the Empress. "Since no one was asking me for it, Aurelia, I...I was holding onto it to try to figure out Malin's notes. The book was the only clue I had to whoever took him away."

"Is that the only reason, child?"

Felix shrugged dispiritedly. "That...and no one would've believed I wasn't the one who stole it."

Giancarlo lifted frowning colorless eyes to Felix. "And the princess? How is she involved?"

"I don't know how N'abranaacht got to her. We were heading to the Quai game to meet her when the Literato did something to Tanis—nearly knocked him unconscious, I vow. I don't know how; the man was a whole stadium away at the time—and when Tanis came back to himself, he said the Literato had Nadia and took off after him. That's when all hells erupted."

The Empress turned wordlessly to the High Lord.

"Tanis...enigma of Adonnai," the latter murmured. He stared fiercely down at the book now lying closed on his lap.

Felix scratched at his head, dislodging a tuft of calico hair, and gazed down at his boots, seeing neither scuffed leather nor marble floor but a stadium in chaos and Tanis running atop the bleachers towards the field, faster than any natural person should've been able to move.

"Your thoughts speak loudly with veracity, Felix di Sarcova."

Felix lifted his eyes to find the Empress regarding him steadily.

The High Lord grunted. "But you've said nothing that will help us find the Princess Heir or the other Adepts who were taken, which you claim you had no part in."

"Because I don't know anything about any of that!" Felix felt a sense of desperation returning. "I was buried under a dozen fat-arsed blokes—begging your pardon, Aurelia—while Tanis sped off to save the princess."

The High Lord's gaze tightened upon him. "And do you know what became of Tanis?"

"No, Your Grace," Felix gave a shuddering exhale, "but if the princess has any chance at all, I know it rests on him."

"The boy is right," came a deep voice from the corner of the room.

Every head turned as one.

Felix saw the zanthyr standing in the shadows, and a wave of relief overcame him.

The High Lord turned rigidly to confront Phaedor. "Pray, how is the boy right?"

The zanthyr emerged into the light, flipping his dagger. He gave the High Lord a rather dismissive once-over and settled his emerald gaze instead on the Empress. "Tanis has drawn Nadia onto his path, and no force in the Empire can retrieve her from it until their threads in the tapestry separate again."

Staring at him with a concerned frown, the Empress murmured, "You would have us rest the hopes of the Empire on a boy of sixteen years?"

"A nameless boy," the High Lord remarked with a deeply furrowed brow, "offering no parentage to speak of."

The zanthyr flipped his dagger. "Tanis is the son of Isabel van Gelderan and Arion Tavestra." He turned the High Lord an arch look, and there was aught of dark victory in it. "The sole heir to Adonnai."

Felix's mouth fell open. *Thirteen bloody hells, Tanis!*

He heard the Empress catch her breath.

The High Lord went white as a sheet.

The zanthyr looked back to the Empress. "Like his mother, High Mage of the Citadel, Tanis is an Adept of four strands. Two immortals have bound themselves to his path. More will follow." He flipped his dagger again. "He is no *mere* boy of sixteen."

Whereupon a swarming sensation overcame Felix. His breath ran off to engage in some other less stressful occupation, the ceiling closed in on him, and darkness clutched him greedily into its depths.

THIRTY-THREE

"The wise man looks both ways before crossing a one way street."
—A favorite Kandori proverb

M*Y...WHAT HAVE YOU gotten yourself into?*
Pelas wasn't sure if he'd heard the words or merely imagined them. He swam up from unconsciousness through stinging pain, whereupon he perceived a cosmic flutter. Layers of thought whipped past as a sheaf of ruffling paper. The plane of existence altered.

Suddenly he perceived the plane shifting as another universe collided with Shail's. The two cubes of framed space drifted inside one another until the starpoints themselves collided...*coincided*—

The intruding universe instantly overcame Shail's—starpoints duplicated, claimed, *owned*, now superimposed—in the same way that Shail had overtaken and claimed Pelas's starpoints.

The revenants scattered wildly, suddenly as voracious to escape as they had been to feed but a moment ago. Pelas lay exposed upon the dull ice. He hadn't enough energy even to move his head, but he saw what the golems were fleeing.

Within the void, darkness was coalescing.

Pinprick stars, as sparks from a fire, swirled into the shape of a man, and a gilded creation birthed through the veil of unbeing.

First emerged a muscled torso of crackled gold, as if an artist had painstakingly painted his form in metallic foil. Then followed an expanse of velvet wings dripping darkness—so dark that Pelas more had an impression of their immensity than actually saw them. He felt a kiss of *deyjiin* upon his brow, and then a hand, helping him to sit up. He blinked several times to make the focus of his eyes align with the perceptions of his mind…

And saw a pale gold face peering into his, nearly human in its fashioning. A round red crystal glowed between the Warlock's raven brows. His void-black eyes were smiling. "Pelasommáyurek."

"Rafael." Pelas inhaled a deep breath of *deyjiin*, which was shedding off Rafael like smoke. "It's been a long time."

The Warlock's black eyes glinted like fire trapped in obsidian. "Has it?" Flinty sparks flared through his raven hair, which danced in tousled waves.

The revenant hyenas were hovering at the edge of Rafael's framed space, hungering as they milled about, waiting for the lion to depart.

"What a fascinating predicament." Rafael turned a curious look back to Pelas. "Even with your penchant for new experiences, I can't fathom what you hoped to gain from offering yourself to a clutch of revenants."

Pelas managed a dubious exhale. "I didn't do this to myself, Rafael."

The Warlock tilted his head slightly. "Who then?"

"Shailabanáchtran."

Boldly, the revenants started inching closer. Rafael's black gaze snapped towards them. His wings flapped once, quick and violent, and raw energy flared. The creatures scattered like beetles. Those who didn't flee fast enough simply evaporated—an effacement Pelas might've managed if he could've duplicated the starpoints of that world the way Rafael had done.

The Warlock looked back to Pelas with the faintest of furrows notching his brow. "You and your brothers find curious ways of interacting with one another." His dark eyes regarded Pelas critically then, hinting of concern. "How badly have they drained you?"

Pelas shook his head. He truly didn't know.

Rafael straightened to his full height and surveyed the space he'd claimed from Shail. "How came you to be trapped on this pitiful plane, Pelasommáyurek?"

Pelas moved gingerly to hands and knees. Then, more slowly, he found his feet and straightened. "Shail overtook me."

The Warlock turned to him with a look of dazed wonder. "I'm not sure which is worse—letting your brother coincide your starpoints, or admitting to it."

"The first, believe me."

Rafael gave a low chuckle. "It's considered the greatest of all blunders for a *reason*, Pelasommáyurek. Did you learn nothing from me during our time together?"

Pelas offered a rueful smile. "Enough to get me in trouble, it would appear."

"You would've been in difficulty indeed if I hadn't been receptive to your calling."

Pelas smiled meaningfully. "Whenever have you not been receptive to my calling?"

A dark sparkle glinted in the Warlock's eyes. "A fair question. Let's leave this plane, shall we?" His wings trembled, and stars shed from their tips. Pelas got the sudden sensation of flying, but only because of the trailing waterfall of stars that spiraled now in a wake behind them.

Starpoints shifted. Space shifted. Shail's plane and its hungering golems vanished.

Pelas stood in a vast chamber of black glass. Stars slowly turned beyond a row of tall obsidian arches, themselves nearly invisible against the background of space. Pelas looked up and saw a nebula staining the glass ceiling a violet-red. "This is new."

Rafael walked across the obsidian floor and up the adjoining wall to a table. He looked over to Pelas as he poured a mercuric liquid into a goblet—an odd thing to witness, watching the stuff flowing sideways—and offered an alluring smile. "One can only do so much in a gravity-based world."

Suddenly Pelas was standing beside him at the table, facing an identical wall of arches. He turned a look back over his shoulder, trying to reorient himself.

Rafael smiled at his expression. "For an immortal child of Chaos, you're oddly fussy about spatial orientation." He extended the goblet to Pelas.

Who gratefully accepted, remarking, "Chaos is no more like Shadow than Shadow is like the Realms of Light, Rafael."

Rafael's dark eyes smoldered. "Shadow is anything I want it to be."

Pelas saluted that truth with his goblet and then downed its contents. The glowing fluid had no taste, but it felt cool in his throat and much restored his vitality. Rafael had unique ways of condensing *deyjiin*.

Quickly feeling more himself again, Pelas cast his awareness outward to find and mimic Rafael's starpoints—not to claim the space but to share it, so he might work *deyjiin* equally. He noted the indistinct glimmer of furniture on the distant ceiling—wall? floor?—and murmured, "It seems like a world of your creation should follow your dictates, gravity or no gravity, as *you* choose."

Rafael sipped from his own goblet and contemplated the tumultuous nebula in front of them. "Theoretically, but once gravity enters the equation, energy tends to want to follow its own laws." Sparks flared through the black flames of his hair, embers glowing and extinguishing. "Fighting against these natural affinities becomes tedious."

Pelas looked to him with unbridled appreciation. He and Rafael had long shared a kindred love for the ingenious and unique; under other circumstances, he might've dallied with him indefinitely. "My gratitude knows no bounds, my friend."

The Warlock received this with an amused look. "Likewise your naivety in regards to your brother, it would appear."

Pelas arched a resigned brow. "You needn't rub it in, Rafael."

The Warlock chuckled. "I haven't begun rubbing it in, Pelas." He looked him up and down with those darkly sparkling eyes, ever hinting of potent and dangerous possibility. "But I will, very soon."

Pelas shook his head. "I can't stay. My brother has something of mine I must retrieve." And he knew exactly where to go to find Nadia. Shail had his own demons of predictability to wrestle with.

Rafael arched a skeptical brow. "You can't even keep your starpoints stable. You think somehow you'll successfully command a portal?"

Pelas handed him back his goblet with a smile. "I'll even let you watch."

THIRTY-FOUR

"If you have to choose between two evils, I say pick the one you've never tried before."

—The Nodefinder Felix di Sarcova

TANIS DREAMED.

He stood on the terrace of Pelas's mansion as the sun was sinking low in the west, its nightly abdication giving birth to that magical time when the very air seemed golden and soft. Tanis felt a little calmer just finding himself in Hallovia, in seeing something he knew to be real. And then—

"Tanis?"

The lad spun. Pelas stood on the far end of the terrace.

Even more powerful than seeing his bond-brother was the feeling of their binding in full force. A wave of relief washed over the lad and he rushed to embrace him. Only then did Tanis realize how desperately he'd been missing him. "What happened to you? Are you safe? Is Nadia safe?"

"I'm fine," Pelas said as he held Tanis, though he spoke the words with an odd sort of hesitation. "I will protect Nadia. Tell me what's become of you. Sinárr hasn't—"

"No." Tanis dropped his arms and exhaled an explosive breath. "He hasn't bound me." Then he frowned up at him. "How can I have reached you?"

"I don't know." Pelas cast an assessing gaze around the terrace, as if searching for proof of some artifice in its crafting. "Sinárr must be facilitating our conversation. I can't reach you in his universe without him willing it—believe me, I've tried."

Tanis felt perplexed all over again. "But why would he help us communicate? He *knows* I only want...ugh." He pushed palms to his forehead and then scrubbed his hands back through his hair. "By all the gods in the known, he's so bloody confusing."

Pelas's gaze narrowed. He drew the lad towards a low stone wall and sat him down. "Tell me everything."

Tanis tumbled through a rushed explanation of what had happened since they'd been torn apart. While he listened, Pelas drew one knee to his chest, hooked his arms around it and frowned deeply.

"Then Sinárr said something I really don't understand." Tanis pushed his hands against his knees and looked up under his brows. "He said Alorin was formed of *deyjiin* and *elae* in perfect balance, but I thought *deyjiin* was a consumptive power and antithetical to our realm."

"No...I think he might be right."

"How is that possible?"

The powerful intensity of Pelas's gaze made it seem as if he was deconstructing the cosmos just so he might answer Tanis's question. After a moment of this, he shifted his eyes back to the lad. "Yes, it makes sense... my brothers and I wouldn't be able to work a power that didn't already exist in the realm—we certainly can't draw it from Chaos. That's an essential reason that your mother and uncle have done what they've done—because they know we can't access the full source of our power while within Alorin's aether. All we have access to is what is already extant in the realm."

While Tanis was pondering this, Pelas rubbed his jaw and continued thoughtfully, "Yes...I see better what Sinárr means. *Deyjiin* is consumptive when wielded in *Alorin* because the two forces coexist in a delicate balance; *elae*'s positive to *deyjiin*'s negative."

Tanis frowned. "It seems like you just contradicted yourself."

Pelas looked back to him. "No, it perfectly follows." He flashed the lad a smile. "If the two forces are in a delicate balance, then wielding *deyjiin* over and above Alorin's natural equilibrium—that is, forcing *deyjiin* out of its natural currents—unbalances the negative and positive forces. *Deyjiin* becomes destructive."

Suddenly he leaned towards Tanis. "Do you see? It's actually no different from what occurs when a wielder works *elae*. Forcing either of the powers out of their natural course alters the balance of the two energies—*and affects the Cosmic Balance to a greater or lesser degree*—that's it." He snapped his fingers, and the light of understanding danced in his eyes.

Tanis could sense the wheels of his intelligent mind turning rapidly, making connections that lay far beyond his own understanding.

"Tanis..." Pelas cast him a keen look, "it's entirely possible that the wielding of *elae* affects the Cosmic Balance only when certain workings destabilize the negative-positive ratio of *elae* and *deyjiin*." His lips curled in a sly smile, and he leaned back on both hands, his gaze sparkling as if with a delicious secret. "I wonder how long the *Sobra* Scholars have been laboring over that conundrum, eh, little spy? I know one or two who would pay dearly to hear the explanation we've just deduced."

Tanis didn't care so much in that moment that they'd just solved a debate that had been raging for millennia; the solution didn't show him the way out of Shadow. The lad sighed dejectedly. "Then Sinárr was telling the truth." Somehow this came as disheartening news. "You need both powers to build a realm, just as he said."

Pelas arched a brow. "Sinárr wants to build a realm?"

Tanis glowered. "Yes. With *me*."

"Well, who wouldn't?"

Tanis frowned in response to his grin. "You know, you're really not helping."

Pelas placed a hand on the lad's knee and squeezed gently. "How can I help you?"

Tanis slumped his shoulders, feeling disheartened again. "The trouble is, I don't think you can. I think I have to figure my own way free of here."

And that was the crux of the matter, Raine's truth.

"Tanis…" Pelas leaned to capture his eye, "if it can be solved, you will find a way."

Tanis exhaled a slow breath and lifted a troubled gaze to him. "And if I can't?"

Pelas looked him in the eye, so that there could be no mistaking his intent. "Then I will tear Shadow apart, world by world, to find you."

The windows of his bedchamber were dark when Tanis woke from his dream, which at least answered the question of whether Sinárr's world saw regular days and nights. Tanis lay in bed for a time feeling stormy. His thoughts whirled like snowflakes, battering him with icy frustration.

Tanis interlaced his fingers behind his head and lay for a time with his elbows pointing towards the ceiling, wishing he could frame his thoughts between those two bony points as easily as Sinárr framed space.

The problem was, he didn't know where to start piecing this picture together. He couldn't connect what he knew with what he didn't understand; he couldn't put the information into any sort of framework that made sense; and he couldn't differentiate between what information was important and what wasn't, so it all merged into one huge snowstorm of confusion.

Everything Sinárr and Mérethe had told him kept running through his head, each conversation carrying equal weight with the others, so that nothing really stood out as *the* important piece to begin with in assembling the puzzle.

'Shadow has no form except what the Warlocks give to it.'

'I knew the moment I saw you that our opposing natures would call to each other.'

'Warlocks cannot tear the binding fabric between the realms…'

'He will make you forget what is real.'

'Most Adepts cannot survive in Shadow for more than a day or two…'

'I like your world.'

'You must agree to be bound.'

'With Mérethe…I felt something similar, though far less strongly so.'

'We create space by first creating a point to view.'

That's exactly what Tanis needed—a little space in which to frame some perspective.

He threw his hands to his sides and stared at the ceiling, which was dimly illuminated by the wavering light of a candle. He felt like that tiny flame, a single source of *elae* sputtering amid the vast void of Shadow.

No…that can't *be right.*

Now more than ever, Tanis felt that he had to have been correct in his initial assertion: if *deyjiin* roamed Alorin, then *elae had* to roam Shadow.

But Mérethe said most Adepts couldn't survive there, even bound to a Warlock, which meant that whatever form *elae* took in Shadow, it was not enough to sustain most Adepts. Yet it was sustaining *him*.

Or was it?

Tanis draped an arm over his head and gazed up at the ceiling again. Why were he and Mérethe the exceptions? Or rather, what similarity put *them* together in one category and other Adepts in another?

In a moment he had it, or thought he might.

'No strand is so wildly variant as the third…' His mother had told him this. But could it really be that simple?

Maybe simple is what he'd been missing. Maybe in expecting the answer to be complex, he'd missed the underlying, fundamental truth.

He recalled his father writing about the Ninth Esoteric—*Pure concept always overwhelms linear translation.* Arion wrote that the Esoteric had many interpretations, but its most basic meaning was that for anything to be fully grasped, it must be reduced to its *simplest* form.

Complexity meant impurity in logic as well as in Patterning, at least according to Arion. In his investigations of magical phenomena, Arion would strip down all the data to its most basic facts, while at the same time disregarding *all* assumptions, no matter how 'agreed-upon' those assumptions were. He believed this was a vital step in any study of unexplained phenomena.

The most basic truths then, once found, would prove workable in both deductive and inductive reasoning—they would explain existing phenomena as well as *predict* phenomena. This was one of many reasons that Arion believed a student should never be taught how to wield a pattern; instead, he should be given the pattern and allowed to extrapolate its uses on his own.

So, if Tanis used the one simplicity he'd landed upon…well, it certainly opened up a whole new realm of possibility. It might even predict phenomena, as his father had claimed.

But to be able to work with his idea, he needed more information.

Tanis threw off his covers and started hunting around for his clothes, determined to speak to Sinárr immediately—

Whereupon he found himself standing on a tower roof in the middle of a winter storm. Braziers burning atop the crenels illuminated the swirling snow.

Sinárr stood on the far side of the flat roof, staring off into the night. Snow clung to his dark cloak and hood and had accumulated in drifts at his feet. Tanis wondered why the Warlock hadn't made the storm avoid the tower the way the rain had miraculously avoided their ship.

Tanis hugged his arms and trudged through the drifts towards Sinárr. The icy wind cut through his linen garments as if he wore nothing, and he was chilled to the bone before he'd even made it halfway across the tower. He wondered why Sinárr had brought him there without a coat. Perhaps it was a sort of punishment for their last conversation, when Tanis had spoken so brusquely to him.

He was shivering by the time he reached the Warlock. Every exhale puffed frost into the night, only to be stolen away by the stinging wind. Tanis hugged his chest and stomped his feet in a futile effort to maintain some circulation.

"I think we should t-talk," the lad stammered. His face was already so cold it was hard to make his lips form words.

The Warlock turned his head sharply, as if Tanis had startled him, and took the lad's measure in a single sweep of his golden eyes. "Perhaps I'm uneducated in your traditions, Tanis…but this seems an odd choice of garments for a snowstorm."

Tanis clutched his arms tighter around his chest and stomped his feet some more. "You didn't give me a c-coat."

"You asked me not to pick your clothing for you."

"I asked you to let me *ch-choose*, not to make me f-freeze for w-want of it."

Sinárr looked him up and down with one raised eyebrow. Then he lifted his gaze to the storm and observed thoughtfully, "I expected you would make for yourself what you required."

Tanis started bouncing in place. He could feel neither his fingers nor his feet and wished Sinárr would quit punishing him and take them someplace else. "Why w-would you expect that?"

Sinárr looked back to him. "Because this is your storm."

Tanis stilled. "*My* storm? But I—one minute I w-was in my rooms, the n-next I was here!"

"You asked me to let you shape my world."

"When I *knew* I was d-doing it! N-not j-just *any* t-time—*oh* for Epiphany's s-sake!" Tanis gritted his chattering teeth and shouted the thought, *Just please take me somewhere warm!*

Daylight blinded him.

Tanis threw an icy arm across his eyes.

The heat from the blazing day felt a furnace against his chilled flesh, yet the warmth was a welcome balm. In the short time it took his eyes to adjust to the sere daylight, the snow in his hair had melted and was dripping into his eyes.

Tanis shook out his wet head and blinked into a glaringly bright afternoon. The sun was veritably baking the high plateau where he stood. Around and below, as far as he could see, spread the ochre-hued walls of an immense canyon.

He walked to a marble railing and peered over—easily a thousand feet down to the canyon floor. Then he turned behind him and saw the towers and spires of an immense palace rising out of the rock.

Looking around, Tanis saw Sinárr sitting at a round table in the shade of a gazebo, so he walked to join him. The temperature dropped at least ten degrees just moving from the sunlight into the shade.

Sitting in an elegant wingback armchair, the Warlock wore a royal blue silk shirt with the cuffs turned back, the fabric bright against his very black skin. He was resting an elbow on the arm of his chair and running a finger along his lower lip, observing Tanis with a quiet intensity in his golden gaze—though the lad felt more like Sinárr was *absorbing* him than observing him.

Tanis paused beside his own chair and eyed Sinárr uncertainly. He still suspected the man was subtly punishing him for becoming so angry during their last conversation.

"Would you like something to eat, Tanis?" Sinárr lifted his chin from his hand to indicate the empty table. "Or do you prefer to conjure it yourself?"

Tanis frowned at him. "You needn't be petulant."

Sinárr cracked a smile. "I was trying to be deferential."

Tanis stared unhappily at him. Every time he thought he had the Warlock's thoughts or motives pinned down, Sinárr moved in a different direction.

The lad plopped down in his chair, pressed his hands to his face and mashed his cheeks towards each other to encourage the frozen muscles to work properly again. Amid this ungainly manipulation, he mumbled, "I'm... *really* hungry."

Sinárr nodded accommodatingly. When Tanis lowered his hands, the table held a host of platters offering so many varied delights that Tanis's stomach growled just from smelling them.

While the lad was serving himself a turkey leg, Sinárr remarked, chin in hand again, "I mislike this lingering discord between us, Tanis. I would that we remedied it somehow."

Tanis paused just before taking a bite of the meat. "Then let me go, Sinárr."

"I cannot, Tanis."

"You *choose* not to."

"A moot distinction. The outcome is the same."

"What do you hope to accomplish?" Tanis lowered the meat back to his plate. "You think you'll somehow convince me to be your slave for all eternity?"

A slight furrow narrowed Sinárr's brow. "A concubine is not a slave."

Tanis arched an eyebrow in challenge. "A moot distinction. The outcome is the same." He returned to his food.

Sinárr's expression became slightly pinched. His lips made a firm line. "If a dog refuses to comply, do you simply give up with training the animal and set it loose in the wild? Is that not worse for the dog?"

Tanis reached to pour himself some wine. "Is that how you see Mérethe? As your pet?" It would certainly explain a few things. He took a drink of wine and asked more deliberately, "Is that how you see me?"

Sinárr dropped his hand into his lap. The furrow between his brow deepened. "You...confuse me, Tanis."

"Likewise, Sinárr."

The Warlock straightened in response to this. "Have I not been solicitous to your needs? Given you everything you asked? Have I not looked the other way when you sought to communicate with Pelasommáyurek, who I cannot but think of as a rival, yet with whom I willingly aided your communication when your sleeping mind sought his in the night?"

Tanis slowly lowered his goblet from his lips. "So you did help us." He shook his head, staring at him. "Why would you do that?"

"You seemed upset. I thought it would calm you to speak with someone you knew and trusted. When you reached for him in your dreaming sleep, I…facilitated the connection."

Tanis thought of the dream scene as it had played out on Pelas's terrace and felt suddenly violated. "You listened to our conversation and painted our words with illusion?"

"No, Tanis. You wove the context of the dream. I merely…" he waved an absent hand, "didn't stop you."

Tanis sat back in his chair. "*I* did that." His gaze tightened. "Like I made the storm? You let me do both? Why?" He took up his wine again and gave the Warlock a tight look over its rim. "More gallant acts of courtship?"

Frustration clouded Sinárr's expression. "I don't understand why you expect such ignobility from me."

"Yes, I wonder why?"

"I gather from your sarcastic tone that you take exception with my actions."

"Sinárr…" Tanis had a hard time keeping the derision out of his voice. "You attacked me in the temple, attacked us again in Shadow, you took me hostage, you're holding me against my will. You've made *eidola* for Shail." He flung out a hand at the man. "By Cephrael's Great Book, you fed off of Mérethe—"

"*Fed* off of Mérethe!" Sinárr sat abruptly forward in his chair. "Did she claim this vile untruth?" His tone had become very dangerous indeed.

Tanis reined back hard on his hauteur, for the look in Sinárr's eyes and the indignation in his tone made it clear to the lad that in *this* presumption, he was very much in the wrong.

The gazebo seemed to tip and teeter violently.

Tanis dropped his gaze and his peremptory tone and sort of scraped out a reply around the disconcertion suddenly choking him. "I…assumed. It was my mistake."

Sinárr sat back with an elbow on the chair arm and one long forefinger framing his temple. He studied Tanis in this fashion for a lengthy time. Finally, he let his hand fall to his lap. "I made no harvester of Mérethe." There was a hint of wounded injustice in his tone, as if Tanis had truly offended him with his accusation. "The very idea of it is inconceivable. That you could imagine such of me only proves how little you understand of Shadow, and of me."

Chagrin fluttered in Tanis's chest, making him reconsider everything he'd been thinking. Here he'd been imagining himself so adept at applying his father's teachings, when in reality he'd made so many assumptions that he couldn't now even list them all.

Tanis forced a swallow. "You're right. I understand very little—only what I've seen or overheard from Shail…or what you or Mérethe have told me." He lifted his eyes to meet Sinárr's. "But she *has* lost her contact with *elae*."

"Yes, I know."

Tanis searched the Warlock's gaze. "But if not from something you did, then why?"

Sinárr settled his chin on his hand again and rubbed one finger along his temple. "That, I don't know."

"Sinárr…" Tanis's tone pulled the Warlock's gaze back to his, "if she's of no use to you anymore, why don't you release her?"

Sinárr dropped his hand again and looked at him as if he'd suddenly sprouted horns. "*Release* her?"

"From being bound to you. Why don't you return Mérethe home, to Alorin?"

Sinárr looked utterly perplexed. "Mérethe *wants* this? You've spoken with her?"

Once again, Tanis saw that the siren Assumption had nearly lured him onto the rocks. He felt as if he'd been caught in a lie. As a truthreader, this was a uniquely and unsettling experience. "I…well, no."

Sinárr arched brows.

Tanis fell back in his chair and pushed palms to his eyes. *Why must you be so bloody confusing?*

Sinárr took up his wine. "It's your opposing nature that so attracts me to you, Tanis. But lest we somehow forget, we *are* from different universes in every possible sense. I suspect confusion at each other's ways is…inevitable."

Tanis wasn't certain that Sinárr had the right of it wholly, but he sensed an important truth somewhere in his statement.

He couldn't help comparing this experience to his early days with Pelas. When he looked at the two experiences objectively, they were oddly parallel. Pelas was an immortal from the plane of Chaos with his own unique philosophies on life, bound to his own purpose, which was antithetical to Tanis's survival. He'd taken Tanis hostage and held him against his will. Yet despite their disparate origins and contentious beginning, Tanis had understood Pelas intuitively, and they'd shared a rapport almost from the beginning.

Why was his experience with Sinárr so different?

Because Pelas was always a child of both worlds.

Perhaps this simplicity again pointed to the answer. Pelas held an innate understanding of *elae* as well as *deyjiin*—he just hadn't known it until Tanis proved it to him.

But Sinárr...he was as singly a child of Shadow as Tanis was of Light. They *were* each other's *inverteré*, their equal opposite. Tanis had to admit the truth in this, though it wasn't the only truth he saw suddenly.

Sinárr was staring into his goblet and tracing a finger along its rim. "Mérethe..." he exhaled a slow sigh. "She became my concubine willingly, and we enjoyed each other for a time, but she blames me for her loss of contact with *elae*, even though my binding should've prevented it." His expression twitched with regret. "Shadow is timeless, yet it's fair to say it's been decades since Mérethe has willingly spoken to me. My advances have been...poorly received. I try to leave her alone."

Hearing this explanation made Tanis feel like he was spinning. No longer teetering on the edge of error, he swirled down a drain of egregious miscalculation.

"But..." Tanis groped for any rationale that would justify his earlier train of thought. "Why not return her to Alorin then?" He made himself look at the Warlock, though it was painful to meet Sinárr's gaze after so badly misjudging him. "Why have you kept her here when she doesn't want to be with you?"

Sinárr regarded him quietly. "You wouldn't ask this if you understood what happens to those who've been bound to us and then abandoned. I would not leave Mérethe to wither so—nor any *eidola* of mine."

A sick feeling beset Tanis. He'd been terribly misguided by badly-reasoned conclusions and even—dare he admit it?—a sort of prejudice against the Warlock, due to accepting observations, even hearsay, without conducting his own evaluation.

This was one of the worst mistakes he could've made. His father would've bowed his head in shame.

It made no difference that all the events Tanis had witnessed seemed to have been pointing him towards one conclusion. He'd still jumped on the horse of assumption and given it its head without even noticing where the bloody animal was running. He suddenly felt like his own ignorance was suffocating him.

I need air—lots *of air.*

A cold wave crashed powerfully around his legs, knocking him sideways. He tumbled into the surf and was quickly swept deeper into the churning water. Finally finding his feet, he surged up out of the icy wash, choking up saltwater, drenched in seawater as much as the terrible weight of his presumption. He had an awful sense of having wronged Sinárr.

The Warlock stood higher on the rocky shore, just beyond the tide line, looking frustratingly immaculate in his blue shirt and blood-red cloak, the colors seeming especially brilliant against the cloudy day.

Tanis gave him a sooty look as he sloshed out of the water, chilled and dripping. "I think you did that deliberately."

Sinárr's lips twitched with a smile. "You seemed a little wilted."

Tanis stripped off his tunic and started wringing it out. He'd been wrong about Mérethe, but there were still some things he *knew* to be true. As he shook out his tunic, he cast the Warlock a sidelong eye. "So why Shail?"

Sinárr tilted his head slightly. "Perhaps I don't understand your question."

Tanis settled his gaze firmly on the Warlock. "Whatever else you think Shail is doing, he's set on harming my world—of this much I'm certain. Why are you helping him?"

"But I've already told you, Tanis. I cannot tear the fabric between the realms—only Malorin'athgul can do this."

Tanis didn't bother correcting him on the error of this statement—he'd seen Phaedor do it countless times—for its implication was more important in that moment. "So Shail gives you access to the Realms of Light. That's the only reason you're allied with him?"

"What greater reason do I need?"

Tanis thrust his arms into his wet tunic and grimaced. "Does binding me to you give you that access?" He shoved his head through the opening and pulled the clammy thing down over himself. It was hardly better than standing bare-chested in the chill wind.

Sinárr looked him over mildly, but there was nothing mild about his answer. "An Adept bound to a Warlock acts as a porthole into the world. A Warlock can follow the Adept's connection to *elae* to find his way inside. With you bound to me, I would have no need for Shail except as a means of restoring you to Alorin."

Tanis held his gaze, considering this. Shail acting alone against them was disheartening, but Shail with a Warlock pinned to his cloak spelled sure disaster. Though still unnerved by the prospect of binding, a new idea colored over Tanis's previously hazy outline to form a different shape. He thought he saw a path towards disrupting Shail's plans.

If he dared follow it.

He shoved wet hair out of his eyes. "I thought you and Shail were allies."

"Allies is too strong a word. We serve each other's purposes."

Upon this utterance, the world started tilting again, but this time Tanis sensed it inclining in a fortuitous direction. Tingling all over, he said a bit weakly, "You would forsake your contract with Shail—or whatever it is you're doing together—for me?"

The Warlock pinned Tanis with an ardent gaze. "Surely you've realized by now that I would do anything to bind with you, Tanis."

Uncomfortable beneath the needle of Sinárr's regard, the lad scrubbed a hand through his sand-filled hair and stared off down the shoreline. He saw Fortune drawing a new course for his potential path, but he felt like he was rushing headlong towards the first curve without any way of braking. *It's moving too fast, and there are still too many things I don't know!*

He lifted his eyes back to Sinárr. "There's this part I still don't understand."

The Warlock gave him a tolerant look.

Tanis was formulating his question when his hair was suddenly dry again and his clothes fresh and clean. He even had a cloak to protect against the wind. It seemed the Warlock had forgiven him his earlier criticism. The lad lifted an apologetic look to Sinárr. "Thank you."

A smile twitched on his lips. "My pleasure."

Tanis drew the heavy cloak closer around himself. "I just need to understand…why do you have this fascination with Alorin?" He flung a hand towards the crashing waves. "Why do you imitate another world when you could make it look like *anything* you wanted?"

Sinárr clasped hands behind his back and shifted his gaze out over the ocean of his creation. His brow constricted slightly. "As to the latter…" he cast him a smile hinting of confusion, "I did this for *you*, Tanis, to surround you with something familiar." He looked the lad over with a sort of injured majesty—or perhaps Tanis was just projecting the injury upon him, having realized now that he'd done him such an injustice. "I perceive your excitement over the new and unique, but I doubt you'd feel so firmly grounded and confident in yourself without the land and the sky and a sense of gravity pulling against you."

Tanis admitted Sinárr could be right about that—he recalled too nearly that feeling of vertigo in the void. "And as to my first question?"

The Warlock shrugged. "I like the sensation of your world."

"What does that mean?"

Sinárr cracked a smile. "Nothing so sinister as your expression implies." He started walking towards the surf. "Your realm is full of sensation." He cast a gaze of invitation over his shoulder, so the lad jogged to join him. "The rich taste of roasted fowl, a lemon's tart cool bite, the refreshing mist cast by cascading water, the shade of trees and the heat of the sun on your baking skin; undulating rocks beneath your feet; hunger, thirst and craving; the painfully vivid colors of the sunset, the delightful terror of a raging thunderstorm…"

He walked them directly towards a wave. Just when Tanis was bracing himself to receive another icy dousing, the water parted and rolled backwards on itself to form a channel for their passing.

"Sensation abounds in your world." Sinárr continued leading them deeper into the parted sea. "You feel the weight of cloth upon your body, its wildly varied caresses against your skin, and always gravity's immutable pulling of your form towards the planetary core. Pressure, temperature, sound—*oh, sound!*" He cast Tanis a marveling look. "Sound is simply a product of force, yet it can be used to create miraculous wonders."

He paused their walk beside a school of fish that was eyeing them through the wall of their watery domain. Sinárr held up a dark-skinned hand for their inspection. "You see all shapes and forms, and a kaleidoscope of motion, even the motion trapped in the apparent solidity of objects." Sinárr leaned towards the fish, bringing his ebony nose nearly to the edge of the wall of water, whose surface towered high above them now. "You even enjoy a wide scale of emotion that causes physical and chemical reactions in your bodies, themselves wondrous to experience." He flashed a smile at the fish. They scattered.

Sinárr looked to Tanis—

The water crashed in upon them.

Tanis felt an instant of panic, but Sinárr placed a hand on his shoulder and grounded him firmly in the sand. Moments later, the tumult of silt and water cleared, and Tanis looked around from the sea floor.

"Here, I make the rules." Tanis heard Sinárr clearly, though water now surrounded them. The lad had no difficulty breathing except through his unreality.

"For you, Tanis, there is much sensation in my universe." Sinárr placed a finger beneath Tanis's chin and gently guided the lad's eyes up to his own. "But only because I *place* the sensation in the illusion I'm crafting for your benefit. For me..." he shrugged and sighed.

The idea of talking under the water was just too surreal. *Can we please go somewhere else?*

And they were back on the balcony overlooking the edge of the world and a dazzling nighttime sky. Sinárr leaned one hip against the railing and regarded Tanis with a quirk of a smile. "You were about to say?"

No longer merely an outline, Tanis's picture of understanding now had color and form. All he needed to finish it was the detail. He looked up at the Warlock. "Your universe has no feeling?"

Sinárr tilted his head slightly. Then he cupped his hands before him, and a geyser of light exploded upwards from them. The light's shifting glow brought an intensity to his features and made his golden eyes sparkle.

"My universe offers perceptions by the thousands, Tanis. For me, the colors of light are a language all their own. To see energy coalesce and merge, solidify and change, is to conceptually *know* every potential wavelength of this power. This is but one of hundreds of ways I perceive my universe."

Sinárr vanished the dancing light and held the lad's gaze in the darkness that poured into the space of its departure. "But *sensation*..." He lifted the velvet edge of his cloak. "To feel this cloak the way you feel it, I have to *place* the sensation there first to then be beheld. My worlds offer back to me only what sensations I place into it."

Tanis wasn't sure that he really understood what Sinárr was trying to describe to him, but he thought he grasped at least a glimmer of it.

Sinárr extended his palm towards Tanis. "Will you give me your hand?"

Only slightly hesitant now, for he understood much better of the Warlock than he had before, Tanis placed his hand in Sinárr's. The Warlock stroked his ebony fingers down across Tanis's palm, tracing it with his gilded nails. The lad no longer misinterpreted the man's fascination with him as some misplaced desire; now he understood that he offered Sinárr a connection to the sensation he craved—a connection to *elae*.

"I've never encountered an Adept like you, Tanis." Sinárr looked up under his brows. "I've never had a concubine who wished to create *with* me, never come upon an Adept with such innate talent for it as you possess. I *want* this co-creation." He exhaled a forceful breath and released Tanis's hand. "As you've seen, I would do anything to gain it."

Turning away from the lad, he spread his hands on the railing, leaned his weight into his arms and gazed out across the valley and the stripe of mercuric sea. Both moons burned high and bright in a sky resplendent with stars. Tanis could tell the Warlock was holding himself in close check.

After a moment, Sinárr exhaled a slow sigh, redolent of disappointment. "I thought you wanted to create worlds with me." He cast Tanis a sidelong look. "At one point...it seemed to me that you did."

"I do."

"But you won't consent to be bound to me?"

"No."

Sinárr looked away from him, radiating frustration.

In their nearness, Tanis felt that resonance building between them again, bringing with it a sense of connection that drew him to the Warlock as much as it magnetized Sinárr to him. Once, the feeling had frightened him. Later, it had confused him. Now he understood what was causing it.

When he first realized his path was leading him to the Warlock, Tanis had no idea why or what he was meant to do—he'd been so focused on rejecting the idea of being bound to Sinárr that he'd missed several important truths. Now he saw them clearly.

Tanis put a hand on the Warlock's arm, amplifying their mutual attraction. "Sinárr."

The man looked desperately to him.

Tanis met his gaze. *There is another way.*

THIRTY-FIVE

"In this world, there are givers and takers. The takers may eat better, but the givers sleep better."

–Yara, an old Kandori woman

RAIN SLASHED THE night as Ean and Sheih ascended the winding stairs of a campanile. All the while he climbed, Ean thought about the pattern of cause and consequence. The more he thought on it, the more he saw the skill as something native to him, an ability long possessed but never before relied upon—never actually recognized.

He recalled a time on his grandfather's ship when he'd looked at a sailor stowing the loose end of a line and seen stormy seas and the mizzen mast breaking. Between broken mast and sailor lay a host of choices and actions. At the time, these images had flown past in his mind's eye as a school of fish beneath the waves—the pattern of their arrangement glimpsed for but a breath and vanished. But two days later, their ship had hit a storm, and the mizzen snapped from stay lines incorrectly secured.

Then, Ean had dismissed his earlier vision as a fluke of chance. Now he saw it as a talent that Arion had also possessed—

No...a talent Arion had honed *to a razor edge.*

Ean emerged from the stairwell into the campanile's bell tower, overlooking a wide plaza. A brazen wind whipped through the tower's vaulted stone arches, danced capriciously in the rafters and swept on, leaving a pool of rainwater beneath the massive iron bell.

Ean moved through one of the open arches out into the rain and walked to the tower's crenellated edge. Cloaked in the fifth, he stared down into the arcaded square, unaware of the lashing rain, only observing the rose-hued funnels of the first strand: lithe spirits reflecting life's purest energy; their whirling cyclones joined earth to sky. Visible beyond these gossamer whirlwinds, the second strand spread its burnished copper sheen across the world. But Ean mostly watched the fourth strand's shimmering tides, for this ephemeral yet powerful energy was the strand most offended by the *eidola's* presence.

And the fourth-strand currents were rippling.

He crouched at the campanile's edge and let the wind bludgeon and buffet him while the rain made a lake of the square far below. He hardly noticed the storm, but he did notice the way Sheih kept staring at him from the deeper protection of the bell room.

Monitoring the currents required only a whisper of his attention, so he concentrated in the meanwhile on making sense of his newfound ability with what Arion had called 'patterns of consequence.'

They were only glimpses, yet each time, with each flashing moment, Ean had conceived the *entire* pattern—a falling domino effect of choices rushing forward into action, reaction, decision and new causation, resulting in a design of final consequence where the felled domino pieces represented the outcome of each individual choice. It seemed almost scientific to him; a logical path of choices and consequences that stippled its shape like raindrops on the desert sand, easily swept away by an unanticipated decision, and yet for that brief moment, entirely valid, as predictable as an equation's mathematical result.

As Ean in that moment walked the living path of this pattern, he traced along the spiral already predicted by those falling domino choices; each new decision led to one already anticipated—but only so long as no one made an *unexpected* choice.

The rain ebbed, and Ean glanced up to see the clouds beginning to break. Sheih emerged from the bell room and came to stand behind him where he crouched at the tower's edge. "Do they come?" Her voice was low, fervent. A viperous anticipation laced her tone.

Ean straightened to his full height and looked down at her masked face. "Get ready."

Her slanted eyes narrowed. "I'm always ready."

The ripples that heralded the *eidola's* coming had grown into waves, the distance between crests shortening, troughs deepening, the creatures' arrival imminent. But Ean couldn't see them anywhere.

He stared out across the darkened plaza using both naked eyes and *elae*-enhanced vision, but no matter how he strained, his sight revealed only storm-washed arcades, shadows supporting shadows, and darkly glimmering pools making mirrors out of stone.

Tension threaded Ean's frame. Why couldn't he see them? Where *were* they?

He moved to the other side of the campanile and looked out over the Upper City. The rapidly clearing storm was now shedding intermittent moonlight on the patchwork of *riads* and the lush darkness of their sleeping gardens. The second strand's currents showed him the lattice of city streets that the night concealed from his mortal eyes. Most of those passageways were empty, for the rain had driven all but the stoutest of humanity inside. Still... no *eidola*.

Yet the fourth-strand currents were veritably *writhing*.

Ean should've been able to see the *eidola*—instinct warned that they were nearly upon him—but somehow they remained hidden among the night's drenched and languorous shadows. He could almost *feel* the creatures, like Arion had been able to feel the Mages hiding in the Citadel's hall...

A curse left Ean's lips, barely formed. He should've seen it from the first! All this time he'd been assuming Dore had sent the *eidola* in pursuit of him... but what if *Darshan* had sent them?

Darshan...who wielded *deyjiin* as the Enemy had wielded it on Tiern'aval—who may indeed have *been* the faceless force of enmity that had claimed Arion's life. And now the clearing storm...

The Prophet had awoken.

And sent his *eidola* in night-cloaks of *deyjiin*.

Ean growled a heated oath.

Sheih stiffened at his side. "What is it?"

He rushed to the tower's edge, catching himself against the low crenels, his mind searching for ideas while his eyes scanned the sleeping plaza. A gritty foreboding churned in his chest.

How could he find them if they were cloaked in *deyjiin*? He didn't know how to wield it; even Arion hadn't been able to combat it. All Ean knew about it was that it was a consumptive power.

So give it something else to consume.

Ean threw together a working with a painter's rapid, careless strokes. He lashed the patterns into a matrix, bound it with the fourth and was about to launch it when he remembered it wouldn't stick to the *eidola* without the first strand added to its design. This he threw on as a pot of paint upended and then shot the pattern off on the arrow of his intent.

His breath hung in his lungs while he watched the glimmering energies fly through the air, watched them impact and splash across the entire plaza in a diffuse shimmer...which rapidly vanished into a mass of deeper darkness oozing along the plaza's north side, just steps from the tower's base.

Shade and darkness!

He hastily formed Dareios's pattern—a complicated matrix much more sophisticated than the rough sketch he'd tossed a moment ago. Meanwhile, the black mass reached the bottom of the tower.

Behind him, Sheih hissed a curse. Steel scraped against stone.

Ean spun. The matrix fell apart in his mind.

Five *eidola* were climbing over the tower's edge. A sixth was already pressing Sheih in a combat of swords, driving her towards the crenellated wall.

Time seemed to hold its breath for the instant Ean deliberated, stricken to stillness by the sudden emergence of two paths clearly sailing forth from the same point of embarkation. There was the slightest chance that Darshan had sent his creatures on the hunt for someone who'd worked *elae* in his city and not for Ean specifically. But if he destroyed these *eidola* without using the matrix to do it…Darshan would recognize him. He would *know* him.

Along one course, Ean saw himself abandoning Sheih to her own fate and securing his escape, living to test his patterns another day. Upon the other course, he fought these creatures long enough to test the matrix and in the doing announced himself to Darshan. It wasn't a particularly palatable choice, but Ean recognized that he *did* have one.

Sheih was furiously battling the one *eidola* and seemed to be holding her own, but now the other five creatures were coming for him, never mind the mass swarming below.

Ean chose a path.

He summoned the pattern he'd used in Ivarnen and threw it at the closest *eidola*. Two of them immediately collapsed into convulsions, but the other three split apart and darted for cover beneath the arches.

Ean drew his sword and went after them, and—

Barely got his weapon up in time to fend off a bolt of *deyjiin*. It sizzled along the skin of his arm, an icy tingle, sharp and stinging. Ean slung the bulk of the power off his blade and set his sights on the lucid, who had jumped up and was clinging to one of the arches.

The lucid rattled a ratcheting cry and power flared, thunder without sound. Ean pushed intention into his fifth-strand shield and absorbed it in a backwards skid of water, but the campanile's iron bell had no such protection. It emitted one ear-splitting toll as it flew off its rafters and crashed through the stone archway. Stone rained in its wake. It smashed through the tower's crenellated edge and tumbled down into the plaza. Bats erupted behind this exodus with shrill cries, and a breath later, the tormented bell landed in a cacophonous clang of shattering bronze.

Ean's ears were still ringing when an *eidola* launched into him. They hit the broken archway together and tumbled across the littered tiles. Ean hugged the *eidola* close and used the contact to find the pattern binding it to life. With a thought, he unworked it.

The creature stilled atop him.

Deyjiin sizzled against his fifth-strand shield—another blast thrown from the lucid. Ean felt the cold power gnawing at his mind and fought back a reflexive revulsion. He shoved the creature's dead weight off him and got to his feet.

Hanging beneath the arch like some kind of mutated bat, the lucid rattled an *eidola* clatter and fired another bolt at him. Ean felt its effects against his shield as a torrent of stones thrown into the pond of his mind. He flung the Ivarnen pattern back at the lucid in aggravation. It hit the creature full in the face, and the lucid fell onto the shattered stones, already convulsing.

Ean was running towards it with the intention of unworking it when another *eidola* launched itself out of the shadows. They tumbled together across broken stones and landed with the thing sprawled on top of him. Ean mashed his hand into its face and ripped the pattern of its existence into shreds. Then he shoved it irritably off. *And good riddance.*

The lucid was still convulsing. Ean dared not spare any more time for it. He ran instead to the tower's west wall, feeling urgency humming through him, and pitched to his knees at its base. Then he summoned once more the patterns of their matrix.

The first strand formed the base and ensured the matrix would attach to the *eidola*; fourth-strand patterns disrupted their thoughts, the fifth strand eroded the link between monster and master; and the second strand would carry the working on the kinetic tides, scattering it as far as the wielder could power it.

Ean focused the aim of his intent—

A blast of thunder without sound struck his fifth-strand shields, knocking him sideways. He managed to release the pattern just as another blow struck him hard enough to make him lose his shields completely. He regained himself just as the lucid ran headlong into him.

Ean caught the creature in his arms, and they both went over the edge.

The lucid bit down at the joining of Ean's neck and shoulder. Pain seared through him, but worse was the sensation of *deyjiin* flowing in, a very deadly sort of poison.

Ean cast a desperate pattern towards the earth while simultaneously seeking the lucid's life pattern; but the pattern binding the lucid to Darshan differed from those binding the other *eidola*, and it wasn't so easily found. Complicating the problem, the icy magic pouring into his veins seared thought from his mind, making concentration all but impossible.

The pain was *so* intense, and the remembered feeling of unmaking so close and horrifying—suddenly he was Arion looking into the face of the Enemy; he was his younger self staring into Rinokh's yellow eyes; he was lost in the darkness of those twisted dreams of malevolent unmaking—

Ean! Focus! Isabel's voice pierced into his mind as sunlight piercing through a storm.

He gulped an agonized gasp.

Then they hit.

The stone swallowed them.

Hauling himself back to awareness on Isabel's lifeline, Ean then swam through the lucid's mind. Seconds were all he would have. If the creature resisted…but it was discomposed at finding itself deep inside the earth sinking through viscous rock. It drank stone into its open mouth and clawed desperately for the surface.

Ean clung to it, riding it back towards the air while his mind swam more deeply in search of the pattern that bound it.

There. A shimmering light amid the darkness of the *eidola's* golem existence. Ean discerned the pattern's beginning and ending and pulled—

And opened the door into another's awareness.

Light—heat—power seared his consciousness. A forceful presence flooded his mind, blinding, overpowering, *suffocating*.

Ean fled this awareness, but he might've been running from the sun in a vast desert. He couldn't outrun it. He couldn't escape it.

EAN VAL LORIAN, the thought blazed in his skull, trembled his ears and hollowed his core, *I RECOGNIZE YOUR MIND.*

The lucid finally clawed into the open air and clutched onto solid stone, as a sailor clinging to flotsam in a storm. Ean made a rope of the fifth and hauled himself away from the creature—and that terrible connection to its master.

As he slid on his back across the plaza's wet stones, he pulled a thread of the lucid's life pattern along with him. The *eidola's* head fell forward with a dull clack, half of its body still sunk in the earth. Ean released the fifth and threw out his arms, and his body slowed to a halt.

He gave a tremulous exhale.

The puddle he was lying in quickly soaked through his clothing, but its ice was pleasurable after the heat of Darshan's awareness. So deeply had the Malorin'athgul invaded Ean's mind that it felt like the man was still there, haunting the recesses of his thoughts.

Feeling a little sick, Ean slowly pushed up into a sitting position. His entire body was shaking. That contact with Darshan had been…indescribable. Oddly, not because of any malevolent intent, but because of the *power* Ean had perceived. The Malorin'athgul's mind was a veritable *star*.

Ean drew his knees to his chest, rested his elbows on them and pressed palms to his forehead. How had Isabel withstood him?

Isabel.

Ean closed his eyes and tried to calm his racing heart. He owed her his life just now. In his most desperate moment, she'd pierced all of his shields, focused him and forced him into action. She'd been there for him when he needed her, even though he'd turned his back on her when she'd most needed his compassion.

Shade and darkness.

But he didn't dare think about Isabel just then, for *Darshan knew he was in Tambarré*. The Malorin'athgul could send a thousand more of those monsters to hunt Ean down, and they would care nothing for who they harmed in the process.

Suddenly urgent to get moving again, Ean pushed shakily to his feet, but then his eyes seemed to notice what his much-abused mind had missed.

Around the tower's base lay a moat of unmoving *eidola*.

The prince blinked, making sure he was actually seeing what his eyes claimed to observe. Then a bold laugh burst out of him. "It *worked*." Ean heard the incredulity lacing his own words. They'd labored so long…it hardly seemed possible. And then, suddenly, he realized that it was.

He threw out his arms and lifted a grin to the heavens. "Sebastian, Dareios—it worked!" His cry echoed back to him from the plaza's arcades, a hundredfold disembodied congratulations.

Suddenly he heard a commotion coming from the shadowed side of the tower. Had an *eidola* escaped his working? Success put power beneath his steps as he ran to investigate, but as he rounded the tower…

Sheih had one of the creatures pinned beneath her and was trussing it in *goracrosta*. A few more pieces of that first glimpsed pattern of consequence finally slid into place.

Ean watched her skillfully trying the creature and felt a cold foreboding settle over him. She'd claimed she wanted vengeance. Ean had assumed that meant killing the creatures who'd killed her partner. He'd never imagined she wanted to capture a *living* one.

"Release that thing and step away from it, Sheih."

Sheih froze with her fingers mid a knot. After a moment's pause, she continued tying it off. "This isn't what it looks like, Ean."

Ean grunted at her familiar use of his name. "So you've finally dispensed with pretense? *This* is the truth, then—what you were really after?"

She turned a look over her shoulder, her dark eyes calculating. "We needn't be at odds. You got what you came for, as did I."

"You said you wanted vengeance."

"Which you exacted for me when you killed the *shaytan'jinn* wielding *deyjiin*."

"*Deyjiin*." Ean arched a brow. "How does a satrap's agent know about *deyjiin*?"

She stood slowly and faced him with a defiant set to her slanted eyes. "How does an unringed wielder defeat three dozen *shaytan'jinn*?"

Ean clenched his jaw. "Step away from it."

Her eyes flashed. "Get your own."

She whispered something—it sounded a curse—and Ean felt a force hit his mental shields and *invert*, like a fléchette that speared thinly through his armor and then expanded. Its barbs slung outwards as it flew, tearing the flesh of his thoughts. It felt like knives were driving into his mind.

Ean staggered back. Somehow he managed to maintain his fifth-strand shield, which was lucky, because two shuriken ricocheted off it to clatter into the tower wall instead.

Sheih cursed him. She was reaching for another blade when Ean finally focused on her inverted pattern and unmade it. Then he grabbed the fifth and bound her arms to her sides—eliciting a gasp and a venomous glare.

One hand hooked the front of her coat and dragged her close. "Who do you really work for?" He added a little compulsion to the question to help her answer along.

Her eyes widened, her jaw clenched. She was resisting him.

Ean pushed more insistently with the fourth—barely a whisper of the compulsion he was capable of, but enough to make her gasp out, "The Sorceresy! We were sent as envoys to procure a *shaytan'jinn*. The Advisor would not sell them to us, so we contrived to steal one. My partner died in the attempt."

Ean felt everything inside him tighten all at once—Arion's memories somehow impressing upon him the import of this news. Beyond Arion's ghostly fury, Ean recalled Isabel speaking of the Sorceresses of Vest, of their *mor'alir* Adepts and their twisted paths of Alir. Yes, this Sheih could be such a one as that.

He asked in a voice gone cold with a long-forgotten anger, "What does the Vestian Sorceresy want with an *eidola*?" He made a dagger of this question so she wouldn't waste his time trying to resist him.

"To study it." She bit the words at him like a cobra spitting venom.

Ean's gaze darkened. "So they can make their own?"

Sheih narrowed her eyes into daggers of malice. "I don't presume to question my mistresses—and neither should *you*." Something both icy and searing lanced his shield into a webwork of fractures. Lightning pain seared his thigh.

A pattern flashed into Ean's mind just before a debilitating pain ruptured thought. Concentration fled before this onslaught, whereupon a memory surfaced—

—*Arion frowned at the curved dagger in his hands and the patterns etched into its steel.* Mor'alir *patterns,* inverteré. *They twisted the lifeforce into unrecognizable shapes, the inverted opposite of true purpose, the worst sort of corruption. The blade hummed viciously in his mind as it trapped and twisted* elae, *its patterns like jagged crags of dead coral twisting riptides out of the currents.*

He lifted a look of horror to Isabel. "They stabbed you with *this? How did you escape it?"*

She took the blade from his fingers and returned it to its place on her wall. "You begin by reverting the pattern to its original shape…"—

Sheih's voice echoed to him as if spoken through a void. "Do yourself a favor, foolish prince. Find a place to hide and stay there. Everyone is looking for you. The whole world is looking for you."

Staggering, blinded by *elae* inverted—*perverted*—Ean sought the pattern he'd seen flash the instant before pain had pounced on him. After what seemed a lifetime, he found the pattern and pushed it concave to itself. Then he sought the pattern's beginning and ending and unraveled it.

The debilitating pain vanished, leaving only a dull ache in his thigh.

Ean's breath returned with a harsh inhale. He found himself on his side with a dagger extending from his thigh and a wide stain spreading down his pant leg. He clenched his jaw and yanked the dagger from his flesh, then grimly looked over the blade.

Patterns similar to the ones Arion had been looking at etched the curved steel, their lines seeming to capture and hold his blood as it dripped towards the narrow tip.

Mor'alir. Inverteré. Ean understood these terms better now. Sheih had used *inverteré* patterns to corrupt his shields and a *mor'alir* dagger to make her escape.

Ean could see every pattern bound into the dagger, even the ones concealed by the leather-wrapped hilt, even the ones pounded deep within the folded steel. Just holding the thing revolted him.

He pushed up to sitting and looked around. As might be expected, Sheih had vanished and taken her contraband *eidola* with her. Ean growled a muted curse. How many minutes had he lost to that Belloth-spawned dagger?

At least he would know those patterns if he ever saw them again, and he would be much better prepared to handle them—handle *her*—the next time.

He removed the straps from around his knees and bound his injured thigh with them instead. All the while, urgency pressed upon his thoughts.

He had to find Sheih, and then he had to get out of Tambarré—and fast, before Darshan could send any more *eidola* after him.

It was then that a whispering presence presented itself for his inspection. Like a courtier with a proposition, it bowed before his awareness and said as it straightened, *Darshan will be expecting you to flee.*

Indeed, the whispering went on to point out that the Prophet would probably have his *eidola* watching every node, every outlet in or out of the city. If Ean's only chance of success was to do the *un*expected, then what could be more unexpected than going after Darshan?

As outrageous as it appeared upon first inspection, Ean quickly began to see the possibility in it. He'd long had the feeling that he and Darshan were destined to meet. Isabel had tried to argue him out of the notion, but Ean was sure that he had to confront the man—and not at some future time when Darshan willed it, but *right then,* that very night, when the Prophet would be least expecting him. The thought impinged itself so determinedly upon his consciousness that he nearly gasped from the force of it.

Yes.

Ean would go to the temple, find the Prophet and confront him.

Surely Darshan's indiscriminate use of compulsion proved that *he* was the faceless enemy behind the Mages' betrayal and Arion's death. How else was Ean ever going to find out what had happened to Arion, save by confronting the man who'd murdered him?

Ean stood and tested the muscle in his leg. It was angry, but it held his weight. Stowing Sheih's *mor'alir* dagger in a spare holster, he turned his gaze towards the acropolis. The Prophet's *al-qasr* was glowing all along the crest, a lighthouse calling its sailors home.

Ean set a course for its shores.

THIRTY-SIX

"The forge of suffering produces the strongest souls. The greatest characters are seared with scars."
– The Elevated Teachings of Jai'Gar

ALSHIBA TORININ, SEAT of the realm of Alorin, sat at a table with a goblet of wine untouched in front of her. Beyond her quiet table, the balustrade of a long terrace arched outwards, offering an uninterrupted view of Illume Belliel's azure ocean.

To left and right of her high vantage, the mansion estates of hundreds of realms studded the lush coastline, while on the terrace immediately above her, the restaurant's other patrons were taking their evening meal. Their quiet chatter sounded a calming hum, mingling every so often with the sound of crashing waves carried up on the breeze from far below.

On the opposite end of the terrace, an older man sat drawing in a sketchbook, capturing the scene in pastel hues, but Alshiba saw not the impressive view, the gleaming waves, nor the richly golden sun falling towards the sea—only a wavering time stream of incomprehensible choices.

Time's leviathan tail undulated backwards to the horizon of her earliest days in the Sormitáge, when she'd merely admired Björn van Gelderan from afar, never imagining he would notice her. From that horizon to now, the serpent's head lengthened, twining through such highs of experience as to leave her breathless from their memory, and diving to lows so deep that the pressure of their depths vanquished all the light from her thoughts.

Alshiba felt that pressure now as a vice around her heart. She could barely breathe through it.

How desperately she missed him. How furiously she wanted to upbraid him.

Like the last time he came to you?

What a joyless and embarrassing confrontation *that* had proven. She'd hardly been able to stand, much less stand up to Björn. The most mortifying part of the encounter was how desperately she'd wanted him to stay.

Stay and reclaim his Seat. *Stay* and guide her in guiding the realm. *Stay* with her, and heal her heart.

In the weeks since Björn's last visit, due in no small part to Franco's halting—if honest—explanations, Alshiba had come to understand better of what Björn was trying to accomplish. What she couldn't understand was why he hadn't trusted her with those truths from the beginning.

By Cephrael's Great Book! How could she still love a man who had so thoroughly betrayed her?

Alshiba exhaled a tremulous breath and sank her forehead into her hands.

'*…He's an easy man to admire, my brother, but a hard man to love…*'

How right Isabel had been to caution her all those years ago! Alshiba would rather have endured the unending punishment of Belloth's thirteen hells than the eternal torment of loving Björn van Gelderan.

"Deep thoughts, Your Excellency…or perhaps a little too much wine?"

Alshiba lifted her head from her hands to find a tall man standing between herself and the sun. Haloed by the afternoon's golden light, with dark hair, a close-cropped beard and a debonair stature, Mir Arkadhi had the kind of striking good looks that gave women of any age thoughts to make them blush. But while he wore charm like a cloak, the Eltanin Seat was also ruthless, cunning and endlessly dangerous—very much the product of a world whose Adepts chose the *mor'alir* path almost exclusively.

"Lord Arkadhi." She nodded to him.

"Lady Torinin." He nodded politely in return, a subtle smile hinting in his crystalline gaze. "May I join you?"

With Björn so heavy in her thoughts, distracting her from what was real, Mir Arkadhi was the last person she wanted to see just then.

Well…perhaps not the very *last person.*

Wordlessly, Alshiba held a hand to the other chair at her table.

Mir seated himself across from her and extended his long legs towards the distant railing and the view. He clinked his own glass against hers and then held it up, eyeing the ruby liquid speculatively. "Shall we share a toast, Alshiba?"

Alshiba eyed him warily. "What would we be toasting?"

"Progress." He angled her a meaningful gaze, his crystalline truthreader's eyes easily holding hers captive. "That elusive minx coveted by all."

Alshiba made sure the shield around her thoughts was secure. Mir was as strong in his talent as Raine D'Lacourte, and far less scrupulous in his use of it.

She didn't need a truthreader's gift to know what topic he was alluding to, however. If it was possible for a realm to be comprised entirely of bankers and their darker cousins—loan sharks and bounty hunters—Eltanin would be that realm.

"I didn't think Eltanin looked favorably upon the Interrealm Trade Measure."

"On the contrary, we're most agreeable to it." Mir sat back in his chair and swirled his wine idly in his glass. "The more commerce, the more Eltanin's services are required."

Mir already had half the Seats on the Council in his thorny debt. She could hardly imagine the horror of Eltanin opening its endless vaults to the Thousand Realms.

Monopoly…tyranny…empire…

Subjugation.

These words practically shouted in her head. She couldn't be altogether certain Mir wasn't the one shouting them, thoughts spearing at her from behind his calculated smile. His goals…her worst nightmares.

Alshiba picked up her wine, already feeling the urge to gulp it. One didn't merely banter words with the Eltanin Seat. Mir put force behind his every thought and cast each with intent to wound.

And he wanted to skirmish. This was evident. He enjoyed a sort of intelligent, deadly jousting.

Alshiba hated it. But marching the battlefield of these machinations was her duty, the helm Björn had so indifferently left behind for her to wear, regardless of how unsuitable and ill-fitting. And on the vast battleground of Illume Belliel's politics, one either learned quickly how to fight in multiple situations and with a host of weapons, or fell quickly to another's lengthy and better practiced pike.

She took a sip of wine and murmured over the rim, "I can see why that would please you."

Mir scratched at his jaw to cover a dark amusement. "There is a refreshing candor to the layered meaning in your words, Alshiba. But you do Eltanin an injustice. We can only be what it is in our nature to become."

"A view assumed by most who choose the *mor'alir* path."

He smiled, but his eyes never lost their dangerous glint. "I take it from your tone that you don't approve of this *mor'alir* path. In Eltanin, there is but one path—the one we walk."

Alshiba smiled wryly into her wine. "Another viewpoint in common with those who walk the path of *mor'alir*."

Mir held his goblet beneath his draping fingers and angled it at her by way of emphasis. "So…Alorin's Adepts believe there is more than one path?" He arched a raven brow. "Educate me."

Alshiba laughed. "Oh no. I would never presume to educate you."

"But you presume to disapprove of me."

She really laughed then. "As if you'd even bother yourself with indifference to my disapproval."

Mir chuckled. "You know…" he draped his arm across the back of his chair and pointed at her with one long finger, "you and I have rarely spoken." He fixed his colorless gaze meaningfully upon her. "Why is that?"

Because Björn warned me away from you before I ever arrived in the cityworld.

She gave him a conciliatory smile. "Alorin has never needed Eltanin's services."

"Ah, but I'm not merely speaking of our respective positions, Alshiba."

Despite his intimation, there were no friendships in Illume Belliel, no genuine advances, only the ploys of politics.

"Mir," Alshiba arched a brow as she took a sip of her wine, "are you propositioning me?"

He seemed slightly startled—and mildly pleased—by her bold question. "What if I was?"

Alshiba lowered her glass slowly. "Then I would say I should need to think lengthily and carefully upon my answer."

Mir's eyes glinted with dark amusement. He lifted his finger again and rolled it around at her. "A daring feint, only to fall back in a hasty retreat? Alshiba…surely you can do better than that."

She swallowed beneath the force of his meaning and offered a careless shrug to cover her unease. "It is as you say. We've never had need of each other's services."

"Ah, but those were *your* words, Alshiba."

Alshiba retreated into her wine. Mir's daggers of insinuation always drew blood. She knew well what services he hoped to gain from her now.

Moreover, *he* saw that she saw it.

Mir smiled deliberately at her. "Implementation of the new measure will be aided by establishing a common currency for trade throughout the realms. Don't you agree?"

She nearly choked on her wine. "A common currency," she fought to keep her expression neutral and her voice even, "…which Eltanin is no doubt prepared to provide."

"Of course. No other worlds' mints are even remotely capable of competing with Eltanin's."

Alshiba could barely believe she'd heard him correctly. "Let me get this straight." She arched a brow rather incredulously—better he saw her surprise than the horror she truly felt. "Eltanin expects to become the *sole* minting institution for the Thousand Realms?"

He flashed a sinuous smile. "Perhaps you have another more qualified realm in mind."

"It would seem safer to diversify," she managed somewhat breathlessly, trying to maintain a balance she didn't feel, "perhaps to choose a metal readily available on all of the realms rather than have all the realms dependent upon the metals of one."

Mir eyed her quietly and fingered his dangling wine glass. "I hope this is not your final position," he said aloud, but his thoughts said, *It would pain me to have to remove you from my path,* while his taunting gaze said, *Then again, I might enjoy it.*

Alshiba felt each of these communications spear into her at three distinct points. Each left her composure bleeding in different ways.

Had she been better rested, had she been able to keep anything beyond wine in her stomach for the past fortnight, she might've fared better against his assault. As it was, she just tried to keep her hand from shaking.

Alshiba forced a smile. "I'm sure whoever is chosen to chair the committee will give every suggestion due consideration."

Mir's crystalline gaze gleamed with dubiety. "The way I hear it, there is only one Seat being considered for the position."

In spite of her best efforts, Alshiba went a little pale. If that was true, it was a frightening responsibility Aldaeon was placing on her shoulders alone. She felt utterly inadequate to the task. The only reason she hadn't turned the Speaker down outright was for fear of who he would be forced to choose in her stead.

"Really?" Alshiba drank her wine to cover her consternation. "I…hadn't heard that."

Mir saw that he'd thrown her—damn the man. His smile became predatory, his gaze viciously amused.

Epiphany give her strength, she hated these games! And the worst of it was, whether you attacked, feinted, placated or surrendered, there was no way to win against Mir Arkadhi. You merely hoped to crawl off the battlefield with most of your limbs still attached.

Mir downed the last of his wine and angled her a look beneath his brows while he refilled his glass from her bottle. "You realize that your predecessor would not have hesitated to claim the committee chair."

The last thing she needed was to be reminded of Björn—or to let Mir trap her into admitting that she'd been offered the position.

Alshiba stared hotly into her wine. "There are many things Björn did that I would not."

Mir gave a dark laugh, but his eyes bore ever more powerfully into hers. "I applaud the care you take in phrasing your ambiguities, Alshiba. I had no idea what I'd been missing—the sublime enjoyment of a *tête-à-tête* with the Alorin Seat." He set down the bottle of wine and raised his glass to her. "I shall endeavor to place us at odds more often."

Alshiba forced a swallow, which Mir no doubt noticed. The bloody man noticed everything.

Sitting back again, he hooked an elbow on his chair and waved airily with his wine. "Perhaps, you're right to be cautious." He eyed her quietly. "The position would doubtless be very difficult...perhaps too strenuous for a woman of your nature? All those predators in the Hall would quickly make a meal out of a pretty little morsel like you."

Beneath the sexual innuendo, Mir layered a host of lustful intentions, images of violent encounters, a ready confession of his own dark hungers.

Alshiba might've been adept at shielding her own thoughts from Mir's attentive mental ears, but she was not so competent at protecting herself from the thoughts he was forcing on her—as ineffective as she would be in trying to stop him from physically doing the same.

He made *this* point clear in his thoughts as well.

Feeling shaky, Alshiba lifted her gaze to meet his. The smile he was leveling her sent a chill down her spine.

Oh, he was simply trying to shake her composure—Alshiba knew this. If only it wasn't working so effectively! If only he wasn't so *good* at it.

Oh, Alshiba, my sweet, I am very, very good at what I do.

He cast this thought of layered innuendo like a spear to which he'd attached a rope of compulsion. Alshiba barely fended it off with a mental gasp. Had it penetrated her shield, it would've snared her mind like a grappling hook, and he could've climbed his rope of compulsion to infiltrate and overcome all of her defenses.

Alshiba could think of nothing more horrifying than her mind, body and thoughts lying at the mercy of Mir Arkadhi. She hastily reassembled the shards of her composure, reminding herself that if she could stand up to Björn van Gelderan, she ought to be able to stand up to Mir.

Except that you didn't stand up to Björn.

Alshiba hastily drank the last of her wine and set down her goblet. Mir refilled it for her with an accommodating smile.

"To be clear…" she summoned a bravado she didn't feel, "letting you refill my glass should not be construed to mean we have forged some accord."

He gave a low laugh. "Well spoken, Alshiba. I dare say I've not yet misconstrued any of your intentions."

No, I dare say you haven't. Indeed, he seemed too clearly to know her mind, despite her best efforts to shield herself.

Alshiba watched the wine swirling in her goblet and felt her head doing much the same. She said too faintly for comfort, "I can't imagine the Speaker agreeing to a plan that would give one realm so much power over the rest."

Mir pushed her wine glass towards her. "And yet, he must've known when he put the measure forth that it would necessarily lead to this end, for Eltanin's offer is the most obvious path to a quick and effortless implementation."

Alshiba accepted the wine but not his insinuation. She didn't for a moment believe that Aldaeon H'rathigian was in collusion with Eltanin. That would've been merely trading one monopoly for another, when the purpose of the measure was to bring new freedoms to all the realms.

Mir sat back and eyed her quietly again, but his perfect smile had a guileful shape. "Do you not think it odd that our illustrious Speaker refuses to say which Seat wrote the measure?"

"Perhaps he wrote it himself."

Mir arched a chastising brow. "Alshiba, you are too canny to believe that."

If only she was canny enough to figure out what in Tiern'aval Mir Arkadhi hoped to gain from this conversation!

Alshiba set down her wine. "It's not unheard of for a Seat to request anonymity to ensure neutrality during the Council's vote."

"But the originators usually step forth after the measure is approved. In all my centuries here, I've never seen one *not* step forward after the fact."

Alshiba frowned at him. "What's your point?"

He draped an arm across the back of his chair again and turned his gaze towards the glimmering ocean. "I see but one rationale for maintaining anonymity at this late juncture." He waved an elegant hand to emphasize his point. "The Seat is either dead…or disavowed," and with this, he cast her a very sharp and very dangerous smile.

Oh, no. Oh, Björn…please, no!

There were so many reasons in that instant why she hoped Mir Arkadhi was wrong, but her every instinct shouted he was right.

Mir casually studied the wine in his glass. "I haven't seen your Fifth

Vestal in many a long century, though I hear he's paid a few illicit visits to you and our illustrious Speaker of late. I seem to recall he and Aldaeon were close friends before Björn abdicated his Seat in favor of playing god." He chuckled and leaned towards her. "Not that *I* presume to disapprove." The smile he gave her in that moment was daggered indeed. "Eltanin rewards men of ambition, even the ones with obvious…what's the word I'm looking for, sweet Alshiba? Ah yes: megalomania."

Alshiba felt weak—cold and weak; of heart and of mind. *Of course* Björn wrote the measure. Who else would've dared to imagine operational statutes in direct opposition to the vested interests that had been working to keep the realms separate and isolated for millennia? And who but Aldaeon would've dared to see it got passed?

And now that both had set themselves so wholly in the line of fire, who else but Alshiba could see it fairly enacted?

Oh, she hated Björn in that moment—hated Aldaeon, *definitely* hated Mir Arkadhi for putting all the facts together and presenting them to her so mercilessly. He knew, as she now knew, that she would unequivocally accept the position.

Alshiba sat back in her chair and let her hands fall into her lap. She turned her gaze out to sea. At least now she understood where all of this had been heading.

"More wine, Alshiba?"

She held up a hand to refuse him but then spun turned a look to her goblet. Yes, she'd drained it. She didn't even remember doing so.

Mir, damn him, was leveling her a satisfied smile, colorless eyes glinting mirthfully. He'd certainly achieved the effect he'd set out to cause. A fine application of the First Law.

"Well then," he exhaled decisively and got to his feet. "I suppose I should leave you to your thoughts. Doubtless you have much to think upon." He cast her a smile of parting, darkly victorious. "As I'm equally sure we'll have much to discuss in the coming weeks." He nodded to her. "Lady Torinin."

"Lord Arkadhi." She couldn't even look at him.

Whereupon, chuckling softly, Mir took his leave.

Alshiba walked Illume Belliel's winding streets back towards her estate, feeling queasy, lightheaded and wholly unnerved. The cityworld's days were long—sometimes the sun set just one hour before midnight—but even so, the streets had grown dark by the time she left the café.

Mir's conversation had so unsettled her that she'd had to consume another two glasses of wine just to stop her hands from shaking. Now they were shaking for another reason.

Whatever was wrong with her, the trouble lay beyond her skill to detect—beyond any of the cityworld's Healers—but she had no doubt *elae* was being used to make her ill.

Perhaps Mir Arkadhi was quietly planning her demise and had merely come to ascertain how well she was faring against whatever dark working he'd set upon her. It would certainly fit his temperament to stand there and jab her with fire-flamed stakes while she was lying helpless and begging for death.

But more unsettling still, what if Mir wasn't the only one who'd figured out she stood to become the Interrealm Committee Chair? The Eltanin Seat enjoyed toying with his prey, but most of the others would simply hire an assassin to eliminate anyone they viewed as competition for their own candidate.

And you're certainly making it easy for them, aren't you?

It occurred to her with a sudden faltering step that walking alone late in the evening without her usual escort was an imprudent choice at the best of times, much less when she'd been offered one of the highest positions of power in the cityworld.

Her knees felt suddenly weak, and a spell of vertigo set upon her. Alshiba stumbled towards the nearest building and clung to its corner, pressing her forehead against the stones while the dizziness faded.

That's when she heard them.

They must've been keeping enough distance that they rounded upon her all at once, not expecting her to have stopped. She heard their footsteps halt and then heard those same feet darting away, as if making silently for the shadows.

So she was being followed. But to what end?

She tried summoning the first strand to show their life signatures on the currents, but found the strand almost entirely beyond her reach.

Oh, Dear Epiphany…

A cold dread slithered down her spine.

She was a *Healer*. If she couldn't reach the first strand…

Alshiba forced a swallow against her queasy stomach. Had it been so long since she'd worked the lifeforce? How could she have not noticed that her connection with *elae* was eroding? Alshiba swore vehemently. If she died now, she would only have herself to blame.

On the brighter side, the realization brought a renewed clarity.

She cast the second strand behind her—it at least was still

responding—to warn her of their next approach, and pulled on the fifth to place a shield around her person—

It felt like immersing herself in flaming oil. She released it instantly with a sharp gasp.

This was very, very bad.

If she'd had any doubt her situation was dire, she doubted no longer.

Trying not to let her own fears panic her, Alshiba pushed shakily off the wall and started down the street again as quickly as she could manage. Her legs felt unsteady, her stomach in a flutter. She dared not reach for the fifth again but had no other means of protection.

No sooner did she start walking than her second strand pattern told her they were once more in pursuit.

Alshiba kept a hand near the wall for support and made herself focus. She was trained in combat. She could use the fourth as a weapon—what she could gather of it; if it would even comply—but it had been so long since she'd fought with the lifeforce, and she was already so weak, that she didn't hold much hope for her chances.

They must've known this. They must've chosen that night to attack her for this very reason.

Perhaps Mir had seen enough in her responses to know that she would never bend to his will. Perhaps someone else entirely stood behind these acts against her. Whoever stood to gain, their men were gaining on her now.

Alshiba tried to push herself into a run, but moving faster made her dizziness so severe that she worried she would lose her balance and fall. She slowed at once back to her halting shuffle. Her stomach was rotating on a sickly spit, making her boiling hot one moment and chilling her the next.

Up ahead, she saw a long rock wall framing both sides of the road, while the cobbled street angled steeply downwards. She wasn't far from her own estate now, but they could catch her long before she reached the safety of its gates.

Oh, if only she could've been thinking more clearly!

That's what happens after weeks without proper food or rest.

Yes, they'd taken care in planning her end. How easy it would be for these men to catch her now, and from there…? A sheer drop from the nearest overlook. She'd be too weak to protect herself from the fall upon the rocks, and very likely too weak to recover from it, even should the Healers find her quickly enough. They would call it a suicide. She could just see Niko van Amstel now—

Stop it! Think what to do!

Alshiba braved a glance over her shoulder. Five men were following her.

They weren't even trying to hide themselves now. They must've noticed how weak she was.

She mustered what she could of the fourth and threw something at them. Ineffectual. It bounced right off their...shields?

No, they weren't wielders, these. They must've been wearing *elae*-enhanced armor beneath their cloaks.

Alshiba reached the long stretch of wall and paused just before it, trying to catch her breath. That stone-lined corridor suddenly seemed a gauntlet from which she likely would not emerge alive. Yet, if she *could* reach the other end...

She dared another glance over her shoulder. Her pursuers seemed much closer than the last time she'd looked. Turning back to the way ahead, Alshiba mustered everything she had, forced a sickly swallow, and threw herself into a sprint.

The men bolted after her in pursuit. Their pounding feet were hitting the stones much faster and harder than hers.

An arrow whisked past her ear. She gasped and ducked as it ricocheted away. Two more arrows whizzed awry of her. It seemed impossible they were missing her at that distance.

Already her breath was coming in painful gasps, her vision was starting to blur and her legs felt leaden. The end of the wall was still so—

Something grabbed her arm and yanked her forcefully sideways, off her feet and—*through the wall?*—into disorienting darkness. Alshiba inhaled to scream but a hand closed hard over her mouth. She struggled, but the arms holding her were like iron.

He held her bound against his strong form in utter darkness and opened a window—

Nay, not a window. He was using the fifth to make the wall transparent to her view. Did he have her *inside* the wall...?

On the street, the men had halted and were turning fast in search of her. They spoke to each other in low, angry voices in a tongue she didn't recognize.

Suddenly they stilled...stiffened.

She felt her captor wielding the lifeforce, but her own connection was too weak to tell what he was doing. When *elae*'s tingling ceased, the men spun and walked back the way they'd come.

Alshiba let out a desperate sob and turned her face into her captor's shoulder. "*Björn!*" His name crossing her tongue sounded both curse and prayer.

He pressed a kiss into her hair. "I'm so sorry they frightened you, love."

"*You* frightened me!" She beat at his chest with her fist, but he only caught her hand in a gentle hold and pressed it over his heart.

"I'm sorry *I* frightened you." He kissed her fingers. "I would never have let harm come to you. I only needed them close enough to cast a pattern over all five at once. Here, come…" He turned her in his arms and drew her—

Into a moonlit garden. Beside her stood a tall, cobblestone wall. So she *had* been inside it.

Björn took her face and with his thumbs smoothed away the tears from her cheeks. The moon illuminated the near foliage and highlighted Björn's features—so aristocratic, so revealing of his damned immutable certainty.

To be standing there with him after all those centuries, to see him in the flesh and be held in his arms after so many untold frustrating dreams…she almost couldn't bear it.

Alshiba sucked in a shuddering breath and pressed her forehead against his coat. She could hardly stand to look at him, she loved him so…she *hated* him so.

By Cephrael's Great Book! She truly wanted to be done with all of it—his betrayal, her confusion, the Council's wretched machinations… She felt so weak, so unprepared to face him. He had no right to own her heart so completely. She'd have gotten more mercy from one of Eltanin's dreadful banks.

"You should've let those men take me, Björn." And she meant it. *Oh why*, when he'd just saved her life—when he'd returned and was holding her in his arms—why did she feel *now* that she simply couldn't go on?

"Never." He tightened his hold on her.

Alshiba turned her cheek against his shoulder and stared hollowly off into the night. Grief clutched her in a vicious grip, such that her lungs refused to function, and what meager air they gathered burned. "The torture of seeing you is far worse than anything they would've done to me."

He tucked her head beneath his chin and gave a slow exhale. "I believe you."

"I hate you so much for what you've done."

"If it's any consolation, it was fair torture watching you sitting with Mir Arkadhi this afternoon."

Alshiba caught her breath. She drew back from him. "…What?" Utterly embarrassing how faint her voice had become.

Amusement glinted in his gaze, but desire fairly burned in it. "Do you really think I would let you be alone *anywhere* with Mir Arkadhi?" He brushed his hand over her hair, his eyes held hers.

"If you cared for me at all you wouldn't be her—"

Björn captured her mouth in a kiss. Light flooded her mind as *elae* flooded her life pattern. She felt suddenly plunged into a sea of *elae's* warmth. Her body became weightless, her mind whirling in a heady rush.

He eventually released her that she might reclaim her breath. "If I thought you believed that," he murmured, running his nose along hers, "I would honor your request."

"Björn…" his gasped name was very nearly a plea—for mercy, for explanation, for release from the wretched agony of loving him. "*Please*, just—"

He kissed her again, more gently that time, and in the same moment lifted her into his arms. This was actually provident, because his second kiss completely stole the strength from her legs. Her world spun.

Alshiba must've blacked out, for when she came aware again, he was carrying her towards her bed in the mansion. Disorientation swirled, a confusion of lamplights and shifting shadows. She dizzily cast her mind for the last thought she recalled…

"How did you know I was with Mir Arkadhi?" her voice sounded so faint to her ears. Was she speaking aloud at all?

Björn threw back the duvet and laid her gently down on the bed. "I've been watching you all day, love." He pressed a kiss to her forehead and brought up the covers over her.

"The artist…" she realized suddenly what he meant, "on the terrace… an illusion…"

Björn sat down on the bed at her side. He brushed a strand of hair from her face and then leaned and pressed a kiss to each of her eyelids. "Sleep, Alshiba…" Then he kissed her mouth. "Sleep, and be well."

So Alshiba did.

THIRTY-SEVEN

"Risk is like the lifeforce; it pervades all matter."
—The Adept wielder Arion Tavestra

TANIS DECIDED HE was either utterly brilliant or insanely stupid…or he supposed, utterly insane. Sitting on the edge of his bed, he pushed a hand through his hair. The third option suddenly seemed the most likely.

Yet his choice *felt* correct.

Of course, he was basing everything on one very big assumption.

No…not assumption this time—inductive reasoning.

Had his father been there, he would've congratulated him…or crucified him. The zanthyr would still likely proceed with the latter.

Mérethe came over holding his boots. "Tanis, are you certain about this?"

He'd told her of his plan the moment he awoke. At the time, he thought he'd seen the barest spark of life surface in her gaze, but now she'd sunken back into her melancholy sea.

"Certain?" Tanis took his boots out of her hands and set them on the floor at his feet. "Not at all."

"Then why are you doing it?"

He shoved a foot into one boot. "Because I think I'm right."

She settled meekly onto a chair across from him and captured her hands between her knees. "It seems a terrible risk."

"What's the alternative, Mérethe? Arguing with him until he binds me against my will out of sheer frustration?"

Mérethe gazed worriedly at him. "You don't really know what you're getting into."

Tanis gave a humorless laugh. "That's a certain truth."

"I know you don't see Sinárr's illusions as dangerous, Tanis."

He glanced up under his brows. "I see the danger, Mérethe."

She pressed her lips together and watched him with her large blue eyes, her hands still captured between her knees like a child's. Then her gaze wandered the room. "That these things around us appear real…" she spoke softly, as if to avoid waking Sinárr's attention to their conversation, "that the people Sinárr creates *act* real, that there's solidity and sensation in his universe…Tanis, these things make Sinárr seem benign, because all of this is so familiar."

Tanis shoved his other foot into its boot and straightened to look at her. "But?"

She let out a tremulous breath. "But he's one of the most powerful Warlocks in Shadow." She searched his eyes with her own. "Don't you see? That Sinárr can make these things solid to our perception, that he can fashion beings out of *nothing* and make them act human…it should frighten us, but instead it makes us complacent. The depth of his understanding of us just adds to his power over us."

Tanis slowly straightened and considered Mérethe's words. While he didn't doubt her veracity, he no longer trusted her conclusions. "*One* of the most powerful Warlocks," he repeated, tasting of the idea, wondering at it.

"He and Baelfeir are arguably equals." She said this as if it should be meaningful to him. "The Warlocks don't spend much time in society with one another, and I can't imagine what would ever bring them into conflict, but were Sinárr and Baelfeir ever given a reason to battle each other…" She let out a slow breath and shook her head. "It would be difficult to say which of the two would prevail."

Tanis heard all of this, but all his ear really stuck on was the unusual name. "Who's Baelfeir?"

Mérethe shoved her hands deeper between her knees and lifted a disconcerted gaze to meet his. "In Alorin, he's more commonly known as Belloth."

"*Belloth.*" Tanis barked an incredulous laugh. "The *Demon Lord?*" You could've hung a coat on his dubiety.

But Mérethe's eyes remained large and very worried.

Tanis couldn't stop the disbelieving smile that claimed his face. It was just so, well…*ridiculous* admittedly wasn't the right word. *Implausible* was better suited.

He pushed off his bed and wandered around the room, feeling Mérethe's eyes following him. "So…what?" He flung a look at her. "The Demon Lord Belloth really exists? That's what you're saying?"

Tanis was having a hard time reconciling this information against all of the curses he'd heard crossing Fynn's lips and the resulting images he'd formed in his own head. Come to think of it, most of those curses had centered around the Demon Lord's loins. Tanis had envisioned a black-skinned, rotund, bald man with a scrotum like two fat hairy bulls, and nearly as big as his own immense belly.

"You would not be smiling if you'd ever met Baelfeir. He's as different from Sinárr as the night from the day."

Tanis frowned at her analogy. It left too much room for interpretation while telling him nothing truly useful.

A child couldn't live in the Middle Kingdoms and not know the Demon Lord Belloth. Parents invoked the Demon Lord's name to threaten their children into good behavior, while the more frightening tales of him were favorites on All Hallows' Eve. The stories spanned the gamut from stealing babies in the night to twisting mortals to his will and driving them to do terrible, treacherous acts. Tanis had never imagined Belloth truly existed.

Now he wondered how many of the stories held some truth. As dark and malicious as those tales were, even a grain of it would be too much.

But true or not, it didn't change his plans.

Tanis squatted down before Mérethe and put his hands on her knees. That time, when he felt the soft wool of her dress, he understood better the skill and power Sinárr wielded to provide him with the sensation.

Tanis met Mérethe's gaze. "If I'm right, if I can make this work…do you want to go home?"

For a moment she merely stared at him. Then her eyes filled with tears, she pressed her lips together tightly and nodded.

Watching the tears brim and fall from Mérethe's blue eyes, Tanis recalled the moment when he'd first met her and the promise he'd made to himself to set her free.

He exhaled a measured breath. *Well…if nothing else comes of this, at least I'll have accomplished that much.*

When he was fully dressed and could find no other reason to delay, Tanis headed out of his rooms onto the marble bridge in search of Sinárr.

If the Warlock was really giving him the freedom to create within his universe, as he'd claimed, Tanis might've simply 'thought' himself to Sinárr's location. But the lad wasn't comfortable jumping around at will—at least not on his own cognizance—and in any event, he wanted to use his last moments before confronting the Warlock to organize his thoughts.

He'd told Sinárr very little the day before, only promising that he saw another path and that he would share it once he'd had time to actually formulate a plan. He'd finalized that plan as he was describing it to Mérethe that morning.

She was right, though. It was a terrible risk. So much depended on the conclusions he'd reached about his and Mérethe's commonality and his strange resonance with Sinárr.

He was also placing enormous faith in an immortal who held an undeniably *alien* view of existence. Yet he'd come to trust Sinárr, even if he wasn't entirely comfortable around him.

He assigned the latter feeling to the disparity in their viewpoints. He still wasn't sure that he could accurately predict Sinárr or know how he would think or feel in certain situations, and that unpredictability kept Tanis off balance in their interchanges. But instinct had been his guide since the very beginning of his path, when it had led him to follow a Malorin'athgul from a café in Rethynnea without cause or caution.

In retrospect, Tanis was grateful to have lived many years with only a bare understanding of his talent, for during those years, he'd been forced to formulate conclusions through thoughtful evaluation—and perhaps a little instinct—rather than on the surety offered by his truthreader's gifts.

Nadia had shared with him how lost her mother currently felt without her Sight to guide her, and how her father the High Lord was hamstrung against the Danes without the currents to tell him what he saw. This frustrated her, because her parents were strong, intelligent people who had seemingly forgotten that they had other abilities besides the ones that involved *elae*.

If Tanis had only had his truthreader's talent to guide him with Sinárr, he would've been totally lost there in Shadow. But the lad wasn't merely a truthreader; he was a wielder personally trained by the High Mage of the Citadel and studied of the writings of one of the most talented Adepts ever to work the lifeforce—his father, Arion Tavestra. Though still young in his practice, Tanis knew well both the Laws of Patterning and the Esoterics, and he had his parents' wisdom to guide him in applying these vital truths.

He was having to use everything he knew now to guide him across the dark expanse of Sinárr's will.

As the V-shaped end of the ravine came into view, Tanis started formulating what he meant to say to Sinárr. But the moment he emerged from the ravine, the entirety of his carefully planned speech vanished.

He could barely comprehend what he saw.

Planets seemed to float in the sky—entire *worlds* encapsulated within the scope of his view. Hulking, ethereal forms, drifting and sometimes even overlapping each other, seeming to occupy the same space while existing instead on a different plane or in a different dimension of agreement.

The white bridge extended a hundred paces beyond the ravine mouth and then simply stopped. Tanis felt like he might step from the marble onto the roseate clouds and climb them to reach the closest hovering planet.

Sinárr came up behind him and placed his hands possessively on the lad's shoulders. Tanis supposed he was going to have to get used to the immortal always wanting to be in physical contact with him. Once, he'd considered it an uncomfortable sexual advance, but now that he understood better of their opposing natures, he saw that the connection Sinárr desired to have with him was simply tactile, not unlike a cat who insisted on sitting on your lap.

In fact, once Tanis thought of it, he realized that his relationship with Sinárr was quite like having a cat: they were of incompatible races, each party thought it was in charge, both approached the relationship from entirely different perspectives, yet each received some benefit in the exchange.

Tanis had only the barest glimpse of what he stood to gain as yet. But he'd seen what his parents were willing to sacrifice for his uncle's game. He gauged the path he'd chosen to be equally worth the risk.

Sinárr murmured close in his ear, "I got the impression you were ready for more…elaborate creation." He nodded towards the worlds hovering impossibly near, defying description, defying *explanation* by any natural laws. "These are other worlds I've made. I thought you might like to see them."

Tanis moved out of the Warlock's hold and turned to face him. "They're different from this one?"

He smiled. "Very."

"Why is this world so different from the others?"

Sinárr cast a thoughtful gaze into the sky. "This is Mérethe's world." A shadow of sorrow flickered across the Warlock's brow. "I'd hoped it would help her feel more at home."

Tanis thought it more likely it had made her miss Alorin more. Frowning slightly, the lad set off down the bridge at a meditative pace. Sinárr fell in beside him with his hands clasped behind his blood-red cloak.

Tanis glanced to the Warlock. "Mérethe said you sometimes keep her in the void."

Sinárr ached brows resignedly. "I cannot force her to see the illusions I make for her benefit."

"But actually you *could*, couldn't you?" When Sinárr made no reply to this, Tanis pressed, "You *could* force her to see anything you desired, since she's bound to you?"

Sinárr cast him a wry smile. "Very well, I *choose* not to."

"You *choose*..." Tanis shook his head, threw up his hands in a gesture of hopelessness and then looked exasperatedly at him. "Will I ever understand you?"

Sinárr appeared humorously baffled. "I confess my confusion at your confusion."

Tanis stopped and turned to face him. "Here's what I know: when I asked you not to dress me, I was applying the First Law of Patterning, *KNOW the effect you intend to create*. The First Law teaches that the moment you abdicate from a position of cause you open yourself to be made the effect of someone else's cause."

"A fascinating truth," Sinárr remarked with an appreciative smile.

"When you refused my request to make worlds the other day, when you said you had never allowed another to guide your intent, *you* were simply applying the First Law."

Sinárr eyed him amusedly. "I'm following your logic."

Tanis narrowed his eyes at him. "Here's my point, Sinárr: I know you didn't choose to let Mérethe see your world, or not, because of any respect for her own determinism."

Sinárr seemed injured by this assessment. "Tanis, I—"

"No, I understand this much about you." Tanis held up a hand to pause the Warlock's protest. "It's actually no criticism. I even compliment you, because I understand better now how you must surely view life. When you've lived an immortal existence, controlling every aspect of your universe—from the composition of the world to the color of the smallest plant upon it, and which in itself is *correct* application of the First Law—when this is all you've ever known, it would never even occur to you that another being should be allowed to decide things for themselves, and *especially* not one from a 'lesser race.'"

Sinárr arched a brow at him. "I perceive a sardonic hue in the color of your compliment."

Tanis gave him a smile and started walking the bridge again. "So why did you allow Mérethe that freedom?"

Sinárr eyed him uncertainly. Then he lifted his gaze towards the planets looming in front of them. "There is only so much pleasure to be gained in creation for oneself alone, Tanis." He angled the lad a sidelong glance. "Personal creation holds a supreme joy, yet there is reward too in sharing one's creation with another, in gaining their admiration or viewpoint, or as I hope to do with you, in forging a mutual creation."

Tanis stopped just shy of the end of the bridge. Leaning slightly out over the edge, he could see more clouds, more *worlds*, stacked up beneath him. The effect was dizzying.

Sinárr laid a hand on the wide marble railing and then trailed a finger along one grey-streaked vein. "I suppose even in my universe, there are some things I don't want to control." He gave Tanis a resigned smile. "Mérethe's appreciation of my creation, or lack thereof, is one of them."

Tanis knew of at least one other who fell into the same category of beings Sinárr didn't want to compel—*himself*. He was counting on it to make his plan work.

He inched closer to the edge of the bridge and stared past the tip of his boots into the endless vista of floating worlds, feeling metaphorically poised on the edge of several eternities. His mouth felt a bit dry, but he managed to say, "So…I have an idea of a way to do this."

Sinárr's arm brushed his own as the Warlock joined his side at the lip of the bridge. "I am yours for the asking, as they say."

Tanis turned to face him. "A mutual binding."

Sinárr shook his head. "Impossible. It requires both parties to be of the same fabric."

"Pelas and I are bound."

"So I suspected when you so easily contacted him in your dreams, but the Malorin'athgul are native to both fabrics: *elae* and *deyjiin*."

Sinárr seemed so certain of what he knew, yet Tanis felt equally sure, because the solution he'd landed on was the only answer that both resolved confusions and predicted phenomena. Sinárr's certainty, rather than disheartening Tanis, somehow strengthened his surety.

He flashed a smile. "Bear with me." Then he tried something he'd never attempted—at least not consciously.

He remembered being in the void and how he'd expanded his awareness outwards in a search for something solid. He'd eventually perceived what his disoriented mind had interpreted as the edges of space—some kind of framework of dimension. Now he knew that what he'd actually been perceiving were the starpoints—not of a single world, but of Sinárr's entire universe.

Tanis searched for those points again in that moment. He wasn't sure he'd be able to find them, but they came to him as soon as he cast his mind in search of them, as soon as he decided to *know*.

He expanded his mind to embrace Absolute Being, as taught by the Esoterics, making his own awareness large enough to encompass this vastly unknowable distance. Then, maintaining this larger awareness of the entire framework, he brought a part of his awareness back to his body.

Now feeling immensely larger than the meager space his body occupied,

Tanis placed one beam of his awareness on the end of the bridge and another beam on the mountain at his back. Then he *pressed* the two edges in opposite directions.

The bridge instantly lengthened from a hundred steps to over a mile in length.

Sinárr's lips spread in a slow, approving smile.

Tanis let go of the larger framework and returned his awareness to his body alone. He turned a look over his shoulder towards the mountains and found them much farther away than he'd expected. He couldn't be sure if he'd stretched the bridge by moving it outwards or if he'd held the bridge in place and moved the mountains away from it. He didn't have the clarity of perception to know which thing he'd changed, but he *had* achieved the end result he'd envisioned—the First Law, well applied.

Tanis placed his hand on the Warlock's chest. Immediately that resonance between them intensified. "Do you feel that?"

Sinárr gave him such a look. "You know that I do."

A smile flickered on the lad's lips. "What you feel, oh Maker of Worlds, is the third strand of *elae*."

Sinárr veritably hissed at him. "Tanis—" he took him by the shoulders.

Tanis took his in return, mirroring Sinárr's hold, effectively locking their forms together. "There are things *you* know, and there are things *I* know." Tanis looked him firmly in the eye so there could be no mistaking his meaning or his seriousness about it. "What you perceived in Mérethe, what drew you to her, and what you perceive in me—the trait she and I share—is *elae*'s third strand."

Sinárr looked mystified. "But you're a truthreader."

The flicker of a smile crossed Tanis's lips. "And a Healer, a Nodefinder…" his smile turned wry, "…a Wildling."

The Warlock searched his gaze in open astonishment. "You work all of these strands natively?"

"Yes."

"This is possible?"

"It's a rare variant trait." Resonance hummed between them as they stood locked in each other's hold. Tanis imagined he could see waves emitting through the aether. "I'm also trained as a wielder, and this has helped me understand the way you use energy and the other esoteric laws that you natively apply."

Sinárr held Tanis's gaze while he pondered his words, golden eyes serious. After a moment, he said, "Explain to me why Warlocks are unable to reach your world if we share a third-strand association."

Tanis released him and took a step back—the resonance was becoming distractingly intense. "No strand is so wildly variant as the third," he replied then, quoting his mother's teaching. "I have my theories as to why, and possibly you and I can test them together, but for now, what I know is that the third strand has certain patterns associated with it—as do all the strands—but unlike the other strands, third-strand patterns are only workable inside the realm of their genesis."

Sinárr shook his head slightly. "I fear I'm no longer following your logic."

Tanis exhaled slowly to ease both the humming sensation in his head as well as his apprehension over what he intended. "Assume I'm right and follow this train of thought with me: Mérethe cannot take the form outside of Alorin—correct?"

Sinárr looked surprised. "This is true. She shared this with you?"

"No, but it logically follows. Third-strand patterns are only workable inside the realm where they naturally evolved. The pattern that allows her to innately shift forms only works within Alorin, which is why she can take the form there but not in Shadow."

"She claims her association with *elae* has left her. I have sensed this withering of *elae's* light and her life."

"Hence your pact with Shail, so you could come and go from the realm at will."

Sinárr gave him an acknowledging nod.

"But Mérethe's connection to *elae* hasn't entirely eroded, else she couldn't take the form at all, and I saw her in Alorin in the form." Tanis stroked his forehead and frowned slightly. "See, I had it all backwards. I thought her trouble stemmed from being bound to you—*she* obviously thinks the same—when actually it's because you took her away from Alorin. The longer she's stayed beyond reach of the realm, the more her connection to *elae* is deteriorating."

"Tanis, this doesn't follow logically." Sinárr clasped hands behind his back and began to pace in an agitated fashion. "If the third strand is so weak outside of the realm, then how can this connection between us be so strong?"

Tanis walked to the other side of the bridge and leaned back against the railing, crossing his arms. "The third strand connects me to Alorin and attracts you to me, but the intensity we feel together, the resonance…" He was still trying to extrapolate the reason for the resonance.

Sinárr turned Tanis a look of focused concentration while he continued pacing. "Taking your argument as fact, my bond should've kept Mérethe's link to Alorin strong. Why has she withered?"

"Because she's an Avieth. Look, Sinárr," Tanis held up a hand to entreat his understanding, "all things in my world are formed of patterns. *Mérethe* is formed of patterns. Her life pattern has two halves—a human half and an Avieth half—but the Avieth half is natively associated with Alorin. When Mérethe departs Alorin, half of what she innately is remains in the realm of her birth."

Tanis smoothed a lock of hair back from his eyes and tried to capture Sinárr's brooding gaze. "Being third strand, Mérethe can survive on the ephemeral presence of the third strand in Shadow, but it's not enough to sustain her connection to Alorin. And your bond…I suspect your working only commands the human half of her."

Sinárr considered this deeply as he paced. Then he pressed his lips together and shook his head. "No…it still has holes, your theory." He spun in a sanguineous swirl and started pacing back in the other direction. "You claim the link that connects the three of us is the third strand. You claim it is too weak of a thread for Warlocks to follow back into the realm of its attachment."

He cast Tanis a speculative eye, deliberately dubious. "Let us pretend this is true—that the third is too weak to sustain you. Yet Adepts from other strands have perished within *hours* of coming to Shadow. They must be bound quickly lest they be lost. Do you take the position then that the other strands in your native composition are sustaining *you* as the sole exception?"

"No, Sinárr." Tanis exhaled a measured breath. "I can survive here because I'm bound to a Malorin'athgul."

Sinárr stopped and stared at him. Then he sat down on the opposite railing and frowned deeply instead.

Tanis stood up. "I can see your starpoints innately because I'm third strand, like you." He slowly crossed the distance between them. "And I can make changes to your world—even with such little understanding of Shadow—because I'm a wielder trained in the manifestations of energy." He stopped in front of the astonished Warlock. "And for all of these reasons, and countless others, I would bind myself to you, Sinárr, if you would equally bind yourself to me."

"Tanis…" Sinárr shook his head slowly, holding the lad's gaze, "it has never been done."

"Do you fear it?"

The Warlock cracked a smile. "I more have no idea how to accomplish it, but I admit a certain apprehension."

Tanis arched a brow. "Why?"

Sinárr stood to better meet his challenging gaze—or rather, to stare down at him, for he was a head taller than the lad—but his eyes were dancing with a sort of dark promise. He fingered the placket on Tanis's coat with a smile hinting on his lips. "Bound to a reckless wielder?"

"Reckless?" Tanis protested.

Sinárr gave him a telling look. "You did not see the results of your last working in Shail's temple that night. Many *eidola* remain buried beneath the mountain."

Tanis had almost forgotten about his desperate attempt to escape Shail or die trying. "Oh…right."

Sinárr stepped closer to Tanis, a looming shadow with eyes of golden light. "But I do not think you make this proposition to me so cavalierly as you would have me believe." He trailed his hand down the lapel of Tanis's coat while leveling a beacon gaze upon the lad. "What is the rest of it?"

Tanis reminded himself that for all he found the cloak of boldness a better fit than timidity, he was throwing down his gauntlet before an immortal who could crush him with a thought. His only real defense was Sinárr's innate sense of restraint.

He had to work some moisture back into his mouth. "A binding between Adepts is a troth."

Sinárr still had hold of the cloth of his coat and was stroking it with his thumb. "So I've been told."

"A promise to each other and to each other's causes."

Sinárr lifted his gaze to meet Tanis's. "And what is this cause you would bind me to, through you?"

Tanis took a deep breath. "The protection of the Realms of Light from any who seek to harm them."

Sinárr gave a deep and haunting chuckle. He looked Tanis over again with a hungering gaze. "I accept."

Tanis gulped a swallow.

"But you knew that I would," Sinárr eyed his discomfiture amusedly, "for I've already told you I would go to any lengths to bind with you." The Warlock ran his hand over Tanis's shoulder and down his arm, his manner both predatory and possessive. "And if you're wrong, and no third-strand link exists…" his hand closed around Tanis's arm while his gaze bound the lad's attention like the sun binding a planet to its orbit, "…we have a troth, regardless."

"Yes," Tanis scraped out.

Sinárr released him. "This is a pleasing arrangement." He clasped hands behind his back and stepped out over the abyss. The bridge lengthened to receive his lowering foot.

Beset by a sudden hollow and nervous energy, Tanis watched the Warlock striding away. "There's one more thing I would ask."

Sinárr eyed him over his shoulder. "We've already concluded our accord."

"This isn't a condition, Sinárr, it's a request."

"Very well, Tanis. Make your appeal."

Tanis watched him strolling on, taking each step as if into nothing, only to find the marble bridge beneath his foot when it landed. "Return Mérethe to Alorin."

Sinárr stilled.

Tanis slowly walked down the bridge to join him. "Mérethe isn't *eidola*. If you return her to Alorin and release her from your bond, she may yet recover her connection to *elae*."

Sinárr frowned deeply at this. "And if she does not?"

"She'll die a natural death."

"Or so you believe." Sinárr searched his gaze, looking troubled by the prospect. "You've spoken to her about this?"

"Yes. I didn't ask her about severing her bond with you, but there's little chance she'll regain her connection with *elae* unless you release her from it, because while it once tied you to Alorin, it certainly still ties her to Shadow."

"And you believe this is draining her due to her Avieth nature."

Tanis nodded.

The Warlock sank into a thoughtful silence. Then he exhaled a slow breath. "I will put the offer to her, but now let us proceed with our collaboration. I've enjoyed the tantalizing promise of you long enough." He moved towards Tanis.

The lad pushed a hand hastily against Sinárr's chest. "I need *elae* to work my side of the binding."

Sinárr frowned at this.

Tanis shook his head to deny the things the Warlock was thinking. "We trust each other now or never."

Sinárr looked the lad over, tasting him with his eyes. "You are a prodigious creature. Very well, I will give you access to *elae* and trust that you won't use it to try to escape me, but..." he arched a curious brow, "have you any idea how to forge this connection? A Warlock and a mortal have never been mutually bound."

"I have an idea of how to begin." Tanis tried not to think on what would happen if he was wrong. "For the rest...?" he shrugged.

Sinárr radiated a sort of dark admiration. "You gamble everything on a guess."

"The greater the risk, the greater the reward." Tanis wished he felt more comfortable with those odds.

The Warlock chuckled. "Your mouth says one thing and your expression quite another. Come then, let's see which of us your Cephrael will serve."

"If I do this right, He'll serve us both." Tanis braced himself mentally for what was to come and blew out an explosive breath. "Give me your hand."

Looking amused, Sinárr placed his hand into Tanis's palm. Tanis knew the Warlock thought he would fail in his attempt. He just wished Sinárr didn't have to act so smug about it.

In the next moment, Tanis felt a shift, like a window opening in the frame of Sinárr's universe, and *elae* flooded in. Tanis closed his eyes and let the lifeforce's warmth wash over him, *into* him. He reveled in the exquisite sensation of fullness after so many barren days, like a withered plant restored of vitality by a hearty watering.

With *elae's* return, Tanis instantly perceived Pelas's mind again. Reaching him would've been as simple as a thought; yet while the urge to contact Pelas was instinctive and strong, Tanis knew it wasn't yet time for their paths to rejoin.

Still holding Sinárr's hand in his, the lad opened his eyes and drew his dagger—*wait, dagger?*—and before the Warlock could wonder at it, he'd pulled the Merdanti tip across Sinárr's palm.

Red blood welled against black skin. Tanis cut his own palm across his own earlier, still-healing scar. Then he mashed his hand into the Warlock's and met Sinárr's gaze. "Open your mind to me."

A flicker of uncertainty crossed the Warlock's brow. "Tanis…you don't know what you're asking."

Tanis forced the thought insistently across to him, *Open your mind to me as mine is open to you, or we can't forge this binding.*

Perhaps it was the tone of Tanis's mental command, or perhaps the fourth flooding into him gave additional weight to his request, but Sinárr shook his head and complied, albeit with a *don't say I didn't warn you* look.

Then Tanis perceived—

Dear Epiphany…

Had he not already conceived of the plane of Chaos through his connection to Pelas—and what a mind-altering experience *that* had proven to be—the vastness of a mind linked to Shadow might've overwhelmed him, even to the point of madness. Sinárr had been right to caution him on this course.

Tanis saw the space Sinárr had framed—an immense, unknowable distance of *galactic* proportions, encompassing entire solar systems—yet Sinárr's universe became but a speck of dust compared to Shadow's infinity. The mortal mind couldn't conceive of so much space with *absolutely nothing* in it.

Tanis felt immeasurably miniscule against such an enormity of nonexistence. The weight of it pressed powerfully against his consciousness. He felt himself shrinking beneath it, dwindling into insignificance, as if the empty space was the Divine All and him, nothing…

No disappearing on me now, Tanis… Sinárr's amused voice recalled him as a wayward kite, reeling him rapidly back from an oblivion of unbeing. *You'll not escape this binding so easily as that.*

Sinárr drew Tanis's consciousness back within his own universe, and Tanis once again perceived the Warlock's starpoints framing space. They anchored and reoriented him. Tanis regained his equilibrium and managed a smile. *Nor you, Sinárr.*

The Warlock nodded accommodatingly. *Let us proceed then.*

Tanis shook off the lingering sensation of unbeing and focused back on his task. His foray into Shadow's void had at least shown him that no energy existed outside of the space the Warlock himself had framed. Which meant he'd been wrong in one of his conclusions, but he still believed he was right overall. He would just have to seek the third strand elsewhere than Shadow's void.

Blood is the catalyst…forming a bond of connection…

With his mother's words as a guide, Tanis dove into the first strand and followed its course, curious as to what he would find. He'd been taught that *deyjiin* was a consumptive power and antipathetic to life and *elae*. Yet Tanis had seen Sinárr create universes with *deyjiin*, and it obviously sustained him the way *elae* sustained Adepts.

Tanis let his awareness drift upon the strands of the first.

Without currents to pull the energy along established channels, *elae* drifted and coalesced according to its own attractive properties. Tanis sank into the energy, letting it curl and undulate around him, and assessed everything he perceived.

He soon observed that his life energy and the Warlock's mingled, even seemed to somehow embrace the other's particles, yet couldn't combine.

But where is the third?

Every strand of *elae* had a unique aspect to its energy: the fifth was elemental, the second kinetic, and so on. Scholars had been warring over the nature of the 'wildly variant' third strand for eons. But Tanis had developed his own theory. He suspected it had something to do with time.

Time, which binds everything and nothing. Time, which exists only as the rate of change or the rate of energy decay. Time, which exists only in our perception because we have decided that things should endure.

If this theory was correct, however, Tanis knew the likelihood of finding a trace of the third strand without the currents of *elae* to channel it was slim to none. This presented a problem, because unless he could find the third strand as a connecting point between himself and Sinárr, he had no way of pinning *elae* to the Warlock, no way of binding Sinárr to him.

Tanis returned his attention to the swirling energies. He watched them embrace and separate, even as he and Sinárr were so often doing.

Interestingly, this was not the way *deyjiin* appeared in Alorin, where it became destructive, unbalanced. But in Shadow, the two energies were exhibiting an obvious sympathetic attraction.

Was he seeing *elae* and *deyjiin* in their truest forms, or some other expression of their innate properties?

Either way, the vacuum of Shadow proved that the two energies—his and Sinárr's—weren't inherently antithetical, merely...opposing. He watched, intrigued, as the undulating tendrils of each energy reached out, swirled together as if to combine, and then sped away, alternately attracted and repulsed.

The lad's eyes widened. His mind leapt to a sudden understanding.

They're magnetizing and repelling.

Revitalized of hope by this realization, Tanis thought again of himself and Sinárr, of their opposing, innate energies that attracted them to each other and then pushed them apart, and of the resonance that built up between them when they were grounded in close proximity.

He considered how Sinárr's starpoints framed space, and added to this the understanding that Shadow held no energy in its vast expanse; the energy only existed within the space that a Warlock had framed. Whereupon, putting all of these facts together, Tanis saw...

He *saw*.

His eyes flew to Sinárr's, and he cast forth the thought, *Bind me to you.*

Needing no prodding to do something he'd wanted all along, Sinárr growled lustfully and wrapped his power around Tanis. Bands of cold energy enveloped the lad's mind. Suddenly he was spinning and bobbing within an enveloping cocoon, all concentration momentarily lost to the disorienting concert of binding threads.

No...not threads. Bands—*sheets* of energy enfolding, twirling him as if he was the spool around which they wound, until he felt them constricting tightly, binding thought within their space.

Tanis recognized immediately that the Warlock's binding was not compulsion, it was simply control. Sinárr now framed the context of Tanis's awareness and could shape it how he would, as he willed.

Tanis still held *elae* within this cocoon, but only because Sinárr allowed it. The lad knew that he existed now at the whim of this immortal, that his every thought might be directed at his command; indeed, he hardly felt that *he* existed anymore at all. It was as though Sinárr had absorbed him into his own consciousness.

And he knew unequivocally that this would be his state of existence from that moment to the end of his days unless he could find a way to equally bind Sinárr to him.

Panic began fluttering at the horror of this possibility, distracting Tanis from his task; yet the lad ultimately still held hope. Sinárr's mind remained open to him, and while the Warlock was undeniably thrilled to have Tanis finally bound to him, he was also waiting patiently to see what Tanis would do with it. Tanis himself still held *elae*. In all, Sinárr had only done what Tanis had asked of him.

With a grave effort of concentration, Tanis pushed off the sense of peril that had accompanied Sinárr's binding and focused instead on the idea that had spurred him to request it.

'*You gamble everything on a guess....*'

Sinárr had never spoken anything more true.

In their first foray into Shadow together, Sinárr had told him that to create anything, it was necessary first to frame space. Tanis knew that he would need to find Sinárr's starpoints if he meant to work any kind of binding on the Warlock. Accordingly, he sought an awareness of those points, as he'd done earlier, but the binding Sinárr had laid on his mind resisted his attempts to penetrate it.

'*When embracing Absolute Being, a wielder permeates...*'

His father had filled an entire journal on Absolute Being. With Arion's teachings guiding him, Tanis imagined himself becoming porous. Instead of attempting to penetrate, he let his mind *permeate* the cocoon of power. He *became* it wholly, until he knew every aspect of its construction...and then he *expanded* through it.

Beyond it. Into the open space of Sinárr's universe.

Excitement hummed through the lad.

Free now of Sinárr's mental binding, yet still very aware of its existence, Tanis sought Sinárr's starpoints. Instantly he regained them and assumed the observation point from which Sinárr himself observed his own universe; Tanis now held a bird's eye view from the edge of space.

Or to put things in his father's preferred analogy: he had a view of the entire game board.

From this broad context of Absolute Being, Tanis looked down on himself and the Warlock, but rather than seeing their fleshly bodies, he saw them as terminals of energy linked by a conduit formed of threads of power—Sinárr's binding.

An exultant grin split the lad's face, for he found what he'd been seeking—*finally*.

And he'd been right.

When Sinárr had woven the link between himself and Tanis, he'd forged the bond and *willed that it would endure*. Thus, within the energy Sinárr himself had made, he'd forged a link of the third strand.

Time.

Tanis knew how to work his own binding now.

First, he permeated Sinárr's starpoints and duplicated them with his own energy, essentially creating his own points in the same space. In Alorin, two energies couldn't occupy the same space, but Shadow wasn't subject to the same physical laws as those that bound the Realms of Light.

Holding his starpoints in coincidence with Sinárr's own, Tanis wove the fourth strand through the conduit Sinárr had created and bound the Warlock's mind, even as Sinárr had bound his.

And the working stuck.

Sinárr's eyes widened. *What is this you do?* He searched the lad's gaze while mentally resisting his binding.

Tanis grinned at him. *I'm keeping our accord. Now stop resisting me.*

Sinárr's jaw dropped open. *I did not think it could be done!*

Tanis smiled drily. *That was apparent.*

He continued on then, weaving his binding into and through the one that Sinárr had initially forged. Having permeated the latter, he knew its construction wholly and was able to easily mirror that construction using *elae*.

This was not the unbreakable reweaving of life patterns that Tanis had worked with Pelas, though his binding with Sinárr would also endure, because he and Sinárr had both willed permanence into the pattern using the third strand.

Whereupon it struck Tanis all over again: *the third strand is Time!*

The lad shook his head, marveling at this truth. The monumental fact that he was forging a mutual binding with a Warlock of Shadow seemed a somehow miniscule feat compared to the excitement of proving his own theory correct.

As Tanis laid the last binding band of his working, he felt the pattern become complete. It was a sudden recognition, a sort of *knowingness* that a pattern had been made into an integral whole. In its own way, forging a unique pattern into being was giving life to something new, for as soon as the final strand of the pattern connected to its beginning, energy started channeling through it to achieve the effect the wielder had intended.

The moment the pattern was whole, it woke in both Tanis and Sinárr's awarenesses. Suddenly Tanis and Sinárr were occupying the same mental space *as equals*. The lad could conceive *deyjiin* as the Warlock did: malleable and ready for shaping.

Deyjiin felt cool while *elae* felt warm; the former held a sort of *roundness*...the way lard made a soup taste creamier. *Deyjiin* had less form than *elae*—mist to *elae's* water—but it would be an electrified mist full of charged particles. Whereas *elae* might be channeled voluminously to fill an eternity of space, Tanis got the sense that each individual particle of *deyjiin* might itself expand to an infinity.

Tanis.

He heard his name on multiple wavelengths and focused his gaze back on Sinárr.

The Warlock looked utterly fascinated. *Do you see? Do you feel this?*

Tanis had been so distracted by the sensation of *deyjiin* that he hadn't noticed the power building up around them. Now he assumed Sinárr's perspective and saw what he was seeing: themselves as two terminals of differing potential, each holding itself apart from the other—and *generating power between them.*

Suddenly they no longer stood on the marble bridge. They no longer *stood* anywhere. Tanis sensed they were now floating in the void, with Sinárr's universe moved …elsewhere. The Warlock was moving them through the raw energy their bond was generating, diving down through a mist of charged particles that Tanis perceived easily yet couldn't actually see. It was…odd…and at the same time exhilarating.

Did you know this would happen, Tanis?

Tanis smiled—or at least, he thought he was smiling. Perhaps it was simply the thought of smiling, conveyed in an instant. *I suspected.*

Sinárr shifted them with a thought. Suddenly they stood within the starry universe with nothing beneath their feet, yet with a sense of orientation. The Warlock was standing with his arms lifted and nebular clouds of voluminous power surrounding him.

"I don't know if you can yet perceive this energy on the level I have seen." Sinárr dropped his arms and looked at Tanis. "The particles are bonded."

Tanis felt heady. "As we are bonded?"

"Much in that way, yes. The particles display a symbiotic affinity—even, one might say, akin to the affinity that exists between you and me."

Tanis grinned. "Intriguing."

Sinárr's eyes narrowed. "You are not at all surprised. How did you know?" *How could you know when I did not?*

"It's because of this." Tanis took Sinárr's hand in his own. This sealed their connection and forced their energies to magnetize and repel and the resonance to build exponentially. A standing wave of energy started blasting around them in a circular flow.

Ironic that he'd been so apprehensive of this sensation before he understood it, so fearful of the feeling of attraction. The resonance had been showing him the solution all along.

He lifted his gaze to the swirling power, grateful to have hold of Sinárr's hand to ground him amid such intensity. It wasn't that they produced more energy through their physical contact; Tanis could simply perceive the energy more clearly now.

"When you place two energy-producing terminals of differing potential in proximity but hold them apart, a flow will occur between them. It became apparent to me what was happening when I realized that Shadow had no energy of its own, only the energy *you* created and *placed into* the space you framed. It followed then that your starpoints were of differing potentials and that's how they were generating energy."

Sinárr shook his head. "Incredible. I've never encountered a mortal who works Shadow so innately."

Tanis smiled and moved slightly away—it was hard to breathe when they stood so close together. He lifted a contemplative gaze to the stars. "I suspected that the third strand was extant here, but what I didn't realize was that you *created* it—" he turned a look back to Sinárr, "you generate the third strand of *elae* when you decide things shall have permanence."

Sinárr arched brows. "I worked *elae*." He sounded dubious.

Tanis grinned. "Be as skeptical as you like, Sinárr, but we're mutually bound. How else can you explain it?"

"Mutually bound." A possessive sort of fascination burned in Sinárr's gaze. "And you've done what you promised—more than you promised, for this is not simply a connection to Alorin, I *feel elae* through your awareness. It is…warm."

"As *deyjiin* feels cool in my mind."

Sinárr placed a hand on Tanis's shoulder, causing again that heady resonance which he craved and the lad endured, and lifted his gaze to the clouds of static power that were continuing to accumulate around them. "This energy between us is unique. I've never seen its like."

Reeling a little, yet exhilarated also, Tanis focused his gaze back on Sinárr. "I think there's just one thing left to do."

The Warlock looked inquiringly to him. "Which is?"

Tanis smiled. "To see what we can create with it."

THIRTY-EIGHT

"It's not work to him. It's a form of art."
—Dagmar Ranneskjöld, Second Vestal of Alorin,
on Björn van Gelderan and the game

Ean walked the streets of Tambarré as dawn was lighting a fire in the eastern sky. Golden rays flamed the clouds, turning the heavens into a riot of dark violet and rose. With the break of day, the city was rousing—shopkeepers unlatching shutters, flower-sellers opening their stalls; the souks were quickly coming alive, likewise the city streets.

That dream where he'd confronted the Enemy and witnessed Arion's death had convinced Ean that learning the truth of Arion's ruin was the only way he'd ever regain all of his talent…the only way he'd ever feel whole; but sitting around waiting for Epiphany or Fate to bestow the knowledge upon him in a divinely inspired dream or a fragmented moment…it seemed as likely as a donkey winning a horserace.

In Tyr'kharta, it was *action* that had restored Arion's knowledge to him. Likewise in Tal'Afaq, and even at Ivarnen. During those times, Ean had assumed it was Isabel's faith in him that had allowed him to pierce the veil of memory, but now he saw it had simply been necessity driving action… action fueling necessity.

Necessity was certainly pushing him now. He felt the sting of its whip with every step he took upon this course of intent, which seemed to have nothing directly to do with their game and yet somehow everything to do with it.

He was nervously trusting to that whispering voice, trusting even more to the pattern of cause and consequence he'd glimpsed the night before.

By sticking to his choices, he was also trusting his instincts. They would either lead him to doom or deliverance, but he'd committed himself to their course as Arion had always done—with an unwavering determination to walk the path to its end.

Or so he kept telling himself. At the moment, unwavering determination was feeling a lot like misgiving.

As Ean observed yet another sunrise, the prince reflected that he couldn't remember the last time he'd slept...or at least the last time he'd slept more than a few hours. Lately, his waking moments of dullness often felt more restful than his sleeping nights—that is, when sleep came at all—but exhaustion was admittedly taking its toll. The days had started blurring together in an ever-lengthening haze; his mind often felt woolly, his thinking muddled. He repeatedly drew upon *elae's* first strand to stay alert.

Fortunately, his feet seemed to know where to go. He walked an uninterrupted path of purpose beneath the *al-qasr's* arching gates—as the whisper promised, the guards manning the mighty portal merely looked past him, unseeing—until he reached the base of the stairs leading up the side of the acropolis. There, Ean lifted his gaze towards the crowning temples at the summit. Somewhere among those impressive structures, Darshan would be waiting.

That whispering voice—so polite, so *compelling*—leaned again to advise, *Hurry now and you could be standing over him before he wakes. The first moment he learns of you will be as you're holding your blade to his neck.*

Before him, a thousand limestone steps notched the mountain, stone waterfalls cascading through terraced gardens. Ean was deliberating which way to go when the doors of a nearby domed structure opened and a procession of acolytes emerged.

Quickly! Over there.

Ean followed the voice's direction and ducked into a cellar stairwell. He watched from cool cement shadows as the acolytes went by, each one carrying a deep basket filled with bread, fruit or vegetables. Ean perceived the silvery imprint of patterns as the procession passed. He couldn't tell if the patterns lay upon each man, the baskets or the food, but he had no time to investigate the mystery, for that whisper urged him on.

As he climbed the stairs, trusting the whisper's instructions to keep him away from undue notice, Ean watched acolytes with downcast eyes scurrying between temples and along terraces like mist fleeing the dawn. They appeared even more fervent to avoid anyone's notice than Ean was.

Bethamin's Ascendants—notable for their shaven and tattooed heads as much as the befouling trails they left on the currents—led streams of cowed adjuncts and scribes, or moved together in smoggy processionals.

Occasionally during Ean's long climb, the morning sun would dim as a grey cloud passed—the silk-shrouded forms of the Prophet's Marquiin, all of them radiating death.

As the whisper promised, Ean moved unnoticed through this inclement populace, but he grew increasingly ill at ease, mostly from observing the patterns that clouded the currents in a perpetual overcast.

When he'd unworked the pattern binding the Marquiin to the Prophet all those months ago, he'd been newly Awakened and hardly understood what he was seeing. Now, he saw too keenly: every person had patterns wrapped about them. Thorny, twisted patterns, they drew the darkest versions of *elae*, mutating what might've been used for good into some vile intent.

The patterns that enwrapped the Marquiin were fourth-strand compulsion woven through with *deyjiin*—corruptive *and* corrosive. Ean knew instinctively that those Adepts would die from this slow poison. Almost worse were the patterns tattooed on the Ascendants. *Those* he couldn't even decipher.

The closer Ean came to the summit, the more destabilized he felt by the currents washing down from the high temples. They carried a rotten stench, like the slimiest bog, rank with dying things.

In Tal'Afaq, the currents had been riotous from the pulsating metamorphosis of men transforming into monsters; Ean had plowed through those thrashing waves on a course of righteous indignation. But this…this was like swimming a sea of excrement, thick with the sludge of debased acts.

Ean couldn't imagine living there—he couldn't imagine anyone *sleeping* there—and especially not truthreaders, who were innately sensitive to the currents of thought. What a hellish nightmare they must've been enduring, even the ones who'd been spared Bethamin's corruptive Fire.

Ean thought about Kjieran van Stone. What courage the man had possessed, walking into this hellhole! He wondered where Kjieran was now—had Raine's working helped him survive Bethamin's Fire? What had become of that brave soul?

The whisper in Ean's head led him to another staircase that angled steeply upwards. On he climbed, baking in the sun's rising heat. A thousand stairs seemed too kind an estimate—they certainly were not kind to his legs. His body ached with exhaustion, his lungs felt raw, and his injured thigh burned. Every one of the thousand times he put his weight on that leg, he cursed Sheih and her *mor'alir* dagger.

The sun was a painfully bright disk hovering directly in front of his eyes when Ean at last reached the summit. He headed for the shade of a grove of eucalyptus trees and sank down behind one of their wide trunks, reaching for his water flask while he caught his breath.

The whisper urged him to hurry.

He was starting to loathe that whisper; even starting to wonder if it was his own mind playing tricks on him—or perhaps more germane to his current condition, if he was losing his wits from lack of sleep. Nonetheless, the whisper's gnawing insistence soon pushed him on again. Ean leaned against the tree and pocketed his flask while he assessed the lay of the Prophet's domain.

Three main temples dominated the acropolis. The largest, central temple was multi-tiered, with many open-air galleries; its highest levels must've offered a commanding view—perhaps all the way to the coast. The temple closest to Ean loomed nearly as large but not as airy, more closely resembling a ziggurat. Its central chamber hosted tall, leaded windows.

Further along the acropolis on its eastern edge, an arcade of arches separated the first two temples from a third. A crenellated tower on the edge of this temple overlooked terraced gardens, which both surrounded and cascaded down the eastern end of the acropolis. The latter temple seemed cloistered, private. Ean felt sure that he was looking upon the Prophet's personal dwelling.

He made his fourth-strand pattern more solid and started off.

This way... Ean followed the whisper's direction to the north side of the acropolis and a path—more goat track than trail—that twined among the orchards growing there.

Thalma's fortuitous eye had traveled with him thus far that morning, but as Ean was passing beneath the largest central temple, Lady Luck turned her gaze towards more interesting fare, and he came upon an apricot orchard flooded with workers. The whisper urged him to ignore them, that they would ignore him in return, but Ean doubted he could fool so many people at once.

Exhaustion clung to him as sweat, and a dull fogginess permeated his thoughts. As he stood staring at the workers uneasily, Ean realized he would have to find another way inside.

High above him, a strip of road hugged the acropolis's stony edge. Unlike the crowded orchard, no one was walking that road. Likewise open and empty lay the promenade of arches leading to the Prophet's residence. Both routes would offer less natural cover, but under the circumstances, they seemed more inviting options.

Ean backtracked and made his way up a footpath to the road, much in defiance of that whispering voice. But he'd begun feeling like the whisper boded of a madness associated with fatigue, and he worried over giving it any more sway. The whisper was practically shouting at him by the time he reached the road, but he clenched his teeth and shoved its warnings aside—

That's when he felt the pattern.

Too late. He sensed it as he was stepping through it. His foot came down on the road, and alarm bells rang from one end of the acropolis to the other.

The whisper swore at him.

Equally swearing at his own lack of foresight—was he not walking in Dore Madden's own domain?—Ean summoned a shield of the fifth and made a desperate dash for the Prophet's residence. Dore's creatures would likely soon be hunting for him, but perhaps not within the Prophet's own chambers, or at least not right away.

As he ran, the prince drew more strongly on the first strand to restore his energies and powered his running steps with the second. In moments, he was plunging into the Prophet's temple.

This way…

The Prophet's residence was far larger inside than it appeared from without, with multiple galleries opening onto each other and numerous chambers that all looked the same. Ean would've been quickly lost without the whisper guiding him.

Elsewhere on the acropolis, men and Marquiin moved rapidly about—Ean could sense the motion of many upon the currents—but the deep chambers of the Prophet's residence possessed a deathly quiet. Even the alarms hardly disturbed the mausoleum silence.

You see…he won't even know you're coming.

Ean had decided that he must be hallucinating…except that the whisper did seem to know its way around the temple. Indeed, a small voice in the back of Ean's mind warned that this whisper knew *too* much, but the two ideas wouldn't quite connect.

Though the whisper urged him to hurry, Ean paused at the atrium floor and searched for patterns and traps, but Dore Madden clearly held no sway there in the Prophet's inner sanctum.

The longer he studied the currents, in fact, the more puzzled Ean became. Elsewhere on the acropolis, the currents had been either choppy with friction or sluggish from the excrement of vile patterns. He'd expected the currents to grow more riotous the closer he got to Darshan, but there he stood inside the Prophet's primary domain, and the currents were strangely…neutral. Ean had no idea what to make of it.

COME NOW.

The voice, no longer a whisper, speared Ean's consciousness as a cold stiletto of command. He went without a second thought.

When next he became aware of where he was, he was standing in a large hall, facing a wall of arches open to the morning breeze and with no idea of how he'd gotten there. A vast gallery spread away to his left, its tall ceilings supported by columns inscribed with patterns unreadable to him.

And walking towards him between two columns...

Ean startled to full awareness with a mental jerk, like the snapping of fingers rouses a dazed man. He stood at first utterly bemused, and then, as understanding dawned, his entire body came alive with painful needles of dread.

Compulsion.

Now he understood that uncanny whisper, the quiet directions, the urgency. *Darshan* had been compelling him all the way from the Lower City—even since that very moment when their minds had touched as Ean had been destroying the *eidola*.

He saw the truth so easily now! Yet while Darshan had been cradling him within the thrall of his will, Ean had suspected nothing. He hadn't been *capable* of suspecting anything; his mind had simply slipped around illogic like water over a rock. And the most frightening part of all was seeing that the Malorin'athgul had compelled his activity through naught but a tenuous connection from *miles* away!

Ean managed a dry swallow and started walking backwards, retreating from Darshan's advance. Forgotten were his thoughts of vengeance for Isabel, or for his loyal men made into *eidola*. Ean forgot everything before the man approaching him.

"Ean val Lorian..." Darshan's voice enwrapped Ean, darkly liquid and formless, but infused with intent, "we meet at last." He came towards Ean wearing an open robe of black silk, and carried a dark scepter, angled low. He must've stood nearly seven feet tall.

His features had that statuesque quality common to the fifth-strand immortal races, but harder, broader, with a squared chin and sharply defined cheekbones. Wavy ebony hair fell long down his back, and his gaze was very, very dark. "I have long wanted to meet the man who claims the lives of my *eidola* with such disregard."

Ean continued his retreat, but for his every step backwards, Darshan seemed to advance two. The prince instinctively made his shield of the fifth more solid, yet he wondered at the same time why he was bothering to shield himself at all. The fifth-strand currents rolled before Darshan as off the prow of a ship. Giant waves engulfed Ean and passed on, leaving him shaken.

By Cephrael's Great Book! How had he gotten himself into this? *More importantly, how in Tiern'aval are you going to get out of it?*

All this time, he'd held an idea in the back of his mind that Isabel should've just taken care of Darshan when they'd met at Ivarnen and saved him the trouble; but the man in the flesh commanded so much more power than Ean had imagined.

Isabel had been right to caution him. He would need every scrap of power he could muster—every possible understanding of his gifts—if he meant to fight this immortal. At the moment, he was woefully ill-prepared.

"Have you nothing to say?" Darshan spun his scepter at his side. He was barely ten paces from Ean now.

A frantic need to escape kept hauling at Ean, ropes of desperation yanking him in every direction except the one aligned with Darshan's approach. Yet he stood rooted.

Shade and darkness!

That time he perceived the compulsion that was forcing him to remain in place—verily, the Malorin'athgul had lassoed him like a steer—but he didn't know how to counteract the working. He could see no patterns, which meant that Darshan was working his compulsion innately.

No, not just innately. As though it was its own strand of the lifeforce.

Darshan stopped about five paces away, his gaze unremitting. Ean realized the man was truly expecting a response to his question.

The prince's skull felt full of wool, his thoughts muddled. He sensed Darshan's mental hand still clutched around his mind, and beneath all else, like the constant clanging of a distant bell, instinct screaming in warning.

Ean did his best to gather his wits under these conditions. "Why did you bring me here?"

Darshan cradled his scepter in muscled arms. "It seems to me you brought yourself here, Prince of Dannym."

"At your behest…" Ean mentally tried to pry his consciousness out of Darshan's mental fist, but succeeded only in minor resistance, "by your compulsion. But to what end?"

Darshan twirled his scepter and starting walking a circle around Ean. "Many moons ago, you severed my connection with one of my Marquiin." An arctic gaze swept Ean, scouring him in a chilling inspection. "Tell me how."

"I unworked the pattern binding him to you—" Ean choked. The words had come without thought to shape them, commanded off a tongue no longer under his control.

As he walked, Darshan clasped hands behind his back and held his scepter between them. He had the manner of a man used to his will going unquestioned. "You *unworked* the pattern." He cast Ean a sidelong look. "Do you mean to say you unmade it?"

"You could call it that." Ean stared at him with his jaw clenched, turning his head as Darshan continued his slow circling. Somehow he had to get free of his mental binding, but first he had to figure out how the man was crafting it.

Hands behind his back, Darshan tapped his scepter against his palm. The slightest tightening of his gaze indicated the speculative nature of his thoughts. "You do on this plane what we do in Chaos?"

What was it in his tone? Not disbelief, surely, for Ean could no more lie to him than he could prevent him stealing the words off his tongue.

"This craft is innate to you?"

"Yes."

Darshan arched a brow. "What other tricks come innately to you?"

Ean clenched his jaw, but still the answer ran headlong into the spear of Darshan's will. "I can see patterns."

Darshan continued his slow circle, scepter tapping in time with his steps. "All kinds of patterns?" He turned him a sudden, piercing stare. "*My* patterns?"

Ean ground his teeth. "Patterns of *elae*." Fighting the compulsion only made him ill and did nothing to stop the words from leaving his mouth. It felt like the answer that time had been ripped out of his gut with a longshoreman's hook.

It seemed the pinnacle of irony that Arion had always been writing his brilliant ideas in those damned journals for posterity, and not a one of them lay to hand for Ean's use now.

So be brilliant again.

It couldn't have been Isabel actually speaking to him, not with Darshan crouching so predatorily over his mind, but her imagined voice encouraged him all the same. Ean forced himself to stop thinking about the shark with its teeth sunken into the back of his skull and tried to come up with some useful ideas for escape.

If you can't see the pattern, what can *you do?*

Well…whether or not he could see the pattern, if *elae* was being channeled through it, then at least a trace of the pattern should be found on the currents.

Find its path. Follow it.

He'd done it before when he'd intuited the pattern of his own talent to give to Sebastian. But *how* had he done it? The moment had been so instinctive…

Darshan completed his circle and arrived in front of Ean once more, still twirling his scepter at his side. Ean noted the stone and realized the scepter was Merdanti.

"I've never heard of an Adept with abilities such as yours." The statement held a leading edge, demanding explanation; likewise the sharp skepticism in Darshan's gaze.

Ean's tongue again offered an answer without consulting him first. "They're common only to Adepts of the fifth."

"The fifth." Darshan looked him over critically. "A fabled strand."

Ean stared defiantly back at him. "As fabled as you and me."

Darshan arched a brow at this.

Ean held the Malorin'athgul's gaze, but mentally the prince was splitting his mind, portioning off a segment for his own uninterrupted use. He only hoped Darshan wouldn't miss the small bit he was claiming for himself.

Arion had been expert at this mental segmentation. He'd had to be to manage so many simultaneous workings—sometimes as many as a dozen different patterns at once, all of them layered with form. Arion had learned to compartment his mind into five lesser minds, or twenty smaller still; yet with a talent such as his, he could accomplish with one twentieth of his mind what baffled the full abilities of most.

Darshan was twirling his scepter in one hand like a waterwheel turning the millstone of his thoughts. "Who else shares your skills?"

This question hit Ean with a pang of dismay. He sealed his lips and clenched his jaw. *He would not—would not—would not—*

"Björn van Gelderan."

Damn you to thirteen hells! Ean wasn't sure in that moment if he was cursing himself or the Malorin'athgul.

"Björn van Gelderan…" Darshan's gaze narrowed. He twirled his staff, spinning…spinning. It seemed now more like a deadly scythe. "Often of late I've heard this wielder's name."

Ean finally finished closing off his mind and dove into *elae's* current stream, seeking the fourth strand, where compulsion patterns would flow.

"I've heard this Björn named betrayer, traitor, villain and Vestal. But others closer to me name him as my enemy." Darshan clasped hands behind his back again. "Tell me what *you* know of him."

Ean urged his mind to swim faster, even as he heard himself replying, "I know he will stop you."

Darshan's head assumed the slightest tilt. "From doing what, pray, does he hope to stop me?"

The words ground themselves out between Ean's clenched teeth, despite his every effort to resist saying them. "From unmaking our world."

"From unmaking your world…" the words came out with the low rumble of thunder warning on the horizon. Darshan started circling again and angled a dangerous stare in Ean's direction. "And how does your Vestal plan to achieve this laughable improbability?"

Ean's heroic effort to stop himself from answering this question endangered his carefully compartmentalized portion of thought. He realized he couldn't both resist the compulsion and seek the pattern of its causation; he likely wouldn't be able to resist the compulsion for long, in any case. Yet giving in to it was agonizing—there he stood offering up the secrets of the entire game! "The First Lord began preparing for you by creating the realm of T'khendar…"

To Ean's utter mortification, the entire story poured off his tongue, every treasonous word accompanied by the crystalline sound of his will shattering. He bled a hopeless dismay.

And then…Cephrael must've turned His fateful gaze away, for Ean reached the end of the fourth-strand tributary current he'd been following, and—

He mentally recoiled. Immediately he shielded his mind's eye from the origin point of that stream, for it lay concealed within the exploding furnace of a star—verily, he could barely look at the blinding light that was Darshan's mind, for it seared too deeply into his own, searing *thought* itself into cinders.

Ean's head started throbbing, his mind's eye blistered, but he forced himself to trudge the last few steps up that stream…

And found the pattern.

It shimmered along the photosphere of a demigod's mind, an ephemeral outline against the solar storm. One glimpse and Ean had absorbed it, duplicated it; in a heartbeat he understood its conceptual makeup.

By his next breath, he'd unmade it.

Darshan swung him a violent stare.

Ean met his gaze for one instant, during which a deeply unsettling understanding dawned for both of them.

Then the prince was summoning a shield of the fifth to protect his body and the fourth to protect his thoughts and was sprinting for the daylight at the gallery's edge.

Darshan growled an oath. Thunder without sound boomed through the chamber. The force blasted Ean off his feet, but his shield absorbed the worst of it. He righted himself with the fifth, found his footing upon landing and kept running.

Until a net sizzled into being directly before him.

Too close, he careened headlong into it. His shield exploded. Light blinded him. Searing pain charged through his head, and the repelling force of the collision flung him backwards.

Ean hit the floor with a painful exhale and slid on his back across the marble tiles. He frantically summoned his shields again. It took almost a dozen beats of his pulsing heart to hold them firmly in place, and many more before he could assure himself that all of his parts were still working properly.

His body slowed to a stop at Darshan's feet.

Ean looked dizzily up to see the man staring down at him. Five sets of dark eyes gazed reproachfully, five mouths pursed in a disappointed line.

"This behavior hardly becomes you, Prince of Dannym."

Necessity gathered Ean's wits. He somersaulted backwards and came up on his feet with his hand on his sword.

And then what? You'll fight him in hand to hand combat?

Ean was desperate enough at that point to try.

But Darshan had other plans. A circle of *deyjiin* geysered up around him, trapping him yet again.

Dizzy, frustrated, all Ean could wonder in that disheartening moment was why the man kept trapping him instead of simply destroying him? Did he mean to merely toy with his prey before consuming it?

'*Come and find me. I'll be waiting…*'

This comportment hardly seemed like the Enemy he remembered…

And then it hit him. Darshan was not—*could not*—be the Enemy of Arion's past. He lifted the Malorin'athgul a look of sudden clarity. "You're not the one I met before…are you?"

Darshan twirled his scepter. "We met every time you claimed one of my *eidola*."

A tentacle of sizzling energy leapt from the net towards Ean and sparked against his fifth-strand shield. The frenetic energy continued dancing between shield and net, tiny filaments of icy death drawn to *elae's* warmth.

Ean expelled his breath in a frustrated hiss. He had to get out of there. Every time *deyjiin* touched his shields, he felt icy needles stabbing his brain, felt himself weakening. To compound matters, Darshan was bombarding him with a wicked volley of compulsion aimed at reclaiming his mind.

But Ean had seen Darshan's innate pattern now; he knew how the Malorin'athgul formulated his intent. So long as his shield held—so long as his strength held—the immortal would not again be able to invade his thoughts.

But neither strength nor shield would hold for long under these conditions.

While Darshan considered him amid a deep and disturbing silence, Ean hastily sought some way of escaping the net. He couldn't unwork patterns of *deyjiin*, even had he been able to see them. Nor would it help him to throw *elae* at the net. *Deyjiin* would only consume the energy.

So if you can't unwork the net and you can't break through it, what can you do?

Ean wondered resignedly why so many of his thoughts had to take on Isabel's tone of voice.

Darshan clasped hands behind his back again and thrust the spear of his attention at Ean. "I have—"

"My lord! My lord are you all right?" A banging on the outer doors of the chamber drew Darshan's eye. It was the chance Ean needed—just an instant free of Darshan's pinioning gaze.

He looked down at his feet and thought, *liquid*.

The floor melted beneath him.

THIRTY-NINE

"Fortune never shares her bed with vengeance."
–Isabel van Gelderan, Epiphany's Prophet

NADIA VAN GELDERAN, heir to the Empire of Agasan, touched her own cheek and drew her finger across her skin, tracing a path that mirrored the dark patterns around Caspar's eyes. "But are they actual tattoos?"

Caspar was sitting cross-legged just a few inches away, on the other side of the invisible wall of deadly static. His eyes were closed and he had his hands clasped in his lap, allowing her to study the patterns masking his face.

Nadia had found him waiting for her when she'd awoken that morning. He'd barely left her side, in fact, since she'd bonded with him.

Bonded with a Marquiin.

A bond could be easily undone, but it was still an incredibly foolhardy act. Never mind that Tanis had done far more reckless things. She wasn't sure she should use Tanis's choices as any sort of yardstick for measuring her own.

"The Prophet fashioned the marks when he made me Marquiin," Caspar answered, eyes still closed. "I don't know how he created them. My eyes became painfully cold, and then I felt the patterns sort of...*uncoil* through my flesh."

Nadia gazed at the patterns with fascination. They clearly weren't native to *elae,* nor did they appear to be *inverteré*—though she knew only scant theory about the latter. But if not native to the Realms of Light...could it be possible she was looking at actual patterns of *Chaos*?

The idea roused a sort of nervous excitement. She couldn't tell if it was a trick of the energy field or the patterns themselves, but they seemed to emit a faint silvery sheen. She shifted closer to the screen, pushing her nose into the static fringes. Stinging needles zapped its tip. "They have a certain luster to them, don't they?"

Caspar opened his eyes and met her gaze. "I wouldn't know."

She drew back to stare at him. "You mean you haven't looked at yourself at all? Not even once?"

"Would you, Nadia?"

The question gave her pause. Once she thought about it, she still wasn't sure what she would've done. She touched her fingers to her own cheeks in lieu of touching his. "They're frightening because they're so different. But they're also rather beautiful."

"I can see my face in your thoughts, Nadia. Perhaps..." but for whatever reason, he didn't voice his thought, only confessed into the shared space of their minds, *I think if you were standing beside me, I could be bold enough to look.*

Nadia could not mistake his intimation. It made her apprehensive...and even slightly fluttery.

Suddenly the howling wind that ever roamed Caspar's mind blew open a shutter into her own, and Nadia rushed to shut it again.

The effort of cordoning off this tumult was draining her strength by the hour. This was one of the risks of the bond she'd allowed—nay...the bond *she'd* forged after catching the desperate lifeline Caspar had thrown at her. But despite that chaos storm, she didn't want Caspar to go away any more than he wanted to leave her side. He was her only friend in that despairing place.

As soon as she shut out the howling mental winds, she felt Caspar shudder and then settle within the refuge of her mind, like a tiny animal sheltering in her arms while a cyclone raged outside. They were both equally trapped in a sanctuary that neither dared leave.

"How long can you endure it?"

She managed a weak smile that she hoped he would find encouraging. "A bit longer yet."

He studied her in silence. Then he held up his hand before the invisible wall. Nadia matched it with her own. His eyes, holding hers, entreated caution. "Please don't weaken yourself because of me."

"I'm not as fragile as I look, Caspar."

"No..." he lowered his hand and gazed off along the barrier, "but the Prophet's storm is everlasting."

"We just—" but whatever she might've said, the words fell unspoken off her tongue, disrupted by the sound of men running.

Caspar moved quickly to his feet. "Something's happening." He darted a look over his shoulder and then back to her. "Your rescuer?"

Somehow she didn't think Pelas would've announced himself so dramatically. Her gaze tightened, and she stared beyond the veiling wall of her prison feeling oddly unsettled. "I'm...not sure."

"I should go look into it."

"No—please." She automatically reached for him and just checked her hand before it touched the deadly field. She entreated him with her gaze instead. "Please stay with me."

He considered her while exhaling a slow breath. Then he nodded. "As you wish." He slowly settled back down into the same cross-legged position, grey robes pooling around him.

She braved a slight smile. "You don't mind staying, do you?"

Caspar looked into her eyes. "There is nowhere I'd rather be, Nadia."

Nadia quickly dropped her gaze. She ought not to feel nervous beneath his stare. She ought not to care how he was looking at her.

Oh, if only her mind might've been free of this torment that she could think more clearly, *see* clearly where lines should be drawn for sake of propriety and even her own troths! But Caspar was providing as desperate a lifeline for her as she was for him, and she couldn't let go of him just yet.

No... Nadia swallowed around a sudden welling lump, the produce of ever ripening fears...*not just yet.*

◆

Ean sprinted through the bowels of the Prophet's temple, keeping his mind and body shielded and his eyes on the currents. His fall from the gallery through melting stone had delivered him onto a level of windowless chambers and servants' quarters, which had been built in labyrinthine fashion around the monolithic blocks that supported the upper temple. Even using the currents as a guide, he hadn't yet found his way out.

This futile flight of yours suits neither of our purposes, Ean. Darshan's stiletto thought stabbed painfully into Ean's consciousness. Unable to gain control of Ean's mind, the Malorin'athgul was exploring new ways to penetrate his shield by fashioning his thoughts into different shapes. *You cannot hide from me in my own temple.*

But Ean didn't intend to hide. He intended to get the hell out of there.

He paused at an intersection of passages and pressed a hand to the wall, hanging his head while his breath burned in and out of his lungs. A constant bombardment of compulsion hammered at his consciousness, a hailstorm against his mental shield. It would've been challenging enough if his sole attention had been upon preventing that storm from shattering the fourth-strand barrier he'd fashioned to protect himself, but he also had to find some way through the temple's minotaur maze, knowing full well that the beast was hunting him.

Ean focused his mind's eye upon the copper-hued labyrinth that spread before him, the product of his second-strand working. He searched the mental overlay of twisting passages while listening to the pounding rhythm of his heart. His hand trembled against the wall. Just holding his shields in place felt like he was hauling one of his grandfather's ships onto dry dock on his back.

Take care, Ean.

Ean ground his teeth. Damn it all, he didn't need Isabel's warnings! He knew perfectly well that if he pushed himself too hard his mind would become a sieve, that he wouldn't even be able to grasp *elae,* much less mold it to his intent. But the only other choice would be to give Darshan free access to his mind.

He could make you into his weapon. He could make you eidola.

The horror of this thought—which echoed against some fear Arion had also experienced—flung Ean into motion again. He took a flight of steps two at a time and turned down a long hallway, running towards the far end where a solitary lamp burned a cold, dim light. The entire level looked deserted. The servants had probably fled at the first sound of the alarm.

Why do you insist upon this cat and mouse effort, Ean? Darshan's thought struck as lightning against his shield.

Ean gritted his teeth and pushed on, wondering what possible reason Darshan could have for apprehending him if vengeance wasn't his aim. The Malorin'athgul had barely seemed to care what Ean had done to his Marquiin and *eidola,* save to understand how he'd done it.

'The currents will show you what is true...' Isabel's words. But they couldn't be showing him the truth, for they defied his every expectation.

Reaching the end of the passage, the prince flung himself around a corner and past an open chamber, large and well lit, just glancing within—

And drew up short.

Inside, a dark-haired girl was just rising to her feet; but it was the energy field in front of her that riveted his attention.

As a moth drawn blindly from darkness towards the light, Ean moved inside the chamber, his every perception glued to that shimmering field. He'd never encountered patterns like the ones captured within this static sheet of energy—patterns which seemed to bind *deyjiin* and *elae* together.

Balanced? The two energies are balanced? He hadn't thought it possible for *deyjiin* and *elae* to coexist.

Barely noticing the girl staring at him from the other side of the field, Ean lifted a hand—

"Be careful," said a male voice to his right.

Ean stepped back and drew his sword.

"Stop!" gasped the girl.

The man—Marquiin?—lifted both hands in quick surrender. He appeared to be unarmed, but Ean kept his sword pointed at him while he glanced brusquely to the girl. "Who are you?"

She looked nervously at his sword and its evident target. "I might ask the same of you, sir."

Ean spared another moment to look her over. Though apparently a prisoner, she was radiating purpose, and when their eyes met…

A sudden powerful sense of kismet flooded him.

Ean shifted his gaze between the female truthreader and the Marquiin, who seemed hardly older than himself. Without understanding why, he exhaled a forceful breath and lowered his sword. "I am Ean val Lorian."

◆

'I am Ean val Lorian.'

Nadia couldn't believe she'd heard him correctly. She wasted several astonished heartbeats trying to accept this truth. "*Tanis's* Ean?" She stared at him while a tingling sensation coursed through her for no reason she could explain. "You're the Crown Prince of Dannym?"

Ean stared at her in return. "*You* know Tanis?" He spun a look between her and Caspar and then stepped closer to the field. A sense of urgency underscored his manner. "Do you know where he is? What's happened to him?"

Nadia gazed wide-eyed at him. "I know *much* of Tanis. I'm Nadia van Gelderan."

Now it was Ean's turn to draw back with widening eyes. "The Princess Heir?"

She managed a flickering smile, more revealing of culpability than hauteur.

Ean was clearly trying to comprehend the machinations behind this improbable meeting. Well, so was Nadia.

"The Prophet took you hostage?" Ean looked again to Caspar, obviously confused by his presence.

"No." Nadia grimaced. "I was a…gift."

Ean turned back to stare at her. "A gift to Darshan? From *whom*?"

An odd sense of relief flooded Nadia upon hearing Ean speak the Prophet's true name. The prince knew of the Malorin'athgul then. "From his brother Shail."

Ean exhaled an oath, and Nadia saw a flurry of thoughts sweep across his gaze. Something in his manner reminded her of her father—whereupon she realized that what she was perceiving in the prince was *elae*'s fifth strand. He must've been shielding himself with it.

"Your Highness, what are you doing here?" She gazed at him with wonder threaded through concern, for Ean looked about as haggard as a man could manage and still be on his feet.

The prince startled back to awareness and looked to her sharply. Then he took a step away and looked over the field, assessing it with a critical eye. "There's got to be a way to get you out of there."

He lifted his sword towards the field.

"I wouldn't do that, if I were you," came a voice from the archway behind Ean.

Nadia caught her breath, and her heart did a little jump, for she knew that voice! She moved to better see around Ean's form.

Pelas stood in the portal. "Opposing polarities, you see…" but his words trailed off as Ean turned to face him, and his expression went slack. "Ean." Pelas sounded horrified.

"*Pelas.*" Ean's tone pulsed with fury—an inexplicable fury that filled Nadia with immediate dread.

Pelas lifted a hand. "Ean, you must let me explain—"

Ean swung for him.

Pelas threw up his hand—he must've summoned some kind of shield, for Ean's sword sliced along it in a wild spray of sparks. "Ean, I don't want to fight you!"

Ean dove at him again. That time his sword struck Pelas's shield with a forceful explosion. The prince skidded backwards towards the energy field and just rooted his footing before slamming into it.

Pelas lowered his hand, looking tormented. "Ean, please—"

Ean leveled his sword at him. "You will not speak to me." Then with a look of fury, he flung his sword into the energy field.

Light flared in a blinding eruption of force. The concussion knocked Nadia backwards off her feet, knocked her breath painfully from her lungs. Her vision went starry and then dark, and the next thing she knew, she was tumbling into chaos.

❖

"I wouldn't do that, if I were you," came a voice from the archway.

Ean froze, at first unbelieving of his ears. Of all the improbable, *impossible* places to meet…

"Opposing polarities, you see…" but Pelas trailed off as Ean turned to face him, and when their eyes met—

A violent and instinctive urge to attack instantly roused within the prince.

He saw himself with his bare hands around Pelas's throat—he saw twenty ways at once to destroy this duplicitous man, who had helped him rescue his brother but then taken Isabel to his bed...*who'd sliced Chaos patterns into her flesh!*

Ean sucked in his breath through clenched teeth, while fury exploded in his chest and loathing blackened his gaze.

Pelas's face went slack. "Ean."

"*Pelas.*" The name tasted like char on his tongue.

Pelas lifted a placating hand. "Ean, you must let me explain—"

Ean swung for his head.

Pelas threw up a shield, and Ean's sword sliced along it in a spray of searing sparks. "I don't want to fight you, Ean!"

But Ean had descended to a plane of frost and fury where reason lay as rime upon the world to be tread upon by vengeance's iron hooves. In Pelas, Ean didn't see a Malorin'athgul, only the man who'd tortured and then bedded his wife.

With fury veiling his gaze, Ean dove at Pelas again, that time putting the fifth into his blade. His sword striking Pelas's shield caused an explosion that flung Ean backwards towards the energy field. He threw the fifth behind himself to recover his footing.

Pelas lowered his hand, wearing a look of abject remorse. "Ean, please—"

Ean leveled his sword at Pelas and aimed his words along its razor edge. "You will not speak to me." Ean couldn't think, couldn't breathe. All he knew was that this man had to feel what he'd felt, had to atone for the harm he'd caused. Suddenly he realized that a deadly weapon lay just behind him.

Ean turned a determined look over his shoulder, solidified his shield, and flung his sword into the static field.

Energy exploded. Air exploded. *Light* itself exploded.

Ean dove for the marble floor, thinking, *dissolve*. He cast the intention broadly.

Perhaps too broadly, for he plunged in a downward rush amid a waterfall of marble dust and hit the floor of the level below with a painful expulsion of breath. His fifth strand shield wavered, and he nearly lost his hold on the fourth-strand shield protecting his mind from Darshan's merciless bombardment, but as his breath was gingerly inching its way back into bruised lungs, Ean managed to reaffix both shields firmly in place. Dazed, he pushed up to hands and knees.

Showers of marble sand were pouring down along the edges of the room as the floor above continued dissolving. Across the chamber, veiled by voluminous clouds of marble dust, the Marquiin was bending over Nadia. The two of them appeared wraithlike and indistinct in the shifting air, amalgams of shadows.

With a blood haze still clouding vision and judgment both, Ean spotted Pelas just rising and threw his intent as a spear. The fifth caught Pelas in the chest and flung him backwards into a column.

An instant later, Ean was atop him.

"*Stop!*"

Ean barely registered Nadia's desperate cry or her hands dragging at his shoulders and arms. He knew only the feeling of his fingers closing around Pelas's throat, and the fathomless apology in the immortal's gaze.

With wrath reigning absolute, reason abandoned Ean for safer pastures; thus, nothing stood to impede him as he searched for Pelas's life pattern. Not even Pelas. He lay still beneath Ean's clenching hands, unresisting; his gaze swore, *I will not harm you.*

Ean's replied remorselessly, *Then you will die.*

He found Pelas's life pattern and started pulling.

❖

When Nadia found her bearings again, she was lying in a cavernous chamber. Pillars carved with patterns supported a groin-vaulted ceiling—at least what part of the ceiling wasn't showering down in cascades of fine marble sand.

Nadia pushed up to sitting and tried to find her breath but only ended up choking on the fog of dust clouding the room. A moment later, Caspar appeared out of the unbreathable haze. His silk robe was torn, his dark hair wore a layer of ashen dust, and his cheek was bleeding, but he otherwise seemed whole.

He squatted beside her and helped her to sit up. "Are you all right, Nadia?"

She took hold of his arm and with his help, found her feet. Then she heard a grunted exhale and turned to see Pelas sliding down a column. An instant later, Ean appeared on top of him and with his hands around his throat.

A razor of terror sliced through Nadia. "*Stop!*" She grabbed Caspar's arm and hauled him after her. "Ean—you don't understand!"

She threw herself atop Ean and tried to pull him off of Pelas. Caspar also grabbed the prince, but he must've held the fifth, for neither of them could budge him from his terrible work.

Nadia perceived two pillars of light, one growing brighter while the other dimmed. She turned a desperate look at Pelas that he might take action himself, but he merely lay still beneath Ean, holding the prince's gaze while his face reddened, as if accepting of this torturous penance.

Frantic, Nadia tried to reach Ean with the fourth—she even tried compulsion—but she couldn't penetrate the prince's mental shield. Finally, she clung to Ean's form, crying madly, saying anything she could think of to get through to him. The idea that Tanis might lose Pelas…it was unconscionable.

"*Please*," Nadia sobbed in the last, "he's *bound* to Tanis!"

❖

Pelas felt himself being unmade…filaments of his own construction becoming unwoven…innate threads pulled out of cohesion. He rather feared if he looked down he'd no longer see his feet; yet he knew this dismantling wasn't so linear. The threads of form that bound him into that shell were part of a pattern that had a beginning and an end. Ean was unworking it from both directions.

I will not harm you.

He'd meant this sentiment, invoked it in his gaze. He wouldn't harm another being who was important to Tanis.

Had he known Isabel was Tanis's mother, he would've driven daggers into his own hands—pinned himself to the stone wall of that tower—before harming her.

Whether or not Ean knew that he'd been—was…is?—Tanis's father; whether or not Tanis even knew it, Pelas had worked out this truth. If being unmade would atone for what he'd done, if his deconstruction would ameliorate the pain he'd caused Ean and Tanis, if it would open a path to eventual absolution, Pelas would endure it.

Even to the end?

He had to ask himself this. There was a very real chance Ean would succeed in this endeavor if he did nothing to stop him. Already his vision was blackening at the edges, already he felt his anchors on this world beginning to drag. This shell could exist without breath for a long time, but he couldn't keep himself bound into form in Alorin without it. What *would* happen if the prince unworked the shell that anchored him to this plane?

I'll have to find my way into the realm again. Construct a new shell.

He'd managed it once, but the hole he'd used all those centuries ago had been plugged by T'khendar's bulk. He'd surmised that much from the pieces of truth Isabel had shared with him, and from the sure certainty that his brother Rinokh would've found his way back by now if the route had still been open.

Then I'll have to use the void. It would take some time—weeks, even months he dreaded losing—but now that he knew Alorin so intimately, at the very least he could find his way back into the realm via the formless dimension of Shadow…

Even as he had the thought, he saw it—the enormity of Isabel and Björn's plan, their nearly incomprehensible foresight. His amazement in this recognition even dampened the pain of Ean's working and gave Pelas a renewed clarity of thought.

They knew we could come back via Shadow.

Rinokh might already have accomplished it if he'd known how to navigate Shadow's void as adroitly as Darshan, Shail and Pelas.

That Björn van Gelderan in his wisdom had seen this truth already, Pelas had no doubt. That he'd included the possibility in his plans, even prepared for it…

Oh, Tanis…your uncle might be the most brilliant man to ever walk the Realms of Light.

It seemed fitting somehow that this might become his last thought in that shell.

As his vision went dark around the edges, Pelas wondered how quickly and closely he could pattern a second shell to resemble the first. He wondered if Tanis would recognize him…

Ean—you don't understand!

The words echoed in Ean's head, spoken by three voices as one: Nadia, Sebastian, Isabel…all those voices of reason sheltered within the confines of his mental shield, protected from Darshan's relentless bombardment, witnessing Ean's requital and Pelas's deserts.

He wondered why they weren't cheering him on.

Sebastian's voice chastised, *Isabel sacrificed your love to bind Pelas to Alorin's welfare, and here you are killing her sacrifice.*

And Isabel all too clearly said, *Do not be quick to judge, Ean.* Her warning stabbed painfully, a hook of momentary recollection that yanked him up from the depths of rage.

Ean lifted his head above the water just as Nadia cried desperately, "He's bound to Tanis—and Tanis to him!"

These words struck him like a spear.

For a moment, all breath ceased and Ean stared, stunned and unseeing, only hearing Nadia's words resounding in his head.

Pelas is bound to Tanis, and Tanis to him?

Ean felt Pelas's life pattern slipping from his grasp.

In his mind's eye, he looked down to find his hands bloodied with *elae*, just like the Enemy's dagger as he'd ripped it from Arion's chest. Ean shoved away from Pelas and fell back on his hands, suddenly repulsed by what he'd nearly done. He turned a horrified look at Nadia. "They're *bound?*" His voice scraped its way out of his throat.

Nadia sucked in a shuddering sob and fell across Pelas. She pressed her ear to his chest and looked up at Ean with tears streaming through the dust on her cheeks. "They worked the Unbreakable Bond!"

Ean felt sick. "Tanis is bound to a *Malorin'athgul*?" It seemed impossible, *wrong*.

Nadia cupped Pelas's face with a trembling hand. "Pelas bound himself to Tanis's path." She smoothed a strand of hair back from the Malorin'athgul's forehead and then looked up desperately at Ean. "He swore to protect him. They're bond brothers now."

Ean covered his face with both hands.

The Unbreakable Bond.

Too well he understood that working. He wanted to say this changed nothing…but it changed everything.

He dropped his hands and looked around the milky darkness, saw at last the destruction he'd wrought in the name of vengeance, and felt sickened by it. Had he kept his anger in check, they might've already escaped.

…*The Citadel fell because my brother felt too deeply*…

Ean clenched his jaw. Ever Isabel's rationality roped him to a post to be flayed by the lash of reason. He hung there now, strapped in the bounds of his own conscience, bleeding remorse. Yet through the astringent clarity of mortification, Ean finally admitted an understanding that he'd been refusing to accept: if Pelas was bound to Tanis, and by extension to Alorin itself, *then they had a Malorin'athgul on their team*…a vortice capable of bending Cephrael's will, weighting Balance in their favor.

Ean knew to the depths of his soul that Tanis would not have bound himself to anyone unworthy. The zanthyr *assuredly* would not have allowed such to occur.

Shocked by the truths he was finally seeing, Ean surged back to Pelas, laid his forehead against the Malorin'athgul's, and sought with his mind the selfsame pattern he'd a moment ago tried to unmake.

That time examining it instead of merely attempting to unravel it, Ean saw that Pelas's life pattern was badly frayed—the coat of a pauper, not a prince. Ean wielded the first strand into him, yet using that ephemeral, creative energy to smooth Pelas's life pattern proved as effective as polishing granite with a feather.

Regret gripped Ean. He couldn't fathom how he could've caused Pelas's life pattern to so deteriorate in so short a time. Sitting back on his heels to ponder this confusion, a simple truth struck him: he *couldn't* have caused it. Pelas must've already been in a debilitated condition before coming to Tambarré.

And you've certainly made things no better.

As guilt's vise tightened around his chest, Ean tried to think of—

At once the answer became apparent. He drew upon the fifth strand and funneled great pulses of it into Pelas's life pattern, though the effort drained him to the point of dizziness.

And then, at last, Pelas opened his eyes.

Nadia let out a little cry and flung her arms around him.

Pelas slowly wrapped his arms around the princess in return, but his eyes sought Ean's, and as they met, his gaze held a grave foreboding. "Darshan is coming."

◆

Nadia turned a fast look between Pelas and Ean, the latter of whom was lifting a tense stare towards the dissolved ceiling and the chamber above.

"He's coming for me," Ean murmured.

"Don't be so certain." Pelas gave a pained exhale. Nadia moved quickly to help him sit up.

Ean looked bemusedly back to him. "But he's your brother."

Pelas put a hand on Nadia's arm with a meaningful look. She got to her feet and then helped him find his. It disturbed her to feel his body shaking, to realize his weakened condition.

Pelas slowly straightened and lifted his gaze overhead, brow furrowed, as if already seeing Darshan standing above them. "Since I escaped from the tower where Darshan had imprisoned me—believing my power lost and under compulsion to harm your Isabel—my brother and I haven't been on the best of terms." He rolled his shoulders and gave a sort of wince. "I'm not on amiable terms with any of my brothers, actually."

"And whose fault is that?" Darshan's deep voice volleyed out of the dim recesses of the chamber, striking arrows of alarm into Nadia.

Ean spun a look to Pelas, but Pelas was already staring past him at a form congealing out of the darkness.

Darshan emerged from the milling, dust-filled shadows as a star birthing from a nebula's core. Seeing him again, Nadia felt breathless. There was just something so overpowering about him.

She flicked her gaze between Pelas and a very tense Ean, fervently hoping one of them was envisioning a way to get them out of there, because she was wholly out of ideas. And Darshan…it was almost impossible to think within the gravity of his attention.

Darshan looked Pelas over and did not appear at all pleased by what he saw. "What in Chaos happened to you?"

Pelas drew Nadia closer against him. "Revenants."

"*Revenants.*" Darshan's tone speared in accusation. "*This* was Shail's solution for containing you?" His dark eyes scanned Pelas as if to find some rebuttal for his claim. "I find it difficult to believe Shail would tread a path of such depravity."

"I find it difficult to believe you find it difficult to believe." Derision honed Pelas's tone to a fine point. "Nothing is beyond Shail. You should know that by now."

"As you should know better than to let him ensnare you in Shadow."

Pelas's gaze was arctic. "Sage advice as always, Darshan."

Darshan's eyes viewed the entire space while he twirled a dark scepter at his side. He shifted a razor gaze to the prince. "And you, Ean val Lorian? You're running out of stone to unmake. End these futile efforts of resistance and submit to me."

Ean was standing with his hands balled into fists and his shoulders as taut as the rest of his stance. "Why should I do that?" His words came out through clenched teeth.

Nadia's mouth fell open. *He's resisting Darshan's compulsion! How strong a wielder must he be?*

Pelas observed the charged energy amassing between his brother and Ean and stiffened. "*Darshan—*"

"Stay out of this, Pelas." Darshan swung his scepter at his side but kept his eyes pinned darkly on the prince. "The anticipation of *our* reckoning is something you should be savoring right now."

Nadia felt icy air suddenly all around her and realized Pelas had summoned *deyjiin*.

No—oh please, no! Pelas was so weakened, she feared he wouldn't survive a confrontation with his brother.

Likewise apparently sensing Pelas drawing upon his power, Darshan turned him a perilous look of warning.

"Pelas, *don't.*" Ean emphasized his communication with a pointed stare. The prince looked haggard and grim, but his grey eyes held such determination that Nadia felt a measure of hope again.

Pelas met Ean's gaze in return and…Nadia couldn't decipher half of what passed between them—clearly they had their own history together—but she did understand when Ean's gaze said clearly, *Get them out of here.*

And Pelas's in return demanded, *You'd better live through this.*

It was only an instant, this interchange of glances and thoughts, yet Darshan perceived it too. He pointed his scepter at Pelas, and a beam of violet-silver light erupted from its tip.

Pelas sucked in his breath and launched away from Nadia, *towards* the beam. He caught it in his fist just as a net of *deyjiin* curtained down. Pelas threw up his other hand and held the net open while its edges sought each other as if to close in a trap. The force exerted by the pulsing net pushed Pelas backwards across the dusty stone.

"Run, Nadia," he growled through clenched teeth.

She stared at him in shock, her mind a sudden blank. *Run? Run* where?

Caspar appeared at Pelas's side.

Pelas glared at him. "*You* cannot—"

But Caspar ignored him and grabbed the net. As his hands closed around the lines of *deyjiin,* he sucked in a fierce and tremulous gasp. Nadia felt him take immediate shelter in her mind. Caspar turned a strained look to Pelas with the net's light casting frightful shadows across his face and asked through gritted teeth, "What do…we do…now?"

The net contracted violently, pulsing with an eerie, silver-violet glow as it tried to close around them.

Caspar fell to one knee.

Nadia pressed both hands to her mouth and inhaled a shuddering breath just short of a sob.

Something whisked past her in a fury of wind.

She followed its fast flight with her gaze and watched Ean grab whatever it was out of the air. He lowered it to shoulder height, leveled at Darshan.

The prince had summoned his blade.

※

To Ean, the path before him seemed to split—*nay,* it fractured into shards of future. Myriad confusing and conflicting threads spiraled haphazardly into uncertain consequence.

The moment Pelas summoned his power, Ean made a decision that planted his feet firmly on one of those paths.

"Pelas, *don't.*" Ean shot him a telling stare, and though he felt threadbare himself, he made sure his gaze conveyed his intent: *Get them out of here.*

At first Pelas resisted—Ean saw a grave protest in his gaze, but Pelas was in no condition to fight his brother. Ean knew this. Pelas knew this. Probably even Darshan knew it.

Ean was exhausted, but at least his life pattern remained whole. Pelas, on the other hand, was a glass pedestal webbed with fractures. The least weight would shatter him. Ean made the words in his gaze clear: *You have no choice.*

Pelas knew better than to argue, though he appeared less than pleased about it. His returning gaze said in no uncertain text: *You'd better live through this.*

Ean intended to. He still had the lifeforce at his command to help him—or so he fervently hoped. It bothered him how difficult it was proving to hold the fifth now; that elemental strand was becoming as willful as the pull of gravity or the implacable ebbing of the tide.

Suddenly Darshan pointed his scepter and launched a spear of light towards Pelas. The latter caught it above his head, and a net shimmered down—the same type of net that Ean had careened into earlier that night.

Ean couldn't free Pelas from the net, but he could possibly give him a chance to escape—for Nadia, for Tanis, for the sake of the Balance, which Pelas might be able to shift in their favor.

He turned his attention to finding his sword. Somewhere among that chaos and ruin, it lay waiting for his call. Phaedor had crafted that sword for him, and Ean knew unequivocally that the zanthyr would've fashioned it to endure even the opposing polarities of Darshan's deadly field.

Ean pulled as much of the fifth as he could hold in preparation for what he meant to do. He made his fourth-strand shield more solid—if he lost that, he would lose everything—and compartmentalized his mind, all while mentally seeking his sword amid the rubble.

Finally perceiving its Merdanti song, he lassoed it with the fifth, heard its vibrating whisper as it sailed through the air, and reached up to grab the weapon just as it flew above his head. His fingers closed around the hilt with a clap of leather. The blade sang a welcome in his mind.

Ean lowered his arm and leveled his blade at Darshan.

Darshan arched a brow. "So this is the path you choose?" He flipped his scepter in the air and caught it in its center. "Only a fool challenges his gods."

"You're no god of mine."

"So be it." Darshan extended his arm before him, aligning the scepter's shaft parallel to Ean, and out of the blunt ends speared dual swords of *deyjiin*. They pulsed with a cold light and cast grimly flickering shadows across Darshan's features and the surrounding hall.

Ean swallowed in spite of himself.

You sure don't see one of those every day, Fynn's voice remarked in the prince's head. Ean wondered contentiously just how many people were going to be paying his head a visit before the day was done.

Darshan advanced upon him with slow regard, reminding Ean unsettlingly of the Sundragon Ramuhárikhamáth in T'khendar's Hall of Heroes, just after the *drachwyr* had apologized for what he meant to do.

Quickening his approach, Darshan lifted his arm overhead and spun his scepter—nay, his dual-bladed staff—and then sliced it downwards. The saber of *deyjiin* struck a pillar, and a large portion of the stone dissolved into sand.

Important safety note, Ean, Fynn's voice observed. *Don't let it touch you.*

Ean just caught himself before snapping a reply—he *would not* be engaging in conversation with these mad voices, spawned of exhaustion and fatigue.

But the moment served as a grim reminder of the very real danger he was facing in trying to work the lifeforce, for these voices were *elae's* warning that his endurance was nearing its end.

As Darshan neared, Ean lifted his blade to the ready, and they embarked upon a well-known prelude to the dance of swords, tracing each other's steps in a predatory circle.

Darshan held his gaze on Ean with an archer's expert fix. He never once removed it while he spun his staff from one hand to the other, his deadly, polarized blades singing a discordant hum. He never once relented in his pounding mental assault, sending a constant barrage of compulsion to break against the ramparts of Ean's mind.

Verily, resisting the compulsion alone would've been contest enough for Ean—who knew if Darshan himself might've been content with it?—but Ean had thrown down the gauntlet, and now only a pool of blood would suffice to name the victor of their contest.

Darshan spun his staff blindingly quick, brought it up spinning over his head, and advanced towards Ean. Ean put the fifth into his blade and spun into the *cortata* as he stepped to meet him.

Blade and staff met-met-met-met, sang as they separated, and meeting again, rang in tympanic thunder. Every time Ean's Merdanti blade touched Darshan's sabers of *deyjiin*, static sparks flew, the currents rippled, and the hair stood up in needles on Ean's arms.

Darshan had long legs, long arms, and took lengthy steps. He flowed with the grace of a demigod and the power of one. His dark gaze never wavered from Ean. His every motion remained controlled, crafted with precision, certain of its placement. Around they danced, continuing their rapid cadence of staff and steel, *deyjiin* and *elae*. *Rap-rap-rap-rap-rap*, a frenzied connection of twirling staff and wielded blade.

With the *cortata's* help, Ean held his own against his dangerous opponent, but every clash of their weapons sent lightning coursing along his bones. Ean only needed to hold Darshan's attention long enough for Pelas to escape, and then he could make his own flight to freedom. But by *Cephrael's Great Book*—what was taking the man so long?

❖

Pelas braced one hand on the floor and thrust the other overhead, holding off the hissing net of *deyjiin* with gritted teeth and a lot of silent cursing. The electrified net was cutting into his palm, and a painful current charged continuously down his arm and into his chest, fluttering his heart.

Still, this was better than revenants.

Beside him, Darshan's Marquiin wasn't faring as well. His hands and arms were covered in blood, a result of the net's static bite, and his face was growing paler by the breath. Nadia seemed to care about him, which roused Pelas's concern for him also.

A quick self-assessment suggested he had just enough strength to summon a portal into Shadow and possibly enough to get them out again. That *possibly* struck a disturbingly chord. He had to turn it into a *probably*. Tanis wouldn't take kindly to his losing Nadia in the void for all time.

The trouble with this solution wasn't how to call a portal while holding off the net, but how to get them all through the portal without letting the net close around them—or bringing the damnable thing along with them into Shadow, where it would become ten times stronger and mean their certain end.

In their favor, Darshan had turned his ravenous attention towards a more interesting meal. Providing that Ean could keep Darshan occupied, Pelas at least didn't have to worry about fighting his brother. Only his brother's net.

While the net sizzled above his head and that relentless, searing current electrified his body, making his muscles twitch erratically or even refuse to function as they should, Pelas thought through the possible scenarios for escape. Working the lifeforce would be impractical while holding a pulsating negative energy source—the net would only nullify *elae*—and the acrobatic feats he favored were quite beyond him at that point. He couldn't push the net off of them because of its magnetic properties, which were trying to force it closed around them. However…he could still possibly put gravity to work on their behalf.

Pelas looked to the grimacing Marquiin. "Can you hold it? Even for a few seconds? If I let go, can you hold it?"

Dark shadows now combined with the tattoos beneath the Marquiin's eyes. A tragedy, this youth; he was young to have had his future so befouled by Darshan's appetites. The young man looked sickly, ready to collapse; his entire body was shaking. But he managed a nod.

Pelas looked to Nadia. "Princess, come closer."

As Nadia was approaching, Pelas looked up beneath the net and assessed their line of fall. Then he looked to the Marquiin. "We have to get back on our feet."

He locked eyes with the youth to help synchronize their motion. Together they pressed back to both feet. Pelas swore beneath the effort. By the time he straightened, his entire body was alive with static.

Looking at the situation newly, this was not that much better than revenants.

"Nadia..." Pelas forced out her name between his clenched teeth. He felt like his teeth were the only thing truly supporting the weight of the damned net. "Come closer."

Nadia inched tentatively up to him. At the behest of his gaze, she slipped her arms around his chest and gasped when static sparked upon her touch.

Pelas struggled to draw in enough breath to speak. His lungs felt petrified, frozen into one shape. He looked grimly to the Marquiin. *By Chaos born*, his timing would have to be perfect or this boy would singe into ash.

"When *we* fall..." he managed, "*you* fall!"

Pelas would've preferred that he went last to hold the net off of them all, but he couldn't frame space while still standing on Alorin's plane. He had to lead them into Shadow. He looked to Nadia. "Ready?"

She swallowed, nodded once.

Pelas summoned a portal an inch in front of their feet. A door-shaped hole seemed to open in the marble floor.

It might've taken an extra two grains of sand through the hourglass for that portal to open far enough for the three of them to pass through it, but to Pelas, they seemed like the slowest two grains of sand that ever fell.

"Now!" He threw himself and Nadia towards the portal. The Marquiin flung himself, too. That single second of fall was the longest moment of Pelas's life.

It was going to be close.

Without their bodies forming a base to brace the net apart, its edges curled powerfully towards each other. Pelas released his hold on the net and grabbed Nadia into the circle of one arm and the Marquiin in the other.

They fell through the portal.

The net snapped closed.

Not necessarily in that order.

❖

Pelas was gone. The net was gone.

It had happened during Ean's overhead parry Darshan's staff. By the time Ean had beaten back the Malorin'athgul's next three moves, Pelas, Nadia, the Marquiin—all had vanished.

Ean was ready to vanish, too.

His second-strand pattern had revealed that freedom lay just beyond the outer wall, and he'd been slowly working their fight closer to said wall in preparation for the next part of his plan. Only...he suspected he was going to need to make Darshan fairly angry to accomplish it.

This idea posed its own challenge. For all Darshan was showing Ean how futile and audacious were his endeavors, the man's tone had barely warmed above a cool indifference. What could he do to actually rile the man?

Fynn's voice snorted. *Well...how bold can you be?*

Ean parried several more of Darshan's strikes in quick succession, feeling each bone-jarring blow rattling his teeth. *Bold enough to get myself killed.*

That was the short answer. He'd be treading a superfine line between audacity and blatant stupidity. It was the same line he walked between causation and collapse. But he'd been holding his own thus far.

Ean drew in a deep breath of *elae*—*This had better work!*—and took a running leap. He threw the second beneath himself and launched over Darshan's head, swinging his sword as he flipped upside down. The razor edge of his Merdanti blade just missed the man's neck.

The effort cost Ean. He landed dizzily, swooned, stumbled and only just got his footing in time to veer backwards and avoid Darshan's whipping saber.

The Malorin'athgul did not look amused by Ean's acrobatics.

Well and good. Let's up the ante.

The prince advanced anew—only he advanced upwards on steps of air, bringing his battle closer to Darshan's own height. He only succeeded in driving the Malorin'athgul back a few steps, but he made large strides towards darkening Darshan's mood.

While enduring a dual bombardment of compulsion and Darshan's whipping staff, Ean sought the fourth-strand channel of awareness the Malorin'athgul was using to attack his mind. That channel forged a link between their consciousnesses. By monitoring that channel, Ean might potentially perceive what Darshan was intending a fraction of a second before he cast the working. That split second might make all the difference.

Ean drank in the fifth and then pushed it into the floor. As he forced thought to *become*, a warning weakness flickered, even as his consciousness flickered.

The marble turned molten under Darshan's feet. The Malorin'athgul wobbled, wavered, and solidified it again with a glare at Ean.

Ean grinned at him.

Darshan's gaze smoldered. "What is it you think to do here, Prince of Dannym?" He swung his staff before Ean could answer.

Ean dodged back, made the floor soft again, and ran up a crescent wall of air while Darshan foundered. That time the Malorin'athgul irritably slung the fifth off the end of his blade, and the floor rippled into ferrite.

Not so easy to manipulate, that ferrite.

Having put some distance between himself and the immortal, Ean was now trying to focus on the central-most version of the three Darshans blurring before his vision. Somewhat accomplishing this, he called up the most egregiously foolish working he could envision.

The fifth, the fourth, the second—they all went into the pattern of his intent, which he layered with form.

Well, here goes...everything.

He threw the pattern at Darshan.

The sphere of force hit the Malorin'athgul in the chest and drove him in a backwards skid across the mottled, brownish floor. A kinetic current glowed beneath his scraping feet.

Darshan threw the fifth to stop himself—an innate working Ean couldn't see but surmised from his slowing motion—and spun to face Ean.

At least...he tried to, but his feet wouldn't budge from their position.

Or more properly, his shoes, which Ean's pattern had changed into iron. The kinetic force of the slide across the ferrite floor had magnetized the shoes to it. Now Darshan was stuck.

He leveled Ean a thunderous glare.

Ean gave a debonair bow. Then he turned and ran towards the wall. He barely had the strength to lift his legs, he was barely managing to hold onto his blade, but he had to look like he had some plan to escape...

A tiny spark pulsed along the channel of thought Ean was monitoring. The prince dove to the floor, landing painfully on his stomach with an arm pinned beneath him. He rolled fast aside.

Thunder without sound shattered the wall in a deafening explosion, opening a hole to freedom.

Ears ringing, Ean struggled to his feet, shoved his sword into its scabbard and launched himself through that hole. He didn't look back.

Only...he hadn't anticipated the drop.

A sheer and lengthy drop, as it turned out—at least five hundred feet straight down into the city below.

Well played, Ean val Lorian. Darshan's thought pierced through Ean's mental shield—nay, it disintegrated the entire shield.

But Ean had larger problems. He couldn't worry about Darshan's compulsion if he was dead.

Falling backwards through the rushing air, Ean threw a rope of the fifth...

He threw a rope of the fifth...

He threw a rope of the fifth!

The fifth yawned at him and returned its obdurate attention to the motion of the world.

The fourth gazed concernedly at his falling form but made no attempt to aid him.

The third called boldly, *Death is only the beginning!*

The first snatched her hand from his discourteous fingers with a gasp.

He reached desperately for the second. It clapped him on the shoulder with a jovial, *Good luck, mate!*

Ean scrambled to look down.

Then he hit.

FORTY

*"Betimes, the greatest courage a man can display
is to admit he does not know."*

—The Adept truthreader Giancarlo of Caladria

DARSHAN STOOD UPON the broken stones of his tower, gazing south into the night while the wind whipped his long hair into his eyes and the electrified currents pulled a static comb across his flesh. A storm was coming towards him, shedding darkness over the Saldarian moors where they met the Nadori desert in estuarial convergence.

Neither province nor kingdom sought to claim those lands. They offered only sparse grass and burning sand in ample measure. The lines thus overlapped, blended, melded one into the other so that none could easily discern where Saldaria ended and M'Nador began. Yet Darshan felt that it ought to be easy to lift one land from the other, to watch the desert stream away in falls of sand as the moors reemerged from beneath the burying earth.

It ought to have been that easy for him to separate truth from falsity, true purpose from delusion.

But it wasn't.

After the events of earlier that day, Darshan's smoldering thoughts had churned endlessly around Ean val Lorian, this Adept who unmade patterns as Malorin'athgul unmade worlds...this being who had supposedly lived and died three lifetimes, sworn to a single cause throughout.

Darshan had learned much from the Prince of Dannym before he'd escaped both his presence and his will. Ingenious, Ean's tricks with the lifeforce. Darshan had never met an Adept who could mold the elements as easily as himself and his brothers.

'The fifth…a fabled strand.' He recalled declaring this to Ean, to which the prince had replied with bold intimation, *'As fabled as you and me.'*

Darshan's eyes narrowed.

Pelas had come to him once, claiming that their innate composition included *elae*'s fifth strand. The conversation had rapidly devolved into another of their combustive arguments. But Darshan well remembered his brother's message: that while they were not children of this world, an essential part of them was connected to it.

Now Ean val Lorian claimed the same.

Darshan considered this with a black and introspective malcontent.

And what of this Björn van Gelderan? Another Adept who could purportedly shape the world to his will—who indeed, had created an *entirely new world* to prevent Darshan and his brothers from unmaking Alorin…at least if Ean val Lorian was to be believed.

What kind of mortal possessed such power? The antithesis, it would appear, of their own?

Darshan's gaze darkened measurably. Too many questions had been thrown into this cauldron of mischief. It was boiling over from a tumult of conflicting truths.

Well…there was one way to resolve some of his questions.

'…Sundragons are Björn's peacekeepers, monitoring Balance in the game. They come and go via the First Lord's sa'reyth. It is a way-station between Alorin and T'khendar…'

Yes, Ean val Lorian had proven *very* informative.

Darshan summoned his power.

Long ages had passed since he'd last assumed the form he used in the Void—centuries of observing this world through the shell he'd poured his essence into as he'd first entered Alorin's plane.

Rinokh, while he'd been among them, had lived almost exclusively as a dragon, and all of Avatar had feared his notice. But Darshan had always considered it faintly abhorrent to imagine bringing his pure, innate form into this puny world.

Now though…now he would claim his true shape again.

Power channeled into him with his breath. Darshan let his head fall back, closed his eyes, and surrendered to the impulse to expand.

Ever it seemed he fought to contain the immensity of his being in a fraction of its necessary space. Now he let himself unfold; his mind blended with a new form, his native form, interweaving thought and shape—*becoming*.

Light and darkness blurred. Power pulsed. Opposing energies collided with violent reactivity and exploded into fragments. Charged particles magnetized into orbit around a dual nuclei of merged polarities—*elae* and *deyjiin* in perfect balance. Darshan seized these fragments of power and shaped his intent, and they reformed into a new combination.

He surged into form.

Liquid darkness undulated atop the tower, blocking out the stars. It rapidly spread along the length of the acropolis; it poured itself into wings and coalesced into a massive body.

Before he could fully manifest, Darshan gave a powerful downward stroke and cast himself off the tower, lest it collapse beneath the weight of his congregating form.

A mighty wind buffeted the city of Tambarré as he surged upwards and into the pregnant clouds. Icy particles clung and froze to his form, sheathing him in pinprick stars, while the massing mists parted in whorls. He left a tunnel a quarter-mile wide in his wake.

Up, Darshan flew—higher, *farther*, until the storm appeared as a blanket across the marbling globe and the air became thin. Above him lay only the endless void of space, and a moon, strung low, as a fisherman's globe bobbing upon the atmosphere sea.

He hung there in that cold place of paucity, amid the blurred boundaries of worlds, and he waited...and he watched.

In the Void, this was his way: to float on the endless tides of unraveling space, observing a star he was about to unmake, tasting—appreciating—its power before he drank in its essence and reduced it to a point of utter darkness so hungry for energy that it gravitated all else into its insatiable core; or, unmaking even this dense mass, until all that remained of the once bursting star were infinitesimal particles of magnetic dust.

Now he hovered similarly within the confines of Alorin's outer atmosphere as he might've if he'd been ripe to unmake this world. But even in his powerful Chaos form, he couldn't unmake the realm from within its own aether.

Oddly, he no longer wanted to.

Oh, these were dangerous waters he was drifting upon, waiting for Balance's tide or a decisive breeze to determine his direction! He gloomily suspected that both of his brothers had already traveled these same mercuric seas.

Beneath him, the globe turned, and a crest of fire licked along the planet's edge. Soon light bathed the land, bouncing color into his void-black eyes. He saw all from his high vantage.

Darshan focused a dissecting gaze upon the rough crest of the Kutsamak

Range, which lay as an abrasion against the smooth, pale Sand Sea of M'Nador. He studied miles of these lands with the smallest shifting of his eyes, watching for a particular glint, and in time…

There.

As if birthed from the aether they appeared, four gilded specks of sunlight, soaring stars in miniature. *Sundragons.*

What else but these fabled *drachwyr* might capture the light unto their forms even as his form congealed the darkness?

Hovering, buoyed by the planet's magnetic tide, Darshan watched them.

They dispersed upon compass lines, claiming territories for their daily inspections. Darshan noted an obvious symmetry and organization to the paths of their flight; some mowed their quadrants in straight lines, others flew a spiral of shrinking concentricity.

The day still clung to the land when one of the females finished her inspection. Darshan watched her circle outward, ostensibly for one last view, and then fly back towards the point where he'd first seen the four of them appear.

He cast his wings powerfully behind him and dove down into daylight's languid sea.

He hardly noticed the tearing wind or the ice that crystallized along his razor form. He descended thousands of feet in heartbeats of time. The *drachwyr* beneath him grew from a star into a bright comet, the comet into a dragon.

Darshan speared through a grouping of thunderheads, and, emerging into the darkness beneath, flung open his wings and hauled to a hover in an instant. The force of his breaking flight cracked as thunder across the land, one more grumble among the rumbling storm.

Still far beneath him, the dragon flew in serene silence. Angled afternoon sunlight bathed her form in gleaming light and cast her undulating shadow to chasing her as she flew over the mountains. Her bronzed and gilded wings dazzled, with the occasional glint of blue sparking from their iridescent tips.

Staying within the shadow of the storm, Darshan followed her. He watched her alight on a mountain ridge and fold in her wings, and in that moment, he pinned a thread of attention to her form—barely a whisper of power, nothing she would notice.

The dragon dissolved into shimmering light; while it lasted, a perpetual starfall.

Interesting…

The *drachwyr,* it appeared, did not have to cram one form into the shell of another, as he did. This raised questions for him, curiosities to be explored at a later time.

Having observed them all throughout the day, however, he'd confirmed one truth: these *drachwyr* were beings of immense power, perhaps even the mirror opposites of himself and his brothers. That Dore said they were no threat to him could only be true if they weren't standing in direct opposition to him.

The curtain of stars finished its shimmering dance, and a woman wearing a blue dress stepped forth from the light. Darshan assured himself that his thread of attention remained secure upon her form.

She took three steps and vanished.

The spool of his attention unraveled in a furious stream as his thread was pulled across a vast distance in an instant. Mentally, Darshan traced the path of the *drachwyr*'s passing across the Pattern of the World to...elsewhere.

Two surging flaps of his wings later, he alighted upon that same ridge.

Blacker-than-black claws sank deep into the hard-packed earth. The land cracked and shifted with a terrestrial groan as he settled the fullness of his weight upon it.

The long afternoon sun cast its rays upon his flesh, and his wings and body hungrily drank in its light. His immense form blocked most of the ridge, as though a great nothingness had overcome it. Darshan exhaled a thoughtful breath. An icy, barren wind scoured the mountainside.

He cast his black gaze out across the scar of ochre-hued mountains, feeling an unusual solemnity. In his mind's eye, he reviewed the *drachwyr*'s shifting of form. Clearly the light had embraced her in symbiosis, as though she was in fact an extension of itself. She had simply *released* one form and claimed another; while a part of him fought in every moment to keep himself in the shell he needed to interact with this world.

The observation gave him more to think about, though one fact remained undeniably certain: How alien he was to this realm.

And how naïve and unready it was to meet such as him.

The darkness that had claimed the mountain closed its eyes. It seemed to explode into serpentine waves and then rapidly implode, sucked back within itself. The undulation subsided into the shape of a tall man, broad of shoulder, with a curtain of long hair as the only reminder of the darkness that was his true form.

Darshan traced again the *drachwyr*'s path in his mind, charting his own course across the Pattern of the World, to elsewhere.

Then he stepped across the node.

※

Amithaiya'geshwen, Bosom of God's Nectar, lifted her blue silk skirts as she walked through the grass up a long hill.

To her left, the sun was setting behind snow-capped mountains and casting long, striated rays between the peaks. Atop the far hill, the copper-hued tents of the First Lord's *sa'reyth* were glowing.

Mithaiya looked left, to the mountains and the too-bright outline of the ridge, the last effort of the falling sun to etch the world with its imprint. Soon the entire valley would lie beneath shadow-streaks drawn by night's charcoal hand. At twilight, Balaji would light the lamps, and the *sa'reyth* would become a mirror of the glimmering stars.

Mithaiya loved the gilded hour but not the twilight. Jaya, conversely, felt the latter a magical time. But in the twilight, Mithaiya sensed an overlapping of boundaries, a no man's land where light and darkness mingled recklessly, as in a ribald fête whose revelers were too soaked with drink to keep their judgment dry. In the twilight, Mithaiya perceived a dangerous convergence of forces, a span of an hour's falling sands where the hard substance of the daylight world grew porous. Who knew what malevolent sylphs might slip through the holes?

Higher up the hill, Vaile appeared above a rise, striding towards her. "*Trath'na maeth, faelle.*" *Good evening, sister.*

Mithaiya answered her, also in Old Alaeic, "And to you, Vaile, sister of my heart."

They met halfway on the hillside and exchanged kisses on each cheek. As they both turned to head back up the hill together, Vaile drew her shawl closer about her shoulders and looked Mithaiya over. Mithaiya in turn frowned at Vaile's shawl.

"You're the first to return." The zanthyr's green-eyed gaze moved past Mithaiya, searching the darkening valley. "Where are the others?"

Mithaiya exhaled a slow breath. "Sweeping their territories twice."

Vaile arched a brow. "What news is this?"

"Radov's army is on the march through the Sand Sea towards Raku."

Vaile arched a disbelieving brow. "The prince thinks to mount an attack on the oasis with all of you on patrol?"

"Would that his intentions were less apparent." Mithaiya blew out her breath.

"There is little enough satisfaction in slaying a lunatic, and even less in slaying a lunatic's army." She swept a curtain of dark hair back from her shoulder and looked to the sky. It was nearing twilight—

Vaile stiffened.

With her next breath, Mithaiya perceived him too.

Her eyes flew to Vaile's. Everything that needed to be said passed in that sudden locking of eyes. Then the zanthyr was reaching over her shoulder for her sword and Mithaiya was bolting for the node to warn the others.

A net of *deyjiin* sizzled into being in front of her.

Mithaiya hissed a curse—every natural sense recoiled from the foul energy—but she drove through it nonetheless. It felt like smothering herself in icy, electric jelly.

Beyond the net, she shrugged off the vile sensation of its touch and kept running.

Fractions of a second later, something cold and very sharp hooked into her back. No, *two* somethings.

Mithaiya cried out, stumbled on her long skirts, and fell to hands and knees in the grass. Liquid fire was burning up and down her spine. She could barely breathe for the pain. It felt like her wings were being ripped away—*no*, sliced away with knives of ice.

Whatever he'd thrown at her was pushing its way deeper inside and spreading a throbbing chill. It must've been some working of *deyjiin*. Nothing else could feel so antithetic to her very essence.

Incredulity claimed the moment.

How had he found them? *Why* had he come here?

She tried to stand again, but just lifting a hand from the earth made her cry out with pain. She stayed there then, sucking in short gasps, trying to find her breath, tears clinging to her lashes, her ears listening urgently for an expected scraping of steel…

Vaile…?

Footsteps through the long grass. *Not* Vaile.

Preceded by a radiating chill, he halted above her.

Mithaiya slowly turned her head to look up at him. He might've been taller than Ramu.

He bent and hooked his fingers under her arm. She sucked in her breath as he drew her to her feet. Pain exploded; likewise her disbelief.

They'd expected and planned for so many scenarios, but a Malorin'athgul striding up to the First Lord's *sa'reyth* had been utterly inconceivable.

He set her, gasping, on her feet and supported her elbow with iron fingers. His hold wasn't rough, but nor was it gentle. And his eyes were very, very dark.

Mithaiya wanted to call her brothers, but reaching their minds across the realms required more concentration than she could muster; she wanted to turn her head to see what had become of Vaile, but movement of any kind brought debilitating pain; and then there was his radiating presence…

Focus, Amithaiya'geshwen! You're not some mortal girl spellbound and awed by an immortal's gaze. It's all up to you now!

Mithaiya pushed away her incredulity, her desire to deny, and concentrated instead on what he might want and what she could do about it.

Power was radiating off of him in waves. She drew upon her own to balance it.

This had an unexpected effect on both of them.

His hold on her arm tightened, but not in anger.

Power pulsed–*flared*…pulsed–*flared*…

With each pulse, the air popped, the grass rippled in circular waves—no, the *land* rippled.

Suddenly she felt his mind in her mind, her mind in his mind. A cold wind swept through the chambers of her thoughts.

He gave her an unsettling smile.

Amithaiya'geshwen.

❖

Darshan stepped off the node into a new realm.

In the distance, the little *drachwyr* was climbing a hill. He moved after her.

His fingers undulated at his sides without his awareness. They were the vestigial filaments of his mighty wings, which in the Void would expand to receive the solar winds, magnetic storms, radiation from a glowing nebula… and translate these perceptions into means of unmaking.

This realm tasted as different from Alorin as salt from sugar, as an orange from a sage plant…as a planet from a star. Perceptions beyond counting brought to him their offerings—gravity's varied inclination, a difference in lunar pull, the air holding a slightly altered combination of gasses; many others. Each new awareness laid itself before the throne of his perception as a gift for him to sample. Here was a smorgasbord for his senses.

Was every realm of light so different from every other? The idea intrigued him mightily.

Abruptly his radiating senses brushed the mind of another. A new kind of mind.

His gaze flew back up the hill towards his prey. The *drachwyr* had vanished over the rise.

Darshan broke into a run.

He regained view of her in time to see two women separating. The *drachwyr* broke for the trees, while the raven-haired woman reached over her back, ostensibly for a weapon he couldn't see, yet did perceive.

He threw a net of *deyjiin* to trap his dragon.

She burst right through it.

With an admiring smile, Darshan cast an anchor of intent along the thread he still had pinned to his *drachwyr* and dragged her instantly to the ground.

He shifted his attention back to the other immortal.

She was coming towards him carrying Merdanti blades in each hand.

His scepter was strapped to his thigh, but this woman…

To his eyes, she appeared as a dark star…a dying star. She might've once offered him some challenge, but he perceived her core eroding from within, as a tree that appeared outwardly strong but inside had been hollowed by parasites. She was weak and brittle now. She posed no threat.

At least…not a physical one.

The woman scraped her blades along each other with her green gaze pinned upon him. She maintained a steady approach, her manner deliberate and deadly.

The smallest tightening of his gaze betrayed his wonder. Surely she was cognizant of the pestilence eroding her core?

He didn't know what other powers she possessed. He hadn't been able to study her as he'd studied the *drachwyr*. So he summoned a different kind of net, boundlessly pliable, one he often cast around a star he was intending to unmake.

He flung this doughy platelet at the female. Made to absorb the riotous energy of a star, the field would absorb anything this immortal tried to throw at him.

Which she did, even as the field was closing around her. A webbed net of energy blossomed outwards into a sphere of iridescent color, violently charged, deadly with trapped force; but the pliable platelet quickly absorbed and metabolized whatever energy she'd thrown into it. The field shrank in around her again.

Satisfied, Darshan turned to look for his *drachwyr*.

She was on her hands and knees in the grass.

He barely had the tips of two mental claws in her back, but to his perception, the gashes ran nearly from her shoulder blades to her waist. They were bleeding radiance.

He stopped over her, and she slowly turned her head to look up at him. Blue eyes like the sparkling iridescence he'd seen upon her wings met his gaze in defiance. Darshan hooked his fingers under her arm and drew her to her feet.

She sucked in her breath with a hiss. Then she drew upon her power.

Perception shifted—wondrously, startlingly.

With her power radiating against his, equal and opposing, the space of their minds intercepted. Suddenly they were as colliding stars, one burning cold, the other hot, their outer atmospheres dangerously interacting, combusting...merging.

He swirled his awareness through the space of her mind and tasted of her name.

It tasted...*good.*

A hungering smile parted his lips. *Amithaiya'geshwen.*

Darshanvenkhátraman, she returned with furious rebuke. Then she added with a mental hiss, *I know who you are.*

His smile widened. "Then you know that you cannot defeat me." He looked her over, seeing a trapped dove rather than the caged lion she pretended. "Not alone. Not without your brothers."

This truth smoldered in her gaze.

"No doubt you're wondering why I've invaded your sanctuary." He lifted his eyes towards a collection of tents, now becoming shadows on the high hill above them. He gleaned much about that place from sharing the space of her mind.

He shifted his gaze back to hers. "I want to speak with your First Lord. You will take me to him." He gave the faintest nudge upon his mental hooks for emphasis.

She gasped. Then she ground her teeth and glared up at him. "Remove your claws. I will do as you ask."

Darshan chuckled. "You doing as I ask, little dove, is an inescapable eventuality. My *claws* shall remain as they are to ensure your willing and swift compliance."

Defiance fulminated in Mithaiya's gaze. The air around them wavered as if with heat. Lines of radiating power extended now for hundreds of paces; her will balanced against his, her power vibrating synchronously against his own.

Power pulsed–*flared*, pulsed–*flared*, each time extending farther, rippling deeper into the fabric of the realm. The distant trees began shaking in rhythm with their battling wills.

Darshan admitted an intense enjoyment in this collision.

Holding her was like holding a star in his arms...a star begging to be unmade. Singing harmonics thrummed though him, electrifying his form, *intensifying* every sense. This was no carnal desire; this was a need so intrinsic it blazed from his very core.

Whatever else Pelas might say about them, there was no denying they had been made to destroy. Holding this creature of light in his arms, she who represented the diametric opposite of himself, Darshan felt an exhilaration so heady he could barely control himself.

Her expression shifted to dismay. Her gaze flicked to the alternately standing and flattening grass, the pulsating land, the trembling trees. She looked back to him entreatingly.

He perceived the fear in her thoughts, the concern in her heart.

She said with a terrible, breathless fear, "We will tear the world apart."

His smile offered a certain irony. "Then you would be wise to take me quickly where I've requested."

Mithaiya's brow furrowed. She stared a moment longer at him. Then she lowered her gaze. A curtain of ebony hair draped her downcast eyes from his view. "Very well," she whispered.

It must've cost her much to submit to him. He couldn't read it in the mental space they shared—the magnetosphere of her mind he well perceived, but her thoughts were protected within her inner atmosphere.

She lifted him a glance, searching of permission.

He nodded her to lead away.

His mental claws were dug deep into her energy. His fingers, he kept firmly around her arm. In this manner they crossed the hill beneath the night, a moving epicenter of pulsating waves.

The node was not close.

Pain colored the ripples of her power. Sometimes she stumbled, gasped…but he kept her on her feet, and she led him without resistance.

He sensed the node as one might perceive a distant window in a wall by the light shining through it.

She stopped before the node and looked up at him, her moonlit features washed in regret. Doubtless she loathed bringing him before the one she served so loyally, especially knowing nothing of his intentions. But the trees were shaking around them as if with a hurricane wind, and the ground was rolling beneath their feet. She had little choice but to obey.

Mithaiya drew in a shuddering breath, and with his hand clasped firmly around her arm, she called her power and drew him across the node—

Furnace heat blasted Darshan.

Brilliance blinded him.

A raging solar wind ripped the *drachwyr* from his fingers as it tore him off his feet. He flew, tumbled, bounced across a lake of near-boiling sand.

He reached for his power, only to gasp at the thinness of its tides. There, in the wash of that creative furnace, *deyjiin* found little purchase. Still, he managed enough to anchor his shell and protect it from the worst of the heat.

Slowly, he regained his feet. Straightening, he looked around. She'd brought him to a planet circling a blazing sun, virtually airless, with an atmosphere more magnetic than gaseous. He felt the pull of the planetary core fighting against the star's voracious gravity; these opposed forces made lead weights of his bones.

Darshan lifted his gaze to the monstrous star looming on the planet's horizon, consuming most of the sky. Reddish-black storms exploded on the sun's boiling surface.

In the nearer distance, the *drachwyr* had shimmered into her dragon form, gilded scales backlit by the sun's fiery halo. She turned her lengthy head to him, and with a righteous glare, opened her muzzle in soundless fury.

Another sun boiled within her maw.

The strong solar wind was burning holes in his shield. Darshan felt an urgency uncharacteristic and rare. His shell could endure much punishment, but he hadn't made it to long withstand *these* conditions.

He collected his power in gasping gulps—as much as he could rapidly gather, for its tides were so languid—and tore the fabric of existence. He threw himself into Shadow's dark and icy waters just as the sun's searing winds tore his shield to shreds. It was the closest he'd ever known of desperation.

Mithaiya's body tumbled haplessly on the solar wind, yet those boiling tides of elemental creation freed her from Darshan's claws of power.

The moment she felt herself free of him, she exploded into the form. Her human body was as elementally intrinsic to the Realms of Light as Darshan's true form was to Chaos.

He had damaged her with his power. This she understood. How badly, she couldn't yet say. But as light congealed into form, she found that she couldn't lift her wings.

Pain racked her. The solar winds blasted that desolate place with their furnace heat, but she still felt cold inside. His power had hollowed a dark place into her core. It would take time to fill it again with light.

Her anger and indignation took the first strides in this direction.

As her form at last solidified and some meager strength returned, Mithaiya turned her head to glare furiously at him.

How dare he invade her home and make demands of her! How *dare* he expect her to betray her oaths! How dare he require *anything* of her!

She roared a soundless cry of blistering rebuke and watched him stumble back, an arm raised against the burning light.

Then he tore the fabric of existence and threw himself into the safety of Shadow.

And good riddance.

Suddenly exhausted, Mithaiya settled her snout onto the boiling sands. She could barely think for the pain coursing through her.

Well…Balaji often said that thought was overrated. Or was it Náiir who said that?

By the light, but her mind felt numb. Her thoughts had frozen into foreign shapes.

As she settled to rest, her large pupils narrowed to mere slits among crystals of variegated blue, their mirrored lenses reflecting the boiling corona that loomed so massively in the otherwise black sky.

The solar wind embraced her, caressed her as a mother comforting an ailing child.

Mithaiya's gilded lids slowly closed, and she willingly submitted to her mother star's ministrations.

PART TWO

"If you must resort to force to win, you've already lost the game."

–The Fifth Vestal Björn van Gelderan

FORTY-ONE

"Stories travel farthest on the wings of impossibility."
–The desert parable, *The Eagle and the Wren*

TRELL CLENCHED HIS jaw as his grey eyes inspected the serpentine path of the Taran River, which wove in and out of view towards the great volcanic peak of Mount Attarak in the east. Behind him, the dark clouds of a storm were moving in, trailing a striated curtain of rain. The flood from that downpour had yet to reach the valley below him, but it was only a matter of time—and not much of that. The Converted Commander Raegus n'Harnalt's men were working feverishly to construct a cable ferry and cross the Taran before rising water levels and the storm stranded them on the wrong side of the river.

Trell had only just met up with Raegus's company in the middle of this effort, and the Converted commander had done his best to greet him amid the urgent rush. "By the Seventeen, but you're a welcome sight, Trell of the Tides!" He'd taken Trell by the arm and promptly explained what he needed from him.

Trell had managed to give the Emir's written missive to Raegus as the commander was all but shoving him back on his horse, but they'd had no chance to read it together or speak of the truths it contained.

A hard uphill climb later, Trell found himself atop the mountain, pinned between mystery and the storm. He turned his head away from the rising wind and murmured to soothe Gendaia, who was shifting uneasily beneath him. Eastward, between his cliff-side vantage and the snowcapped volcano lay miles of forested mountains concealing deep ravines, ancient ruined cities and the moldering bones of Cyrene kings. If he squinted, he could just make out a hulking stone fortress that could only be Khor Taran, the fist at the end of the mountain's arm.

Verily, the fortress loomed there, taunting him, goading—*gloating* even—smug in its certainty that Trell would never free the men being held behind its walls, sure that his meager forces could never threaten its impregnability.

But that was his first problem—they weren't *his* forces to command, not until this company completed their initial mission to free the region from Saldarian marauders, the undoubted work of whom currently lay all around him. Everywhere Trell looked in the hillside town, the doors of stone cottages hung open, gates sprawled unhinged, vegetable gardens lay trampled.

Raegus had tasked him to inspect the hillside town, something the commander himself had intended to do before the coming storm made crossing the river a more pressing concern. "Look for survivors!" Raegus had called to Trell as two of his men were dragging him away to help with another matter. "Look for anything to point us in the direction of those responsible!" From the frustration in the commander's voice, Trell had gotten the idea that this wasn't the first such town Raegus's company had come across.

The glaring light of afternoon shed long shadows across the town's steep and narrow streets, all with an imposing view of Mount Attarak, but it failed to illuminate any rationale for the town's abandonment. The only living thing Trell had encountered was a lone chicken clucking its way across the road.

"Trell!" the Avataren Loukas n'Abraxis ducked beneath the low lintel of a cottage door and strode back up the hill towards where Trell sat his horse. Loukas held a length of black wood in his hand. "I found something."

Learning that Loukas was traveling with Raegus's company had been a welcome surprise. In fact, Trell could hardly think of anyone he'd have been happier to reunite with. Though not Converted—Loukas was one of the Emir's hired consultants—he, Ware and Graeme had been Trell's closest confidants at the Cry. The Avataren had been the first man Raegus had called that day to accompany Trell on his investigation of the town.

Like many Avatarens, Loukas had a fey look about him. His slender frame and angular features, drawn sharply beneath a shock of auburn hair, made him seem rather a porcelain doll, more suited for velvet court chairs than the dust and blood-filled roads of war. The Converted joked relentlessly at his expense—all the more for he was nearly useless with a blade—but Trell had never encountered a finer combat engineer.

Reaching Trell and their horses, Loukas leaned elbows across his saddle and held out the broken end of a black quarrel to Trell. "What do you make of this?"

Trell took the bolt and looked over the shaft and fletching. His gaze tightened.

The last time he'd seen a quarrel of that make, the bolts had been showering down from a high ridge in the Kutsamak. That had been just minutes before he'd sent Alyneri off with an ailing Fynnlar to seek safety at the First Lord's *sa'reyth*…moments before he'd fought and then faltered beneath a wielder's compulsion…instants before he'd come face to face with his brother Sebastian, both knowing and not knowing his countenance in the same heartbreaking moment.

Trell handed the broken bolt back to Loukas and cast a tight gaze out across the abandoned town again. "It's a Saldarian quarrel."

"Ah…well, at least our suspicions are confirmed." Loukas remounted and turned another look around, his green eyes speculative. "We suspected Saldarians were taking these people, we just can't figure out where they're taking them, or why—"

"For nothing constructive, that's the path proving true." The Converted soldier Tannour Valeri of Vest trotted his horse around a corner and over to them. He wore the cloth of his scarf wrapped about his ebony hair and shoulders in the fashion of his eastern homeland rather than the turbans favored by the Seventeen Tribes. This amounted to everything Trell knew about the Vestian.

Tannour's pale blue eyes tightened on Loukas, a narrowing that accentuated both their almond shape and the darker rim of blue limning their edges. "May I see the bolt, Loukas?"

Loukas wordlessly handed it over to Tannour. Trell wondered what history lay between them, for any time they came into contact with one another, the air became uncomfortably charged.

Tannour examined the broken bolt. "This is the fifth of such towns we've found, Trell—did our *A'dal* tell you?"

Trell shook his head. "As you saw as we were leaving, he was pressed for time."

"Five towns, not a single inhabitant remaining—alive *or* dead. No trace of where they've gone, no tracks leading away from the towns, certainly no evidence to indicate an entire populace's departure, and never a quarrel or blade left behind. We're chasing ghosts through the Taran Forest while the trees laugh at our folly." He tossed the bolt indifferently back to Loukas. "It's shades of foretelling up and down the path."

Trell looked bemusedly to his friend.

Loukas explained, "He means it bodes badly for what has happened as well as what's to come. You'll have to excuse Tannour, Trell. He can't but speak in Vestian parlance."

Tannour snapped off a brusque reply in his native Vestian—one of the few languages Trell didn't speak—and spun his horse away and down the hill.

Loukas stared after him. "He says he'll go search the east gate." But if told from the Avataren's strained expression, this was clearly not all Tannour had said.

The wind chased down the street in pursuit of the Vestian, a herald of the storm's imminent arrival. Trell pushed a hand to hold his hair back from his eyes and pondered the mystery of their surroundings. Tannour had spoken the right of it; the town had clearly been abandoned in a rush, yet there was little evidence of their departure outside the town walls. Were the Saldarians *flying* the townspeople off on winged horses? "Has Raegus any sense of where these people are being taken, or for what purpose?"

"East. That's all we know." Loukas glanced to the sky and the rapidly advancing clouds and pulled up the hood of his cloak.

"East." Trell looked back across the valley towards the distant, stony outcropping that was Khor Taran. It was supposedly a Nadori fortress, not a stronghold for Saldarian mercenaries…so why did he have such a sneaking feeling that Khor Taran was where they would find both the townspeople and his father's men?

Wishful thinking…

"What are you thinking?" Loukas's tone drew Trell's attention back to him. The Avataren narrowed his gaze suspiciously. "I know that look."

Trell blinked. "I have a look?"

"You have a hundred of them if you have one, Trell of the Tides. One to represent each of the thoughts you never voice to the rest of us. It took me two years to learn the language of your looks."

Trell cracked a smile and turned away again. "I was thinking… wondering, if we might find our missing townspeople at Khor Taran," and he nodded towards the fortress.

Loukas followed his gaze, whereupon his green eyes narrowed with speculation. "What's at Khor Taran for you besides missing townspeople?"

Trell's smile widened culpably as he looked back to his friend. It had been a long time since he'd spent time with someone who intuited his mind so readily—that is, someone other than Alyneri. "I've missed you, Loukas."

Loukas actually might've blushed a little. "Trell…" he fingered his reins, his expression becoming pensive, "whatever the Emir sent you here to do, you know the entire company would follow you without a whisper of protest—"

The clatter of hooves on cobblestones drew both their gazes higher up the street just as a Basi rider came storming around the corner, both rider and horse mud-spattered. Trell recognized the scout, Saran, with whom he'd worked on several campaigns for the Emir.

Saran seemed to bring the wind with him, for it gusted past him and continued on down the street, ripping at Trell's cloak and setting the doors and shutters of the abandoned homes to squealing on their hinges.

"*A'dal*—I mean," Saran corrected himself, "*Ama-Kai'alil*, the water is rising in the Taran. Raegus, our *A'dal*, needs you all back." His words held urgency's sharp bite, and indeed, as evidence of such need, the first drops of rain began falling.

Trell exchanged a look with Loukas and then told Saran, "We'll return at once."

"And by Jai'Gar's will, in all haste." The scout spun his horse around, heeled the animal back into a canter and sped away.

Loukas quickly rounded up Tannour while Trell collected the other two men who'd accompanied him, and then they were all following Saran's example.

The way beyond the town carved a leaf-strewn tunnel through the trees. Tangled limbs towered over their heads. Churned mud lay beneath their horses' hooves. The forest at first offered an oppressive silence, but then the pattering rain reached them and rapidly grew into a downpour.

The wind shook the limbs overhead, raining leaves and debris. The damp scent of moss and earth clung to the air and cloyed in their lungs, while a prickling sense of things gone awry only grew more emphatic beneath the rumbling thunder. The trail was steep and soon became slick. The horses slid often. Gendaia snorted her indignation continuously as Trell guided her down the mountainside.

Save for Gendaia's complaints, they rode in silence beneath the drumming rain, bound to solidarity less by mutual pact than by a growing tension and a shared sense of self-preservation.

By the time they regained the river, the water level had noticeably risen. Gone were the placid green waters from the time of Trell's arrival. In their place ran an angry tumult, rapidly approaching a flood.

They dismounted into mud at the staging point, where four men were loading pack animals onto the last raft, joining half a dozen Converted already there, who were trying to soothe and secure their uneasy horses. Two other rafts full with men and horse were already mid-river in pursuit of the opposite shore.

Rain fell in sheets between the forested hills that bound each side of the wide river. Long, grey veils blurred the figures swarming the distant bank.

The rain thrummed in Trell's ears. The river roared. Riversong shouted at him to make haste.

Saran was already guiding his horse onto the raft, and the rest of them again followed his example. The last to board, Trell reached for the guide rope that they would use to haul the raft across the water, made sure all of the men lined up before him had hold of the rope also, and then nodded to the men manning the mooring lines. "Let's go!"

The moment the raft was released, every able man hauled upon the guide rope to heave the craft across the current. Even with the combined strength of over a dozen men, the river still threatened to drag them downstream.

Trell used all of his strength to pull on the wet rope, hand over hand. The rough hemp abraded his palms. Water sloshed across his boots. The raft rocked and bounced through the waves. He was drenched and sweating only moments after leaving the shore.

The angry Taran wrenched at the craft. Muddied waters carrying a host of submerged threats attempted continuously to drag them from their course. Trell and the others held the raft to a wavering line with white knuckles and force of will. They were overmatched, fighting against the river's power with mortal strength, but Trell prayed that Thalma, the Goddess of Luck, wouldn't turn a blind eye to them just yet.

Elsewhere on the raft, men were swearing—or praying. It was hard to tell the difference from watching their mouths alone, for the combined noise of storm and river transposed even shouted words into whispers.

On the opposite bank, men were waving their arms. Trell couldn't hear them for the roaring and Naiadithine's cacophony raging in his skull. He could hardly spare attention to whatever the men on shore were trying to tell them, for like the others on the raft, he was focusing his every effort on just placing one hand before the other, on pulling one more time…

A prickling sense urged a glance upstream—

The uprooted tree coming towards them seemed a dark leviathan, bristling with broken limbs.

Trell's breath froze in his lungs. Then it exploded out of him. "*Faster!*"

The few who heard him widened their eyes and increased their efforts. The raft was near enough to the opposite bank for them to see the concern on the faces of the line of men who were trying with equal desperation to haul them in.

For an instant as the bobbing tree sped towards them, Trell thought it might just miss…

The current or aught else pitched the tree into the raft. Sharp limbs raked across Trell's back. Then the massive trunk slammed them sidelong.

Men and animals staggered. Trell shouted to keep hauling, but the tree had caught upon their raft and now was dragging them downstream.

Loukas shoved his way to the edge and began chopping with his sword—not at the limbs which were caught on the raft, as two others were frantically doing, but at the ropes that bound the logs together at the raft's far end. The other two quickly caught on and helped, while Trell and Tannour rallied the rest for a final press towards shore.

Abruptly the two logs which were bound together broke away, and it seemed as if the leviathan would move on to consume more interesting fare, but the long end of the tree trunk must've struck against something deeper in the river, for suddenly the rooted end erupted towards them.

A flail of deadly spikes struck through the core of the passengers. The raft rocked dangerously, dislodging horses and their owners. One horse gave an equine scream and reared, knocking several others awry, and finally tumbled backwards into the water.

It's flailing head struck Loukas, and he went into the water with it.

Before he knew himself, Trell was shoving his sword at the nearest man and unfastening his cloak as he dove in after Loukas. Tannour or Saran might've called his name just as his head hit the murky waters.

Something rough scraped along his back. Formless things bumped against his arms and legs. Trell swam for the surface through the flotsam of miles of forest, conscious of the current dragging countless submerged dangers along its watery course around and beneath him.

He broke the surface and slung wet hair from his eyes. Far behind him now, the raft had nearly reached the shore. Trell treaded water and looked for Loukas.

The horses and their owners he spotted further downstream, misplaced sea animals swimming for a last stretch of beach. Around Trell, the river was full of broken things.

He caught the echo of his name and spun his head to see men scrambling over rocks, chasing him along the shoreline. They were calling to him, waving him towards that last outlet. There was no way he could reach it, not with the current so strong.

The rain stung his eyes. The water's chill stole his breath. Downstream, the river tumbled into whitewater. Trell caught sight of a dark head bobbing over the first of those waves. He put urgency into his arms and legs and swam through the rain after Loukas.

The current quickly dragged him into a churning cauldron. Trell shoved his feet in front of him, sucked in a breath at the bottom of a wave and then suffered repeated lashings directly in his face through the first section of rapids.

He recovered his breath right before the river dove again and pitched him into another series of punishing waves. Trell just tried to keep his feet downstream—better his boots ram into a submerged rock than his head—but the river made a toy of him, and he tumbled from one angry wave to the next.

Oddly, it was a familiar terror, this elemental flood making an easy pawn of his body. As another wave consumed him, dragging him under, he submitted to it, as he'd always done. The river swung him around a bend into a ravine where high walls soared on both sides. The land continued dropping away, quickening the river's pace. Further ahead, an anvil-shaped rock split the river in twain.

A wave smashed Trell in the face. He sailed over a short falls, dropped through froth and tumbled out the chute at the other end. He came up choking and coughing, his nose and lungs burning. The current was carrying him right towards the rock.

If he timed it right, he could find respite there; wrong, and the current would smash him against immovable stone, trapped beneath the water.

He'd hardly had time to think since jumping in, but now he offered a heartfelt plea. *Goddess, I pray you*—the river sucked him into another set of rapids and bludgeoned him with churning waves; there was no opportunity for breath, no chance of influencing his course towards or away from the rock, only Her grace would carry him safely—*look fondly upon me one more time...*

Trell came up sputtering and choking and with the massive rock looming.

Then the current shoved him chest-first into it, the air exploded from his lungs, his body scraped across sharp stone, and his boot caught on something and stuck—

He felt a split-second's desperation as the force of the current tumbled him sideways and onto his back—

A hand grabbed his arm, wrenching at his shoulder.

Trell reached fast with his other hand, and Loukas grabbed both of his arms and hauled him back up. "*Trell!*"

"My boot—" Trell gasped hoarsely. The river still held him trapped against the stone, but at least he could breathe now.

Loukas clambered higher on the rock, wrapped both arms around Trell's chest and held him still against the current, while Trell reached down and freed his foot from his boot. A breathless minute later, the Avataren hauled him out of the water.

Trell collapsed beside Loukas atop the angular rock.

Foolish...but brave... the river seemed to whisper with a mother's approving smile. A wave lapped at Trell's foot as though a caress.

Trell rolled onto his side and focused on trying to make his waterlogged lungs work properly again. Had he been foolish to launch himself into a flooded river? Certainly. But what else could he have done? He'd already sacrificed one friend to the Cry when Graeme fell to his death. Did his Goddess really require him to sacrifice another?

"*By Fiera's flaming hair*, Trell!" Loukas only swore in the name of Avataren fire goddess when he was really discomposed. He gave a breathless exclamation and fell exhaustedly onto his back. "By my soul, what were you *thinking*?"

Trell coughed up more water and managed hoarsely, "I was thinking you might need my help."

"You shouldn't have put yourself in harm's way for me!"

Trell met his gaze evenly. "Wouldn't you have done the same?"

"That's not fair." The Avataren's expression twisted and he looked away, swallowing. "I'm not the Emir's adopted son."

Or a prince of Dannym, Trell's conscience reminded, *or a Player in the First Lord's game.* Yet if his path was meant to end this war, then he certainly wanted Loukas n'Abraxis walking that path with him.

Trell spent the next four breaths thinking about not moving and the four after that working up the will to do so. Then he gingerly pushed up to his hands.

His lungs ached, he could tell from the way his back burned that it was a mangled mess, and a bad scrape on his elbow was bleeding through his shirt, but nothing appeared to be broken except his judgment.

Wincing a little at this thought, he shifted around into a sitting position, noting as he did that Loukas had already had the presence of mind to doff his boots. The Avataren's bare feet looked very white against the dark, wet stone.

Trell dragged his remaining boot out of the water and freed his foot from it. He dumped the former into the river and watched it sweep away downstream to be quickly swallowed by the first frothing wave. The river was tumbling just as furiously ahead of them as it had been behind—perhaps more so.

"Let's find a way to live through this," Trell said quietly, not at all certain of their chances, "then you can chastise me."

Still lying on his back, Loukas pushed palms to his eyes. "They'll blame me, you know," he grumbled, "Raegus and all the rest of them." With his damp clothes clinging to him and accentuating his slender form, he seemed very much the stranded wet cat. "Tannour will probably garrote me in my sleep."

"Come, Loukas," Trell nudged him with a smile and a tap on his arm, "put that engineering mind of yours to work and help me find a line of passage through these rapids."

"*'Come, Loukas,'*" Loukas mimicked with palms still pressed to his eyes, "*'figure out a way for us to cross this impassable river.'*" His arms flopped down at his sides and he turned Trell a flat look. "*'Come, Loukas, devise a means of destroying this bridge so that no one will be able to rebuild it.'*" Loukas exhaled a forceful breath and heaved himself up. "*'Come, Loukas, figure out how to rig a zipline to ferry all of us five hundred paces across this bottomless canyon.'*" He crawled up the rock while leveling Trell a baleful, green-eyed stare. "*'Come, Loukas, construct a siege engine with these twigs and this pile of sand.'*"

Trell chuckled. "I'm getting the impression that you feel I ask impossible things of you." He eyed his friend humorously as the latter sat down beside him. "What was your plan then?"

Loukas hugged his knees to his chest. His auburn hair clung to his head, shadows hung beneath his eyes, and his lips had taken on a bluish tinge. Despite his levity, there was little of hope in his gaze. He shrugged. "Wait here until the water levels dropped."

Trell angled a look at him. "The likelihood of surviving even one night—"

"Offers better odds than swimming that gauntlet," he nodded towards the way ahead.

Trell looked back to the river. It churned through the canyon in a brown froth while waterfalls tumbled down from both sides of the rocky ravine, muddy streams forged by the storm. Rain still pelted the river, still stung their skin and numbed Trell's bare head with its constant drumming. With the dropping temperature, a pervasive chill had already claimed his flesh, and the night hadn't even settled upon them yet.

He didn't trust at all in the Wind God Azerjaiman's mercy. How much did he trust in Naiadithine's?

"The night will kill us if we stay here." Trell pushed dripping hair back from his eyes. His head was throbbing, his hands and thoughts growing increasingly numb as concentration fled to warmer locales. Directly below their bare feet, the two streams of the river met again in a boiling wave. "But there's the slightest chance that we can survive the river."

Loukas barked a dubious laugh. "There's the slightest chance I'll be elected the next emir of the Seventeen Tribes. I'd take that bet over this one."

Trell heard the wariness in Loukas's voice. Surely it ought to ring in his own as well…

Nothing so pleases one's gods as a leap of faith, Trell of the Tides.

Trell caught his breath.

Had he really just *heard* those words, or had he merely imagined them, his numbed mind starting to show more deleterious effects of the chill that had hold of his body?

Yet he couldn't strike from his consciousness the feeling that the river had truly *spoken* to him, not merely a divine whisper, but actual concepts conveyed—if not with words, then at least with an understanding that translated into thoughts, whole and complete.

'Nothing so pleases one's gods as a leap of faith...'

In reflecting on this idea, as well as the surprisingly droll tone of its conveyance, it occurred to Trell that every time he'd asked Naiadithine for Her aid, he'd felt guilt in doing so, as though his efforts were preying upon Her goodwill, or taking advantage of the grace She'd bestowed upon him.

But what if that wasn't how Naiadithine viewed it?

Riversong had never sounded so cacophonous, and he'd never understood it more clearly.

That's when the truth hit him: Ramu had Awakened him to an awareness of *elae*, and now the riversong made *sense*. Nay, far more than this...

For an instant's hesitation, all of Trell's mortal apprehension at the idea of conversing with a god bubbled to the surface, bringing an effervescent discomfort to his stomach and a lightness that made his head swim.

Was he really going to do this? Deliberately try to communicate with a *god*? It seemed impossibly arrogant that he would try, and absolutely, beyond a doubt imperative that he should.

And with his next inhale—slow and deep, a soldier's focusing breath to summon calm—he admitted to himself that he'd always known how to reach Naiadithine, that indeed, the submission She required had been his native inclination every time the waters had claimed him, as if She'd marked him somehow as Her own from the moment of his birth, blessing him with the innate knowledge of how to summon Her in times of need.

Whether or not this was true—*however* he'd come by the grace of Her goodwill—Trell called upon it then, both opening his mind, as Alyneri and others had taught him, and opening his heart, as Naiadithine required of those She'd graced.

*Greetings, my Goddess...*he let the welcome flow away on the rushing waters, let the current pull open the doors of his heart.

And only a breath later, she answered him.

*Trell of the Tides...*Naiadithine's true voice sounded the liquid chime of crystalline waters, as multifaceted as a waterfall's veils beneath the shifting sun. Laughter hinted in her tone, and affection. *What took you so long?*

Even anticipating Her reply, wonder gripped Trell chest in a tight hold. A disbelieving laugh choked out of him, drawing Loukas's curious gaze.

He felt warmth come up beneath his chilled cheeks and knew his face must've been turning pink. *You might've chosen a smarter champion, My Lady. I'm a little slow in figuring things out.*

But ever earnest in the effort. For an instant, the rushing waters seemed to carry her smile and more besides...a sense of *Her* that was as perceptible to him as if Fhionna stood upon that very rock, letting him see the admiration in her eyes, or taste of her attraction in a kiss. The waters churned past him, heralding the Goddess's favor. *What do you desire from me, Trell of the Tides?*

Trell glanced to Loukas, who was staring strongly at him now, pointedly asking for explanation for his silence, or perhaps for the flush that had come to his cheeks, or his undoubtedly dumb-faced grin. Trell held up a finger, begging a moment's patience in the lingering mystery. *Safe passage, My Lady.*

Is that all? Trell couldn't be sure, but he got the impression Naiadithine was smirking at him. Nor could he quite discern the undercurrent of Her tone—did She *want* him to want more from Her?

Trell tried to keep his focus beneath the pounding rain—which was dulling his faculties with its ever-present, hypnotic thrumming on his skull—and somehow force a coherent thought through the heady spinning that had claimed him as a result of actually *communicating* with a god.

He dragged both hands back through his hair and inhaled deeply. *Perhaps... something to keep us afloat?*

Way ahead of you, Trell of the Tides.

Something banged into the rock behind him.

Trell and Loukas both spun. Then they launched at the same time to grab onto the little skiff that the water was both pushing onto the rock and trying to drag away. A moment's labored scramble, and they had the heavy thing pulled to safety out of the current.

Loukas fell back on his hands and turned to Trell a disbelieving look. "What..." he waved at boat, rock, river and him, "*what* just happened here?"

Follow the water, Trell of the Tides... Naiadithine's farewell felt a chaste kiss, as a parting grace.

Trell flung the hair from his eyes—*oh, to be free of this accursed rain!*—and winced slightly. "I think She wants us to follow the river." He got to his feet.

"*Who?*" Loukas pinned him beneath a hammering stare. For all he had the build of a minstrel, his gaze could sure give a man a pounding. "*Who* wants us to follow the river?"

"Naiadithine." Trell put one foot carefully in the boat to steady it.

"The River Goddess?" Loukas's voice sounded a bit shrill, but he might've just been trying to be heard over the raging water.

Trell looked to him. "Get in, Loukas." He held the skiff while Loukas climbed in, glaring profoundly at him the while and muttering oaths in at least six languages. Trell bent down and tried to work free some of the debris clinging to the rudder, whereupon Loukas remarked darkly, "Are you familiar with the Akkadian parable about the prince and the tiger?"

Trell looked up under his brows. "The one where the prince gets eaten or where the tiger loses her ruby?"

Loukas speared him with a stare. "The one where the prince learns it is a dangerous—never mind insanely stupid!—idea to seek the favor of a god."

"Oh, that one." Trell grinned at him. "Hold on now." He grabbed the rim of the boat and launched them off the rock.

The current instantly caught and slung the skiff around, slung Trell into the bottom, and before he could get his bearings or claim his seat, they were tossing and pitching down the rapids, smashing through waves when they weren't being deluged by them, both of them holding hard to each side of the little boat, the rudder forgotten and useless in any case against such a torrent.

At one point where breath was possible, Loukas spun Trell such a look—*And you thought we could swim this and survive?*

Trell grinned through the hair plastered to his face. Loukas had a point.

How long they rode the river, Trell couldn't say, for each moment passed with that heightened sense of timelessness that comes when a man is fighting for his life. Hours passed as minutes; minutes stretched into hours. Never is time more malleable than when a man has the sense that each ticking second could become his last.

Finally the canyon broadened again and the river flattened out. Trell saw a stretch of flooded trees downstream where the water became smooth. He pointed through the rain. "We can make that eddy!" Well...they could if they swam harder than they'd ever swum before, and if nothing lay hidden beneath the churning waves, and if the river graced them with extraordinary luck. "But we have to swim!"

Loukas considered the trees briefly and then nodded. He appeared determined, but Trell worried for him. His body was shaking, his face was very pale and his lips were blue.

Trell pulled off his belt and rethreaded it through its buckle. Then he shoved one arm through the loop and waved to Loukas to do the same, shouting to be heard over the rain, "So we don't get separated!"

It was a tenuous link, but if there was a better way to keep them together with the materials and time they had available, Trell couldn't think of one.

Loukas hooked his arm through the belt and nodded to him.

They jumped out of the boat.

The current carried the little skiff fast away. Loukas could barely keep his head above the waves, so Trell kept the belt firmly within the hook of his left arm and used his right to maneuver them both towards shore, kicking as hard as he could manage.

It was a harrowing few minutes.

He finally reached the eddy where the current eased, and soon thereafter—and to his immense relief—he had them into shallower waters. With his own teeth chattering, Trell wrapped his arms around Loukas and half swam, half-dragged him onto land.

There they collapsed, side by side, in the mud. Cold, slimy earth had never felt more welcome.

The last few minutes of swimming had cast a fog over Trell's thoughts. His body was shaking forcefully, yet he could barely find the energy to move. He hugged closer to Loukas and tried to inch both their bodies further up the hillside. A grey twilight had claimed the river, darkness the trees…

Trell must've lost consciousness, because when he became aware again with a sudden start, he was staring at a pair of muddied boots. His gaze traced their line up to a belt sporting a pair of daggers and a wickedly fat scimitar, farther up over an embroidered *kameez* and vest beneath an expensive cloak, to the three chin braids that marked the man a member of M'Nador's nobility. A tattoo of thorns collared his neck, marking him an heir within the Council of Princes, but the shiny, trident brand of a thief stood out starkly against one of the inked thorns, ruining its line.

Rolan Lamodaar. Trell heaved a sigh of relief and let his head fall back in the mud. He'd been on several campaigns with Rolan before being assigned to the Cry. He'd never encountered a man who hated Radov abin Hadorin more.

Rolan grunted amusedly. "You two have got to be the luckiest bastards Thalma ever saw fit to grace."

Trell wanted to agree with him, but he couldn't make his lips form words just then.

"N-not Thalma," Loukas stammered, his voice barely audible. "N-naiad-dithine."

At this, one of Rolan's shaggy black eyebrows hitched an inch higher than the other. He bent to help Trell up, and together they dragged Loukas to his feet. It took a few attempts to get him to stay upright, and then he just stood there with his shoulders hunched, teeth chattering, hugging his chest and shivering.

Rolan planted a hand on his scimitar and looked Loukas up and down. "I thought you didn't believe in our gods, Loukas n'Abraxis."

Chin to his chest, Loukas managed faintly, "I'll believe anything T-Trell tells me to b-believe."

Rolan looked to Trell with his rearing bear of an eyebrow seeking explanation for this statement.

Trell wrapped an arm around Loukas's icy shoulders. "Don't listen to him. He's delirious."

"No doubt." Rolan goaded Loukas with his gaze. "I would've thought Valeri would've been the one went into the Taran after you, n'Abraxis. Or maybe I've been reading him wrong and he was relieved to let the river claim you."

Trell shook his head. "Tannour didn't see him fall."

Rolan—or at least his eyebrow—appeared unconvinced. "In any case, n'Abraxis is lucky you went in for him, Trell of the Tides, and we're all damned fortunate you made it out still breathing."

"Rolan!" A male voice called to them from further up the hill.

"*Balé!*" he answered in the desert tongue. *Yes.* "I found them!" Rolan clapped Loukas hard on the arm and added with a grin, "Hang in there, Yashar," which was the name of a cat with nine lives from a famous Akkadian parable.

Soon, men were flooding down the hill, Loukas was being wrapped in blankets, someone placed a heavy blanket around Trell's shoulders as well… but as they were encouraging him away, he looked back to the river, which lay darkly now beneath night's blanket. Riversong still sang loudly in his thoughts.

'It is an ephemeral, perilous state to be beloved of a god,' thus the saying went.

Every story Trell had ever heard warned that a mortal need seek no better way to an alacritous death than to court or be courted by a god. If the god of his desire didn't do him in, another god, stricken by jealousy or greed or simply the whimsical caprice that often infects immortality, most assuredly would.

The Goddess Naiadithine had saved Trell's life so many times…thus far she'd asked nothing of him in return, though he'd given her multiple offerings from his own gratitude. But now that Trell had *somewhat* met her— at least gotten more of a sense of Her, a perception of Her…corporeality, if such could be said, and in the least the experience of an actual interchange of communication between them—he was beginning to suspect that Her benevolence would in fact come at a price.

What troubled him most in this thought was wondering if it would be a price he'd be willing to pay, and if not…well, he didn't like to contemplate the consequences of denying a god, especially one to whom he so many times owed his life.

FORTY-TWO

*"Just because it can be done doesn't mean it should be done,
and what should be done cannot always be accomplished,
but where the two coincide—this must be done."*
– The Akkadian Emir Zafir bin Safwan al Abdul-Basir

LATER THAT NIGHT, after Trell had ensured Loukas was being well cared for and was attending to himself—which mainly involved sitting beside Rolan's campfire wrapped in blankets and being fussed over needlessly by everyone from the company's Healer to the cooks—Raegus's valet showed up and hovered at the edge of the firelight, beyond the reach of Rolan Lamodaar's long arm, if not beyond the spear of his gaze.

"What is it, Rami?" the Nadorii prince waved the boy into his lighted domain.

The lad stepped forward tentatively, a youth of ten and three at best, with large, dark eyes and a hairless upper lip. Those large eyes darted between Trell and Rolan as if unsure which of the two he should address. In the end, he sort of spoke to the air between them. "The *A'dal* is asking for Pr—Trell of the Tides."

"Pr-Trell?" Rolan's dark eyes scrutinized the lad while his tone taunted. "Is that a new prefix? Will you be calling me Pr-Rolan?"

The boy went red in the cheeks. He shifted a desperate gaze to Trell.

Trell set down his bowl of stew and pushed to his feet. "I guess that's my cue."

"Try not to let Raegus beat you to a pulp, Pr-Trell." Rolan's dark eyes glinted with amusement. "You're about to get an earful, as Sherq blows west."

Trell followed Rami to a large tent. He nodded to the two men standing guard, neither of whom he knew—though both seemed to recognize him, if told from the way they straightened at his approach—and ducked inside behind the boy.

An antechamber opened to the left into a bedroom partially concealed by drapes and to the right into a living area. Raegus n'Harnalt was seated behind a camp desk situated between two wrought-iron braziers. Two more burned at the opposite corners of the room. The air was blessedly warm.

The Avataren had a knife scar on one cheek that looked new. It disappeared beneath his dark, close-shorn beard. Raegus looked up as Trell entered. Then he came around and clasped shoulders with him, whereupon they each pressed a fist to their hearts in the traditional desert greeting between commanders.

"Trell of the Tides." Raegus smiled and motioned him towards a chair across the desk from his own. "I read the Emir's missive." There were at least a thousand things implied in his tone, and as he sat down again, his blue-eyed gaze held a flinty spark.

Trell lowered himself slowly into his chair.

"You're all right?" the commander asked. He sounded angry enough to have possibly wished the opposite.

Trell watched him warily. He wasn't about to tell him that his hands were still shaking at odd times, or that the inside of his head felt like an over-used punching bag. "It was nothing a bowl of stew couldn't cure."

"Well and good," Raegus leaned towards him with thunder in his gaze, "because *take me for a Sorceresy slave* but that was the stupidest bloody fool thing anyone could've done, and I certainly didn't expect it from you!"

Trell drew back slightly in his chair.

Raegus slammed his palm on the desk. "What in Jai'Gar's holy name were you *thinking*, throwing yourself into the Taran like that? Do you have *any* idea how much trouble I'd be in if anything happened to you?" He picked up the Emir's letter and shook it at him. "Never mind what this says—I don't even want to think about what *this* says—the Emir looks upon you as one of his sons, Trell, and everyone here bloody knows it. If something were to happen to you while attached to my company, the Emir would have my balls in a sling, and that would just be the appetizer."

"Raegus," Trell felt numbed by his words, "he couldn't possibly hold you accountable for my—"

"No-no-no-no-no." Raegus fell back in his chair and glowered darkly at him. "You *know* how our *Su'a'dal* thinks. He would've asked me, why did I place the son-of-his-heart in a position where he felt he had to make such a choice? Why weren't *my* men faster in responding? Why wasn't *I* there, putting *my* life before yours? He would painfully remind me that such is what Jai'Gar requires of His Converted. There's no escaping that responsibility."

Trell held the other commander's gaze, recognizing the truth in his words, disturbed that he'd disappointed and aggrieved him. "Raegus, I deeply apologize for putting you in such a position."

The Avataren grunted. "Well…I accept your apology." He scrubbed at his jaw and considered Trell like a magister assessing a horse thief when he knows the man is just going to go right back out and steal another horse. "Who'd you pull out of the water anyway?"

"Loukas n'Abraxis."

Raegus's hand froze on his jaw. "Loukas n'Abraxis." It fell to his lap. "My only combat engineer—well, *fethe*." It was Avatar's most versatile curse word. "I guess I ought to be thanking you instead of busting your balls, eh? Or I suppose you can be thanking yourself soon enough."

Trell gave him a curious look.

Raegus arched brows, challenging his ignorance, and held up the Emir's missive again. "Do you know what this letter says?"

Trell frowned at his tone. "I can guess at some of it."

"I'm to turn command over to you."

"Once the Saldarians have been taken in hand," Trell stressed.

Raegus snorted. "Do you really think our *Su'a'dal* would place *you* beneath my command? Hero of the Cry? Son-of-his-heart? A *prince* of Dannym?"

This news hit Trell powerfully. "Raegus, I never imagined—"

"Bloody hells, Trell, you're one of the val Lorian heirs?" Surprise threaded strongly through his tone. "And the *fethen* Dannish soldiers are our allies now to boot? I had to read that damned letter three times just to be sure I was reading it right."

Silence bound Trell's tongue like astonishment bound his thoughts. He *should've* seen this coming, knowing the Emir as he did, and it bothered him greatly that he hadn't. Had he been gone from the war for so long that his greatest weapons of instinct and prediction, both of which he'd honed to a fine point, had become rusted from lack of use?

"I see you really didn't know." Raegus gave a droll grunt. "So we're both on the punishing end of Ha'viv's rod. He is having His way with us something fierce today."

Trell misliked the imagery of the Trickster God's 'rod', for it invoked memories of Taliah that he would much rather have forgotten. He exhaled a slow breath. "I suppose another apology serves neither of us."

Raegus pushed out of his chair. "No need," he waved at the room while walking towards a cabinet boasting several bottles of wine, "though I'll miss the accommodations, but I couldn't have done what you did at the Cry, Trell. *Fiera's ashes*, it was all I could do to hold the lines after you left."

He poured two glasses of wine and handed one to Trell. Then he stood there, considering him with his dark brows inching towards one another. "You'll fit right in with this motley crew. The company is chockablock with disenfranchised princes. I can name five off the top of my head—most of 'em with chips the size of boulders on each shoulder, one going by the name of Indignation and the other Affront. Had to make them into my officers, because the gods know they won't follow orders, even to save their own necks." He drank his wine, still pinning Trell with a speculative gaze. "Is that what's next for you? A kingdom of your own?"

"I honestly don't know."

Raegus grunted. "The Emir says he'll award me a sheikdom if I can return you in one piece." He looked Trell over dubiously. "I guess our *Su'a'dal* doesn't trust in your sense of self-preservation any more than I do."

Trell cracked a smile. "I suppose I deserve that."

"More than a little." Raegus retook his chair. "What did you find in the town?"

"Loukas uncovered a Saldarian quarrel."

The Avataren perked up at this. "You're sure it's Saldarian?"

"Quite."

He nodded. "Anything else?"

"Outside of a wandering hen, there wasn't much else to see—leastwise nothing you haven't seen before, according to Tannour."

"It's damned eerie, is what it is—five towns with folk and all just outright disappeared?" He took a long drink of his wine and then studied Trell with a pensive scowl. "Did Tannour tell you about our first skirmish?"

Trell shook his head.

"The Lord Rhakar found the bastards to begin with and Prince Farid led us right to them using the nodes. There might've been fifty Saldarians camped in this clearing long about thirty leagues behind us now, but *fethe* if the place didn't reek of four times that many men, just rank with the smell of liquor and piss. Half of 'em were drunk on their arses, but the others fought like angry badgers and us the raccoons taking over their den.

"There wasn't any question that these were the bastards that'd been causing all the trouble. If it wasn't the plunder they had just sitting there as a perch for flies, you'd have told it from the reek of the dead they'd piled up on the east side of camp, so the wind would blow away their stench. I rode in thinking this would be the shortest campaign of my career, started shooting off my mouth about how we were cleaning up this region and that meant the end of all of them…"

He shot back the last of his wine and pushed out of his chair again. "You want something stronger? *Fethe* if I don't need it."

Trell followed him with his gaze, watching as Raegus pulled out a decanter of amber liquid from inside the cabinet and poured it to the very brim of the glass.

"That's when we found the rest." He took a long swallow of the bourbon, topped off his glass and came back over to his chair. "We thought we had them rounded up, when Saran comes storming in with his mount all lathered and says I'd better come and see. Would that I could erase the sight from my head, Trell."

He sat down heavily in his chair, but the sigh that crossed his lips was heavier still. "The rest of the hundred and fifty that belonged to that stench we found a mile away, chasing their horses in a racetrack circle. Had the mud good and churned up. Every one of those horses was dark to the teats with it—except it hadn't rained for days, and there wasn't any way that earth was water-wet. They had two score or more hostages corralled to one side. Seems they were making sport of trampling them one at a time—sometimes two, in the case of the women and children." Raegus took another long swallow and then stared into the drink. "What the Mage did on the Khalim Plains was more humane than this."

Trell clenched his jaw. "I see."

"And they saw us, by Ha'viv's ill eye." Raegus shot him a look of fury, the memory clearly hot in his thoughts. "They promptly shoved the rest of the hostages into the middle of the field, screaming and crying, full of pitiful pleading—not a soldier was among them, you know, that went without saying—and all of us glared at each other's arrows like two low-city gangs facing off.

"The leader and I exchanged some words—nothing I'm proud of, you needn't hear it repeated—meanwhile, I've got men flanking their position in the trees. When I gave the signal for attack, I expected the bastards to break left and right and head directly into the men I had on their flanks..." he took another long draw that finished off his drink, and when he lowered the glass, his eyes were shadowed, "but they rode right over those people... trampled them into the earth, laughing as they went. They speared through our lines, and by the time I rallied my men, the blackguards had vanished."

Raegus set down his empty glass and lifted a troubled gaze to Trell. "I found out later they stormed back through their camp and grabbed who and what they could, brief and bloody, and then tore off into the trees again. We followed their trail for about a mile before it disappeared."

Trell straightened in his chair. "A hundred and fifty men and horse disappeared?" He frowned over the possibilities. "They crossed a node?"

"Unless their *fethen* horses could fly."

"So they have a Nodefinder with them—or a wielder?"

Raegus shrugged. "Either one would explain how a single band of slug-thugs could be harrying so much of the region." He turned his glass beneath his fingers, rotating it on the table. "We've been chasing their dust ever since, town to town, finding no evidence save the fact that there's nothing to find. Somehow they're always one step ahead of us."

Trell frowned at this. "Could someone in the company be keeping them appraised of our movements?"

Raegus waved resignedly with his glass. "I admit thinking as much myself, though how they'd be communicating eludes logic. But we've got Converted in our number as well as consultants like your Loukas n'Abraxis, plus all the grooms and cooks—it's a damned king's entourage I'm dragging through these hills."

He grunted, shot Trell a dry half-smile. "Can't say it disappoints me to hand this problem to Your Highness. The kindest bed in the world isn't worth the price of a clap-ridden whore if sleep avoids it like the plague." He waggled his empty glass in the air pointedly. "I aim to sleep well tonight though."

Trell thought he understood the darkness haunting Raegus's gaze. Five towns and all of the people taken…what *were* the Saldarians doing with those innocents? It seemed almost a purposeful taunt, and at least a malevolent mystery. Certainly enough to deny sleep to any good man. "Rest tonight is doubtless deserved, Commander."

"Hey, hey—none of that." The Avataren lifted a finger off his glass and made a circle with it at Trell, his eyes shadowed now with exhaustion as much as the memories that plagued him. "*You're* the commander of this motley troop now. I'd give you this chair but I'm too bloody tired to haul my arse out of it just yet. While you and your pretty engineer were taking a swim, the rest of us were setting up camp in that blasted storm."

Trell rose and went to pour himself more wine. "When do you want to tell the company?"

"Up to you, *A'dal*."

"Tomorrow then." He leaned back against the chest and observed Raegus, who was slouched now in his chair with his lids half-mast. "Tannour said you managed to get something out of one of the Saldarians."

"For what it's been worth. We sure haven't caught up with them again."

Trell sipped his wine. He was finally starting to feel more himself—at least his hands had stopped shaking, and though his head felt a little fuzzy, he suspected it was from the wine more than the river. He narrowed his gaze at the dark liquid, thinking of the pattern of things so far and what he knew of Saldarian tactics. "I don't think you will catch them. Not until they're ready."

Raegus forced his eyes open. "What do you mean?"

Trell met his gaze. "I think they're leading you on a merry chase to give them time to prepare."

"For?" He shook his head bemusedly.

Trell's brows narrowed as he worked to make the pieces fit. They did when placed in a certain order. "We'll give the men tonight to recover from the storm, but I want to be off again by midmorning."

"Off to where?"

Trell downed his wine. "Khor Taran." He set down his goblet and made for the exit.

Raegus pushed up after him. "*A'dal—*" he motioned to the desk and all it signified, but his gaze conveyed even more than this.

Trell shook his head, smiled. "I'll bunk with Rolan tonight. Give you one last go at that king's bed." He added with a wry grin, "Sorry there's no one to join you there."

Raegus grunted. "I'd pay a courtesan's fee just to *sleep* in it for once." He pushed hands in his pockets and frowned at Trell. "Dawn then? I'll summon the troops."

"Let's give them their ham and porridge first. Men are more amenable to change when their bellies are full—in case anyone is inclined to protest in your honor."

As it happened, no one was, though they honored their former commander with a round of jeering, which in the case of the Converted, was as good as a toast. The real toast of the occasion, however, came when Trell told the men his true name.

Every soldier there knew some story of Trell of the Tides, adopted son of their Emir, hero of the Cry, and when they broke into applause and jesting shouts of *'All hail Prince Trell, King of the Converted!'* Trell felt deeply moved.

"I have stories to share with all of you," he called to the assembled crowd, "not the least of them how our kingdoms are now allied against the forces of Radov abin Hadorin and his wielder, Viernan hal'Jaitar."

This announcement met with a cacophonous response. Trell listened carefully to the catcalls that floated to the top of the froth, gauging the general tone of their response by the slant of their jests. He'd taken care to name Radov and hal'Jaitar specifically, directing the Converted's enmity at the men who were their enemies, rather than an entire nation.

Trell held up a hand to calm them. "Tonight, we'll celebrate in honor of

Raegus n'Harnalt," and he motioned to the other commander and gave him a slight bow, "but today we travel—fast and hard."

Raegus stepped forward into the murmuring. "You heard your *A'dal*. Break it down!"

As the men were jogging off to strike camp, Trell went in search of Loukas. He found the Avataren standing outside Rolan Lamodaar's tent with Tannour Valeri and two others. The latter excused themselves before Trell could learn their names. He gazed after them, realizing that he had his work cut out for him if he meant to know all the men as he'd known his company at the Cry—especially if he meant to do it before they reached Khor Taran.

Trell looked back to the others. They'd gone silent, curiously so. He met each of their gazes, wondering what they weren't saying, and then focused a smile on Loukas. "How are you feeling?"

"Much improved, Your Highness."

Trell heard himself so named from his friend's tongue and worried where this was headed. "Loukas—"

Loukas dropped his gaze. "I'd better go break down my tent."

"After what you went through yesterday, surely someone else—"

"No..." Loukas flicked his gaze between Tannour and Rolan, "I should do it. That is..." he looked back to Trell, "unless that's an order."

Trell frowned slightly. "No."

Loukas dutifully touched fingers to his lips, then laid the same hand across his heart. He darted another unreadable glance at Tannour and headed off.

Trell stared after him in stunned silence.

That was the Avataren Sign of Obeisance...

If he'd ever seen Loukas make that gesture before, he certainly hadn't been able to connect it to its meaning, for his lessons on the manners and courtesies of Avatar—extensive lessons, as it happened—had been buried beneath Raine D'Lacourte's truthbinding.

This time, however, Trell instantly recognized the Avataren genuflection.

He exhaled a slow breath as he stared after his friend. *The great mystery of Loukas n'Abraxis...*

He'd shared the front lines with the Avataren engineer for two years, and in all that time, Loukas hadn't once spoken of the events that had driven him to seek refuge in the Akkad.

Some Converted were all too willing to boast about the acts that had forced them to flee their homelands, while others spoke only haltingly of their former circumstances, but Trell had never met a man more close-mouthed about his past than Loukas n'Abraxis.

That he'd been raised by a privileged family was obvious from his education—he spoke more languages than Trell and could calculate advanced mathematics in his head faster than Trell could write the formulas—but that kiss of fingers and touch to heart...it indicated that Loukas had spent time in the courts of Avatar's Fire Kings. Suddenly Trell was very interested in having a look at Raegus's list of disenfranchised princes.

"What is it?"

Trell shifted his gaze to find Tannour observing him peculiarly. The dark-haired Vestian nodded in the direction Loukas had just gone. "N'Abraxis touched his heart, and you departed us for elsewhere." His tone held an oddly possessive edge.

Trell wondered if Tannour also recognized the Avataren Sign of Obeisance—he suspected that he did—and if his name might also be on Raegus's list along with Rolan Lamodaar, who made no secret of his noble status, even flaunting his wealth when he wasn't gambling it away.

Trell shifted his gaze between the two men. "Keep an ear to the chatter. I'd like to know if anyone takes exception to my command...or my station."

Rolan quirked a grin at him, his teeth very white against his dark skin and even darker beard with its jeweled braids. "This was no great shock, Trell of the Tides. Anyone who's ever seen a Kingdom Blade knew you had to be from Dannym's noble class. Not a man here hasn't heard that rumor."

Trell stared at him. How had he failed to hear that rumor about himself? Or had he heard it and simply dismissed it out of hand? He shifted his gaze to Tannour inquiringly.

Tannour shrugged. "We all expected this when you arrived to take over."

"When I—" But Trell's protest that in fact he hadn't come to take over froze on his tongue. It served little point to argue what was plain to the eye. "Then..." he shook his head slightly and glanced again in the direction Loukas had gone, "why is he—"

"Pay no attention to n'Abraxis," Rolan remarked. "He's been moody ever since joining this troop," and he looked pointedly, if not quite accusingly, at Tannour.

The latter's pale blue eyes tightened slightly. "If you'll excuse me, *A'dal*, I must go break down my tent also." He cast a stiletto stare at Rolan. "I haven't the funds to keep servants at my beck and call." He spun in a swirl of desert robes.

"And whose fault is that, Valeri?" Rolan called after him. He watched him stalking off in a direction opposite from Loukas and blew out a forceful breath. "Azerjaiman's winds, I'd hate to be the confessor for that pair."

"What do you mean?"

Rolan looked around as if searching for someone. "Nothing I can prove...but you watch those two long enough, you can tell someone's arrow has pierced them both—whether it was Inithiya's or Ha'viv's, only they can say."

Inithiya's arrow implied love, the Trickster God Ha'viv's implied betrayal. Trell wasn't certain either of those answers fully explained the odd friction between the two men.

Appearing to give up on whoever he was looking for, Rolan shifted his gaze back to Trell. "Maybe you should ask n'Abraxis. He would probably confide in you."

Trell shook his head. "We were on campaign together for years. He never said a word to me about his past."

"Ah, but I'll bet you never asked him directly." At Trell's bemused frown, Rolan added meaningfully, "You haven't been here to hear him talking about you for so many sweepings of the sun." He flashed a devilish grin. "Any time he wanted to drive Valeri from the fire, n'Abraxis would just start talking about you."

Trell frowned slightly at this. "What do you know about Tannour?"

Rolan chewed at a hangnail on his thumb. "Rumors mostly. Some say he was a prince, some say he assassinated a prince..." he grinned at Trell. "You can't trust the rumors, but you watch Tannour with a blade and see if you don't wake up at least once in the night with a hand to your throat, just making sure it's still in one piece."

Just then one of Rolan's servants came rushing up. He looked about twenty, at least half Rolan's age. Trell had met him the night before and knew him to be soft-spoken, with unusually long lashes framing quiet, dark eyes.

Rolan swung out an arm to stop the servant from going into his tent. "Where have you been, Yusef?"

Yusef held up a pair of Rolan's boots as if to shield against his stare. "We ran out of polish, *Sidi*." He managed an awkward bow in accompaniment to the proper title for his master, the upheld boots somewhat limiting his motion. "I had to borrow some from Sandarin Correanos's man."

Rolan took Yusef by his vest and pulled him close. "That polish had better not have lard in it, like Sandarin is always going on about. I won't be walking around with fat from a pig's arse slathered on *my* boots."

"No, *Sidi*." Yusef dropped his gaze, cowering beneath Rolan's piercing stare. "Only beeswax and almond oil."

Rolan stared at him circumspectly for a moment longer. "Good." He released him. "Go help Naseem break camp."

"*Balé, Sidi*." He ducked hastily inside.

Rolan frowned after him and crossed his arms. "He's a distant cousin on my mother's side. Came to me bearing a letter from my mother that was more threat than introduction. Sometimes I think he's more trouble than her gratitude is worth."

"He seems to want to please you," Trell murmured.

"I don't know…" Rolan's gaze narrowed, as towards an unwelcome visitor, "do you ever get a feeling of something slime-ridden crawling down your spine? That feeling of being watched?" When Trell nodded to this, Rolan grunted. "Sometimes I'll get that sense and look around and he'll be standing in the shadows somewhere… just *staring* at me with those big lamb eyes."

Trell gave him a quirk of a grin. "Don't you require your servants to be in constant attendance to your needs?"

"*Balé*, but I don't require Yusef to be so damned spooky about it." He pried at the hangnail on his thumb again. "I would offer to gift his services to you if I wasn't so sure my mother would put a blood-price on my head. I've enough of Radov's bloodthirsty lot after me as it is."

"A blood-price?" Trell invited Rolan with his gaze and started walking back towards the command tent. "I thought, with…" his eyes strayed to Rolan's neck.

"You mean the brand, of course—as if that would be the end of Radov's vengeance. Nay, Trell of the Tides, that hawk-nosed bastard hal'Jaitar has reserved a special cell in his carefully constructed Shamshir'im hell just for me." Rolan clapped a hand on Trell's shoulder. "Did I ever tell you about the third time I tried to kill Radov?"

Tell turned him a hard look. "How many times have you tried to kill him?"

"Six…" Rolan puckered his face with thought. "Seven? One of my attempts might count as two. I think hal'Jaitar accuses me of nine, but I'd hang myself if I failed nine bloody times to kill that whore-humping lump of camel dung, even though he is protected by a wielder and a hundred Talien Knights. But time number three, now that was something…" and as he walked Trell back to the command tent, Rolan proceeded to tell him why the Ruling Prince of M'Nador prayed regularly to the Seventeen Gods for Rolan Lamodaar to meet with an appallingly gruesome end.

❖

"*Master…*"

Viernan hal'Jaitar paused in his reading of a report. He wrapped his right hand around a ring on the third finger of his left hand, and his eyes went unfocused.

"*What have you learned, Kifat?*"

The Shamshir'im wielder on the other end of the bonded line must've tightened his hold on his own *elae*-enhanced ring, for his words became sharper in Viernan's mind. *"News, Master—wonderful, hateful news."*

Viernan had neither the time nor patience for enduring Kifat's paradoxes that day. *"What news?"*

"Trell val Lorian travels with a company of Converted. They're chasing a band of Saldarians like hounds on a hare through the whole of Abu'Dhan. But they're finding the hare not so ready to be caught—"

Viernan bit back a curse. *"I don't care about the hare! How do you know it's truly the prince?"*

"A brother Shamshir'im travels with the company. He's been reporting to me on an insurgent you wanted watched. He says there is no doubt of Trell val Lorian's identity—apparently the prince announced it to the entire company."

Viernan allowed himself a triumphant smile. *Finally*, Cephrael had turned His inauspicious eye elsewhere than Viernan's activities. Yet...he found it strange that Sundragons and a zanthyr had rescued the val Lorian prince from Darroyhan only to drop him right back into the fray, unless...

Khor Taran.

Viernan's dark eyes narrowed dangerously. The fortress had to be the linchpin in this mystery. He wondered...could there be some new alliance between the Akkad and Dannym? Would this explain the rampant mutiny among the Dannish troops? Or perhaps the prince merely hoped to rescue his father's soldiers to reestablish himself in the line of succession?

Of one thing Viernan was suddenly quite certain: the Dannish soldiers somehow factored into the prince's activities.

"Master, what shall I advise our agent to do?"

Viernan's gaze took on a viperous gleam. *"Kill him."*

"And if he cannot manage the act without compromising his position?"

"You will have to intervene—but carefully, lest you draw the unwanted attention of the prince's immortal allies. The prince must be stopped before he can lead an attack on Khor Taran."

The Shamshir'im wielder gave the equivalent of a mental snort. *"He's no Adept to challenge me."*

"Do not underestimate him!" Viernan's warning carried a venomous bite, poison flowing as violent thoughts packaged within a piercing intent. There was naught but a skeleton crew holding Khor Taran now. Still, had it been any other opponent, he might not have blinked, but Trell val Lorian by all accounts had waged some nefarious deal with Cephrael, and Viernan greatly misliked those odds. *"If you must destroy everything to destroy him, do so."*

"By your will, Master..." the wielder's voice began fading, the connection growing fainter, *"so shall it be done."*

Viernan released his ring and severed the contact with his Shamshir'im. He hoped the man had felt the point of his thoughts forcefully enough, because he would see the entire Fortress of Khor Taran and everyone in it burned to ash before he'd allow Trell val Lorian to rescue a single one of his father's men.

FORTY-THREE

"We might as well be playing Blind-Man's Bluff with a handkerchief around our eyes."

–The truthreader Cristien Tagliaferro, on *deyjiin*

SEBASTIAN VAL LORIAN paced in the shade of an obsidian temple raised from the volcanic ridge that supported it. Desert spread as far as he could see in every direction save south, where a violent storm was darkening the horizon.

It was always there, this storm, in every Dreamscape meeting he'd had with Isabel van Gelderan. He'd never asked her about it—whether the storm was real or imagined, or what those jagged red scars in the firmament signified; whether the constant flashes of lightning were natural or the result of a magical battle, or why, if the sun was high above them, was the lip of the world limned in blood-red flame?

Some things Sebastian didn't want to know.

Maybe that was callous of him, or careless. He preferred to think of it as trust, *faith*, that if Isabel needed him to understand something, she would tell him; that if she needed his help, she would ask for it. She'd certainly never hesitated in the past.

It was because of one such request—his most important task—that Sebastian had sought her dreams this time. She'd instructed him in the necessary patterns, taught him how to find her consciousness in the vast expanse of the aether. But time between Alorin and T'khendar wasn't synchronous, so he'd been waiting in Dreamscape for quite a while—pacing, rather, with his hands behind his back and his thoughts as the churning waves beneath his waterwheel steps. A long time trying not to look at the storm, fighting the magnetic draw it had upon his attention.

"Hello, Sebastian."

Sebastian turned with an instant welling of hope. Hope always welled in the instant of her greeting, partly as a result of the impression of Isabel's mind joining his in Dreamscape, a sense of *her*, which roused such protectiveness on behalf of his brother, such gratitude on his own; but partly also this hope derived from a glimpse of possibility, an instant's view of a different path from the one they'd been walking for so long.

But Sebastian saw in the calm acceptance of her expression, in the set of her shoulders—held slightly straighter than they had to be, as if the overused brace for her endurance—that the one thing he most cared about hadn't changed.

"Isabel." He hadn't meant for her name to carry such disappointment. Sebastian greeted her with a kiss on each cheek and a touch to her arm. "He hasn't contacted you then?"

"Not in the sense you mean it."

"He is young. Give him time."

Her colorless gaze chided him. "He is an old soul." She wasn't wearing her blindfold anymore. He'd never asked her about that either.

Isabel looked past him to the storm, and something shifted in her gaze—recognition perhaps, or resignation. "I'm spending far too much of my time here these days." She cast him a smile, redolent of apology. "I would that my dreams took me elsewhere, but Dreamscape is unpredictable. Sometimes we see things as we want them to be, other times as we expect them to be. Rarely exactly as they are."

"I wouldn't mind conversing elsewhere, to be perfectly frank. The storm is…"

"Disturbing?" She offered understanding with her gaze and touched his arm—

They stood in a wood of dappled sunlight, with a blue lake glimmering in the distance. The tree tops soared high above them on thick branches softened with moss. High in the emerald canopy, one might walk a path of those wide, tangled limbs and never touch the carpet of grass beneath. The air held morning's early crispness, an effect heightened by the birds singing in the treetops.

Isabel smiled. "Better?"

"Quite." He looked her over. "I hope for you also."

She arched brows resignedly. "We walk the path we walk, Sebastian." She touched his arm by way of invitation and set off through the trees towards the lake, her mood pensive. The green dress she wore emphasized the air's emerald cast, and the elaborate plait in her chestnut hair mirrored the twining limbs above. She looked like she belonged there among those ancient, magical trees, a steward of the forest.

"This was my favorite wood as a child." Isabel glanced at him over her shoulder. "I spent many hours here seeking dryads, holding conversations with the trees…hiding from Phaedor." A fleeting smile graced her lips, whispers of old amusements.

"Did you ever find them? The dryads, I mean."

"Every day…but only in my imagination. Phaedor claimed the dryads would never reveal themselves to a child who made so much noise in the woods." A shadow crossed her brow, chasing the lightness from her expression. "I wonder sometimes if Phaedor didn't doom us with his prescience."

She glanced uncertainly to Sebastian. "When Arion and I worked the Unbreakable Bond, Phaedor warned us that our paths would ever be diverging and converging. There's a fine line between prediction and postulation, between perceiving a consequence and causing that consequence to become. It's the intention beneath the statement; a simple slip, the slightest misthought, and prediction becomes a curse."

"You don't think Phaedor caused this."

"No." She smiled in reassurance. "But my path would be easier to accept if he had." Isabel pressed fingers to her brow, rubbed it as if to banish a persistent ache. "These are private fears, Sebastian. I normally wouldn't speak of them, but my fortitude is low, my brother is away, and the man I'm bound to for eternity is refusing my contrition." She winced slightly and cast him a glancing smile, full of sorrow. "It was easier to be apart from him in death than to live separated by contention."

They emerged from beneath the trees into the bright of day. The lake spread before them, azure and sparkling in the bosom of steep emerald mountains. Behind them rose granite peaks capped with snow.

"Forgive me." She looked softly to him. "You didn't seek my dreams to hear my laments."

"On the contrary, Isabel. I wish there was more I could do."

She gave him another glancing smile. "I confess, you're a better ear for my sorrows than my brother. Björn knew Arion, but he doesn't know Ean. Not really, not as the man he is now. He's kept his distance for several reasons, but most of all to prevent his influence on the tapestry from affecting Ean's path. Would that I'd had his strength of will."

"Ean wouldn't be here today without you. He knows that." He touched Isabel's arm to emphasize his words. "He doesn't want to be without you at all."

She regarded him with a delicate sadness. "He will not accept my attempts to contact him."

Sebastian thought of his last conversation with Ean. "You broke his heart, Isabel. Young men can heal from the wounds of battle far faster than from the wounds of love."

They walked down a hill towards a marble path and accompanying railing, which followed the line of the lake.

Isabel hugged her arms. "I remember the moment I first knew Ean was near." She glanced to Sebastian. "I felt him the instant he walked into my brother's game room in T'khendar. I felt his eyes find me."

She pressed curled fingers to her lips and lifted her eyes to the mountains, as if seeking escape from her memories in those remote reaches. "You cannot know how hard it was not to run to him, Sebastian—his attention was practically hauling me across the room like a ship dragging its anchor. It was all I could do to resist, to let our reunion come in its time." She looked resolutely back to him. "*This* is the strength my brother possesses which I do not, to watch Arion Return again and again, to watch him *die,* again and again—three times *again*—"

Isabel pressed her lips together tightly, and for a time she stared away from him, her shoulders held rigidly, her mouth set with firm defiance.

"All those years..." she confessed after a while, still not looking at him, "I held so desperately to my memories of Arion. They were all I had to protect myself from his loss, but in doing so..." she met his gaze with confession offered in her own, "in trying to guide Ean, in skirting that line so closely—all the while fearing I would drive Balance's dagger into his heart yet again—in trying to *protect* him, I might've wounded him in the worst possible way."

"Isabel..." Sebastian wrapped an arm around her shoulders. But what could he say to comfort her that she didn't already know? She leaned against him, accepting of his support. Her body felt frail in the circle of his arm, too slender to bear the weight she was carrying, and from what Sebastian understood of the problems in T'khendar, Ean's anger was the least of those, if perhaps the one that stabbed most deeply into her heart.

He tried to reassure her, though she hadn't asked for it—didn't seem to need it, truthfully, only his ear lent in compassion. "Ean is resilient. We can at least count on that."

"He is astonishing." She turned slightly to better meet his gaze. "I don't know if you realize just how astonishing."

Her words instantly recalled to him a midnight plunge from the Palace of Andorr, a head-over-heels tumble into night's abyss, limbs entangled with his brother's, their two minds in a struggle of wills as they plunged towards the earth—Ean's against Dore Madden's compulsion. Sebastian smiled softly. "I have an idea, yes." He offered her his arm then, which she accepted, and they started strolling the path around the lake.

Isabel returned her colorless eyes to the way ahead. "We all experience tragedies that overwhelm us." She appeared so strong to him in profile, so dauntless, but Sebastian shared her Dreamscape thoughts; he knew *she* was feeling overcome. "Such experiences make us afraid—of repeating the same mistakes, of straying too far from the comfortable known, of adventuring anew. It becomes increasingly difficult to set aside our fears upon our next attempt, because those moments of loss are so constricting. Too easily we let past failures prevent us from finding future success."

She looked portentously to Sebastian. "But your brother, despite everything that's happened—dying three times for our game, Sebastian!—despite all Ean has endured, what can only be powerful failures for him, remembering so many of them as he does…that he *continues on* despite all of this?" She exhaled forcefully. "I've never encountered anyone so brave."

Sebastian smiled softly to himself. Bravery, his littlest brother had in ample supply. Prudence, on the other hand, *perspective*… He shifted his gaze back to her. "But surely, Arion—"

"Arion had the benefit of education," her gaze conveyed the import of this fact. "over a century of practice and study. He *knew* he could do impossible things. Ean has neither that experience nor Arion's strength of conviction. He simply embraces the challenge along with the recognition that he might've failed that very same challenge in the past, sometimes more than once."

She shook her head and gazed tragically at him. "I fear I've slighted him in the worst possible way, for I've denied him the admiration he's due in his own right. It is *Ean* working these feats now—not Arion. I well know this, yet well have I failed to say it. There are so many things I admire about him that I've never told him. Would that I'd spent more time praising him and less time fearing my influence on his path."

"You only did what you thought was right, Isabel. What more can anyone ask?"

"More." She turned him a look. "Far more." Then she sighed, slow and thoughtful. "You're right to remind me of his youth, though. I look back on the first hundred years of my life and think how young I was throughout that time, yet Ean has but twenty name days in his current shell. Age is incidental to a wielder who's worked the Pattern of Life." She glanced his way, and some of the tension eased from her brow. "Have you worked it, Sebastian?"

"Not yet, my lady."

"But you intend to?"

Sebastian cast a half-smile off towards the hills. "I think Ehsan will not give me much choice in the matter."

"Then you intend to wed her, bind with her?"

His smile turned droll. "I think she won't give me much choice in that, either."

"I would love to attend you both for that ceremony."

Sebastian blinked. "We…would be *honored*, Isabel."

She smiled and they continued their walk. In time, the lakeside path led to a marble gazebo, which seemed the perfect ornament to crown the slight peninsula extending there. With the sun, the breeze, the green mountains and the dazzling water, Sebastian thought he'd never been anywhere so beautiful. An impassioned sigh escaped him. "I never imagined I would have a chance at life again." He shifted his gaze to meet Isabel's. "I owe you for that."

"You owe your brother for that. From the moment he perceived you at Tyr'kharta, Ean knew only you. You'd drawn him onto your path."

Sebastian shook his head. "I don't have that power."

"His love for you has that power."

He dropped his gaze to his hands, realizing not for the first time that he owed Isabel and Ean for the fact that he even *had* hands instead of mangled appendages useful as a torment and little else.

Which contemplation brought him to the point of his visit. "Isabel," he stopped and turned to face her, "we think we may have found a combination of patterns that will stop the *eidola*. Ean's gone to Tambarré to test it."

Only a flicker on her brow suggested any concern over this news. Then a smile manifested, so bright that it alone was fair acknowledgment for all of their hard work. "Well done, Sebastian." She cupped his cheek with her hand, tenderly, yet with such conveyance in her gaze as only the High Mage of the Citadel might've summoned. "Describe the matrix to me."

She took his arm again, and they continued their pastoral stroll, passing through a wood and across an arching bridge while he spoke of first-strand bindings, fourth-strand interruptors and fifth-strand molecular destabilization.

Beyond the bridge, a flight of marble steps led down, following the line of a cascading waterfall. Isabel hugged his arm more closely as they descended. "How will you convey the pattern broadly across an army of *eidola*?"

"We're still working on that, but we have some ideas." They emerged from the trees to a whole new view of the lake, and—

Sebastian halted. Directly across an inlet from where they stood, the whorls of a grand iron gate demarked a boat landing. Beyond this elegant entrance, steps led up to gardens, gardens to fountains, waterfalls to terraces, and terraces to an immense marble mansion framed perfectly by forested hills and the jutting mountains beyond.

"*What* is that?"

Isabel hooked a stray strand of hair behind one ear. "That is the Palazzo di Adonnai, my brother's house in Caladria."

He turned her a look. "*That's* not a house."

She smiled. "His home, then." She drew him on towards the mansion. "Home is perhaps a fairer appellation, in any case, for Adonnai has always been our refuge. It's where we go to restore our hearts, our hopes, to dream newly, free of the plague of past failures. It's where my brother and his Council of Nine planned this game that has overtaken our lives. It's where…" but whatever she'd meant to say, the words kept their own counsel behind her soft smile.

Sebastian looked upon the palazzo and marveled anew at Björn van Gelderan—Vestal, wielder, philosopher…brother. Maker of the Game. He *really* needed to meet this man who'd bound him and his brothers so fully to his pattern, like a painter swirling tri-colored paint upon a vast canvas.

He shoved his hair back from his eyes and flicked his gaze to Isabel. "You know, I've never met the man I've sworn to serve."

She sought meaning in his gaze and found it, no doubt. A slight nod, a faint smile. "I will see what can be arranged."

He blew out his breath. "And Dareios and I will continue working on this task you've given us meanwhile."

She took his hand and squeezed it with gratitude in her gaze. "Thank you, Sebastian." She kissed his cheek and murmured, "Thank Dareios for me also…"

Sebastian roused to dawn's lambent kiss upon the world…and Ehsan, stirring a curl in his hair with her finger. He rolled onto his back to better enjoy her beauty in the soft morning light—in any light, actually. Or no light. Ehsan was light enough in his heart.

She had her head propped in her hand while her lush, dark hair hugged her bare form. Her repose was as perfectly poised to elicit his desire as if an artist had positioned her for painting.

Sebastian let his eyes wander from the tattoo of the *Khoda Panaheh* on her forehead—sacred declaration that she'd worked the Pattern of Life—along her lovely nose, straight and slightly rounded, to her lips, full and soft, then lifted to her large blue eyes and dark eyebrows, perfectly formed with a hint of irreverence in their aspect.

Ehsan arched one of them in that moment. "Well…what did she say?"

"She said…" but he paused the automatic answer on his tongue and shifted his head slightly. "How did you know I was in Dreamscape with Isabel?"

She twined his hair tighter around her finger, taut, like the cords of his heart. "Whenever you converse with the Lady Isabel, your sleeping lips assume a particular shape." Her gaze conveyed affection, but also challenge, her silent way of saying she was his…but only so long as *she* willed it.

"What kind of shape?"

Ehsan's blue eyes gleamed with secretive amusement. "A peaceful one, Prince of Dannym."

A peaceful one. He supposed that was fair. He always slept better when Ehsan slept beside him—that is, in those times they were actually sleeping—but there were still just as many nights when he woke in a cold sweat, dreaming he was back in Tambarré, bound beneath *goracrosta* and Dore Madden's malice.

His thoughts must've bled into his expression, for she leaned and kissed him beneath a curtain of soft hair. Against his lips, she murmured, "Some wounds take longer to heal."

Sebastian swept her hair back to better admire the heart-shaped curve of her jaw. "I told Isabel about the matrix. She was grateful, and pleased."

"Rightfully so. You and my brother have proven yourselves many times over with this achievement. Any news of Ean?"

Sebastian exhaled a sigh. "He still hasn't contacted her." They had no new word of him either—nothing since he'd left for Tambarré.

Ehsan tightened her finger within the curl of his hair, a tiny torment, shades of the desirous ones she compelled out of him during their nights together. She eyed him amusedly. "I'm not sure how I feel about your entertaining another woman in your dreams."

"Princess," he grabbed her around the waist and pulled her atop him, "my dreams belong only to you."

Much later, after they'd pleasured each other, fed each other and bathed together, Sebastian stood naked before a standing mirror, frowning at his reflection.

Ehsan had been using her Healer's gifts to repair his damaged leg, encouraging the bone to straighten by meticulously mending the frayed threads of his life pattern. Beneath the corded muscle of his thigh, the bone still seemed slightly askew, but his leg no longer pained him, and he was walking now without a limp. He supposed, in the end, it hardly mattered what the leg looked like so long as it worked properly.

Ehsan came up behind him, dressed in a jeweled sari the same shade of royal blue as her eyes. She wrapped her arms around his chest and trailed kisses along his neck. Sebastian watched her reflection in the mirror.

Her lips reached his jaw and the thin white line traced there, all that was left of the scar that had once marred his face. She smiled at his reflection. "It is become hardly visible since our last Healing."

Sebastian's eyes tightened. "It's the first thing I see."

"Yet you grow no beard to hide it." Her eyebrow challenged him as much as her tone.

Sebastian frowned at her reflection.

Ehsan laughed at him with her eyes. "I know the scar means something to you—I see that in your responses. But what can the past mean that the future cannot overwrite?"

Sebastian exhaled a slow breath and considered her point. He knew why he didn't hide the scar he so hated. Because doing so would be to admit it had defeated him—it and all it stood for, the horrors he'd endured in N'ghorra, Dore Madden's torments... everything that had happened to him since Viernan hal'Jaitar sent Raliax of Saldaria to kill him.

Ehsan pressed her cheek against his. "The first thing you see, Prince of Dannym, is any perceived failing in yourself." Her blue eyes chided him more gently than her tone. "Yet in truth, this imperfection only adds to your perfection."

His brows assumed a dubious shape. "I'm afraid you're going to have to explain that one, Princess."

She held his reflected gaze with her very blue eyes. "Only a man who has endured hardship can know true compassion. What you endured as Işak'getirmek may have changed you, but not necessarily for the worse. Ostracism breeds humility, and out of loss blossoms tolerance. All men are born bold, but they cannot know courage until they've learned fear. In his failings, a man becomes more ideal."

He took her hand and pressed a kiss to her palm. "Who is this man you keep going on about? I worry I should count him a rival."

She laughed as he turned to face her. "He's the one you would see if you but listened less attentively to Doubt's ill mutterings."

Sebastian slipped his arms around her. "Very well, Princess, I shall endeavor to make you proud. How else am I to win your hand?"

"A decidedly relevant question you should be asking yourself daily." She cupped his face and kissed his mouth, trailing her fingers along his chin as she withdrew.

Sebastian admired her hips as she walked away.

Ehsan paused in the portal and glanced back at him, her gaze full of promise—the sort of gaze that implied they had only just begun exploring the delights of their courtship. She nodded with the hint of a smile. "Prince Sebastian."

"Princess Ehsan."

Then she glided from the room.

Dareios was already at work in his laboratory when Sebastian arrived. The rising sun had cleared the Dhahari range and was now a too-bright ball in direct line of sight of Dareios's lab. The Kandori prince was shading his eyes with one hand when Sebastian entered.

"Ah, Sebastian, *sobh bekheir.*" *Good morning.* "What excellent timing you have. Come, stand there," and he pointed to a position across his workbench.

Sebastian dutifully planted himself in the indicated spot between Dareios and the sun, whereupon his host returned to etching a small leather scabbard he'd been holding. "What news from Isabel?"

Sebastian pushed hands in his pockets while the sun warmed his back. "She's happy with our progress."

"And Ean?"

"She hasn't heard from him either." He eyed Dareios humorously, wondering, as he had many times, if their discussions served more formality than function. Surely the truthreader had gleaned all of this already from his thoughts.

Dareios's lips hinted at a smile. "If one presumes to know all, Sebastian, it severely limits the opportunity for conversation. Ah!" He held up the scabbard with a look of triumph. "Let's see how we've done. Hold this, if you will." He handed Sebastian the sheath. Then he picked up a Merdanti dagger and threw it through the open balcony doors. It soared across the terrace and vanished beyond the railing.

"I really hope no one was standing in the courtyard," said a voice from the doorway.

Sebastian turned to see Dareios's cousin, Bahman, leaning against the door frame. Dark-haired and caramel-skinned, with the *Khoda Panaheh* marking his forehead, Bahman often seemed a leaner, less bejeweled reflection of Dareios, save that his large brown eyes ever harbored an irreverent gleam. This morning he also wore an insouciant smile.

"Prudent as ever, Bahman. Would that you'd been here but twenty seconds earlier to offer your wisdom." Dareios held a hand towards the leather scabbard Sebastian was holding. "But, as you see, your cautions were ultimately unfounded."

Sebastian looked back to the scabbard to see the Merdanti dagger that Dareios had just thrown suddenly sheathed there.

"It worked." Bahman sounded mildly surprised.

Dareios shot Bahman an amused smile as he retrieved the dagger and scabbard from Sebastian. "I basked in your confidence as I was preparing the pattern, Bahman."

"It shouldn't have worked." Bahman sauntered into the workshop with hands in his pockets. "There's no precedent for electromagnetic induction in a bonded pair."

"That is precisely why our efforts are called experimentation, Bahman."

"What's a bonded pair?" Sebastian asked.

"The items are bonded much the way Adepts are," Dareios replied, "with a strand of *elae* pinning them together. Which strands of *elae* are used determines the type of symbiosis the two items share. In the case of this dagger, the bond engenders second-strand magnetic connectivity with its sheath."

Dareios pulled the dagger from its sheath and eyed it circumspectly. "What isn't clear is why the induction on this one only works when the dagger is unimpeded. Lodge it into wood, like so..." he flung the dagger into a chair leg, which caused the chair to scrape loudly across the stone floor, and the wildcat Babar, who was sitting on it, to flatten one ear and hiss at him, "and *voilà*..."

The dagger remained pinned in the wood.

Dareios sighed. "Do you see, Bahman?"

"The laws of physics in action. A miraculous proof, cousin." Bahman wandered over and yanked the dagger out of the chair, eliciting another affronted hiss from Babar. He shooed her off and sat down in her stead, which did not improve his favor in her eyes.

Bahman twirled the dagger through practiced fingers while the wildcat observed him indignantly from the floor, her ears flattened and tail twitching with a decidedly vindictive rhythm.

"It must have something to do with motive force." Bahman crossed a sandaled foot over one knee and balanced the dagger on the back of his hand. Unlike his cousin, who never left his rooms without enough jewels on ears, fingers and clothing to furnish a small kingdom, Bahman wore an embroidered blue kurta and shalwar, their only jewels his flashing smile. "Second-strand induction technically can't override inertial velocity."

Dareios leaned both hands on the worktable and frowned at him. "Somehow a bonded pair overcomes this."

Sebastian thought he had the gist of what they were talking about. "If there's already a pattern to produce a bonded pair, and with that pattern the dagger returns to its sheath in every situation, why not simply use that pattern?"

"Because it already exists as its own proof, Sebastian." Dareios shifted his gaze to him. "The focus of our scientific inquiry is in reproducing the effect to understand *why* the bonding pattern works."

Bahman was spinning the dagger around his hand and balancing it each time on the back of his fingers. "I can run a few velocity tests."

"That would be a start."

Bahman flipped the dagger, caught it as he stood, and pointed it at Dareios as he started out of the room. "And the arrows are ready."

The truthreader flashed a smile and looked meaningfully to Sebastian. "How's your arm for archery, Prince of Dannym?"

The three princes, Sebastian, Dareios and Bahman, were trying to find a way to cast their matrix broadly across many *eidola* at once—that is, for someone other than Ean to do so, and assuming, of course, that the matrix had the intended effect of disrupting the *eidola's* connection with their master. All those things being equal, this problem still wasn't enough to fully occupy Dareios's industrious mind. He was generally pursuing at least a dozen different projects simultaneously. In this spirit, the late morning saw Sebastian on a practice field testing another of the Kandori prince's hypotheses.

Bahman, a skilled metallurgist and bladesmith, had layered patterns into hundreds of arrows, each pattern slightly varied from the next, to find the most effective patterns for penetrating *eidola* flesh. Since they didn't have any *eidola* for target practice, Bahman had set up targets of Merdanti stone in one of the Moon Palace's archery yards.

Sebastian hadn't practiced archery since leaving Dannym, but he found his rhythm again easily enough. After firing off a score of arrows, his arm was warming and he was hitting the bull's-eye each time—that is, when the various patterns on the arrows enabled them to penetrate the enchanted stone.

As when Sebastian was occupied with any display of skill, Dareios's sisters collected like colorful birds in the shaded arcades to watch him. Although he more perceived than heard their whispers, he definitely heard their light laughter—or at least Ehsan's, whose voice more than once distracted him enough to make him miss his mark.

After his third such miss, Sebastian dropped a smile to his feet, drew his next arrow, fixed his gaze on the bull's-eye and shut out all perception except the tension in the bow, the position of his nocked arrow, and his sight along the shaft. He envisioned the arrow's spinning flight all the way into the stone, where several earlier arrows were crowded in the center, their fletching like the tail-feathers of a hawk, and he recalled another time he'd sighted down an arrow towards a target...

The blue-fletched arrow *thocked* into the center of the target beside the dozen Sebastian had already lodged there. He reached for another from the quiver at his thigh and nocked a new arrow to his bow.

The Calgaryn air held autumn's crisp bite, but the sun was yet high in the west and the sky clear. It was one of those glorious days destined to become fond recollection after the grey skies of winter set in.

Sebastian had the yard to himself that day because the bulk of his father's men were down at the harbor receiving a ship of Avataren dignitaries. Solitude of any kind was rare in his father's castle—most of the time it had to be hunted out and hoarded like mice stockpiling corn kernels in the walls—and it rarely lasted long enough.

As case in point, as Sebastian strode to retrieve his arrows from the target, rapid footsteps caught his ear. He glanced over to see their languages tutor heading his way along one of the yard's bordering arcades. The tutor still wore the flared, knee-length coats of his Agasi homeland despite living in Dannym for nearly fifteen years.

Reaching Sebastian, he bobbed a bow. "Good afternoon, Prince Sebastian."

"Master di Falco." Sebastian pulled the last of his arrows out of the bullseye. "Have I confused the days for our lesson?"

"No, no." The tutor dropped his gaze to his boots. "No, I was wondering if you'd seen your brother…" he glanced up with a pained expression, "or if you knew perhaps where he might've gone?"

Sebastian returned his arrows to their quiver and headed back to the firing line. "That very much depends on which brother we're discussing."

"It's Prince Trell, Your Highness. He's…missing." The tutor muttered something in his native Caladrian—one of the few languages he hadn't been teaching the princes of Dannym. Sebastian suspected this was so the man could swear at them unrestrainedly when they pushed his patience beyond its limits, which Sebastian admitted was probably often, especially with Ean. But what nine-year-old wanted to be conjugating verbs in five languages when the sunshine was calling?

Yet their tutor was asking him about Trell, who actually excelled at languages.

"I haven't seen him." Sebastian eyed the tutor inquiringly. "Did something happen?"

The Agasi gave a pained wince. "Ah…it is my fault." He pushed his thumb across his opposite palm as if trying to press ink out of his flesh. "We've been working on a greeting for the Avataren delegation that will be arriving shortly.

Prince Trell presented it to His Majesty about an hour ago. The presentation went...poorly."

"That hardly sounds like Trell."

"It's my fault. I never should've let him attempt one of the High Court Orations."

Sebastian arched brows. "He actually *asked* to present an Avataren Oration? You used to make me memorize those damnable speeches to punish me."

The tutor frowned at him. "*Learning* is never punishment, my prince, but I take your meaning."

"So what happened?"

"Prince Trell accidentally substituted the gesture of loyalty for the Sign of Denial and then lost the meter of the speech, resulting in many flubs. Then he mistook His Majesty's gesticulation—" The tutor pressed clasped fingers to his lips and shook his head.

Sebastian was starting to get an idea of how things must've devolved from there. "Father was angry?"

"Oh, he had every right to be. If Prince Trell had presented before the Avataren delegation, they would've taken grave insult. His Majesty's anger was rightly directed at me," he exhaled a slow breath, "but you know your brother. He took His Majesty's censure as his personal failure. The moment the king dismissed us, Prince Trell bolted away beneath a black dispirit, and I haven't been able to find him since."

Sebastian considered the tutor quietly. "I think I have an idea where he might've gone. I'll try to talk to him."

"Thank you, my prince. Please help him understand this was my failure, not his."

Sebastian aimed him a half-smile. "I doubt Trell will accept that, but I'll see what I can do."

Half a turn of an hourglass later, Sebastian climbed out a window and inched his way around the side of a tower with bare toes and fingertips clinging to parallel strips of stone barely wide enough for a raven's perch.

That was the easy part.

The difficult part involved navigating the near vertical tiled roof, inching down the other side in the mossy shade of a stack of chimneys, and then climbing a notched spine in the wall to reach a particular section of rooftop where multiple angles conjoined into a sort of bowl, which offered a perfectly framed view of the western mountains.

As Sebastian had suspected, his brother was seated there, barefoot, as

Sebastian was, hugging his knees and staring out at the layered blue-green ridgeline. He turned his head when he heard Sebastian.

"What—" Trell's his grey eyes widened beneath his shock of unruly dark hair, "how did you know I was here?"

A grin tugged at a corner of Sebastian's mouth. "You think you're the only one who ever found this spot?" He settled down beside his brother and mirrored Trell's position, hugging his knees. "Something tells me you had a rough afternoon."

"Word of my fine achievement has spread already?" Trell turned a bitter stare away from Sebastian with his thirteen-year-old jaw clenched tightly.

Sebastian considered him for a moment. "You know, Ysolde told me a story once." His mother's Companion, the Fire Princess Ysolde Remalkhen, was always telling them stories of her homeland of Avatar. Most of them seemed pretty farfetched, but something in the way she told them always made you wonder if they might be true. "She said the Fire Kings invented the Orations to keep fools from afflicting their court. If a man couldn't memorize five hundred lines of verse in sequence with an equal number of conflicting hand gestures, he was too unintelligent to be bothered with."

Trell cast him a grim look. "So I'm too unintelligent to be bothered with? Is that your meaning?"

"My *meaning*, little brother, is that the Orations aren't easy even in your native tongue—much less your third language." Sebastian gripped him on the shoulder. "But you can't let one day's failure set you spinning. This is hardly an appropriate attitude for one of His Majesty's ambassadors."

Trell's grey eyes narrowed. "What're you talking about?"

"Why do you think father wants you learning so many languages? He intends to make you his ambassador when you're older—send you around the realm to negotiate treaties on behalf of the Eagle Throne."

"You're making that up."

"I would never lie to you, little brother. Why do you think you've been betrothed to a Kandori princess practically since birth? That's always been father's plan for you—the learned middle son, skilled diplomat and world traveler—just like Grandpère arranged for Uncle Ryan." Their father's younger brother, Prince Ryan, had married one of the Empress of Agasan's great nieces and had been Dannym's Ambassador in Agasan since before any of the boys were born.

Trell still looked unconvinced. "Ean is learning all of the same languages. As did you."

"Me, obviously, because I'm going to be king. And Ean…" Sebastian pointedly did not look at the muffin-top of tousled cinnamon curls and grey eyes hovering on the other side of the notched wall. "I'm not sure Ean will live long enough to find out father's plan for him, the way he goes about things."

A disgruntled puff preceded the rest of Sebastian's youngest brother as Ean clambered over the wall. "You're just saying that because you knew I was there." He settled his nine-year-old body down between Sebastian and Trell, but slightly higher up on the roof.

Trell glowered at him. "You're not supposed to be up here, Ean."

"*You're* up here."

"I'm older than you."

"But I'm a better climber."

Trell angled him a fast stare. "No, you're not."

"Yes, I am."

"Ean, I climbed to the top of Mieryn Bluff four minutes faster than you did."

"Only because you have longer legs."

"Which *objectively* makes me a better climber."

Ean wiped his nose on his sleeve. "I don't think that's a fair comparison."

"Ean..." Sebastian looked his littlest brother up and down. "Why do you smell so weird?"

Ean sniffed inside his tunic and hauled up a bare foot to sniff between his toes. Then he lifted grey eyes to Sebastian with youthful inquiry. "What do I smell like?"

Sebastian and Trell both answered together, the latter with a look of disgust, "*Weird.*"

While Ean tried to figure out what piece of clothing was emitting the unusual smell, Trell heaved a ponderous sigh and looked back to the view. "I never should've tried to present that Oration. Master di Falco encouraged me, but I knew I wasn't ready."

"Well, no wonder you failed."

Trell frowned up at him. "What do you mean?"

Sebastian turned his gaze west, towards the fiery line the falling sun was making of the mountains. "You have to *know* you're going to accomplish something, even if you don't yet know how you're going to accomplish it." He angled his brother a telling look. "No matter the obstacle, or how great the opposition, you have to know you can overcome it. Otherwise you've defeated yourself before you've even begun. Our greatest enemies lurk within our own decisions and thoughts, for success or failure always begins there."

"He's right, you know."

All the boys turned with startled intakes of breath.

Their father was standing behind them on the steeply angled tiles, hands in his pockets, barefoot as they were, regarding them all with a hint of a smile and the royal eyebrow inching upwards as if to answer their surprise with, *Did you boys really think I wouldn't know about this spot?*

Sebastian saw his father in the gilded light of the falling sun and felt such admiration for him. All of Gydryn val Lorian's sons had inherited some of his physical structure—Trell and Sebastian had their father's dark hair, Ean seemed to have his jaw, and all three of them had his nose and grey eyes—but Sebastian wanted so much to possess the other of their king father's qualities: his deep understanding of the motivations of men, his calm assurance under pressure, his integrity and regal bearing...

"You can't let a single failure dishearten you, Trell." His father seated himself beside Ean, who shifted over to make room for him with wonder large in his eyes. "And you certainly shouldn't take it personally."

Trell glowered off into sunset's fire-limned clouds. "How am I supposed to take it?"

Gydryn clasped hands around his bent knees and considered his middle son. "Let me tell you a story." He cast Sebastian a pointed look, inviting his recollection. "Once upon a time, three princes set off to find their fortune. They took the road into the west, as the land of the setting sun in those days was wild and untamed, and the princes knew that Fortune waited there. After traveling the road for many days, they reached a dark, impassable wood, and a sign that read, 'Beware: a jealous failure guards this way. Pass on and perish.'"

"I bet it was a trick," Ean nodded sagaciously, "pirates or something." Pirates were Ean's current fascination.

Trell rolled his eyes. "They're not going to run into pirates in the middle of the forest."

"You never know. Pirates are tricky."

Trell gave him an irritated look. "Just let Dad tell the story."

"Now...the princes had heard about this wood," their father continued, "for no one had ever passed beyond its borders." He leaned towards Ean as though to share a secret with him and added, "At least, no one who'd returned to speak of it."

Ean looked significantly to Trell and mouthed, *pirates.*

"But the princes, being princes, were possessed of a certain perseverance which took up more than its share of space in the coach of good sense, such that they'd had to leave reason and judgment behind at the last station. So they ignored the warning and headed into the wood anyway."

Ean puffed a deprecating exhale. "Stories never end well when they head into the wood anyway."

"Like *you* would've turned back." Trell rolled his eyes again.

"'Cause I'm not a coward!" Indignation swelled Ean's nine-year-old chest.

Sebastian nudged Trell lightly with his foot. "I think you're both missing the point of the story."

Trell continued glaring at Ean. "Maybe if Ean would quit adding his own subplots."

"What's a subplot?" Ean looked to his father. "Is it like punctuation? 'cause I still don't get why people are so worked up about commas."

Their father eyed his youngest son quietly. "Would you like to hear what happened to the princes, Ean?"

Ean nodded and settled into large-eyed silence.

"The princes continued into the forest, which grew shadowed and treacherous. The further they traveled the road, the less of a road it became. They encountered many dangers, but none so great as the one they faced when the road finally ran out." Their father lowered his voice, setting a new tone for his tale. "There they stood before the vast unknown, with no path to guide them…and that is where an ominous darkness reared to block any further advance."

Gydryn looked around at each of his sons. All of them were bathed now in the gilded glow of sunset. "Out of this darkness, a great and villainous voice spoke. 'I am Failure,' it said. 'Choose the form I shall take and meet your end.'"

"A pirate would've said 'demise.'" Ean noted, earning another glare from Trell. "Pirates use big words to show they're not stupid."

Gydryn placed a hand on Ean's shoulder, which quieted him. "Now, the first prince was secure in his youth and sure of his strength. He tossed his cloak back from his shoulders and told the darkness, 'Come, old man. You shan't find me a ready victim.'

"So the darkness funneled itself into an old man, white-haired and stooped. The prince drew his sword and charged Failure, and for a time, the young man held the upper hand. But time drew on, as time is wont to do, and eventually the prince's limbs aged, his youth diminished. For all his stamina, still Failure blocked the road. Finally his strength abandoned him; whereupon Failure raised his stooped and aging head and cut the prince ruthlessly down."

"I knew nothing good could come from going into the wood," Ean announced.

"The darkness abandoned the form of the old man and hovered once again before the two remaining princes. 'I am Failure,' it said. 'Choose the form I shall take and meet your end.'

"Now, the second prince was cunning and secure in his intelligence—"

"How smart could he be if he went into the wood?" Ean protested.

Trell clenched his teeth. "Father, *please* make him be silent."

Their father placed his hand again on Ean's shoulder. Ean crossed his arms and scowled at Trell.

King Gydryn continued, "Now, the second prince was cunning and secure in his intelligence. He told the darkness, 'Come, fool, and be yourself claimed.' So the darkness assumed the shape of a drooling fool. The second prince drew his sword and engaged him, but despite all his cunning and wit, he couldn't best Failure. When the prince faltered, the fool cut him down."

Ean grumbled, "This is a horrible story."

"Finally, left all alone in the wood, the third prince faced the black wall of Failure. He knew strength wouldn't save him, nor youth, nor intelligence, though each of these he also possessed. He was sure of only one thing: that he didn't want to seek Fortune alone. So he held out his hand to Failure and said, 'Come, friend. Let us pass on together.' So Failure took the prince's hand, and they walked side by side into the west."

All three boys sat quietly, thinking on their father's message. "So…the prince made a friend of failure?" Ean asked in a small voice. "Why?"

"Because failure always walks beside us," Sebastian murmured.

"Because we elect our enemies, Ean." His father nodded to Sebastian's point. "We choose who to conceive of as opponents, and in so doing, we give them the power to become our downfall."

Much later, after wearing out his arm on the archery yard, Sebastian sat at a banquet table beneath the stars, surrounded by a froth of princesses and princes, heirs, their children, cousins, brothers- and sisters-by-marriage, and Dareios and Ehsan's father and mother, Jorin and Niga Haxamanis.

The clan had descended on the Moon Palace to celebrate one of the nephews' name days—Sebastian couldn't say which nephew, or which sister, brother or cousin he belonged to; nor did he know how many name days the nephew had gained—and necessarily swept Dareios, Bahman and Sebastian into the celebration.

As he sat between Ehsan and Dareios, drinking his wine and listening to the hum of conversation buzzing around him, Sebastian marveled at the switchback turns in the course of his life. From prince to prisoner, slave to madman's puppet, to this place of…

Freedom didn't quite encapsulate it, yet freedom is what he felt when he looked to his future.

A hope which he'd vaguely sensed when battling Ean at Tyr'kharta, which he'd barely dared believe in upon waking at the Palace of Andorr, had now grown into a conviction of purpose, a *path* of purpose that no man—not even Dore Madden—could ever knock him from again.

He'd given his oath to Isabel, binding himself to her and her brother's cause, yet Sebastian was finding more freedom in being bound to Björn's game than he'd ever felt in any action he'd pursued as prince or emissary.

And despite all he'd gone through—N'ghorra's efforts to break his will along with his body, and Dore's most fervent attempts to degrade him—Sebastian had come through all of this to gain the love of a beautiful woman. He found this the most astonishing twist of all.

Yes…he still saw his twisted leg and scarred face as flaws—he might always look upon them so—but he also saw in them evidence that his will could endure any and all attempts to dominate it. He felt strong in his growing ability as a wielder, and strong in his purpose, stronger than he ever could've foreseen while sitting on the roof with his father and brothers imaging what Fortune lay in store for them in the west.

FORTY-FOUR

"There is a certain cavalier attitude that sets in when all you can really do is inconvenience one another."

—The zanthyr Leyd, on immortality

FELIX DI SARCOVA shoved both hands into his hair and scratched furiously at a sudden itch at the back of his skull, right where the Literato N'abranaacht had struck him on the day he'd found Felix snooping in his apartments.

It was so odd, seeing the man lying there now, all still and silent, his dark hair swept back from that widow's peak and his thin lips oddly slack, like an old woman's. If you didn't know him, you could almost think him peaceful. Felix noted that N'abranaacht's long nose still flared in disdain, though. Even death couldn't wipe away his supercilious air.

And he certainly *looked* dead.

Actually…thanks to all the preservation patterns layered across him, he hardly looked a day riper than when he'd been clawing Felix by the back of the neck like a disobedient pup.

Bleeding Sanctos on a sword, had that been a rat's breakfast! Who knew what would've become of him if Tanis hadn't been there to save his stupid arse!

Felix glowered down at the literato, who was laid out like a bloody prince awaiting a hero's burial, all decked out in opalescent robes, with his long hair in a neat and shining braid across his broad chest. He wasn't wearing that Palmer's hood anymore—what need, now that half the Empire had seen him battling a demon?

And that was exactly the point, wasn't it?

Bloody N'abranaacht. From looking at him now, it was hard to tell how the literato had died, though the rumor—now that Felix was free of the Tower to hear the rumors—was that it had been a spectacular battle and had provided far better entertainment than the Quai game...unless you were rooting for the Danes.

Lord and the Lady.

Two hundred Adepts missing, and all people could talk about was the Literato N'abranaacht. Everywhere Felix had gone in Faroqhar that day, people had been talking about the literato's battle with the demon, or his pattern, the one he'd claimed had Awakened him in the last hours of his life...the one that had allowed him to work the fifth in front of thousands of people.

They went on and on about how N'abranaacht had braved the wilds of Myacene—him, a *na'turna* with no Adept talent—to find the pattern amid the ruins of an ancient civilization and bring it back to the Sormitáge in the hopes it would help revive the Adept race. There was even talk that the Empress intended to give him a posthumous title for his service, though Felix knew that was hogwash.

In any event, by the time evening rolled around, Felix would've rather eaten a stew made from Belloth's necrotic scrotum than listen to another gushingly enthusiastic account of the Literato N'abranaacht's immense bravery.

Where's the bloody bravery when the demon you're killing is your own bloomin' underling?

Oh, but he had to hand it to N'abranaacht. The man had orchestrated one of the worst attacks in Faroqhar's history and then turned the tide of gossip and rumor solely to his own heroic shores. He was lying there dead and still had people fawning all over him.

Only...Felix was fairly sure that N'abranaacht wasn't dead.

He lifted his gaze to the Palmer standing behind the marble slab where the literato's body was laid out. She wore their order's traditional white hood and flowing robes, only her eyes free to look upon the world—a custom which was supposed to be an inverse representation of having 'blind faith in their path.'

The Palmers were a religious order that followed the writings and tenets of Epiphany's Prophet—which usually made them a neutral voice in the religious disputes that often raged through the Sormitáge halls—yet Felix didn't think he could ever trust a Palmer again, not after learning that N'abranaacht had been masquerading as one for the last however many bloody decades. Talk about living with a scorpion in your shoe!

As he looked to the Palmer, feminine eyes met Felix's, and she nodded to him, kindly like, as if Felix was one of the hundreds standing in line to pay their respects to N'abranaacht because he actually respected the man.

The slight tightness in her gaze, however, encouraged him to finish saying his goodbyes and move quickly on, because, well, there *were* hundreds of people standing in line behind him, all of whom the zanthyr had basically cut in front of when he'd walked Felix directly onto the dais.

Phaedor was standing there still, like a stone rolled over the king's tomb, blocking off the entire dais to give Felix time to look over the literato's body. Nobody had raised a word of protest—at least not out loud.

Felix supposed that was one of the perks of being widely known as Björn van Gelderan's zanthyr. People might despise you, but nobody was fool enough to challenge you.

Phaedor probably would've stood there all night, just flipping his dagger and ignoring all the hateful stares aimed at his back, but Felix had seen enough. He glanced to the zanthyr by way of saying *let's get the hell out of here* and descended the dais down the far side. The dark shadow that was Phaedor rejoined his side soon thereafter.

There was something thrilling and yet deeply unsettling about walking beside the zanthyr. It was kind of like crossing a thin strip of icy bridge over a wide abyss, with the wind and the elements doing their damndest to knock you off into oblivion. Since Felix was used to walking death's precipitous edge—eight older brothers and a Nodefinder's innate sense of recklessness had seen to that—he rather enjoyed the sensation.

As they were heading out of the temple, he saw that the line of people waiting to pay their respects to N'abranaacht extended down the steps, through the lamp-lit piazza, and around the corner of another building. You had to be pretty damn devoted to stand in a line that long so late into the night just to see a dead guy.

Felix looked at all the people queued up and made a face. "I mean...that can't be good."

"A safe assumption when speaking of Shailabanáchtran."

Felix shifted his gaze to the zanthyr. "You know, he sure *looked* dead."

"Looks can be deceiving."

"How?" Felix hardened his gaze on him. "*How* can looks be deceiving?"

He'd spent only a day with the zanthyr so far and already he was desperate for a straight reply. Phaedor's idea of an answer was a bowlful of hints smothered with ambiguities. You had to dig and dig through all that tasteless mush to find even a morsel that had some substance to it. No wonder the High Lord winced every time the zanthyr came in the room.

They reached the bottom of the temple stairs and started across the piazza beneath a starry sky, whereupon Felix grumbled, "I think I understand why Tanis said you could be infuriating."

The zanthyr cast him a sidelong eye speared between his raven curls. "I think I understand how you will find your way into an early grave."

"Ha. Very ha." Felix searched his mind for some kind of retort, but an uncomfortable thought struck him instead. "Wait—" he did a double take at the zanthyr, "was that prophecy just now? Were you speaking of my actual future? Or…I mean, were you just, you know, making a point?"

The zanthyr summoned one of his dark daggers out of nowhere and began flipping it as they walked. This drew a lot of attention. "The future belongs to no man, and every man."

"Wow, I love it when you talk in paradoxes." Felix looked ahead wearing a pinched expression. "It's just *so* much fun trying to figure out what the hell you're talking about."

"I'm relieved you appreciate my charms."

"Yeah, I know that tone from you."

Phaedor grinned at him. "Is that so?" He flipped his dagger again.

"*And* I know the meaning of that smile." Felix shoved hands in his pockets and hunched his shoulders. "I'm onto you. I'm no fool."

"I don't keep company with fools."

Felix gave a skeptical grunt. "You're sure good at making us think you do. Must be thrilling, staring down upon the fools of the world from Know It All Peak."

The zanthyr's chuckle sounded much like the low rumble of distant thunder. "It does get rather lonely up there."

As they walked past the long line of people waiting to see N'abranaacht, every head turned to stare at the zanthyr. It was like a ripple effect, heads turning in sequence all the way down the line, one after another, like the zanthyr was hooking each man or woman's attention and dragging it after him. Except, of course, that the zanthyr acted like he didn't notice any of their shameless staring, despite practically the entire piazza gaping at him.

"So…N'abranaacht." Felix made his N'abranaacht face. Like the way the zanthyr had a particular smile he offered in place of certain answers, Felix was developing grimaces and expressions to reflect his opinion on important subjects. The N'abranaacht face was the one he would use for heinous traitors masquerading as popular public attractions. "Is he dead then…or not?"

The zanthyr flipped his dagger. "I expect we have seen the last of the Literato N'abranaacht."

Felix harrumphed disagreeably. "Now see," he shoved his finger towards the zanthyr, "you *say* one thing, but you mean something else entirely. *Sancto Spirito*, I'll bet you can't say just *one* bloody thing and mean *it* and it alone. I'll bet you don't even know how to be forthright."

"Perhaps you should teach me."

"And there you go again." Felix leaned forward to capture the zanthyr's amused gaze. "You didn't just mean that I should teach you. You meant that I'm the last person who should be lecturing you on being forthright." Felix shoved hands back into his pockets. "Like I said, I'm onto your tricks."

The zanthyr grinned. "Rue the day."

"So…" Felix scrunched his upper lip towards his nose and his nose towards his upper lip. It was his 'thinking of something unpleasant' face, or possibly his 'taking a shite' face. They'd looked rather similar when he was practicing them in the mirror. "The Literato N'abranaacht's done for, but we haven't seen the last of that Shail fellow, by Cephrael's ill eye. *That* was your meaning. But that wasn't all of your meaning." Felix sucked on a tooth while he speculated on the rest of the zanthyr's meaning. "Something significant about N'abranaacht…about the N'abranaacht *disguise*." He looked suddenly to the zanthyr. "That's it, isn't it? Shail killed off the N'abranaacht disguise because he was done with it. Which means…" He frowned while trying to figure out what it could mean.

The zanthyr flipped his dagger.

Felix watched the black blade whipping through the air a few times. "Yeah…so how long did you say Shail had been masquerading as a Palmer?"

"Centuries."

Felix blew out his breath. "I don't get it. Why give it up now? You told me—I mean, you *strongly implied*—that the Adepts he took from the Sormitáge were hardly even worth considering. So what did he really accomplish by causing such chaos at the Quai game?"

"That is the pertinent question."

Felix shoved his hands deeper into his pockets. "I hate it when you say that."

The zanthyr cast him an amused look. "There is one time-tested way to move a figure from obscurity to notoriety and ensure his cause—however shallow or insignificant—is carried forward by the masses."

Felix thought about all of the obscure, insignificant causes that his cousin Phoebe and his mother had routinely prattled on about—the plight of Llerenas-Onstaz pottery makers, who made crappy pots, so of course no one would buy them, and the Gideon birds on Palma Lai, who were too stupid to fly to an island that wasn't routinely blowing itself up, and some weird frog that was eating its way through all the flower bulbs and endangering the Ijssmar Tulip Festival…

Felix assumed his thinking hard face again. "I'm not sure I see your point."

The zanthyr gave him a droll look that said he was quite sure Felix was never going to see his point even if he speared him hard in the arse with it. "A simple formula: you make a martyr out of him."

Felix hissed an oath in his native Caladrian that translated roughly into *I'll be Belloth's ball-sucker!* He stared at the piazza stones, unseeing, as the memory of events at the stadium flashed before his eyes.

"He made a martyr of himself—*certo*, it's practically punching you in the face, it's so obvious." He looked back to the zanthyr. "And now, everything that was supposedly important to N'abranaacht is important to the masses of Faroqhar." Felix shook his head and exhaled a slow breath. "It's bloody brilliant." He made the N'abranaacht face again and scowled at the night shadows on the pavement. "You know...I really despise that guy."

The zanthyr flipped the hair from his eyes and his dagger into the air. "You are not alone in this view."

"So what's the cause that Shail pushed to the forefront by killing off the N'abranaacht disguise?"

"That is the fateful question, Felix di Sarcova." Phaedor turned his emerald gaze on Felix. "Let us hope the High Lord is asking it as well."

As it turned out, the High Lord di L'Arlesé was mostly asking why Felix di Sarcova needed to be included in their private discussions, especially when he clearly would have preferred to have excluded the zanthyr as well; but the Empress had asked for Phaedor's counsel, so generally the High Lord's eyes were alone in making this plea each time they strayed towards Felix in a rather pinched and weary fashion.

Then again, the pinched weariness he saw in the High Lord's expression might've just been commiseration, for surely they were both suffering from the malady known as Björn van Gelderan's zanthyr—the High Lord probably more so than Felix. The zanthyr had a knack for finding the weak points in a man's armor where his critiquing bolts might penetrate to their deepest mark. Felix had experienced this; fortunately, he wasn't very sensitive about his weaknesses.

The High Lord on the other hand...

Felix well knew that stodgy, aristocratic type, even if he didn't well know Marius—though he enjoyed the impertinence of thinking of him as 'Marius' instead of 'Your Grace'—and a man like Marius, who was so wrapped in dignity that it took him a half-turn of the hourglass just to peel off enough layers to take a shite...a man like that didn't well appreciate having his nose pushed into his failures like a pup being house-trained.

While Felix had been getting his things moved from the Sormitáge to the Imperial Palace—*do you hear that, Tanis? The Imperial Palace!*—cleaning himself up, and visiting N'abranaacht—all beneath the zanthyr's watchful eye, which Felix rather imagined served to keep both Felix and the zanthyr out of the High Lord's hair—the Empress and her consort had been meeting with officials from the war ministry.

By the time Felix returned with the zanthyr from their visit to N'abranaacht, the Empress had adjourned to her private apartments, but she'd left word that they were to be admitted.

The High Lord received Phaedor into his home with a long suffering expression and Felix with a look of strained patience. It could not have been clearer how immensely irritated he was by the zanthyr's imposition on his private time with his wife.

Marius directed Felix to a chair with a warning look that said *keep silent*. As Felix was making a wallflower of himself, the Empress turned from a cabinet with two goblets in hand. She extended one to her consort with a sigh. "It is worse even than I imagined."

Marius accepted the proffered wine and retreated to the mantel.

"This is my failure." The Empress's regretful tone mirrored her gaze. "If I had trusted your instincts, Marius, we would not be at such a desperate crossroads."

The High Lord gave a slight wince. "Valentina—"

"No, Marius, you told me months ago that something strange was occurring with the nodes out of Daneland."

Marius regarded her gravely. "I didn't know what it meant—I still don't."

"But you warned me the Danes meant to revolt." The Empress slowly moved from the cabinet towards a grouping of chairs, her motion across the thick carpets silent save for the whisper of her silk skirts. "That this attack could happen—that my daughter-heir could fall prey to it—these tragedies rest solidly upon my shoulders." She paused before a chair and lifted a troubled gaze to her consort. "All of Alorin is talking about this event they're calling 'the Quai Fiasco.' More than *two hundred* Adepts taken, Marius!"

Marius laid a hand on the mantel, but Felix got the idea he was setting his patience there as well, the better to stare in the face of it. "I am well aware of it, Valentina."

She claimed a chair and arranged her skirts discontentedly. "*Ineptus.* That's the word circulating on the streets. Our elite have become a source of ridicule."

"The Adeptus stands ready."

"Yes, too ready now that it is far too late." She regarded him vexedly. "What I cannot fathom is how the Danes orchestrated any of this when they have no trained Adepts. This will be the argument thrown back at me by the Patrician Senate. They'll want more than a toss of divining sticks pointing north. They'll want proof that the Danes have the missing Adepts."

Marius dropped his gaze to his goblet and slowly swirled his wine. "Is there any doubt in your mind that Ansgar sits behind this act?"

She considered him as she sat back in her chair. "If he does, why has my Sight shown none of his intent? Even the strongest wielders cannot hide from the Sight."

Phaedor remarked from the shadows, "When the Alorin Seat and his sister the High Mage of the Citadel were investigating early signs of imbalance in the realm, Isabel discovered that when a Malorin'athgul laid his mark across the path of a mortal bound to the tapestry, that mortal's path became obscured or even completely inaccessible to the Sight."

Marius frowned at the zanthyr. "You want us to believe *this* is why Valentina cannot see Ansgar's path?"

Phaedor flipped his dagger. "The truth speaks, regardless of my opinion about it."

"I rather think it speaks only when it suits your opinion."

"Marius." Valentina's tone entreated his forbearance. Her gaze laced across Felix before coming to rest on the zanthyr in his darkened corner. "If only we had some proof that the Danes truly stand behind this treason—a trail linking to them across the nodes, or some sighting of the Adepts that were taken; even proof of this Malorin'athgul—something beyond the words of an adolescent, something concrete to bring to the Patrician Senate."

"The proof is all around you," the zanthyr observed, green eyes aglow, only the motion of his flipping dagger occasionally catching the light from the low-burning fire or the room's amber-glass lamps, "that is, should you choose to look beyond the deception cast specifically for your eyes."

The High Lord thrust his goblet onto the mantel. "Isn't deception your own established trade? It was no mythical creature throwing *deyjiin* at the stadium—"

"And no *na'turna* literato who worked the fifth to slay it." The zanthyr's words cracked sharply with rebuke.

Marius's expression hardened. "The Literato N'abranaacht was a valuable and productive Arcane Scholar in the Sormitáge for many decades."

The zanthyr arched a derisive brow. "Beneath your nose, all that time."

"Now he's a celebrated hero—"

"For slaying his own servant."

"—and now that the man lies dead, you do nothing but cast aspersions across his name."

"*Some* man lies there," the zanthyr remarked from beyond the glint of his flipping dagger, "not Shailabanáchtran."

The High Lord threw up both hands. "For all we know, *you* could be in collusion with this so-called Shail—"

"Marius, this prejudice is unproductive." The Empress set down her wine and closed her fingers around the sculpted knobs of her chair arms. "Invading Danes we may file as commonplace, but how they crossed a twisted node—or corrupted it thereafter such that no one else could cross it—*this* must be lodged with the arcane. Likewise the demon creatures and their sorcery, which resembled *deyjiin* too nearly by all accounts." Her gaze shifted to the zanthyr. "A *na'turna* literato is pedestrian, but one who works *elae*'s fifth strand in front of thousands is unqualifiable. And I can barely think about Nadia for its effect on my rationality." She pressed fingertips to her brow. "It is difficult to frame these events into any cogent context."

Marius eyed the zanthyr with a dark rumination. "Rest assured it all frames within the context of *his* motives, Valentina."

The Empress studied her consort with a furrow between her brow. "Phaedor doesn't walk the tapestry as you and I, Marius." She cast an unreadable gaze at the zanthyr. "He has a different view—potentially a broader view."

Marius worked the muscles of his jaw. "Did *he* tell you that?"

She gave him a soft smile. "No, *mio caro*…my father."

In the silence that descended while they held each other's gaze, an uncomfortable energy built in the room. Felix noted that the zanthyr stood as remote from the two monarchs' argument as a mountain from the deliberations of climbers attempting to scale its heights.

"The attack at the Quai game constitutes an act of war." Valentina riffled her fingers on her chair arms, deliberately, her gaze unfixed yet clearly focused on the stream of her thoughts. "It cannot go unpunished, lest the Empire become the laughingstock of the realm. Even if another stands behind this aggression, surely there can be no question in their minds that the Empire will retaliate against Daneland, and yet…"

"I know your mind, Valentina." Marius took his wine and left the mantel. "It seems nearly scripted—this invasion, our expected retaliation."

She focused her gaze on him. "I fear we could be walking into a trap."

The zanthyr flipped his dagger. "It is certainly a trap."

The High Lord cast him a strained look that was part entreaty and part *stay the hell out of our conversation*. To the Empress, he replied, "The Empire has always responded to acts of aggression with the might of the Adeptus."

"I think that's Phaedor's point," she noted, frowning.

The High Lord set his empty goblet down on a table and turned in a slowly deliberate manner to face her. "If we know it's a trap, then we prepare for it. We bring our entire force to bear—"

"The very act he's expecting," Phaedor remarked.

Marius spun and slammed his hands on the table between himself and the zanthyr. "What would *you* have us do? Speak plainly or speak not at all!"

The zanthyr emerged from the corner like Night taking form. "I would have you remember who you are."

Marius's fingers tightened against the wood. Anger simmered in his gaze. "Meaning?"

The zanthyr began strolling the lengthy shadows beyond the reach of lamps and firelight. "If Valentina's Sight eludes her, if the currents are muddled, then you both must use *other* perceptions. Mortals have fifty-two, but a wielder's depth and scope of perception is limited only by the Eleventh Esoteric."

The High Lord straightened from the table, his expression drawn in long, deep lines.

"Ansgar is but one of many pikes aimed against you." The zanthyr's emerald gaze closed the distance between himself and the High Lord. "Each pike is long enough to keep your attention focused on the spear at its tip, rather than on the enemy wielding the shaft. Should you ever look far enough down the length of any of these pikes, you would discover this truth yourself."

"Malorin'athgul." Marius tracked the zanthyr's progress around the room with his gaze. "A name only, lacking proof."

The zanthyr turned him a critical stare. "The proof is carried upon the unreadable currents flooding out of the north, as I warned."

"Yes, your many warnings," the High Lord's tone stung with asperity, "shouting of alarm, signifying nothing."

"So long you've delayed causative action against the one who works against you that he stands now within arm's length of the Diamond Throne."

At this remark, the High Lord looked very much like he was grinding an unspoken curse between his teeth.

Tanis had told Felix that the zanthyr acted as a mirror. That it was a game of his to reflect back at people whatever attitude they directed towards him. In dealing with Felix, the zanthyr's manner became flippant and droll; towards the High Lord, severe and relentlessly practical.

"He has lived beneath your banner," the zanthyr continued, eyeing Marius through the spill of his wavy hair. "He's studied you; he's studied your literature, your sacred works, your magic. He knows your methods, and he has observed the ebb and flow of your politics. This man knows *you*, High Lord of Agasan, even though you don't know him. Trust that he has well predicted your decisions and already made plans to outmaneuver you. He is an opponent quite beyond your ken."

Marius straightened in defiance of this challenge, and his gaze hardened.

"Reverse this scene and stand in my place if you dare: *your* kingdom has been invaded, *your* daughter and heir taken—"

"Nadia's absence will be remedied shortly."

The High Lord looked like he was ready to explode. "—*your* people witnessing impossible feats that even your best scholarly minds cannot explain; and here comes another, who claims—if not foreknowledge, at least an arcane understanding, but instead of offering clarity, this stranger of questionable loyalties simply dangles tantalizing morsels of truth. He offers no real advice. He tells you *nothing*, yet implies that he knows all."

The zanthyr caught his dagger by the point and aimed the hilt at Marius. "What I know is inconsequential, Marius di L'Arlesé. It is what *you* know, and what *you* choose to do with that knowledge, that changes the pattern on the tapestry."

The High Lord stared at him, clearly at a loss for words.

The Empress shifted in her chair. "Are you advising us to move against the Danes or not, Phaedor?"

The zanthyr flipped his dagger. "All the answers to this mystery will be found in Kjvngherad. You must seek your proof there."

Marius bristled. "You just said we shouldn't—"

Phaedor speared a look at him. "I just said you mustn't do what he *expects* you to do. You've no choice but to go to Kjvngherad. It is the manner by which you will proceed there that must be carefully…" but the zanthyr's words faded as his attention seemed to shift…

He ran for the doors.

They flew open before his approach, and he passed the startled Praetorians in a blur, a dark arrow of intent.

Felix automatically launched up to follow but stopped himself when he saw that no one else was moving. The High Lord's Caladrians appeared just beyond the doorway, their gazes inquiring, awaiting command.

"But…" Felix turned a fervent look around. "Shouldn't we follow him?" He searched the many pairs of eyes staring at him. "Don't you see? He clearly *meant* for us to follow him or he would've just disappeared."

Felix turned to the High Lord rather desperately, knowing better than to leave without being given leave, but feeling the zanthyr getting farther ahead with every breath of delay. "Your Grace, don't you remember what he said just now?" His eyes beseeched Marius's understanding. "Why else would he—"

"Get after him!" Marius flung the order, and his Caladrians scrambled to obey.

Felix darted after them without waiting for further permission. He soon overtook the stockier Giancarlo and found himself neck and neck with

Vincenzé, who seemed very indignant at the idea of letting an upstart youth like Felix get the better of him in a footrace.

The zanthyr led the chase through the personal apartments of the imperial family, down long marble passages and across galleries shadowed by night, and finally outside into the moonlight and across the family's private grounds. Felix lost sight of him for a time but finally spotted him again at the bottom of a terraced hill, a darker shadow poised before a large fountain. The latter's waters had been stilled for the night, but the silver-dark pool reflected the zanthyr's form back against the starry sky.

Vincenzé came to a panting halt near the zanthyr and shoved hands onto his knees. "What...?" but the rest of his words went by the boards while he caught his breath.

Felix saw the slight tightening around the zanthyr's eyes, so he found a seat on the fountain's edge and kept his mouth shut.

Giancarlo came jogging up. He pushed hands on his hips, threw back his head, and sucked heaving gulps of air loudly into his lungs.

Far in his wake came the High Lord, leading a wedge of Praetorians whose armor gleamed darkly in the moonlight.

Felix was just thinking this had better be good or the zanthyr was surely done for, when the night rippled and...*split*—Felix didn't know how else to put description to it—and a darkness unlike anything Felix had ever seen carved a jagged scar down through the air.

He jumped to his feet.

The High Lord arrived just as the scar was forming the shape of a door.

Hissing an oath, Vincenzé threw himself in front of the High Lord and drew his sword—

Which the zanthyr grabbed by the blade and ripped from his hand—

Whereupon three figures stumbled out of the darkness.

One man collapsed to his knees and hung his head.

A second, taller figure toppled and was caught by the zanthyr, who promptly vanished with him.

The third inhaled a desperate gasp and threw herself into the High Lord's arms.

The Princess Nadia was home.

FORTY-FIVE

"Hell offers better company."
—The Adept truthreader Thrace Weyland,
on the Temple of Tambarré

Ean roused to the taste of dirt in his mouth and throbbing pain pretty much everywhere else…which, looking at things optimistically, seemed to indicate he was probably still alive.

Towards the end of his fall, his descent had somehow slowed to a few degrees shy of terminal, and the slate roof he'd careened down had managed the rest. Ean remembered scraping down sharp tiles, bouncing off a ledge and flipping haphazardly over an open yard…crashing through a thatched barn roof and down past several bales of hay, and finally splashing into the muck of a horse's stall—thankfully sans occupant—where he remained, many hours later.

That he woke with his mind within his own control meant the link with Darshan had been severed by his unconsciousness. With any luck, the Malorin'athgul thought him dead.

Get up, Ean. Get up—get up—get up—

He did finally get up. It was a fundamentally joyless experience.

So was walking, and thinking…breathing…*being*.

Ean staggered out of the barn rubbing his neck and looked up at the sheer eastern edge of the acropolis, which towered over the steep-roofed manor and the adjoining farmstead that had so kindly broken his fall. He couldn't see much of Darshan's temple from that angle. He was looking forward to seeing *much* less of it as soon as possible.

Ean oriented himself to the city and headed off, exhausted, aching, reeking of manure and too tired to care about anything but finding a safe place to sleep. He carefully refrained from calling the lifeforce. He hoped the intervening hours had repaired the tiff he'd caused between *elae* and himself, because he wouldn't last long in Darshan's city without the use of his talents.

By the time he reached the inn where he'd secured a room the day before, the sun was setting amid boiling flame in the west and another storm was blowing in from the south, darkening the horizon.

Ean lifted a shaking hand to open the gate but then paused with his fingers on the high handle and hung his head. Had it really only been less than a day's time since he'd walked out of that selfsame gate, sure purpose and possibility were guiding him true? He could barely separate the days from the nights anymore, only counting the unclocked hours of sleep by the depth of the ache behind his eyes.

With a great effort of will, Ean pushed through the gate and wound his exhausted way among the high-walled gardens. The inn's doors stood open to the storm's cooling breeze, so he let himself inside, waved a haggard hello to the startled innkeeper, and tromped wearily upstairs to his room.

One of the stewards caught up with him at the second floor landing.

"*Rabb'an*, good evening…"

He kept talking, but Ean's ears were past listening, his brain past understanding any words other than sleep. He let the older man lead him to his rooms and then sat slouched in a chair while two chambermaids drew a bath for him. He must've dozed in that state, because when he came aware again, he was alone and water was steaming in the copper tub. The room smelled of lavender, which was a far cry fairer than himself.

The next half hour became a blur of heat and drowsy half-awareness. He had the wherewithal to put a warding on the room—fiery, searing pain in his skull!—that he might sleep undisturbed. Then he wrapped himself in the robe they'd left for him, staggered—still dripping—over to the bed, and collapsed onto it, asleep even before his body hit the mattress.

Arion turned a page in his journal and wrote on the new line,

> *I think there is a hidden solution to the understanding of all Patterning in this thing we call Absolute Being. The more we strategize T'khendar's creation, the more this becomes apparent to me.*
>
> *The First Esoteric tells us Absolute Being is 'the entire concept of actuality,' while the Twenty-first Esoteric instructs that 'Actuality is monitored by the wielder's point of view; reality is monitored by collective thought agreement.'*

For any wielder of elae, understanding the distinction between actuality and reality cannot be underestimated—

"It is a great tragedy of our time that we have an incomparable day birthed for our appreciation and Arion can't keep his nose out of that journal of his."

Arion looked up to see Cristien Tagliaferro grinning at him. The truthreader usually seemed the brooding poet, with that curling auburn forelock ever falling into his eyes and his sensual mouth and cleft chin—that is, when he wasn't engaged in some taunt of Arion.

They were sprawled in the grass on a hillside overlooking a deep blue lake framed by emerald hills, with the jutting crags of the Navárrel forming an impressive white and charcoal backdrop. It was the kind of view an artist would've given his left hand to paint, yet just one of many offered at the Palazzo di Adonnai.

Would that they'd had more time to appreciate the villa's luxuries and diversions, but they'd been holed up in Björn's study for over a month, working round the clock to strategize what could only be called a desperate gamble—all their brilliant plans for which had come to a screaming halt when they'd tried to isolate a focal point for the working.

It was the Seventeenth Law: *'The use of talismans must focus force without limiting scope.'* No talisman known to man would be capable of focusing the force necessary to create an entire world, whole cloth, out of Alorin's aether. To wield a talisman of such capability, they would have to craft *it* first, an undertaking which would be nearly as arduous as the primary working in question. Thus their frustrating stalemate.

The sunny day was providing a much needed respite; time to regroup, reconsider, renew; time to let their minds wander, to think through all they'd discussed and potentially find new avenues of approach.

Arion smiled and looked back to his journal. "We each take our respites in different ways, Cristien."

Reclining on the blanket opposite Arion tending a large basket of food and wine, the Nodefinder Parsifal d'Marre cast Cristien his satyr's grin. "Cristien would be enjoying himself much more if a certain Vestal had also been invited to Björn's council."

Cristien made some kind of retort, but Arion had already set his pen back to his page and was drawing upon *elae*'s fifth and third strands—the faintest pattern of permanence, he barely noticed it—to continue writing in this magical ink,

—in importance. As reality depends upon the agreement of others, reality

then has already disappeared from a wielder's purview, per the First Law; for reality lies on the scale of causation below the line between cause and effect. Verily, if something requires another's agreement to be so, that is the level of effect, not the level of cause.

Actuality, then, is determined by the wielder's point of view; thus actuality is the only level of causative interest to the wielder, for this is the level at which one becomes the point of causation, the point of origin, the place from which anything in the wielder's imagination can—

"Nonetheless, Cristien does have a point." Parsifal nudged Arion's leg with his boot to gain his attention. "What is it that you're always writing in those journals of yours, Arion? Share it with us, since it's captured your interest so completely as to deny all else the blessing of your notice."

Arion closed his pen inside his journal and raised his gaze to meet Parsifal's. "Originally my journals were a repository for the patterns I was experimenting with," he shifted his attention between Parsifal and an attentive Cristien, "…but now I think I will leave them for my son."

Parsifal's eyebrows shot up, resembling fuzzy caterpillars inching to touch one another. "You have no son."

Arion smiled softly down at the leather journal and laid his right hand, each finger bound by two Sormitáge rings, across the cover. "One day I might."

A dubious grunt echoed from overhead. Arion turned his head to see Markal Morrelaine standing behind him. Dressed all in black, and with his mane of white hair, he stood out like an iron post against the blue sky.

Arion's welcoming smile hinted of challenge. "You doubt my virility, Maestro?"

"I merely doubt you'll live long enough to procreate, the way you go about things."

Arion grinned at him. "That's why I have more rings than you—because of the way I go about things."

Markal came and settled himself dead center in their midst, forcing both Parsifal and Cristien to change positions to accommodate his broad frame. The effect was somewhat like a bear choosing a raccoon den for his rest and ousting the raccoons in the process.

Markal accepted a goblet of wine from an offering Parsifal and settled his scrutinizing gaze on Arion. "Having more rings than me doesn't make you wiser, Arion. Only bolder."

Arion rolled onto his back and clasped hands behind his head. The sky above really was an impossible shade of blue. "Boldness and wisdom rarely walk hand in hand, Maestro. That's why I keep you around—to wisely remind me of all the things I'm not supposed to be able to do."

The Nodefinder Anglar Tempest and the truthreader Voss di Alera came striding down the grand staircase from the palazzo, mid some heated debate. Arion couldn't remember a time when the two of them *weren't* mid some debate. Those two were like vinegar and baking soda: ever in a froth when combined.

"Ah, perfect!" The heavily bearded Anglar extended a hand to the group on the lawn and turned his bright blue eyes on Voss. "Who better to provide us with a definitive answer?"

Voss cast them all a taunting grin, wide and sharp on his jester's face. "Yes, but we should ask Arion, for I'd like our question answered this century, and the maestro couldn't find brevity if it was chained 'round his neck."

"Nor you, prudence, Voss di Alera," Markal rumbled.

Voss threw himself down beside Arion. "Prudence is overrated, Maestro."

"So is impudence, Voss."

"Maestro, we would be honored to gain your wisdom in the resolution of our debate." Anglar took a seat beside Parsifal, who was just then pouring wine for the two newcomers. Anglar pushed his dark hair back from his forehead and then accepted the wine. "So..." he extended his goblet towards Markal, "the Thirteenth Law says *'intention monitors solidity, solidity monitors structure.'*"

"But the Seventh Esoteric says, *'solidity is monitored by Absolute Being,'*" Voss inserted, "which implies that within the bounds of Absolute Being you could have *any* structure, regardless of solidity—"

"But according to the Fourteenth Law," Anglar cut in, "equal opposing forces will nullify structure, so solidity is still paramount to—"

"You forget that the Fourteenth Esoteric says, *'exact duplicating thought, with the same energy, in the same time, will nullify reality.'*" Voss held up a lecturing finger. "So obviously solidity is only *apparent*, not absolute—"

"Which is exactly to my point, Voss."

"Maestro," Parsifal murmured as the two men continued debating, "hadn't you best intervene?"

"To what purpose?" Markal cast a mordant eye across the arguing pair and drank his wine. "They merely volley rules, not reason."

"Anglar, you both have it right." Reclining on his back, Arion idly blew a wisp of the fifth into a puffy cloud floating overhead and instantly vaporized it. "Matter is far more malleable than most people realize; it's merely energy particles that have become so compacted that they've solidified. The fifth strand, for example, takes this sluggish energy and mobilizes it. Patterning is just the ability to mold energy to our will in a new way, a method of imposing *new* thought to the agreed-upon physical laws that bind matter together."

"But the Seventh Esoteric—" Voss began.

Arion rolled onto his side. "Yes, Voss. Too much energy in too little space results in solidity; but give that energy space to move again by *creating new* space through Absolute Being, and you can do anything with it."

Voss directed a triumphant look at Anglar.

"But Anglar is on point when referencing laws governing the interaction of energy outside of Absolute Being. Solidity does determine what structure the elements can assume in that case, because of the associative properties of energy."

Anglar arched an imperious brow.

"But within Absolute Being?" Arion cast a smile across the group, "*within* it, you can change the very laws that govern matter."

Into the thoughtful silence that followed this speech, Parsifal raised his wine and remarked, "And that's why the Alorin Seat chose Arion Tavestra to sit upon his council."

"As if Björn would've invited Arion if he hadn't been courting his sister," Cristien teased with a wink. "Rowed wielders are a dime a dozen."

Arion regarded him amusedly. "Ah, but I have a row and five, Cristien, and I guarantee before this is over, I'll have my second row."

"Oh sure," Voss waved an airy hand, "they say once you have your first row, it's all downhill from there."

Anglar was regarding Arion with a quiet intensity. "If you get your second row, he'll make you one of his generals."

Parsifal grunted. "The Alorin Seat never would've overlooked Markal's star pupil. Cristien's just jealous because his lover, Raine, wasn't also invited to sit on Björn's council."

Cristien gave him a frustrated stare. "Raine and I are not lovers."

Parsifal winked at him. "But you would be if he would have you."

"What do you know of love, Parsifal?" Voss tossed a stem of long grass at him. "The closest you've ever come to it is with that mongrel beast you call a horse."

Parsifal lifted a finger off his goblet. "That's true. Horses are more predictable than women—*or* vestals," he added with a grin at Cristien. He raised his goblet to the sun and studied the liquid within it speculatively. "Women are much the same as wine, my friends. The bottle may be shapely, but you never really know if the vintage is sweet or sour until you pop the…cork…" his gaze strayed beyond Arion's shoulder, and he murmured, "Speaking of eccentric vintages."

Arion turned to see Malachai ap'Kalien approaching—blonde, broad-shouldered and thin as a winter twig.

"Lady's light, man," Voss shook his head resolutely. "Why don't you eat something, for all our sakes? You're as like to blow away with the next breeze."

"You're one to talk." Anglar eyed Voss disagreeably over the rim of his goblet. "An anorexic goat has more meat on its bones."

Voss looked down at his lanky frame, noticed a bit of something on his vest and scraped at it with a fingernail.

"What? No comeback?" Cristien elbowed him.

Voss tossed his hair from his eyes. "*Anglar's* the one's been intimate with anorexic goats. But hey, you know…" he lifted his goblet to Anglar, "to each his own, mate."

"What I would like to see you own, Voss di Alera, is a modicum of productivity," Markal grumbled.

"But a modicum would only leave you wanting more, Maestro." Voss leaned on one elbow and crossed his long legs at the ankles. "I wouldn't want to elevate your expectations."

"There's little fear of that."

"Well…I did it." Malachai dropped to his knees in the grass and sank back on his heels. His brown eyes were lambent, like polished pebbles, and his pale countenance held an uncommon light.

Arion's instincts roused instantly in alarm.

"Did what?" Parsifal extended a goblet of wine towards Malachai.

Malachai seemed not to notice it, for his eyes were pinned on Arion, as Arion's were fixed on him while alarm bells of consequence sounded painfully in his head.

Malachai tugged on his nose. "I told him I would do it."

Cristien must've caught something of Malachai's thoughts, for he straightened and stared at him. "Malachai, you didn't—"

"I told him I would be the focal point for the working." Malachai lifted his gaze to include the whole of the group. "I will be his talisman."

A startled silence marched in the train of their collective surprise.

Then chaos erupted—multiple exclamations of "*Are you insane?*" from the others, voiced with varying degrees of civility.

Arion saw a new pattern of cause and consequence spiraling forth, a crystalline design spreading before his vision, superimposed against his friend's shining face and the others' rather desperate ones. The vision filled him with foreboding.

"If something goes wrong..." Arion placed a hand on his friend's leg. "Malachai, you'll be the first one to be hit."

Malachai pushed his long blonde hair back from his face with both hands. His gaze grew distant. "To be on the forefront of it, Arion...to ride the forward edge as life itself begins, the dawn of a new world..." a faint furrow creased his brow but vanished as he smiled and focused his gaze on Arion. "I would give anything to surf the breaking wave of that moment."

Markal's grunt held a decided undertone of ironic skepticism.

Arion cast him a reproachful stare.

"Hold on, hold on!" Voss held up his hands to quiet the argument that had erupted between the others. "What are we saying here?" He turned his colorless eyes around to include everyone, his tone one of insistence more than inquiry. "Nothing's going to go wrong. I mean...what could go wrong? The Alorin Seat has assembled the greatest minds in the realm," Voss touched a hand to his heart and gave a humble nod, "my own included."

Markal shifted agitatedly. "If your mind displayed half as much talent as your ego, you might actually find something valuable to contribute to this council."

Voss clenched a long stem of grass between his teeth and angled a grin at Markal. "Technically, I'm only a *consulting* member of the Council of Nine."

"Praise Epiphany for small blessings."

Arion sat up and returned his journal to his satchel. His mind was spinning with new possibilities now. Malachai as the focal point changed everything. He lifted his gaze to Markal. "Maestro, you know Voss is right."

Voss grinned audaciously at this, earning a black stare from Markal.

"But not in the sense that nothing can go wrong," Arion added thoughtfully, more to himself than the group, "rather...that we won't allow anything to prevent us from achieving the effect we're intending to achieve."

Markal drank his wine mid a stormy contemplation. "Do you know why he collected all of you?" He cast a challenging gaze around the assembly of Adepts, many of whom looked hardly more than twenty and eight, though most of them had seen sixty name days or more. "Why all of *you*? Why not maestros and scholars with established reputations in their field?"

When even Voss offered no answer to this, Markal grunted dubiously. "You're young for your accomplishments, *too* young yet to have learned that there are things you cannot do. He needs that idealism to have any hope of success."

"What does he need from you then, Maestro?" Voss inquired with a cheeky grin.

"Doomsday warnings," Cristien grumbled.

"Practicality," Anglar observed more soberly.

Markal draped his arms over his bent knees and dangled his empty goblet beneath one hand. "Rest you assured: whatever hope we have, it is the slightest, barest thread of it. What he intends…the chances of success are so miniscule as to be nonexistent." He cast a stern look across all of them. "Let me not hear you say nothing can go wrong. *Everything* can go wrong."

Cristien muttered into his wine, "Doom and gloom, as I said."

Malachai shook his head, his gaze distant but luminous. "Even if I die in the attempt, Maestro…to have lived to see such a momentous event, to have laid my name upon it, made my mark; to even be associated with this illustrious cause, my legacy assured…" He gave him a vivid smile. "Nothing is more meaningful to me."

Markal growled, "The immortal delusions of youth."

Arion frowned at him. "A wielder is limited by what he can envision, Maestro." He handed his goblet to a brooding Parsifal, who absently refilled it. "The Alorin Seat needs us because you cannot envision the creation of a world without also conceiving of thousands of possible catastrophic ramifications. The simplicity is that we must have the courage to push through any obstacle to achieve the effect we intend to create. There's nothing else to consider."

"Only the thousands of possible catastrophic ramifications," Cristien grumbled.

"There *will* be ramifications." Markal aimed a pointed stare at Cristien. "The waves of our pebble cast into Alorin's aether will permeate far. There may come a point when we have to consider not *can* it be done, but *should* it be done?"

Arion shook his head. "I disagree, Maestro."

"Of course you do, Arion. Wielders always disagree with caution when they've never faced a force bigger than themselves."

Arion accepted his goblet, now refilled, back from Parsifal and drank from it. Caution versus courage was an old argument between himself and the maestro. He fingered his goblet contemplatively. "There is no excuse for failure once the First Law has been observed."

Markal exhaled malcontent in a forceful breath. "While wielding the lifeforce, things can change, Arion. A wielder must be constantly assessing and reassessing against Balance to determine if the effect he intended is actually the effect he's achieving. Occasionally there comes a time when you have to decide that the effect you intended will *not* be achieved."

Arion shook his head. "A wielder who fails to achieve the effect he intended just didn't display enough fortitude, courage, or conviction to see it through."

Markal pelted him with a black agate gaze. "One day you may come up against a force that even you cannot overcome. *Then* you may talk to me of fortitude, courage and conviction…"

—the dream shifted—

Arion clenched his teeth as a blast of *deyjiin* exploded against his fifth-strand shield. A sizzling chill speared his mind, numbing his edge, while the exhaustion of battle, of working *elae* constantly for untold hours, had begun to bring a sluggishness to his thoughts.

Arion spun and slammed his sword against the Enemy's again. A geyser of sparks erupted as blades charged with opposing energies scraped and separated, *elae's* fire meeting *deyjiin's* ice. The eruption illuminated the weld chamber's crumbling ceiling.

Arion pivoted and lunged. The Enemy sidestepped and slung Arion's blade off his own in another flaming eruption of sparks.

A constant barrage of compulsion battered Arion's consciousness. He channeled it into his blade and back at the Enemy as needle-sharp threads, but the latter's mental shields were viscous on the surface and bedrock beneath. Arion's threads found little purchase there.

The Enemy threw a new pattern at him, an explosive combination of the second and fourth. Arion split it with the arrow of his intention and the pieces fell in twain. The air was choked with fractured patterns.

Choked as well by dust and smoke and *deyjiin's* acrid ash. As Arion parried another advance, a huge section of the ceiling fell and shattered on the floor. Shards of stone pelted Arion's shields, and a cloud of marble dust engulfed him. The entire chamber was coming down around their battling forms. The walls had become webbed with cracks. Even as Arion watched, a section of plaster crumbled down upon itself, leaving a cottage-sized pock in the wall.

Arion split another of the Enemy's patterns before it was fully formed and brought up his blade to meet the man's next powerful swing. Sparks geysered.

Arion wiped his brow with his upper arm, pushed the hair and sweat from his eyes and tried to maintain his focus. Is this what Isabel had foreseen so long ago? That he would face an immortal there at the last, when all else was falling into an abyss—Malachai gone mad from *deyjiin*, the best of them lost, T'khendar a wasteland unable to support *elae*—and perhaps amid such despairing times, he would falter?

Arion still couldn't comprehend what she'd foreseen, couldn't fathom the truths she'd told him, the years they would be apart because of a choice he'd already made. He didn't believe he was destined to the path she'd seen him walking, not when every step was still his to choose.

The ground shook, tossing Arion and the Enemy apart. Arion used the fifth to right himself just as a pillar fell, carrying the last of the light. Iron crashed into stone and pitched the chamber into darkness.

Arion let the currents show him what was true.

The weld appeared as a swirling whirlpool of liquid bronze webbed with lightning streaks of darkness. *Unstable*, but he had few choices left. The paths spiraling before him were diminishing with every clash of his and the Enemy's blades, with every piece of stone tumbled from the crumbling walls.

Another pillar rocked on its base and then started falling directly towards them. Arion dove half a dozen steps to the chamber floor while simultaneously wrapping the fifth around the monolith of stone. A thought drove it towards the Enemy.

The Enemy dove for Arion and cast *deyjiin* off his blade at the pillar.

It exploded into marble ash.

The floor shook again, and a fissure split the weld.

Arion rolled to his feet and sprinted through clouds of choking dust to engage the Enemy before the man could regain the advantage. He drove him back, back towards the weld—

He summoned the second strand in a pivotal instant.

Light sprang into being as Arion moved their battle onto the Pattern of the World.

FORTY-SIX

"When vindictiveness and gall meet prudence on the battlefield, prudence ever proves the weaker opponent."
–Nadori Commander Nassar abin Ahram, *al-Amir* of Ramala

AT CAMP THAT night, the Converted celebrated in honor of Raegus n'Harnalt. The cooks slew several lambs for the occasion and made a stew with olives that had the men licking their bowls, but the biggest highlight of the evening—much to Trell's surprise—was his promised story about how the kingdoms of Dannym and the Akkad became unlikely allies.

From his father's daring attempt to remove his forces from under the nose of Viernan hal'Jaitar, through hal'Jaitar's plot to assassinate King Gydryn and his rescue by Prince Farid, to the Dannish soldiers finding their way behind 'enemy' lines to Nahavand and the subsequent peace between their kingdoms, Trell told the story in heroic fashion. If he filled in a few details here and there that he wasn't entirely certain about, surely he could be forgiven under the right of poetic license. Certainly the cheering that followed his tale sounded approving.

Much later, after Trell had made his rounds through camp and visited Gendaia bearing apple gifts, he lay in his tent courting sleep while listening to the murmur of his princely name flowing across the lips of his men.

Too soon, he woke again, or so it felt to him as he lay there sensing morning's approach, yet knowing darkness still held the world in thrall. Discipline alone drove him from the warmth of his bed.

He dressed and moved silently through the camp, past still-smoking firepits and the folded shadows of tents, walking unnoticed amid the susurrant currents of two hundred sleeping men. His body would have happily rejoined their slumbering flow, but his mind had awoken and was too active to allow sleep to find him again.

Something Alyneri had said was still troubling him. He'd contacted her via their bond and shared what had happened so far on his journey. But after he spoke of the flood and jumping in after Loukas, a sort of stillness had overcome her thoughts, the mental equivalent of silence settling upon their conversation.

What is it? What did I say? The last thing he wanted was to become estranged from her while they were apart, and he sensed that something he'd said had upset her.

Trell... he perceived more than heard her mental sigh, *you did promise that you wouldn't take needless risks with your life.*

This was needful, Alyneri.

Was it? Her tone chided him lightly, but there was plenty of challenge in it, too. *Because the way you described it to me, you might've simply stayed on the raft, asked the River Goddess to send a boat to your friend, and accomplished the same end.*

Trell had initially frowned at this. Now he frowned again while he walked the camp.

I know heroics are in your nature, she'd put a soft smile in her voice as she'd said this, *but it requires far more bravery to allow others to risk their lives when you would rather risk your own. It takes a strong leader to make a knowing sacrifice.*

Her words had invoked images of loss and brought a painful sharpness to his thoughts. *You don't have to educate me on sacrifice, Alyneri. I know what it means to lose men on the battlefield.*

But the First Lord's game is far larger than one battlefield, Trell, she'd reminded him. *Imagine if the Mage acted as you and put his life on the line every time some danger had to be confronted? I'm sure he* would *rather be there, leading the charge—doubtless the game would be finished that much faster if he was—but at what cost, Trell? The chance of losing him altogether? Then where would we all be?*

Trell knew that Alyneri's point wasn't about him saving Loukas. She wanted him to take a broader view, to stand back and assess the entire game board and acknowledge his role in it. But Trell considered this case entirely about Loukas. He couldn't turn his back on a friend in need. How could he, and maintain his own integrity the while?

And what about the rest of the company's need? his conscience argued, Alyneri's advocate. *What happens to them if you fall? Do the needs of the one outweigh the needs of the many?*

He couldn't deny the validity of this point. If he fell while saving one man, what would happen to his father's men? Was one life worth the cost of thousands simply because that one life belonged to a friend?

The very question brought immense conflict to Trell's heart, because it pointed to a question even more disturbing; namely, what cost was he willing to pay to maintain his own integrity? And what would be the cost of compromising it?

Trell reached the edge of camp and the two sentries standing watch—Thierry and Ferrault, brothers expatriated from Veneisea. He nodded to them, said good morning in their native tongue, inquired of the night's happenings, learned things had been uneventful save for Thierry losing a bet to Ferrault on the nature of an animal that had been making an unholy racket most of the night, and continued walking the line of the camp with swirling thoughts dragging like a river's current against his feet.

Dawn was turning the air a misty grey when Trell finally found a clearing that suited his needs. He doffed his cloak, and with his breath steaming in the chill air, started running through the *cortata*.

Every time he worked the Adept dance of swords, he felt immense gratitude to Alyneri for teaching it to him. From the very first day, when he'd been watching Alyneri transition smoothly from form to form, her every motion connecting seamlessly to the next, and attempting with his own motion to copy hers...since that initial attempt, he'd embraced a mental calm while working the pattern's forms, a heightened focus both of attention and awareness. Even his breath submitted to the *cortata's* rhythm, such that his entire body felt balanced—and it would stay that way for hours, for as long as he continued working the pattern.

Alyneri had explained how the pattern of the *cortata* collected and combined *elae's* strands to fuel his energies. While he'd understood the theory, all he'd experienced in the beginning was a sense of forces in balance. Now that he could perceive *elae*, however, he could feel the lifeforce funneling into him, as if his every step absorbed it from the earth, every breath refined it from the air. He felt himself moving through clouds of *elae* even as the pattern gathered more of it around him.

Trell cut his blade across and down to the right, crouched as he turned in a slow circle, and straightened again as he brought up his sword crosswise from low to high—a form known as Cardinal Skims the Water. This flowed through Searching the Sea and Crouching Leopard into Holding the Moon—an unusual combination, for Green Dragon Emerging from the Water was much favored in place of the other three—yet it intrigued him to find the same sword forms he'd learned as an adolescent mirrored within the *cortata's* movements. No doubt what he dubbed the 'mortal' version of the forms had been derived from the *cortata*, and not the other way around.

Something in this recognition seemed profound to him, in the way truth pervaded all cultures and beliefs, even when disguised within differing dogmas. What was it the First Lord had said to him once? *'Truth is the ultimate solution.'*

Trell had understood 'solution' in that context to mean resolution, but now…now he was beginning to think Björn had meant 'solution' as in *solubility,* solvent…truth not only resolved, it *dissolved*—bitter hostilities, brittle misunderstandings, the feuds of nations.

His father and his *Su'a'dal* were a perfect example of this. The truth, raining upon the rancorous construct that had buffeted their two kingdoms, had washed it clean, and a sparkling new city, diverse in belief yet united in purpose, had emerged.

Many thoughts later, Trell moved through the *cortata's* final form—a combination of Black Dragon Whips His Tail and Comet Chases the Moon—a spinning, thrusting, slashing maneuver that made his sword a truly deadly extension of his intent. Then he stepped out of the pattern and opened both arms, blade held low and off to the side, and bowed as if to a sparring partner.

Clapping, slow and deliberate, drew his gaze behind him.

Rolan Lamodaar stood at the edge of the clearing. He wore loose-fitting but expensively embroidered *shalwar kameez,* the tunic's placket open to better display the muscular lines of his chest. His tattooed collar of thorns stood out starkly behind the three braids of his beard. He'd foregone his usual *keffiyeh*, choosing instead to queue his long ebony hair at the back of his neck.

"That must've been every form illustrated in the Book of Swords and a fair few I've never seen before." Rolan hefted his blade and spun it in a figure-eight, warming his arm. "You didn't tell us we'd be working our forms this morning, *A'dal*."

Trell lifted his gaze to the barely blushing sky and then cast a smile at Rolan. "How did you know I was here?"

Rolan arched a bushy ebony brow. "After the stunt you pulled two days ago? Someone has to keep an eye on you." He motioned to Trell with his blade. "Shall we have at it again? It's colder than Shamal's frosty arse out here."

Trell flicked a smile at Rolan's irreverent reference to the Wind God's northerly son. Then he gave an accommodating nod and took up his position to repeat the *cortata*.

The first time he'd worked the sequence hard and fast, the better to generate some heat—for Rolan spoke truth; it was bloody cold out there—but as he began it a second time, Trell worked the forms with deliberate and slow precision, extending every motion to its fullest.

The first round had warmed him, but the second quickly had him sweating. Sitting in a crouch and turning a slow circle while holding his blade extended to the fullest stretch of both arms…this was far harder than performing the same motion quickly, where momentum carried him through. And there were countless such difficult positions in the *cortata*, poses or sequences that challenged one's dexterity to its fullest.

Ne'er a muscle could relax while the dance was in play, for all had a role in stabilizing and supporting each position and the flow into the next. Trell had the benefit of weeks of practice at the sequence—his breath remained even, his mind calm and focused—but Rolan was quickly huffing behind him.

By the time they finished the sequence, the sun had risen and a crowd had collected. Trell rounded the last stretch of Comet Chases the Moon and stepped out of the pattern with a low sweep of his blade. He bowed to a damp-chested Rolan, who bowed in return.

Applause drew both of their gazes.

Raegus n'Harnalt, Tannour Valeri and an imposing man Trell hadn't yet met stood in a line to the side of the clearing. Just behind them, Loukas hovered in a pod with Rolan's servant Yusef and the valet Rami, whose service Trell had inherited along with Raegus's embarrassingly large tent and several other accoutrements belonging to his new command.

"How is it that Rolan claims such special favor from our *A'dal*?" demanded the imposing man, who spoke in a voice as deep as his mahogany skin was dark. He had the frame of a giant and wore a similarly imposing scimitar at his belt, but something either in his gaze or his smile hinted of a good-natured humor. Trell liked him immediately.

Rolan handed his sword to Yusef and took a towel from him. "Some of us sleep with one eye and both ears open, Nyongo Kutaata."

Nyongo grinned at him with teeth that seemed very large and white against his dark skin. "Some of us need to." He bowed to Trell. "*A'dal*, with your permission, we three will join you tomorrow in the dance of swords."

"You four," Trell pinned his gaze on Loukas, "and I would be honored."

Loukas looked mortified, while Tannour became rigidly stone-faced.

Nyongo eyed them both rather amusedly. "Tomorrow then." He bowed again, and the group dispersed.

"Loukas, a moment please," Trell murmured, "and Raegus—"

The other Avataren looked back over his shoulder.

Trell retrieved his scabbard and sheathed his blade. "Ready the men to move."

Raegus pressed a fist to his heart. "Your will, *A'dal*." He departed after the others.

"Rami, you can go also." Trell belted on his blade, looking up under his brows as he did. "Loukas and I need to speak a moment."

"Your will, *Sidi*. I should ready Gendaia to ride for you?"

"Yes, thank you."

The boy bobbed a bow and ran off.

"Your Highness needs to speak to me? That sounds portentous." Loukas affected a levity he clearly didn't feel—Trell could sense his nervousness from across the clearing.

Trell's gaze tightened slightly. "Loukas…" He retrieved his cloak and swung it around his shoulders. With the arrival of dawn, some of the night's chill had departed, but Trell could still see his breath on the air. "Remember the other day when we were swimming for our lives, and I was calling you Loukas and you were calling me Trell?"

Loukas regarded him warily. "If memory serves."

Trell walked over to him. "And do you know what's changed since that day?"

Loukas's pained expression reflected countless possible answers. "What?"

Trell clapped a hand on his shoulder. "Nothing."

Loukas exhaled a slow breath. "Trell—"

"And so begins the lengthy but ultimately futile protest." Trell started walking back towards camp. "It's lonely at the top, Loukas." He gave him a voluminous look, full of all the things he shouldn't have to say.

Loukas followed him with a deeply furrowed brow, but finally he pressed fingers to his lips, placed his hand over his heart and bowed his head.

Trell smiled quietly. "Now that that's settled…"

Loukas blew out his breath and aimed a narrow stare at him. "I hate being a foregone conclusion."

Trell cast him a sidelong grin. "So, you know we head for Khor Taran."

"Yes." Loukas arched a brow, perhaps made wary by Trell's tone. "What don't I know?"

"Only that a thousand of my father's men are being held there."

Loukas hissed an oath. "What? How? *Why?*" Then he must've remembered Trell's story of the night before. "Ah, no, I get it. Were they trying to escape?"

"Viernan hal'Jaitar's Shamshir'im trapped them before they could cross into Akkad-held lines. I've come south to free them."

"Of course you have." Loukas considered him with a tense gaze. "How many Nadoriin at Khor Taran?"

"A thousand or so."

Loukas blinked at him. Then he barked a laugh. When Trell merely held his gaze, not laughing in return, Loukas's green eyes widened considerably. "You're seriously expecting to take on…" he gave Trell a startled look. "This is…I mean—even for *you*…" Loukas scrubbed at his jaw, frowning ponderously, and pushed both hands roughly back through his auburn hair. "Trell—*Fiera's flaming hell*, are you really expecting two hundred of us to take down a thousand men?"

"Plus the Saldarians that I'm fairly certain are using Khor Taran as their base of operations. We can't forget them. They're the whole reason the company is in this region to begin with."

"So…" Loukas was beginning to look a little ill, "potentially *twelve hundred* men—"

"And possibly—*probably*—a wielder." Trell knuckled his growth of beard. He'd been thinking it through, and magic seemed the most likely means of holding that many trained soldiers captive. He arched a brow and muttered, more to himself than Loukas, "This *is* Viernan hal'Jaitar we're dealing with."

"Ha! Right." Loukas gave a faintly hysterical laugh. "Viernan hal'Jaitar and his Shamshir'im—wielders, trained assassins, *torturers*." He spun Trell an imploring stare.

Trell chuckled.

"By all the gods in all the lands." Loukas audibly moaned. "And you're telling *me* all this, why?"

"So you can be thinking of ways to defeat them."

"So *I* can…" He fell to cursing.

Trell imagined you could curse rather inventively when you spoke nine languages.

Once Loukas had recovered himself, some several minutes later, he glowered at Trell. "Who else is complicit in this insanity?"

"Raegus." Trell gave him a wry smile. "I know how much you enjoy the challenge of my impossible tasks."

Loukas fell to brooding upon this utterance, speaking only in loud glares and silences that shouted of accusation. As they were nearing camp, he said, low and rather fiercely, "Trell…do you really mean for me to practice swords with you tomorrow?"

"Tomorrow and every day thereafter."

Loukas speared an agonized look at him. "But you know how terrible I am with a blade."

In point of fact, Trell couldn't remember ever seeing the engineer draw his sword, but he well recalled the talk among the men of Loukas's ineptness at wielding it. He'd never pressed Loukas for answers about his background—how could he have pushed another to speak of theirs when he knew so little of his own?—but now, with Loukas radiating such constant unhappiness, Rolan's words nagged at him.

"If you're truly as dreadful with a blade as you claim to be, it will be good training for you."

Loukas frowned at him.

"You learn a lot about a man when you train with him," Trell eyed him sidelong, "and I've only a short time to get to know my officers before we'll find ourselves on the battlefield together."

Loukas came to a sudden halt. Trell thought he meant to protest again, but he said instead, "You would make *me* one of your officers?"

Trell reached back for him and dragged him into motion again. "I would make you more than that. Come. As Alyneri would say, we must make hay while the sun shines."

As it happened, the sun never did show its face that day. A sullen rain turned up instead and kept them company all the long hours, quickly turning their march into a slog. Several wagons got stuck, they lost a horse in a bog—nearly lost its rider, too—and had to change course around a flooded lake, losing several hours of travel.

On a cheerier note, while the wagons were stuck, the cook happened upon a field of mushrooms and was all atwitter at making a stew of them that night for the troops.

Sensing a general malcontent spreading among the men, Trell ended their march early, and they made camp beneath a steady drizzle that finally stopped just as the last pole of the last tent was being lifted into place.

Trell raised his gaze to the clearing sky and wondered if the Trickster God Ha'viv was having His fun with them. He half considered blaming Rolan, who was far too creatively blasphemous with his cursing. Trell didn't know if Ha'viv was as attentive to the mortal world as Naiadithine, but if there was a sure way of gaining His attention, Trell imagined that blaspheming His name, as Rolan so often did, would probably do the trick.

Trell saw the men settled and lining up for the stew before attending to Gendaia and then himself. He'd just finished cleaning up and donning dry clothes when a heavy wind battered the canopy of his tent and roused a commotion outside.

What now? Trell grabbed his cloak and threw it on as he ducked out to investigate. The men were all standing with their eyes glued to the west and a palpable apprehension filled the air, thick enough to drag at Trell's curiosity as he strode in the direction of their gazes.

And then the clouds parted and the world suddenly grew brighter, like a lamp was being carried down a darkened corridor—that is, if the lamp was a star and the corridor all the world. Whereupon the star emerged from the trees, and Trell understood what had so captured the men's attention.

He swept a hand to his heart and made a gallant bow. "Lady Jaya."

"Prince Trell." Jayachándranáptra, Rival of the Sun, reached for Trell's hands and kissed him on both cheeks. An embroidered tangerine sari wrapped her form in elegance and then draped across one shoulder to trail behind her, while a headdress of citrines held her golden hair, the gemstones dangled across her brow a dazzling orange-gold—almost the exact color as her eyes. The sun was half-mast to the horizon, but Jaya lit their camp with her radiance.

She looped her arm through Trell's and looked to the sea of male faces. "So this is your company."

"Lady Jaya, may I present the forces of our *Su'a'dal*." He held a hand to them. Then he raised his voice to be heard. "Soldiers of the Emir, may I present the Sundragon Jayachándranáptra, Rival of the Sun."

Into the silence of their astonishment, some of the men bowed, some made awkward attempts at bowing, but most simply stood there gaping at her.

That the Sundragons could take human form was a well-kept secret—Trell himself hadn't known until he'd visited the First Lord's *sa'reyth*—but clearly Jaya was unconcerned with upholding that secret now, for the wind he'd heard must have been her dragon form soaring above their camp, and even an imbecile could've made the connection when she appeared out of the forest only minutes later.

Trell turned Jaya a smile. "You seem to have made quite an impression on them, my lady."

Jaya eyed them all demurely. "They're very sweet to flatter me with their surprise, but perhaps we might go somewhere we may speak in confidence."

Trell bowed to her wishes. "This way." As he was escorting her to his tent, he asked in a low voice, "Should I call my officers?"

Jaya was nodding politely to the men as she passed them. "We have matters to discuss that will concern them." She smiled and nodded to the next two Converted, who mustn't have realized they were staring at her like a pair of carp, for surely they would've closed their mouths if they had.

As they were passing Rolan's cerulean and gold tent and its bowing prince and servants, Trell murmured to the Nadoriin, "Get Raegus and the others and join me in my tent."

Rolan looked up under his brows by way of acknowledgment.

Reaching his own tent, which was larger yet less grandiose than Rolan's, Trell swept aside the drapes and escorted Jaya into the partitioned section he used as his study. Walking to a cabinet, he asked, "Can I offer you anything, my lady?"

"Thank you, no." She pulled a pair of rolled canvases out of… somewhere and extended them to him.

"What's this?" Trell crossed the room to take the canvases from her.

"A map of the land surrounding the fortress. The most accurate you will find anywhere, as we've drawn it from our view in the sky; and a diagram of Khor Taran—the best we can create for you without walking its streets and passages ourselves."

Trell stared at the rolled-up maps feeling like she'd just bestowed the entire Kandori fortune upon him. "*Thank you*, Jaya."

"It is the least we can do." She seated herself primly on one of the folding camp chairs, making it appear the seat was designed for the specific purpose of displaying her perfection.

Trell set the maps on a long table and went to pour himself some wine. "You won't mind if I…"

"By all means, Trell of the Tides. We needn't stand on ceremony, though I'm touched by your gracious welcome."

Just then Rolan and Raegus entered, with Tannour and Loukas close on their heels.

"Ah, perfect timing." Trell made quick introductions, and then the men took seats around Jaya. Trell smiled at the arrangement. For all the world it appeared as if Jaya was holding court and they were her knights.

"Jaya is here with information about Khor Taran." Trell took his seat behind his desk. "You four are the only ones who know that we're marching directly for the fortress. However, most of you don't know that a thousand of my father's men are being held there."

"Now *that* makes sense." Rolan blew out an affirming breath. At Trell's confused look, he shrugged and explained, "Our *Su'a'dal* wouldn't have sent the son-of-his-heart to round up a degenerate lot of bandits."

"We've all been wondering why he sent you here," Tannour added.

Trell acknowledged their perceptivity with a nod. "This company's mission beneath Raegus's command was to deal with the Saldarians. My mission is to free my father's men. If my suspicions are correct, we'll take care of both with the one assault."

"Jai'Gar willing," Raegus murmured.

Trell held a hand to Jaya. "My lady, if it pleases you…"

She nodded to him and then looked to all the men. "My brothers and I have been watching Khor Taran for some time. It sits, as you know, as the fist at the end of Mount Attarak's south-westerly arm. Three of the fortress's five sides sit atop sheer cliffs. The fortress can only be attacked from the north, and the majority of its defenses are aligned to that direction. The currents indicate the recent addition of a wielder at the fortress. It is safe to assume the Dannish soldiers are being held under magical duress."

Trell knew well enough how easily that could be accomplished. When Sebastian had overcome him in the Kutsamak, he'd found himself lying flat before he knew what hit him.

"*A'dal?*"

Trell turned his head to see the servants Rami and Yusef standing in the draped partition. Rami held up a tray with several goblets and a large bowl. "Would you take refreshments and your meal now, or—"

"Oh, yes, you must," Jaya said. "I didn't realize you hadn't supped, Trell."

"It's fine, Jaya—"

"No, no. 'Tis meet they should care for their *A'dal* and his officers."

"Very well." Trell had no interest in arguing the point. He was hungry enough to eat his boots. "Have you all eaten?"

"I have, *A'dal*," Raegus said. Then he grinned. "Two helpings."

"Some refreshment for you then." Trell smiled and waved the servants to come in.

Rami walked the line of Trell's guests offering each of them a goblet and bowl from his tray, while Yusef made a beeline for Rolan. "*Sidi*, your stew. Naveed made it himself—"

"Ah, no," Rolan pushed the tray away. "Mushrooms and I have a long-standing disagreement. *A'dal,* you should have this. Naveed's stew is favored of the gods."

Trell glanced from an suddenly rigid Yusef to Rami, holding the tray with Trell's food. His eyes looked over the rail-thin youth. "Perhaps you would take my meal, Rami?" The lad certainly looked like he could use an extra helping of everything.

"*Shukraan, Sidi.*" The boy bobbed a delighted bow and departed.

Yusef set his tray down before Trell with a smile that seemed somewhat forced. Then he bowed and departed. Tannour got up and closed the drapes in the wake of his exit.

Trell spooned his steaming stew to cool it. "If you have any other intelligence to offer about the lay of the fortress, Jaya, perhaps you can share it with Loukas. I've tasked him with the entire problem of winning the battle," he winked at Loukas. "He'll no doubt appreciate any intelligence to help even the odds."

"I'll be happy to consult with him." She nodded amiably to Loukas before shifting her gaze back to Trell. "There is more news, if you will hear it."

Trell had a mouthful of meaty mushrooms, so he mumbled, "Please," and motioned with his spoon for her to continue. It really was excellent stew.

Jaya let out a portentous breath. "Radov is amassing his army in obvious preparation for a renewed attack on Raku Oasis. The Ruling Prince himself has been spotted among a party heading for the outpost of Ramala. He's even pulled the majority of his forces from Abu'Dhan."

Trell perked up. "Then…"

"Yes, your task becomes easier. There are fewer than five hundred men holding the fortress now."

Trell fell back in his chair. "That is…amazing news, Jaya."

She smiled graciously. "Such a windfall is needed though, for I don't know how much additional help we'll be able to give you, Trell. Rhakar and I must stay on the front lines until such time as we can determine Radov's ultimate motive."

"Other than stupidity, you mean, my lady?" Rolan muttered.

Jaya settled her cool gaze upon the Nadoriin. "The Ruling Prince has exhibited less than admirable judgment in the past, but since the massacre upon the Khalim Plains, he hasn't risked his army in a press for the oasis. Now he brings his entire force to bear. Stupidity alone cannot account for this, Rolan Lamodaar."

"Something has changed." Trell pushed his bowl away and scrubbed at his jaw. "Radov must have some new device, something foul dreamed up by hal'Jaitar no doubt…" he lifted his gaze to her significantly, "something he thinks will eliminate you all as a threat."

Jaya held his gaze soberly. "This is exactly our concern, Trell."

"But surely, my lady…" Tannour cast a disbelieving smile around at them all, "you don't *actually* fear it—whatever it might be—this dubious threat?"

"We are powerful but not infallible, Tannour Valeri. Arrogance accounts for far more losses than victories in the annals of history."

"If Radov intends to move on the oasis," Raegus said, "our *Su'a'dal* will need us back as soon as…possible…" his face suddenly became pasty, and his head lolled forward.

Trell jumped from his chair, but Rolan was faster to catch their falling friend. He laid Raegus down on the floor while Jaya knelt and placed her hands on his head. A moment later, she looked up at Trell. "He's been poisoned."

They all processed this, and then everyone looked to the bowls of stew. Loukas blanched, while Tannour looked relieved that he hadn't yet touched his.

"Trell..." Jaya's eyes were wide upon him.

"I feel fine." He called for his valet and got no answer. A cold foreboding settled upon him. "Rolan—"

The Nadoriin was already making for the drapes. "Say no more, *A'dal*. I'll see to the men."

"I'll go help him." Tannour darted out.

Loukas gathered up the bowls and set them on the table. "I'll find Rami."

Trell looked him over. "Are you well?"

"Enough," Loukas replied, though he'd begun to sweat. "I ate only a little."

Trell nodded. "Thank you then." He looked back to Jaya and a very pale Raegus. "What can you do for him, Jaya?"

The *drachwyr* had her eyes closed and her hands on Raegus's head. "I'm mending his pattern so the poison can't attack him further, but it will still run a course through his system."

Knowing his friend would recover dampened Trell's agitation only slightly. "I need to speak to the cook. Are you—"

"Yes, go. I'll do what I can to make him more comfortable."

Trell was out of his tent in a flash.

The camp was in turmoil, with many men retching outside their tents and others moaning from within. Those unaffected were doing what they could, but most appeared unsure what to do. Trell grabbed the first of those he came upon and sent him in search of the company's Healer while he ran towards the cooking tents.

He found the head cook trapped against his wagon, cringing beneath the point of Rolan Lamodaar's fat-bladed scimitar. The cook's four assistants were lined up beside him, each one looking more fretful than the next. Rolan looked ready to slay them all.

He nodded to Trell upon his arrival and then looked back to the cook. "Now you can tell our *A'dal* this concoction of lies," he pushed a little harder with his sword into the cook's chest and growled, "but don't expect him to swallow it the way you expected all of us to eat that hell-spawned stew."

The cook turned a pleading gaze to Trell. He was an older Basi, more than twice Trell's age, and balding beneath his turban. He had a round face and a butcher's forearms, but gentle eyes.

"*A'dal*, beneath Jai'Gar's eye," he raised clasped hands as in prayer, "I picked the mushrooms myself. I *know* which ones are safe to eat. I was tasting the stew throughout its preparation—my assistants may vouch to this—yet here *I* stand."

"*Yes…*" Rolan drawled with a daggered gaze, "here *you* stand."

The cook wetted his lips. "*A'dal*, I've served thousands of meals to these brave men. Why would I seek to harm them now?"

He had a point. Trell had already considered the idea that there might be a spy in their camp, but the likelihood it was their devout Basi cook seemed small.

"Rolan…" Trell motioned for the Nadoriin to lower his blade. Then he asked the cook, "Could anyone else have gotten to the stew?"

The man's expression became even more fretful. "Just we five—"

"*A'dal!*" The man Trell had sent in search of the Healer rushed up. "Madaam Chouri and the…the lady dragon are seeing to the men taken ill."

"*Shukraan*. See what you can do to help them."

The man nodded and rushed off again.

Trell looked back to the cooks. Then he frowned at them. "*Someone* poisoned the stew, Master al'Fazim. If you gave them no opportunity, then one of you is clearly responsible."

"*Master*," one of the cooks whispered.

All eyes turned to him, including his master's, which appeared quite unforgiving of his interruption.

The man looked pained beneath the spearing stares but he managed, "What about the rosemary?"

Master al'Fazim threw up both hands. "The rosemary! You are brilliant to remember that unpleasant moment, Bazel." The cook looked quickly back to Trell. "Young Lalim couldn't find the rosemary, *A'dal*. Bazel, Dahi, Muhid—we all searched for it. We had to take everything off the wagon. I feared we would not have the stew ready in time." He gave a deep exhale. "It was a tragic moment when we realized…" he opened palms to the heavens resolutely, "we simply had none."

"So, during that time…?" Trell posed.

"Yes, we were all away from the pots. Oh!" he crushed his head between his palms. "May Jai'Gar forgive us our careless inattention!" He clasped his hands and bowed his head, his lips murmuring a silent prayer. The other cooks instantly mirrored him.

Trell cast a sidelong look at Rolan. "We'll need to search elsewhere for our poisoner. Master al'Fazim," his tone drew the cook's gaze back to him, "the Prime God is more likely to forgive when he sees effort to atone. Perhaps you and your assistants can consult with Madaam Chouri to see if there is any antidote you might brew to help ease the men's discomfort."

The cook nodded gravely. "Your wise will be done, A'dal." He glanced nervously at Rolan and then shooed his assistants away to see to the task.

"So…" Trell regrouped with Rolan as the cooks were shuffling off, "some of the men who ate the stew are sick, others not. Your stew, which your man Naveed made himself, was free of it—for which you and your man have my gratitude."

Trell cast a narrowed gaze out across the camp. "Whoever our culprit, he mustn't have been able to poison all the stew before the cooks returned. But the question remains, who was his target?"

Rolan sheathed his sword, his expression thunderous. "All of us, it would appear."

"Yes, that's definitely how it appears." Trell cocked a brow at him.

Rolan considered him with evident speculation. "Half a dozen men here have hefty prices on their heads, A'dal, myself included."

"Yes, I thought of that." Trell motioned to him to follow and headed back to his tent. "What chance the Saldarians we've been chasing had some role in this?"

"Could be. Could also be a grudge carried too far."

"Perhaps some quiet questioning to both ends would be prudent."

"Your will, A'dal."

As they reached the center of camp, Trell looked around at the general state of the men and blew out his breath. "We'll need to stay here another night. I won't march them in this condition."

"I'll spread the word." Rolan ducked a bow and departed.

While Jaya and Madaam Chouri attended to the sick, Trell walked the camp, checking in with every man, explaining what they'd learned, reassuring them personally that better precautions would be taken to preserve their health, that they might find a glorious death on the field of battle, not in their beds. And he promised them the culprit would be found and made accountable for his actions.

Many men volunteered their assistance in this effort, but the last thing Trell wanted was the inevitable avalanche of suspicion that would follow such activity. He advised the men instead to stay alert for anything suspicious or out of the ordinary, and to communicate such to their chain of command—or directly to himself if they feared their superiors were somehow involved.

Trell ended his rounds where he'd begun them, at Raegus's side. The Avataren had recovered some of his color and was nursing a goblet of something when Trell entered his tent. Trell cracked a smile as he shut the tent flaps behind himself. "What—in your cups again already?"

"*Blaaagh*," Raegus shook his head. "It's foul, whatever it is. Almost worse than that *fethen* poison, this stuff."

"It seems to be helping. Your fair humor is back."

Raegus belched and then grimaced. "If torture can be termed as help." The once-commander's expression fell into gravity. "How is it out there?"

Trell pulled up a chair and told him all.

When he had the whole story, Raegus asked, "Will you question the men to find the culprit? Conduct a search?"

"No."

"No?" Raegus sharpened his gaze on him. "What am I missing?"

Trell leaned back in the folding chair and draped his hands over the iron arms. "Since you told me about the Saldarians and how they seem to stay one step ahead of the company, I've suspected there was a spy among us."

"A spy." Raegus scrubbed at his jaw, mulling this over. "But why act now? Why this?"

"That's what I don't yet know." Trell rubbed his thumb absently on the knobby end of his chair. "*If* a spy sits behind this poisoning, he must be smart to have lasted this long beneath your observation. He'll only have hidden the evidence in someone else's packs, or long divested himself of it entirely. Searching for him at this point seems futile. And in truth, I don't want the distraction. I told the men to be on the lookout for anything suspicious."

Raegus grunted. "I wouldn't have been so forthright with them. Soldiers need to know what direction to march and who to swing their swords at. Little else."

Trell pinched the bridge of his nose between his thumb and middle finger. "The surest way to attempt to control a man is to lie to him." He dropped his hand and looked back to Raegus. "I think men can sense that—on some level, they know that you're just trying to manipulate them, that you don't care if they have a thought, that their thoughts don't matter."

"I vow *you* can sense it." Raegus snorted. "I'm not sure the rest are so perceptive."

Trell regarded him resolutely. "If we were a thousand strong, I would agree with you, but we're two hundred, Raegus, and we'll be facing at least five hundred men holding a fortified position, *and* their wielder, whose presence exponentially increases our chance of failure. I don't just need soldiers. I need *thinking* men."

Trell sat forward and braced elbows on his knees. "In a game of Kings, one soldier, pointed in one direction, is the equivalent of a pawn. He can take the enemy one to one. But a thinking man—a Sorcerer or a Knight—if played well, he could take ten pieces off the board before he falls. If I have two hundred thinking men, and each one poses a match for ten of the enemy, *now* we have a fighting chance."

Raegus held Trell's gaze for a long moment. Then he looked back to the goblet in his hand, grimaced, and drank the rest of it down. "*Gah—*" he shook his head again and pressed a fist to his ribcage, "far be it from me to question you."

"I hope you will never cease doing so." Trell stood and laid a hand on the Avataren's shoulder. "Thank you for your prayers. I'm grateful for your counsel. Who knows…" he cast a shadowy smile to the heavens, "Inanna may actually be listening. I hear She has a soft spot for lost causes."

Raegus managed a grim grunt. "I think you're confusing the Goddess of War with Her brother Shamash."

Trell smiled at him. "We can pray to the Traveling God, too. When you're pitting yourself against the impossible, it never hurts to have a few immortals on your side."

<hr>

"It did not succeed."

The unwelcome words from the spy scalded the wielder Kifat's mental ears. He fixed his hand more firmly around the ring he wore and focused on the spy's voice on the other end of the bonded line. *"How could you fail? You said you had the proper poison!"*

"The poison did its duty," the spy replied tightly, mind to mind, *"but a Sundragon came to the aid of the company in time to save many lives. The act wouldn't have resulted in our goal in any case, for Rolan Lamodaar gave the prince his own bowl, which his personal cook had prepared. This unfortunately could not be prevented."*

Kifat hissed a curse, which echoed back to him from the stone walls of his tower chambers. His master, Viernan hal'Jaitar, would be outraged that Trell val Lorian still lived, and the Consul was not a man who let failure go unpunished. *"Do you have some other means of reaching the prince yourself?"*

"Not without compromising my position."

"But you haven't compromised yourself with this poisoning?"

"No. I left one of the pots untouched, so a number in the company were spared any sickness. That I was among them raised no brows."

"That was prudent thinking." Kifat turned his ring on his finger, pondering his choices. His master had been clear on what he must do if the val Lorian prince actually reached Khor Taran, but perhaps they hadn't exhausted every avenue yet.

Kifat focused back on the spy. *"Where are you now?"*

"Halted for the night while the company recovers. But we've kept a steady south-eastward advance thus far."

"You're near the mountain then?"

"Yes."

Kifat's lips parted in a smile. He sensed victory on the horizon after all. The Prophet's Saldarians had left camps like boils all across Mount Attarak's north-lying shadow. The mercenaries had proven something of a nuisance to Kifat since they arrived in the area, but now they could make themselves useful.

"Report to me tomorrow with the company's exact location," he told the spy. *"I will have my own surprise ready for our heroic Prince of Dannym."*

FORTY-SEVEN

*"Anything truly decent in life is either illegal,
immoral or life-threatening."*

–The royal cousin Fynnlar val Lorian

DAWN GREETED THE world with a lover's gentle kiss, sending a blush across the heavens and a sighing wind through the trees. The sunrise found Trell working the *cortata* in a high meadow overlooking the towering peak of Mount Attarak. The others of his council shadowed his movements—Loukas, Tannour, Nyongo, Rolan. Even Raegus had dragged himself from his sickbed to practice swords with his *A'dal*.

Though he hadn't slept himself, or perhaps because of it, Trell arrived while darkness still gripped the land, and he worked the first time through his forms fast and hard. By the time his officers started arriving with the first paling of the sky, he felt energized again.

Somewhere beneath him, among the trees and the tents of his Converted, Jaya and the Healer were still tending to the ill. It had been a long night for everyone. Yet for Trell, it made those lessons in the *cortata* that much more vital. These were the men he'd chosen to depend upon, even as they were depending upon him. He was duty bound to offer them every advantage he could muster.

And as he taught them, he observed them.

He saw where they struggled and where they excelled. He noted the sequences that challenged them and how they met those challenges. Rolan and Raegus, both seasoned men nearly twice his age, accepted each challenge, addressing them but not combating them. If they failed to finish a form, they merely found the movement again to the best of their ability and kept going, their focus intact.

But Nyongo found grave difficulty in facing his own imperfection; he struggled any time he hit a position he couldn't execute perfectly. He'd soon moved himself to the very back where he could accompany his practice with a steady stream of invective in his native Shi'maan tongue.

Tannour and Loukas were another matter entirely.

Every time Trell turned so as to view the men behind him, his gaze went automatically to Tannour. The Vestian worked his forms with a dexterity that was both elegant and deadly, the sinuous motion of a viper coiling to strike. One would have to know the forms intimately to notice the difference in Tannour's technique, but Trell often saw him make a turn of ankle or wrist, a twist of his blade after he'd stabbed it—subtle shifts of motion that were the method of a man trained to strike once and make it a killing blow. And the sections Rolan and the others struggled with, Tannour sailed through. Either he was just that talented of a swordsman, or he'd studied the *cortata* before.

Trell couldn't help but perceive strains of Taliah in Tannour's motions, these flourishes that were decidedly Vestian in flair and in some way echoic of their famous curved blades. Trell thought he could see the *mor'alir* influence in the way Tannour worked the *cortata,* and he well understood Rolan's comment about Tannour's swordplay haunting his dreams.

He would've liked to observe the currents of *elae*, as Alyneri was learning to do, that he might see how these embellishments Tannour was putting onto each sword form were changing the *cortata*'s pattern, for surely they were. Instead, he admitted his fascination with the way the man moved, and he gave thanks that Tannour was fighting on his side.

Perhaps more surprising to him than Tannour—for he'd expected uniqueness from the Vestian as a result of Rolan's comment—was watching Loukas. It took Trell at least half the sequence before he figured out why Loukas's wary, methodical movements seemed so incongruous to him. Finally, he hit upon the understanding.

Loukas was working the *cortata* with slow and careful precision, staying just a heartbeat behind everyone else, struggling—not because the motions were new to him but because they *weren't*; because he was attempting with his every breath to make something incredibly familiar seem foreign; because he was trying to hide the fact that he actually knew the sequence intimately… perhaps even better than Trell.

Loukas's position as a combat engineer often put his life in greater peril than the men faced in open combat, and while the Converted teased him relentlessly over his lack of skill with a sword, they never challenged his courage. But Loukas might've forgone all of that by proving he knew his way around a blade.

Trell couldn't imagine why he would rather earn their ostracism than their respect, but instinct told him it had something to do with Tannour—if only from the way the two men were studiously *not* looking at one another while the rest were carefully observing and learning from each other's movements.

Trell finished the final form and stepped out of the *cortata*. Turning to face the others, he swept his sword to the side and bowed low.

They mimicked his motion.

Whereupon applause brought all of their heads around to the south.

Perhaps three dozen men were standing or sitting along the line of the trees. Some hardly looked capable of moving, yet their expressions all reflected that particular light that illuminates a man's face when he fixes on a challenge he simply can't forgo.

Plenty of jesting accompanied the applause, calls to one or another of Trell's protégés asking if they could have the next dance. Plenty of laughter, too.

Trell opened his arms to the audience of soldiers. "All right then, do you want to learn it?" A low chorus of assent came in reply, and a dozen or men so started up the incline. Trell shook his head at the rest of them. "Inanna preserve us, you're a sorry lot. Half of you still look like Madaam Chouri's grinding your balls beneath her pestle."

That got the remaining ones on their feet.

"Well, all right—come up and prove your mettle. No swords. You'll learn the sequence first." Trell looked to Raegus. "I'm going back to camp to see about those who couldn't make it up the hill for the show."

Raegus looked confused. "But, *A'dal*, who will lead us?"

Trell looked purposefully to Loukas. "Loukas has it best."

All of the men turned as one and stared at the Avataren. Tannour's mouth fell open.

Loukas gave Trell a look so desperately pleading that it stabbed at his conscience, but he had to do what was best by the company. He held the Avataren's gaze and gave the slightest shake of his head. *No,* he wouldn't change his mind.

Loukas closed his eyes briefly. Then gave a forceful exhale and started towards the front. Tannour stared at him with dark reproof the entire way.

Raegus cleared his throat. "You heard our *A'dal.* Line up behind n'Abraxis."

The men found their places.

Loukas visibly swallowed. He pulled at the placket on his tunic and straightened his shoulders. "So…no blades, like our *A'dal* said. We work the sequence. Follow my motion." He began the *cortata* anew, leading Trell's officers and three dozen soldiers through Cardinal Skims the Water and executing it perfectly.

Trell let out a slow breath and headed back to camp.

He knew he wasn't doing Loukas any favors with this action—certainly Loukas would see it that way—but the engineer clearly had the sequence better even than Tannour and was thereby best suited to teach the rest of the company. Besides, whatever dark drama was unfolding between Tannour Valeri and Loukas n'Abraxis, Trell had no intention of playing a part in it.

Trell met Jaya as she was coming out of Madaam Chouri's tent. Though she hadn't slept, she looked every bit as radiant as she had upon her arrival.

"My lady," Trell took her hands in his, "my men and I thank you for all your efforts here."

"Your Healer is wise and capable, Trell of the Tides. See that she's well cared for and your company will be also."

"I surely will, my lady. I take it you're leaving us now?"

"Before I wear out my welcome." A brief smile lightened her mood. "My brothers call me back. I'm not sure how long it will be before one of us can visit again."

"I understand the situation, Jaya. We all have to play our positions."

His words for an instant gave her pause. Then she cupped his face tenderly. "Such wisdom. I confess, at first I protested Vaile's choice to go to Darroyhan for you, but now I see she was wiser than I was."

Trell wasn't sure how to interpret her comment, though he thought Jaya had meant it kindly. He offered his arm to her in escort, and she took it with a smile that didn't quite touch her eyes.

The camp was much calmer than it had been the night before. Many men were up and about tending to their gear or just breathing air that wasn't thick with sickness and the stinking broth Madaam Chouri had ordered to ease their ills. Every man they passed bowed deeply to Jaya.

"Was it the Balance, my lady?" Trell asked. When she glanced to him inquiringly, he clarified, "The reason you didn't want Vaile to go to Darroyhan—was it because of Balance?"

A shadow befell Jaya's expression. "I don't know if you will ever understand what she did for you."

He searched her gaze. "Do you think it's possible for me to be more appreciative than to know I owe her my life? Or to show her my gratitude more fully than to do everything she asks of me? If there's more I can do, Jaya—I beg you, tell me."

Jaya's expression softened, and she leaned and kissed his cheek. "You are worthy, Trell—worthy of all she's done, and an unworthy target for my disquiet."

She started walking again with a gentle tug on his arm. "The creature that assaulted Vaile at Darroyhan…" she glanced to him, seeking his recollection—as if he could ever forget the moment. "Vaile should've been able to recover from its attack by now, even from something so foul as *deyjiin* channeled directly into her undefended core."

Trell heard the hesitation in her voice. "But?"

Jaya cast him a sidelong glance, burdened with regret. "I fear she doesn't want to." She added tremulously, "We all fear it so."

Trell thought back to his first meeting with Vaile and the deep melancholy she'd revealed to him. "She's been lonely for a long time, hasn't she?"

"Vaile wed herself to sorrow many ages ago." Jaya offered a smile through her exhale, though it failed to dispel the shadows from her gaze. "Our thoughts are powerful things, Trell. A wielder knows better than anyone that our thoughts determine our success or our failure. Our thoughts, our viewpoints, shape our world, and we shape ourselves to conform to our thoughts."

They passed a line of compulsively bowing Converted, and Jaya summoned a smile for their pleasure, but she drew herself closer against Trell's escorting arm. "Immortality can be a wondrous gift, but it can also be…" she compressed her lips, "it can be a terrible curse. Some complain about the Returning and the loss of memory that accompanies a mortal's death and reAwakening, but when you pass through the Extian Doors, you shed the mistakes of an entire lifetime—all of your errors, misdeeds, betrayals…you're given a chance to live again, to live *better*, without the drowning weight of your mistakes."

Jaya puffed a strand of golden hair from her eyes and glanced at him with a hint of irritability behind her gaze. "Mind you, Náiir would argue that one is never truly free of past deeds, but this is neither here nor there. Are you taking my point, Trell?"

"Indelibly, Jaya."

"Good." She considered him with kindness carving a deep furrow between her brows. "It's important that you understand these things, for one day you…" she seemed to bite back her words, shook her head and said instead, "One day it may be something you need to consider. Immortality means *never* forgetting. The compounding losses of decades, centuries, *millennia* build until their weight becomes unbearable. You have to find a way to free yourself of them or they'll suffocate you."

She gripped his arm tightly, as if fearing to sink into the deep waters of memory. "One hopes…" she began more faintly, "one hopes for more moments of pleasure than pain, but they don't equal out—no, they never seem to balance each other. The tragic memories are frequently so much more powerful than the fair and transient moments of joy—or at least they feel so when you're suffering grief's lasting scourge. And those memories compound and build until very soon they're towering over us, casting their lengthy shadows so far that we cannot even see the daylight around their edges."

Trell placed a hand over Jaya's and gripped it tightly. "What can I do?"

She lifted a startled look to him. Then she smiled with gentle appreciation. "Nothing. Merely understand. I haven't seen Vaile care for anyone in a long time the way she cares for you and Alyneri."

They'd reached the edge of camp and the path Jaya had arrived on the day before. She took Trell's hands in hers, looking down at them with the citrine stones as dazzling yellow-orange stars on her brow and her hair shining with that radiant golden glow. She seemed to want to say more, but in the end, she just kissed him on each cheek, smiled in her solemn way, and took her leave.

Trell watched the skies and listened for the wind of her departure, but she mustn't have wanted to announce her leave as she'd announced her arrival the day before, because only a lonesome breeze sighed through the trees.

"*A'dal*...?" Rami's hand on Trell's shoulder woke him.

He sat up stiffly, only then realizing that he'd dozed off in his chair. On the table before him were several maps of the Abu'Dhan region, including Jaya's diagram of Khor Taran. After he'd left Jaya, he'd returned to study the maps.

Trell pressed palms to his eyes. "What time is it?"

"They just rang the bell for dinner, *A'dal*." Rami towered over Trell's seated form, for he had the sort of lanky-limbed physique that came to boys whose bones were growing faster than their bodies or brains could keep up with. "But there is...that is, there might be a problem."

Trell sat back in his chair. "What kind of problem?"

Rami scratched uncertainly at his head, slightly dislodging his turban in the process. "The kind it is appropriate for our *A'dal* to solve?" he suggested hopefully.

Trell looked him over. "I see." He slowly pushed out of his chair, registering grave protest from nearly every part of his body, and tried to shake his mind free of the hold sleep still had on it. "Does this problem require a weapon?"

"Jai'Gar willing, I pray not." Rami handed Trell his cloak.

Trell accepted it with a curiously arched eyebrow.

The boy gave a disarming shrug. "The night grows cold."

"This is all very mysterious, Rami."

"Some things are better left to the eyes than the tongue, A'dal."

Trell cast him a smile while fastening the clasp on his cloak. "That's quite a wise thing to say."

"Would that it was my wisdom, but it is my mother's." The boy followed him outside the tent. "She says this to me most often when I am trying to take food from the table before the meal. No manner of protest or debate—no matter how logical or well thought out—can swerve her from her surety of this wisdom."

"That's true for women in general, I think, Rami."

The boy heaved a ponderous sigh. "Women are the Great Unknown."

Trell eyed him humorously. "Is that another of your mother's proverbs?"

"No. That one is my father's. But he also says 'be the last to the field and the first to the couch' so I'm not sure I can always trust in his wisdom."

Rami led Trell on a beeline to wherever this problem existed, weaving quickly in and around tents, most of which appeared to be unoccupied, perhaps since the dinner bell had already been rung.

Trell noted the problem the moment he arrived in the center of camp.

The cook and his assistants were all lined up behind the cook pots, while a great cluster of men had gathered near the central fire, with a grumbling malcontent passing like wraiths among them. The head cook was fidgeting dyspeptically.

Trell turned to Rami with a gaze that asked, *what exactly do you expect me to do?*

The boy extended a soup bowl.

Trell stared at it for an instant and then lifted him a smile. "You know…I don't think Raegus realized what he had in you." He took the wooden bowl determinedly and strode to the first of the pots, with Rami close on his heels.

The cook's assistant looked immensely relieved to see them. "May I serve you, A'dal?"

"Please."

The assistant sloshed stew into his bowl and then into Rami's.

Trell moved to the next pot and its attending cook.

The man brightened instantly. "May I serve you, A'dal?"

"Please." Trell extended his bowl.

And so it went, down the line of pots, until Trell and Rami had been served a little from each.

With every eye upon them, they crossed the no-man's land between cooks and men, wordlessly seated themselves around the central fire, and set to eating. By the time they were halfway into their stew, long lines had formed before each cook pot.

Trell and Rami shared a look and clicked their bowls together.

Trell ate and drank with the men that night, pleased to get to know some of them better, warmed by the stories of their courage, and reassured by the passionate way so many of them described their lives since joining the Emir's Converted.

When all had eaten and the stars were out, someone called for a story. This quickly became a deluge of requests for Trell to tell them another tale, so of course he felt obliged to do so.

Thus, the later evening saw Trell telling his men how the Emir had sent him to seek his name and his past. He spoke hauntingly of the cave-in at Naiadithine's shrine, and recalled the names of those who'd been lost with gravity and a solemn prayer to Inithiya, which most of the men joined with him in offering.

But then he had them laughing as he told of his experiences at the Mage's *sa'reyth*, and how the Mage had made a gift of Gendaia and sent him west to the Cairs. And there were catcalls aplenty as he walked them through his meeting with the pirate Carian vran Lea in that blinding blizzard in Olivine.

The moon was well to its zenith before he finished regaling them with his adventures traveling with the pirate. He went to sleep to the murmur of his princely name whispered in concert with those of Nodefinders and a dragon enchantress.

The next morning as Trell was heading out, again before dawn, to run through the *cortata* before the others came, he noticed a peculiar quiet in the camp. His still-waking mind only partially registered this, in the way one recognizes sounds during a dozing sleep but doesn't really connect them with action; or in the awareness of a conversation being carried on nearby while engrossed in one's own business, listening without really hearing.

He quickly forgot about the quiet camp, for the early morning had that crisp clarity only found in the mountains, where the sky is as blue-black glass, depthless and cold, and the air forms sharp crystals in a man's lungs.

As Trell neared the high meadow, a waxing moon was hovering low to the horizon, half-blocked by the immense, dark majesty of Mount Attarak, whose peak stood out, silver-limned against the sky.

Trell emerged onto the meadow bathed in that same silver light, but where emptiness should've opened above him, shadows shifted. One of them separated itself from the whole. In time, Rolan's form resolved.

That's when Trell realized that the camp hadn't been quiet; it had been utterly *silent*. And the shifting mass of shadows before him was his entire company ranged across the meadow.

Rolan rested his sword against his shoulder. "Ready when you are, *A'dal*."

Trell gazed in wonder upon the dark mass of men. "Is this...*everyone?*" He could hardly believe they would all rouse themselves before the dawn for this, for him.

"The sentries maintain the watch, but they've worked out a rotation."

A wordless gratitude filled Trell as he looked upon them all. "Very well," he lifted a hand to Rolan, "line them up and we'll begin."

"You heard your *A'dal!*" Rolan waved his sword in circles over his head. "Form up!"

Thus did a surprisingly cheerful dawn find two hundred men working slowly through the Adept dance of swords on a high meadow beneath a boundless sky. The wild lupine that dotted the hills seemed to trap the color from the roseate clouds in its petals of clustering pearls, so that for a time, the long grass and the heavens both wore a mantle of variegated rose.

As Trell led his men through the sequence for the second time, he knew an uncommon satisfaction. Perhaps it was so many minds and bodies joined in forging the *cortata's* pattern, or perhaps it was simply a glimpse of future and the limitless potential it held.

The day followed as the dawn—bright, sanguine, possibility so crisp in the air that Trell could almost taste it. They followed the Taran River through a wide valley for most of the day and made up much ground lost in the days before.

The hours seemed to pass quickly, and not just due to their ground-eating march. The men were talkative in a way that only bright sunshine and fair skies invokes—the sort of fluid, rambling conversation that accompanies a lope.

Trell moved up and down the lines during the day, but no matter where he walked or rode, he overheard the same conversations spun together like a whirlwind of leaves: mutterings of the spy in their midst, wild conjecture about Loukas n'Abraxis, and perhaps loudest and foremost of all, bawdy speculation on what Trell and the lady dragon had been doing in his tent.

At camp that night, Trell had barely begun his meal of stew, taken while standing and frowning over Jaya's map of Khor Taran, when Rami rushed in, bursting to show him some new discovery. Trell let the boy drag him excitedly off, and then, for the rest of the night, as he'd tended to his duties and saw to the men, he kept thinking about what his valet had found.

Finally, as the men were settling down and the moon was rising large in the east, its luminous orb glimpsed through limbs of fir and birch, Trell floated in a pool of liquid heat, listening to the song of the river while he let three days of mud and horse dissolve from his skin and the knots of hard riding melt out of his bones.

The hot springs had indeed been a boon discovery, one he never would've known about if not for Rami's proclivity for wandering off, but now that Trell knew such places existed along the River Taran, he would advise the boy to keep a devilish watch.

Riversong sang loudly in his thoughts. Trell opened his heart to the river and sought Naiadithine. *My Goddess...*

Trell of the Tides.

Submerged as Trell was, Naiadithine's harmonic voice permeated him. He *felt* her words, his name, chiming in molecule of his being. A current of cooler water threaded around him, siphoned off from the larger flow to cool the bubbling pool where he lay immersed. Without that flow, the water would've scalded instead of soothed, even as Naiadithine's presence certainly would've scalded without the buffer of the river to disperse Her power.

You have questions in your heart, Trell.

Trell sighed beneath this truth. The things he wanted to ask Her were things he felt he never should—that even asking them would be an affront to Her goodwill.

You've never withheld your heart from me. Why do you do so now?

In a moment of misgiving, he asked himself the same question. Why *did* he fear asking Her? Because he feared offending Her, thus losing Her benevolence? Her graces were never his to begin with, only Hers to bestow.

Trell tried to shape his thoughts with truth. *I owe so much to you, my Goddess, I fear I can never repay the kindnesses you've shown me.*

Nay, Trell of the Tides, you're afraid I will ask of you a price you cannot pay. Though free of anger, Her words carried a thunderous edge, as a waterfall's churning roar.

Trell blew out his breath and sank all the way beneath the water. Why did he imagine he could keep any truth from Her? Why did he try?

Fear my will, fear me, she offered calmly but pointedly, *they are the same—*

Suddenly her attention shifted. It was as palpable to him as a cold current threading among the warmer stream. And when her attention shifted back...

A host is approaching from the south. Their thoughts are vile.

Her words as much as the forceful intention beneath them cast him surging up out of the water. *How far away?* he asked as he climbed from the pool.

Minutes, as the river runs.

Trell ran for his clothes.

FORTY-EIGHT

"Our thoughts shape our reality. Our thoughts shape all the world."
—The Adept wielder Malachai ap'Kalien

PELASOMMÁYUREK WOKE TO silence. *Utter* silence. A silence that could exist only beyond the unraveling fringes of the cosmos where nothingness became allness. The unmitigated silence of Shadow. For a dazed moment, he wondered if he'd been taken there and the bed and room were but constructs.

Absent was the distant yet omnipresent cosmic roar that usually underpinned his every thought. He could no longer perceive gravity's thundering timpani, the screaming whir of planets flying around their suns, or the fiery static of the solar wind. His mind felt…lighter.

Pelas looked down at his chest and arms, which lay bare against the soft sheets. The injuries he'd sustained battling Darshan's net had been healed; but more significant than this, he sensed that his native energies had been replenished, the pattern of his shell made whole again. This was no small feat after a bout with revenants. And he perceived, too, that his connection with Tanis had been restored—yet…that wasn't the only connection he perceived.

Pelas exhaled a slow breath. *Tanis, what've you done to me?*

Thinking through the things he'd done on the lad's behalf, it was hard to believe that any one being could've had such an impact on him. Yet for Tanis, he'd promised to protect a world from unmaking and forsworn his brothers in the process. He'd even fought them in pursuit of this cause and undoubtedly would again. For Tanis, he'd bound himself to the mortal tapestry…and he wasn't the only immortal to do so.

Pelas lifted his gaze to a dark form standing before a parting of the room's heavy drapes. It took a moment to focus words through the veil of healing sleep that was still enveloping his consciousness. "He's bound with the Warlock, hasn't he?"

"Yes." Phaedor's purr-growl resonated in the silent room.

By Chaos born, Tanis. That made three immortals bound now to the lad, and through him, to each other. Pelas could barely wrap his mind around the potential ramifications, and his was a mind skilled at wrapping itself around the vastness of stars.

He let his gaze explore Phaedor's shadowed form while ruminating on the unique experience of that moment—to be sharing that oddly silent space in solidarity with Tanis's zanthyr... And yet, to refer to Phaedor in this fashion anymore—should the latter now refer to *him* as Tanis's Malorin'athgul? The thought made him smile.

When last they'd met, they'd been rivals, or so it had seemed to Pelas at the time, when he'd followed Tanis into an abandoned courtyard on the night of the solstice and found the lad clutching the zanthyr, much the lost son embracing his father.

But he and Phaedor were rivals no longer, if ever they had been. The river of Pelas's bond with Tanis ran strong in his mind, anchoring him to the Realms of Light in ways constantly new and intriguing; but Pelas also now kenned a distant connection to Sinárr, as two men knowing a meeting of gazes across a wide river, yet too far to actually focus on each other's eyes.

And between Pelas and Sinárr, somehow present but not, like a shifting stream of sunlight that appeared and vanished, yet always with the sure understanding that its source remained constant...Phaedor's linked presence.

"Is Tanis..."

"With Sinárr, for a time yet."

"Yes, I sensed that somehow." Pelas frowned slightly. "A new perception." He contemplated the zanthyr quietly. "Your influence, perhaps?"

Phaedor cast him an unreadable look over one shoulder. "Perhaps."

Pelas pushed himself upright and then sank back against the pillows at the head of the bed. He was finding it difficult to push off the lingering effects of the Healing sleep; his eyelids felt too heavy at their corners. He lifted his gaze back to the zanthyr, who was standing in profile to him. "This was your Healing, I presume?"

The slightest wry curl lifted one corner of the zanthyr's mouth. "There were few others qualified to repair a Malorin'athgul's shell."

That's a certain text. Pelas nodded to him earnestly. "Thank you."

The shadow of a smile teased upon the zanthyr's lips. "You're welcome."

Pelas looked around again, trying to understand what he was perceiving...and not perceiving. The bedchamber wore opulence as a matter of course. Interestingly, when he tried to perceive the energy of the luxurious items that filled the room, *they* resonated predictably; yet they might've existed in the vacuum of Shadow for all the supportive energies that should've resonated along with them.

He looked back to the zanthyr. "There is a peculiar silence here."

"The room is warded."

"Against the very turning of the cosmos?" Pelas layered an amused skepticism into his tone.

Phaedor turned to him. "In a sense." He pushed the fifth into the curtains and sent the folds of heavy silk scraping back. Light poured in from three walls, revealing a vista of blue water, steep green hills, and forbidding, snowcapped mountains. Phaedor came towards him. "To heal you properly, I needed time's effects to pass us by unnoticed."

Pelas arched appreciative brows. "So this entire room is caught out of time?"

Phaedor shook his head. "The whole palazzo."

Pelas's brows rose another half inch. "That's a nice trick." He looked the zanthyr over carefully. "Your working?"

Phaedor smiled. "Another's. The patterns are layered into the palazzo stones. You will see." He took up a robe from a bench at the foot of the bed. He must've withdrawn his veil of Healing sleep at the same time, for Pelas finally felt a wakeful resurgence. "The staff will be here soon with your meal."

Pelas eyed him contemplatively as he reached to take the robe. "The *palazzo* staff...just where have you brought me?"

"The Palazzo di Adonnai."

A slow smile claimed Pelas's features. "So the fabled place is real."

"Most legends have their source in truth."

"Including your own." Pelas shook his head, still grinning. "Björn van Gelderan's infamous zanthyr, protector of the Vestal's nephew." He eyed Phaedor intently. "What a marvelous new experience this is going to prove."

"You would have it no other way."

This statement of truth caught Pelas by surprise. "I suppose you're right." He narrowed his brows slightly as he held the zanthyr's gaze. An understanding was dawning. "Just how long have you been watching me?"

The zanthyr cast him a shadowy smile. "Long enough. Come," he moved towards the bedchamber's double doors, "your breakfast is arriving."

Pelas wrapped himself in the robe just as Phaedor was opening the doors to admit a woman with grey hair in a meticulous bun.

"Ah! Thank you, my lord." She nodded to Phaedor as she swept inside carrying a silver tray laden with domes and made a beeline for a linen-draped table positioned before the windows. Another woman, plumper and younger, followed in her wake carrying the tea service. She eyed Pelas coquettishly as she passed.

Pelas smiled at her.

The older woman set down her tray on the table and looked up in time to see the blush on the younger woman's cheeks. She looked to Pelas, whereupon her eyes went a little rounder, and she promptly turned back to Phaedor. "My lord, you can't bring the likes of *him* here and not have the maids all in a fuss. They're too long away from the society of handsome men." She ran her eyes over Pelas once more and added faintly, "But the Lady shame me if this one doesn't give Náiir a run for his money."

"I do apologize, Madaé Lisbeth," Phaedor said.

Her creased blue eyes softened upon him. "I suppose you shall be forgiven. First you bring young Tanis back to his mother's beloved Villa Serafina, and now..." she glanced to a still smiling Pelas and seemed to lose her thought. "Well..." she briskly pressed out her skirts and made a point of composing her expression to a suitably unremarkable equanimity, "I suppose a little excitement never hurt anyone. The Lady knows we haven't had much since the *drachwyr* left the palazzo to rejoin His Lordship in the east."

Phaedor extended a hand to the older woman and told Pelas, "Madaé Lisbeth is the seneschal of Palazzo di Adonnai. Madaé, may I present Pelasommáyurek."

Pelas took Madaé Lisbeth's hand and gazed into her eyes as he kissed the back of it. "Surely the elegance of this room reflects your influence, Madaé Lisbeth."

She stared at him for a startled moment. "My goodness..." a faint flush came to her cheeks. "Whoever would've thought that when His Lordship was here plotting against you four that one of you would be sleeping between his linens and bound to his treasured nephew?"

"I would be greatly surprised if your master didn't have the thought at least once, Madaé Lisbeth." Pelas kissed her hand again and then released her. His gaze strayed amusedly to the table and the meal, which the maid had been doing her best to set out while staring at him in blushing wonder.

Madaé Lisbeth looked back to Phaedor, seeming a little piqued herself. She pressed the back of one hand to her cheek. "You might've warned us he was so charming, my lord, and so handsome."

Phaedor gave a little bow. "My humblest apologies, Madaé Lisbeth."

She shook her head. "I'll need to warn off the maids..." her blue eyes strayed to the younger woman, who was now flushing vividly. "Raine's truth, he'll have them all standing nude before him just for the pleasure of his gaze." She turned determinedly back to Phaedor. "Birger should attend upon him."

"A wise decision, Madaé," the zanthyr murmured.

"And what do you know about it?" She flung a chiding look at him. "You'd welcome the diversion of every female in the palazzo dancing to a Malorin'athgul's tune."

He bowed to her again, that time with a smile. "You know me well, Madaé."

"Too well, I'd say." She cast a sharp look at the maid and waved her out of the room. Then she bobbed a discreet curtsy to Pelas. "Be welcome, my lord. We're at your service. Doubtless the Lord Phaedor will acquaint you with the house…" she looked as if she meant to say something more, but then she just nodded politely and took her leave.

As she was shutting the doors, Pelas murmured, "An intriguing woman." He shifted his copper-eyed gaze back to Phaedor. "She's no Adept. Is it the house then that's prolonged her life?"

"Time passes differently here." Phaedor extended a hand towards the table of food.

Pelas kept his eyes on the zanthyr as he walked to break his fast. "How differently?"

"Time is inexact, for it depends heavily upon individual perception." Phaedor strolled after Pelas. "A week here could see but a day passing beyond these lands, or a leisurely day spent beneath this sun might know the changing of a season in Alorin. It much depends upon one's need. The only surety is that time's spool is still winding. You'll know when the world is calling you back, for the thread goes taut."

Pondering this fascinating concept, Pelas held out a hand in invitation, and they sat down together at the table. As he was pouring himself some tea, Pelas looked Phaedor over inquiringly. "I would offer to share this meal, but I see the way the currents spiral about you. Food isn't a requirement for your shell—because it's not a *shell*, is it? You don't inhabit it for a brief span of eternity and then claim another. You didn't craft it, like my brothers and I did, from thought and energy and intent."

"That is correct."

Pelas began serving himself. "Your two forms *are* your essence? They're pure energy forms, even as ours are in the Void?"

"Yes."

Pelas looked up under his brows. "And I'll posit a guess that *elae* and *deyjiin* are balanced in the pattern of your forms, as they're balanced in ours. That's why you can work both powers."

The zanthyr nodded quietly to this truth.

"Your forms are native to the Realms of Light—tied to them also, I imagine?"

Phaedor laid his arm on the table. One strong finger nudged a serving dish out of the path of his hand. "Zanthyrs could navigate Chaos, but the ending of things is not in our nature."

"Ah…" Pelas sat back in his chair and studied the zanthyr. "So we're alike in form, but opposing in divine purpose?" He frowned slightly. "No, not opposing… differing."

The zanthyr nodded again.

Pelas sipped his tea contemplatively. The ideas percolating in his head were fundamental truths around which many others revolved. Only since Tanis came into his life had he begun to see these truths *as* truths, for Shail had intentionally misled him and Darshan to keep them far afield of his own activities.

"Three immortal races, each with a role to play in the cosmic balance." A new thought occurred to him, and he lifted his gaze back to meet Phaedor's again. "Is it our coming to Alorin that disrupted the Balance, or our *intent*?"

"A valid question." Phaedor flipped his hair from his eyes and held Pelas's gaze. "The First Law is the First Law for a reason."

"Yes, the all-important Laws." Pelas frowned into his tea. "Isabel admonished me that if I'd better understood the Laws of Patterning, I might've solved my brother's compulsion myself." But thoughts of Isabel quickly led him elsewhere. He lifted his gaze back to the zanthyr. "You came for her in Myacene, after…"

"Yes."

Pelas set down his teacup. Tanis had forgiven him for harming his mother, but Pelas had much to accomplish yet to make himself worthy of Isabel's sacrifice. "How…is she?"

"If you would know, ask her."

Pelas drew back slightly, but then he understood. "Ah, of course." He'd forgotten that Tanis possessed another bond, an older bond to both of his parents. Phaedor was suggesting that bond was available to Pelas now as a channel of communication.

Pelas shook his head slowly, still awed by the lad's powerful impact. "It's staggering what Tanis has done." He studied the zanthyr quietly. "Did Isabel know her son would…" but he couldn't even begin to define the enormity of what Tanis had already accomplished.

"Isabel would not have risked a pregnancy without purpose, knowing what she knew."

"About us, you mean?"

"You were only part of the equation. Isabel had already foreseen her husband's death. She would never have allowed Arion's son to grow up without knowing his father." He lifted a finger towards the food to remind Pelas to eat it instead of ponder it. "The idea was unconscionable to her."

Pelas dutifully started eating—unlike the zanthyr, *his* shell required sustenance—but his mind was a whir. "Yet Arion Tavestra died at the Citade—*ah*…I see." The truth occurred to him so simply. He gazed at the zanthyr with a wondering admiration, hardly noticing the flavors upon his tongue for the heady understandings unfolding in the galaxy of his mind. "That was a magnificent risk you and she took."

"Isabel is known for taking risks."

The layers of subtext in that comment gave Pelas a discomfiting twinge. He considered Phaedor with deep regard. "So you took Tanis, what…three hundred years into the future? How did you find your way back?"

Phaedor arched a brow. "You have seen how brightly shines her star."

Pelas blew out his breath, for that answer had been too obvious. Isabel could ground a man through all of eternity. He returned to his food and let his thoughts drift beyond Isabel's gravity.

"Divine purpose…" he nodded slowly as he considered the idea newly, "this is the greatest contention between Darshan and myself." Pelas drew a spiral with his fork in the air. "If I can conceive of another game beyond the game of unmaking, then surely I can choose to play that game or not, as *I* determine. Otherwise, I wouldn't have the ability even to conceive of following another purpose."

"This is axiomatic."

"But not to Darshan."

"Your brother wouldn't harbor such confusions if he'd studied the mortal tapestry."

Pelas blinked at him. Then he set down his fork and shook his head. "I want to view this tapestry with your understanding."

"It begins with understanding there is something there to view."

Pelas sank back against his chair. Copper eyes held emerald green. "I thought the immortal races had no paths in the mortal tapestry."

Phaedor nodded to this truth. "You've bound yourself to Tanis's thread in the pattern, but his path through it will never *belong* to you, for you can leave it at any time." He tossed the hair from his eyes and leaned forward to level Pelas a potent look. "Why do you think they fear us so desperately? Because we can jump from one path to another, influence it, and move on."

Pelas ran a finger beneath his lower lip. "So what you're telling me is that you've found a way to track a Malorin'athgul's *influence* through the mortal tapestry."

Phaedor's emerald eyes gleamed. "Just so, Pelasommáyurek."

"My, my, my..." Pelas shook his head. "For your view, Shail would destroy multiple worlds."

"It is not by destruction that he would gain this view."

This comment gave Pelas pause for a lengthy span of thought.

Suddenly too full with ideas to eat anything more, he rose from the table and headed out onto the terrace. Beyond a marble railing, a glittering lake bound the sunlight into a watery net. The air felt crisp in his lungs and the sun strong upon his face; his breath frosted with every exhale.

The cold places of this world reminded him of Chaos in visceral ways—Darshan hadn't been wrong about that. The sensation of ice crystallizing around his body in the blackness of the Void, or shedding itself in veils of refracted light as he sped through a galaxy's core...the feeling of hovering on the solar wind while he embraced a dying star...these were experiences as part and parcel to his existence as thought itself.

Yet while the game of unmaking remained one he could enjoy—relish even, in its purity of purpose—he saw other games he would rather be playing now; newer games...*creative* games.

Pelas leaned on the railing and breathed deeply of the mountain air.

With so many eons on the track behind him, he took most experiences in stride, but *this* experience—treating with another immortal in equal allegiance? Even with his brothers he'd never known such harmonious partnership.

And beneath that new sense of unanimity, a driving urgency replaced gravity's usual pull. The energy of Pelas's consciousness now hummed with *purpose*. More incredible still, it hummed a song of *his* choosing.

How fascinating, these many new awarenesses, among them a sense of the rightness of things. Could it be he was perceiving Balance itself? Even more intriguing to ponder, had he always possessed such an awareness? Had the ethereal song he was now hearing simply been drowned out by the dynamic cacophony of Creation, the former's melody having become clear at last, thanks to this oddly silent place?

He admitted a clarity of thought previously unavailable to him, bombarded as he had always been by elemental perceptions that formed the woof and warp of his cosmic essence. But *he* was caught out of time now, like the palazzo, his consciousness removed from the supersonic motion of the cosmos and placed in a sort of stasis where thought might percolate without undue molecular influence.

No wonder Björn had seen so far into the future during his years of planning at this palazzo. From such a vantage, the right sort of man might see around time's curve into many distant tomorrows.

Pelas became aware of Phaedor's presence in the doorway and turned him a glance...and a smile. "These are interesting roles we've chosen: protector, brother. What role will Sinárr choose, do you think?"

Phaedor emerged from the shadowed doorway into the brilliant day, flipping a Merdanti dagger. "That very much depends on how jealous you make him."

Pelas barked a laugh. "Jealousy is in Sinárr's nature, isn't it? But they're all absurdly possessive, the Warlocks of Shadow." He leaned back against the railing and crossed his arms. A rising breeze blew his long hair across his face, and he swept both hands back through it to hold it out of his eyes. "They've never created anything they didn't control utterly. It's why they have no society to speak of." He gave another thoughtful laugh. "The gods help us if they ever learned to share."

Something flashed in Phaedor's consciousness upon this comment. His mind went suddenly still.

Pelas pulled his blowing hair around to the side to better regard him. "What is it?"

"A perception." The zanthyr came and stood beside him at the railing, facing outwards over the glittering lake while the wind tossed his wavy raven hair into his face. "Do you see it?"

Pelas could sense Phaedor's direction of attention, but he couldn't hone in on it or recognize its meaning. "I haven't yet the facility you've developed."

"Your statement..." the zanthyr's eyes tightened slightly, "if Warlocks learned to share...it makes me wonder, who would teach them?"

"Understanding the threat they would become if they ever worked in concert?" Pelas arched brows. Then his expression fell. "Yes, I see your point." He exhaled a slow breath and rubbed the scruff shadowing his jaw. It would be just like Shail to unite a notoriously independent and solitary race through some enticing treachery—and giving Warlocks access to the Realms of Light would be enough to bring together a disturbing number of them.

Shailabanáchtran meant Maker of Storms, and his younger brother embraced the meaning of his name to its fullest. Pelas had committed himself to defeating Shail's end game, even though he still didn't know what that end game entailed.

"You will discover it."

Pelas shifted his gaze back to the zanthyr. It was a unique experience having his mind read so completely.

Phaedor flipped his dagger. "There are few capable of threatening your brother's plans, but you are uniquely qualified to do so."

Pelas gave a slight wince. "So far I've only shown myself qualified to be outwitted." He studied the zanthyr. "Why do you think so?"

Phaedor's emerald gaze spoke volumes. "Because your brother has elected you as his enemy."

Pelas frowned. "Game theory. I admit my novice understanding."

"You must advance it quickly, for understanding the game provides the foundation for intelligent choices."

Pelas studied the zanthyr intently while a new understanding percolated in his thoughts. "That's why you brought me here."

Phaedor motioned with his dagger towards the palazzo. "You will find the Fifth Vestal's library more than adequate to your needs."

"A study," Pelas nodded his understanding, "beginning perhaps with the theory of games?"

"The song will lead you to the important subjects."

The song…

The zanthyr viewed the mortal tapestry in ways that defied explanation. The threads of the living pattern seemed almost to speak to Phaedor—shouted even. Was *this* the song the zanthyr was referring to? Or was it some other force, perhaps the one Pelas had heard humming in his consciousness already?

Whatever its source, Pelas wanted the zanthyr's skill of prediction. He would need it if he hoped to outsmart his brother.

Phaedor straightened away from the railing. A new energy underscored his manner now, an obvious desire to depart. Pelas wondered what the zanthyr was seeing in the tapestry, what thread was calling to him.

"Time passes differently here," Phaedor reminded him with a pointed look, "but be diligent in your pursuits. Timing is—"

"Everything." Pelas nodded his understanding. He was seeing many things in a different light. He would need to shine that light on many more old conceptions to bring them into new focus. He looked up under his brows as the zanthyr was pocketing his dagger. "I've just one last question before you go."

The zanthyr glanced up inquiringly.

Pelas crossed his arms and gave him a meaningful smile. "Who's Náiir?"

FORTY-NINE

"If you would hold your heart protected, let no one inside, for once that boundary is breached, it will ever be vulnerable."
–Ysolde Remalkhen, Fire Princess of Avatar

ALSHIBA ROUSED TO firelight's shadow-spirits dancing on the wide-beamed ceiling. Midwinter's chill clung to her bedchamber, making ice of the shadows at the edges of the room, but where she lay beneath a heavy eiderdown, she felt almost too warm. She hadn't been to her family's chalet in Avatar's great mountains since the fall of the Citadel. Odd that her dreams would've taken her there now.

Alshiba pushed up from beneath the eiderdown and noticed that her finger was conspicuously missing an important ring. A younger self, then, had drawn her to this past.

Across the room, Björn was tending the flames of her fire.

Ah, no... that sounded wrong even in her head. Would that it hadn't been so aggravatingly true. She angled a narrow gaze at him. "Who's weaving this dream?"

He looked over his shoulder as he straightened. "You are." Then he smiled—*damn him*—and pushed hands in his pockets. "I'm just a willing participant."

"If this was my dream, you wouldn't be in it." But she knew this was a lie, and so did he.

Alshiba looked down at her hands, trying to understand. This felt like Dreamscape, but with an odd resistance between layered consciousnesses, as a dream within a dream. She lifted her gaze back to meet his. "You're Healing me, aren't you? Forcing deep sleep?"

"Yes." He stood backlit by the flames in the oversized hearth; golden light wreathed the outline of his familiar form. It was actually painful, looking at him.

Alshiba closed her eyes and laid her head back against the pillows. "Where am I really?"

"In your bed in Illume Belliel."

She swallowed. "And where are you?"

"Right beside you."

Alshiba looked up at the painted beams that crisscrossed the plastered ceiling. The angst and longing she usually experienced around Björn felt distant to her, less friends than family members holding a heated discussion in another room, probably about her; the kind of discussion she would just as soon not interrupt—let them think she was still sleeping...alone.

She recognized a younger version of herself in these thoughts, a freer self whose greatest concern had been her father's grumbling disapproval. Björn had changed that—changed *her*—when he'd chosen her for Alorin's First Vestal. In between those youthful years of insignificant consequence and her life now, she'd spent many winters in that chalet, that bedchamber...winters of stolen solitude, long nights of darkness where she'd laid blissfully with Björn's fine form stretched alongside her.

It hurt just thinking of those moments now.

But not enough to stop them from scrolling through her dreaming mind, as if to force their imprint upon her sleeping consciousness and reshape the dream.

Alshiba looked back to him. "You must be holding me in a very deep sleep for me to dream of this place."

"It's not easy." He came over and leaned his shoulder against the bedpost, hands still in his pockets, and regarded her with one of those come-hither smiles that always made her embarrassingly flustered. "You're fighting me every step of the way."

"That sounds about right."

He turned his gaze off towards the darkened windows, which wore winter's frost without and the fog of warmth within. "Since we're going to be here for a while, what would you like to do?"

"What do you mean?"

He turned a smile back to her. "Shouldn't we make the most of it?"

Alshiba narrowed her gaze at him. Then she checked beneath the covers to make sure she was actually dressed—she couldn't trust her younger self to know discretion or modesty if they were two suitors carrying on a fistfight right in front of her—but finding herself clothed, she climbed out of bed.

"You know I love this place," she angled him a pointed look as she headed for the dressing screen, "and you *well* know how libertine I was before I met you."

Björn followed her with his very blue eyes, his smile more forthcoming than his thoughts. "Alshiba, this is *your* dream."

She harrumphed dubiously.

While she dressed, the hundreds of phrases Seth had used to upbraid her for loving Björn sounded a clamorous protest in her skull. Yet in three hundred years of Seth's raging and her own willful denial, she hadn't managed to alter the course of her heart by a single degree; its compass always pointed to Björn.

Part of her consciousness kept straying to the now, to all that had happened and all he'd done, but her younger dream-self resisted these efforts, insistently recalling her from what was real, encouraging a lover to return to bed.

Björn eyed her appreciatively when she reemerged. She knew what he saw—her younger self dressed in form-fitting hunting leathers, shamelessly self-possessed, as equally confident of her talent as of the effect she had on men. Alshiba stared down at her younger self and wondered if any part of that girl remained.

He was wearing his winter cloak when she looked back to him. Björn extended his hand invitingly. "What shall we hunt today?"

Alshiba looked to the windows. Daylight was glaring against the frost. Just below, bathed in the early morning light, her King's board waited on a table between a pair of chairs. Two empty wine glasses stood beside it. She went and stared down at the game.

Now she remembered that he'd moved his piece. After three hundred years…he'd made his next play.

Alshiba stared down at the chequered tiles and their marble pieces. "In all of the hours I spent studying that board, in any of the scenarios I explored, I never envisioned putting *that* piece there."

"And that is why you fail."

She lifted her gaze to him. "Because I can't predict you?"

"Because you won't let your imagination take you beyond the boundaries of what is logical into the improbable, the *impossible*…" he took her chin in his hand and looked into her eyes with passionate insinuation in his, "the great expanse of the uncharted unknown."

"A wielder is limited by what he can envision." The First Law sounded a curse crossing her tongue; his hand felt an iron branding her heart. In Illume Belliel he was repairing her life pattern. In her dreams, he was scoring it forever with the imprint of his own—

"Good shot!"

Alshiba spun a triumphant smile at him and swung out of her saddle. She landed in the snow and ran through the bracing air, feeling his equally bracing gaze admiring her as she moved.

She had a sense of things having come before, of nights spent together, of the hunting they'd been at since dawn; but in the way of dreams, she couldn't recall the experience of any of this.

Alshiba held up the winter hare with a brow arched in triumph. Her arrow, fletched red, had taken the creature through the heart. His, fletched in blue, fell just shy of the mark.

"Now I *know* I'm dreaming." She came back towards where he sat his horse. "Only in my dreams would I best you in any contest." She pulled both arrows from the hare and tossed the limp animal up to him.

He put it into his saddlebag along with the others. "That's what dreams are for, love."

"What," she angled him a skeptical look as she remounted, "revealing our elevated opinions of ourselves?"

He undressed her with his eyes. "Envisioning new realities."

She laughed—

Björn caught her hand before she could escape him and dragged her back down on the fur rug, trapping her long, bare legs beneath one of his own. They'd been days in that room together, seeking no other pleasure than the other's shape, thriving on each other's breath.

The fire felt hot against her back, the rest of her satiny beneath a silk dressing gown. Björn ran his hand along her hip, letting admiration flow from his touch, his cobalt eyes dark with visualization…

How mortifying, these moments, recalled from their lives together, bits of memories she was holding up for his inspection, her treasured mementos, tokens from before his remorseless abandonment.

Alshiba wished the dream would stop, but he was holding her in that deep sleep state where she had no control over the unfolding images.

His gaze grew quieter, if such a thing could be said of a man's eyes alone; yet Björn spoke volumes in a glance. His quiet meant only apology. He ran his thumb across the back of her hand. "There was no other way, Alshiba."

Her older self and younger self pushed to be the first through the door to reply. Her younger self won.

Alshiba rolled onto her back, letting the silk robe fall as it willed, inviting his gaze. "You read too much into my dreams."

His eyes explored the shadows of her body beneath the silk, and his breath came faster for it. He returned hot eyes to hers. "What would you have me read into this?"

She gave a languorous sigh and turned her head to smile at him. "A foray into missed opportunities." She slipped out of his reach before he could catch her back again.

He rolled onto his stomach and watched her as she walked to a cabinet and poured more wine. She could feel his eyes exploring her curves; she knew the desirous places his mind was dwelling. Her younger self had been so certain of her power, so sure she held his heart in her hand.

Oh, she'd been shameless in her youth, but the unfolding centuries had hardly made an honest woman of her—sleeping with a man she'd neither married nor bound, who held no ties to her beyond his word, no responsibility save for a troth they'd renewed in their lovemaking each day.

This truth made his betrayal somehow worse…that they'd had no contract beneath court or law, nothing binding him to her but his own heart. He'd always been free to leave her side. She'd just never imagined that he would.

Her younger self had never imagined he would want to.

She felt him coming up behind her. The heat of his gaze warmed her more strongly than the fire. His hand slipped up across her breast and then trailed up her neck. He inclined her head back into his shoulder while his other hand sought the heat between her legs. "Alshiba," he breathed against her ear, "I never *wanted* to."

She awoke in silence. Beyond the windows of her dimly lit bedchamber, night greeted her with stillness and solitude. Alshiba squeezed her eyes shut again and turned a pained grimace into her pillow. By Epiphany's Blessed Light, if she had a silver crown for every unsatisfying dream she'd had about Björn van Gelderan, she might've rivaled Eltanin for wealth.

The effects of the dream notwithstanding, she sensed immediately the change in herself. Gone was that lingering malaise. She felt alert for the first time in weeks. Her stomach growled a terse welcome to her wayward appetite, which was sneaking in the back door as if from a night of carousing, contrite and seeking absolution.

A sigh escaped her, echoic of regret. Her gaze found the ornate ceiling and the nymphs painted there. At least someone was regularly frolicking in her bedchamber.

"We can do something about that, you know."

Alshiba tensed. She'd expected him to be gone—she'd assumed he was. Now, as she looked to a dimly lit corner, she saw him reclining on his side on the couch with a book open before him. His shirt was undone, his feet bare. His curls were slightly longer than they'd been in her dream. It really was obscene of him to be so ridiculously good-looking.

She pushed a strand of hair from her face with a weak hand. She hadn't said her last thoughts out loud…had she? "Do something about what?"

He looked up under his brows. "That growling stomach of yours." He smiled innocently. "What did you think I meant?"

"You know perfectly well what I thought you meant."

He rose and crossed the room to her bedside. The picture of that moment reflected a thousand others: herself in bed while Björn reclined on the couch, working or reading through all hours of the night—he'd only ever stayed in bed to be with her—and then, finding her awake, striding towards her with a rather relentless ardor darkening his gaze. Watching him coming towards her like that again now made her body come alive in places it had no right to recall.

Björn sat down on the bed close at her side. She looked upon his face, one she'd known so intimately, which had known *her* so intimately, before which she'd surrendered every part of herself, to which she'd revealed her deepest desires. A face she'd thought of in the highest esteem, the face she'd come to equate with everything brilliant in the world, the one she saw when she thought of betrayal; just a face, *his* face, the target of her vehement censure, subject of centuries of her adoration.

He smoothed a strand of hair back from her eyes. *His* eyes, holding hers, made her breath quicken. "How would you like it, Alshiba?"

She froze beneath the question. A dozen different ways she would like it flaunted themselves before her imagination. "…What?" the word sounded embarrassingly breathless.

"The food." He looked over her discomfiture with quiet amusement. "Should I bring the food to you, or you to the food?"

"You should go." She looked him up and down while hauling brusquely back on her runaway imagination. "You've been working the lifeforce. They'll know you're here."

He twined a lock of her hair around his finger. "Only if I want them to."

"Then I should go." She felt like she couldn't breathe beneath his gaze. "The Council—"

"Franco is sitting in for you."

"I may still make it for part of the evening session." But she didn't move to leave. He had her heart twisted around his finger as surely as her hair. She dragged breath into her lungs and put heat into her gaze. "I should summon the knights." But she didn't move to do this, either.

He caressed her cheek with the back of his fingers. "I will consider my work complete when you're well enough to do so."

Something in the way he said this...alarm trilled uncomfortably in her core. "How long did you keep me asleep?"

"Three days."

She stared at him. "Healing me the entire time?"

He nodded.

He'd had her subdued that long and she still wasn't fully well? "How..." her voice came more faintly than she would've liked. *Dear Epiphany!* "How bad was I?"

He stroked his hand down her cheek, her neck, along her collarbone...quickening her heart painfully. "Do you really want to know?"

"Of course."

He removed his hand to his lap. "The Healers you consulted described your pattern as being frayed. In truth, it was disintegrating. By the time I started upon you, it had deteriorated to mere threads."

Alshiba choked. "You...*rewove* my life pattern?"

"Thread by thread."

Even recognizing this was Björn making such a statement, it seemed an impossible feat—and a horrifying truth. How could she still be herself if so much of her life pattern had eroded?

Perhaps he read the concern in her gaze. "There are few patterns on the mortal plane that I know better than yours, Alshiba." He traced the line of her collarbone with his thumb again, bringing tingles with his touch. "I explored it from multiple angles every time we—"

"Yes, I get it." She brushed her hair from her face to cover her disconcertion. "So...my illness. Did you determine the cause?"

He held her gaze steadily. "I found enough *atrophae* in this mansion to kill five Adepts."

Shock stole the words from her tongue.

He took her hand, entwined his fingers through hers, and gazed contemplatively towards the windows and the moonlit sea beyond. "They weren't counting on your being as strong in the lifeforce." He turned a smile back to her. "Or as headstrong."

Alshiba tried not to imagine her fate if Björn hadn't arrived to aid her when he had. It seemed almost more frightening to ponder in retrospect. "Who did this? Was it...?" But she didn't want to say where her thoughts had led her; she didn't want to believe Niko was capable of such treachery, or think that she'd knowingly brought the viper into her own house.

"The work was Eltanin."

Alshiba blew out her breath. "That's revealing of five strands of nothing."

A slight tension in his gaze conveyed his agreement. "My contact here is looking into it further."

She eyed him tersely at this. She'd known he maintained spies in Illume Belliel, alliances, *allegiances* that had weathered Malachai's genocide, as well as her very vocal vilification of him, with steadfast aplomb. Yet in all of her years in the cityworld, she'd found no clue to the identity of these personages—neither a telling look nor a stray comment, not even a shadow of favorable inclination to lead her to their door. Whoever they were, they wore a flawless mask across their duplicity.

Björn brushed his lips against the back of her hand. Not possessively—that had never been his way—but with an undeniable sense of ownership, less as property than responsibility, devotion…troth. He had as much right to hold her hand this way as she had to desire him to.

Alshiba pressed her lips together. She no longer had the strength to play the role she'd chosen for herself in his game of betrayal and sacrifice. "What I really want right now…" but she saw in his eyes as he lifted them back to her that he already knew what she wanted.

She turned her head towards an antechamber adjoining her bedroom and saw steam rising from a copper tub. Alshiba exhaled a sigh, and her gaze softened as she looked back to him. "How did you know?"

He smiled and brought her hand to his lips once more. "Because I know you."

He left to arrange for a meal while she bathed. As she stripped out of her sleeping gown to climb in the tub, she wondered if he'd undressed her after she'd collapsed on the night of his rescue. Thinking of his hands touching her bare form certainly would've made more sense of her dreams. Not that she didn't dream of him often, just rarely in an amiable context.

She was brushing out her damp hair when he returned, carrying a tray of food. He must've had her staff standing by to prepare such a meal so quickly. But of course, he would've had everything in place well in advance of her waking. Björn had always predicted her every need. He was too damnably perceptive, just one of the many attributes that made it so difficult for her to evacuate him from her heart.

She watched him heading for a table by the windows. "Who undressed me?"

He paused and cocked his head slightly. "Just now, or…?"

"The night you brought me home."

"Ah." He set the tray down. "Your attendants. I would never presume."

Alshiba shook her head. "I would that you had."

He lifted his gaze to her wonderingly.

She pushed a palm to her forehead. "That sounded different in my head."

She walked to the table and sat down. "If you had, it would just make sense of my dreams."

"Dreams…" he smiled inquiringly at her while setting out the food, "was I in them?"

"As if you need ask."

He grinned. "Were *you* in them?"

Alshiba crossed her arms. "You knew Aldaeon would offer me the Interrealm Committee Chair."

Björn set aside the last silver dome and sat down across from her.

Alshiba held a hard look upon him.

He shook his head amusedly. "Was there a question in there somewhere?"

"You wrote the measure, you knew Aldaeon would put it to a vote, and you knew I would accept the chair."

He searched her gaze with smiling eyes. "And?"

She somewhat fell back in her seat. "Why?" Frustration propelled her forward again. "*Why*, Björn?"

He knew what she was asking—far more than this inquiry alone. He laid a hand on the table—his right hand, with his oath-ring, diamond bright, glinting on his middle finger—and pointed at her. "You eat, I'll speak."

She eyed him narrowly. "The whole truth?"

"As much as you can stomach, Alshiba."

She picked up her fork. Björn lifted a goblet of wine.

He sat back and watched her as she started to eat, a resolute understanding shadowing his gaze, as of consequences known, choices owned, willingly accountable but far from contrite. "We originally built T'khendar to seal a hole in Alorin's aether, but soon it would become the realm's bastion, a fortress against their unmaking…"

Thus followed the story of their endeavor—his and Isabel's and his Council of Nine—to protect the realm from the very real threat of Malorin'athgul and right the cosmic Balance.

The night lengthened as Björn unwound his side of events, from the onset of Malachai's tragic madness, through their discovery of *deyjiin*, to what he knew of Arion Tavestra's fall at the Citadel. He made no apology for Arion's decision to slay the Mages, nor even gave her a reason for it, only admitting that he'd claimed the act as his own; and he told her how he and Cristien Tagliaferro had found the Fifty Companions hiding in the Citadel's catacombs, and what he'd done about it. Finally, he confessed to her how he intentionally tricked her, Raine and Seth with misinformation, and how they'd twisted the nodes leading to T'khendar to protect Alorin as much as to prevent others from harming themselves in attempting to follow them there.

But he did not tell her why he couldn't have trusted her with these truths from the outset.

Darkness still clutched the land when he was finished, yet the night felt thin—Alshiba felt thin. She'd eaten all she could hold, but only hollow bereavement filled her.

It didn't matter anymore how wrong she'd been about him—all of her and Raine's suppositions, their conjectures, their vehement claims—Björn had *intended* them to misunderstand. He'd drawn the outline of their reactions long before he'd departed; they'd merely colored in the shapes as if per his own instructions.

Of course his ring gleamed as brightly as the day of its forging. Despite all of the heartbreak, the tragedy, the anguish and loss…he'd remained true to Alorin throughout. But he had not remained true to her.

The worst part of it was that in some way—in *whatever* way he used to justify keeping everything from her—he'd probably been right to do so. Much of the frustration she'd experienced during the lengthening centuries had simply been the contesting of one irresolvable fact: that despite all semblances, Björn could only be acting in the realm's best interests.

Alshiba exhaled a slow breath and rose from her chair. Her legs felt unsteady beneath her heart's uneven rhythm. Understanding posed an impotent comfort for her grief. She laid a hand on the back of her chair, unable to look at him, not *wanting* to look at him unveiled of all her misjudgment.

"If you love me, as you claim," she voiced quietly, "you'll stop coming here. The aftereffects of your visits are too devastating."

He came up behind her and laid his hands on her shoulders. His words fell softly across her ear. "As soon as you're Healed."

Healed? She leaned back against his chest, feeling like her heart was breaking and breaking. Only it wasn't her heart, it was some essential part of herself that she could never regain. She hardly had room for breath for the suffocating loss. "Why can't I hate you?" She turned in his arms. "Why won't you let me hate you?"

He brushed her cheek with his thumb. "Because it's not the truth."

She wrapped her arms around him, in spite of her inclination to push him away. If only she could stay there with her head pressed to his chest and think of nothing, recall nothing…no reprimands, no demands, no drums of duty calling her integrity to act. Let her thoughts be quiet and her heart know a stolen, impractical, all but *impossible* moment of peace; let her find rest within the strength of his arms holding her.

She blinked against burning eyes. "What now?"

"Now?" He ran his lips across her hair and then sank his hands into it, drawing her head back to look up at him. "Now..." his gaze became molten, "we must resolve a depressing foray into missed opportunities."

Alshiba caught her breath.

He pushed on before she could upbraid him for pretending innocence of her dreams. "I've rewoven your life pattern. You'll need to study it yourself now, learn its pathways."

Only an idea so momentous could've distracted her from the remonstration she'd been preparing for him. She stared at him, dumbstruck. It was one of those well-known ironies that Healers couldn't see their own life patterns—the forest for the trees, and so forth—but if she could *see* it...if she knew how to find it...in the future she could Heal herself.

"You're—" she paused with her mouth open and changed course mid-sentence, "offering to show me my own life pattern?" She pulled back from him, her eyes widening. "By Epiphany's Light—*how?*"

He smiled down at her. "The visualization works on the same principal as a binding. We would need your blood, or we could..."

Her eyes hardened, his suggestion too clear. "No."

He ran his nose along hers. "*Alshiba...*"

Her heart launched into a painful cadence, draining determination from her voice. She pressed her forehead to his chest. "I can't believe you're asking this of me."

He gave a low chuckle. "You *want* me to ask this of you."

Epiphany give her strength—she'd only needed one good reason. He'd given her an irrefutable one.

He didn't wait for her to speak the words. He knew the desires of her heart—Lady's light, it was beating its consent loudly enough for her staff to hear it at the other end of the mansion.

In a breath he'd lifted her in his arms. A few long strides carried her to the bed.

"But I'm so tired," she protested as he laid her down.

He hovered above her with desire making his eyes gloriously dark. "I think we can fix that."

And planting his mouth on hers, he proceeded to do so.

Their hands found each other deftly. They knew each other's ways. She hardly noticed their mutual disrobement, only the moment when her bare form knew the full weight of his.

He moved into her, body and mind, and as he pulled her up beneath him, he drew her thoughts into his own. Light blinded her, and then a rushing channel of *elae* resolved into view. As a river rounding a bend towards a mountain, her life pattern appeared for an instant, looming before her vision, but then they vanished into it, *became* it, charging blissfully into the canyon of her pattern upon the waters of the first strand.

He navigated the river of her life pattern as an expert guide, showing her all of its twists and bends, coursing headlong down the tumbling thread of her existence. But this was not all he did.

Upon the ship of his intention he pulled the first, second, third, fourth, fifth—every strand of *elae*—miles-long pennants streaming from the mast. He wove them as he sailed—sewed—stitched anchors within her pattern, the lengths of each fluttering in between, as ribbons loosely basted.

Until the moment when the motion of his hips synchronized with the motion of his intent, and then, all at once, he pulled those ribbons tight. Alshiba arched beneath him, against him, her mind bound now with kaleidoscopic lights, color, *sound*—

The harmony of the strands flooding through Björn's mind into hers made a concert of their lovemaking, the sweet melody of aesthetics counterpointing the darker shades of sensations both painful and exquisite.

He'd never made love to her like this. He composed a symphony of the lifeforce, and played the strands as if he worked them all innately. She'd never asked him if he did—she'd never imagined he could—

His desirous growl ripped her back into the moment, the motion, the force of his body thrusting into hers and his power coursing the channels of her pattern. Björn wasn't going to let her think about anything but the harmonious interweaving of his lifeforce, mind and power with hers.

Alshiba felt him stripping her life pattern of the distraught energy that had darkened her light for so long. He seared her, cleansed her, unmade and rewove her upon studier truth, scoured her down and filled her up anew…

Over and over, until she became, once again, a star to mirror his own.

FIFTY

"An idea isn't responsible for the people who believe in it."

—Yara, an old Kandori woman

THE DAY BID farewell to Tambarré and night claimed the world while Ean slept, caught in the throes of true dreams. All the long night, the dead fish of memory bobbed to the surface, until the sea of Ean's awareness became clogged with unwelcome truths.

When the day dawned anew, Ean felt its warm summons brightening the horizon and sought to wake. Sunlight filtered between the slatted wooden shutters of his room, illuminating dust motes and glinting off silver lamps, but though it cast its light across Ean's sleeping eyes, it couldn't draw him out of the dark depths of dreaming.

Oh, he tried to find his way back to those sun-streaked waters! But his countless nights without sleep and his days of continuously working *elae* had assured an eventual reckoning, an untimely trade that had finally caught up with him during the dark hours of exhaustion.

Dreams now held Ean's awareness in thrall while they unraveled their unpleasant imaginings—not the deep, lasting dreams of restful sleep, but the disjointed, fitful dreams of a mind trying to wrest itself free of a possessive will...

"Björn won't do it." Arion shut the door behind himself and walked to the mantel and a waiting carafe of mulled wine. He sloshed it into a goblet and turned a frustrated look to Isabel. "He says he loves me too much."

Perfectly positioned on a settee, Isabel kept her gaze on her project, which currently involved two long needles and a large ball of yarn. "If I do what my brother will not, does that mean I don't love you enough?"

"Love is a specious excuse to deny my request."

Her mouth curled upwards at the corners. "I realize the experience of having your way thwarted is new to you, Arion, but my brother rarely denies you anything, much less for specious reasons."

Arion eyed her while he drank his wine. After a time, he draped an elbow on the mantel. Two thin gold bands glinted on every one of his fingers. "And you, Renaii...why will you deny me?" He only used that name for her when he wanted to remind her of his utter and complete devotion, or when he was intending something dangerous and desired her blessing on the endeavor.

The faintest of furrows came to Isabel's brow. "I thought we agreed I wouldn't look down your path...that you wouldn't ask me to."

"I'm asking you now."

The furrow in her brow became ever so slightly deeper.

Arion dropped his arm and leaned his shoulder against the mantel instead. "If our roles were reversed...Isabel, if *you'd* seen something you couldn't make sense of and it was within my power to assist you, do you doubt I would do it?"

She set her needles down in her lap and looked up at him. "No." Then she picked up her needles again and started winding the yarn around one of them. "But you're not exactly known for prudence."

"Nor you for reticence, High Mage."

One corner of her mouth curled amusedly. She flicked her colorless gaze up to him and then back to her work. "For most, to know their future is to become the effect of it."

"I'm not most people, Isabel."

"Arion, even you may not be immune to the phenomenon. Prophecy puts a person at the effect of their own decisions. They think the future is set."

"Have you ever known me to be the effect of anything? I'm the one who causes the effects, going forward to—"

"Achieve the effect one has intended despite any and all odds, yes." She lifted a smile up at him.

Arion draped an elbow on the mantel again, drank his wine and considered her.

There were times when he felt so stricken by his love for Isabel van Gelderan that he could barely look at her; at other times, her beauty and brilliance so awed him that he couldn't look away. She would find him staring at her, utterly enraptured, with embarrassing regularity.

Abruptly he clapped his empty goblet down on the mantel and turned to pace in the open space between them. "Isabel...I *must* know. The things I've seen..." He shoved both hands through his hair, beset by the intricate patterns of cause and consequence that had been haunting him for days. They appeared before his vision again, seeming more corporeal than armchairs and furnishings—patterns of arabesques drawn of glass in the air, each swirl representative of choice and action.

"I wish I could describe it to you." He lowered one hand, the other still being pinned to his head as if to help suppress his confusion. "I've never seen such spiraling paths forming so complex a design. If I but understood my *own* path, I could see the whole of it—Isabel..." he spun and dropped to his knees before her and took her knees to gain her crystalline gaze. "Think of what it might mean to the game to know these things."

Her brow furrowed deeply as she regarded him. "We cannot know what the Malorin'athgul will do. They have no paths. The Sight cannot predict them."

"But their steps cross *my* path—this much I'm sure of! This much *you're* sure of." He gazed intently into her eyes. He understood what he was asking of her. He prayed she loved him enough to take that risk. "If I but knew the rest of my path...Isabel, I could predict them. We'd know what we're going to be facing. We could plan far in advance of the curve of time."

Her expression grew troubled. "What if we look together and you don't like what you see?"

He squeezed her knees. "It doesn't matter if I like it; it matters only that I'll know the truth of what will be."

"What *will* be..." A tension came into her tone. "The only true future is what you cause to become, Arion."

"Which I can't do nearly as well if I don't know what I'm going to face."

She looked back to her needles and yarn with one arched brow. "Whose reasoning is specious now?" It was only one delicate eyebrow lifted with inquiry, but there was plenty of challenge in it.

Arion pushed back to his feet and resumed his pacing. He shoved hands behind his back and shot her looks of perilous importance every few steps, all of which she calmly ignored. How could she just sit there looping string into knots when such a momentous dawn of possibility brightened their horizon?

After a moment of stalking stormily back and forth and not getting due attention for it, he strode to refill his goblet and then turned exasperatedly to her. "Why in Epiphany's name is the High Mage of the Citadel *crocheting*?"

She arched a brow without looking up from her work. "Technically, I think this is knitting."

He opened his arm and bowed to her point. "Fine. Why is the High Mage of the Citadel *knitting*?"

She smiled while looping her needle again. "I've been given to understand this is what noble ladies do when they're with child."

It took Arion an embarrassing breath of time to process those words. Then he flung his goblet aside, jumped over a low table and grabbed her up by the shoulders. He searched her eyes with a sort of wondrous exhilaration bursting in his core. "Isabel…you're going to have a baby?"

She smiled at him.

Incredulity gripped him as he stared at her. Then he fastened a fervent kiss upon her mouth, swept her into his arms, and started carrying her determinedly off.

Isabel saw where he was heading and laughed. "I do believe this is how we got into this situation to begin with, my lord."

Arion threw the fifth into the doors and carried her through them towards their bed chamber.

Isabel protested with amused exasperation, "My lord, I'm already *with* child."

He growled hungrily into her ear, "Let's make another."

"I'm given to understand that Nature requires us to finish making this one first."

Arion blew the fifth to close the doors behind them and pressed her down beneath him on the bed. He hovered over her, his arms braced at her sides. He could hardly breathe, the room was so choked with possibility.

He captured her laughing gaze with his own. "Will you do it, Isabel? By Cephrael's Great Book—if not for me, if not for *us* even, will you do it for our son?"

Staring into his eyes, she asked him across their bond, *So sure that our child will be a boy?*

You sense it as well as I. That pattern is clear.

She held his gaze. Then she closed her eyes and opened her mind, her thoughts…her *will* to him. This invitation echoed another more carnal one, a deeper resonance that had already formed a humming energy between them.

To feel Isabel's mind unfolding, enveloping his unto her own, blending, *merging*…to feel her surrender to him and yet somehow by that very action encourage his own surrender to her…even the rush of wielding the lifeforce paled by comparison. Isabel drew Arion into the shared space of awareness where their minds resonated harmoniously; the plane of binding where they would exist eternally together.

Arion closed his eyes and laid his forehead against hers, exhaling a tremulous breath. "Will you do it, Isabel? Will you look down my path?"

She lifted her mouth to meet his and gave her answer in a kiss...

—the dream shifted—

Arion swam in a river of light.

He and the Enemy bobbed upon the raging current of the Pattern of the World, their bodies parted by its rushing stream. Further behind him on the river, the Enemy's face formed a furious mask. Arion wondered what his own revealed.

He cast another anchor towards the Citadel's weld, but the hooks found no purchase. Either he'd missed—*unlikely*—or the weld itself had been destroyed.

The Pattern's river tore at him, waves of power ripping at his consciousness, at his very being. To ride that current with neither anchor nor destination was to become unmade by its power.

Arion hastily cast more anchors to the nearest points he could find— one to Tal'Shira, one to the weld in Tregarion, and one long to the north. He felt each of them hook and catch. The lines went taut.

Arion suddenly stood still while the river rushed around him. He turned amid that golden light, seeking the Enemy.

The latter had anchored himself as well, for he was approaching Arion now across the swirling flood. The Enemy spun his blade, cutting the currents, *staining* them, so that they carried downriver to Arion the smoldering char of his touch.

"A modestly impressive attempt," his eyes glinted darkly from a face sketched by the Pattern's glow into rigid angles, "but ultimately futile."

The kinetic river swarmed around them, ever trying to rip Arion from his anchors, or rip his anchors from their grounding nodes. Fighting amid that rushing stream would be a test of all of his skill.

Arion tightened his hold on his blade and readied himself. "They say he who laughs last, laughs best."

"You will not be laughing when I claim your consciousness for my own use." The Enemy's dark eyes licked over Arion. He felt their touch as the cold, sharp edge of a blade slicing along his flesh, even as he felt the man's daggers of compulsion stabbing for a hold on his consciousness. "Soon, you will know no laughter but that which I command from your throat."

Arion raised his blade with both hands. "Thrilling, to be so underestimated."

The Enemy lifted his lip in a snarl. Their weapons clashed in a geyser of sparks.

On the bed of the realm's kinetic river they fought, striding across sands of power, raising the silt of the second strand in their wake. Every clash of their blades made ash of the lifeforce, clouds which were quickly ripped away on the currents. Every step dragged against Arion's anchors while the current continuously tried to rip him downstream.

Arion bobbed in a delicate equilibrium of forces, even as he bobbed in the cosmic Balance, caught in a channel of opposing tides. Choices… choices spiraled…and ended. Their paths were too short, nearly concluded before they'd begun. The choices whose threads still extended far into the pattern of consequence had dwindled to a scant half-dozen. Arion misliked all of them.

He'd only brought their battle onto the Pattern of the World as a stopgap, a borrowed moment to strategize his next play, but the *sheer force* hauling upon his consciousness—never mind the Enemy, the Pattern would be the death of him!

The Enemy's spiny tentacles of compulsion resumed their efforts to overwhelm Arion's fourth-strand shields. Every breath became an effort of will, as labored as that of a beleaguered swimmer caught in a riptide.

Arion clenched his jaw and swung again for the Enemy. The latter avoided, parried and struck back. Arion caught the blade overhead on his own and swung out from beneath it, striking as he turned. The Enemy met Arion's blade with a downward stroke of his weapon and slung him off balance. Arion recovered with a curse and plunged back to engage him anew.

The Pattern of the World tore at both of them…

—the dream shifted—

Kaleidoscopic light bombarded Arion, a deadly concoction of compulsion woven through with *deyjiin*. Every touch of it speared his mind. He tasted the blood of his own thoughts dripping dying life onto his tongue.

He could barely see, barely *think*. Fragmented patterns clogged the currents; the ashes of hope clogged his lungs.

He and the Enemy tumbled together on the raging current, locked in a deadly embrace.

He'd had to sever two of his anchors. It was that or lose his fourth-strand shield altogether and succumb to the Enemy's compulsion.

Perhaps…had he just been fighting an immortal who wielded *elae*, had the Enemy not *also* wielded *deyjiin*…Arion might've stood a chance.

But to endure the continual dual bombardment of these conflicting and polarizing powers...

Deyjiin was attacking every particle of *elae*—furiously, agonizingly, each molecule engaged in its own war for dominion. The very air was combusting, *fusing*, exploding.

The myriad strands of choice had become two.

Dangling amid that rushing river, clinging to the last of his anchors, Arion knew which one he would choose. It was impossible for him to choose any other. He saw this now. Perhaps this is what Isabel had always known.

The Enemy clung to him with iron hands while his mind clawed hooks of searing ice into Arion's mental shield. The raging tide of the Pattern of the World ripped at both of them.

Arion might've released his anchor and ridden the tide to a safe harbor, but to think of letting the Enemy walk free...to abandon the game when there was still a chance to turn the tide...to simply *turn his back* on the First Law...

Arion! Isabel's mental call along their bond cast a spear into his heart, even from so great a physical distance, even with the Pattern of the World raging around him.

I'm sorry, Isabel. Arion steeled his will against the compulsion patterns bombarding him and his heart against the woman he loved. *You cannot stay with me for this.* He couldn't think of her, couldn't think about what he would be losing if he failed. To do so meant losing the battle then and there.

Arion closed his mind to the woman he loved and chose his path.

Ean woke with a low groan mumbled into the mattress and flopped over onto his back. Now he remembered why he hadn't been sleeping. He threw an arm across his eyes and lay for a time, trying to push off the misery of waking to the realization of what he'd done.

He'd long suspected that Arion had knowingly abandoned Isabel—the idea had haunted him from the outset—yet he'd never imagined that in this same choice he'd also been abandoning his son.

Isabel, we had a son?

Ean exhaled a tremulous breath and pushed both palms to his eyes. *Shade and darkness...why hadn't she told him they'd had a child together?*

Probably because your son died centuries ago, having never known his father.

It seemed the likely truth. Isabel only withheld things about his past to spare him pain, and if his son had still been alive...

No, it was too torturous to ponder other scenarios. The joy Arion had known in that part of the dream still felt too visceral, too exhilarating and new. Ean shoved the memories aside out of self-preservation and tried to find something less tormenting to think about.

It took quite a while.

Finally, he found his way back to the confrontation with Darshan and the strange confluence of paths at the Prophet's temple. The Princess Heir of Agasan, *two* Malorin'athgul, Tanis of Giverny and himself...somehow all of their paths had intersected in that place. Or at least, well...he'd crossed Tanis's path by extension through Pelas and the Princess Nadia van Gelderan.

Ean exhaled a slow breath, marveling at how far-reaching was Björn's game...how *spiraling* all of their paths! He'd never imagined that the innocent young truthreader traveling among his company might be a Player in the First Lord's game, yet if the lad was mutually bound with a Malorin'athgul, how could he be anything else?

Ean couldn't help wondering what circumstances had driven Tanis all the way across the Empire to meet the Princess Heir. And by what strange twists of consequence had Tanis gained the binding troth of Pelasommáyurek, for whom Isabel had sacrificed so much? Trying to envision the possible connections boggled his mind.

Yet it seemed appropriate somehow. Tanis was special—anyone could see that. He'd gained Ean's affections from their very first meeting—far more deeply than Ean had realized at the time.

But for Tanis, he'd let Pelas live. For Tanis, he'd set aside his own grievances, forgone vengeance in Isabel's name—*thirteen hells*, for Tanis's sake he'd even *allied* with the man who had tortured and bedded his wife! Ean pushed both hands into his hair and gave an explosive exhale. What *wouldn't* he have done for the lad?

And yet...whatever lay between him and Isabel, Tanis and Pelas—these relationships weighed against each other in the balance of sacrifice—it also felt right that Tanis's welfare and happiness should prove more important to him than his own.

After a lengthy argument with his body about the need to do something beyond lying very still, Ean finally roused himself into an upright position. It took another round of contentious discussion before he could make himself get out of bed to ring for the inn's staff.

They attended him quickly once he removed the warding from the room.

As he was breaking his fast to the accompaniment of cicadas singing to the evening beyond his open balcony doors, Ean pondered his meeting with the Prophet.

Now that he had the mental capacity to inspect his and Darshan's interaction, Ean recognized several truths he'd been unable to acknowledge at the time. Of fundamental importance: what if the currents had not been lying about Darshan?

He simply hadn't *wanted* to believe what he was seeing. What was that Kandori saying? *'The eyes will not see what the mind does not want.'*

Yet it was a sure truth that Darshan had been leading him around Dore's wards and keeping him beneath the notice of Marquiin and Ascendants alike. Darshan's whispered compulsion had brought Ean directly to his location without rousing any alarms—or would have, if Ean hadn't finally defied its directions.

But *why?*

The more he looked it over, the more Ean got the uncomfortable impression that Darshan had carefully managed his visit to the temple for a specific purpose, one that had little to do with his activities as the Prophet. It wasn't lost on Ean that Dore Madden had been conspicuously absent.

Another thing Ean hadn't wanted to admit at the time: the patterns surrounding the first two temples had been belching a continuous sludge into the currents, but the currents around Darshan's temple had run clean.

If the Prophet's patterns were a view into his intentions, why weren't the same patterns extant in his residence? Why weren't the currents in that place roiling and riotous?

'The currents will tell you what is true.'

Isabel's words, an axiomatic fact. If the currents weren't lying, then Darshan's patterns, and the patterns Ean had long associated with the Prophet Bethamin, were not synonymous.

He recalled what he'd observed of the man. Darshan had barely spared a glance for the Marquiin who'd been with Nadia; he couldn't have cared less that one of his own was helping her.

But if the Prophet wasn't outraged at Ean, why the relentless pursuit? Why all of the attempts on his life? Why take Ean's men hostage in order to lay a trap for him? Darshan hadn't seemed at all concerned about the things Ean had done. But someone cared. *Someone* wanted Ean dead. *Someone* was taking vindictive pleasure in making monsters out of men, orchestrating atrocities in the name of a god. *Someone* was running things at the temple of Tambarré.

Ean was starting to think that someone wasn't the Prophet.

He sat back in his chair and rubbed the back of his neck. His pondering had delivered him to the edge of a question: What if the attempts to lure and kill him were serving a purpose beyond Dore's personal vengeance? What if each of the attempts to kill him had really been misdirection, feints to make Ean look everywhere to find his enemy but at the one *true* place where the enemy resided?

His troubles had all begun the moment he returned to Dannym, but clearly someone had been working against him lifetimes before that point. What if someone had recognized his life pattern pressed on an invitation all those months ago? And what if, in that recognition, that someone had known him as Arion Tavestra and a potential enemy—'*Come and find me. I'll be waiting.*'—and taken steps to eliminate him, while himself hiding in the shadows of other men's hatreds?

And it had worked. Ean had only been looking at the arrows shooting towards him, or perhaps at the archers firing at him, but he'd never thought to look for the man who'd given the order to fire those arrows.

Suddenly, this all seemed so clear to him. So self-evident.

All this time he'd only been looking at his own pieces on the board. He needed to start looking at *both* sides of the board. He needed to understand the Player sitting across from him.

The Enemy.

Thus far, Ean had faced three Malorin'athgul. That left but one face to the Enemy: Shailabanáchtran.

…*Come and find me. I'll be waiting*…

And Shail had been waiting, each time Arion had Returned; waiting to destroy him again, and again, and again.

This time had to end differently. This time Ean was determined to make *new* choices. This time, he *couldn't* fail, or there would be no more future for any of them in which to act.

Ean knew one thing unequivocally: in all of his confrontations with Shail, whether he'd won or succumbed boiled down to one simple truth: Shailabanáchtran worked *deyjiin*. If Ean couldn't work that power, if he couldn't learn how to apply the Laws of Patterning to it, he would *never* be able to defeat Shail. To imagine any other outcome was lunacy.

Ean knew three men who could potentially teach him.

Asking the First Lord seemed like a step backwards, a move off the field onto the sidelines and out of the zone of play.

That left the zanthyr, and Pelas.

While he packed up his things, he planned.

His brother and Dareios waited for news of his success, but he'd find neither teachers of *deyjiin* nor opposing Players by rejoining Sebastian in Kandori.

At some point during his adventures in Tambarré, one of the steps he'd taken had set him on a path that forked firmly away from his brother; indeed, looking at the pattern of consequence he was treading now, that path he'd walked beside Sebastian seemed to have ended even before he left Kandori. Ean knew he couldn't now return there and still hold his position as a Player.

So...he would send word to Sebastian and Dareios of the success of their matrix. They could move forward with the plans they'd already devised in pursuit of Isabel's task.

But that left him...where?

With the whole world on the lookout for you. Dore's two hundred talents had seen to that. No city in the Middle Kingdoms would be safe for him with that kind of price on his head.

But Ean didn't intend to remain in the Middle Kingdoms. He couldn't—not if he meant to learn how to work *deyjiin*.

He knew where he had to go, but first, he had one last thing to do.

The prince picked up his sword and looked it over. As his unfortunate foray with Sheih had proven, the eagle-carved crossguard with its sapphire pommel stone was easily recognizable, and anyone who knew a Kingdom Blade could identify him by it. Carrying his blade for the world to see had dumped him onto Sheih's path. He wouldn't make that mistake again.

He dared do nothing to alter the weapon itself. The zanthyr had laid patterns all through the steel when he'd remade it into a sentient blade, and some of those patterns Ean still didn't understand. But the identifying hilt...*this* he could change.

He focused first on the grip and crossguard and *permeated* the metal. Verily, in his mind, he *became* the metal. He knew its innate composition as if it were his own; he saw how the molecules of energy had been bound into form.

These he shifted with a thought—*darken*—and the hilt became as grey as the storm clouds over the sea—a little of the detailed molecular restructuring Arion had been so fond of. With a bit more layering of form, Ean morphed the design of the hilt and cross guard so it resembled a phoenix more than an eagle.

For the pommel stone, he formed a clear thought in his mind of the effect he intended to achieve—the First Law; Markal would've been so proud—but rather than impelling the thought, *forcing* the currents to comply, Ean let his intention sort of float away, as a toy boat set upon *elae*'s tides. Gently, quietly, the intention whispered along the currents until it had infused them with intent.

A twisting spire of smoke appeared within the sapphire's core. Dancing, spinning, it drew the rich color of the stone into its depths. Indigo waned to cobalt, cerulean to sky, until only the faintest glisten gave memory to the color it had once been.

In place of the sapphire, an incandescent stone remained, water-clear, emitting a faint, cobalt sparkle when it caught the light. It very much reminded him of Isabel's eyes. Perhaps that vision of her gaze had been his true inspiration for the stone.

His job complete, Ean flipped the weapon around and caught it by the hilt. It was hardly recognizable now, even to his own eyes. He assessed his work with a sense of accomplishment, yet with a pang of sadness as well.

His Kingdom Blade had been his last physical tie to the family that had birthed and raised him, yet it had never been more clear to him that his path lay with Isabel and Björn.

Like it or not, wherever it might lead, to tragedy or victory…across betrayal's dark moors and whatever trials lay ahead, their path was his path, their game was his game. Not simply because Arion had chosen it—though Ean was doubly bound to it because of Arion's choices. No, this was his path because he knew the consequences of not walking it, and those weren't consequences he was willing to live with.

Ean gave one last look around his room. Then he sheathed his blade, slung his pack up over his shoulder and set a course for the Pattern of the World.

FIFTY-ONE

"Legends and facts are not meant to coincide."
—Dareios Haxamanis, Prince of Kandori

MINUTES, *AS THE* river runs.

Trell jerked his britches up over his damp skin while envisioning possibilities of intent, defense, counterattack and retreat and feeling every heartbeat too keenly. He was donning his shirt when a rustling in the trees made him jump for his sword. He swung it around just in time to pin Rami at the point of his blade.

His young valet froze with towels in hand and misgiving luminous in his startled gaze.

Trell exhaled an oath and lowered his weapon. "Run to Raegus. Tell him to sound the alarm. Men are coming."

Rami dropped the towels and sprinted back the way he'd come.

Trell belted on his sword and jammed his feet into his boots. Speculation crowded up against the urgency already pressing on his thoughts. Whose vile intentions had the river overheard? They were only days from Khor Taran. Was this a force of Nadoriin come to eliminate them before they could threaten the fortress? Saldarians finally seeking revenge? Or bounty hunters hard upon the scent of one of his expatriated princes?

Trell reached for his cloak—

Trell of the Tides!

He sensed them in the same moment he perceived Naiadithine's warning. Trell drew his blade and spun.

Dark forms emerged from the trees into the moonlit clearing, while other shadows were approaching through the steam rising from the hot springs. "Lo, is that *him*?" a voice asked in the desert tongue, the accent distinctly Saldarian.

"It has to be," another said, "he's just as described. Fortune favors us tonight, men."

Trell counted twenty in a glance. *Twenty against one.* He let out a slow exhale.

"Take him," the leader growled.

Trell rushed them first. He felled one man with a crosswise blow that split his chest and another with a slash through the shoulder that nearly severed the arm. Then he broke for the river.

"I said *take* him!" the leader snarled.

Four shadows chased Trell through the luminous mist. He found flat ground near the river and fought all four, using elbows and feet as extensions of his blade. One man fell back with a broken nose, the second with his thigh opened to the bone. The last two worked in concert, jabbing and slashing at him, trying to find a lapse in his guard. The *cortata* sang counterpoint to their motion. Trell blocked high and low, dodged and sidestepped, perceiving in the *cortata's* melody where their swords would come at him.

He drove one of them backwards into the river, and the dark water swept him instantly away. The last attacked with a furious cry. Trell blocked an overhand blow, spun underneath it and brought up his blade across the man's back. A kick sent him sprawling into the river, and the Taran hungrily swallowed him, too.

Trell jumped over one of the steaming pools and found his footing on a narrow strip of land that ran between the hot springs. There, they couldn't all swarm him at once. He moved through two more forms of the *cortata*, keeping the pattern active. *Elae* sang in his thoughts, riversong in his ears.

In the darkness beyond the rising steam, his attackers were shouting at each other. Elsewhere in the night, a lone horn bellowed. Trell clenched his jaw. He'd wanted to be in camp with his men when the attack came.

More forms resolved out of the mist. Trell exhaled a slow breath, infused it with determination, and lifted his blade to meet them.

✦

Loukas n'Abraxis walked the edge of camp with hands shoved in his pockets and his thoughts as far away as sleep's embrace. He always had a hard time finding his rest whenever Tannour's tent lay only a dagger's throw from his own.

That night he'd found it especially difficult, what with the entire company now knowing he'd trained in the *cortata*, and this after so many years of feigning uselessness with a blade.

Everywhere Loukas went, he heard men whispering his name. Rather than endure their evident speculation, he sought solitude by the river. Eventually he found a rock overlooking the dark water and seated himself there, hugging his knees.

He could still feel the piercing stare Tannour had leveled him when Trell had told the company Loukas would be teaching them the Adept dance of swords. But what else could he have done, save what the *A'dal* required? Tannour demanded impossible things of him.

—*"You're always doubting me." Tannour let go of his hold on the rock and hung by one arm to cast Loukas a level look, disturbing in its candor. The chimney of stone they were climbing fell away fifty paces below their twelve-year-old feet.*

Loukas winced up at him. He wished Tannour wouldn't hang like that, where the slightest slip of fingers would cast him to his death. He himself had both hands and feet firmly driven into every available crevice, and still his heart was pounding. He wetted his lips, which were dry from the climb as much as from the fear that kept trying to drag his eyes downward. "I don't doubt you."

"You think because I'm not learning to speak as many languages as you, or dance swords like you, that I'm not as smart as you."

"Don't be absurd. I know how smart you are. Just because I'm asking you to hold tighter onto the damned rock doesn't mean I don't think you're smart. Fiera's breath, you're so touchy."

Tannour was still hanging by one arm, but now he was grinning at him. "You Avatarens, so high and mighty."

Loukas scowled at him with twelve-year-old aggravation. "Just climb, won't you? I don't care how you fethen *do it—"*

"That was quite a show you put on today."

Loukas started at the near voice, which registered to his ears as keenly as his own. He let out his breath and glanced to Tannour, then swallowed tightly and looked back to the river.

"Loukas n'Abraxis, Avataren prince, combat engineer, speaker of nine languages, expert dancer of blades…" Tannour was leaning against a tree with his arms crossed and gazing at him with that calculating half-smile, the one that always made Loukas feel empty inside—the one he used to punish him.

Loukas flicked a look to him and away again. "What was I supposed to do?"

"I don't know…think of something brilliant. Isn't that what you're always claiming the *A'dal* brings out in you?"

Loukas clenched his jaw. "Your words, not mine."

Tannour arched a brow in dark humor. "They'd be yours if you spoke with any candor."

Loukas flashed him a spiked glare. "And how am I meant to speak candidly and still hide all of *your* secrets?"

"Is that what you were doing today? Hiding my secrets?"

"*Fiera's breath*, Tannour." Loukas made fists at his sides. "I would the river had never risen sometimes."

He expected Tannour to bristle at this comment—it was the one they lobbed at each other when frustration made fools of their tongues—but Tannour only exhaled a slow breath and shifted to lean back against the tree. "That would've been easier, wouldn't it?" He pushed hands in his pockets, and his raven brows performed a show of ponderous contemplation. "Never owing each other anything, never caring…the path proving false." His blue eyes found Loukas's. "But you'd still be a prisoner of your pride."

Loukas gnashed a curse between his teeth. *Fethe*, but Tannour could ply him to the ends of his wits. He was seeking some retort that didn't make him seem utterly contemptible when Rami came storming down the path.

Tannour caught him in his arms, fast as the wind. The boy yelped and reared in a wild horse panic.

"Easy, lad." Tannour steadied Rami beneath his hands. "What's got you so spooked?"

Rami tried to pull free, but Tannour was deceptively strong. Loukas knew this better than most. "The *A'dal* says men are coming!" Rami gave the Vestian a frustrated glare. "Let me go! I must warn the others!"

Tannour released him, and Rami bolted off down the path.

Loukas stared at Tannour feeling oddly short of breath. "How can the *A'dal* know such a thing when you don't?"

But Tannour had already gone to that place Loukas could never follow him. "Get your sword, Loukas," he murmured tightly. Then he vanished into the trees.

❖

Rolan Lamodaar had just concluded some personal business in the woods and was returning to his tent when Trell's young valet, Rami, came barreling into him.

"Whoa—" Rolan grabbed the boy before they both lost their feet. "Where's the fire, *walad*?"

Rami's brown eyes were wide as saucers. "The *A'dal* says bad men are coming, *Sidi*. We must wake the company!"

Rolan gave him a once-over, decided he was telling the truth, and inwardly swore. "Come with me." He dragged the boy through the camp to a particular tent, swept aside the flap and stormed inside. "Raegus!"

Raegus shot upright on his cot. "What the *fethe*—"

Rolan shoved Rami forward. "Tell him."

"*A'dal* says bad men are coming!" Rami spurted.

Rolan tossed a shirt at Raegus and ducked out of the tent, dragging Rami in his wake. Outside, he centered the boy in front of him. "Where's the *A'dal*?"

"By the river."

Rolan pointed down the line of tents. "Wake the men—quietly—and tell each of them to spread out and wake the others. Everyone should meet at the center of camp."

"*Balé, Sidi!*" Rami darted off.

Raegus emerged from his tent, belting on his sword. "The men?"

"Rami's waking them."

"What's this about an attack?"

"You know as much as I do."

"Well, *fethe*." Raegus looked as if he'd been enduring too many long weeks being teased by the strumpet Sleep. He cast a wary look off into the trees. "Who do you think it is?"

Rolan grunted. "Does it matter?"

Raegus looked him over. "How is it you're so prepared?"

Rolan was still fully dressed, with both daggers and scimitar at his belt. He grinned at the other man. "Inanna favors me."

"*Fethe*, if you don't have the most irreverent tongue of any man not long for this world. You *must* be favored of the gods with the things you get away with saying."

Rolan rested a hand on his sword. "I will live to see my name avenged and that unwholesome get of a gout-eaten camp whore, Radov abin Hadorin, disgraced." He leaned towards Raegus meaningfully. "Inanna has shown me this vision."

Tannour came jogging up wearing so many straps and weapons he looked like a pincushion for knives. He was carrying the scarf that usually wrapped his raven head, so Rolan clearly saw the three lines of tattooed script running down the side of his neck. He never had learned what the symbols meant.

And he had no idea how the Vestian had donned all of that gear so fast. "Blood of Inanna, man, do you sleep like that?"

Tannour's pale blue eyes flicked to Rolan with their usual calculating gleam. Tannour was one of those who made Rolan never want to turn his back on him, despite his promising vision from the War Goddess.

"What's this about a supposed attack?" Tannour was absently checking his knives in their various sheaths. "And how did they find us? The scouts haven't crossed anyone's path in days."

"*A'dal* says so, so it must be." Raegus shifted his gaze past Tannour and motioned someone else towards the center of camp.

"But who's out there? What have they come for?"

"Besides our heads?" Rolan inquired.

"We don't know, Tannour." Raegus looked back to him with impatience hardening his gaze. "All we know is what the *A'dal* told us."

The Vestian flicked an assessing look between Rolan and Raegus. "Where is the *A'dal*?"

"By the river."

"What's he doing there?"

"*Fethe* if I know, but it must be important or he'd be here."

"Then shouldn't we—"

"What we should do, Tannour Valeri, is prepare for attack like the *A'dal* instructed." Raegus pinned Tannour with an uncompromising stare. "Get the men to the center of camp and see to their readiness."

Tannour regarded him with evident frustration. "How can ready ourselves when we have no idea what's coming at us?"

Raegus blew out his breath. "Inanna's blood, Tannour—go find out then!"

Tannour gave him a sarcastic bow and loped off.

"*Fethen* princes." Raegus glowered after him. "What I wouldn't give to have two hundred men who simply followed orders."

Rolan cast him a sly half-smile. "I follow your orders."

"Sure," Raegus looked him over vexedly, "so long as my orders align with what you're already planning to do." He looked past Rolan, ostensibly to someone trying to gain his attention, whereupon he nodded brusquely to them and muttered to Rolan, "The men are assembling. Let's go."

❖

Tannour moved as wind through the darkness, invisible in his black garments and with his head wrapped in a shroud of concealing silk. With his eyes bound to blindness, he'd learned how to listen to the night; he knew the language of Air. Now, as he moved silently through the forest, alert and listening, Air's currents spoke of a host coming up from the south. They were almost upon them.

So the prince was right.

How by the Ghost Kings had Trell val Lorian learned of this approaching force? Tannour seriously doubted their illustrious prince kenned the language of Air.

Vibration and waves, breath and motion—Tannour read the air's disturbance and noted that a small company had split off from the larger group. He concealed himself behind a tree and waited for them to pass. Then he stole towards the main host approaching.

Sensing they were closing in, Tannour caught the limb of an oak and swung himself silently up onto the limb. He moved into concealment and crouched there, listening to Air's whispers. Soon dark shapes began passing beneath him, as a school of fish through shadowed waters; and like bad fish, Tannour recognized their stink. *Saldarians.*

He counted their number with increasing enmity. This had to be the same force they'd been chasing for weeks in their game of cat and mouse.

As the last of the Saldarians passed beneath his limb, Tannour lowered himself headfirst and then somersaulted soundlessly down. A few steps and he had his quarry around the neck and a push-dagger piercing the side of his neck.

Incapacitate-trap-interrogate.

Tannour clapped a hand over the other's mouth. His hand flashed down for two quick jabs to the man's back, low and fierce, and stifled his scream while supporting his fall.

Tannour instantly straddled him. One hand pressed hard across the Saldarian's mouth while another whisked, exchanging daggers. He spun a *skorpjun* blade through his fingers, angled it just so, and slipped the razor steel fluidly between the man's ribs. Only a strangled cry disturbed the air, it's wavelength too low to carry far.

One had to be careful when wielding a *skorpjun* dagger so as not to let the wickedly hooked tip stab the heart; but inserted just so, twisted just so, the needle end caused the heart to palpitate viciously and brought a frantic sense of impending death unlike any other experience on the living paths.

Tannour knew this first-hand, for his instructors had used the technique on him, that he might properly respect its power.

He twisted his *skorpjun* blade just so.

The man beneath him screamed into Tannour's hand. Tannour brought his mouth close to his captive's ear. "Who sent you? Answer me and the pain goes away. Cry for help and it gets *much* worse." He removed his hand.

"...*Kifat,*" his captive rasped.

"Kifat. Who is that? A Nadoriin?"

The man shook his head, his eyes squeezed tight from pain. "...We... we..."

"Wielder?"

His captive nodded. "…Shamshi—" a sudden wail broke for freedom.

Tannour clapped his hand across the Saldarian's mouth again. "This Kifat. He's Shamshir'im?"

His captive nodded fervently as he struggled for breath.

"Located where—Tal'Shira?" Tannour followed a hunch. "Khor Taran?"

Again, the Saldarian nodded. His tearing eyes begged mercy, while his body shook beneath Tannour's binding thighs. He sucked in his breath in halting gasps.

Tannour squeezed the man's jaw to make him pay attention. "Who's the target?"

His captive sucked in a shallow, shuddering breath. "…prince…"

"*Which* prince?"

He had to repeat the question three more times before the Saldarian found his answer.

"…Dannym."

A parade of curses marched silently across Tannour's tongue. How by the Two Paths had these bastards learned the prince was traveling with their company? They'd met neither hide nor hair of anyone since Trell had joined them.

Tannour considered his choices. Always the Two Great Paths spread before him: *hal'alir* with its bright boulevards and *mor'alir* with its shadowed alleyways. The moment called up ghosts of memory shouting violent threats; his ears still bled from that vitriol. Ephemeral chains bound him far more soundly than iron. The path had chosen him, but he hadn't chosen the path.

He focused back on his whimpering captive and probed him with a few more questions to uncover anything else he knew. Then gaze and decision narrowed to a point. A final thrust of his *skorpjun* blade pierced the man's heart.

The Saldarian arched in a soundless scream.

Tannour brought his lips close to the man's ear. "For speaking true, the Great God of the Black Sky shall bring you quickly to the Ghost Kings."

A flick of his wrist slipped his dagger out of the man's heart. Then he was up and running on the wind before the Saldarian's last sigh fled his chest.

❖

Trell sidestepped a thrusting blade and slammed his down over his assailant's, hoping to dislodge his hold or at least jar him off balance, but the man recovered smoothly and came at him anew.

Trell danced back along the narrow bridge of land fending off powerful blows. A luminous fog had risen, confining visibility to the man directly before him. He had no idea how many others remained.

Even with the *cortata*, he was tiring. How many had he cut down—not merely dispatched but battled and bested with determination clenched between his teeth? His lungs felt aflame and his arms oddly insubstantial, as though their muscle was formed of chaff instead of flesh. Was it nine men now that he'd killed? A dozen surely remained.

A blade flew past his nose. Trell veered back and brought up his weapon to block it. Steel clashed, scraped, separated. The river shouted a constant warning, mixing with the echoes of fighting from elsewhere in the night.

Trell's attacker pressed him in a retreat. This opponent was stronger than the others, more skilled, and far fresher for the fight than Trell. Backing across the uneven path, the prince lost his balance, and the man's weapon slashed his side.

Trell stumbled back, drawing his opponent after him. Luminous mist swirled in his wake. His side was already on fire. Somehow he managed to complete another form of the *cortata*.

The other growled and charged at him. Trell sidestepped blade and attacker. An elbow to the latter's kidney had him staggering. A punch to his jaw forced him to one knee. Trell ripped the man's sword from his hand and kicked hard. His opponent toppled backwards into the hungry river.

Trell sucked in a shallow breath. The maneuver hadn't done his side any favors. It was throbbing, protesting the least motion now, and blood was gluing his shirt to his flesh.

Of course, they rushed him then. Trell fended them off, but barely. He was stumbling as often as he was parrying their blows, and his breath came ragged when he could find it at all. There were too many cornering him, their press too tight. He couldn't keep up the *cortata*.

A blade flew towards his head. He dodged and then had to dodge again as a different razor edge speared into the space of his escape. A sword slashed for his side, and he spun out of its path while somehow blocking another. The fog grew thicker with each forceful exhale. Trell fought shadows. Only their blades held substance, shining as they flashed towards him.

He tried to find deeper breath and found instead the vice of pain. Two men pushed in on him, forcing him stumblingly back. Too late, Trell realized others were coming up behind him. He threw himself sidelong to avoid the sword thrusting for his spine.

Pain exploded violently down his injured side. He sprawled awkwardly, braced on one hand, gasping for breath while agony wracked him. He couldn't make his body move.

"Be done with it," a voice said.

Shadows resolved out of the fog. A shadowed blade lifted above him. The river screamed.

Three *thocks* drummed a guttural staccato.

Three men grunted sharp exhales.

A body landed beside Trell, convulsing, with a barbed steel star stuck in his throat. Two others fell still and staring with similar stars lodged in their foreheads.

Fighting began anew among the mist. Clashing blades and the thud of falling bodies forged a disharmonious counterpoint to the riversong. Whoever Trell's mysterious defender was, he posed threat enough to draw the rest of the Saldarians to him.

Which was fortuitous, because Trell was in no shape to threaten anyone. He maneuvered himself back against a rock and pressed a hand over the wound in his side. His stomach turned violently at the pressure of his own touch, and he sat thereafter just trying to coax breath back into his lungs.

A breeze swept through and dispelled some of the mist, enough for Trell to make out five men standing in ready crouches with their blades held defensively before them, staring at a lone figure bending over one of the fallen. They held their swords with uncertain action, as if they stood facing a demon instead of a man.

The dark figure pulled two knives out of the dead man and straightened. As he turned, Trell stared.

He's fighting them blind?

An eyeless mask wrapped the figure's head like a burial shroud.

The figure's bloodied daggers caught the moonlight—deadly, curved knives with a second, separate fang extending. He spun his blades into his grip and launched towards the remaining Saldarians.

They raised their swords, but as children feigning battle with a knight. The dark figure dodged a slashing sword, twirled and sliced the man's throat. Another whirling spin, and two more men tumbled with their throats slit open.

The last two banded together to take him the stranger. The dark figure dodged their slashing blades as if he knew the choreography of their swordplay. He spun and sidestepped and lashed out right and left. The Saldarians collapsed with strangled cries.

Trell could hardly process the scene. His defender had claimed a dozen men in a matter of minutes—and done it completely blind.

The figure spun and rushed over to him.

"A'dal!" Trell's faceless savior crouched before him. Quick motion unwove the swaths of silk masking his face, and Tannour shook his head free. "How bad is it?" He looked Trell over and then lifted pale blue eyes to meet Trell's. "Can you walk?"

Trell managed a humorless smile through gritted teeth. "Doubtful."

The Vestian considered him for a moment's concern. Then he darted soundlessly away.

Lightheadedness combined with a rapid pulse told Trell he was losing too much blood. He knew these symptoms well. Taliah had once kept him in a state of physical shock for several days, healing him just enough each time to keep him from escaping into unconsciousness. But Taliah wasn't a prudent memory to invoke just then. Trell concentrated instead on the Vestian. "How did you find me?" His voice sounded faint, even to his own ears.

Tannour was cutting one of the dead men's shirts into strips. "I have a certain skill set, Your Highness. Details are better left unspoken." He soaked the bandages in the mineral springs and returned to Trell's side. "If you will permit me...?" He held up the wrappings.

It took a grave force of will for Trell to remove the pressure of his hand from his side. Blood pulsed the moment he did so.

Tannour gently tugged at Trell's torn shirt to assess the wound beneath.

"How bad is it?" Trell cracked a grim smile. "You tell me."

"Well..." Tannour glanced up under his brows, "you'll certainly be giving Madaam Chouri a challenge. That's the path proving true." He began wrapping one of the strips around Trell's ribs.

Trell laid his swimming head back against the rock. "What of the others?"

"I wasn't with them. The fighting has stopped. That's all I know."

If he hadn't been with their company, then how did he know the fighting had stopped? That was the question that occurred to Trell, but following a lucid thread beyond this way stop of logic was impossible. He managed instead, "You saved my life, Tannour."

"Gods willing, I'm working on it, Your Highness." Tannour tied off the strip of cloth—tightly.

Trell's eyes flew to his. There might've been a little more accusation in his gaze than he'd intended.

Tannour quirked the shadow of a smile. "Can't have you bleeding out before we reach the Healer, can we?" He started binding the wound with a second strip.

Trell clenched his teeth and gazed wordlessly at the Vestian. Here was a man he'd known but a few days—a man he hardly knew at all in fact—yet who'd brooked no question of fighting over a dozen others, risking his life to save Trell's. Gratitude brought a different sort of tightness to his chest.

Tannour must've seen something of this in his gaze, for he gave a dubious grunt. "I can't say my motives are entirely altruistic, Your Highness. If something were to happen to you, I'd be the first one they looked to.

Rolan Lamodaar would never believe I didn't somehow have a hand in the act, and our *Su'a'dal* would crucify me."

"Even so, Tannour..." Trell put a *thank you* into his gaze, which Tannour acknowledged with a shadowed smile.

The Vestian tied off the last strip and sat back on his heels. "Well, that should get you to Madaam Chouri at least." He blew out his breath and looked around, but as his eyes took in the score of dead littering the shoreline, something overcame his expression. "Your Highness..." he shifted his pale blue eyes back to Trell, "in return for my aid, or simply by your willing grace, may I ask a boon of you?"

"Of course."

Tannour suddenly radiated a potent apprehension. "Would you keep this between us? My involvement, my actions here?"

Trell blinked at him. "No one is going to believe I felled over twenty men single-handedly, Tannour."

"Trust me, *A'dal,* your men will believe anything you tell them."

Trell studied the Vestian and saw real fear behind his gaze—*this* man, who'd just felled a dozen others in a matter of minutes while bound into *blindness*...yet something surely had him worried. Trell hoped he wasn't making an agreement in a moment of weakness that he would regret when clarity returned. "Very well."

Tannour let out his breath. He darted off and started retrieving his throwing stars.

"But..." Trell spoke as best he could in his condition, "when all of this is behind us, Tannour, you must explain to me why you want this secret kept..." he determinedly summoned breath and strength to his voice to finish, "and what it has to do with Loukas n'Abraxis."

Tannour's hand froze on the last of his shuriken. He lifted his eyes to meet Trell's across the night.

"Blood of Inanna!" Rolan's oath carried to them from atop the slope leading down to the river. "Raegus! The *A'dal's* over here!"

Several curses and some loud scrabbling later and the Nadoriin was standing over Trell and staring down at him with a hand gripping his scimitar and his chin braids twitching agitatedly. "Why do I keep finding you like this?"

Rolan turned his attention to Tannour, who was slowly coming back to Trell's side. "And *you.*" One of his bushy eyebrows arched for his hairline. "If it's not n'Abraxis it's you bound up in the *A'dal's* misadventures." His tone thrust a sharp hook of suspicion at both of them.

A loud disturbance in the forest quickly resolved into Raegus and

Loukas leading a mass of dark forms. Raegus hastened over to Rolan's side. "The *A'dal*—"

"Is in need of Madaam Chouri *again*," the Nadori prince remarked with considerable disapproval.

Raegus squatted beside Trell. "*Huhktu's bones*, you'll be the death of me." The moon cast dark shadows beneath the Avataren's cheekbones and made hollows of his eyes. He looked Trell over and then turned meaningfully to Rolan. "Help me get him up."

Trell lifted a hand. "I can walk—"

"And Inithiya is my lover!" Rolan barked. "Take his other side, Raegus."

As they were carefully maneuvering Trell's body into their linked arms, Raegus asked Tannour, "What *fethen* happened here?"

Tannour was restoring his head scarf to its more usual drape. "The *A'dal* was set upon by these men. I found him like this."

Raegus speared a look at Trell.

"You're saying the *A'dal* killed every one of these men?" Rolan's tone wasn't *quite* challenging Tannour's claim.

"Did I not make that clear the first time, Lamodaar?"

The others were looking around at the dead, obviously counting them, and their eyes became very wide. Loukas, on the other hand, looked ill. He murmured, "I'll go alert Madaam Chouri," and hurried off.

Rolan and Raegus got Trell situated in the basket of their arms and started up the hill after Loukas. Every step they took felt like a spear stabbing Trell's side. He sucked in shallow breaths amid a swirling haze of pain. "Where are all those magic carpets when you need one?"

Rolan angled challenge on the beam of his gaze. "I thought you were blessed of Naiadithine. How did this happen?"

"I wasn't fighting them *in* the river."

"Twenty against one..." Rolan snorted dubiously, "I think I would've figured out a way to walk on water. The gods can't help us when we don't seek their aid, *A'dal*."

"Gods are gods," Raegus grumbled. "They do as they please."

"Nay, Raegus n'Harnalt. The gods fear Fate's will the same as you and I."

"The only thing I fear is your *fethen* blasphemy." Raegus looked to the heavens as if expecting a lightning spear to come lancing towards them at any moment. His upward gaze caused him to slip on the incline.

Pain flared through Trell's entire side, freezing his breath. He fought back a powerful surge of vertigo by focusing on something else. "Tell me... of the men."

"You'll be proud of them, *A'dal*," Rolan guided them beneath a splay of overhanging limbs. "They fought well beneath Inanna's eye."

"Beneath *Her grace*," Raegus corrected with a pointed glare at Rolan. "Ha'viv knows how those bastards got so close without our sentries spotting their approach—"

"They had a wielder helping them," Tannour murmured from somewhere beyond Trell's view. "He guided them into camp by some arcane means."

Raegus gave a deprecating grunt. "That would explain it." To Trell, he answered, "Madaam Chouri had some gashes to mend—none so marked as yours, *A'dal*—and a few burns, some cracked ribs…Nyongo dislocated his shoulder taking down four of them. I vow, it was almost a pleasure to see those Saldarian bastards felled after the joyless chase they've given us."

"How many did we lose?"

"Eleven," Raegus answered soberly, "but considering the Saldarian numbers…"

"If they'd caught us unawares, as they intended," Rolan remarked, "they might've stabbed us all in our sleep and only Ha'viv would be the wiser, but we were ready when they came at us." He cast a voluminous look at Trell. "You saved many lives tonight, *A'dal*."

Except the eleven that he hadn't.

Trell let out a measured exhale. "We must honor our dead—and honor the Goddess Naiadithine," he managed faintly. "Our gratitude belongs to her. She warned me of the attack."

Both Raegus and Rolan stared at him at this. Thankfully they reached camp before either of them could question him further on exactly how conversant he was with the Seventeen Gods.

Madaam Chouri was a round woman with greying hair and a propensity for patterned headscarves that always seemed to match her bright blue eyes. She was waiting for Trell outside his tent and held back the flaps for their entrance.

"Bring him in, bring him in." She directed Rolan and Raegus through one of the draped partitions to where someone—probably Rami—had set up a cot. The two men took great care in laying Trell upon it. Even so, he held his jaw clenched tightly the while.

"*Balé*, now away." Madaam Chouri waved them off. "Loukas n'Abraxis, come hither…" Loukas moved out of a shadowed corner, and the Healer started in with a list of orders for him.

Tannour entered in the middle of this and took up the position Loukas had just vacated. They patently ignored one another.

"*A'dal!*" Rami appeared in the opening and rushed quickly to Trell's side. "Please, *Sidi*, you cannot die—"

"Gods be deaf, child!" Madaam Chouri scourged him with a glare.

Rami fell to his knees beside Trell's cot. "If you die, I'll have to go back to serving the old *A'dal*—"

"Eat your words, boy." Raegus glowered at him.

"—who eats too many onions and then farts all the night." Rami cast Raegus a look of abject indignation. "He fills the tent with fumes that make me fear even to light a candle. Every morning I must air the canvases before packing the tent away." He gripped the edge of Trell's cot and looked entreatingly to him. "You wouldn't wish this punishment upon me, would you, *Sidi*? I've served you well, haven't I?"

Madaam Chouri grabbed Rami's ear and encouraged him elsewhere. "Give the *A'dal* some room to breathe, child."

Rami retreated out of reach of her pinching fingers. "He doesn't need room, Madaam Chouri. He needs a stiff drink. My father is always saying this is the solution to all ills—camel bites, overcooked stew, shrewish women who talk too much, impudent boys who talk even more…" he sighed. "It is a long list."

Trell observed the boy fondly, though he only managed a smile by way of a pained exhale. "With Madaam's help, I hope to make it through, Rami."

"I will pray to the Seventeen for you, *A'dal*."

"*Balé*, child. Go say your prayers elsewhere." Madaam Chouri pulled up a stool at Trell's side and started cutting away Tannour's makeshift bandage. She looked up under her brows at Loukas. "I must clean the wound before I heal it. Bring me the hot water, Loukas."

He did so, and she dipped a cloth into the steaming bowl and began soaking Trell's wound with a different sort of heat. Trell clenched his teeth and tried to imagine he was back at the *sa'reyth*, stretched out in bed beside Alyneri—that is until Rolan's words recalled him to the pain of the moment.

"Valeri," the Nadoriin's tone wasn't *entirely* judgmental, "tell the *A'dal* what you learned on your little scouting foray."

"It had better have been fruitful," Raegus added in a tone that *was* entirely judgmental, "since we stood alone against them, sorely missing your sword. Even n'Abraxis pitched in when you were nowhere to be found—surprised us all out of our *fethen* shorts."

Tannour looked at Loukas like a black stain upon his honor but he answered coolly, "They came for the *A'dal*."

Raegus blew out his breath. "How in Inanna's name did the bastards even know His Highness was traveling with us?"

Rolan muttered, "I thought sure this was the same Saldarian crew we'd been chasing."

"It doubtless was," Tannour said. "They've been colluding with a wielder out of Khor Taran. The larger force came as distraction, while the twenty men the *A'dal* slew were on a special mission to find and assassinate His Highness. I saw them break away from the main host, but I had no idea at the time that they were hunting the *A'dal*."

Raegus gave an even more colorful curse than usual.

"So how *did* they know His Highness was traveling with us?" Rolan wanted to know.

"I wondered the same thing. The man I questioned could only tell me that they were sent here by a Shamshir'im wielder who's lording over Khor Taran."

Khor Taran…

Why it clicked only then, Trell couldn't say, but he immediately knew the true source of their troubles: *Viernan hal'Jaitar.*

Consul to Radov, wielder of merit, master of the Shamshir'im—he might've heard only *Khor Taran, Shamshir'im* and *wielder* and could've put it all together.

Trell clenched his jaw and closed his eyes, stung by the lash of self-reproach. He never should've announced his true name to the company. There hadn't been any need for it, just the hubris of candor when a cautious reserve would've served everyone better. Now he looked upon that choice and tasted bile.

Eleven lives lost for the luxury of truth, for his lack of foresight—*thirteen hells*, he hadn't even *considered* the potential consequences! It was inexcusable.

Somehow Viernan hal'Jaitar had gotten word of his presence within the company. It almost didn't matter how the wielder had learned of it. It was Trell's doing, through and through. And once the wielder had learned of Trell's location, he'd started working to thwart Trell's obvious aims—Raine's truth, Trell had made it easy for him!

Even more galling to his conscience, his intuition had hinted at a spy in the company from the outset. Why hadn't he followed a path of logic backwards from that observation to conclude who the spy might be working *for*?

Gods above, he deserved far worse than he'd gotten…and those eleven men far better than he'd delivered them. Poor victims of his misjudgment—how naïve he'd been!

Trell recalled his conversation with an ailing Raegus and saw portent veritably shouting his name, yet he'd been deaf to its warnings. And now *eleven men* had lost their lives because of his own misguided sense of invincibility. This truth cut deeper than the wound burning his side.

Madaam Chouri finally lifted the last piece of the bandage from Trell's wound. He felt a tug, and then the draining warmth of blood spilling free. She pressed a dressing over his wound and looked to Rami. "Make yourself useful for more than noise, child, and fetch that bottle and the honey beside it."

He rushed to retrieve said items from a near table. As he walked back across the room, he sniffed at the bottle and made a face. "Are you sure this is fit for our *A'dal*, Madaam Chouri?"

"Calendula, chamomile and garlic for cleaning, bird pepper to thicken the blood, juniper, lavender and honey for healing. A potent mixture." She took the bottle from Rami and held it close to Trell's wound. "Are you ready, *A'dal*? Perhaps you'd like that stiff drink the boy spoke of first?"

"I'll be fine, Madaam Chouri. Do what you must."

"Loukas," she lifted her gaze to him, "hold the *A'dal's* shoulders and keep him still. This is going to burn—there's no way around it."

Loukas pressed down on Trell's shoulders. As his eyes met Trell's, his anguished look said clearly, *I should've been there for you.*

Then Madaam Chouri poured the fiery astringent over his wound and Trell was swallowing a muffled cry. He closed his eyes and thrust his head back against the cot, listening to the roar of his heart as she continued pouring liquid fire into his flesh. Would that her treatment could cure him of misjudgment!

While Trell was trying not to pass out, the Healer said, "Do you see how quickly the bleeding stops, child? That's the bird pepper doing its work." She dabbed around the wound with a damp cloth.

Trell eventually found his breath again and opened his eyes. Loukas was still standing over him, still pressing down on his shoulders, still looking tormented. Trell met his gaze and managed, "I'm all right," yet the words came out strained, regretful in a way he hadn't intended.

Loukas released him, but his eyes kept straying to Trell's side, and each time he looked, his expression became more twisted.

"The honey now, Rami." Madaam Chouri held out her hand for the jar and proceeded to coax the thick fluid slowly and liberally into Trell's wound. Then followed new bandages, expertly applied. Finally she washed her hands and sent Rami away with the bowls and other things. Her gaze found Trell's again. "That will keep the fever off until my Healing can take its full effect."

Trell swallowed, nodded. "Thank you, Madaam Chouri."

Her blue eyes gazed upon him with concern and apology. "I would I had the Lady Jaya's power to Heal you overnight."

"I'm grateful for your aid in any capacity."

"As I am to Jai'Gar for the grace of His Healing power. If you're ready, we'll begin that process now." She settled her hands on Trell's head and closed her eyes.

"Madaam Chouri." Trell's tone summoned her gaze back to his. "You should know, for several months I was tortured by a *mor'alir* Adept."

Into the startled silence following this pronouncement, Raegus and Rolan exchanged a glance, Loukas hissed a muted oath, and Rami murmured a prayer. Everyone stared at Trell, but no one stared harder than Tannour.

"You'll find the scars of those months upon my life pattern." Trell held the Healer's gaze soberly. "I just didn't want you to be shocked when you came across them."

Madaam Chouri's brows lifted so high they vanished beneath her headscarf. She sat back to gaze wonderingly at him. "Only a Healer could know such things. How can you?"

A smile softened Trell's strained expression. "Because I'm bound to one."

Rolan barked a disbelieving oath. "Bound to an Adept! You never cease to amaze, *A'dal*. Blessed of a goddess, confidant of dragons—you couldn't invent a better story if you'd all the genius of the Immortal Bard himself."

Raegus shook his head and pointed at Trell. "Remember what I said about that sheikdom." Then he clapped Rolan on the shoulder and encouraged him towards the partition. "Let the Healer do her work. Valeri, n'Abraxis—both of you, out."

Loukas squared his shoulders. "I'm staying."

Raegus glared at him. Then he shifted his glare pointedly to Tannour, who was standing in the corner.

Tannour crossed his arms. "If n'Abraxis stays, I stay."

Raegus's hands twitched at his sides as if itching to give both of them a good paddling with the flat of his blade.

"Let them stay." Trell didn't want to be the cause of more friction between the two men, or provide fodder for whatever feud was already driving them.

"There," Rolan tugged on Raegus's arm, "the *A'dal* has spoken. Let's share a drink to the gods, you and I. Much better use of your arm than the wasted effort of trying to flog insubordination out of that pair."

"Fine." Raegus gripped the hilt of his sword as if it was a lightning rod for his frustration. "You two can guard the *A'dal* for the rest of the night."

"That's the plan," Tannour remarked coolly.

Trell heard Raegus growl to Rolan as they were departing, "Will *anyone* miss him if I turn him in for the bounty on his insolent head? Surely I've earned it…"

Then Madaam Chouri placed her hands on Trell again, and he felt *elae's* warmth channeling into him. A lulling sleep settled over him, encouraged by the tingling in his side and Trell surrendered to her ministrations.

FIFTY-TWO

*"He endeavors to know absolutely nothing about
as many things as possible."*

—Cassius of Rogue, on Fynnlar val Lorian

"THIS ISN'T EXACTLY inspiring confidence." Alyneri tightened her grip on Carian's right shoulder. All she could see while standing upon the Pattern of the World were the blurred outlines of indistinct shapes, but she could feel the kinetic current sawing through her readily enough.

"Torture Tuesdays," Fynn grumbled from Carian's left.

Carian grunted. "I've got it all in hand. Don't you worry that pretty little head of yours, Princess."

"It's not my head, it's my arse," Fynn complained.

The pirate took Fynn's hand from his left shoulder and Alyneri's from his right, and moved his two 'passengers' around to stand in front of him. "Just a little further now…and here we are. Off you go…"

Alyneri stepped off the node into a wide courtyard lined in climbing roses. "Oh, how lovely." She smiled at all the bright pink flowers.

Arriving beside her, Fynn looked around, scrubbing at his arse. That is, until a guard stepped out from behind a trellis and took him roughly by one arm.

Alyneri drew up stiffly. "Kindly unhand Lord Fynnlar val Lorian!"

Her tone, if not her affronted glare, drove the guard into indecision. He released Fynn but kept a hand on his sword while he looked them up and down. "Which is the Espial among you?"

Fynn indignantly brushed at the sleeve of his coat. "Grammatically that should be '*who* is—"

"*I* am, mate." Carian sauntered off the node jingling the coins in his pockets.

The guard's gaze tightened on the pirate while his hand tightened on his sword. "Show me your ring."

"You must be blind, man." Carian extended both of his hands, which were so covered in rings that Alyneri could barely distinguish his fingers beneath the jewels and gold. "Come closer then, my handsome. Have a look-see."

The guard studied him like a shopkeeper eyeing a dirty street child. He warily inched closer—

The pirate grabbed him around the neck and dragged him across the node, choking off the guard's half-uttered yelp as they vanished.

Alyneri turned an accusing stare on Fynn.

He raised both hands. "I had nothing to do with it this time."

The sound of running feet turned them both around.

Fynn drew his sword and placed himself in front of Alyneri just as four armed men came rushing into the nodecourt. He shot her a bemused look over his shoulder. "Did they have a bell on that other guy, or…?"

Carian reappeared behind them, sans guard, saw the new guards and opened his arms beneath a saucy grin. "Now, now, poppets, I think we started off on the wrong foot—"

Abruptly he drew his cutlasses and laid out two guards before they realized his intention. The remaining two backed away with their swords upraised, but they looked very uncertain about using them.

Carian pinned both of his blades together beneath one arm, pulled a leather pouch from within his vest and began rolling himself a smoke. "Now, you both look like bright mice—brighter at least than these bilge rats here," and he kicked at one of the fallen, eliciting a low moan. "I've just claimed them in the name of the Admiral of the Nodefinder Rebellion. If you don't want your blood joinin' theirs in a pretty mosaic on these here stones, you run back to Big Rat Niko and tell him the rebellion controls this node now, like the other nodes we've taken from him."

Carian puffed his roll alight via some means Alyneri couldn't discern and exhaled a cloud of smoke in the guards' direction. "You got all that?"

They nodded vigorously.

The pirate nodded towards the exit.

They bolted. The two fallen men helped each other up and hobbled after them.

Carian clenched his smoke between his teeth and sheathed his cutlasses.

"See?" He grinned at Alyneri around the smoking weed. "Told you I had it all in hand."

Fynn glowered at him. "Just go get the coach, will you?"

Carian gave him a saucy salute and strolled back across the node to retrieve their carriage and driver, who was waiting at the other end of the node until Carian had 'cleared' the path for travel.

Alyneri meanwhile regarded Fynnlar beneath an arched brow. "Remind me again why we're doing this."

"Politics." He shoved his sword back into its scabbard.

"I misspoke. Remind me again why *I'm* doing this."

Fynn gave her a wan smile. "Benevolence?"

"Benevolence feels strangely unscrupulous."

"I'll tell you what's unscrupulous." He waved emphatically towards the node. "All of this in and out, off and on, climb-up-climb-down, now-it's-time-to-fight-again-Fynnlar nonsense. When's a bloody man supposed to sleep?"

The horses came clomping across the node, so Alyneri and Fynn moved out of the way to make room for the animals, coach and Carian, who was hanging off the step.

The pirate jumped down and opened the door as the coach swayed to a stop. "Your Grace." He gave Alyneri a surprisingly debonair bow.

"Captain vran Lea." She eyed him circumspectly as she climbed back into the carriage.

Fynn followed after her, grumbling, "I thought the point of hiring a coach was to let a man sleep, vran Lea." He threw himself onto the seat across from Alyneri. "You make me pay to hire the damned thing, but I might as well have been riding my own bloody horse for all the rest I've gotten."

The pirate swung inside and onto the seat next to Fynn. He rapped on the partition for the driver. The coach started off with a lurch and a sway.

"The sooner you secure Cassius's participation for the rebellion, Fynnlar, the easier our return." Carian opened a window and blew smoke in its general direction—mainly because Alyneri was glaring pointedly at him to do so. "This journey would've been a lot smoother if we could've used Cassius's nodes to get to his estate."

"Yeah, and whose fault is that?" Fynn propped his feet on Alyneri's seat, crossed his arms and closed his eyes.

She pushed his boots off. They hit the floor in a thump of heels. It had become a constant battle of diligence for her, keeping her cushion free of dusty boots.

Fynn adjusted himself into the corner.

Carian grinned and blew smoke towards the window.

Alyneri sighed.

The driver continued driving.

"Remind me again why I agreed to do this?" Alyneri leaned closer to her window to better see the countryside passing by. Veneisea's Rogue Valley was known for its beauty, and while she highly doubted this excursion with Fynn and Carian would prove the best use of her time, she couldn't complain about the scenery.

She'd gotten to see much of the countryside, in fact, since Carian could only use the nodes to get them as far as Veneisea. He claimed that was as close to Cassius's estate as he dared, being that he wasn't currently in Cassius of Rogue's good graces. Fynnlar had pointed out that Carian had never gained Cassius's good graces, in reply to which the pirate had launched into a lewd exploration of possible ways that Fynn had acquired Cassius's 'graces'…and the conversation had devolved from there. Alyneri had been ignoring them for most of the drive.

Fynn roused himself to answer, "Niko's mandate means a lot of money for the vested interests, Your Grace—loads of money to the Nodefinder's Guild." He sounded uncharacteristically sedate now that they were closing in on Cassius's estate. He kept staring out the opposite window with his unruly dark hair shadowing his eyes. "But entire fortunes lost by merchants who can't afford Guild rates to hire ringed Espials to move their wares; livelihoods lost by Nodefinders who can no longer make a living plying their Maker-given trade." He aimed a sidelong look at her. "The rebellion aims to circumvent all that."

"Think of it like a game of Shari." Carian pushed hands behind his head and propped his boots on Alyneri's seat. "You're trying to not only take your opponent's stones but also ensure your own stones occupy the majority of the board."

"Yes, I understand that part." Alyneri pushed the pirate's boots off her cushion. "But how does Cassius of Rogue fit into it?"

"Well, see—" Carian reached for his pouch of tobacco.

"I said no more of that in here." Alyneri gave him an uncompromising look. "Not if you want my assistance with this charade, or whatever wool you're planning to pull over this poor Cassius person's eyes."

Carian barked a laugh. "The man's more of a pirate than Fynn and me combined, Princess."

"Cassius of Rogue runs his own mini-guild, Your Grace." Fynn rested his chin glumly on his hand. Alyneri couldn't imagine why he was so morose except to suppose it was because he didn't have any more wine. "If the rebellion can gain the use of his network of nodes, our Nodefinders can travel up and down the Middle Kingdoms, avoiding Niko's goons completely, and the continental commerce can carry on unimpeded."

Alyneri shifted her gaze between the two of them. "The surprising altruism in all of this aside, it still doesn't explain why you needed *me*."

Carian gave Fynn one of those *Go on, tell her* kind of grins.

Fynn glowered at him. Then he turned and glowered out the window. "Cassius has a soft spot for Healers. We thought you could, you know… butter him up a bit."

Alyneri arched a mistrustful brow. "Just how are you expecting me to *butter him up*, my lord?"

"Just…you know…" Fynn winced a little, "try to be *nice* to him."

"Nice." Her tone was somewhat lacking for warmth.

Carian grinned at her. "Some people do manage it, Princess."

She speared a look at him. "I'm perfectly capable of being nice to those deserving of…" she waved for a word, found nothing better, "niceness."

The pirate propped his feet on her seat again. "He won't make it easy for you."

Alyneri shoved his boots back onto the floor.

"The man's only profession is tormenting people," Fynn muttered. "He's richer than the Empress and has all the scruples of a Dane in raiding season."

Their coach trundled between a pair of wrought-iron gates and plunged into the darkness of a tunnel beneath the wall. Alyneri felt a moment of disorientation as the coach jolted in the darkness, and then they emerged onto a promenade lined in cherry trees.

After an impressively long drive, the coach pulled to a halt before a mansion. Carian clambered out and started rolling himself a smoke. A morose Fynnlar stepped down and helped Alyneri outside into a bright afternoon.

"Ah, Lord Fynnlar!" A liveried manservant with the nut-brown coloring and rounded nose of a Bemothi came down the steps from the mansion. "I didn't recognize your coach at first. My master has been eagerly anticipating your visit." His gaze shifted to Alyneri. "And who's this, another of your—"

"*No*, she's not one of them." Fynn waved the man irritably away. His mood seemed only to have blackened since turning onto the drive.

The pirate exhaled a bluish cloud from where he was leaning against the coach. "This is Alyneri d'Giverny, Duchess of Aracine, mate."

"Ah, Your Grace, you honor us with your visit. Please follow me at your convenience." He snapped his fingers at a pair of grooms, who rushed over and started unloading their baggage from the back of the coach.

As Alyneri was making to follow the manservant, Fynn said in a low voice, "I would advise Your Grace to be careful what you share with Cassius.

Give him an inch and he'll have you girded up by the balls, or..." he frowned at his choice of phrase, "well, you know."

"He doesn't much stand on ceremony," Carian said by way of agreement, his words floating to her out of the bluish haze surrounding his head, "and he ain't easy to read."

Fynn grunted. "He'll take your measure in a glance and thereafter try to throw you from your horse."

Carian flicked ash from his smoke. "And never, ever make a bet with him."

Alyneri shifted a humorous gaze between them both. "He sounds so familiar somehow." She wondered why they were both just standing there. "Aren't you coming inside?"

Carian eyed the steward who was waiting by the door. "In a minute."

The man bowed apologetically. "My master prefers that the pirate should smoke outside of the mansion, Your Grace."

"Very well." Alyneri headed up the steps and inside, through an impressive three-story foyer into—

Well...it wasn't the largest party she'd ever seen, but it might've been the most diverse.

Alyneri felt transported back to Rethynnea's famous Thoroughfare as she stood beneath the carved marble archway. Looking down a long gallery, she saw the colorful cloth of multiple nationalities and heard the rhythmic cadence of multiple languages being spoken in concert. "It appears your master is hosting an afternoon party." Alyneri smiled at the manservant beside her. "I hope we're not interrupting."

"Not at all. Please make yourself at home. I'll let him know you've arrived."

The moment he left, a steward came over bearing a tray of bubbling wine. Alyneri accepted a glass of the golden liquid, feeling slightly out of place and a bit underdressed. Fynn had told her they'd be traveling to Veneisea, so she'd donned a bustled silk dress and jacket appropriate to that kingdom's customs, but she might've arrived in one of her desert gowns and felt equally at ease. She would've blended in with several honey-haired Avataren women who were strolling the gallery sipping Cassius's golden wine.

Elsewhere, she saw pale and powdered Veneisean high-born dressed in elaborate lace and satin speaking with golden skinned Bemothi in colorful silk kurtas. Khurds in jeweled turbans shared couches with dark-eyed Nadoriin, the latter's heads and shoulders draped in patterned *keffiyehs*—the two kingdoms' frictions apparently overlooked for the chance to converse in their own language.

And she saw other races less familiar to her but equally as

distinctive—long-haired, blonde men in black coats with silver rings piercing noses and brows lounged beside women wrapped in tangerine gauze like delicate confections; warrior-types wearing sleeveless leather vests to better display the tattoos decorating their muscular arms strolled beside almond-eyed women in platform shoes and satin gowns nearly too tight to walk in; Highlanders in plaid kilts conversed with dark-eyed men with moustaches that flared as widely as the hems of their coats…the list seemed endless.

As did the supply of golden wine, for nearly everyone held a glass.

As she drank her own, it surprised her that she could feel so… comfortable, so sure of herself. Confident, even—*her*, Alyneri, only daughter of the striking Melisande d'Giverny, ever the subject of gossip and criticism, ostracized and generally unwelcome among other ladies of Dannym's court…

Yet now, none of that mattered.

Now she was a Healer learning to Pattern, *elae*-bound to Prince Trell val Lorian, sword-sister of a zanthyr, a princess of Kandori and a descendant of an immortal *drachwyr*. What carping criticism could possibly cloud her truth now?

As she pondered the shifts in her own self-image, Alyneri recognized that this newfound confidence stemmed in no small part from her training with Vaile. What was it about being physically strong that made her feel as though she had more agency in her own life?

Certainly she felt more secure knowing she could reach Trell in any moment via their binding, and Vaile also, via the bonded dagger the zanthyr had given her, which she wore in a hidden sheath strapped to her calf. But it wasn't *having* the dagger that made her feel secure; it was *knowing how to use it*, knowing that she could defend herself and those she loved. For the first time since her mother died, Alyneri felt like her life was truly her own.

"It is quite the congregation, is it not?"

Alyneri turned to see a man wearing a wide-brimmed, aubergine hat plumed with ostrich feathers coming up beside her. He was tall enough that his hat might've equally shaded her face from the sun. His long velvet coat, blood-red with a fox fur collar, hung open over a white shirt unbuttoned to his waist, where leather pants hugged his hips and muscular thighs. The shirt stood out brightly against his chocolate skin.

The contrast of light and dark continued in his expression, which seemed to her both whimsical and slightly challenging, an enigmatic smile enhanced by a truthreader's candid gaze. And his crystalline eyes amid his chocolate skin were as dazzling as the large diamond studding his ear. He lifted his glass to her but nodded towards the assemblage. "Rather remarkable, when you think upon it."

Alyneri thought *he* was rather remarkable. Then she wondered if he'd caught her thought. His secretive smile certainly seemed to hint of that he had.

She looked back to the gallery. "I was reminded at first of Rethynnea."

"A fair comparison." He sipped his wine while he surveyed the guests. Two Sormitáge rings glinted on his ring finger, and another banded his pointer finger. Becoming a stacked truthreader *and* a ringed Espial was no small accomplishment. "Rethynnea plays host to outcasts and pirates, expatriates, freedom-seekers, freedom fighters…you might say it harbors a special strain of humanity."

She cast him a puzzled look. "I'm not sure I understand the comparison you make."

He nodded to the guests. "They've come here because all other avenues are closed to them. If you will permit my presumption, I would hazard to say you look across this gathering and see Nadoriin, Avataren, Bemothi. *I* see Nodefinders blocked from using their innate gifts, Healers fleeing Eastern prejudices, Adepts at odds with their various guilds, merchants seeking means of conveying their…unique…wares outside the auspices of port authorities and tax collectors."

"So this isn't a fête?"

He smiled, shrugged. "I wouldn't go so far as to say that. It's a fête comprised of uninvited guests. A party of convenience, you might say; a neutral gathering of the like-minded and equally malcontent. A place for forming mutual alliance against oppression."

"*Oppression*." She smiled dryly. "Something tells me you and I construe this word differently."

He looked her over speculatively. Then he smiled. "Let me show you something." He led on without waiting for her accord. Being a truthreader, perhaps he already knew she would follow.

And she did, smiling beneath a wondering gaze as she trailed behind his flamboyant hat with its ostrich feathers beckoning like a lady waving a kerchief out the rear window of a coach.

The feathers drew Alyneri outside where more guests lounged, gamed or strolled the extensive grounds. On the terrace, servants were clearing away the remains of high tea. The late afternoon sun had fallen behind the mansion and was casting the gardens in shadow, but the air beyond the mansion's shade appeared very bright. The colorful clothing of diverse races dotted the extensive grounds. For a gathering that wasn't a fête, it certainly looked like one.

"All of these people came here unbidden?"

Strolling beside her, he waggled a hand. "With a few exceptions."

"They're all welcomed generously, it would appear."

"Our host looks upon each of his guests as potential business associates. A little wining and dining goes a long way in establishing the necessary rapport."

"Drunken guests make poor negotiators."

He flashed a smile of perfect white teeth, very bright against his ebony skin. "That assessment rather depends upon which side of the negotiating table you're sitting on."

"So our host is less about altruism than opportunism?" Alyneri inquired, smiling.

"Our host is a business man. He spent two lifetimes acquiring wealth—not merely in gold but in location. His nodes are beyond the reach of kings or guilds." He added with a wink, "He is his own vested interest."

A servant approached holding a box and two goblets on a silver tray. Alyneri's flamboyant guide set down his empty goblet and opened the box, out of which he drew a *siqaret*, but one unlike any Alyneri had ever seen. Expertly rolled in black paper and printed all over with gold patterns, it had an alien elegance to it.

He cast her an inquiring look. "Will you smoke?"

"No, thank you."

"I thought not—and especially not these." He placed it to his lips and lit it with a thought—Alyneri perceived the slightest flare on the currents—and when he inhaled, the gold patterns flared to life all the way back to the gold-wrapped filter. He exhaled pale smoke scented with cloves and some...*other* herb that she couldn't place, but which made her heart flutter uncertainly.

He handed her a fresh goblet from the steward's tray and took the other for himself, then motioned them along the terrace once more. They passed two Veneisean women napping on lounge chairs and two men, presumably their counterparts, hunched over a King's game, powdered wigs askew and silk coats unbuttoned. Both men were scowling at the board. So many people who'd apparently come to Cassius of Rogue with pressing business...but if they'd come on business, why were they still there, lounging about?

Alyneri shook her head and muttered, more to herself than to him, "What are they all still doing here?"

He surveyed the scene as if to view it through her perspective. "Our host is a busy man. Some of his guests wait to make their proposals. Others await his decision. He has many proposals to consider." He drew upon his *siqaret*, gold patterns flaring. "Some decisions affect more than just himself. Some negotiations affect other negotiations already underway. Sometimes deals must be re-negotiated, based on new deals. He's found it efficacious to encourage involved parties to remain and partake of his hospitality until all related negotiations are concluded." He turned her a pointed smile. "He didn't get this far by carelessly making enemies at every turn."

No, I'm sure you didn't.

If Cassius heard this thought of hers, he gave no indication of it, but merely waved with his *siqaret*. "This is not to say he is universally adored. That would be asking too much. A hawk doesn't adore the huntmaster, nor a kenneled wolf its keeper. And his fees can be exorbitant," he gave her a knowledgeable nod to this truth, "but then, sometimes, so are the profits that his business partners stand to gain through the use of his network."

She smiled in return. "So you make your home in Veneisea, but you don't exactly espouse the Virtues?"

"You speak, of course, of our *host*."

When Alyneri merely held his gaze, he exhaled. "I find it so much more edifying to talk about myself in the third person." He took a long draw from his *siqaret,* those gold patterns burning all the while, though never seeming to burn up, and let the smoke filter up lazily around his head.

"What were we speaking of? Ah, yes, the Virtues…" he cast her a sagacious eye. "I don't think the Veneiseans aspire to emulate the Virtues so much as hide behind them. They're convenient buffers against inconvenient obstacles like morality and conscience. Veneiseans hang the Virtues as fenders along the beam of their ships and sail on past conscience's quay without giving it a second glance."

"Such an environment would seem suitable to your purposes, if you'll forgive my saying."

"On the contrary, your candor is refreshing, Your Grace." He waved airily. "I prefer a nation of hypocrites, to be honest. The Veneiseans can be depended upon to flagrantly violate any virtue they profess to follow, and vilify anyone whose vices resemble the slightest shadow of their own. Yet… imagine how tedious life would be if everyone practiced what they preached. Who would ever find anything to gossip about?"

Alyneri blinked at him. Did he really believe the things he was saying? He was a truthreader, so he couldn't lie, yet some of his opinions were startling, to say the least.

She understood now what Carian had meant when he said Cassius was hard to read. It was as if he spoke in mirrors, mercuric views espoused from a façade that flashed with mirrored sides. Equally depthful and shallow, philosophical and mundane, flamboyant and pragmatic…the man was a consistent paradox.

And Alyneri had no doubt that her host had worked as diligently upon crafting this illusion of himself as he had upon honing his craft—truthreaders were excellent, natural illusionists, after all—and as he had upon building his network of nodes.

They turned a corner at the terrace's end and walked to a balcony overlooking—well, they must've been facing east, from the direction of the sun, and yet…

A boxwood maze embroidered the sloping hill, beyond which lay a stripe of forest and then a deep valley that looked *nothing* like the one she'd traveled through to get there. Mountains jutted in the distance, snowcapped and forbidding.

Alyneri looked swiftly to him. "When did we cross a node?"

"The tunnel beneath my walls."

Alyneri felt pricked by paradoxes again. "So we're not even *in* Veneisea?"

He gave her another of his enigmatic smiles, full of sage wisdom, hinting of mischief. "Well, the *node* is. But look there, Your Grace." He directed her attention to the vista. "Do you know what you look upon when you gaze across that valley?"

"Other than surprise?"

A half-smile tugged at his lips. "That," and he pointed with his *siqaret*, "is the Seam."

"Which is?"

Another draw, another flare of intoxicating smoke. Alyneri tried to step aside from its path. She was starting to feel slightly lightheaded just breathing in the fringes of it. What must it be doing to him?

"The Seam is one of Alorin's wonders—nodes aligned thick as a lode of gold, strung all through this valley. So many that all of them haven't even been mapped."

Alyneri thought of the hovering sphere in the rebellion's headquarters, which she'd seen so many times. The node points on the world grid were aligned geometrically. What he was describing didn't seem possible.

"You're right. It's quite impossible," he nodded to her unspoken thought, "which is why it's held my curiosity for decades."

"And why you built your home overlooking it?" She arched an inquiring brow. "For study?"

"If by study, you mean so he can constantly find new ways to exploit it," came Carian's voice from behind her, "then yeah. Study away, mate."

"Ah, Carian, Fynnlar." Cassius turned with a smile that seemed more hungry than amiable. "I wondered where you two had wandered off to. My steward alerted me to Her Grace's honoring presence but barely mentioned yours."

"That's because the bastard locked us out of the house." Fynn scowled in the steward's generally assumed direction. "We had to walk all the way around the gardens to find a way inside."

"My staff well know I do not associate with pirates," Cassius said with stern look at Carian.

"Maybe not of the *genuine* variety." Carian's smoke roll bobbed on his lips, shedding ash on his vest.

"Nor do I appreciate that foul-smelling weed of yours, vran Lea."

"The pleasing aroma adds to the experience." Carian plucked his smoke from his lips and shoved the burning stub towards Cassius. "And tabac don't mess with your head like that alien stuff you're so addicted to."

"Contraband *siqarets* from Eltanin." Fynn spoke the words with reverent awe. "One case of those things sold on the black market and I could buy a nice island in the Palma Lai archipelago, build a mansion for myself and my wine-conjuring dragon…" he swayed slightly on his feet, perhaps beneath the heady weight of this contemplation.

Cassius snapped for a servant, who rushed out of the shadows immediately. "Get Lord Fynnlar some wine. Can you not see he's nearly falling down with sobriety?"

The servant bobbed a bow and rushed off.

"I hope he returns with two goblets on that platter, mate," Carian said.

Alyneri handed the pirate her glass while simultaneously waving off the smoke from Cassius's *siqaret*. "I've never heard of Eltanin. Is it a city?"

"That's gratitude for you." Fynn sullenly eyed Alyneri's goblet, now in Carian's hand.

"Eltanin is another realm, Princess." Carian saluted with Alyneri's wine and tossed back a large swallow. "One of the few realms that welcomes intrepid Nodefinders to its shores—so long as they're willing to ply its wares to the highest bidder elsewhere in the Thousand Realms."

Alyneri's head was starting to spin a little—from the wine, Cassius's drugged smoke or all the startling information, she couldn't quite say. "But I thought…isn't it forbidden to travel between the realms?"

Carian grinned. "Yup."

"And aren't you imprisoned or executed if ever caught?"

"Yup."

"But that's where the real money is, Your Grace." Fynn sighed despondently. "Why couldn't I have been born a Nodefinder—or at least why couldn't one of my cousins have the talent? I might've exploited them so profitably…" his eyes strayed longingly after the vanished servant. "Well, maybe not Sebastian, but the *other* two—"

Carian blew a smoke ring at Cassius. "It's how *this* one made his fortune, sure as silver."

Cassius flashed his brilliant white smile. "The Guild has never been able to prove that."

"Because you're not one of the brethren." Carian looked him over inhospitably. "You're a bloody imposter-truthreader-wielder-I-don't-*know*-what."

"Don't be fooled by the colorless eyes, Your Grace," Fynn grumbled. "Cassius is a rogue from balls to bones."

"A rogue whose services you seem rather desperate to employ, Fynnlar." Cassius strode over to a grouping of couches, flung his hat onto a table, then seated himself and extended both arms along the cushioned back. His *siqaret*, with its black wrapper and glowing golden patterns, emitted a thin trail of smoke from between his fingers. It hadn't burned down even a fraction.

Carian followed after him. "Mate, you know Niko's edict is going to inconvenience you sooner or later—probably sooner, the way he's running things." He flopped onto a couch across from Cassius. "The long arm of Niko's greed won't long ignore the ripe pluckings of your network."

Cassius took a draw on his *siqaret*, considering Carian the while. "But your offer is laughable." He blew out pale smoke. "Even charity has its cost."

"No good deed goes unpunished." Fynn fell into an armchair and rolled his head around on the cushioned back. "That's why I try to stay away from them—except on Tuesdays."

Alyneri seated herself across from Cassius. "How did you and Lord Fynnlar meet?" She had the sneaking suspicion that Fynn had once been one of Cassius's 'guests.'

"Your instincts guide you well, Your Grace." Cassius drew deeply of his *siqaret*. "Fynnlar and I go way back—how long ago was it now that you first came to me?"

Fynn harrumphed. "Can anyone really remember past last week?"

Alyneri smiled. "Last week seems a generous estimate for you, my lord."

"You support my point exactly, Your Grace."

Cassius took another draw. "Seven years and several ventures later, here we are." His colorless eyes observed Fynnlar as if knowing intimately of his measure, "two peas in a lucrative pod."

"You and I have different ideas of lucrative," Fynn grumbled.

Alyneri clasped fingers around her knee. "I'm so interested in hearing about Lord Fynnlar's business dealings. None of us knew he'd ever held any sort of gainful employment."

Carian snorted.

Cassius still had Fynn pinned beneath his gaze. Now he added a meaningful smile. "There is a side to Lord Fynnlar that most people never see."

The royal cousin squirmed in his chair. "You needn't get personal, now."

Cassius looked to Alyneri. "You might be surprised to learn of the many dear ladies our Fynnlar has aided—"

"Shouldn't we get to the reason we came all this way?" Fynn protested shrilly.

Cassius cast him a smile, predatory in its aspect. "I suppose, if we must. Before we proceed any further into our negotiations, produce for me the items I required of you, Fynnlar." He waved his *siqaret* absently. "I confess my doubt that you've met my stipulations, but let us see the evidence."

Fynn sat up and opened his satchel, muttering ungraciously about people who use the royal *we*. From its depths he pulled a bundle wrapped in velvet, which he set on the low table between himself and Cassius. "Behold, *objet d'art de votre désir*."

Cassius arched a dubious brow and unwrapped the bundle. Inside lay an ostrich feather dyed a most eye-offending shade of chartreuse. He sat back with a hand to his brow. "No, *no*, the color is *terrible*—*w*rong, beyond wrong!"

"You said you wanted Castelvetrano Green." Fynn turned Alyneri a sulky glare. "The damnable color can only be distilled from the ink of an octopus found off the shores of Tal Verran, in the middle of the Fire Sea. Do you *know* how much I had to pay for that bloody feather?"

Alyneri looked to Cassius. "The realm is imperiled and you're concerned about a feather for your hat?"

"Ah, Your Grace..." his sigh could only have been more patronizing if it had been offered along with a spoonful of honey, "the world is always entertaining the next new crisis once people have become bored with the last new crisis, but a hat is never fashionable without the right feather."

He regarded said feather like a housekeeper eyeing a dead mouse. "I suppose this will have to suit." He dropped it on the velvet and sat back again. "And my next requirement? Where is this painting by a blind man of the blind man's parrot who is now dead?"

Fynn pulled a rolled canvas from his satchel and tossed it out to unfurl across the table.

Alyneri stared bemusedly at the oddly misshapen image painted there. "The blind man is dead?"

"No, Your Grace, the parrot." Cassius gave her a faintly chiding look. "How could a parrot paint a painting of itself?"

"But it hardly looks like a parrot."

Cassius shook his head at her. "Let us not be so alacritous to judge others. How do we know what the blind man sees?" He waved with his *siqaret*. "This will suit, Fynnlar. And the breed of rare, exotic animal? I don't suppose you have one of those hidden in your bag?"

"I brought you Alyneri."

Alyneri turned Fynn a disbelieving look.

Carian chuckled. Cassius's lips spread in a delighted and not altogether auspicious smile—at least as far as Alyneri was concered.

That's when the servant rushed up with a goblet and a wine bottle on a silver tray.

Fynn grabbed the goods and glared at him. "What took you so long, man? Did you press the grapes yourself?" He drank half the contents of the goblet in one go. Then he fell back in his chair again. "Oh, don't stare at me like that, Your Grace. I could've spent thousands hunting down a damned llama that pisses gold thread—and gone to exorbitant trouble to acquire it—but you *know* he wouldn't have accepted it in the end."

Cassius waved with his *siqaret*. "I cannot be seen to accept gifts from Fynnlar val Lorian. The man is a known associate of pirates." He nodded to his servant, and the man promptly removed the feather and the painting. Alyneri almost expected the manservant to take her in hand as well.

"I'm confused." She met her host's gaze. "You *don't* care about the feather and the painting…or you do?"

Cassius winked at her. "It's the thought that counts."

"It's the aggravation that counts," Fynn grumbled. "So?" He eyed their host disagreeably.

"So…" Cassius pushed to his feet and gazed down at him. "I shall consider your request. In the meantime, my staff will show you to your rooms so you can prepare for dinner, which I believe tonight is—" he looked to another of his hovering servants.

The man bowed slightly. "The lamb, sir."

"The lamb." Cassius smiled at Alyneri as he said this, making her wonder if he was making some obscure reference to herself. Then he swept up his hat from its chair and donned it as he took his leave.

Alyneri called after him, "Just how long will you be 'considering' our request?"

Cassius turned his head and looked her over appreciatively. "Not one instant past the point I tire of your intelligent company, Your Grace." Then he smiled a very bright, very predatory smile and departed.

Fynn growled an oath and fell back in his chair. "Well, you've gone and done it now, Your Grace." He rolled his head around as if it pained him. "I said butter him up—not make him *like* you. Now we'll all be stuck here til bloody Samhain."

Alyneri blinked. "I beg your pardon?" Samhain was half a year away yet.

Fynn waved with his goblet. "Don't you see where we are? He lives in the middle of bloody nowhere."

"It ain't as bad as all that." Carian had stretched himself out on the couch and had his smoke propped between his lips, slowly becoming a pillar of ash. He mumbled around it, "You can find the node on the world grid. You just can't find the grid again once you've crossed the node."

Fynn held up a hand to him as if this proved his point.

Alyneri looked bemusedly between the two of them. "What am I missing?"

Fynn drank his wine and glared off in the direction Cassius had gone.

Carian tucked his hands behind his head and closed his eyes. "What you're missing, Princess, is that Cassius lives on the end of a one-way road as far as the nodes are concerned. We crossed it the moment we passed beneath his walls. Now we're his guests until he decides our business is concluded and returns us to the grid."

Alyneri thought she must've heard him incorrectly; yet at the same time, it made sense out of the many odd personages 'taking advantage' of Cassius's hospitality.

Carian opened one eye to peer at her and then closed it again. "Y'might as well make yourself at home. As keen as he clearly is for your company, we could be here a good long while."

FIFTY-THREE

*"Freedom cannot be lasting without vigilance and
the indomitable will to fight back."*

–Farid al Abdul-Basir, Prince of the Akkad

"ISABEL." SEBASTIAN VAL Lorian crossed the black stone terrace in Dreamscape to take Isabel's hands in his own. "How are you? I've been trying to reach you—"

"I haven't been sleeping much lately. I hope you don't mind my intruding on your dreams instead."

"On the contrary, it's a great relief to me." Sebastian noticed how pale she looked beneath the sere desert sun—even a dreamed one. "Ehsan and Dareios were also going to try to reach you in their dreams tonight."

A faint smile hinted on her lips. "Yes, I received their callings. For a moment it seemed as if half of Kandori was banging on my bedchamber door, wanting admittance."

Beyond the obsidian pavilion where they stood, the same violent storm that always haunted their Dreamscape meetings was darkening the southern horizon. The black band of clouds flashed violently with lightning, while above this dark turbulence, fiery veins split the firmament into a fragile webbing, lines of blood through a fractured blue sky.

Sebastian couldn't tear his eyes away from the unsettling scene. "Is that what's been occupying your days?"

Isabel followed his gaze back over his shoulder. Her eyes tightened. "The Malorin'athgul Rinokh is seeking a way into the Realms of Light."

"*One* creature is causing all of that?"

"He attacks T'khendar directly from Chaos, where his power is greatest. We give thanks that he is alone in this effort."

The longer Sebastian stared, the greater grew his horror. Isabel cupped his face and turned his eyes to hers. "They were created to unmake worlds, Sebastian. This is the battle we of T'khendar fight…but it needn't be yours."

Suddenly they stood upon a marble terrace overlooking an immense white city. Across the surrounding valley, a ridge of imposing mountains reared upwards to scrape the sky. Countless waterfalls fell from those heights, their lengthy white trains vanishing into mist among the undulating canopy of trees.

Isabel now wore a corseted gown in the deepest cobalt beneath a silk over-robe, its layers as light and airy as gossamer. A steady breeze caught and lifted the gown into floating streams behind her. With her chestnut hair bound in a net of sapphires, she seemed a lady painted of an artist's imagination, ethereal and fey. Sebastian had hardly noticed what she'd been wearing before. Now he couldn't look away.

Isabel looked down at herself with a wry expression somewhere between apology and humor. "If you'd seen what I've really been wearing these many weeks, you might forgive my dreaming about soft silk."

He shook his head. "My brother doesn't realize what he's missing out on, that's all." *His brother…* but he'd long stopped asking her about Ean.

"Isabel," he searched her gaze, "what I saw back there…"

She gave a resigned exhale. "We expected this would happen, Sebastian, yet now that the moment is nigh…" A brief weariness took the place of her words. She started them walking beside the railing, and her thoughts became pensive in the Dreamscape aether, honey-thick and opaque to his understanding. "When my brother and his Council of Nine first built this world, they were idealists. They swore they were planning for as many outcomes as possible, but if you spoke to them, if you saw the potent light dancing in their eyes, you knew they believed everything would go exactly as they intended." Her brow furrowed faintly. "Now, those who survived know better."

"Perhaps a more cautious outlook will prove fortuitous in the end."

"Or catastrophic." She gave him a troubled look. "A wielder is limited by what he can envision, Sebastian. This is the all-important Fifth Law. If the tragedies that shadow our past make us too afraid to envision an impossible future, our enemies will eat us alive—for they do not suffer the same losses or know the same defeats."

She stopped at the railing and looked out over the world her brother and his Council had made—a beautiful world, by Sebastian's estimation.

"This is why I almost wish that Ean remembered nothing. Even if it meant also not remembering me."

"Ean would be lost without you."

She turned to face him. "Yet he's been as hindered by me as by his memories."

"His memories..." Sebastian thought surely he must've misunderstood her. "You'd have him play the game knowing nothing? Without even the Laws of Patterning to guide him?"

"What Ean most needs, he knows innately." She challenged his protest with an arched brow. "The Fifth Law is almost self-defeating. While the Laws help us codify and understand this power we call *elae*, at the same time, to some degree they restrict our viewpoints about what we can do with it. We say the limit to a wielder's ability is what he can envision—the sky is the limit, yes. But is it?" She looked him up and down. "What the Laws of Patterning tell us, we believe—there is Balance in all things, *elae* has five strands. But in the East, in Avatar and Vest, kingdoms where the *Sobra* hasn't yet found a foothold, they work Alorin's lifeforce beneath entirely different rules. Not all of the things their Adepts can do are explainable within our known Laws."

Sebastian recalled too late that he was arguing doctrine with the High Mage of the Citadel. He gave her an apologetic grin. "Point taken, my lady."

Isabel dropped her gaze. "Forgive me." She reached for his hand and held it more tightly than he expected. "Our world is coming apart at the seams. With my brother gone, I fear it's taking a toll on my disposition."

"Your point is a good one, Isabel."

She squeezed his hand. "But I might've made it more gently." She looped her arm through his and started them walking again. "Tell me of your news. I could well use a cheerful thought to buoy my demeanor." She cast a rueful smile off across the city. "Doubtless Dagmar and Raine would appreciate it, too."

Sebastian worried for her, but he knew she sought no sympathy, only his ear to listen, his arm to escort her. At the most, his shoulder to lean on. "As I told you earlier, we got a letter from Ean detailing everything that happened to him in Tambarré, but more importantly, the letter confirmed that our matrix can sever the *eidola's* link with its master. We've been testing arrows as an initial means of delivering these disruptor patterns to the creatures, and now we think we've isolated the order for proper crystallization."

Patterns locked within a matrix interacted similarly to elements in crystals—within a pattern's structure, molecules of energy formed into specific bonded shapes, much as chemical elements bonded during the process of crystallization. Hence the borrowed use of the word by Patternists.

"How have you tested them?"

"Well, that's just it..." Sebastian scratched at his head.

He'd been arguing back and forth with himself about that very point. They'd tested the arrows on Merdanti stone, but they couldn't really know if they'd nailed the disruptor sequence until they tested them on actual *eidola*. Without Ean to aid them in that effort, Sebastian felt that task should fall to him, but Ehsan and Dareios both argued strongly against it, since seeking out *eidola* would necessarily place him in the same arena as Dore Madden.

Sebastian didn't relish confronting a man who still haunted his dreams almost nightly, but would he ever be able to rest easy knowing Dore was alive and possibly—probably—plotting against him and his brother?

He realized Isabel was still waiting for his reply and grimaced slightly. "I guess you could say I haven't sought to fill Ean's shoes on the testing field. But perhaps I should?"

He'd hoped the open tone of his inquiry would encourage her to offer her oracular talents on their behalf, but it had the opposite effect.

"Prophecy cannot be a sounding board for your decisions, Sebastian. The paths are too jumbled now, all of our threads too closely intertwined." She stopped walking and turned to him with a grave determination steadying her. "Yet even were they as far distant as the seas from each other, I wouldn't do as you ask."

Disheartened by her refusal but trying to understand, Sebastian pressed, "Not even for Ean?"

Her gaze tightened. "I haven't consciously sought to know Ean's path in this life." She looked away from him. "Only once did I do this for Arion, and it's an act I'll grieve to the end of my days."

Sebastian felt her sorrow as though his own, her feelings open—or perhaps betrayed—by the closeness of their minds in Dreamscape. "Why, Isabel?"

She cast him a look, critical with self-rebuke. Then she started them walking again, tugging on his arm, both apology and entreaty. Her tone, when she spoke again, told only of sorrow.

"Our paths aren't set in stone, Sebastian, yet there is a sort of predictability that comes into play once we've made a certain choice. Even without a gift for prophecy, if a man looks far enough along a potential line of consequence proceeding from any one decision, he can predict a whole series of ramifications deriving from that choice. One's path is predicated on decision. If the person changes his or her mind at a pivotal juncture, that path of consequence ceases to exist and a new one branches out."

She searched his gaze, assessing his understanding. "While our paths aren't predestined, our viewpoints shape us so deeply that in many cases our paths almost seem inevitable. When I looked down Arion's path, much against my better judgment, I saw that certain viewpoints were guiding him to make specific choices. Unfortunately, these were not viewpoints he was likely to change. Thus the instant I saw where his path was leading, I knew also that his death was inevitable."

Sebastian's feet dragged him to a halt. "Shade and darkness, Isabel."

"He fought with me the entire way, of course." A melancholy smile hinted on her lips. "He believed he could somehow still change what I'd seen. Even my brother tried to outmaneuver my foretelling. But I knew...I knew that to alter the outcome, Arion would've had to change who he was—*compromise* who he was—and that was something he would never do."

Sebastian could hardly fathom the emotional toll of such an experience. He could say nothing to comfort her, knowing the path her foretelling had stitched in the tapestry, the path his brother was still walking.

She saw understanding in his grim expression. "My brother loved Arion too much, and in that love refused to warn him of his path. I loved him too much, and in my warning doomed him to walk an immutable one. Arion died for his part in these mistakes. I must live with mine. I cannot yet decide which of us is paying the heavier cost."

Sebastian drew her into his arms. "Isabel...I'm sorry."

"These are old wounds." Her eyes as she withdrew found a shadow of humor. "But *you* must be a glutton for punishment, receiving me as often as you do, knowing the darkness of my dreams."

He touched her arm. "You're my brother's wife. I would weather any storm with you for as long as I must to keep you safe."

One corner of her mouth curled with a smile. "I can take care of myself, Sebastian, but I appreciate the chivalry in your offer. To that end," a different light manifested in her weary gaze, "an emissary of mine will be visiting you soon to retrieve something I left in your care—"

A pounding on his door roused Sebastian from Dreamscape with a startled inhale. He sat up in bed, still hearing Isabel's last words.

Bang! Bang! Bang!

"*All right*, I'm coming." Sebastian threw off his covers and staggered through the darkness to the door, only to fumble to find the latch.

Whereupon the impatient door became amorphous, and a shadow stepped through the wood.

Sebastian drew stiffly back.

Every lamp and candle blazed to brilliant life, illuminating a countenance he'd seen only once from afar, and even then too close for comfort; a face that had haunted his steps—never mind his dreams—for weeks thereafter.

"Rhakar," Sebastian choked out.

Rhakar arched a brow. "Prince Sebastian." He moved past him into his chambers without further invitation. "The Lady Isabel requests her staff be returned to her."

Sebastian pushed both hands through his hair, trying to get a grip on the startled apprehension that was making his insides squirm like gelatinous goo. Perhaps, as Isabel had claimed, Rhakar held no grudge against him for releasing the Labyrinth on him during their first meeting in the Kutsamak, but Sebastian's guilty conscience wasn't so sure. It made a strong case for his departing the room instantly and without explanation.

Rhakar finished looking around and turned his yellow-eyed gaze on Sebastian.

Sebastian stared at him.

"Her staff, Prince of Dannym?"

"Oh...right." Sebastian grabbed a robe and motioned towards the door. "Its, um, this way."

He led Rhakar through the moonlit halls of the Moon Palace, his every step dragging the memory of an earlier life, an echo of the days when the *drachwyr* had dogged his trail, following him from node to node after their altercation in the Kutsamak. The path of the man called Işak'getirmek had ended at the Castle of Tyr'kharta. That's where Sebastian's path had merged with Ean's—at least according to Isabel—and forever shifted the course of his life.

But Rhakar had been in the Kutsamak, and he'd been at Tyr'kharta, and here he was now...

Perhaps he was being overly sensitive to paths and foretellings after Isabel's Dreamscape speech—certainly she'd made her opinion clear on the matter—but he couldn't help remembering the look in her eyes as she'd said it.

Sebastian trusted Isabel, but he didn't entirely trust Epiphany's Prophet. If she *had* looked down his path—especially after what had happened with Arion—she certainly wasn't going to *tell* him about it.

He glanced to the *drachwyr*. The moon was setting in the west, shining angled light between the pillars of the arcade and limning Rhakar's strong nose and brow in silver.

Sebastian swallowed and turned ahead again. "I just have one question I can't get past."

"What's that, Prince of Dannym?"

Sebastian glanced at him again. "You're not holding that Labyrinth business against me, are you?"

"Why would you expect me to?"

Sebastian frowned at him.

Rhakar shifted his gaze back to the moonlit passage ahead. "In our youth, my sister Mithaiya and I flung the Labyrinth on each other more frequently than mud. And if I didn't take care to ward my dreams, I would wake to find myself trapped in the maze."

"I take your point." For all Sebastian had felt an awkward guilt over wielding such a vicious trap as the Labyrinth on Rhakar, the *drachwyr* clearly viewed it as a child's game.

Ean had told him much of Ramu and a little of Rhakar, and the Kandori practically seemed to worship the Sundragon Náiir, sire of their princely line, but Sebastian's only experience with immortals came from his limited interaction with the Prophet, who Rhakar, at that moment, reminded him of too nearly. Were they not both cut from opposite sides of the same cloth, the *drachwyr* and the Malorin'athgul?

Feeling unsettled by the comparison, Sebastian walked the rest of the way in silence, which apparently suited Rhakar just fine.

Dawn had taken over her watch by the time they reached Dareios's laboratory. Sebastian walked through the early grey light and retrieved Isabel's staff from its place in the corner. Holding it, realizing he was about to relinquish it into the care of another, gave him a strange and awkward sense of loss, as if he'd failed somehow. Whether that failure related to Isabel, his brother, or Captain Rhys val Kincaide, who was still healing from an ordeal Sebastian was entirely responsible for causing, he couldn't say.

He handed the staff to Rhakar.

The Sundragon gave him an acknowledging nod and flipped the staff over his shoulder into some kind of holster on his back.

Perhaps it was a trick of the early light, but Sebastian got the sense of the *drachwyr's* greatsword looming there also, with its hilt fashioned as a dragon's wings. Upon this thought, a memory flashed to mind—his first sight of Rhakar in human form as he'd come striding towards him across the desert.

He played the Labyrinth as a child's game!

Sebastian crossed his arms and leaned against the wall. "You could've ended my path in the Kutsamak without a second thought."

Rhakar was securing Isabel's staff firmly behind him. He arched a brow that said clearly, *And?*

"Why didn't you?"

"I saw from the first you were a Player."

Sebastian straightened off the wall. "How could you possibly see something like that?"

Rhakar looked at him like he couldn't be seriously asking this question. "You all have auras about you, the First Lord's Kingdom Blades."

The familiar phrase gave Sebastian pause. "Kingdom Blades? As in—"

"It is his epithet for all of you."

Something in this knowledge made Sebastian feel oddly warm, and…unexpectedly empty. The phrase reflected a part of his life he hadn't yet restored—if indeed it could be restored at all, Ehsan's claims notwithstanding. He accepted that people called him 'prince,' but he made no claim to his father's throne.

Verily, even if he survived the coming conflict, which was a very big *if*, Sebastian couldn't see himself back in Dannym. The years lay too long between them—that youthful Prince Sebastian and the man he was now—too long and deleterious; acid years that had etched away the fine marble exterior of Gydryn val Lorian's firstborn son, leaving a pocked slab that hardly resembled the original.

Rhakar's yellow eyes narrowed upon him. "The First Lord doesn't waste time with broken pieces, Sebastian val Lorian."

Sebastian wasn't sure how to take this comment—had it been spoken in reassurance or warning?

"You each have your roles to play, the four of you—"

Sebastian raised a hand to pause him. "I beg your pardon—did you say the *four* of us?"

"Your brothers and another Player whose name would be meaningless to you." Rhakar held his gaze with his startling yellow eyes, so like the sun when it burned low in the west. "Your threads in the tapestry have never glowed so brightly, nor your paths been so closely entwined. The four of you are like the Nodefinder's Seam, a starry core of strands packed so tightly that your light outshines all others. What each of you do now will inevitably affect the others' paths." Rhakar headed for the balcony. Sebastian followed as a matter of course.

"You called us Kingdom Blades, which implies…" Sebastian shook his head, tried to clarify his question. The Sundragon's words had…well, they'd wakened something in him—not unease; rather, a sense of *necessity*, something of perilous importance, an action he suddenly felt compelled to take. Only he had no idea what it was. "What can you tell me of my brothers?"

"Of Ean, I know only that his thread is tangled among darker strands." Rhakar stopped at the railing and turned to him. "Trell, I left not long ago in the hands of the Akkadian Emir and your King Father."

Sebastian stared at him. "Say that again?"

"As your paths are interwoven, so accordingly are the workings of the wielders Dore Madden and Viernan hal'Jaitar, the Duke of Morwyk, and your father." Every name spoken off Rhakar's tongue pulsed with power in the saying, as though each was a portent of future events. "Against all odds, your father found his way to safe harbor with the Akkad's Emir, who is a good man, as mortals go, and very much in the Mage's service. Your father withdrew his forces from M'Nador and sent them to the fortress of Nahavand, behind Akkad-held lines, where they await his return ere they all depart for Dannym."

Sebastian spun beneath this news. "And Trell?"

"Your middle brother forges towards the Fortress of Khor Taran in Abu'Dhan to rescue a thousand of your father's forces tricked into captivity by Viernan hal'Jaitar. He draws and binds many threads to him. His pattern through the tapestry grows thick."

Sebastian wondered with an uncomfortable twinge how Rhakar would describe his own thread. He nodded wordlessly, hoping his gaze conveyed thanks enough.

The *drachwyr* gave a nod in reply. Then he planted a hand on the railing and slung himself over it.

Sebastian rushed after him. He caught the railing with both hands and sort of hung there, squinting painfully against the rising sun as he watched a gilded dragon flying away into the dawn.

FIFTY-FOUR

"Not even the purest soul is exempt from a mixture of madness."
–The Adept Socotra Isio, Sormitáge Scholar

EAN STEPPED OFF the node and felt a pattern flare and expire—a ward of some kind. He didn't notice its exact purpose, for his attention went immediately to the rainbows of light enveloping him.

The afternoon sun was casting long rays through the dome and crystal columns of the gazebo where he'd arrived, so that Ean stood amid a monument of light. Beyond the too-bright columns spread a lake, whose stone retaining wall mirrored the scalloped shape of the structure at its center. Fountains sprayed out of statues set at each petal point in the wall, making a dance of shifting rainbows across the lake.

At Ean's feet, inscribed in Old Alaeic in the marble floor, were the words: *'I'ci anu eliannae. I'ci anu terrae.'* *Here began the light. Here began the world.*

Ean's Adept senses, as well as his own memory, told him that the words were not carved into the stone; rather, the entire marble slab had curled itself to form the shape of each letter, such that the inscription existed all the way through.

—*'Make this promise to me, Arion, here upon Epiphany's Altar, and I shall believe you.'*—

Isabel's words, suddenly and unexpectedly recalled, brought an immediate ache to Ean's eyes and an even greater one to his chest, for he remembered then that she'd said those words to Arion when last they'd stood together in that place.

He could still feel the energy of that moment, the expansive sense of their minds bound and entwined, *elae* flooding them both; Isabel's disconcertion woven through with love, and Arion's thrumming anticipation.... Ean had no idea what promise she'd been requiring him to make on such sacred ground, but for some reason, he didn't think it was one he'd kept.

Who had raised the gazebo from the lode of crystal far below it? This was one of the Sacred City's most enduring mysteries. According to legend, the gazebo had been standing long before Emperor Hallian the First built his palace overlooking the hills and sea and pronounced the lands *faroe qhar'* or *fairest view*. It was easy to understand why the Agasi believed Epiphany must've been birthed on that very spot.

No path led from gazebo to land, so Ean made the water hold his weight and walked across it. The ripples of his passing bled into waves from the fountains, making new patterns where they joined.

Beyond the lake, a sculpture garden bordered a boxwood maze. The individual shapes cut into the hedges were new to Ean, but he remembered every twist and turn in the maze's design. And past the towering boxwoods, he knew what he would find—flower gardens alternating with orchards and promenades, trellis-lined paths dripping roses or fruit, temples hiding beneath clusters of wisteria; and all of it forever blooming, there in the endless spring of the Sacred City.

The path he took through the maze led him to the private gardens of the imperial family. Arion had walked those grounds often during his years at the Sormitáge, when Isabel had maintained residence at the palace.

The Empress's Praetorians were waiting for him when he emerged from the boxwoods.

A score of swords descended towards Ean in a steel fan of deadly points. A dozen archers stood in a staggered half-moon behind the first line, crossbows loaded and aimed.

Ean slowly raised both hands and said in Agasi, "I mean no harm. My name—"

"Prince Ean?" A female voice preceded a veiled figure pushing her way through the line of guards. "Can it *be*?" She grabbed onto the arm of the nearest one. "Lower your weapons! I know this man."

The leading Praetorian turned her a defiant look. "Princess—"

"*Lower your weapon*, Lieutenant." Nadia's command warned that she *would* be obeyed, while a higher harmonic of the fourth cast a feather-light encouragement to comply quickly.

The Praetorian lowered his sword, but he looked severely defiant about it.

Ean held a shield of the fifth and would've let them keep their weapons where they willed, but he didn't want to offend the princess after such a valiant rescue.

Nadia pushed through the line and came towards him. She wore an opalescent veil bound by a circlet of emeralds, and a dress the color of shaded grass, but even had she been wrapped in muslin, Ean would've known her by her signature on the currents.

She stood before him with astonishment raising a momentary barrier between them, her gaze full of bewildered wonder. Then she threw her arms around his neck and hugged him fiercely.

The Praetorians instantly restored their weapons in aim at Ean's head.

The prince raised both hands while Nadia hugged him. "Please…I have no intention of harming anyone here."

The lieutenant motioned with his sword. "Be it so, lower your shield."

Ean smiled meaningfully at him. "Lower your weapons."

Nadia turned stiffly to the Praetorian. "Lieutenant di—"

"Princess, come away from this man." The Praetorian's face was as stone, and his eyes were harder still.

"Lieutenant di Corvi, *this man* is the Crown Prince of Dannym and personally responsible for my rescue from Tambarré. You will treat him as my honored guest!"

At this statement, declared so emphatically by a ringed truthreader who could not lie, the lieutenant clenched his jaw and lowered his sword. The rest of the Praetorians followed suit. Sheathing his weapon, the lieutenant murmured, "Our apologies, Your Highness." He neither looked nor sounded the least apologetic.

Ean nodded soberly. "And mine, Lieutenant. You attended your duty well."

"The Princess's wishes notwithstanding, Your Highness, I must ask how you came to be in the private gardens of the imperial family." It was more accusation than question. None of the Praetorians seemed of a mind to budge their semicircle of containment.

"I used the node at Epiphany's Altar."

Silence descended. The Lieutenant exchanged an unreadable look with another of his men. He might've doubted Ean's veracity, but he couldn't doubt the truthreaders among his company bearing witness to it—never mind the Princess Heir.

The lieutenant clasped hands behind his back. "For now, Your Highness, I must ask you to remain with the princess."

"It is my only aim, Lieutenant."

Nadia gave Ean a wondering stare by way of *Come with me* and led him away on the path. The Praetorians followed a dozen steps behind, heavy steps clinking of suspicion.

When the guards were presumably far enough behind, Nadia swept her veil back from her face and turned to Ean. "When the alarms sounded from the gardens, we thought..." but she swallowed whatever she'd thought. "You must know the entire city is on high alert since the Danes' invasion."

Ean blinked. "The Danes invaded Faroqhar?"

"It's a long story." She looked him over with her colorless eyes, a truly lovely girl with a hint of the fey in her makeup. Her expression revealed amazement, but her gaze held shadows that Ean recognized too nearly; they were the footprints of Players whose actions had forever changed her.

Perhaps perceiving this thought, Nadia turned profile to him. "I worried we would never see you again."

"I feared the same myself for a time, Princess."

"But...clearly you escaped." She searched his gaze, seeking explanation.

"Or he let me leave." Ean arched brows. "I'm still uncertain which."

Nadia stopped at the base of a staircase and considered him with her lips pressed together. "Your Highness..." but whatever she'd wanted to say, the Praetorians' clomping arrival dissuaded. Nadia gave him a constrained smile instead and murmured, "This way." She started up the stairs.

Ean might've done much, said much to ameliorate her uncertainty surrounding his appearance, but he was being bombarded by memories—Isabel laughing, teaching him patterns, taunting him...kissing him. Her reflection watched him from the waters of every fountain. Vines and stems twined themselves in mimicry of her hair. Urns captured the curve of her hip; a statue, her inviting smile. Isabel was everywhere in that garden. Her energy had so permeated it that evidence of her thrived there still, three centuries later.

Ean had expected to remember that place, but he hadn't anticipated the feeling of the memories unfolding in his mind with fain recollection; as if they'd been building for centuries just waiting for the door to be reopened; *favorite* memories, moments of pleasure that Arion had clung to when all else had gone dark.

Ean hadn't expected that he would experience such aching loss at being in that place without Isabel, and he'd never imagined he hear his soul calling with desperate relief, *At last I'm home!*

He knew where the path was leading long before they entered a walled courtyard where climbing roses were overtaking a pavilion. There, beneath a blossoming fragrance, a table draped in white linen had been set with a meal. A man seated there in the shadows. His shoulder-length dark hair draped his features, but even without seeing his face, Ean knew him from the way the currents made jagged ridges around his form.

The Marquiin looked up as they arrived and quietly got to his feet. His well proportioned brow bore the Prophet's dark tattoos.

The prince came to a standstill.

The Marquiin looked uncertainly to Nadia. She looked to Ean. "Your

Highness…perhaps you remember the Marquiin who helped me in Tambarré. This is Caspar."

Ean forced himself through the energy of his own surprise. "Well met, Caspar." He managed a smile and moved slowly towards him, his gaze fixed on the patterns curling across Caspar's brow. "Are you aware that your tattoos are no longer active?"

Caspar exchanged a look with Nadia and then returned his gaze to the prince. His eyes were nearly the same storm-grey shade as the prince's own. Ean found this far more disturbing than the tattoos.

"The Prophet did something to—well, in the end, he made me sane again."

"The Prophet made you *sane*." Ean hadn't meant for the statement to sound so choked with disbelief. He lifted an apologetic hand. "I beg your pardon, I didn't mean—"

"It doesn't matter. Whatever he did, it still wasn't enough." The hollowness in his tone gave testimony to this truth.

Nadia placed a hand on Caspar's shoulder and lifted her gaze to Ean. "They live in a storm." Consternation flickered across her brow. "A constant, maddening storm."

Ean observed the currents surrounding the two truthreaders. "The two of you are bonded?"

Nadia nodded.

"That was…valiant."

"Or foolish—according to my mother." She tightened her hand on Caspar's shoulder. "But she wasn't *there* when…" but whatever *when* Nadia was referencing, the words never came in description of it.

Caspar laid his hand over Nadia's.

Ean wondered what hope there was for Caspar if Darshan himself couldn't undo the harm his patterns had caused. And patterns bound the Marquiin as a web cocooning a spider's prey. Ean could unwork them, but not safely…not and still have much of *Caspar* left to speak of.

Nadia donned a brave smile. "Would you join us, Your Highness?" She motioned to a chair across the table. Caspar rose to help the princess into her own seat, and she said as she was adjusting her skirts, "The Prophet sent Caspar to treat with me and answer my questions."

"It's why he made me sane again." The Marquiin said. "That much I understood from him. He didn't want to frighten the princess. He wanted me to converse openly with her."

Nadia added portentously. "The Prophet told Caspar he would make no more Marquiin."

Ean slowly sank down in his chair and breathed more than spoke, "Why would he do that?"

Caspar retook his chair. "Things were changing in the temple even before the princess arrived." He settled his hands in his lap and held himself in a manner that seemed very formal for the setting, even somewhat antiquated. "Talk in the temple spoke of the Prophet having portentous dreams. Some of his acolytes spoke to me of how he'd changed, how they…desired his bed now, when ever before they'd feared being chosen for the duty." He dropped his gaze to his lap. "Everyone feared being chosen."

Nadia shook her head. "There's so much we don't understand about the Prophet. Most everything, actually."

The three of them sat in silence for a time after this pronouncement, unsure how to proceed into conversation. Finally, Nadia straightened purposefully. "Forgive my impatience, Your Highness—"

"Ean," he said absently.

"Ean," she corrected with a slight smile, "but would you mind explaining what you're doing here?"

He met her gaze with his own troubled one. What could he tell her? What *should* he tell her? "I guess the simplicity is that I need your help."

She shook her head. "But how did you *get* here?"

"The node—"

"There *is* no node at Epiphany's Altar."

"Regretfully, Princess—"

"Nadia."

"Nadia," he amended, "there *is* a node, or more accurately a weld, for the well of the second strand runs deep in that place. You won't find the weld on any map, but it can be traveled by those who already know its location on the world grid."

Nadia drew back in her chair, staring at him. "And how by the Lady do *you* know its location?" Her words were crisp with startled unease.

Ean cast a wistful gaze around the pavilion. He remembered luncheons taken there amid the autumn wind, and evening parties beneath strings of hanging globes. Arion had toasted Isabel numerous times beneath that dome—he recalled golden wine sparkling from dozens of upheld glasses. Even more often they'd danced in darkness beneath the stars to music playing in their minds alone. "I lived here for many years…long ago."

"*You…*" Nadia stared at him, clearly at a loss for words.

After a moment, Ean focused upon her again. "Nadia," he laid his hand flat upon the table, half expecting to see each finger bound by two gold rings, "I know all of this is unexpected and…strange, but our paths connected in Tambarré, and connected for a time they remain."

He looked down at the table again, his attention being caught by his bare fingers, thinking how fallacious it was to say his name was Ean val Lorian. "I don't know what you know or how much you understand, Nadia, but you're Tanis's friend, and I'm Tanis's friend..." he lifted his gaze and took a chance on her understanding, "and Tanis and I are both Players in the game against those who would see our world unmade."

"Malorin'athgul," she whispered with wide, knowing eyes.

"Pelas, Shail, Darshan, Rinokh." Ean sat back in his chair with a heavy exhale. Suddenly he saw not the long light filtering through the pavilion roof but Rinokh's great dragon eye staring at him through an obsidian wall in a valley that shook with unmaking. "The eldest is vanquished, the middle brother bound now to our side of the game," he focused back on Nadia, "but the other two—"

"Must be *stopped*." Caspar's words snapped as if with *deyjiin's* static bite.

The sun sank lower behind the trees. In the filtered light, motes illuminated as fireflies. A silence settled over the pavilion.

"Everything is so upended." Nadia seemed both somber and uncomfortable. "The High Lord, my father, left on a ship bound for the Dane's city of Kjvngherad with Phaedor, and—"

Ean's pulse skipped a beat. "The *zanthyr* Phaedor?"

"Yes. He brought Tanis to the Sormitáge. It's how Tanis and I met...of a fashion." She took up her wine but then only stared into it. "But Phaedor's gone with my father to retaliate against the Danes, even though it was Shail—"

"*Shail.*" Ean sat stiffly forward. "Nadia, I beg of you, start at the beginning."

While Caspar poured more wine, Nadia spoke to the prince in quiet words: everything she knew about Tanis, Felix and Malin van Drexel, the attack at the Quai game, the Warlock Sinárr, and Pelas and Tanis's brave rescue at the temple.

She told him how Pelas had pulled *deyjiin* from her veins to draw her back from death, and how Tanis had healed her of its deleterious effects at Pelas's mansion.

And she told him how Pelas had sworn himself to Tanis's path, and how they'd worked the Unbreakable Bond together, the latter a truth which again speared Ean deeply.

In the last, Nadia gazed pensively into her wine as she explained, "Pelas told Tanis that he would choose his own brothers this time. He said he would—"

"Choose better for myself than our Maker chose for me."

Ean slowly turned his head to see Pelas ascending the steps of the pavilion.

The Malorin'athgul wore a ruby-red coat over dark pants. His raven hair had been pulled into a queue, though a few loose strands framed his face, and he carried a cane with a ruby capstone the same exquisite color as his coat.

Ean studied him on the currents. This was not the same Pelas he'd fought beside in Tal'Afaq, for the currents were swirling about him now in very different patterns.

The prince slowly got to his feet. He was careful not to summon the lifeforce.

Pelas paused beneath the archway. His copper eyes looked Ean over. An undeniable tension claimed the space between them, and silence filled in everywhere else. Then the slightest of smiles hitched one corner of the Malorin'athgul's mouth.

Pelas looked down at the cane in his hand. "I wondered if you would come." He glanced up at Ean as he moved slowly through that no man's land buffering their mutual apprehensions. "I saw the possibility but not the rationale."

Ean's gaze tracked Pelas's progress around the table. "Saw the possibility… where?"

Pelas took Nadia's hand and kissed it. "Princess." He nodded to Caspar and then opened his hand to indicate the one empty chair. "With your permission, Ean?"

Ean slowly sank back down in his own seat. "I came here to find you, not fight you."

Pelas cast him the ghost of a smile. "Evidently." He spread the folds of his coat to either side of his chair as he sat. The cane he set on its point beside him, letting the fifth brace it and reminding Ean with a discomfiting twinge of Isabel's staff.

Pelas poured some wine. "I only just returned here myself, in time to see the zanthyr off and thank him again for restoring me, and make more promises—" he glanced at Nadia with a rueful smile, "ones I hope to be able to keep this time."

Ean dropped his gaze and worked hard to keep his thoughts aligned with his new perspective. A month ago, he would've been enraged to hear that Phaedor had healed this man who'd brought such harm to Isabel. A week ago, he would've known a powerful resentment upon hearing Pelas say that he shared the zanthyr's confidence. Now he only marveled at the connections that bound them all to the game and to each other.

Nadia looked between the two of them uncertainly. "Should we…eat something?" But no one made a move towards any food.

Ean stared out into the courtyard, which was quickly being overtaken by shadows. So many emotions and memories were pummeling him, he was finding it difficult to separate them. "It's harder being here than I anticipated." He flicked his gaze to Pelas and away again.

"She is everywhere in this place," Pelas murmured by way of understanding. Then he saw the look on Ean's face and raised an apologetic hand. "I'm sorry, I shouldn't have…"

"Truth is truth," Ean replied tightly. "Why should it be any less clear to you?"

Silence made its entrance again, dragging an unwilling tension across the stage.

"Forgive me for interposing," Nadia made a tentative advance into the silence, "but Ean…*when* were you here? Dannym's ruling nobility haven't visited the Imperial Palace in decades."

Ean shifted his eyes to meet Pelas's. "You must know." He hadn't meant it to sound like such an accusation. "So tell her."

Pelas held Ean's gaze with a slight furrow between his brows. "Princess…" he looked to Nadia, "when the prince walked these gardens before, his name was Arion Tavestra."

Nadia covered her mouth with both hands.

Caspar looked around the table at all of them. "Who is Arion Tavestra?"

"One of the greatest wielders of the Fourth Age." Pelas regarded Ean steadily, his gaze conveying far more understanding than the prince ever imagined to see there. "And the eternal soulmate of Isabel van Gelderan."

Caspar let out a low whistle. "The High Mage of the Citadel."

Nadia collared her throat with one hand. "But aren't they both…" Understanding flooded her expression, though Ean couldn't imagine why the news so distressed her. "But the Lady Isabel isn't *alive*…"

Ean looked away again. He felt speared by every pair of eyes. "She lives, Nadia."

"By the Lady's Light, *where*?"

"For the last three centuries in T'khendar," he looked resolutely back to her, "with her brother."

Nadia's mouth fell open, and her hand slipped from her throat to cover her heart instead. She shifted her colorless eyes to Pelas, looking inexplicably stricken. "He knew…didn't he? He knew that they lived?"

Pelas nodded soberly.

"But…" her bottom lip trembled slightly, "why didn't he tell me? Tanis didn't tell me *anything* about them!"

Ean rubbed his forehead. "Why would Tanis know anything about Isabel van Gelderan or Arion Tavestra?"

"His training with Phaedor took many forms, Ean." Pelas cast a look at Nadia that Ean couldn't interpret, but which made her face grow even paler.

Then he leaned and refilled the prince's goblet. "You haven't seen him since you parted ways—in Rethynnea, I recall. You may be surprised by what he's learned in the intervening months."

"I'm sure I would be." Ean made an effort to push off the memories of himself and Isabel and focus instead on his purpose for coming there. He met Pelas's gaze tensely. "Can we talk?"

Pelas glanced to Nadia. "Princess, with your leave?"

"By all means." Nadia's eyes were voluminous with some secret understanding that Ean was obviously missing.

He downed his wine and stood. Pelas followed, and they exited the courtyard together into the open gardens, where the trees and every stem, leaf and bush were aglow.

"The golden hour." Pelas gave Ean a smile. "A painter's favorite time of day. The light, you see." He was walking with his hands behind his back and his cane clasped between them.

"How well does Immanuel di Nostri know these gardens?"

"I crafted marble for their fountains, but I never walked the imperial grounds with your familiarity."

"*My* familiarity." Ean puffed a dubious exhale.

Pelas glanced to him. "But you've come far in regaining your ability since Tal'Afaq, haven't you, Ean? The currents embrace you differently. You're not the same wielder I met in my brother's fortress."

Ean looked him over soberly. "I had the same thought about you a few minutes ago."

And the truth was, they'd become friends at Tal'Afaq—uncommon friends, if Ean dared admit the immediate feeling of kinship he'd shared with Pelas; but that esteem he'd developed had only heightened his initial sense of betrayal. Had he never cared, never admired, he would've felt only a pressing need to avenge Isabel. But he'd fought side by side with Pelas. The man had carried Sebastian's broken body in his arms. It had been *personal*, his betrayal.

Pelas shifted his hold on his cane, adjusting course with the current of Ean's thoughts. "Ean…if I could change the past—"

"I don't want to talk about it. I'm trying to let the past lie where it belongs—in the past." If only Arion's memories would let him. Ean pressed fingers to the bridge of his nose. "I'm trying very hard to maintain perspective. You cut Chaos patterns into my wife's flesh…" he took a measured breath and let it out slowly, "but you also carried my brother's naked form in your arms. Sebastian would not be free now without your aid."

"Nor I without Isabel's."

Ean's feet suddenly refused to take another step. He stared at his boots and clung to reason with what felt like his last effort. "Whatever else Isabel has chosen," he said slowly, using the entire force of his will to ground himself and keep his voice calm, "she chose to help you and sacrifice her troth to me in the process. I thought..." he gave a powerful exhale and glanced to Pelas. "In the beginning I really thought it would destroy me, knowing this, but I can't go on blaming her for it now, not knowing what I..."

When only silence continued onward, Pelas dipped his head with quiet inquiry.

The prince met his gaze soberly. "Isabel bound herself to Arion Tavestra, Pelas. She didn't bind herself to me," —*Lady's light*, how that truth drained him in the knowing— "not really to me for *me*. The troth she made to Arion, the troth he made to her..." Ean let out his breath slowly. "What I've come to realize is that those promises haven't changed, but they're not the same troth I thought *I* was making. She sacrificed *our* troth for the game when she helped you, but I don't think she betrayed her troth to Arion at all. I think Arion would've done the same..." Ean pressed his lips together and shook his head. "No, I'm *certain* Arion would've done the same—that he *did* do the same thing to her three hundred years ago."

Compassion colored Pelas's gaze. "I'm sorry, Ean."

Ean regarded him feeling a conflict of guilt. That the immortal could stand there earnestly offering sympathy when Ean had tried to *unmake* him... Contrition tightened his throat. "I owe you the greater apology. What I did to you in Tambarré—"

"Was justified. My brothers and I have done far worse things to one another." Pelas thumbed the ruby knob on his cane and considered the prince with a furrowed brow. "I'm bound to the game now, Ean—at least for as long as Tanis is playing it. Whatever force of intent I bring with me, whatever skill or power I possess...it is yours for the asking."

Ean let out his breath slowly. "I want you to teach me to work *deyjiin*."

Pelas stared at him for a moment's startled pause. Then he shifted his cane to his other hand. "I confess..." a marveling smile hinted on his lips, "of all the things I thought you might ask of me, this is one I never guessed." He pinned Ean with a long look then, full of wary disquiet. "I understand why you want to pursue this ability, but the endeavor is fraught—"

"Your brother has three times claimed my life with this power."

At this, Pelas stared at Ean with concern carving deep lines through his expression.

"Unless I can learn to wield *deyjiin*, to combat it, I won't ever be able to defeat him."

"Which brother was it—" but then Pelas waved away the answer. "Never mind. It was Shail. Of course it was." He worked the muscles of his jaw and stared off, ostensibly chewing on the bitter root of his own experiences. After a long moment of this, his copper eyes shifted and held Ean's. "*Three* times?"

Ean stared sootily at him.

"Ah, I meant only…" Pelas eyed the long line of his cane musingly. "You see, three is the number of times Shail has grievously, even disastrously, fooled me." He lifted him a grim smile. "If I include all of the years Shail was holding my attention with one hand while stabbing me in the back with the other, that number is exponentially increased."

Ean arched brows resignedly. "Should I feel honored or disheartened that he's outsmarted us both?"

"Let it motivate us equally. Whatever my youngest brother is planning, we're aligned in our intention to stop him."

"Then you'll teach me?"

"It was never a question of willingness." Pelas contemplated his cane for a moment more, then started them walking again, his brow shadowed now by private concerns. "It's just…" he cast chariness on his glance, "the only way I know for a mortal to work *deyjiin* is to first be bound to an immortal."

Ean puffed a dubious exhale. "Not likely."

"So you see," Pelas eyed him intriguingly, "it will be a challenge for both of us, this learning."

"Fair enough. When do we start?"

Pelas considered him. Then his lips parted with a smile. "Follow me."

FIFTY-FIVE

"Jump, and trust that you will know how to spread
your wings as you fall."
—The desert parable, *The Eagle and the Wren*

TRELL ROUSED TO the false darkness of heavy draperies closed against the day. The tea Madaam Chouri had made him drink had given him dark and troubling dreams, or perhaps they'd come as a result of the frustration he still felt at himself. In any case, the tea had been potent enough to keep him asleep while they'd washed the muck of battle from his limbs and moved him into his bed.

As he lay staring into the shadows of his tent and listening to the hum of activity from elsewhere in the camp, Trell explored his bandage with careful fingers and found the wound beneath it much improved. He suspected his quick healing had as much to do with Madaam Chouri's skill as with the Mage's masterful manipulation of his life pattern all those months ago.

Had it been whim or prescience that had prompted the Mage to strengthen Trell's life pattern the first time he'd Healed him? Whatever his purpose for doing it, Björn's act had already saved Trell's life several times.

The First Lord planned so far in advance of events that Trell envisioned him as walking Time's unfolding forward edge, with only a tenuous link binding him to the present. Yet when you spoke to him, when he fixed his gaze upon you…there was no debating but that Björn was *right there* with you, giving life his full attention, giving *you* his full attention, experiencing every moment to its utmost.

Trell knew the First Lord didn't know exactly what would happen in the game, but he planned for so many contingencies that it certainly appeared that he did.

That's what Trell had to do. He had to take a broader look, a longer look, a wide enough look to predict what the enemy had in store for them. And he felt an acute urgency to do it now that he knew Viernan hal'Jaitar was sitting on the other side of the gaming board.

The curtains parted to admit a head. "Ah, *Sidi*, you're awake!" Rami's hovering young face beamed at him. "Might I bring you the soup Madaam Chouri prepared for you?"

What Trell really wanted was a shoulder of lamb drenched in gravy, with carrots and potatoes and a couple of loaves of bread, and maybe a bottle of wine all to himself. He gave a quiet sigh. "The soup will be fine, Rami."

"*Balé*." The boy vanished behind the drapes.

Loukas entered at his exit. "Welcome back to the land of the living. How are you feeling?"

"Better. What time of day is it?"

"Past four turns in the afternoon. Raegus said to let you sleep. We needed the day to return things to rights, in any case."

Trell looked over his friend, noting the disheveled state of his clothing as much as the circles beneath his eyes. "I hope you slept."

"A little." Loukas gave him a tired smile. "Enough." He perched on a camp chair and rested elbows on his knees. "Tannour found a survivor from among the enemy last night. He questioned him and learned that someone in our camp is communicating with the wielder at Khor Taran. We still don't know how, exactly."

Trell let out a slow exhale. "I suspected as much."

"Raegus and Rolan have been circling each other all night trying to decide what to do about it."

"I have some ideas to that end. What of our fallen men?"

"The funeral pyre is ready. Raegus was waiting for you before lighting it. He thought you'd want to say a few words."

"I do, certainly."

"Raegus had the men pile the dead Saldarians in a ditch. Said that was better than they deserved."

"For men who made sport of trampling women and children, I'd have to agree."

In the quiet that followed, Trell noted once again the odd melancholy behind Loukas's gaze, which had become more pronounced as a result of last night's sleepless vigil. The most confusing part was how Loukas seemed to endure this sorrow so complacently, as though he felt he deserved whatever malicious affliction was draining his vitality.

"Loukas…" Trell's meaningful tone summoned his friend's gaze.

Loukas broke eye contact and rose from his chair. "Madaam Chouri was planning to check on you again. I should let her know you're awake."

Trell considered him seriously. Trying to get Loukas to talk to him was like squeezing blood from a stone. "Can you summon Raegus and Rolan while you're out, and Tannour as well?"

"Tannour is waiting to see you." The Vestian's name tinged Loukas's tone with an odd disharmony. "I'll get the others."

Just then Rami came through the curtains with Tannour close behind him. The latter had changed back into his usual desert garb and headscarf. He breezed past Loukas without a glance.

Loukas clenched his jaw, staring forward. Then he turned and pushed through the drapes.

Trell exhaled a sigh.

"Here we are, *Sidi*." Rami set the footed tray down across Trell's lap. "Madaam Chouri's famous soup, which smells very strange to me, but I am assured it is good for the healing."

Rami helped Trell sit up and adjusted the tray across his lap. "My mother is very fond of soup," the boy planted hands on his slender hips and gazed at Trell, "but my father prefers the meat stew—preferably lamb, when the sheep are compliant; goat when they are not. He complains when our dinner is soup, to which my mother always explains that he who would eat the fruit must climb the tree, after which my father usually replies he is no woman to sit on the eggs, to which my mother answers it is better to wear out one's shoes than one's sheets, or in my father's case, one's arse, which—"

"By the two Paths, you prattle like a brainless woman." Tannour's *get-out-of-here* stare could've melted stone.

It certainly melted the boy's enthusiasm. He cast a rather uncertain look at Tannour before bowing to Trell and murmuring sheepishly, "I'll just be outside if you need me, *Sidi*."

"Thank you, Rami."

Tannour approached as Rami was departing.

Having seen the Vestian in action the night before, Trell understood better of why Rolan held him in such cautious regard. Yet for all he moved as smoothly as a cloud's shadow across the land, hardly even disturbing the air with his passing, there was something brittle about Tannour. It wasn't just the way the planes of his face seemed smoothed across sharp angles, or how his raven brows drew straight, thick lines above his pale blue eyes. There was a studied contrivance to his manner, as though he'd exhaustively drilled the motions of hand and body and voice, as though comportment had been forced upon him with lashes and blows. Tannour struck Trell as like a shell bleached and tumbled in the surf, battered by circumstance into a mutated shape that was all razor edges.

Pretending not to notice Trell's obvious study of him, the Vestian clasped hands behind his back. "How's your wound, *A'dal?*"

"Better, thank you." Then he added with pointed emphasis, "*Thank you.*"

Tannour acknowledged this with a silent glance, potent with unspoken truths. "I questioned a man last night. Did n'Abraxis tell you?"

The same disharmonic chord rang in Tannour's voice upon speaking Loukas's name as when Loukas had spoken Tannour's.

Trell started eating his soup. "Was the Saldarian able to tell you how the spy was communicating with Khor Taran's wielder?"

"No, but my guess is a bonded pair."

"What's a bonded pair?"

"It can be any two things, but the items are bonded the same as Adepts. For example…" Tannour pulled something from his pocket and tossed it to Trell.

Trell caught it out of the air and looked it over—a simple gold band with an onyx stone. "A ring?"

"I pulled that off the leader of the crew that attacked you." Tannour passed behind the head of Trell's bed and around the other side, as though scouring the shadows for hidden threats.

"You think they were using this?"

"I'm not an expert, but I know enough to tell that there's residual power in that ring."

Trell held the ring up to the light. How deviously simple! And the bonded item could be any ordinary thing. He felt slightly vindicated in his decision not to hunt for the spy, though admittedly, doing next to nothing about him had been a dreadful mistake, and one he wouldn't be making again. "Could this ring allow us to talk to the wielder?"

"It's slightly more complicated than that. When the leader died, the bonded link died with him. All that's left is a trace of what once was." Tannour held a hand to the low chair Loukas had been sitting in. "May I, *A'dal?*"

Trell gave a surprised exhale and looked wonderingly at him. "You saved my life, Tannour. Please, be at your leisure."

"In Vest one never presumes." He repositioned his sword as he seated himself. "Some men count it no favor, the saving of their lives."

"Some men…" Trell regarded him quietly, letting silence more than words lead the charge of his inquiry.

Tannour folded his hands around the sculpted chair arms. He scraped the knobbed end with his thumbnail, a furrow between his brows and his attention angled off. But he was as intelligent as he was perceptive. He knew what Trell was asking with his silence.

After a time, he replied quietly, "It's because I don't wish for death that I begged you to keep my secret."

Trell wondered what history would drive a man like Tannour Valeri to hide himself from the world. "Who here knows you were trained as an assassin?"

Tannour's gaze shifted fast back to his. "Yourself," he answered, tight and low. "The former *A'dal*." He gave a slight wince. "One other."

Trell read that to mean Loukas n'Abraxis. "And Rolan Lamodaar?"

"He suspects, but I wouldn't put it past Rolan to know the truth. Raegus shares everything with Rolan."

Something in this statement snared Trell's attention. He set it aside for future contemplation and concentrated instead on eating the last of his soup, trying hard to imagine it was lamb and failing utterly.

When he'd taken as much as he could stand, he set down his spoon and rested back against the pillows to relieve his aching side. Tannour was staring off into the gloom again, his gaze astringent, hands still gripping the knobby ends of the chair.

Some men shouted their crimes by the lines on their faces; others within the hollows of their eyes. Tannour wore none of the telltale signs of viciousness or cold indifference that might've been expected of an assassin. He seemed to Trell like a doll composed of dry sticks bound into form by injustice.

"Is your life in danger because of a man you killed?"

Tannour scraped at the iron knob with his thumbnail. "It's because I wouldn't kill a man that my life is forfeit."

Trell cocked his head sideways. "Last night I watched you slay a dozen men."

Tannour flung a forceful look back at him. "For *you* I killed those men; for the others of our company who they would've slain. Blood shed with valor splashes the Mirror Path, Your Highness. This is very different from killing for *them*. I…" but he bit back whatever else he'd meant to say.

When he spoke again, his voice had become lifeless, hardened, like the white-scarred flesh where blood no longer flows. "My name is on a list you *never* want to see your name written on—"

A sudden, whipping wind battered the tent canvas. The trees outside shook in a frenzy. Trell looked to the ceiling. "Is that—"

Tannour shoved out of his chair. "It certainly sounds like it."

Men started shouting outside.

Tannour looked quickly to him. "With your leave, *A'dal*?"

"By all means."

Tannour bolted. Trell called for Rami.

The boy appeared just as Trell got both of his feet over the edge of the bed. The motion sent pain stabbing through his side, but he wouldn't countenance meeting one of the *drachwyr* in a sick bed. Too many times already he'd occupied that position beneath their gazes.

Trell had just gotten his pants on—gingerly, gritting his teeth—when a rising commotion announced the *drachwyr*'s imminent arrival. Trell slipped his arms into a loose linen shirt and emerged from his tent in time to see Náiir striding towards him, followed by Tannour and a host of others.

Náiir wore his fighting blacks and carried his dragon-hilted greatsword behind one shoulder, and though he was not so tall as Ramu, he radiated a formidable threat. When his gaze fell upon Trell, however, he broke into a wide grin.

"So you haven't departed us after all!" Náiir took Trell by both shoulders and looked him over with smiling eyes. "My sister was quite distraught. I'm relieved to be able to convey in return that her fears were for naught."

Trell regarded him bemusedly. "How did you—"

Náiir motioned Trell back towards his tent. "It seems that my many-times great niece, your sweet Alyneri, perceived distress across your bond and tried to reach you. When she failed, she told Vaile via their bond, Vaile told my sister, and my sister ordered me to seek you out posthaste. Now I ordinarily ignore Jaya's orders on principle," he angled Trell a grin, "but for you, Trell of the Tides, I would always make an exception."

"I appreciate that more than you know, Náiir." Trell would have to thank Alyneri later, when solitude allowed for conversation across their binding. He motioned to his tent. "Will you share a drink with me?"

"That's most kind of you." Náiir ducked inside.

Trell looked to his waiting officers and shook his head slightly, for he'd sensed that the *drachwyr* wished to speak alone.

Raegus arched a brow with a look that said clearly, *This can't be good.* He turned and waved off the crowd. "Back to it, then! You've seen the A'dal is risen and well. Be ready for his address when his guest departs!"

Inside his tent, Trell found Rami hovering hesitantly between partitioned spaces, staring at Náiir, who'd found his way into the room Trell used as his office.

Trell laid a hand on the boy's shoulder. "Will you bring us some wine, Rami?"

"Rather, just two goblets," Náiir called from the other room with a smile.

Trell headed through the partition as the boy rushed off. Náiir was wandering the space, taking note of the chests, braziers, camp chairs and overlapping carpets, and Trell's work table covered in maps.

"These accommodations aren't so dismaying." Náiir hooked a leg over one corner of the table Trell was using as a desk and clasped hands in his lap. "Jaya led us to believe you were sleeping in fly tents on the bare earth. She was incensed."

Trell found the nearest chair and slowly lowered himself into it. His side was radiating an angry ache all the way down to his knee. "I feel like a sultan, traveling with all of this."

Náiir grunted. "You should see Radov's compound. He could house an entire town beneath the canvas he's set up north of Ramala. We watched from the skies as countless oxen labored to haul four immense wagons through the desert sands. The heaviest one was transporting his bathtub."

Trell somewhat choked out, "Bathtub?"

Náiir flashed a sharp smile. "Forged of solid gold."

"*A'dal?*" Rami was hovering in the partition holding two empty goblets and looking confused.

"Ah, good. Bring them to me, child of the Fourth Tribe of Ishmar."

Rami dutifully crossed the room towards Náiir, but as he passed Trell, he turned him a bewildered look that clearly asked, *fourth tribe of who?*

Náiir took the goblets and dismissed the boy with another of his sharp smiles, the kind that said, *I might be handsome, but in my other form, I can squash you with one toe.* Rami very nearly fled.

Náiir focused on the goblets, and a sanguineous liquid swirled up to fill them. He handed one to Trell.

Trell arched brows. "When did you start making wine?"

Náiir gave him a lazy half-smile and settled back onto the edge of the desk. "About a century before Ramu and Balaji."

"So *you* started the debate?" Trell stared at him for an instant. Then he drank the wine. It was a *very* good Volga.

"My brothers have yet to master my technique." Náiir winked at him. "Now you know a truth shared only by a few. To your health, Trell of the Tides." He raised his goblet to Trell and they both drank anew. But as Náiir lowered his cup, his expression sobered. "So…what happened to you?"

Trell told him in brief sentences while Náiir drank his wine.

"Viernan hal'Jaitar." Náiir grumbled an oath. "Would that a Whisper Lord might've claimed him in the First Lord's name and saved the rest of us the immense misfortune of his involvement. I asked Loghain once if he might, as a favor to us, make the 'mistake' of executing hal'Jaitar earlier than his Calling." The *drachwyr* made an airy wave. "You've seen these Nadori wielders with their black *keffiyehs* and silk robes. They all look alike. Loghain could've passed it off as an honest mistake. The First Lord would've forgiven him."

Levity drained from his expression as he frowned down into his goblet. "Now Viernan hal'Jaitar has brought M'Nador's forces once again to those bleak sands north of Ramala, and the princedom to the edge of ruin."

"The Khalim Plains," Trell murmured.

"Where last M'Nador forced the Mage's hand so disastrously." Náiir's gaze as it lifted back to meet his bespoke a night of storms. "Now the desert air carries the electric charge of Radov's fermenting malcontent. We wait to confer with Ramu upon his return from T'khendar. We don't know what Radov waits for."

"No attacks as yet?"

"They sit. The Emir's forces sit. Archers wait with arrows nocked on both sides of that no man's land, which neither force yet dares cross. The stalemate has become a stalking."

"What kind of force has Radov mustered?"

Náiir cast him a telling look. "They are ten thousand strong, Trell."

Trell sucked in his breath. "Where did Radov get that many men?"

"Allies unknown to us undoubtedly. If that sour mass somehow presses past *our* defenses, the Emir's forces will have difficulty holding the oasis against them."

Trell understood this with painful clarity. By all the gods, but his reasons to complete his mission rapidly only seemed to be compounding! He shifted in his chair, stifling a wince. "Can you tell me anything of the magic being worked at Khor Taran? The wielder there is already proving problematic."

"The currents show a constant flow of the fourth channeling into the lowest tier of the fortress—likely where they're holding your father's soldiers. The consistency of flow suggests static compulsion patterns—that is, the wielder is not himself constantly working them. They must be painted or carved or otherwise fixed into the room itself. The good news with this kind of working is that if you can destroy one of these patterns, the circle will break; but beware entering the space yourself until you do, Trell, for you could become prey to whatever malicious working holds the rest in thrall."

Trell glowered into his wine. "So it'll be a cinch then."

Náiir grunted. "If it makes you feel any better, Rhakar routinely relieves himself while flying over the fortress. If he sees the wielder below him, he takes special aim." He downed the last of his wine and then settled his gaze more seriously upon Trell. "But there is something else you should know."

The gravity in this pronouncement gave Trell a stab of foreboding. "Yes?"

Náiir stared into his goblet while more wine swirled upwards, clearly not seeing the dark liquid but another memory, much reviled. "Something happened at the *sa'reyth*." He lifted a direct gaze to meet Trell's. "Vaile was injured, and we cannot find Mithaiya."

Trell lowered his wine from his lips. "What happened?"

"A Malorin'athgul found his way to the *sa'reyth*. His every step left deep indentations in the cosmic fabric. Vaile described him but couldn't tell us his name, which is...troubling."

Incredulity pinned Trell against the back of his chair. "Did Vaile fight him?" He could hardly fathom this news. "How was she injured?"

"He threw something around her—an energy field of unfamiliar construction. She exhausted herself into unconsciousness trying to escape from it. Rhakar found her and with not inconsiderable effort managed to free her from it." Náiir's gaze grew dangerous and dark. "They were created in the Genesis to *unmake stars,* Trell. They have abilities beyond our ken—not *meant* for our ken—even as the Realms of Light were not meant for theirs. This is Balance at its utmost *unbalanced*."

Trell's wine sat forgotten in his hand; his breath hung leaden in his lungs. "And Mithaiya?"

Náiir pressed his lips together and shook his head. "We don't know what happened to her. Vaile saw nothing of what transpired after the Malorin'athgul trapped her. We believe he may have taken Mithaiya across a node, or..." his brow pinched, "there are other possibilities. We perceive our sister via the binding we all share, but none of us have been able to reach her."

Trell exhaled a slow breath. The constant discomfort in his side mingled with a new disconcertion, making his entire body throb with pain. "Is there anything I can do?"

Náiir regarded him wonderingly. "All of this is to explain why we may not be able to aid you again, and you ask to help us...instead..." Abruptly his gaze narrowed. He rose purposefully from the desk. "You said you were healed. Why have you kept your injury from me?"

Trell hadn't realized until that moment that he'd been holding back a wince...or he supposed, *not* holding it back, since the radiating pain had infused his expression. "You've already done so much—"

Náiir very nearly hissed at him. He went to one knee beside Trell, laid a hand on his shoulder and locked eyes with him. "Have you any idea the storm that would meet me if I left here without ensuring you were well and whole? And here all this time you've been hiding your infirmity?"

Even while Náiir was still talking, Trell felt *elae* channeling into him with such power that it made Madaam Chouri's Healing of the night before feel like a trickling brook next to a river in flood. No...a tidal wave.

A heady disorientation overcame him; his side prickled powerfully, and heat flooded outward from where pain had once reigned. Rather than the subtle intensification he'd experienced during other Healings, this one burst into being, an explosion that seared through his life pattern and forced repair with whiplash intensity.

Then it was over. The room slowly stopped rotating. Náiir stood, and Trell felt...

Restored hardly described the sensation. He felt like *elae* had wrapped itself around his bones. He rather imagined he could withstand the force of a mountain collapsing atop him.

Trell shifted his eyes to meet Náiir's gaze. "*Thank you*," he choked out.

"Don't mention it—except to my sister," Náiir added with a wink. "Jaya fancies herself a better Healer and eschews my methods as uncouth. I find my own approach more expedient. Why spend five minutes when the deed can be accomplished in two?"

"A worthy question," Trell somewhat gasped.

Náiir settled him a look of stern reprimand. "You must seek aid when you need it, Trell. A good commander never fears utilizing every resource available to him and must do so ruthlessly. The game intensifies. Never let yourself forget that we're closing in on the finish, for better or worse."

Trell exhaled a slow breath and nodded his understanding. Then, newly decisive, he rose from his chair—happily divested of all pain; verily, he felt as strong as a bear!—drank Náiir's excellent wine in several deep swallows, and set down the goblet with finality.

That done, he looked at Náiir with a determined glint in his gaze. "Before you leave, there is one last thing I'd like your help with, if you're willing."

The *drachwyr* grinned. "Finally! Someone who gives my advice its due regard." He gave a little bow. "At your service, Prince of Dannym."

Trell led him out of the tent.

Loukas and the others got to their feet as Trell emerged.

"Summon the men," Trell told them. "It's time to honor our dead."

The sun had fallen behind the mountain and the forest lay in shadows by the time the men had all gathered around the funeral pyre. Bundles of wood jammed the lowest tier and interwoven logs the second, while upon the third lay the bodies of the eleven men who'd lost their lives to Saldarian blades.

Trell walked to the pyre and faced his men, feeling in return the weight of their focused attention. He raised his voice to be heard by all.

"Courage is a word that tempts us—dares us—to live bolder, to strive harder, to test our mettle against the clock of Fate and race Destiny to life's last horizon. Courage is the measure of our willingness to persevere beyond right or reason; to forge a shape from the formless aether of impossibility. Courage shouts, and courage is silent. It derives from the fears that whisper louder than any battle cry. It thrives in those choices to deny instinct, to stand firm when all would have us quivering, to live on when Death sings a serenade of escape. Courage shines in enduring when all reason is shouting submission, and in submitting when all else would demand we persevere."

Trell held a hand to the pyre behind him. "Tonight, the men we honor sit at Inanna's banquet table—" He paused and then offered a wry smile. "Let's be honest. They're probably drinking themselves into a stupor on Huhktu's wine, ogling Inithiya, and lewdly propositioning Qharp."

This earned a round of chuckles among the men.

"With their courage, our comrades purchased honorable passage into Annwn. Now we must raise our courage and allow them to enjoy the spoils they've earned in the Afterlife."

The men murmured concordance at this.

"Do not chain them with our grief. Let us instead take up their weapons and carry forward…"

Hearty agreement met this statement.

"…and with every step, honor the courage they taught us as they stormed bravely beyond life's horizon."

The men gave a collective cry.

Trell looked to Náiir. "Would you honor us with flame, Náiir?"

Náiir pressed a hand across his heart. "The honor is mine, Trell." He looked to the pyre with a moment's contemplation.

Blue-white funnels of fire shot upwards to engulf the entire three-tiered structure. The men quickly pressed themselves back to the far edge of the clearing, for the heat from these spires was so intense that the sand beneath the pyre soon started boiling. Only Náiir remained near, haloed in the corona of his geysering flame, and Trell, at his side, safe within his protective sphere.

When the smoke billowing from the pyre's center abated and all had burned away, the columns of blue-white fire reached for each other, and the tips of their flames became entwined. Out of this tangle emerged a spire, spreading wings of flame too bright to look upon.

The roar of the flames became almost painful then, and the heat so intense that it crisped the leaves on the trees edging the clearing.

Then, all at once, the flames vanished.

But something remained.

As the spots cleared from Trell's vision, he gazed at a soaring monument of glass. Eleven twisted spires, each as thick as a tree trunk, reached three stories high. At their top, the glassy flames interwove beneath the talons of a great winged bird. An eagle.

The men stood in mute silence.

Trell looked to Náiir, utterly at a loss for words. The *drachwyr* pressed a hand to his heart. Trell turned to his men and cleared his throat. "We have honored them." Determination filled his voice. "Now let us prove our own honor!"

The men emerged from the safety of the trees murmuring agreement.

Trell told them, "A wielder sits behind the aggression that brought us here today. The same man holds a thousand of my father's men hostage. *He* is the target for our vengeance! Focus your eyes to the south. In the morning we ride, and he shall hear the thunder of our coming!"

A rousing shout went up, which quickly fell into an alternating chant of *'Trell of the Tides, King of the Converted! Trell of the Tides, Prince of Dragons!'* As the men were breaking up, the chant faded into talk of the Dannish soldiers being held at Khor Taran and this so-called wielder who thought to take on their *A'dal*.

Trell looked back to Náiir with gratitude weighty in his gaze and gave him a brief but tight embrace.

"May you ever remain in Fortune's favor, Trell of the Tides," Náiir said into Trell's ear. Then he flashed one of his more dashing smiles and headed off beneath the singed trees.

Raegus and Trell's other officers joined him at the monument, crossing from browned grass into a circle of living green that extended about five paces around Trell. They all looked a bit round-eyed.

While Tannour knelt and ran his hand across the glassy surface where the sand had been boiling, Raegus stared up at the towering monument and visibly swallowed. "It this what you meant when you said it never hurts to have a few immortals on your side?"

Trell sighed. "Not exactly."

"He didn't have to do this." Loukas looked bemusedly to Trell. "Why did he do this?"

"Because he could." Tannour speared Loukas with an unapologetic stare. "Because it's the power they were born to."

"I think this was his way of honoring them." Trell let out a slow exhale, deeply touched by Náiir's creation. It would stand for centuries as a reminder to all who knew its tale, a memorial for every man who'd given his life in service of another's cause. Trell vowed that he would make those sacrifices mean something.

He looked to Raegus and Rolan. "Let it be known—quietly—that the *drachwyr* came today with news that the Emir has summoned two thousand men out of Duan'Bai and that they're even now marching on Khor Taran. We will rendezvous with them on the plains south of the mountain."

"Huhktu's bones!" Rolan hissed. "Is that what he told you?"

"Not at all." Trell met every one of their confused gazes with a level one of his own. "But it's what I want our resident spy to tell the wielder at Khor Taran. So speak among yourselves of these plans, and do it where others can overhear."

They all nodded to this.

Trell looked to Raegus. "On your ride tomorrow you'll need to collect wood—wagonloads of it. If I recall correctly, trees in the lowlands south of the fortress are sparse."

Raegus looked bewildered. "Wood?"

"For campfires."

He blinked at Trell. "For the nonexistent army we're not actually meeting up with?"

"Exactly. Find a campsite within a day's march of the fortress—defensible, and well hidden—and send a scout to wait for me by the river. That's how we'll find you."

Rolan arched a bushy black brow. "*We?*"

"Loukas and I are riding out tonight."

Loukas turned him a swift look. "We are?"

Trell gripped the engineer's arm. "Saddle your horse. We ride for Khor Taran."

FIFTY-SIX

"Man suffers no greater deception than his own convictions."
–Darshanvenkhátraman, Destroyer of Hope

DARSHAN STOOD GAZING out across a vista of rolling green hills bordered by a great mountain range. The undulating emerald landscape reminded him vaguely of a nebula's voluminous clouds, while the snowbound crags somehow seemed to mimic the points of distant stars. The symmetry of this construction reflected a beauty Darshan could appreciate.

He looked to Kjieran. "There is much to admire in this view."

Kjieran stood farther along the hill with the grass blowing long about his knees. In his acolyte's colorless gaze, Darshan saw those untouchable, bright stars that ever beckoned from beyond the Void. No matter how long or far he'd soared through the immense reaches of Chaos, those stars had remained beyond his ken. He'd long wondered why. Now he knew they'd been the stars of the Realms of Light.

The spring breeze made Kjieran's black hair dance around his shoulders, and the sun shining strongly on his face gave a radiance to his skin. Darshan reflected that Kjieran held his own sort of beauty, one that he found no parallel for in Chaos. Perhaps that was why he'd been so drawn to him from the start, because the truthreader's essential construction was so antithetical and alien to his own.

A subtle smile hinted on Kjieran's lips.

Darshan arched a brow at him. "What is this thought you're keeping from me?"

Kjieran turned back to the view, still wearing that secretive smile. "There's something different about you."

Darshan looked down at himself, though he suspected Kjieran wasn't referencing his clothes. Yet he'd never dressed himself so—in a knee-length coat of finely woven flax, Agasi in design. Kjieran wore a similar coat, but with less embroidery around the cuffs and hem. Darshan angled skepticism on his gaze. "Who's weaving this dream?"

Kjieran looked him over and grinned. "Perhaps we both are." He started off down the hill.

Darshan followed, clasping hands behind his back.

"These are the mountains of Tirycth Mir." Kjieran affected a breezy manner as he glanced Darshan's way. "They're the tallest and longest mountains in Agasan. These hills demark the western edge of the Solvayre."

Darshan cast his gaze across the jutting mountains—forbidding, gloriously wild and remote. They cast no shadow across this part of the land. Perhaps the sun found it too beautiful to cast into shadow.

Kjieran exhaled a long, contented sigh. "I have so many memories from my childhood here…or I did, once, when I could remember them. I can't reach most of them now."

"What do you mean?"

Kjieran angled a look at him. "When I place my attention where those memories ought to be…all I see is you."

Darshan frowned. He considered Kjieran's last comment as well as his earlier one. In truth, the entire Dreamscape felt different. Perhaps, as Kjieran had said, they were both weaving the dream that day.

Darshan's dreams had often ridden a heady edge—desire at war with betrayal, lust and fury courting one another with explosive disapprobation—while the dream now felt oddly peaceful, as if their two minds had finally achieved an equilibrium.

"The Goddess said I would be able to find the Returning…" A furrow twitched between Kjieran's brows as he strolled. His thoughts had clearly traveled elsewhere.

But Darshan halted, rooted by the word. "*Goddess?*"

Kjieran turned back to face him and pushed hands into his pockets. "I dreamed of her, there before the end." He looked Darshan over. "I assumed you knew."

Talk of goddesses immediately roused Darshan's possessive will. "What did you assume I knew?"

Kjieran's colorless gaze became distant again. "I felt you so strongly in my thoughts there at the end. It seemed that you must surely know my mind completely." A contemplative thought hung in the silence. He gave him an apologetic glance. "I thought you knew that I'd come to you under false pretenses; that I never stopped serving my king. A truthreader's oaths to a liege are as binding as the pattern you worked to seal me to yourself, my lord."

Darshan felt that old betrayal come surging towards the surface anew, but the aether of Kjieran's dreaming slowed its ascent. Where he usually found a dagger of sharp censure ready to hand, now it had to drive through Kjieran's own rationale. By the time it reached Darshan, Kjieran's viewpoint had dulled its edge.

Darshan started walking again, his mind pensive now, mulling over the changeling dream and the new ideas he was suddenly able to recognize and understand. As they rounded another hill, a new vista opened with a new shift of perspective, much like what Darshan was experiencing just then. "The landscape of your dreams colors my understanding." He cast his acolyte a sidelong eye and clasped hands behind his back again. "I see grave purpose in your choices. I did not see this before."

"That's true." Kjieran agreed quietly.

"This causes me conflict."

Kjieran glanced to him. "I understand that, too." The look in his eyes showed that he did indeed understand the implications, yet the smile twitching on his lips betrayed an uncharacteristic amusement at it.

Darshan frowned at him.

Kjieran returned his smiling attention to the view. "If I have any say in the Returning, I would like to find my new life here."

Darshan considered this for a time. "Do you have such say?"

"I don't know." Kjieran flashed a wry smile. "For all we understand about the Returning, much of it remains a vast unknown. If anyone could've spoken on such matters, it would've been Isabel van Gelderan."

The name pulled a pause in Darshan's step. "Why?"

"She's Epiphany's Prophet." Kjieran pushed his wind-blown hair from his eyes and lifted his face to the sky. He wore a soft smile, as if drinking in the pleasure of the sun's warmth. "Some legends speak of Cephrael as choosing the time you will die and Epiphany the time you'll Return. Others speak of both of them as manning the gates of Annwn, the Extian Doors, portal to the Returning."

"Epiphany..." Darshan explored the patterns of Her name. "Is She the goddess you spoke of just now?"

"Yes."

"And She spoke to you?"

"I *saw* her there, at the end." Kjieran's expression seemed nearly beatific as he recalled that moment. Then he focused back on Darshan. "Didn't you see Her also?"

Darshan gave a rueful grunt. "Apparently the goddess found my presence unsuitable."

Kjieran dropped a smile to his toes at this.

Darshan looked him over circumspectly. "You seem different as well."

"I suppose I must." Kjieran exhaled a measured breath. "Through the time I've spent in your dreams, I've come to understand you better also, my lord."

"Have you?"

Darshan was feeling a pulsating dissatisfaction that intensified with every step they took down the hill together. The old Kjieran had often roused feelings of betrayal, but this Kjieran, with his dazzling eyes and ready grins, only roused Darshan's desire. He clenched his jaw and looked back to the view. "I feel like you're holding me hostage."

Kjieran burst into laughter. "*I'm* holding *you* hostage?" He shot Darshan a quick, flashing smile that only made Darshan ache all the more.

He regarded Kjieran beneath a brooding malcontent. "Because you chose death over an eternity with me." It was the first time he'd ever spoken this hateful truth.

Kjieran stopped walking and turned to face him. His crystalline eyes offered apology and something else that Darshan couldn't decipher, yet which drew a taut thread through him. They stood barely a hand's width apart, yet Darshan felt as if Kjieran was entirely out of his reach. "I wouldn't make the same choice today, my lord."

A puff of disbelief escaped Darshan. "I'm meant to trust this now, when you dissembled before me for so long?"

Kjieran gave a sudden grin that he quickly smothered as he dropped his gaze, but Darshan suspected the smile had merely gone underground. He looked him over speculatively. "You hide your thoughts from me again. Go on then, speak your mind."

A shadow of that smile returned as Kjieran looked back to him. "I was only thinking…would you ever have imagined that someone in your temple didn't serve you wholly?"

Darshan's gaze darkened as he took Kjieran's meaning. "You are a vexatious spirit."

A broad grin split Kjieran's face. He started walking again, inviting Darshan to follow with an amused glance. "My lord, you must admit the truth in my statement. You're utterly blind to the idea that anyone could be other than as you assume them to be. You cast compulsion with your gaze and mold the world to your intent and make everyone in it take the shape of your expectations."

This truth, so boldly stated, gave Darshan pause. He stared hard at Kjieran.

Seeing that his words had hit the mark, Kjieran laid his hand on Darshan's arm and said more gently, "You've never given any of us the chance to be other than as you decided we are."

For a long moment, Darshan held his gaze in silence, with each inhalation feeling that spear of truth penetrating more deeply, with each exhalation feeling pierced by painfully acute threads of promise.

"And what if I did?" Even as he said the words, he couldn't quite believe they were crossing his tongue. "What if I walked through the world and looked with different eyes…would you walk with me?"

Kjieran opened his mouth to respond but then simply stood there, grounded by surprise. He searched Darshan's gaze, gleaning meaning and understanding through their shared dream. "I…would try, my lord." He pushed a hand through his hair and blew out an explosive breath. "Lord and the Lady…" he lifted a momentous look back to Darshan. "I have no idea how to go about finding you in the waking world."

Darshan felt those threads of promise disintegrating.

Kjieran reached for his hand. "But let us try at least. When you wake, reach out to me—perhaps in the way you contact your brothers?"

Darshan considered him deeply; likewise what he was committing himself to doing. "Very well. I will call upon you, Kjieran. Do not disappoint me."

Kjieran held his gaze with large eyes. "I very much hope not to, my lord."

Darshan rose from his bed and walked outside beneath a shadowed gallery where a storm was lashing the stones. It seemed he summoned storms with his dreams even when they weren't tumultuous.

And before the dream…he hardly remembered stumbling out of Shadow, or crawling into bed with the flesh of his shell still smoking from exposure to Mithaiya's sun.

And how is the little drachwyr *faring, I wonder?*

Was she still drinking in her mother sun's light, repairing the damage he'd done to her? His claws of *deyjiin* had dug in deep and drained her badly. In retrospect, perhaps he shouldn't have barged into her territory issuing demands. A little of Pelas's favored diplomacy might've served his purposes better.

Beyond the rain-swept portico, the storm was making night of the day. Long sheets of rain charged across the land, while charcoal clouds blanketed the distant mountains.

The wind tore at Darshan's singed and tangled hair but caressed his bare flesh, leaving the impression of a damp kisses while electrically charged particles tingled his skin. The latter had taken on a bronze hue since his unexpected foray to Mithaiya's molten planet, but otherwise his shell had healed well.

He couldn't say the same about his hair.

A subtle smile lifted one corner of Darshan's mouth. The little *drachwyr* had gotten the better of him, no doubt. He admired her for that.

'The moment you step out of that temple of yours, you'll be far out of your depth.' Shail's warning held new meaning for him now. He'd never imagined there would be others on this plane who could challenge him.

Darshan walked to the edge of the gallery and leaned a muscled shoulder against a column, his gaze seeing not the storm-washed world but the bright day he'd left behind in Kjieran's dream.

For the first time, he'd woven a dream of equal sharing with Kjieran van Stone. He'd shared his acolyte's thoughts, *felt* Kjieran's purpose—a purpose so strong and unwavering that the truthreader had clung to its mast amid the raging waves of Darshan's fury and weathered the storm all the way to his tragic end. Kjieran had saved the lord he was sworn to while with every breath betraying and defying the lord he was bound to.

These were *undeniable* truths.

Whereas before he'd been tiptoeing around this admission, now he knew it definitively. He could no longer say Kjieran had no purpose save to die. Purpose had driven Kjieran as desperately and willfully as a row master upon a slaver's galley.

The wind whipped Darshan's charred hair into his eyes. Tangled strands bound his face and blurred his vision, like these truths now bound and blurred his thoughts. Nay, not merely his thoughts—his entire view of the realm's existence.

For if Kjieran van Stone could so prove himself possessed of purpose, could not other creatures of this realm potentially as well? Was it possible that he'd been drawn to Kjieran because he'd sensed within him a purpose as singular of will as his own?

Indeed...possessed of purpose *and* an immortal soul.

Darshan walked from gallery to storm-swept terrace, letting the whipping rain sting his skin and echoes of lightning dance in his core where a hollow feeling had begun spreading, a reminder of things as yet unsettled.

This game was not so simple as it had once appeared to him. The stark clarity of singular purpose had become diffuse in the light of varying perspectives, and now a host of indistinct truths lingered on his periphery.

'If you ever left your ivory tower, perhaps you'd see the truths you're so plainly missing.' Pelas's words.

Darshan exhaled a slow breath. *Perhaps you've the right of it after all, brother.*

Reaching the end of his terrace, he stepped up on the marble wall and stood with feet spread, braced against the wind. A simple thought drew the lightning, and a jagged streak speared down from the charcoal clouds, splitting rain into sizzling vapor as it leapt for his outstretched arms.

The flash turned the world into negative, even as its force charged through his shell, leaving thorny black streaks in his flesh to mark its passing. Raindrops exploded into ozonic mist, and steam rose from his skin. A tidal wave blasted through the currents.

As the lightning's effects were fading, Darshan lowered his arms. That hollow feeling in his core remained, unaltered by the elements; its cause was not a lack of energy but of conviction.

He stepped backwards off the railing, landed with a splash and returned to his chambers. Time to follow through on his promise and find out if Kjieran would make good on his.

As he walked beneath the gallery, Darshan sought Kjieran the way he would seek his brothers. He first found the threads of binding that linked their souls. Then he sought Kjieran's awareness across that ethereal connection.

But unlike when contacting his brothers, Darshan couldn't sense any awareness on the other end of the cord. This troubled him, but he cast forth the calling nonetheless.

Kjieran...?

His feet slowed, expectation dragging his steps, yet he regained his chambers without a spark of recognition from Kjieran's end.

Now he felt foolish. How many times had he sought Kjieran's awareness right after his acolyte's death? How often had he called to him? How many nights had he sought him, only to dive instead into tormenting dreams? And in every foray, he'd found only emptiness, absence...death.

Darshan exhaled a slow breath and forced himself to accept the obvious truth: no sentient life remained beyond the dark cloak of death. Kjieran was a ghost haunting his dreams, nothing more.

He braced a hand against a column and lowered his head. Rainwater dripped into his eyes while his hair made a dark cast of his shoulders. How could he still feel so hollow when loss bound his chest and throat so tightly?

Abruptly he straightened and pressed on, crossing the gallery back to his chambers. He'd already decided upon his course of action and would continue forward, with or without Kjieran beside him.

He opened himself to the hundreds of bonds linking to his consciousness and cast a thought across two of them, as the plucking of dual harp strings, to summon his acolytes.

They were waiting for him when he re-entered his bedchamber, two men kneeling with downcast eyes and long hair of blonde and brown, their bodies well proportioned, hands pressed to their knees.

These two must've been the ones who'd tended to him while he was unconscious. They'd stripped him of his burned clothing and bathed him in his sleep. He almost smiled upon imagining their expressions when they'd found him.

Darshan looked them over speculatively. "Come. I have need of you both."

He strode into his dressing chamber and assessed his form before the tall mirror. His shell had healed well from his foray to that burning planet, but his hair…in places it had simply melted, fused into thick and tangled cords, while other sections had been singed away. Even sopping wet from the rain, he could tell it would not recover.

"It must be cut."

One acolyte fetched a chair for him while his partner went for scissors. The former stood behind him and drew the mass of tangled hair behind Darshan's back. Then he held his hands beside Darshan's neck, just above his shoulders. "About here, my lord?"

Marveling at the sorry state of his hair, Darshan determined that Mithaiya had surely taken the point in their tête-à-tête. A subtle smile touched his lips. "I think…a little higher."

They cut his hair above the line of fracture, shorter in back and longest in front, so that when he lifted his head to look at himself, uneven damp strands fell around his cheekbones while the foremost strands clung to his jaw. Then his acolytes brought him the clothes he requested. In the last, he stood before the mirror in another of Pelas's gifted coats, this one a damask of burnished gold, worn over an embroidered white shirt whose long cuffs skimmed his knuckles.

Darshan pushed both hands through his hair to sweep the long strands back from his face. Then he stood there staring at his reflection. With his raven hair cut short and wearing the garments of an Agasi nobleman, he hardly recognized himself.

Yet it seemed appropriate. A new image in honor of the new vision—*a truer vision?*—he was determined to gain of the world.

Part of him wished that Kjieran could've seen him, could've perhaps adopted this image to replace the one of the Prophet Bethamin, which memory his acolyte associated with so many moments of despair. Though he wasn't sure that this version of himself was that much of an improvement over the old one. Neither were a true expression of his real form.

But you look quite handsome.

The voice speaking into his mind halted both Darshan's breath and his thoughts.

His first impulse was that he'd imagined the voice. Next, he suspected Pelas was playing a trick on him. Even so, his heart beat faster. Hope drove him to speak, despite his suspicions. *Kjieran…? Is it truly you?*

How many voices do you have in your head, my lord? Darshan heard Kjieran's amusement, felt his smile. These were common impressions when speaking to his brothers across their bond. He stared at his reflection and was startled to find such emotion revealed in it.

For the first time, he admitted to himself that this was no haunting but a continued thread of connection to the Adept he'd bound to his soul. Yet it puzzled him almost to the same degree of intensity.

Kjieran, I called to you, but you didn't answer me.

I heard you, my lord, but…I couldn't find you. I had nothing to lead me to you, only a voice out of the formless void.

Then how—?

Just now, when you were thinking of me…you were sharing your thoughts, sharing what you saw—whether or not you meant to.

Darshan's brow furrowed slightly.

I don't know how to explain it, my lord, but when you shared your thoughts with me, it was like a window of light opened into the dark void. When I looked through it, I found you on the other side.

Darshan considered this idea. *This is not how I communicate with my brothers.*

Bindings take many forms, Kjieran offered. *Ours feels to me less like a line strung between us and more like a mutual, shared space we can both access from opposite sides.*

Darshan thought on this but reached no immediate conclusion. *There are things I would better understand, Kjieran—the nature of our dreams, for example, and the nature of the binding I worked upon you. Who could answer such questions?*

The Sormitáge has scholars dedicated to such studies, my lord.

Darshan's gaze at his reflection tightened slightly. *The Sormitáge…*

Where his brothers had dedicated so much of their time in this realm to their own individual, disparate pursuits. There was a definite irony to be acknowledged here.

Yet…once he aligned his thoughts towards the idea, he felt a sort of *inclination*, almost a tugging—or perhaps a slight yearning? It was hard to decipher the exact feeling—drawing him westward.

Certainly he needed to better understand the Adept Returning. Even had he any idea how to release Kjieran from his thrall, he wouldn't leave such a thing to chance. Kjieran's body was already deceased. Darshan was obviously holding his spirit on that plane—but *why? How?*

Yes, a trip to Agasan's famed Sacred City was definitely in order.

Darshan turned from the mirror and faced his acolytes. In his mind, he found the threads of binding that subsumed their determinism to his own. He placed a hand on each of their shoulders while placing a mental knife to those binding strings. "I release you from your oaths to me."

They must've felt it, the quivering snap of those threads parting, but he couldn't tell if their shocked expressions were a result of his working or his words.

"My lord!" They both gasped and fell to their knees before him.

Darshan saw tears trailing down their cheeks. From the sense of hope that suddenly flooded the currents, he assumed with a dry resignation that they were tears of joy.

He wasn't sure what possessed him then—certainly the idea had never occurred to him before that moment—but he took hold of each of the hundreds of strings within his harp of compulsion, myriad threads of binding to Marquiin scattered around the realm, and with a razor-edged thought, severed every one.

The rain suddenly ceased against the temple roof.

His acolytes stared open-mouthed at him.

What had they experienced? What had they perceived? Surely the currents had carried something of what he'd just done.

He hooked a finger beneath each of their chins and encouraged them to their feet. "Let it be known forthwith: Nothing of the Prophet remains to serve here. I do not know if I will ever return."

Then he spun away from their shocked expressions, and strode out beneath a clearing sky to determine what he could see of the world without the veil of his own expectations.

FIFTY-SEVEN

"Not taking life too seriously is the surest way to get out of it alive."
–The pirate truthreader Hadrian of Jamaii

EAN CAUGHT *DEYJIIN* on his blade and winced. The toxic power sizzled through his fourth-strand mental shield, injected acid into his thoughts and corroded the intent he'd just summoned. He quickly wrapped the fifth around the expanding power and cast it from his mind; his grunted exhale carried the noxious taste of sulfur.

Of course, the latter could've been a result of the volcano belching smoke into the otherwise clear sky a dozen miles from where he and Pelas were sparring. The Palma Lai archipelago played host to many active volcanoes, the fiery jewels of its lengthy chain. All around them, dark peaks scraped the ocean horizon, alternately oozing fire or fumes.

The islands apparently had far more patience for the earth's dyspeptic flatulence than Ean could muster, especially with *deyjiin* constantly crackling in his brain, but Pelas's choice of a battlefield was purposeful. Palma Lai was one of the few places in the realm where they could work their powers indiscriminately and not call attention to themselves on the currents. And gaining the attention of one of Pelas's brothers was the last thing either of them wanted.

The tropical sun was bearing down with unrelenting intensity, baking Ean's bare chest and arms along with the dark rock beneath his feet. They sparred on the high plateau of an old lava flow, which thrust a shriveled and barren arm across the lush island. After a morning of battling *deyjiin*, Ean was beginning to feel like his mind resembled that blackened swath rather too closely.

Pelas swept his foot through the dark earth and spat dust from his mouth. "If you let it touch your thoughts, Ean, that's going to happen."

You don't say. Ean tried to clear his mind of *deyjiin*'s lingering tingle. He was attempting to find an ability within himself to compel the power the way Björn could, or at least a better means of controlling and channeling it, but thus far, *deyjiin* seemed to be doing most of the controlling. "Let's do it again."

Pelas grinned predatorily at him. "Your wish is my command, Prince of Dannym." He pushed *deyjiin* into another pattern and cast it forth with the flick of a thought.

Ean cast his own intent into a spear and ripped the pattern apart just before it hit his shields. The detritus of the exploded pattern bombarded his mind with spiny needles of pain.

The prince pushed a palm to his forehead and hissed a frustrated oath.

Also stripped to the waist beneath the punishing sun, Pelas shoved hands on his hips, just above the waistline of his pants, and looked up at Ean under his brows. Strands of his long hair clung damply to his skin. Both of them wore a sheen of sweat. "I thought you wanted to find a way to combat *deyjiin* other than unworking it?"

Ean glowered at him. "The pattern came too quickly at me."

"Or you think too slowly." Pelas aimed a knowing grin at him. "You *did* ask me to make this realistic—"

"I know what I said." Ean paced a tight circle. He could see the pattern of causation branching forth from this learning. He knew he was on the right course, but despite his efforts, he didn't seem to be making any *headway* upon that path. The distant spirals of consequence stayed just as indistinct, no matter what he did.

Pelas retied his long hair into a messy knot behind his head, observing the while, "We've tried this your way all morning, Ean. Perhaps we should try it my way for a time?"

His way—an intimate sharing of minds. Ean dragged his fingers through sweat-dampened hair and lifted his head to stare between his elbows up at the sky. A long trail of fulminous smoke led back to the nearest volcano and its cauldron of liquid fire. That belching hole seemed more inviting to him than the inside of Pelas's head.

"Fine." Ean dropped his arms to his sides and a sooty contemplation towards the Malorin'athgul. "Let's try it your way."

Pelas grinned. "I'll try to make it as painless as possible."

"Just make it fruitful."

Pelas approached him bare-footed across the black and blistered earth, assessing Ean with a shrewd glint in his copper eyes. "It will be a new experience at least, this sharing of each other's minds."

"Seems to me you have a few too many others sharing that space already."

Pelas chuckled. "You have no idea, Prince of Dannym." He extended his hand and clasped wrists with Ean. "A light bond, temporary," Pelas met his gaze intently, "central between us; a common space for the sharing of thought. Would you like to do the working?"

Ean had already claimed *elae*'s fourth strand to do so.

Pelas opened his mind to the prince, and light unfolded like a sudden, blinding break in the clouds. Ean molded the fourth into a field beneath that blazing light, forging a central space, neutral ground where each might place ideas for the other to inspect. Then he retreated to the shady solitude of his own mind.

Pelas crossed his arms and considered Ean while they each explored the mental space newly created between them.

Ean had no idea what his mind seemed like to Pelas, but the Malorin'athgul's felt as slick as an oiled blade, and surprisingly…benign, so different from Darshan's razor intent. He sensed *deyjiin*'s presence within Pelas's constitution, but the Malorin'athgul was keeping the power contained behind the immutable wall of his own consciousness.

"So…" Pelas looked the prince up and down with a taunting smile, "shall we try it with blades?"

Ean blinked against the sun as he spun and caught Pelas's bolt of *deyjiin* on his sword. The sentient weapon sang, his muscles tensed, and cold power sizzled against his shields. The prince wrapped the fifth around *deyjiin* and slung it off to his right. The black earth behind him shivered into an ashen blight several feet in diameter. The landscape now sported a rash of such craters.

Pelas skipped forward with his weapon swinging. Ean raised his in both hands to block it. Their Merdanti blades clashed in a rapid staccato that echoed back from the scree slope behind them. *Elae* sang in Ean's mind. *Deyjiin* hissed against his shields. Sparks fanned in shimmering, deadly tails.

Pelas spun out of contact and threw a web of *deyjiin* in the wake of his departure. Ean pierced it with a hooked spear and flung it away. He advanced into Pelas's guard, thrusting low. The Malorin'athgul slammed his blade down across Ean's and aimed an elbow for his jaw. Ean veered back, and Pelas sent his sword scraping narrowly past Ean's ribs. Ean parried and struck anew. Pelas blocked him, their blades clashing beneath his flashing smile.

Instinct told Ean that the solution to battling *deyjiin* resided in the Ninth Law—*Do not counter force with force; channel it*—but he hadn't yet landed on the exact form of that solution. Sharing the space of Pelas's mind was helping him understand how the Malorin'athgul was shaping his power to his intent. Pairing this with a view of the currents, Ean was staying half a breath ahead of him—most of the time.

The Malorin'athgul threw another *deyjiin* net. Ean dodged left while slinging a pattern of containment back at Pelas. It caught his leg as he was turning and nearly trapped him, but Pelas dove with the momentum and somersaulted back to his feet. As he was rising he fired a third sizzling web off his blade.

Ean made a rope of the fifth and yanked himself out of harm's way just before the web closed around him. It sizzled instead into the rocky earth where he'd been standing, leaving a man-sized, ashen crosshatching.

Heart racing, Ean held his blade low and paced a slow circle in time with the Malorin'athgul, reflecting that there was nothing quite like a series of narrow escapes to remind you that you were alive. He cast Pelas a sharp smile. "I thought I asked you *not* to make it easy for me."

Pelas tossed his hair from his eyes and wryly watched Ean circling him. "Just having some fun."

Ean grunted. *No,* it wasn't fun fighting Pelas. It was *thrilling.*

And so it went, the two of them battling in concert, seeking solutions for Ean to combat *deyjiin*. The sun observed their dueling as it trekked across the firmament. At times, its heat helped combat *deyjiin*'s numbing effects, but at others it dragged at Ean's thoughts and weighted his limbs. Always when Ean was slow to respond, Pelas stung him for it—but this only motivated him the more.

Above all else, their sparring heightened Ean's appreciation for Arion's skill. What *discipline* he'd exhibited in his fight with Shail at the Citadel! To combat first the Mages, then the Paladin Knights and *then* Shailabanáchtran? To summon, compel and *repel* so much force for such a lengthy span of hours? Ean could barely conceive of how difficult it had been, and he'd lived through Arion's memory of it.

Ean dragged his damp hair out of his face and walked a short line away from Pelas. His head felt like a much-abused pin cushion, and the ache in his limbs encouraged little beyond utter stillness, but the *cortata* kept him fuelled, and the understanding he'd gained of *deyjiin* had him mentally exhilarated.

Ean turned to face Pelas and waved absently with his sword. "I feel like we need to up the ante."

Pelas grinned wonderingly at him. "Because…?"

Because Shail would've thrown everything he had at Ean. Because nothing short of a near death escape would give him any sense of future success. The prince opened palms to the sky. "I'm still standing, aren't I?"

Pelas eyed him in amusement while the wind blew the dampness out of his long hair. "Come then." He motioned for Ean to ready himself.

Still wearing an *I-hope-you-know-what-you're-doing* look, Pelas began a pounding advance of overhead blows. Beneath this he a new working of *deyjiin*. It hit Ean's fifth-strand shields like a lightning bolt and sent him skidding backwards through the raw earth, raising a voluminous cloud of ash. In the same breath, Pelas summoned a wall of *deyjiin* behind Ean, forcing him into a sideways dance. Then three more walls rose at right angles to the first, bringing Ean up short within a box of dancing, deadly light.

Ean stood, breathing hard, and assessed the walls' construction via their shared mental space. This was the first time he'd been able to study an extant working of *deyjiin*—usually the power simply blasted him and dispersed. This time he saw how Pelas was forming the barriers but…

"There are no patterns binding the energy to form." He shifted his gaze to focus on Pelas through the wavering energy. "Is that because the working is innate to you, or because of some other reason?"

Pelas approached the wall. "I've never thought to ask that question. When I made the walls just now, I simply willed them to form."

"That doesn't tell us much." Ean crossed his arms and mentally studied the energy. "Adepts think in the patterns that are innate to them—the patterns are formed automatically by the process of their thoughts."

Pelas considered him curiously. "What are you thinking, Ean?"

"I don't know. There's just something about it…" Ean narrowed his gaze contemplatively, whereupon both gaze and his thoughts sharpened to a point. He focused fast back on Pelas. "Do you *ever* use *deyjiin* in a pattern?"

"No patterns that are native to these realms."

"Because *deyjiin* would consume *elae*, right?" He snapped his fingers. "That's the thing. I've been going about this the wrong way, trying to find some pattern that would allow me to channel *deyjiin*. But yours is a *consumptive* power…" He stared purposefully at a bemused Pelas while fashioning a new intent—a new pattern hastily fashioned, broad stokes of the fifth across a three-dimensional canvas. Then he released it.

The walls became a sizzling veil of sparks and evaporated.

Pelas arched brows. "How—" he studied Ean's working in their shared mental space. "*How* did you do that?"

"It's the Ninth Law." Grinning, Ean approached him. "See, I've been trying to find a way to rechannel *deyjiin* using a pattern, but *deyjiin* doesn't create, it consumes. It's interesting to watch. I've observed that once you've released the power, it becomes solid in the shape of your intent. It *becomes* your intent and that intent is immutable. Conversely, *elae* is always in motion; it can always be rechanneled.

"It occurred to me that I had to stop trying to force *deyjiin* to take a new shape—a new intention, because it won't. It was like trying to push square blocks through a round hole. I have to let *deyjiin* maintain its current shape but give it something *else* to consume."

Pelas eyed him keenly. "Another pattern."

"Yes, I used the fifth for this one. The shape of your intent required *deyjiin* to consume my life pattern, but my hypothesis is that any pattern of similar complexity will do."

"Impressive, Ean." Pelas cast him a dangerous smile. "Let's see how far your theory goes, shall we?"

Over the next few hours, Ean used every trick available to him from Arion's arsenal, and with his newfound understanding of *deyjiin*, he even succeeded in marking Pelas twice—thin stripes of blood as his winning ribbons—but these were not nearly so rewarding as the Malorin'athgul's conceding grin.

True to Ean's earlier request, Pelas kept finding new and ingenious ways of challenging the prince's ability. Ean had just rolled out from beneath another of those deadly nets when Pelas spun *deyjiin* into a spiral, which he flung at Ean.

The prince caught the first part of the corkscrew on his blade, but the force of its impelling slung him around, so that he only narrowly avoided Pelas's descending sword. Ean used the fifth to stabilize his footing and adjusted his shields to dissolve *deyjiin's* corkscrew. But instead of dissipating against his mental shield, as he'd expected, the spinning point *bored through* it. *Deyjiin* speared into his mind. And on the heels of this, as a line threaded to that spiral hook—*compulsion*.

This wasn't the Labyrinth or even one of Dore's matrices—it was the formless, *innate* compulsion of a Malorin'athgul, and once it clamped its jaws, it became impossible to shake off.

Ean perceived immediately that Pelas's compulsion was as individual from Darshan or Shail's as Pelas was himself individual from his brothers; thus, the pattern Ean had derived to protect himself from Darshan's compulsion would be useless against Pelas.

Ean felt the compulsion expanding through his thoughts, needle tendrils as clinging vines, with each new hold casting forth additional branches, ever multiplying. He couldn't contain it fast enough—

An idea came to him. Outrageous, foolhardy. His favorite kind.

Ean hastily portioned off the part of his mind not yet overcome by the compulsion. Eventually those vines would penetrate the walls he'd erected, but he gained a few moments of clarity. Ean used the small, free portion of his mind to gain a view of the trapped side of his mind—in effect, he was attempting to see the entire compulsion that was trapping him. Then Ean summoned the lifeforce into that tiny free portion of his mind.

Pelas responded as the prince had anticipated—with a spear of *deyjiin*. Ean dodged this mental spear and caught it in its passing. He couldn't change the intent of the working, but he wagered he could rechannel it with the same intention along a new course, as a river diverted.

Clenching his teeth—*Lady's light, this is going to hurt*—Ean redirected Pelas's arrow of *deyjiin* into the trapped portion of his mind, *directly* into the compulsion that held his mind enthralled—

Pain seared his consciousness.

Blackness blanketed his vision. His thoughts went white…

When he regained consciousness, the blue sky was forming a wide dome above him, his body felt like a tree had fallen on it, and a mace was pounding his brain into mush. A hand appeared before his blurring vision. It took an embarrassing span of time to make his arm lift to take hold of it.

Pelas pulled Ean up into a seated position. "Well, that was…interesting." The Malorin'athgul crouched down in front of him and regarded him with amused copper eyes. "Suicidal, but definitely unexpected."

Ean gave him a pained smile. "I aim to please."

"It appeared more like you were aiming at self-immolation." Pelas helped him up.

The moment Ean regained his feet, the world became a spinning kaleidoscope trying to upend the contents of his stomach. Ean grabbed Pelas's shoulder to steady himself. "On second thought…"

"Yes, a break might do us both some good." Pelas scooped up their swords and helped the prince towards the jungle trail.

The sweat had dried on Ean's skin by the time they emerged from beneath the mantle of palm trees onto a breezy beach, where black sand formed a crescent between high cliffs. Ean trudged down to the aqua water and fell in.

The sea bottom angled sharply down so that deep waves immediately lifted and buoyed him, while a current drew him away from shore. Ean perceived the waves' immensity, their dormant power, and beyond these closer perceptions, the tumultuous churning of the volcanoes, which were flooding the currents of the fifth with chaotic pulses.

He must've floated there for half a turn of the hourglass, letting the fifth channel through him, sensing the elements…trying to encourage his head to stop pounding. When he finally swam back to shore, Pelas had a large fish and two lobsters cooking over a fire. Ean fell onto his back in the sand beside him.

In the last few days, he'd made new connections to the things Isabel had been saying all along—that a wielder's thoughts shaped his reality, that the Laws were a wielder's surest security. He'd seen these truths in what had happened with Darshan, and proven them again that day.

Ean still didn't know the whole of Arion's betrayal, but he saw already that Arion's fixation on going forward to achieve the effect he'd intended despite all opposition had made a murderer of him in his last hours.

The value of Arion's outlook was that once you committed yourself to the path, *you were committed to the path*. You couldn't give sway to *any* doubt. Yet this viewpoint had proven just as dangerous as it had been vital to Arion's success.

Ean exhaled a slow breath, mulling over these truths. It took a lot of courage to walk one's path fully committed to the outcome. Doubts had a way speaking to your innate fears and cajoling your uncertainties, so that such voices felt like friends when in truth they were undermining your every action.

How many doubts must Isabel have faced down while trapped in that tower with Pelas, cut off from *elae* and any aid, her only hope the certainty she placed in her path?

And yet…where else did any real certainty come from save through the belief in one's own ability?

Ean blew out his breath and draped an arm across his eyes.

"You know, you achieved a lot today, Ean." Pelas angled him a look. "That trick you devised for rechanneling *deyjiin*…I don't think anyone has ever intuited that—not even one of us."

Ean turned his head to meet Pelas's gaze. He refrained from saying that it still might not be enough, since Pelas knew this as well as he did, and said instead, "Thank you." He put earnest meaning into his words. For all he'd tried to unmake the Malorin'athgul's shell barely seventy-two hours ago, Pelas had helped him achieve something even Arion had never managed.

Pelas got to his feet, took up the spits in one hand and extended the other to the prince. "Come, Prince of Dannym. Dinner is ready, and we'll be more comfortable eating at the house."

Ean let Pelas haul him to his feet. He extinguished the fire with a glance and followed the Malorin'athgul through the trees. "If that fish tastes as good as it smells, I could definitely be on the road to forgiving you."

Pelas angled an amused half-smile over his shoulder. "I imagine that's a rather lengthy road."

"Well, that depends."

"On?"

Ean nodded to the spits in Pelas's hand. "On how good the fish is."

What Pelas called a 'house' was in actuality a mountain cliff that had been fashioned into a honeycomb of garden terraces and shaded rooms separated by volcanic glass shutters. As Pelas led Ean up a set of stairs hewn from the uneven rock, the prince perceived the currents permeating the space and intuited how the house had been constructed.

He let out a low whistle. "You fashioned all of this with *elae*?"

Pelas hooked a smile at him. "It isn't the Palazzo di Adonnai, but it will do for our purposes."

Ean cast a wondering gaze across the house. "What were you doing, living way out here?"

Pelas set their dinner on a stone worktable and headed inside. He returned carrying a tray with glasses, a bottle of wine and other items. "There have been times during my venture here in Alorin when I needed to isolate myself from the world, Ean." His pleasant smile made light of this statement, but his eyes conveyed a singular disquiet.

Ean sank down on the edge of a stone chair, even as realization sunk into his understanding. After a moment of silence, acknowledgment of the import of his words, Ean asked quietly, "How did he do it?" He searched the Malorin'athgul's gaze. "How did Darshan lay compulsion on you without your knowledge?"

Pelas's copper eyes narrowed speculatively. "*Goracrosta*, I suspect." He handed Ean a glass of wine. "Anything can be done beneath its auspices—including erasing one's memory of the violation."

Ean was all too aware of the vile acts that might be worked against an Adept bound in *goracrosta*. "Dore committed unforgivable crimes against my brother using that stuff. I can only imagine what…" he grimaced and shook his head. "I mean, with Dore Madden whispering in Darshan's ear…"

Pelas arched brows resignedly. "To be perfectly honest, Ean, I count myself lucky that Shail relegated the problem of me to Darshan to deal with." He began filleting the fish. "You may find this hard to believe, but my brother Darshan actually operates with an inherent restraint—he only uses what force he needs to accomplish his intention."

Ean paused his goblet of wine just shy of his lips. "Surprisingly, I've had the same thought about him."

"So you understand my meaning then. Shail, in contrast, thrives on imbalance. He never feels so alive as when surrounded by chaos." Pelas came over and handed Ean a plate.

Ean started on his meal. It was *very* good fish.

While Pelas settled onto a sofa across from Ean, the prince regarded his host quietly, thinking over the things they'd spoke of as well as the things left unsaid. "When you and I clashed at Tambarré..." he lifted his eyes to meet Pelas's again, "I couldn't have wrought such destruction on your life pattern. That was Shail who did that, wasn't it?"

Pelas pulled at one ear. "Indirectly." He drank his wine and assumed a thoughtful repose, one arm draped along the back of the couch and an ankle propped across his knee. "Darshan and I both found order in unmaking, a sense of balance in the act, if you'll forgive my unintended pun. We would hover on the edge of the Void and work in tandem to dissolve the unraveling aether. But Shail..." his gaze tightened, "my younger brother was forever putting himself in the center of exploding stars, where forces beyond your imagining were reacting against each other. Shail fed on that chaotic energy. It was like lifeblood to him."

He downed his wine and then settled his gaze firmly on the prince. "If Shail had been the one compelling me, he would've put me under his total, unrelenting control. I would've become his puppet, and he would've been able to channel the entire force of my ability towards his aims."

A cold foreboding settled over Ean upon hearing this, for it mirrored Arion's own fears while he'd been battling Shail on the Pattern of the World. Ean cast a pained expression off into the night.

Pelas rose to retrieve the bottle of wine and refilled Ean's goblet and then his own. He sat down beside him with a slow exhale. "I'm starting to understand Phaedor's reputation, his reticence to speak of the things he sees."

"Influence, not interference." Ean angled him a sidelong look. "I'm well aware of his views on the matter."

Pelas considered him quietly. "There are things I would tell you, Ean. Events I see on your path, yet to speak them aloud...it would create a sense of permanence about them, when in truth, they're merely shadows."

Ean set his empty plate aside, leaned back and crossed his arms. "What things?"

Pelas scratched his head. "For example, I see the value to you in this undertaking with *deyjiin*, but at the same time I wonder..." Pausing, he took up his bottle and stood, smiling faintly by way of invitation, but also a clear request for a moment to marry his thoughts with safer words.

Ean followed him onto a patio on the north side of the house, facing the line of volcanoes. That pillar of smoke that had been belching from the central peak all day had finally waned to a thin spire, while three adjacent islands were now rimmed in flame. The sky wore twilight's depthless cobalt, with a sprinkling of bright stars.

"When I was in Adonnai, I read extensively of Björn van Gelderan's library, even of his own writings." Pelas turned to sit on the terrace wall, facing Ean. "The more glimpses I get of Björn's vision, the more I want to meet the man who could see so far around the curve of consequence." He set the bottle down and looked Ean over with the slightest challenge in his gaze. "But Björn van Gelderan is your brother by Isabel, and surely you recall the route to Adonnai."

Ean flicked a glance at him. "What's your point?"

Pelas made an expansive gesture with his goblet. "Why haven't you availed yourself of the same wisdoms?"

The question struck Ean with a powerful and unexpected sense of loss. He'd never thought much on it before, but the idea of returning to Adonnai after all that Arion had done there, after all of their magnificent planning, the dreams devised, the hopes and ideals explored...and after the appalling tragedies that had come to pass... It had been hard enough returning to the Sormitáge. To think of going back to *Adonnai*? He shuddered to imagine the emotional cost.

Ean gave a slow exhale and turned a tight gaze off into the night. "I just can't bring myself to do it."

"You don't want to know?"

Ean speared an anguished look at him.

"Ah...I see." Compassion threaded Pelas's exhale. "It's not that you don't want to know, it's that you don't want to remember." He arched brows resignedly. "This I understand."

Ean frowned. "How could you possibly understand that?"

Pelas arched a brow, challenging his dubiety. "For countless years I resisted the truth of my brother's compulsion—refused to believe he could've done something so vile to me. I wasn't willing to accept that truth—I didn't want to know such a thing, *especially* if it was true. I fought the knowing tooth and claw." He looked off over the darkening sea, contemplatively, as if his memories were a ship sailing the horizon, capturing his attention with their passing. "I understand now that the only way to overcome the compulsion was to accept it." He shifted his gaze back to Ean. "Not to accept and succumb, but to treat it as if it was my own creation. Rather than resisting it, I had to let it permeate me. *Do not counter force with force; channel it.* This was the lesson your Isabel taught me."

"I'm learning the value of the Ninth Law myself." Ean aimed a rueful smile down into his wine. "I suppose I *have* come a long way since Markal's repeated attempts to drown me."

Pelas set down his goblet. "Speaking of, I think a night swim would do us both good. What say you?"

Ean gazed at him, keen to the peaceful silence emanating from the shared space of their minds, wishing he could find a similar quietude in his own thoughts. That pattern of consequence still extended before him looking exactly the same as it had yesterday, as if he'd spent every moment since then caught out of time. Making his peace with Pelas, setting his intention upon a path—even learning to better combat *deyjiin*—none of these had advanced him along that road. What choice had he missed that he remained stranded there, oddly unable to make any headway? What should he have been doing instead?

"It seems like such a fallacy." The prince shifted a tight gaze out over the mercuric sea. "This day, this place, *our* solidarity, this strangely idyllic escape when the realm is on the verge of—" He pressed his lips together, feeling the weight of the game and a driving need to find and understand his own role in it.

Pelas pushed hands in his pockets. "You take your respites where you can find them, Ean. Memories of those moments are sometimes all you have to get you through the long stretches where there is no light to be found by purchase or prayer."

Ean shifted his gaze to meet Pelas's, having perceived the raw feeling that had threaded the immortal's words. Yes, they understood each other far more than they had any right to. For some inconceivable reason, Cephrael had thrown them together at Tal'Afaq. Looking at all that had happened since, Ean couldn't now imagine that their meeting had been merely chance.

Who was he to challenge a pattern his gods had seen fit to weave?

He took another drink of his wine. "A swim…in the dead of night?"

"Have you ever seen the ocean lit by *elae's* currents, Ean? It's a sight unlike any other this side of Shadow."

"Shadow?" Ean focused more sharply upon him. "What do you know about Shadow?"

Pelas's eyes fairly danced. "I know much." He headed off, trailing that comment as a dangling carrot.

Ean downed his wine, set down his glass and followed him. "Like what?"

Already headed down a set of steps, Pelas shot a grin over his shoulder. "Let me tell you about a friend of mine named Rafael…"

FIFTY-EIGHT

"War is only profitable for bankers and blacksmiths."
—Valentina van Gelderan, Empress of Agasan

TRELL INCHED FORWARD on elbows and stomach to join Loukas at the edge of the cliff. The combat engineer had found a perfect vantage from which to study the Fortress of Khor Taran. Reaching it had only required scaling a rope down a hundred feet of sheer rock and then shimmying lengthwise across a thin spire of ledge over a five hundred foot chasm.

But having gained the point, Trell realized why it had to be *this* spot from which they studied Khor Taran, for while the vantage offered a detailed view of several sides of the pentagonal fortress, more importantly, the cliff extending above them kept them shaded from the morning sun. The soldiers upon the fortress walls would only see shadows on that side of the cliff, while the sun's rising rays were angled to miss the lens of their spyglass, preventing any telltale glint.

Stretched out beside him on the ledge, Loukas wordlessly handed said spyglass back to Trell. He closed one eye and peered through the tube. The fortress came into stark definition. Having studied maps and diagrams until he knew every twist of the fortress's layout, as well as the surrounding topography, Trell was now getting his first real look at the place.

Built into the end of Mount Attarak's lengthy southern arm, the fortress consisted of three tiers, each separated by a crenellated wall boasting wide ramparts and mounted crossbows. In case anyone was bold or foolish enough to attempt scaling those cliffs and walls, arrowslits marked intervals all along the fortress's exterior. The only approach for an army of any size would have to be from the north, where an unassailable wall would dishearten even the most stalwart siege engine.

Yes, if you were going to hold a thousand men captive, you could hardly dream up a more perfectly impregnable place.

"So...there's the problem of getting in," Loukas ticked off their challenges on his fingers while Trell studied the fortress, "and once we're inside, there's the problem of finding your father's men, freeing them from whatever spell has been cast over them, as well as from the prison itself, and then finding a way out. Then there's the problem of escaping with a thousand men, who may or may not be in any condition to fight or flee, down a winding mountain road, probably pursued by five hundred Nadoriin and any remaining Saldarian hounds."

"Don't forget the wielder," Trell murmured with his magnified gaze on the winding mountain road leading to the fortress.

"Right," Loukas blew out his breath. "There's the problem of the wielder, who exponentially magnifies the severity of the other problems." He looked to Trell vexedly. "Your propensity for attracting insurmountable obstacles defies logic."

Trell cast him a sidelong grin. "Admit it. You missed me."

A half-smile teased on Loukas's lips. His mood had much improved since leaving the camp, even though the shadows under his eyes had deepened. But sleep was a luxury neither of them could afford until solutions were found and their plans determined.

And Loukas had spoken sooth. How were two hundred men going to get into a fortress that would only yawn at an attack from five thousand? Trell's every waking moment had been directed towards this question—many of his sleeping moments, too. The one thing he knew for certain was that it couldn't be through open confrontation.

Loukas looked back across the gorge. "So...what are you thinking?"

Trell studied the cliffs above the mountain road. "Two days."

Loukas turned him a look. "Two days...to ponder our misfortune? To make sacrifices to the gods...?"

"Two days to prepare an avalanche for our egress." He handed the spyglass back to Loukas. "There. My part is done."

Loukas frowned at him.

"You get us in, I get us out. That's the deal."

Loukas lifted the spyglass and resumed his study of the fortress. "Somehow I always get shorted on this deal of ours."

"Only if you consider combat the easy part."

"It *is* the easy part," Loukas muttered.

"Well, I suppose it would be, when you know the *cortata* better than the back of your hand."

"Says the man who rides a dragon."

Trell had told Loukas the story of his escape from Darroyhan—the highlights, at least—to keep them alert during their night ride. He cast him a sidelong smile. "I'm not sure Náiir would appreciate your reference. He *carried* me. I didn't *ride* him."

"Tomato, *tomahto*."

Trell pointed a finger at the mountain. "Take a look higher up there, just above the northeast wall. What do you see?"

Perhaps a hundred feet above Khor Taran's northernmost tower ran a conduit that appeared manmade. It hugged the line of the mountain until it vanished out of view.

"I think it's an aqueduct, or possibly a millstream." Loukas followed the conduit's path with his magnified gaze. "Cyrenaic, I would imagine. The water is most likely sluiced off the Taran while the river is running at a higher elevation and redirected over the mountain to power the grain mills in Abu'Dhan."

"Are those men up there?" Trell noted some ant-like figures milling around one of the aqueduct's supports.

Loukas found them with the spyglass. "Yes, but they don't look like guards. Actually...I don't see patrols anywhere near there." He lowered the glass and looked significantly to Trell.

Trell gave him a devious smile. "Not a one."

Midday found them on the mountain's easterly slopes. The terrain was rocky and too steep for the horses, so they hid them near a spring and took the climb on foot.

An hour or so later, they came upon a trail that had seen heavy use. They were close enough now to Khor Taran that they could glimpse its walls through openings in the canopy of trees, and the proximity made Trell cautious.

He looked up and down the trail, which curved quickly out of view at both ends, and glanced to Loukas. "Let's—"

"Right."

They took cover in some tall bushes and waited, watching and listening for any movement.

After a time, Loukas muttered under his breath, "Where's Tannour when you need him?"

Trell cast him a curious eye. "What do you mean?"

"Oh...but didn't he—" Loukas searched Trell's gaze, whereupon his expression became slightly chagrined. He looked back to his window of leaves, radiating a confused disconcertion. "I thought he would've told you."

"Told me what?"

Loukas exhaled a slow breath. "Tannour speaks the language of Air. The Vestians call it the Blind Path. In Avatar, we call them *nabhahkaranta*."

Trell recalled his Avataren. "Airwalkers?"

"*Nabhas* can mean sky or air, mist, vapor, clouds...Avataren is a rather indecisive language. It's as if each one of the Fire Kings wanted his own colloquial use of the word included in the official dictionary, so one word ends up having fourteen different meanings. Fiera forbid you should use the wrong meaning in the wrong king's court."

"Rue the day." Trell grinned, for he knew well the complexities of Avataren etiquette. "So airwalking...is it a form of wielding?"

"I'm not sure. Tannour's always been very mysterious about it—all of Vest is mysterious about it, actually. The Blind Path is like some proprietary trick of hand that you have to be inducted into their brotherhood to learn the truth of. All I know is if there were men anywhere within a league of us, Tannour would know it." Loukas looked up and down the road again. "I think it's safe to cross."

"I agree." Trell pushed out of the bushes. "But I don't want to cross it." He set off up the road.

Loukas stared after him exasperatedly. "Has prudence *never* visited you?" He shoved out of the bushes and jogged to catch up.

Trell aimed him a sidelong grin. "If I'm not in two or three life-threatening situations a day, I begin to wonder if I'm still alive."

"I wonder *how* you're still alive," Loukas grumbled.

Trell's grin widened. "I wonder that myself sometimes. But tell me more about airwalkers."

"I honestly don't know much, Trell. You grow up hearing stories, but I couldn't speak to their truth. There are long-standing animosities between Avatar and Vest. Prejudice permeates the stories on both sides of the Ver."

"The Ver?"

"The River Ver draws the southern boundary between Avatar and Vest—at least in the part of the kingdom where I'm from."

"So you don't know much for certain," Trell remitted. "What *do* you know?"

Loukas aimed him a look of frustration. "About airwalking...or Tannour?"

Trell smiled meaningfully. "Either, as they apply."

Loukas puffed a grumbling exhale. He kept his green eyes on the stony path, brows slightly furrowed, as if deliberating how to answer. He was long in responding, and still seemed hesitant when he did. "Tannour described it as a calling—that is…you can't learn the Blind Path. It has to be inside you. You don't choose the path, the path chooses you and all that. In Avatar, there are legends of airwalkers leading legions through the sky."

"So *is* it or isn't it a form of wielding?"

"I wish I could tell you." Loukas puffed his auburn hair out of his eyes. "Magic in the east isn't looked upon the same as in the Middle Kingdoms or the West. Wielders, Adepts, *elae*, the capabilities I hear spoken of so prevalently here, it all has little correlation to the magic worked in the eastern kingdoms. In Avatar, the *baddha* don't have the same training, and they certainly don't have the same freedoms."

They reached a section of recently broken trail where the earth looked to have simply slid off itself. Trell climbed from rock to rock with Loukas close behind. "If Avatar doesn't look upon *elae* in the same way, how did you learn the *cortata*?"

"From the *baddha talavāra* that served my family."

Trell straightened on a boulder as Loukas was gaining his footing. "'Bound sword?'" He scrubbed at his head. "I'm a bit out of practice on my Avataren."

Loukas aimed a shadowy smile at him. "At last—one language you don't speak perfectly."

"Says the man who speaks every language known to the educated races." He made jumping steps to cross the gaping earth and started up the next section of trail.

Loukas lagged behind, staring after him. "I don't speak Gorul."

Trell laughed and called back over his shoulder. "Does *anyone* speak Gorul?"

"Some Fhorgs, I think." Loukas jogged to catch up. "In any case…'bound sword' is the literal translation for *baddha talavāra*, but the word has many meanings and connotes much more…" Loukas looked up the trail ahead of them and slowed. "Is that—"

"Yes, a cave I think."

The road ended in a mountain wall and a huge, jagged hole in the rock face. Fire pits, churned mud and other evidence of a large camp of men surrounded the wide opening. Beyond the clearing, the trees pressed up against the mountain wall, preventing any view of their surroundings, but Trell was betting they were within a longbow's shot of the fortress's lower ramparts.

The cave opening had become partially blocked by a fall of rock that looked to have tumbled recently—a reminder, perhaps, that this volcano might've been sleeping, but it was still very much alive.

Trell drew up short as they neared, his attention snared by a boot extending from beneath the rock fall. As he looked closer, he saw a leg still attached to it.

"*Saldarians.*" Loukas gave a deprecating grunt.

Trell turned him a look. "You can tell the man's origins from his boot?"

"Who else would leave their dead so disgraced?"

Trell conceded his point.

Loukas bent to inspect the body. "He can't have been here more than a day or two—three at the most."

Trell cast a narrow gaze towards the cave. "If the cave became unstable, it would explain why they abandoned this place in such a rush."

Loukas eyed the cave disagreeably. "I suppose you're going to want to investigate it." He pushed back to his feet and headed towards the opening, muttering in mimicry of Trell's voice, "*Don't fret, Loukas. If the mountain falls on us, I'm sure you can figure a way to dig us out with this broken dagger and this piece of string.*'"

With Loukas grumbling and Trell chuckling, they descended into the cave. Within, the opening quickly broadened to a wide cavern. Light streamed in from other openings elsewhere in the mountain wall. Trell took up a torch he found on the ground and lit it from the dying flame of a flickering oil lamp bolted into the wall.

"Do you think the Saldarians were using this for their base?"

"Could be, or at least a regular waystop. But they wouldn't have all fit in here. By Raegus's estimation, there were at least two hundred of them, and five villages' worth of people unaccounted for."

"Do you think they might be holding them in the fortress?"

"I don't know what to think." Trell looked around. To his right, the cavern angled down into chill darkness, but to his left…

A short walk took them into a tube of sorts, with walls almost perfectly rounded but oddly ridged.

"This isn't manmade." Loukas was walking close to the wall, examining the rock.

"Lava, I suspect. The legends speak of Mount Attarak spreading arms of fire."

They followed the tube long enough for Trell's hopes to rise…and then crash in a tumble of broken possibility as they came upon another rock fall that blocked the tunnel completely.

Loukas shoved hands on his hips and cocked his head. "Do you think this cave connects to the fortress?"

"I think it just might—or did, once. Náiir says the entire mountain is riddled with caverns. I was hoping we could use this one to get inside, but the mountain seems to have had other ideas." He turned and started back the way they'd come. "I guess we'll have to fall back to plan A."

"I didn't realize we had a plan A."

Trell turned him a look. "We had a plan A."

Loukas narrowed his eyes at him. "We had the barest ghost of possibility for a plan A."

"Tomato, *tomahto*."

Loukas somewhat ground his teeth. "An *idea* is not a plan, Trell."

"I'm the commander, you're my combat engineer. I have ideas, you have plans."

"Your ideas are more like fantastical conjecture married with insanity," Loukas grumbled.

"Which you find a way to implement practically to our extreme benefit," Trell quipped with a grin.

Loukas puffed a dubious exhale. "I'm making no promises about that aqueduct until I see it up close. We have no idea how deep or fast that water is running."

Trell gave him a meaningful look. "Then we'd better get up there, hadn't we?"

Night had fallen by the time they headed back to camp, leading the horses beneath the illumination of a waning moon. Those silvery rays were captured by the singing river on their left and the snow-capped peak lording over the night, such that both glowed with luminescence. A cast of stars had taken their places in the firmament and now watched the lands of men as actors distracted by a rowdy audience, waiting to see what drama would unfold beneath heaven's vault.

Or perhaps in wait for another's cue? Trell thought to himself as he saw Cephrael's Hand suddenly appear in the eastern sky, half-occluded by the volcano's peak but sparkling vividly in a space that a heartbeat before had offered only the infinite night.

"*Fiera's breath*, how does it do that?" Loukas was also staring at the constellation.

"Just appear like that, you mean?"

"Real stars don't just appear and disappear," Loukas growled in uneasy protest, "and they don't *move*. But that constellation…one day it's rising in the east, the next day in the west—the demon stars come and go and as they *fethen* please."

As Trell continued gazing at the constellation, a smile hooked one corner of his mouth. He gave the *angiel* a nod of greeting. *Good evening, my lord.*

The stars almost seemed to blink back at him in reply.

"Did you see—" Loukas turned suddenly to Trell with the look of a man who had seen things that clearly could not be explained. "Do not tell me that you entertain a relationship with Cephrael, too." Under his breath, he added, "*That* would certainly explain a few things."

Trell let his smile spread to both sides of his face. "The constellation and I go way back."

"Is that a fact?"

Trell shifted a sobering gaze to him. "Those stars kept me company every night during my imprisonment at Darroyhan."

"You had long conversations, the two of you?"

Trell smiled at his dubious yet slightly unsettled tone. "In a sense, you could say we did."

Humming along at their side, the river gurgled amusedly at them.

"Trell..." Loukas regarded him with a pensive frown, "have you ever thought about why those stars move? *How* they move? I mean, what motivating force could possibly be causing the stars to move? If we're to believe each of those lights are other worlds, distant suns, yet these seven just fly themselves through the firmament on a *fethen* whim—"

Trell finally looked away from the constellation to meet the Avataren's gaze. "I don't think the *angiel* is prone to whimsy. His actions only seem capricious because we see but a portion of His pattern. You and I are at the tiniest tip of an arabesque, each of us but single threads in a vast tapestry. How can a thread be expected to see or understand the greater pattern it's weaving?"

When Loukas said nothing, only stared oddly at him, Trell flashed a smile. "Was it something I said?"

Loukas looked back to the way ahead. "I've just never heard you speak of such things before."

Trell grinned. "Do I sound crazy?"

Loukas's brow constricted. "You sound like Tannour."

They reached a bend in the river where a wide, sandy beach glinted darkly with moonlight. If the Taran hadn't told Trell that a man was crouched there, bleeding his thoughts into the water, Trell never would've noticed the scout. He raised a hand, even though he couldn't see him. "Is that you, Saran?"

A shadow separated itself from a clump of bushes. "*A'dal.*" Saran strode forward. Only as he neared could Trell discern his eyes amid the amalgam of shadowed cloth that wrapped him. "Inithiya blesses us to see you returned. The Avataren, our former *A'dal*, has been gnawing his nails."

"Let's get back forthwith then, shall we?"

Saran pressed a fist over his heart and went for his horse.

The moon was well past its zenith and the men abed when the scout finally led them into camp. They'd passed six sentries along the mountainous trail leading to their hidden campsite. Raegus was taking no chances, and for good reason—they were within a half-day's ride of Khor Taran and easy prey if spotted by the wrong eyes.

The wrong eyes... Trell cracked a smile at this irony. Assuredly a spy still walked among them, still reported to the wielder on their activities, but Trell was betting the man would make no more forays against them now that they were so close. He would wait instead for them to come to him, knowing they would have to.

They sat on opposite sides of the board, Trell and this wielder whom Tannour had called Kifat, both of them wrestling over the same prize. The onus was on Trell to play the game in a way the wielder couldn't predict.

As Trell and Loukas made their way into camp, the only light beneath the moon and stars came from Trell's command tent, whose soft glow appeared as a cobalt radiance amid a mushroom field, their tents like man-sized versions of the giant boulders that concealed the mountainside clearing.

Trell ducked inside his tent and nearly tripped over Rami, who was lying across the narrow strip of passage like a cat in wait.

The boy sat up, rubbing one eye. Then he realized who was standing in front of him in the darkness. "*Sidi*, you're back!" He scrambled to his feet. "I'll get you some dinner."

Trell walked into the next room and found Tannour, Raegus and Rolan dozing in low-slung chairs. The latter of the three was snoring loudly.

As Trell was heading for his desk, Raegus started awake in his chair and saw Trell. "Gods be thanked." He gave an explosive puff and relaxed again.

Trell smiled faintly. "That exhale seemed rather weighty with relief." He slung himself into the chair behind his desk. "Did you so fear for me?"

Raegus smacked Rolan on the arm.

Rolan snorted awake with a glare, followed Raegus's gaze to notice Trell, and then looked momentously back to Raegus. "He's back."

Raegus arched both brows.

Rolan nudged a still sleeping Tannour with his boot.

Tannour blinked awake, saw Trell, and roused promptly. "Ah...you're back."

Trell rubbed at his forehead. "Why do all of you sound so amazed by this fact?"

"Well, we can't exactly count on n'Abraxis to keep you out of trouble," Raegus said at the very moment that Loukas walked in.

Loukas scowled at him. "I'd like to see you do better. I vow even the gods aren't up to the task."

An entering Rami returned with food for Trell and Loukas—warm stew, a loaf of bread and a chunk of hard cheese with bowls of olives and figs. Simple fare had never looked better.

Trell carried his bowl over to the map table and ate his stew while studying the map of Khor Taran and the surrounding area. The others followed him first with their eyes, then with rather resigned exhales. Soon they'd all gathered around.

Rami moved among them offering wine.

Trell lifted his gaze to Raegus. "Have we spread the word of the forces coming from Duan'Bai?"

"Aye. Quietly, as you ordered. The men were whispering widely of it on the march today."

"Good. We can expect our spy to have told the wielder at Khor Taran. By now, they'll be expecting us."

"And this is desirable…why?" Rolan sounded doubtful.

Trell munched on his stew and studied the map, comparing places his eyes had seen that day with their topographical representations, marrying landmarks with ridge points. "Have any of you wondered why the Nadoriin haven't come out to hunt us down?" He lifted his gaze to meet all of theirs. "Khor Taran's wielder has known of our whereabouts for days, perhaps weeks. Why haven't the Nadoriin marched out of their fortress to wipe us from their domain?"

Into the silence that followed his question, Tannour remarked, "A bear can't be bothered to swat at a fly."

Trell nodded to his point, then looked inquiringly for other ideas.

"Five hundred men in a fortress that size," Raegus offered, "they'd all be needed there to hold it."

"That's what I've been thinking. It may also be true that the wielder, the Saldarians and the Nadoriin of Khor Taran are not necessarily on amiable terms with each other, or aligned with each other's purposes."

Rolan grunted into his wine. "There's an understatement. Like Vest to Avatar are M'Nador and Saldaria. I'd take a Vestian over a Saldarian any day of the week."

"Thank you, Lamodaar." Tannour's gaze had somewhat frosted over.

"Let's suppose the Nadoriin have been ordered to hold the fortress," Trell continued, "while the wielder has orders to hold my father's men, and the Saldarians…well, whatever their orders, they're at least out of our way for the moment."

"I vow we all knew some vindication that night," Raegus commented, eyes on the map, "but it was joyless. Never did find the leader, and the minute the tide turned against them, the *fethen* bastards ran off. Didn't even try to help their wounded."

Rolan rumbled, "Rats make better bed partners."

"The Saldarians lie behind us on the path for now," Trell said. "Let us fix our eyes to what lies ahead." He motioned with his spoon to the map area south of the fortress, a wide valley that curved to the west. "This is where the Emir's forces will set up camp."

Raegus scratched at his head. "The *imaginary* forces from Duan'Bai?"

"Exactly." Trell looked to Loukas, who was standing across the table from him staring absently down into his goblet. "How many men to set up and light a hundred bonfires, Loukas? *Loukas?*"

The Avataren started back to the present. "Sorry." He pressed a palm to one eye. "A hundred fires? How fast do they need to be lit?"

"All within the first hour of nightfall."

"How long do they need to burn?"

"At least two hours. Three is better."

Loukas made some quick calculations in his head. "Forty-six—no. Forty-seven."

"You're sure it's not forty-eight?" Rolan inquired drolly.

Loukas wiped wearily at one green eye, missing his sarcasm entirely. "Of course, that's assuming the bundles are prearranged and we have enough oil to start them all quickly."

"How much oil to how many logs, n'Abraxis?" Rolan wanted to know.

"Assuming a standard median porosity and size, we're looking at approximately twelve to—" but then he noticed Rolan grinning at him and gave the man an aggrieved look.

Trell set down his empty bowl. "Fifty of us to draw out five hundred Nadoriin." He crossed his arms and studied the map, tracing with his eyes their imagined lines of entry, exit and retreat. "Twenty-five of the strongest to free my father's men." He scrubbed at his jaw. "What will you do about our egress, Loukas?"

"Blasting powder at the ridge, but if they're chasing us—"

"Right. We'd need cavalry to hold them back."

"That's assuming the other Nadoriin don't return from the valley and outflank us." Loukas met his gaze. "That's a pretty big assumption, Trell."

"Then we have to make it impossible for them to return on that road. Make them go through the cave, only to find it blocked."

"That's a lot of blasting."

Trell held his gaze meaningfully. "Or…if we can arm my father's men…"

Loukas shook his head. "They may not be in any shape to fight after such a long captivity."

"True, but you know how it alters the odds."

"By eighty-two percent."

"Exactly."

"Well, not *exactly*." Loukas pushed his auburn hair back from his face. "The percentage has nonterminating decimals…"

"Did I miss something?" Raegus looked around the group. "Like the part where we talked about how we're getting into this practically unassailable fortress in the first place?"

"Tell them the plan, Loukas."

Loukas gave a sort of wince. "Fiera forgive us for calling it a *plan*." He shoved both hands back through his hair. "So there's this aqueduct…"

While Loukas talked them through the 'plan'—the men's eyebrows arching incrementally with each new revelation—Trell observed the game board and knuckled his growth of beard.

The best laid plans really only went as far as the first clashing of swords. From that moment forward, chance and luck determined how men would fall, how events would play out, and if consequence would take the direction you'd predicted.

Trell wished he'd had more time to study each potential piece and put it through an equation of cause and consequence to determine the odds of outcome. Instead, he felt the grains of the hourglass slipping away. Each instant took Radov closer to Raku, the Emir closer to war, and his father further from his reach. Each second gave the wielder, his enemy, more time to plot against him.

"You can't be serious!" Raegus's shocked exclamation drew Trell from his thoughts.

He looked to the Avataren, who was gaping at him, and arched brows resignedly. "I'll admit we have some challenges still ahead of us."

"*Some* challenges?" Raegus's eyes looked ready to pop from his skull.

"*If* the Nadoriin buy our deception," Rolan muttered, "*if* they send as many men as we're expecting them to send in pursuit of our nonexistent army, *if* we can exit the aqueduct safely *and* get into the fortress unnoticed… *if* all of that occurs, none of it—"

"Accounts for the *fethen* wielder," Raegus finished heatedly.

Trell's gaze found Tannour, who had been uncharacteristically silent thus far. "I have a different idea about how to handle Kifat."

Loukas blew out his breath. "You know…despite everything, it will probably all go off perfectly." He walked to the liquor chest to pour himself a drink.

Raegus followed him with his gaze. "That's an unusual optimism from you, n'Abraxis. Why will it all come off perfectly?"

Loukas drained his glass, clapped it down on the cabinet and turned Trell a portentous stare. "Because our *A'dal* is in collusion with Cephrael."

Raegus assumed the look of a man who was sure he must've missed something.

"I saw the constellation bow to him." Loukas refilled his glass. "*Cephrael's Hand*. I watched it appear out of nowhere tonight and bow to the *A'dal*."

"It bowed to you?" Rolan's black bear eyebrows reached for each other.

Trell glanced from Rolan to Loukas uncertainly. "It didn't bow to me."

Loukas put meaning into his gaze. "At the very least it winked at you."

"Cephrael's Hand *winked* at you?" Raegus asked.

Trell cast him a sidelong eye. "I highly doubt it winked at me."

"Then why did it follow us here?"

"The constellation *followed* you?" Raegus and Rolan exclaimed together.

"It's high above us right now." Loukas was holding Trell's gaze, fully expecting some explanation from him for what he'd witnessed. The trouble was, Trell couldn't explain it either.

His head felt as heavy as iron, and weariness was burning his eyes. This was no time for speculating about divinities. He spread his hands and leaned on the table. "Superstition isn't going to see us through the next many hours. Our success or failure hinges on this plan, exactly timed, meticulously executed." He straightened and pointedly held Loukas's gaze. "We should seek rest with what's left of the night. We've a day and a half at most to prepare."

"Your will, *A'dal*." Rolan pressed fist to heart and headed off, clapping Raegus on the arm as he went.

Raegus cast Trell a wondering stare and trudged after Rolan. Tannour rose to follow them.

"Tannour, may I have a word?"

The Vestian halted a few steps from the door.

"Trell…" Sudden contrition threaded Loukas's tone. He was staring at the glass in his hand. "I shouldn't have—"

Trell eyed him quietly. "Get some sleep, Loukas."

The engineer nodded, set down his glass, and eyed Tannour unreadably as he left.

Trell walked to the liquor chest. "Wine, Tannour?"

"No, thank you, Your Highness."

Trell poured a goblet for himself, saying while he watched it filling, "We didn't finish our conversation the other night."

"No," Tannour agreed tightly.

Trell turned a look over his shoulder. Tannour was standing there very much seeming bound by reticence and unease, his dark hair falling across his cheekbones, the planes of his face drawn in ashen lines.

Trell moved to a chair across from where Tannour was staring at his toes. "I need to know if you're capable of doing what I require of you."

"I'll do anything you ask of me, *A'dal*."

"Your willingness, I trust. But can you accomplish it?" Trell slowly lowered himself into the chair, feeling exhaustion's ache in every pore. "This is what I must know. Loukas called you an airwalker. Explain this to me."

Silence wrapped Tannour so deeply that he almost seemed to vanish into it. He stared forcefully at the carpet for a long time. Then he drew in a deep breath and let it out slowly. "Some things are just understood in Vest: the first son takes the father's place, the second son serves his family's estates, and the third son, if there is a third son, is sent to the Sorceresy for training." He lifted burning eyes to Trell. "I am the third son."

"I know very little about the Vestian Sorceresy."

"They prefer things that way," Tannour quipped acidly.

"But I knew well of one of their *mor'alir* Adepts."

"Yes, so you said."

"Are you a *mor'alir* Adept, Tannour?"

"No, *A'dal*."

"What are you then?"

Tannour clasped hands roughly behind his head and made a vice with his elbows before his face. He stood this way for several long breaths. Then he dropped his hands to his sides and moved to claim a chair across from Trell.

"The Sorceresy teaches that you don't choose the path, the path chooses you." He lifted pale blue eyes to meet Trell's gaze. "I was thirteen when the path chose me. That's the age I was sent to the Sorceresy, as all third sons are. They tested me, as they test everyone—a month of torment and trials, trickery, wicked games of mind and malice that you wouldn't wage upon your worst foe—and after a time, though I doubt it took them the entire time, because they enjoy torturing young boys for their entertainment, they determined I could learn to speak the language of Air."

He sank elbows onto his knees. "This language is called *ver'alir*, the Blind Path, a rare path. It lies between *chrys'alir*, the Mirror Path, and *mor'alir*, the Path of Shadows."

"Loukas spoke of Avataren legends of airwalkers leading legions among the clouds." Trell studied Tannour's downcast stance. "Can you work *elae's* fifth strand, Tannour?"

Tannour lifted his head from his hands. "I wouldn't know it if I did, *A'dal*. We aren't taught with any such terminology."

"What can you do?"

Tannour gave him a regretful look. "It is death to speak of it."

"You can trust my discretion—"

"No, *A'dal*," Tannour pressed his lips together, "I mean this as the literal truth. I would *die* if I tried to speak of these things."

Upon this utterance, a memory flashed in Trell's mind—his body broken, beaten, strapped to a trunk; and a hostile face before his own, shouting with foul breath and fouler words, demanding thoughts Trell's tongue refused to carry, no matter how desperately he tried to speak them...

This was not a memory he relished, yet as he tried to ease the tension that suddenly constricted his shoulders, as if those straps still bound him backwards across the arching wood, Trell was at least grateful that he *did* in fact remember it.

He regarded Tannour with quiet understanding. "They've truthbound you."

The Vestian shrugged. "This is a foreign terminology. I trust in Your Highness's assessment."

Trell settled his goblet on a table. "The wielder at Khor Taran is a problem piece upon our game board. By nature of being a wielder, he's more powerful than any of us. But I wonder...is he more powerful than you?"

Tannour slowly lifted his gaze. "If you're asking me if I will take him on, the answer is yes."

"But can you defeat him?"

Tannour worked the muscles of his jaw, masticating a cold yet unaccountable anger that reflected in his gaze. "Yes."

Trell accepted this without questioning it further. "You said your life was in danger, your name upon a list."

Tannour blew out his breath and fell back in his chair. "They wanted me to kill a man." He turned and stared heatedly off towards the curtains. "I suppose it's true that it resonates for me...*ver'alir*, the Blind Path." He looked at his open palm, ran his other fingers across it. "I feel it calling every time I use my knife. And with every life I claim, I feel my feet binding more firmly to the path. Yet to kill for *them*..." he slung Trell a look of storms, "this is to bind yourself to *ver'alir* forever and all time. Worse, it would bind me to *them*—" Tannour bit back whatever else he'd intended to say and sat in a silence of his own enforcement, radiating disconcertion and injury, chords of injustice playing sharp counterpoint to a thrumming resentment.

Trell studied him quietly. "Because you defied them, they placed a bounty on your life?"

Tannour dragged a hand back through his hair. "The bounty comes from the ones who hired me, the ones I failed. The Sorceresy wants me because..." he blew out a forceful breath. "Suffice it to say that if they ever found me—"

"They would kill you?"

His eyes flew back to Trell's. "They would make me a *puppet,* their little marionette assassin. My mind would no longer be my own. I would no longer be *me.*"

Trell felt a chilling understanding upon hearing this. He saw suddenly his eldest brother's face superimposed across Tannour's and knew too well the possibility of which Tannour spoke.

Trell wouldn't wish such a fate on any man…not even Viernan hal'Jaitar—not even Taliah. It was the worst conceivable cruelty to him to deny a man his own will and at the same time force him to recognize his subjugation in every moment of every day.

He observed Tannour's downcast eyes. "This is why you wanted me to keep your actions in confidence?"

Tannour looked like he was being made to chew nettles. "Even among outcasts," he said through clenched teeth, "*assassins* aren't fit company. If the others knew, they'd look upon me no better than Radov's Shamshir'im."

Trell frowned. "I don't think less of you because of your past, Tannour. No one among the Converted would."

He lifted him a bitter gaze. "N'Abraxis does."

"That lies between you and Loukas, and I'm guessing it began long before you and he sought the Emir's goodwill."

Tannour looked away, which was admission enough.

Trell considered him for a moment. Then he pushed out of his chair. "These titles we hang upon ourselves—prince, assassin, A'dal—in truth, they're no different from other names, less respectable: failure, incompetent, coward. We hang ourselves by our imperfections and forge blades of self-abnegation far more damaging than steel. The daggered words of pettiness and envy only harm us because we let them. We're our own wardens, jailors and headsmen, Tannour. *We* decide what defines us."

Tannour held his gaze for a long time in silence, his expression unreadable save for the slight furrow between his brows.

For some reason, in holding his gaze in return, Trell was reminded of Ean, who he hadn't seen in so many long years. He wondered if his younger brother, third-born of the val Lorian sons, was struggling to define himself as Tannour was, seeking a path of his own choosing yet unable to escape the bombarding expectations of others. Had Ean found ways to define himself, or had he let others' assumptions forecast the direction of his path?

One thing Trell knew for certain—Ean would be just as headstrong about making his own choices as Tannour seemed to be. The thought made him smile.

Trell cast it in the Vestian's direction. "You should get some sleep."

Tannour's gaze upon him tightened slightly. "I will if you will."

Trell's smile widened. "I give you my word I shall find my bed before the sun rises."

"That leaves a lot of room for interpretation."

Trell winked. "The smartest negotiations generally do."

Tannour accordingly pushed from his chair and made his way towards the exit, but he paused just shy of the opening. "You know…" he looked over his shoulder at Trell, solemn and serious, "none of us doubted n'Abraxis tonight."

Trell arched brows by way of inquiry.

"About the constellation." He held Trell's gaze seriously for a moment longer. Then he bowed and departed.

Staring after him, Trell heard Rolan's words, spoken out of the mist of memory, *'The gods can't help us when we don't seek their aid.'*

Trell dropped his chin to his chest and closed his aching eyes. He didn't know if the *angiel* Cephrael was out there somewhere, listening to their hearts as Naiadithine did, or watching their goings on beneath the auspices of seven unearthly stars. He didn't know if the constellation had actually acknowledged him earlier, or if it had simply been a trick of dark clouds; but whether the *angiel* was listening or watching, or was simply a figment of men's hopes, Trell had no compunction about asking for His aid.

Because of all the gods, Cephrael knew how much he was going to need it.

FIFTY-NINE

"The only difference between an historian and a bard is how skillfully the lies are crafted."
–The Adept Nodefinder Vincenzé of Caladria

THE FOUR MOST notable architectural buildings in the Sacred City of Faroqhar were also some of the city's most important: the Tower, a spire of pale green marble where operatives of the Order of the Glass Sword conducted their clandestine operations; the crenellated Fembrand, fortress, home and training grounds of the Imperial Adeptus; the sprawling marble-columned Forum, where the Patrician Senate met in their daily administration of the Empire; and crowning the highest hill with its gold and crystal domes seen for miles in every direction, the Sacred City's prized jewel—the Imperial Palace.

Within the cool marble confines of the latter, Valentina van Gelderan, Empress of Agasan, sat back in her chair and stared at Liam van Gheller, Endoge of the Sormitáge, certain she must've heard him incorrectly.

"I'm sorry, did you say *petition*?" She tightened her gaze upon him. "Someone is petitioning the Order of *Sobra* Scholars to overturn their own ruling?"

The Endoge gave a minor wince. "Forgive me, Aurelia, but the petition will actually be addressed to you."

Her eyes widened considerably. "They want *me* to overrule the *Sobra* Scholars and declare a pattern safe to work?" It had never been done. It never would be done. The Sormitáge was the ultimate word; judge, jury and executioner in matters of Patterning. "Who are these fools?"

Liam passed a hand across his bald pate. "The movement is gaining uncommon support from both sides of the populace, Aurelia, Adept and *na'turna* alike."

"I thought it was a petition. Now you tell me it's a movement?"

"The Adepts who approached me want to be allowed to work the pattern on those in need."

"Those in need." You could've cut her dubiety with a knife.

The Endoge looked wan. "The leaders of the movement *claim* they've identified many unAwakened *na'turna*. They believe the Literato N'abranaacht's pattern will waken their ability."

"Preposterous." Valentina pushed out of her chair and cast him a severe look as she walked to the sideboard.

The Endoge followed her with his gaze. "The *Sobra* Scholars agree, Aurelia, but half of Faroqhar saw the Literato N'abranaacht working the fifth. He claimed with his dying breath to an audience of hundreds that this pattern had Awakened him. The Sormitáge Tribunal ruled the pattern too speculative for broad use and refused to give their sanction, but it is, nonetheless, hard to refute the possibility of the pattern having done something to give N'abranaacht access to the fifth."

Access he'd long possessed and hidden from the world, Valentina inwardly groused.

It was still a shock to her, the spiraling events that had culminated in a fabled Malorin'athgul rescuing her daughter-heir, but she'd spoken to the one called Pelasommáyurek, read his words with her power, observed him on the currents. She and Marius could no longer deny the truths Phaedor had long been claiming.

Valentina slowly poured wine into two crystal glasses, watching the sanguineous liquid swirl and fill, trying to find any perception to lead her through this sudden quagmire—demons wielding *deyjiin*, hundreds kidnapped, her consort heading north into some kind of trap, trusting that Phaedor and a hundred men could do what all of the Adeptus apparently could not, and now this pattern rearing its ugly head…

She sensed these were but pieces in a much larger puzzle, the broader game playing out on the mortal tapestry—her great-uncle's game, no doubt—but her purview must necessarily remain the Empire and its wellbeing. Would that such a view wasn't so stilted.

Valentina exhaled a pensive breath. Her Sight in this area had become a lake of fog. The currents showed only events already passed, giving no hint towards future. Instinct was shouting so loudly it kept her awake at night, yet its maddening screams formed nonsense words, and reason bade her ignore them.

She turned with goblets in hand and rejoined the Endoge. Their chairs were set before tall mullioned doors which stood open to admit the breeze. A line of Praetorians stood watch on the terrace beyond the fluttering curtains, but they would hear nothing of Valentina's conversation, for the ancient wards surrounding the room allowed neither a whisper of sound nor a fragment of thought to pass their boundary.

She handed Liam a goblet and seated herself with a frown. "Whether Adept or *na'turna*, the educated peoples of Alorin understand the impact the demise of the Adept race would have on the realm. *Na'turna* depend heavily upon our skills and craft for defense, Healing, merchandising, trade—you well know how long is the list, Liam. The realm depends upon our skills for its very way of life, and all have suffered from the race's decline." Valentina sat back in her chair and fixed her colorless gaze on the Endoge. "A pattern that could Awaken Adepts even after they've passed their adolescent years? I can see why both sides of the populace would support it."

Liam exhaled a ponderous sigh. "Too many see its value, too few its danger."

Valentina considered him while her mind explored the implications of the pattern's use. "What are the terms of this petition?"

"They're asking for detailed testing and study, human trials, experimentation on *na'turna*—with volunteers of course—"

"And return us forthwith to the darkest days of the Quorum." Valentina grunted into her wine. "*They* claimed all of their torture and sacrifice used willing volunteers."

"The Sormitáge equally fears such a return, Aurelia. It's been centuries, yet our studies keep the Before close in our minds. The Quorum with its dark undertakings, Warlocks from the Shadow Realms commanding armies of mortals bound to their will…" He shook his head. "Even Malachai's scourge upon our race did not compare to those black times."

Black times—*devastating* times—when free will was held as a currency in trade. Alorin had been hard-pressed to defend itself against Warlocks when at its Adept prime. Should such immortals find a way back into the realm now, they would tread the fabric all but unimpeded, binding men to their will in a single glimmering glance, playing vicious games with humanity for their own entertainment.

Nadia had described encountering a Warlock while being held hostage by the Malorin'athgul Shail. This news had disturbed Valentina almost more than losing two hundred Adepts, for she feared that where one such creature walked, more would surely follow.

Liam traced a hand across his bald head again, an agitated gesture from a man who was rarely discomposed. "We scholars remember, Aurelia, but others…suffice it to say the movement in support of this pattern gains more followers by the day. The new Second Vestal Niko van Amstel has lent his approval to the petition, and his opinion carries considerable weight among the younger generations."

Valentina brushed a stray strand of hair from her brow. *Well, this is certainly an elaborate mess.*

Epiphany bless the day Phaedor had returned to the Empire. Without his warnings and counsel, she might've been desperate enough to entertain notions of this pattern's potential. Now she worried more about its potential to create havoc.

Valentina lifted her gaze back to the Endoge. "What do we know about the pattern?"

"Literato N'abranaacht claimed to have found it among some ruins in Myacene."

"Belonging once to the Quorum of the Sixth Truth, no doubt." *Or worse.* If he was really a Malorin'athgul, who knew where the pattern had originated?

Liam traced an eyebrow with a finger. "The *Sobra* Scholars have yet to pinpoint its origins. It's unlike any of the other Quorum patterns found to date."

"Even had the pattern been discovered under less questionable circumstances, we would still have reason to be suspicious of it."

The Endoge shifted in his chair. "This is why I've come to you, Aurelia. This pattern defies our understanding. The Order of *Sobra* Scholars has requested that you put it to the Council of Realms for their review."

"I *could* present the matter to the Alorin Seat," Valentina wasn't sure why the idea made her uneasy. "It would delay any imperial ruling on the petition, which might be a boon." She considered the idea more fully, letting her mind wander along as many threads of consequence as she could imagine.

But every thread doubled with a strand of doubt. *By the Lady's blessed light*, would that Phaedor had not been so acute in his criticisms! For too long she'd depended on her Sight to guide her, to the exclusion of all other perceptions. Now those awarenesses were drowned beneath a cacophonous uncertainty. What her Sight *could* tell her was that a darkness was coming. She watched its approach as a squall crossing the open sea, spreading veils of shadows, consuming the sky.

Feeling oddly unbalanced, Valentina lifted her gaze back to the Endoge. "Who has access to the pattern?"

"The *Sobra* Scholars, but it's possible N'abranaacht's disciples may have obtained a copy."

Valentina's brows rose considerably. "Disciples?"

"Self-proclaimed in the wake of the literato's death." The Endoge winced into his wine. "They're calling him the Martyr of Myacene."

"Epiphany preserve us." It didn't take the Sight to predict where this path was heading. Valentina sat forward in her chair and captured the Endoge's colorless gaze with her own. "Liam, it's vitally important that this pattern is studied, but it must be done by the Adeptus engineers and the Order of the Glass Sword's Patternists, who are knowledgeable in the combat arts."

The Endoge frowned as he held her gaze. "With due respect, Aurelia, were not your engineers trained by my maestros?"

"Yes, but as you might imagine, their training became more specialized after they left the Sormitáge." She set down her glass and regarded him severely. "I have a strong suspicion there is more to this pattern than meets the eye. To my knowledge, the Sormitáge does not walk *elae's* dark paths."

He drew back. "Assuredly not."

"But the order has much experience with them, Liam. Its operatives have vital reason to be knowledgeable about all of the Paths of Alir." Valentina let out a low exhale as she sat back in her chair again. "And I very much suspect *inverteré* patterns are somehow involved with this pattern of our intrepid literato." Two pairs of colorless eyes held one another. "I would like you to personally ensure a rendering is delivered immediately to Francesca da Mosta for the Adeptus to review, Liam."

The Endoge rose from his chair, bowed with a murmured, "Your will be done, Aurelia," and departed to do as his Empress had tasked him.

❖

Shailabanáchtran stepped out of Shadow into the laboratory hidden in his Sormitáge apartments and cast his gaze around the icy room. *Inverteré* patterns hung in the air, suspended in a balance of forces, while the perpetual rift in the cosmic fabric behind him funneled *elae* into Shadow and gave his Warlock colleagues easy access to the realm.

His eyes scanned the dim room while his mind studied the currents, seeking energetic impressions of disturbance. But all remained the way he'd left it.

He'd placed N'abranaacht's rooms in the care of one of his puppets, of which he had many scattered around. He need not compel all of their minds at the same time, as he'd once manipulated the Hundred Mages; rather, he could simply trigger the dormant compulsion when he had need of a particular puppet's perspective, and wear his eyes around the world as the puppet acted upon his bidding. When Shail later withdrew from his puppets' minds, such men and women had no memory of his occupation, no concept of having done anything beyond their own will.

Shail employed compulsion liberally in carrying out his games, but he considered it an inelegant tool. It was simply expedient, pragmatic; why walk when you could ride? But he found little merit in its use.

Pride came in walking among thousands of learned Adepts, interacting with them, *deceiving them every day*, making each one think he was naught but a lowly *na'turna*—him! A god among fleas! And requiring no power whatsoever to fool them into thinking he was their equal; simply their own ignorance, their pathetic inclination to ignore unwholesome acts, their mortal propensity to see only what they *wanted* to see, what they *wished* to believe; and to believe only those things that made them feel stronger, smarter, less aware of their innate uselessness.

Shail thrilled in this deceit. He derived a sublime, almost divine, pleasure in making all the world think he was other than he was.

Pelas for all of his failings had at least convinced the mortals he was only a simple artist; yet he'd never run in the circles Shail had navigated. No one looked to an *artist* expecting to find strains of Adept power. No, Pelas's Immanuel di Nostri was an effective but ultimately uninspired disguise.

Shail found his puppet standing in the drawing room awaiting his arrival, a glassy-eyed statue in flowing Palmer's robes. He was a handsome man of perhaps five and twenty years, fair-haired and beardless, as was the Palmer's way, with hazel eyes and a sensual mouth. Yes, quite a nice looking young man. People would follow him. They would *believe* him. There was an earnestness to his gaze—when not vacant in wait of Shail's overtaking—that could be quite compelling.

Shail traced his fingers along the man's jaw as he studied him. He recalled what it felt like to look through those sweet eyes, to know what his puppet knew, to *feel* his passions, *yearn* for his ideals, and with every breath, to watch him betraying the things and people who meant the most to him.

Shail exhaled contentedly. The innocent ones were always the sweetest to claim, the low-hanging fruit so ripe for the reaping, juicy unspoiled berries plucked from the bush with all of their goodness bursting beneath his compulsion's probing tongue.

The uninitiated might expect the corrupt or dissolute to be quicker to compel, but so often their minds had petrified, rutted from trundling too long upon the muddy paths of false ideals, now hardened into aberrant shapes. Such minds had to be broken before they would properly conform to his desires, and who but a madman like Dore Madden had time or inclination for such labored pursuits? No, a mind free of evil intention was far easier to corrupt.

Shail ran his thumb down the Palmer's eyelids, closing each. He had big plans for this one, and soon.

He took the man's chin in his hand and roused the puppet's consciousness with a thorny mental hook. *What have you seen since last I was here?*

The puppet rewound his thoughts through the moments since Shail had last scoured his mind. Shail watched his unspooling memories with a narrowed gaze.

Wait—a face in the crowd, surrounded by flashes of steel. *Who was that?*

"The Princess Nadia," the puppet said dully, his answer lifelessly reeled up through layers of compulsion. "She's been seen often of late on the Sormitáge campus in the company of a Marquiin of the Prophet Bethamin."

A Marquiin? Shail worked the muscles of his jaw. What was Darshan up to now? When Shail had given Nadia as prize and peace offering to his brother, the possibility Darshan would release her never crossed his mind. What did it mean that the princess had returned to Faroqhar in the company of one of Darshan's puppets?

He considered a few threads of possibility. Then he sank into an armchair and called the mortal tapestry into mental view. Toying with the threads of this endlessly pliable fabric had become his favorite pastime. If Pelas had spent more time drawing on *this* canvas, they might've actually gotten on well together.

Sometimes Shail found it effective to push his will along a specific thread of the mortal tapestry, but usually he preferred the outcome when he simply sketched an outline of his intention and let Balance fill in the rest of the picture.

Releasing one such intention into the tapestry to let Balance get to work, Shail then reclined in his chair, closed his eyes, and poured his consciousness into his puppet. The man's eyes flew open. But a very different being now gazed through their lens upon the world.

Operating the puppet's body as if his own, Shail retrieved the Palmer's hood from its place on a hook and fastened the mask across his borrowed face.

Let's go for a little stroll, shall we?

❖

The Princess Nadia walked with Caspar down a cloister linking the Sormitáge's Physical and Theoretical Sciences building with the Hall of *Sobra* Scholars. The sunlight was casting long, diffuse rays between the columns, lending a peaceful cast to the afternoon, but Nadia's mind still knew a tempest. No matter where they were, she and Caspar endured *deyjiin*'s raging wind together, Nadia's bond acting as a tiny sanctuary amid the maddening storm.

She'd thought she would grow inured to the perpetual tempest of Bethamin's Fire, or at least more accustomed to it, but she felt it always, heard it always, as if she and Caspar sheltered within a dome's lantern while the wind and rain raged around them.

How he endured it, Nadia didn't know. *She* at least could shut it out by closing off the bond, but she only did this in moments of great desperation, for doing so abandoned Caspar to weather the storm alone.

Because Caspar had been Marquiin, her Praetorians didn't trust him—especially the wielders among her guard—though he'd given them no reason to doubt his loyalty to her. They seemed to fear he would do or say something to corrupt Nadia, however, and were far too interested in her private conversations with him.

When her mother had announced she would allow Nadia to retain the bond with Caspar, he'd practically prostrated himself with gratitude. He was willing to endure any necessary strictures. But Nadia considered her Praetorians' eavesdropping a sore infringement on her personal freedoms.

Accordingly, she'd taken to conversing with Caspar via their bond and doing her best to look like she wasn't conversing at all.

She glanced at him as he was walking a polite distance from her, solemn within the halo of her Praetorians, his eyes covered by a patterned Merdanti mask that they'd just had fitted to him. Sormitáge artisans had crafted the mask and engraved it with patterns in the hope of counteracting some of the more deleterious effects of Bethamin's Fire, but there was no way of knowing how long it would take before the mask had any effect...or if it ever would.

But they had hope now—unlikely, *improbable* hope. She'd barely believed him when he'd told her the Prophet had severed his mental connection with him. Caspar could offer her little more than this, for he understood nothing more himself, but the fact that the Prophet had done it at all...

Nadia cast him the private inquiry, *Do you notice any difference yet?*

Caspar kept his gaze forward. *From the mask or the Prophet's broken binding?*

Either...both.

The broken binding feels...strange, empty. I fear for the other Marquiin who were not so lucky as me, the ones still mad from Bethamin's Fire. I can't imagine what this has done to them.

Nadia exhaled a slow breath. *He's such a mystery, your Prophet, Pelas's brother. You will tell me if you notice any change in the storm?*

A smile hinted on Caspar's lips. *I have a feeling you will know as soon as I do, Princess.*

Nadia shifted her gaze to study him out of the corner of her eye, noting how refined he appeared in his charcoal coat with his raven hair cut just above his shoulders; how the dark mask emphasized his straight nose and pale complexion. She doubted the Praetorians could tell she was looking at Caspar from beneath her veil. Probably even Caspar couldn't tell.

The smile on his lips became slightly more pronounced. *I can tell, Princess.*

You know, she thought primly back, *it's impolite to read another's thoughts—or don't they teach the Truths in Myacene, where you're from?*

He turned his eyes to her. *Your gaze is like heat on my skin.*

Nadia caught her breath and looked quickly forward again.

When only silence lingered between them, Caspar ventured, *Have I offended you?*

No, she hastened the thought to reassure him. *It's just…* She cast her gaze across the bright piazza, wishing everything wasn't so tangled. If she hadn't crossed the line of propriety and forged a bond with Caspar, she wouldn't now be feeling such a conflict of emotions about him.

'*If you hadn't bonded with him…*' she heard her father's voice in reply, '*you mean, if you hadn't cared for his suffering? If you hadn't extended a hand in mercy? If you hadn't done everything your mother ever taught you in considering another's welfare above your own…if* you *hadn't been you?*'

Princess…? Nadia—

Caspar's insistent thought called her gaze back to his. She found him watching her from behind the ornate mask, his eyes apologetic, his thoughts even more so. Caspar brushed her hand with his own. *I have no aims, Nadia.* He held the thought before her that she might easily read the truth in it. *It's just…I hide from all the world—even from myself.* He looked away with a tight swallow. *I don't want to hide from you, too.*

She looked forward again, feeling numb and oddly bereft at the same time, hardly aware of her feet moving in cadence with the Praetorians' heavy steps. A sigh escaped her.

If only there might've been *somewhere* in the realm that she could feel herself again. Since crossing paths with the Literato N'abranaacht, she'd become a leaf caught in a cyclone, tumbled from Quai game to temple to Shadow to Tambarré—even when she landed she couldn't be sure of safe harbor.

She only truly felt secure when Pelas was near, though even in Pelas's company she couldn't quite banish the fluttering apprehension that had become her constant companion.

But Pelas had been gone with Prince Ean for several days now. Her father the High Lord was sailing north to confront the Danes for their treachery, and her mother hadn't the time to speak with her—not unless she wanted the one open slot on the Empress's docket, a quarter-turn of the hourglass stolen between a formal protest from pig farmers and a hearing on tax complaints from Vestian privateers. The only attention Valentina had spared for Nadia was a brief interlude wherein she'd assessed Caspar as a non-threat and then threatened both of them within a inch of their lives if they spoke a word about the Literato N'abranaacht's true identity.

Nadia supposed her mother had her reasons for harboring this secret, but she worried that in the meantime their enemy was becoming a national hero.

They were just then passing by the *Piazza della Studioso,* an expansive plaza of fountains and cafés between the Hall of *Sobra* Scholars and the Sormitáge's main administrative building. Near the plaza's largest fountain, a man was standing on a protester's plinth, addressing a crowd.

Nadia tapped her leading Praetorian on the shoulder. "Lieutenant di Corvi, I would like to hear what that man is saying."

The lieutenant accommodatingly turned off the cloistered walkway and marched them into the piazza.

"...found anything dangerous about it, don't you think they'd have told us?" the man was declaring loudly as Nadia and her Praetorians neared.

Someone asked a question, to which the man pointed emphatically. "Now, *you've* the right of it, good sir!" He lifted his gaze to the crowd, which may have numbered fifty Adepts by then. "My man here says if the *Sobra* Scholars had learned anything to discredit the literato's pattern, said defaming information would've been plastered on every door and bulletin board from here to the Agasi Sea. They'd be shouting it from the Sormitáge steps and crying it through the streets. You know I speak the truth!"

Do you know what he's talking about, Nadia?

Yes, unfortunately. Nadia felt a hollow foreboding. She managed a brief mental explanation to Caspar while the man on the statue continued talking.

"...claims the pattern shouldn't be worked, my friends, but we all saw the great Literato N'abranaacht—a known *na'turna*—fighting that demon with *elae's* fifth strand. I was there when he gave his dying confession. I heard him tell how the pattern had Awakened him! We know it's safe to work, my friends. Our brave literato is proof of this!"

Nadia heard the truth in his words—he *believed* wholly what he was saying.

Felix and I attended a talk that N'abranaacht gave on this pattern, Nadia told Caspar. She felt sick as she recalled that day, thinking of N'abranaacht's impressive and knowledgeable lecture and how he'd so effortlessly fooled every Adept in the room—many truthreaders among them, *herself* among them—into thinking he was *na'turna*.

"My colleagues and I have written a petition…"

Nadia touched the Praetorian's shoulder again and asked faintly, "Lieutenant, can't we stop this?"

The soldier shifted his weapon at his hip, indicative of his equal disfavor, and his gaze tightened. "He's breaking no laws, Princess, and the crowd is calm. Citizens have the right to assemble, providing there's no disruption of the peace."

Nadia's every sense was shouting. She searched her mind for any avenue by which they might stop the man from talking. She landed on an idea. "How do we *know* he's a citizen of the Empire? Perhaps we should ask to see his papers?"

The lieutenant considered her. Then he gave a brusque nod and raised his hand to the man. "You there! Citizen!"

The Praetorians fell into a phalanx behind their lieutenant and marched forward amid a thunderous clomping, with Nadia and Caspar at their core.

The crowd saw the Praetorians approaching and began to disperse—in true Sormitáge style, far enough to appear uninvolved, but still close enough to observe and overhear—while the man atop the speaker's platform slowly descended the steps and tugged his coat straight, looking apprehensive. He smiled weakly as the Praetorians halted before him. "Is there some problem, Lieutenant?"

"Your papers, citizen." Lieutenant di Corvi held out his hand expectantly.

As the man was reaching inside his coat, a flash of sunlight drew Nadia's gaze across the piazza. "Is that…?" she lifted her veil to get a clearer look and saw a willowy man in violet robes heading towards her.

Caspar's gaze followed hers. *Who is that, Princess?*

It's the Endoge of the Sormitáge. But what could Liam van Kheller possibly want with her?

The Praetorians smartly shifted ranks to admit the Endoge. Nadia nodded her head in polite greeting. "Lord Liam, good afternoon."

"Your Highness." He bowed respectfully while also extending her a mental welcome, an invitation to share the space of their 'public' minds, a respectful practice among ringed truthreaders and a gracious offering. "We were all relieved to learn of your safe return."

"Thank you, Lord Liam." Nadia extended a hand to Caspar. "Your Excellency, may I introduce my friend to you?"

"Yes, Caspar of Myacene, I believe?" The Endoge nodded to him. "I've been hearing much of you of late, and of the patterns that mark you."

Nadia felt Caspar mentally cringe at this remark. "I thank you for your support in the creation of this mask, Your Excellency," he murmured.

The Endoge studied him with a look of shrewd contemplation. "Our knowledge of the Prophet Bethamin's Marquiin has been thin, to say the least. I hope you will not begrudge us more of your time to allow further study."

"It would doubtless behoove us both, Your Excellency." Caspar clasped hands behind his back and bowed slightly, in the manner of his people. His Agasi was so flawless that one would never guess he was from Myacene. "However, the thread of my life, such as it is, belongs to the princess to weave."

The Endoge shifted an inquiring look to Nadia.

"We shall certainly make the time, Lord Liam," she affirmed with a smile. "Working in concert with your scholars, we may even find a cure for Bethamin's Fire."

The Endoge nodded. "This is my hope, Princess. Many would benefit from our combined efforts." He regarded her then with obvious reservation.

"Was there something else, my lord?"

"Princess..." an odd reticence threaded the Endoge's usually forthright manner, hesitancy interwoven with contrition, "the Empress told me some of what happened to you after the attack. I cannot apologize enough for—"

"Surely you don't blame yourself for what occurred at the Quai field."

"On the contrary, I am most distraught over it, Princess."

Lieutenant di Corvi released the citizen back to his own affairs. Nadia noticed the man departing, and a frown overcame her expression. "Have you heard about this petition, Lord Liam?"

"I have, unfortunately, Princess. I've just come from presenting a report to the Empress upon it, in fact." The Endoge's colorless eyes took on a shadowed cast. "Who would've thought a simple pattern found by one of our more obscure Arcane Scholars would gain such unwelcome notoriety?"

Nadia grunted. "The Literato N'abranaacht, I guarantee you." She shifted her gaze back to the Endoge. "Did my mother tell you why I was at the Quai game to begin with, Lord Liam? Did she speak of my investigation with Tanis di Adonnai and Felix di Sarcova, or share what we learned about the literato?"

"She did not mention any such to me, Your Highness."

Nadia, what are you doing? Caspar sounded alarmed.

Nadia set her jaw and her determination. *What my mother should've done.* She settled a flinty look upon the Endoge. "Is there somewhere we might speak in private?"

Viewing the world through the borrowed eyes of his Palmer, Shailabanáchtran walked the Sormitáge's Grand Passáge with his masked visage twisted into an expression of malcontent.

What was Darshan up to, sending Nadia back to Faroqhar with one of his Marquiin in tow? Had he put the princess under his own compulsion? Might *he* now be walking behind her eyes, even as Shail was walking behind the Palmer's? Or was he watching through the Marquiin's corrupted gaze? Had Darshan sent Nadia back as his spy?

And what was Darshan *thinking,* sending her back with a Marquiin at all—shouting to all the world that Nadia had some connection to the Prophet Bethamin? The lack of subtlety in this arrangement disturbed Shail on numerous levels, for Darshan rarely acted imprudently.

What vexed Shail the most in all of this was that he wouldn't be at odds with Darshan if not for Pelas's meddling. It irritated Shail beyond reason to find his elder brother suddenly allied with Pelas, when Pelas had been blatantly and egregiously ignoring their purpose for centuries. And now, because Pelas made a few ill-founded claims…now Darshan had decided that *Shail* was acting against their purpose. *By Chaos born,* it infuriated him.

What Darshan didn't see—was *incapable* of seeing, really—was that the act of unmaking had infinite forms and expressions; some were just more rewarding to explore than others.

Shail could unmake stars in his sleep. But to unmake societies from within…to meticulously break down the social constructs, the ties of trust that bound these mortals together into civilization, to watch them devolve into contention and chaos…*this* was a sublime interpretation of their purpose.

Darshan lacked vision. That was ever his problem. He saw only one avenue, one perspective—*his own*—and he followed but one mundane path of purpose; yet there were infinite interpretations possible to those with inventive minds.

Brooding on this, Shail walked his Palmer towards a pair of carved bronze doors which were surrounded by a vomitous amount of green marble—his brother's work, all.

It offended Shail beyond reason to see Pelas putting his considerable talent towards such a useless mortal industry as *art*; then again, the menial labor of chipping stone was nearly all Pelas was useful for these days.

Through the bronze doors, the Palmer whose eyes Shail wore emerged into the *Piazza della Studioso*, a busy gathering place at any time of day or night. As he descended the steps, two observations struck Shail at once:

First, a man standing on a plinth addressing a crowd and the phalanx of Praetorians heading towards him. And second, the veiled figure walking amid their flashing livery—the Princess Heir—and the masked man beside her, clearly his brother's Marquiin spy.

Oh, how ripe this moment! Balance remained as true to him as ever.

He sent his Palmer flowing across the piazza towards the speaker. The crowd had begun to disperse beneath the oncoming Praetorians, but there were still plenty of onlookers to blend in with while Shail deliberated what mischief he might stir up. The opportunity seemed too fine to let the moment pass untroubled.

Whatever he did, it would be a simple thing to abandon his Palmer after the fact. The man would simply go about his day thinking that he'd lived it as he usually did, and if anyone questioned him about an uncharacteristic choice, he would simply invent something to explain away the inconsistency in his action.

So fascinating, this aspect of the human mind, that the part of the consciousness that computed and analyzed *required an explanation* for even the most inexplicable occurrences! No matter how outrageous a man's actions, no matter how unreasonable, reactionary or preposterous his choices, he would manufacture some way of rationalizing them. Shail didn't even have to do anything to this end. It was like these mortals were made to be manipulated.

He'd just landed upon an idea of devious merit when he noticed a man dressed all in black crossing the piazza. His Palmer's eyes revealed this stranger to be younger than his confident stride would indicate—perhaps only twenty years. Shail would've found the man unremarkable save for the way the crowd shifted out of his path, a telltale sign of an Adept shielded in *elae*'s fifth strand.

So… the man was a wielder, despite his young years, and accomplished, it would appear, to already be wielding the fifth with confidence.

The Palmer whose eyes Shail wore couldn't see *elae*'s currents, but Shail suspected they would be carrying evidence of the wielder's passing. More surprising still, the man appeared to be heading directly towards Shail's Palmer.

Shail moved his puppet backwards by several steps to blend in with other onlookers. The oncoming man in black shifted course ever so slightly to follow him. Yes, he had Shail's puppet pinned in his sights.

Intriguing. What could this wielder have seen in his puppet to draw him so unwaveringly across a crowded square?

Shail turned his Palmer around and moved him quickly back towards the main building. There were a hundred empty galleries in that monstrosity of limestone and gilt where he could confront the wielder unmolested. Shail was curious to know what had first drawn his attention.

He reached the steps and turned his puppet's gaze over his shoulder. Yes, the wielder was still following him. *Excellent.* He enjoyed a good game of cat and mouse, especially when the mouse thought it was the cat.

Shail pushed his Palmer up the steps and through his brother's bronze doors, into shadows.

SIXTY

*"Pray not to be sheltered from dragons
but to be fearless when facing them."*

—A popular Malchiarri saying

"MADAM SCHOLAR?"

Socotra Isio turned from placing a book on its shelf to find an intern standing in her office doorway. Socotra tried to remember the girl's name—Mariel? Marie? It was so hard keeping track of all of the Maritus students working on their theses beneath the auspices of the Order of *Sobra* Scholars. Socotra herself was sponsoring seven students and she could barely remember their names.

She eyed the cart beside her stepladder and the dozens of books stacked there, then peered at the girl above her spectacles. What chance she could finagle the intern into putting away all of these books for her? "Yes, what is it?"

"A man, Madam. He says he has questions on the Returning."

Socotra sighed. Weren't they teaching these interns anything anymore? "Ordinary inquiries should be directed to the citizens' library or advised to attend a Palmer's Mass."

"Yes, Madam." The girl dropped her gaze, and a slight flush came to her cheeks. "It's just…" she shuffled her feet with a diffidence that would've earned Socotra a fast reprimand from her mother, "he's not an ordinary man."

Socotra arched a brow. "What makes him unordinary?"

"Oh, no, it's just…well, he's rather extraordinary, Madam Scholar."

Both of Socotra's eyebrows arched that time, doubtless pushing her wrinkled forehead up in indecorous mounds. She'd long stopped paying attention to mirrors for the stranger they always showed staring back at her. "He's an Adept then?"

"He didn't say, Madam." The girl seemed distracted by her memory of the man. She twined a strand of dark hair around her finger. "He's really… tall."

"Oh, for Epiphany's sake." Parade a handsome man before a teenage girl and she becomes as useful as frozen butter. Socotra came down off her stepladder—she remembered a day when the maneuver hadn't required so much concentration—and retrieved the next book to be put away on the shelf. "Send him to Maestro Restari. It's his day to entertain inquiries."

"Maestro Restari is in class, Madam Scholar."

Socotra carefully climbed back up the ladder again. "Maestro di Priori then."

"He's in a meeting, Madam. The gentleman asked to speak with a *leading Sobra* Scholar."

"Oh, he's a gentleman now, is he?" Socotra pushed the book into place and leaned an elbow on the bookshelf to study the intern. "And he wants to speak with a *leading Sobra* Scholar." She sighed and came down off the ladder again. "He's some kind of lord, I presume?"

No telling what this nobleman wanted. She'd unhappily learned through the years that being one of the Sormitáge's foremost *Sobra* Scholars too often involved dealing with nobles with inflated ideas about the value of their own opinions on subjects they knew absolutely nothing about.

"He's certainly dressed like a nobleman, Madam, but he didn't give any title."

Socotra eyed the intern vexedly. "Did you manage to find out *anything* about him, Marie?"

"It's Margarie, Madam Scholar." The intern twirled her hair. "He did say something about being an acquaintance of some famous artist…Immanuel di Nostri, I think?"

Socotra's insides tightened as if she'd just been doused in ice-water. *Lady's light,* how embarrassing! Just hearing Immanuel's name did ridiculous things to her, especially since his recent visit.

She waved brusquely at the intern to cover the moment's discomposure. "You might've started with that, Margarie. Take me to him then."

The girl led away at a brisk pace which soon had Socotra straining to keep up—old bones resented being bounced and jostled like apples in an open cart, and hers were pushing four centuries, even if she might've passed for sixty name days beneath the moon. Such was the power of the Pattern of Life, that working it but twice had propelled her into a future she'd never imagined wanting to see.

"Lady's light, child!" Socotra's tone summoned the girl to heel. "There's little chance of him being gone before you return if he came here for answers. Hasten slowly."

Margarie flushed. "My apologies, Madam Scholar." She continued at a more sedate pace.

Socotra had left her office so quickly that she'd forgotten to don her Palmer's wimple and hood. *Ah well…*

To make up for the indiscretion, she gave the intern a long lecture on the immodesty of haste, well timed to conclude just as they reached the doors separating the public and private spaces of the Sormitáge's immense Hall of *Sobra* Scholars.

Carved of alabaster and nearly fifty feet high, the doors were replicas of the Extian Doors as depicted in the *Sobra I'ternin*. Bursting with myriad expressions of life, the exquisitely sculpted doors seemed to have captured all manner of animals and men complete, their bodies entwined harmoniously in their ascent towards Annwn. Socotra had never once passed through the doors without admiring their detail. It made every morning bittersweet, thinking of the artist who'd sculpted them.

She allowed herself a private smile upon this reflection. *He* was every inch as exquisite as his art.

The doors opened with a flow of *elae*, swinging inward to reveal a man standing before their parting as if he'd been inspecting them from the other side. He was indeed quite tall.

"Here is the gentleman, Madam Scholar," the intern gushed—as if Socotra couldn't have figured this out for herself.

The gentleman wore a damask jacket of burnished gold over an embroidered white shirt whose long cuffs skimmed his knuckles. He wore his short raven hair swept back from his broad forehead. The lines of his nose, cheekbones and squared chin displayed a symmetry of form almost too perfect for Nature to have had much hand in their creation, which immediately made Socotra suspicious of *his* nature.

He was standing with his feet planted slightly apart and holding a sculpted black cane behind his back, the stance of a man comfortably in command—certainly of a man comfortable in his own skin. He gave the impression of a personage who lived by no other's grace. Despite her arrival, his gaze remained fixed on the sculpture above the doors.

Socotra saw something in his eyes as he studied the lintel. Not so much appreciation as recognition; less admiration than…resignation?

"This work," he glanced down to her—truly startling, the effect of his gaze settling upon her; almost as a shock of power scoring along her core. Only one other man had ever affected her thusly, and she was standing beneath his handiwork. She better understood the intern's reaction to him now. "Whose is it?"

Her eyes tightened. "I think you know." She looked him over discreetly. "I am Socotra Isio. I'm told you have questions on the Returning. I'll answer what I can."

"Shall I reserve a gallery, Madam?" Margarie was staring at the gentleman as if she would've rather reserved a bedroom.

"We'll speak in my office." Socotra looked the blushing intern over resignedly. "Find one of my interns," —*one of the male ones*— "will you, Margarie? Stefan or...Ronald, Rikard—"

"Richard?"

"Yes, that one, and have him bring tea for us."

Margarie bobbed a curtsy. "Yes, Madam Scholar." She cast a fleeting, wistful look at the gentleman visitor—who hadn't once appeared to notice her—and whisked away.

Socotra frowned after her. Then she shifted her gaze and frowned at the stranger, who still had not offered his name. "Well..." her aging eyes had rarely encountered a man of such self-possession, "you'd best come with me."

He followed her in silence, though she remained acutely aware of his presence walking in her wake, but even more so of the effect his presence was having on the mortal tapestry.

In her years spent pursuing the Palmer's faith, Socotra had learned to perceive the mortal tapestry in the way raedans learned to read the currents of *elae*. She'd determined through observation that some men glided through the world leaving a slender thread in the pattern. Some let the world glide around them, hardly weaving any thread at all. Still others chopped up the fabric, tilling the aether of Balance, leaving ruts of disharmony.

But *this* man...it was as if he caught and pulled the tapestry with him in his passing—verily, its gossamer threads practically *clung* to him. He dragged them along behind himself in a flowing train of consequence, with his every step reshaping the pattern.

Socotra knew a vortice when she saw one.

She led him into her office. He stopped just inside the double doors and looked around—at her two floors of bookshelves, at the wall of windows overlooking the piazza, at the large hearth that always had a small blaze going, even on warm days.

There were certain benefits to being good at what you do. Socotra's father had taught her that truism from her earliest years, when she'd still been spending her days running barefoot in Malchiarr's cloud forest, never thinking she would stray beyond those mountains of mist; fresher days, when it had seemed impossible that she might betray her faith with one oath or restore it with another; long before she could've imagined sharing her bed with a man like Immanuel di Nostri.

Socotra walked to her cart of books and picked up a stack of them. "Here," she extended the books to her guest. "You can make yourself useful while we wait for the tea."

He leaned his cane against a bookcase and accepted the books without comment.

Socotra waved towards the higher shelves. "Up there—alphabetically."

With careful attention, he studied each book's binding and then placed it on the appropriate shelf, most of which she'd have needed to climb four ladder steps to reach. However, the last and largest book gave him pause.

He extended the cover towards her. "This language is foreign to me."

Socotra looked at the book in his hands. The gold lettering tooled into the leather was shifting continuously through every alphabet known to man. Socotra grunted and took it from him. "Seems the book doesn't know what to make of you either." In her hands, the lettering resolved into Malchiarri. "This one goes up there." She pointed to a dark opening on the highest shelf, into which he obligingly restored the book.

So intriguing, this striking man with his provocative stare and unsettling radiance of power.

Socotra had always been the curious sort, but experience had taught her patience, especially when dealing with immortals. And this man was fifth strand or she'd give up her university tenure and go back to weaving baskets in Malchiarr.

She handed him another stack of books.

And so it went, trading books with glances, the passing of each an opportunity for conversation, each of her invitations silently but politely denied.

He didn't strike her as a man who spoke of idle things to fill the empty spaces of silence. He seemed the kind of man for whom words were decisions, pieces in a King's game, each one carefully weighed, chosen and placed deliberately upon its square.

She'd just returned the last book to its shelf when Richard arrived with the tea. He hovered in the doorway holding the tray, his blue eyes fixed on the stranger with a mixture of curiosity and ready suspicion. "Madam Scholar?"

"Yes, yes," she pushed hands against her lower back, remembering a time when her body had been a vehicle instead of a hindrance, "we'll take the tea by the windows."

Socotra turned to her oddly grandiose guest. Her thoughts kept comparing him to Immanuel, but though she suspected they were bound to the same strand, the two men were as dissimilar as night and day.

She had to lift her head to meet her guest's gaze. "You do drink tea, I suppose?"

He took up his black cane from where it had been resting against the bookshelf. It was a gorgeous piece of sculpture, as elaborate as a king's scepter, and if it wasn't Merdanti, Socotra would eat her wimple.

He nodded slightly to her. "If you are offering, madam."

"I'm offering." *Somewhat against my better judgment.*

Was that a twitch in the corner of his mouth? The hint of a smile aimed at her passing thought, plucked from the aether? Immanuel had always seemed to know her mind as surely as any truthreader.

Then again, maybe she'd just imagined the twitch. Her guest wasn't exactly a basket of ready grins.

Richard was setting out the tea when Socotra reached the table. Beyond the tall windows of her office, daylight drenched the world, and the trees lining the building's edge were bright with spring's gloss. To her perception, the man radiating behind her glowed brighter still.

"I'll take things from here, Richard. Close my office doors on your way out."

"Yes, Madam Scholar." He glanced at the stranger as he departed, speculation hot in his young gaze. Doubtless there would be quite some talk among the Maritus students that night.

Her guest was observing the second floor of her library and hardly seemed to notice Richard's exit.

Socotra settled into her armchair, feeling manifestly old. What was it about handsome men that made a woman so suddenly aware of her years? "So…" she extended a hand for her guest to join her at the table, "how do you know Immanuel di Nostri?"

He seated himself in the armchair and crossed his legs as he sat back, fixing his brown eyes upon her. "Is this to be the manner of our treating, Socotra? You ask me a question, I ask you a question?"

His deep voice enfolded her like a bolt of velvet power, wrapping her whole and complete to reshape her to its design. *Lady's light…* Socotra forced an even breath. Had the intent of compulsion laced his words, she would've been putty beneath them.

She leaned to pour the tea and was pleased to find her hand far steadier than her heart. "You would prefer it some other way?"

The slightest shadow narrowed his brow. "I am merely...uninstructed in the delicacies of social engagement."

Socotra set down the tea pot, sat back in her chair and studied him. She'd known men who commanded power by nature of position, and men who compelled it by nature of ability, but in her several hundred years of life, she'd encountered only one man who *was* power—whether or not he'd ever admitted this truth to her.

She nudged her saucer away from the table's edge. "Etiquette is for wives and politicians. I prefer the stiff drink of candor."

He clasped long fingers in his lap and studied her in return—a heart-quickening experience to be sure. "And how much candor can you drink, Socotra?"

"A good deal more than we'll have tea for." She took up said tea, really wishing it was a stiff drink instead. "You might start with your name."

He gave a nod to this simplicity, but his eyes never left hers. "My name is Darshanvenkhátraman."

"That's a mouthful." The foreign name felt sharp in her thoughts, as words of power, those with patterns underlying their arrangement, are wont to do. Her order had derived many such words from their study of the *Sobra I'ternin*. "What is its meaning?"

His lips twitched with an almost-smile. "It means Destroyer of Hope."

"Your mother had a sense of humor, I see." She took a sip of tea and scalded her tongue, much the way her credulity was feeling round about then. "Is there a short version to this mouthful?"

His gaze looked her over with the faintest glimmer of what might've passed for amusement for him. "Darshan."

"Very well, Darshan." Socotra set down her tea before her hands started shaking. A woman couldn't sit four feet from a man radiating such power and not be affected by him—she'd hazard that even the Empress would've chosen to keep her hands in her lap. "What questions do you have about the Returning?"

"Just at the moment, I have questions about you, Socotra Isio."

Socotra's heart fluttered in spite of her years.

Every immortal she'd ever encountered had a sense of predation about them. Even Immanuel had given her looks that made the hair on her arms stand on end. Yet if Immanuel embodied the qualities of a jaguar, this one took the form of a panther—far darker and appallingly dangerous. But she'd survived encounters with such cats in Malchiarr; she knew how to tread lightly around them.

Taking her silence for acquiescence, or perhaps not caring if he had her agreement or not, he took up his teacup and eyed her over the rim. "How does an Adept of your quality become one of the Sormitáge's foremost *Sobra* Scholars?"

"Of my quality?" A bemused smile flickered on her lips. She wasn't sure if she should be flattered or insulted. "You mean a Wildling?"

"I speak only to the impression of your lifeforce on the currents."

"Ah. Well," she gave a resigned grunt, "a few centuries of study and a lot of groveling."

He waggled a finger towards something behind her. "And these accoutrements?"

She turned to see her wimple and veil on their headrest by her desk. "The Palmer's drape is a ritual of faith." She looked back to him. "Studying the *Sobra* is my profession."

"Yet does this faith not derive also from this profession?"

"Certainly the *Sobra* forms the basis for our religious dogma." Socotra held a hand to draw his attention to the left side of her library. "But most of these works are the writings of Epiphany's Prophet, important texts to my faith."

"How so?"

"The writings of Epiphany's Prophet transcend the *Sobra's* axioms in the way the Esoterics transcend the Laws of Patterning. Epiphany's Prophet has helped us understand how the axiomatic patterns of the *Sobra* apply to all of life, not merely to Patterning."

"Epiphany's Prophet…" he sipped his tea, "the enigmatic Isabel van Gelderan."

Something in the way he said her name, some intimacy in its construction… Socotra wondered if he'd crossed paths with the Citadel's High Mage, and recently.

Most of the world thought Isabel van Gelderan had perished with the Hundred Mages on Tiern'aval. Having lived through the Citadel's fall, Socotra knew better of this untruth.

She straightened her robe across her knee. "Without the writings of Epiphany's Prophet, we Palmers would never have learned to see the mortal tapestry."

He tilted his head slightly. "You can see the tapestry?" He returned the cup to its saucer. "Speak to me of this ability."

"*Sight* is too strong a word. It's a perception, not something one views with mortal eyes." Socotra reached for her tea and was glad to find her hand steady again. "In her writings, Epiphany's Prophet teaches us how to find this perception and hone it, even as a *raedan* learns to read the currents of *elae*."

"Are they not the same energies—the tapestry and the currents?"

"Yes, but they're not the same canvas, Darshan."

"Intriguing, Socotra." He set down the cup and saucer and flowed to his feet. Walking to the windows, he lifted aside the sheer curtains and gazed out over the broad piazza. "How does an Adept Return?" He turned her a look in caution. "Give me not the mythology, the religious speculation. What are the mechanics involved in this process?"

Socotra fixed her gaze on the tall figure blocking out the daylight. "Adepts are bound to the mortal tapestry via the patterns inherent in their makeup." She let her eyes admire the long line of Darshan's form and wondered where a man like him had been all these years to go unnoticed and unremarked. "Those patterns bind them to a particular strand of *elae*. There is much dissention among us exactly *how* the patterns bind an Adept, but evidence suggests that the patterns that enable an Adept's innate ability are not merely confined to their bodies but are somehow scripted to their immortal souls, for Adepts always return to the same strand, even when the gender of the body changes."

Darshan let the curtains fall back in place and turned away from them. "That much was clear to me."

She shook her head. "Then perhaps I'm not—"

"How does the Adept *Return*?" He clasped his hands behind his back and strolled the wall of bookshelves. "Death has claimed the Adept's corporeal form and your *angiel* Epiphany his soul. *Then* what occurs?"

Socotra smoothed a strand of hair back from her face. "We have only speculation."

Her leveled her an intense look. "I will accept your speculation."

She took a few moments to organize her thoughts while her heart found its natural rhythm again. Many of her colleagues feared treating with the immortal races, for their combined long history was riddled with tragedy—usually for the mortals. But Socotra had always found it thrilling. Not since Immanuel's last visit had her heart worked so hard to keep afloat. She was rather enjoying it, in a suicidal sort of way.

"If the mortal tapestry is woven of the energy of life," Socotra began, "then it follows that Adepts are bound to the tapestry—in spirit, in *essence*... we can only infer this truth, yet the axioms support it."

She looked him over to gauge his reaction, but his gaze revealed nothing of his thoughts. "We believe that when an Adept dies, the tapestry pulls their spirit back into itself, and..." she opened palms in apology, "we can only assume that the tapestry restores the Adept to life when it is time for his thread to surface and begin weaving its path in the pattern anew."

Hearing this, Darshan turned to face her. His dark hair fell forward, draping angular cheekbones, softening his features but not the potency of his gaze. "What would prevent an Adept from Returning?"

"Balance, I suppose?" She set down her empty cup and sat back heavily in her chair. "Our race is dying. We suspect the Adepts are still Returning but not Awakening."

He waved off this answer. "There is no mystery in this to me." He took up his cane and started walking again, gesturing with it as he inquired, "What would prevent an Adept from returning to the tapestry after death? What could trap him here?"

The concept startled her. She followed him with her gaze. "Do you speak of ghosts? Spirits held to this plane?"

His gave her a voluminous look.

Socotra sat stunned. Between breaths, she held up fascination in one hand and prudence in the other and allotted them careful consideration. Then she tossed prudence over one shoulder—it only ever served longevity, and what was the point of a long life without risk and the wonders it reaped?

"Is this Adept by chance bound to you, Darshan?"

He turned her a swift and penetrating stare. His words followed on danger's breath, icy against the back of her neck. "Why do you ask me this?"

She rallied her composure from where it had scurried to hide in the next room. "My eyes may be old, but they're not blind," her voice sounded embarrassingly weak, "and I know a vortice when I see one."

He studied her with a deep and meaningful stare. Then he released her from his pinioning gaze and returned to his chair with an immortal's grace of movement. The cane he left standing on its point. "Tell me about these vortices."

Socotra let out her breath slowly. She still had her youthful temerity but not the physical resilience that had once held hands with it.

As she looked at Darshan, remaining acutely aware of his power in a way that kept her walking the knife-edge of vigilance, it wasn't lost on her that he could've been directed to any of a hundred different scholars, save that she alone happened to be in her office. That this man, who was somehow connected to—and certainly of the same ilk as—Immanuel di Nostri had found her...there had to be some kismet in this crossing of threads.

That was the thing about the tapestry, though. So many times, you never knew the moment was important until you looked back upon it and saw how it connected to the rest of the pattern. Ironically, or perhaps by divine design, in the way that Healers couldn't heal themselves, no mortal could see the long view of their own path. They could speculate, they could postulate, they could pray, decide, act with faith or without it, but no manner of postulation would give them an actual view of their path, only a view of its potential. Even Seers had difficulty looking down their own threads.

Socotra cleared her throat and focused her thoughts. "Vortices weave no thread through the pattern; rather, they attract and bend the paths of others to suit their aims, forcing change in the tapestry's design. They summon those they'll need to accomplish their objectives, whether or not they know they'll need those people at the time."

She looked him over speculatively, thinking of herself and how she'd clearly tumbled into his gravity. "You, Immanuel di Nostri…you're both wells in the tapestry's fabric. You attract other threads to yourselves as stars attract planets."

He considered her with a quiet and unsettling intensity. "You have assumed much about my nature, Socotra." She couldn't tell from his comment how he felt about this. His gaze narrowed slightly. "Did Immanuel speak to you of us?"

Socotra gave a dubious laugh and pushed up from her chair. Talk of Adept ghosts bound to immortal vortices required stronger stuff than tea.

"Immanuel di Nostri is the most close-mouthed man I've ever met." She reached her sideboard and turned him a look over her shoulder. "More tightlipped than you by far."

He frowned at this.

Socotra poured two glasses of brandy. "You've drawn me onto your path, Darshan. Let us speak candidly. You came here for answers. Take advantage of my expertise." She returned to the table and offered him a glass and a smile. "That was something Immanuel was very skilled at."

Darshan accepted the brandy with an unreadable gaze. "I don't doubt it." He watched her as she retook her chair.

"So," she settled in again, "this Adept, the dead one who hasn't Returned…"

His eyes tightened. "He is bound to me."

Even though she'd expected it, the truth was still thrilling to ponder. "With the fifth?"

Darshan nodded.

Socotra marveled at the territory they were heading into. "An unbreakable binding?"

Again, he nodded.

She took a drink of her brandy and schooled herself to sip instead of gulp. As the liquor warmed her stomach, she walked herself through what she understood. "You must still be in communication with him, else how would you know he hasn't gone through the Extian Doors?"

"It appears that we are still able to reach each other," he agreed.

Socotra stroked her chin. "I freely admit, these are uncharted waters. Only a handful of Adepts in recorded history have ever dared work the Unbreakable Bond—Isabel van Gelderan and Arion Tavestra being the most famous of them—but none of them were immortals."

Darshan paused his brandy halfway to his mouth. "That is a bold presumption, Socotra."

Socotra gave a low chuckle. "We've a saying in Malchiarr: *because a leopard suffers a butterfly to land upon its nose doesn't make the leopard appear a butterfly.*"

She lifted a finger from her glass to aim it at him. "Immanuel would never admit it to me, but I always knew he was fifth strand." She set down her glass and spied her guest shrewdly. "I cannot say what race of immortality claims you both—none that I've ever heard of, to be sure—but only a fool imagines we know all there is to know of creation."

He arched a raven brow. "It doesn't bother you, knowing you treat with something unknown?"

"It intrigues me greatly, Darshan."

After a moment's consideration, he lifted the brandy to his lips. "You are a fascinating woman. I can see why my brother enjoyed your company."

She blinked at him. "I beg your pardon?"

His eyes explored her unapologetically as he drank. She got the distinct impression he was resculpting her flesh in his mind as perhaps it had once appeared. "You would've provided a welcome escape for him."

"Your *brother*." Socotra drew back in her chair with inquiry sharp in her gaze. "Do you..." —she'd dared suppose they were of the same ilk, now dare she ask it?— "speak to me of Immanuel di Nostri?"

"He has another name which he answers to, but now I recall he mentioned you." Darshan set down the brandy glass and sat back in his chair. "Your name becomes familiar to me in the way one refashions a lost memory after it's been invoked by another." He captured her eyes anew with his own dark and compelling gaze. "You were his lover for a time."

Only an immortal would think of a handful of decades as 'for a time.'

Darshan rose from his chair and walked to the windows again, his manner pensive, his thoughts reshaping the cosmic fabric before her very eyes. "I see where your logic would take us: a vortice, an unbreakable binding...I am indeed holding Kjieran on this plane."

Socotra couldn't tell if he was pleased or distraught by this truth. "It does follow, I'm afraid," she admitted.

Darshan again lifted the sheers and gazed out into the piazza. In the distance, a crowd had gathered around a man who was speaking atop a protester's plinth. Darshan rested one hand on the window and inquired without looking at her, his voice reflective, "How do I release him?"

"I do not know." He looked over at her, and she shook her head in apology. "However..." she wondered if she dared suggest it.

The faintest lift to one raven brow encouraged her to continue.

Socotra exhaled a slow breath. "I might suggest asking Epiphany's Prophet." She raised a placating hand before he could summon his ready suspicion. "Another presumption, I'll admit, but you gave me the impression that you and she had crossed paths in recent months."

He drew back slightly. "*I* gave you this impression?"

She smiled. "You leave deep footprints in the fabric, Darshan."

He tightened his gaze upon her. "Socotra—"

But whatever he'd meant to say he abandoned, for something beyond the windows drew his gaze suddenly back to it. So riveted did he instantly become that she rose to discover for herself what he was observing.

"Do not." His tone alone pushed her back down in her chair. Darshan scraped the sheers fully aside and then stepped back from the windows. His extended hand summoned his cane through the air. It clapped as it struck his palm, and Merdanti stone remolded itself into a dual-ended scepter.

He leveled a stare at her, dangerous and dark. "Stay away from the windows." Then with the barest glance, he made the glass amorphous and stepped through.

Socotra pushed out of her chair in an instant.

She reached the reforming windows in time to see him leap down two stories and go striding across the piazza, dragging innumerable threads of the tapestry behind him.

SIXTY-ONE

"I care not what becomes of me, only what becomes of it."
— The wielder Malachai ap'Kalien, on T'khendar

Sleeping beneath a star-studded sky, lulled by the slosh of waves against the black sands, Ean dreamed of another life…

Arion paced the path skirting the lake surrounding Epiphany's Altar, electrified by the charged polarities of outrage and disbelief. The moon shone from high above to imbue the crystal gazebo with a luminous glow, while the lake lay still beneath sleeping fountains, a mirror of the heavens.

Yet he couldn't appreciate the glorious night, for his mind remained in the chamber where the attack had occurred. Too clearly he saw it still— *inverteré* patterns cob-webbing the air, others set to explode the moment she worked *elae*, innocuous shelves filled with *atrophae* to drain and enervate her. A cunning and deadly trap set for the Citadel's High Mage.

How many of the Hundred Mages had been directly involved, and how many were simply complicit? Of course they'd all pled their innocence, but this hardly constituted proof; they all knew enough to evade fourth-strand readings.

If Arion had been allowed his way, every one of them would've been summoned before a truthreader tribunal—to Shadow with their indignant protests and attempts to hide behind their offices!—on pain of death, if needed, and dragged in chains if he had to.

How could this have happened? How could he have failed to see a pattern of such deadly cause and consequence? How could *Isabel* have failed to see it? The one thing he was sure of was that Dore Madden had orchestrated the entire affair. That much he'd seen in the pattern. If only it had shown him direct action instead of ambiguous intent!

Arion shoved a hand through his hair and turned to pace in the other direction. One would think a man as depraved and despicable as Dore Madden couldn't be so bloody successful. But he was *incredibly* successful. And Arion knew why: Dore simply didn't conceive that there was anything he couldn't or shouldn't do.

That was the essence of success as a wielder. But in the case of a man like Dore Madden, with a moral compass attuned solely to self-interest, it made him unpredictable, and immensely dangerous.

Isabel's imminent arrival pulled Arion's attention back to the moment. He rushed to meet her at the bottom of the stairs and took her hands in his.

For a moment, words failed him. The horror of almost losing her felt too raw. Then he pressed a kiss to each of her palms and enfolded her in his arms. "*By Cephrael's Great Book*, Isabel, if I hadn't been there—"

"But you were." Her breath fell softly across his ear; her mind caressed his with reassurance.

Arion took her by the shoulders. "I'm supposed to leave for Adonnai, but I cannot *think* of—"

"No, you must go. What you do there is too important." Her colorless eyes were as luminous as the gazebo, her manner radiating a similar calm, much in contrast to the agitation coursing through Arion. "We can't let these things distract us from the higher purpose."

"An attempt on your life is hardly a *distraction,* Isabel, and you and I both know they'll try again."

"It seems likely." She kissed him and ran her nose lightly along his. "But I will never again allow myself to be blinded to the truth."

Arion frowned at this. Blinded was exactly the reason they were there. "Isabel..." he looked her over uncertainly, "are you sure about this?"

She took his hand and drew him towards the lake. "If memory serves, this was your idea."

"*Metaphorically.* A show of strength." He put the fifth beneath his steps and followed her out across the water. "To walk not only unafraid but blindfolded against their evil, proof that you stand remote from their treasons—untouchable, *incorruptible.*"

"And I agreed with the value of this metaphor."

"But Isabel, *this*—"

She stepped from lake to gazebo. Light erupted in a dance of spiraling, prismatic patterns. Arion followed her beneath the crystal dome, frowning deeply.

Isabel took his hand and wove her fingers through his, even as her mind was interwoven with his mind, their life patterns forever entwined. "Arion, I looked into Dore's eyes and let myself be deceived." She sought understanding in his gaze. "I wanted to believe he could be redeemed. I wanted to think some good remained in him."

Concern and his own reservations sharpened Arion's unease. He traced his thumb across her cheek. "Compassion is a Healer's curse."

"Even so, you warned me."

He shook his head. "I hardly understood what I saw. You were right to challenge my conclusions."

"Was I? Events would convince me otherwise." She took his hand from her face and opened his palm. Her thumb traced his lifeline, while her mind traced a path backwards through choice. "I couldn't see anything on Dore's path to prove his deception, so I denied your instincts—I denied my *own* instincts." Isabel squeezed his hand in hers, the slightest emphasis of her fury. "Now we have no idea how far the corruption has spread, how many Adepts were allowed to purchase their rings, how deeply the Mages' misinformation has penetrated the Sormitáge Orders. I have much work ahead of me in restoring truth." She fixed her colorless gaze upon him. "This was a necessary lesson, Arion, and this..." she exhaled a slow breath, "this is a necessary sacrifice."

Arion pressed his lips together. There was nothing to be done for it. She'd decided, and in that decision, she'd chosen her path. The most he could do now was support her in her choice.

Isabel held out a long strip of cloth to him.

Frowning deeply, Arion took the cloth while she turned and readied herself. The idea of never again looking into her eyes summoned a knot to his throat, but he lifted the strip and draped it across her eyes. She adjusted the blindfold into place.

"You will become a symbol to all of us," Arion forced the words through an ache in his chest, "an icon representative of hope and truth, *elae* embodied." He tied the cloth behind her head and lowered his hands to her shoulders. The crystal gazebo was blazing so brightly he had to squint. "You will become—"

She turned in his arms and lifted her blindfolded gaze to him. "Epiphany's Prophet."

—⬦—

Ean woke to Pelas's hand on his shoulder. Beyond the open wall of his room, sunlight was glaring off the sea. "*Gah...*" His head felt like someone had been kicking it all night. "What time is it?"

Pelas straightened above him. "Early afternoon. You seemed to need the sleep."

But definitely not the dreams.

Pelas gazed intently at him. "Do you feel it, Ean? The tapestry is calling us back."

Ean mostly felt the protest of overtaxed and much-abused muscles. He pressed palms to his eyes and stifled a groan. "Calling *you*, maybe. Me, it would rather spit out." He swung his legs over the side of the bed, pushed elbows to his knees and sank his head into his hands. The dream felt heavy in his mind, thick with Arion's confusion, his loss webbed with guilt.

All this time, Ean had thought the blindfold was a result of Isabel's promise to Arion…that it had something to do with his Return, that when they were bound anew she would remove it. He'd resented her still wearing it without realizing why.

Yet in the end, her promise hadn't been to all the world. And Arion—he'd been so caught up in his personal loss over not seeing her eyes that he'd hardly considered *Isabel's* sacrifice. *Shade and darkness,* to *never* look freely upon the world again?

He dropped his hands and looked up at Pelas. The Malorin'athgul was already dressed for a return to Faroqhar, looking splendid in a coat of muted plum, his long hair neatly queued. Pelas arched a brow at him. "Rough night?"

Ean rubbed his eyes and stood up. "Rough year." He took up his shirt and slipped it on, casting a look at Pelas as he went for his pants. "You can feel the mortal tapestry?"

"A new perception Phaedor opened to me. But I wonder, Ean, can you not feel it also?"

Ean looked up under his brows while donning his pants. "Why would I?"

Pelas leaned against the wall and crossed his arms. Beyond him, the sea and sky appeared so deeply blue, it was difficult to separate the two. "In my understanding, Balance and the fifth strand are inseparable."

Ean sank down on the bed to don his boots. "You and Phaedor have no paths in the tapestry. It follows you'd be able to view its pattern—at least, it explains some things." He lifted his eyes to meet Pelas's gaze. "Not so for me."

"But your path through the tapestry is thick, Ean. You bind many threads to you. Perhaps you cannot see the overall pattern in the same way," Pelas waved a hand vaguely, conceding his point, "but could you not perceive something of it?"

Ean frowned, considering the idea. He knew Balance played heavily in his life. He was bound to Balance in part for being a fifth-strand Adept, but even more so due to Arion's choices and actions, for each time he'd died tragically and Returned, Balance had woven him more firmly into its fabric. Now his every action tugged upon the Balance to some degree.

He thought he saw Pelas's point. While he was pulling against the Balance on one end, mustn't it be pulling against him on the other? If he but learned how to perceive that force, could it direct him towards the right path, the right actions—choices that wouldn't violate any cosmic equilibrium, yet could still result in achieving the effect he intended?

Pelas handed him his coat, and Ean slipped arms into it slowly, pensive now, for he was seeing an important truth. Both memory and instinct told him a violation of the Balance was central to why Arion had ultimately lost. It would be hugely beneficial if he could learn to perceive such signals.

Ean glanced to Pelas as he belted on his sword. "It's the Fifth Law, isn't it? *'A wielder is limited by what he can envision.'* That includes what he can envision himself envisioning, per the Eleventh Esoteric—that is, in this case, what he can envision himself *perceiving*."

"I believe you have firmly grasped my point." Pelas looked him over with a smile. "Ready?"

"As ever."

Pelas tore the fabric and escorted Ean into Shadow. As the portal was closing them into unmitigated darkness, the prince asked, "You can go anywhere traveling through Shadow?"

"Only to places you've been before. To open the portal on the other side, I must envision a clear and detailed concept of the space I want to arrive into—an application of both your First Law and the First Esoteric. It would be dangerous and ultimately futile to attempt a traverse through Shadow without this image in place."

Light split the darkness before them, and Ean stepped into daylight, automatically summoning the currents—

He spun to Pelas. "Is that—"

"I'm not sure." Pelas's eyes tightened. "Something's not right."

"We should—"

"Split up, yes."

They headed off in opposite directions.

As Ean took wary steps in pursuit of his vague premonition of unease, he wondered…could that feeling be the Balance speaking? If his every action tugged at Balance to some degree, *shouldn't* he be able to feel its force tugging at the opposite end? And if he was limited only by what he could envision—per the Laws and Esoterics—then why not envision such godlike power for himself?

Because it doesn't work unless you actually believe *it, Ean.* Fynn's voice had a way of speaking Ean's thoughts any time they became suitably sardonic.

Unfortunately, the Fynn voice had a point.

He was never going to be able convince himself that he had godlike power, but he might be able to convince himself that he could draw the people he needed to help him onto his path. That seemed well within Isabel's explanation of how she and Ean bound many threads to themselves. Yet while this idea intrigued him, he had no clue how to consciously go about it.

He was apparently quite competent at wandering aimlessly through the Sacred City, though, because before he knew it, he was crossing a *sogliá're* and emerging onto the Sormitáge campus.

Where he came to a standstill.

Looking around at the immense buildings with their lawns as expansive manes; marbled paths, the veins of the university, pulsing with a constant stream of students and scholars; wide boulevards winding among groves of ancient trees shading boarding houses and dormitories…

Ean stood in that moment feeling a strange duality of lives. In one breath he saw the famous university for the first time; in the same breath he knew his own intimate connection to it, a breathtaking reunion with a place that had been as deeply woven into his being as he was into its. Arion had spent more than a century haunting these halls, studying, experimenting, honing his craft; arguing with friends and combating Markal Morrelaine's pessimism. Ean could almost feel Arion's energy still radiating from the limestone paths, in the way he'd felt Isabel in the imperial garden. Almost.

It didn't take him long to discover that the Sormitáge was a city unto itself. Too easily one could become lost among the maze of courtyards, walls and cloisters, in one moment traversing a brightly lit tunnel beneath a walkway expecting to find the building's front at its end, only to discover yourself in a private courtyard instead. Sadly, if unsurprisingly, Arion's mental map hadn't survived the transition into Ean's head.

Even so, lost or not, the day was bright, the campus was beautiful and awash with colorful flora—not to mention the myriad Adepts milling or rushing about—and if he'd had a better idea of what he was looking *for,* he might've truly enjoyed the moment.

Ean couldn't say with any certainty that a divine force was guiding his tour across the campus—he could've simply been moving on the path of least resistance—but in the spirit of optimism, he entertained the notion that Balance was leading him in the right direction.

He finally found his way out of a maze of arcaded courtyards into a broad piazza separating two massive halls. Both structures boasted impressive domes, but the one across the piazza from Ean had a cluster of them surrounding its central bulb.

Ean sat down on a set of wide marble steps and studied the currents beneath the comings and goings of Sormitáge life. When he shifted his perspective to view the world through the fifth strand, he saw something fascinating.

In the energy of the fifth, Adepts glowed as bright stars among the radiant, sweeping tides of *elae's* other strands, while *na'turna* appeared far dimmer by comparison. The prince had never been among such a concentration of Adepts before. Seeing so many of them now, watching how the currents swarmed around them...Adepts were *magnets* for the lifeforce. No wonder it was so easy for them to manipulate *elae*, whereas *na'turna* like Markal, or his brother Sebastian, had to labor for years sometimes even to sense the lifeforce.

He recalled tales from the days of the Quorum of the Sixth Truth, when *na'turna* had been relegated to the lowest caste of society because they couldn't natively sense *elae*. Those had been dark times for the realm. Yet seeing this view of *na'turna*, as the Quorum's members might've also viewed them—fifth-strand Adepts all, like himself—he could almost understand how the Quorum might've developed those prejudices.

He was studying a core of stars that had collected around the darker, shadowed radiance of a plinth, when he noticed a matrix of light caging one of the dimmer, *na'turna* stars. The matrix was so utterly unusual that it took Ean a moment—and a shift of his view of the currents—to realize what he was seeing:

A man wrapped in patterns. And not just any patterns. *Compulsion* patterns.

Apprehension quickened Ean's pulse. Suspicion leapt to a fearful question: had Darshan sent this man in search of him—or, more likely, in search of Nadia?

Ean slowly got to his feet. The matrix surrounding the *na'turna* was so stark that Ean marveled no one else could see it, but then, he alone in that galaxy of stars possessed the variant trait of seeing patterns.

He descended the steps and started across the piazza, walking within a bubble of force that encouraged people out of his path long before he reached them, giving him an unimpeded view of the man who had become his unsuspecting quarry.

The latter moved out of a cluster of onlookers and headed towards the larger building. Ean put the second into his steps and within seconds was walking twenty paces behind the *na'turna*. The prince followed him through a pair of soaring bronze doors into palatial elegance.

Columns of marble supported friezes where life-sized statues acted out a drama fifty feet above the mortal one; and above this march, the marble arched like the branching limbs of trees into an exquisitely painted groin-vaulted ceiling and its multiple domes.

With mortal eyes, Ean noticed these tributes to the creativity of man, but his wielder's gaze remained fixed on the matrix shouting man's depravity ahead of him. The *na'turna* wore a Palmer's masked hood and robes, as did many who traversed the crowded passages, but Ean easily singled out this Palmer from the others by the cage of compulsion he wore.

The Palmer turned down another passage and slipped through a pair of double doors midway down. Ean reached the doors soon after him. He searched the entrance for patterns and then followed the *na'turna* inside.

A long gallery extended into shadows. The Palmer was skirting the inside wall, the other providing the only source of light via tall windows overlooking a shaded garden, but to Ean's *elae*-enhanced vision, the room might've been lit by a thousand torches.

In three steps, he'd caught up with the man. With his fourth step, he grabbed the *na'turna's* shoulder and spun him around. Hazel eyes stared from beneath the Palmer's hood, unfocused—but *someone* was watching.

Ean pushed his palm into the man's chest and dove into his mind. It was like walking into a cage of kaleidoscopic light. He sought the pattern that bound the man's consciousness, speeding along a rushing channel of the fourth, but when that river course opened upon the delta of another mind, an entirely *unexpected* mind—

Recognition's spear impaled them both.

The prince reared mentally back—staggered physically back from the Palmer with bells of alarm shaking his certainty. And beneath these…the echo of haunting laughter.

Behind him, the air rippled.

Ean spun and drew his sword. A portal split the fabric. The same laughter that was echoing in Ean's skull made its chilling arrival as the actual man stepped out of Shadow. His blood-red robes rippled like the currents as he strode into the realm

Tall and broad of shoulder, his features reflected an immortal's symmetry, but the aspect of his brow, the flare of his nose, his thin lips and sharply angled chin—every part of his face seemed to have been molded by contempt.

"Shailabanáchtran." The name burst out of Ean's constricted chest, interwoven with disquiet. The one immortal he hadn't expected, the *last one* he wanted to confront just then.

Shail's contemptuous chuckle resolved into a cold smile. "*Ean val Lorian.*" He spoke the name as if savoring the shape of the letters upon his tongue. "Or should I say Arion Tavestra?" Darkly predatory eyes licked over Ean. "Do you even know the answer?"

Chagrin had Ean clenched in its icy hand. He'd been hoping Balance might lead him, but was *this* really where Balance had been taking him?

"*'Come and find me...'*" Ean ground out the words beneath an exacting stare. "Have you been waiting?"

Shail's smile slowly widened. "Fascinating." He looked Ean over again with dark eyes that Ean remembered too well from Arion's last moments. "So you really have recovered some of who he was. But how much do you recall?"

Enough to know he wasn't prepared for *this* encounter. He moved opposite to Shail's approach, pacing him in turn.

"I've sought you the realm-wide, Prince of Dannym. I freely admit, I never imagined we would meet here on Arion's old stomping grounds."

"I should've known *you'd* be here, haunting the scene of the crime."

Shail's smile became a disdainful sneer. "You inherited Arion's insolence, I see." His eyes smeared condescension across Ean's form. "All this time, you've been the proverbial thorn in my side, and here with my least effort, you come right to me. It is astonishing how desperate the world is to submit to my will."

Ean tightened his hold on his sword. "You won't find all of us quite so willing."

"No?" Shail smirked. "In the end, Arion seemed willing enough. He begged, as I recall."

Ean believed Arion might've begged for a host of things there at the end, but he doubted any of them aligned with what Shail was implying.

Shail halted and crossed muscular arms. "You do realize you've died already three times by my hand?"

Ean held onto his fortitude and the Malorin'athgul's gaze, though neither came to him easily. "They say the fourth time's the charm."

Shail barked a skeptical laugh. "Can you not see the futility of this endless cycle?" He waved vaguely to emphasize his point. "Returning again and again with no memory of your prior life; reborn as a wailing, helpless babe; damned to a perpetual amnesia, growth, and relearning of skills many times mastered and forgotten. The perverse futility of so-named *parents* doting on eternal beings trapped into mewling, drooling forms..." Disgust wrinkled his lip. "What use is it to perpetuate this cycle?"

With no further warning, Shail wrapped his power around the prince.

Ean felt it seeping through his shields, *permeating* them, darkly toxic and treacherously inviting, a mesmerizing power he seemed powerless to combat. This wasn't compulsion, it was enthrallment, captivation, *seduction*. All of his work with Pelas to battle *deyjiin*—yet these were traps of *elae* wielded as expertly as anything Arion had done!

Shail watched Ean wrestling with his working, wearing a smile of foregone conclusion. "What perverted creator designed this way of life for you?"

Cold power caressed Ean's mind. *Submit*, it encouraged, *give up—give in.*

"Where is the purpose in your existence?"

Spiny thorns stabbed at Ean's thoughts, muting reason's clear edge, luring disheartenment to the fore. *Let another be in charge...shed the weight of your obligations...*

Ean fought to maintain control over his thoughts, but Shail's working unbalanced reason, exchanging rationality for irresponsibility, honor for ignobility. And it had melted right through his shields!

If you would know peace, relinquish your hold, submit *to me...*

Now the power teased, waking strange and unwelcome desires. It was a courtesan's smile of invitation, a licking tongue of arousal. *You could know pleasure unlike anything you've known before, if you only submit...submit...*

Shail effortlessly held Ean in his gaze and Ean's mind—horrifyingly—in the thrall of his will. "Who would *choose* such an eternity?" he posed, and his power echoed the question with a thousand sweet caresses, a nursemaid stroking a sick child into sleep...or death. *Release yourself, free yourself. Why endure this futile effort?*

Ean felt his fingers loosening around his sword. The frightening part was how *right* it felt to let it go. He *wanted* to let go, and yet...

—*No!*—

Ean fought it with every ounce of will.

A vague recollection, so faint beneath the veils of Shail's compulsion, floated to him. *'...the only way to overcome the compulsion was to accept it...I had to let it permeate me. Do not counter force with force; channel it. This was the lesson your Isabel taught me...'*

Ean's fingers were growing looser, his sword heavier, his own thoughts harder to hold. He desperately cordoned off the tiny corner of his mind where rationality was cowering and hung there, gripping desperately to indecision's slippery rope. Submit to this? Accept it? Could he trust Pelas enough to act on his advice against his own instincts? Did he trust *Isabel* enough?

Across the space of their *tête-à-tête*, Shail was smiling darkly, the outcome in his mind already assured.

Feeling even his small corner being overtaken now, Ean forced a swallow. If this was going to be the last thought he ever had as himself, it had best be a meaningful one. He cast the thought along their bond, *Isabel...I trust you.*

Then he embraced Absolute Being and opened himself fully to Shail's power...

His consciousness was instantly consumed.

Ean let those compulsive waves permeate him, terrified it would be the last sensation he ever recalled...but within that surrender, within the open willingness to *be* consumed...

Suddenly Ean realized that while the compulsion was permeating him, he was also permeating it—and for every particle of energy pummeling his consciousness, he created one just like it of his own.

His sword was slipping from his fingers.

Ean collected all of the energy of Shail's working in one mental arm, and all of his own energy, an exact duplication of Shail's working, into the circle of his other. Then, with a singular focused effort, he channeled the full force of this combined power into his blade.

His fingers gripped with sudden strength.

His arm brought the weapon to bear upon Shail, and a laser of power lanced through the air.

The Malorin'athgul dodged in a whirl of silk.

The windows behind him shattered.

Shail turned among the sound of falling glass and leveled Ean a severe stare. Then he slowly reached over his shoulder and drew his Merdanti blade. "So I see you're not without *some* skill." He strode back across the shattered spray. "But how *much*?"

Abruptly he cast a bolt of *deyjiin* at Ean. The prince deflected it off his blade, and the marble floor disintegrated into a puff of chalk.

Shail began stalking him. "I see you've accomplished the level of ability of any Maritus student." He tossed another pattern at Ean, wickedly fast.

Ean spun out of its path and threw a mental dagger to shred it in passing. He knew Shail was testing him, determining how much of an adversary he would prove this time around.

This time around…

Ean watched the Malorin'athgul circling him, his malice making waves upon the currents, utterly delighted at the prospect of killing Ean a fourth time…and a deep-rooted anger sparked inside the prince—anger at all of the times this immortal had gloried in his death, at the cruel and calculating acts he'd worked against Isabel, and the heartless hold he'd waged over the Hundred Mages.

Perhaps Balance *had* thrown them together—it certainly appeared that way—but while Shail was viewing their encounter as a foregone conclusion, Ean didn't have to agree with his assessment.

Shail spun his weapon in a figure-eight and grinned. "How would you like to die this time?"

Determination and disquiet formed the woof and warp of Ean's outlook as he watched the man circling him. He raised his blade and made a shield woven of every strand of *elae*. "Let's meet the Demon Lord together."

Shail gave a low laugh. "Oh, Prince of Dannym…you have no idea what you're asking." He launched at him.

Their blades clashed with sound and light. Broken glass shivered across the floor. The curtains shredded themselves on the shattered windows. Shail beat Ean back in a fast, precise attack—every stroke accompanied by harpoons of the fifth.

The prince felt them skidding across his shields, seeking any notch in which to catch and haul. Chains of compulsion linked each harpoon to Shail's will, so that if even one found its mark, Ean would be caught.

The prince compartmented his mind to keep equal attention on his shields and Shail's flashing blade, and portioned off a third section to devise some way out of there. If the man had killed him three times, it followed that he knew all of Arion's tricks. Ean's best hope would be inventing some new ones.

They crossed the floor embroiled in their clashing dance, with the lifeforce thrumming and the very air shivering around them. Sentient Merdanti blades sang while the currents whipped an agonized accompaniment. Shail nearly landed a fatal blow, but Ean managed to yank himself out of reach with a lasso of the fifth. His feet scraped broken glass into a shivering wake as he came to a skidding halt.

Shail pointed his weapon with rancor blackening his gaze. "At least prove yourself worthy of my interest. Provide *some* challenge for me." He crossed ten paces in a breath and swung for Ean's head.

The prince locked blades in a geyser of sparks, *elae* and *deyjiin* singing discord onto the currents. Shail forced both blades back towards Ean's throat and brought his face close enough for the prince to see the sparks reflecting in his eyes. He held Ean there beneath the razor edge of his malice while his compulsion pelted Ean's shields.

Ean finally managed to shove him off and moved into their predator's circle again, holding his blade low. As he walked, he recalled to mind every pattern Pelas and Darshan had ever thrown at him. These he fashioned into a matrix—inelegant, haphazard, but functional—and into it he threw as much power as he could summon.

Shail was still sneering at him when he released his working.

The air flashed—split, *fractured*.

The currents seethed.

Shail flung up his own shields, even as the working flung him backwards in a wild spray of shattered glass. For a moment he vanished beneath glittering dust, the roiling currents and a collision of exploding patterns.

Ean chased after Shail, spearing his awareness towards the Malorin'athgul. In the space of a thought, he latched onto his mind—with all of the compulsion Shail had poured onto Ean, he'd laid a fast track back to his own awareness, a practical map guiding Ean through his shields.

When Arion had found the same opening, he'd used it to attempt to unwork Shail. Ean intended something very different.

Before Shail regained his shields, the prince poured his awareness into the Malorin'athgul's mind and reached for Absolute Being. In effect, he was embracing Shail's mind and bringing it within the confines of his own space where he could do anything he wanted with it.

Shail roared. He launched towards Ean with his blade glowing violet.

They collided in a thunderous clash that shattered every crystal left on the chandeliers and sent plaster raining down on them. Blinded by dust as much as Shail's barrage, Ean could only trust to his compartmented mind to keep the immortal's sword from scoring a killing blow while he continued expanding his hold on Absolute Being, kept reaching outwards to surround Shail's mind entirely with his own. It was a dizzying effort, trying to embrace a star, yet if he could expand his awareness to fully contain it—

A hand suddenly clamped around Ean's throat.

Ean jerked back to awareness to find his own hands at his sides and Shail's eyes inches away, boring into his.

Shade and darkness! What had just happened?

The Malorin'athgul's fury radiated through Ean in punishing waves. He managed the barest wheezing inhale. His entire body had gone numb.

The part of his mind that still held to lucidity recognized that Shail had somehow overtaken Absolute Being and was holding *him* captive now—exactly what Ean had been trying to do.

Thirteen hells! He'd fallen entirely within the Malorin'athgul's control! But *how*?

Shail's iron hand tightened around Ean's throat. He pulled the prince's body closer and pressed his lips to Ean's ear. An icy breath heralded ominous words. "Let me show you how *I* remember your end…"

Light seared Ean's consciousness. A barrage of images lanced agony across his mind. Stars whirled, streaks of shattering light, color broken into fragments, fragments into razor shards…

The world spun…or they were spinning, sealed together in mind and deed.

Time had fractured.

The only thing not spinning was the dagger clutched between them.

On the other side of their shared grip, Arion's features were twisted with effort, making his face almost unrecognizable between the pulsating light and the centrifugal force pulling against his flesh.

Shail's long hair whipped and spit around them, electrified with static by the kinetic wind, every end a stinging lash. And like Ean in the now, Shail then had Arion pinned within the space of Absolute Being.

"There is only submission now." Shail forced the thought into Arion's

mind—Ean's mind—both of their minds reeling beneath that thrumming demand, separated by the centuries, yet bound to the same moment. "You will become my pawn—the magnificent Arion Tavestra, my puppet-wielder, Bringer of the End of Days…"

Arion wrestled for control of the dagger. His jaw was clenched and his hair clung damply to his brow. Arion's blue eyes held anguish and outrage…and in the deepest shadows of his gaze, abject apology.

There was no denying that look, no denying what Arion intended. Even Shail recognized it for what it was.

"No!"

Arion plunged the dagger into his own heart…

Abruptly the spinning kaleidoscope vanished, replaced by a hazy battleground clogged with the detritus of broken patterns. Ean sucked in a rasping inhale, but only the barest slip of air scraped down his throat, teasing his burning lungs with the memory of breath.

Blackness became indistinct blotches that finally resolved into Shail's face, close before his own. So many malicious thoughts glimmered behind those cruel eyes. Had Ean seen Darshan's indifference there, he would've been grateful for it.

Shailabanáchtran clasped both hands around Ean's throat and lifted him off his feet. His body hung agonizingly between iron palms, legs dangling, his neck and shoulders screaming, his breath wheezing painfully and fast.

"Do you still want to meet the Demon Lord, Prince of Dannym?" Ean thought he could see the glint of *deyjiin* behind the immortal's dark eyes… or perhaps it was just his fading eyesight, blighted by breathlessness and the storm of power stirring a hurricane through his thoughts.

He couldn't have drawn enough breath to speak, even had Shail wanted an answer. But he didn't, in fact, for he threw Ean forcefully and cruelly aside, a toy flung by an angry child.

The prince flew sideways through blinding stars—

And across the boundary of a silver-limned doorway. It winked shut with a singular finality, leaving Ean falling…falling…endlessly falling through a darkness so vast that all awareness fled from it.

SIXTY-TWO

"What he's forgotten about elae would fill a hundred tomes."
—The Second Vestal Dagmar Ranneskjöld,
on Björn van Gelderan

PELASOMMÁYUREK STEPPED ONTO a terrace of the Sormitáge's sprawling Theoretical Sciences building, following a thread in the tapestry that kept changing before his eyes.

Everything he'd learned in his recent research about the mortal tapestry warned against attempting to directly alter its weaving; such efforts usually resulted in unanticipated and unfortunate outcomes. The tapestry wove itself into a pattern only it understood. Trying to preempt the shape of that pattern would only cast the threads spiraling in new directions, forming whorls of consequence between the moment of misdirection and the eventual point at which the pattern restored itself to its original path of intent.

Who was weaving this infinite pattern? Was it some divinity? Or was the tapestry's design merely a product of choice and action, predictable only to the degree that choice and action could be predicted, and able to be influenced to the same extent?

One might as easily ask how fixed was the course of a river, and what would be the ramifications of redirecting it. Many speculated, but no one *knew*.

Pelas would've liked to have spent an evening, or a hundred of them, discussing the mortal tapestry with Socotra, now that he'd gained a new understanding of it. He still hoped one day to do so. But some things were already clear. That Shail had learned about the mortal tapestry seemed an obvious truth. That he would be using the tapestry to shape events to his will went without saying. But had Shail learned to read the tapestry to determine *their own* influence? This was the gauntlet Phaedor had thrown at Pelas's feet—a skill the zanthyr had already mastered over millennia of studying the pattern. But Pelas hadn't an infinity of time to answer that challenge himself.

In that very moment, the influence of a Malorin'athgul is what he thought he was seeing on Nadia's path. It appeared to him as a warping—not of the thread itself, so much as the space around the thread, or…even a hollowness where substance should've been. He wasn't sure he'd have noticed anything had he not been monitoring Nadia's path so closely.

But was the warping a product of his own influence, or a result of one of his brothers? And would he ever be able to spot something so insubstantial on a thread that wasn't as intimate and familiar to him?

He'd just reached an arcade connecting two wings of the building when the thread shifted again. Pelas came to a halt. At first, he thought the warping had vanished from Nadia's thread, but when he prudently broadened his view, he saw instead that the warping effect had expanded and was now influencing an entire section of the tapestry.

He hadn't taken any action.

So who had?

A chime must've rung, for students began flooding out of the building at both ends of the walkway. Pelas moved closer to a column while mentally studying the tapestry's pattern, searching for…

Then he saw it.

In the same moment, the currents went berserk.

Pelas shoved through the flood of students and finally drew up on the wide steps leading down to the piazza, blinking against the bright afternoon sun and searching for a familiar head among the hundreds milling there.

How long did he have? Minutes? A collection of seconds?

At last spotting a figure veiled in white, he anchored time behind him and rushed towards her, slowing time so greatly that he might've run circles many times around each person he passed on his way to Nadia's side. Pelas reached her and released his time-anchor in the same instant. "Princess." He touched her arm.

Nadia gasped. The Marquiin beside her jumped. Her Praetorians reached for their swords.

Pelas took Nadia by the elbow. "Princess, you must leave here at once."

A dozen concerns flashed through Nadia's colorless gaze. She nodded significantly to her Praetorians and moved off beneath Pelas's prodding. He started them walking fast—faster than Nadia would've liked, if told from her round-eyed gaze and the way her stride didn't quite keep up with his—but not as fast as he needed. With her came Caspar and the Sormitáge's Endoge.

Nadia made a hasty but unnecessary introduction as they all rushed off. "Immanuel...I—I assume you know Lord Liam?"

Pelas nodded to him. "Your Excellency."

The Endoge looked bewildered.

"His Excellency and I were about to adjourn elsewhere for a more private conversation."

"An excellent idea, Your Highness."

Nadia took Pelas's arm with a rough whisper. "What's *happening?*"

Seconds had become instants. It wasn't going to be enough—

The last grain of falling sand bounded down.

The fabric shifted.

Shail spoke mirthfully into Pelas's mind, *Why are you heading off so hastily, brother?*

Pelas grabbed Nadia and spun her behind his body. At the same time he threw up a silver-violet dome of *deyjiin* around them all.

Collective oaths hissed out of the Praetorians. They drew up short and looked accusingly at him. Caspar looked alarmed. "Who is it? Is it—"

"No." Pelas turned a dark look to the Marquiin. "My younger brother. You will find even less to appreciate in him."

"*Shail?*" Nadia threw back her veil and stared around the piazza. "Is Sinárr with him?"

Pelas could protect Nadia and her guard. It was the rest of the people crowding the piazza who worried him. Shail wouldn't hesitate to harm them for no better reason than because it would aggravate Pelas. Verily, the greater the chaos, the greater Shail's amusement.

Pelas couldn't yet see his brother, but he sensed he was close. The tapestry was practically sinking beneath their collective weight.

Shailabanáchtran. Pelas greeted him tightly as he searched for his brother among the crowd. *So thoughtful of you to pay us a visit. I still have to thank you properly for the experience you gave me. I made many new friends.*

Enjoyed it, did you? Shail seemed inordinately pleased about something, which probably meant he'd just completed some vindictive coup. *I'm sure the revenants will love having you back.*

Pelas finally saw his brother coming towards him through the distant crowd. To the world, he remained invisible, but Pelas easily saw through Shail's shield of *deyjiin*.

He released his hold on the Praetorians' swords and turned a severe look to their commander. "Let no one leave this dome."

Lieutenant di Corvi's glare said clearly, *As if we could!*

Pelas cloaked himself in night and stepped through the curtain of *deyjiin*.

A crowd of onlookers had gathered around it. If even one got too curious and touched that shimmering curtain, it would be the last thing they did; but Pelas knew no better way of keeping Nadia safe while he confronted his brother.

He started off across the piazza on a collision course for Shail, uncomfortably aware of the tapestry rippling beneath his feet. *I'm surprised you're not still licking wounds, Shailabanáchtran, considering your many recent disappointments.*

Shail gave him a sinuous smile, hidden to all but Pelas's eyes. *You've simply given me another chance to school you, brother—fulfill that penchant of yours for bloody punishment.*

Shail walked with his Merdanti blade held low. The currents seethed as a river of asps beneath his every step. *When will you see that there is nothing you care for that I cannot take away? Your truthreader paramour; the Princess Heir—soon I shall claim her again...perhaps more properly this time.*

Pelas clenched his jaw. Shail only wanted Nadia because she was important to him. For the same reason, she would never be safe from his brother's malice.

Shail was walking invisibly past the tables of a piazza café when he gave Pelas a particularly devious smile. The fourth-strand currents flared—a layered compulsion, cast wide—and fighting broke out in his wake.

Diners overturned their tables attacking others of their own party. Dishes and glasses became weapons, chairs bludgeons. Further chaos erupted in an expanding wave as people fled the sudden confusion.

Give me the princess, Pelas. Shail came on, smiling darkly. *I want to revel in the look on your face when you hand her over to me again—beaten again, bested* again, *my own little dancing marionette brother.*

Pelas tightened his grip on his blade and looked quickly around the wide piazza. Somehow he had to clear the place of people or they would all become weapons to be used against him. Moreover, he was certain that whatever chaos Shail caused there, it would only feed into the efforts of his larger plan. His brother was nothing if not calculating.

A storm would clear the piazza quickly, but real storms took time to summon. The *wind* on the other hand...

Elae could be wielded countless ways to create wind—changing the density or temperature of the air to result in higher or lower pressure, adjusting the balance of atmospheric forces, restructuring molecular adhesion—but a fifth-strand Adept need only think, *blow.*

And blow it did.

A gale force wind scoured the piazza, ripping cloths from tables, overturning chairs, sending everyone running for cover. A marauding giant could not have done a better job of sweeping humanity from the space. Even Shail was momentarily caught in the charge.

Pelas used the moment to release his shield around Nadia and was rewarded with the sight of her Praetorians spiriting her away.

Until Shail threw up a wall of *deyjiin* in front of them.

The Praetorians veered back while the wind raged around them and Adepts ran like panicked mice. The gusting wind snared an unfortunate fellow off his feet and tumbled him headlong into Shail's wall. The ash of his passing swirled out the other side, raising even greater alarm among the witnesses.

The Praetorians turned and rushed Nadia and the Endoge parallel to the shimmering wall, but Shail threw up three more walls in rapid succession, boxing them within.

"Do you see, Pelas?" Shail made his voice heard above the raging wind, but his patronizing smile needed no amplification. "Whatever you possess, I can take away." The walls of the cube began pushing inwards. All of humanity fled.

Pelas hissed an oath and released the wind. He would need the full focus of his attention if he meant to combat his brother—

Abruptly Shail's *deyjiin* walls vanished.

The Praetorians hoisted Nadia and ran.

Shail spun, snarling, and lifted his hand—

The world went still. Silent. *Frozen.*

Whatever working Shail had intended was ripped out of his hands as a toy from a disobedient child.

Apprehension strung a tight thread through Pelas. He slowly turned to face the cause of this new shift in the fabric. His skin was alive with needles of warning.

The fountains had gone glassy beneath a suddenly cloudy sky. The air felt electric in his lungs.

Across the piazza, Darshan was approaching.

Shail growled a muted curse.

※

Darshanvenkhátraman crossed the piazza with the tapestry undulating beneath his steps and his gaze fixed on his perplexing middle brother. An hour ago, Socotra Isio had asked him about their relationship and he'd hesitated in answering her. After what he'd done to Pelas, he could hardly name himself a friend.

In the near distance, he observed his two brothers facing off—Pelas's wind, Shail's targeted compulsion, the currents boiling between them and chaos spreading in the streets.

In previous times, he would've let them resolve their own differences, at best standing firm on the side of Shail's contention. Now all Darshan could think of was how Shail had given Pelas over to revenants. Such an unconscionable act seemed a far greater indignity to him than any ill he'd ever himself worked against Pelas…but he wondered if Pelas would think the same.

Darshan ripped away Shail's *deyjiin* box, allowing the little princess to escape. Then he cast his own intent broadly to encourage the rest of the mortals out of the space. He preferred to school his brothers in private, and Shail would only make bystanders into distractions.

With the piazza cleared and the world stilled beneath his slicing gaze, Darshan halted at an angle to his brothers, the better to regard them both. Shail stood immersed in a cloud of acrimony, Pelas in silence, but his expression made a window of his thoughts, and his thoughts were… surprising.

For a moment as their eyes met, Darshan saw Pelas as Pelas saw himself—artist and explorer, seeker of experiences new and exhilarating; a creative soul more than a devouring one. For eons, Pelas had infuriated him with his dilettante disregard for their purpose. Now, a part of Darshan wondered if Pelas had had the right of it all along.

By Chaos born, but that was the foulest tasting crow he'd ever tried to swallow.

The three Malorin'athgul stood deep in the well their presence had created in the mortal tapestry, enveloped by Darshan's imposed silence, warily gauging one another's intent. The electric air held a potent charge. The currents had gone flat and now seethed with friction. Around them, the fabric grew thinner.

Pelas regarded him curiously. "This is a new look for you."

"Yes, I seem to be hearing that a lot." Darshan shifted his attention to Shail. "You and I have much to discuss, Shailabanáchtran."

Shail's stare was void-black, his stance taut; clearly he was itching to attack either or both of them. "You're meddling where you don't belong, Darshan."

Darshan arched a brow. "You encouraged me out into the world."

"*I* warned you against it."

"Ensuring by the very nature of your warning that I would do the opposite." Darshan spun his scepter in his hand and then gripped it tightly, contemplatively, holding Shail firmly beneath the point of his gaze. "But I don't think you expected me to see what I've seen."

Shail growled, "I *expect* you to stay in your sandbox and play with your toys!"

"With Dore Madden as my keeper?" Darshan looked him over sardonically. "Yes, your expectations are all too clear."

Shail's anger pulsed on the currents. "I won't warn you again, Darshan."

"Warn me? Against the carefully constructed trap you have waiting for me, as surely as you had revenants waiting for our brother?" The disapprobation in his tone could've sheared granite. He started towards Shail with the currents clinging to him, dragging threads of consequence, tilling the tapestry. "Or do you reference the deceit you've been spinning these many centuries? What *exactly* won't you warn me against that I don't already know?"

Power flared as Shail's answer.

Lightning splintered the sky. The *air* itself exploded.

Darshan threw up a shield—

—that startlingly merged with another's.

He spun his head to find Pelas suddenly at his side, hand extended, holding a shield of protection around them both. Their combined shield sizzled beneath Shail's continuing bombardment.

Pelas searched his gaze wonderingly. "*Darshan, what...?*" but surprise clearly stole the words off his tongue.

Darshan regarded his brother with an ever-tightening gaze. "After all I've done to you...you come to my aid?"

Pelas gripped his shoulder, the first time in decades when his touch hadn't been connected to a blow, and asking via the intimacy of their bond, *Do you know me not at all?* His brow furrowed deeply. *You would have my forgiveness if you but asked!*

Darshan looked back to Shail. Whatever reckoning he owed his middle brother would not happen there that day. "Go, Pelas." He moved away from him. "Go do whatever it is you're doing here."

"Until this moment, I thought I was stopping you."

Leave this place, Pelas, Darshan drew the dome of his shield with him, *or Shail will make a target of you to punish me.*

Pelas cast him a fleeting thought and went.

Darshan turned his attention away from his middle brother and strode purposefully towards Shail. Power rained chaotically around him, Shail's formless hate eating through the world's canvas. Darshan tightened his gaze on his youngest brother.

Shailabanáchtran, cease this tantrum.

To emphasize this behest, he drew upon his own power in equal proportion to Shail's and sent a magnetic pulse flaring back through the bombardment. Each molecule of Darshan's energy bonded with one of Shail's.

To the naked eye, a shimmering darkness overcame the raining light.

Then Darshan seared both powers from the aether. A violent flash of light and sound shattered every window in the surrounding buildings. Daylight returned, grey beneath the clouds of a storm now churning above them.

Shail looked at him through the sound of raining glass. His lips twitched with an acerbic smile. "Always so peremptory, brother." He spun his sword and started towards Darshan. "That's ever been your problem, you know. You think all of existence should account to you."

"Did you not say we were gods, Shailabanáchtran? He who can unmake creation is evidently senior to it."

Shail gave a trenchant smile. "You cannot unmake me."

"That remains to be seen, since I haven't tried."

"And *would* you?" Shail twisted injury into a hateful stare. "All these years, I've done your bidding, come when you summoned, listened to your incessant sermonizing…but Pelas—*Pelas* does none of these! Yet upon his forked words you turn against me!"

"You've called my hand through your own actions, Shailabanáchtran."

"*Brother*," Shail's sneering tone sent the currents flooding away from him. "I see the way you look at Pelas. He could betray you endlessly and you would *still* seek his love."

This comment gave Darshan pause, only because he wondered if it might be true.

Shail's ire was stirring the storm into action. Wind scoured the empty piazza, splaying eager droplets of rain. "Everything I've done has been in pursuit of our purpose!" he shouted. "How can you imagine anything else of me?"

Lightning pulsed in the darkness above, highlighting Shail's expression of malcontent. "You've become deluded, *brother*." He pointed his sword at Darshan while rain pelted them both, his gaze as black and unforgiving as the storm clouds above. "*You* ally with an enemy and name him friend."

And he attacked.

Darshan stepped forth to engage him.

Thunder sounded as their weapons clashed, and the storm amplified the story of their battle to the distant masses—faces behind broken windows, mortal toys hovering in shadowed doorways, unwelcome guests on a playground they'd claimed for themselves.

Lightning repeatedly struck the pavement around their battling forms, each time tainting the air with stone dust and the tang of ozone. The wind whipped their hair into their eyes and tore at their clothing. The currents became as molten rock.

Shail rode fury's relentless wave, giving Darshan no opening to take the offensive. He plunged spears of compulsion towards Darshan's mind like berserkers stabbing an enemy king, and he tore at Darshan's shields with malice's fanged and venomous teeth.

Darshan held an impregnable shield and spun his staff to block his brother's advances, coldly considering how best to contain him. Brute force would not overwhelm Shail. He would need to be more cunning than that.

He pulsed the fifth to force them apart and simultaneously threw a net of *deyjiin*.

Shail skidded backwards across the slick pavement and only just caught the net on his blade. He paused there, breathing hard, glaring blackly at Darshan while he held his sword with both hands to support the dangling net of power.

Then he slung it back at Darshan.

Darshan dodged left—

And tumbled through a silver-limned portal Shail had summoned out of his line of sight.

◆

Shailabanáchtran, Maker of Storms, closed his portal and lifted his face to the rain. When he lowered his gaze again, gone was the persona of injured hate projecting envy and resentment with every exhale. In its place spread a mocking smile.

They all just make it so easy.

He sheathed his blade with finality. The storm he allowed to rage on, the better to commemorate the day the Balance shifted forever in the Realms of Light.

SIXTY-THREE

"Bravery is being the only one who knows you're afraid."
–Gydryn val Lorian, King of Dannym

TRELL SLUNG DRIPPING hair from his eyes and watched from the shadows of a boulder as his men slipped one by one over the edge of the aqueduct and vanished into the deeper shadows of a vertical scar splitting the mountainside above him. He'd just completed the descent down that fissure with his body nearly numb from the aqueduct's icy water, but between his pounding heart and the exertion required by the descent, his flesh now felt as steamy as his breath.

A hundred feet below his hidden vantage, torches glowed on Khor Taran's walls, and lamplight made a patchwork of the structure's towers. A circle of deeper darkness wreathed the silent fortress, while the River Taran drew a silvery thread across the far distant valley.

Trell didn't expect any part of that night's effort to come easily. The aqueduct had posed their first challenge. It waters were swift, and its slick sides had offered but one slim chance of escape. Yet Trell had felt more excitement than apprehension while riding that current, for he had Loukas n'Abraxis at his side, and together they'd accomplished many impossible things.

While he waited for his men to join him, Trell stared through the mist of his steaming breath and assessed the fortress they would soon be invading.

Even now, Rolan was leading fifty men beneath the first stars of night in a mad rush to create both deception and diversion, and hopefully to draw most of five hundred men down to the plains to investigate a nonexistent army.

Raegus was waiting in the hills for the Nadoriin to raise the inevitable alarm, whereupon he would attack from the north to split the forces remaining inside the walls. And Tannour...it was left to him to eliminate the wielder from the equation altogether.

Trell and Loukas, Rolan, Raegus and Tannour. They were all gearwheels independently turning in the many parts of Trell's clockwork plan, their actions separate yet interconnected, each one intrinsic to an outcome for the others. And of course, everything depended upon Trell first finding his father's men, freeing them from whatever compulsion held their will in thrall, and then somehow fighting his way out of the fortress with a thousand men in tow.

Risk upon risk, if-this-then-that; their gambit carried chance across a fluctuating equation whose factors were always shifting. But instead of focusing on Chance's diminishing remainder, Trell preferred to think of Fortune's rising potential. *If* they could successfully get into the fortress, find his father's men, free them, and arm them...*then* their force would become over a thousand strong.

Everything depended on his men playing their positions brilliantly, yet this was no more than the First Lord was expecting of him...trusting in him to somehow end the war.

For some reason, this realization made Trell feel connected in a way that he found oddly heartening. All of the Mage's Players were allied in this vast motion, entire sections of the pattern shifting and changing, yet somehow still acting in concert, working together—whether or not they even realized it—to weave a new design into the tapestry. And in so doing, changing the world.

The very idea of it made his skin tingle...though, it could've also been the wind, which was not exactly being kind to any of them.

"Trell..." Loukas's whisper reached him. "The men are ready."

Trell joined the others where they'd gathered in the shadows at the base of the fissure. "Nine men on the upper walls that I saw," he told them in hushed tones as they all gathered close in the deep darkness. Their faces were but slashes of charcoal on black canvas, their eyes like agates. "Once we're inside the walls, you know your roles."

"Your will, *A'dal*," they whispered so softly that the wind carried none of their words.

Trell gathered his resolve and searched their gazes in the darkness. "We're about to forge a new reality against chance and reason. In this endeavor, what we see is what will become. Let no one divert you from our goal. Let nothing shift your mind. Hold our objective firmly in your thoughts. We're going to carve a new truth out of impossibility." He pressed his fist to his heart.

They mirrored him as one.

For the space of an inhaled breath, Trell hovered in the moment before the dice roll, that instant where infinite possibility and failure were interwoven, chance held in perfect balance.

Then he set off, casting those cubes a-tumbling, and led his men from the safety of shadows to see how their dice would land.

❖

Tannour Valeri walked the Blind Path wrapped in shadows, himself a shadow, seeing nothing, yet seeing all. The air gave shape to his blinded vision, forming itself around objects, predicating orientation upon spaces instead of solids, cohesiveness rather than separateness. He perceived the distances between bouncing waves—sound, light, heat, motion—and they provided context to his understanding. He saw not with human eyes, nor heard with human ears, but with countless other sensory channels honed to interpret a version of the material world without solidity.

Air carried him. Air bound him. He sacrificed worldly vision to use this gift, but he'd never needed his eyes when communing with Air. Air showed him all.

From the hillside above Khor Taran, he perceived the fortress breathing; the activity of daily life pumped circulation through every cavity and hall, down the bones of passages and deep into the bowels. Air's bellows filled every room to Tannour's view as sand poured into a honeycomb, outlining shape. He knew every space where air laid claim, and the number of men inhabiting each.

He might've told Trell immediately where to find his father's soldiers—oddly, they were fewer than expected—but Trell was somewhere in the aqueduct higher on the mountain above him, beyond his purview, and in any case, freeing the Dannish soldiers was not his mission.

He should've focused on his mission then, but pieces of his mind remained with Trell. Communing with Air always brought a certain detachment—

Detachment? Is that how he was thinking of it now? That dissolution of self, of substance…the dispersal into the aether which had so frightened him upon his first attempt that it had taken him weeks to recover his mind? *Detachment, is it now?*

—but thinking of Trell grounded him as a flagpole grounds a pennant. *Ver'alir* might flurry his fabric, rip at him, shred his form, but it could never tear him fully free—not with Trell tethering him.

To walk the path of *ver'alir* without a grounding tether was to forever disperse into the aether, to lose one's humanity upon the airborne tides, absorbed by communion. A tether provided the airwalker with a purpose for living, a compelling reason to return to his mortal shell. Once, Loukas had been Tannour's tether…long ago. He hadn't dared commune with Air since losing him as such.

But now he had Trell. It had shocked him, actually. After so many long months listening to Loukas's nearly rapturous boasting of Trell of the Tides, to then discover that the man actually lived up to his reputation…

Tannour had wanted to hate Trell. He'd expected all along that he would. Instead, to his immense surprise, the man had become his new tether, and a stronger grounding force than Loukas had ever provided him.

'Air is caprice,' Tannour's instructors had explained. *'Do not seek to confine or predict it, only to ken each new direction as it shifts.'*

Tannour certainly could not have predicted this shift—gaining a new tether in someone he barely knew; restored to his full ability by a man for whom he'd only ever known jealousy.

Before him, Khor Taran heaved a bulging exhale and disgorged a flooding displacement. Tannour recognized the heartbeats of hundreds of men rushing out of the fortress. Enough, perhaps, to even their odds if Luck would carry her fair share.

Tannour whispered down the mountain while the fortress was still exhaling men and breezed inside on Khor Taran's inevitable inhale. He hovered just within the yard then, wrapped in a motionless whirlwind, himself the whirlwind. He was a trick of the light, if glimpsed at all then easily forgotten—a shadow cast by nothing, insubstantial.

Now Khor Taran's heartbeat reverberated in his consciousness. Tannour cast his awareness outwards on the thinner bands, higher wavelengths, listening—

It was not the right word, *listening*. His ears had no part in it.

—for the ratcheting reverberations of men's language, repetitive and predictable impressions in the fabric, the invisible transcript of speech.

As the educated blind could read with fingertips the studded impressions of letters, Tannour read similar impressions on the wavelengths of air, sifting through them for the one name he needed. He let all else dissolve around his perception as wet sand through his cupping fingers, washed away by the ebbing water to reveal the tiny prized shell beneath.

Kifat…

There was the name. Once…and again. The sparkling shell glimpsed among the sand, washed over and gently dragged off, but he had its location pinned.

Tannour rode air's currents then, letting the natural flows pull him towards his quarry as a raft floating upon the tides. He might've sped there, but he dared create no displacement himself, and riding the current gave him time to better discern his enemies.

Shadows appeared before him, gossamer layers of minute motion—heartbeats, the trembling filaments of expanding lungs, blood's radiating warmth—all of which cast the air into predictable waves. Tannour breezed past these men unseen, an inchoate shadow. Through the fortress he whispered, a feather caught and carried by the wind

—if a feather was a deadly shadow that had its own will—

into a tower, foremost of the five. Up a winding staircase, drawn now by the heartbeat of the man he sought. Its cadence was strong, steady. The man yet had no idea Tannour had come to claim him for the Ghost Kings.

He rode air's currents up the curving stairs and was reminded...

—*'But why must you walk* ver'alir?' *Loukas's words were spoken in hushed tones on a dark tower stair, much like the one he was ascending then. 'Why can you not walk the Path that Casts Infinite Reflections? Or at least the Mirror Path?'*

'I didn't ask *to walk* ver'alir!' *Tannour had protested desperately. 'I would walk* hal'alir *or* chrys'alir *if I could, but the path chooses you, Loukas. You don't choose the path!'*

Loukas fell back against the stairway wall and slid down onto the step, wearing an expression of abject horror. He lifted his green eyes to meet Tannour's. 'Don't you realize what this means?'—

Tannour pushed away the memory with his jaw tight. He never could think about Loukas n'Abraxis without grinding resentment between his teeth. As often as Tannour found himself thinking of Loukas, it was a wonder he had any teeth left to grind. But walking *ver'alir* always opened windows into the darkest places of his soul. There was no hiding from the Blind Path.

Tannour rounded a landing where the staccato of speech was rippling the air. He paused just shy of an iron-bound, wooden door—cold, slow waves melded with wood's radiating warmth, the latter nearly indistinguishable from the ambient temperature, yet with a timber that bespoke of living origins, echoes of harmonic resonance...

Air brought him the words—

"...coming here even now." A male voice, charged with friction. "If these Converted succeed in freeing the mutineers, five hundred Northmen will be hungering for the blood of those who imprisoned them."

"We bound them at *your* instruction," came a reverberating growl.

"I do not think they will note the distinction. Would you, Lazar?" A pause while waves of contention buffeted the air. "Despite your sentries' claims, this band of Converted *are* coming—they may already be inside the walls. And now you've fallen for this diversion and sent more than half your men away—"

"At last accounting, *Kifat* did not have command at Khor Taran," growled the voice of Lazar.

"Neither long will Lazar hal'Hamaadi, I suspect."

A scrape of steel made spines in the airwaves. "Hold your tongue, Shamshir'im, or I'll cut it from your mouth."

"You'd take better aim to point your anger at our enemies." Contempt underscored Kifat's tone. "These Converted may have a wielder with them, Commander. I surely see the signs of a fearful working brewing in the aether."

Tannour knew these words were a lie, both because *he* was one of those Converted, and because of the disharmonic undertone that accompanied Kifat's words. But he doubted the man called Lazar hal'Hamaadi could tell the truth from a lie when spoken off a wielder's tongue.

"I would act now if you mean to catch them before the moment is past you," Kifat sneered.

Lazar growled an oath. The speech impressions ended.

The tower inhaled-exhaled a broad-chested figure that greatly displaced the air. He flung the door open and stormed out, followed by many others. Angry waves accompanied the clanking jingle of mail and the stomping of boots.

They paused in the hall, inches from Tannour, their heart-rates elevated, rapid exhalations fueling fury.

"Do you think he speaks true, *al-Amir*?" a soldier asked while waiting for the rest of the men.

"He's Shamshir'im," growled the tallest of them—Lazar, if told from his voice. "What do *you* think?"

Tannour whispered past their exiting forms into the tower room.

Air claimed much of the hexagonal space inside. It spoke to Tannour of windows and walls, and of static energies casting waves into the aether. Some gathered in corners like floating vapors, traps with long tendrils flailing outwards, luring innocent death. Others hovered as wispy webs waiting for the fly to snare itself in treacherous strands. Myriad varying wavelengths reverberated, each one the melody of a different pattern.

On the far side of the room, the wielder Kifat stood before a south-facing window. Air encased a dark-haired man with a hooked nose and bullish jaw. He was leaning on the window base seeping filaments of tension into the air.

As the last exiting soldier slammed the door, Tannour retreated from communion with Air. Pulling out of communion always left him slightly disoriented, a pale version of himself, hollowed by *ver'alir's* darkly scouring winds. The longer he walked the Blind Path, the longer it took to recall his own humanity.

Bound again to solidity—

Solidity...did he ever actually lose solidity? It was impossible to know. He was not himself when he walked the path—

Tannour stood in the shadows, waiting to see how long it would take before the wielder noticed him.

Four beats of his heart later, Kifat spun. Surprise flared his nostrils. Air sucked sharply into his lungs. A fanged smile borne on crooked teeth slowly claimed the wielder's face, but his quickening heart—and the host of new patterns that suddenly coalesced into being around him—betrayed his unease. So he'd recognized Tannour from his shroud—a telling clue to his identity for any who'd faced a *ver'alir* assassin... although few survived such encounters to speak of what they'd seen—if not from some other arcane means. Doubtless he still thought Tannour disabled, tetherless and unable to commune. That would explain why he wasn't more afraid.

"My, my...Tannour Valeri." Kifat dragged the long folds of his robes away from his feet as he left the window. "I set a trap for a rabbit and caught a fox."

Tannour thought this statement a little premature.

"I expected the val Lorian prince to seek me out." Kifat ran his eyes across Tannour hungrily, as if already contemplating how to spend the bounty on his head. "But then, I didn't know *you* were among this company of irritants. My master will be so pleased to finally have you in his hands. He's been looking for you for a *very* long time...the one man who knows the true face of the traitor Thrace Weyland."

"Is that what hal'Jaitar told you?"

"Don't prevaricate with me!" Kifat speared him with a daggered glare. "You had Weyland under your knife. Every Shamshir'im felt the kiss of your blade upon his traitorous throat."

"You will know it soon yourself, Kifat."

"But you didn't follow through," the wielder snarled. "My master paid the Vestian Sorceresy an extravagant fee for your services—a prized *airwalker*, famous among the paths. But you...*you* did not do as they promised us. You didn't kill Weyland."

Tannour stood remote upon *ver'alir's* shadowed shores. "I will never kill for them."

"And you will die for it!"

Kifat's fervor became suddenly familiar. Tannour remembered meeting him; the wielder had been one of many Shamshir'im who'd fallen over themselves to tell Tannour everything they knew about Thrace Weyland, all but drooling at the chance to rid their brotherhood of Weyland's interference.

"I should've guessed you'd conceal yourself among Abdul-Basir's kennel." The wielder's lip curled in a sneer, as though this affectation would somehow mask the stench of his unease, and he continued his slow circuit of the tower, as if Tannour would believe the air empty of danger.

Tannour's blind gaze followed the wielder via Air's displacement. "Your spy, Kifat…tell me about him."

The fanged smile returned. "The spy, the spy—this *spy* you've been force-feeding lies. I knew Abdul-Basir couldn't afford to send two thousand men against us when my master's liege marches on Raku. I told the fortress commander as much. Soon, I think, he shall regret his deafness—"

"The spy." Tannour made air reverberate his voice through the room. "Tell me his name."

The wielder spun in a swirl of dark robes. Black fury flashed in his gaze. "I will tell you *nothing*."

"You'll tell me everything," Tannour's liquid voice resonated with certainty, "and then beg to tell me more."

Kifat snarled a curse. He flung his arms wide, and furniture split away from the center of the tower, shrieking as it scraped across stone to bang against the walls. "How did Weyland turn you?" He slowly advanced on Tannour. "Compulsion? Bribery? Thrace Weyland was the least of us, but I am pleased to school you in a real wielder's power."

He slung off his outer robe, revealing a molded breastplate, and pulled a serrated knife from its sheath at his belt. Tannour drew a black-bladed dagger—

cold Merdanti steel beneath his form-fitting calfskin glove, so oddly solid

—and approached the wielder in turn. He might've thrown one of his shuriken and ended the man with well-placed aim, but he wanted answers before he sacrificed Kifat to the Ghost Kings.

"I accept your invitation of tutelage." Tannour spun the dagger through his fingers. "Let us tread *san'gu'alir* together." He struck with Air fuelling his strength.

Kifat blocked with a vambraced forearm and slashed for Tannour's throat. Air rippled in advance warning of his motion. Tannour slipped aside, simultaneously striking again. The wielder blocked him, more narrowly that time. Tannour struck high, low, high—his stabbing blade splitting air. The wielder dodged, blocked and flung a pattern at Tannour, displacing Air.

Tannour sidestepped, and the pattern blasted the wall instead. Kifat growled and swung for Tannour's throat. Tannour twisted and struck his knife backhanded, slicing through the meat of Kifat's forearm. The wielder hissed and jumped out of range.

So went their dance of flashing knives: retreat and advance, advance and retreat, the ebb and flow of razor edges splitting air into agitated waves, razor patterns aimed as arrows requiring Tannour to dodge.

He stabbed high and found his weapon blocked, dropped his blade into his lower hand and slashed for the wielder's gut. Kifat twisted wildly. Tannour advanced into his retreat, flipped his blade, caught it out of its spin and struck—muscle parted with flesh—tossed it back to his right hand and struck anew—more blood flowed—flipped his dagger into the air and spun beneath it, catching and stabbing at a stumbling Kifat, slicing along a rib.

He struck again, dodged again…back and forth, tossing his blade from hand to hand, twisting, spinning to avoid the wielder's patterns, his footsteps marking a dance led by Air's pulsing displacement.

Kifat finally backed away, breathing hard, his clothing bloodied. Bravado told one tale, but the wielder's pounding heart bespoke another. The Blind Path brooked no dissembling.

Always the uninitiated underestimated the Blind Path. Always they thought Tannour's shrouded eyes a hindrance. They assumed he was walking blind, fighting blind. Always, they learned the error of these assumptions.

Tannour had chased the wielder deep into the thick of his extant patterns. Invisible energies surrounded him now, frenzied moths casting choppy waves. He perceived the vibrating patterns and kenned each one's intent by the frequency of its energies.

Kifat swiped at his jaw where a jagged red line was seeping blood down his neck. Tannour knew the wielder entertained many similar wounds, lovebites of their embittered dance.

He flipped his dagger and caught it, flipped and caught it, the millwheel of his intent. Air bound tension between them…bound them both to opposite ends of an inevitable outcome. The Blind Path demanded sacrifice.

"The spy…" Tannour's dagger flipped-spun-sealed loudly against his gloved palm while *ver'alir* hummed its song of blood in his consciousness, "tell me about him."

Kifat ground hatred between his crooked teeth. "This is barely begun, Valeri."

Tannour hooked a half-smile beneath his shroud. "I agree."

"You will get *nothing* from me!" The wielder threw his power—

Trell led his men down a narrow road in Khor Taran's lower fortress. The stars cast indifferent light on the narrow passage of hard-packed clay and dirt. The high walls of outbuildings loomed on both sides. Their feet met uneven stones and their eyes sought substance from shadow.

The alley road ended at a granary, a structure Trell remembered from Jaya's diagram, where he suspected he would find his father's men. Just shy of that intersection of lanes, he held up his hand to pause the group.

Diagonal to their position, across the broken stones of a rutted road, the granary jutted two stories, its roof falling just shy of the battlements of the lower fortress wall. Five men stood watch before the granary's barred doors.

"Security seems a little excessive for a grain house," Loukas remarked low and droll in Trell's ear. "Must be some very unruly wheat."

"Or very big rats," offered another man, which spawned low chuckling.

Above the granary, Nadori soldiers policed the ramparts and manned a large, mounted crossbow that could just as easily be aimed down into the fortress proper as outside of it. The distance too great and the moon too bright to risk crossing there.

Trell motioned his men to fall back. They hugged the darkest shadows while a patrol wandered past. Then they slipped back the way they'd come.

Threads of tension bound the night so tightly that Trell felt like he was running through webs of coarse muslin. Every passing second dragged at his awareness, for each anticipated an alarm sounding in the next.

Having studied Jaya's map until he knew it blind, Trell led the men on a winding route through the alleys of the lower fortress until they'd circled around to approach the granary from the north, out of view of the men guarding the doors. Trell had tossed the dice against Chance that there would be an entrance on that side of the building. To his relief, a staircase led up to a second floor landing.

They eliminated the sentries in skilled silence and then forced the door. Trell's men slipped inside, one by one. The smell of excrement and unwashed bodies assaulted them.

'Beware entering the space yourself…for you will become prey to whatever malicious working holds the rest in thrall…'

Náiir's warning added another layer to Trell's apprehension. He motioned to his men to spread out. Most took the stairs leading down to the main floor, while Trell and Loukas crossed the loft to a railing overlooking the warehouse. Beneath them, the shadowed outlines of men formed an undulating sea.

"Trell, there's not—" but Loukas smothered the rest of it in a curse.

Trell clenched his jaw, knowing well what Loukas had observed. There couldn't be more than five hundred men in that space, a far cry from the thousand he'd been expecting.

But whether one thousand or five hundred, the soldiers sat in utter stillness, eyes open but obviously unseeing. Their hands lay dully in their laps. Most wore soiled tunics and britches, but some still wore their swords. A particularly cruel taunt, perhaps?

Holes in the floor along the left side—possibly once holding urns—had been converted into privies and accounted for the stench. The air was heavy enough to burn their lungs.

"*Fiera's breath.*" Loukas turned Trell a look of horror framed with implication.

Obviously some kind of working was pinning the soldiers to immobility—no man in his right mind would sit there and calmly endure such a punishing stench—but his own men were exploring the room without any ill effects. So how *had* the wielder formed his working?

Trell headed for the stairs, keen to the eerie human sea, pricklingly aware of the presence of magical workings, yet frustratingly obtuse to their construction. Between them and the front doors, five hundred men sat enveloped in death's own silence.

Something struck him in this thought. He halted Loukas with a hand on his arm. "Look at them. Look at their positions."

"You mean how they're chained in groups of five? Do you think it's important?"

"I don't know." Trell could *almost* grasp a significance… He continued down the stairs.

"Maybe five were as many as they could secure to one chain," Loukas offered from behind him.

"Maybe." But Trell had never seen men so oddly shackled, and the closer he came, the stranger they appeared. Braided silver ropes bound each man's wrists and then connected to a similar band collaring their necks. The same rope linked the band on each man's wrist to his neighbor's, until the circle completed itself with all five men linked together.

When Trell lifted the soldier's bound arms to get a better look at the rope, the man kept his arms in the air until Trell lowered them again. The soldier made no effort to move of his own accord, nor even acted as though he knew Trell was there.

Trell and Loukas regrouped in the shallows of that unnerving sea, surrounded by dull-eyed soldiers sitting in daisy-clusters of docility. He pushed off a frustrating sense of time's insistent ticking.

Loukas rubbed his brow. "If some pattern is holding their minds, why isn't it affecting us?"

Trell shook his head. "That's the question, isn't it?" He crouched to study the rope up close. Multiple silver strands had been intricately braided…

Multiple strands.

Could each strand of braided rope represent a strand of *elae*? Could the ropes *be* the pattern?

Quickly Trell drew his dagger and tried to sever the rope binding one soldier's wrist. He sawed at it with fervor, but the rope didn't even warm beneath the dagger's edge.

Trell turned a significant look to Loukas.

The Avataren's eyes were wide. "*Fethe*, Trell. If your blade can't sever it…"

Trell settled a determined gaze on a hanging lantern. "Maybe fire can."

❧

With Air-fuelled sight, Tannour watched the energies from the nearest pattern come funneling towards him. He whispered a fraction of an inch to his right. The spear of power splintered the door behind him.

Kifat threw two more patterns at him, rapid fire. Tannour angled his body slightly to avoid one and then the next. Stone and wood shattered instead of blood and bone.

Kifat cursed him vehemently. Barbed words, they notched a sharp staccato. Now the wielder's sweat filled the air with musk and his heart beat a rapid rhythm of fear. He threw another pattern.

Tannour stepped an inch to his left. The wall behind him exploded.

Four more patterns came in quick succession.

Tannour leaned slightly left or right, and the deadly energies whispered past him. The last pattern disintegrated a large portion of the stone wall and opened the room to the night.

Tannour returned his blinded gaze to the wielder. "You're destroying your tower."

Kifat screamed rage into the air. He shoved fists at his sides, thrust forward his neck and shouted, "*I'm not afraid of you!*"

"I do not require your fear." Tannour started towards him.

A web above him hummed, collecting energy unto itself. Its waves whispered of wielder's compulsion. Tannour communed with Air, and his body vanished to worldly sight.

Kifat slashed wildly with his knife. He threw pattern after pattern—deadly energies these, embodying vicious devices—but Tannour walked *ver'alir*, and the patterns whispered harmlessly past him.

Kifat threw out long arms of power and hooked stone, wood, furniture.

These he pitched as desperate weapons. The air became a frenzy of flying, shattered things—sharp implements of pain, heavy rock to crush skull and bone—but Tannour walked *ver'alir,* and the deadly storm swirled harmlessly around him.

He reappeared directly before the wielder.

Kifat slashed at him.

Tannour caught the wielder's arm in one hand and his throat in the other. His howl became a choked gurgle. Tannour forced him backwards over a plinth of air and pinned him there, arched awkwardly across the invisible barrier, his arms drawn back into a painful extension and bound at the wrists with ropes of air.

"They told my master you could no longer c-commune," Kifat gasped. "They told us you had no tether!"

Tannour stroked a gloved hand down Kifat's arching throat. His voice barely disturbed Air's sudden stillness. "I found a new one." He methodically sliced the buckles off the wielder's breastplate and tossed the leather carapace aside.

"Wait—*wait!*" Kifat smeared the spittle on his lips with a darting pink tongue. "We can help each other."

Tannour sliced the wielder's robes down the center and ripped them aside, baring Kifat's chest, clearing a canvas for his knives. He exchanged one dagger for a different one from a cache within his vest.

Kifat struggled, but air bound him more surely than stone. Now desperation flushed his face but bled the color from his chest. Now his heart announced his fear to any who would hear it. "Release me—I'll tell you what you want to know!"

"You'll tell me anyway, as I warned you." Tannour began marking meridian points on the wielder's chest with tiny crosscuts of blood. He could make them shallow or deep. These were deep.

"I can offer you gold!" Kifat's eyes were round, his red face sweating. "Power! I can—"

"We've come too far on the path together to turn back now."

The wielder's desperation formed rigid waves. "I am Shamshir'im! You'll pay dearly—"

Tannour cut another deep X. Kifat started cursing.

'You'll pay dearly...'

Didn't he know Tannour paid dearly every time he walked *ver'alir*. The path demanded...*unconscionable* things of him. He paid in sleepless nights and blood vigils and most desperately in a loss of his humanity.

Then again, the man shouting obscenities at him was a Shamshir'im wielder. How much humanity could *he* have possessed?

Tannour cleaned his blade with a whisper of air and swapped it for a steel needle, uniquely constructed, as long as his forearm and hollow. While the wielder damned him in two languages, Tannour readied the needle at the precision junction of one of the crosspoints he'd marked. Then he inserted it between Kifat's ribs—but carefully, so as to puncture the lung at just the right angle.

Kifat's vitriol was abruptly replaced by a long bout of strangled choking.

Tannour's instructors had assured him that this technique simulated the sensation of drowning. He tried not to think too hard on the methods by which they'd perfected the procedure. The Sorceresy's torturers—researchers, they called themselves—walked *mor'alir*. The Path of Shadows didn't only demand pain, punishment, sacrifice…it *reveled* in them.

Kifat's eyes grew bloodshot. Pain, fear, and the grim light of understanding also made them wet. He coughed, choked, struggled for breath. "What…have you…done to me?"

A dark smile twitched in a corner of Tannour's mouth, but of course, all Kifat would've seen was a man's head shrouded in black silk, as blind and mouthless as the bundled dead.

"Now…" Tannour plucked a thin dagger from his arsenal of blades and drew the razor point down Kifat's chest, his air-fuelled gaze contemplative, "let's see what you know."

SIXTY-FOUR

"What he lacks in aptitude he makes up for in ambition."
— Raine D'Lacourte, on Niko van Amstel

NIKO VAN AMSTEL slouched in a chair in a drawing room of his Bemothi estate with his fist shoved against his jaw and malcontent churning turbulence in his stomach. He bet Alshiba never had to deal with the issues he was facing. Likely even Björn van Gelderan hadn't had to handle so many troubling problems as those plaguing Niko at present. He felt the weight of the entire realm resting on his shoulders.

Of course, they *were* broad shoulders. Strong. A fitting support for his handsome countenance. Vestals should be fine-looking specimens of the race. Only fools and Fhorgs worshiped ugly gods.

Niko hadn't expected godhood to require so much effort, though. Dagmar had always seemed to strut around the realm—or ride, he supposed, on the famous steed Caldar, who galloped on hooves of gold—and the strand-brothers bowed to him, virgins begged to become the vessels for his seed, and queens preened beneath his cool, green-eyed gaze.

But Niko could paint his entire horse in gilt and still not gain the worshipful reverence of his strand—*shade and darkness*, if he believed the rumors, fully half the strand was rebelling against him!

They're but children, your unruly flock, a soothing voice of reason reminded him. It might've been his mother's, though Epiphany knew the Lady van Amstel had never conversed with reason when she was alive. *They cannot know what's best for them. You must be their shepherd and guide them to make the right choices.*

Niko thought of the rebellion's unknown leaders, whose faces were blanks in his mind. He didn't want to guide them. He wanted to throttle them. He wanted to see their bland, featureless heads bulge and pop beneath his strangling hands. He wanted to watch their eyes bleed, their tongues blacken. He wanted to hear their wheezed choking. He wanted—

"Niko, damn it, have you heard a bloody word I've said?"

Niko focused back on the Nodefinder Demetrio Consuevé, who was sprawled on a couch across from him with one hose-covered leg draped over the couch's upholstered arm and his other leg splayed wide, so as to give Niko the full-frontal view of his oversized codpiece.

Lifting his gaze from this unpleasant contemplation, he fixed it instead on Consuevé's waxed moustache and goatee, a style far out of vogue beyond the borders of Rimaldi, where the man made his home. Niko reflected that he was going to have to find more fashionable attendants if he meant to be taken seriously in Alorin's royal courts.

His eyes tightened on Consuevé. "Perhaps if you had something valuable to offer." All the man had ever provided mankind was a use for moustache oil.

Consuevé gestured with his goblet. "It's not my bloody fault that the stinking maps don't exist. I'm not the one who sank Tiern'aval into the goddamned Bay of Jewels."

Niko made a scoffing noise. "I find it difficult to believe that no weldmaps survive anywhere in the realm." Never mind that Dore had been telling him this for months. Dore didn't know everything. He eyed Consuevé up and down. "You're saying there are none to be found for purchase anywhere? Not even on the Eltanin black market?"

"Aye, there's some." Consuevé's dark eyes gleamed wickedly. "But *you* want the kind showing the welds linking to the other realms. One of *those* you couldn't buy for all the wealth in Eltanin's vaults—hell, if they could find one, be assured those greedy Eltanin bastards would keep it for themselves."

This explained why Dore was pushing him so hard to acquire Dagmar's weldmap. But Dore might as well have demanded that Niko make the sun rise in the west—Raine's truth, it would've been easier to accomplish.

Raine's truth…

Niko glowered at the vestal ring on his hand. When were people going to start swearing by *his* name? Currently they mostly seemed to be cursing it.

Dore had promised him a lode of luxury in Illume Belliel. All Niko had hit with his digging so far was disapproval. It was almost enough to convince him to return to his old life, where he could simply be rich and popular, a patron of artists and host of the realm's most illustrious perpetual party—Cassius of Rogue had nothing on him.

Dore was used to people despising him, but Niko saw his hard-won popularity—*hard*-won might've been slightly self-aggrandizing; everyone just naturally loved him—slipping like sand through his fingers. The injustice of it made his eyes burn.

Verily, he was doing them all a favor, wasn't he? Stepping up when no one else would, trying to revert Malachai's legacy and overcome the inertia of Björn van Gelderan's indifferent abandonment…and all he had to show for his efforts were death threats.

Niko frowned ponderously at Consuevé. "What if we offered more money?"

"I'm telling you, it won't matter."

"Could the Karakurt perhaps—"

"Bloody Sanctos on a stake, Niko—the maps *don't exist. Cassius of Rogue* couldn't get one of these damned maps for you, even if you paid him with a whore that squirted rubies out of her twat."

Niko frowned at this crude visual. He was really going to have to find someone more cultured to accompany him when he started being invited to court.

He shifted agitatedly in his chair. "One map exists. Dagmar's map. Legend says he had it with him when he vanished to T'khendar after the Citadel fell."

Consuevé snorted. "Sure. Are *you* gonna risk you life traveling twisted nodes between the realms to go retrieve it?"

Apparently that's exactly what Dore expected him to do since Franco wouldn't.

If only he could send someone else in his stead, someone more… expendable.

Niko thumbed the stone on his ring, pondering expendable resources. The jewel really did look clouded—it had looked clouded ever since Viernan hal'Jaitar had pointed it out. He wondered if the man had cursed him.

"Franco Rohre could get Dagmar's map for us." Niko lifted his gaze to Consuevé. "He *could*, but he won't."

Consuevé sat forward. "Wait—isn't bloody Rohre *your* deputy? Can't you just order him to do it?"

"No." Niko's eyes narrowed to sullen slits. "Alshiba made sure of that."

Consuevé sat back, eying him meaningfully. "You've really got to do something about her."

Indignation darkened Niko's gaze. "What exactly am I meant to *do* about her, Consuevé?" Never mind that he was already trying his damnedest. People had no idea of the grave effort he was making on the realm's behalf. The obdurate woman really should've died by now. He'd put enough *atrophae* in her rooms to dispose of a herd of cattle.

"There's got to be a way to get Rohre beneath your thumb." Consuevé twirled a corner of his moustache. "He's not that hard to figure out. Pull the right strings, and he'll dance like a marionette. You just need to find the right strings."

Niko brooded on this.

"And really, you can't let the bastard get away with serving a traitor without making him pay a blood-price for it. When I had him beneath the point of my blade, Rohre all but admitted to being sworn to Björn van Gelderan." Consuevé sucked on his tooth, thinking hard. After an annoying while of this, he asked, "Does Alshiba know?"

"Does it even matter what she knows?" Niko cast a scathing look in the general direction of the node to Illume Belliel. "Björn made her his whore for three hundred years, betrayed and abandoned her, and despite this, she's still infatuated with him. She's become the laughingstock of the entire Thousand Realms. To think of a woman like that holding the Seat…it's a wonder they let Alorin maintain its thrones on the Council."

Consuevé finally pulled his leg off the couch and propped his feet on Niko's table instead. "If only Lord Abanachtran had given me leave to show Rohre the sharp side of my steel."

"You did show him the sharp side of your steel."

"Yeah, but only once. Traitors like Rohre…you've got to stab them a dozen times for every one poke that kills an honorable man."

"We can't kill Franco until he gets us Dagmar's map or we'll have to deal with Dore." Niko made it a point to never have to deal with Dore.

"But you said Franco won't get you the map."

Niko glared at him. "Why else do you think *you're* here? You're the expert on ignoble methods of coercion."

Consuevé pondered this with a slow nod. "What about getting one of your Eltanin mates to compel him? Didn't you say you and the Eltanin Seat were in like thieves?"

"I don't recall putting it so crudely." He made a face as he tried to imagine possible ways of getting Franco Rohre together with Mir Arkadhi so as to give Mir a chance to put Franco under compulsion. The contemplation just made his head ache.

Niko puffed a plaintive exhale. "It's this rebellion. I can't *think* for the audacity of it." He narrowed his gaze on Consuevé. "I ordered you to take the matter in hand!"

Consuevé twirled his moustache. "Yeah, and Dore Madden ordered you to get Dagmar's weldmap. It's hell, wading through the morass of other men's shite, ain't it?"

"What have you done about it, Consuevé? Have you the names of the leaders at least? This Admiral fellow—" Niko bit back a curse. When he got his hands around the one they called the Admiral, he was going to throttle him very, *very* slowly. He might drag it out for days…

"I've got nothing that will cheer you." Consuevé pushed up to go refill his wine. "No one will speak this so-called Admiral's real name, even under the knife. I wager they've been truthbound on it. Gannon Bair is their rumored leader, and he's as indiscriminate with truthbindings as a whore with her tricks. Carian vran Lea's the only vocal one of the bunch—and he's damned vocal, let me tell you—but we can't touch him."

Niko's expression had lifted. Now it fell into petulance. "Why not?"

"He's a *pirate*, Niko. If we go after him, we'll have the whole goddamned island of Jamaii ready to keelhaul us. They'll sink a whole ship just to make sure we go down with it, probably chained to the goddamned mast."

Niko shifted on needles of aggravation. "I don't care about Carian vran Lea. I want this Admiral, this arrogant, insolent *pretender* who dares to imagine himself the equal of his betters—"

"Raine's truth," Consuevé muttered.

Niko lost his train of thought.

He followed Consuevé's motion around the room with a narrowed gaze. "What are you talking about?" He knew why *he* believed this Admiral fellow was so audacious, but why did Consuevé?

"Well, it's obviously a lie, isn't it?" Consuevé sat back down with an airy wave. "What they're saying about him?"

Niko drew back from the edge of what he perceived to be a potentially threatening truth. He dropped his voice. "What are they saying about him?"

Consuevé propped a foot over one knee. "That he's plus-crossed a node. That he can make double-backs in his sleep. That he has three rings—"

"*Three* rings?" Niko quivered all over.

"Bloody ridiculous, isn't it?" Consuevé missed entirely Niko's sudden riveted stare. "Only the Great Master has three rings. And who's really going to believe this Admiral bloke got his rings from the Citadel's High Mage when the woman's been dead for centuries? They must think the whole strand's composed of imbeciles and idiots."

"You never told me the Admiral had three rings."

"Don't be a fool and swallow the shite they're shoveling. It's just a lot of posturing to position their candidate more strongly beside the Great Master, as if by saying this Admiral's got three rings it implies he also has the Great Master's blessing. Everybody sees through that shite."

Everyone patently didn't or half the strand wouldn't be in rebellion.

But three rings. *Three* rings?

He knew a man who had three rings…

Niko's eyes narrowed to slits. But Franco Rohre wouldn't have those rings for much longer. Not once Niko got his hands around his throat. He would feed him those rings and watch him choke on the gold.

Abruptly the doors banged open amid a ruffled protest, "Milord, you *cannot*—"

Niko spun in his seat to see a tall, dark-haired man wearing a crimson kimono painted with gold birds striding into his drawing room. Two hulking Avatarens with scimitars at their belts followed after him. Last came his butler, looking browbeaten. Niko glared at the butler. "Get out."

He went.

"Ah, Niko, what a pleasure it is for us to see you again."

Niko couldn't stand people who spoke in the royal *we,* but that was the least of the reasons he despised the Karakurt's associate, Pearl. He also despised him because he titled himself Speaker of the Karakurt's Will and strutted about everywhere as if he held all the power of his mistress.

"It's been too long since our last conversation." Pearl walked to Niko's sideboard and helped himself to some of his wine. The brutes meanwhile took up a position behind Niko's chair. Consuevé, damn him, was just sitting there, useless as always.

"I don't need you pecking at me, Pearl." Niko sat back in his chair again, pondering all the reasons he despised Pearl. "Dore's already said everything there is to be said."

"Oh, we don't think he's said *everything*." Pearl came over and stood above Consuevé, smiling his corpse smile until the man got the hint and moved over. The Karakurt's second-in-command seated himself sinuously and crossed his legs. He wore black silk pants beneath his ornate kimono, and woven sandals over split-toed socks. Something about him always made Niko wonder if he was a eunuch—maybe it was the kohl lining his eyes.

Pearl held up his goblet to Niko. "The Lord Abanachtran sends his regards."

By *regards*, Pearl meant the Lord Abanachtran had sent him, which was itself a communication of the Lord's actual regard for Niko. If he'd had any esteem for Niko at all, he would've sent someone else.

Niko summoned a supercilious smile. "What do you want, Pearl?"

"What do any of us want?" Pearl waved vaguely with his goblet. "Peace, prosperity…" He fixed his kohl-ringed eyes on Niko. They were even blacker than the spider tattoo on his forehead. "The ring and the weldmap."

Niko pushed out of his chair—he couldn't sit across from the horrid man and not want to choke the life out of him. "I don't have them yet."

"The Lord Abanachtran is growing tired of your yets."

Niko flung him a black glare. "He's asking for things that can't be gotten! I can't conjure a weldmap out of thin air. And Alshiba's ring is the only one that will safely allow anyone other than a vestal to enter Illume Belliel. She's not going to simply *give* it to me."

"Then take it from her, Niko."

Consuevé—damn him—grunted to the efficacy of this course of action.

Niko poured some wine, eyeing Pearl the while. The man wasn't threatening so much as unsettling, the way finding a spot of dark liquid on your silk Veneisean carpet can unsettle you when you don't know what caused it or how it got there. Pearl was a dark spot of something icky congealed on Niko's couch.

"I'll get him what he wants," Niko groused. "I just need more time."

Pearl cast his dark gaze around Niko's drawing room, leaving a coat of slime on everything. Niko was going to have to replace all the furniture now.

"It would be a shame to see all of this crumble—this estate, your life of luxury." Pearl let his corpse gaze come to rest on Niko and sipped his wine. He had a way of drinking his wine that made you feel like he was drinking something else. "And it *will* crumble, Niko. If you fail him, he'll smear your destruction across the Middle Kingdoms and make you watch the while. Or, I suppose…" Pearl paused, and his black eyes became electric with wicked amusement, "he could always give you as a gift to the Fifth Vestal."

Niko choked on his wine.

Pearl rose and slinked over to Niko, stopping close enough that Niko could see the wrinkles beneath his tattoo. The man was not nearly as youthful as he projected from afar. "What the Lord giveth, the Lord can taketh away, and the Lord has been far more patient with you than any of his other agents, Niko."

Niko brushed wine from his coat irritably. "Even so, I need more time."

"You have twenty-four hours."

"*Twenty*—" Niko choked on the impossibility. He gaped at Pearl, wanting to rail and protest, but all he managed were embarrassing strangling noises.

"You chose to play with the big boys, Niko." Pearl's raccoon smile conveyed just how much he was enjoying watching this game. "Now it's time to gird up your little boy loins and start running, or they'll crush you like a too-ripe melon." He waggled a finger at Niko's chin. "It would be a shame to ruin that pretty face."

He handed Niko his empty goblet and strode away, adding without turning, "Excellent wine, by the way. I'll entreat the Lord Abanachtran to spare your wine cellar when he lays waste to your estate. My mistress appreciates a good vintage."

The Avatarens slammed the doors behind their exit.

Consuevé blew out his breath. "I hate that effeminate bastard."

Niko leaned on the sideboard, not trusting to his knees or his stomach.

Twenty-four hours!

Only twenty-four hours to get Franco Rohre *and* Alshiba strapped to the whipping post of his will?

Thirteen bloody hells. He'd better get to work.

SIXTY-FIVE

"Against boredom even the gods struggle in vain."
—The zanthyr Leyd

VIERNAN HAL'JAITAR PACED beneath the colored glass globes hanging from the beams of Prince Radov's tent, with every step feeling Cephrael's noose tightening around his neck. His nails dug into the flesh of his palm, curled around the paper he clenched in his hand. Anger made his eyes burn.

Outside Radov's compound, the desert wind was scouring their campsite and laying waste to anyone who dared venture forth, but deep inside, beyond a beaded curtain, the Ruling Prince was taking a bath and talking loudly to his absinthe. The Shamshir'im messenger who was awaiting Viernan's reply pretended not to notice.

Viernan himself noticed hardly at all, for the words of the letter in his hand had become a doleful chant.

'Dannym's soldiers found at Nahavand.'

Nahavand. *Nahavand, of all confounded places!*

What a cunning ploy on Gydryn val Lorian's part to send his men to Nahavand, knowing Viernan would never seek them there—would never even imagine looking *across* enemy lines for the missing army of his supposed ally!

Oh, he'd played his hand expertly, had Dannym's fickle king. How long had he known Viernan was acting against him? How much had he learned of M'Nador's complicity in the capture and torment of his sons? And how deeply did Gydryn ken the alliance between Radov, Bethamin and Morwyk? These indigestible questions churned acid as they turned endlessly in Viernan's gut. He spun and paced in the other direction, dragging a whirlwind wake with his thoughts.

Would that he might've washed his hands of every val Lorian once and for all. The fool men just didn't know when to give up and die! He notched them on his list of most loathed, along with gypsies, zanthyrs and Thrace Weyland.

The discordant notes of a bullfrog's nighttime melody accosted Viernan's ears. Radov was singing to his absinthe now. Viernan caught the Shamshir'im wincing and speared him with a venomous stare. By what right did such a man judge his prince?

Perhaps he claims the right in absentia, a voice goaded. Sadly, Viernan couldn't deny that Radov seemed to have abdicated all claims to reason.

'*If Morwyk needs ships, let him have the damned ships!*' Radov had spoken over the rim of his glass as he once would've spoken over the shoulder of his mistress while taking her, his mind obviously elsewhere.

The Ruling Prince's mind was always elsewhere these days.

Viernan had tried to reason with him. '*But, my prince—*'

'*No, Viernan, what do we need with a fleet of ships? They can't help us reclaim Raku. I need soldiers, not boats.*'

'*But with the bulk of your army moving on Raku, my prince, you'll be leaving Tal'Shira unprotected.*'

'*Who's going to invade Tal'Shira? No, Viernan. Morwyk's giving me half his army. Give him as many damned ships as he wants.*'

Viernan could feel his hold on events slipping as sand through his fingers, grating in the gaping wound Radov had made of his reign.

Now they were marching all of their men into the very same conflict which had, upon their last engagement, resulted in corpses from the front lines to the horizon. Even Viernan had shuddered as he'd gazed over the ashen dead that had littered the Khalim Plains, the result of a single working of Abdul-Basir's damnable Mage.

Then had come the dragons…

After which, the two armies had squatted a constipated stalemate while M'Nador's hopes for reclaiming Raku and the Kutsamak ulcerated. Now their troops were marching back to that no-man's land with rusted steel and cankered fortitude, their arses still plugged by the ill humours spawned by the dragons' fell breath.

It troubled Viernan immensely not yet knowing this 'plan' for eliminating the Sundragons, upon which M'Nador's sure victory hinged. It troubled him placing all their eggs in Dore Madden's crocodilian nest. It troubled him still *more* having no idea if Gydryn val Lorian was alive.

The world was falling to pieces beneath his feet.

'...If it was Cephrael returned me to your doorstep, Viernan, you can be certain He had his reasons...'

Trell val Lorian's words had become a curse that haunted Viernan's every waking hour. His every sleeping one, too. Would that he might've rolled back the hands of time and strangled the impudent prince while he'd sat across a pot of tea from him. Now his own daughter had paid the blood-price for his hubris.

Of course, better Taliah than *himself*, but he missed her skills.

The sound of flapping canvas mingled with the howl of the wind and the scrape of sand abrading oiled cloth. Viernan didn't envy the Shamshir'im, who would be riding through that storm with new orders for Viernan's guild of spies...providing, of course, that Dore's emissary actually arrived with the recipe for ridding themselves of the malady called Sundragons.

Already Viernan had thrice flipped the hourglass beyond the time when the emissary was meant to appear with his so-called solution.

Pshaw! If anyone else had made such a claim, Viernan would've dismissed it outright, but it had been spoken across the withered lips of Dore Madden, a man who'd dared attempt to bring down even the High Mage of the Citadel and would've managed the near-impossible feat if not for Arion Tavestra.

Arion Tavestra...bloody Arion Tavestra. Just thinking the dead wielder's name brought the taste of char to Viernan's tongue. Tavestra was another one who just couldn't tell when it was time to lie down and die—

The flaps of Radov's tent blew open in a blast of stinging sand.

A cloaked figure breezed through the opening.

Viernan spied him with a mordant eye while his Shamshir'im rushed to pin the tent flaps closed again. "You're late."

"I don't mark the hours by your convenience."

The stranger pushed back his hood. Emerald green eyes pierced into Viernan's from between strands of oily raven hair. The zanthyr shifted his gaze around Radov's tent and sprouted a supercilious smile. "Ooh, I feel so *clandestine.*" He pushed past a wordless Viernan, obviously making for a chest sporting a collection of crystal decanters.

Viernan finally summoned his voice back from the canyon of disgust where it had been retching. "*You're* Dore's emissary?" He would've welcomed a rotting corpse over the zanthyr Leyd.

The creature turned with a full glass of Radov's most expensive bourbon in hand—not that the Ruling Prince would notice; he hadn't imbibed anything but absinthe for months—but the effrontery raised Viernan's hackles.

"Viernan hal'Jaitar." The zanthyr sipped his bourbon—the prince's bourbon—and eyed him over the rim with a malicious humor dancing in his emerald eyes. "Fancy finding you still wandering around upright."

"As opposed to slithering, as is your wont?" Of all the creatures with which to forge an unlikely alliance, Dore *would've* picked the most vile to ever disgrace the realm. The zanthyr Leyd accounted for more than half the reason Viernan despised zanthyrs, and the man himself knew it and blatantly gloried in it.

Of all the capricious stories told about zanthyrs—pledging allegiance to each of two feuding dukes and then selling their secrets to the other; wooing the princess-heir of a dynasty away from her betrothed and tumbling two kingdoms into chaos; inserting himself as an advisor to a merchant prince and destroying his dynasty—if it would result in catastrophe and cause irreparable harm, Leyd was sure to be behind it.

The creature had caused so much trouble in his long history that Viernan couldn't understand why his brethren hadn't gotten rid of him. Even if it was true that a zanthyr's immortality was tied to the life of the realm...there had to be *some* way to eliminate the malevolent man—like sinking him to the bottom of a volcano and encouraging it to cool. Surely it would take a creature like Leyd at least a *few* decades to dig himself out again.

"This is quite the little soiree you're spinning together out here in the dust, Viernan." Leyd peeked through the beaded curtain between the two Talien Knights standing guard and arched an amused brow at the drunken prince now snoring in the bathtub. He turned a knowing grin back to him, full of goading.

Viernan's skin tried to crawl off his bones.

Leyd continued his stroll of the room. "Two score *eidola* plus the gathering thousands...perhaps your army will actually make it to the walls of Raku this time."

Viernan stared blackly at him. "Do you ask so you can inform the Emir of our plans?"

"Now why would I do that..." he waved airily with his glass, though his green eyes held a daggered perspicacity, "when I've brought you the means to eliminate their best defense?"

"As if that would give you pause." Viernan crossed the room to his map table. "Let's see it then, this windfall you claim to offer us."

Leyd cast him a smile that was all fangs. He pulled something from inside his cloak and tossed it on the table.

Viernan's brows shoved upwards almost to the line of his *keffiyeh*. He lifted his eyes from the rectangular glass lying on the wood and fixed them once more on Leyd. "I haven't seen a *simulacra* outside of the Sormitáge in..."

"Centuries?" A corner of Leyd's mouth curled patronizingly. "Some of us still recall how to make them."

A *simulacra* enabled a fourth strand flow of *elae* to waken an illusion of the patterns forged within its glass confines. Viernan touched the glass and summoned the fourth, whereupon a three-dimensional pattern shimmered into being a handspan above the table.

Viernan's eyes widened considerably.

Leyd smirked. "The *drachwyr* rendezvous near Raku every third phase of the moon. It's the only time they're all together here in Alorin. You have to work this matrix when they're *all* together—are you hearing me, Viernan?"

Viernan tore his eyes away from the illusion to spear Leyd with his gaze. "Like a caterwauling grimalkin in rut."

Leyd's grin broadened. "You really are a vicious old bastard, aren't you?" He took Viernan by the shoulder with his iron fingers. "You'll need more than bravado to carry this through though."

Viernan recalled several other reasons why he despised zanthyrs. He jerked free of Leyd's hold. "Spare me your condescension." He returned his attention to the pattern—nay, the matrix of patterns. It was as ingeniously terrifying as one of Dore Madden's contrivances. Some of the patterns were so complex that Viernan had no idea what they were meant to do.

Leyd hunkered down beside the table and pointed to a swirling central pattern that the others appeared to be linked through. "This fifth-strand one is for pinning it to them—the pitch to make the feathers stick. *This* one…" his lip rose with malicious amusement, "is for disorientation." Then he straightened again and grinned at Viernan. "When they return, they'll be fire-spittin' mad. It goes without saying that your forces must gain the oasis before that happens."

If it goes without saying, why are you saying it? Viernan studied him with dark circumspection. "This seems a low betrayal, even for you."

The zanthyr tossed back the bourbon and went to refill his glass. "You know how they say love is the cause of all disasters among the gods?" He looked up beneath his brows while he poured his next drink. "It's not love, old man. It's boredom."

As Viernan stared at the zanthyr, a niggling, nagging part of him warned that *this* was what his life amounted to—centuries of courtship with the debased and vile, culminating in this abominable creature who stood as an affront to his own divine purpose.

Shaking his head, Viernan returned his attention to the matrix.

It made his eyes hurt—never mind his head—trying to contemplate the difficulty of working it. He counted the patterns of the illusion. Then he turned Leyd a mordant stare. "This is *nine* patterns woven through a tenth for binding."

Leyd drank his bourbon. "And?"

Viernan bristled. "I would need nine wielders!"

"Did you think it would be easy?" He slammed down his drink and was suddenly looming over Viernan, pushing him back with the force of his stare. "Did you expect to blink your eyes and say a magic word and the *drachwyr* would vanish? You're pitting yourself against *immortals*, you decrepit old man! Rise to the challenge, or give up while you can still crawl back to your filthy bughole and cower with the rest of your Shamshir'im fleas."

Only when his spine started shouting with pain did Viernan realize he was bent backwards over the table, supporting himself with both hands against the weight of the zanthyr's enmity and breathing fast for the effort.

Leyd stared him down a moment longer. Then he straightened, flicked his eyes to the spy—who was pressed as close to the door as possible, smartly trying to remain invisible—and headed over to the liquor chest again. "If you intend to thrust your stick into this anthill, Viernan hal'Jaitar, you'd best know the fury you'll be stirring up."

Viernan stared blackly at him. He blamed Dore Madden for...well, for just about everything. Would that he might've used Leyd's patterns on *him*. "A single wielder cannot work this matrix."

Leyd snorted. "Even Arion Tavestra couldn't have worked my matrix."

Viernan flung him a glare. "Huhktu's bones, but we could all rise to the stars on the hot air of your self-opinion." He slipped the *simulacra* into a pocket inside his robes. "And what of the Emir's Mage?"

Leyd poured himself another bourbon. "What of him?"

"He could do again what he did upon the Khalim Plains."

Leyd turned to him, swirling his drink. "And?"

Viernan ground his teeth. "Know you anything of his whereabouts?"

Leyd shrugged. "I know he's not at the *sa'reyth*—hasn't graced everyone there with his immaculate presence for ages." He lifted a finger from his glass to waggle it at Viernan. "But I can guarantee if he was at Raku with the Emir and his pups, your little party would've been over long before the entertainment arrived."

Viernan supposed this was the best he was going to get from such a creature. He offered a smile of poisoned sugar in return. "You've delivered your ill work and drunk of my prince's hospitality. We needn't trouble each other any longer."

Leyd eyed him amusedly—that is, if a creature forged entirely of venom and malice could look amused. He swirled the bourbon in his glass. "You know, there's a particular sublevel of the thirteenth hell reserved for mortals like you, Viernan."

Viernan spied him coldly. "I would rather endure an infinity immersed in Belloth's foul humors than share another minute of air with you."

The quirk of a grin sprouted on Leyd's face. He saluted Viernan with his glass. "The next time I see Baelfeir, I'll be sure to tell him you said that." Then he downed the bourbon, cast a vicious grin at the Shamshir'im spy, tossed his glass at Viernan and vanished.

Viernan let the crystal bounce on the carpet. He half expected the glass to start smoking.

He turned a glare to his Shamshir'im messenger. "Look sharp. We've no time to waste."

He walked to his desk and rapidly scrawled the spy's instructions. But even as he was penning a summons for every able wielder at his command, his hand paused, the quill poised, its sharpened tip dripping ink onto the parchment while he saw everything come crashing down—his Shamshir'im destroyed, Tal'Shira fallen, Radov vanquished and with the prince his own power…and he wondered if it might be time to seek a new benefice.

Then he shook off the ill vision, finished penning his instructions and brusquely offloaded his spy into the howling night.

SIXTY-SIX

"No one likes perfect people. They too readily illuminate everyone else's inadequacies."

–The Adept Cassius of Rogue

DARSHAN HIT THE peaked roof with a hard expulsion of breath. His shoulder went instantly numb, and his staff flew out of his fingers. Instinctively, he reached for *deyjiin*—

Tumbling behind his staff, he careened down the tower's slate roof towards an abyss of dusky clouds. He reached for *deyjiin*...

He flew off the roof and crashed onto a ledge, almost caught a handhold before gravity pulled him past the lip. He reached for *deyjiin*...

A hand caught his flailing arm.

Darshan hit up hard against the side of the tower and then dangled there, held as much by another's hand as by the grimmest shade of wonder. He stared down past his boots to the rose-milk clouds misting beneath him, then looked up at the hand clamped around his wrist. A narrow rescue.

"Give me your other hand!"

Darshan saw only the man's fingers fastened around his wrist, an arm bound in a blue coat, and beyond these, the stone ledge rimming the tower. He thought he recognized the tower.

He swung up his other hand, and the man took it in a hard grip. He hauled Darshan up over the narrow ledge, grunting with effort.

Darshan fell back against the tower wall with his legs hanging over the edge, still trying to get his bearings. This couldn't be Shail's Shadowspace or he would've easily found his brother's starpoints. Yet to find *this* tower there...

A hand clasped his shoulder. "Are you all right?"

Darshan swept his hair back from his face and looked up at his rescuer.

The man fell back—scrambled back?—and pinned himself against the open doorway, staring hotly at him.

Darshan frowned faintly at the clouds surrounding the tower, wondering what traps Shail had placed beneath their sunset stain. He unbuttoned his coat with one hand while a sardonic smile hinted on his lips. *Shailabanáchtran…you have really outdone yourself.*

Darshan glanced over his shoulder to the man still gaping at him. "Thank you for the rescue."

Ean slowly sank down against the door. "So this isn't—"

"My doing?" Darshan arched a droll brow. "No, Ean val Lorian. We are both my brother's prisoners, it would appear." He got to his feet and moved past Ean into the tower.

Everything inside was as he recalled, right down to the candlesticks and cup on the mantel; every dagger and blade aligned upon their velvet drape, the rumpled bedcovers on the ebony four-poster, even the deep white lines scoring the stone walls, which Pelas had scrawled as he'd paced. Had Shail been planning this eventuality even then?

Ean followed him inside and gazed bemusedly around. "Do you know where we are?"

"Shadow." Darshan walked to the table and began stowing Pelas's daggers in their velvet pockets—that is, Shail's recreations of Pelas's daggers. "This was the tower where I imprisoned my brother."

Ean turned him a swift stare. "You mean Pelas?" The prince looked around the space again, and Darshan saw his larynx lift and fall. "And… Isabel?"

Darshan arched brows by way of his answer.

Ean watched him stowing Pelas's daggers. "Are those the actual…"

"These are recreations. The real tower and everything in it was destroyed."

Ean sank down onto the hearthstone, looking dazed. "Why did he send us here…together?" That last word sounded a bit choked.

Darshan rolled up the knives in their velvet casing and began securing the ties. "My brother enjoys throwing two cocks into the ring to see which will peck and claw the other to death. He considers it efficient management of resources."

Ean's expression twisted. "Isn't that what you did when you gave Isabel to Pelas?"

"Yes." Darshan looked up under his brows. "We often think alike, my youngest brother and I."

The prince rubbed his forehead and then pushed both hands back through his hair. His coat was undone, his shirt partially unbuttoned, but he still had his sword. That was a boon.

"So…" Ean scrubbed at his head, "you can take us out of here, right?"

Darshan's gaze tightened. "Not exactly." He left the roll of knives and began searching the drawers for anything else that might prove useful. "Not yet."

"But you would."

Darshan lifted his gaze to him.

"You *would* take me with you." Both question and accusation burned in his gaze.

Darshan slowly straightened. "Yes, Prince of Dannym."

Ean blew out his breath and slumped back against the wall. "I thought as much." He shook his head. "I shouldn't have survived that fall from the acropolis. *Elae* had abandoned me." He fixed his gaze on Darshan again. "*You* saved me…slowed my fall."

Darshan went back to searching the drawer. "You wouldn't have saved me just now if you'd recognized me."

Ean gave a pained grimace. "I don't know." He frowned off out the door. "Maybe. I knew you'd spared my life in Tambarré. I just didn't know why." Grey eyes fixed on him again. "I still don't."

Darshan closed the drawer and began searching through the next one.

Ean rolled his head around on the wall. "How did Shail do this? The way Pelas described Shadow to me…I thought you had to open the portal and lead the way in? All of that about framing space—"

"This space has clearly been framed by a Warlock."

Ean rubbed at one eye. "So…did the Warlock build the tower, or—"

Darshan shoved the drawer closed and straightened again. "My brother engineered this place with myself in mind. Such excoriating irony suits his temperament."

Ean's brows narrowed as he registered the meaning of Darshan's words. "So we're stuck here." The furrow deepened. "Together."

Darshan eyed him amusedly. "Yes, Ean val Lorian."

Ean let his head fall back against the wall again. He looked exhausted, and dark circles shadowed his eyes. "Better together than alone in this place, I suppose." He shot Darshan a haunted look. "I can't even *feel elae*."

Darshan studied him for a moment. Then he plucked a glass and a bottle from the cabinet and poured wine as he walked. He offered the glass to Ean.

Ean stared at it, looking mystified.

"The idea is more useful than its truth, I'll admit." Darshan pushed the wine towards him more insistently.

Ean took the glass but then just gazed perplexedly at it. "What truth is that?"

"That it doesn't exist."

Ean frowned. "I see." Though his expression said he clearly didn't. He drank half the glass in several quick swallows, then pressed the back of his hand to his mouth. "It tastes real enough."

"Yes," Darshan's gaze tightened slightly, "that is the danger of Shadow." He sent his awareness outwards again, seeking the edges of framed space. He could *almost* perceive them...

"I have a fair idea why Shail tossed *me* into this place," Ean set down his empty glass and slumped against the wall again, "but why did he trap you here?"

Darshan watched him with a tightness behind his eyes. The prince already looked pale. "At the moment we must concern ourselves with finding a way out." He picked up the roll of knives and the few other things he'd collected and dumped them into a satchel that had been lying on a chair. "How much do you understand about Shadow, Prince of Dannym?"

Ean grunted. "Not enough."

"But you understand the idea of framing space."

"In the context of Absolute Being, yes."

Darshan held his gaze significantly. "There is no space in Shadow save what a Warlock or other frames. I should be able to perceive the edges of that space, the anchors the Warlocks call starpoints—these are fixed points of dimension, between which space exists." He shouldered the satchel and motioned for Ean to follow him outside. "That I cannot find the edges of space indicates *this* space lies within another one, a cube within a cube, if you will. We need to reach that outer cube."

Ean pushed up from the hearth to follow him. "How do we do that?"

Darshan paused at the rim of the ledge and looked over his shoulder to the prince. "We jump."

Ean's expression well conveyed his opinion of this idea.

Darshan surveyed their surroundings once more, seeking any new hint of meaning in their construction, some clue to Shail's intent. "The tower where I imprisoned my brother had no door; likewise no satchel such as this for Pelas's use—what need, when I had him trapped? Yet everything else about that tower has been meticulously recreated, down to the smallest detail." He searched Ean's gaze and was pleased to find understanding there. "This is one of Shail's games. I regret that he's caught you up in it, for surely *this* game was designed for me, formulated to test my strengths, not yours. Shail has set the parameters of this little entertainment; now he'll be watching to see how far I can make it—*we* can make it—across the actual field of play."

Ean glowered down past his boots into the mist. "I actually think I loathe your brother."

"He does have a way about him."

"Three times." Ean speared a tormented look at him. "That's the count of my deaths by Shail's hand." He gave a forceful exhale. "I guess I should consider it lucky that this time he sent me here instead."

Darshan's expression tightened. He extended his hand to Ean.

After a long hesitation, the prince clasped wrists with him and met his gaze. "This is surreal."

"Welcome to Shadow, Prince of Dannym."

"I meant—"

Darshan jumped.

The world became a hazy, rose-tinged nothingness—he recognized it as an overlapping layer where one Warlock's framed space crossed another's. He and Ean fell out of the mist between bands of blinding light—

They stood in a forest of black trees growing in neat, symmetrical rows. Darshan released Ean's wrist and turned a slow circle, observing the shifting lines as rows merged, separated and merged again beneath his rotating perspective. An undulating carpet of fuchsia-hued grass covered the dark earth. The lines of trees extended as far as the eye could see in every direction, merging into infinity.

Deciding one row was as good as the next, Darshan set off between the trees while mentally seeking the starpoints of that realm.

Ean followed wonderingly. "I've never seen pink grass before." He squinted off into the distance. "Can Warlocks make anything they want, any way they want it?"

"It is, I believe, an expression of your Fifth Law."

"*A wielder is limited by what he can envision.*" The prince was walking with his hand resting on his sword. He turned him a curious frown. "But that only applies to Alorin's space."

"By whose estimation?"

Ean frowned harder at this.

While he walked, Darshan continued expanding his awareness outwards in search of the edges of framed space. He perceived many overlapping layers, as of multiple canvases hung to some but not all of the same hooks. Finally he found the starpoints of the specific canvas across which he was walking and merged his awareness with them.

Deyjiin instantly opened to him.

Darshan sent his power radiating outwards across the canvas of framed space then, in search of a specific but subtle hum.

A short time later, he perceived that they were nearing another fold where the canvases of framed space overlapped, though to his eyes, the trees continued endlessly on. "A moment, Ean, if you will." He turned to face the way they'd just come.

"What is it?" Ean joined him in staring back along the path they'd been following. "Is someone coming?"

"It's truer to say some*thing*...ah, here we are." A whistling sound grew in volume and whisked among the trees until something dark came flying at them.

Ean hissed and ducked.

Darshan caught his scepter out of the air with a hard clap. He looked it over, reacquainting himself with the living, mutable patterns that held it to form. Then he wrapped his power around the enchanted stone, stretched it into a walking staff, and glanced to the prince. "Now we may proceed."

Ean regarded him bemusedly. "I'm so glad you took care of that."

Darshan arched a brow at him. "Do you lead me to believe you would've left *your* weapon behind in this world?"

"I see your point."

They crossed through the overlapping barrier of worlds, stepping from the forest of black trees into a landscape where the trees were as wide as hills, with roots arching several stories high and limbs lost in cloud. Shallow green pools spread beneath the trees, interspersed with islands of moss and breezy blue grass.

Ean scrubbed at his jaw. "So you have your power back, I take it."

Darshan was in that moment finding the starpoints of this new canvas. It didn't take him long, since two of the dimension points were held in common with the world they'd just departed. "In a sense." He planted his staff and started off.

"What do you mean 'in a sense'?" Ean lengthened his stride to catch up with him. "In the sense of getting us the hell out of here?"

Darshan arched a rueful brow. "Not in that sense."

"What then?"

"I can perceive the starpoints of this world and in so doing perceive *deyjiin*, but this...there is a confusing confluence of dimensions in these worlds. They veil and overlap each other. Until I can coincide the outermost starpoints, I won't be able to tear the fabric."

Ean rubbed his forehead. "I'll pretend I understood what you just said."

"Until I can perceive the outermost ring of starpoints framing this space, I will continue to be the effect of the interior environment, Ean.

I'm subject to whatever laws the Warlocks have established for the world—much as my brothers and I are subject to the laws of the Realms of Light when in your world."

Ean grunted. "I'm not sure you're subject to much of anything in Alorin."

Darshan turned him a meaningful gaze. "Were we not, Prince of Dannym, we would have already unmade it."

It must've been drawing on afternoon—that is, had time been sequential in the various worlds—when they passed from the humid land of lakes onto a frost-covered plain devoid of any landmark save a large sun and an even larger planet falling beneath the horizon. The chill air attacked their skin and made fog of their every exhale.

Ean stared into the distance, scrubbing at the back of his head. "Are you sure we're headed the right way?"

Darshan arched a rueful brow. "I am sure of little here, save that wherever I'm heading is where we're meant to go."

"That's deep." Ean turned a glower off to the horizon. "You should've written that in Bethamin's book."

"I perceive in your tone a peculiar dissatisfaction at my response."

"Even so?" Ean looked him over with intelligent grey eyes. "Such a doctrine of belief would imply we've been brought together for a reason."

"A specious conclusion."

"No. A logical one." The frozen earth crunched beneath Ean's steps. "To say with any certainty that wherever you're heading is where we're *meant* to go is a statement of faith in your path."

"Malorin'athgul have no path."

"In the *mortal* tapestry." Ean stared pointedly at him. "But having and acting upon a purpose connotes action intended to deliver you to a specified future. That's a path."

"By this definition I accept your point." Darshan looked him over speculatively. "Why does the idea disturb you?"

Ean abruptly stopped and turned to face him. "It bothers me because neither of *us* foresaw or planned this consequence. I don't even think your brother expected it until the opportunity presented itself. Yet you claim to be walking some path in pursuit of your intention, and I…I thought I was walking mine before I wound up here. I even thought Balance might've been…" but he bit back whatever else he'd wanted to say.

"Keeping to your metaphor of paths, why would you imagine you're not still walking yours simply because it brought you to Shadow?"

"So you see my point then."

Darshan studied him in the growing dark. Ean stood gripping his sword firmly, yet without evident hostility; more a clutching at some reality that made sense to him. "I'm not sure that I do."

Ean shifted beneath agitation's weight. "My point is…who brought us together?"

"Who…" Darshan eyed him quietly, "as in what force, or what divinity?"

"Take your pick."

Darshan cast his gaze across the prince, and beyond him, the featureless expanse. The sun was nearly gone, the world growing colder with every inch of its descent. He perceived quite some distance in any direction before reaching another canvas. "Let's settle over there," and he nodded towards a section of plain where grass grew long enough to soften their repose.

They made camp encased in a dome of *deyjiin,* which provided light as well as protection from the wind…and other things that roamed in Shadow. Darshan used his power and fashioned chairs from the frost, so that if Ean couldn't eat, drink or be warm, he could at least sit comfortably.

He didn't look comfortable, however. *Deyjiin*'s flickering light made hollowed shadows around the prince's eyes, and he sat with his elbows plugging into his knees, supporting his head in his hands.

Darshan watched him carefully while he fingered his scepter, returned now to its original shape and positioned between his feet. "If I could do more, Ean…"

Ean waved him off. "I know. Starpoints. Coinciding. I get it."

"Do you?"

Ean slouched back in the low-slung chair. "It's basically a fourth-strand construct—not all that different from the Labyrinth." He waved nebulously. "You're caught within its reality so long as your mind is trapped within the pattern. You have to permeate the pattern to escape that reality, and while you're in it…well, you're basically a slave to its design."

"An adequate comparison."

Ean eyed him askance. "So how *are* we going to get out of here?"

"I'm working on that."

In fact, Darshan was seeking the exterior starpoints with his every breath, but so far he hadn't found the outermost rim of framed space. What he had found, however, brought a tightening around his eyes.

Ean clasped hands behind his head and let it hang back, braced by disquiet. He looked at Darshan between the steeple of his elbows. "Are you ever going to tell me why you saved me in Tambarré?"

Darshan thumbed his scepter pensively. After a time, he said, "I'd hoped you could provide some answers."

"Answers." The prince sounded dubious. He sat slumped in his chair with malcontent making a severe line of his brows. "I could use some of those myself. For instance, what did you do to Kjieran van Stone?" When this question met with Darshan's silence, a purposeful determination hardened Ean's gaze. "Did you kill him?"

Darshan rubbed the back of his neck, and once again registered surprise at his missing hair. He thought of Ean's metaphor of paths, and Socotra Isio's discussion of vortices, and he thought on how his own decisions had shaped his future action. He'd *intended* that Ean would come to him, and Ean had.

In this intention, had he reshaped Ean's path to conform to his own? Had he connected them cosmically through cause and intent? He'd certainly done *something*, for now he and the prince were navigating Shadow together. Darshan couldn't see how this confluence aligned with his still-shifting purpose, but he was certain somehow that it did.

He looked down at the scepter in his hands and ran his thumb along the patterns carved around its end. "I bound Kjieran to me."

Ean roused. "Bound, how?"

"A pattern of Dore Madden's…a form of the Unbreakable Bond, but one-sided. I bound him against his will."

Ean's eyes widened. He lanced a thunderous look at him.

"Kjieran was the first *eidola* I made and the only one I fashioned using that pattern, the only one I bound to my own soul. I…" Darshan exhaled a slow breath, "I wanted to make him immortal."

Ean's waxing anger waned into incredulity. "You were in love with him."

Darshan arched resigned brows. "Kjieran chose death over eternity with me. He betrayed me multiple times along the path to his eventual immolation, but the worst of those betrayals for me lay in his choice to end his life."

"Thirteen hells." Ean fell back in his seat again. He stared at Darshan while a deep furrow notched his brows. After a time, he remarked, "That's one hell of a binding to work on a man without his consent."

"So I have come to understand."

Ean blew out his breath. "Your understandings come too bloody late!"

Darshan ran his thumb along his scepter, contemplatively, one part of his mind still exploring the threads of consequence that had united his path with Ean's. "You may be surprised to learn that Kjieran's death did not sever our connection."

Ean blinked. "You mean—" he sat roughly forward again, "he's still in communication with you?"

"Yes."

"*How?* He didn't go into the Returning?"

Darshan's gaze tightened. "These were the very questions that drew me to the Sormitáge. Those, and how to restore Kjieran to life again."

At this, the prince fell back and stared open-mouthed at him. Then he pushed palms to his temples. "*No-no-no-no-no*—the *eidola*, the Marquiin, those *appalling* Ascendants—you've wrought nothing but torment and death. Why would you *restore* Kjieran? It goes against—"

"Everything I've apparently stood for?" Darshan cast resignation on his gaze. "As you said, Ean, many understandings have come to me too late."

"*By Cephrael's Great Book,* Darshan!" Ean launched out of his seat and paced several quick steps beneath *deyjiin's* dome. As the lightning in his gaze faded, he shook his head and pinned him with a gaze of clouded wonder. "If not for what happened in Tambarré, I would never believe this conversation is real."

He threw himself back down in his chair and stared at Darshan in brooding silence, rubbing his jaw. "So…what does this mean? You're on our side now?"

"I admit a certain lack of clarity in how to go about accomplishing my purpose."

Ean gave a muttered curse. "What about Dore Madden?"

"Dore has always been Shail's creature."

Ean's eyes explored the veil of *deyjiin* gleaming above him. Then his gaze found a particular focus and his fingers slowed on his jaw. "It was Pelas, wasn't it? This—this…" he waved at him, "whatever *this* is."

Darshan shook his head. "I admit Pelas has long been trying to sway my intentions—"

"No, no…you don't see it." He rolled his head from side to side along the back of the chair, his expression full of grave comprehension. "Isabel knew, or at least she suspected. She saw a possibility that I was incapable of envisioning." He pushed his palms to his forehead again. "No wonder she chose to save your brother!"

Darshan perceived the prince's radiating emotions, his confusion and misgiving, feelings of loneliness, estrangement, and beneath all else, a tormenting sense of guilt. He was coming to understand human emotions far better than he ever desired to, and finding more empathy through his own experience than he cared to admit.

"When I laid the compulsion on Pelas, I wove it into the pattern of his existence." He held his gaze on Ean as evidence that he understood this was a crime against his brother. "For Pelas to somehow have managed to deny it—much less overcome it—when it had become so much a part of his being, is testimony to your Isabel's ability as much as to my brother's tenacity."

Ean turned to him seriously. "If the pattern is that interwoven, I wouldn't even be able to unwork it. It will be with him until the end of his days." His tone conveyed the enormity of this truth.

"Yes…" Darshan arched brows, "I have forever altered my brother's immortal composition."

Night claimed the Shadow world as the dream claimed Ean's sleeping mind…

Arion stood at the balcony railing looking out over the nascent world he and the others had made. A storm had just emptied itself upon Niyadbakir, cleansing its palaces, bridges, and towers. The dark city sparkled. Further across the barren valley with its mist-filled hollows and volcanic earth, a line of jagged mountains was tearing the ashen clouds into strips.

Though the naked eye saw naught but bedrock and harsh, stabbing light, Arion knew that T'khendar was alive. The fifth thrummed its heartbeat through every inch of stone and earth; the air tingled with it. Yet the fifth was the only strand of *elae* to be found there.

Ah, but Arion saw such promise in this world! What he could've done with the basalt city, the granite peaks! When *elae* filled this land, Niyadbakir would become a city of impossible beauty. Björn would see to that.

The thought gave him pause.

Gah! If only his own future still held the same promise of possibility! But the pattern of consequence had become a tangled bramble. Soon, so many bright paths would intersect that all he saw was light, and beyond that burning core…

Arion's throat felt tight when he thought upon it.

But this potential was the least of their loss. Tragedy's bloody flag flew high over the battlefields of their endeavor now. They'd planned for so many contingencies, thought through as many scenarios as their inventive minds could muster, yet still they hadn't foreseen this madness.

A door opened behind him.

Arion turned from the railing to see Isabel emerging. Her pale blue dress appeared grey in the storm-light. Its color now more truly reflected their hopes. She closed the door quietly, then lifted her blindfolded gaze to him. "I thought you'd gone."

Arion collected her into his arms. She felt too thin against him, a fragile bird draped in heavy silk. He pressed a kiss to her hair. "You didn't seriously imagine I would leave you here?"

Isabel slipped her arms around him, too weary-worn with grief and exhaustion to reply.

Arion stroked her hair, feeling vestiges of his own sorrow threatening. "How is he?"

She exhaled a tremulous breath. "Destroyed." Grief choked her voice. "Consumed. We can do nothing for him."

Arion turned burning eyes out over the blackened city. His heart felt charred. "If we took Malachai to Alorin—"

"*Elae* cannot combat this devastation, Arion." She withdrew from his arms and walked slowly to the railing. The blindfold could no longer conceal the ever-widening shadows around her eyes. "We don't yet understand enough about *deyjiin*, but nothing good has ever come from violating the Ninth Law."

A damp wind clutched at their clothing and made chestnut flames of Isabel's hair. She gave a shuddering exhale and dropped her chin to her chest. "I wish you'd gone."

Arion collected her into his arms again. "Why?"

"Our son needs you as much as I…more, perhaps."

"He's been cooing in my head all night across the bond. He's had much to say about Madaé Giselle's barley milk."

She turned within the circle of his arms to look up at him. "Björn thinks our bond with Phaedor is protecting us from *deyjiin*, but Arion…you shouldn't linger in this place."

"The fifth is everywhere here, Isabel."

"You need more than the fifth to sustain you."

"No," he drew her close and pressed a kiss to her hair, "only you."

She pulled back stubbornly. "We need you at your strongest."

Arion managed a grin. "But *I* only need—"

"Don't be cavalier. If we've learned anything from the tragedies of this endeavor, it's that we cannot accurately predict every possible outcome."

Arion adjusted her blindfold gently across her eyes, his gaze upon her thoughtful. "What does Björn want to do?"

"What else can we do?" She gave another tremulous exhale and let her lingering grief disperse. "We must do our best to protect Alorin from what we've done. Go through with this charade with the Vestals, make sure no one tries to find their way here. My brother thinks he can solve the riddle of *deyjiin*, given time."

Arion heard the leading edge in her words. He searched her hidden gaze. "But?"

Her brow furrowed. "But...Björn wants to twist all the welds. If something happens to you in the events to come...you may not find your way back."

Arion touched his thumb to her lips, where soon he intended his own lips to be. He let his gaze convey the fullness of his desire. "You think a few twisted welds will keep me from your side?"

"*Arion...*" Her disconcertion sent jagged waves through their bond.

It wasn't just his insouciance that disturbed her, it was everything else—T'khendar overcome with *deyjiin*, Malachai overcome as well; his resulting insanity and the wave of mad rage that had so violently and explosively decimated their race; and the looming fate that stole sleep from her every night—some confrontation that Isabel believed Arion would not survive.

Oh, she tried to hide her surety from him. She lectured him on their paths. She said every choice offered new possibility, opportunity to change one's course. But she couldn't hide from him the truth that had consumed her hope—that somewhere along the way, he'd already made the choice that would take him to his end.

Well...maybe he had set himself upon an inexorable course. This didn't mean he had to believe himself lost to it.

He and Björn had pursued many avenues in search of understanding of Isabel's prediction, seeking ways for Arion to prevail; but even more personal than any choice he might make for the game, Arion couldn't believe he would ever make a decision that would take him away from Isabel's side, or from his son's.

Isabel was just watching him—listening, perhaps? He wasn't trying to hide his thoughts from her.

She lifted herself and kissed him, and for an instant their bond resonated with a different energy. As she withdrew, she pulled off her blindfold.

Arion caught his breath. "Isabel—"

"I will make this promise to you, Arion, if you will look me in the eye and make a promise to me." Isabel's resolute tone bound his tongue to stillness, while her colorless eyes, staring so intently and shockingly into his, bound his soul to her will. "I swear to you that you will know your son, and he will know you; you will see him grow and become a man. But *you must* promise me that you will not pit yourself against the Balance as Malachai and we have here done." She searched his gaze for willingness as much as pressured him to agree. "Promise me that you'll do nothing to compromise the integrity of your honor, that you'll do nothing to draw Cephrael's eye against you."

Arion stared wonderingly at her. "Do you truly think me so imprudent, Isabel? I know better than to attract Cephrael's gaze in censure—"

She laid her fingers across his lips, and her eyes became glassy as she whispered, "Desperation makes fools of us all."

He radiated a gentle protest. "Have you ever seen me desperate?"

Isabel gazed at him for a moment more. Then she dropped her eyes. "I never imagined *I* would know such desperation as I felt just moments ago, staring at that brave soul lying in agony, watching Malachai being *unmade*, knowing I could do nothing to help him…"

Isabel pressed palms to her eyes, then looked away, out into the churning storm, tightly holding back her grief. "Malachai may never find his way back to the Returning."

Arion understood now what fear had taken hold of her. "I won't let that happen to me, Isabel. If I can promise you anything, I promise you that."

She turned her tears into his shoulder.

Arion felt every bit as distraught as Isabel was over Malachai's fate. Their friend had done terrible things in the throes of his madness, but even he deserved a new chance at life in the Returning.

The first pattering of rain sounded in the distance. The next storm was blowing in.

"Please take us out of here." Isabel's voice sounded barren.

Arion lifted her into his arms and murmured against her hair, "Where would you go, my love?"

"Home. Adonnai." She pressed her face into his chest. "I just want to be myself for a little while longer, to be a wife to you and a mother to our son."

And although she didn't speak it, Arion heard her concluding thought as though Destiny Herself had spoken it.

…*before you're both taken from my arms.*

As sunlight sliced across the Shadow-world, Ean struggled to wake. A lassitude had settled over him during the night, as though the life had been draining from him all the while.

In that incognizant state between waking and dreaming, Ean reached out to Isabel, for she was and always had been his heart's greatest desire. He knew that *elae* was beyond him, that *she* should've been beyond him, yet he sensed their connection, or…at least *some* connection, an ethereal link to an awareness not his own. His mind, struggling towards consciousness, clung to this link desperately.

Isabel…?

An icy pressure on his shoulder roused him.

Ean forced his eyelids apart and focused blearily on Darshan's three faces until they combined into one. There was a tightness behind the man's eyes that hadn't been there before. He squeezed the prince's shoulder again. "Daylight has claimed the world, Ean."

Ean managed to push himself up, only to have to immediately brace his pounding head in his hands. His arms trembled; his breath came shallowly and with pain. His eyes felt full of sand and kept shying away from the sun.

He'd parted with Pelas excited by the prospect that Balance might lead him. But had his path really been leading him *here*? He couldn't understand why Balance had pitched him into this improbable hell.

Oh, he understood that it was surreal. He understood the complete inconceivability of everything Darshan had confessed to him last night. And he understood that his inability to envision greater realities such as Darshanvenkhátraman's indecision, which Isabel had surely foreseen, limited him profoundly. But he didn't understand where it was all leading. The pattern of consequence just…dead-ended.

And yet…he now recalled that Isabel had made a promise to him all those centuries ago—'*I swear to you that you will know your son, and he will know you; you will see him grow and become a man…*'—and despite every reason not to, some part of Ean clung to the hope that she'd somehow kept that promise. That meant his path couldn't end there in Shadow because he hadn't yet met his son. But if she *had* followed through as promised, then where *was* his son?

A hand appeared in front of his face.

Ean looked up at Darshan.

By what strange twist of fate had his enemy become his ally? He let the man haul him to his feet. Then he grabbed onto his iron arm until his head stopped spinning, except…it never fully stopped spinning.

Ean drew in a ragged breath and looked around, finding naught but empty moors furred with sparse grass as far as his eyes could see. The sun had already burned off most of the frost, and the day was growing hotter by the breath. He tried to ignore his hollow stomach; likewise the hollowness that was the haunting reminder of a missing part of his essential self.

He scrubbed at his jaw. "How far did you say to the next tavern?"

Darshan almost smiled. "Just a world or two away."

"Yeah…" Ean tugged his jacket down and adjusted his sword belt wearily, "that's what I thought you'd say."

They headed off.

The sun never rose more than halfway to its zenith and was somehow always directly shining into Ean's eyes. As they were trudging across the flat expanse, which was becoming more sand than grass, Ean proposed, "Why don't you work some *deyjiin* magic and shield us from the sun?"

Darshan turned his head and assessed the fiery orb angling its heat at them. "I've experienced worse."

"You unmake *stars*."

A smile twitched in one corner of the Malorin'athgul's mouth. "Encasing us in *deyjiin* might lessen the sensation of heat, but it would not benefit your constitution."

"It would certainly benefit my disposition towards you."

Darshan flicked the shadow of a smile in his direction. Then he clasped his scepter behind his back and gazed off, and his eyes narrowed slightly—an expression Ean had witnessed him make several times that morning. This time he concluded its meaning. "What is it? What aren't you telling me?"

The Malorin'athgul eyed him sidelong. "We're being followed...tracked. I'm summoning them from across the linked worlds."

"I take it they're unfriendly, whoever they are."

Darshan's gaze became pinched. "You could say that, yes."

"Then might I ask why you're summoning them?"

"They sense my lifeforce on this plane, Ean." He looked around, giving the impression that he was seeing far further than the boundaries of moors and sky. "I'm drawing them from...everywhere."

Ean shook his head sadly. "Just when I was starting to like you."

The sun paced their travels like a loping wolf, shedding its blistering light across a world without wind or water.

"About these things that are following us..." Ean had been brooding on the topic for much of the morning. "I've seen the power you command. What could possibly pose a challenge to you here?"

"Shadow operates on different rules, Ean. The problem is less the breadth of power available to me than how it may be used. I am not the god of this universe."

"What does that mean?"

Darshan glanced at him. "He who makes the world, makes the rules—unless you can coincide the starpoints and gain equal control."

Ean dragged both hands through his sweat-dampened hair. "But you can't coincide the ones here—whatever that means?"

"Coincidence is a form of duplication, and yes...and no." He lifted his gaze to the pale sky. "I've been able to match this canvas's starpoints enough to draw power through them—duplication—but I cannot completely coincide them—which means to make them my own. Something is preventing my doing so."

"Something...your brother?"

"Indirectly, perhaps. Shail wouldn't have put me here if he expected an effortless return." He arched a rueful brow. "I'm fairly sure he expects me not to return at all."

The lassitude Ean had felt upon waking only intensified in the relentless heat. By the time afternoon arrived and the skyline of a distant, glimmering city came into view, Ean was having to focus every ounce of his will just to make one foot move before the other. The grasslands had long given way to desert. It had been hours since he'd found the breath for speech.

It was difficult to maintain hope amid that sea of sand, in an alien realm made by an unknown being, with nothing living and no glimpse— barely even a *memory*—of *elae*. Even the heat felt wrong. But he clung to something, even if it was only a shadow of hope, the tiniest seed of it planted in a dream…the hope of meeting his son.

If they *could* meet somehow, well, it would at least redeem one of Arion's mistakes—the one Ean found the hardest to bear.

He'd come to recognize a certain equity in Arion's and Isabel's choices; they hadn't betrayed each other, even if Ean had felt betrayed, because their troth had always been first and foremost to the game.

But for Arion to have abandoned his son, who shared no such promise with him…this Ean couldn't stomach.

Perhaps that's what fueled his will in those enervating hours—the determination to survive Shadow and reunite with his son. This purpose hugged the core of his being, more personal than any aspect of the game. He even found a whisper of faith that this couldn't be his end, because Isabel had made a promise to Arion, and Isabel always kept her promises.

This is what it means to walk your path: to trust in your decisions, to have faith in the future, to see possibility despite all reasons not to.

It almost sounded like Isabel's voice encouraging him. What he wouldn't have given to hear her in true in that moment, to tell her everything he'd realized, to beg her forgiveness for not trusting her more…to ask her about their son.

The ache behind his eyes made it difficult to see anything clearly. Ean cast a pained gaze at the endless sands, the too-bright sky. Behind him, the planet they'd seen last night was blocking out half of the horizon. How could there be all of *this* and not a whisper of *elae*?

Lady's light, Isabel…

His vision spun. The world tilted—

Darshan caught him as he fell.

Ean's head lolled against Darshan's body. His right arm hung limply at his side, unwilling to budge even to push the hair from his eyes. "Is it the heat," he managed weakly, "or…?"

Darshan's gaze tightened. "It is not so simple as that." He hefted the prince into his arms and started walking again.

Ean summoned breath enough to whisper up at him, "What's happening to me?"

He saw the Malorin'athgul's jaw tighten. "Shadow is killing you."

The next many hours became a blur of too-bright light and silence, the odd feeling of floating in Darshan's iron arms, and the paradox of a cold heat that had no relationship to life. At one point Ean roused to find that the mirage of a distant city had resolved into saucer-shaped towers with glittering spires that scraped the sky.

The next time the prince came aware, he was lying in a bed—at least, it was soft like a bed. Beyond the translucent walls, the onion domes of the near buildings seemed strung haphazardly, as toy tops dangling on a child's mobile. Varying shapes and sizes populated the view, glimmering with metallic iridescence in the orange light of the setting sun.

"Where…?" Ean's voice scraped painfully out of his throat. His body felt fashioned of fragile parchment.

"This was the Warlock's domain." Darshan stood in dark silhouette before the sunset, his tall, broad-shouldered frame well suited to a palace constructed for a demigod.

It might be said that Death when He arrived extended lassitude in one hand and peace in the other, for Ean was having trouble summoning the defiance he ought to have been feeling as he lay there facing his end. Anger's heat seemed a remote, cold star and far beyond his reach. Even grief hovered distantly, an alluring fisherman's ball bobbing on dark waters.

To think that after everything he'd endured, everything he'd relearned, all that he'd planned—the radiant hope of actually *succeeding*—that he should still find his end as inexorably as the sun setting on another day; that the dark foreshadowing which had forever haunted his path could once again prove true, that *nothing* he'd done had changed any of it, had mattered in the least, but that he'd walked to another inevitable, brittle end…

Since Arion's first misdeed—whatever it truly had been, for Ean trusted Shail's version not at all—Balance had stitched his brilliant thread in the tapestry away from a glorious course and had begun sewing his strand among tragic and misshapen patterns instead. A part of Ean had always feared that his life pattern remained lost there within those dark whorls, each time recalled into the same spiral to walk its dwindling path anew; each time reaching the same twisted endpoint. How could he ever find again the tapestry's bright threads?

All this time he'd thought he'd been fighting Geishaiwyn and Whisper Lords, Dore Madden, Malorin'athgul and monsters made from men, but in reality he'd been fighting against Balance.

...And that was a battle he could never win.

His throat was too dry even to swallow, but his eyes at least still worked. He shifted them to the dark form that was Darshan and scraped out, "Did you know?"

The Malorin'athgul turned his head. "That this place would destroy you?" He left the window, trailing shadows. A somber solicitude cloaked his manner. "I had hoped I would find an exit sooner. I was naïve to imagine my brother would make it that easy." He sat down on the bed next to Ean with apology darkening his gaze. "This is not the end I had envisioned for you."

Ean dragged breath into his lungs; the air weighed too heavy in his chest, so that he could hardly push it out again to ask, "Who will do it, if I don't?"

Darshan laid a hand upon his thigh. "Do what, Prince of Dannym?"

Ean whispered, "Make right everything I've done...all the mistakes, the battles I've left unfinished."

"Battles..." a slight frown marred his brow, "as with my brother?"

Ean grimaced. "I have a role to play. It can't end here, only to do it all again when I Return—*if* I Return...who knows what happens when you die in Shadow?"

Darshan studied him with a focused intensity behind his dark gaze. "Could you not choose some other course, some other purpose?"

Ean gave a laughing wheeze. "Could *you*?"

Darshan frowned deeply at this.

"It *can't* end here."

...This is what it means to walk your path...to see possibility despite all reasons not to...

Ean closed his eyes. As Arion had experienced while battling Shail on the Pattern of the World, Ean's choices had narrowed to two. Incredible, the paths a man was willing to tread to avoid death.

No, it wasn't fear of death that drove Ean to possibility's precipitous edge. It was unwillingness to fail everyone he loved yet again. It was determination to know his son. It was his own conviction to achieve the outcome that Arion and Björn had envisioned, and which Björn and Isabel had been continuing on towards while Arion floundered in the shadows of the Returning.

Ean shoved intention into his fingers and fumbled them towards Darshan. With surprising gentleness, the man took his hand in his own.

Still not quite believing he was choosing this path, Ean met his gaze. "I see a way."

Darshan tilted his head. "A way…?"

"Bind me to you."

Darshan drew back, staring at him. "Ean, you cannot mean—"

"I do." He gripped the Malorin'athgul's hand with everything he had. "If you bind me to you, I'll live."

"You'll live bound to *me*." Darshan looked him over severely. "Can you truly live with that?"

The prince managed a grim smile. "Can you?" He wanted to say more, but the effort had stolen the last of his energy. He lay there instead, his vision stained now with dark veils, the colors of the tapestry's whorls that had trapped Arion in their pattern.

Then the world started spinning, weaving darkness amid the light. Ean's fingers twitched against the immortal's hand.

He cast farewell on her name.

Isabel…

SIXTY-SEVEN

"Be careful what you wish for."
—A favorite joke among Warlocks

ISABEL...?

Tanis woke to an echo of his father's entreaty.

Less the sound of his voice, it was more a perception of *him*, a sense of him reaching out to Tanis's mother, or...at least, it *felt* like his father calling from the other end of their bond; but Tanis had been so young when last Arion had spoken to him, mind to mind. He couldn't say for certain that he'd perceived anything at all. He may have simply dreamed it.

Whether dreamed or real, however, the experience left him feeling unbalanced. That disorienting sense of the world tilting beneath his feet hadn't bothered him since binding with Sinárr. His first inclination was to wonder if the feeling was Alorin calling him back...but when he set his intention in that direction, the disorientation only got worse.

Tanis wished he better understood the peculiar sensation that he might more effectively interpret its message; the only conclusion he'd reached about it was that it heralded change—*momentous* change. Understanding this in no way made the feeling less formidable or his stomach less queasy.

Tanis slid a foot out of bed and rested it on the floor. Fynn was always explaining this was the best way to stop the world from spinning around you when you were nearly passed out drunk. He tried breathing deeply, which his Lady Alyneri had always said was the better hand of patience, a phrase which Tanis had never quite understood.

While he waited for that unbalanced feeling to calm, Tanis thought about the world-building he'd been doing with Sinárr.

The Warlock had promised him that creating worlds would offer a joy unlike any other, and so far he'd made good on that promise. In fact, Tanis knew an impossible joy in the activity; the pure joy of creating provided a thrill beyond imagining—far beyond even the rush of wielding. A compelling, intoxicating, *addictive* exhilaration that made it hard to think about anything else.

At least...that had been the case until that unbalanced feeling had shaken him awake. It was so dramatic that Tanis began to wonder if it was *his* feeling at all.

He hadn't reached out to Pelas since before he'd bound with Sinárr, but suddenly he really missed his bond-brother's company and the connected calm he felt when they were together. Now that Tanis and Sinárr were equally bound, Tanis had full access to *elae,* so he closed his eyes and sought Pelas, casting his own thoughts across the interwoven conduit of their binding to give a polite rap on the door of Pelas's mind.

His bond-brother immediately opened his thoughts, warmly welcoming him, enveloping him with the affection he always flowed across their bond.

Tanis...

Tanis made an anchor of Pelas's thoughts and wove shape around them. Dreamscape opened between them.

A narrow strip of beach angled between cold, high cliffs, while in the deeper water, a reef broke the waves into tumbling surf. Tanis knew if he looked at a certain angle, he'd see glimpses of Pelas's Hallovian mansion.

Pelas came towards him from further down the windy beach. He lifted his gaze to survey the cliffs and then fixed a smile on Tanis. "This is elaborate." He shifted his own clothing to resemble Tanis's, so that as he reached the lad, he was wearing a dark sweater and pants, with his raven hair blowing long about his shoulders.

Pelas smiled and touched a finger beneath Tanis's chin. "I like this new you, effortlessly weaving us into Dreamscape."

Tanis hugged him. "I just wanted to see you."

"I am grateful that you did." Releasing him, Pelas pushed hands in his pockets and smiled at him. "How are you, little spy?"

Tanis exhaled a slow breath. "There's a lot I should tell you."

"What, you have more surprises for me?" Pelas grinned. "Not *another* immortal waiting in the wings to bind with you, I hope."

"I think three is my limit." It was the first time they'd spoken of his binding with Sinárr, and apparently all that needed to be said about it. Tanis reflected it was a wondrous experience to hold another's trust so completely. He glanced to Pelas in invitation and started walking the shoreline. "Are you well?"

Pelas eyed him humorously. "Do you mean since my bout with my brother's revenants or since Ean val Lorian's unworking?"

"Both. Wait—" Tanis's eyes widened, "did you say revenants?" His eyes grew wider, his voice slightly shriller. "Do you mean Prince Ean tried to *unwork* your life pattern?"

Pelas winked. "No harm was done that your zanthyr couldn't repair."

Tanis really gaped at him then. "*Phaedor* Healed you?"

"In Adonnai—"

"Okay, stop talking." He held up a hand. There was no way he could keep up with that many momentous revelations at once. "I beg you, start at the beginning."

Pelas wrapped an arm around his shoulders and gave a low laugh. "I will tell you all, little spy."

The story he recounted for Tanis would've rivaled the best tales of even the Immortal Bard Drake di Matteo. Tanis listened raptly with a wonder that sharpened to apprehension, elevated to dismay and finally resolved into astonishment. As they walked and Pelas spoke, Tanis tossed lone pebbles into the waves, notching their progress down the timeline of their separation. Pelas ended his tale by explaining how he'd left his brothers to battle each other at the Sormitáge and had taken Nadia to safety.

Tanis angled him a wondering look. "I hadn't imagined that even you could get into so much trouble."

"Well, I *have* bound myself to your path, Tanis." Pelas regarded him warmly. "But explain to me this feeling of imbalance that has you bobbing all about as in a stormy sea. Even I feel a bit queasy."

"That's just it. I can't explain it." Tanis flung another pebble and watched it skip through the surf. "I've experienced something like this before. It usually heralds change."

"Change…" Pelas looked him over with dancing copper eyes, "which on your path precedes epic misadventure."

"*Epic*." Tanis made a face. The word had an uncomfortable flavor with its naming—reminding of Quai games and exploding temples and perilous eternal bindings with immortal demigods.

He flung another stone and frowned after it. "Surely there's nothing wrong with being ordinary. Lord Fynnlar speaks at length on the merits of mediocrity."

"There must be a middle between the extremes," Pelas said by way of amused agreement, "but I doubt we'll find it on your path, little spy."

Tanis sighed and flung another stone.

"When did it start, this feeling?"

"This morning."

"Interesting."

Tanis eyed him sidelong. "What's interesting?"

Pelas looked him over. "I'm wondering how much of what you perceive colors my perception and how much of my perception colors yours. Ean and I just returned to the Sormitáge to investigate a thread in the tapestry that's vibrating rather madly for attention."

Tanis considered his words. Then turned his gaze out across the white-capped waves. "I'm not sure this is my own feeling, but I thought…"

Pelas arched a brow inquiringly. "You thought?"

Tanis puffed an explosive exhale. "I thought I heard my father reaching out to my mother across their bond." When Pelas said nothing to this, Tanis looked back to him. "But how could that be? If my father was calling my mother on *their* bond, why would *I* have heard him?"

Pelas's mind became suddenly quiet and his gaze serious. He looked out towards the breaking waves, letting the wind blow his hair into his eyes. "Whyever indeed?"

Tanis knew well enough when his bond-brother was hiding important knowledge from him. He looked him up and down narrowly. "I'm not sure you spending time with Phaedor is such a grand idea."

Pelas chuckled. "One day when it's safe to do so, I will show you the tapestry as Phaedor has opened it to me. It's…*vast*, Tanis. You could waste away eternity studying it." Suddenly his smile fell into sobriety, and he fastened his eyes intently on the lad. "But having seen it, the weight of responsibility becomes immense, for one such as me cannot look upon this fabric without also seeing how easily it might be manipulated."

Tanis held his gaze soberly in return. "My father could see the tapestry—I mean, at least some expression of it. He could see patterns of action and consequence and follow their course beyond the curve of time." He scooped up another stone and flung it into the sea. "My mother says my father has Returned, and Phaedor says he's not as I remember him." He turned to Pelas. "Do you think my father is really out there somewhere?"

Pelas returned his gaze softly. "Very much so, Tanis."

Tanis wondered what Pelas wasn't telling him. "Do you think we'll ever meet?"

The faintest furrowing of his brow was the only indication that this question caused Pelas some concern. "I think…"

"Never mind." Tanis cast him a resigned look. "You don't have to answer that."

Pelas exhaled a slow breath. "I would if I dared."

"Now you're *really* sounding like Phaedor." He blessed his bond-brother with a grin and laid a hand on his arm. "Thank you."

Pelas arched brows. "For?"

Tanis shrugged, smiled. "Walking my path with me?"

Pelas held his gaze, but it was the resonance of feeling through their bond that gave his words their emphasis. "Until the end of time, Tanis."

Feeling calmer if not exactly reassured, Tanis dressed and went to find Sinárr. He might've appeared instantly wherever Sinárr was by merely thinking it—for in truth, Shadow possessed neither *when* nor *where*—but Tanis preferred to walk at least part of the way to give some sense of normalcy to his very unusual existence.

There was something to be said for convincing yourself of your own illusions. Now that he could see the world as Sinárr saw it, Tanis had to consciously decide it was real in order to feel that same solidity and permanence he'd experienced upon first waking in Shadow. He was beginning to understand Alorin's lure.

When he ran out of path, he shifted himself to Sinárr's location by deciding he was wherever Sinárr was. Yes, it was as easy as that, yet it had taken Tanis an embarrassing number of tries before he'd realized that it really *was* that simple.

Upon this decision, cloud forest became jungle. Tanis emerged out of the shade of palm fronds onto a sparkling pink-sand beach. Tropical mountains jutted around them, and more lush islands dotted the aqua sea.

Sinárr had a meal set for them beneath a breezy tent. Sinárr being Sinárr, however, the peaked gold and violet tent might've belonged to a sultan, and the table was lavishly decorated in shimmering pearlescent cloth set with abalone dishware.

Tanis found the Warlock seated at the table wearing a radiant white silk shirt that stood out brightly against his very black skin. His shirt cuffs showed gold where they were turned back, and his ruby cufflinks matched a large ring upon his finger.

"Good morning, Tanis-mine."

"Good morning, Sinárr." Tanis pulled out a chair. "How went your conversation with Mérethe last night?"

"She's still undecided, while I am equally uncertain of what is best for her."

"But you'll return her to Alorin if she decides she wants to go?"

"Yes, as I promised you. *If* she decides she wants to return. It is not so easy giving all this up in the end, as you may well find."

"Yes, I'm already seeing that." The idea of never building worlds again posed such a potential loss that Tanis couldn't even bear to consider it now.

If he'd had any real idea what he stood to gain, he wouldn't have hesitated to bind with Sinárr.

Sinárr reached for a silver pot. "Tea, Tanis?"

"Please." Tanis sat back in his chair and watched the Warlock pouring for him. The silver shone as if newly polished, and the glasses and flatware were sparkling in the early morning sunlight. A breeze stirred the colorful fringe draping the curtains, and the jungle was humming with sounds of life. Sinárr had really outdone himself that morning. The question on Tanis's mind was *why*.

He turned an admiring look around. "This is elaborate."

The Warlock's eyebrow twitched as he set down the pot. "You would prefer we ate somewhere else?" He handed Tanis his tea.

"No, it's quite beautiful, only…" Tanis settled him a look. "All of this wouldn't have anything to do with the fact that I reached out to Pelas this morning, would it?"

Sinárr sat back and clasped hands in his lap. "You're free to communicate as you choose, Tanis. I've never sought to compel your will."

Tanis smiled at him. "No…only my affinities."

Sinárr rested an elbow on his chair arm and ran a finger along his jaw, considering Tanis with an earnest but slightly injured gaze. "You and I are bound…but earlier when you needed reassurance, it was not my counsel you sought. How *should* I feel about that?"

Tanis smothered a grin. "I just think it's a little unnecessary…your being jealous of Pelas."

"I merely wonder that you did not think to come to me."

"Really?" Tanis grinned up at him beneath arched brows. "You wondered at that?"

Sinárr's expression fell into a fragile disappointment. "You agreed to our binding."

"You didn't give me too many choices about it, Sinárr."

"But creating worlds brings you great joy. I've perceived this truth in your thoughts."

Tanis popped a grape into his mouth and grinned around it. "I wouldn't trade it for anything." He served himself a piece of a duck and cherry tart and started in on it while mulling over the Warlock's reaction. "It's not just Pelas, is it?" Tanis made a swirling motion with his fork. "There's something deeper here. I can sense it, but I can't quite put my finger on what's really bothering you."

Sinárr's golden eyes studied the lad. "You inquire into something that sits at the heart of who we are, I think."

Tanis held his gaze gently. "So tell me, that I may understand you better."

Sinárr met this appeal with silence. Tanis felt a faint misgiving coming across the bond, as a wavering pitch in the resonance that continuously bounced between them.

After a moment, Sinárr ran a gilded fingernail along his bottom lip. "Do you think this place is beautiful, Tanis?"

"It's lovely, Sinárr."

"I created it for you."

"Yes, I gathered that."

Sinárr leaned forward slightly. "But do you understand *why* I made this beautiful place, the glorious table, these fine foods, for you?"

Tanis set down his fork and sat back in his chair. "I would imagine they're gifts. You're courting me, as Mérethe would say."

"Courtship is an essential aspect of our existence. We Warlocks are constantly courting one another with our creations—*constantly.*"

"That's..." Tanis paused to ponder this new idea, "unexpected." He frowned slightly. "Why?"

Sinárr sat back again. "I've told you that we're not a collected society, but while there is rarely collaboration between Warlocks, there are...associations, games, and even a form of barter and trade."

Tanis tried to wrap his head around this idea. What could they possibly trade in when nothing in Shadow truly existed?

Sinárr held a hand towards the world he'd created. "If I fashion this illusion for you, what do you imagine I hope to gain in return?"

"You mean, other than binding me for all eternity?"

Sinárr gave him a droll smile. "Yes, Tanis, other than this."

Tanis put honest thought to the question, for clearly it was important to Sinárr. He recalled that Sinárr hadn't wanted to compel Mérethe into seeing his illusions. It had confused him at the time, but now Tanis thought he better understood. "When you make an illusion for me, I get the enjoyment of it, and you get..." he frowned slightly, "I don't know—my appreciation, perhaps?"

Sinárr merely watched him with his forefinger stroking his bottom lip, giving Tanis time to work out the truth for himself. That's when the lad realized that Sinárr had already given him the answer, days ago. '*...Creation holds a supreme joy unlike any other experience, yet there is reward too in sharing one's creation with another, in gaining their admiration...*'

"It's admiration, isn't it?" Tanis could tell by the Warlock's gaze that he had the right of it. "But why should that matter so much?"

Sinárr lifted his chin from his hand. "Admiration, attention, these are our currencies, such as they exist."

"You *trade* in admiration." Tanis drank his tea while he tried to process that revelation.

"Admiration is one of the most powerful forces, Tanis. I will show you today why it is so important—that is, if you choose to continue our lessons."

"Sinárr," Tanis angled a voluminous look at him, "I'm here with you, aren't I?"

Sinárr rested his chin on his hand again. "For the time being," he remarked morosely. "I can sense the disturbance in your energies."

"Well, it doesn't mean what you clearly think it means."

"I have no idea what it means. You haven't shared your thoughts with me."

Tanis chuckled. "Will you stop pouting? We have a world to build together, remember?"

"Yes, Tanis," Sinárr fixed a suddenly ardent gaze upon him, "I remember."

Tanis finished his breakfast quickly. Downing the last of his tea, he pushed back from the table and grinned at Sinárr. "Shall we?"

Sinárr came over and drew Tanis close against his own form—his preferred stance while they built worlds together, which the Warlock greatly enjoyed and Tanis rather stoically endured. The table fell away, the beach fell away, and the illusion surrounding them dissolved into darkness.

Frame your starpoints, Sinárr spoke into Tanis's mind.

Tanis felt a jolt of excitement upon this command. They'd built the beginnings of a world together already, but it had been inside Sinárr's framed space. To build something in his own space would offer an altogether different thrill.

Tanis put up a starpoint and instantly duplicated it. Then he made six more and shoved them all apart, framing a cube.

Now impress within each starpoint that they will remain in this relationship. One frames space and time in the same thought.

Remind me again why that is so?

Right now you're consciously holding your starpoints apart. When you move your attention to creating within the space you've framed, if you haven't directed the starpoints to remain as they are, they will either collapse or vanish. You must direct them to endure, giving time to their property, and you must direct them to remain stationary and hold the same angular relationship.

Tanis did both of these things.

Sinárr radiated approval. *Now, what will you put into the space you've framed?*

Tanis got the idea of a tower of stars. He fashioned it in his mind and willed it into being.

The tower formed quickly, sculpted out of the stuff of Shadow, a shaft of sparkling brilliance derived from raw energy coalescing and combining. Tanis finished off the spire at the top and was mentally stepping back to admire his work, when—

No! What happened? The lad cast a startled query to Sinárr—the equivalent of a look of dismay. *Why did it disappear?*

You did not give your tower permanence.

I willed that it would endure! Tanis protested.

But then you admired it with the same energy, in the same time, seeing all that it is and was and could be—for you are its maker and know its composition intimately—and erased it by so doing. We call this phenomenon 'effacement.'

The idea of this so-called *effacement* seemed pretty farfetched to him. *So because I admired it, it vanished?*

Sinárr duplicated Tanis's starpoints so he could share the creative space with him.

When you have an energy flow, such as sound, for example, flowing upon a specific wavelength—he pushed an undulating wave of blue-white energy through the empty space before them—*and if you match this flow with the same kind of energy at the same wavelength in the exact opposite vector*—he added another flow of energy coming towards the first—*where the two meet, they will erase each other.*

Watching Sinárr's demonstration, Tanis expected the two energy flows to collide into an eruption of power. But instead, just as Sinárr had stated, a dark emptiness resulted where the two exact opposing flows met.

This is nullification. It is similar to the way effacement works, except that effacement is a result of admiration.

I'll pretend I understand this.

Tanis heard Sinárr's deep chuckle. *As you admired your tower—you, its maker, observing it in the same space of its creation, with the same energy with which you created it—you unknowingly duplicated every aspect of it exactly as it was in that moment and nullified it in the doing. This is effacement.*

So... Tanis scratched his head—a singularly odd experience in Shadow's void, where he saw neither head nor hand but felt the scratching nonetheless. *How do I make it endure my own admiration?*

A valuable exploration, Tanis-mine. Let us start by making something that isn't yours. *A building perhaps—something from your world that you know is not your own invention.*

For some reason, recreating something from Alorin there in a space of his own framing felt somehow disingenuous, artful...counterfeit. Tanis couldn't bring himself to do it.

As he searched for something to create then, he recalled Pelas's illusion of the tree city. *This* thing of Shadow, Tanis felt comfortable recreating in his own space.

Like a potter grabbing an armful of clay to place on his wheel, Tanis swept his mind through the space he'd framed, gathered his energy, and began shaping it into the tree city.

Crafting illusion from the aether of Shadow was very different from the way he went about it in Alorin. There, he merely envisioned what he wanted and threw up the energy of the fourth strand solidly enough for another to see.

In Shadow, he sculpted energy into form with beams of intent. His mind became his arms and hands, moving invisible bands of imaginative decision to arrange the energy and force it to assume the shape he desired. As he achieved the form he wanted, he pushed energy into it until there was so much energy in the space that it became compact and appeared solid.

Before his eyes, the tree grew. From lengthy roots, through trunk of stacked buildings, to branching streets, the white tree city assumed shape—

Tanis... misgiving threaded Sinárr's sudden query, *what is this?*

Enveloped in the majestic energy of creation, Tanis heard Sinárr, sensed his disturbance, yet at the same time he really only knew the tree, the feel of his energy surrounding him, and the heady whirlwind of *making.*

Tanis finished solidifying the tree and admired his handiwork. He knew he could admire the tree without fear of erasing it, for it was not really his creation at all.

No, it is another's. Sinárr sounded inordinately displeased with him.

Suddenly a new space surrounded them with its bright stars beyond counting. They were in Sinárr's universe again. Tanis realized that Sinárr had coincided his starpoints—stolen them, in a sense, and he perceived the loss of his own space as forcefully as if someone had pulled a potato sack down over his body and scooped him up inside.

Now they stood upon a strip of glossy darkness, as a bridge, circling his tree city. He turned to Sinárr, feeling startled and confused. "What did I do wrong?"

Emanating displeasure, the Warlock walked a few paces away from him and studied the tree city, which appeared twice as big now as it had when Tanis was constructing it.

Then Sinárr turned his head and studied Tanis intently. Energy accumulated in clouds around him, invisible to view but needle-sharp in Tanis's perception, crackling with static. After a long moment of this uncomfortable inspection, Sinárr slowly let out his breath. "I can see you knew not what you were doing."

Tanis perceived his disapproval but couldn't interpret it. "I don't understand what I did wrong."

Sinárr came back to his side and brushed his hand across Tanis's hair, a gesture of forgiveness. He allowed the energy of his displeasure to dissipate. "Taerenhal." He looked back to the tree. "That is the name of this city. It belongs to Rafael." The Warlock's golden gaze shifted back to the lad. "I suppose Pelas showed it to you?"

"We were playing a game of illusions. This was one of his creations."

"Which is why you've been able to duplicate it so perfectly."

"I don't understand why you're upset with me."

"No," Sinárr ran his hand across the lad's hair again, "I can see that you don't."

He drew Tanis into the circle of his arm and turned them to face the radiant tree. "Illusion is one of the most accurate forms of duplication, Tanis. Had Pelas sculpted this tree in stone, we would find many inconsistencies from the original. Instead he presented you a highly accurate rendering from his conception, which you then accurately recreated."

Apprehension fluttered uncomfortably in Tanis's chest. "Then, what—"

"Things created in Shadow are not just *things*, Tanis. The starpoints that framed the space of a thing's original making remain attached to it. When you recreate in Shadow something made by another Warlock, it approximates also the starpoints of that Warlock."

Tanis was itching to move away from Sinárr, for the resonance always built powerfully between them whenever they were in physical contact, but the Warlock's hold upon him was firm. Tanis rather suspected Sinárr was punishing him in this way, for while the Warlock enjoyed that heady interchange, it always made Tanis feel uncomfortably charged, as with a restless unease.

"What am I missing?"

"Think it through, Tanis."

Tanis thought he'd be able to think a lot better if he was standing further away from Sinárr, but he imagined Sinárr wouldn't appreciate hearing that sentiment at the moment. Putting his mind to work on the problem then, Tanis reviewed the last few minutes. He'd stirred Sinárr's disquiet when he'd crafted the tree.

"If by making the tree, I approximated the starpoints of Rafael…what does that do?"

"We anchor our universes with starpoints. What happens when you approximate mine?"

"I can see your universe."

"*Exactly*. Your space and mine become the same space. Starpoints can be duplicated or approximated, which facilitates the sharing of space, or they can be coincided, which—"

"Is what you did to my space just now when you claimed it for your own." Sinárr stroked Tanis's head. "For your protection."

"Yes, so you said," Tanis grumbled.

Sinárr chuckled. "Rafael is one of the strongest among us, Tanis-mine, but also perilously inquisitive and a keen observer of Alorin's children. He will find you…intriguing, to say the least. I had hoped to keep you beneath the beam of his notice a little while longer."

Tanis recalled Mérethe telling him that Sinárr was as powerful as Baelfeir. "But surely Rafael is no threat to you."

Sinárr arched a brow. "We are all threats to each other should we choose to be, but what would we ever have reason to argue over?" Sinárr released him, allowing Tanis to put some distance between them and the resonance of power to dissipate.

Tanis admitted Sinárr's point. The contentions that so often plagued the races of Man—money, land, power, freedom, beliefs—could never be problems to an immortal who created his own worlds. Warlocks had every freedom they could desire.

Except the freedom to wander the Realms of Light.

The thought sent a twinge of unease flittering down Tanis's spine.

"When you approximate the starpoints of another Warlock, Tanis, the space becomes coincident." Sinárr strolled the bridge and glanced at the lad over his shoulder. "This is the method we use to communicate to one another, to summon each other across the void. When you were building Rafael's city, you were also unknowingly approximating his starpoints, calling out to him. I didn't think it wise to allow Rafael to greet you in your own space, considering—"

His attention shifted swiftly to a patch of coalescing darkness. "Ah," Sinárr cast a voluminous look at him. "Rafael comes."

SIXTY-EIGHT

"There is no higher court than conscience."
—Valentina van Gelderan, Empress of Agasan

FRANCO ROHRE CLOSED the door behind himself and walked through the antechamber towards Dagmar Ranneskjöld's personal study. Another long day embroiled in Illume Belliel's politics had his head tied in knots. He understood why the First Lord had written the Interrealm Trade Measure, how it would restore to the realms freedoms that had long been usurped by various Council factions and vested interests. But Franco wasn't at all sure that the Council of Realms itself would survive the measure's implementation.

The problems surrounding it seemed to grow exponentially, day by day, while the Council grew more fractured in opinion, more fractious in dealing with one another's demands and criticisms. The Speaker was calling for order more frequently, and each time the hall took longer to calm. If hostilities continued building as they were, someone was going to end up with their head on a pike. It concerned Franco a great deal whose head that might be.

Yours is certainly worthy, his conscience goaded. *It's a shame they can only jam it on one pike instead of the many it deserves, though.*

His concerns weren't aided in knowing that at that very moment the First Lord was in Alshiba's apartments working to Heal her from the deleterious effects of *atrophae*. If anyone got wind of his presence in the cityworld…

Or that back in Alorin, countless of his brethren were gathering support in his name for a nomination to the Vestal Seat, in challenge of Niko. If *Niko* ever got wind of that…

But mostly Franco worried about Alshiba. She'd become a ghost haunting his thoughts, a torment in his dreams.

Coveting his liege's woman will do that to a knight.

Franco gritted his teeth. *Oh, I'm a knight now?*

His conscience gave an inconsequential shrug. *Poetic license.*

Brooding on the fidelities of knights, Franco pushed through the double doors into Dagmar's study, and drew up short.

Surprise for an instant stole words from his tongue. Then he pulled the doors closed behind himself. "What are you doing here, Niko?"

Niko turned a page in the large book he was reading and replied without looking up, "I might ask the same of you, Franco."

Franco held up the book in his hand and the note that had accompanied it. "Alshiba asked me to return this for her."

"Maybe she asked me to return something, too."

Did she ask you to sit behind the Great Master's desk and peruse his books at your leisure?

Franco gave him an odd look as he crossed to the bookshelves. "I thought you were in Alorin."

"I thought you and I were allies. I guess we've both been duped."

Oh hahahaha he knows! The mad voice of his conscience shrieked with laughter.

Franco slowed in putting the book back in its place on the shelf. "What do you mean?"

Niko looked up. "Dagmar's weldmap? Have you forgotten so soon the *only* thing I've asked of you as my deputy?"

Franco frowned. "Niko—"

"You gave us your word, Franco."

"My word?"

"*Dore and myself*—don't look so mystified." Niko *tsked* his forgetfulness like a school marm scolding a recalcitrant child. "The day you attended my dinner for the Fifty Companions, you were quite definite in your allegiance." He flipped another page in the book, rather sharply this time. "I would think you'd be more appreciative, even if honoring your commitments is too great a burden. I've asked so little of you in return for naming you my deputy—and you *agreed* to help us."

Franco slowly leaned against the bookshelf, the better to keep the wall at his back and Niko in clear view. Nothing about this meeting felt right. "I agreed to act as my conscience dictated, Niko."

Niko glanced up again. "Ah, yes. That is what you said." His veiled smile seemed a little too hungry for comfort. "Leaves so much room for interpretation, doesn't it? The famous truthreader doublespeak. Who knew you were so adept at it?" He looked back to the book, waving vaguely. "Doubtless you've gained three rings in that talent as well. Perhaps you should instruct me in the technique. I never learned it myself."

Because you've all the intelligence of a clam, his conscience snickered, *who flings open its mouth when the sand comes barging in, only to let in more sand.*

Feeling uneasy, Franco looked around the space. The curtains were closed across the archway leading to the adjoining solar, lending a dingy cast to the otherwise windowless office. Or perhaps it was just the expanding shadow of Niko's querulous mood.

"We should take our conversation elsewhere. These are the Great Master's private chambers."

"They'll be mine soon enough. Besides," he tapped the book lying open in front of him, "Dagmar has a copy of the *Vestal Codex* in his library." Niko licked a finger and turned another page. "Rethynnea's Guild Master had a copy, but it was stolen several moons ago." Niko looked up to meet his gaze. "But you don't know anything about that, do you?"

"I told you no the first time you asked me." Of course, he knew all about it *now*.

Niko gave him a slow and—coming from him—rather unnerving smile. "See... there it is again." He waggled a finger at him. "The careful doublespeak. Amazing that I never noticed it before. Do you ever say anything you actually mean?"

Franco kept a careful hold on his temper. Niko wasn't himself, and whatever was going on with him felt dangerous.

"I see that you intend to stay. I'll be going then." He made for the door.

"Doesn't it bother you, Franco?"

His words halted Franco mid-stride. He stiffened, braced for the next insult.

"Seeing how much has been lost?" Niko fell back in his chair—Dagmar's chair—and exhaled a ponderous sigh. "It doesn't bother you?"

Franco turned his head with a frown.

Snared like a fly in a web.

Shut up!

"Reading the Codex reminds me of the greatness that once was." Niko entreated him with his gaze, which appeared surprisingly sincere. "Wouldn't you like to see Alorin restored? Don't you want our race to flourish again?"

"Of course I do."

Niko sighed. "So do I." He sounded uncharacteristically earnest. "I've just been reading about the training required to be considered for a vestalship. There are so few Adepts who gain their first row anymore—I don't even have my first row. Do you?"

Franco shook his head.

"See?" Niko gave a grim smile. "Neither of us are truly qualified. We have so much work ahead of us to restore the realm. At the very least we need to establish a new Citadel."

Franco stared wordlessly at him. This hardly seemed the same Niko who'd sulked off to Alorin after Alshiba's rebuke. Had some other entity taken over his shell in the intervening weeks?

And yet...they'd been friends during Franco's early years in the Sormitáge, back when Niko's renown was appealing enough that Franco overlooked his hauteur, desirable enough that he tried to convince himself there was something beneath the surface of his smile. Back when he'd had enough self-esteem to care what people thought of him; a long time back, when he'd been naïve enough to imagine Niko's popularity would transfer to him, if only they were seen to be friends.

But while that Niko had been no less superficial, he'd had bright ideas, bright ideals, a vision for the ways things could be that seemed to Franco a far cry better than they were. Perhaps...was it possible some of that old Niko had resurfaced?

Franco sank down on the back of a chair. "How do we establish a new Citadel without any mages?"

Niko blew out his breath. "Yes, that's the problem, isn't it?" He gave him a rueful smile, acknowledging the folly. "But even if we don't have mages, shouldn't we try? The deaths of the Mages has kept us from doing *anything* for three centuries. Now our knowledge itself is dying, poor victim of the race's intellectual enervation."

Hearing his own words so nearly out of Niko's mouth paused Franco's breath.

"Shouldn't we do something before the knowledge is completely lost to us, Franco? While at least a few of us who trained beneath those great men and women are alive to contribute what we know? While we're still capable of carrying forward their torch?"

Franco sat speechless, stunned by the rationality of this view. Of course, the First Lord and Markal Morrelaine were already doing that very thing in Illume Belliel under Isabel's watchful eye, but Niko didn't know that.

Franco crossed his arms. "Who would instruct?"

"Well, I suppose the Companions could to start with, and any of the Sormitáge maestros who desired a stronger presence. If there are others qualified that you know of, please tell me." Niko rose from his chair and wandered the room, hands in his pockets, looking and sounding surprisingly...*sane.* "I mean...isn't this what we wanted all along, Franco—the whole reason we marched behind Dore's doomsday vitriol?" He gave him an earnest smile, reflective of their days of friendship which Franco had himself just been recalling. "Wasn't it to have our own voice? An opportunity to explore our talents *our* way, instead of following always the ruts of everyone else's passage?"

"Yes..." Franco answered, hesitant to walk down that catastrophic road again, "but you saw where that got us." The question was, where was Niko going with all of this?

Niko turned him a forceful stare. "*Yes*, I saw—Malachai's war. Genocide. A race dying. A realm in chaos. A Seat who abandoned us. Another who's done nothing but mourn his abandonment—and all because *we* failed!"

"We failed," Franco felt a rather frantic incomprehension, "to...?"

Niko threw up both hands. "To kill the Mages—what else, Franco?"

Ah, the lunatic rises from Reason's ashes. I knew it couldn't last.

Niko went on, half grumbling, half extemporizing, pacing in time with the cadence of his thoughts, "Björn obviously took care of the Mages for us in the end—imagine him slaying his sister after all Arion Tavestra went through to save her from Dore?—but...well, at least he's done our work for us now. It's late, I'll admit. Three hundred years late. But regardless, the slate is clean. We can start fresh."

Franco pressed fingers to his temples, reeling as much from Niko's words as his inconstancy to a troth with reason.

"And it starts here, Franco. With *us*—united."

Here it comes.

"*New* vestals to replace the broken ones. The Second, sadly, the *Fifth* for a surety. We'll have to look for someone to replace Raine if he doesn't come around. And of course, Alshiba. She's the most fractured of all of them."

Franco had listened to about as much as he could take. He heard Carian vran Lea's plea to Dagmar shouting in his head, *'Let me kill him! Why can't I kill him? I'll make it quick!'*

I wouldn't make it quick, Franco thought with his jaw clenched tightly.

Anger kept trying to make fists of his hands. He forced his fingers to relax at his sides, but to stand there and let the man accuse *him* of duplicity, while with his every breath, Niko was so openly plotting to depose all of the realm's vestals?

—To be fair, he didn't say anything about Seth—

Franco really wanted to hit something. He wished it could've been Niko.

Niko helped himself to some wine, giving Franco time with his thoughts. He looked rather desperately around, seeking some anchor of rationality, something to ground him to his purpose for being there, to remind him of his oaths to the First Lord and Alshiba.

What he saw instead were changes in the office that he'd missed upon first entry. Niko must've been using the space for quite some time, clearly without Alshiba's knowledge or leave.

Niko took up his wine and sat leaned against the sideboard. "We could do great things together, you and me. I would keep you on, of course, as my deputy. You needn't worry." He drank his wine and had a thought in the middle of his swallow. "Oh—here's something that will cheer you. I'm working on a way to release us from our oaths."

Franco felt lost. "What oaths?"

"To the Fifth Vestal." Niko looked at him like he was surprised Franco had to ask. "The man is a traitor and, frankly, a terrorist. Twice he's invaded Alshiba's apartments as well as the Speaker's own. It's unconscionable that we Companions should still be bound to any shadow of his will. I know a man who can release us from those oaths. Won't that be a relief?"

Franco felt like the rug had been pulled out from under him. No, the floor. No, the ground for miles around. He choked out, "Who could *possibly* break an oath-binding laid in by the Fifth Vestal?"

Niko sipped his wine with a smug sort of smile. "You wouldn't know him."

Franco's gaze was hot. "Wouldn't I?" He'd been putting a lot of thought into who Niko could've found to replace the Fifth Vestal. Only one man seemed to fit the bill, and he was not a *man* in any sense of the word. "What about Alshiba?" he asked with his jaw tight and his hands tighter at his sides. "I suppose you already have her replaced, too?"

Niko seemed to backpedal a bit. "Now, now...let's not be hasty, Franco." He lifted a finger off his goblet and pointed meaningfully at him. "No, we have to kill her first. That's where the *atrophae* come—"

Franco didn't remember crossing the room or drawing his dagger. He only really became aware of himself when he found Niko beneath him on the floor and his blade at the man's treacherous throat. "Go on," Franco growled. "Tell me the rest of your plan."

Niko tried to swallow past the pressure of Franco's blade and choked instead. "I will if you will," he gasped.

Franco arched a brow, dangerous and dark.

"Admit it," Niko's voice barely scraped past Franco's blade. "You serve him. You're sworn to Björn—" he winced as Franco pressed the blade harder into his neck. "Just...one truth."

Franco could barely see through the bloodhaze clouding his vision. "I serve him," he hissed, low and fierce, "*proudly,* as you—"

A numbing force shocked through him all at once, a lightning strike of immobility. Breath froze in his lungs—everything froze.

Niko scrambled out from underneath his rigid form, toppling Franco onto his side in the process. He couldn't move, couldn't breathe, could barely even *think*.

"See?" Niko indignantly tugged at his coat. Franco heard a scraping sound—curtains being drawn back. "I told you I could get him to confess."

"Indeed you did. Fine work, my friend." A man's voice, deep and full-bodied—if such could be used to describe the timbre of a sound. But he did speak as though he was a fine wine, with a sort of fluid and intoxicating depth to his tone, each word offering multiple meanings, inviting of a desirous complexity. Franco only knew one man with a voice like that.

The working holding him immobile lessened to allow him to breathe. He gasped just as a pair of shoes planted themselves in front of his eyes—expensive shoes, shining beneath immaculately tailored pants.

"I am surprised at how well your formula worked, though," Niko muttered from above him.

"Bully them, confuse them, anger them," the man with the red-wine voice chuckled softly. "Three corners of a kite. Nudge up one, then another, then the next, then the first, round and about until the kite is toppling and your victim practically tumbles into confession. Three points to gain an admission of fault from any reasonable man."

"Franco serves a heinous traitor," Niko grumbled, "how *reasonable* can he be? Still, it worked like you said it would."

"Like a charm."

I'd like to shove a very large charm down his smug Eltanin throat.

Franco stared into the rug, cursing his stupidity. He should've walked out when he had the chance!

Yes, Franco Rohre, said the mental voice of the truthreader standing above him, whose expert working was pinning him to frozen life, *you certainly should have.*

Doors slammed open, followed by running feet.

"He's here, the traitorous dog! Isn't that right, *Admiral?*" Niko punctuated his call to arms with a kick of Franco's immobilized leg. "Bind him! Take him!"

Hands grabbed Franco's arms and hauled him to his feet. The immobilizing working fell away in time to be replaced by the icy bite of *goracrosta* around his arms.

*Hmm...*the mad voice in Franco's head tapped its finger to its lips thoughtfully, *I'm starting to think it wasn't Alshiba who sent that book after all.*

While the guards were binding his wrists behind him, Franco tossed the hair from his eyes and met Mir Arkhadi's crystalline gaze.

"Franco." Mir nodded with quiet amusement.

"Mir." Franco knew where this was headed now. "Be careful rooting around in my head. You may snare more thorns than even you can enjoy."

"Yes, I've heard all about your dangerous mind." Mir very much looked like he was relishing the challenge. He nodded to the guards to take Franco away.

"I want to know everything." Niko grabbed Mir's arm. "*Everything* he knows—especially about Dagmar's weldmap."

"We shall leave no stone unturned, you have my word."

And then they were carting Franco away for a private date in Mir Arkadhi's dungeon.

SIXTY-NINE

*"To stand before the light of truth and admit what it reveals...
these are the greatest pursuits of man."*

–Aristotle of Cyrene

EAN BOBBED WITHIN a river of disorientation. Freezing waves stole his breath, pummeling light his vision. Power soaked his core until he knew he was drowning in it. He flailed for wakefulness as for the surface of that power, for breath and for life. Was it memory, or was it happening in that very moment—this dying, drowning sense of being swept into the vast beyond?

He couldn't separate time's segments. Infinity was all that had been and would be in a loop of *now* that never let *now* become *then*. He found no handhold of yesterdays to anchor him, for the river was rushing him too quickly on, and his hands...his frozen, *burning* hands—

Ean woke with a harsh inhale. He pushed palms to his eyes, but he still couldn't shield himself from the blinding light. His head was swarming, yet his mind felt fractured. Multiple awarenesses stacked themselves in layered shards, but none of those awarenesses understood each other. An emptiness so vast as to dwarf comprehension hovered just beyond his mind. Ean's bemused and battered consciousness spun within these layered perceptions, observing them...wondering at them.

He finally dragged his mind back beneath his own control to focus on one clear thought: *Why am I alive?*

Pain throbbed in his palm.

He blinked until his bleary eyes found his palms—his left palm...and a cut, still raw. Whereupon the layered awarenesses aligned beneath a sudden, rather horrifying memory—

Breath halted in his lungs. Ean threw an arm over his eyes and stifled a groan of realization—in the same moment feeling immensely grateful that he was alive and absolutely terrified at what that meant.

You chose this path, cousin, Fynn's voice smirked. *You asked him to bind you.*

Yes, but I didn't think he'd actually do it!

The Fynn voice snorted derisively. *That's why they say never to make a deal with Death when you're standing on His doorstep.*

Thank you for that very helpful observation—

"Do you always carry on conversations with yourself this way?"

Ean dropped his arm to look at Darshan. The Malorin'athgul was sitting in a low-slung chair, stroking a finger along his bottom lip and observing him—*damn him*—with quiet amusement.

Ean pushed an arm over his eyes again. His entire body felt numb and at the same time, electrified. He had no idea how that was possible. "Lady's light…" he breathed more than spoke, "you're probably wondering what you got yourself into with this binding."

The Malorin'athgul stroked at one eyebrow. "Actually, I was wondering if this sort of display might've been Kjieran van Stone's true reaction upon realizing he was bound to me."

Ean was trying to get a grip on the enormity of what he'd done—of what Darshan had done for him, at his request. "You saved my life. And I'm grateful—*thirteen hells*, I'm so astonished I'm speechless." This truth, compounded with the cosmic perceptions he'd been awakened to, had him reeling. "The reality is just a little hard to wrap my head around."

Indeed, possibility was a rearing monolith splitting the sky into forked potentialities, light and dark in positive and negative, reflections of intent. Ean had gambled everything on the tenuous hope that Darshan possessed more humanity than his actions as the Prophet would suggest. But it was done now, whatever the outcome, whatever Darshan's intention beneath the act—whether charitable or aught else. Ean was bound to him now and subject to everything that binding implied.

By Cephrael's Great Book! He prayed he'd made the right choice!

The Malorin'athgul rose from his chair and idled towards the windows. "There are worse things than being bound to one of us, Ean."

Processing this, Ean exhaled a slow breath and looked back to him curiously. "Like what?"

Darshan turned a telling look over his shoulder. "You could be bound to a Warlock." He halted before the window, which soared nearly three times his own considerable height. Beyond him, the onion-dome towers of the alien city sparkled with painful brightness.

Looking out at the city, it took Ean a moment to discern what seemed different about the view. He sat up and swung his legs over the edge of the bed to study it, and soon realized that he was seeing more than light reflecting off of solid objects; he was seeing the city's towers as *solidified energy*, a dazzling spectrum of variegated masses, as though viewed through the lens of *elae*'s fifth strand—only it couldn't be the fifth he was looking through now. For some startling reason, Darshan was sharing his awareness with Ean, and his was a very different perspective.

Indeed, when he chose to become aware of it, Ean got the distinctly uncomfortable perception that *he* was actually somewhere else entirely, or else… rather, that what appeared to be there wasn't actually there, but the only *there* was his body, suspended out of space and time in a dimension that had neither, while his mind wove illusion into form around him.

The prince looked to Darshan and swallowed. "Tell me how you bound me."

Darshan's tall form made a dark silhouette before the sparkling city. He clasped hands behind his back. "I crafted its intent to mirror the binding I share with my brothers. This was the only way I knew to forge such a link with *deyjiin*."

Ean was just rising from the bed. Now he sank back down again on its edge.

Darshan had spoken so matter-of-factly, yet this was a staggering truth—a staggering *gift*. He had a thousand questions in that moment, yet the only one that scraped past his incredulity was, "*Why?*" Ean stared perplexedly at the man. "Why would you do such a thing for me? Why bother sparing my life at all?"

Darshan turned over his shoulder. "You expressed uncertainty about your path leading you here, about us being here together. I harbor no such uncertainties."

Ean sank elbows onto his knees and tried to reconcile this statement with the truths he was perceiving through their binding, recognizing in the same moment that the immortal was giving him free access to his thoughts so that Ean might gain this understanding.

The prince scrubbed at his jaw. Amazement and wonder were running neck and neck with gratitude, all of them chasing after possibility. He couldn't see any paths of consequence—of course not, for they were patterns of *elae*—but he could *sense* myriad spirals unfolding.

"I perceive your lingering discomposure, Ean, but we haven't much time left to prepare." The Malorin'athgul looked to him. "Binding your life pattern to my own required much use of my power. The working has made a beacon across the linked realms." His gaze tightened. "We must ready ourselves. They're coming."

Ean shook his head. "Who's coming?"

"Revenants. Golem creatures."

Ean came alert. "*Eidola?*"

"*Eidola* would be preferable; they're bound to the Warlock that created them and may still be controlled and directed. Revenants are the discarded entities the Warlocks have brought to life and then abandoned. They no longer know any consciousness, only hunger."

"That's…horrifying." Ean got unsteadily to his feet. "What do they hunger for?"

"*Deyjiin.* They could feed for millennia off of one such as me." Darshan placed his hand on the window, Ean felt his thought as a mental snap, and the glass vanished. A scorching wind blasted into the room, whipping hair and clothing. "Shail left our brother to a clutch of these creatures." Darshan turned him a look that spoke volumes. "Pelas had just escaped them when you tried to unmake him in my temple."

Ean winced and shoved a hand to hold back his hair and his chagrin. "That wasn't my best moment."

It occurred to him as he joined the Malorin'athgul at the window's edge that through his binding with Darshan he was now also connected to Pelas and Shail…and Rinokh. The potential ramifications kept branching the more he thought about them, and not all of those outgrowths were easily digested.

"I assume you can't use *deyjiin* against these revenants?"

"Correct. It would only make them stronger."

"So how do we fight them?"

Darshan lifted a calculating gaze out across the city. "For now, with the strength of sword and staff." He turned to face Ean. "You must duplicate the starpoints of this realm so you can draw your own power here."

The prince blinked at him. Then the truth sank in. He shook his head slowly while a welling astonishment gradually consumed him. "*By Cephrael's Great Book…*" he gave an incredulous exhale, "you're telling me I can work *deyjiin?*" He'd never imagined Darshan would bind him in a way that allowed him access to his own power.

Darshan looked back to the city. "It is fortunate you're of the fifth—'as fabled as you and I,' I believe you said—for in *elae*'s fifth strand, the two powers achieve balance."

Ean considered deeply of his words. "That field you placed around Nadia back in Tambarré. It was formed of both powers, wasn't it? Balanced somehow. That's what you're talking about?"

"Yes. Even bound to me, you would not be able to work my power were you not also a fifth-strand Adept…or *eidola,* mutated by the fifth." Darshan leveled him a deeply penetrating stare. "Perhaps we too will find balance in this unanticipated union."

Ean managed a swallow around a continuously-increasing disbelief. "So…matching starpoints. How do I do that?"

Darshan extended his hand. "Join minds with me and I will show you the manner of it."

Ean looked at his hand, feeling like the foundations of every his expectation of the man were being shaken. Then he clasped wrists with Darshan.

The Malorin'athgul opened his mind—that mind which had felt like a sun upon Ean's first contact. It still blazed as brightly, but now Darshan's binding protected Ean from the searing star of his awareness. Darshan drew him within the corona of his thoughts and then exploded his awareness outwards to encompass the starpoints of that world.

Ean saw balls of light framing space in a cube, almost exactly like what he envisioned when he framed space in Absolute Being. He understood immediately what he needed to do. He communicated this understanding to Darshan with the instant timelessness of thought, and Darshan stepped mentally aside.

Duplicating the starpoints of that realm felt natural in a way that Ean found incredibly stimulating, for he realized he was using *deyjiin* to do it. The power felt light and cool in his mind, so different from *elae*—the lifeforce had a warm viscosity, while *deyjiin* seemed as a weightless, cohesive mist— yet it responded similarly to his intent. The moment he duplicated the final starpoint, *deyjiin* flooded through him.

Darshan veiled off his mind and left the prince standing once again in his own mental space. Without Darshan's sun, Ean felt colder and unexpectedly hollow. Older preconceptions were cascading away now, caught by a constant current of revelation. Ean looked to him and swallowed. "Words are proving inadequate for everything I want to say."

The ghost of a smile touched Darshan's lips. Then he stepped out the window and walked across the open air towards a tower across the street.

Ean had done the same thing a thousand times with *elae*. He didn't yet have the same confidence with *deyjiin*. He retrieved his sword and belted it on while alternately watching Darshan striding through the empty air and staring down into street far below. Then he called to the Malorin'athgul, "You're sure about this?"

"What applies to one applies to all, Prince of Dannym." Darshan's voice floated back to him.

"*'What applies to one applies to all.'*" The prince muttered the Second Law under his breath. *Well, here goes nothing.* He focused his intent...

A fateful step later he was walking across solidified air. His wielder's self-respect refused to admit the relief he felt each time his boots found purchase beneath his will, but his heart did a little triumphant dance in the privacy of his chest.

Reaching the next tower, Ean clambered around the sloped roof towards Darshan with his mind hard at work trying to sort what felt like a mountain of assumptions into new categories of truth. "If you could manipulate the fabric of this world so easily, why did we walk all that way through the desert?"

The Malorin'athgul was staring out over the endless sands with the wind blowing his hair back from his face, looking much the god surveying his domain. "I didn't want to call the revenants' attention to us. In your condition, you couldn't have withstood an attack."

Ean halted near him and found a stable footing. "And now?"

Darshan nodded towards a dark line rimming the horizon. "They're nearly here. Soon we will see what you can withstand."

Ean squinted at it. "That doesn't look so promising."

Darshan gave him a somewhat unnerving smile. "Certainly not of any experience either of us stands to appreciate."

Ean frowned at him. "You don't seem too worried about it."

The Malorin'athgul's eyebrow inched upwards, arch in its aspect. "In the countless millennia of my existence, do you imagine revenants are the worst things I've faced?"

"Well, when you put it like that..." Ean threw himself down on the edge of the roof to await the revenant apocalypse. The sun, once again, was shining directly in his eyes.

But now he could do something about it.

He focused his intention on the air overhead and made it solid...except somehow it remained transparent. So he tried making it opaque...but it still didn't stop the light from blinding him. He tried giving it property—color—but then the particles wouldn't solidify.

In Alorin, he could've used the elemental fifth to solve the problem a number of ways, but this wasn't *elae's* fifth strand; *deyjiin* was formless energy without any inherent aspect or quality.

Ean latched onto this simplicity and tried creating something whole cloth—a parasol—out of the formless aether, but while the energy itself would congeal into a semblance of form, the fabric of the world would not shift to accept the thing he was trying to shape. He couldn't make it solidify, and felt instead a tugging resistance, like the realm's fabric was trying to snap itself back.

"It resists your efforts." At Darshan's comment, the prince looked to where the Malorin'athgul stood staring out at the desert. "Shadow has—not necessarily different laws from Alorin," he said without turning, "but Shadow's are often higher-order laws. Your Alorin is a realm of solid energy. But nothing you or I could make here would be solid enough to provide shade."

"Or hold off revenants," Ean murmured, catching the thought.

Darshan cast him a sidelong eye. "Even though we've duplicated the starpoints of this world and can reach its energy, we remain within the compartment of a Warlock's framed space and are subject to its laws—the *Warlock's* laws. Until I can find and coincide the exterior-most starpoints—the maze beyond this maze, if you will—we'll remain bound by the rules the Warlock established for his world."

Beyond them, the dark line was spreading rapidly across the sand.

"In my temple in Tambarré," Darshan said, "you told me of your First Lord, this Björn van Gelderan, who claimed my brothers and I could not unmake your world from within."

Ean warily watched the revenants overtaking the horizon. "And?"

Darshan shrugged. "It is evidence of this same law in application in Alorin. Within the realm, we are bound by its rules. In Shadow, the most powerful Warlocks are those who are capable of not merely duplicating others' starpoints but *coinciding* them, such that they can become the god of any universe."

"That's what you intend to do when you find the starpoints of the outermost sphere of these worlds?"

"Yes. Then I may tear the fabric and return us to Alorin's space."

In Ean's estimation, that couldn't happen soon enough.

He observed the dark horizon creeping ever closer and felt a chill, despite the heat of wind and sun. The creatures were spearing across the desert like a flock of birds, with a chevron out and in front of the mass of others—the first wave.

"About that..." Ean rubbed the back of his neck, "any estimate on when you think you'll have those starpoints in hand? An hour? A year? I'd like to have an idea of how long I'm going to be golem food."

Darshan clasped hands behind his back and turned his face into the wind. "Pain is a transient inconvenience."

"Oh, thank you for that wisdom. I'll try to take solace in it while I'm being eternally devoured by soulless entities."

A smile flickered on Darshan's lips. "Shail expected you would die here, Ean. He expected I would want you to, even as I expected Pelas to slay your Isabel." He turned seriously to him. "I never imagined Pelas was capable of resisting my compulsion; it never occurred to me that he might release her. If anything true can be said of all of us equally, it is that we constantly underestimate each other."

Darshan returned his penetrating gaze to their oncoming enemy. Much of the desert now wore a cloak of darkness. "Come, Prince of Dannym." His gaze flicked to Ean and away again. "Let's see where this game is leading us."

He stepped off the building.

Ean watched Darshan's form streaking down towards the earth, far, far...*far* below, until he landed in a voluminous eruption of dirt and dust. The prince shook his head. One thing he could say with certainty about Darshanvenkhátraman—he wasn't short on courage.

Ean took a deep breath and leaped off after him.

While he was falling, the prince tried to focus on gravitating *deyjiin* to slow and cushion his descent. But it was a long way down, and he had an unfortunate span of wind-filled, teary-eyed falling to *not* think about the last time he'd experienced a similar downward rush.

He landed on a cushion of power amid a violent explosion of earth—what had appeared as a puff to him from high above was closer to a forty-foot geyser. Ean coughed his way out of the dust clouds with his eyes tearing and his throat burning.

He found Darshan waiting for him at what passed for a street corner in that alien city. The prince looked down at his own dusty and disheveled appearance and then up at the Malorin'athgul, with his raven hair and burnished gold coat so pristine, and waved vaguely at him. "Does nothing stick to you, or...?"

"This is all illusion, Prince of Dannym—or hadn't you realized that yet?" He flashed a dark smile and started off down the street.

Ean called after him, "Just so you know, that whole 'Shadow is killing you' thing felt pretty real to me." He jogged to catch up.

Darshan led a fast route towards their enemy. Ean was speculating on how long just the two of them would last against the oncoming horde when Darshan extended his Merdanti staff horizontally before him. Ean felt the click of a thought, and lightning flames of *deyjiin* speared out both ends of the staff.

Where power struck stone—or whatever material formed those oddly reflective buildings—the structure instantly vaporized. Walls began to disintegrate, the towers themselves to waver, their foundations to simply dissolve.

Ean placed a hand on Darshan's shoulder, gaining his gaze—and realizing again as their eyes met that he was *bound* to this immortal, the knowledge flooding him with a still-unsettled anticipation—and requested, mind to mind, *Let me see how you're doing this.*

The Malorin'athgul obligingly shared his awareness, and the prince studied the flow of power through Darshan's thoughts, observing how he sculpted *deyjiin* to his intent. Darshan in turn looped a thread of power around Ean, keeping him within a protective sphere while he strode along. He held his staff before him in his left hand, while his right hand pushed tidal forces around in massive waves, shoving the toppling structures hither and yon, leaving piles of monolithic stone blocks and rubble several stories high in his wake.

He razed the city in this fashion, walking an uninterrupted pace. The roaring in Ean's ears was rivaled only by the depth of the obscuring dust clouds that soon surrounded them; but Darshan walked them effortlessly through this, encased in his bubble of *deyjiin*—yet a fourth compartmented working he managed in concert with the other three: the flames of *deyjiin* erasing the foundations, the thrashing waves of power, and Ean, held protectively close.

They halted at the city's edge. When the tsunami of dust finally settled and Darshan lowered his protective dome, at least a dozen blocks of city had been destroyed and their broken materials repurposed into the towering walls of a rubble maze.

The prince turned rather abused eyes out across the desert. The creatures were close enough now that he could see them as separate entities instead of a solid swath of darkness. Their numbers were beyond counting.

"Maybe this is my mortality talking," *or the fact that I've nearly died already too many times in this life and don't relish the idea of experiencing it again*, "but these don't look like such great odds to me."

Darshan eyed him sidelong. "Balance bends to my will."

"Balance...but this is Shadow."

"All of the cosmos bows to Balance, even as all of creation bows to the laws of energy—what you Adepts call your Laws of Patterning." When Ean merely stared wordlessly at him, Darshan remarked, "You appear surprised by my understanding."

Ean shook his head. "I'm...you..." It took quite a bit for him to formulate words, and longer still to speak them without an undertone of reprimand. "You formed a religion that persecutes Adepts and corrupted truthreaders into walking nightmares of themselves—and all along you knew *elae*'s Laws?"

Darshan looked back to the desert. "Those are just games, Prince of Dannym."

"*Games.*" Ean's voice held an accusing edge. "Destroying Adepts was a game to you?"

Darshan settled him an arresting stare. "As defeating me and my brothers is a game to your Björn van Gelderan."

Ean exhaled a measured breath, for he recognized the truth in the parallel

Darshan had drawn. "The game of being the Prophet Bethamin…" he grasped critically for Darshan's point of view, "the game of Balance…" He lifted him a look. "The game of unmaking?"

"Existence holds no value without a game, Ean. Immortals understand this better than most."

Then the first wave of revenants was upon them, and they'd no more time for talk.

Darshan stepped forward swinging his long Merdanti staff and took seven of the golems down with one blow. Ean swung for the next one—

And they were suddenly in the thick of it, surrounded on all sides by *eidola*-like creatures with empty black eyes. Darkness crowded Ean's vision. The too-bright sun bore down from on high.

Darshan dragged Ean into the stream of his own thoughts, unifying their action. The prince suddenly saw through two perspectives—no, *three*, for Darshan was holding that world's starpoints and viewing the battle from above as well as through his body's eyes. Ean found the view both disorienting and really bloody fascinating, although he admitted a certain disheartenment at seeing how many revenants there truly were.

Whenever any of them got too close, the press too intense, Darshan would explode *deyjiin* through the ranks to blast the creatures back. This gave them room to fight but also made the revenants incrementally stronger.

And so it went—the constant press, dark weapons flashing, *deyjiin* exploding, carcasses of dead things piling up in mounds, the air thick with an alien hunger, Ean's lungs burning with another sort of need—on and on *and on*.

And the revenants kept coming. By the thousands.

SEVENTY

"There is no glory to behold in war. The glory is all moonshine, dust, a trick of the light reflecting off sharp blades and dull reason."
—The Fourth Vestal Raine D'Lacourte

THE NADORI REGIMENT Commander Nassar abin'Ahram stood in the grey light before dawn watching a line of black-cloaked men treading a sinuous path through the tents, heading his way. Beyond them, down in the valley, Prince Radov's army camp spread as a rash across the smooth desert sands, with one bulging conglomeration of pustules that was the Ruling Prince's compound lording over the high ground in the center.

May Jai'Gar forgive my insolence. Nassar pressed his palms together and glanced to the smoke-colored heavens. He should not think of his own prince so derogatorily, but he couldn't watch the army camp amassing on the Khalim Plains and not recall the horror that had overtaken those lands two years prior. An ashen death, as if the Demon Lord of old had walked there, claiming each man with an effacing touch that drained the life from his very bones.

The ashes of those men still painted the plains in great strokes of charcoal and grey. Erasing winds would whip the dunes and blow in new sands to make a fresh coat upon the old, but even the great sandstorms that left villages buried in their wake couldn't cleanse that ashen field.

The ghosts of the men who'd died that night still roamed there too. Inithiya hadn't claimed their spirits—no one knew why. Rumor said if you braved a sandstorm upon the Khalim Plains, you would see those meandering ghosts outlined in sand, their bodies continuously whispering into dust, then as on the day death claimed them.

And now Radov was leading M'Nador's fine soldiers across those scarred lands to make ghosts of thousands more.

May Inanna bless their swords, perhaps the dawn would see a different end than what had come before. Their prince had certainly seemed to think so when he'd addressed the war council the night before. He'd spoken lengthily if…ineloquently on their superior position, their brilliant plan and their infallible secret weapons. Much to Nassar's dismay, he did not ask the favor of the gods upon these declarations, so Nassar imagined They probably would not bestow it.

This saddened him, because no matter which side claimed to have Inanna's favor, many men would die. Inithiya and Huhktu would soon be busy ferrying the dead, and this was not an outcome that Nassar, nor any who sought peace, favored.

He wondered at their prince's logic. He was risking M'Nador's *entire* army to claim a single stronghold. It was one the Council of Princes coveted, yes; but if Radov regained the oasis at the cost of the army, how would he hold it when the Emir's forces attacked anew? Did he really imagine the Council of Princes would let him keep his throne if he threw away the kingdom just to reclaim a few palaces?

It is never that simple.

Nassar knew this. The oasis was the foothold on the Kutsamak, a mineral and gem-rich swath of inhospitable earth. But even with a toe lodged firmly in Raku, they would not long hold the Kutsamak without an army.

There has always been war in the Kutsamak.

Nassar exhaled a long sigh. This was true; the Kutsamak knew feuding like the rivers knew water. If the denizens of that unpropitious landscape had spent more time irrigating and less time attacking each other with farm utensils the entire mountain range would be an oasis. Nassar supposed the only real difference between war between tribes and war between nations was the count of the dead.

The procession of men coming towards him was close enough now that he could see the patterns stitched into the fabric of their black robes. Nassar wondered if there was some deeper meaning in the fact that wielders always wore black.

The first wielder reached him, pressed his palms together and bowed. "Peace be upon you." He was not Nadori—possibly Avataren. All Nassar knew about him or any of the nine men was that they were Shamshir'im.

Nassar mimicked the wielder's motion and murmured the traditional reply.

"I am Torqin. You're the *al-Amir* of Ramala?"

"I am Nassar abin'Ahram. The space has been prepared for you per the consul's specifications."

"As good as your word." Torqin cast a meaningful look behind him at the other black-robed men. "The consul said as much of you."

Nassar would've preferred that Viernan hal'Jaitar said nothing of him at all. Verily, hal'Jaitar was the leader of the unscrupulous Shamshir'im, who imagined themselves above princely law—even above the gods. Nassar would that Viernan hal'Jaitar had never even learned his name.

He took them to the bunker his men had dug into the mountainside and covered with muslin dyed in shades of ochre, russet and ash. One could barely differentiate the bunker from the surrounding hillside when standing right on top of it, much less from the top of the escarpment… or the skies. At least, that was the outcome Viernan hal'Jaitar was hoping for—some concealment for his wielders while battling the Sundragons that day. Doubtless they would work their own patterns of protection, but magic sometimes failed. Camouflage was more dependable.

Inside was cool, the night's fair breeze trapped beneath the stained gauze covering. The wielders spread themselves along the forward edge and fixed their gazes on the high walls of Raku atop the escarpment, which appeared a darker shadow two miles distant. Between crenellated walls and Nassar's camp, Radov's forces were already amassing, lining up beside the men of Morwyk. In all, they were ten-thousand strong. By dawn, the desert would be an undulating sea of determination and flashing steel, and not nearly enough piety among them for Nassar's taste.

"What now?" asked one of the wielders.

Torqin clasped hands behind his back. Nassar noted that his right hand sported a thin gold band on every finger. "Now?" He fixed his gaze to the east and the coming dawn. "Now we wait."

❦

The attack came with the dawn, well timed so the Akkadian archers had the Nadori sun to contend with as much as the Nadori soldiers. First the Nadoriin attacked the bulwarks with their spikes and sharpened stakes, but they were so numerous, and their commanders so insistent, that the bulwarks were soon overrun, the dead making a carpet for the living to storm over unimpeded.

Next they met the naptha trenches, whose fire held them back for a time. But the commanders drove the soldiers over these as well, in much the same fashion.

"He cares nothing for them." Jayachándranáptra, Rival of the Sun, hugged her arms and gazed out across the battle with a furrow between her brows.

Beyond the outer walls of the oasis, swaths of oily smoke billowed up to stain the dawn skies while the blood of brave men stained the sands. Archers lined the walls, three rows deep, already busy making pin-cushions of the Nadoriin. Behind them, the rest of the Emir's soldiers were amassed and waiting.

"It's war, Jaya." Náiir joined her at the crenellated wall. Like her, he wore his fighting blacks and carried a dragon-hilted greatsword on his back. "Soldiers fight, they die."

She eyed him tetchily. "Thank you for clarifying that truth. I haven't been observing it for the last million cycles of the sun." Abruptly she blew out an aggravated breath and lifted her gaze to the skies. "*Where* is Ramu? I would we stopped this insanity."

"We cannot intervene until they breach the walls. You know that."

"I don't *know* that." She shot him a frustrated look. "Balaji isn't always right."

"He's more often right than wrong."

"That is utterly irrelevant." She returned her gaze to the battle. "Balaji said the tapestry is thick here. Thick enough to hold our weight."

"But many branches of consequence extend forth from this battle, Jaya. If we break one with a misplaced step…" Náiir wrapped his arm around her shoulders. "I worry for Mithaiya, too. Like you, I would rather be searching for our sister than watching men tear each other limb from limb. But we cannot rush the hours. We have to choose every step carefully."

Jaya watched the smoke billowing a quarter mile away. She could smell blood burning in it. Her eyes tightened. "Ramu may say differently."

"Ramu will not overrule Balaji in matters of Balance."

Jaya flung a look at him. "Why can't you be agreeable and side with me for once? You *always* take Balaji's side."

"That is because I am a better cook than you, Jayachándranáptra."

Jaya turned to see Balaji and Rhakar coming along the wall.

"Well said, brother," Náiir turned with a smile. "A man's mind and allegiances reside in his stomach."

Jaya harrumphed. "Your mind resides a good deal lower than your stomach."

"We cannot understand what we are unwilling to ourselves become, Jaya."

"If being a male involves scattering your seed like a pollinating pine, I would rather live without the knowledge."

"And so begins our descent into unknowing, our fall away from godliness."

Jaya flicked him a look. "Stop trying to distract me by talking about philosophy."

Náiir winked at her. "Is it working?"

A horn sounded, harsh beneath the rosy dawn.

"The Nadoriin have reached the walls." Balaji frowned slightly.

"Finally. We can end this now." Jaya looked expectantly to her brother.

Balaji continued frowning.

Along the lower wall, the Emir's soldiers were fighting off Nadoriin scrambling up scaling ladders, while on the battlefield, catapults appeared, trundling through the smoke.

Jaya felt a desperate urgency. "Why are we all still standing here? Balaji, you said—"

"I know what I said, Jaya." Balaji watched the battleground with a focused intensity. Yet his gaze was misleading, for though he stared out at the battle, he was surely studying the mortal tapestry instead.

"What is it?" she asked. "What do you see?"

"A knot in the fabric," Rhakar muttered.

"Of course it's knotted." Jaya flung a hand to the lower wall. "Thousands of mortal threads are ending!"

Rhakar crossed his muscled arms and looked to Balaji. "We should wait."

Balaji shifted him a look of agreement.

Jaya threw up both hands and spun away from them. That's when she saw her favorite brother approaching. "Finally!" She turned them a triumphant stare. "Ramu comes to bring some sense to all of you." She started off to meet him.

"That's not very complimentary, Jaya." Náiir called after her. "I'm far more handsome than Ramu. I should be your favorite brother."

"You might be if you were more agreeable," she tossed back.

"More *amenable*, you mean?"

Jaya took Ramu's arm. "At last you've come to bring reason to this insanity."

"Which insanity?" Ramu eyed her speculatively. "The battle, or our brothers?"

Two such brothers gave Ramu looks of greeting, but Balaji continued staring out into the smoking valley. "Do you see it, Ramu?"

"Yes," Ramu said gravely, joining his side.

"*Yes*," Jaya grumbled, "thousands of men are killing each other when we could stop it."

Balaji shifted a troubled look to her. "If we act now, Jaya, more will die."

"More than are dying already?"

Náiir shifted a look between Balaji and Ramu. "What do the currents tell you?"

"The currents are in a storm," Rhakar remarked over crossed arms.

"Yes, to my eyes also."

Balaji's frown deepened. "There is an inexplicable darkness in the tapestry."

Ramu exhaled a decisive breath. "I fear we must walk it to find the light at the end."

"Enough dithering." Rhakar threw himself over the wall.

❖

The wielder Torqin clenched his jaw and held tight to the pattern poised in his mind. Holding *elae's* third strand in a static pattern was like trying to restrain a raging bull. He felt kicked all to hell, and he hadn't even *worked* the damned thing yet.

"What's bloody taking them so long?" another of his wielders hissed under his breath.

Their simple instructions to wait for the Sundragons to take to the skies were not so easily accomplished when it meant holding patterns in their consciousness for over an hour. But they would have only seconds to act, and it took more than seconds to conceive of *these* patterns properly. It took more than courage to conceive of them at all. They were attempting an attack upon immortal fifth-strand creatures. Torqin had never felt so close to his own mortality.

Another pointed. "Look there! Is that—"

Torqin raised a hand to the others. "Wait. They must all be together."

They watched from their high, hidden vantage as first one and then four more dragons emerged through the oily smoke rising from the naptha pits.

"There's only five," one of the others said uncertainly.

Where is the sixth? "Wait!" Torqin cautioned.

"We cannot wait!" The wielder beside him turned with fear in his eyes. "They'll incinerate the prince's army." Under which circumstances they all knew hal'Jaitar would incinerate them.

"He said all *six* had to be present," Torqin growled, but he felt the same urgency to release his pattern, the same need to be done with this business.

"It has to be now," said the wielder on the end. "I cannot hold the fifth any longer."

A chorus of hissed consent followed this statement.

"Five is better than none," one of the others pointed out.

"Very well." Torqin prayed he wasn't signing his own death warrant. "We proceed."

They all joined hands and linked minds through the bond they'd created for the purpose of this working. The wielder holding the fifth-strand pattern placed it in the shared space for the rest to view. They each then layered their patterns upon it—rapidly, almost frantically now that the end was so close in sight—until the matrix floated in their shared minds.

They studied it then, each from his own perspective, to be certain all the patterns were correctly interlaced. They knew its aspect well, having practiced this rendering almost continually for nearly a fortnight.

"It is done," said the wielder of the fifth. "Aye," agreed the next, and on down the line, until Torqin added the final *aye* and they counted in their minds together, *Three, two, one—*

❖

"All is in readiness, Your Majesty."

Gydryn val Lorian turned his head to nod to the steward. "Tell Prince Farid I'll be right there."

The man pressed palms, bowed and departed.

Gydryn looked back to the valley. From his vantage at the Emir's palace, he gazed out across a flashing sea of steel, row upon row in orderly columns, five hundred to a block, block upon block arrayed across the sand.

Ten-thousand strong. That was the assessment from men with sharper eyes than him. The Nadoriin were nearly a mile distant, but the wind still carried the tang of oiled armor and aggression—never mind the stench of burning flesh—to him from the south, where columns of smoke darkened the sky.

Was this the scene he was destined to face from the walls of Calgaryn Palace? All their futures writ so clearly, those who stood to oppose the unstoppable trinity of Radov, Bethamin and Morwyk? Across that flashing sea, easily as many banners waved with Morwyk's colors as with Radov's, flaunting their alliance now that all the cards were face-up on the table. And once they'd reclaimed Raku for M'Nador, would this army turn its strength against Dannym?

Gydryn exhaled a slow breath. Had he been able to sit his horse sooner, he wouldn't have been there to see this assemblage, and would've slept better for it. Watching such a force marshalling against a man of decency and honor made him feel too keenly for his own neck.

It had taken him far to long to recover his strength, too long to write letters to those who needed to hear from him, too long to face another journey across the desert with the memory of the last one a pall upon his courage. And now that all was finally in readiness for his departure to

Nahavand, too long to pull himself away, to commit to the course of action they'd all agreed upon.

In his heart, he wanted to help Zafir—in the very least, he owed him *his* sword—but if he brought his forces from Nahavand to bolster Raku's soldiery, who would stand to defend Calgaryn against Morwyk? The Duke of Towermount could not long hold the city alone.

These were bitter choices he was facing. His kingdom or Zafir's. His responsibility to his people versus his responsibility to the man who'd saved his life, without whose selfless action he would have no chance to help his people at all. Where did honor reside? He felt he would be compromising it no matter what choice he made.

Farid was waiting for him in the palace atrium—pacing, actually, with all the patience of a caged leopard. The Nodefinder prince had the look of a leopard, too; all hard muscle beneath the soft covering of his desert robes, a close-shorn beard hugging his jaw, his shoulder-length dark hair pinned close beneath his turban. He spun in a whirl of robes at Gydryn's approach. "Your Majesty, I regret we can no longer delay. My father fears for your life."

"You didn't invite Radov's army to crowd your walls, Prince Farid. How far to the node?"

"It lies beyond the city. We must hurry. Your honor guard is assembling by the west gate."

The king followed down the passage after Farid, still feeling a convalescent's uncertainty in his limbs. While determination held him upright and grit drove him forward with his will set on reaching Nahavand and Calgaryn beyond, a part of him remained there in Raku, in the Emir's war room, forever paused in that moment when he'd looked across the map table and seen his son's courage, the admiration those seasoned commanders held for him, and the look of respect in the Sundragon Rhakar's yellow eyes.

Gydryn would never forget that moment. He felt bound to it, bound *in* it, for it was the moment hope had been reborn—not for himself so much as for his kingdom. It was the moment when he realized that Trell could lead should he himself fall; the moment when he knew that no matter what happened to him, Dannym's future was assured. And oh, how tempting in this realization to stay and offer his sword, for what it was worth, trembling limbs and all! As far as the world was concerned, Gydryn val Lorian was dead, his life already forfeit, his choices made and that path walked.

Before his reunion with Trell, Gydryn saw no future for himself but the road that returned to Calgaryn. Now he saw many potential futures. With two strong sons alive to carry forward his line—

Oh, these were dangerous thoughts. Cowardly thoughts? Brave thoughts? He couldn't decide. Responsibility yoked him in both directions.

They reached the horses and mounted with silence lengthening between them, but in the distant city, horns were bellowing. The morning wind carried echoes of shouting, fighting; deceptively innocent whispers, drained of emotion.

Farid cast a tight gaze to the east. "We should be able to make it. The Mage's dragons patrol the skies." Yet he sounded uncertain. He swung into the saddle in a swirl of robes and looked to Gydryn as he took up his reins. He was a fierce prince, Zafir's middle son, hardly older than Trell yet with a severe intensity to his gaze, as of earnestness honed by responsibility to its most extreme edge. "You're ready, Your Majesty?"

"As I'll ever be, Prince Farid."

Farid set his heels to his horse and rode hard for the west gate.

❖

Ramu—

Jaya!

Balaji!

Anchor yourselves!

Ramu felt the pattern hit and cling to him like bitumen. A force speared through his shields into his mind, spreading instant confusion. Other patterns blasted thought from his reach, blasted his body upwards into the sky. No, elsewhere.

A familiar disorentation swirled.

No...else*when*.

Anchor yourselves! Ramu hastily threw an anchor into time. He continued whirling backwards...forwards? He couldn't say into what *when* he was headed, couldn't stop time's spool unwinding, only perceive its unraveling threads amid the swirling, kaleidoscopic light.

Balaji...?

Jaya...?

Náiir...?

Rhakar!

None of his siblings answered his summons. They'd all been scattered, tumbled through time.

Ramu's anchor held and eventually he slowed, but the kaleidoscope remained. Wherever the working had cast him lay between the bindings of universes, beyond the collective reality, into a where/when unbound by agreement, without the shared solidity birthed of mankind's unified concept of time and space.

This was an ingenious working, elaborate and well structured. An inventive intellect had devised it, one that well understood fifth strand immortals and their native shields. Such patterns lay far beyond the ken of Viernan hal'Jaitar.

Balaji…?

Jaya…?

Náiir…?

Rhakar…?

Ramu cast harpoon thoughts through the aether of space/time in search of his siblings' minds. While those hooks sailed forth, he grabbed hold of the taut line of his time anchor and began dragging himself back along it.

But he knew already that he hadn't cast his anchor soon enough. The moment of their departure was too far behind them now. Without an anchor in that moment, they would never regain it.

Perhaps one of his siblings had realized sooner what had occurred and anchored themselves closer to the moment. He didn't hold out much hope for this.

Eventually their minds would find each other. *Eventually* had many interpretations.

Ramu kept hauling on his line.

※

Nassar abin'Ahram stood beneath an awning along with several other commanders, the Consul Viernan hal'Jaitar and Prince Radov, watching in wonder, watching in horror, as the Mage's Sundragons flew through the billowing smoke of battle and abruptly vanished, ripped from the aether in five dark swirls, as if sucked into a vortex.

"Ha! I knew it would work!" Radov threw down his glass in a triumphant smashing of crystal. He immediately called for another one. "I told you it would work, Viernan."

"My prince is ever wise," drawled Viernan hal'Jaitar. He looked to the commander beside him. "I counted five dragons. You?"

"There may have been five of them before they vanished, Consul."

Viernan looked to Nassar. "How many dragons did your eyes count, Nassar abin'Ahram?"

"Five, my lord."

Viernan turned his gaze back to the battle. "Five." His dark eyes tightened. "Five, indeed."

"Viernan, what are you waiting for?" Radov threw back the entire glass of absinthe and then choked through a wheezing exhale, "Call out the other things." He extended his glass to his steward to be refilled while still partially bent over.

Something that might've passed for emotion made a brief appearance within the consul's frown. Then he snapped his fingers to one of his waiting Shamshir'im, and the man bolted off like all the demons of thirteen hells were chasing him.

"The other things…" Nassar heard himself murmur. He hadn't meant to say it out loud, but the dread coursing through him had forced the words off his tongue.

He'd seen the 'other things' during yesterday's tour of camp. The Consul kept them corralled like bulls in a warded tent, out of view of the general army as well as sealed off from *elae*'s currents. Nassar had observed them at their milling rest, sluggish flies trapped in a glass jar—curiosities for wanton boys or weapons for wanton princes.

The comment earned him a sharp stare from hal'Jaitar.

Prince Radov turned with unsteady legs and a fixed smile. "Our secret weapons, Commander. They'll be inside the oasis in a matter of minutes. Watch. You'll see."

Nassar would watch, but he very much doubted that he would enjoy what he saw.

❖

Farid al Abdul-Basir, Prince of the Akkad, gripped his saddle with his knees and spared a look over his shoulder. The wind churned by his speeding horse turned the scarf from his turban into a whip. He absently secured the trailing end across his face while his eyes searched the walls.

Horns were blaring through the oasis, bursts of communication passing from one unit to another, warning of incursion, summoning reinforcements. They told their story of the battle.

The currents told a different one. And whatever was coming towards them, it had the currents in a roiling fury.

Farid turned forward again and held their course towards the western gate. Beside him, Trell's king father clung to his horse. He looked a bit uncertain in the saddle, but Farid found no uncertainty in his gaze. As they raced west, Farid felt Fate racing with them.

The horses ran into a tunnel beneath a wall and they plunged into darkness. That's when Fate struck them a blow.

Farid drew back hard on his reins, forcing his mount and Gydryn's to come to a skidding, clattering halt on the sandstone-paved road. In the bright daylight beyond the tunnel's crescent, men were fighting.

But *what* were they fighting? Whatever it was, *elae's* currents avoided the thing in choppy ridges of revulsion.

Even as Farid watched, the black-skinned creature smashed in a man's skull, kicked another into the air to land out of Farid's view, and crushed a third's windpipe in its fist.

"Shade and darkness!" Gydryn swore.

Farid bit back a curse of his own and urged them on. They stormed out of the tunnel, careened around the creature as it was battling two soldiers, and stormed down a promenade. Around the oasis, more black things were dropping from the walls. Men were fighting atop the ramparts, others in the city streets, but the bulk of his father's forces were arrayed to the east.

Had the eastern attack simply been a diversion while the real attack came from the rear? And where were the Sundragons?

Long before they reached the west gate, Farid feared they would find the way blocked. True to his suspicions, the unit that had been intended to ride as Gydryn's honor guard were now all involved in fending off two of the creatures. Farid watched a third one scale the wall with its bare hands and then launch itself into the clump of fighting men, taking several of his father's soldiers down beneath it.

This then was how the monsters had gotten inside the walls—they'd simply dug their hands into the sandstone!

Farid flung a look into the skies. By the Seventeen—*where* were the Sundragons?

He bit back another curse and turned to Gydryn. "I can't get you out this way." He might not be able to get him out at all. But could he get him somewhere safe?

Would anywhere be safe?

"Back to the palace!"

Farid spun his horse around and stormed back the way they'd come. His father's elite guard were protecting the palace. They wore *elae*-enhanced armor crafted by the Mage and carried Merdanti blades. If they couldn't hold these creatures off, no one could.

Their flight drew the gaze of a pair of the monsters, and they broke away to chase them. He did curse then. Perhaps the gods would forgive him this one indiscretion, under the circumstances. He drew his sword and urged his horse faster.

They barreled through the center of the soldiers fighting near the tunnel. Farid leaned in his stirrup and made a blow for the creature in their midst. His strike took a chunk out of the creature's neck, but it felt like he'd slammed his blade against a rock. The blow reverberated all the way into his shoulder.

A glance back just before they dove into the tunnel showed that at least the monster was down—his father's men were chopping at it like boys with hatchets—but the other two demons were still chasing him.

Out of the tunnel, Farid turned them onto the main boulevard and gave his horse its head. The animal needed no encouraging to lengthen its gait. Doubtless it was as aware of the evil things chasing them as Farid was. The king proved more able than he appeared and kept his horse apace with Farid's.

The palace walls had just come into view when Farid heard the horns. So the damnable things had gotten to the palace ahead of him. He said a quick prayer for his father and struck left, making for the harem gate.

It was open—abandoned—and they clattered through unimpeded. The things were *still* chasing them.

Inanna give us wings!

They sped the horses across a lawn, clumps of grass flying in their wake, and through a narrow archway into a walled garden where tall trees shaded a sacred spring. Farid spun his own mount around to face the things coming after them.

The first bolted through the gate and took a running leap. Farid kneed his war-trained horse sideways, and the demon speared through the grass, churning a furrow of dark earth. It rolled back to its feet and came at him again.

Farid laid it flat with a blow to its head. But before he could recover in the saddle, a force like a falling boulder rammed into him, something hard struck his head, and he tumbled from his horse, blinded by pain's black and debilitating veil.

❖

Gydryn watched the black-fleshed creatures come swarming over Raku's walls and experienced a sickening dread. Radov had truly made a pact with darkness, for who else but the Demon Lord could've raised such things out of the ashes of men?

Farid struck down a creature as they flew through a melee, wielding his Merdanti sword—black-bladed in a gold hilt—and leaning half-out of his saddle to do it. They put some distance between them after that, but Gydryn wondered if anywhere would be safe from the creatures. Beyond the two chasing them, many more were scrambling, fighting, running atop the walls. It was like the oasis had become infested with ants—if ants possessed the strength of beasts.

And when not engaging Akkadian soldiers or Converted, the demons made dark streaks in the same direction as Farid, heading for the palace.

Horns sounded just as he and the prince sped beneath an arch into a walled garden, with the first of the creatures fast on their heels. Farid leaned in his saddle and laid the demon flat, but he'd barely recovered before the second foul thing was upon him. They both tumbled to the ground, with the Akkadian prince landing beneath the demon and far from his sword.

Gydryn finally overcame incredulity to find his anger. Before he knew himself, he was off his horse and had the prince's blade in both hands. He hadn't counted on it being so heavy, though. It took everything he had to lift it over his head. Gravity gave him a needed assist as he brought it down on the back of the demon's head, just as the creature was clawing for the prince's throat.

A dull crack signaled the demon's end, and it toppled to one side. They didn't bleed, these things, but only oozed an unwholesome, tarry sludge.

The weight of Farid's descending blade pulled Gydryn down onto one knee. The king braced himself against the hilt and bent to the prince. "Farid?" He shook him hard.

The prince roused with a startled inhalation. Then he saw Gydryn and blew out his breath. "Your Majesty." He quickly sat up. "Are you injured?"

"Only my pride."

The prince's dark eyes fixed on his Merdanti weapon lodged in the earth. "You used my blade to kill that creature?"

Gydryn gave a sort of wince. He hadn't thought himself so infirm as to barely be able to lift a sword.

The ghost of a smile touched Farid's lips. "This is a sentient blade, Your Majesty. It wakens to a flow of *elae*. Beneath the lifeforce, it feels an extension of my own arm, but without it? It's a wonder you managed to lift it at all."

"Yes, that's what I was thinking."

They each rose. Farid sheathed his blade and frowned at the demon. "But without it, I doubt you'd have made a dent in whatever this thing is." He cast a troubled gaze over his shoulder to the pool behind them, where the shadows of deep water reflected the two tall jade pillars standing at the center. "This is a sacred place." His dark eyes darted to the king and away again, betraying conflict in their cast. "I cannot decide if Jai'Gar spared us here, or if we've offended Him by killing such a thing as this before His sacred spring."

Gydryn didn't believe in a god who would care one way or another what men did in front of a pool of water. "You're familiar with the concept of acting without asking and begging forgiveness later, Prince Farid?"

The prince looked gravely to him by way of his answer.

Gydryn nodded to the dead thing that had once clearly been a man. "This is one of those times when it seems appropriate."

Farid's brow furrowed deeply at this.

That's when the creature Farid had first laid out pushed up on one arm and gave a ratcheting cry to the heavens.

Raine's truth, hearing that clattering demon-call sent a chill coursing through Gydryn.

Farid launched towards the thing and took its head off with slash of his blade, but not before that call had sent its echo ricocheting through the cloisters. They had time in their locking of gazes to imagine the worst potential the next few minutes could present to them, and then more of the creatures were dropping from the walls.

Farid put himself between Gydryn and the oncoming demons.

Gydryn placed a hand on his shoulder. "If my sons display half your courage, Prince Farid, I will die a proud father."

The prince spared a tight glance for him. "I would we both survive this day, Your Majesty." He glanced heavenward, as if seeking favor of the gods, or perhaps seeking the Sundragons, who were conspicuously absent.

Gydryn drew his sword. His blade might do no more than irritate the creatures, but that wouldn't stop him from using it while strength remained in his limbs. "I may not be of much help to you, Farid, but I'll keep them off your back. You have my word."

Farid gave him a grim nod. Then the creatures were upon them, and no more words mattered.

Gydryn swung for the first demon's head. It veered back, and the tip of his blade skittered across its cheekbone, leaving a faint tracing, as of stone scraped across stone. So mortal weapons *would* mark them, just not grievously.

Farid had more luck, being possessed both of youthful vigor and a Merdanti blade. He felled his first monster as Gydryn was parrying another swing from the villain accosting him. It beat at him with bare hands, trying to get to his flesh, his neck, anything it could rip asunder, and if he gave those black fingers a chance to close around his blade, they would try to rip it out of his hands.

Gydryn pounded at the thing determinedly, but the creatures quickly had them backed up against the edge of the deep pool. There were two on the ground now but many more trying to get past their swords. It was all the king could do to hold the monsters back.

Behind him, the towering jade Pillars of Jai'Gar cast colorful shadows on the water. Gydryn had hardly given the desert gods a second thought until Trell declared himself blessed of one. Now, as he battled before the sacred pillars, said to be Jai'Gar's eyes into the world, Gydryn admitted a willingness to pray to all the Seventeen if they'd only provide some divine intervention.

The sounds of running feet rebounded from the arcade bordering the garden, and then a shout. Gydryn felt a twinge of hope that guards were coming to their aid, but then a troop of harried Converted rushed into the garden. They all seemed to spot Farid at the same time—or at least to spot his black-bladed Merdanti sword—and poured towards him in a wave.

The demons turned from Gydryn and Farid, who had not made soft targets of themselves, and rushed the Converted like rampaging bulls.

Farid stormed after them in pursuit. Gydryn was twenty years and a breath slower.

In moments it became a bloodbath.

Gydryn and Farid shifted from defending one to defending many. If the king's blade could only drive them back, at least he kept them off the few behind him, many of whom were already wounded. But for those he protected, just as many he could not. He fought within a chaos unlike any battle of his days. Betimes the creatures stole a blade and slashed at a man until they became drenched in his bits. Other demons simply tore and shredded with clawed fingers, ripping flesh and limbs. Men tumbled into the pool, staining its waters.

Farid's was the only blade capable of truly harming the things, though Gydryn had learned that with a well-placed blow he could at least fell them for the space of a few breaths. But Farid fought as though every man there was his responsibility. Gydryn could see this in his gaze, in the tension of his jaw, in the way he swung his sword and drove himself after every creature as if personally offended by the aberration of its existence.

And the king watched helplessly, in the way one knows a sort of prescience when past experience crosses present events, as Farid extended himself across danger's lip.

The prince beat one of the creatures back until the two of them moved out of the scrabbling fray, towards the pool. The moment Farid's back became an open target, two demons abandoned their victims and jumped on him.

Gydryn choked on urgency as he rushed to the prince's aid, bashing through anything in his path, even *leaping* the fallen to reach the prince before the creatures ripped him apart. He rammed his shoulder into one of the monsters and it tumbled in a tangle with him. Gydryn got out from beneath it, but the demon grabbed his leg and then clawed its way up his back. Bloody fingers slashed for his throat.

The king felt wet warmth pouring down his chest. Stars overcame his vision, dizziness his balance, and he tumbled limply into the pool.

SEVENTY-ONE

"They say Cephrael could feel the Balance shifting. It would pull His gaze towards man or beast, towards those who were causing the disturbance. A rare gift."

–Excerpted from *Genesis Legends,
Tales from the Before*

THE PATCH OF darkness spreading through Sinárr's universe expanded until it blocked most of Tanis's vision. Then another Warlock emerged.

His muscular torso shone as though an artist had painted him in gold foil, while liquid-dark pants draped his legs. He stepped into Sinárr's universe trailing an expanse of velvet wings. As he approached across Sinárr's bridge, his shoulder-length raven hair shed flinty sparks.

"Rafael, I bid thee welcome." Sinárr bowed low to him.

"Sinárr." Rafael stepped into a bent knee and bowed in return. His wings flared behind him, blocking out a swath of stars and raining silvery *deyjiin*. Tanis had never seen anyone so impressively intimidating.

Rafael straightened, and his wings folded into a cloak behind him as he approached. "I'm pleased by your summons." His striking features emitted a golden radiance beneath his dark eyebrows and tousled hair. A round red crystal glowed between his brows. "Though I confess a slight confusion." He shifted void-black eyes between Sinárr and Tanis.

Tanis cleared his throat. "That would be my fault, sir. I summoned you without understanding what I was doing. Please accept my humblest apologies for troubling you."

"*You* summoned me?" Rafael studied Tanis more intently. "Ah...but I've seen *you* in another's thoughts of late." He directed a telling glance towards Sinárr, as if delighting in some dark entertainment. "Many mysteries become newly clear to me."

"Undoubtedly, Rafael."

Rafael looked Tanis potently up and down. The feel of the Warlock's hypnotic gaze licking over him soon had all the hairs on Tanis's body standing on end. He fought the inclination to hide behind Sinárr.

One corner of Rafael's mouth curled upwards, hinting at a formidable interest. "What name am I meant to assign to this alluring creature, Sinárr?"

Sinárr placed a hand on Tanis's shoulder. "Rafael, may I present Tanis to you."

Tanis very much misliked the phrasing of that introduction.

Rafael's obsidian eyes glinted with an alluring luster; unfortunately, Tanis couldn't be sure that he wasn't as unnervingly captivated by Rafael as the Warlock was by him. The lad suddenly recalled the stories from the Before, which spoke of Warlocks having mesmerizing power over mortals—frightening stories, where men committed atrocious act against themselves or each other to entertain their Warlock masters.

Upon their first meeting, Sinárr had magnetized Tanis's interest in a way that had frightened and disturbed the lad. Tanis had thought the experience singular to Sinárr. Now, seeing Rafael, he reconsidered that assessment.

Rafael touched a finger of crackled gold beneath Tanis's chin and looked deeply into his eyes, studying him through the magnifying glass of his curiosity. "*You* permeated Pelas's thoughts like you now permeate Sinárr's." He arched a raven brow with dangerous fascination. "Explain this to me if you will…Tanis."

Tanis glanced to Sinárr. Knowing the Warlock as he did, he could tell that complicated rules of etiquette were governing this meeting—Sinárr was practically radiating solicitude—but Tanis understood little of the politics of Warlocks.

He dropped his gaze to his hands. "Sinárr and I are bound, sir."

"*Bound*." Rafael turned a narrow stare on Sinárr. "A concubine?"

"The binding is mutual, Rafael."

Rafael reared back with a flaring pulse of his wings. *Deyjiin* rained from them in a sparkling veil. "You tell me this impossibility without prevarication?" His obsidian gaze speared Sinárr. "You worked a mutual binding with a child of Light?"

"Rafael, it is so."

Rafael swung back to Tanis and studied him twice as intently as before. His hair sparkled with dark embers, and his wings continued dripping *deyjiin*. A threatening energy coalesced around him. "And you…Tanis," something in the way Rafael said his name made Tanis want to crawl under a couch, "what is your relationship with Pelasommáyurek?"

Tanis sensed he was standing on very dangerous ground indeed. He had to work a little moisture back into his mouth. "We worked the Unbreakable Bond, sir."

Again the wings flapped their disbelief, raining a starfall of *deyjiin*. Rafael grabbed Tanis's arm and pulled him close. "Pelasommáyurek bound himself to *you*?"

Tanis was feeling bombarded by confusing parallels of power—Sinárr's, Rafael's, his own energies, perhaps—he didn't understand the cause, but he felt bounced and jarred and torn in multiple directions, as if buffeted by a damaging wind.

Rafael lifted his darkling gaze to Sinárr. "I would speak more of these matters. May I host you both?"

Please, no!

Sinárr bowed his head. "We would be honored, Rafael."

Whereupon Tanis felt a nudging at his mind and became aware suddenly of Rafael's starpoints, as if the Warlock had just turned up the lamps to their fullest intensity.

Sinárr wrapped his mind protectively around Tanis and directed him in duplicating Rafael's starpoints, a master painter guiding an apprentice's hand. Tanis knew how to do this on his own, yet he was grateful for Sinárr's assistance, because something in the action…again, he perceived a definite etiquette involved.

He sensed it in Rafael's invitation, in Sinárr's modest response, in the way they approximated each other's starpoints with amity, tiptoeing with whisper touches. The interchange reminded Tanis of the propositions occurring on the fringes of a court ball, a polite flirtation of advance and withdrawal.

Yet he perceived so much more surrounding these intricacies also, for he understood that these were vital details which differentiated an action that was essentially the same whether offered in amity or aggression. More interesting still was recognizing an intimacy in this duplication, as if Rafael had offered a coveted invitation to a private room, one refused at grave peril. They handled one another's starpoints with kid gloves…and their universes combined.

Existential planes shifted.

Tanis felt a nearly toppling sense of imbalance.

He blinked, and the world had changed.

Now they stood among the brightly colored whorls of a nebula so vast it defied description. An obsidian glass bridge extended away into clouds studded with stars, worlds unto themselves, but Rafael directed them towards a staircase as wide as a river, which descended an incomprehensible length through star-clouds painted in gossamer hues.

As they walked, Rafael placed a hand on Tanis's shoulder, oozing power with his touch, guiding the lad possessively to his side. Tanis shot a rather desperate look at Sinárr, but the Warlock merely nodded for him to go with Rafael.

What if I don't want *to go with Rafael?* Tanis cast Sinárr a private plea.

You invited him, Tanis. Sinárr sounded less irritated now, though a faint note of reprimand still underscored his tone, as that of a possessive friend suddenly forced to share his intimate meal with many unwelcome others. Tanis was fairly sure Sinárr thought of him as the meal more than the friend.

You realize I didn't mean *to summon Rafael, right?*

And yet you did. These are the consequences you must bear. Warlocks don't treat one another rudely. It simply is not done.

Tanis cast a grumbling look over his shoulder. *Punishment doesn't seem beyond you, though.*

"Tanis, Tanis..." Rafael spoke his name as if trying to dissect its many flavors. "Imagine my surprise at learning that you summoned me—*you*, a child of Light, molding Shadow as though *elae*, duplicating my own starpoints?" His power called to Tanis differently than Sinárr's, but no less coercively, and his obsidian gaze sparkled with beguiling invitation, compelling Tanis to partake of its dangerous darkness.

Tanis didn't think looking deeply into Rafael's eyes would be at all a good idea. He observed the impossible starscape surrounding them instead. "I hope I didn't offend you, sir."

"On the contrary, my curiosity knows no bounds." Rafael shifted his wings behind him in a whisper of velvet fluttering that shed *deyjiin* in a chill mist. A kiss of burning ice laced across Tanis's cheek. "And what did you think of my tree city of Taerenhal?"

Tanis recalled Sinárr's lecture on the importance of admiration. "I thought it a wondrous work, sir."

A half-smile tugged at Rafael's mouth. "I see Sinárr has been instructing you in our ways...how to charm a Warlock and win his benevolence."

The lad managed an uncomfortable swallow. "I rather think it's the other way around, sir." He had no doubt that Rafael was trying to charm him and likely would've already had him in thrall if not for the protection of Sinárr's binding.

Rafael turned forward again wearing that hint of a smile. He was undeniably bewitching and outrageously intimidating. Tanis didn't wonder that Pelas had made friends with him.

As if reading of his thoughts—and perhaps he had, for they were in *his* universe after all—Rafael posed, "Pelasommáyurek…" he arched a brow in fey challenge, "you know him well?"

Tanis was starting to wonder if Rafael might perceive him as a rival for Pelas's affections. He might not have understood the complicated etiquette of Warlocks, but it didn't take a genius to observe how jealously possessive they were. "I haven't known him long, sir…not nearly so long as you have."

Rafael clasped hands behind his back and turned an unreadable look off into the vista.

They floated on together—there was no other way of describing the motion of their progress, for Tanis felt none of gravity's pull, yet *some* force assuredly held their feet to the dark-glass steps—with Rafael's wings flowing once more as a cloak behind them.

Tanis watched the Warlock striding along, a god strolling within the universe of his own creation, and saw himself in Rafael's eyes—a mortal Adept boy, yet one that had somehow claimed the heart of an immortal who Rafael himself desired… It was like one of those theatrical Cyrenaic dramas that pitted mortals against their gods, the kind of play that never ended well for the mortal.

"I admit my bemusement at learning that Pelas bound himself to you." Rafael's tone implied more than bemusement; more like complete bewilderment.

Tanis felt the world shifting beneath him again, hinting of portentous change. He gave the Warlock a wan smile. "I'm still coming to grips with it myself, sir."

Rafael frowned. "I sense an earnest candor beneath this confession, yet my impression was that your binding with Pelas was mutual. Did you not bind yourself to him in the same working? Why, if you were so uncertain of him?"

Tanis rubbed at one eye. "It seemed like the right thing to do at the time."

Rafael drew back with a faint flutter of wings. "That's quite a risk to take with your eternity, mortal child." He looked him over speculatively. "And now what is your view of this decision?"

"Now…" Tanis exhaled a slow breath, "now I'm sure of it."

Rafael paused mid-stride to observe him. Then he lifted his gaze to Sinárr, who was just coming up on Tanis's other side. "However did you come across this boy, Sinárr?"

"Shailabanáchtran had him in hand, a lure for his brother."

"Shailabanáchtran." Rafael's tone made the name sound unclean. His gaze narrowed dangerously. "Pelas would've been in a dire crisis if I hadn't come to his aid—after *you* coincided his starpoints, Sinárr. I assume to retrieve your treasured Tanis here."

"Whenever have you not come to Pelas's aid, Rafael?"

Dark flames shot through Rafael's hair, shedding bright embers into the firmament, as with sparks in the smoke tumbling upwards from a fire. He leaned closer to Sinárr with his wings rising threateningly behind him. "Do you know what Shailabanáchtran did to his brother after you coincided Pelas's starpoints?"

Sinárr shook his head slightly, keen to Rafael's ire. "He didn't discuss his intentions with me."

Rafael's aggressively shivering wings riled *deyjiin* into massive silver clouds. "He left Pelas prey to a clutch of revenants."

Sinárr drew back. "I had no idea—"

"That your ally would stoop so low?"

Sinárr's gaze darkened to a smoldering consideration. "We are allies no longer, Rafael. My bond with Tanis makes any pact with Shailabanáchtran unnecessary."

Rafael's wings abruptly calmed. "That is well," he turned away, "for I find the offense unforgivable."

The world shifted again.

Suddenly Tanis stood in a palace of darkly translucent glass floating within a nebula. He looked down to the singularly unnerving experience of watching gaseous clouds of every imaginable color churning beneath his feet, stars shifting in and out of view with the shifting vapors, and of realizing that he was looking upon entire *worlds*, yet so distant as to seem as pearls, or pebbles, or naught but specks of glittering dust.

Tanis understood better of Warlocks in that moment. Their courtship of admiration involved elaborate displays of *imagination*. The result was world upon world, each more ingenious and inventive than the last.

Sinárr clasped hands behind his back and cast an admiring gaze around the palace. Its walls and vaulted ceiling held just enough solidity to discern their elegant shape without blocking the view of the immense star-clouds surrounding them. "You have outdone yourself, Rafael."

In the shift from stairway to palace, Rafael's wings had become a velvet cloak again. It draped long now from his gilded shoulders and trailed across the floor. "I thank you graciously, Sinárr."

Tanis added, "My admiration knows no bounds, sir." It seemed obvious that he'd never seen its like, so he didn't say this, though he certainly thought it.

Rafael arched a brow. "He speaks on two planes, this one, as a zanthyr's duplicitous speech, yet with earnest intent."

"Tanis speaks with wisdom beyond his years, Rafael. You needn't hold it against him."

"If I were to hold anything against your Tanis, Sinárr, wisdom it would not be." Rafael settled Tanis an unnerving smile, then led away through an arcade of arches, out onto a terrace formed of the same darkly translucent glass.

Sinárr held a hand for Tanis to lead the way.

The lad pushed his feet into motion after Rafael and his gaze in a protest towards Sinárr. *You're enjoying this far too much.*

Sinárr clasped hands behind his back. *I admit a certain satisfaction in this instructive lesson, Tanis-mine.*

Instructive in what—how petulant you can be about sharing me?

Sinárr gave a mental chuckle. *It is my hope you will gain more yet than this understanding alone.*

Beyond the terrace, an extravagant staircase led down to a fountain spewing diamond waters, only…the gleaming droplets were too viscous for water; more like melted glass. And beyond the huge fountain, the churning rose-violet-blue-green nebula blocked the starscape like the imposing mountains of the Navárrel.

Surreal did not begin to describe it.

"A wielder is limited by what he can envision." Rafael appeared beside Tanis and extended a goblet filled with a darkly sparkling drink—though his gaze was more darkly alluring still. "Is that not the saying in your Alorin?"

The liquid whispered effervescently in Tanis's thoughts, promising experiences unimagined. Rafael's gaze promised more.

Sinárr took the drink out of Rafael's hand, breaking the momentary enchantment. Tanis sucked in a relieved breath.

"Tanis isn't ready for your heady enthrallment, Rafael." Sinárr held up the cup in gratitude and then drank deeply of it. His golden eyes shone more brightly thereafter.

Rafael smiled wryly while trailing a liquid gaze across Tanis. "He seemed desirous enough."

"As if you gave him any choice."

Rafael turned his smile on Sinárr. "As much choice as you likely gave the lad in binding with you." He seated himself in a chair.

Sinárr took a chair across from the other Warlock. "We needn't argue over which of us is more humane, Rafael. You will always win that debate."

"That's encouraging," Tanis muttered.

Rafael's dark eyes danced between them. "The lad is wondering now if he bound himself to the right Warlock. Perhaps he should bind with me also, that he might make a more informed decision."

Tanis perceived a terrifying invitation in this offer. He felt suddenly like the Warlocks had declared open season on his affections—though surely Rafael's only interest in binding with him was to become bound to Pelas by extension.

"I think three immortals is my limit, sir." Tanis sank down on a chair between the two of them, wondering if he should've accepted that drink.

"*Three?*" Rafael turned a portentous stare upon Sinárr.

Who gave a resigned sigh. "There is a zanthyr as well."

Rafael clapped a hand to his cheek and fell back to regard Tanis with intense speculation. "Malorin'athgul, zanthyr, *Warlock*...each bound to you, and by extension your cause, whatever it may be..."

Sinárr nodded to the edge on his tone, demanding answer, as much as to his perception. "In return for Tanis's binding, I've promised to protect the Realms of Light."

Rafael's eyes widened upon Tanis. "You *are* a portentous youth." He studied him for a moment longer before aiming a considering look at Sinárr. "Speaking of joined realms, do you have recent cognizance of Wylde?"

"I have not seen it since its genus, when Baelfeir invited my involvement and I declined."

"As did I, suspecting his motives, but many did not, as you know."

Hearing the true name for the Demon Lord Belloth spoken with camaraderie made all the hairs stand up on the back of Tanis's neck. That sense of unbalance exponentially worsened. Tanis croaked out, "Baelfeir, sir?"

"There are two camps among us, Tanis-mine." Sinárr traced the arm of his glass chair with a forefinger while a slight furrow narrowed his ebony brows. "Rafael and I have always shared the view that a Warlock should act responsibly for his creations—that is, when they no longer claim his interest or admiration, he should efface them back into the aether. But there are those among our kind who, when bored with it, simply abandon a thing they've given life to. Sometimes such worlds have gained admiration from other Warlocks, which imparts a permanence, or even a solidity, to them; yet they discard those creations without care to what happens to them thereafter. You might say that Baelfeir heads this other camp."

Rafael's dark hair became as riotous flames. "His games darken the aether." Coming from a Warlock of Shadow, this was an ominous accusation indeed.

Tanis was starting to feel a little queasy from the way the world had started pitching—to the left, to the right, forward and back, as if he was pinned upon a spinning top that was winding itself unevenly down. "What games might these be, sir?"

Rafael suddenly speared a look at him—

And Tanis found himself seated with the Warlocks at a dark glass table in the center of a rotunda. Obsidian columns soared in a circle around them, so tall as to appear to be holding up the nebula's shifting, striated clouds.

"Now, Tanis," Rafael's gaze sent hooks of inquiry into the lad's mind to snare the thoughts he sought, while a formidable smile reeled them all to the surface, "what is this you keep doing to my floors?"

Tanis realized that his perceptions must be impinging on Rafael's universe; the Warlock was simply preventing the disruption from actually altering the space.

Rafael reached for a decanter of crystalline liquid. "This time, I think you would do well to imbibe my offering, Tanis."

Tanis shot a rather desperate look at Sinárr.

Sinárr merely nodded accommodatingly. "As you will, Rafael."

Rafael pushed a goblet over to Tanis, then clasped hands in his lap and observed him with dark fascination.

Tanis felt suddenly like a penned prisoner waiting for some dangerous predator to be released while spectators looked on with riveted attention. The lad lifted the goblet like the prisoner might take up his uncertain spear. Then he cast a defeated look between the two immortals and drank the contents.

The fluid had about as much flavor as liquid light, but *sensation* permeated it. One swallow wakened senses Tanis didn't know he could experience, and in parts of him he'd hardly ever noticed before. Just one sip left him flushing and embarrassed—for as Rafael had perceived Tanis's feelings of imbalance, so would he *certainly* have shared in his experience of that drink.

Rafael was eyeing him with veiled amusement.

Tanis quickly set down the goblet again and lifted bright eyes—the heat behind them made them feel like burning lamps—and a flushed expression to Rafael. "I'm sorry about tilting the floors, sir."

The Warlock gave him a wry smile. "I'm merely impressed you can manipulate Shadow. No mortal has proven capable in the past."

"The boy just intuits it," Sinárr remarked.

Rafael pushed the goblet insistently back towards Tanis. "But *why* are you tilting my floors?"

That one swallow was still stirring uniquely unsettling sensations; Tanis couldn't imagine taking another draught of it. "I have feelings I can't explain, sir," much like what the drink was doing to him, only less disturbing, "a sort of unbalanced, tipping sensation—as you perceived—that sometimes inclines in a certain direction," Tanis managed a swallow against the effervescence in his stomach, "...or not."

"Inclines you in a direction towards...?"

The lad lifted a frown to Rafael. "Action, I suppose? Choices. It's rather ambiguous, this feeling."

"What kinds of choices?"

Inexplicable ones, Tanis thought, recalling how the perception had first led him to escape from Sinárr and then inclined him to bind with him.

Rafael must've perceived this thought, for he cast a grin across the table at the other Warlock. "So this perception seems to be leading you true, Tanis?"

"I'm not sure what you mean by *true*, sir, but it's quite impossible to ignore, in any case."

"I imagine not, what with so many immortals bound to your path." Rafael settled his void-black eyes on Sinárr. "Do you perceive it as I do?"

Sinárr held his gaze. "That Tanis senses the cosmic Balance? It seems rather clear."

Tanis didn't see how this was at all clear.

Rafael tapped a finger on his table while his gaze considered Tanis with new ardor. "You are quite the treasure."

"I wouldn't bind myself to the Realms of Light merely for the experience of it, Rafael. That's your and Pelasommáyurek's intrigue."

Tanis was still stuck on their earlier comment. "But...why do you think I'm perceiving the cosmic...Balance?" He almost couldn't get the word out, the statement seemed so improbable.

"It follows, Tanis." Rafael waggled a finger at his glass to indicate he should drink again. "Your *angiel* Cephrael was bound to each of the immortal races, an act which wakened his perception to the cosmos." He looked back to Sinárr. "I would still like to know which of us bound himself to the *angiel*. My money, as they say, is on Persephus, though he won't admit it to me."

Tanis stammered, "I-I thought that was just a myth." The idea made him highly uncomfortable—probably since he was haplessly on his way towards accomplishing the same. "Could—"

Rafael raised a finger to halt him. "Not another word," and he pointed to the glowing goblet.

Tanis reluctantly took another swallow of the drink. He admitted it did slightly settle that sense of imbalance, but it *unsettled* so many other feelings that he wasn't sure it was worth it.

He set down the goblet with his face flushing hotly and...other parts also…not quite able to look Rafael in the eye. "That can't be true, can it?" He turned between Rafael and Sinárr. "About Cephrael?"

"Why wouldn't it be?" Rafael asked.

"There are many myths in our world that aren't true, sir."

"Is that a fact?" Rafael leaned towards him with a meaningful smile. "How do you know?"

Tanis drew back in his chair as if pressed there by Rafael's challenge. He felt like he often did after the zanthyr had ripped to shreds one of his more illogical conclusions.

"What myths in your world are untrue?" Rafael arched a brow. "Myths of *us*?" He sat back again and waved vaguely. "I grant, some of Baelfeir's stories have become exaggerated, which thrills him no end and fuels his tiresome boasting—for instance, I have no knowledge of his ever building a temple from the skulls of kidnapped children, or keeping fifty human virgins chained to his loins."

"Twenty at most," Sinárr muttered disagreeably.

"Your Alorin was always his preferred world." Rafael tapped a finger absently on the tabletop, his gaze narrowed in recollection. "He found Alorin's children most easily bound to his will. It was his favorite game, seeing how many mortal minds he could control at once."

Talk of the Demon Lord made Tanis feel off-kilter again. He just wished he could figure out in which direction Balance wanted him to lean—if in fact it was Balance pushing him hither and yon.

Rafael suddenly speared another look at him. "Now that *is* intriguing." He shifted in his chair to better study him. "In what direction is the floor leaning this time, Tanis?"

Tanis shook his head, feeling terribly queasy. "It happens every time you mention…the Demon Lord."

"Baelfeir." Sitting back again, Rafael laid one hand, palm-up, on the arm of his chair and curled his fingers in and out, reminiscent of a cat flaring and sheathing its claws. He lifted a dangerous gaze to Tanis. "Warlocks have no society, such as it is, yet Baelfeir has made a game of forming one. He gathered to him—you might call them a family of sorts, a congregation…a collection. They've merged universes and built worlds in concert with one another—something that has never before been done. They call this conglomeration Wylde." He shifted a voluminous gaze to Sinárr. "But once their interest in a world is lost, they abandon it, leaving revenants behind to muddle the aether."

Sinárr's golden eyes reflected the same indignation that Tanis perceived in Rafael's tone. "How *many* worlds?"

Rafael's gaze tightened. "Beyond counting."

Tanis felt the floor suddenly tipping him violently—and it was finally leaning in one obvious direction.

"Sir?" His voice sounded a little weak against his suddenly pounding heart, frail compared to the sense of momentous portent gripping his chest. "Could we...go there?" He looked entreatingly to Sinárr. "Now?"

SEVENTY-TWO

"Man plans and the gods laugh."

–A popular desert saying

THE NADORI COMMANDER Lazar hal'Hamaadi walked Khor Taran's lower ramparts with a scowl rutting his bearded face and his deep brown eyes surveying the fires in the valley.

Whether distraction or diversion, those fires had to be investigated. He could've done no less in his duty as the fortress commander. And if he was sending his men out into the night, he *had* to send them in force.

Yet the wielder Kifat's words—*warning*—still rankled. Ever since arriving at the fortress, the untrustworthy man had asserted his superiority, though what power he claimed flowed down a different channel of command than Lazar's own.

Nadori military commanders were not subject to orders from the Shamshir'im, but this didn't keep the Shamshir'im from using the commanders in their machinations. This is what was troubling Lazar at that moment. Kifat could be trusted about as far as a weasel in a henhouse, and maybe not even as far as that.

Inanna, Goddess of War, watched over M'Nador's soldiery, but the Shamshir'im walked firmly within the crafty and ill-disposed auspices of Ha'viv the Trickster God. Lazar misliked the whole bloody business Kifat was mixed up in—holding the Dannish soldiers prisoner, especially when Dannym was supposedly M'Nador's ally, and who-knew-what ill dealings with that band of Saldarian refuse.

If not for the fact that the Dannish soldiers had attempted to mutiny, showing their ignoble color, Lazar would've ousted Kifat and the lot of them from his fortress.

Now, as he came in view of the granary where Kifat was holding the King of Dannym's men, Lazar felt that same ill apprehension that always overcame him whenever he went near the place. His own men protested even entering the storehouse, though it was necessary to feed the prisoners and escort them in groups to the privies. But you couldn't be around them and not stare morbidly, what with the way the Northmen moved so unnaturally, like life-size dolls made of soft clay. It was bloody unnerving.

So he didn't begrudge his men their complaints when their turn came for the duty, and he was privately relieved that his own position exempted him from the rotation.

A grey dawn was shedding light into the alley beside the granary as Lazar strolled past, drawing his eye. He expected to see two soldiers at their posts but noticed instead a set of empty steps. His gaze dragged him to a halt while he searched for answers. Eventually he found them in the guise of two dark forms crumpled in the shadow of a wall.

Lazar hissed a curse. So Abdul-Basir's Converted hounds *were* inside his fortress, after all, like rats in the walls!

Well…he knew how to flush vermin into the open.

Lazar ran down the parapet shouting orders to his men.

❖

Trell and Loukas selected an officer for their first attempt to break the spell. Loukas held up the braided silver rope that connected the officer's wrist to the collar at his neck, while Trell held a torch beneath it. White smoke blossomed upwards.

Loukas withdrew from it violently. "*Fethe*," his eyes widened, "it smells like—"

"I know." It smelled like burning blood.

The rope should've caught the flame, but it only molted smoke.

"Try pulling, Loukas."

Loukas strained to tear the rope in two. Trell even pressed the flame directly on it to help him. At last the silver threads started to fray, and the rope burst in a puff of foul-smelling smoke.

Both Trell and Loukas looked to the soldier, but the man's eyes remained glazed.

Grimacing, Loukas waved his hand to clear the air. "Hard to imagine anything smelling worse than this place already does."

Trell let out a slow breath. "Let's try the other rope."

They moved to the soldier's other side and repeated the process. Even after the second rope split, still he merely stared ahead.

Loukas motioned to the band at the officer's wrist and the link of rope that chained him to the man beside him. "We'd best try breaking the link between them."

That link was barely the span of a man's two fists. Trell handed Loukas the torch and took up both men's hands. He held their arms apart, pulling taut the braided rope that connected their wrists. This did not leave much room for error.

Loukas carefully set the flaming torch against the rope chain linking them.

When it started smoking, Trell started pulling their hands in opposite directions. After a strenuous effort and a curse or three, the rope split apart.

An audible snap echoed through the room.

Trell laid the soldiers' arms back down and studied the officer for any sign of life.

Gradually his blue eyes blinked and came into focus. "Wh…what've you done to me?" His voice was hoarse, his consonants clipped in the accent of the north.

"We're here to help." Loukas handed him his canteen, which the officer accepted in a daze. "You've been bewitched."

"Aye—my dreams were dark." He winced as he handed the canteen back to Loukas. His eyes shifted between Loukas and Trell. "Who are you?"

"I'm Loukas n'Abraxis of Avatar, and this man is your own Prince Trell val Lorian, who has just freed you from a wielder's compulsion."

You could see the confusions compounding in the officer's blue eyes. "But…our prince is dead."

"Radov abin Hadorin certainly wanted you to think so." Trell squatted down beside the officer. "I've spent the last five years in the Akkad, protected by the man my father thought was his enemy, when Dannym's true enemies have been masquerading as our allies all along."

The officer stared at him. Meanwhile, the other four men who'd been linked to him began recovering.

The officer studied Trell's face. Then his blue eyes lifted to the sword behind Trell's shoulder, a Kingdom Blade, like his own.

"I'm here to rescue you at the behest of my father," Trell said. "We all fight now for the same cause."

Uncertainty still clouded the officer's brow. He angled a look from Trell's sword down to the rope chains around his wrists. "What is all this?"

Trell cast his gaze to include the other men, who'd roused now and were watching the exchange with cautious eyes. "The ropes you wear held your will in thrall to a Shamshir'im wielder."

The Dannish soldiers exchanged looks at this.

Slowly, the officer nodded. "Aye, I recall it now. The bastards made me watch while my men fell prey to it one by one, until the end, when my own vision went—"

"Dark," one of the men said hollowly.

"Everything just blurred." Another looked around at his mates as if for confirmation of a similar experience. "It all seems an ill dream after that."

One of them asked, "Where are we?"

"The thirteenth level of hell," another said grimly, gazing at the dim sea of unmoving forms.

"Raine's truth," several others grumbled in unison.

"You're at the Fortress of Khor Taran on the border of Abu'Dhan." Trell settled a significant look on all of them. "A *Nadori* fortress. You and the rest of my father's men are the captives of a Shamshir'im wielder sworn to Viernan hal'Jaitar, Dannym's true enemy."

One of the men blew out his breath. "*Daw*, it *must* be Raine's truth. Magic rope and wielders and the ghost of our dead prince—who could possibly make up something so cockeyed?"

"Hold your tongue, Donovan." The officer flashed him a sharp look of warning.

"Cockeyed is a kind way of describing the wrongs you've endured." Trell angled his compassionate gaze to include all five men. "You have my word I will explain more when time permits, but right now, the rest of the men need our help."

The officer regarded him with a deep furrow between his brows. He might've seen thirty name days, if told from the faint lines etching the corners of his blue eyes. A beard hugged his lean jaw. For all he'd been months in captivity, he maintained an air of nobility.

The other men looked to him, clearly waiting to follow his lead. Finally, he seemed to make up his mind and pressed a fist to his heart. "Captain Gideon val Mallonwey at your service, Your Highness."

"And I," said the soldier named Donovan. The rest quickly offered their service as well.

Trell gave them a grateful nod, then shifted his gaze back to Gideon. "Val Mallonwey…" he frowned slightly.

The hint of uncertainty roused once more in Gideon's gaze. "Do you know not my family name?"

Trell shook his head. "For a long time, my memory was lost to me—a result of a truthbinding from Raine D'Lacourte and some very nasty interrogation by a Saldarian mercenary, which I'd rather not recount. It's a long story. But I do recall your name, of course. You're the nephew of Duke val Mallonwey, eldest son of his sister, the Lady Miranda."

The clouds in Gideon's gaze cleared. "Aye, Your Highness."

"Well met, Gideon." Trell held his hand to him.

Gideon clasped wrists with him. "It is my honor, Your Highness." He let Trell pull him to his feet.

As the other men stood, Loukas cast a despairing gaze across the sea of heads. It had taken nearly ten minutes to free those five, and nearly five hundred still needed their ministration. He blew out a forceful breath. "Fiera's fiery hell, this is going to take forever."

❖

"*Fire!*"

Lazar hal'Hamaadi watched with deliberate hard-heartedness as half a dozen fire-flamed crossbow bolts lodged themselves in the granary roof.

"*Fire!*"

Another volley shattered the high windows on their downward flight.

"*Fire!*"

Upon the third fiery volley, Lazar assumed a confident smile. The Akkadian Emir's arrogant dogs would not long stay within the granary once flame started raining down around them. Already Lazar's men were lining up in front of the building waiting for the hounds to emerge, choking and blistered. His men would make short work of teaching them humility.

Khor Taran, Crown of Abu'Dhan. This was *his* fortress. To think of Akkadian hounds invading *Khor Taran*—his impenetrable, undefeated *Khor Taran*? In all of his years there, no force had *ever* breached its walls. The gall of these Converted made his blood boil.

"*Al-Amir?*" One of his subordinate officers moved to speak close—a sure sign he meant to question his orders. "We burn out the dogs, but what of the prisoners?"

Lazar kept a steely gaze leveled on the granary. Smoke was already rising from the roof of the burning structure. "Mutineers. What of them?"

The junior officer dropped his gaze. "But they shall perish—"

"*They* are traitors, and prisoners of the Shamshir'im." He turned the man an uncompromising stare. "Let Kifat spare them if he so—"

The explosion ripped Lazar's words off his tongue.

Nay, it ripped his very breath from his lungs!

He spun to the north. Disbelieving eyes watched as an avalanche of water came raging down the mountain, darkly chalky in the grey dawn. The wave of churning water crashed around the northernmost tower like a storm-maddened sea against a lighthouse, and tumbled on in muddied whorls into the upper fortress, washing away everything in its path—men, wagons, racks of arms. Nothing withstood it.

Lazar was still staring in mute disbelief when the raging water churned down through the stairway tunnels and began flooding the middle fortress. In moments, it would reach the lower fortress and his men.

Lazar shouted orders as he ran.

❖

Within Khor Taran's northernmost tower, a cyclone spun a constant vortex. In the center of this soundless whirlwind, Tannour questioned the wielder Kifat—invisible, protected, isolated from all save Time's countdown towards consequence. The cyclone's walls of spinning air caught and trapped any sound, so no one would hear the wielder's screams.

But at the moment, the wielder's screams were not the issue.

"*What* did you say?" Tannour placed his finger over one of the holes in the hollow needle piercing Kifat's chest. If a captive was reticent to answer his questions, Tannour could play that needle like a pipe, to his captive's acute agony. But in Kifat's case, he was simply impatient.

One black-gloved hand played the needle while the other held Kifat's arching throat, which was vibrating with a moan. Tannour brought his mouth closer to the wielder's ear. "What did you say about Trell val Lorian?"

Kifat's eyes were streaming tears. Air bubbled through his bloodied mouth. "…stopped…all costs…"

Tannour heard dual strains of truth in these answers, chords of duplicity. The wielder was holding something in reserve—a truth, a trick? He couldn't yet say.

'The scales holding application of pain and relief from pain must be carefully weighed. Overabundance of either defeats the interrogator.'

Relief from pain reflected many colors. Tannour found it more effective to layer different kinds of pain upon a baseline torment, rather than to relieve all pain completely, which only bolstered the strong-willed. T'was better the captive understood that pain could always be intensified, such that they came to look upon the first torment as a kindness—sought relief in it, in fact. An interrogator who played the harp-strings of pain with expert fingers made quick work of his duty.

'Men respond to torture with varying resilience. You must learn your captive intimately to know which torments he cannot endure.'

This truth of the path was why expert interrogators spent hours, even days, working over a captive before questioning him. But Tannour didn't have that kind of time. What he did have was certainty that the man caught in the Arch of Submission was a Shamshir'im wielder; thus, everything he said was suspect.

Straightening away from Kifat, Tannour chose another needle, this one designed to stimulate the nerve channels. He felt for the meridian point on the wielder's bleeding chest, near the shoulder—

The earth trembled beneath the tower.

"Too late..." a blood-filled gurgle rasped out of his captive. Kifat choked on his laughter, coughed, sputtered, grinned around bloody teeth, "...*too late*."

Tannour banished his cyclone. Instantly he learned what its reflective walls had prevented him from perceiving—horns of alarm and a rumbling which rapidly grew in strength, casting foreshadows of its truth.

Tannour braced himself with Air for the impact.

The cascading wave smashed into the tower, swarmed around the circumference and continued on. The river of the aqueduct was now dumping directly down into the fortress.

"Goodbye...prince...," Kifat gurgled.

Displaced air confirmed the wielder's boast. The waters were quickly finding channels through the three-tiered fortress. They would continue to build and deepen until the waters spilled over the ramparts and made a fountain for the gods out of the Fortress of Khor Taran.

Tannour clenched his jaw against a rising frustration. All of his skills would be useless in aiding Trell, for water walked no path. Yet to do nothing...

'*Once embarked upon ver'alir, stay the course. There is but one route through.*'

This truth of the path, Tannour had learned agonizingly well.

The Blind Path was less a craving than a hunger, a *knowing* that the path must be fed, and that it fed upon sacrifice. These darker wavelengths which coursed *ver'alir*... Tannour didn't know if they resonated within him because of something native to his construction, or if some resilience in his nature made him capable of withstanding that resonance when others could not. In any case, *ver'alir's* resonance rang an undeniable harmony within his soul, a dark harmony—regretted, even loathed at times—yet as often equally desired; an aching harmony, as the recollection of a haunting melody, beautiful and melancholy, barely remembered from a dream.

Tannour returned his attention to the man gurgling with laughter in front of him. Kifat would not find his next acts nearly so humorous.

Trell flinched away from the shower of glass as much as from the flaming arrow that had caused it. The latter struck the floor in an explosion of sparks an inch from where he was crouched. Already the smoke from the burning roof was clouding the rafters. Trell felt its acrid bite with every inhale.

Elsewhere in the granary, the men were in action. Every able bodied soldier they freed instantly set to freeing others, but many of the king's men still sat in docile wreaths.

Another volley of arrows streaked down through the shattered windows.

Trell finally succeeded in splitting the silver rope he'd been burning through and looked to the soldier beside him. "Get them up." He left the man to attend the task and called for Loukas while making for the front doors. Along the way, he ripped two burning bolts out of the floor by their fletching and tossed them into one of the privies.

Loukas caught up with him halfway to the front. "Trell!"

Trell dodged back from an arrow, and it *thunked* into the wood in front of his foot. He yanked it out of the floor, pitched it into the privy and kept going. "How many soldiers are left, Loukas?"

"A hundred or so."

"And how many are armed?"

"Two score, maybe? I lost count in this confusion."

Trell eyed the rafters—or rather the roiling clouds of black smoke that were entirely consuming the rafters. "We can't wait any longer." He turned a grim look to his friend. "Get the officers and every man with a weapon to the front. Everyone else should arm themselves with anything they can find. Assign as many men as can be spared to the rear of the column to escort the soldiers still under compulsion. The Nadoriin will assuredly be—"

An explosion sounded a powerful concussion.

The ground shook beneath them.

"*Daw*—what was that?" The Dannish officer Gideon straightened out of a near grouping of soldiers, torch in hand.

Trell turned swiftly to Loukas.

Loukas looked wan. "Do you—"

Trell shook his head.

"I should—" he hooked a thumb over his shoulder towards the doors.

Trell gave him a voluminous look of agreement.

Loukas sprinted for the doors.

Trell's every sense was screaming in alarm. "Gideon, get your men to form up ranks, armed officers to the front."

"Soldiers of Dannym, form up!" Gideon rushed through the crowd of milling, disoriented men, shouting instructions.

Trell ran after Loukas.

A horn sounded from elsewhere in the fortress, a deep and scornful cry, as if the mountain itself was bellowing in rage. Reaching the front of the granary, Trell pushed through the parted doors—

And came up short behind Loukas.

Water was flooding the streets. Easily two dozen Nadoriin were awash in it, their lines scattered, all of them grappling for each other and struggling against the current.

Trell grabbed Loukas by his coat and hauled him back inside before the Nadoriin recovered themselves or an archer got off a lucky shot.

Loukas slammed the doors and turned breathlessly to Trell. "The aqueduct—"

"Those men we saw the other day." Trell arched brows in understanding. "They must've been setting charges."

"The fortress alarms—"

"Their signal."

"All that water," consternation flooded the Avataren's green-eyed gaze, "and this place like a sealed urn…"

Shouting came from elsewhere and everywhere.

Trell took Loukas's arm. "Come on, we've got to move."

※

Raegus n'Harnalt was readying his men to respond to the alarm from Khor Taran when an explosion echoed from ridge to ridge. Moments later, the ground rocked beneath him.

What the fethe….?

He set heels to his horse and stormed along the ridge, following the sound back towards its origins near the fortress. The others of his men were arrayed among the trees. He shouted orders to hold their positions as he thundered past.

Dawn's early grey light was diffusing itself around thunderheads in the east, the harbingers of a coming storm. The wind fought against him as he sped along a wide dirt path. He followed the track to an overlook where, just the day before, he and Trell had planned out the stages of their attack and egress. He threw himself off his horse and jumped-slid-clambered to the furthest point of the overlook—

He swore in his native dialect, and then again in the desert tongue for good measure.

A powerful waterfall was churning down the mountain out of what used to be the aqueduct. The deluge had spawned a mudslide that was piling up against the fortress gates, clearly already deeper than a man was tall.

Raegus swore again. He and Trell had planned an avalanche to block those doors and wipe out the road, but *after* their men and the Dannish soldiers had escaped the fortress. What in *Fiera's* name was he going to do now?

A sudden loud crack brought his gaze swiftly back to the north tower. Even as he watched, the water gushing around the tower became milky, and then the base seemed to simply…wash away. The length of the tall tower tipped…tipped…toppled—

Slammed down across the middle fortress wall. The water found a new course and flooded down into the lower tiers.

Raegus cursed and ran for his horse.

❖

Air told Tannour of the tower's crumbling base before it actually began tipping. He yanked his needles free of Kifat's chest and sprinted up the rapidly inclining floor towards the hole the wielder had blasted in the wall. He ripped off his head-shroud and dove into open air just before the tower crashed down across the middle wall.

Tannour hit the water along with a shower of pelting rock. Waves surged around him, tumbled, dragged and sucked him under. *Ver'alir* could offer no help against this.

The churning current dragged Tannour into a channel towards a stairwell, now a funneling flood. He bobbed up and found air for a brief moment before the water sucked him into the frothing vortex the river had made of the tunnel beneath the wall.

❖

With the Dannish Captain val Mallonwey's help, Trell made fast work of organizing the ranks, even among the chaos of the quickly flooding granary. At least the water had quenched the fires on the floor.

As the men were lining up, Trell felt that peculiar energy that comes in times of great need—heated apprehension rising beneath cold determination, forming a thunderous storm of urgency. There was hardly time for inspiring speeches, yet he had to say *something* to guide them through the chaos surely to follow.

With the smoke pressing down from above and the water rising from below, Trell climbed up on an urn and raised his hands for quiet.

"Soldiers of Dannym!" He felt every set of eyes shift and fix upon himself. The air was hot where he stood, acrid and difficult to breathe. He worked hard to put strength into his voice. "I thank you for your courage and your trust. I tell you truly—I don't know what we'll face out there. I know many of you are still disoriented, confused, angry—and you've every right to be. I know my men and I are strangers to you, but I give you my word, we will stay the course at your side! Fortune looks favorably upon men of honor, and Luck graces the brave. If we work together, we *will* overcome!"

"Just point us towards the bastards, Your Highness!" someone called. Others fervently joined in this sentiment, and a thunderstorm of demands for retribution quickly overcame the room.

"They shall know Dannish steel!—"

"We'll bathe in their blood!—"

"Death to the Nadoriin!—"

Trell raised his hands to quiet them. "You seek blood for the wrongs waged against you, and rightly so, but today I bid you focus on one life—*yours*—and that of the man next to you—"

Another horn sounded, louder than the first.

He spun an urgent look from the doors back to the men. "Soldiers of Dannym, this fortress is dying, and we're far from free of its final throes. Let us not perish with it! His Majesty needs you with him in Nahavand. This was your mission, and my mission it remains."

Trell jumped down with a splash and sloshed for the doors. Loukas quickly found his side. "Bold words. Very inspiring. Just how in Fiera's name are you expecting to get us out of here?"

Trell cast him a sidelong eye. "I was expecting you to get us out of here."

"No-no-no—" Loukas shook his head emphatically, "*I* get us in, *you* get us out. *That* was the deal."

"I'm starting to feel shorted on this deal of ours."

"*Trell…*" all the levity had drained from Loukas's voice.

Trell paused behind the line of armed men who would be first through the doors and met his friend's gaze. "If anything happens to me, I'm counting on you to get them out." Trell looked to the men lined up behind him and shoved his sword high. "For His Majesty—courage and honor!"

"*Courage and honor!*" hundreds of voices echoed.

Then the doors were flying open and the mass of men was shoving forward into churning brown water. The current pushed them towards a wide boulevard in the shadow of the wall separating Khor Taran's middle and lowest tiers. Archers were there, firing down into the melee.

Trell heard the battle before he reached it, saw the arrows flying down into the emerging crowd of soldiers, listened to their cries of pain. One black-shafted arrow splashed down in front of him. Another hit to his right, striking a near man in the arm. Trell grabbed him before he fell and supported him while he recovered his footing. He returned a look of gratitude limned in pain.

Then the front lines had blurred enough to reach Trell, and he raised his sword to meet a Nadoriin with a missing eye. The latter fell quickly, and Trell moved to the next. The water was surging around his knees.

As Trell fought, submerged things caught on his boots, tripped him, made him stumble. When he needed to dodge swiftly, the water dragged at him. When he needed to hold his position, the current shoved him forward. They were battling the water as much as each other, and men fell as often to the churning froth or its buried dangers as to another's blade.

Dannym's officers fought free of the ropes that had bound them, even though the braided links still shackled their wrists and necks, but many of the king's foot-soldiers remained partially chained together. They fought as best they could with such a handicap. Sometimes their linked wrists proved a boon, but other times, when one of their number fell to a blade, or the water caught a man in a violent embrace, the entire group went down.

Out of the corner of his eye, Trell saw Loukas fighting a Nadori soldier wearing a chequered *keffiyeh*. The latter stood a head taller and much broader than the Avataren, yet Loukas seemed to be holding his own.

Suddenly the way cleared for a burly Nadoriin, who shoved through the melee towards Trell with the brown water surging around his thighs. His bearded face was drawn in deep lines, and he carried shades of fury in his gaze. He wore the braided *agal* of an officer around his *keffiyeh*.

Trell raised his blade to meet him.

Their swords clashed, locked. The Nadoriin growled in his own tongue, "*Akkadian dogs!*"

He shoved Trell off and swung anew. Their blades struck-reverberated, struck-reverberated—powerful blows fuelled by a powerful anger.

The officer might've overpowered Trell more easily—for he was taller and broader—but the *cortata* sang in Trell's thoughts, putting strength into his limbs and unexpected force beneath every blow.

Something caught at Trell's feet—both of their feet.

Suddenly the current had him *and* the Nadoriin, their boots tangled in netting or aught else—Trell couldn't say, except it was threatening his balance. They both stumbled, staggered, tried to maintain their footing and continue their battle until neither became possible. The Nadoriin fell with a splash, yanking Trell into the stream after him.

Men fought to either side as the current swept them on together. Two arrows nearly found their mark—one scraped Trell's ear as it splashed into the water. Half a foot to the left and it would've struck the Nadoriin. He loudly cursed the archer for a fool.

Trell saw where the current was taking them nearly at the same time the Nadoriin did. The powerful flow of water, forging its own path as ever was water's wont, had churned away at stone and plaster until a gaping hole had opened in the fortress wall where it abutted the mountain itself. Now a waterfall emptied down into cavernous darkness.

"What's down there?" Trell scrabbled furiously for some kind of handhold.

The Nadoriin, who was swim-splashing beside him with the same fervent intention, swung him a stare, perhaps surprised that he spoke his language. "Caverns! Death!"

"Work *with* me!" Trell tried to claim some footing, but whatever was around their feet was creating a powerful draw. Taking a chance that the Nadoriin preferred his own life over Trell's death, the prince shoved his sword into the scabbard on his back and dove for a doorway with both hands.

He missed. The current swept them on.

The Nadoriin had better aim, or a stronger jump, and succeeded in hooking his arms around a fencepost. Trell grabbed onto his thigh.

A sudden commotion among the archers on the walls drew both of their gazes upwards. Men started shouting. Then the mass of archers fled, just as the top of a falling tower came into view. It struck the wall in a violent explosion of splintering stone.

Water came surging across the ramparts in the tower's wake, making waterfalls of the crenels, while angry waves stormed down the stairway tunnel nearest Trell—

And swept Trell and the Nadoriin towards the waterfall.

❖

Loukas watched the falling tower with a sort of horrified fascination. That is, until the resultant flood swept him off his feet. He grabbed for balance at the man nearest him, who happened to be Gideon, while all around them, men toppled like sticks in the surf. The Dannish soldiers maneuvered well in the suddenly chest-high water, but the desert-bred Nadoriin clung to anyone who appeared able to swim.

Both Loukas and Gideon realized this advantage in the same moment. Gideon struck off through the flood, shouting new orders to his men, while Loukas turned to rally the Converted—

And saw a dark form tumbling down the rushing cascade that had once been a stairwell. A grave foreboding beset him.

Loukas lurched after the body, half-swimming, half-running against the current. He only just caught the man before the stream dragged him off. Blood stained the water around his body.

Feeling like an entire volley of arrows had just struck his chest, Loukas turned the man over...

Gideon sloshed back to his side. "Ah...the wielder." He sounded not the least regretful to see him dead. And very dead he was. Tannour had clearly been at him for hours.

Loukas grimly released the body to the current and let out his breath, relieved that the wielder hadn't been Tannour. But then, where *was* Tannour?

And for that matter, where was Trell?

Loukas cast a fast look across the battle, though it seemed less a battle now than a rout, with the well-trained Dannish soldiers—and apparently capable swimmers—taking rapid command of the scene.

Yet his sense of foreboding only deepened as he searched for and failed to find a particular visage among the fray. "Where's the *A'dal*?" he turned swiftly to Gideon. "Where's Trell?"

SEVENTY-THREE

*"The First Law of Patterning is also the first law of the game.
You can't just say the effect you want to create is to 'win the game.'
This isn't an effect, it's a state of being."*

–The Agasi wielder Markal Morrelaine,
to Cristien Tagliaferro

EAN HAD LOST count of the hours he and Darshan had been battling the revenants, only noting that the sun had passed its zenith and that they'd slowly been working their way back towards the maze. Darshan drew fuel from Shadow and Ean from him.

His lungs burned and his arms ached, yet strength never left them. A cold energy was funneling through his form; insubstantial, but it kept him strong. Like a river, however, the channels along which it flowed were growing ever wider, ever deeper, such that Ean had begun to feel hollow and oddly… corrugated; honeycombed, like the things dying all around him.

Indeed, the revenants were as fibrous shells, their insides webbed like some sort of noxious weed. While still animated, they crawled over one another to get at Ean, hungry to feed on him, and they needed but a hand or mouth—a fraction of skin-to-skin contact—to do so. Every time he touched one, it became an instant race to slay the thing before it drank of his lifeforce. But once he'd cut them down, they crumbled like brittle black chalk.

Darshan seemed to view their endeavor as a battle of attrition—himself the Great Immortal against the hundreds of thousands that comprised the revenant horde. Ean could see them through Darshan's bird's-eye view. In all the time they'd been battling, they'd hardly carved through a fraction of the ranks that waited to get at them. The prince was starting to feel as though he would be battling out his eternity right there, just trying to keep the bloody things off of him.

Darshan's staff came whirling past Ean's head. He ducked in time to see a creature that had launched itself towards him meet with the flying end of the weapon. The revenant wind-milled back into the crowd, felling dozens in its passing. Ean resumed his own battling; he stabbed and slashed with his blade, spun and chopped and batted; he crushed faces with his elbows and throats with one *deyjiin*-fuelled hand.

Behind them, the city gleamed bronze in the sere sunlight.

How long-lived were the days in this alien realm? How many hours had they spent slaying and slashing, as farm workers threshing the wheat?

Ean tried to take Darshan's perspective on their battle. If he spent a year or a hundred fighting off these things, it would consume but an eye-blink in the endless span of his immortality. But the prince had begun to feel a sort of gnawing urgency to finish this and move on—he *felt* the game calling him, a cosmic coach shouting to him to resume his place on the field, and beneath this, a growing vehemence towards all things Shail.

At its highest tide, determination fueled Ean through the grueling hours. But when determination ebbed low, he thought of the years he'd wasted, the times he'd sacrificed himself on the altar of reckless stupidity, only to bring himself to *this* point, where he was endangering everything yet *again*.

But these thoughts came as shadows, as thoughts will when body and mind are married with action and intent, or when activity becomes repetitive to the point of exhaustion, when labor no longer needs thought to drive it and the mind becomes freed of mechanical restrictions to fear for future and dither over hope; when shields of conviction become enervated, allowing through— if not the bloody strikes of swords, then at least the more permeable lashings of regret.

Throughout, Darshan fought with cold dispassion, making his every action count. He used the fallen as weapons, propelling individuals into the crowd with his staff, or scattering piles of them with *deyjiin* to fell even more; and his mind, looped with Ean's, remained focused, determined, undivided of intent.

But every once in a while, Ean perceived a grittiness there, as a gristle beginning to form on the burning edges of his patience. Perhaps he could sustain revenants in feeding for millennia, but could he fight them for that long?

And why had he built the damned maze if he never intended to use it?

Darshan gave a mental grunt and said across their binding, *For a man whose life I have twice saved now, you exhibit an astonishing lack of faith.*

Ean slashed a revenant in twain and shot a razor grin over his shoulder. *So you* do *have a plan?* He batted another creature away with the flat of his blade.

The Malorin'athgul twirled his staff and sent five revenants catapulting into the crowd. He cast an arch look at Ean. *You will see its beginnings...now.*

He slammed the end of his staff into the earth.

A violent wave of power sheared the sand of revenants for a hundred paces in every direction. United of mind, Ean and Darshan ran together into the maze, the hares luring the hounds. Whereupon Ean learned that revenant hounds could run inhumanly fast.

Darshan led the chase through the rubble walls, which towered four or more stories above them. Due to the low angle of the sun, they ran in shadows, while a hungering mass of cadaverous forms pursued them; the revenants tumbled and frothed and clambered over each other after the beacon light of Darshan's lifeforce.

Twice the creatures nearly overtook them. Twice Darshan had to blast them back. Each time thereafter the revenants ran faster.

The maze ended in a wide plaza enclosed by high rubble walls and surrounded by standing towers many times as tall. Darshan took a running leap and launched himself to the top of a nearby tower. Ean threw *deyjiin* beneath his steps and followed.

The Malorin'athgul grabbed Ean's arm as he landed and braced him until he found his footing on the tower's steep side. Far below, revenants were oozing into the plaza, their pace slowing as the channel filled. They amassed against the rubble walls and clung there like pitch. Soon they would push each other upwards, as water filling a bowl. The desert beyond the maze wore a carpet of black.

Ready, Ean?

Darshan pointed his staff at the mouth of the maze. Ean felt his intent an instant before *deyjiin* lanced out towards the maze's opening. The prince shielded his eyes from the beam and listened to the roar of walls collapsing. The thunder of destruction grew closer, louder, as Darshan raked his lightning power all across the maze, until the tidal wave of toppling walls at last reached the plaza. The revenants became frantic then—but horribly, Ean perceived that their frenzy stemmed from hunger for that energy which was even then sealing their demise.

Darshan changed the intent of his working and erased the foundations of the four buildings surrounding the square. The towers toppled. Glass and metallic-tiled domes collided in ear-shattering crashes. Choking dust inundated the sky.

Ean watched Darshan wreaking this potent destruction, and though the

Malorin'athgul's gaze revealed only concentration, yet the prince perceived through their bond a reflection of his emotion in that moment:

Joy. This undertaking brought him *joy*.

That's when Ean understood a terrible truth about the immortal he was now bound to: destruction was the duty the Maker had birthed Darshan from the aether of Chaos to perform, the act in which he felt the most aligned with his purpose. Ean might've known such a powerful sense of self in overcoming some extreme challenge of battle or wielder's skill; but he saw in Darshan's resonating—if coldly dispassionate—vitality the incontrovertible truth that these beings had not been engendered to carry out any act of creation.

What strength of will must it have required then to even *conceive* of an action other than destruction? Theirs was not the simple choice a mortal made between right or wrong. For a Malorin'athgul, to participate in a creative endeavor would have to be a conscious and consistent defiance of his most essential nature.

A furnace wind finally cleared the dust of destruction away. Where had been towers remained mountains of crushed stone, with thousands of revenants buried beneath them. Ean shaded his eyes with one hand and surveyed the carnage of the alien city. "Well…what now?"

Darshan planted his staff before him. "We wait for the next wave."

"Outstanding." Ean sat down in the shade of a spire. Was he really going to be trapped there until they killed every one of those damnable creatures? "What about the starpoints?" He leaned his head back against the copper tiles and tried to drag his yipping frustration to heel. "I thought you were getting us out of here eventually."

"*Eventually* has many interpretations." Darshan cast him a trenchant look. "*Eventually* all of the revenants filling these worlds will be destroyed."

"Right, I get it."

"I cannot coincide the exterior starpoints of these worlds." Darshan lifted his gaze to the sky and his brow narrowed slightly, as with contemplation. "I don't know precisely why."

Ean pressed palms to his eyes and tried to envision some other solution than escape. He knew so little of the workings of Shadow…

A wielder is limited by what he can envision. The Fifth Law all but sneered at him.

"There is a chance I could escape this realm if I abandon this shell."

Ean dropped his hands to look at Darshan. "Wouldn't you still be restricted by the Warlock's starpoints?"

"There is a chance I could unwork them. We are more powerful in our native form." Darshan twirled his Merdanti staff in one hand, looking thoughtful, contemplative…and really damned impressive.

"But you don't want to do that."

Darshan's eyes tightened. "This is likely what my brother is hoping I will do—which is exactly why I mustn't." He began pacing the outer edge of the tower while spinning his staff. "Since our original path into your realm is blocked by way of your Björn van Gelderan's ingenuity, my only means of re-entering Alorin is via Shadow—but without a shell, this becomes problematic."

"Can't you make another shell?"

"Assuming I can escape these Shadow worlds and return to Alorin at all? Yes…but not quickly." He tossed his spinning staff into his other hand without disrupting its circle or the thoughtful meter of his steps. "Whether I'm trapped in Shadow or removed to Chaos, my brother's aims are equally served."

"Well, we can't have that."

Darshan tilted his head slightly. "What is this new thought you're hiding from me?"

Ean scrubbed at his growth of beard. "I was just wondering…what if I could unwork them?"

"The starpoints?"

"The revenants."

Darshan arched brows. "As you've unworked my *eidola*."

"Something like that."

The Malorin'athgul shook his head. "It cannot be done while we're subject to the starpoints of this realm." Abruptly he spun to face the city's edge. His spinning staff slammed home in his palm, sounding a distant clap of thunder. "They're coming." He turned Ean a look. "Get ready."

When the next wave of revenants reached the maze, Darshan and Ean went down to meet them. There was no other path, save to keep fighting, and as Darshan had said, *eventually* they would destroy all of the creatures.

Ean was really starting to mislike that word, *eventually*.

They fought atop a mountain of rubble with the revenants crawling up the hillside like ants. Ean bashed and slashed with a sword fuelled by *deyjiin*, but there was no end to their numbers, and only so much light in the day… only so much fortitude in his soul.

This from the man who claims to have died three times for the same cause? Darshan had his back to Ean as they fought, but his tone came through loud and clear.

Ean kicked a revenant in the face and slashed another into pieces. *Glibly spoken by the immortal who has never tasted death and never will.*

I have tasted death, Prince of Dannym. Darshan sent several revenants flying with a swing of his staff and glanced to Ean. *I have known it far longer and more intimately than you could ever imagine.*

Really? Ean shot him a sharp and challenging smile in return, *because I can imagine a lot.*

Darshan swept his staff low and upended half a dozen revenants. They tumbled down the incline, taking three times as many others with them. His smile, cast over the top of his whirling staff, became equally pointed. *I imagine you do have a certain context of experience that many mortals are lacking.*

Ean knocked a revenant flying and speared a sooty look in his general direction. *Ha, very ha.*

It was then that he heard a low rumble. The rubble shifted beneath his feet—and revenants erupted out from beneath them in a clambering geyser. Within seconds, a veritable tower of the creatures fell upon Darshan.

The resulting avalanche flung Ean off his feet. He landed on the side of the mound and tumbled down the incline into the dark pool that was the revenant horde. His head slammed against something hard, and before he could rouse from the starry spots blinding his vision, a score of the horrid things had descended on him. They dragged him deeper into the pool of their brethren, down into darkness.

In seconds, mouths, elbows, hands—any bit of themselves they could press against him, they had. The prince felt each *revenant's* touch as an icy sting that only became more intense as more of them found purchase. His body grew cold, pinned beneath their accumulating forms; his skin instantly rose in welts beneath their probing touch. Different mouths found his fingers; many more his face and throat. Numbness pulsed a pale cadence in concert with a drumming staccato of pain.

Ean!

Ean wanted to answer Darshan's mental call, but his own thoughts already felt too distant. He suspected such would only worsen as the revenants fed off his energy. How soon before he lost the ability to focus on anything beyond pain and despair? *And by Cephrael's Great Book*—how had Pelas managed to escape these things?

…what applies to one applies to all…

Had Darshan gotten the thought across to him, or did the reminder find its own way to the forefront of his muddled thoughts? In any case, Ean heard the words in a repetitive chant.

…what applies to one applies to all…

Recalling him to lucidity.

…what applies to one applies to all…

Suddenly realizing how the Law might apply in the context of Shadow, Ean tried using *deyjiin* to compartment his thoughts. His binding with

Darshan gave him access to the power, but his native instincts as a fifth-strand Adept guided him in working it. Not understanding why it was possible but relieved at finding that it was, the prince portioned off the pain, lassitude and disorientation resulting from the revenants' feeding into a separate section of his mind.

With those distractions thus compartmented, analytical thought returned to him. So also came the very real fear of remaining trapped beneath these things for all eternity. Darshan had said it wasn't possible to unwork the revenants, but the Malorin'athgul didn't understand everything that Ean could do.

Suspended upside-down, as immobile as a bulb buried in the dirt, Ean managed to drag his fingers free of clinging mouths and closed his hand around a revenant wrist. Using this contact, he cast the free part of his mind in search of the pattern that bound the revenant to existence.

This is Shadow. There are no patterns here.

But if what applied to one applied to all, then the Eleventh Law—*All things are formed of patterns*—must also apply.

Ean knew he hadn't an infinity of time to solve this mystery. Already he could sense the barrier portioning off his mind thinning. How long would his will survive—how long would his *mind* survive—if both he and Darshan were being simultaneously drained?

Ean flung his awareness through the revenant's consciousness—as much as such an entity could lay claim to consciousness—seeking anything that resembled a pattern. But this was no human; it wasn't even *eidola*. It seemed little more than an accumulated mass of energized clay lumped into humanoid shape.

Yet *some* lifeforce had to be animating it…driving it; *something* instilled it with this ravenous need. So where was that intention within the fabric of its existence? And if it *was* an instilled intention, mustn't it assume *some* design? All Ean saw within the revenant's awareness were liquid shadows.

Ean had shared minds with both Pelas and Darshan; he'd witnessed them using their power innately, molding it to their intent. He'd seen no patterns associated with those workings. But all those months ago, when he'd found the pattern that enabled his own ability to see other patterns, in that deriving he'd proven that even innate workings assumed some design.

What was it he'd learned about Warlocks that seemed suddenly relevant? His mind was getting dull around the edges, the borderlands between analytical thought and numb disability narrowing, the two compartments of his mind beginning to merge.

Ean desperately forced himself to focus.

Innate…something about innate—no, *inverteré*. Warlocks worked *inverteré* patterns. And that was important…why?

Something reminded him of Darshan's imprisoning field around Nadia—*deyjiin* and *elae* in balance. They were opposites, the two powers, create and destroy, positive to negative.

Positive to negative…

Ean realized exactly what he was seeing when he looked at the shadows within the revenant's awareness.

In searching for patterns, he'd been looking for the kind of shadows cast upon the water; instead, he should've been focusing on the shadows filtering beneath the surface—*inverteré*. These were the patterns native to Shadow.

Ean again dove beneath the waves of the revenant's consciousness, seeking those shadows—patterns in negative. He'd just found what he thought he was looking for when that wall portioning off his mind finally fell.

Pain, numbness, shock—a host of blighting sensations flooded him. Ean mentally dragged his awareness into the equivalent of a lifeboat—nay, a piece of a boat, flotsam on the surf—and started swimming towards the pattern. He latched onto it with everything he had…but he still didn't know how to unmake it.

Until he remembered the Fourteenth Law: '*Exact duplicating forces, in opposition, will nullify structure.*'

If everything Patterning-related formed itself to the opposite in Shadow, then unmaking a Shadow-pattern was accomplished by making another one.

Suddenly certain he'd landed on the right answer, Ean duplicated the shadowed pattern he was seeing in the revenant, only he formed it in reverse.

Become became *un-be*.

Then he released his pattern of intent—not once, but as many times as he could duplicate, focus and cast it before the storm of lassitude overcame him.

Except…

The lassitude waned instead of his awareness. And where he expected to feel pain, he sensed only the pressure of inanimate bodies encircling him. Just beyond this brittle barrier, more creatures were worming through each other, trying to reach him. Ean started swimming.

Or perhaps *climbing* better described his rather frantic crawl towards the surface. Whenever he touched a live thing and felt its telltale sting, he cast his pattern anew. He must've cast it a hundred times before his head broke free of the pile and daylight blinded him.

Ean sucked in a breath of relief and looked around. The boiling froth to his right had to be Darshan. He was deep in the pit and blasting *deyjiin* repeatedly to work his way out.

I thought you said not *to do that,* Ean thought to him as he started towards him.

Darshan's voice floated back to him on the bond, suitably sardonic. *If you have a better plan, Prince of Dannym, I'm open to hearing it.*

Ean threw his pattern of unmaking in a circle around himself to form a sort of shield, and in this guise ran across the mass of revenants, making stepping-stones of heads and shoulders, using *deyjiin* to stabilize his crossing, spreading a wake of stillness. *Darshan, I'm coming for you. Don't blast me into oblivion.*

To which the immortal mentally grunted a dubious reply.

As he ran, possessed of a certainty of action he'd long missed, Ean perceived that finding this new ability was changing the pattern of consequence of his own path back in Alorin, but he also sensed that using it was weakening him there in Shadow. It would be a close thing—reaching Darshan before he drained himself too nearly; Darshan freeing himself from the froth before he made the revenants strong enough to pin him down.

Ean's head was pounding and his body was feeling frighteningly thin by the time he broke through the sphere of creatures trying to get to Darshan. The Malorin'athgul dragged him within the circle of his whipping staff and kept trudging up the incline towards the mound where they'd first taken their stand.

Ean felt every pulse of *deyjiin* as a thunderclap in his skull. Every muscle in Ean's body ached. It was no wonder he felt so drained with Darshan shaking the fabric of the world with every pulse of power and Ean drawing his power from him.

Darshan cast him a scant eye between pulses. "How did you escape them?"

"Long story."

Darshan slammed his staff. *Deyjiin* pulsed. They were nearly to the rim of the mound. "When our work is finished here, I will be intrigued to hear it."

But would their work ever be finished?

Ean was finally comprehending just how much trouble they were in. Even should they escape that city, the revenants would follow them to the next one—even to another Shadow world. They could spend their eternity hovering in the clouds above city, desert, jungle or moor, fed by *deyjiin*, contemplating their fates and arguing over the greater meaning of existence, but when they finally came down again—because there was nowhere else *to* go—the revenants would be waiting. Ean felt trapped in one of those dreams where you ran but never made any headway towards your goal.

They reached the top of the mound and Darshan exploded a pulse of power that sheared the revenants back for several hundred feet. Ean saw a glimmer of steel and jogged over to his sword. The pounding in his head made his skull feel three times larger than it should, and when he leaned down to pick up his blade, he almost fell.

Lady's light, there had to be some other way out of this besides slaying every demon in Belloth's hell, but to save his life, Ean couldn't see one. The idea of escaping that place, reuniting with Isabel and meeting his son—it was all that kept him upright.

Staving off a crippling sense of futility, Ean picked up his blade and swung anew.

SEVENTY-FOUR

*"Love is an empty eagle who feasts on the young, the foolish,
the trapped and the taken 'til either gorge be stuffed
or prey be gone. Love makes prey of all."*

– The Adept truthreader Voss di Alera

ALSHIBA HAD NO idea how long she and Björn made love. It might've been one night, or a night and a day and many nights again. She only knew it was over when a grey light seeped into the world and he rose from her bed to greet it.

Admiring Björn as he crossed the room, feeling her old self again, and yet far from herself, perhaps never again the self she'd once known, Alshiba realized that she'd been wrong to ever imagine Björn was hers. After showing her what he could do—her own life pattern placed in her hands!—he'd proven that he belonged to the realm, or perhaps to many realms, but never just to her.

This idea didn't assuage her loss, but it brought a small measure of peace, an understanding that his choices actually cast no reflection on hers. She couldn't have acted otherwise than she had. Nor he, as he had—not and each of them remain themselves whole. And he'd demonstrated that he loved her still, had always loved her; his more confusing actions aside, that he always would.

Standing at the windows with his back to her and his form profiled by the dawn, Björn might've been another man, one who didn't scald her with his gaze or tear her heart with his choices. There was such a man in her life, if she was willing to admit him into her heart, if Björn would give him some room.

Alshiba let out her breath slowly. "What have you been doing to me?"

He turned a half-smile over his shoulder. "If you didn't recognize that activity, love, it's been far too long."

"You weren't just Healing me all this time. You were changing my life pattern." She rolled onto her back and stared at the nymphs on her ceiling. No longer flaunting their own lovemaking, they were whispering behind their hands, staring down at her with wide, scandalized eyes. She recalled her younger self and arched a daring brow at them. "I can sense it."

Björn returned his gaze beyond the window and said quietly, "Just a little extra protection for the days ahead, love."

"The days ahead," she cast him a narrow look, "of which you've told me so little. As much, in fact, as you told me before. We stand upon the same precipice, you and I, staring into the same beyond. Will you trust me this time?"

"It was never a matter of trust, Alshiba." He returned to the bed and pressed her down beneath him, pressed her head into the pillow with a kiss. Then he draped himself alongside her and propped his head in one hand. His other explored her hip in a possessive caress, while his eyes studied hers with quiet intensity. "I knew if I told you my plans, you would never go along with them."

"Damn you, Björn." She bit back a stronger curse and tasked him with a stare of injury instead. "I would've done anything you asked."

He held her gaze, profoundly serious. "I would've asked you to stay here and guide the realm in my stead."

For a moment while those words sank in, Alshiba stared at him. Then she closed her eyes beneath an avalanche of understanding.

Björn kissed one of her closed eyelids. "Perhaps I did betray you in not granting you that trust," he kissed her other lid, "in imagining you would consider our relationship, or me, more important than the realm."

Alshiba turned her face away from him. Her throat felt dry, her chest hollow. "You should go. It's nearly dawn."

He stroked her face with the back of his fingers. "Do you want me to go?"

She cast censure on the spear of her glare. "I want my heart to be whole again."

By all the gods, she hated what he did to her—this discomposed, dismembered *mess* he made of her conviction!

"Alshiba," Björn dragged her eyes to him as he rose from the bed, dragged her attention with him as he retrieved his pants from the floor. "You still don't see it, do you?" He dressed himself with the same ruthless efficiency with which he'd built a world and guided the realm and shattered her heart. "You've held the Seat now for three hundred years. You're a trusted member of the Council; you're doing everything I could've required of you and far more than I could've asked of you..." he came and leaned both hands to either side of her on the bed, bringing his gaze close and his thoughts closer, so that she felt both of them impinging strongly upon her, "but if I had not *broken* with you, how could any of them have trusted you?"

He withdrew then, leaving her cringing beneath the lash of this truth, and continued buttoning his shirt, his jaw tight. "Sometimes we have to be our own pawns of sacrifice."

Alshiba watched him dressing with burning eyes. Somehow she managed to find her voice. "This was your goodbye, wasn't it?"

He cast her a look. "In the sense you mean it, yes."

Silence bound them both while he finished dressing. In the end, he came and sat beside her on the bed. The folds of his coat hung open, undone, like herself.

Björn took her palm and kissed it. His blue eyes, gazing into hers, made her soul cry. "One day, love..." He looked her over without regret, as though already envisioning some other time, some far distant future. "One day, perhaps Epiphany will grace us to meet in the Returning, and what was done will be undone, and what was said will be forgotten, and we can love anew." He held her gaze, studied her expression, and finding no resistance to his intent, claimed a long kiss from her. With their breath mingling, he murmured against her lips, "Epiphany has a soft spot for star-crossed lovers."

Grief bound Alshiba's throat too tightly, so that her words were squeezed of all life by the time they crossed her tongue. "I would not ask for that."

He withdrew far enough to meet her gaze. "You don't have to. It will be my prayer."

Her heart caught in her throat. She swallowed as she watched him walking towards the balcony. The thought of never seeing him again seemed suddenly more than she could bear. "Do you—"

He looked over his shoulder.

Alshiba pressed tears from her eyes with her palms. "Do you think She listens to you?"

Björn's grave expression lightened with his answer. "When the mood suits Her."

Then he was out onto the balcony and gone in a blurring blink of tears.

An instant later, a knock came at her bedchamber doors.

Alshiba sucked in a shuddering breath. She pushed palms to her eyes again and called mutedly for entry.

"Your Excellency?" Her chambermaid opened the door and bobbed a curtsy. "The Speaker has summoned you. Some knights are here to provide escort and any assistance you may need."

Assistance...because Aldaeon still believes I'm ill.

Alshiba gathered her robe and her conviction. "Tell them I'll be ready as soon as I can."

"Yes, Your Excellency."

"Oh, and Mariel?"

"Yes, Your Excellency?"

"Alert them that there is something I must do along the way."

A pair of Paladin Knights opened the doors for Alshiba, and she glided inside the Speaker's office with the heavy silk of her white dress floating just above the tiles, her steps uninterrupted.

That is, until she rounded the corner and came to an abrupt halt. She turned a scathing look to the Speaker, who was seated behind his desk. "What is the meaning of this?"

Aldaeon H'rathigian had his long fingers folded in his lap and a grim expression lengthening the shadows beneath his cheekbones. He returned his gaze to an ailing Franco, who was clearly only standing upright because of the two knights supporting him. Niko, the Eltanin Seat Mir Arkadhi, and another truthreader were seated in a grouping of chairs, while her Third Vestal Seth Silverbow was standing at the glass doors, glaring out at the knights guarding the balcony.

"Franco has admitted to serving Björn van Gelderan, Alshiba," the Speaker answered.

With dread gripping her, Alshiba scanned the others in the room, taking their measure in a glance. From the bruises on Franco's face and his dazed stare, it was obvious what had been done to him—that is, if Mir's darkly satisfied expression wasn't telling enough. Alshiba felt a driving urge to rush to Franco, while in the same breath she ached to choke the life out of Niko and Mir. The resulting conflict made her hands twitch at her sides.

She turned with indignation stiffening her stance. "Under *torture*? In such a civilization as ours?"

Aldaeon scratched defeatedly at one temple. "They had reason to believe he'd been truthbound."

"Since when does torture release a man from a truthbinding?" she demanded heatedly.

"He confessed, Alshiba." The Speaker's gaze sought her understanding. "The means may have been unorthodox—"

"*Unorthodox,*" her eyes flared dangerously.

"—but we cannot now discount the information gained thereby."

Alshiba knew she had to keep a tight rein on her emotions. First Björn's goodbye and now this—seeing Franco so undone. It nearly suffocated her. She managed to calm her twitching hands. "Confessions under duress can hardly be trusted."

"He confessed first, Alshiba." Niko sounded inordinately smug, and his improper familiarity rankled all the more. "To my face and before these others." He held a hand to Mir Arkadhi and the other truthreader.

She turned a razor eye on all three of them. "If Franco confessed, Niko, pray why was he tortured?"

"For the other things he hadn't confessed, obviously." It was clear from his tone that he considered this a perfectly reasonable course of action. "And there were a good many things he hadn't come clean on, believe you me. For instance, *Franco* is this so-called Admiral of the rebellion that so many of the brethren are supporting, the one trying to usurp *my* candidacy." He snorted haughtily. "We'll have those rebels in hand in quick order now, with Cephrael as my witness."

Franco is the Admiral? The news made her want to cheer, and to weep.

Alshiba kept her gaze level, but anger was making her insides quiver like a thin blade. "Why would Franco confess anything to the pair of you?"

Mir opened his palms to the heavens and gave her a smile of benign resignation, but his colorless gaze felt like blades scraping her skin. "Conscience, perhaps, Lady Torinin? Guilt? The forest of men's motivations requires endless exploration."

While Eltanin's requires little at all to understand. She made sure her thought was loud enough for every truthreader in the room to hear it.

Alshiba turned back to the Speaker. "By last accounting, it is action, not *oaths*, that establishes a crime in our society." She turned a rigid gaze on the Eltanin Seat. "Why, if a man were to be judged and tried by his thoughts alone, Your Excellency, Lord Arkadhi would be partaking of the gaoler's hospitality until the end of his days."

I do like the way you think, Alshiba, Mir cast her a private smile.

She replied with a cold stare. *Speak aloud or speak to me not at all!*

Aldaeon shifted slightly in his chair. "Franco will need to stand before a *formal* tribunal," his emphasis was clearly aimed at Niko and Mir, "to account for his oaths and actions, but if he's innocent of wrongdoing against the cityworld's canon, no punishment will be meted against him. But I believe you mistake the purpose of this gathering, Alshiba. The unfortunate circumstances aside, Franco has provided us with the information we needed to be able to send Paladin Knights to T'khendar."

Alshiba spun to Franco in astonishment, but his dazed gaze didn't register her concern—he hardly seemed aware of anything at all.

"I summoned all of your vestals here for the required vote. If all are in accord, the mission of the Paladin Knights will be to rescue Alorin's Second and Fourth Vestals and bring Björn van Gelderan back for trial."

"Yes!" Niko shoved to his feet. "Too long have those responsible for our race's decline gone unpunished!"

Seth grunted from his place at the window. Alshiba stared severely at him.

"We all see this truth, do we not?" Niko stalked about, waving his hands as if trying to rouse a sluggish congregation into song. "Too long have our enemies flourished while Alorin withers! Fewer Adepts are born each year. Now, I must ask you, Speaker, is this fitting? Is it *just*?" He paused for effect, but Aldaeon looked confused as to whether Niko expected him to answer. He straightened as if to reply but then Niko pressed on. "No, Your Excellency! I tell you, it is *not* just. It is *not* right. Our mother world should not succumb in an effort to feed the voracious hunger of its undesired spawn!"

The Speaker's colorless eyes tightened with a wince.

"Eloquent," Seth remarked.

Alshiba had heard this speech at least three times. "Niko—"

"I swore upon this ring to oversee the proper use of my strand." Niko helpfully shoved his oath-ring towards the Speaker, even though Aldaeon wore one of his own. "I swore to my people that these atrocities *shall be ended!*"

"Niko—" Alshiba gave a strained exhale.

Niko rushed forward and slammed his palms on the Speaker's desk. Aldaeon recoiled in his chair. "Your Excellency, it's time to do what should've been done three centuries ago. Illume Belliel must rally its forces to destroy the abomination that is T'khendar and see the Balance righted!"

Seth turned Alshiba a look that accused, *This is the man you've chosen to replace Dagmar?*

Amid the strained silence that followed, Niko finally seemed to notice the affronted stare the Speaker was leveling at him. He straightened and looked down at his ring. "Or...I suppose, bring back the Vestals for questioning, as Your Excellency determines."

Aldaeon stared at Niko until he retook his chair. Then he shifted a troubled gaze to Alshiba. "I admit, the circumstances under which Franco provided this information were unfortunate, Alshiba, but now that we have the knowledge, I *am* duty bound to act upon it. Björn van Gelderan has twice caused an uproar in the city. He admitted to me during one such disruption that Dagmar and Raine are alive in T'khendar...I see no other choice."

"No," Alshiba let out a slow exhale, feeling dread like a too-tight rope binding her chest, "I don't either. But the nodes into T'khendar are twisted. How—"

Niko snorted. "There's a node leading directly from the cityworld to that godforsaken place—can you believe Björn's audacity? Franco told Mir all about this so-called Sylus node. He even volunteered to take us there himself…that is, after Mir gave him the proper encouragement. Tell her what he said, Mir."

"I would rather hear from Franco." Alshiba turned a furious gaze from Niko back to Aldaeon. "Honestly, Your Excellency, why is my Deputy Vestal being treated this way? He should be in an infirmary, not held in arms like a criminal."

The Speaker winced slightly. "Franco is here to cast his vote, Alshiba—or I should say, he has given it. Yours is the only vote outstanding."

"He didn't seem to want to sit down earlier," Niko remarked smugly.

I take full responsibility for that. Mir's voice felt like scalding oil pouring into Alshiba's mind. A host of unwelcome images accompanied this admission—Mir's willing confession.

Alshiba had never hated anyone like she hated Mir Arkadhi in that moment. She made a tight coil of her conviction. "I will give my vote of consent," she told Aldaeon levelly, "but only on the condition that Franco is Healed before he's required to travel."

"Of course, Alshiba. I'll summon my Healer—"

"I'll see to him personally, but thank you for the offer."

"Do you really think that's wise?" Niko clucked with disingenuous solicitude. "I mean…with your recent illness and so forth."

It was all she could do to keep the daggers out of her gaze. "I feel much restored of spirit today, Niko."

You seem quite remarkably restored, in fact, Alshiba dear.

Alshiba shifted a frosty stare to find Mir regarding her with a hand draped beneath his chin and his eyes gleaming with amused speculation.

"You can attend Franco in my adjoining chambers, Alshiba." Aldaeon motioned to his knights, and they set off carrying a semi-conscious Franco between them.

With the meeting clearly adjourned, Mir glided from the room with his usual grace, but Alorin's candidate vestal and Alshiba's biggest mistake came over and took her hand in his. "Do take care for your health, oath-sister—"

"She's not your bloody oath-sister!" Seth spun a glare over his shoulder. "*You* haven't sworn the oath."

Alshiba leveled Seth a pleading look.

He turned to glare out the windows again.

Alshiba withdrew her hand from Niko's clutching fingers, which oddly dragged at her oath-ring as if to remove it with their departure. "Thank you for your concern, Niko."

He gave an insincere smile. "We would all be quite distressed were anything to happen to Your Excellency, especially while engaged in the activity of Healing a traitor's Espial." He bowed to her and departed.

The moment the doors shut behind Niko, Seth spun heatedly. "I'm not spending my eternity oath-bound to *that* insufferable snot."

"Epiphany willing, you won't have to." Alshiba looked to Aldaeon. "You should know, I've formally withdrawn my recommendation of Niko and have named Franco instead. I filed the motion on my way here this morning."

"About bloody time," Seth grumbled.

Her gaze entreated his silence, but in truth, it startled her that he had agreed so readily to Franco's nomination.

Aldaeon sank his head into his hand and regarded her gravely. "My, that does complicate things."

"Yes, I suppose it does." Alshiba held the Speaker's colorless gaze while a whirlwind of concerns made a tangle of her mind. "Aldaeon…" suddenly she saw another hall in another time, and a sea of Shades prostrated before a madman's throne, "you recall what happened the last time the Council sent the Paladin Knights in search of Björn."

"Unfortunately, I do. That's why this time we'll be sending two hundred knights instead of fifty. Mir lobbied heavily for a considerable force, in light of their quarry."

Alshiba leaned both hands on the Speaker's desk. "You *know* him. You know what he's capable of," she took a leap of faith and added, fierce and low, "you know what he's *actually* doing in T'khendar!"

Seth hissed an oath from behind her.

Aldaeon laid fingertips on his desk and pressed himself tall. Alshiba straightened away from the august force of his presence. "I know Björn," he replied austerely and with the slightest tinge of reprimand in his tone, an acute reminder that his integrity remained absolute, "well enough to know he acts according to his conscience and expects us to do the same. Now," his tone softened a fraction, but his gaze conveyed much more, "see to your Vestal, and let us get on with this unpleasant business of betraying my friend in the name of justice."

❖

Franco roused to the taste of blood souring in his mouth. The last thing he remembered with any clarity was being strung up in one of the many devices Mir kept in his dungeon for his dark entertainments. Then the *mor'alir* truthreader had poured himself into Franco's mind like an oiled snake, and the only thing Franco remembered after that was pain.

No…that wasn't true. He recalled many of Mir's dark torments. The man had taken steps to ensure that he would. It was another of Mir's little private amusements—anything to subjugate or enthrall others to his will.

Franco's mind felt like a battleground after the battle had been fought—churned and blood-muddied, littered with the torn remains of broken thoughts. Had Mir taken anything the First Lord had bound him on? Franco honestly couldn't say. The truthreader had tilled his mind so badly that its landscape was unidentifiable.

He didn't recognize the room where he'd awoken, but from the angle of the sun shining in through the windows, the day had matured. He turned his head and saw Alshiba sitting nearby. She was staring out the windows, her gaze distant, lips pressed together tightly.

Franco held out his hand to her. "My lady." His words felt thick on his tongue. "Are you well?"

She turned with a sudden smile. "You're awake." She moved to his bed and took his hand in hers. Gentle fingers brushed his hair back from his eyes. "In all my years, I've never had to work the kind of Healing I just did to restore you. Mir...*twisted* your life pattern. It took me hours to untangle it."

Franco thought that was probably the least of what Mir had done. "He's a *mor'alir* Adept." He managed a tight swallow. "I feel like he made an *inverteré* pattern out of me."

She exhaled a slow breath, holding his gaze with apology heavy in hers. "I'm afraid I may not have..."

"Found everything he did to me?" Franco was sure she hadn't. Alshiba was a strong Healer, but it would take someone with the First Lord's skill to unwork that many inside-out knots. "I'm sure you've Healed me enough for what I have to do."

Her brow constricted. They both knew what that 'doing' entailed.

"My lady, about this Admiral business—"

"You did what I should've done from the first." Sudden determination brought new strength to her tone. "But I've taken care of that now."

Franco tensed. "What do you mean?"

"I've formally withdrawn my advocacy for Niko and named you as Dagmar's successor instead."

As if she wasn't already in enough danger! Oh, if he ever got his hands on Mir Arkadhi—

But Mir had made certain Franco could never exact the vengeance he was due. To even attempt to harm Mir would cause Franco debilitating pain. Amazing what a truthreader could do to a man when conscience and discretion no longer ruled the use of his talent.

Alshiba rose. "I'll give you a moment to dress."

Franco reached for her hand. "Stay...if you would." He looked down at the outline of his legs beneath the sheet. Thinking of what Mir had done to him made them quiver.

"Of course."

He hated that he had to reveal such weakness to her, but the fact remained that even with her Healing, he didn't trust his legs to hold his weight.

Alshiba retrieved his clothes and set them on the bed. Then walked to the windows while he dressed.

Franco moved to the edge of the bed and looked up as he was donning his pants. "When did he leave?"

It was a moment before she answered, though she certainly knew of whom he was asking. "This morning, five seconds before Aldaeon's summons. His timing was as impeccable as ever." Surprisingly, the bitterness that would've darkened her tone before revealed only shades of resignation instead, even… admiration.

Franco found this more telling of the reparative force of her time spent with the First Lord than anything she might've told him. "But he finished his Healing. You feel restored, my lady?"

"I did…" she turned a look over her shoulder, "until I saw what Mir had done to you."

The meaning in her eyes…oh, it had never been clearer to him—startling, yes, *surprising* certainly, welcome even, and yet acutely painful.

If only Mir had known how deeply he'd destroyed Franco with his petty torments! The First Lord had finally shared everything with Alshiba; yet now, on the cusp of what should've been their long overdue moment of candor, along had come Mir Arkadhi with his devastating games to make honesty impossible yet again.

Franco worked the muscles of his jaw, holding back a fury that had no outlet. For what Alshiba couldn't know, and what Franco couldn't tell her—couldn't even *hint* at—was that Mir had revealed their entire plan to him, there in that dark room reverberating with pain, and then he'd truthbound him on it, so he couldn't warn her—couldn't even mention it in a way that would rouse her caution.

This was Mir's twisted sense of humor at work, another of his dark games—thorns of malice set to work their way slowly into Franco's heel until they became too excruciating to endure.

Alshiba dropped her gaze. "If you don't feel the same—"

"I *do*." The force of this confession drove him across the room with surprising strength. He took her hand and met her gaze—Mir's games be damned! "Alshiba…I've been bound to you since the first moment you Healed me. Would that I'd had the courage to tell you sooner."

A soft smile touched her lips, echoic of an ages-old grief, redolent of hope. "I know now hardly seems the time."

Franco cupped her face. "Will there ever be a better time?" Then he kissed her.

She clutched him almost desperately close. This was no gentle kiss from either of them, yet Franco felt incredible relief in it, and even more in finally laying claim to her affections. He drew her into his arms afterwards, feeling suddenly as if he'd wanted nothing else in centuries save to hold her. She hugged him tightly while their racing hearts beat echoes of each other.

"I knew it also in that moment," she whispered, "though I couldn't—"

"I know." Franco pressed a kiss into her hair, feeling her arms tight around him. So he'd staked his claim, but would she believe his feelings were true after tonight had played out, after she'd been betrayed anew, this time by the secrets *he'd* been forced to keep from her?

The entire situation reeked of the callous irony of the gods. Franco knew that somewhere Cephrael was laughing, and Mir Arkadhi was laughing with Him.

❖

Alshiba kept trying to pull herself out of a daze, but the day's events were so difficult to frame into context—at dawn to have awoken in the arms of the man she loved and by sundown to be sending two hundred wielders to hunt him down as a fugitive? To have at last learned the truth of Björn's actions, only to be forced to act against him? To have finally admitted her feelings to Franco, only to soon watch him being carted away to await a formal tribunal?

Now she stood within the grounds of Alorin's embassy—how ironically fitting that Björn had built a portal to T'khendar within the protective patterns of his own estate—watching as two hundred knights prepared to bring her Fifth Vestal back to Illume Belliel, dead or alive. She imagined most of them would prefer dead.

How could she stand there and let them carry on with this? She *knew* why T'khendar was so vital now. Without it, the Malorin'athgul would have direct access to the Realms of Light! And without Dagmar, Raine and Björn there to shore up the world's magnetic grid against the immortal actively trying to unmake it, T'khendar would fall in short order.

A desperate grief clenched inside her. If she stood to defend Björn now, if she told Aldaeon *everything*, he would only think her still besotted. She'd accomplish nothing save ruining her position with the Council.

By all the gods, why did Björn always have to be so insufferably *right* in his predictions? He'd broken with her to ensure they trusted her. What good now would come of destroying her reputation? The knights would still march off to war. Franco would still go on trial. Björn would still be dragged back in chains, her other Vestals under extreme suspicion—and she'd be in no position to help any of them. The only thing she'd gain from trying to head this off was a clear conscience.

'...Sometimes we have to be our own pawns of sacrifice...'

Alshiba clenched her jaw. *Sometimes I really despise you, Björn.*

Only sometimes, love?

By the time they arrived at the staging area, the sun had fallen behind the trees and the gardens wore a cloak of shadows. Men filled those gardens now, most of them armored. Franco moved into their midst to prepare the node for travel.

While half of Alshiba's mind lamented, the other half was scrambling to think of a way to protect Franco. She didn't for a moment believe that Niko would wait for a Council Tribunal to determine Franco's guilt or innocence. Nor was Franco the only one who was likely going to need help and protection.

Alshiba spotted Seth's fiery red hair amid the masses and made her way over to him. Drawing him out to the fringes of the lake of knights, she warded the space and leveled him a determined look. "You need to get involved in this rebellion."

The Avieth crossed his arms, making his massive biceps strain against the green suede of his tunic. "You're different." His tawny-gold eyes studied her. "Are you going to tell me what's been going on around here?"

"Yes, if you'll hear it." She eyed him askance and then cast her gaze across the others. "But not now. Not here."

Seth's muscles flexed as he considered what she was asking of him. "All right." He settled into decision as a hawk upon its perch. "What rebellion are we talking about?"

She told him in broad strokes. In the last, her gaze shifted to Niko, who was standing amid a pod of knights, separate from the larger group. "He'll go after them—all of them, every Nodefinder who's backing Franco. I had no idea Niko was so conniving. Perhaps it's his association with Mir Arkadhi. Perhaps he's always been this way. I only know we can't let him destroy what's left of the strand to avenge himself against Franco." She shifted her gaze back to Seth. "And I have a feeling Alorin is going to need your help in that effort."

Seth considered her with all the receptiveness of a knotted oak. Then he gave a nod of accord. Alshiba let out her breath in relief.

Seth eyed her tetchily. "You know, if you'd asked *me* before proposing the slime-ridden bastard, I might've advised you better to begin with."

Her gaze softened in apology. "I know, Seth. I've been unfair to you. None of us cares more about the realm than you." It was almost true. *Elae's* third strand bound Seth more tightly to Alorin than any of the other vestals. Only Björn had proven himself more willing to sacrifice in the realm's best interests.

Seth's tawny gaze scanned the assembly, fierce and predatory. "I've dreamed about this day." He shifted his eyes back to hers. "It doesn't feel like I imagined it would."

Alshiba put as much understanding into her expression as she could manage.

He looked critically upon the assemblage. "Think I'll skip the coup d'état." Those tawny eyes looked her over for a moment more. "Be careful, sister. There's a foul wind blowing here."

She watched him walk away, feeling hollow.

※

Franco saw Niko coming towards him through the crowd and wished he'd cut the man's throat when he'd had the chance. Niko led his little pod of knights beneath a flag of self-importance, waging a collision course for Franco like a victorious king claiming the battlefield, but Franco's gaze was tracking Mir Arkadhi, who was following behind Niko's knightly goons, the stalking viper whispering through the verge.

Mir had orchestrated this entire affair. He'd advised Niko what to say to trap Franco into confession, he'd sought the audience with the Speaker, he'd demanded the knights be sent to T'khendar with no time to waste. Verily, Mir had murmured the entire plan into Franco's ear while his fourth-strand *inverteré* patterns twisted his mind into unrecognizable shapes.

The question was, *why*. Why was Mir involved? Alorin had nothing to offer Eltanin—Niko certainly had nothing to offer Mir—and Mir Arkadhi never extended a toe beyond the door of self-interest.

Niko halted before Franco wearing a smug, cat-ate-the-canary smirk. Doubtless he felt safe indeed with two hundred Paladin Knights lined up behind him and Mir Arkadhi's compulsion pinning Franco's hands behind his back. "Let's see this node of yours then, *Admiral*." Niko looked to the knights and raised his voice with command. "Five go with us to inspect the scene. Then we'll return for the rest of you. Ready yourselves, Knights of Illume Belliel!"

Franco rolled his eyes. Somehow Niko had failed to notice that readying themselves was the only activity the knights had been engaged in for the entire afternoon.

Niko shoved Franco's shoulder. "Well, go on then."

Franco turned a black stare to Mir, letting the truthreader know by way of his unbroken gaze that no matter what Mir thought, no matter what evil he'd worked on his mind, this wasn't over.

Mir smiled, very much the wolf that ate the cat that ate the canary. "After you, Franco."

Franco exhaled a slow breath and took them across the node into T'khendar.

And that was one.

They emerged in a park overlooking Niyadbakir. The setting sun was bathing the white city in shades of gilded rose and limning the surrounding mountains in flame.

"No, *no*, this isn't *T'khendar*." Niko spun a furious look around. "T'khendar is fire and basalt, red skies and a boiling sun!" Niko grabbed Franco by his coat. "Where've you brought us, you conniving piece of—"

Franco slammed his fist into Niko's jaw and heard a satisfying crack. Niko hit the ground at the same time that fiery pain stabbed through Franco's stomach, doubling him over. He shoved hands on his knees and sucked in his breath, but despite the compulsion making a daggered agony in his gut, he still grinned up at Mir and managed, "Worth it."

Mir sighed and motioned to the knights—Eltanin men all, and deep in Mir's pocket. "Rouse the Vestal, if you would be so kind." While a couple of them attended to Niko, Mir shifted his colorless gaze across the glowing vista. A faint smile touched his lips. "So he really did it."

It seemed an odd sort of thing to say, under the circumstances.

Still doubled over, Franco sent a strained look up at him. "Satisfied?"

Mir shifted his eyes back to him. "Hardly. We've work to do yet, you and I." Abruptly he caught Franco beneath his jaw and hauled him upright.

Franco felt like daggers were slicing his insides open—until suddenly they weren't. Mir had removed whatever compulsion had been causing the pain.

The Eltanin Seat offered a chilly smile. "Can't have you distracted from your important work, can we?" He looked to the knights awaiting his instruction—no one had any confusion about who was actually in charge. "You know what to do."

Four of them turned and ran off. The fifth was still trying to rouse Niko. Franco really hoped he'd broken his jaw.

Mir released Franco's throat and took his shoulder instead. "Ready when you are, Franco."

Feeling very much like it was Cephrael's portentous hand resting on his shoulder instead of Mir's, Franco took them back across the Sylus node into Illume Belliel.

And that was two.

He blinked as they emerged into the cityworld and met the glaring sun, which was now angling directly at them from beneath the trees. He searched for Alshiba and caught her gaze just as the knight was helping Niko off the node behind him.

Alshiba saw Niko and her eyes widened. She covered her mouth and turned away to hide a smile. And that made it worth it, too.

Mir nodded meaningfully to the knights' commander.

He drew his sword and raised it in the air. "Paladin Knights—onward!" A gauntleted fist clapped against his breastplate. Two hundred knights echoed him.

Mir held a hand to Franco. "Looks like that's your cue. Don't forget our little arrangement."

As if he could. Mir had implanted a failsafe that would trigger if Franco tried to escape Illume Belliel while standing on the Pattern of the World—because this time, Franco wouldn't be *going* so much as *becoming*. He would become the gateway, a bridge over the Pattern of the World, his mind alone holding the connections open between Illume Belliel and T'khendar, allowing the knights to cross between realms in a single step.

Franco almost wished Mir was going with them.

With a measured exhale, he stepped on the node and opened the route, watching silently as the Paladin Knights charged into T'khendar.

And that was three.

※

Alshiba stood between a brace of Paladin Knights, waiting with bated breath for Franco to step back off the node. The clearing felt empty without the massing tide of armed men, with just a pair of knights separating her from Mir and Niko.

"He might've broken my jaw, the *sneaking weasel*!" Niko was stomping back and forth like an irate child while Mir murmured calming words—or possibly threats. One never knew with Mir Arkadhi.

The moment Franco emerged off the node, Niko swung for him. Franco had no time to react. Alshiba saw Niko's hand flash, saw Franco double over—

Fury exploded inside her. She grabbed the fourth and sent a bolt spearing at Niko.

Mir blocked it with his own working and spun her an *are-you-out-of-your-mind?* stare. He pulled Niko roughly off Franco. "By the seven scales," he hissed, "you have all the intellect of a dull-witted bovine." He shoved Niko far from Franco.

That's when Alshiba saw the bloodied dagger in Niko's hand.

Franco collapsed to his knees and then onto his side.

"Franco!" She rushed towards him, but the knights caught her by both arms and held her back. She flung them a glare and a command with compulsion beneath it, "*Release* me!" But they held her fast, probably because they were both shielding themselves with the fifth. "I am the Alorin Seat. You will do as I command—"

"Actually, Lady Torinin," Mir approached wearing a chilling smile, "these knights only follow my commands."

Niko wiped his dagger on a handkerchief and tossed the bloodied linen onto Franco. "We don't need the traitor now. Your men will find the weldmap, Mir."

'Your men…'

A dreadful understanding crashed over Alshiba. The pod of knights that had accompanied Niko and Mir across the node…so they'd been Eltanin men too, and obviously loyal to Mir. And *'the weldmap'* could only be referring to Dagmar's infamous map.

No wonder Mir Arkadhi was involved! You could buy an entire realm with the money Dagmar's weldmap would fetch on Eltanin's black market.

Suddenly it became so clear to her, Mir's plan. Sending the Paladin Knights after Björn was just a diversion, a bit of trickery to turn the Speaker's attention—and Björn's attention—in one direction while Mir's goons stole a priceless treasure in another.

She settled a corrosive stare on Mir and tried not to think about Franco lying frighteningly still. "Do you care at all if Björn is brought to justice? Or was this entire affair just smoke-screens and artifice?"

Mir's expression resolved into dark admiration. "Oh, well done, Alshiba."

Niko meanwhile crossed to her and grabbed her hand. There was a terrible light in his eyes, or perhaps a terrible darkness. He leaned improperly close, forcing Alshiba to turn her face away, and murmured into her ear, "I've been wanting to do this for a very long time." Then he tore her oath-ring off her finger.

Stepping back, he held up the ring and eyed it triumphantly before shifting a narrow glare to the knights holding her. "Bind her and the traitor in *goracrosta*."

Abruptly, rough hands pulled Alshiba's arms behind her back, and a static bite quickly tightened around her wrists. She felt her connection to *elae* slowly draining off.

The other knight grabbed Franco's unresisting arms and started winding silver rope around his wrists. He looked up beneath his helm as he did so. "What do you want to do with this one?"

Niko considered Franco's fallen form while sucking on a tooth. His gaze took on a vengeful gleam. "Throw him on the node."

Alshiba gasped. "Niko, *please*!" Bound in *goracrosta*, Franco wouldn't be able to navigate the Pattern of the World. It would rip him apart.

Niko pocketed her ring. "Don't worry, Your Excellency. You won't have long to mourn him." He nodded pointedly to the knight standing behind Alshiba, and he dragged her into motion. "Get rid of her somewhere deep," Niko called after them. "For *good* this time!"

Alshiba turned a desperate look over her shoulder. The other knight had Franco up on his feet. As she watched, he gave him a hard shove. Franco fell onto the node and vanished.

❖

Popular theory describes a plus-crossed node as four leylines pinned to one nodepoint. But such was technically *not* a plus-crossing, because four leylines could mean traveling the nodepoint eight times, if the four leylines were traveled in both directions.

Plus-crossing actually meant the node was set with four specific lines of travel that could only be traveled in *one* direction before switching to the next line of travel.

But since Franco and Dagmar were the only two Nodefinders to have ever successfully plus-crossed a node, and since said nodes had always been constructed for questionable purposes, they felt the less their brethren understood about plus-crossing, the better.

When Franco was plus-crossing the Sylus node, he programmed the node to switch to different destinations each time it was traveled, said destination set per Isabel's instructions.

The plus-cross initially triggered when Franco took Mir and Niko across to T'khendar. The second line triggered when they returned to Illume Belliel. The third switched on when the Paladin Knights crossed into T'khendar, and the fourth…

Franco had always been concerned about the fourth switch, because Isabel had directed him to make the leyline charge on the instant it recognized his life pattern. This bothered Franco immensely, because all the wrong people would need was the right combination of mishaps, and he could simply *fall* across the node directly into Björn's palace in Niyadbakir.

Which is, in fact, what occurred.

Franco landed in a crumpled pile of agony, suffering in that moment as much from Mir's implanted failsafe than the dagger Niko had shoved in his gut.

Alarms were sounding, *resounding*, echoing off the city's alabaster walls. He heard shouting and running footsteps coming closer. Then soft hands cradled his head—*Isabel*.

A shadow fell across his brow. Franco opened his eyes see the First Lord bending over him. "Alshiba—" Franco gasped to him.

"Don't worry. Mir will keep her safe."

"*Mir!*" Franco could barely choke out the words past the compulsion clenching his chest, "he's *with* Nik—"

Abruptly something tore inside him, another of Mir's traps waiting for the right trigger.

"He's losing too much blood." Isabel's voice, out of Franco's view.

Björn nodded to her.

Strong hands lifted Franco up. Swooning darkness spilled across his vision.

"Be well, my friend," Björn said, but all Franco saw as they rushed him away was the look of concern in the First Lord's eyes.

❖

Alshiba walked in a dream, a nightmare veiled in loss and treachery, where her steps only dragged her backwards and her furious screams emerged as strangled, threadbare gasps.

Björn gone. Franco gone. *Elae* gone. Her ring stolen, her Seat likely soon usurped, and no one the wiser thanks to Mir Arkadhi's devious scheming.

He was following her now, probably to make certain the knight actually carried out his assignment and threw her off a very high cliff. This time, she knew unequivocally that Björn would not be there to save her.

The location the knight chose was on her own estate. The better to make it look a suicide, no doubt. She could hear the gossip-mongers now: *'Alorin Seat Takes Her Own Life After Node to Forbidden Realm Discovered Beneath her Nose.'*

You have quite the sense of humor, Alshiba. Mir's quiet mental laughter made the hairs stand up on her arms. *It really will be a shame to see you gone, and without even that dinner I'd hoped for.*

Alshiba clenched her jaw. It did no good to spar with Mir. He enjoyed the tussle as much as the teasing.

Alshiba, do you have any idea how many Seats want you removed from the Council? Mir bent his head to capture her gaze. *Any idea at all? It's not personal. It's simply that the Speaker has his mind set on you chairing the Interrealm Trade Committee, and a great many others find that a terribly unmanageable arrangement.*

"And I suppose *you're* better suited?" Her gaze made a daggered accusation of her words.

Mir arched an amused brow. "Most anyone else would be better suited, my dear. A woman whose only desire is the man who abandoned her three centuries ago is hardly a candidate for extortion or bribery. Imagine, someone with actual moral fiber chairing the most important committee on the Council? Everyone would be forced to treat honestly and above-board with one another. The Council's entire infrastructure would probably implode."

The knight stopped on a bridge nestled in the bosom of two hills, a high overlook where the sea sluiced through a natural arch and made a churning cauldron of the rocky inlet far below. He dragged Alshiba to the bridge's edge and hefted her into his arms.

This can't be happening!

She was fighting a debilitating incredulity, unreality at war with desperation, a sense of Fate reaching out for her while she scrambled frantically backwards from its obdurate hand. Surely, surely there was *something* she could do! But when the knight readied himself to dump her into the abyss, all of her ideas fled like night shadows beneath the dawn.

"Over so fast?" Mir came up beside the knight. "Let's make it interesting, shall we?" He reached for her.

"*Damn you, Mir!*" She fought against him but only made herself look ridiculous.

Mir sliced through the rope binding her arms behind her back—though the *goracrosta* still cuffed her wrists, ensuring *elae* remained far from her grasp. She struggled desperately then, but the knight quickly pinned her arms anew, and Mir only laughed.

Then he grabbed her wrists and yanked her out of the knight's hold and over the edge—

Alshiba gave a choked cry.

Her body swung in a frightening arc. Mir held her up, dangling beyond the railing, himself leaning precariously over it, holding her arms while her feet kicked the empty air and her head went numb with fear. Her stomach had already fallen to the rocks below.

Alshiba gave him a violent look of terror. "*Mir—*"

"Goodbye, Alshiba."

And he dropped her.

SEVENTY-FIVE

"The pattern weaves as it wills."

–The zanthyr Vaile

CAUGHT BY THE swift current, Trell saw the opening looming in the fortress wall, spilling into a cavern and the deep darkness of the mountainside. Whatever hidden entrapment had bound his foot to the Nadoriin's was acting as a powerful undertow and preventing Trell from using his feet to kick out of the current. The officer was keeping himself afloat, but his flailing arms testified to an unfamiliarity with water's ways.

Suddenly Trell's back struck up against something blunt—a post of some kind. An instant later the Nadoriin slammed into him. Trell grabbed him before the current could rip him off and away.

The officer glared as though insulted. "You shall never be forgiven for what you've done!"

It took Trell an embarrassing second to process his words. "You think *we* caused this flood?"

The Nadoriin struggled against Trell's anchoring hold. "I would strike you down in Inanna's name!"

"The *wielder* did this!"

"He claimed the same of you!" He swung for Trell.

Trell dodged and in so doing nearly lost his footing. He grabbed for the wood behind him again, and the Nadoriin's next fist connected with his jaw.

Stars blanketed his vision. The current surged greedily around them, clutching at them both. If not for the pole, the river would've already swept them over the falls.

The Nadoriin threw another punch at him. Trell caught the man's fist in his hand and used the officer's momentum to pull him close. He held his gaze and said fiercely in the desert tongue, "We mean no harm to you and your men. We came for Dannym's soldiers only!"

"*Mutineers.*" The Nadoriin's fury overruled his reason. He grabbed for Trell's throat, and they fell into the river.

Yet…as the brown water surged over his face and Trell went down beneath the officer's heavy form, he glimpsed possibility—unlikely, *improbable*, yet an opportunity presented with such clarity that it wiped all other possibilities from his mind.

The last time Trell had experienced such a moment, he'd been in the Kutsamak facing similar overwhelming odds. The vision then had been but a breath glimpsed, but it had bolstered his resolve through all that was yet to come. That first vision had retreated into the obscurity of shadowed memories now, but Trell recalled that moment. He remembered that *feeling*.

He and the Nadoriin came up together, sputtering, with Trell still clutching the larger man and the latter still trying to choke him. The current was sweeping them towards the falls again. Trell could see in the Nadoriin's gaze that he'd abandoned hope of all save vengeance.

Trell clutched him as they bobbed, just feet now from the hole emptying into the mountain's belly. What could he do? Nothing. Whether or not Jai'Gar's justice was served, they were both going over.

The cavern loomed.

They shot through the opening. Trell fell amid whitewater into darkness—

A hand caught his arm. Hope surged and then shattered as momentum ripped him away—

Only to be caught again by—not a hand, no, but some other force. His body slammed against the rock wall, and then the netting still tangled around his ankles slammed the Nadoriin around upside down beneath him. Agony flamed up and down his side. The officer gave a muted cry and went still.

They were both dangling there on the waterfall's edge, hung in the darkness by an invisible force.

Trell blinked up through the spray.

Tannour was clinging to the rough stone of the cavern wall with one hand and one foot jammed in a crevice. The other hand was reaching towards Trell, as if holding the invisible rope wrapped around his wrist and arm.

"*Your Highness.*" Tannour's expression mirrored that same mixture of panic and horror that had liquefied Trell's insides.

"Tannour." The name rather exploded out of him, loud with gratitude, thrumming with relief. They were far from saved, yet had it been Náiir smiling above him, he would've known no more hope than he felt in seeing Tannour holding him up with what could only be *elae*'s fifth strand.

Tannour glanced to the opening, far above. "Well…this is an interesting problem."

Critical might've been a more suitable word. They *were* rather stuck. Tannour was clearly unable to climb without releasing Trell, and the dead weight of the unconscious Nadoriin was tugging all of them towards the empty depths.

Trell felt the man's weight as pins in his ankle and a shoulder already flaming. "Can you pull me to you, Tannour?"

"I don't think so." Tannour gave a slight wince. "That is…I've never used the ropes for this purpose. I can't think how to—"

"No, I understand." Trell looked down at the Nadoriin swaying beneath him. The tangle of netting, combined with the man's weight, was already cutting off circulation to his foot. He had an idea, but it required the Nadoriin as a conscious participant.

Trell tried to concentrate on something other than the stabbing pins now working their way up towards his knee. "Can you do anything to rouse the Nadoriin?"

Tannour's voice floated down from above. "Possibly."

Soon the man's body started swaying in a widening arc. The pendulum motion pulled agonizingly on Trell's shoulder and ankle. Then the Nadoriin's face splashed into the waterfall—once, twice—

He sputtered. Coughed. Growled a curse.

The swaying slowed, save now for the Nadoriin's flailing.

"Inanna's Shield!" Trell called to him in the desert tongue, using the most honorable form of address one could pay a Nadori officer. "Give me your name and I'll give you mine, and let us speak beneath Jai'Gar's eye."

The officer stopped flailing, which seemed to indicate he was considering Trell's proposal. Perhaps the knock on the head had restored his reason, or at least a sense of self-preservation.

After a lengthy silence, the Nadoriin's deep voice replied out of the darkness, "I am Lazar hal'Hamaadi, *al-Amir* of Khor Taran."

"I am Prince Trell val Lorian, and above us is Tannour Valeri, a Vestian who serves in my company of Converted, and the reason we're still alive."

Lazar's silence that time lasted even longer. "Trell val Lorian." His body swayed slightly, shooting pain through Trell's entire side. "I heard you were dead."

"Viernan hal'Jaitar would like the world to think so. We didn't flood your fortress, Commander. The Shamshir'im wielder did that wicked work."

The silent blackness beneath him seemed a reflection of the Nadoriin's stare. After a time, he asked, "And why would he do that?"

"To keep me from freeing my father's men." When Lazar made no reply to this, Trell forced through his pain, "Because Viernan hal'Jaitar will stop at nothing to see me dead. He's tried drowning me, torturing me, imprisoning me—you might say our mutual enmity runs deep. But you are not Viernan hal'Jaitar, and I am neither of my fathers, and if we're going to make it out of here, we'll need to work together."

"Beneath Jai'Gar's eye you speak these things?"

It was an insult to question the oath once given, but Trell *had* invaded Lazar's fortress. "May I stand beneath the Pillars unclothed." This phrase had significant ramifications if spoken duplicitously.

Lazar grunted. "You speak too well of our tongue to be a kenneled hound. I accept your words beneath Jai'Gar's eye, though I fear Inanna will withdraw Her spear from my hand."

"May she forgive us both duty's calling—" A stabbing pain shot through him, and Trell sucked in his breath. "Lazar," he somewhat gasped, "can you lift yourself to take hold of my legs?"

The Nadoriin seemed to consider this while he swayed in silence and Trell gritted his teeth. Then he heaved himself upwards. Every motion on Trell's ankle sent knives stabbing through his tortured joints. Three attempts…*four*…finally strong hands closed around Trell's boots.

Trell let out a shuddering exhale and lifted his gaze. "Tannour?"

"Your Highness?"

"Can you push us towards that ledge?" Trell could just make out a slim stone shelf gleaming in the cavern's dim light.

While Tannour made a pendulum of them again, Trell ground out through clenched teeth, "Lazar, try to get a hold wherever you can."

The next few minutes were as harrowing as they were agonizing. The ledge was shallow, and handholds were few. It took several attempts for Lazar to find purchase, and many minutes more before he'd maneuvered himself into a sitting position where he could grab for Trell and drag him onto the ledge as well.

At last they both found precarious seating. Tannour released his fifth-strand binding around Trell's arm, and the prince hugged the much-abused appendage to his chest while his eyes teared and his breath came in painful shards.

Trell looked down at the tangle of netting that bound his and the Nadoriin's ankles. "Commander, any chance you can cut us free?"

"I have no blade."

Trell still wore his sword, but there was no way he could draw it and keep his position on the narrow slice of stone supporting him.

"Use mine." Tannour's voice floated down from above, followed in short order by a dagger.

Lazar hissed a curse commonly used against wielders and drew away from the floating dagger as if from a snake.

"Tannour is a Vestian airwalker, not a wielder." Trell caught the dagger with his good arm and handed it over, hilt first. "Can you do the honors?" The pain beneath his words was answer enough as to why he himself couldn't.

Studying him beneath a deeply furrowed brow, the Nadoriin slowly took the dagger. He stared at it for a time, then he lifted dark eyes to Trell. "You might've cut me free while still hanging back there. Inanna would not have shamed you. I tried to drag you down to death."

"Forgive me for speaking so bluntly, Commander, but my honor resides in my own acts." Trell shook his head with a slight smile. "Not in yours."

Lazar held Trell's gaze while he fingered the dark-bladed dagger. Then he bent and cut the netting from their feet.

Trell could just make out the Vestian's silhouetted form, still clinging to the stone about five feet above their ledge. "Tannour, how do you suggest we get out of here?"

"Can you climb, Your Highness?"

With an inoperable arm and a potentially broken—certainly useless—ankle? He gave a pained grimace that might've passed for a smile only in the darkness. "Not easily."

Tannour growled something in Vestian that sounded a curse. Trell wasn't sure who he was cursing. "I might be able to—"

"I will carry you." Lazar met Trell's surprised gaze with grave regard. "If you can hold to my back, I will get you to the top. You have my word, Prince of Dannym."

"I can secure you both, Your Highness," Tannour said.

Trell held Lazar's gaze, feeling a welling admiration. It was a brave man who shook the hand of an enemy, but a greater one who offered him his aid. He realized that Lazar was still waiting for his reply. "Sorry, I was just..." he shook his head, smiled. "Thank you."

"We spoke beneath Jai'Gar's eye. He is watching."

The Nadoriin carefully found his footing on the ledge and then slowly and with unexpected care, helped Trell to do the same.

The process of wrapping himself around the burly commander proved less comfortable and far more heart-pounding in its management, but finally he called to Tannour that they were ready and felt something ephemeral hug around his form, securing him to the Nadoriin.

Lazar hissed another oath and turned a suspicious stare over his shoulder. "You swear he's no wielder?"

Trell smiled at him. "May Huhktu claim my bones before my time."

Lazar shook his head. "I've never met a Northman who speaks so well of our tongue." He started climbing, asking as he reached for the first handhold, "Where did you learn it?"

"Duan'Bai."

Lazar gave a choked exhale. He plugged his foot into a crevice and heaved them up with a grunt of effort. "Duan'Bai—*you*?" His voice became strained with effort as he asked, "Didn't the Khurds slay your brother Prince Sebastian?"

"A ploy orchestrated by Viernan hal'Jaitar to draw my father's forces into M'Nador's war."

Lazar slipped a handhold and only just grabbed it again in time. He hugged the rock wall for a moment, breathing hard, and glanced back at Trell. "This is a truth?"

"Yes."

His eyes widened, serious and intent. "Explain it to me."

While Lazar climbed, Trell told him, "Five years ago, Radov abin'Hadorin decided I would prove a nuisance to his warmongering and sent a crew of Saldarian mercenaries to invade my ship, interrogate, and kill me. After questioning me thoroughly—and quite ungently, I assure you—they roped me to a trunk and threw me into the Fire Sea."

Lazar shifted his weight and hauled them up to the next ledge. "How did you survive?"

"Our Goddess Naiadithine took pity on me and delivered me safely to the Akkad."

"*Inanna's ashes.*" Lazar blew out an explosive breath and turned another stare over his shoulder. They'd passed the section where Tannour had been hanging when he'd first caught Trell. The Vestian had climbed well above them now and had nearly reached the mouth of the cavern.

Lazar's gaze as he stared at Trell was darkly troubled. "Your words are treason. I would they shouted with less veracity."

"As do I, Commander. Radov's greed has shattered my family and imperiled my father's throne."

The Nadoriin cast him another look before starting his climb again. "And your birthright?"

Trell clung to him with one arm and both legs, feeling the pressure of a different weight upon his heart. "The Eagle Throne is my brother Sebastian's to claim. I walk a path askew of my fathers."

"Fath*ers*?" Lazar spoke the emphasis through a hard exhale as he hauled them up to the next handhold.

"My fathers: King Gydryn val Lorian, and our Emir, Zafir bin Safwan al Abdul-Basir. It's…a long story."

The Nadoriin gave a dubious grunt. "So you've been in the Akkad since…the Goddess," he almost seemed to choke over the word, or at least the idea of it, "spared you?"

"More or less." Trell winced into the darkness. "With a brief tour through Darroyhan before I escaped."

"*Darroyhan*." The Nadoriin slipped his foothold. Trell felt Tannour's binding constrict while Lazar hastily found a new place for his foot. He tried not to think on what would've happened if Tannour hadn't been roping them with the fifth.

Clutching hard to the rock face then, and with his rapid breath mirroring Trell's in equal parts alarm and relief, Lazar somewhat gasped, "How in Inithiya's name did you escape Darroyhan?"

"With help from a Sundragon and a zanthyr." Trell exhaled a slow breath to calm his own racing heart. That had been a very near thing. "It's another long story."

Lazar again paused to turn him a wide-eyed stare. "You're a walking fable, Prince of Dannym." Then he hauled them up with another heave of effort.

And Tannour came into view beside them. An unreadable smile flickered on the Vestian's lips. He told Lazar, "He is no fable. He is our *A'dal*."

Left of Tannour, the cavern opening appeared a blister of light surrounded by rough plaster and then enveloping darkness. Tannour clung beside the hole in an impossibly awkward position, like some improbable spider; the kind of position only an experienced rock climber could assume with any confidence.

The Vestian lengthened his limbs to push his head around the opening, a mere foot above the rushing water, whereupon Trell heard a voice shout, "It's Tannour!"

❖

When the water had first clutched Tannour into its embrace, it had also ripped him from *ver'alir*. He'd tumbled, spun, become entangled and trapped, dizzied and water-blinded until finally it had spat him out for breath, only instants before the current clutched him and dragged him over a waterfall into the darkness of a cavern inside the mountain.

The fall was...very far. Yet now capable of breath and with air back in his grasp, Tannour bound himself to *ver'alir* and sensed the bottom before he hit—with just enough time to commune and reduce what might've been a bone-shattering splat to a rather ungentle and certainly ungraceful stumble-trip-roll across the cavern floor.

He stood for a while then, encased in *ver'alir*, letting his racing heart settle, recognizing that had he taken an instant longer to commune, this place would've marked his end, thinking for a painful moment what that would've meant in the broader context of his life. Then he thanked the Ghost Kings and in total darkness, set to climbing.

Air told him where pockets of stone would fit his fingers and feet. Air supported him when one of those proved too shallow or fragile. Air might've carried him all the way to the summit, but to commit to an elemental communing, such as airwalking itself, would be to bind himself forever to the path.

You don't think hal'alir *is still open to you after what you've done?*

Tannour didn't know, and he certainly didn't care to think on it just then. Thinking on it any time brought a strain to his breath. He focused instead on the vertical climb, which he found far less taxing than pondering how dark his soul might've become by treading *ver'alir*.

He was nearly to the summit when Air brought him his *A'dal's* voice raised in exasperation, and a few heartbeats later, his *A'dal*.

Tannour flung a hand to grab Trell's arm and caught it but couldn't hold him. As he felt his hand slipping, he flung a rope of air—desperate, thinking fast, or hardly thinking. Trell was his tether. But he was also his friend. Tannour didn't know if it would work—he'd never used air-bindings for any constructive purpose, but he understood their nature and he hoped...

Trell slammed around beneath him, taut in his line. Tannour whispered a prayer of thanks under his breath. Twice invoking the Ghost Kings in less than an hour. It was a momentous day.

As they resolved what to do and started climbing, Tannour listened to Trell's words and marveled at the prince's candor with the Nadoriin—nay, not merely a Nadoriin, but the *al-Amir* of the fortress they had invaded!

Twice as he climbed he felt the binding thread he'd kept on the two men constrict and pull against his hold. That was twice the prince would've owed him a life had he been keeping count in the Vestian way, or three times by an Avataren accounting. Tannour no longer tracked the tally he and Loukas had once kept on each other, but he bet Loukas knew it down to the decimal point.

But Tannour didn't want to think about Loukas. He had a new tether now. What did he care about Loukas n'Abraxis?

Only…everything.

Tannour clenched his jaw and threw himself upwards to hook his fingers in the rock where it abutted the plaster wall. He hung there with his arms long over his head and his shoulders hugging his ears while the waterfall gushed in all its elemental power beside him.

Water very likely coursed its own path of Alir. But that was the thing about the Vestian Sorceresy—they didn't tell you a path even existed until the path had chosen you.

'Need to know…' Tannour supposed it was a common enough phrase in the espionage community; of course, the Sorceresy believed its operatives only *needed* to know what they *wanted* them to know.

Tannour slung up his leg and wedged himself sideways between plaster, wood supports and stone in a semi-crouched position that would allow him to press out around the edge of the hole and assess their options.

Trell and the Nadoriin joined him soon thereafter, with the latter radiating confused conflict and his *A'dal* merely radiating pain. Tannour felt it as his own—his air-binding had caused it, after all—but how was he to have known that the *A'dal* was dragging around by the ankle a Nadoriin weighing upwards of fifteen stones?

Air brought him voices above the rush and roar of falling water. Near voices. *Familiar* voices. Tannour ensured that Trell and the Nadoriin were stable just below him and then lengthened his hold to peer out around the side of the hole.

The scene that met him was…

Astonishing didn't quite describe it. Four Converted were heading their way, navigating the strong current with ropes around their waists and more than five times as many men anchoring each of them from surer positions further back. Loukas was in the lead. No doubt Loukas had come up with the idea.

"It's Tannour!" one of them shouted. Not Loukas, though Tannour was sure that Loukas had seen him, because air shouted the sudden quickening of Loukas's pulse.

Tannour called out to them, "The *A'dal* is with me!"

A voice shouted something from further away. One of the men closer repeated the words. "He asks about their *al-Amir*."

"I also have Lazar hal'Hamaadi!"

The men conveyed this back to others, whereupon a cheer rose up, Nadori in nature. The Nadoriin must've surrendered or otherwise fallen to the Dannish soldiers after the tower collapsed, for king's men and Trell's own had charge of the scene.

Yet for all their effort, they wouldn't be of much use to Tannour unless he could somehow lob himself, Trell and the *al-Amir* beyond the swift-moving current at the edge of the falls. He scanned his eyes across the shattered tower and the wall crushed beneath it. It gave him an idea.

Tannour ducked back inside. "*A'dal*," he looked down to Trell, who he'd kept purposefully bound to the Nadoriin—Tannour sensed Trell's radiating pain and didn't trust his *A'dal* to confess the truth of his condition. "I have an idea."

"I'm all ears for it, Tannour."

"There is some risk involved. I don't know if it will work."

"You've gotten us this far, Vestian," Lazar remarked, which seemed almost a compliment.

"Well enough. By your leave." Tannour pushed himself back out to see around the cavern's edge and called to the men, "Hold your positions. We're coming out!" The last thing he needed was for one of the men to get too close to the falls and lose themselves to the current, which grew increasingly wicked the nearer one got to the rim.

Tannour should've felt nervous—he was risking his *A'dal* and the Nadori commander, never mind himself—but he walked *ver'alir,* and the emotions that coursed the Blind Path, of themselves tumultuous and passionate, left no room for unease. He hadn't dissembled, though. He had no idea if it would work.

He took a moment to focus his intention—he was attempting to do things with Air that no airwalker to his knowledge had ever done—but his mind kept straying with thoughts of Trell.

Tannour finally understood Loukas's fervent adoration for their *A'dal*. There was much to be said for a leader who expected impossible things of you. Trell made you *want* to rise to the challenge. You became more than you were because of him.

Taking a deep breath of resolve, Tannour sent a binding of Air in an arrow shot towards the tower. He made his arrow loop through a shattered window and boomerang back towards him out another. He caught this end as it returned.

One end of this ephemeral rope he kept firmly in his grasp. The other end he secured around Trell and the Nadoriin.

"That feels...interesting." Lazar remarked.

Tannour kept his eyes on the tower. Already its integrity was starting to fracture beneath the pressure of his binding. He prayed it would last them long enough. "Now's the time to pray to your gods, Commander." And without giving him time to do so, Tannour hauled on the air-binding.

Lazar and Trell both swung up past him. Soon they emerged through the cavern's opening into free air, their boots dangling inches above the water.

Everyone watching either gasped or cursed.

Tannour ignored the storm of startled consternation that followed—soldiers yelling to each other, debating whether or not to try to reach the A'dal, despite Tannour's admonishment not to—and concentrated instead on pulling.

Slowly, Trell and Lazar floated towards the lines of Converted. Tannour clenched his jaw and mentally hauled on his pulley, trying not to think about all the things that could go wrong, or how *fethen* angry Loukas would be if he dropped the A'dal to get sucked back down over the waterfall.

Air brought him waves of elemental discord emitting from the tower—plaster, wood and stone in fractious contention. Every inch of force he applied weakened the collapsed tower, so that groans of wood and cracking mortar soon reached his awareness, even if no mortal ears might yet hear them.

Tannour kept steadily pulling until his charges were within reach of Loukas and the men, whereupon he released his air-binding. Trell and Lazar splashed down well behind the point of safety.

But the backlash of releasing the binding whipped through the tower. The structure gave a great, heaving shudder and just...*melted* in a tumble of stone and chalky water.

Tannour had no choice but to cast himself upwards on Air. He shot out through the hole in the wall before the debris from the collapsing tower blocked him inside. But he'd underestimated the force needed to propel himself far enough to reach the Converted. He saw even before he splashed down in the water that he wouldn't clear the current—it would drag him right back under, just in time for an avalanche of stone to fall atop him.

Tannour cursed his mis-estimation as he hit. The waves from the collapsing wall shoved him further afield of his aim. Then another wave overwhelmed him and he lost Air completely.

Prepare yourself to meet the Ghost Kings, Tannour Valeri—

A hand closed around his wrist.

The current dragged at him, but the hand held him firmly. Submerged, blind, Tannour strained to grab for the another handhold. Finally, his fingers closed on the man's other hand. He heard a fractured shout, broken by water's refraction.

A force began pulling him against the current.

He surged to the surface with a gasp.

The hands dragged him close...*clutched* him close. Tannour felt himself and the other being hauled back, as if on a roped line, while water deluged his face. Finally the hauling eased and Tannour found his feet. He slung wet hair from his eyes and looked to the man who'd saved him.

"*Fiera's breath*, Tannour." Loukas's green eyes were voluminous with meaning: remarks he didn't dare say, feelings he didn't dare confess, sorrows they both knew too nearly—all that history over all those years; the experiences they'd shared, the lashes Tannour had endured, which had cut far deeper than any flail he'd wielded in return, Loukas's rejection as acute punishment...

And then Trell was at his side, shouting his praises, with what seemed like a thousand other men, and Tannour let the world carry him away from Loukas n'Abraxis's pinioning gaze.

※

With the hole into the caverns blocked by the collapsed tower, the water levels in the lower city started rising quickly. A stormy dawn observed this filling pool. The coming rain would turn the aqueduct's waterfall into a torrent.

Trell tasked Gideon with moving the soldiers up onto the walls for safety, while Lazar saw to his own men. All other contentions were momentarily set aside in lieu of the two commanders' pact beneath Jai'Gar's eye. Trell was himself half-hobbling, half-swimming for the nearest stairwell when something changed in the water.

He perceived the riversong the instant before She spoke to him.

Trell of the Tides...

Trell stilled. *Everyone* stilled.

Had they all heard Naiadithine's summons because they stood within the swarming waters of Her domain? Or because She'd simply willed it so?

The flood waters began swirling. Men cleared from the path of this vortex with alacrity, backing themselves into buildings and each other to give the water its way. Soon a great whirlpool spun before the startled eyes of the men. As the waters turned, ever widening, silt drained away until the whirlpool became as glass and mirror-clear.

And within this mirror, Naiadithine showed them—

Battle as Trell had never seen, viewed from within a wide pool, as a window onto another world. Except this world was familiar to him. He recognized the sacred pool several breaths before the Converted started murmuring aggressively among themselves, a full minute before one of them dared say in hushed awe, "It's *Raku*."

Was it because She showed them the battle filtered through Her perspective—a god's perspective to which they were now privy, embraced as they were within Her auspices—that they couldn't look upon the scene with a view to glory, only with a sense of grave dismay as men were cut down and fell into the pool, staining its sacred waters with their lifeblood?

Or maybe it was because everywhere among those men, demons ran, spreading chaos. Travesties of men, they cut and slashed or merely tore mortals limb from limb. Trell recognized their likeness to the thing that had accosted him at Darroyhan, the same thing that had cast *deyjiin* into Vaile.

And then a new type of consternation beset Trell, as a man tumbled into the pool amid clouds of blood. As his turning body sank beneath the surface, his face came into view...

Dannym's soldiers gave a collective gasp.

Trell felt his heart sinking along with his father's form. *Why* was he still in Raku? He was meant to be in Nahavand by now!

Do you see? Naiadithine asked him—asked *them*.

And though She did not say the words but spoke in concepts in the way of gods, they all knew She was asking: *do you see the blood of men shed for the greed of men? Do you see the blood shed for the grace of gods who care nothing for the vanities imposed upon them? Do you see the harm done to the tapestry? The frayed threads, the broken lines, designs in the pattern that simply end, forever unfinished?*

Do you see *what war has wrought?*

Then the vision faded, the whirlpool stilled, and all of the men who'd stood witness to that moment were left only with the combined horror that had echoed from her essence into their own.

And a final warning, spoken to all, spoken to one:

Trell of the Tides...you must end this war.

Whereupon Trell knew at last what the Goddess required of him in return for her many graces.

SEVENTY-SIX

*"When you can see beyond the curve of consequence,
the path becomes clear."*

–The Adept wielder Arion Tavestra

WHEN RAFAEL MOVED himself, Tanis and Sinárr from his own universe to the outskirts of the Warlock universe known as Wylde, Tanis experienced a moment of disorientation. But as Rafael realigned his starpoints, swirling darkness resolved into space—starless, yet far from empty.

The lad found himself standing between the two Warlocks on a translucent bridge, facing a wall of worlds. The latter shifted before them in veils of color and perspective, each one layered over the next, as a vast window comprising hundreds of stacked panes of glass. Starpoints framed the 'corners' of each pane, making them all unique.

Far distant of the wall of worlds, beyond view but not beyond perception, another set of starpoints framed the space the worlds occupied. If the worlds were a book, these latter starpoints would've been the table upon which the book was lying.

"They have built much since last I viewed Wylde." Sinárr sent his bridge unfolding towards the wall of worlds.

Rafael looked to Sinárr with golden embers sparking in the raven flames of his hair. "It is an ingenious collaboration, but I find aspects of its existence unsettling."

"I share your unease." Sinárr clasped hands behind his back and morphed his dark bridge into a viewing platform. "There are too many linked determinisms beneath Baelfeir's own."

Tanis walked to join them at the railing that was forming as they spoke. He felt like Sinárr's entire bridge was tilting sideways. "What do you mean by linked determinisms?"

Sinárr turned his golden gaze to Tanis. "Baelfeir invited the Warlocks to build worlds within his starpoints—a collaboration they've named Wylde, the first of its kind. You might consider it the Warlocks' attempt to mimic the Thousand Realms of Light. This idea is how he convinced many of them to join in the effort."

He placed a hand on Tanis's shoulder. "As soon as the Warlocks created space within Baelfeir's starpoints, however, *their* starpoints became Baelfeir's. A Warlock could decide that within his world he wanted a certain structure and intent, but ultimately, if in conflict, its rules would bow to Baelfeir's."

Rafael placed his hand on Tanis's other shoulder—Tanis was starting to feel a bit like an amphora they each wanted to claim. "Essentially, young Tanis, Baelfeir has coincided every starpoint within his framed space. This makes it impossible for anyone *in* the worlds to coincide his exterior-most starpoints in return."

Tanis turned with a puzzled frown. "Why?"

"Baelfeir's starpoints are not representative of a single determinism anymore." Starlight limned Sinárr's dark complexion, imparting a silvery cast to his features and accentuating the furrow marring his brow. "To coincide Baelfeir's starpoints, you would have to duplicate *also* all of the starpoints beneath them. This is nearly impossible, for they represent too many determinisms all linked together—much like your Alorin, where millions have agreed upon the same illusion to create a lasting reality."

Rafael's wings twitched, shedding a rustling starfall. "Duplicating Baelfeir's exterior starpoints will allow us to move in and out of Wylde and its worlds, but we will only be able to make limited changes to those worlds, since we haven't actually coincided all of the starpoints." He settled a telling look upon the lad. "There is only one god of Wylde."

Tanis gulped disconcertion. "Baelfeir."

Two sets of unearthly eyes pinned on him in voluminous acknowledgment.

Tanis looked with misgiving back to the shifting veils of worlds. They really were like a book to his perception, a closed book whose hidden story yet beckoned. Tanis duplicated Baelfeir's exterior-most starpoints and then, without really understanding what he was doing, he opened the book of Wylde and began shifting through the pages—rapidly. Worlds riffled past.

Rafael turned a wide-eyed stare at Sinárr.

The latter shrugged. "The boy just intuits it."

"Tanis," Rafael shifted his wings agitatedly, dripping *deyjiin* stars, "you must reconsider my proposal. Being bound to only three immortals is an underwhelming accomplishment for one of your talent."

Tanis stopped the pages at a desert world. Suddenly it seemed as if Sinárr's bridge was trying to dump him down into it.

"Tanis, the floor…"

But the lad missed whatever Rafael said, for he was already grabbing the starpoints of that world as though they were two hanging rings, and swinging himself inside.

When his slight disorientation settled, Tanis found himself on a saucer-shaped rooftop overlooking an alien city. Much of the place lay in ruins, while what had at first seemed a blackened plain turned out to be a mass of *eidola*-like creatures. They'd overtaken the rubble of the city and were swarming around one of the tallest mounds. It took a few seconds of focusing through his bemusement to realize that a battle was occurring there.

"Are those—" Sinárr came up behind Tanis with smoke wreathing his form.

"Revenants, yes." Rafael appeared on Tanis's other side with his wings fully extended.

Sinárr cast his golden gaze across the melee. "They seem to have collected here from many different worlds. Without coinciding Baelfeir's exterior starpoints, we won't be able to efface them back into the aether."

"You chose an oddly immutable world to visit, Tanis," Rafael remarked. "The aether here is nearly petrified."

Tanis was staring at the seething mass of revenants and feeling as unnervingly bounced and jarred as if Destiny had roped him to a runaway coach. "I think *they* chose it, sir."

Rafael followed Tanis's gaze to the mound boiling with revenants. "Ah…" Understanding colored his exhalation. "This reeks of Shailabanáchtran's particular malodor."

Sinárr inquired, "Who is the mortal?"

Tanis swallowed. "Prince Ean."

"Your Prince Ean?" Sinárr arched brows. Then he frowned. "That is very peculiar."

Urgency now had Tanis doubly unbalanced. "We have to get them out of there."

"They seem rather firmly ensconced."

"The Malorin'athgul has anchored himself." Rafael shifted his wings. "I can retrieve the mortal, but—"

Tanis felt like the world was sliding off its axis. "We have to help both of them."

"Darshanvenkhátraman is no friend to Pelas." Rafael arched his velvet wings threateningly behind him, framing his golden torso with darkness, forging a striking display. "Let him find his own way."

Tanis held his gaze. "This won't please Pelas, sir. He's forgiven his brother."

Rafael drew back, staring hard at him. "No…you would not lie to me." He looked back to the melee and exhaled a sigh. "I fear we must do this tedious thing, Sinárr." A powerful stroke of his great wings propelling him into the air, a gilded demon, a fallen angel, both terrible and darkly beautiful. *Deyjiin* streamed behind him in a sparkling wake.

Tanis looked somewhat desperately to Sinárr. "I can't *think* for the—"

Sinárr placed a hand on his shoulder. "I perceive the tumult that has you unbalanced." He dissolved into smoke and whisked towards the fray.

Yet Rafael had barely reached the horde before the revenants began attacking him as furiously as they'd been after Darshan. They threw themselves into the air, so that the black sea became choppy with revenant spray. Rafael spun, dove and dodged, trailing silvery whorls of *deyjiin* that stilled every revenant they touched, but Tanis saw quickly that even with such power as this, Rafael would have to fly for hours—days—back and forth across the horde to dispel them all.

He was hovering now above the mound, trying to reach Prince Ean and Darshan inside what amounted to a funnel of revenants, for every time the Warlock swooped in close, the creatures made ladders of each other to reach him.

Sinárr meanwhile whisked through the ranks. Yet even without form, they managed to cling to him. When too many had accumulated, Sinárr would solidify and then vaporize again, dragging the revenants into nothingness with him.

Every few minutes, Darshan would release a pulse of *deyjiin* and force the revenants back, but this only gave him and Prince Ean a moment to breathe and room to swing their weapons. No room for Rafael to land. Not enough space for escape.

Tanis watched this frenzy feeling like he was clinging to a skiff in a hurricane sea. That unbalanced sense had become nearly overwhelming. He leaned against the side of the dome and clung to the tiles, lest the precariously wavering tower tip him off into the revenant waves.

And yet in truth, what had him most reeling was the *absurdity* of the situation.

In a universe where anything could be anything, a boundless place without scope or limitation, it seemed utterly unreal to him that *this* was the only solution they could find—to fight these creatures as mortals, with force and effort and blunt aggression.

Sinárr had told him early on that to control anything, you had to be willing to *be* it entirely. This was a theory underlying the duplication and coinciding of starpoints, as well as effacement—it was practically one of the Laws of Shadow, if such could be said to exist.

'You cannot control something you cannot duplicate,' Sinárr had said, *'all you can really do is fight it.'*

And that was all they were doing—fighting these revenants—because the Warlocks were unwilling to duplicate a thing they found so repulsive, so offensive to their moral sensitivities; unwilling to *be* them, to understand them. Unwilling even to *try* to communicate with them or ken them with any sort of intimacy—certainly not with the intimacy required to duplicate and share each other's starpoints.

It occurred to Tanis in a moment of violent seasickness that perhaps the Balance wasn't inclining him towards Prince Ean and Darshan at all, but towards these others—these forgotten, discarded beings, the produce of indifferent gods, who no one in all of creation would ever try to help.

Whereupon, the tilting floor finally slammed down, level at last.

Tanis looked around at the desert world and knew suddenly that *it* had been abandoned, just like these revenants. The only ones owning the world now were the beings standing there at that moment—and possibly Baelfeir, elsewhere, via his overarching starpoints, his table to this book of worlds.

Baelfeir had made certain no one could coincide the starpoints of his universe. Thus he'd made it impossible to change the fabric of the desert world.

But what if the world itself was no longer a part of Wylde? Then they wouldn't need to coincide Baelfeir's starpoints at all.

Tanis thought about how he'd duplicated the starpoints of that world, and he wondered, what would happen if he just…*shifted* them? If he just ripped this page right out of the thousand-page world-book and put it down on a different table…would anyone even notice it was gone?

The Warlock who'd created the world clearly wasn't owning it anymore, and Baelfeir obviously wasn't paying attention, or he would've already come to find out what two foreign Warlocks and a child of Light were doing in Wylde.

So Tanis took a deep breath and concentrated….

A smile claimed his features.

So simple. Everything in Shadow was just *so* simple. It had all shifted while nothing at all had shifted. Yet Tanis looked at the revenants now and he *knew* them, the way Sinárr knew his mind when he brought Tanis into his own universe.

New understanding guided Tanis's next intention. He framed starpoints down on the bed of rubble and opened a portal.

Light speared out in gleaming brilliance.

The sea of roiling inhumanity froze.

Then it surged through the portal in wave upon dark wave.

Instantly forgotten were the Warlocks, the Malorin'athgul, Prince Ean. Tanis's portal shone more brightly than all of them, and the revenants shoveled themselves through it with unreserved abandon.

Sinárr soon reappeared at his side, molting smoke. "Tanis…" he was observably breathless, and not from fighting revenants. He took the lad's shoulder sharply. "What did you do?"

Tanis tugged at one ear. "I guess you could say I, uh…stole it?" He scrubbed at the back of his head and gave Sinárr a culpable look.

"You *stole* it." Sinárr's golden gaze felt like heat burning his skin—a merciless, sun heat, the kind that melted planets. "You moved the entire world out of Wylde?" His pulsating shock could've pounded a mountain into chalk. "To *where*?"

"To my own universe."

Sinárr gave some kind of choked curse in the language of stars. The words seared Tanis's thoughts, such that they felt charred on all their edges. "And then?"

"Then…" Tanis let his breath out slowly, "I opened a portal into one of the new worlds we've been building together."

Sinárr spun a swift and probing stare at Tanis's portal. The revenants were still funneling through it in a flood that would likely continue for many hours. He looked bewildered when he turned back to the lad. "*Why?*"

"They only wanted the energy of life."

"Tanis," he sounded slightly frustrated, but more concerned, "you cannot restore life to these entities once they've been severed from their Warlock."

Tanis watched the flood of creatures with a furrowed brow. "Maybe they're just shadows of what they once were, Sinárr. I don't know, but I doubt anyone has tried to restore them with *elae*," he turned to him significantly, "and *our* world has both. Here, they're only hungering. At least there they have a chance for something else." He let his gaze stray across the revenant sea and added soberly, "It seemed more humane, in any case."

Sinárr gripped his shoulder. "Baelfeir will eventually realize this world is gone, even if its own creator does not."

"We don't have to keep it, Sinárr. What would we do with it, in any case? As soon as the revenants are through the portal, I'll move the world back to Wylde."

Tanis's attention drifted then to the others coming towards them on a bridge Rafael was unfurling across the open air. The Warlock was striding smoothly with his wings hovering in an almost possessive curl around the imposingly tall Darshan, seeming more jailor than rescuer. And walking a few paces in front of them...

Apprehension clogged Tanis's chest and anticipation his throat. With his entire body suddenly tingling, he watched Ean approaching—

And saw that his prince was covered in welts and barely standing upright.

"Your Highness!" Tanis ran to him.

"I'm all right, Tanis." Ean took hold of the lad and looked him over, his grey eyes incredulous and so full of warmth. His fingers gripped and released on Tanis's shoulders as if to reassure himself the lad was actually there. "I can't believe it's really you."

Suddenly Tanis felt his younger self again, that youth of Calgaryn who wore admiration for his prince as proudly as the coat Ean had gifted him. He thought of the impossible road he'd traveled since they'd last seen each other, thought of everything he'd learned about them both in that time, and gave a quiet smile. "It's been a long time, Your Highness."

Ean just gazed at him, still smiling, his eyes glassy.

Tanis had so many things to say to him, to tell him—*ask* him—but all he seemed able to do just then was grin.

"Words can't communicate how overwhelmed I am to see you." Ean ran his hand along Tanis's arm. "Shadow is all illusion, but you *are* here, aren't you? I'm not dreaming you up in some wild hallucination from the bottom of a pile of revenants?"

"I'm here." Tanis managed a smile despite the unnerving perception that the prince had been speaking from recent experience; that would also explain why he seemed so unstable on his feet.

Ean was still gripping his shoulders, looking mildly haunted but at the same time amazed. "Darshan said that Balance pervaded the cosmos. I'm ashamed to say I doubted him, but now—well, what else explains this impossible meeting than that Cephrael brought us together?" He shook his head with slow incredulity. "Lady's light...Tanis—how did you find me?"

Because you called. Tanis stared wordlessly at him, wondering with a pang of uncertainty why Ean wasn't aware of their bond. Was it because the prince was cut off from *elae*?

Into their reunion Rafael and Darshan arrived, with the former murmuring, "…should not have happened—would not have happened unless all of the Warlocks had withdrawn their vitality from these worlds."

Whereupon Tanis heard Darshan's deep voice inquire, "It begs the question, Rafael, if they're not here, where have they gone?"

As if the Malorin'athgul's arrival had enervated him, Ean looked to the others. "Forgive me, I think—"

His knees buckled.

Darshan caught him in his arms.

"*Sinárr!*" Tanis spun urgently to the Warlock, who shifted them immediately away.

SEVENTY-SEVEN

"The most glorious moments are not those of success, but rather those moments when out of despair you feel rise in you a challenge posed to life itself."

–Errodan val Lorian, Queen of Dannym

NASSAR ABIN'AHRAM WATCHED the dark death moving through the Akkadian ranks, feeling gravely conflicted. Jai'Gar instructed loyalty, but He also said that a pious man must look upon his neighbor as his own brother. When Nassar's time on this earth was done and Inithiya brought his spirit before Jai'Gar, the Prime God would call forth all men whom Nassar had treated with in his life. *'Were you treated well, treated fairly?'* the Prime God would ask them. *'How fared you by this man once called Nassar abin'Ahram?'* Jai'Gar would hear their claims and judge Nassar by his acts.

He would be judging Radov abin'Hadorin, too. In death, all men stood humbled before their gods, whether or not they'd ever known humility in life.

Now Nassar looked upon the battle waged by his Ruling Prince, and he wondered what virtue Jai'Gar would deem in this act. Would He find prudence in waging war to claim power for power's sake? Would He see justice in making abominations of men, or temperance in allowing them to slash and slay unhindered, unrestricted, as wild animals on a rampage?

He had no idea what was happening with the creatures Radov had loosed directly on the oasis, but the twenty-five pushing through the front lines were leaving a frightful wake of death.

Nassar was no stranger to battle. As a pious man, he always prayed for peaceful resolution, but there were times when peace must be carved from the immobile mass of fanaticism, and when the only possible justice required an eye for an eye. He saw a crude balance in men fighting men, in the clean combat of swords and shields; and though brutal and always tragic, there had been moments in his career when those dark and smoking clashes held a sort of dark majesty for him. Battle was man at his basest and shouted of the failure of higher reason, but he admitted it was sometimes necessary.

But what he was witnessing that morning on the Khalim Plains wasn't battle. It was slaughter.

※

Farid felt the impact when Dannym's king barreled into one of the creatures trying to throttle him. He twisted to avoid its clawing fingers and brought up his legs around the demon's chest. Then he threw himself over backwards, threw it over backwards, somersaulting as the thing flew off him. It dove back for Farid at the same time that Farid dove for his sword. By Jai'Gar's will, Farid moved faster.

He brought up his blade just as the creature fell atop him. His breath left him in a painful expulsion, and he watched through pinpoint stars as whatever dark life possessed the creature expired. Not a strain of humanity remained in its dying stare.

Farid finally regained his breath and managed to shove the creature off of him. The one he'd clashed with earlier was regaining itself. Half of its arm was missing. It hardly seemed to notice.

Behind Farid, the others were still fighting, but far fewer of them were on their feet than had first begun.

Farid pushed his boot into the dead creature's shoulder and yanked his blade free. Then he did a fast scan of the scene. Several demons had seen him rise and were coming towards him now, but another truth struck far more forcefully and with immediate alarm.

Where was the king?

※

Ramu…?

Jaya…?

Náiir…?

Rhakar…?

Amithaiya'geshwen, the Bosom of God's Nectar, opened her eyes, and her large pupils flashed to slits, forming a narrow band among crystals of variegated blue, their lenses reacting to the boiling corona that loomed so massively in the otherwise black sky.

She lifted her snout and inhaled the solar wind, and her body shivered to wakefulness, gilded scales riffling from head to spiked tail. She tested her wings and found them strong. The star inside her combusted with restored vigor.

Balaji...

She cast the thought to the brother whose voice had awoken her. Doubtless they'd all been wondering where she'd gone, what had happened after Darshan had dared invade the Mage's *sa'reyth*, dared accost her with his power, shaking the world fabric as a storm whips a flag. How long had she been asleep on that metal planet, healing from the wounds he'd inflicted? She hoped her lesson in kind had shown him the better of some manners.

Balaji...?

He should've answered her by now.

She cast a hook for his awareness along the bond they shared, a polite summons for his attention...

Still no answer? Had he not *just* called to her?

Something was very wrong. Mithaiya reassessed the timbre of Balaji's first address. She'd thought the faint distress was concern for her, but what if it derived from some other cause?

Had Darshan found his way back to the world faster than she had?

Balaji! Ramu! Rhakar! Náiir! Jaya!

She sent summonses spearing towards all of her siblings, and after a startlingly lengthy breath of time, she perceived a faint reply.

...aiya...

Ramu's call. So distant, yet...

Mithaiya challenged her own perceptions. Ramu seemed to be calling to her not across the cosmos but across the *years*. Had she been gone so long?

But no, something had to have been done to shift her and her siblings out of the same time stream. Darshan hadn't manipulated time during their altercation, and neither had she, which meant...

Mithaiya shook the third strand to get its attention and sent it seeking her siblings. She found her favorite brother first. *Ramu!*

Mithaiya. Relief coursed his mental tone. *Where are you? Do you remain in Alorin's time?*

Yes. I've been asleep—healing.

Well that you were, else we'd all be scattered across the ages and might never find our way back to the same moment. I've anchored to you now and will seek the others.

Confusion spun rings in Mithaiya's head. *Ramu, whatever hap—*

Later, my sister, for if I'm not mistaken, you're desperately needed in Raku.

Mithaiya roused to at once.

Be certain of what course you take there, Mithaiya. Balance hinges by a thread.

Mithaiya shook out her wings. *I will, brother. Find the others.* She launched herself towards the node.

※

Spinning a fast look around, Farid saw the rippling pool and the shadow beneath the surface and felt his heart sinking with it. For the space of an indrawn breath, he debated. It was hardly a deliberation. He sheathed his sword and dove in.

His dive brought him close to the king. Farid grabbed him around the chest and kicked hard for the surface while also taking them deeper into the pool, towards Jai'Gar's pillars at the center. The creatures had avoided the pool thus far, probably because they couldn't swim. More likely they would sink like stones.

Farid surged to the surface with Gydryn heavy in his arms, wondering by what odd twist of will the Prime God had made him the protector of Dannym's king, and kicked backwards towards the pillars, hugging Gydryn against his chest.

By some miracle of luck he got the king's limp form up onto the stone platform where the pillars rested. The creatures that had been chasing him were standing at the pool's edge making an unholy row with their clattering shrieks and ratchet screams. But since they were on the edge and he was beneath Jai'Gar's eye, Farid mostly ignored them.

The king was bleeding heavily from a gash along his neck. Farid tore a strip from his robes to stanch the wound, then tried rousing the king. After several attempts, Gydryn's eyes fluttered. Then followed a perilous bout of choking and coughing, during which Farid did his best to keep pressure on the king's wound.

Finally, Gydryn inhaled a shuddering breath and lifted bloodshot eyes to him. Farid saw gratitude there, and amazement, and not a little disbelief. "You already saved my life once," the king managed with a choked gasp.

"And you saved mine, Your Majesty."

Gydryn lifted his eyes to the pillars overhead. "Either there's divine will in this, Farid, or one of us needs to find a new line of work."

That's when one of the creatures jumping up and down in fury on the pool's stone rim slipped and fell in with a gigantic splash. Farid watched it sink instantly to the bottom. It laid there for a moment as if startled, or confused. Then, horrifyingly, it found its feet and started walking.

Gydryn looked grimly to Farid. "That could be a problem."

Mithaiya flew off the node into the sere Nadori daylight, banked her wings and flew south towards the thunderhead of smoke roiling above the walls of Raku. Her anger had already been roused by the emotions seeping across the bond from Ramu and her siblings. Seeing the currents, that simmering fury geysered to all new heights.

What atrocities against the lifeforce were being worked here, and by whom?

She intended to discover those answers. She intended many things that day.

Mithaiya studied the currents as she soared towards the oasis, seeing much of what had come before and what was still to come if she took no action. Ramu had urged caution from her, warning that the Balance hung by a thread, but the creatures wreaking havoc on the currents were offenses against Nature itself. She would be justified even if she erased every one of them from the aether.

Which was exactly what she intended to do.

Gydryn pressed the wad of cloth to his neck and watched the creatures lining up at the rim of the pool. Beyond them, the Converted who'd rushed the courtyard had either found their end in blood or fled anew. Now the seven remaining demons were free to stare at Farid and Gydryn—or more unnervingly, at the creature wading across the bottom of the pool towards them.

Farid doffed his soaking cloak and shrugged out of his wet layers until he wore only a linen tunic and pants. He squatted on his heels beside Gydryn then, his hand resting on the hilt of his blade. Both of their gazes went to the creature beneath the water.

"It won't be able to reach this platform," Farid said, though he sounded too uncertain for Gydryn to take his words to heart. "We're at least ten feet above the bottom."

"What if it tries to climb the supports? Or knocks them down and us with them?"

Farid exhaled a slow breath of unease. "Jai'Gar willing, it's not that smart."

As it happened, the creature on the pool floor stood in the shadow of the pillars staring up at them for a long while. Eventually a clattering racket erupted amid the demons on shore, and then one of them jumped into the pool after the first. The others quickly followed.

"What are they—" Farid stared down into the water, watching with a puzzled frown as they strode across the pool floor. Then his eyes widened. "Your Majesty, hurry away from the edge—*please*." He took Gydryn's arm and half-supported, half-hauled him back to the safety of the pillars.

Gydryn leaned against the stone, keeping pressure on the wound at his neck, and tried to ignore the queasiness in his stomach. He managed a rather sickly swallow. "What are they doing, Farid?"

Farid was peering down over the platform's edge again. He turned the king a look, portentous and grave. "They're making a ladder of each other."

Gydryn leaned his head against the jade pillar and closed his eyes. The world spun dizzily.

Farid didn't have to tell him their odds of survival now. He saw it clearly enough—the small platform that had been their refuge would quickly become a liability. Gydryn himself was already one. He'd lost his blade, but even had he still possessed it, he wasn't possessed of enough strength to wield it.

He opened his eyes and settled them on the Akkadian prince. "I'm sorry I placed you in such danger. If not for my infirmity, my delays, none of this would be."

Farid regarded him gravely. "Your deeds are mine and mine are yours, Your Majesty. This is the will of Jai'Gar." He turned back to the pool, and Gydryn saw his jaw tighten. "They come."

A dark head appeared at the platform's lip. Farid kicked it back into the water and took the second creature with his blade, but the third demon grabbed Farid's lower legs and the fourth surged out of the froth to hijack his balance. The prince tumbled onto his back.

He beat at them with his sword, but they clawed their way up his form nonetheless. The first one onto the platform fixed its dead eyes on Gydryn.

The king said a prayer—of gratitude, contrition, grief for choices made in error and those errors of indecision; prayers for his sons, their protection... their forgiveness. Then he turned a burning gaze upon the demon and roared at it. He poured all of his fury and frustration into his cry, all of his breath, his very soul, until his lungs emptied themselves and his throat scraped hoarse and raw.

Farid was still thrashing at the platform's edge, but the one with eyes on Gydryn found its feet and moved towards him. Even before it reached for him, he knew it was his end—

Blinding light flared, and a dark figure plummeted out of the sky. It struck the *eidola* that had been coming for Gydryn and knocked it to the platform with a satisfying crash. As Gydryn's eyes recovered, he saw a woman crouched atop the creature's chest, dressed all in black and with a greatsword strapped to her back.

The demon grabbed for her as she straightened, as indifferent to its clawing hands and flailing feet as a fisherman to a fish flapping on the chopping block. She stared down at it.

Gydryn felt a radiating heat that was shockingly intense. He had to turn his face away—but not before he saw the demon's stone body crust over like charcoal.

She stepped off it resolutely and turned to the next. A solitary kick sent one of the two that was grappling with Farid flying head over heels across the water. It crashed through the pool's stone rim and dug a trench through the grass. She cast the spear of her gaze after it and seared it to ash.

The other creature leapt for her. She caught its throat in her outstretched hand, and a wave of ash overcame its dangling body. She tossed it away. Two steps brought her to the edge of the pool. She cast a relentless gaze down into the water where the other demons had collected. The pool came to a rapid boil, and soon an oily residue floated to the surface.

Steam was rising from the pool when she knelt at Farid's side and cradled his head in her hands. "Farid?" She laid a hand on his brow and appeared to concentrate. After a moment, she lifted her blue eyes to Gydryn. "You are the king, father of Trell?"

Gydryn managed a nod.

"Can you walk, King of Dannym?"

Gydryn looked at the steaming pool. "Not across water, Lady dragon."

A brief smile graced her features. "I am Mithaiya." She lifted Farid into her arms and straightened. Her lithe form appeared fragile compared to the broad-shouldered prince, but she held his body as easily as if he'd been a child. "Come, King of Dannym. Today you will walk on water."

Even as Gydryn was wondering if she'd meant that literally, she stepped off the platform and started walking across the pool. The water simply solidified beneath her feet and stayed solid, still as glass, while ripples streamed away from her steps. A long black braid hung down her back, tracing the line of a greatsword.

She turned a pointed look over her shoulder, whereupon Gydryn realized he'd been staring instead of following and amended that as fast as the vertigo still consuming him would allow.

Mithaiya was laying Farid on the grass when the king finally climbed over the rim of the pool. She came and placed her hand on his own brow then. Her blue eyes captured his astonished gaze while her other hand caught his shoulder to prevent his startled pulling away, and he remained locked in her hold for an instant that felt like an hour.

Gydryn had no words to describe that timeless moment wherein he became the receptacle of a Sundragon's power. The intense prickling he felt at his neck and the clawed flesh of his back paled in comparison to the throbbing heat pulsing everywhere else. He felt electrified, yet painlessly so; rather, as though every molecule in his body had become charged with life.

As she released him, breath surged into his lungs. He gasped and staggered back. His dizziness had become a heady vitality.

"I've closed your wounds and restored your life pattern," Mithaiya told him resolutely. "Watch over Zafir's treasured son until I return."

Gydryn gazed wondrously at her, still grasping to believe in this impossible salvation. "You may depend upon it, my lady."

Mithaiya gave him that brief smile, comet-fleeting but hinting of the brilliance of an exploding star. Then she rushed away.

Gydryn knelt and laid a hand on Farid's shoulder. The prince was covered in blood, but he seemed to be breathing easily. Gydryn lifted his gaze to the towering jade Pillars of Jai'Gar, the Prime God's remote eye into the realm of men, and sitting there upon the damaged lawn, with a dragon's energy circling his core and gratitude consuming his heart, he cried.

SEVENTY-EIGHT

"Betrayal has many faces. Forgiveness has but one."
—Attributed to the *angiel* Epiphany

TANIS WAS DOZING in a chair by the bay windows when Mérethe entered the infirmary carrying a silver tray. "Hello, Tanis."

"Hello, Mérethe." Tanis shook himself more awake and sat up straighter in the chair. He narrowed his gaze at the tray. "What's all this?"

Mérethe looked down at the cups and goblets with their varied contents. "Red and white wine, tea, water, something Rafael conjured that I don't advise you to drink, and possibly," she sniffed at a tiny cordial glass, "well… it smells like anise."

"Are we having a party?"

"Sinárr wasn't sure what you might want." Her blue eyes glanced to Prince Ean, who lay sleeping in the bed, and back to Tanis. "He thought you might be worried for him."

"No, I'm not worried for him. Tell Sinárr not to worry for me."

As if hearing them speaking of him, Ean stirred. Val Lorian grey eyes opened sleepily on Mérethe, whereupon the prince roused himself to give her a smile. "Ah, hello there." He looked dashingly disheveled.

Mérethe very nearly blushed. She set down her tray on a table beside Tanis. "I'll leave you to get reacquainted." She bobbed a bashful, "Good day, Your Highness," and hurried from the room.

Tanis scrubbed at his jaw. "And that was Mérethe."

Ean grinned speculatively after her. "She's an Avieth?"

"Yes. Sinárr's concubine…or she was…is." He gave a slight grimace. "It's complicated."

"Isn't it always?" Ean cast a smiling gaze around the room. "This looks familiar." He let his eyes come to rest on Tanis. "The first time we met, you were sitting in that very chair."

"Well...almost the same chair." Tanis looked down at it. "I've made this one more comfortable than the real one. Her Grace had this theory about the relationship between cushioned chairs and laziness...it was a rather lengthy hypothesis."

Ean sighed. "Sometimes I really miss Alyneri." He glanced down at his bare chest and arms, and a puzzled frown hinted as he looked up again. "Who Healed me?" His gaze sharpened on the lad. "You?"

Tanis pulled at one ear wearing a culpable smile. "In Her Grace's absence, I took it upon myself. I thought you'd prefer my attempts over Darshan's."

Ean shook his head wonderingly. "So you're a wielder now too, *and* bound to a Malorin'athgul..." A strained recollection overcame his expression. "Doubtless you know that Darshan bound me to him to save my life. I'm still trying to wrap my head around that."

Tanis looked over his prince. "How do you feel, Your Highness? Fit for a walk?"

Ean's tense gaze softened. "In Alyneri's garden?"

Tanis grinned. "Not exactly."

Ean drew in a deep breath and let it out. "How do I feel?" He appeared to think it over. Then his eyes crinkled. "I feel damned relieved, to be honest. *Whole* in a way I haven't felt in a long time. Well enough, I'd say, for a walk."

"Good." Tanis retrieved a pile of folded clothes. "These are for you."

The prince eyed him as he took the bundle. "Did you conjure these, too?"

"No." The lad wandered over to the window while Ean dressed. "Sinárr is better with clothes than I am. I wanted them to actually fit you."

Ean cast his grey eyes around the room while pulling on his pants. "But this place is obviously your doing."

Tanis pushed hands in his pockets and leaned back against the windows. "I thought it would be..." but he didn't quite know how to say what he'd hoped it would be.

Ean put warmth into his gaze. "It is. But we *are* still in Shadow."

"Yes. This is..." Tanis shoved a forelock of ashen hair back from his eyes. "Well, it's sort of my world *and* Sinárr's world. We've been building it together."

Ean sank back down on the edge of the bed. "Say that again?"

"Right..." Tanis rubbed at one eye. This was the hard part—well, one of the hard parts. "I worked a mutual binding with Sinárr so that we could build worlds crafted of both *elae* and *deyjiin*."

Ean stared harder. "So…" he scrubbed at his jaw, "you're bound to a Warlock…too."

Tanis grinned sheepishly. "That's right."

Ean looked dumbfounded. "Does Pelas know?"

"The last time we spoke he asked if I was planning to bind with any other immortals. That was before Rafael started propositioning me."

Ean stared at him for a moment longer. Then he reached for his shirt while a smile slowly claimed his features. "Just how many immortals *are* you bound to, Tanis?"

"Only three, Your Highness. I haven't bound with Rafael. I'm hoping to somehow…not."

"*Three.*" Ean barked an incredulous laugh. "Who's the third? Cephrael Himself?"

"Oh, it's Phaedor."

"Of course it is." Ean eyed him wonderingly as he reached for his boots. "And when did you bind with Phaedor? After we split up in Rethynnea?"

"No, sir. He bound himself to me when I was a child."

Ean slowed. "I see." He frowned at the boot in his hands for a moment, and Tanis perceived a whirlwind confusion tear through his thoughts. Then he shoved his foot all the way in. "Well, I suppose you should tell me of the others. What plans have you all concocted while I was unable to speak for myself?"

"Rafael took Darshan to his universe to have words with him about his brothers, and Sinárr is…elsewhere. We have the day to ourselves, so to speak."

Ean straightened. "So to speak…because there is no day?"

"Basically." Tanis tapped his knuckles absently against his palm. "But if you consider that reality as we know it is only solidified illusion—per the Twenty-first and Twenty-second Esoterics—then Shadow doesn't seem quite so strange."

Ean just stared at him for a silent while with a grin splitting his features. Then he sobered his smile and waved at Tanis. "So where will you be taking me for this walk?"

Tanis joined his side as they were heading for the infirmary door. "That's the thing about Shadow." They walked out the door into the hall, and—

—emerged on the top of a cliff overlooking the sea. "You can do things like this."

Ean surveyed the granite cliffs with their deep green mantle of firs, the churning surf, and the tall sea stack in the distance. Striated clouds blanketed the heavens, darkening underneath, yet the sun shone through in many places and illuminated the charcoal waters into patches of glorious blue.

The prince laid a hand on Tanis's shoulder. "*This* beach." His eyes danced. "Why *this* beach?"

Though the day felt cooler beneath the heavy clouds, Tanis stood warm in his prince's esteem. "I always wanted to swim out to that rock. Her Grace would never allow it."

"Alyneri is too practical for her own good." Ean arched a brow, both invitation and challenge, and took off down the steep trail, nearly at a run.

Tanis ran after him, already grinning.

Ean was stripped down and diving into the waves by the time Tanis got to the beach, so he shifted them both into a pair of swim trunks—some clothes were easier to manage than others—and dove in after him.

Tanis followed Ean's lead and swam beneath the breaking waves, and soon they were far from the shore but only halfway to the sea stack. As they were treading water and catching their breath, Tanis asked him, "Was it really this far? Maybe I should—"

Ean grinned and flipped the hair from his eyes. "Don't change a thing." Then he started off again, arm over arm, dragging his body through the deep waves at a punishing pace.

Tanis was a strong swimmer, but he couldn't keep up with Ean. The waves were high, the current strong, and his prince had a way of reading the water that surpassed familiarity; it was his innate association with the fifth, imparting an underlying sense of all things elemental—even those recreated through the power of Shadow. And he swam *fast*.

The sun was shining through a break in the clouds when Tanis finally reached the sea stack. Already out and balanced on a ledge, Ean grabbed Tanis's hand and hauled him out of the water before the waves could smash him against the rocks.

Finding his footing, Tanis looked back towards the shore, which was mostly hidden by the tumbling surf, and let his eyes travel over the jagged cliffs looming above the beach. He dragged his wet hair back from his face and turned Ean a smile. "It's just how I thought it would be."

Ean clapped him on the shoulder. "You need to see it from higher up." He started off along a ledge above a colony of razor-sharp barnacles. "When Trell and I swam out here as kids, we found a path of sorts around the side. Let's see if it's still here."

Tanis made sure that it was.

They climbed the harrowing path, which angled steeply over the jagged rocks at the sea stack's base, scraping knees and toes and tearing their hands on the rough stone, but Tanis wouldn't have traded the pain for anything.

Ean was again first to the top, and he held a hand back down to Tanis. Soon they stood side by side with their chests rising and falling fast, staring first out at the deep sea and then back at the Calgaryn coastline.

Tanis had no idea how that line of cliffs actually appeared from the sea stack. He'd crafted it from his imagination—a postulation of possibility married with pieces of memory—but whether it existed as such in Calgaryn or only in Tanis's imagination, the mountainous coast he'd created boasted a rugged and forbidding beauty.

The wind whistled around the rock and blew the sun away, but it also dried their skin. They sat on a ledge while the birds circled overhead, and they talked of their adventures and reminisced about the zanthyr.

Later, as they sat hugging their knees with the briny wind blowing their hair into their eyes, Ean turned to Tanis with warmth in his gaze. "Pelas told me you'd grown, not just in stature but in ability. I had no idea. I never imagined—I never could've conceived of all that you've become."

Tanis dropped a smile towards his toes. "Your Highness—"

"Don't you think it's time you started calling me Ean? I left the life of Dannym's prince behind quite some time ago."

Tanis's brow furrowed at this. There were truths he needed to get to, for both of them, but he didn't quite know how to navigate those waters—mainly because he didn't yet understand why his father didn't know him. The lad rested elbows on his knees and squinted towards the horizon. "Pelas told me you tried to unwork his life pattern."

After a moment of silence, Ean said, "Did he tell you why?"

"He said he'd done something to betray your trust."

Ean radiated a sudden discomfort, and Tanis perceived a deeper unrest still beneath the surface of this. "You're his bond-brother, Tanis." Ean's grey eyes shifted to meet his. "I'm sure you know about the compulsion he was under."

"Yes."

"And I assume…" he gave a slight wince, "I imagine he told you about the woman who helped him overcome it."

"Isabel van Gelderan."

"Isabel…" Ean exhaled a slow breath, tinged of disharmony. "I am bound to her, Tanis, and she to me. We worked the Unbreakable Bond centuries ago when I answered to another man's name. To free Pelas from his compulsion, she chose to betray our troth."

Tanis dropped his gaze to his hands. He understood now what Pelas and his mother both had glossed over in recounting their versions of the incident. "It was the Ninth Law," he murmured. "She would've applied the Ninth Law." Tanis looked back to Ean. "I'm sorry. That must've been very hard for you."

Ean blew out his breath and somewhat fell back on the rock. "It doesn't matter now. I've made my peace with Pelas." He rolled his head to look at Tanis. "It has to be your influence I saw in him. He's—thirteen hells, we have a *Malorin'athgul* bound to our side of the game now, Tanis. Who would've imagined?"

Tanis was fairly sure he could name several people who had imagined it, but he kept this to himself. "So you've forgiven Pelas. Have you forgiven Isabel?"

Ean arched resigned brows. "Yes—no…I mean, her acts don't require my forgiveness." He gave a pained grimace. "It's complicated."

"Isn't it always?"

Ean tossed a soft grin in his direction. Then his expression sobered into thoughtfulness. "At first…in the beginning I struggled to forgive her, I'll admit, but now it's more about forgiving myself, I think."

"How is that, Your Highness?"

Ean sat up to better meet his gaze. "You perceive it. I know you must. You've always been keen to my mind, Tanis, more than most…better than most." He sank forward and braced elbows on his knees, staring out at the distant cliffs. "Darshan drew me to Tambarré, drew me to himself; he'd bound my path to his intent long before he bound me with his power. I know this has changed everything, Tanis—I perceive the paths of consequence shifting even without *elae* to show me their design. But I think the reason I can't move forward into that future is because I still don't know everything that lies behind. There's a betrayal at the end of Arion's path—I can sense it. I know it's the key to understanding so much more than I currently do, but for the life of me, I can't recall that truth!"

Ean hung his head. "I probably don't need to tell you any of this. What with your being a truthreader and the fact that I'm in your world here—Raine's truth, you've probably read every thought that's come to me."

Tanis was watching him with compassion making a vise around his chest. "I sense your turbulence."

Ean cast him a rueful smile. "How could you not?" He straightened and laid a hand on Tanis's shoulder. "We can talk more of this as you will, only right now…I just want to enjoy this day with you. Can you do that for me, Tanis? It's been so long, I hardly remember what simple happiness feels like."

Tanis exhaled a slow breath and silenced his own impatience. "Of course, Your Highness." He let his gaze wander towards the horizon, thinking of another time, centuries ago, when he'd sat happily in his mother's arms admiring the sea. "My mother once told me that it's important to enjoy moments of respite when they present themselves." He glanced to Ean and away again. "She said those are the times when Fate isn't requiring greatness of us."

Ean's hand tightened on Tanis's shoulder. "Your *mother*? You finally met your mother?"

"She taught me most everything I know about truthreading, and much about Patterning."

"How? *When*?" Ean took him by both shoulders. "Don't keep such momentous things from me!"

Tanis held his gaze, feeling oddly choked. "I wouldn't dream of it, Your Highness." He stood and focused on the beach, anchored both the sea stack and the shoreline firmly in his thoughts and then...*folded* the illusion, as if bringing together two edges of a painted canvas.

Suddenly they stood on the beach, only now the cliffs had been hollowed out to house a domed gazebo with towering columns tiled in abalone. Beneath the dome waited a linen-draped table set with a meal.

Tanis stood there sort of smiling at it.

Ean let out a low whistle. "That's beautiful. Is this another of your creations?"

"It's Sinárr's." Tanis turned him a grin. "He always knows when I'm hungry." He led the way up the stairs.

Ean followed, but at the top, he paused and stared at the table with its elegant display of delicacies. At compass points around the central table, iron filigree braziers glowed, filling the cave with warmth. "Is this...but it's not real, is it?" The prince lifted a puzzled look to Tanis. "It can't be real."

Tanis sat down in a chair. "The first law of Shadow: it's as real as we decide it will be."

Ean came and sat down across from him. "Is that really the first law?"

Tanis started helping himself to a pheasant pie fragrant with apricot and sage. "To be honest, Shadow has a lot of first laws. It depends on which Warlock you ask."

"I see." Ean served himself from a tagine of lamb and olives. "So, you were about to tell me of meeting your mother. When did this miracle come to pass?"

"After the zanthyr came for me in Rimaldi."

Ean paused the serving spoon halfway to his plate. "You were in Rimaldi?"

Tanis smiled. "That's another long story, Your Highness."

"All right, fair enough." Ean motioned for him to continue. "So the zanthyr retrieved you from Rimaldi..."

"And took me to my mother's house..."

Tanis told his prince then how he'd discovered the patterns on the walls of his bedroom, how each one had revealed another of his mother's lessons, and some of what she'd taught him.

Ean listened raptly, his smile wide and his gaze marveling. At one point he remarked upon her ingenuity, whereupon Tanis had to admit to him how foolish he'd felt when the zanthyr had asked him if he *really* thought that his mother had put those very important lessons on his *walls*.

Ean laughed out loud. "No?" He clapped a hand down on the table, his eyes bright. "Where were they, then?"

Tanis smiled softly. "Just memories stored in patterns in my mind, like gifts for opening in my later years. Returning home had wakened those patterns, and the memories of her lessons came back in the form of illusions. Many lessons returned over time—years of lessons, actually."

Ean shook his head wonderingly. "But weren't you just a babe when you became a ward of the Lady Melisande?"

"I was two years old when Phaedor brought me to live with Her Grace's mother."

"Two." Ean sat back in his chair and stared at him. "But...did you say the zanthyr brought you?" He rubbed at his forehead. "How did I not know that?"

Tanis imagined the answer to that lay in his father's occluded memories. "After a few months at my mother's home, Phaedor took me to the Sormitáge—that is..." he flashed a sheepish grin, "actually, the High Lord of Agasan came to see Phaedor, and the zanthyr ingeniously commandeered the High Lord's ship to take us to Faroqhar."

"That must've been something to see." Ean shook his head and drank his wine. "So you enrolled in the Sormitáge..."

Thus did Tanis tell his prince the tale of his time in Faroqhar. Over the course of the evening, as they moved from the gazebo to a balcony at Sinárr's villa, Tanis detailed his adventures—from his invocation examination with the Endoge, to his investigation with Felix and finally the battle at the Quai field.

As Tanis spoke of Shail's capture and Pelas's rescue, they were sitting beneath the stars on Sinárr's balcony overlooking the edge of the world. Beyond their high vantage, a luminous sea extended to the edge of creation. Three moons in different phases made an arc in the west, while high above, a pair of twin planets hovered, nearly translucent, against the backdrop of space.

When Tanis finished catching Ean up on his experiences, the prince sat still for a long time, drinking his wine and studying the lad with a furrow between his brows. "So, because of you," Ean began slowly, "two of our most powerful enemies have not only become allies but have now been eternally bound to the game on our side." The portent in his tone, likewise the intensity of his admiring gaze, felt a little overwhelming to the lad.

Tanis pushed his hair from his eyes. "I had some help."

Ean arched brows at him significantly. "Not much, I'd say."

Tanis held his position with polite insistence. "I had my mother's teachings…and my father's."

When Ean only stared at him at this, Tanis dropped his gaze to his goblet. "This betrayal that sits in your past…why do you think you can't remember it?"

Ean gave a forceful exhale and pushed to his feet. He walked to the railing and stared out across the Shadowscape. "Tanis, this may seem unreal to you…" he paused, looked around, and then cast him a wry smile, "or not, but I've died three times for this game—each time Returning, each time trying again to take my place as a Player, each time falling prey to Shailabanáchtran's malice."

Ean turned to lean back against the railing and regarded Tanis with a deep furrow between his brows. "Arion made a choice in his last hours, and it's condemned *me* ever since. Why can't I remember?" He tapped his fingers on the balustrade while his frown deepened. "Honestly, I think it scares me—I don't even know why. It's not like I can change anything about it, *do* anything about it, and yet, just aiming my attention towards that memory makes me cold." Ean gave a troubled exhale and shook his head. "Shail showed me something from his own recollection, but I don't trust it."

Tanis studied him with quiet concern. "What things do you know are true?"

Ean crossed his arms. "I had a dream where Isabel asked me—asked Arion—to promise not to pit myself against the Balance. In that memory, I didn't make that promise, but I believe that later I did."

He came back over and sat down on the couch next to Tanis, resting elbows on his knees. "Arion Tavestra slew the Hundred Mages at the Citadel—*I* did that, not Björn." He lifted a burning gaze out across the sea. "But because he was my friend…Arion's closest friend…Björn took responsibility for Arion's choices as though they were his own, even though he hadn't been there, even though he had *no idea* why Arion had done it—or if it was even the right thing to have done. He simply trusted that it was a choice Arion had to make."

Ean slumped back against the cushion. "But I don't know, Tanis. Shail had the Mages under compulsion, but if Arion had *looked* for another way, might he have found one? He slew them ruthlessly, driven by fury at what they'd done to Isabel…hardly considering the personal consequences, and I believe in so doing, he drew Cephrael's blighting eye." The prince looked gravely to the lad. "Beyond this surety, the rest of that night is jumbled. I can't even remember the name of my own—" He pressed his lips together tightly and turned his gaze away.

Tanis felt Ean's radiating torment on multiple wavelengths. "Your Highness—"

"Ean," he protested faintly.

"—if you're willing, I could work a Telling to help you recover your memory."

Ean turned swiftly back to him. "You can do that?"

Tanis knew unequivocally that he could, but he said only, "It's worth a try."

"Of course, then—yes." An almost desperate willingness radiated from Ean. "I'm in your hands, Tanis. Do what you will with me."

Fighting a sudden nervousness of his own, for Tanis knew at least some of what he'd find in Ean's memory, the lad placed his hand over the prince's brow in the truthreader's hold. "Open your mind—"

—*to me*. Ean had done it before Tanis even finished the request.

The lad summoned *elae* through the link he shared with Sinárr and bound his thoughts with Ean's in the powerful patterns of *elae*'s fourth strand, working the Telling as his mother had taught him.

*Recall Arion's battle with Shail. Find its beginning…*and when he sensed-saw that Ean had done this, *Move through it and show me what occurred.*

Thus did Ean recall Arion's final battle for the first time through the fourth strand's unadulterated lens of truth.

Arion swam in a river of light. He could barely see, barely *think*. Fragmented patterns clogged the currents; daggers of compulsion fractured his thoughts. He and the Enemy rode the raging current of the Pattern of the World, locked in a deadly embrace.

He'd had to sever two of his anchors. The last one, the node in the far north, still held. Balance had a sense of humor after all, it would seem.

An hour ago he might've released that anchor and ridden the Pattern's tide to a safe harbor, but an hour ago he'd been unable to conceive of letting the Enemy walk free, or of abandoning the effect he'd intended to create, of *turning his back* on the First Law…

How could he call himself a wielder if he made such a choice? It would be denying everything that he was, everything he knew. He would be denying *himself*.

Arion understood then that this was the choice Isabel had foreseen, the choice she'd known so unquestionably that he would make…the one he'd already made…the only one he could ever make.

An hour ago, two paths had extended before him.

Now both lay in shards. He leapt from one decision to the next, each time hoping the landing might reveal a new consequence, an opening to some future beyond the one reflected in the Enemy's eyes.

The Pattern of the World tore at his mind. The Enemy tore at it more violently.

Every time the man's compulsion had overcome one of Arion's shields, he'd been forced to retreat behind the next one. He'd compartmentalized his consciousness so many times, he hardly knew what part of *him* remained.

They now clutched a dagger between them. Two men, each with a foot upon a single stake, teetering violently, forging a tug of war with Balance.

Arion had hold of the Enemy's life pattern. He was unworking it.

The Enemy had hold of Arion's last shield. He was unmaking it.

Balance would decide which one would prevail, but Arion already suspected which of them Cephrael had chosen as the victor.

There came a point when a man knew the battle couldn't be won, yet he kept fighting anyway, because that's all he could do. For a soldier, this was a courageous act, but for a wielder…for him, it would always prove catastrophic, because the moment a wielder *knows* that he can't achieve the effect he intends, he can't.

In that place of knowing stood Arion. He *knew* the Enemy was more powerful, and he couldn't shake that knowingness. It had poisoned all of his efforts, corrupted his certainty, broken his resolve.

The only recourse he had to keep the Enemy from compelling him into becoming his weapon was his native skill of unworking; yet using it in combat was tantamount to using the fifth in combat.

And so he had…

And so he knew where Balance would cast its favor.

Oh, Isabel…I am so gravely sorry.

She'd known, because she knew *him*. He should've listened to her.

Arion fought against the compulsion bombarding him, fought to continue unraveling the Enemy's pattern, fought to keep desperation's claws out of his thoughts. Amid the many compulsive patterns overtaking his mind, among the disheartening illusions and lies trying to corrode his efforts, he clung to one truth: *Isabel had promised him that he would know his son.*

The Enemy's gaze burned into Arion as they struggled, nose to nose, for control of the dagger. The man needed but a grace of Arion's blood to bind him unbreakably. No longer merely a pawn to be used and discarded then, but a puppet to be manipulated, leveraged, broken and punished until eternity's clock wound down.

The Pattern of the World raged, spearing Arion's eyes with painful shards of light. Balance rang a reverberating warning. *Elae* screamed for him to act.

Isabel had told him to what time and place she would send their son if Arion fell, as she'd foreseen. He finally felt vindicated in dredging that truth so ruthlessly out of her.

Arion reached out along the bond with his son and anchored himself to his child's awareness. He threw a second anchor into Time to hook upon a far-flung future that Isabel had foreseen. He cast a third desperate anchor to the north, and Calgaryn.

Then he clenched his jaw, and his determination, and forced the three streams to coincide.

Time sucked him violently forward.

The Enemy almost lost hold of him. Arion had hoped that he might, but the man clung to him as Time skipped them along its undulating stream, both Arion's life pattern and the Enemy's bared to the elements, intertwined…tangled.

The Enemy's anchors hauled them back in time. Arion's hauled them forward. He felt himself being torn apart across the centuries—his very life pattern ripped to shreds.

Arion had but a brief window left to act, seconds…fractions of seconds.

The Enemy was dragging his consciousness back to his own time. Arion couldn't prevent that. But without his body, the Enemy couldn't bind him either.

With a final surge of determination, Arion plunged the dagger into his own chest while simultaneously anchoring his body in his son's future time. Then he released his hold on the Pattern of the World, and the node in Calgaryn reeled him in.

But the forces rushing through it were too violent. The node expanded—*exploded*. The floodgates opened back into the Pattern of the World, and the river became a sea.

Where the node had been now pulsed a powerful weld.

It sucked Arion into its vortex and spit his body forcefully out into the future, even though he felt his consciousness being pulled backwards into the past. For a moment in the shattered continuum, Arion existed in two places. The Enemy existed in two places.

Time stretched.

Existing simultaneously in both moments, the Enemy rose above Arion. His eyes gleamed darkly in the shadowed tunnel where they'd landed after the weld spit them out.

Arion watched the Enemy pull the dagger out of his chest. Blood choked his throat. "This isn't…the end of me."

The Enemy gave him a sharp smile. "Come and find me. I'll be waiting." He licked his thumb and pressed it to Arion's bloodied lips.

Deyjiin flooded into Arion. Every molecule in his body screamed.

The Enemy vanished back down Time's stream, dragging Arion's soul with him.

Arion fought that current as long as he could, but *deyjiin* was devouring his body, turning it into crust, an ashen shell, and without it, he had no more anchors. With a last force of will, his last effect to create, Arion willed that his body would become a beacon for his soul, to find his way back to his son when time's clock struck the year.

He cast a final apology along two binding threads, but he was so weak, his pattern so torn, and Time's clutching current roaring so loudly in his mind, he didn't know if either would hear him.

Isabel…Tanis, my son…I love you.

Then, with his last dying breath, Arion bound his memories for his future self to unravel and surrendered to the darkness.

Tanis gently released *elae* and removed his hand from the prince's brow. His own eyes were wet, but Ean's were wetter. He met the lad's gaze.

"*Tanis…*" Ean sucked in a shuddering breath. Then he hugged him fiercely.

Ean clutched his son close, reeling with the impossible course of their separate journeys, marveling at the pattern of cause and consequence that had resulted in their unlikely reunion, recognizing Isabel's hand in its design.

That he'd held out hope of meeting his son—that he'd placed all of his faith in this potential—only to have his son personally answer that call… Ean blessed the choice that had placed him on that path and every choice thereafter. For the first time in his life, he regretted nothing.

How impossible it all seemed, and yet how *correct*. All of the connections fit—Isabel's foretelling, Arion's desperate gamble in sending his body forward in time, Phaedor taking Tanis to be raised close to where his father would resurface...and that body discovered in the Calgaryn catacombs, which had appeared on the same night Ean had returned to the mainland, the very night their paths had all connected—that had been Arion's body, the catalyst for everything else that followed. Yes, it all made sense. And now with his memory no longer occluded, Ean perceived a desperately missed bond of awareness.

He cast gratitude and love upon it. *Tanis.*

The lad pulled back, his colorless eyes suddenly bright. *Father.*

Ean smiled wordlessly, wondrously, at him. *Is it strange for you to call me that?*

Tanis shook his head around a wide smile. *Not at all. Your mind feels the same to me now as it did when I was a child.* He searched Ean's gaze. *Is it strange for you?*

Ean blew out an amazed breath. *I never knew how much a part of me had missed our connection until this moment.*

They sat smiling at one another, exploring the binding, letting it fill with the energy of their reconnection as a stream swelling in a sudden flood—only these were floodwaters of admiration, appreciation, joy, love. Tanis shared his own memories with Ean, glimpses from his childhood, moments of tenderness with his father eliciting emotions that made Ean's eyes wet anew.

But in the wake of their reunion bobbed a terribly truth, one that darkened the waters of the prince's joy. He held Tanis's gaze for a moment longer and then stood, driven by a tumultuous energy that spiked the bond with charged particles.

As he walked to the railing, he tried to think of a way to apologize to his son for what Arion had done. Because of Arion's choices, Tanis had grown up knowing neither of his parents.

Ean closed his hands around the railing and then pushed away from it, unsure how to even begin expressing his contrition.

Tanis rose tentatively behind him. "There was another place I wanted to show you...if you'd like to see it."

Ean turned to face him. "Of course." He swallowed around the tightness in his throat and managed a smile. "I'd go anywhere with you."

Abruptly the world around Ean shifted.

He stood looking out upon a pebbled beach, a star-studded sky, a sea darkly luminous with moonlight. The soft roar of the waves churning the stones served as a reminder of Time's inexorable march.

Ean felt a stab of recognition, deeply poignant. "I remember this place," he breathed more than spoke. Verily, the scene struck a powerful chord in his soul. "Arion loved this beach."

"I know." Tanis aimed a smile at him and started off along the shoreline.

"You know?" Ean jogged to catch up with him. "How do you know?"

"I have memories, too." Tanis gazed out to sea as if seeing some of those memories in the play of moonlight upon the waves. "They were dreams at first, like yours, but after I remembered my parents' names, everything came back."

Ean exhaled a slow breath. "So you knew about Arion." He searched his son's face. "Did you know about me?"

Tanis looked back to him. "I didn't know you were him until I saw you in Wylde, but I suspected." Tanis radiated solicitude over a lingering excitement, soothing Ean's turmoil with his own calm energy. "When I realized that Phaedor had taken me forward in time, I started to wonder why he would've delivered me to Dannym in *this* specific time. Three hundred-something years?" He tossed a winsome smile at Ean. "It's rather an unlikely number, you know? I spent a long time thinking it over, and the only rationale that made any sense was that Phaedor brought me to this time so that I could be with you."

Ean folded his fingers behind his head and walked with his head tilted back and self-abasement dragging his steps. "Tanis…this is my third time through the Returning, but for you—Tanis, for you it's the same lifetime!" Abruptly he dropped to his knees in the sand. "How can you ever forgive me for something like this?" He searched his son's face. "How can I ever make it right?"

Tanis knelt down before him and met his gaze soberly. "Because dying like that isn't penance enough?"

For a moment, Ean stared at him. Then he gave an explosive exhale and fell back in the sand.

Tanis laid down beside his father and joined him in staring up at the stars. "Arion believed that all of his postulated effects were aligned to achieve the game's purpose, and because he believed unequivocally that his and my uncle's game served the greater good, he truly believed all of his decisions were aligned to serve the greater good as well. He *had* to go forward and achieve them…he had no choice but to do that."

Ean turned him a swift stare. "You speak as though you truly knew him…me…Arion." Confusion threaded his tone, astonishment his gaze.

Tanis cast a soft smile into the sky. "Do you remember the journals?"

Ean pushed up on one elbow. "Don't tell me you have those journals!"

Tanis grinned. "My mother left them for me at our home in Caladria, protected from time by the patterns that preserved the house—your patterns. I've read every one of the journals, most of them several times." He folded an arm behind his head and smiled up into the starry night. "I have your Sormitáge rings, too. I imagine if you try them on, you'll find they fit."

"Blessed Epiphany." Ean fell back in the sand. After a moment, he took Tanis's hand and gripped it tightly, feeling relief, joy and an impossible sense of hope humming through every thread of his soul.

Tanis... Ean's thought sounded choked with wonder, even to his own ears, *she really did keep her promise.*

Tanis squeezed his hand in return, radiating happiness. *She always does.*

EPILOGUE

"YOU WANT ME to do what?"

Raegus n'Harnalt's disbelief hit Loukas in the chest with the force of a blunt-tipped arrow. Either that, or the dull burn in his esophagus came from trying to stomach Trell's indigestible expectations.

To their right, the gushing waterfall was pouring down from the aqueduct. The eastern ridgeline burned with the sun's morning light, but dark clouds were blowing in fast from the south. When the storm hit them, the rain would make a deluge of the waterfall and a three-tiered fountain of the fortress.

They all had to be out of there before the storm hit.

This presented Loukas with a unique challenge. Though all of the men were working side by side—Dannish soldier, Converted, Nadoriin—they still hadn't found a way *out* of the fortress.

The portcullis was too heavy and clogged with mud to be lifted by its chains, but Loukas thought if they could find a way to brace the portcullis in the center, they could make a fulcrum of the braced point and the thing would hinge and fall across the top of the mud. It might even make a lattice of sorts for helping them tread over the worst of the sludge.

Loukas called down from the high wall to Raegus and his men, who were sitting their horses on the far side of the mud slide. "Use the ropes and the horses to create a fulcrum…" but he bit off his own words. Trying to explain physics by shouting from a forty foot wall over a hundred feet of mud to a man who had never studied mathematics was about as useful as cursing at the clouds for raining on you.

Loukas thought of two people he would *really* like to be cursing at just then, but neither of them were available to receive his complaints. Trell was on the lower wall with Lazar hal'Hamaadi; and Tannour...well, shortly after floating Trell and the Nadori commander out of the caverns—and if *that* hadn't raised a thousand words of speculation, Loukas didn't know what would—Tannour had collapsed. Trell had sent him off to be looked after.

But Loukas *really* didn't want to think about Tannour just then.

"*What did he say?*" Raegus called from across the scar of mud.

"Are you all right, Loukas?" Gideon val Mallonwey placed a hand on his arm.

Loukas shook himself back to the moment. "Yes. Sorry." He gave an apologetic wince. "I was just...wishing we had someone down there who could explain my idea to Raegus."

The Shi'ma warrior Nyongo Kutaata sauntered up with his sword caught behind his massive shoulders like a beam for hauling buckets. "And what is it you need explained, *Chamagi'tiito?*"

Gideon tilted his head at him. "I'm afraid I don't know this word."

Nyongo flashed a grin of very white teeth, bright against his ebony skin. "It means 'little-mouse-who-doesn't-know-his-own-strength.'"

"It's not my favorite sobriquet," Loukas muttered.

"Ah...I see." Gideon smiled amusedly at Loukas before returning his gaze to Nyongo. "Well, you see, the Avataren and I are not entirely in agreement on the best way to clear the portcullis. Loukas thinks we need to brace the portcullis near its center hinge, attach ropes to the top and use the horses to pull it down across the mud."

Gideon leaned out over the crenel to view the massive slope of mud piled up against the portcullis, blocking them in. "My feeling is that even if we got the portcullis off somehow, we'd still never out get through all of that. I can't help but wonder if perhaps we can jump...make a sort of slide of the mud."

"Is that all?" Nyongo shoved his sword into the hands of a nearby Converted. While Loukas gazed at him perplexedly, he looped a rope about his substantial girth, handed one end of the rope to a bewildered Gideon, and promptly launched himself over the wall.

Gideon uttered an oath, grabbed for him and missed.

Loukas flung himself partway over the crenel in time to see Nyongo vanishing deep into the mud. "Haul him back up!" He grabbed the trailing end of the rope along with Gideon and the others.

"Shadow take me if he don't outweigh a bear," one of the Converted hissed between clenched teeth. Too slowly the rope scraped back across the crenel's stone edge.

Loukas knew Nyongo had risen from the mud when he heard Raegus shout, "*Are you out of your* fethen *mind?*"

When Loukas looked out over the crenel again, Nyongo was swim-sliding through the mud towards Raegus. He reached the edge of the mud field, got to his feet and waved up at them. Raegus launched into a rife scolding liberally peppered with *fethe* and *fethen*.

Loukas looked pointedly to Gideon.

"Right." The captain scrubbed at the back of his head. "So...we should pull down the portcullis then."

"That's a marvelous idea, Captain. Can you get them started?"

"Yes," Gideon said through a sigh. He looked disappointed that his idea hadn't proven the better one. "Nyongo!" he called down to the Shi'man. "Tell him Loukas's plan!"

Nyongo waved an acknowledgment and started explaining to a frowning Raegus how they were going to pull down the portcullis to get the men out.

Loukas headed off to see to other tasks.

Most of seven hundred men were atop the walls industriously going about whatever business Gideon or Lazar had set them to—searching for the missing, salvaging what they could of the fortress's arms and supplies, helping to restore each other to rights. Many of the Dannish soldiers were lined up along the west ramparts taking turns burning off their cuffs and collars.

As Loukas walked the wall, the only thing more constant than the buffeting wind was the talk among the men of Trell and how the Goddess Naiadithine had spoken to him. Unfailingly he saw questions in their eyes as they watched him go by. But Gideon had commanded his soldiers to ask no questions and stay alert to ways they could 'assist the prince's men in securing our departure.' So no one stopped Loukas, though he could tell many of them wanted to.

It was odd walking among so many unknown faces, himself unknown to them save perhaps to those who'd seen him standing at Trell's side. He could always tell which ones they were, for they'd give him a nod or some other acknowledgment, subtle if potent—a definite recognition of his status as their prince's friend.

He reached a bastion at the joining of walls and climbed five stairs to its elevated rooftop, which gave him an unimpeded view of the river valley. Earlier in the morning, they'd spotted a dark swath coming up from the south—the Nadoriin host returning. Lazar had signaled them to wait there, and the soldiers had paused their march where the valley split eastwards around the mountain's arm.

"Do you think they can see us?"

Tannour's unexpected voice made everything inside Loukas clench up. He looked to him, reflecting that Tannour made his chest ache far more painfully than anything Trell had ever tasked him to do. "I suppose. It's probably a sight, all these strangers crowding the walls of their fortress. What must they be thinking?"

"I think they're probably thinking, 'Where'd that bloody waterfall come from?'"

A faint smile manifested on Loukas's lips.

Tannour seated himself on the crenel and propped up one booted foot. The wind tossed his dark hair about his shoulders in a way that accentuated the sharp angles of his face. Loukas rarely saw him bare-headed, for he always wore his head scarf as the Vestian nobility wore it—which was his right.

Tannour leaned back against the merlon and caught his knee between interwoven fingers. He could make any position look comfortable, even as a twelve-year-old hanging a hundred feet above a fall to his death.

Loukas looked back to the valley, feeling hollow. "How are you feeling?"

"I've been worse. I've been thinking about how you saved my life down in the water."

Loukas swallowed. "And?"

"I don't know," a dark smile hinted on Tannour's lips, "maybe that makes us even."

Loukas cast him a look. "It makes us far from even."

"I suppose you're right." He cocked a raven brow. "Depends on who's counting, doesn't it?"

Loukas turned away from him. He was determined not to let Tannour rile him that morning, especially not when Trell was depending on him to remain focused. "I saw the wielder's body. Did you learn anything from him?"

"He told me all, as they all do." His smile grew chilling. "The man was undone long before the tower fell on him."

Loukas clenched his jaw. "Do you have to be so *fethen* pleased about the grim things you do?"

"Sorry…" Tannour regarded him with a quiet intensity. "I never did master the art of Avataren dissembling, as you have. I suppose I just didn't recognize your lessons at the time for what they were."

Loukas turned him an even stare. "Have you come just to torment me, or for some fruitful purpose?"

"Tormenting you bears fruit," Tannour looked him over with a shadowy gaze, "just not the kind you find particularly palatable."

Loukas cast him a spiked glare. "Stop it."

Tannour made the Avataren sign of obeisance, which only frustrated Loukas more. Grinning then, he spied a look around. "Where's the *A'dal*?"

Loukas let out his breath. "Meeting with Lazar about how to keep the entire fortress from flooding."

Tannour abruptly straightened. "*Fethe*, you might've led with that."

"And deny myself the immense pleasure of your barbed lashes?" The rebuke struck from his lips before he could stop it.

Tannour's expression sobered, proof that he'd taken well enough both of Loukas's meanings—the less obvious striking the deeper cut. "Where is he, then?" Tannour's voice had assumed that cold distance which Loukas had come to know so well.

Loukas returned his gaze to the valley, but all he saw was regret. "Down on the lower wall."

Tannour started off without another word.

Loukas called after him, "What can you do?"

Tannour paused on the steps and looked over his shoulder, his pale gaze full of accusation and injury. "You always doubt me." Then he simply vanished.

Loukas stared at the space where he'd been for a long time, but it was even longer before he murmured through a tightness in his chest, "I never doubt you."

◆

Much later, as a thunderstorm was raging outside Trell's command tent and his camp was playing host to hundreds of guests, Trell sat behind his desk listening to a different kind of storm raging inside—ideologies and ideals battling for agency amid the convex scales of morality, honor and obligation. Men once at cross-purposes had been forced into unity, not by king or country but by the undeniable will of a god who cared nothing for bindings of blood or oath. The men argued now as much with their own consciences as with each other.

Trell observed those collected there and thought of their strengths—Raegus n'Harnalt and Rolan Lamodaar: able men, competent leaders; the Nadori Commander Lazar hal'Hamaadi, whom Trell had learned to be a man of reason and rationality, though their initial meeting might've led him to assume otherwise; Gideon val Mallonwey: bright and capable, and already so loyal to him; Loukas n'Abraxis: his closest friend among that group, and brilliant beyond his own estimation.

Had Loukas not solved their escape from the fortress with minimal effort? Such a simple solution, pulling down the portcullis and using it as a lattice, a sort of snowshoe across the worst of the mud, allowing upwards of seven hundred men to walk out of the fortress unscathed.

And Tannour Valeri, who had found him and Lazar in the lower fortress and in quick order 'softened' places in the wall—strategic spots where a crack would allow the water to escape without weakening the fortress's structural integrity—such that the Fortress of Khor Taran sprouted enough leaks to mitigate the waterfall and the coming storm and prevent the upper levels from flooding. They might even be able to restore the fortress one day, once the aqueduct had been repaired.

Trell saw these men as his greatest resources—weapons if they must be so used—in ending the war. They were weapons he never would've gained had he not embarked upon the task to free his father's men. And marching behind those weapons were nearly a thousand Nadoriin and Dannish soldiers, the beginnings of his own army. His force for peace.

The men arguing around him wielded ideas as swords, points made and debated as blades scraping and separating. They argued ethics and obligation. They thrust duty against morality and looked surprised when the two resoundingly clashed. The blade of reason collided with myth and met unexpectedly firm resistance.

The night drew on, and Trell listened. He let them debate, argue, talk themselves in circles until they'd exhausted every idea, explored every option they could present; until they found themselves frustratingly back at the beginning, a fork in the road he'd once been standing at but had now left confidently behind.

He reached for his wine with his good arm. The other wore a sling on orders of Madaam Chouri, who had healed both his shoulder and his ankle but bade him keep from using either for several days. He would have plenty of time to heal before they arrived at their next destination, which was the Saldarian camp where the rest of his father's men were being held. This intelligence had come to him compliments of Tannour.

Setting down his wine, Trell raised his hand to gain the others' attention. They looked to him and quieted.

"We cannot help them in Raku." This comment Trell directed at Gideon, who'd been pushing hardest for this objective; the captain's concerns lay with his liege, Trell's king father. "We're more than a week's forced march from the oasis, Gideon. I'm the first to feel my father's loss—both of my fathers were undoubtedly involved in that battle—but we're too far away to offer them any aid."

Trell looked to Rolan and Raegus. "Nor can we engage Radov's forces at Ramala and draw out their flanks. Whatever battle is ongoing in that arena, it must run its course without our interference."

Trell turned his attention to Lazar. "I won't ask you or your men to fight your own, but I will ask you to lend me your assistance in whatever way your consciences permit."

Lazar crossed his arms and considered Trell. "What do you intend?"

Trell cast his gaze across everyone in the room, all of them good men, men he trusted. Men he could depend upon. Many of them men who would lay down their lives for him. The weight of this responsibility was never far from his thoughts, or his decisions.

"We cannot help them in Raku," he repeated, including all of them in his gaze, "but here's what we know: that we have to end this war somehow; that the front lines are now centered around Ramala and that Radov has moved all of his forces there; that the Ruling Prince himself is there—likely Viernan hal'Jaitar as well; and that they're fully occupied with the Raku campaign…" he looked around at all of them again, taking a moment to meet each gaze, and finished the thought, "…leaving Tal'Shira undefended."

Their silence was testimony to their reason.

"*Trell*," Loukas scraped out his name through his disbelief, "you're not thinking—"

Trell met his gaze. "Yes, Loukas. We're going to take Tal'Shira."

※

In the cityworld of Illume Belliel, the center of the starry spiral that was the Thousand Realms of Light, the second strand currents flashed, and a tall man stepped off a weld.

He pocketed the silver ring that had brought him there—a stolen ring, a coveted ring—and lifted his dark gaze to the stars. In time, that gaze floated languorously across the sparkling cityworld, observing how its lights seemed a mirror of the night sky…imaging how those lights would look once chaos broke out.

A slow smile claimed the man's features.

He spun in a swirl of blood-red silk and walked away from the nodecourt, far enough to clear the wards that protected the cityworld from unwelcome guests entering that way. But his guests would not be entering that way.

He concentrated.

A silver line split down through the air and quickly broadened into a glossy darkness blacker than the night. When the portal reached the shape and size of a door, the man swept a hand before him and bowed in invitation. "Come, my friends."

Darkness spilled through the portal.

It took many forms, many densities. It poured into the cityworld as smoke from a burning house. Gradually the smoke assumed many shapes, all as unique as the imaginations that had chosen them. Some claimed solidity; others misted, faint as ghosts but possessed of power, as lightning in the storm.

The last to emerge stood the tallest of all. He had black hair, glossy like the darkness, and eyes that sparked an electric blue. Everyone who gazed upon him saw a different face. A few of them even appeared human.

But Shailabanáchtran just saw a Warlock. "Welcome, Baelfeir. Welcome back to the Realms of Light."

Baelfeir looked around and flashed a lightning smile.

KEEP IN TOUCH

"Melissa loves hearing from her readers with feedback, comments, or just discussion of Alorin and its peoples. For updates on book five, the final installment in *A Pattern of Shadow and Light*, or other conversation, follow Melissa's blog at http://melissamcphail.com/blog.

Melissa would love to hear from you. Find her here:

http://MelissaMcPhail.com

http://Facebook.com/CephraelsHand

http://Twitter.com/MelissaGMcPhail

http://Goodreads.com/MelissaGMcPhail

Appendix

1. The Strands of *Elae* and Their Associated Adepts [chart]
2. Glossary of Terms
3. The Sormitáge Ranks
4. The Laws of Patterning
5. The Esoterics
6. Dramatis Personae

THE STRANDS & THEIR ASSOCIATED ADEPTS

⋄ FIRST STRAND ⋄
CREATIVE ENERGY

Healers
Seers

Variant trait:
Foretelling

VESTAL
Alshiba Torinin

⋄ SECOND STRAND ⋄
KINETIC ENERGY

Delvers
Espials
Nodefinders

Variant trait:
Dreamwalking
Twisted Nodes

VESTAL
Dagmar Ranneskjöld

⋄ THIRD STRAND ⋄
ENERGY OF TIME & FORM

Avieths
Fhorgs
Holven
Malchiarri
Nymphs
Shi'ma
Tyriolicci
Warlocks

Variant trait:
Timeweaving
Shapeshifting
Animal Magnetism

VESTAL
Seth "Silverbow" Nach Davvies

⋄ FOURTH STRAND ⋄
ENERGY OF THOUGHT

Truthreaders

Variant trait:
Illusions

VESTAL
Raine D'Lacourte

⋄ FIFTH STRAND ⋄
ELEMENTAL ENERGY

Adepts of the Fifth
Drachwyr
Malorin'athgul
Zanthyrs

Variant trait:
Seeing patterns
Unworking patterns

VESTAL
Björn van Gelderan

GLOSSARY OF TERMS

Underlining within definitions denotes words that may be found in this glossary.

Adendigaeth (aden´– di gay´uth) [Old Alæic] 1 Rebirth, regeneration 2 A festival in celebration of the Winter Solstice lasting varying lengths but traditionally ending on the Longest Night.

Adept (a´-dept) n. [Old Alæic] 1 One born with the instinctive ability to sense and compel one of the five strands of *elae* 2 A race of such persons, each with attributes intrinsic to the strand of *elae* that modified them *[an Adept of the third strand]* 3 A Healer, Nodefinder, truthreader, or Wildling.

Alir (ah -leer´) n [Agasi] 1 lit: heart-light 2 The path followed by an Adept during the course of his life; also referred to as the path of destiny, especially in the vernacular of the Palmers 3 Indicating either of the Two Great Paths of *elae* able to be followed by an Adept inducted into the Vestian Sorceresy. See Paths of Alir.

Angiel (ahn gēl´) n. [Old Alæic] The Maker's two blessed children, Cephrael and Epiphany, who were made in the Genesis to watch over His worlds.

Annwn (an´ wen) n. [Old Alæic] The Otherworld where all life was formed and where the Maker resides. At the gates of Annwn stand the Extian Doors. On the Longest Night, the *angiel* open the Extian Doors to allow all the waiting souls to journey through Annwn, that they may learn the secrets of death and Return.

Ascendant n. [Cyrenaic *ascendere,* to climb] A priest or cleric serving the Prophet Bethamin. Ascendants are marked by tattoos denoting their rank and function.

Atrophae n. (at´ tro fay) [Cyrenaic átroph, not fed] A cursed object created with *mor'alir* patterns designed to bring harm or illness. An *atrophae* can be formed of anything into which a pattern can be indelibly inscribed.

Avieth (ay´ vee uth) n. [Old Alæic, bird] A third strand Wildling race of shapeshifters with the ability to asssume two distinctly separate forms: human and hawk.

Awaken (ah wā´ ken) v. [Old Alæic] Adepts who have Returned Awaken to their inherent abilities usually during the transition of puberty but sometimes as early as two years of age.

Balance (bal´ans) n. [<Veneisean <Cyrenaic, *bilanx* two+scale] The term used to describe the highest force of cause and effect in the realm of Alorin; the natural laws of the realm which define how far the currents may be twisted out of their natural paths by wielders of *elae* before manifest retribution is incurred by the wielder. These laws are of much consideration among the various Adept guilds and a topic of intense speculation and theorization.

Catenaré (ca-ten ah´-ray) n. [Old Alæic, *catēna*, a chain] The second ranking of Adept enrolled at the Sormitáge University. Adepts wear the Catenaré cuff until they pass their Invocation Trials to advance to Maritus status, usually a span of five to ten years of study.

Celantia (se lan´ tee-ya) n. [Markhengari, box] A box formed of constantly shifting patterns developed by the Elf realm of Markhengar, often used for the capture and imprisonment of criminals.

Cephrael (sef´ray-el) n. [*Sobra I'ternin*] The Maker's blessed son. Ascribed as the Hand of Fate, Cephrael is responsible for administering the Maker's ultimate justice. See also *angiel*.

Companions – See Fifty Companions

Deyjiin (day´zhen) n. [Old Alæic] The power that roams Chaos and the dimension of Shadow, antithesis of *elae*.

Devoveré (de-voh ver´-ay) n. [Old Alæic, to vow] The fourth ranking of Adept enrolled at the Sormitáge University. Adepts are awarded their Devoveré ring (often called a Sormitáge ring) upon successful completion of the Devoveré Trials. Gaining a Devoveré ring automatically entitles an Adept to membership in the guild respective to their strand.

Docian (dos´ see-an) n. [Old Alæic *docilis,* readily taught, equivalent to *doc* (*ēre*) to teach + *-ian*] The first ranking of Adept enrolled at the Sormitáge University. Adepts wear the Docian collar from their earliest years until they pass the Invocation Trials to advance to Catenaré status.

Drogue wolf (droag) n. [Origin unknown] A sentient animal, larger and more intelligent than a common wolf, which roams the mountains of Agasan. It is most often found in the Navárrel, the Geborahs and the wild ranges of the Hallovian plateau.

Drachwyr (drak´wēr) n. [Old Alæic] An Adept of the fifth strand of *elae*: the *drachwyr* were banished to the icy edges of the realm in the year 597aV. Also called a Sundragon.

Eidola (eye dohl´ la) n. [Old Alæic, *eidolon,* phantom] A mutated lifeform that possesses great strength and is difficult to harm and kill. It receives its lifeforce and animation from a binding to a superior life form, such as an immortal.

Elae (e-lā´) n. [Old Alæic, *elanion,* life, force; the power of life] 1 The itinerant (roaming) energy that, in its accumulation and formation, creates the pattern that becomes the foundation of a world 2 Pertaining to any of the five codified strands of this energy, each with distinctly separate attributes.

Epiphany (ē pif´fany) n. [*Sobra I'ternin*] The Maker's blessed daughter. Epiphany is the speaker of the Maker's will and is often turned to in prayer by those seeking divine blessing. See also *angiel*.

Espial (espy´-al) n. [Cyrenaic *espyen* <es- + *spähen,* to spy] See also Nodefinder. The term used to describe a Nodefinder of the highest degree who has gained license from the Espial's Guild to travel between the realms.

Fhorg (forg) n. [origin unknown] One of the Wildling races most notably known for their use of blood magic.

Fifty Companions n. [Colloquial] The name given in reference to the Adept survivors of the Battle of the Citadel on Tiern'aval.

Hal'alir n. [Agasi, light of the heart] In the Vestian Sorceresy, 'The Path That Casts Infinite Reflections.' Adepts following *hal'alir* wield the lifeforce primarily towards constructive or creative aims.

Healer (hēl´er) n. [Old Alæic *haelan* > *hal* whole] An Adept of the first strand of *elae* who has the ability to see the life patterns of living things and compel the creative forces of the first strand to alter them.

Khoda Panaheh (lay) n. [Kandori, "God protects"] 1 A tattooed mark upon the forehead which is gained when an Adept of the royal lines of Kandori takes the oath of immortality and works the Pattern of Life.

Leis (lay) n. [Old Alæic *leis*] The shortest pathway available to a Nodefinder when using the Pattern of the World to travel, often connecting spaces within a small geographic area.

Literato n. [Old Alæic *literati*, learned, scholarly] A scholar at the Sormitáge University whose focus is on research of the strands of *elae* or into the history of the realm or the Adept race.

Maestro n. [Old Alæic, master] A teaching scholar at the Sormitáge University.

Maritus (Mer'i-tus) n.. [Old Alæic *maritum*, act worthy of praise] The third ranking of Adept enrolled at the Sormitáge University. Adepts wear a Maritus bracelet until they've completed their thesis and passed the Invocation Trials to advance to Devoveré status, often a span of five to ten years.

Marquiin (mar kwen') n. [Myacenic, chosen] A truthreader who has been chosen by the Prophet Bethamin to be cleansed in a "purifying" ritual involving, in part, the insertion of Bethamin's Fire into the Adept's mind.

Merdanti (mer dan'tē) n. [Agasi] 1 An impossibly hard black stone named for the region of Agasan in which it is found 2 A weapon forged using the fifth strand of *elae* and made from this stone.

Malorin'athgul (muh lor'en – ath'gool) n. [Old Alæic, they who make the darkness] A race of beings from beyond the known Realms of Light who were birthed by the Maker to balance Creation by unmaking the universe at its far unraveling fringes while it is constantly expanding at its core.

Mor'alir n. [Agasi, dark of the heart] In the Vestian Sorceresy, 'The Path of Shadows'; Adepts following *mor'alir* wield the lifeforce towards destructive aims.

Na'turna (nah toor'nah) n. [Old Alæic < *nare turre*, of the earth] A non-Adept; mortal.

Node (nod) n. [Old Alæic *nodus*, knot] The points where the Pattern of the World conjoins. Nodes connect places in vastly different geographic regions and allow a Nodefinder to travel great distances within a few steps. In the realm of Alorin, nodes also connect to the neighboring realm of T'khendar due to the nature of the latter's formation.

Nodefinder (nod-fin'der) n. [Old Alæic *nodus*, knot + *findan*, find] Adept of the second strand of *elae* who sees the points where the Pattern of the World conjoins (called nodes) and can use these points to travel vast distances; see also *espial*.

Quorum of the Sixth Truth n. [Origin Unknown] A defunct order of fifth strand Adepts that held power in Cyrenaic times. The quorum are believed to have been involved with extensive experimentation on Adepts and *na'turna* in pursuit of understanding of their native gifts.

Order of the Glass Sword n. Agasan's spy network.

Palmer n. [Caladrian, pilgrim] A religious order devoted to the study of alir and the influence or interference of destiny or fate upon an individual's path.

Paths of Alir n. [Agasi, heart-light] (also called the Two Great Paths) Referring to any of the valid paths an Adept inducted into the Vestian Sorceresy can follow. The commonly known paths are *chrys'alir*, the Mirror Path; *hal'alir*, The Path That Casts Infinite Reflections; *mor'alir*, The Path of Shadows; *san'gu'alir*, The Path of Blood; and *ver'alir*, The Blind Path (a rare path).

Patterning (pat´ərn·ŋ) v. [Veneisean *patrun*, patron, hence something to be imitated, pattern] The codified methodology encompassing the use of patterns to compel the strands of *elae* to move against their natural course, an action (also called *wielding*) which is often erroneously referred to as magic.

Qhorith'quitara (Cor´ith kee-tar-ah) n. [Old Alæic] The collection of apocryphal books derived from the *Sobra I'ternin*.

Raedan (ray´ dan]) n. [Old Alæic *raedan*, to guess, read, counsel] 1 One trained to read the currents of *elae* and thereby able to discern the workings of patterns and their effects throughout the realm.

Realm (relm´) n. [Veneisean, *realme* (altered by assoc. with *reiel*, royal) < Cyrenaic, *regere*, to rule] 1 A kingdom 2 One of the thousand linked worlds, each represented by an elected Seat and four Vestals in the governing cityworld of Illume Belliel 3 The realm of Alorin.

Return (Returned, Returning) (rē turn´) n. [Veneisean, *retorner*] An Adept who has died and been reborn. See also Awakening.

Revenants n. [unknown] The remnant entities created by the Warlocks of Shadow and then abandoned; vampiric creatures who feed off the lifeforce of the living.

Sanctos n. [Caladrian *sanctus*, hallowed] In the Caladrian belief, sanctified ancestral spirits who watch over their descendants.

Shamshir'im (sham´sheer - eem) n. [Nadori *saber*, sword + *'im*, belonging to] The name for M'Nador's espionage network of spies, wielders and assassins headed by the Adept wielder and consul to Prince Radov, Viernan hal'Jaitar.

Simulacra (sih´muh - lack´rah) n. [Agasi *simulācrum*, likeness] A glass device for capturing and presenting patterns in three dimensions. Patterns forged within the glass will waken to a fourth strand flow of *elae*.

Sobra l'ternin (soh´brah - e - turn´en) n. [origin unknown] The ancient text, most often attributed to the *angiel* Cephrael, which details the natural laws of patterns in thaumaturgic application. The book is itself written in patterns and has yet to be fully translated. Many Orders are dedicated to its study, translation and adaptation for use in the Adept Arts.

Soglia-varcarés / soglia're (So´-lee AHR´-ay) [Caladrian, bridge across the earth] Nodes or leis magically constructed into permanent portals that anyone can travel with or without a Nodefinder present and with or without any Adept talent. *Soglia'res* bridge two specific points, only those two points, and cannot be used to travel anywhere else but between those two points.

Sorceresy (also Vestian Sorceresy) The predominant school of Adept learning in the far eastern land of Vest. The Vestian Sorceresy believes all Paths of Alir have equal merit, but they're known for their Blackshard Council and its extensive exploration of *mor'alir* (the Path of Shadows).

Stanza segreta (Caladrian, secret room) The term given to a leis which a Nodefinder has pinned to his personal life pattern or to an object in his possession, the use of which allows the Nodefinder to secret away or store items for later use. Colloquially called a "coach."

Strand (strand´) n. [Agasi, *strônd*] 1 Any of the parts that are bound together to form a whole *[the strands of one's life]* 2 Referring to any of the five composite aspects of *elae* and its five attributive fields of energy (respectively: strand 1:creative energy, 2:kinetic energy, 3:variant energy, 4:energy of thought, 5:elemental energy).

Tethys – Goddess of the Sea worshipped by sailors, especially from the Island of Jamaii.

Thread (thred) n. [Old Alæic *thræd*, to bind] A colloquial term used when speaking of a group of four men of a specific race, as opposed to a string, which is a grouping of six.

Tiern'aval (teer´- navol´) n. [origin unknown] An island city, one of the Free Cities of Xanthe, which vanished at the end of the Adept Wars circa 597aV. The city's fate remains a mystery.

T'khendar (tuh – ken´dar) n. [origin unknown] The realm created by the Adept wielder Malachi ap'Kalien out of Alorin's own aether, which sacrilegious act resulted in fierce denouncement from the Council of Realms and indirectly, his later madness.

Truthreader (trooth´ rēd er) n. [Old Alæic *treowe,* true + *raedan*] An Adept of the fourth strand of *elae* who is able to hear (and sometimes see) the thoughts of others and is thereby able to discern the time, place and form of any occurrence in their memory, i.e. its truth.

Tyriolicci (teer´e-oh – lee´chee) One of the Wildling races of the Forgotten Lands. See Whisper Lord.

Vestal (vest´-al) n. [Cyrenaic, *vestir,* to endow] 1 An Adept elevated and empowered with the responsibility of enforcing the laws, regulations, activities and codes of his respective strand of *elae,* and of overseeing all Adepts subject to it 2 One of five highly-trained and advanced Adepts elected as voting members of the Council of Realms, ranking just below the Seat of the realm in authority.

Weld (weld) n. [Cyrenaic, *welden,* to be strong] The most major joints in the Pattern of the World. All leis and nodes connect through a weld, thus a weld allows travel to any location. Welds also form the joints between the realms and thus allow travel from realm to realm.

Whisper Lord n. [Collq.] One of the Wildling races (also called Tyriolicci) known for their frenzied fighting style and ability to make small skips through time.

Wielder (wēld´ər) n. [Cyrenaic, *welden,* to be strong < Old Alæic, *valere,* a show of strength] A person of any race who uses patterns to compel one or more strands of *elae,* thereby influencing the strand's properties to create the effect he has postulated; a sorcerer in the realm of Alorin. Adepts and men alike become wielders through intensive training and study.

Wildling (wahyld´-ling]) n. [Old Alæic *wilde*] 1 (Collq) An Adept of the third strand of *elae* 2 Any of the twenty-seven non-human races whose native abilities are attributed to the third strand of *elae* but who may or may not be possessed of paranormal abilities.

Zanthyr (zan´thur) n. [Old Alæic] An elusive Adept of the fifth strand of elae; zanthyrs can shapeshift between two forms: one human, one animal. Many have been seen to work *elae*. The extent of their abilities is unknown.

THE SORMITÁGE RANKS

(in ascending order)

The Docian Collar: yoked to the honest study of elae. Adepts wear the Docian collar from their earliest years until they pass the Catenaré Invocation Trials, often a span of five to eight years.

The Catenaré Cuff: chained to the dutiful service of elae. Adepts wear the Catenaré cuff until they pass the Maritus Invocation Trials, usually a span of three to four years.

The Maritus Bracelet: married to the courageous exploration of elae. Adepts wear the Maritus bracelet until they've completed their Maritus thesis and passed the Devoveré Invocation Trials for their strand, usually a span of five to ten years.

The Devoveré Ring: devoted to the just and virtuous practice of elae. Adepts are awarded their Devoveré ring upon successful completion of the Devoveré Trials.

A stacked Adept– referencing an Adept who has gained more than one ring in the discipline of a single strand.

A bracketed wielder – referencing an Adept who has gained a Devoveré ring for each strand of *elae* and thereby wears a ring on every finger of his or her right hand. A bracketed wielder has ascended from Docian to Devoveré on every strand of *elae*.

A rowed wielder – having gained a bracket on both hands. A rowed wielder has ascended first from Docian to Devoveré in every strand, then again ascended through the same ranks specializing in the wielder's craft of Patterning, learning to apply the Laws and Esoterics to each strand of *elae*, as well as building his or her repertoire of associated patterns.

THE LAWS OF PATTERNING

(1-17)

1. KNOW the effect you intend to create.
2. What applies to one applies to all.
3. Create newly each effect.
4. Positive determinism is necessary to achieve the intended effect.
5. A wielder is limited by what he can envision.
6. Energy responds to positive thought. Corollary: Patterning is most effective at the level of thought.
7. A wielder succeeds in the alteration of energy, space and time in inverse proportion to his agreement with the material universe.
8. All patterns are the result of effort channeled along a specific vector; thus, patterns are the product of force.
9. Do not counter force with force; channel it.
10. Energy cannot be unmade, merely transformed.
11. All things are formed of patterns.
12. A pattern need not be perfect, but the wielder's concept of it must be.
13. Intention monitors solidity, solidity monitors structure.
14. Exact duplicating forces, in opposition, will nullify structure.
15. Talismans magnify intent.
16. Talismans form the bridge of cause and effect.
17. The use of talismans must focus force without limiting scope.

THE ESOTERICS

(Covered so far)

1. Absolute Being is the entire concept of actuality. Corollary: Absolutely Being is the exact form, material composition and position in space as modified by time.
2. Patterns lie within the boundaries of Absolute Being.
3. The wielding of Form must encapsulate Absolute Being.
4. Time results from the application of an intention that matter and space will persist. Thus, time and space are monitored by Absolute Being.
5. Absolute Being must equal the scope of a wielder's concept of effect.
6. Absolute Being is necessary to the creation of space. Corollary: Energy cannot exist without Absolute Being.
7. Solidity is monitored by Absolute Being.
8. Absolute causation is fundamental to Absolute Being.
9. Pure concept always overwhelms linear translation.
10. A wielder is limited by what he can envision himself envisioning.
11. Space, energy, time and form are the result of thought applied as intention.
12. Energy can be unmade only within the space of Absolute Being; corollary: a wielder can unmake his own energy but not the energy of another.
13. Exact duplicating thought, with the same energy, in the same time, will nullify reality and actuality.
14. Doubt of intention results in diminished effect on a gradient scale.
15. The strands are divisions of energy as applied towards creation of life, form, time, thought, elements. Thus, all Laws of Patterning follow also the laws of energy.
16. Actuality is monitored by the wielder's point of view. Reality is monitored by collective thought agreement.
17. Illusion becomes reality when a) collective agreement is achieved on the existence of the illusion and b) when enough agree that the illusion should persist.

DRAMATIS PERSONAE

The Five Vestals

Alshiba Torinin—the First Vestal and Alorin Seat, an Adept Healer
Dagmar Ranneskjöld—the Second Vestal, a Nodefinder
Seth Silverbow nach Davvies—the Third Vestal, an avieth of the Wildling races
Raine D'Lacourte—the Fourth Vestal, a truthreader and *raedan*
Björn van Gelderan—the Fifth Vestal, also called the First Lord

The Malorin'athgul

Darshanvenkhátraman (Dar´shan – vin ka´tra mahn) called Darshan whose name means Destroyer of Hope; also known as the Prophet Bethamin
Pelasommáyurek (Pe´las – oh my´yur eck) called Pelas whose name means Ender of Paths; also known as the artist Immanuel di Nostri
Rinokhálpeşumar (Rin´och – cal pesh´oo mar) called Rinokh whose name means The Mountain That Flames
Shailabhanáchtran (Shale´ – ah bah nock´trun) called Shail whose name means Maker of Storms

The Sundragons (Drachwyr)

Dhábu'balaji'şridanaí (Da´boo – ba lah´gee – shree´da-nye) called Balaji whose name means He Who Walks the Edge of the World
Şrivas'rhakárakek (Shree´vas – rah kar´akeck) called Rhakar whose name means The Shadow of the Light
Jayachándranáptra (Jai´ah – shan´dra – nap´tra) called Jaya whose name means Rival of the Sun
Ramuhárikhamáth (Rah´moo – hareek´amath) called Ramu whose name means Lord of the Heavens
Amithaiya'geshwen (Ami-thi´ya – gesh´win) called Mithaiya whose name means The Bosom of God's Nectar

Náeb'nabdurin'náiir (Ni eb´– nab dur´en – ny´ear) called Náiir whose name means Chaser of the Dawn

The Seventeen Gods of the Akkad

Jai'Gar—the Prime God
Azerjaiman—the Wind God
Sons of the wind god—North son, Shamal; South son, Asfal; East son, Sherq
Daughter of the Wind God—West daughter, Qharp
Shamash—God of Travelers and the Poor
Inanna—Goddess of War
Naiadithine—Goddess of Water
Enlil—God of Earth and Agriculture
Inithiya—Goddess of Love and Restoration (Spirit)
Angharad—Goddess of Fortune (Fate)
Thalma—Goddess of Luck (Virtue)
Huhktu—God of Bones
Baharan/Baharani—the two-headed God of Blood/Goddess of Birth
Ha'viv—the Trickster God, patron of thieves

On Tanis's Travels

Sinárr—a Warlock from the Shadow Realms
Mérethe—an avieth bound to Sinárr
Rafael—a Warlock from the Shadow Realms
Baelfeir—a Warlock from the Shadow Realms, aka Belloth the Demon Lord

Agasan's Imperial Household

Valentina van Gelderan—Empress of Agasan
Marius di L'Arlesé—High Lord of Agasan, Consort to the Empress
Nadia van Gelderan—Princess Heir of Agasan
Giancarlo—a Caladrian truthreader in the service of the High Lord

Vincenzé—a Caladrian Nodefinder and wielder in service of the High Lord

Francesca da Mosta, Commander of the Imperial Adeptus

Lieutenant di Corvo, First in the Princess Nadia's Praetorian Guard

At the Sormitáge

Liam van Gheller—Endoge of the Sormitáge

Felix di Sarcova della Buonara—a Devoveré Nodefinder studying at the Sormitáge

Malin van Drexel—(missing) a Nodefinder working on his Maritus thesis

Isahl N'abranaacht—(aka Shailabanáchtran) a literato at the Sormitáge University Monseraut Greaves—Imperial Historian and a maestro at the Sormitáge University

On Ean's Travels

Isabel van Gelderan—Epiphany's Prophet, High Mage of the Citadel, sister to Björn

Dareios Haxamanis—a Prince of Kandori

Ehsan Haxamanis—a Princess of Kandori

Sheih—a *mor'alir* Adept from the Vestian Sorceresy

Björn's Council of Nine

Björn van Gelderan—the First Lord and Alorin's Fifth Vestal

Cristien Tagliaferro—a truthreader

Anglar Tempest—(deceased) a Nodefinder (revived as a Shade)

Dunglei ap'Turic—(deceased) an Adept wielder

Parsifal D'Marre—(deceased) a Nodefinder

Arion Tavestra—(deceased) a fifth strand Adept, one of Björn's three generals

Markal Morrelaine—a *na'turna* wielder, one of Björn's three generals

Ramuhárikhamáth—a *drachwyr*, one of Björn's three generals

Malachai ap'Kalien—(deceased) a fifth strand Adept from Daneland

The Fifty Companions (Those Known to be Living)

Pavran Ahlamby—a truthreader
Usil al'Haba—a Nodefinder
Elien ap'Gentrys—an Adept wielder
Gannon Bair—a truthreader
Karienna D'Artenis—an Adept Healer
Laira di Giancora—an Adept Healer
Mian Gartelt—an Adept Healer
Viernan hal'Jaitar—an Adept wielder
Socotra Isio—a Nodefinder
Ledio Jerouen—an Adept Wildling
Dore Madden—an Adept wielder
Mazur of Elvior—an Avieth of Elvior
Franco Rohre—a Nodefinder
Delanthine Tanner—an Adept wielder
Thessaly Vahn—an Adept Healer
Devangshu Vita—a Nodefinder
Niko van Amstel—a Nodefinder

On Franco's Travels

Alshiba Torinin—an Adept Healer, First Vestal of Alorin and the Alorin Seat
Franco Rohre—an Adept Nodefinder and Deputy Vestal
Niko van Amstel—an Adept Nodefinder and Vestal Candidate

Aldaeon H'rathigian—an Adept truthreader, Seat of the elf realm of Markhengar and Speaker of the Council of Realms
Mir Arkadhi—an Adept truthreader, Seat of the realm of Eltanin

Members of the Nodefinder Rebellion

Carian vran Lea—an Adept Nodefinder and pirate from Jamaii

Gannon Bair—an Adept truthreader, member of the Fifty Companions

Ledio Jerouen—a Whisper Lord, member of the Fifty Companions

Mazur of Elvior—an avieth, member of the Fifty Companions

Franco Rohre—an Adept Nodefinder, member of the Fifty Companions

Devangshu Vita—an Adept Nodefinder, member of the Fifty Companions

Cassius of Rogue—an Adept Nodefinder

The Ruling Prince of M'Nador and His Allies

Radov abin Hadorin—Ruling Prince of M'Nador

Viernan hal'Jaitar—Radov's Consul and wielder (see the Fifty Companions)

Taliah hal'Jaitar—(deceased) daughter of Viernan; a *mor'alir* Adept

Nassar abin'Ahram—Commander of the forces at Ramala

Leilah n'abin Hadorin (called Lily)—Radov's disavowed daughter, princess of M'Nador

Korin Ahlamby—Leilah's betrothed

The Prophet Bethamin (*aka* the Malorin'athgul Darshan)

Dore Madden—an Adept wielder serving the Prophet (see the Fifty Companions)

Raliax—**(deceased)** a Saldarian mercenary serving Dore Madden

Demetrio Consuevé—an Adept Nodefinder

The Karakurt—a female truthreader, leader of an infamous ring of assassins

Pearl—**the** Speaker of the Karakurt's will

Thrace Weyland—an Adept truthreader and purveyor of information

In the Akkad

Emir Zafir bin Safwan al Abdul-Basir—Akkadian Emir, Unifier of the Seventeen Tribes

Rajiid bin Yemen al Basreh—Prime Minister of the Akkad

Farid al Abdul-Basir—Nodefinder son of Zafir, a prince of the Akkad

Men of the Emir's Converted

Loukas n'Abraxis—a combat engineer from Avatar, member of the Emir's Converted

Tannour Valeri—an assassin from Vest, member of the Emir's Converted

Rolan Lamodaar—an expatriated prince from M'Nador, member of the Emir's Converted

Raegus n'Harnalt—a commander among the Emir's Converted, originally from Avatar

Nyongo Kutaata—a Shi'ma warrior, a member of the Emir's Converted

On Trell's Earlier Travels

Yara—an old Kandori woman

Lord Brantley—(deceased) Earl of Pent, liegeman to the Duke of Morwyk

Ghislain D'Launier—a famous courtesan in Rethynnea

Haddrick—an Adept truthreader and pirate of Jamaii, cousin to Carian vran Lea

D'Varre—Guildmaster of the Nodefinder's Guild of Rethynnea

The Royal Family of Dannym

Gydryn val Lorian—King of Dannym

Errodan Renwyr n'Owain val Lorian—Queen of Dannym

Sebastian val Lorian—Prince of Dannym, oldest son and heir to the Eagle Throne

Trell val Lorian—Prince of Dannym, the middle son

Ean val Lorian—Prince of Dannym, the youngest son

Ryan val Lorian—brother to Gydryn, Dannym's Ambassador to Agasan

Fynnlar val Lorian—son of Ryan, the royal cousin

Ysolde Remalkhen—the Queen's Companion; a Fire Princess from Avatar

Creighton Khelspath—(deceased) ward of Gydryn, blood-brother to Ean (now a Shade)

The King of Dannym's Cabinet & Guard

Morin d'Hain—Spymaster

Donnal val Amrein—Minister of the Interior

Mandor val Kess—Minister of Culture

Vitriam o'Reith—truthreader to King Gydryn

Kjieran van Stone—(deceased) Agasi truthreader; killed on assignment in Tambarré

Rhys val Kincaide—Lord Captain of the King's Own Guard

Jasper val Renly—a captain in the Dannish army in M'Nador, elder brother to Bastian

Bastian val Renly—a lieutenant in the King's Own Guard, younger brother of Jasper

The Peerage of Dannym & Their Households

Gareth val Mallonwey—Duke of Towermount and General of the West

Tad val Mallonwey—heir to Towermount

Katerine val Mallonwey—daughter of Gareth, engaged to Creighton Khelspath

Lisandre val Mallonwey—daughter of Gareth

Loran val Whitney—Duke of Marion and General of the East

Killian val Whitney—heir to Marion

Melisande d'Giverny—(deceased) mother to Alyneri
Prince Jair—(deceased) Prince of Kandori, father of Alyneri
Alyneri d'Giverny—Duchess of Aracine, an Adept Healer
Tanis—an Adept truthreader, Melisande's ward
Farshideh—**(deceased)** a Kandori midwife, seneschal of Fersthaven

Stefan val Tryst—Duke of Morwyk
Eugenia val Tryst—wife to Stefan
Darren val Tryst—an Adept Nodefinder, Stefan's son

Lightning Source UK Ltd.
Milton Keynes UK
UKHW011842121021
392112UK00007B/432/J